STEPHEN CRANE

STEPHEN CRANE

PROSE AND POETRY

Maggie: A Girl of the Streets
The Red Badge of Courage
Stories, Sketches, and Journalism
Poetry

THE LIBRARY OF AMERICA

Texts reprinted from the University of Virginia Edition of *The
Works of Stephen Crane*, edited by Fredson Bowers, volumes I, III,
V, VI, VII, VIII, IX, and X, published by the University Press of
Virginia, are Copyright © 1969, 1976, 1970, 1970, 1969, 1973, 1971,
and 1975, respectively, by the Rector & Visitors of the University
of Virginia.

The paper used in this publication meets the minimum
requirements of the American National Standard
for Information Sciences—Permanence of Paper for
Printed Library Materials, ANSI Z39.48–1984.

Distributed to the trade in the United States
and Canada by the Viking Press.

Library of Congress Catalog Card Number: 83-19908
For Cataloging in Publication Data, see end of *Notes* section.
ISBN 0-940450-17-8

Fourth Printing
The Library of America—18

Manufactured in the United States of America

J. C. LEVENSON
WROTE THE NOTES AND SELECTED
THE CONTENTS FOR THIS VOLUME

This volume prints texts from volumes I, III, V, VI, VII, VIII, IX, and X of the University of Virginia Edition of The Works of Stephen Crane edited by Fredson Bowers and published by the University Press of Virginia, with the permission of the publishers.

Grateful acknowledgment is made to the National Endowment for the Humanities, the Ford Foundation, and the Andrew W. Mellon Foundation for their generous support of this series.

Contents

Each section has its own table of contents.
For a complete listing of stories and sketches, see Index of Titles.

NOVELS AND NOVELLAS

Contents

MAGGIE
A GIRL OF THE STREETS

(A Story of New York)

Chapter I

A VERY LITTLE BOY stood upon a heap of gravel for the honor of Rum Alley. He was throwing stones at howling urchins from Devil's Row who were circling madly about the heap and pelting at him.

His infantile countenance was livid with fury. His small body was writhing in the delivery of great, crimson oaths.

"Run, Jimmie, run! Dey'll get yehs," screamed a retreating Rum Alley child.

"Naw," responded Jimmie with a valiant roar, "dese micks can't make me run."

Howls of renewed wrath went up from Devil's Row throats. Tattered gamins on the right made a furious assault on the gravel heap. On their small, convulsed faces there shone the grins of true assassins. As they charged, they threw stones and cursed in shrill chorus.

The little champion of Rum Alley stumbled precipitately down the other side. His coat had been torn to shreds in a scuffle, and his hat was gone. He had bruises on twenty parts of his body, and blood was dripping from a cut in his head. His wan features wore a look of a tiny, insane demon.

On the ground, children from Devil's Row closed in on their antagonist. He crooked his left arm defensively about his head and fought with cursing fury. The little boys ran to and fro, dodging, hurling stones and swearing in barbaric trebles.

From a window of an apartment house that upreared its form from amid squat, ignorant stables, there leaned a curious woman. Some laborers, unloading a scow at a dock at the river, paused for a moment and regarded the fight. The engineer of a passive tugboat hung lazily to a railing and watched. Over on the Island, a worm of yellow convicts came from the shadow of a grey ominous building and crawled slowly along the river's bank.

A stone had smashed into Jimmie's mouth. Blood was bubbling over his chin and down upon his ragged shirt. Tears made furrows on his dirt-stained cheeks. His thin legs had begun to tremble and turn weak, causing his small body to reel. His roaring curses of the first part of the fight had changed to a blasphemous chatter.

In the yells of the whirling mob of Devil's Row children there were notes of joy like songs of triumphant savagery. The little boys seemed to leer gloatingly at the blood upon the other child's face.

Down the avenue came boastfully sauntering a lad of sixteen years, although the chronic sneer of an ideal manhood already sat upon his lips. His hat was tipped with an air of challenge over his eye. Between his teeth, a cigar stump was tilted at the angle of defiance. He walked with a certain swing of the shoulders which appalled the timid. He glanced over into the vacant lot in which the little raving boys from Devil's Row seethed about the shrieking and tearful child from Rum Alley.

"Gee!" he murmured with interest, "A scrap. Gee!"

He strode over to the cursing circle, swinging his shoulders in a manner which denoted that he held victory in his fists. He approached at the back of one of the most deeply engaged of the Devil's Row children.

"Ah, what deh hell," he said, and smote the deeply-engaged one on the back of the head. The little boy fell to the ground and gave a hoarse, tremendous howl. He scrambled to his feet, and perceiving, evidently, the size of his assailant, ran quickly off, shouting alarms. The entire Devil's Row party followed him. They came to a stand a short distance away and yelled taunting oaths at the boy with the chronic sneer. The latter, momentarily, paid no attention to them.

"What deh hell, Jimmie?" he asked of the small champion.

Jimmie wiped his blood-wet features with his sleeve.

"Well, it was dis way, Pete, see! I was goin' teh lick dat Riley kid and dey all pitched on me."

Some Rum Alley children now came forward. The party stood for a moment exchanging vainglorious remarks with Devil's Row. A few stones were thrown at long distances, and words of challenge passed between small warriors. Then the Rum Alley contingent turned slowly in the direction of their home street. They began to give, each to each, distorted versions of the fight. Causes of retreat in particular cases were magnified. Blows dealt in the fight were enlarged to catapultian power, and stones thrown were alleged to have hurtled with infinite accuracy. Valor grew strong again, and the little boys began to swear with great spirit.

"Ah, we blokies kin lick deh hull damn Row," said a child, swaggering.

Little Jimmie was striving to stanch the flow of blood from his cut lips. Scowling, he turned upon the speaker.

"Ah, where deh hell was yeh when I was doin' all deh fightin'?" he demanded. "Youse kids makes me tired."

"Ah, go ahn," replied the other argumentatively.

Jimmie replied with heavy contempt. "Ah, youse can't fight, Blue Billie! I kin lick yeh wid one han'."

"Ah, go ahn," replied Billie again.

"Ah," said Jimmie threateningly.

"Ah," said the other in the same tone.

They struck at each other, clinched, and rolled over on the cobble stones.

"Smash 'im, Jimmie, kick deh damn guts out of 'im," yelled Pete, the lad with the chronic sneer, in tones of delight.

The small combatants pounded and kicked, scratched and tore. They began to weep and their curses struggled in their throats with sobs. The other little boys clasped their hands and wriggled their legs in excitement. They formed a bobbing circle about the pair.

A tiny spectator was suddenly agitated.

"Cheese it, Jimmie, cheese it! Here comes yer fader," he yelled.

The circle of little boys instantly parted. They drew away and waited in ecstatic awe for that which was about to happen. The two little boys fighting in the modes of four thousand years ago, did not hear the warning.

Up the avenue there plodded slowly a man with sullen eyes. He was carrying a dinner pail and smoking an applewood pipe.

As he neared the spot where the little boys strove, he regarded them listlessly. But suddenly he roared an oath and advanced upon the rolling fighters.

"Here, you Jim, git up, now, while I belt yer life out, you damned disorderly brat."

He began to kick into the chaotic mass on the ground. The

boy Billie felt a heavy boot strike his head. He made a furious effort and disentangled himself from Jimmie. He tottered away, damning.

Jimmie arose painfully from the ground and confronting his father, began to curse him. His parent kicked him. "Come home, now," he cried, "an' stop yer jawin', er I'll lam the everlasting head off yehs."

They departed. The man paced placidly along with the apple-wood emblem of serenity between his teeth. The boy followed a dozen feet in the rear. He swore luridly, for he felt that it was degradation for one who aimed to be some vague soldier, or a man of blood with a sort of sublime license, to be taken home by a father.

Chapter II

EVENTUALLY THEY ENTERED into a dark region where, from a careening building, a dozen gruesome doorways gave up loads of babies to the street and the gutter. A wind of early autumn raised yellow dust from cobbles and swirled it against an hundred windows. Long streamers of garments fluttered from fire-escapes. In all unhandy places there were buckets, brooms, rags and bottles. In the street infants played or fought with other infants or sat stupidly in the way of vehicles. Formidable women, with uncombed hair and disordered dress, gossiped while leaning on railings, or screamed in frantic quarrels. Withered persons, in curious postures of submission to something, sat smoking pipes in obscure corners. A thousand odors of cooking food came forth to the street. The building quivered and creaked from the weight of humanity stamping about in its bowels.

A small ragged girl dragged a red, bawling infant along the crowded ways. He was hanging back, baby-like, bracing his wrinkled, bare legs.

The little girl cried out: "Ah, Tommie, come ahn. Dere's Jimmie and fader. Don't be a-pullin' me back."

She jerked the baby's arm impatiently. He fell on his face, roaring. With a second jerk she pulled him to his feet, and they went on. With the obstinacy of his order, he protested against being dragged in a chosen direction. He made heroic endeavors to keep on his legs, denounce his sister and consume a bit of orange peeling which he chewed between the times of his infantile orations.

As the sullen-eyed man, followed by the blood-covered boy, drew near, the little girl burst into reproachful cries. "Ah, Jimmie, youse bin fightin' agin."

The urchin swelled disdainfully.

"Ah, what deh hell, Mag. See?"

The little girl upbraided him. "Youse allus fightin', Jimmie, an' yeh knows it puts mudder out when yehs come home half dead, an' it's like we'll all get a poundin'."

She began to weep. The babe threw back his head and roared at his prospects.

"Ah, what deh hell!" cried Jimmie. "Shut up er I'll smack yer mout'. See?"

As his sister continued her lamentations, he suddenly swore and struck her. The little girl reeled and, recovering herself, burst into tears and quaveringly cursed him. As she slowly retreated her brother advanced dealing her cuffs. The father heard and turned about.

"Stop that, Jim, d'yeh hear? Leave yer sister alone on the street. It's like I can never beat any sense into yer damned wooden head."

The urchin raised his voice in defiance to his parent and continued his attacks. The babe bawled tremendously, protesting with great violence. During his sister's hasty manœuvres, he was dragged by the arm.

Finally the procession plunged into one of the gruesome doorways. They crawled up dark stairways and along cold, gloomy halls. At last the father pushed open a door and they entered a lighted room in which a large woman was rampant.

She stopped in a career from a seething stove to a pan-covered table. As the father and children filed in she peered at them.

"Eh, what? Been fightin' agin, by Gawd!" She threw herself upon Jimmie. The urchin tried to dart behind the others and in the scuffle the babe, Tommie, was knocked down. He protested with his usual vehemence, because they had bruised his tender shins against a table leg.

The mother's massive shoulders heaved with anger. Grasping the urchin by the neck and shoulder she shook him until he rattled. She dragged him to an unholy sink, and, soaking a rag in water, began to scrub his lacerated face with it. Jimmie screamed in pain and tried to twist his shoulders out of the clasp of the huge arms.

The babe sat on the floor watching the scene, his face in contortions like that of a woman at a tragedy. The father, with a newly-ladened pipe in his mouth, crouched on a back-less chair near the stove. Jimmie's cries annoyed him. He turned about and bellowed at his wife:

"Let the damned kid alone for a minute, will yeh, Mary? Yer allus poundin' 'im. When I come nights I can't git no rest 'cause yer allus poundin' a kid. Let up, d'yeh hear? Don't be allus poundin' a kid."

The woman's operations on the urchin instantly increased in violence. At last she tossed him to a corner where he limply lay cursing and weeping.

The wife put her immense hands on her hips and with a chieftain-like stride approached her husband.

"Ho," she said, with a great grunt of contempt. "An' what in the devil are you stickin' your nose for?"

The babe crawled under the table and, turning, peered out cautiously. The ragged girl retreated and the urchin in the corner drew his legs carefully beneath him.

The man puffed his pipe calmly and put his great mudded boots on the back part of the stove.

"Go teh hell," he murmured, tranquilly.

The woman screamed and shook her fists before her husband's eyes. The rough yellow of her face and neck flared suddenly crimson. She began to howl.

He puffed imperturbably at his pipe for a time, but finally arose and began to look out at the window into the darkening chaos of back yards.

"You've been drinkin', Mary," he said. "You'd better let up on the bot', ol' woman, or you'll git done."

"You're a liar. I ain't had a drop," she roared in reply.

They had a lurid altercation, in which they damned each other's souls with frequence.

The babe was staring out from under the table, his small face working in his excitement.

The ragged girl went stealthily over to the corner where the urchin lay.

"Are yehs hurted much, Jimmie?" she whispered timidly.

"Not a damn bit! See?" growled the little boy.

"Will I wash deh blood?"

"Naw!"

"Will I"—

"When I catch dat Riley kid I'll break 'is face! Dat's right! See?"

He turned his face to the wall as if resolved to grimly bide his time.

In the quarrel between husband and wife, the woman was victor. The man grabbed his hat and rushed from the room, apparently determined upon a vengeful drunk. She followed to the door and thundered at him as he made his way down stairs.

She returned and stirred up the room until her children were bobbing about like bubbles.

"Git outa deh way," she persistently bawled, waving feet with their dishevelled shoes near the heads of her children. She shrouded herself, puffing and snorting, in a cloud of steam at the stove, and eventually extracted a frying-pan full of potatoes that hissed.

She flourished it. "Come teh yer suppers, now," she cried with sudden exasperation. "Hurry up, now, er I'll help yeh!"

The children scrambled hastily. With prodigious clatter they arranged themselves at table. The babe sat with his feet dangling high from a precarious infant chair and gorged his small stomach. Jimmie forced, with feverish rapidity, the grease-enveloped pieces between his wounded lips. Maggie, with side glances of fear of interruption, ate like a small pursued tigress.

The mother sat blinking at them. She delivered reproaches, swallowed potatoes and drank from a yellow-brown bottle. After a time her mood changed and she wept as she carried little Tommie into another room and laid him to sleep with his fists doubled in an old quilt of faded red and green grandeur. Then she came and moaned by the stove. She rocked to and fro upon a chair, shedding tears and crooning miserably to the two children about their "poor mother" and "yer fader, damn 'is soul."

The little girl plodded between the table and the chair with a dish-pan on it. She tottered on her small legs beneath burdens of dishes.

Jimmie sat nursing his various wounds. He cast furtive glances at his mother. His practised eye perceived her gradually emerge from a muddled mist of sentiment until her brain burned in drunken heat. He sat breathless.

Maggie broke a plate.

The mother started to her feet as if propelled.

"Good Gawd," she howled. Her eyes glittered on her child

with sudden hatred. The fervent red of her face turned almost
to purple. The little boy ran to the halls, shrieking like a
monk in an earthquake.

He floundered about in darkness until he found the stairs.
He stumbled, panic-stricken, to the next floor. An old woman
opened a door. A light behind her threw a flare on the ur-
chin's quivering face.

"Eh, Gawd, child, what is it dis time? Is yer fader beatin'
yer mudder, or yer mudder beatin' yer fader?"

Chapter III

JIMMIE AND the old woman listened long in the hall. Above the muffled roar of conversation, the dismal wailings of babies at night, the thumping of feet in unseen corridors and rooms, mingled with the sound of varied hoarse shoutings in the street and the rattling of wheels over cobbles, they heard the screams of the child and the roars of the mother die away to a feeble moaning and a subdued bass muttering.

The old woman was a gnarled and leathery personage who could don, at will, an expression of great virtue. She possessed a small music-box capable of one tune, and a collection of "God bless yehs" pitched in assorted keys of fervency. Each day she took a position upon the stones of Fifth Avenue, where she crooked her legs under her and crouched immovable and hideous, like an idol. She received daily a small sum in pennies. It was contributed, for the most part, by persons who did not make their homes in that vicinity.

Once, when a lady had dropped her purse on the sidewalk, the gnarled woman had grabbed it and smuggled it with great dexterity beneath her cloak. When she was arrested she had cursed the lady into a partial swoon, and with her aged limbs, twisted from rheumatism, had almost kicked the stomach out of a huge policeman whose conduct upon that occasion she referred to when she said: "The police, damn 'em."

"Eh, Jimmie, it's cursed shame," she said. "Go, now, like a dear an' buy me a can, an' if yer mudder raises 'ell all night yehs can sleep here."

Jimmie took a tendered tin-pail and seven pennies and departed. He passed into the side door of a saloon and went to the bar. Straining up on his toes he raised the pail and pennies as high as his arms would let him. He saw two hands thrust down and take them. Directly the same hands let down the filled pail and he left.

In front of the gruesome doorway he met a lurching figure. It was his father, swaying about on uncertain legs.

"Give me deh can. See?" said the man, threateningly.

"Ah, come off! I got dis can fer dat ol' woman an' it 'ud be dirt teh swipe it. See?" cried Jimmie.

The father wrenched the pail from the urchin. He grasped it in both hands and lifted it to his mouth. He glued his lips to the under edge and tilted his head. His hairy throat swelled until it seemed to grow near his chin. There was a tremendous gulping movement and the beer was gone.

The man caught his breath and laughed. He hit his son on the head with the empty pail. As it rolled clanging into the street, Jimmie began to scream and kicked repeatedly at his father's shins.

"Look at deh dirt what yeh done me," he yelled. "Deh ol' woman 'ill be raisin' hell."

He retreated to the middle of the street, but the man did not pursue. He staggered toward the door.

"I'll club hell outa yeh when I ketch yeh," he shouted, and disappeared.

During the evening he had been standing against a bar drinking whiskies and declaring to all comers, confidentially: "My home reg'lar livin' hell! Damndes' place! Reg'lar hell! Why do I come an' drin' whisk' here thish way? 'Cause home reg'lar livin' hell!"

Jimmie waited a long time in the street and then crept warily up through the building. He passed with great caution the door of the gnarled woman, and finally stopped outside his home and listened.

He could hear his mother moving heavily about among the furniture of the room. She was chanting in a mournful voice, occasionally interjecting bursts of volcanic wrath at the father, who, Jimmie judged, had sunk down on the floor or in a corner.

"Why deh blazes don' chere try teh keep Jim from fightin'? I'll break yer jaw," she suddenly bellowed.

The man mumbled with drunken indifference. "Ah, wha' deh hell. W'a's odds? Wha' makes kick?"

"Because he tears 'is clothes, yeh damn fool," cried the woman in supreme wrath.

The husband seemed to become aroused. "Go teh hell," he thundered fiercely in reply. There was a crash against the door and something broke into clattering fragments. Jimmie partially suppressed a howl and darted down the stairway. Below he paused and listened. He heard howls and curses, groans and shrieks, confusingly in chorus as if a battle were raging. With all was the crash of splintering furniture. The eyes of the urchin glared in fear that one of them would discover him.

Curious faces appeared in door-ways, and whispered comments passed to and fro. "Ol' Johnson's raisin' hell agin."

Jimmie stood until the noises ceased and the other inhabitants of the tenement had all yawned and shut their doors. Then he crawled upstairs with the caution of an invader of a panther den. Sounds of labored breathing came through the broken door-panels. He pushed the door open and entered, quaking.

A glow from the fire threw red hues over the bare floor, the cracked and soiled plastering, and the overturned and broken furniture.

In the middle of the floor lay his mother asleep. In one corner of the room his father's limp body hung across the seat of a chair.

The urchin stole forward. He began to shiver in dread of awakening his parents. His mother's great chest was heaving painfully. Jimmie paused and looked down at her. Her face was inflamed and swollen from drinking. Her yellow brows shaded eye-lids that had grown blue. Her tangled hair tossed in waves over her forehead. Her mouth was set in the same lines of vindictive hatred that it had, perhaps, borne during the fight. Her bare, red arms were thrown out above her head in positions of exhaustion, something, mayhap, like those of a sated villain.

The urchin bended over his mother. He was fearful lest she should open her eyes, and the dread within him was so strong, that he could not forbear to stare, but hung as if fascinated over the woman's grim face.

Suddenly her eyes opened. The urchin found himself looking straight into that expression, which, it would seem, had the power to change his blood to salt. He howled piercingly and fell backward.

The woman floundered for a moment, tossed her arms about her head as if in combat, and again began to snore.

Jimmie crawled back in the shadows and waited. A noise in the next room had followed his cry at the discovery that his mother was awake. He grovelled in the gloom, the eyes from out his drawn face riveted upon the intervening door.

He heard it creak, and then the sound of a small voice came to him. "Jimmie! Jimmie! Are yehs dere?" it whispered. The urchin started. The thin, white face of his sister looked at him from the door-way of the other room. She crept to him across the floor.

The father had not moved, but lay in the same death-like sleep. The mother writhed in uneasy slumber, her chest wheezing as if she were in the agonies of strangulation. Out at the window a florid moon was peering over dark roofs, and in the distance the waters of a river glimmered pallidly.

The small frame of the ragged girl was quivering. Her features were haggard from weeping, and her eyes gleamed from fear. She grasped the urchin's arm in her little trembling hands and they huddled in a corner. The eyes of both were drawn, by some force, to stare at the woman's face, for they thought she need only to awake and all fiends would come from below.

They crouched until the ghost-mists of dawn appeared at the window, drawing close to the panes, and looking in at the prostrate, heaving body of the mother.

Chapter IV

THE BABE, Tommie, died. He went away in a white, insignificant coffin, his small waxen hand clutching a flower that the girl, Maggie, had stolen from an Italian.

She and Jimmie lived.

The inexperienced fibres of the boy's eyes were hardened at an early age. He became a young man of leather. He lived some red years without laboring. During that time his sneer became chronic. He studied human nature in the gutter, and found it no worse than he thought he had reason to believe it. He never conceived a respect for the world, because he had begun with no idols that it had smashed.

He clad his soul in armor by means of happening hilariously in at a mission church where a man composed his sermons of "yous." While they got warm at the stove, he told his hearers just where he calculated they stood with the Lord. Many of the sinners were impatient over the pictured depths of their degradation. They were waiting for soup-tickets.

A reader of words of wind-demons might have been able to see the portions of a dialogue pass to and fro between the exhorter and his hearers.

"You are damned," said the preacher. And the reader of sounds might have seen the reply go forth from the ragged people: "Where's our soup?"

Jimmie and a companion sat in a rear seat and commented upon the things that didn't concern them, with all the freedom of English gentlemen. When they grew thirsty and went out their minds confused the speaker with Christ.

Momentarily, Jimmie was sullen with thoughts of a hopeless altitude where grew fruit. His companion said that if he should ever meet God he would ask for a million dollars and a bottle of beer.

Jimmie's occupation for a long time was to stand on street-corners and watch the world go by, dreaming blood-red dreams at the passing of pretty women. He menaced mankind at the intersections of streets.

On the corners he was in life and of life. The world was going on and he was there to perceive it.

He maintained a belligerent attitude toward all well-dressed men. To him fine raiment was allied to weakness, and all good coats covered faint hearts. He and his order were kings, to a certain extent, over the men of untarnished clothes, because these latter dreaded, perhaps, to be either killed or laughed at.

Above all things he despised obvious Christians and ciphers with the chrysanthemums of aristocracy in their button-holes. He considered himself above both of these classes. He was afraid of neither the devil nor the leader of society.

When he had a dollar in his pocket his satisfaction with existence was the greatest thing in the world. So, eventually, he felt obliged to work. His father died and his mother's years were divided up into periods of thirty days.

He became a truck driver. He was given the charge of a pains-taking pair of horses and a large rattling truck. He invaded the turmoil and tumble of the down-town streets and learned to breathe maledictory defiance at the police who occasionally used to climb up, drag him from his perch and beat him.

In the lower part of the city he daily involved himself in hideous tangles. If he and his team chanced to be in the rear he preserved a demeanor of serenity, crossing his legs and bursting forth into yells when foot passengers took dangerous dives beneath the noses of his champing horses. He smoked his pipe calmly for he knew that his pay was marching on.

If in the front and the key-truck of chaos, he entered terrifically into the quarrel that was raging to and fro among the drivers on their high seats, and sometimes roared oaths and violently got himself arrested.

After a time his sneer grew so that it turned its glare upon all things. He became so sharp that he believed in nothing. To him the police were always actuated by malignant impulses and the rest of the world was composed, for the most part, of despicable creatures who were all trying to take advantage of him and with whom, in defense, he was obliged to quarrel on all possible occasions. He himself occupied a down-trodden position that had a private but distinct element of grandeur in its isolation.

The most complete cases of aggravated idiocy were, to his mind, rampant upon the front platforms of all of the street cars. At first his tongue strove with these beings, but he eventually was superior. He became immured like an African cow. In him grew a majestic contempt for those strings of street cars that followed him like intent bugs.

He fell into the habit, when starting on a long journey, of fixing his eye on a high and distant object, commanding his horses to begin, and then going into a sort of a trance of observation. Multitudes of drivers might howl in his rear, and passengers might load him with opprobrium, he would not awaken until some blue policeman turned red and began to frenziedly tear bridles and beat the soft noses of the responsible horses.

When he paused to contemplate the attitude of the police toward himself and his fellows, he believed that they were the only men in the city who had no rights. When driving about, he felt that he was held liable by the police for anything that might occur in the streets, and was the common prey of all energetic officials. In revenge, he resolved never to move out of the way of anything, until formidable circumstances, or a much larger man than himself forced him to it.

Foot-passengers were mere pestering flies with an insane disregard for their legs and his convenience. He could not conceive their maniacal desires to cross the streets. Their madness smote him with eternal amazement. He was continually storming at them from his throne. He sat aloft and denounced their frantic leaps, plunges, dives and straddles.

When they would thrust at, or parry, the noses of his champing horses, making them swing their heads and move their feet, disturbing a solid dreamy repose, he swore at the men as fools, for he himself could perceive that Providence had caused it clearly to be written, that he and his team had the unalienable right to stand in the proper path of the sun chariot, and if they so minded, obstruct its mission or take a wheel off.

And, perhaps, if the god-driver had an ungovernable desire to step down, put up his flame colored fists and manfully dispute the right of way, he would have probably been immediately opposed by a scowling mortal with two sets of very hard knuckles.

It is possible, perhaps, that this young man would have

derided, in an axle-wide alley, the approach of a flying ferry boat. Yet he achieved a respect for a fire engine. As one charged toward his truck, he would drive fearfully upon a side-walk, threatening untold people with annihilation. When an engine would strike a mass of blocked trucks, splitting it into fragments, as a blow annihilates a cake of ice, Jimmie's team could usually be observed high and safe, with whole wheels, on the side-walk. The fearful coming of the engine could break up the most intricate muddle of heavy vehicles at which the police had been swearing for the half of an hour.

A fire-engine was enshrined in his heart as an appalling thing that he loved with a distant dog-like devotion. They had been known to overturn street-cars. Those leaping horses, striking sparks from the cobbles in their forward lunge, were creatures to be ineffably admired. The clang of the gong pierced his breast like a noise of remembered war.

When Jimmie was a little boy, he began to be arrested. Before he reached a great age, he had a fair record.

He developed too great a tendency to climb down from his truck and fight with other drivers. He had been in quite a number of miscellaneous fights, and in some general barroom rows that had become known to the police. Once he had been arrested for assaulting a Chinaman. Two women in different parts of the city, and entirely unknown to each other, caused him considerable annoyance by breaking forth, simultaneously, at fateful intervals, into wailings about marriage and support and infants.

Nevertheless, he had, on a certain star-lit evening, said wonderingly and quite reverently: "Deh moon looks like hell, don't it?"

Chapter V

THE GIRL, Maggie, blossomed in a mud puddle. She grew to be a most rare and wonderful production of a tenement district, a pretty girl.

None of the dirt of Rum Alley seemed to be in her veins. The philosophers up-stairs, down-stairs and on the same floor, puzzled over it.

When a child, playing and fighting with gamins in the street, dirt disguised her. Attired in tatters and grime, she went unseen.

There came a time, however, when the young men of the vicinity, said: "Dat Johnson goil is a puty good looker." About this period her brother remarked to her: "Mag, I'll tell yeh dis! See? Yeh've edder got teh go teh hell or go teh work!" Whereupon she went to work, having the feminine aversion of going to hell.

By a chance, she got a position in an establishment where they made collars and cuffs. She received a stool and a machine in a room where sat twenty girls of various shades of yellow discontent. She perched on the stool and treadled at her machine all day, turning out collars, the name of whose brand could be noted for its irrelevancy to anything in connection with collars. At night she returned home to her mother.

Jimmie grew large enough to take the vague position of head of the family. As incumbent of that office, he stumbled up-stairs late at night, as his father had done before him. He reeled about the room, swearing at his relations, or went to sleep on the floor.

The mother had gradually arisen to that degree of fame that she could bandy words with her acquaintances among the police-justices. Court-officials called her by her first name. When she appeared they pursued a course which had been theirs for months. They invariably grinned and cried out: "Hello, Mary, you here again?" Her grey head wagged in many a court. She always besieged the bench with voluble excuses, explanations, apologies and prayers. Her flaming face and rolling eyes were a sort of familiar sight on the island.

She measured time by means of sprees, and was eternally swollen and dishevelled.

One day the young man, Pete, who as a lad had smitten the Devil's Row urchin in the back of the head and put to flight the antagonists of his friend, Jimmie, strutted upon the scene. He met Jimmie one day on the street, promised to take him to a boxing match in Williamsburg, and called for him in the evening.

Maggie observed Pete.

He sat on a table in the Johnson home and dangled his checked legs with an enticing nonchalance. His hair was curled down over his forehead in an oiled bang. His rather pugged nose seemed to revolt from contact with a bristling moustache of short, wire-like hairs. His blue double-breasted coat, edged with black braid, buttoned close to a red puff tie, and his patent-leather shoes, looked like murder-fitted weapons.

His mannerisms stamped him as a man who had a correct sense of his personal superiority. There was valor and contempt for circumstances in the glance of his eye. He waved his hands like a man of the world, who dismisses religion and philosophy, and says "Fudge." He had certainly seen everything and with each curl of his lip, he declared that it amounted to nothing. Maggie thought he must be a very elegant and graceful bartender.

He was telling tales to Jimmie.

Maggie watched him furtively, with half-closed eyes, lit with a vague interest.

"Hully gee! Dey makes me tired," he said. "Mos' e'ry day some farmer comes in an' tries teh run deh shop. See? But deh gits t'rowed right out! I jolt dem right out in deh street before dey knows where dey is! See?"

"Sure," said Jimmie.

"Dere was a mug come in deh place deh odder day wid an idear he wus goin' teh own deh place! Hully gee, he wus goin' teh own deh place! I see he had a still on an' I didn' wanna giv 'im no stuff, so I says: 'Git deh hell outa here an' don' make no trouble,' I says like dat! See? 'Git deh hell outa here an' don' make no trouble;' like dat. 'Git deh hell outa here,' I says. See?"

Jimmie nodded understandingly. Over his features played

an eager desire to state the amount of his valor in a similar crisis, but the narrator proceeded.

"Well, deh blokie he says: 'T'hell wid it! I ain' lookin' for no scrap,' he says (See?) 'but' he says, 'I'm spectable cit'zen an' I wanna drink an' purtydamnsoon, too.' See? 'Deh hell,' I says. Like dat! 'Deh hell,' I says. See? 'Don' make no trouble,' I says. Like dat. 'Don' make no trouble.' See? Den deh mug he squared off an' said he was fine as silk wid his dukes (See?) an' he wanned a drink damnquick. Dat's what he said. See?"

"Sure," repeated Jimmie.

Pete continued. "Say, I jes' jumped deh bar an' deh way I plunked dat blokie was great. See? Dat's right! In deh jaw! See? Hully gee, he t'rowed a spittoon true deh front windee. Say, I taut I'd drop dead. But deh boss, he comes in after an' he says, 'Pete, yehs done jes' right! Yeh've gota keep order an' it's all right.' See? 'It's all right,' he says. Dat's what he said."

The two held a technical discussion.

"Dat bloke was a dandy," said Pete, in conclusion, "but he had'n' oughta made no trouble. Dat's what I says teh dem: 'Don' come in here an' make no trouble,' I says, like dat. 'Don' make no trouble.' See?"

As Jimmie and his friend exchanged tales descriptive of their prowess, Maggie leaned back in the shadow. Her eyes dwelt wonderingly and rather wistfully upon Pete's face. The broken furniture, grimey walls, and general disorder and dirt of her home of a sudden appeared before her and began to take a potential aspect. Pete's aristocratic person looked as if it might soil. She looked keenly at him, occasionally, wondering if he was feeling contempt. But Pete seemed to be enveloped in reminiscence.

"Hully gee," said he, "dose mugs can't phase me. Dey knows I kin wipe up deh street wid any tree of dem."

When he said, "Ah, what deh hell," his voice was burdened with disdain for the inevitable and contempt for anything that fate might compel him to endure.

Maggie perceived that here was the beau ideal of a man. Her dim thoughts were often searching for far away lands where, as God says, the little hills sing together in the morning. Under the trees of her dream-gardens there had always walked a lover.

Chapter VI

PETE TOOK NOTE of Maggie.

"Say, Mag, I'm stuck on yer shape. It's outa sight," he said, parenthetically, with an affable grin.

As he became aware that she was listening closely, he grew still more eloquent in his descriptions of various happenings in his career. It appeared that he was invincible in fights.

"Why," he said, referring to a man with whom he had had a misunderstanding, "dat mug scrapped like a damn dago. Dat's right. He was dead easy. See? He tau't he was a scrapper! But he foun' out diff'ent! Hully gee."

He walked to and fro in the small room, which seemed then to grow even smaller and unfit to hold his dignity, the attribute of a supreme warrior. That swing of the shoulders that had frozen the timid when he was but a lad had increased with his growth and education at the ratio of ten to one. It, combined with the sneer upon his mouth, told mankind that there was nothing in space which could appall him. Maggie marvelled at him and surrounded him with greatness. She vaguely tried to calculate the altitude of the pinnacle from which he must have looked down upon her.

"I met a chump deh odder day way up in deh city," he said. "I was goin' teh see a frien' of mine. When I was a-crossin' deh street deh chump runned plump inteh me, an' den he turns aroun' an' says, 'Yer insolen' ruffin,' he says, like dat. 'Oh, gee,' I says, 'oh, gee, go teh hell and git off deh eart',' I says, like dat. See? 'Go teh hell an' git off deh eart',' like dat. Den deh blokie he got wild. He says I was a contempt'ble scoun'el, er someting like dat, an' he says I was doom' teh everlastin' pe'dition an' all like dat. 'Gee,' I says, 'gee! Deh hell I am,' I says. 'Deh hell I am,' like dat. An' den I slugged 'im. See?"

With Jimmie in his company, Pete departed in a sort of blaze of glory from the Johnson home. Maggie, leaning from the window, watched him as he walked down the street.

Here was a formidable man who disdained the strength of a world full of fists. Here was one who had contempt for brass-clothed power; one whose knuckles could defiantly ring against the granite of law. He was a knight.

The two men went from under the glimmering street-lamp and passed into shadows.

Turning, Maggie contemplated the dark, dust-stained walls, and the scant and crude furniture of her home. A clock, in a splintered and battered oblong box of varnished wood, she suddenly regarded as an abomination. She noted that it ticked raspingly. The almost vanished flowers in the carpet-pattern, she conceived to be newly hideous. Some faint attempts she had made with blue ribbon, to freshen the appearance of a dingy curtain, she now saw to be piteous.

She wondered what Pete dined on.

She reflected upon the collar and cuff factory. It began to appear to her mind as a dreary place of endless grinding. Pete's elegant occupation brought him, no doubt, into contact with people who had money and manners. It was probable that he had a large acquaintance of pretty girls. He must have great sums of money to spend.

To her the earth was composed of hardships and insults. She felt instant admiration for a man who openly defied it. She thought that if the grim angel of death should clutch his heart, Pete would shrug his shoulders and say: "Oh, ev'ryt'ing goes."

She anticipated that he would come again shortly. She spent some of her week's pay in the purchase of flowered cretonne for a lambrequin. She made it with infinite care and hung it to the slightly-careening mantel, over the stove, in the kitchen. She studied it with painful anxiety from different points in the room. She wanted it to look well on Sunday night when, perhaps, Jimmie's friend would come. On Sunday night, however, Pete did not appear.

Afterward the girl looked at it with a sense of humiliation. She was now convinced that Pete was superior to admiration for lambrequins.

A few evenings later Pete entered with fascinating innovations in his apparel. As she had seen him twice and he had different suits on each time, Maggie had a dim impression that his wardrobe was prodigiously extensive.

"Say, Mag," he said, "put on yer bes' duds Friday night an' I'll take yehs teh deh show. See?"

He spent a few moments in flourishing his clothes and then vanished, without having glanced at the lambrequin.

Over the eternal collars and cuffs in the factory Maggie spent the most of three days in making imaginary sketches of Pete and his daily environment. She imagined some half dozen women in love with him and thought he must lean dangerously toward an indefinite one, whom she pictured with great charms of person, but with an altogether contemptible disposition.

She thought he must live in a blare of pleasure. He had friends, and people who were afraid of him.

She saw the golden glitter of the place where Pete was to take her. An entertainment of many hues and many melodies where she was afraid she might appear small and mouse-colored.

Her mother drank whiskey all Friday morning. With lurid face and tossing hair she cursed and destroyed furniture all Friday afternoon. When Maggie came home at half-past six her mother lay asleep amidst the wreck of chairs and a table. Fragments of various household utensils were scattered about the floor. She had vented some phase of drunken fury upon the lambrequin. It lay in a bedraggled heap in the corner.

"Hah," she snorted, sitting up suddenly, "where deh hell yeh been? Why deh hell don' yeh come home earlier? Been loafin' 'round deh streets. Yer gettin' teh be a reg'lar devil."

When Pete arrived Maggie, in a worn black dress, was waiting for him in the midst of a floor strewn with wreckage. The curtain at the window had been pulled by a heavy hand and hung by one tack, dangling to and fro in the draft through the cracks at the sash. The knots of blue ribbons appeared like violated flowers. The fire in the stove had gone out. The displaced lids and open doors showed heaps of sullen grey ashes. The remnants of a meal, ghastly, like dead flesh, lay in a corner. Maggie's red mother, stretched on the floor, blasphemed and gave her daughter a bad name.

Chapter VII

A<small>N ORCHESTRA</small> of yellow silk women and bald-headed men on an elevated stage near the centre of a great green-hued hall, played a popular waltz. The place was crowded with people grouped about little tables. A battalion of waiters slid among the throng, carrying trays of beer glasses and making change from the inexhaustible vaults of their trousers pockets. Little boys, in the costumes of French chefs, paraded up and down the irregular aisles vending fancy cakes. There was a low rumble of conversation and a subdued clinking of glasses. Clouds of tobacco smoke rolled and wavered high in air about the dull gilt of the chandeliers.

The vast crowd had an air throughout of having just quitted labor. Men with calloused hands and attired in garments that showed the wear of an endless trudge for a living, smoked their pipes contentedly and spent five, ten, or perhaps fifteen cents for beer. There was a mere sprinkling of kid-gloved men who smoked cigars purchased elsewhere. The great body of the crowd was composed of people who showed that all day they strove with their hands. Quiet Germans, with maybe their wives and two or three children, sat listening to the music, with the expressions of happy cows. An occasional party of sailors from a war-ship, their faces pictures of sturdy health, spent the earlier hours of the evening at the small round tables. Very infrequent tipsy men, swollen with the value of their opinions, engaged their companions in earnest and confidential conversation. In the balcony, and here and there below, shone the impassive faces of women. The nationalities of the Bowery beamed upon the stage from all directions.

Pete aggressively walked up a side aisle and took seats with Maggie at a table beneath the balcony.

"Two beehs!"

Leaning back he regarded with eyes of superiority the scene before them. This attitude affected Maggie strongly. A man who could regard such a sight with indifference must be accustomed to very great things.

It was obvious that Pete had been to this place many times

before, and was very familiar with it. A knowledge of this fact made Maggie feel little and new.

He was extremely gracious and attentive. He displayed the consideration of a cultured gentleman who knew what was due.

"Say, what deh hell? Bring deh lady a big glass! What deh hell use is dat pony?"

"Don't be fresh, now," said the waiter, with some warmth, as he departed.

"Ah, git off deh eart'," said Pete, after the other's retreating form.

Maggie perceived that Pete brought forth all his elegance and all his knowledge of high-class customs for her benefit. Her heart warmed as she reflected upon his condescension.

The orchestra of yellow silk women and bald-headed men gave vent to a few bars of anticipatory music and a girl, in a pink dress with short skirts, galloped upon the stage. She smiled upon the throng as if in acknowledgment of a warm welcome, and began to walk to and fro, making profuse gesticulations and singing, in brazen soprano tones, a song, the words of which were inaudible. When she broke into the swift rattling measures of a chorus some half tipsy men near the stage joined in the rollicking refrain and glasses were pounded rhythmically upon the tables. People leaned forward to watch her and to try to catch the words of the song. When she vanished there were long rollings of applause.

Obedient to more anticipatory bars, she reappeared amidst the half-suppressed cheering of the tipsy men. The orchestra plunged into dance music and the laces of the dancer fluttered and flew in the glare of gas jets. She divulged the fact that she was attired in some half dozen skirts. It was patent that any one of them would have proved adequate for the purpose for which skirts are intended. An occasional man bent forward, intent upon the pink stockings. Maggie wondered at the splendor of the costume and lost herself in calculations of the cost of the silks and laces.

The dancer's smile of stereotyped enthusiasm was turned for ten minutes upon the faces of her audience. In the finale she fell into some of those grotesque attitudes which were at the time popular among the dancers in the theatres up-town, giving to the Bowery public the phantasies of the aristocratic theatre-going public, at reduced rates.

"Say, Pete," said Maggie, leaning forward, "dis is great."

"Sure," said Pete, with proper complacence.

A ventriloquist followed the dancer. He held two fantastic dolls on his knees. He made them sing mournful ditties and say funny things about geography and Ireland.

"Do dose little men talk?" asked Maggie.

"Naw," said Pete, "it's some damn fake. See?"

Two girls, on the bills as sisters, came forth and sang a duet that is heard occasionally at concerts given under church auspices. They supplemented it with a dance which of course can never be seen at concerts given under church auspices.

After the duettists had retired, a woman of debatable age sang a negro melody. The chorus necessitated some grotesque waddlings supposed to be an imitation of a plantation darkey, under the influence, probably, of music and the moon. The audience was just enthusiastic enough over it to have her return and sing a sorrowful lay, whose lines told of a mother's love and a sweetheart who waited and a young man who was lost at sea under the most harrowing circumstances. From the faces of a score or so in the crowd, the self-contained look faded. Many heads were bent forward with eagerness and sympathy. As the last distressing sentiment of the piece was brought forth, it was greeted by that kind of applause which rings as sincere.

As a final effort, the singer rendered some verses which described a vision of Britain being annihilated by America, and Ireland bursting her bonds. A carefully prepared crisis was reached in the last line of the last verse, where the singer threw out her arms and cried, "The star-spangled banner." Instantly a great cheer swelled from the throats of the assemblage of the masses. There was a heavy rumble of booted feet thumping the floor. Eyes gleamed with sudden fire, and calloused hands waved frantically in the air.

After a few moments' rest, the orchestra played crashingly, and a small fat man burst out upon the stage. He began to roar a song and stamp back and forth before the foot-lights, wildly waving a glossy silk hat and throwing leers, or smiles, broadcast. He made his face into fantastic grimaces until he looked like a pictured devil on a Japanese kite. The crowd laughed gleefully. His short, fat legs were never still a moment. He shouted and roared and bobbed his shock of red wig until the audience broke out in excited applause.

Pete did not pay much attention to the progress of events upon the stage. He was drinking beer and watching Maggie.

Her cheeks were blushing with excitement and her eyes were glistening. She drew deep breaths of pleasure. No thoughts of the atmosphere of the collar and cuff factory came to her.

When the orchestra crashed finally, they jostled their way to the sidewalk with the crowd. Pete took Maggie's arm and pushed a way for her, offering to fight with a man or two.

They reached Maggie's home at a late hour and stood for a moment in front of the gruesome doorway.

"Say, Mag," said Pete, "give us a kiss for takin' yeh teh deh show, will yer?"

Maggie laughed, as if startled, and drew away from him.

"Naw, Pete," she said, "dat wasn't in it."

"Ah, what deh hell?" urged Pete.

The girl retreated nervously.

"Ah, what deh hell?" repeated he.

Maggie darted into the hall, and up the stairs. She turned and smiled at him, then disappeared.

Pete walked slowly down the street. He had something of an astonished expression upon his features. He paused under a lamp-post and breathed a low breath of surprise.

"Gawd," he said, "I wonner if I've been played fer a duffer."

Chapter VIII

As thoughts of Pete came to Maggie's mind, she began to have an intense dislike for all of her dresses.

"What deh hell ails yeh? What makes yeh be allus fixin' and fussin'? Good Gawd," her mother would frequently roar at her.

She began to note, with more interest, the well-dressed women she met on the avenues. She envied elegance and soft palms. She craved those adornments of person which she saw every day on the street, conceiving them to be allies of vast importance to women.

Studying faces, she thought many of the women and girls she chanced to meet, smiled with serenity as though forever cherished and watched over by those they loved.

The air in the collar and cuff establishment strangled her. She knew she was gradually and surely shrivelling in the hot, stuffy room. The begrimed windows rattled incessantly from the passing of elevated trains. The place was filled with a whirl of noises and odors.

She wondered as she regarded some of the grizzled women in the room, mere mechanical contrivances sewing seams and grinding out, with heads bended over their work, tales of imagined or real girl-hood happiness, past drunks, the baby at home, and unpaid wages. She speculated how long her youth would endure. She began to see the bloom upon her cheeks as valuable.

She imagined herself, in an exasperating future, as a scrawny woman with an eternal grievance. Too, she thought Pete to be a very fastidious person concerning the appearance of women.

She felt she would love to see somebody entangle their fingers in the oily beard of the fat foreigner who owned the establishment. He was a detestable creature. He wore white socks with low shoes.

He sat all day delivering orations, in the depths of a cushioned chair. His pocketbook deprived them of the power of retort.

"What een hell do you sink I pie fife dolla a week for? Play? No, py damn!"

Maggie was anxious for a friend to whom she could talk about Pete. She would have liked to discuss his admirable mannerisms with a reliable mutual friend. At home, she found her mother often drunk and always raving.

It seems that the world had treated this woman very badly, and she took a deep revenge upon such portions of it as came within her reach. She broke furniture as if she were at last getting her rights. She swelled with virtuous indignation as she carried the lighter articles of household use, one by one under the shadows of the three gilt balls, where Hebrews chained them with chains of interest.

Jimmie came when he was obliged to by circumstances over which he had no control. His well-trained legs brought him staggering home and put him to bed some nights when he would rather have gone elsewhere.

Swaggering Pete loomed like a golden sun to Maggie. He took her to a dime museum where rows of meek freaks astonished her. She contemplated their deformities with awe and thought them a sort of chosen tribe.

Pete, raking his brains for amusement, discovered the Central Park Menagerie and the Museum of Arts. Sunday afternoons would sometimes find them at these places. Pete did not appear to be particularly interested in what he saw. He stood around looking heavy, while Maggie giggled in glee.

Once at the Menagerie he went into a trance of admiration before the spectacle of a very small monkey threatening to thrash a cageful because one of them had pulled his tail and he had not wheeled about quickly enough to discover who did it. Ever after Pete knew that monkey by sight and winked at him, trying to induce him to fight with other and larger monkeys.

At the Museum, Maggie said, "Dis is outa sight."

"Oh hell," said Pete, "wait till next summer an' I'll take yehs to a picnic."

While the girl wandered in the vaulted rooms, Pete occupied himself in returning stony stare for stony stare, the appalling scrutiny of the watch-dogs of the treasures. Occasionally he would remark in loud tones: "Dat jay has got glass eyes," and sentences of the sort. When he tired of this amusement he would go to the mummies and moralize over them.

Usually he submitted with silent dignity to all which he had to go through, but, at times, he was goaded into comment.

"What deh hell," he demanded once. "Look at all dese little jugs! Hundred jugs in a row! Ten rows in a case an' 'bout a t'ousand cases! What deh blazes use is dem?"

Evenings during the week he took her to see plays in which the brain-clutching heroine was rescued from the palatial home of her guardian, who is cruelly after her bonds, by the hero with the beautiful sentiments. The latter spent most of his time out at soak in pale-green snow storms, busy with a nickel-plated revolver, rescuing aged strangers from villains.

Maggie lost herself in sympathy with the wanderers swooning in snow storms beneath happy-hued church windows. And a choir within singing "Joy to the World." To Maggie and the rest of the audience this was transcendental realism. Joy always within, and they, like the actor, inevitably without. Viewing it, they hugged themselves in ecstatic pity of their imagined or real condition.

The girl thought the arrogance and granite-heartedness of the magnate of the play was very accurately drawn. She echoed the maledictions that the occupants of the gallery showered on this individual when his lines compelled him to expose his extreme selfishness.

Shady persons in the audience revolted from the pictured villainy of the drama. With untiring zeal they hissed vice and applauded virtue. Unmistakably bad men evinced an apparently sincere admiration for virtue.

The loud gallery was overwhelmingly with the unfortunate and the oppressed. They encouraged the struggling hero with cries, and jeered the villain, hooting and calling attention to his whiskers. When anybody died in the pale-green snow storms, the gallery mourned. They sought out the painted misery and hugged it as akin.

In the hero's erratic march from poverty in the first act, to wealth and triumph in the final one, in which he forgives all the enemies that he has left, he was assisted by the gallery, which applauded his generous and noble sentiments and confounded the speeches of his opponents by making irrelevant but very sharp remarks. Those actors who were cursed with villainy parts were confronted at every turn by the gallery. If one of them rendered lines containing the most subtile distinctions between right and wrong, the gallery was immediately aware if the actor meant wickedness, and denounced him accordingly.

The last act was a triumph for the hero, poor and of the masses, the representative of the audience, over the villain and the rich man, his pockets stuffed with bonds, his heart packed with tyrannical purposes, imperturbable amid suffering.

Maggie always departed with raised spirits from the showing places of the melodrama. She rejoiced at the way in which the poor and virtuous eventually surmounted the wealthy and wicked. The theater made her think. She wondered if the culture and refinement she had seen imitated, perhaps grotesquely, by the heroine on the stage, could be acquired by a girl who lived in a tenement house and worked in a shirt factory.

Chapter IX

A GROUP OF URCHINS were intent upon the side door of a saloon. Expectancy gleamed from their eyes. They were twisting their fingers in excitement.

"Here she comes," yelled one of them suddenly.

The group of urchins burst instantly asunder and its individual fragments were spread in a wide, respectable half circle about the point of interest. The saloon door opened with a crash, and the figure of a woman appeared upon the threshold. Her gray hair fell in knotted masses about her shoulders. Her face was crimsoned and wet with perspiration. Her eyes had a rolling glare.

"Not a damn cent more of me money will yehs ever get, not a damn cent. I spent me money here fer t'ree years an' now yehs tells me yeh'll sell me no more stuff! T'hell wid yeh, Johnnie Murckre! 'Disturbance?' Disturbance be damned! T'hell wid yeh, Johnnie—"

The door received a kick of exasperation from within and the woman lurched heavily out on the sidewalk.

The gamins in the half-circle became violently agitated. They began to dance about and hoot and yell and jeer. Wide dirty grins spread over each face.

The woman made a furious dash at a particularly outrageous cluster of little boys. They laughed delightedly and scampered off a short distance, calling out over their shoulders to her. She stood tottering on the curb-stone and thundered at them.

"Yeh devil's kids," she howled, shaking red fists. The little boys whooped in glee. As she started up the street they fell in behind and marched uproariously. Occasionally she wheeled about and made charges on them. They ran nimbly out of reach and taunted her.

In the frame of a gruesome doorway she stood for a moment cursing them. Her hair straggled, giving her crimson features a look of insanity. Her great fists quivered as she shook them madly in the air.

The urchins made terrific noises until she turned and disappeared. Then they filed quietly in the way they had come.

The woman floundered about in the lower hall of the tenement house and finally stumbled up the stairs. On an upper hall a door was opened and a collection of heads peered curiously out, watching her. With a wrathful snort the woman confronted the door, but it was slammed hastily in her face and the key was turned.

She stood for a few minutes, delivering a frenzied challenge at the panels.

"Come out in deh hall, Mary Murphy, damn yeh, if yehs want a row. Come ahn, yeh overgrown terrier, come ahn."

She began to kick the door with her great feet. She shrilly defied the universe to appear and do battle. Her cursing trebles brought heads from all doors save the one she threatened. Her eyes glared in every direction. The air was full of her tossing fists.

"Come ahn, deh hull damn gang of yehs, come ahn," she roared at the spectators. An oath or two, cat-calls, jeers and bits of facetious advice were given in reply. Missiles clattered about her feet.

"What deh hell's deh matter wid yeh?" said a voice in the gathered gloom, and Jimmie came forward. He carried a tin dinner-pail in his hand and under his arm a brown truckman's apron done in a bundle. "What deh hell's wrong?" he demanded.

"Come out, all of yehs, come out," his mother was howling. "Come ahn an' I'll stamp yer damn brains under me feet."

"Shet yer face, an' come home, yeh damned old fool," roared Jimmie at her. She strided up to him and twirled her fingers in his face. Her eyes were darting flames of unreasoning rage and her frame trembled with eagerness for a fight.

"T'hell wid yehs! An' who deh hell are yehs? I ain't givin' a snap of me fingers fer yehs," she bawled at him. She turned her huge back in tremendous disdain and climbed the stairs to the next floor.

Jimmie followed, cursing blackly. At the top of the flight he seized his mother's arm and started to drag her toward the door of their room.

"Come home, damn yeh," he gritted between his teeth.

"Take yer hands off me! Take yer hands off me," shrieked his mother.

She raised her arm and whirled her great fist at her son's face. Jimmie dodged his head and the blow struck him in the back of the neck. "Damn yeh," gritted he again. He threw out his left hand and writhed his fingers about her middle arm. The mother and the son began to sway and struggle like gladiators.

"Whoop!" said the Rum Alley tenement house. The hall filled with interested spectators.

"Hi, ol' lady, dat was a dandy!"

"T'ree to one on deh red!"

"Ah, stop yer damn scrappin'!"

The door of the Johnson home opened and Maggie looked out. Jimmie made a supreme cursing effort and hurled his mother into the room. He quickly followed and closed the door. The Rum Alley tenement swore disappointedly and retired.

The mother slowly gathered herself up from the floor. Her eyes glittered menacingly upon her children.

"Here, now," said Jimmie, "we've had enough of dis. Sit down, an' don' make no trouble."

He grasped her arm, and twisting it, forced her into a creaking chair.

"Keep yer hands off me," roared his mother again.

"Damn yer ol' hide," yelled Jimmie, madly. Maggie shrieked and ran into the other room. To her there came the sound of a storm of crashes and curses. There was a great final thump and Jimmie's voice cried: "Dere, damn yeh, stay still." Maggie opened the door now, and went warily out. "Oh, Jimmie."

He was leaning against the wall and swearing. Blood stood upon bruises on his knotty fore-arms where they had scraped against the floor or the walls in the scuffle. The mother lay screeching on the floor, the tears running down her furrowed face.

Maggie, standing in the middle of the room, gazed about her. The usual upheaval of the tables and chairs had taken place. Crockery was strewn broadcast in fragments. The stove had been disturbed on its legs, and now leaned idiotically to one side. A pail had been upset and water spread in all directions.

The door opened and Pete appeared. He shrugged his shoulders. "Oh, Gawd," he observed.

He walked over to Maggie and whispered in her ear. "Ah, what deh hell, Mag? Come ahn and we'll have a hell of a time."

The mother in the corner upreared her head and shook her tangled locks.

"Teh hell wid him and you," she said, glowering at her daughter in the gloom. Her eyes seemed to burn balefully. "Yeh've gone teh deh devil, Mag Johnson, yehs knows yehs have gone teh deh devil. Yer a disgrace teh yer people, damn yeh. An' now, git out an' go ahn wid dat doe-faced jude of yours. Go teh hell wid him, damn yeh, an' a good riddance. Go teh hell an' see how yeh likes it."

Maggie gazed long at her mother.

"Go teh hell now, an' see how yeh likes it. Git out. I won't have sech as yehs in me house! Get out, d'yeh hear! Damn yeh, git out!"

The girl began to tremble.

At this instant Pete came forward. "Oh, what deh hell, Mag, see," whispered he softly in her ear. "Dis all blows over. See? Deh ol' woman 'ill be all right in deh mornin'. Come ahn out wid me! We'll have a hell of a time."

The woman on the floor cursed. Jimmie was intent upon his bruised fore-arms. The girl cast a glance about the room filled with a chaotic mass of debris, and at the red, writhing body of her mother.

"Go teh hell an' good riddance."

She went.

Chapter X

J IMMIE HAD AN IDEA it wasn't common courtesy for a friend to come to one's home and ruin one's sister. But he was not sure how much Pete knew about the rules of politeness.

The following night he returned home from work at rather a late hour in the evening. In passing through the halls he came upon the gnarled and leathery old woman who possessed the music box. She was grinning in the dim light that drifted through dust-stained panes. She beckoned to him with a smudged fore-finger.

"Ah, Jimmie, what do yehs tink I got onto las' night. It was deh funnies' ting I ever saw," she cried, coming close to him and leering. She was trembling with eagerness to tell her tale. "I was by me door las' night when yer sister and her jude feller came in late, oh, very late. An' she, the dear, she was a-cryin' as if her heart would break, she was. It was deh funnies' ting I ever saw. An' right out here by me door she asked him did he love her, did he. An' she was a-cryin' as if her heart would break, poor t'ing. An' him, I could see by deh way what he said it dat she had been askin' orften, he says: 'Oh, hell, yes,' he says, says he, 'Oh, hell, yes.'"

Storm-clouds swept over Jimmie's face, but he turned from the leathery old woman and plodded on up stairs.

"Oh, hell, yes," called she after him. She laughed a laugh that was like a prophetic croak. "'Oh, hell, yes,' he says, says he, 'Oh, hell, yes.'"

There was no one in at home. The rooms showed that attempts had been made at tidying them. Parts of the wreckage of the day before had been repaired by an unskilful hand. A chair or two and the table, stood uncertainly upon legs. The floor had been newly swept. Too, the blue ribbons had been restored to the curtains, and the lambrequin, with its immense sheaves of yellow wheat and red roses of equal size, had been returned, in a worn and sorry state, to its position at the mantel. Maggie's jacket and hat were gone from the nail behind the door.

Jimmie walked to the window and began to look through

the blurred glass. It occurred to him to vaguely wonder, for an instant, if some of the women of his acquaintance had brothers.

Suddenly, however, he began to swear.

"But he was me frien'! I brought 'im here! Dat's deh hell of it!"

He fumed about the room, his anger gradually rising to the furious pitch.

"I'll kill deh jay! Dat's what I'll do! I'll kill deh jay!"

He clutched his hat and sprang toward the door. But it opened and his mother's great form blocked the passage.

"What deh hell's deh matter wid yeh?" exclaimed she, coming into the rooms.

Jimmie gave vent to a sardonic curse and then laughed heavily.

"Well, Maggie's gone teh deh devil! Dat's what! See?"

"Eh?" said his mother.

"Maggie's gone teh deh devil! Are yehs deaf?" roared Jimmie, impatiently.

"Deh hell she has," murmured the mother, astounded.

Jimmie grunted, and then began to stare out at the window. His mother sat down in a chair, but a moment later sprang erect and delivered a maddened whirl of oaths. Her son turned to look at her as she reeled and swayed in the middle of the room, her fierce face convulsed with passion, her blotched arms raised high in imprecation.

"May Gawd curse her forever," she shrieked. "May she eat nothin' but stones and deh dirt in deh street. May she sleep in deh gutter an' never see deh sun shine agin. Deh damn—"

"Here, now," said her son. "Take a drop on yourself."

The mother raised lamenting eyes to the ceiling.

"She's deh devil's own chil', Jimmie," she whispered. "Ah, who would tink such a bad girl could grow up in our fambly, Jimmie, me son. Many deh hour I've spent in talk wid dat girl an' tol' her if she ever went on deh streets I'd see her damned. An' after all her bringin' up an' what I tol' her and talked wid her, she goes teh deh bad, like a duck teh water."

The tears rolled down her furrowed face. Her hands trembled.

"An' den when dat Sadie MacMallister next door to us was

sent teh deh devil by dat feller what worked in deh soap-factory, didn't I tell our Mag dat if she—"

"Ah, dat's anudder story," interrupted the brother. "Of course, dat Sadie was nice an' all dat—but—see—it ain't dessame as if—well, Maggie was diff'ent—see—she was diff'ent."

He was trying to formulate a theory that he had always unconsciously held, that all sisters, excepting his own, could advisedly be ruined.

He suddenly broke out again. "I'll go t'ump hell outa deh mug what did her deh harm. I'll kill 'im! He tinks he kin scrap, but when he gits me a-chasin' 'im he'll fin' out where he's wrong, deh damned duffer. I'll wipe up deh street wid 'im."

In a fury he plunged out of the doorway. As he vanished the mother raised her head and lifted both hands, entreating.

"May Gawd curse her forever," she cried.

In the darkness of the hallway Jimmie discerned a knot of women talking volubly. When he strode by they paid no attention to him.

"She allus was a bold thing," he heard one of them cry in an eager voice. "Dere wasn't a feller come teh deh house but she'd try teh mash 'im. My Annie says deh shameless t'ing tried teh ketch her feller, her own feller, what we useter know his fader."

"I could a' tol' yehs dis two years ago," said a woman, in a key of triumph. "Yesir, it was over two years ago dat I says teh my ol' man, I says, 'Dat Johnson girl ain't straight,' I says. 'Oh, hell,' he says. 'Oh, hell.' 'Dat's all right,' I says, 'but I know what I knows,' I says, 'an' it'ill come out later. You wait an' see,' I says, 'you see.'"

"Anybody what had eyes could see dat dere was somethin' wrong wid dat girl. I didn't like her actions."

On the street Jimmie met a friend. "What deh hell?" asked the latter.

Jimmie explained. "An' I'll tump 'im till he can't stand."

"Oh, what deh hell," said the friend. "What's deh use! Yeh'll git pulled in! Everybody 'ill be onto it! An' ten plunks! Gee!"

Jimmie was determined. "He t'inks he kin scrap, but he'll fin' out diff'ent."

"Gee," remonstrated the friend, "What deh hell?"

Chapter XI

ON A CORNER a glass-fronted building shed a yellow glare upon the pavements. The open mouth of a saloon called seductively to passengers to enter and annihilate sorrow or create rage.

The interior of the place was papered in olive and bronze tints of imitation leather. A shining bar of counterfeit massiveness extended down the side of the room. Behind it a great mahogany-appearing sideboard reached the ceiling. Upon its shelves rested pyramids of shimmering glasses that were never disturbed. Mirrors set in the face of the sideboard multiplied them. Lemons, oranges and paper napkins, arranged with mathematical precision, sat among the glasses. Many-hued decanters of liquor perched at regular intervals on the lower shelves. A nickel-plated cash register occupied a position in the exact center of the general effect. The elementary senses of it all seemed to be opulence and geometrical accuracy.

Across from the bar a smaller counter held a collection of plates upon which swarmed frayed fragments of crackers, slices of boiled ham, dishevelled bits of cheese, and pickles swimming in vinegar. An odor of grasping, begrimed hands and munching mouths pervaded.

Pete, in a white jacket, was behind the bar bending expectantly toward a quiet stranger. "A beeh," said the man. Pete drew a foam-topped glassful and set it dripping upon the bar.

At this moment the light bamboo doors at the entrance swung open and crashed against the siding. Jimmie and a companion entered. They swaggered unsteadily but belligerently toward the bar and looked at Pete with bleared and blinking eyes.

"Gin," said Jimmie.

"Gin," said the companion.

Pete slid a bottle and two glasses along the bar. He bended his head sideways as he assiduously polished away with a napkin at the gleaming wood. He had a look of watchfulness upon his features.

Jimmie and his companion kept their eyes upon the bartender and conversed loudly in tones of contempt.

"He's a dindy masher, ain't he, by Gawd?" laughed Jimmie.

"Oh, hell, yes," said the companion, sneering widely. "He's great, he is. Git onto deh mug on deh blokie. Dat's enough to make a feller turn hand-springs in 'is sleep."

The quiet stranger moved himself and his glass a trifle further away and maintained an attitude of oblivion.

"Gee! ain't he hot stuff!"

"Git onto his shape! Great Gawd!"

"Hey," cried Jimmie, in tones of command. Pete came along slowly, with a sullen dropping of the under lip.

"Well," he growled, " what's eatin' yehs?"

"Gin," said Jimmie.

"Gin," said the companion.

As Pete confronted them with the bottle and the glasses, they laughed in his face. Jimmie's companion, evidently overcome with merriment, pointed a grimy forefinger in Pete's direction.

"Say, Jimmie," demanded he, " what deh hell is dat behind deh bar?"

"Damned if I knows," replied Jimmie. They laughed loudly. Pete put down a bottle with a bang and turned a formidable face toward them. He disclosed his teeth and his shoulders heaved restlessly.

"You fellers can't guy me," he said. "Drink yer stuff an' git out an' don' make no trouble."

Instantly the laughter faded from the faces of the two men and expressions of offended dignity immediately came.

"Who deh hell has said anyt'ing teh you," cried they in the same breath.

The quiet stranger looked at the door calculatingly.

"Ah, come off," said Pete to the two men. "Don't pick me up for no jay. Drink yer rum an' git out an' don' make no trouble."

"Oh, deh hell," airily cried Jimmie.

"Oh, deh hell," airily repeated his companion.

"We goes when we git ready! See!" continued Jimmie.

"Well," said Pete in a threatening voice, "don' make no trouble."

Jimmie suddenly leaned forward with his head on one side. He snarled like a wild animal.

"Well, what if we does? See?" said he.

Dark blood flushed into Pete's face, and he shot a lurid glance at Jimmie.

"Well, den we'll see whose deh bes' man, you or me," he said.

The quiet stranger moved modestly toward the door.

Jimmie began to swell with valor.

"Don' pick me up fer no tenderfoot. When yeh tackles me yeh tackles one of deh bes' men in deh city. See? I'm a scrapper, I am. Ain't dat right, Billie?"

"Sure, Mike," responded his companion in tones of conviction.

"Oh, hell," said Pete, easily. "Go fall on yerself."

The two men again began to laugh.

"What deh hell is dat talkin?" cried the companion.

"Damned if I knows," replied Jimmie with exaggerated contempt.

Pete made a furious gesture. "Git outa here now, an' don' make no trouble. See? Youse fellers er lookin' fer a scrap an' it's damn likely yeh'll fin' one if yeh keeps on shootin' off yer mout's. I know yehs! See? I kin lick better men dan yehs ever saw in yer lifes. Dat's right! See? Don' pick me up fer no stuff er yeh might be jolted out in deh street before yeh knows where yeh is. When I comes from behind dis bar, I t'rows yehs boat inteh deh street. See?"

"Oh, hell," cried the two men in chorus.

The glare of a panther came into Pete's eyes. "Dat's what I said! Unnerstan'?"

He came through a passage at the end of the bar and swelled down upon the two men. They stepped promptly forward and crowded close to him.

They bristled like three roosters. They moved their heads pugnaciously and kept their shoulders braced. The nervous muscles about each mouth twitched with a forced smile of mockery.

"Well, what deh hell yer goin' teh do?" gritted Jimmie.

Pete stepped warily back, waving his hands before him to keep the men from coming too near.

"Well, what deh hell yer goin' teh do?" repeated Jimmie's ally. They kept close to him, taunting and leering. They strove to make him attempt the initial blow.

"Keep back, now! Don' crowd me," ominously said Pete.

Again they chorused in contempt. "Oh, hell!"

In a small, tossing group, the three men edged for positions like frigates contemplating battle.

"Well, why deh hell don' yeh try teh t'row us out?" cried Jimmie and his ally with copious sneers.

The bravery of bull-dogs sat upon the faces of the men. Their clenched fists moved like eager weapons.

The allied two jostled the bartender's elbows, glaring at him with feverish eyes and forcing him toward the wall.

Suddenly Pete swore redly. The flash of action gleamed from his eyes. He threw back his arm and aimed a tremendous, lightning-like blow at Jimmie's face. His foot swung a step forward and the weight of his body was behind his fist. Jimmie ducked his head, Bowery-like, with the quickness of a cat. The fierce, answering blows of him and his ally crushed on Pete's bowed head.

The quiet stranger vanished.

The arms of the combatants whirled in the air like flails. The faces of the men, at first flushed to flame-colored anger, now began to fade to the pallor of warriors in the blood and heat of a battle. Their lips curled back and stretched tightly over the gums in ghoul-like grins. Through their white, gripped teeth struggled hoarse whisperings of oaths. Their eyes glittered with murderous fire.

Each head was huddled between its owner's shoulders, and arms were swinging with marvelous rapidity. Feet scraped to and fro with a loud scratching sound upon the sanded floor. Blows left crimson blotches upon pale skin. The curses of the first quarter minute of the fight died away. The breaths of the fighters came wheezingly from their lips and the three chests were straining and heaving. Pete at intervals gave vent to low, labored hisses, that sounded like a desire to kill. Jimmie's ally gibbered at times like a wounded maniac. Jimmie was silent, fighting with the face of a sacrificial priest. The rage of fear shone in all their eyes and their blood-colored fists swirled.

At a tottering moment a blow from Pete's hand struck the

ally and he crashed to the floor. He wriggled instantly to his feet and grasping the quiet stranger's beer glass from the bar, hurled it at Pete's head.

High on the wall it burst like a bomb, shivering fragments flying in all directions. Then missiles came to every man's hand. The place had heretofore appeared free of things to throw, but suddenly glass and bottles went singing through the air. They were thrown point blank at bobbing heads. The pyramid of shimmering glasses, that had never been disturbed, changed to cascades as heavy bottles were flung into them. Mirrors splintered to nothing.

The three frothing creatures on the floor buried themselves in a frenzy for blood. There followed in the wake of missiles and fists some unknown prayers, perhaps for death.

The quiet stranger had sprawled very pyrotechnically out on the sidewalk. A laugh ran up and down the avenue for the half of a block.

"Dey've trowed a bloke inteh deh street."

People heard the sound of breaking glass and shuffling feet within the saloon and came running. A small group, bending down to look under the bamboo doors, watching the fall of glass, and three pairs of violent legs, changed in a moment to a crowd.

A policeman came charging down the sidewalk and bounced through the doors into the saloon. The crowd bended and surged in absorbing anxiety to see.

Jimmie caught first sight of the on-coming interruption. On his feet he had the same regard for a policeman that, when on his truck, he had for a fire engine. He howled and ran for the side door.

The officer made a terrific advance, club in hand. One comprehensive sweep of the long night stick threw the ally to the floor and forced Pete to a corner. With his disengaged hand he made a furious effort at Jimmie's coat-tails. Then he regained his balance and paused.

"Well, well, you are a pair of pictures. What in hell yeh been up to?"

Jimmie, with his face drenched in blood, escaped up a side street, pursued a short distance by some of the more law-loving, or excited individuals of the crowd.

Later, from a corner safely dark, he saw the policeman, the ally and the bartender emerge from the saloon. Pete locked the doors and then followed up the avenue in the rear of the crowd-encompassed policeman and his charge.

On first thoughts Jimmie, with his heart throbbing at battle heat, started to go desperately to the rescue of his friend, but he halted.

"Ah, what deh hell?" he demanded of himself.

Chapter XII

IN A HALL of irregular shape sat Pete and Maggie drinking beer. A submissive orchestra dictated to by a spectacled man with frowsy hair and a dress suit, industriously followed the bobs of his head and the waves of his baton. A ballad singer, in a dress of flaming scarlet, sang in the inevitable voice of brass. When she vanished, men seated at the tables near the front applauded loudly, pounding the polished wood with their beer glasses. She returned attired in less gown, and sang again. She received another enthusiastic encore. She reappeared in still less gown and danced. The deafening rumble of glasses and clapping of hands that followed her exit indicated an overwhelming desire to have her come on for the fourth time, but the curiosity of the audience was not gratified.

Maggie was pale. From her eyes had been plucked all look of self-reliance. She leaned with a dependent air toward her companion. She was timid, as if fearing his anger or displeasure. She seemed to beseech tenderness of him.

Pete's air of distinguished valor had grown upon him until it threatened stupendous dimensions. He was infinitely gracious to the girl. It was apparent to her that his condescension was a marvel.

He could appear to strut even while sitting still and he showed that he was a lion of lordly characteristics by the air with which he spat.

With Maggie gazing at him wonderingly, he took pride in commanding the waiters who were, however, indifferent or deaf.

"Hi, you, git a russle on yehs! What deh hell yeh's lookin' at? Two more beehs, d'yeh hear?"

He leaned back and critically regarded the person of a girl with a straw-colored wig who upon the stage was flinging her heels in somewhat awkward imitation of a well-known danseuse.

At times Maggie told Pete long confidential tales of her former home life, dwelling upon the escapades of the other members of the family and the difficulties she had to combat in order to obtain a degree of comfort. He responded in tones of philanthropy. He pressed her arm with an air of reassuring proprietorship.

"Dey was damn jays," he said, denouncing the mother and brother.

The sound of the music which, by the efforts of the frowsy-headed leader, drifted to her ears through the smoked-filled atmosphere, made the girl dream. She thought of her former Rum Alley environment and turned to regard Pete's strong protecting fists. She thought of the collar and cuff manufactory and the eternal moan of the proprietor: "What een hell do you sink I pie fife dolla a week for? Play? No, py damn." She contemplated Pete's man-subduing eyes and noted that wealth and prosperity was indicated by his clothes. She imagined a future, rose-tinted, because of its distance from all that she previously had experienced.

As to the present she perceived only vague reasons to be miserable. Her life was Pete's and she considered him worthy of the charge. She would be disturbed by no particular apprehensions, so long as Pete adored her as he now said he did. She did not feel like a bad woman. To her knowledge she had never seen any better.

At times men at other tables regarded the girl furtively. Pete, aware of it, nodded at her and grinned. He felt proud.

"Mag, yer a bloomin' good-looker," he remarked, studying her face through the haze. The men made Maggie fear, but she blushed at Pete's words as it became apparent to her that she was the apple of his eye.

Grey-headed men, wonderfully pathetic in their dissipation, stared at her through clouds. Smooth cheeked boys, some of them with faces of stone and mouths of sin, not nearly so pathetic as the grey heads, tried to find the girl's eyes in the smoke wreaths. Maggie considered she was not what they thought her. She confined her glances to Pete and the stage.

The orchestra played negro melodies and a versatile drummer pounded, whacked, clattered and scratched on a dozen machines to make noise.

Those glances of the men, shot at Maggie from under half-closed lids, made her tremble. She thought them all to be worse men than Pete.

"Come, let's go," she said.

As they went out Maggie perceived two women seated at a table with some men. They were painted and their cheeks had lost their roundness. As she passed them the girl, with a shrinking movement, drew back her skirts.

Chapter XIII

J IMMIE DID NOT RETURN home for a number of days after
the fight with Pete in the saloon. When he did, he ap-
proached with extreme caution.

He found his mother raving. Maggie had not returned
home. The parent continually wondered how her daughter
could come to such a pass. She had never considered Maggie
as a pearl dropped unstained into Rum Alley from Heaven,
but she could not conceive how it was possible for her daugh-
ter to fall so low as to bring disgrace upon her family. She
was terrific in denunciation of the girl's wickedness.

The fact that the neighbors talked of it, maddened her.
When women came in, and in the course of their conversa-
tion casually asked, "Where's Maggie dese days?" the mother
shook her fuzzy head at them and appalled them with curses.
Cunning hints inviting confidence she rebuffed with violence.

"An' wid all deh bringin' up she had, how could she?"
moaningly she asked of her son. "Wid all deh talkin' wid her
I did an' deh t'ings I tol' her to remember? When a girl is
bringed up deh way I bringed up Maggie, how kin she go
teh deh devil?"

Jimmie was transfixed by these questions. He could not
conceive how under the circumstances his mother's daughter
and his sister could have been so wicked.

His mother took a drink from a squdgy bottle that sat on
the table. She continued her lament.

"She had a bad heart, dat girl did, Jimmie. She was wicked
teh deh heart an' we never knowed it."

Jimmie nodded, admitting the fact.

"We lived in deh same house wid her an' I brought her up
an' we never knowed how bad she was."

Jimmie nodded again.

"Wid a home like dis an' a mudder like me, she went teh
deh bad," cried the mother, raising her eyes.

One day, Jimmie came home, sat down in a chair and be-
gan to wriggle about with a new and strange nervousness. At
last he spoke shamefacedly.

"Well, look-a-here, dis t'ing queers us! See? We're queered!

An' maybe it 'ud be better if I—well, I t'ink I kin look 'er up an'—maybe it 'ud be better if I fetched her home an—"

The mother started from her chair and broke forth into a storm of passionate anger.

"What! Let 'er come an' sleep under deh same roof wid her mudder agin! Oh, yes, I will, won't I? Sure? Shame on yehs, Jimmie Johnson, fer sayin' such a t'ing teh yer own mudder— teh yer own mudder! Little did I tink when yehs was a babby playin' about me feet dat ye'd grow up teh say sech a t'ing teh yer mudder—yer own mudder. I never taut—"

Sobs choked her and interrupted her reproaches.

"Dere ain't nottin teh raise sech hell about," said Jimmie. "I on'y says it 'ud be better if we keep dis t'ing dark, see? It queers us! See?"

His mother laughed a laugh that seemed to ring through the city and be echoed and re-echoed by countless other laughs. "Oh, yes, I will, won' I! Sure!"

"Well, yeh must take me fer a damn fool," said Jimmie, indignant at his mother for mocking him. "I didn't say we'd make 'er inteh a little tin angel, ner nottin, but deh way it is now she can queer us! Don' che see?"

"Aye, she'll git tired of deh life atter a while an' den she'll wanna be a-comin' home, won' she, deh beast! I'll let 'er in den, won' I?"

"Well, I didn' mean none of dis prod'gal bus'ness anyway," explained Jimmie.

"It wasn't no prod'gal dauter, yeh damn fool," said the mother. "It was prod'gal son, anyhow."

"I know dat," said Jimmie.

For a time they sat in silence. The mother's eyes gloated on a scene her imagination could call before her. Her lips were set in a vindictive smile.

"Aye, she'll cry, won' she, an' carry on, an' tell how Pete, or some odder feller, beats 'er an' she'll say she's sorry an' all dat an' she ain't happy, she ain't, an' she wants to come home agin, she does."

With grim humor, the mother imitated the possible wailing notes of the daughter's voice.

"Den I'll take 'er in, won't I, deh beast. She kin cry 'er two eyes out on deh stones of deh street before I'll dirty deh place wid her. She abused an' ill-treated her own mudder—her own mudder what loved her an' she'll never git anodder chance dis side of hell."

Jimmie thought he had a great idea of women's frailty, but he could not understand why any of his kin should be victims.

"Damn her," he fervidly said.

Again he wondered vaguely if some of the women of his acquaintance had brothers. Nevertheless, his mind did not for an instant confuse himself with those brothers nor his sister with theirs. After the mother had, with great difficulty, suppressed the neighbors, she went among them and proclaimed her grief. "May Gawd forgive dat girl," was her continual cry. To attentive ears she recited the whole length and breadth of her woes.

"I bringed 'er up deh way a dauter oughta be bringed up an' dis is how she served me! She went teh deh devil deh first chance she got! May Gawd forgive her."

When arrested for drunkenness she used the story of her daughter's downfall with telling effect upon the police justices. Finally one of them said to her, peering down over his spectacles: "Mary, the records of this and other courts show that you are the mother of forty-two daughters who have been ruined. The case is unparalleled in the annals of this court, and this court thinks—"

The mother went through life shedding large tears of sorrow. Her red face was a picture of agony.

Of course Jimmie publicly damned his sister that he might appear on a higher social plane. But, arguing with himself, stumbling about in ways that he knew not, he, once, almost came to a conclusion that his sister would have been more firmly good had she better known why. However, he felt that he could not hold such a view. He threw it hastily aside.

Chapter XIV

IN A HILARIOUS HALL there were twenty-eight tables and twenty-eight women and a crowd of smoking men. Valiant noise was made on a stage at the end of the hall by an orchestra composed of men who looked as if they had just happened in. Soiled waiters ran to and fro, swooping down like hawks on the unwary in the throng; clattering along the aisles with trays covered with glasses; stumbling over women's skirts and charging two prices for everything but beer, all with a swiftness that blurred the view of the cocoanut palms and dusty monstrosities painted upon the walls of the room. A bouncer, with an immense load of business upon his hands, plunged about in the crowd, dragging bashful strangers to prominent chairs, ordering waiters here and there and quarreling furiously with men who wanted to sing with the orchestra.

The usual smoke cloud was present, but so dense that heads and arms seemed entangled in it. The rumble of conversation was replaced by a roar. Plenteous oaths heaved through the air. The room rang with the shrill voices of women bubbling o'er with drink-laughter. The chief element in the music of the orchestra was speed. The musicians played in intent fury. A woman was singing and smiling upon the stage, but no one took notice of her. The rate at which the piano, cornet and violins were going, seemed to impart wildness to the half-drunken crowd. Beer glasses were emptied at a gulp and conversation became a rapid chatter. The smoke eddied and swirled like a shadowy river hurrying toward some unseen falls. Pete and Maggie entered the hall and took chairs at a table near the door. The woman who was seated there made an attempt to occupy Pete's attention and, failing, went away.

Three weeks had passed since the girl had left home. The air of spaniel-like dependence had been magnified and showed its direct effect in the peculiar off-handedness and ease of Pete's ways toward her.

She followed Pete's eyes with hers, anticipating with smiles gracious looks from him.

A woman of brilliance and audacity, accompanied by a mere boy, came into the place and took seats near them.

At once Pete sprang to his feet, his face beaming with glad surprise.

"By Gawd, there's Nellie," he cried.

He went over to the table and held out an eager hand to the woman.

"Why, hello, Pete, me boy, how are you," said she, giving him her fingers.

Maggie took instant note of the woman. She perceived that her black dress fitted her to perfection. Her linen collar and cuffs were spotless. Tan gloves were stretched over her well-shaped hands. A hat of a prevailing fashion perched jauntily upon her dark hair. She wore no jewelry and was painted with no apparent paint. She looked clear-eyed through the stares of the men.

"Sit down, and call your lady-friend over," she said cordially to Pete. At his beckoning Maggie came and sat between Pete and the mere boy.

"I thought yeh were gone away fer good," began Pete, at once. "When did yeh git back? How did dat Buff'lo bus'ness turn out?"

The woman shrugged her shoulders. "Well, he didn't have as many stamps as he tried to make out, so I shook him, that's all."

"Well, I'm glad teh see yehs back in deh city," said Pete, with awkward gallantry.

He and the woman entered into a long conversation, exchanging reminiscences of days together. Maggie sat still, unable to formulate an intelligent sentence upon the conversation and painfully aware of it.

She saw Pete's eyes sparkle as he gazed upon the handsome stranger. He listened smilingly to all she said. The woman was familiar with all his affairs, asked him about mutual friends, and knew the amount of his salary.

She paid no attention to Maggie, looking toward her once or twice and apparently seeing the wall beyond.

The mere boy was sulky. In the beginning he had welcomed with acclamations the additions.

"Let's all have a drink! What'll you take, Nell? And you,

Miss what's-your-name. Have a drink, Mr. ——, you, I mean."

He had shown a sprightly desire to do the talking for the company and tell all about his family. In a loud voice he declaimed on various topics. He assumed a patronizing air toward Pete. As Maggie was silent, he paid no attention to her. He made a great show of lavishing wealth upon the woman of brilliance and audacity.

"Do keep still, Freddie! You gibber like an ape, dear," said the woman to him. She turned away and devoted her attention to Pete.

"We'll have many a good time together again, eh?"

"Sure, Mike," said Pete, enthusiastic at once.

"Say," whispered she, leaning forward, "let's go over to Billie's and have a heluva time."

"Well, it's dis way! See?" said Pete. "I got dis lady frien' here."

"Oh, t'hell with her," argued the woman.

Pete appeared disturbed.

"All right," said she, nodding her head at him. "All right for you! We'll see the next time you ask me to go anywheres with you."

Pete squirmed.

"Say," he said, beseechingly, "come wid me a minit an' I'll tell yer why."

The woman waved her hand.

"Oh, that's all right, you needn't explain, you know. You wouldn't come merely because you wouldn't come, that's all there is of it."

To Pete's visible distress she turned to the mere boy, bringing him speedily from a terrific rage. He had been debating whether it would be the part of a man to pick a quarrel with Pete, or would he be justified in striking him savagely with his beer glass without warning. But he recovered himself when the woman turned to renew her smilings. He beamed upon her with an expression that was somewhat tipsy and inexpressibly tender.

"Say, shake that Bowery jay," requested he, in a loud whisper.

"Freddie, you are so droll," she replied.

Pete reached forward and touched the woman on the arm.

"Come out a minit while I tells yeh why I can't go wid yer. Yer doin' me dirt, Nell! I never taut ye'd do me dirt, Nell. Come on, will yer?" He spoke in tones of injury.

"Why, I don't see why I should be interested in your explanations," said the woman, with a coldness that seemed to reduce Pete to a pulp.

His eyes pleaded with her. "Come out a minit while I tells yeh."

The woman nodded slightly at Maggie and the mere boy, "Scuse me."

The mere boy interrupted his loving smile and turned a shriveling glare upon Pete. His boyish countenance flushed and he spoke, in a whine, to the woman:

"Oh, I say, Nellie, this ain't a square deal, you know. You aren't goin' to leave me and go off with that duffer, are you? I should think—"

"Why, you dear boy, of course I'm not," cried the woman, affectionately. She bended over and whispered in his ear. He smiled again and settled in his chair as if resolved to wait patiently.

As the woman walked down between the rows of tables, Pete was at her shoulder talking earnestly, apparently in explanation. The woman waved her hands with studied airs of indifference. The doors swung behind them, leaving Maggie and the mere boy seated at the table.

Maggie was dazed. She could dimly perceive that something stupendous had happened. She wondered why Pete saw fit to remonstrate with the woman, pleading for forgiveness with his eyes. She thought she noted an air of submission about her leonine Pete. She was astounded.

The mere boy occupied himself with cock-tails and a cigar. He was tranquilly silent for half an hour. Then he bestirred himself and spoke.

"Well," he said, sighing, "I knew this was the way it would be." There was another stillness. The mere boy seemed to be musing.

"She was pulling m'leg. That's the whole amount of it," he said, suddenly. "It's a bloomin' shame the way that girl does. Why, I've spent over two dollars in drinks to-night. And she goes off with that plug-ugly who looks as if he had been hit in the face with a coin dye. I call it rocky treatment for a fellah like me. Here, waiter, bring me a cock-tail and make it damned strong."

Maggie made no reply. She was watching the doors. "It's a mean piece of business," complained the mere boy. He explained to her how amazing it was that anybody should treat him in such a manner. "But I'll get square with her, you bet. She won't get far ahead of yours truly, you know," he added, winking. "I'll tell her plainly that it was bloomin' mean business. And she won't come it over me with any of her 'now-Freddie-dears.' She thinks my name is Freddie, you know, but of course it ain't. I always tell these people some name like that, because if they got onto your right name they might use it sometime. Understand? Oh, they don't fool me much."

Maggie was paying no attention, being intent upon the doors. The mere boy relapsed into a period of gloom, during which he exterminated a number of cock-tails with a determined air, as if replying defiantly to fate. He occasionally broke forth into sentences composed of invectives joined together in a long string.

The girl was still staring at the doors. After a time the mere boy began to see cobwebs just in front of his nose. He spurred himself into being agreeable and insisted upon her having a charlotte-russe and a glass of beer.

"They's gone," he remarked, "they's gone." He looked at her through the smoke wreaths. "Shay, lil' girl, we mightish well make bes' of it. You ain't such bad lookin' girl, y'know. Not half bad. Can't come up to Nell, though. No, can't do it! Well, I should shay not! Nell fine-lookin' girl! F—i—n—ine. You look damn bad longsider her, but by y'self ain't so bad. Have to do anyhow. Nell gone. O'ny you left. Not half bad, though."

Maggie stood up.

"I'm going home," she said.

The mere boy started.

"Eh? What? Home," he cried, struck with amazement. "I beg pardon, did hear say home?"

"I'm going home," she repeated.

"Great Gawd, what hava struck," demanded the mere boy of himself, stupefied.

In a semi-comatose state he conducted her on board an up-town car, ostentatiously paid her fare, leered kindly at her through the rear window and fell off the steps.

Chapter XV

A FORLORN WOMAN went along a lighted avenue. The street was filled with people desperately bound on missions. An endless crowd darted at the elevated station stairs and the horse cars were thronged with owners of bundles.

The pace of the forlorn woman was slow. She was apparently searching for some one. She loitered near the doors of saloons and watched men emerge from them. She scanned furtively the faces in the rushing stream of pedestrians. Hurrying men, bent on catching some boat or train, jostled her elbows, failing to notice her, their thoughts fixed on distant dinners.

The forlorn woman had a peculiar face. Her smile was no smile. But when in repose her features had a shadowy look that was like a sardonic grin, as if some one had sketched with cruel forefinger indelible lines about her mouth.

Jimmie came strolling up the avenue. The woman encountered him with an aggrieved air.

"Oh, Jimmie, I've been lookin' all over fer yehs—," she began.

Jimmie made an impatient gesture and quickened his pace.

"Ah, don' bodder me! Good Gawd!" he said, with the savageness of a man whose life is pestered.

The woman followed him along the sidewalk in somewhat the manner of a suppliant.

"But, Jimmie," she said, "yehs told me ye'd—"

Jimmie turned upon her fiercely as if resolved to make a last stand for comfort and peace.

"Say, fer Gawd's sake, Hattie, don' foller me from one end of deh city teh deh odder. Let up, will yehs! Give me a minute's res', can't yehs? Yehs makes me tired, allus taggin' me. See? Ain' yehs got no sense? Do yehs want people teh get onto me? Go chase yerself, fer Gawd's sake."

The woman stepped closer and laid her fingers on his arm. "But, look-a here—"

Jimmie snarled. "Oh, go teh hell."

He darted into the front door of a convenient saloon and a moment later came out into the shadows that surrounded the side door. On the brilliantly lighted avenue he perceived the forlorn woman dodging about like a scout. Jimmie laughed with an air of relief and went away.

When he arrived home he found his mother clamoring. Maggie had returned. She stood shivering beneath the torrent of her mother's wrath.

"Well, I'm damned," said Jimmie in greeting.

His mother, tottering about the room, pointed a quivering fore-finger.

"Lookut her, Jimmie, lookut her. Dere's yer sister, boy. Dere's yer sister. Lookut her! Lookut her!"

She screamed in scoffing laughter.

The girl stood in the middle of the room. She edged about as if unable to find a place on the floor to put her feet.

"Ha, ha, ha," bellowed the mother. "Dere she stands! Ain' she purty? Lookut her! Ain' she sweet, deh beast? Lookut her! Ha, ha, lookut her!"

She lurched forward and put her red and seamed hands upon her daughter's face. She bent down and peered keenly up into the eyes of the girl.

"Oh, she's jes' dessame as she ever was, ain' she? She's her mudder's purty darlin' yit, ain' she? Lookut her, Jimmie! Come here, fer Gawd's sake, and lookut her."

The loud, tremendous sneering of the mother brought the denizens of the Rum Alley tenement to their doors. Women came in the hall-ways. Children scurried to and fro.

"What's up? Dat Johnson party on anudder tear?"

"Naw! Young Mag's come home!"

"Deh hell yeh say?"

Through the open doors curious eyes stared in at Maggie. Children ventured into the room and ogled her, as if they formed the front row at a theatre. Women, without, bended toward each other and whispered, nodding their heads with airs of profound philosophy. A baby, overcome with curiosity concerning this object at which all were looking, sidled forward and touched her dress, cautiously, as if investigating a red-hot stove. Its mother's voice rang out like a warning trumpet. She rushed forward and grabbed her child, casting a terrible look of indignation at the girl.

Maggie's mother paced to and fro, addressing the doorful

of eyes, expounding like a glib showman at a museum. Her voice rang through the building.

"Dere she stands," she cried, wheeling suddenly and pointing with dramatic finger. "Dere she stands! Lookut her! Ain' she a dindy? An' she was so good as to come home teh her mudder, she was! Ain' she a beaut'? Ain' she a dindy? Fer Gawd's sake!"

The jeering cries ended in another burst of shrill laughter.

The girl seemed to awaken. "Jimmie—"

He drew hastily back from her.

"Well, now, yer a hell of a t'ing, ain' yeh?" he said, his lips curling in scorn. Radiant virtue sat upon his brow and his repelling hands expressed horror of contamination.

Maggie turned and went.

The crowd at the door fell back precipitately. A baby falling down in front of the door, wrenched a scream like a wounded animal from its mother. Another woman sprang forward and picked it up, with a chivalrous air, as if rescuing a human being from an oncoming express train.

As the girl passed down through the hall, she went before open doors framing more eyes strangely microscopic, and sending broad beams of inquisitive light into the darkness of her path. On the second floor she met the gnarled old woman who possessed the music box.

"So," she cried, " 'ere yehs are back again, are yehs? An' dey've kicked yehs out? Well, come in an' stay wid me teh-night. I ain' got no moral standin'."

From above came an unceasing babble of tongues, over all of which rang the mother's derisive laughter.

Chapter XVI

PETE DID NOT CONSIDER that he had ruined Maggie. If he had thought that her soul could never smile again, he would have believed the mother and brother, who were pyrotechnic over the affair, to be responsible for it.

Besides, in his world, souls did not insist upon being able to smile. "What deh hell?"

He felt a trifle entangled. It distressed him. Revelations and scenes might bring upon him the wrath of the owner of the saloon, who insisted upon respectability of an advanced type.

"What deh hell do dey wanna' raise such a smoke about it fer?" demanded he of himself, disgusted with the attitude of the family. He saw no necessity for anyone's losing their equilibrium merely because their sister or their daughter had stayed away from home.

Searching about in his mind for possible reasons for their conduct, he came upon the conclusion that Maggie's motives were correct, but that the two others wished to snare him. He felt pursued.

The woman of brilliance and audacity whom he had met in the hilarious hall showed a disposition to ridicule him.

"A little pale thing with no spirit," she said. "Did you note the expression of her eyes? There was something in them about pumpkin pie and virtue. That is a peculiar way the left corner of her mouth has of twitching, isn't it? Dear, dear, my cloud-compelling Pete, what are you coming to?"

Pete asserted at once that he never was very much interested in the girl. The woman interrupted him, laughing.

"Oh, it's not of the slightest consequence to me, my dear young man. You needn't draw maps for my benefit. Why should I be concerned about it?"

But Pete continued with his explanations. If he was laughed at for his tastes in women, he felt obliged to say that they were only temporary or indifferent ones.

The morning after Maggie had departed from home, Pete stood behind the bar. He was immaculate in white jacket and apron and his hair was plastered over his brow with infinite correctness. No customers were in the place. Pete was twisting his napkined fist slowly in a beer glass, softly whistling to himself and occasionally holding the object of his attention between his eyes and a few weak beams of sunlight that had found their way over the thick screens and into the shaded room.

With lingering thoughts of the woman of brilliance and audacity, the bartender raised his head and stared through the varying cracks between the swaying bamboo doors. Suddenly the whistling pucker faded from his lips. He saw Maggie walking slowly past. He gave a great start, fearing for the previously-mentioned eminent respectability of the place.

He threw a swift, nervous glance about him, all at once feeling guilty. No one was in the room.

He went hastily over to the side door. Opening it and looking out, he perceived Maggie standing, as if undecided, on the corner. She was searching the place with her eyes.

As she turned her face toward him Pete beckoned to her hurriedly, intent upon returning with speed to a position behind the bar and to the atmosphere of respectability upon which the proprietor insisted.

Maggie came to him, the anxious look disappearing from her face and a smile wreathing her lips.

"Oh, Pete—," she began brightly.

The bartender made a violent gesture of impatience.

"Oh, my Gawd," cried he, vehemently. "What deh hell do yeh wanna hang aroun' here fer? Do yeh wanna git me inteh trouble?" he demanded with an air of injury.

Astonishment swept over the girl's features. "Why, Pete! yehs tol' me—"

Pete glanced profound irritation. His countenance reddened with the anger of a man whose respectability is being threatened.

"Say, yehs makes me tired. See? What deh hell deh yeh wanna tag aroun' atter me fer? Yeh'll git me inteh trouble wid deh ol' man an' dey'll be hell teh pay! If he sees a woman roun' here he'll go crazy an' I'll lose me job! See? Ain' yehs got no sense? Don' be allus bodderin' me. See? Yer brudder come in here an' raised hell an' deh ol' man hada put up fer it! An' now I'm done! See? I'm done."

The girl's eyes stared into his face. "Pete, don' yeh re-mem—"

"Oh, hell," interrupted Pete, anticipating.

The girl seemed to have a struggle with herself. She was apparently bewildered and could not find speech. Finally she asked in a low voice: "But where kin I go?"

The question exasperated Pete beyond the powers of endurance. It was a direct attempt to give him some responsibility in a matter that did not concern him. In his indignation he volunteered information.

"Oh, go teh hell," cried he. He slammed the door furiously and returned, with an air of relief, to his respectability.

Maggie went away.

She wandered aimlessly for several blocks. She stopped once and asked aloud a question of herself: "Who?"

A man who was passing near her shoulder, humorously took the questioning word as intended for him.

"Eh? What? Who? Nobody! I didn't say anything," he laughingly said, and continued his way.

Soon the girl discovered that if she walked with such apparent aimlessness, some men looked at her with calculating eyes. She quickened her step, frightened. As a protection, she adopted a demeanor of intentness as if going somewhere.

After a time she left rattling avenues and passed between rows of houses with sternness and stolidity stamped upon their features. She hung her head for she felt their eyes grimly upon her.

Suddenly she came upon a stout gentleman in a silk hat and a chaste black coat, whose decorous row of buttons reached from his chin to his knees. The girl had heard of the Grace of God and she decided to approach this man.

His beaming, chubby face was a picture of benevolence and kind-heartedness. His eyes shone good-will.

But as the girl timidly accosted him, he gave a convulsive movement and saved his respectability by a vigorous side-step. He did not risk it to save a soul. For how was he to know that there was a soul before him that needed saving?

Chapter XVII

UPON A WET EVENING, several months after the last chapter, two interminable rows of cars, pulled by slipping horses, jangled along a prominent side-street. A dozen cabs, with coat-enshrouded drivers, clattered to and fro. Electric lights, whirring softly, shed a blurred radiance. A flower dealer, his feet tapping impatiently, his nose and his wares glistening with rain-drops, stood behind an array of roses and chrysanthemums. Two or three theatres emptied a crowd upon the storm-swept pavements. Men pulled their hats over their eyebrows and raised their collars to their ears. Women shrugged impatient shoulders in their warm cloaks and stopped to arrange their skirts for a walk through the storm. People having been comparatively silent for two hours burst into a roar of conversation, their hearts still kindling from the glowings of the stage.

The pavements became tossing seas of umbrellas. Men stepped forth to hail cabs or cars, raising their fingers in varied forms of polite request or imperative demand. An endless procession wended toward elevated stations. An atmosphere of pleasure and prosperity seemed to hang over the throng, born, perhaps, of good clothes and of having just emerged from a place of forgetfulness.

In the mingled light and gloom of an adjacent park, a handful of wet wanderers, in attitudes of chronic dejection, was scattered among the benches.

A girl of the painted cohorts of the city went along the street. She threw changing glances at men who passed her, giving smiling invitations to men of rural or untaught pattern and usually seeming sedately unconscious of the men with a metropolitan seal upon their faces.

Crossing glittering avenues, she went into the throng emerging from the places of forgetfulness. She hurried forward through the crowd as if intent upon reaching a distant home, bending forward in her handsome cloak, daintily lifting her skirts and picking for her well-shod feet the dryer spots upon the pavements.

The restless doors of saloons, clashing to and fro, disclosed animated rows of men before bars and hurrying bar-keepers.

A concert hall gave to the street faint sounds of swift, ma-chine-like music, as if a group of phantom musicians were hastening.

A tall young man, smoking a cigarette with a sublime air, strolled near the girl. He had on evening dress, a moustache, a chrysanthemum, and a look of ennui, all of which he kept carefully under his eye. Seeing the girl walk on as if such a young man as he was not in existence, he looked back trans-fixed with interest. He stared glassily for a moment, but gave a slight convulsive start when he discerned that she was nei-ther new, Parisian, nor theatrical. He wheeled about hastily and turned his stare into the air, like a sailor with a search-light.

A stout gentleman, with pompous and philanthropic whiskers, went stolidly by, the broad of his back sneering at the girl.

A belated man in business clothes, and in haste to catch a car, bounced against her shoulder. "Hi, there, Mary, I beg your pardon! Brace up, old girl." He grasped her arm to steady her, and then was away running down the middle of the street.

The girl walked on out of the realm of restaurants and sa-loons. She passed more glittering avenues and went into darker blocks than those where the crowd travelled.

A young man in light overcoat and derby hat received a glance shot keenly from the eyes of the girl. He stopped and looked at her, thrusting his hands in his pockets and making a mocking smile curl his lips. "Come, now, old lady," he said, "you don't mean to tell me that you sized me up for a farmer?"

A laboring man marched along with bundles under his arms. To her remarks, he replied: "It's a fine evenin', ain't it?"

She smiled squarely into the face of a boy who was hurry-ing by with his hands buried in his overcoat, his blonde locks bobbing on his youthful temples, and a cheery smile of un-concern upon his lips. He turned his head and smiled back at her, waving his hands.

"Not this eve—some other eve!"

A drunken man, reeling in her pathway, began to roar at her. "I ain' ga no money, dammit," he shouted, in a dismal voice. He lurched on up the street, wailing to himself, "Dammit, I ain' ga no money. Damn ba' luck. Ain' ga no more money."

The girl went into gloomy districts near the river, where the tall black factories shut in the street and only occasional broad beams of light fell across the pavements from saloons. In front of one of these places, from whence came the sound of a violin vigorously scraped, the patter of feet on boards and the ring of loud laughter, there stood a man with blotched features.

"Ah, there," said the girl.

"I've got a date," said the man.

Further on in the darkness she met a ragged being with shifting, blood-shot eyes and grimey hands. "Ah, what deh hell? Tink I'm a millionaire?"

She went into the blackness of the final block. The shutters of the tall buildings were closed like grim lips. The structures seemed to have eyes that looked over her, beyond her, at other things. Afar off the lights of the avenues glittered as if from an impossible distance. Street car bells jingled with a sound of merriment.

When almost to the river the girl saw a great figure. On going forward she perceived it to be a huge fat man in torn and greasy garments. His grey hair straggled down over his forehead. His small, bleared eyes, sparkling from amidst great rolls of red fat, swept eagerly over the girl's upturned face. He laughed, his brown, disordered teeth gleaming under a grey, grizzled moustache from which beer-drops dripped. His whole body gently quivered and shook like that of a dead jelly fish. Chuckling and leering, he followed the girl of the crimson legions.

At their feet the river appeared a deathly black hue. Some hidden factory sent up a yellow glare, that lit for a moment the waters lapping oilily against timbers. The varied sounds of life, made joyous by distance and seeming unapproachableness, came faintly and died away to a silence.

Chapter XVIII

IN A PARTITIONED-OFF SECTION of a saloon sat a man with a half dozen women, gleefully laughing, hovering about him. The man had arrived at that stage of drunkenness where affection is felt for the universe.

"I'm good f'ler, girls," he said, convincingly. "I'm damn good f'ler. An'body treats me right, I allus trea's zem right! See?"

The women nodded their heads approvingly. "To be sure," they cried in hearty chorus. "You're the kind of a man we like, Pete. You're outa sight! What yeh goin' to buy this time, dear?"

"An'thin' yehs wants, damn it," said the man in an abandonment of good will. His countenance shone with the true spirit of benevolence. He was in the proper mode of missionaries. He would have fraternized with obscure Hottentots. And above all, he was overwhelmed in tenderness for his friends, who were all illustrious.

"An'thing yehs wants, damn it," repeated he, waving his hands with beneficent recklessness. "I'm good f'ler, girls, an' if an'body treats me right I—here," called he through an open door to a waiter, "bring girls drinks, damn it. What 'ill yehs have, girls? An'thing yehs want, damn it!"

The waiter glanced in with the disgusted look of the man who serves intoxicants for the man who takes too much of them. He nodded his head shortly at the order from each individual, and went.

"Damn it," said the man, "we're havin' heluva time. I like you girls! Damn'd if I don't! Yer right sort! See?"

He spoke at length and with feeling, concerning the excellencies of his assembled friends.

"Don' try pull man's leg, but have a heluva time! Das right! Das way teh do! Now, if I sawght yehs tryin' work me fer drinks, wouldn' buy damn t'ing! But yer right sort, damn it! Yehs know how ter treat a f'ler, an' I stays by yehs 'til spen' las' cent! Das right! I'm good f'ler an' I knows when an'body treats me right!"

Between the times of the arrival and departure of the

waiter, the man discoursed to the women on the tender regard he felt for all living things. He laid stress upon the purity of his motives in all dealings with men in the world and spoke of the fervor of his friendship for those who were amiable. Tears welled slowly from his eyes. His voice quavered when he spoke to them.

Once when the waiter was about to depart with an empty tray, the man drew a coin from his pocket and held it forth.

"Here," said he, quite magnificently, "here's quar'."

The waiter kept his hands on his tray.

"I don' want yer money," he said.

The other put forth the coin with tearful insistence.

"Here, damn it," cried he, "tak't! Yer damn goo' f'ler an' I wan' yehs tak't!"

"Come, come, now," said the waiter, with the sullen air of a man who is forced into giving advice. "Put yer mon in yer pocket! Yer loaded an' yehs on'y makes a damn fool of yerself."

As the latter passed out of the door the man turned pathetically to the women.

"He don' know I'm damn goo' f'ler," cried he, dismally.

"Never you mind, Pete, dear," said a woman of brilliance and audacity, laying her hand with great affection upon his arm. "Never you mind, old boy! We'll stay by you, dear!"

"Das ri'," cried the man, his face lighting up at the soothing tones of the woman's voice. "Das ri', I'm damn goo' f'ler an' w'en anyone trea's me ri', I treats zem ri'! Shee!"

"Sure!" cried the women. "And we're not goin' back on you, old man."

The man turned appealing eyes to the woman of brilliance and audacity. He felt that if he could be convicted of a contemptible action he would die.

"Shay, Nell, damn it, I allus trea's yehs shquare, didn' I? I allus been goo' f'ler wi' yehs, ain't I, Nell?"

"Sure you have, Pete," assented the woman. She delivered an oration to her companions. "Yessir, that's a fact. Pete's a square fellah, he is. He never goes back on a friend. He's the right kind an' we stay by him, don't we, girls?"

"Sure," they exclaimed. Looking lovingly at him they raised their glasses and drank his health.

"Girlsh," said the man, beseechingly, "I allus trea's yehs ri', didn' I? I'm goo' f'ler, ain' I, girlsh?"

"Sure," again they chorused.

"Well," said he finally, "le's have nozzer drink, zen."

"That's right," hailed a woman, "that's right. Yer no bloomin' jay! Yer spends yer money like a man. Dat's right."

The man pounded the table with his quivering fists.

"Yessir," he cried, with deep earnestness, as if someone disputed him. "I'm damn goo' f'ler, an' w'en anyone trea's me ri', I allus trea's—le's have nozzer drink."

He began to beat the wood with his glass.

"Shay," howled he, growing suddenly impatient. As the waiter did not then come, the man swelled with wrath.

"Shay," howled he again.

The waiter appeared at the door.

"Bringsh drinksh," said the man.

The waiter disappeared with the orders.

"Zat f'ler dam fool," cried the man. "He insul' me! I'm ge'man! Can' stan' be insul'! I'm goin' lickim when comes!"

"No, no," cried the women, crowding about and trying to subdue him. "He's all right! He didn't mean anything! Let it go! He's a good fellah!"

"Din' he insul' me?" asked the man earnestly.

"No," said they. "Of course he didn't! He's all right!"

"Sure he didn' insul' me?" demanded the man, with deep anxiety in his voice.

"No, no! We know him! He's a good fellah. He didn't mean anything."

"Well, zen," said the man, resolutely, "I'm go' 'pol'gize!"

When the waiter came, the man struggled to the middle of the floor.

"Girlsh shed you insul' me! I shay damn lie! I 'pol'gize!"

"All right," said the waiter.

The man sat down. He felt a sleepy but strong desire to straighten things out and have a perfect understanding with everybody.

"Nell, I allus trea's yeh shquare, din I? Yeh likes me, don' yehs, Nell? I'm goo' f'ler?"

"Sure," said the woman of brilliance and audacity.

"Yeh knows I'm stuck on yehs, don' yehs, Nell?"

"Sure," she repeated, carelessly.

Overwhelmed by a spasm of drunken adoration, he drew two or three bills from his pocket, and, with the trembling fingers of an offering priest, laid them on the table before the woman.

"Yehs knows, damn it, yehs kin have all got, 'cause I'm stuck on yehs, Nell, damn't, I—I'm stuck on yehs, Nell—buy drinksh—damn't—we're havin' heleva time—w'en anyone trea's me ri'—I—damn't, Nell—we're havin' heluva—time."

Shortly he went to sleep with his swollen face fallen forward on his chest.

The women drank and laughed, not heeding the slumbering man in the corner. Finally he lurched forward and fell groaning to the floor.

The women screamed in disgust and drew back their skirts.

"Come ahn," cried one, starting up angrily, "let's get out of here."

The woman of brilliance and audacity stayed behind, taking up the bills and stuffing them into a deep, irregularly-shaped pocket. A guttural snore from the recumbent man caused her to turn and look down at him.

She laughed. "What a damn fool," she said, and went.

The smoke from the lamps settled heavily down in the little compartment, obscuring the way out. The smell of oil, stifling in its intensity, pervaded the air. The wine from an overturned glass dripped softly down upon the blotches on the man's neck.

Chapter XIX

I N A ROOM a woman sat at a table eating like a fat monk in a picture.

A soiled, unshaven man pushed open the door and entered. "Well," said he, "Mag's dead."

"What?" said the woman, her mouth filled with bread.

"Mag's dead," repeated the man.

"Deh hell she is," said the woman. She continued her meal. When she finished her coffee she began to weep.

"I kin remember when her two feet was no bigger dan yer tumb, and she weared worsted boots," moaned she.

"Well, whata dat?" said the man.

"I kin remember when she weared worsted boots," she cried.

The neighbors began to gather in the hall, staring in at the weeping woman as if watching the contortions of a dying dog. A dozen women entered and lamented with her. Under their busy hands the rooms took on that appalling appearance of neatness and order with which death is greeted.

Suddenly the door opened and a woman in a black gown rushed in with outstretched arms. "Ah, poor Mary," she cried, and tenderly embraced the moaning one.

"Ah, what ter'ble affliction is dis," continued she. Her vocabulary was derived from mission churches. "Me poor Mary, how I feel fer yehs! Ah, what a ter'ble affliction is a disobed'ent chile."

Her good, motherly face was wet with tears. She trembled in eagerness to express her sympathy. The mourner sat with bowed head, rocking her body heavily to and fro, and crying out in a high, strained voice that sounded like a dirge on some forlorn pipe.

"I kin remember when she weared worsted boots an' her two feets was no bigger dan yer tumb an' she weared worsted boots, Miss Smith," she cried, raising her streaming eyes.

"Ah, me poor Mary," sobbed the woman in black. With low, coddling cries, she sank on her knees by the mourner's chair, and put her arms about her. The other women began to groan in different keys.

"Yer poor misguided chil' is gone now, Mary, an' let us hope its fer deh bes'. Yeh'll fergive her now, Mary, won't yehs, dear, all her disobed'ence? All her tankless behavior to her mudder an' all her badness? She's gone where her ter'ble sins will be judged."

The woman in black raised her face and paused. The inevitable sunlight came streaming in at the windows and shed a ghastly cheerfulness upon the faded hues of the room. Two or three of the spectators were sniffling, and one was loudly weeping. The mourner arose and staggered into the other room. In a moment she emerged with a pair of faded baby shoes held in the hollow of her hand.

"I kin remember when she used to wear dem," cried she. The women burst anew into cries as if they had all been stabbed. The mourner turned to the soiled and unshaven man.

"Jimmie, boy, go git yer sister! Go git yer sister an' we'll put deh boots on her feets!"

"Dey won't fit her now, yeh damn fool," said the man.

"Go git yer sister, Jimmie," shrieked the woman, confronting him fiercely.

The man swore sullenly. He went over to a corner and slowly began to put on his coat. He took his hat and went out, with a dragging, reluctant step.

The woman in black came forward and again besought the mourner.

"Yeh'll fergive her, Mary! Yeh'll fergive yer bad, bad chil'! Her life was a curse an' her days were black an' yeh'll fergive yer bad girl? She's gone where her sins will be judged."

"She's gone where her sins will be judged," cried the other women, like a choir at a funeral.

"Deh Lord gives and deh Lord takes away," said the woman in black, raising her eyes to the sunbeams.

"Deh Lord gives and deh Lord takes away," responded the others.

"Yeh'll fergive her, Mary!" pleaded the woman in black. The mourner essayed to speak but her voice gave way. She shook her great shoulders frantically, in an agony of grief. Hot tears seemed to scald her quivering face. Finally her voice came and arose like a scream of pain.

"Oh, yes, I'll fergive her! I'll fergive her!"

THE RED BADGE
OF COURAGE

An Episode of the American Civil War

Chapter I

THE COLD PASSED reluctantly from the earth, and the re-
tiring fogs revealed an army stretched out on the hills,
resting. As the landscape changed from brown to green, the
army awakened, and began to tremble with eagerness at the
noise of rumors. It cast its eyes upon the roads, which were
growing from long troughs of liquid mud to proper thor-
oughfares. A river, amber-tinted in the shadow of its banks,
purled at the army's feet; and at night, when the stream had
become of a sorrowful blackness, one could see across it the
red, eyelike gleam of hostile camp-fires set in the low brows
of distant hills.

Once a certain tall soldier developed virtues and went res-
olutely to wash a shirt. He came flying back from a brook
waving his garment bannerlike. He was swelled with a tale he
had heard from a reliable friend, who had heard it from a
truthful cavalryman, who had heard it from his trustworthy
brother, one of the orderlies at division headquarters. He
adopted the important air of a herald in red and gold.

"We're goin' t' move t' morrah—sure," he said pompously
to a group in the company street. "We're goin' 'way up the
river, cut across, an' come around in behint 'em."

To his attentive audience he drew a loud and elaborate plan
of a very brilliant campaign. When he had finished, the blue-
clothed men scattered into small arguing groups between the
rows of squat brown huts. A negro teamster who had been
dancing upon a cracker box with the hilarious encouragement
of twoscore soldiers was deserted. He sat mournfully down.
Smoke drifted lazily from a multitude of quaint chimneys.

"It's a lie! that's all it is—a thunderin' lie!" said another
private loudly. His smooth face was flushed, and his hands
were thrust sulkily into his trousers' pockets. He took the
matter as an affront to him. "I don't believe the derned old
army's ever going to move. We're set. I've got ready to move
eight times in the last two weeks, and we ain't moved yet."

The tall soldier felt called upon to defend the truth of a
rumor he himself had introduced. He and the loud one came
near to fighting over it.

A corporal began to swear before the assemblage. He had just put a costly board floor in his house, he said. During the early spring he had refrained from adding extensively to the comfort of his environment because he had felt that the army might start on the march at any moment. Of late, however, he had been impressed that they were in a sort of eternal camp.

Many of the men engaged in a spirited debate. One outlined in a peculiarly lucid manner all the plans of the commanding general. He was opposed by men who advocated that there were other plans of campaign. They clamored at each other, numbers making futile bids for the popular attention. Meanwhile, the soldier who had fetched the rumor bustled about with much importance. He was continually assailed by questions.

"What's up, Jim?"

"Th' army's goin' t' move."

"Ah, what yeh talkin' about? How yeh know it is?"

"Well, yeh kin b'lieve me er not, jest as yeh like. I don't care a hang."

There was much food for thought in the manner in which he replied. He came near to convincing them by disdaining to produce proofs. They grew much excited over it.

There was a youthful private who listened with eager ears to the words of the tall soldier and to the varied comments of his comrades. After receiving a fill of discussions concerning marches and attacks, he went to his hut and crawled through an intricate hole that served it as a door. He wished to be alone with some new thoughts that had lately come to him.

He lay down on a wide bunk that stretched across the end of the room. In the other end, cracker boxes were made to serve as furniture. They were grouped about the fireplace. A picture from an illustrated weekly was upon the log walls, and three rifles were paralleled on pegs. Equipments hung on handy projections, and some tin dishes lay upon a small pile of firewood. A folded tent was serving as a roof. The sunlight, without, beating upon it, made it glow a light yellow shade. A small window shot an oblique square of whiter light upon the cluttered floor. The smoke from the fire at times neglected the clay chimney and wreathed into the room, and this flimsy chimney of clay and sticks made endless threats to set ablaze the whole establishment.

The youth was in a little trance of astonishment. So they were at last going to fight. On the morrow, perhaps, there would be a battle, and he would be in it. For a time he was obliged to labor to make himself believe. He could not accept with assurance an omen that he was about to mingle in one of those great affairs of the earth.

He had, of course, dreamed of battles all his life—of vague and bloody conflicts that had thrilled him with their sweep and fire. In visions he had seen himself in many struggles. He had imagined peoples secure in the shadow of his eagle-eyed prowess. But awake he had regarded battles as crimson blotches on the pages of the past. He had put them as things of the bygone with his thought-images of heavy crowns and high castles. There was a portion of the world's history which he had regarded as the time of wars, but it, he thought, had been long gone over the horizon and had disappeared forever.

From his home his youthful eyes had looked upon the war in his own country with distrust. It must be some sort of a play affair. He had long despaired of witnessing a Greeklike struggle. Such would be no more, he had said. Men were better, or more timid. Secular and religious education had effaced the throat-grappling instinct, or else firm finance held in check the passions.

He had burned several times to enlist. Tales of great movements shook the land. They might not be distinctly Homeric, but there seemed to be much glory in them. He had read of marches, sieges, conflicts, and he had longed to see it all. His busy mind had drawn for him large pictures extravagant in color, lurid with breathless deeds.

But his mother had discouraged him. She had affected to look with some contempt upon the quality of his war ardor and patriotism. She could calmly seat herself and with no apparent difficulty give him many hundreds of reasons why he was of vastly more importance on the farm than on the field of battle. She had had certain ways of expression that told him that her statements on the subject came from a deep conviction. Moreover, on her side, was his belief that her ethical motive in the argument was impregnable.

At last, however, he had made firm rebellion against this yellow light thrown upon the color of his ambitions. The newspapers, the gossip of the village, his own picturings, had aroused him to an uncheckable degree. They were in truth fighting finely down there. Almost every day the newspaper printed accounts of a decisive victory.

One night, as he lay in bed, the winds had carried to him the clangoring of the church bell as some enthusiast jerked the rope frantically to tell the twisted news of a great battle. This voice of the people rejoicing in the night had made him shiver in a prolonged ecstasy of excitement. Later, he had gone down to his mother's room and had spoken thus: "Ma, I'm going to enlist."

"Henry, don't you be a fool," his mother had replied. She had then covered her face with the quilt. There was an end to the matter for that night.

Nevertheless, the next morning he had gone to a town that was near his mother's farm and had enlisted in a company that was forming there. When he had returned home his mother was milking the brindle cow. Four others stood waiting. "Ma, I've enlisted," he had said to her diffidently. There was a short silence. "The Lord's will be done, Henry," she had finally replied, and had then continued to milk the brindle cow.

When he had stood in the doorway with his soldier's clothes on his back, and with the light of excitement and expectancy in his eyes almost defeating the glow of regret for the home bonds, he had seen two tears leaving their trails on his mother's scarred cheeks.

Still, she had disappointed him by saying nothing whatever about returning with his shield or on it. He had privately primed himself for a beautiful scene. He had prepared certain sentences which he thought could be used with touching effect. But her words destroyed his plans. She had doggedly peeled potatoes and addressed him as follows: "You watch out, Henry, an' take good care of yerself in this here fighting business—you watch out, an' take good care of yerself. Don't go a-thinkin' you can lick the hull rebel army at the start, because yeh can't. Yer jest one little feller amongst a hull lot of others, and yeh've got to keep quiet an' do what they tell yeh. I know how you are, Henry.

"I've knet yeh eight pair of socks, Henry, and I've put in all yer best shirts, because I want my boy to be jest as warm and comf'able as anybody in the army. Whenever they get holes in 'em, I want yeh to send 'em right-away back to me, so's I kin dern 'em.

"An' allus be careful an' choose yer comp'ny. There's lots of bad men in the army, Henry. The army makes 'em wild, and they like nothing better than the job of leading off a young feller like you, as ain't never been away from home much and has allus had a mother, an' a-learning 'em to drink and swear. Keep clear of them folks, Henry. I don't want yeh to ever do anything, Henry, that yeh would be 'shamed to let me know about. Jest think as if I was a-watchin' yeh. If yeh keep that in yer mind allus, I guess yeh'll come out about right.

"Yeh must allus remember yer father, too, child, an' remember he never drunk a drop of licker in his life, and seldom swore a cross oath.

"I don't know what else to tell yeh, Henry, excepting that yeh must never do no shirking, child, on my account. If so be a time comes when yeh have to be kilt or do a mean thing, why, Henry, don't think of anything 'cept what's right, because there's many a woman has to bear up 'ginst sech things these times, and the Lord 'll take keer of us all.

"Don't forgit about the socks and the shirts, child; and I've put a cup of blackberry jam with yer bundle, because I know yeh like it above all things. Good-by, Henry. Watch out, and be a good boy."

He had, of course, been impatient under the ordeal of this speech. It had not been quite what he expected, and he had borne it with an air of irritation. He departed feeling vague relief.

Still, when he had looked back from the gate, he had seen his mother kneeling among the potato parings. Her brown face, upraised, was stained with tears, and her spare form was quivering. He bowed his head and went on, feeling suddenly ashamed of his purposes.

From his home he had gone to the seminary to bid adieu to many schoolmates. They had thronged about him with wonder and admiration. He had felt the gulf now between them and had swelled with calm pride. He and some of his fellows who had donned blue were quite overwhelmed with privileges for all of one afternoon, and it had been a very delicious thing. They had strutted.

A certain light-haired girl had made vivacious fun at his martial spirit, but there was another and darker girl whom he had gazed at steadfastly, and he thought she grew demure and sad at sight of his blue and brass. As he had walked down the path between the rows of oaks, he had turned his head and detected her at a window watching his departure. As he perceived her, she had immediately begun to stare up through the high tree branches at the sky. He had seen a good deal of flurry and haste in her movement as she changed her attitude. He often thought of it.

On the way to Washington his spirit had soared. The regiment was fed and caressed at station after station until the youth had believed that he must be a hero. There was a lavish expenditure of bread and cold meats, coffee, and pickles and cheese. As he basked in the smiles of the girls and was patted and complimented by the old men, he had felt growing within him the strength to do mighty deeds of arms.

After complicated journeyings with many pauses, there had come months of monotonous life in a camp. He had had the belief that real war was a series of death struggles with small time in between for sleep and meals; but since his regiment had come to the field the army had done little but sit still and try to keep warm.

He was brought then gradually back to his old ideas. Greeklike struggles would be no more. Men were better, or more timid. Secular and religious education had effaced the throat-grappling instinct, or else firm finance held in check the passions.

He had grown to regard himself merely as a part of a vast blue demonstration. His province was to look out, as far as he could, for his personal comfort. For recreation he could twiddle his thumbs and speculate on the thoughts which must agitate the minds of the generals. Also, he was drilled and drilled and reviewed, and drilled and drilled and re-viewed.

The only foes he had seen were some pickets along the river bank. They were a sun-tanned, philosophical lot, who some-times shot reflectively at the blue pickets. When reproached for this afterward, they usually expressed sorrow, and swore by their gods that the guns had exploded without their per-mission. The youth, on guard duty one night, conversed across the stream with one of them. He was a slightly ragged man, who spat skillfully between his shoes and possessed a great fund of bland and infantile assurance. The youth liked him personally.

"Yank," the other had informed him, "yer a right dum good feller." This sentiment, floating to him upon the still air, had made him temporarily regret war.

Various veterans had told him tales. Some talked of gray, bewhiskered hordes who were advancing with relentless curses and chewing tobacco with unspeakable valor; tremen-dous bodies of fierce soldiery who were sweeping along like the Huns. Others spoke of tattered and eternally hungry men who fired despondent powders. "They'll charge through hell's fire an' brimstone t' git a holt on a haversack, an' sech stom-achs ain't a-lastin' long," he was told. From the stories, the youth imagined the red, live bones sticking out through slits in the faded uniforms.

Still, he could not put a whole faith in veterans' tales, for recruits were their prey. They talked much of smoke, fire, and blood, but he could not tell how much might be lies. They persistently yelled "Fresh fish!" at him, and were in no wise to be trusted.

However, he perceived now that it did not greatly matter what kind of soldiers he was going to fight, so long as they fought, which fact no one disputed. There was a more serious problem. He lay in his bunk pondering upon it. He tried to mathematically prove to himself that he would not run from a battle.

Previously he had never felt obliged to wrestle too seriously with this question. In his life he had taken certain things for granted, never challenging his belief in ultimate success, and bothering little about means and roads. But here he was con-

fronted with a thing of moment. It had suddenly appeared to
him that perhaps in a battle he might run. He was forced to
admit that as far as war was concerned he knew nothing of
himself.

A sufficient time before he would have allowed the prob-
lem to kick its heels at the outer portals of his mind, but now
he felt compelled to give serious attention to it.

A little panic-fear grew in his mind. As his imagination
went forward to a fight, he saw hideous possibilities. He con-
templated the lurking menaces of the future, and failed in an
effort to see himself standing stoutly in the midst of them.
He recalled his visions of broken-bladed glory, but in the
shadow of the impending tumult he suspected them to be
impossible pictures.

He sprang from the bunk and began to pace nervously to
and fro. "Good Lord, what's th' matter with me?" he said
aloud.

He felt that in this crisis his laws of life were useless. What-
ever he had learned of himself was here of no avail. He was
an unknown quantity. He saw that he would again be obliged
to experiment as he had in early youth. He must accumulate
information of himself, and meanwhile he resolved to remain
close upon his guard lest those qualities of which he knew
nothing should everlastingly disgrace him. "Good Lord!" he
repeated in dismay.

After a time the tall soldier slid dexterously through the
hole. The loud private followed. They were wrangling.

"That's all right," said the tall soldier as he entered. He
waved his hand expressively. "You can believe me or not, jest
as you like. All you got to do is to sit down and wait as quiet
as you can. Then pretty soon you'll find out I was right."

His comrade grunted stubbornly. For a moment he seemed
to be searching for a formidable reply. Finally he said: "Well,
you don't know everything in the world, do you?"

"Didn't say I knew everything in the world," retorted the
other sharply. He began to stow various articles snugly into
his knapsack.

The youth, pausing in his nervous walk, looked down at
the busy figure. "Going to be a battle, sure, is there, Jim?" he
asked.

"Of course there is," replied the tall soldier. "Of course there is. You jest wait 'til to-morrow, and you'll see one of the biggest battles ever was. You jest wait."

"Thunder!" said the youth.

"Oh, you'll see fighting this time, my boy, what'll be regular out-and-out fighting," added the tall soldier, with the air of a man who is about to exhibit a battle for the benefit of his friends.

"Huh!" said the loud one from a corner.

"Well," remarked the youth, "like as not this story'll turn out jest like them others did."

"Not much it won't," replied the tall soldier, exasperated. "Not much it won't. Didn't the cavalry all start this morning?" He glared about him. No one denied his statement. "The cavalry started this morning," he continued. "They say there ain't hardly any cavalry left in camp. They're going to Richmond, or some place, while we fight all the Johnnies. It's some dodge like that. The regiment's got orders, too. A feller what seen 'em go to headquarters told me a little while ago. And they're raising blazes all over camp—anybody can see that."

"Shucks!" said the loud one.

The youth remained silent for a time. At last he spoke to the tall soldier. "Jim!"

"What?"

"How do you think the reg'ment 'll do?"

"Oh, they'll fight all right, I guess, after they once get into it," said the other with cold judgment. He made a fine use of the third person. "There's been heaps of fun poked at 'em because they're new, of course, and all that; but they'll fight all right, I guess."

"Think any of the boys 'll run?" persisted the youth.

"Oh, there may be a few of 'em run, but there's them kind in every regiment, 'specially when they first goes under fire," said the other in a tolerant way. "Of course it might happen that the hull kit-and-boodle might start and run, if some big fighting came first-off, and then again they might stay and fight like fun. But you can't bet on nothing. Of course they ain't never been under fire yet, and it ain't likely they'll lick the hull rebel army all-to-oncet the first time; but I think they'll fight better than some, if worse than others. That's the way I figger. They call the reg'ment 'Fresh fish' and everything; but the boys come of good stock, and most of 'em 'll fight like sin after they oncet git shootin'," he added, with a mighty emphasis on the last four words.

"Oh, you think you know——" began the loud soldier with scorn.

The other turned savagely upon him. They had a rapid altercation, in which they fastened upon each other various strange epithets.

The youth at last interrupted them. "Did you ever think you might run yourself, Jim?" he asked. On concluding the sentence he laughed as if he had meant to aim a joke. The loud soldier also giggled.

The tall private waved his hand. "Well," said he profoundly, "I've thought it might get too hot for Jim Conklin in some of them scrimmages, and if a whole lot of boys started and run, why, I s'pose I'd start and run. And if I once started to run, I'd run like the devil, and no mistake. But if everybody was a-standing and a-fighting, why, I'd stand and fight. Be jiminey, I would. I'll bet on it."

"Huh!" said the loud one.

The youth of this tale felt gratitude for these words of his comrade. He had feared that all of the untried men possessed a great and correct confidence. He now was in a measure reassured.

Chapter II

THE NEXT MORNING the youth discovered that his tall comrade had been the fast-flying messenger of a mistake. There was much scoffing at the latter by those who had yesterday been firm adherents of his views, and there was even a little sneering by men who had never believed the rumor. The tall one fought with a man from Chatfield Corners and beat him severely.

The youth felt, however, that his problem was in no wise lifted from him. There was, on the contrary, an irritating prolongation. The tale had created in him a great concern for himself. Now, with the newborn question in his mind, he was compelled to sink back into his old place as part of a blue demonstration.

For days he made ceaseless calculations, but they were all wondrously unsatisfactory. He found that he could establish nothing. He finally concluded that the only way to prove himself was to go into the blaze, and then figuratively to watch his legs to discover their merits and faults. He reluctantly admitted that he could not sit still and with a mental slate and pencil derive an answer. To gain it, he must have blaze, blood, and danger, even as a chemist requires this, that, and the other. So he fretted for an opportunity.

Meanwhile he continually tried to measure himself by his comrades. The tall soldier, for one, gave him some assurance. This man's serene unconcern dealt him a measure of confidence, for he had known him since childhood, and from his intimate knowledge he did not see how he could be capable of anything that was beyond him, the youth. Still, he thought that his comrade might be mistaken about himself. Or, on the other hand, he might be a man heretofore doomed to peace and obscurity, but, in reality, made to shine in war.

The youth would have liked to have discovered another who suspected himself. A sympathetic comparison of mental notes would have been a joy to him.

He occasionally tried to fathom a comrade with seductive sentences. He looked about to find men in the proper mood. All attempts failed to bring forth any statement which looked in any way like a confession to those doubts which he privately acknowledged in himself. He was afraid to make an open declaration of his concern, because he dreaded to place some unscrupulous confidant upon the high plane of the unconfessed from which elevation he could be derided.

In regard to his companions his mind wavered between two opinions, according to his mood. Sometimes he inclined to believing them all heroes. In fact, he usually admitted in secret the superior development of the higher qualities in others. He could conceive of men going very insignificantly about the world bearing a load of courage unseen, and although he had known many of his comrades through boyhood, he began to fear that his judgment of them had been blind. Then, in other moments, he flouted these theories, and assured himself that his fellows were all privately wondering and quaking.

His emotions made him feel strange in the presence of men who talked excitedly of a prospective battle as of a drama they were about to witness, with nothing but eagerness and curiosity apparent in their faces. It was often that he suspected them to be liars.

He did not pass such thoughts without severe condemnation of himself. He dinned reproaches at times. He was convicted by himself of many shameful crimes against the gods of traditions.

In his great anxiety his heart was continually clamoring at what he considered the intolerable slowness of the generals. They seemed content to perch tranquilly on the river bank, and leave him bowed down by the weight of a great problem. He wanted it settled forthwith. He could not long bear such a load, he said. Sometimes his anger at the commanders reached an acute stage, and he grumbled about the camp like a veteran.

One morning, however, he found himself in the ranks of his prepared regiment. The men were whispering speculations and recounting the old rumors. In the gloom before the break of the day their uniforms glowed a deep purple hue. From across the river the red eyes were still peering. In the eastern sky there was a yellow patch like a rug laid for the feet of the coming sun; and against it, black and patternlike, loomed the gigantic figure of the colonel on a gigantic horse.

From off in the darkness came the trampling of feet. The youth could occasionally see dark shadows that moved like monsters. The regiment stood at rest for what seemed a long time. The youth grew impatient. It was unendurable the way these affairs were managed. He wondered how long they were to be kept waiting.

As he looked all about him and pondered upon the mystic gloom, he began to believe that at any moment the ominous distance might be aflare, and the rolling crashes of an engagement come to his ears. Staring once at the red eyes across the river, he conceived them to be growing larger, as the orbs of a row of dragons advancing. He turned toward the colonel and saw him lift his gigantic arm and calmly stroke his mustache.

At last he heard from along the road at the foot of the hill the clatter of a horse's galloping hoofs. It must be the coming of orders. He bent forward, scarce breathing. The exciting clickety-click, as it grew louder and louder, seemed to be beating upon his soul. Presently a horseman with jangling equipment drew rein before the colonel of the regiment. The two held a short, sharp-worded conversation. The men in the foremost ranks craned their necks.

As the horseman wheeled his animal and galloped away he turned to shout over his shoulder, "Don't forget that box of cigars!" The colonel mumbled in reply. The youth wondered what a box of cigars had to do with war.

A moment later the regiment went swinging off into the darkness. It was now like one of those moving monsters wending with many feet. The air was heavy, and cold with dew. A mass of wet grass, marched upon, rustled like silk.

There was an occasional flash and glimmer of steel from the backs of all these huge crawling reptiles. From the road came creakings and grumblings as some surly guns were dragged away.

The men stumbled along still muttering speculations. There was a subdued debate. Once a man fell down, and as he reached for his rifle a comrade, unseeing, trod upon his hand.

He of the injured fingers swore bitterly and aloud. A low, tittering laugh went among his fellows.

Presently they passed into a roadway and marched forward with easy strides. A dark regiment moved before them, and from behind also came the tinkle of equipments on the bodies of marching men.

The rushing yellow of the developing day went on behind their backs. When the sunrays at last struck full and mellowingly upon the earth, the youth saw that the landscape was streaked with two long, thin, black columns which disappeared on the brow of a hill in front and rearward vanished in a wood. They were like two serpents crawling from the cavern of the night.

The river was not in view. The tall soldier burst into praises of what he thought to be his powers of perception.

Some of the tall one's companions cried with emphasis that they, too, had evolved the same thing, and they congratulated themselves upon it. But there were others who said that the tall one's plan was not the true one at all. They persisted with other theories. There was a vigorous discussion.

The youth took no part in them. As he walked along in careless line he was engaged with his own eternal debate. He could not hinder himself from dwelling upon it. He was despondent and sullen, and threw shifting glances about him. He looked ahead, often expecting to hear from the advance the rattle of firing.

But the long serpents crawled slowly from hill to hill without bluster of smoke. A dun-colored cloud of dust floated away to the right. The sky overhead was of a fairy blue.

The youth studied the faces of his companions, ever on the watch to detect kindred emotions. He suffered disappointment. Some ardor of the air which was causing the veteran commands to move with glee—almost with song—had infected the new regiment. The men began to speak of victory as of a thing they knew. Also, the tall soldier received his vindication. They were certainly going to come around in behind the enemy. They expressed commiseration for that part of the army which had been left upon the river bank, felicitating themselves upon being a part of a blasting host.

The youth, considering himself as separated from the

others, was saddened by the blithe and merry speeches that went from rank to rank. The company wags all made their best endeavors. The regiment tramped to the tune of laughter.

The blatant soldier often convulsed whole files by his biting sarcasms aimed at the tall one.

And it was not long before all the men seemed to forget their mission. Whole brigades grinned in unison, and regiments laughed.

A rather fat soldier attempted to pilfer a horse from a dooryard. He planned to load his knapsack upon it. He was escaping with his prize when a young girl rushed from the house and grabbed the animal's mane. There followed a wrangle. The young girl, with pink cheeks and shining eyes, stood like a dauntless statue.

The observant regiment, standing at rest in the roadway, whooped at once, and entered whole-souled upon the side of the maiden. The men became so engrossed in this affair that they entirely ceased to remember their own large war. They jeered the piratical private, and called attention to various defects in his personal appearance; and they were wildly enthusiastic in support of the young girl.

To her, from some distance, came bold advice. "Hit him with a stick."

There were crows and catcalls showered upon him when he retreated without the horse. The regiment rejoiced at his downfall. Loud and vociferous congratulations were showered upon the maiden, who stood panting and regarding the troops with defiance.

At nightfall the column broke into regimental pieces, and the fragments went into the fields to camp. Tents sprang up like strange plants. Camp fires, like red, peculiar blossoms, dotted the night.

The youth kept from intercourse with his companions as much as circumstances would allow him. In the evening he wandered a few paces into the gloom. From this little distance the many fires, with the black forms of men passing to and fro before the crimson rays, made weird and satanic effects.

He lay down in the grass. The blades pressed tenderly against his cheek. The moon had been lighted and was hung in a treetop. The liquid stillness of the night enveloping him made him feel vast pity for himself. There was a caress in the soft winds; and the whole mood of the darkness, he thought, was one of sympathy for himself in his distress.

He wished, without reserve, that he was at home again making the endless rounds from the house to the barn, from the barn to the fields, from the fields to the barn, from the barn to the house. He remembered he had often cursed the brindle cow and her mates, and had sometimes flung milking stools. But, from his present point of view, there was a halo of happiness about each of their heads, and he would have sacrificed all the brass buttons on the continent to have been enabled to return to them. He told himself that he was not formed for a soldier. And he mused seriously upon the radical differences between himself and those men who were dodging implike around the fires.

As he mused thus he heard the rustle of grass, and, upon turning his head, discovered the loud soldier. He called out, "Oh, Wilson!"

The latter approached and looked down. "Why, hello, Henry; is it you? What you doing here?"

"Oh, thinking," said the youth.

The other sat down and carefully lighted his pipe. "You're getting blue, my boy. You're looking thundering peek-ed. What the dickens is wrong with you?"

"Oh, nothing," said the youth.

The loud soldier launched then into the subject of the anticipated fight. "Oh, we've got 'em now!" As he spoke his boyish face was wreathed in a gleeful smile, and his voice had an exultant ring. "We've got 'em now. At last, by the eternal thunders, we'll lick 'em good!"

"If the truth was known," he added, more soberly, "*they've* licked *us* about every clip up to now; but this time—this time—we'll lick 'em good!"

"I thought you was objecting to this march a little while ago," said the youth coldly.

"Oh, it wasn't that," explained the other. "I don't mind marching, if there's going to be fighting at the end of it. What I hate is this getting moved here and moved there, with no good coming of it, as far as I can see, excepting sore feet and damned short rations."

"Well, Jim Conklin says we'll get a plenty of fighting this time."

"He's right for once, I guess, though I can't see how it come. This time we're in for a big battle, and we've got the best end of it, certain sure. Gee rod! how we will thump 'em!"

He arose and began to pace to and fro excitedly. The thrill of his enthusiasm made him walk with an elastic step. He was sprightly, vigorous, fiery in his belief in success. He looked into the future with clear, proud eye, and he swore with the air of an old soldier.

The youth watched him for a moment in silence. When he finally spoke his voice was as bitter as dregs. "Oh, you're going to do great things, I s'pose!"

The loud soldier blew a thoughtful cloud of smoke from his pipe. "Oh, I don't know," he remarked with dignity; "I don't know. I s'pose I'll do as well as the rest. I'm going to try like thunder." He evidently complimented himself upon the modesty of this statement.

"How do you know you won't run when the time comes?" asked the youth.

"Run?" said the loud one; "run?—of course not!" He laughed.

"Well," continued the youth, "lots of good-a-'nough men have thought they was going to do great things before the fight, but when the time come they skedaddled."

"Oh, that's all true, I s'pose," replied the other; "but I'm not going to skedaddle. The man that bets on my running will lose his money, that's all." He nodded confidently.

"Oh, shucks!" said the youth. "You ain't the bravest man in the world, are you?"

"No, I ain't," exclaimed the loud soldier indignantly; "and I didn't say I was the bravest man in the world, neither. I said I was going to do my share of fighting—that's what I said. And I am, too. Who are you, anyhow? You talk as if you thought you was Napoleon Bonaparte." He glared at the youth for a moment, and then strode away.

The youth called in a savage voice after his comrade: "Well, you needn't git mad about it!" But the other continued on his way and made no reply.

He felt alone in space when his injured comrade had disappeared. His failure to discover any mite of resemblance in their view points made him more miserable than before. No one seemed to be wrestling with such a terrific personal problem. He was a mental outcast.

He went slowly to his tent and stretched himself on a blanket by the side of the snoring tall soldier. In the darkness he saw visions of a thousand-tongued fear that would babble at his back and cause him to flee, while others were going coolly about their country's business. He admitted that he would not be able to cope with this monster. He felt that every nerve in his body would be an ear to hear the voices, while other men would remain stolid and deaf.

And as he sweated with the pain of these thoughts, he could hear low, serene sentences. "I'll bid five." "Make it six." "Seven." "Seven goes."

He stared at the red, shivering reflection of a fire on the white wall of his tent until, exhausted and ill from the monotony of his suffering, he fell asleep.

Chapter III

WHEN ANOTHER NIGHT CAME the columns, changed to purple streaks, filed across two pontoon bridges. A glaring fire wine-tinted the waters of the river. Its rays, shining upon the moving masses of troops, brought forth here and there sudden gleams of silver or gold. Upon the other shore a dark and mysterious range of hills was curved against the sky. The insect voices of the night sang solemnly.

After this crossing the youth assured himself that at any moment they might be suddenly and fearfully assaulted from the caves of the lowering woods. He kept his eyes watchfully upon the darkness.

But his regiment went unmolested to a camping place, and its soldiers slept the brave sleep of wearied men. In the morning they were routed out with early energy, and hustled along a narrow road that led deep into the forest.

It was during this rapid march that the regiment lost many of the marks of a new command.

The men had begun to count the miles upon their fingers, and they grew tired. "Sore feet an' damned short rations, that's all," said the loud soldier. There was perspiration and grumblings. After a time they began to shed their knapsacks. Some tossed them unconcernedly down; others hid them carefully, asserting their plans to return for them at some convenient time. Men extricated themselves from thick shirts. Presently few carried anything but their necessary clothing, blankets, haversacks, canteens, and arms and ammunition. "You can now eat and shoot," said the tall soldier to the youth. "That's all you want to do."

There was sudden change from the ponderous infantry of theory to the light and speedy infantry of practice. The regiment, relieved of a burden, received a new impetus. But there was much loss of valuable knapsacks, and, on the whole, very good shirts.

But the regiment was not yet veteranlike in appearance. Veteran regiments in the army were likely to be very small aggregations of men. Once, when the command had first come to the field, some perambulating veterans, noting the length of their column, had accosted them thus: "Hey, fellers, what brigade is that?" And when the men had replied that they formed a regiment and not a brigade, the older soldiers had laughed, and said, "O Gawd!"

Also, there was too great a similarity in the hats. The hats of a regiment should properly represent the history of head-gear for a period of years. And, moreover, there were no letters of faded gold speaking from the colors. They were new and beautiful, and the color bearer habitually oiled the pole.

Presently the army again sat down to think. The odor of the peaceful pines was in the men's nostrils. The sound of monotonous axe blows rang through the forest, and the insects, nodding upon their perches, crooned like old women. The youth returned to his theory of a blue demonstration.

One gray dawn, however, he was kicked in the leg by the tall soldier, and then, before he was entirely awake, he found himself running down a wood road in the midst of men who were panting from the first effects of speed. His canteen banged rhythmically upon his thigh, and his haversack bobbed softly. His musket bounced a trifle from his shoulder at each stride and made his cap feel uncertain upon his head.

He could hear the men whisper jerky sentences: "Say— what's all this—about?" "What th' thunder—we—skedad-dlin' this way fer?" "Billie—keep off m' feet. Yeh run—like a cow." And the loud soldier's shrill voice could be heard: "What th' devil they in sich a hurry for?"

The youth thought the damp fog of early morning moved from the rush of a great body of troops. From the distance came a sudden spatter of firing.

He was bewildered. As he ran with his comrades he strenuously tried to think, but all he knew was that if he fell down those coming behind would tread upon him. All his faculties seemed to be needed to guide him over and past obstructions. He felt carried along by a mob.

The sun spread disclosing rays, and, one by one, regiments burst into view like armed men just born of the earth. The youth perceived that the time had come. He was about to be measured. For a moment he felt in the face of his great trial like a babe, and the flesh over his heart seemed very thin. He seized time to look about him calculatingly.

But he instantly saw that it would be impossible for him to escape from the regiment. It inclosed him. And there were iron laws of tradition and law on four sides. He was in a moving box.

As he perceived this fact it occurred to him that he had never wished to come to the war. He had not enlisted of his free will. He had been dragged by the merciless government. And now they were taking him out to be slaughtered.

The regiment slid down a bank and wallowed across a little stream. The mournful current moved slowly on, and from the water, shaded black, some white bubble eyes looked at the men.

As they climbed the hill on the farther side artillery began to boom. Here the youth forgot many things as he felt a sudden impulse of curiosity. He scrambled up the bank with a speed that could not be exceeded by a bloodthirsty man.

He expected a battle scene.

There were some little fields girted and squeezed by a forest. Spread over the grass and in among the tree trunks, he could see knots and waving lines of skirmishers who were running hither and thither and firing at the landscape. A dark battle line lay upon a sunstruck clearing that gleamed orange color. A flag fluttered.

Other regiments floundered up the bank. The brigade was formed in line of battle, and after a pause started slowly through the woods in the rear of the receding skirmishers, who were continually melting into the scene to appear again farther on. They were always busy as bees, deeply absorbed in their little combats.

The youth tried to observe everything. He did not use care to avoid trees and branches, and his forgotten feet were constantly knocking against stones or getting entangled in briers. He was aware that these battalions with their commotions were woven red and startling into the gentle fabric of softened greens and browns. It looked to be a wrong place for a battle field.

The skirmishers in advance fascinated him. Their shots into thickets and at distant and prominent trees spoke to him of tragedies—hidden, mysterious, solemn.

Once the line encountered the body of a dead soldier. He

lay upon his back staring at the sky. He was dressed in an awkward suit of yellowish brown. The youth could see that the soles of his shoes had been worn to the thinness of writing paper, and from a great rent in one the dead foot projected piteously. And it was as if fate had betrayed the soldier. In death it exposed to his enemies that poverty which in life he had perhaps concealed from his friends.

The ranks opened covertly to avoid the corpse. The invulnerable dead man forced a way for himself. The youth looked keenly at the ashen face. The wind raised the tawny beard. It moved as if a hand were stroking it. He vaguely desired to walk around and around the body and stare; the impulse of the living to try to read in dead eyes the answer to the Question.

During the march the ardor which the youth had acquired when out of view of the field rapidly faded to nothing. His curiosity was quite easily satisfied. If an intense scene had caught him with its wild swing as he came to the top of the bank, he might have gone roaring on. This advance upon Nature was too calm. He had opportunity to reflect. He had time in which to wonder about himself and to attempt to probe his sensations.

Absurd ideas took hold upon him. He thought that he did not relish the landscape. It threatened him. A coldness swept over his back, and it is true that his trousers felt to him that they were no fit for his legs at all.

A house standing placidly in distant fields had to him an ominous look. The shadows of the woods were formidable. He was certain that in this vista there lurked fierce-eyed hosts. The swift thought came to him that the generals did not know what they were about. It was all a trap. Suddenly those close forests would bristle with rifle barrels. Ironlike brigades would appear in the rear. They were all going to be sacrificed. The generals were stupids. The enemy would presently swallow the whole command. He glared about him, expecting to see the stealthy approach of his death.

He thought that he must break from the ranks and harangue his comrades. They must not all be killed like pigs; and he was sure it would come to pass unless they were informed of these dangers. The generals were idiots to send them marching into a regular pen. There was but one pair of eyes in the corps. He would step forth and make a speech. Shrill and passionate words came to his lips.

The line, broken into moving fragments by the ground, went calmly on through fields and woods. The youth looked at the men nearest him, and saw, for the most part, expressions of deep interest, as if they were investigating something that had fascinated them. One or two stepped with over-valiant airs as if they were already plunged into war. Others walked as upon thin ice. The greater part of the untested men appeared quiet and absorbed. They were going to look at war, the red animal—war, the blood-swollen god. And they were deeply engrossed in this march.

As he looked the youth gripped his outcry at his throat. He saw that even if the men were tottering with fear they would laugh at his warning. They would jeer him, and, if practicable, pelt him with missiles. Admitting that he might be wrong, a frenzied declamation of the kind would turn him into a worm.

He assumed, then, the demeanor of one who knows that he is doomed alone to unwritten responsibilities. He lagged, with tragic glances at the sky.

He was surprised presently by the young lieutenant of his company, who began heartily to beat him with a sword, calling out in a loud and insolent voice: "Come, young man, get up into ranks there. No skulking 'll do here." He mended his pace with suitable haste. And he hated the lieutenant, who had no appreciation of fine minds. He was a mere brute.

After a time the brigade was halted in the cathedral light of a forest. The busy skirmishers were still popping. Through the aisles of the wood could be seen the floating smoke from their rifles. Sometimes it went up in little balls, white and compact.

During this halt many men in the regiment began erecting tiny hills in front of them. They used stones, sticks, earth, and anything they thought might turn a bullet. Some built comparatively large ones, while others seemed content with little ones.

This procedure caused a discussion among the men. Some wished to fight like duelists, believing it to be correct to stand erect and be, from their feet to their foreheads, a mark. They said they scorned the devices of the cautious. But the others scoffed in reply, and pointed to the veterans on the flanks who were digging at the ground like terriers. In a short time there was quite a barricade along the regimental fronts. Directly, however, they were ordered to withdraw from that place.

This astounded the youth. He forgot his stewing over the advance movement. "Well, then, what did they march us out here for?" he demanded of the tall soldier. The latter with calm faith began a heavy explanation, although he had been compelled to leave a little protection of stones and dirt to which he had devoted much care and skill.

When the regiment was aligned in another position each man's regard for his safety caused another line of small intrenchments. They ate their noon meal behind a third one. They were moved from this one also. They were marched from place to place with apparent aimlessness.

The youth had been taught that a man became another thing in a battle. He saw his salvation in such a change. Hence this waiting was an ordeal to him. He was in a fever of impatience. He considered that there was denoted a lack of purpose on the part of the generals. He began to complain to the tall soldier. "I can't stand this much longer," he cried. "I don't see what good it does to make us wear out our legs for nothin'." He wished to return to camp, knowing that this affair was a blue demonstration; or else to go into a battle and discover that he had been a fool in his doubts, and was, in truth, a man of traditional courage. The strain of present circumstances he felt to be intolerable.

The philosophical tall soldier measured a sandwich of cracker and pork and swallowed it in a nonchalant manner. "Oh, I suppose we must go reconnoitering around the country jest to keep 'em from getting too close, or to develop 'em, or something."

"Huh!" said the loud soldier.

"Well," cried the youth, still fidgeting, "I'd rather do anything 'most than go tramping 'round the country all day doing no good to nobody and jest tiring ourselves out."

"So would I," said the loud soldier. "It ain't right. I tell

you if anybody with any sense was a-runnin' this army
it——"

"Oh, shut up!" roared the tall private. "You little fool. You
little damn' cuss. You ain't had that there coat and them pants
on for six months, and yet you talk as if——"

"Well, I wanta do some fighting anyway," interrupted the
other. "I didn't come here to walk. I could 'ave walked to
home—'round an' 'round the barn, if I jest wanted to walk."

The tall one, red-faced, swallowed another sandwich as if
taking poison in despair.

But gradually, as he chewed, his face became again quiet
and contented. He could not rage in fierce argument in the
presence of such sandwiches. During his meals he always
wore an air of blissful contemplation of the food he had swal-
lowed. His spirit seemed then to be communing with the
viands.

He accepted new environment and circumstance with great
coolness, eating from his haversack at every opportunity. On
the march he went along with the stride of a hunter, object-
ing to neither gait nor distance. And he had not raised his
voice when he had been ordered away from three little pro-
tective piles of earth and stone, each of which had been an
engineering feat worthy of being made sacred to the name of
his grandmother.

In the afternoon the regiment went out over the same
ground it had taken in the morning. The landscape then
ceased to threaten the youth. He had been close to it and
become familiar with it.

When, however, they began to pass into a new region, his
old fears of stupidity and incompetence reassailed him, but
this time he doggedly let them babble. He was occupied with
his problem, and in his desperation he concluded that the stu-
pidity did not greatly matter.

Once he thought he had concluded that it would be better
to get killed directly and end his troubles. Regarding death
thus out of the corner of his eye, he conceived it to be noth-
ing but rest, and he was filled with a momentary astonish-
ment that he should have made an extraordinary commotion
over the mere matter of getting killed. He would die; he
would go to some place where he would be understood. It

was useless to expect appreciation of his profound and fine senses from such men as the lieutenant. He must look to the grave for comprehension.

The skirmish fire increased to a long clattering sound. With it was mingled far-away cheering. A battery spoke.

Directly the youth could see the skirmishers running. They were pursued by the sound of musketry fire. After a time the hot, dangerous flashes of the rifles were visible. Smoke clouds went slowly and insolently across the fields like observant phantoms. The din became crescendo, like the roar of an on-coming train.

A brigade ahead of them and on the right went into action with a rending roar. It was as if it had exploded. And there-after it lay stretched in the distance behind a long gray wall, that one was obliged to look twice at to make sure that it was smoke.

The youth, forgetting his neat plan of getting killed, gazed spell bound. His eyes grew wide and busy with the action of the scene. His mouth was a little ways open.

Of a sudden he felt a heavy and sad hand laid upon his shoulder. Awakening from his trance of observation he turned and beheld the loud soldier.

"It's my first and last battle, old boy," said the latter, with intense gloom. He was quite pale and his girlish lip was trembling.

"Eh?" murmured the youth in great astonishment.

"It's my first and last battle, old boy," continued the loud soldier. "Something tells me——"

"What?"

"I'm a gone coon this first time and—and I w-want you to take these here things—to—my—folks." He ended in a qua-vering sob of pity for himself. He handed the youth a little packet done up in a yellow envelope.

"Why, what the devil——" began the youth again.

But the other gave him a glance as from the depths of a tomb, and raised his limp hand in a prophetic manner and turned away.

Chapter IV

THE BRIGADE was halted in the fringe of a grove. The men crouched among the trees and pointed their restless guns out at the fields. They tried to look beyond the smoke.

Out of this haze they could see running men. Some shouted information and gestured as they hurried.

The men of the new regiment watched and listened eagerly, while their tongues ran on in gossip of the battle. They mouthed rumors that had flown like birds out of the unknown.

"They say Perry has been driven in with big loss."

"Yes, Carrott went t' th' hospital. He said he was sick. That smart lieutenant is commanding 'G' Company. Th' boys say they won't be under Carrott no more if they all have t' desert. They allus knew he was a——"

"Hannises' batt'ry is took."

"It ain't either. I saw Hannises' batt'ry off on th' left not more'n fifteen minutes ago."

"Well——"

"Th' general, he ses he is goin' t' take th' hull cammand of th' 304th when we go inteh action, an' then he ses we'll do sech fightin' as never another one reg'ment done."

"They say we're catchin' it over on th' left. They say th' enemy driv' our line inteh a devil of a swamp an' took Hannises' batt'ry."

"No sech thing. Hannises' batt'ry was 'long here 'bout a minute ago."

"That young Hasbrouck, he makes a good off'cer. He ain't afraid 'a nothin'."

"I met one of th' 148th Maine boys an' he ses his brigade fit th' hull rebel army fer four hours over on th' turnpike road an' killed about five thousand of 'em. He ses one more sech fight as that an' th' war 'll be over."

"Bill wasn't scared either. No, sir! It wasn't that. Bill ain't a-gittin' scared easy. He was jest mad, that's what he was. When that feller trod on his hand, he up an' sed that he was willin' t' give his hand t' his country, but he be dumbed if he was goin' t' have every dumb bushwhacker in th' kentry walkin' 'round on it. So he went t' th' hospital disregardless of th' fight. Three fingers was crunched. Th' dern doctor wanted t' amputate 'm, an' Bill, he raised a heluva row, I hear. He's a funny feller."

The din in front swelled to a tremendous chorus. The youth and his fellows were frozen to silence. They could see a flag that tossed in the smoke angrily. Near it were the blurred and agitated forms of troops. There came a turbulent stream of men across the fields. A battery changing position at a frantic gallop scattered the stragglers right and left.

A shell screaming like a storm banshee went over the huddled heads of the reserves. It landed in the grove, and exploding redly flung the brown earth. There was a little shower of pine needles.

Bullets began to whistle among the branches and nip at the trees. Twigs and leaves came sailing down. It was as if a thousand axes, wee and invisible, were being wielded. Many of the men were constantly dodging and ducking their heads.

The lieutenant of the youth's company was shot in the hand. He began to swear so wondrously that a nervous laugh went along the regimental line. The officer's profanity sounded conventional. It relieved the tightened senses of the new men. It was as if he had hit his fingers with a tack hammer at home.

He held the wounded member carefully away from his side so that the blood would not drip upon his trousers.

The captain of the company, tucking his sword under his arm, produced a handkerchief and began to bind with it the lieutenant's wound. And they disputed as to how the binding should be done.

The battle flag in the distance jerked about madly. It seemed to be struggling to free itself from an agony. The billowing smoke was filled with horizontal flashes.

Men running swiftly emerged from it. They grew in numbers until it was seen that the whole command was fleeing. The flag suddenly sank down as if dying. Its motion as it fell was a gesture of despair.

Wild yells came from behind the walls of smoke. A sketch in gray and red dissolved into a moblike body of men who galloped like wild horses.

The veteran regiments on the right and left of the 304th immediately began to jeer. With the passionate song of the bullets and the banshee shrieks of shells were mingled loud catcalls and bits of facetious advice concerning places of safety.

But the new regiment was breathless with horror. "Gawd! Saunders's got crushed!" whispered the man at the youth's elbow. They shrank back and crouched as if compelled to await a flood.

The youth shot a swift glance along the blue ranks of the regiment. The profiles were motionless, carven; and afterward he remembered that the color sergeant was standing with his legs apart, as if he expected to be pushed to the ground.

The following throng went whirling around the flank. Here and there were officers carried along on the stream like exasperated chips. They were striking about them with their swords and with their left fists, punching every head they could reach. They cursed like highwaymen.

A mounted officer displayed the furious anger of a spoiled child. He raged with his head, his arms, and his legs.

Another, the commander of the brigade, was galloping about bawling. His hat was gone and his clothes were awry. He resembled a man who has come from bed to go to a fire. The hoofs of his horse often threatened the heads of the running men, but they scampered with singular fortune. In this rush they were apparently all deaf and blind. They heeded not the largest and longest of the oaths that were thrown at them from all directions.

Frequently over this tumult could be heard the grim jokes of the critical veterans; but the retreating men apparently were not even conscious of the presence of an audience.

The battle reflection that shone for an instant in the faces on the mad current made the youth feel that forceful hands from heaven would not have been able to have held him in place if he could have got intelligent control of his legs.

There was an appalling imprint upon these faces. The struggle in the smoke had pictured an exaggeration of itself on the bleached cheeks and in the eyes wild with one desire.

The sight of this stampede exerted a floodlike force that seemed able to drag sticks and stones and men from the ground. They of the reserves had to hold on. They grew pale and firm, and red and quaking.

The youth achieved one little thought in the midst of this chaos. The composite monster which had caused the other troops to flee had not then appeared. He resolved to get a view of it, and then, he thought he might very likely run better than the best of them.

Chapter V

THERE WERE moments of waiting. The youth thought of the village street at home before the arrival of the circus parade on a day in the spring. He remembered how he had stood, a small, thrillful boy, prepared to follow the dingy lady upon the white horse, or the band in its faded chariot. He saw the yellow road, the lines of expectant people, and the sober houses. He particularly remembered an old fellow who used to sit upon a cracker box in front of the store and feign to despise such exhibitions. A thousand details of color and form surged in his mind. The old fellow upon the cracker box appeared in middle prominence.

Some one cried, "Here they come!"

There was rustling and muttering among the men. They displayed a feverish desire to have every possible cartridge ready to their hands. The boxes were pulled around into various positions, and adjusted with great care. It was as if seven hundred new bonnets were being tried on.

The tall soldier, having prepared his rifle, produced a red handkerchief of some kind. He was engaged in knotting it about his throat with exquisite attention to its position, when the cry was repeated up and down the line in a muffled roar of sound.

"Here they come! Here they come!" Gun locks clicked.

Across the smoke-infested fields came a brown swarm of running men who were giving shrill yells. They came on, stooping and swinging their rifles at all angles. A flag, tilted forward, sped near the front.

As he caught sight of them the youth was momentarily startled by a thought that perhaps his gun was not loaded. He stood trying to rally his faltering intellect so that he might recollect the moment when he had loaded, but he could not.

A hatless general pulled his dripping horse to a stand near the colonel of the 304th. He shook his fist in the other's face. "You 've got to hold 'em back!" he shouted, savagely; "you 've got to hold 'em back!"

In his agitation the colonel began to stammer. "A-all r-right, General, all right, by Gawd! We-we 'll do our—we-

we 'll d-d-do—do our best, General." The general made a passionate gesture and galloped away. The colonel, perchance to relieve his feelings, began to scold like a wet parrot. The youth, turning swiftly to make sure that the rear was unmolested, saw the commander regarding his men in a highly resentful manner, as if he regretted above everything his association with them.

The man at the youth's elbow was mumbling, as if to himself: "Oh, we 're in for it now! oh, we 're in for it now!"

The captain of the company had been pacing excitedly to and fro in the rear. He coaxed in schoolmistress fashion, as to a congregation of boys with primers. His talk was an endless repetition. "Reserve your fire, boys—don't shoot till I tell you—save your fire—wait till they get close up—don't be damned fools——"

Perspiration streamed down the youth's face, which was soiled like that of a weeping urchin. He frequently, with a nervous movement, wiped his eyes with his coat sleeve. His mouth was still a little ways open.

He got the one glance at the foe-swarming field in front of him, and instantly ceased to debate the question of his piece being loaded. Before he was ready to begin—before he had announced to himself that he was about to fight—he threw the obedient, well-balanced rifle into position and fired a first wild shot. Directly he was working at his weapon like an automatic affair.

He suddenly lost concern for himself, and forgot to look at a menacing fate. He became not a man but a member. He felt that something of which he was a part—a regiment, an army, a cause, or a country—was in a crisis. He was welded into a common personality which was dominated by a single desire. For some moments he could not flee no more than a little finger can commit a revolution from a hand.

If he had thought the regiment was about to be annihilated perhaps he could have amputated himself from it. But its noise gave him assurance. The regiment was like a firework that, once ignited, proceeds superior to circumstances until its blazing vitality fades. It wheezed and banged with a mighty power. He pictured the ground before it as strewn with the discomfited.

There was a consciousness always of the presence of his comrades about him. He felt the subtle battle brotherhood more potent even than the cause for which they were fighting. It was a mysterious fraternity born of the smoke and danger of death.

He was at a task. He was like a carpenter who has made many boxes, making still another box, only there was furious haste in his movements. He, in his thought, was careering off in other places, even as the carpenter who as he works whistles and thinks of his friend or his enemy, his home or a saloon. And these jolted dreams were never perfect to him afterward, but remained a mass of blurred shapes.

Presently he began to feel the effects of the war atmosphere—a blistering sweat, a sensation that his eyeballs were about to crack like hot stones. A burning roar filled his ears.

Following this came a red rage. He developed the acute exasperation of a pestered animal, a well-meaning cow worried by dogs. He had a mad feeling against his rifle, which could only be used against one life at a time. He wished to rush forward and strangle with his fingers. He craved a power that would enable him to make a world-sweeping gesture and brush all back. His impotency appeared to him, and made his rage into that of a driven beast.

Buried in the smoke of many rifles his anger was directed not so much against the men whom he knew were rushing toward him as against the swirling battle phantoms which were choking him, stuffing their smoke robes down his parched throat. He fought frantically for respite for his senses, for air, as a babe being smothered attacks the deadly blankets.

There was a blare of heated rage mingled with a certain expression of intentness on all faces. Many of the men were making low-toned noises with their mouths, and these subdued cheers, snarls, imprecations, prayers, made a wild, barbaric song that went as an undercurrent of sound, strange and chantlike with the resounding chords of the war march. The man at the youth's elbow was babbling. In it there was something soft and tender like the monologue of a babe. The tall soldier was swearing in a loud voice. From his lips came a black procession of curious oaths. Of a sudden another broke out in a querulous way like a man who has mislaid his hat.

"Well, why don't they support us? Why don't they send sup-
ports? Do they think——"

The youth in his battle sleep heard this as one who dozes
hears.

There was a singular absence of heroic poses. The men
bending and surging in their haste and rage were in every
impossible attitude. The steel ramrods clanked and clanged
with incessant din as the men pounded them furiously into
the hot rifle barrels. The flaps of the cartridge boxes were all
unfastened, and bobbed idiotically with each movement. The
rifles, once loaded, were jerked to the shoulder and fired with-
out apparent aim into the smoke or at one of the blurred and
shifting forms which upon the field before the regiment had
been growing larger and larger like puppets under a magi-
cian's hand.

The officers, at their intervals, rearward, neglected to stand
in picturesque attitudes. They were bobbing to and fro roar-
ing directions and encouragements. The dimensions of their
howls were extraordinary. They expended their lungs with
prodigal wills. And often they nearly stood upon their heads
in their anxiety to observe the enemy on the other side of the
tumbling smoke.

The lieutenant of the youth's company had encountered a
soldier who had fled screaming at the first volley of his com-
rades. Behind the lines these two were acting a little isolated
scene. The man was blubbering and staring with sheeplike
eyes at the lieutenant, who had seized him by the collar and
was pommeling him. He drove him back into the ranks with
many blows. The soldier went mechanically, dully, with his
animal-like eyes upon the officer. Perhaps there was to him a
divinity expressed in the voice of the other—stern, hard, with
no reflection of fear in it. He tried to reload his gun, but his
shaking hands prevented. The lieutenant was obliged to assist
him.

The men dropped here and there like bundles. The captain
of the youth's company had been killed in an early part of the
action. His body lay stretched out in the position of a tired
man resting, but upon his face there was an astonished and
sorrowful look, as if he thought some friend had done him
an ill turn. The babbling man was grazed by a shot that made

the blood stream widely down his face. He clapped both hands to his head. "Oh!" he said, and ran. Another grunted suddenly as if he had been struck by a club in the stomach. He sat down and gazed ruefully. In his eyes there was mute, indefinite reproach. Farther up the line a man, standing behind a tree, had had his knee joint splintered by a ball. Immediately he had dropped his rifle and gripped the tree with both arms. And there he remained, clinging desperately and crying for assistance that he might withdraw his hold upon the tree.

At last an exultant yell went along the quivering line. The firing dwindled from an uproar to a last vindictive popping. As the smoke slowly eddied away, the youth saw that the charge had been repulsed. The enemy were scattered into reluctant groups. He saw a man climb to the top of the fence, straddle the rail, and fire a parting shot. The waves had receded, leaving bits of dark *débris* upon the ground.

Some in the regiment began to whoop frenziedly. Many were silent. Apparently they were trying to contemplate themselves.

After the fever had left his veins, the youth thought that at last he was going to suffocate. He became aware of the foul atmosphere in which he had been struggling. He was grimy and dripping like a laborer in a foundry. He grasped his canteen and took a long swallow of the warmed water.

A sentence with variations went up and down the line. "Well, we 've helt 'em back. We 've helt 'em back; derned if we haven't." The men said it blissfully, leering at each other with dirty smiles.

The youth turned to look behind him and off to the right and off to the left. He experienced the joy of a man who at last finds leisure in which to look about him.

Under foot there were a few ghastly forms motionless. They lay twisted in fantastic contortions. Arms were bent and heads were turned in incredible ways. It seemed that the dead men must have fallen from some great height to get into such positions. They looked to be dumped out upon the ground from the sky.

From a position in the rear of the grove a battery was throwing shells over it. The flash of the guns startled the youth at first. He thought they were aimed directly at him. Through the trees he watched the black figures of the gunners as they worked swiftly and intently. Their labor seemed a complicated thing. He wondered how they could remember its formula in the midst of confusion.

The guns squatted in a row like savage chiefs. They argued with abrupt violence. It was a grim pow-wow. Their busy servants ran hither and thither.

A small procession of wounded men were going drearily toward the rear. It was a flow of blood from the torn body of the brigade.

To the right and to the left were the dark lines of other troops. Far in front he thought he could see lighter masses protruding in points from the forest. They were suggestive of unnumbered thousands.

Once he saw a tiny battery go dashing along the line of the horizon. The tiny riders were beating the tiny horses.

From a sloping hill came the sound of cheerings and clashes. Smoke welled slowly through the leaves.

Batteries were speaking with thunderous oratorical effort. Here and there were flags, the red in the stripes dominating. They splashed bits of warm color upon the dark lines of troops.

The youth felt the old thrill at the sight of the emblems. They were like beautiful birds strangely undaunted in a storm.

As he listened to the din from the hillside, to a deep pulsating thunder that came from afar to the left, and to the lesser clamors which came from many directions, it occurred to him that they were fighting, too, over there, and over there, and over there. Heretofore he had supposed that all the battle was directly under his nose.

As he gazed around him the youth felt a flash of astonishment at the blue, pure sky and the sun gleamings on the trees and fields. It was surprising that Nature had gone tranquilly on with her golden process in the midst of so much devilment.

Chapter VI

THE YOUTH awakened slowly. He came gradually back to a position from which he could regard himself. For moments he had been scrutinizing his person in a dazed way as if he had never before seen himself. Then he picked up his cap from the ground. He wriggled in his jacket to make a more comfortable fit, and kneeling relaced his shoe. He thoughtfully mopped his reeking features.

So it was all over at last! The supreme trial had been passed. The red, formidable difficulties of war had been vanquished.

He went into an ecstasy of self-satisfaction. He had the most delightful sensations of his life. Standing as if apart from himself, he viewed that last scene. He perceived that the man who had fought thus was magnificent.

He felt that he was a fine fellow. He saw himself even with those ideals which he had considered as far beyond him. He smiled in deep gratification.

Upon his fellows he beamed tenderness and good will. "Gee! ain't it hot, hey?" he said affably to a man who was polishing his streaming face with his coat sleeves.

"You bet!" said the other, grinning sociably. "I never seen sech dumb hotness." He sprawled out luxuriously on the ground. "Gee, yes! An' I hope we don't have no more fightin' till a week from Monday."

There were some handshakings and deep speeches with men whose features were familiar, but with whom the youth now felt the bonds of tied hearts. He helped a cursing comrade to bind up a wound of the shin.

But, of a sudden, cries of amazement broke out along the ranks of the new regiment. "Here they come ag'in! Here they come ag'in!" The man who had sprawled upon the ground started up and said, "Gosh!"

The youth turned quick eyes upon the field. He discerned forms begin to swell in masses out of a distant wood. He again saw the tilted flag speeding forward.

The shells, which had ceased to trouble the regiment for a time, came swirling again, and exploded in the grass or among the leaves of the trees. They looked to be strange war flowers bursting into fierce bloom.

The men groaned. The luster faded from their eyes. Their smudged countenances now expressed a profound dejection. They moved their stiffened bodies slowly, and watched in sullen mood the frantic approach of the enemy. The slaves toiling in the temple of this god began to feel rebellion at his harsh tasks.

They fretted and complained each to each. "Oh, say, this is too much of a good thing! Why can't somebody send us supports?"

"We ain't never goin' to stand this second banging. I didn't come here to fight the hull damn' rebel army."

There was one who raised a doleful cry. "I wish Bill Smithers had trod on my hand, insteader me treddin' on his'n." The sore joints of the regiment creaked as it painfully floundered into position to repulse.

The youth stared. Surely, he thought, this impossible thing was not about to happen. He waited as if he expected the enemy to suddenly stop, apologize, and retire bowing. It was all a mistake.

But the firing began somewhere on the regimental line and ripped along in both directions. The level sheets of flame developed great clouds of smoke that tumbled and tossed in the mild wind near the ground for a moment, and then rolled through the ranks as through a grate. The clouds were tinged an earthlike yellow in the sunrays and in the shadow were a sorry blue. The flag was sometimes eaten and lost in this mass of vapor, but more often it projected, sun-touched, resplendent.

Into the youth's eyes there came a look that one can see in the orbs of a jaded horse. His neck was quivering with nervous weakness and the muscles of his arms felt numb and bloodless. His hands, too, seemed large and awkward as if he was wearing invisible mittens. And there was a great uncertainty about his knee joints.

The words that comrades had uttered previous to the firing began to recur to him. "Oh, say, this is too much of a good thing! What do they take us for—why don't they send supports? I didn't come here to fight the hull damned rebel army."

He began to exaggerate the endurance, the skill, and the valor of those who were coming. Himself reeling from exhaustion, he was astonished beyond measure at such persistency. They must be machines of steel. It was very gloomy struggling against such affairs, wound up perhaps to fight until sundown.

He slowly lifted his rifle and catching a glimpse of the thickspread field he blazed at a cantering cluster. He stopped then and began to peer as best he could through the smoke. He caught changing views of the ground covered with men who were all running like pursued imps, and yelling.

To the youth it was an onslaught of redoubtable dragons. He became like the man who lost his legs at the approach of the red and green monster. He waited in a sort of a horrified, listening attitude. He seemed to shut his eyes and wait to be gobbled.

A man near him who up to this time had been working feverishly at his rifle suddenly stopped and ran with howls. A lad whose face had borne an expression of exalted courage, the majesty of he who dares give his life, was, at an instant, smitten abject. He blanched like one who has come to the edge of a cliff at midnight and is suddenly made aware. There was a revelation. He, too, threw down his gun and fled. There was no shame in his face. He ran like a rabbit.

Others began to scamper away through the smoke. The youth turned his head, shaken from his trance by this movement as if the regiment was leaving him behind. He saw the few fleeting forms.

He yelled then with fright and swung about. For a moment, in the great clamor, he was like a proverbial chicken. He lost the direction of safety. Destruction threatened him from all points.

Directly he began to speed toward the rear in great leaps. His rifle and cap were gone. His unbuttoned coat bulged in the wind. The flap of his cartridge box bobbed wildly, and his canteen, by its slender cord, swung out behind. On his face was all the horror of those things which he imagined.

The lieutenant sprang forward bawling. The youth saw his features wrathfully red, and saw him make a dab with his sword. His one thought of the incident was that the lieutenant was a peculiar creature to feel interested in such matters upon this occasion.

He ran like a blind man. Two or three times he fell down. Once he knocked his shoulder so heavily against a tree that he went headlong.

Since he had turned his back upon the fight his fears had been wondrously magnified. Death about to thrust him between the shoulder blades was far more dreadful than death about to smite him between the eyes. When he thought of it later, he conceived the impression that it is better to view the appalling than to be merely within hearing. The noises of the battle were like stones; he believed himself liable to be crushed.

As he ran on he mingled with others. He dimly saw men on his right and on his left, and he heard footsteps behind him. He thought that all the regiment was fleeing, pursued by these ominous crashes.

In his flight the sound of these following footsteps gave him his one meager relief. He felt vaguely that death must make a first choice of the men who were nearest; the initial morsels for the dragons would be then those who were following him. So he displayed the zeal of an insane sprinter in his purpose to keep them in the rear. There was a race.

As he, leading, went across a little field, he found himself in a region of shells. They hurtled over his head with long wild screams. As he listened he imagined them to have rows of cruel teeth that grinned at him. Once one lit before him and the livid lightning of the explosion effectually barred the way in his chosen direction. He groveled on the ground and then springing up went careering off through some bushes.

He experienced a thrill of amazement when he came within view of a battery in action. The men there seemed to be in conventional moods, altogether unaware of the impending annihilation. The battery was disputing with a distant antagonist and the gunners were wrapped in admiration of their shooting. They were continually bending in coaxing postures over the guns. They seemed to be patting them on the back and encouraging them with words. The guns, stolid and un-daunted, spoke with dogged valor.

The precise gunners were coolly enthusiastic. They lifted their eyes every chance to the smoke-wreathed hillock from whence the hostile battery addressed them. The youth pitied them as he ran. Methodical idiots! Machine-like fools! The refined joy of planting shells in the midst of the other battery's formation would appear a little thing when the infantry came swooping out of the woods.

The face of a youthful rider, who was jerking his frantic horse with an abandon of temper he might display in a placid barnyard, was impressed deeply upon his mind. He knew that he looked upon a man who would presently be dead.

Too, he felt a pity for the guns, standing, six good comrades, in a bold row.

He saw a brigade going to the relief of its pestered fellows. He scrambled upon a wee hill and watched it sweeping finely, keeping formation in difficult places. The blue of the line was crusted with steel color, and the brilliant flags projected. Officers were shouting.

This sight also filled him with wonder. The brigade was hurrying briskly to be gulped into the infernal mouths of the war god. What manner of men were they, anyhow? Ah, it was some wondrous breed! Or else they didn't comprehend—the fools.

A furious order caused commotion in the artillery. An officer on a bounding horse made maniacal motions with his arms. The teams went swinging up from the rear, the guns were whirled about, and the battery scampered away. The cannon with their noses poked slantingly at the ground grunted and grumbled like stout men, brave but with objections to hurry.

The youth went on, moderating his pace since he had left the place of noises.

Later he came upon a general of division seated upon a horse that pricked its ears in an interested way at the battle. There was a great gleaming of yellow and patent leather about the saddle and bridle. The quiet man astride looked mouse-colored upon such a splendid charger.

A jingling staff was galloping hither and thither. Sometimes the general was surrounded by horsemen and at other times he was quite alone. He looked to be much harassed. He had the appearance of a business man whose market is swinging up and down.

The youth went slinking around this spot. He went as near as he dared trying to overhear words. Perhaps the general, unable to comprehend chaos, might call upon him for information. And he could tell him. He knew all concerning it. Of a surety the force was in a fix, and any fool could see that if they did not retreat while they had opportunity—why——

He felt that he would like to thrash the general, or at least approach and tell him in plain words exactly what he thought him to be. It was criminal to stay calmly in one spot and make no effort to stay destruction. He loitered in a fever of eagerness for the division commander to apply to him.

As he warily moved about, he heard the general call out irritably: "Tompkins, go over an' see Taylor, an' tell him not t' be in such an all-fired hurry; tell him t' halt his brigade in th' edge of th' woods; tell him t' detach a reg'ment—say I think th' center 'll break if we don't help it out some; tell him t' hurry up."

A slim youth on a fine chestnut horse caught these swift words from the mouth of his superior. He made his horse bound into a gallop almost from a walk in his haste to go upon his mission. There was a cloud of dust.

A moment later the youth saw the general bounce excitedly in his saddle.

"Yes, by heavens, they have!" The officer leaned forward. His face was aflame with excitement. "Yes, by heavens, they 've held 'im! They 've held 'im!"

He began to blithely roar at his staff: "We 'll wallop 'im now. We 'll wallop 'im now. We 've got 'em sure." He turned suddenly upon an aide: "Here—you—Jones—quick—ride after Tompkins—see Taylor—tell him t' go in—everlastingly—like blazes—anything."

As another officer sped his horse after the first messenger, the general beamed upon the earth like a sun. In his eyes was a desire to chant a pæan. He kept repeating, "They 've held 'em, by heavens!"

His excitement made his horse plunge, and he merrily kicked and swore at it. He held a little carnival of joy on horseback.

Chapter VII

THE YOUTH cringed as if discovered in a crime. By heavens, they had won after all! The imbecile line had remained and become victors. He could hear cheering.

He lifted himself upon his toes and looked in the direction of the fight. A yellow fog lay wallowing on the treetops. From beneath it came the clatter of musketry. Hoarse cries told of an advance.

He turned away amazed and angry. He felt that he had been wronged.

He had fled, he told himself, because annihilation approached. He had done a good part in saving himself, who was a little piece of the army. He had considered the time, he said, to be one in which it was the duty of every little piece to rescue itself if possible. Later the officers could fit the little pieces together again, and make a battle front. If none of the little pieces were wise enough to save themselves from the flurry of death at such a time, why, then, where would be the army? It was all plain that he had proceeded according to very correct and commendable rules. His actions had been sagacious things. They had been full of strategy. They were the work of a master's legs.

Thoughts of his comrades came to him. The brittle blue line had withstood the blows and won. He grew bitter over it. It seemed that the blind ignorance and stupidity of those little pieces had betrayed him. He had been overturned and crushed by their lack of sense in holding the position, when intelligent deliberation would have convinced them that it was impossible. He, the enlightened man who looks afar in the dark, had fled because of his superior perceptions and knowledge. He felt a great anger against his comrades. He knew it could be proved that they had been fools.

He wondered what they would remark when later he appeared in camp. His mind heard howls of derision. Their density would not enable them to understand his sharper point of view.

He began to pity himself acutely. He was ill used. He was

trodden beneath the feet of an iron injustice. He had pro-
ceeded with wisdom and from the most righteous motives
under heaven's blue only to be frustrated by hateful circum-
stances.

A dull, animal-like rebellion against his fellows, war in the
abstract, and fate grew within him. He shambled along with
bowed head, his brain in a tumult of agony and despair.
When he looked loweringly up, quivering at each sound, his
eyes had the expression of those of a criminal who thinks his
guilt little and his punishment great, and knows that he can
find no words.

He went from the fields into a thick woods, as if resolved
to bury himself. He wished to get out of hearing of the crack-
ling shots which were to him like voices.

The ground was cluttered with vines and bushes, and the
trees grew close and spread out like bouquets. He was
obliged to force his way with much noise. The creepers,
catching against his legs, cried out harshly as their sprays were
torn from the barks of trees. The swishing saplings tried to
make known his presence to the world. He could not concil-
iate the forest. As he made his way, it was always calling out
protestations. When he separated embraces of trees and vines
the disturbed foliages waved their arms and turned their face
leaves toward him. He dreaded lest these noisy motions and
cries should bring men to look at him. So he went far, seek-
ing dark and intricate places.

After a time the sound of musketry grew faint and the can-
non boomed in the distance. The sun, suddenly apparent,
blazed among the trees. The insects were making rhythmical
noises. They seemed to be grinding their teeth in unison. A
woodpecker stuck his impudent head around the side of a
tree. A bird flew on lighthearted wing.

Off was the rumble of death. It seemed now that Nature
had no ears.

This landscape gave him assurance. A fair field holding life.
It was the religion of peace. It would die if its timid eyes were
compelled to see blood. He conceived Nature to be a woman
with a deep aversion to tragedy.

He threw a pine cone at a jovial squirrel, and he ran with
chattering fear. High in a treetop he stopped, and, poking his

head cautiously from behind a branch, looked down with an air of trepidation.

The youth felt triumphant at this exhibition. There was the law, he said. Nature had given him a sign. The squirrel, immediately upon recognizing danger, had taken to his legs without ado. He did not stand stolidly baring his furry belly to the missile, and die with an upward glance at the sympathetic heavens. On the contrary, he had fled as fast as his legs could carry him; and he was but an ordinary squirrel, too—doubtless no philosopher of his race. The youth wended, feeling that Nature was of his mind. She re-enforced his argument with proofs that lived where the sun shone.

Once he found himself almost into a swamp. He was obliged to walk upon bog tufts and watch his feet to keep from the oily mire. Pausing at one time to look about him he saw, out at some black water, a small animal pounce in and emerge directly with a gleaming fish.

The youth went again into the deep thickets. The brushed branches made a noise that drowned the sounds of cannon. He walked on, going from obscurity into promises of a greater obscurity.

At length he reached a place where the high, arching boughs made a chapel. He softly pushed the green doors aside and entered. Pine needles were a gentle brown carpet. There was a religious half light.

Near the threshold he stopped, horror-stricken at the sight of a thing.

He was being looked at by a dead man who was seated with his back against a columnlike tree. The corpse was dressed in a uniform that once had been blue, but was now faded to a melancholy shade of green. The eyes, staring at the youth, had changed to the dull hue to be seen on the side of a dead fish. The mouth was open. Its red had changed to an appalling yellow. Over the gray skin of the face ran little ants. One was trundling some sort of a bundle along the upper lip.

The youth gave a shriek as he confronted the thing. He was for moments turned to stone before it. He remained staring into the liquid-looking eyes. The dead man and the living man exchanged a long look. Then the youth cautiously put one hand behind him and brought it against a tree. Leaning upon this he retreated, step by step, with his face still toward the thing. He feared that if he turned his back the body might spring up and stealthily pursue him.

The branches, pushing against him, threatened to throw him over upon it. His unguided feet, too, caught aggravatingly in brambles; and with it all he received a subtle suggestion to touch the corpse. As he thought of his hand upon it he shuddered profoundly.

At last he burst the bonds which had fastened him to the spot and fled, unheeding the underbrush. He was pursued by a sight of the black ants swarming greedily upon the gray face and venturing horribly near to the eyes.

After a time he paused, and, breathless and panting, listened. He imagined some strange voice would come from the dead throat and squawk after him in horrible menaces.

The trees about the portal of the chapel moved soughingly in a soft wind. A sad silence was upon the little guarding edifice.

Chapter VIII

THE TREES began softly to sing a hymn of twilight. The sun sank until slanted bronze rays struck the forest. There was a lull in the noises of insects as if they had bowed their beaks and were making a devotional pause. There was silence save for the chanted chorus of the trees.

Then, upon this stillness, there suddenly broke a tremendous clangor of sounds. A crimson roar came from the distance.

The youth stopped. He was transfixed by this terrific medley of all noises. It was as if worlds were being rended. There was the ripping sound of musketry and the breaking crash of the artillery.

His mind flew in all directions. He conceived the two armies to be at each other panther fashion. He listened for a time. Then he began to run in the direction of the battle. He saw that it was an ironical thing for him to be running thus toward that which he had been at such pains to avoid. But he said, in substance, to himself that if the earth and the moon were about to clash, many persons would doubtless plan to get upon the roofs to witness the collision.

As he ran, he became aware that the forest had stopped its music, as if at last becoming capable of hearing the foreign sounds. The trees hushed and stood motionless. Everything seemed to be listening to the crackle and clatter and ear-shaking thunder. The chorus pealed over the still earth.

It suddenly occurred to the youth that the fight in which he had been was, after all, but perfunctory popping. In the hearing of this present din he was doubtful if he had seen real battle scenes. This uproar explained a celestial battle; it was tumbling hordes a-struggle in the air.

Reflecting, he saw a sort of a humor in the point of view of himself and his fellows during the late encounter. They had taken themselves and the enemy very seriously and had imagined that they were deciding the war. Individuals must have supposed that they were cutting the letters of their names deep into everlasting tablets of brass, or enshrining their reputations forever in the hearts of their countrymen, while, as to fact, the affair would appear in printed reports under a meek and immaterial title. But he saw that it was good, else, he said, in battle every one would surely run save forlorn hopes and their ilk.

He went rapidly on. He wished to come to the edge of the forest that he might peer out.

As he hastened, there passed through his mind pictures of stupendous conflicts. His accumulated thought upon such subjects was used to form scenes. The noise was as the voice of an eloquent being, describing.

Sometimes the brambles formed chains and tried to hold him back. Trees, confronting him, stretched out their arms and forbade him to pass. After its previous hostility this new resistance of the forest filled him with a fine bitterness. It seemed that Nature could not be quite ready to kill him.

But he obstinately took roundabout ways, and presently he was where he could see long gray walls of vapor where lay battle lines. The voices of cannon shook him. The musketry sounded in long irregular surges that played havoc with his ears. He stood regardant for a moment. His eyes had an awestruck expression. He gawked in the direction of the fight.

Presently he proceeded again on his forward way. The battle was like the grinding of an immense and terrible machine to him. Its complexities and powers, its grim processes, fascinated him. He must go close and see it produce corpses.

He came to a fence and clambered over it. On the far side, the ground was littered with clothes and guns. A newspaper, folded up, lay in the dirt. A dead soldier was stretched with his face hidden in his arm. Farther off there was a group of four or five corpses keeping mournful company. A hot sun had blazed upon the spot.

In this place the youth felt that he was an invader. This forgotten part of the battle ground was owned by the dead men, and he hurried, in the vague apprehension that one of the swollen forms would rise and tell him to begone.

He came finally to a road from which he could see in the distance dark and agitated bodies of troops, smoke-fringed. In the lane was a blood-stained crowd streaming to the rear. The wounded men were cursing, groaning, and wailing. In the air, always, was a mighty swell of sound that it seemed could sway the earth. With the courageous words of the artillery and the spiteful sentences of the musketry mingled red cheers. And from this region of noises came the steady current of the maimed.

One of the wounded men had a shoeful of blood. He hopped like a schoolboy in a game. He was laughing hysterically.

One was swearing that he had been shot in the arm through the commanding general's mismanagement of the army. One was marching with an air imitative of some sublime drum major. Upon his features was an unholy mixture of merriment and agony. As he marched he sang a bit of doggerel in a high and quavering voice:

> "Sing a song 'a vic'try,
>   A pocketful 'a bullets,
> Five an' twenty dead men
>   Baked in a—pie."

Parts of the procession limped and staggered to this tune.

Another had the gray seal of death already upon his face. His lips were curled in hard lines and his teeth were clinched. His hands were bloody from where he had pressed them upon his wound. He seemed to be awaiting the moment when he should pitch headlong. He stalked like the specter of a soldier, his eyes burning with the power of a stare into the unknown.

There were some who proceeded sullenly, full of anger at their wounds, and ready to turn upon anything as an obscure cause.

An officer was carried along by two privates. He was peevish. "Don't joggle so, Johnson, yeh fool," he cried. "Think m' leg is made of iron? If yeh can't carry me decent, put me down an' let some one else do it."

He bellowed at the tottering crowd who blocked the quick march of his bearers. "Say, make way there, can't yeh? Make way, dickens take it all."

They sulkily parted and went to the roadsides. As he was carried past they made pert remarks to him. When he raged in reply and threatened them, they told him to be damned.

The shoulder of one of the tramping bearers knocked heavily against the spectral soldier who was staring into the unknown.

The youth joined this crowd and marched along with it. The torn bodies expressed the awful machinery in which the men had been entangled.

Orderlies and couriers occasionally broke through the throng in the roadway, scattering wounded men right and left, galloping on followed by howls. The melancholy march was continually disturbed by the messengers, and sometimes by bustling batteries that came swinging and thumping down upon them, the officers shouting orders to clear the way.

There was a tattered man, fouled with dust, blood and powder stain from hair to shoes, who trudged quietly at the youth's side. He was listening with eagerness and much humility to the lurid descriptions of a bearded sergeant. His lean features wore an expression of awe and admiration. He was like a listener in a country store to wondrous tales told among the sugar barrels. He eyed the story-teller with unspeakable wonder. His mouth was agape in yokel fashion.

The sergeant, taking note of this, gave pause to his elaborate history while he administered a sardonic comment. "Be keerful, honey, you 'll be a-ketchin' flies," he said.

The tattered man shrank back abashed.

After a time he began to sidle near to the youth, and in a diffident way try to make him a friend. His voice was gentle as a girl's voice and his eyes were pleading. The youth saw with surprise that the soldier had two wounds, one in the head, bound with a blood-soaked rag, and the other in the arm, making that member dangle like a broken bough.

After they had walked together for some time the tattered man mustered sufficient courage to speak. "Was pretty good fight, wa'n't it?" he timidly said. The youth, deep in thought, glanced up at the bloody and grim figure with its lamblike eyes. "What?"

"Was pretty good fight, wa'n't it?"

"Yes," said the youth shortly. He quickened his pace.

But the other hobbled industriously after him. There was an air of apology in his manner, but he evidently thought that he needed only to talk for a time, and the youth would perceive that he was a good fellow.

"Was pretty good fight, wa'n't it?" he began in a small voice, and then he achieved the fortitude to continue. "Dern me if I ever see fellers fight so. Laws, how they did fight! I knowed th' boys 'd like when they onct got square at it. Th' boys ain't had no fair chanct up t' now, but this time they showed what they was. I knowed it 'd turn out this way. Yeh can't lick them boys. No, sir! They 're fighters, they be."

He breathed a deep breath of humble admiration. He had looked at the youth for encouragement several times. He received none, but gradually he seemed to get absorbed in his subject.

"I was talkin' 'cross pickets with a boy from Georgie, onct, an' that boy, he ses, 'Your fellers 'll all run like hell when they onct hearn a gun,' he ses. 'Mebbe they will,' I ses, 'but I don't b'lieve none of it,' I ses; 'an' b'jiminey,' I ses back t' 'um, 'mebbe your fellers 'll all run like hell when they onct hearn a gun,' I ses. He larfed. Well, they didn't run t' day, did they, hey? No, sir! They fit, an' fit, an' fit."

His homely face was suffused with a light of love for the army which was to him all things beautiful and powerful.

After a time he turned to the youth. "Where yeh hit, ol' boy?" he asked in a brotherly tone.

The youth felt instant panic at this question, although at first its full import was not borne in upon him.

"What?" he asked.

"Where yeh hit?" repeated the tattered man.

"Why," began the youth, "I—I—that is—why—I——"

He turned away suddenly and slid through the crowd. His brow was heavily flushed, and his fingers were picking nervously at one of his buttons. He bent his head and fastened his eyes studiously upon the button as if it were a little problem.

The tattered man looked after him in astonishment.

Chapter IX

THE YOUTH fell back in the procession until the tattered soldier was not in sight. Then he started to walk on with the others.

But he was amid wounds. The mob of men was bleeding. Because of the tattered soldier's question he now felt that his shame could be viewed. He was continually casting sidelong glances to see if the men were contemplating the letters of guilt he felt burned into his brow.

At times he regarded the wounded soldiers in an envious way. He conceived persons with torn bodies to be peculiarly happy. He wished that he, too, had a wound, a red badge of courage.

The spectral soldier was at his side like a stalking reproach. The man's eyes were still fixed in a stare into the unknown. His gray, appalling face had attracted attention in the crowd, and men, slowing to his dreary pace, were walking with him. They were discussing his plight, questioning him and giving him advice. In a dogged way he repelled them, signing to them to go on and leave him alone. The shadows of his face were deepening and his tight lips seemed holding in check the moan of great despair. There could be seen a certain stiffness in the movements of his body, as if he were taking infinite care not to arouse the passion of his wounds. As he went on, he seemed always looking for a place, like one who goes to choose a grave.

Something in the gesture of the man as he waved the bloody and pitying soldiers away made the youth start as if bitten. He yelled in horror. Tottering forward he laid a quivering hand upon the man's arm. As the latter slowly turned his waxlike features toward him, the youth screamed:

"Gawd! Jim Conklin!"

The tall soldier made a little commonplace smile. "Hello, Henry," he said.

The youth swayed on his legs and glared strangely. He stuttered and stammered. "Oh, Jim—oh, Jim—oh, Jim——"

The tall soldier held out his gory hand. There was a curious red and black combination of new blood and old blood upon it. "Where yeh been, Henry?" he asked. He continued in a monotonous voice, "I thought mebbe yeh got keeled over. There 's been thunder t' pay t'-day. I was worryin' about it a good deal."

The youth still lamented. "Oh, Jim—oh, Jim—oh, Jim——"

"Yeh know," said the tall soldier, "I was out there." He made a careful gesture. "An', Lord, what a circus! An', b'jiminey, I got shot—I got shot. Yes, b'jiminey, I got shot." He reiterated this fact in a bewildered way, as if he did not know how it came about.

The youth put forth anxious arms to assist him, but the tall soldier went firmly on as if propelled. Since the youth's arrival as a guardian for his friend, the other wounded men had ceased to display much interest. They occupied themselves again in dragging their own tragedies toward the rear.

Suddenly, as the two friends marched on, the tall soldier seemed to be overcome by a terror. His face turned to a semblance of gray paste. He clutched the youth's arm and looked all about him, as if dreading to be overheard. Then he began to speak in a shaking whisper:

"I tell yeh what I'm 'fraid of, Henry—I 'll tell yeh what I 'm 'fraid of. I 'm 'fraid I 'll fall down—an' then yeh know —them damned artillery wagons—they like as not 'll run over me. That 's what I 'm 'fraid of——"

The youth cried out to him hysterically: "I 'll take care of yeh, Jim! I 'll take care of yeh! I swear t' Gawd I will!"

"Sure—will yeh, Henry?" the tall soldier beseeched.

"Yes—yes—I tell yeh—I 'll take care of yeh, Jim!" protested the youth. He could not speak accurately because of the gulpings in his throat.

But the tall soldier continued to beg in a lowly way. He now hung babelike to the youth's arm. His eyes rolled in the wildness of his terror. "I was allus a good friend t' yeh, wa'n't I, Henry? I 've allus been a pretty good feller, ain't I? An' it ain't much t' ask, is it? Jest t' pull me along outer th' road? I 'd do it fer you, wouldn't I, Henry?"

He paused in piteous anxiety to await his friend's reply.

The youth had reached an anguish where the sobs scorched

him. He strove to express his loyalty, but he could only make fantastic gestures.

However, the tall soldier seemed suddenly to forget all those fears. He became again the grim, stalking specter of a soldier. He went stonily forward. The youth wished his friend to lean upon him, but the other always shook his head and strangely protested. "No—no—no—leave me be—leave me be——"

His look was fixed again upon the unknown. He moved with mysterious purpose, and all of the youth's offers he brushed aside. "No—no—leave me be—leave me be——"

The youth had to follow.

Presently the latter heard a voice talking softly near his shoulder. Turning he saw that it belonged to the tattered soldier. "Ye 'd better take 'im outa th' road, pardner. There 's a batt'ry comin' helitywhoop down th' road an' he 'll git runned over. He 's a goner anyhow in about five minutes—yeh kin see that. Ye 'd better take 'im outa th' road. Where th' blazes does he git his stren'th from?"

"Lord knows!" cried the youth. He was shaking his hands helplessly.

He ran forward presently and grasped the tall soldier by the arm. "Jim! Jim!" he coaxed, "come with me."

The tall soldier weakly tried to wrench himself free. "Huh," he said vacantly. He stared at the youth for a moment. At last he spoke as if dimly comprehending. "Oh! Inteh th' fields? Oh!"

He started blindly through the grass.

The youth turned once to look at the lashing riders and jouncing guns of the battery. He was startled from this view by a shrill outcry from the tattered man.

"Gawd! He's runnin'!"

Turning his head swiftly, the youth saw his friend running in a staggering and stumbling way toward a little clump of bushes. His heart seemed to wrench itself almost free from his body at this sight. He made a noise of pain. He and the tattered man began a pursuit. There was a singular race.

When he overtook the tall soldier he began to plead with all the words he could find. "Jim—Jim—what are you doing—what makes you do this way—you 'll hurt yerself."

The same purpose was in the tall soldier's face. He protested in a dulled way, keeping his eyes fastened on the mystic place of his intentions. "No—no—don't tech me—leave me be—leave me be——"

The youth, aghast and filled with wonder at the tall soldier, began quaveringly to question him. "Where yeh goin', Jim? What you thinking about? Where you going? Tell me, won't you, Jim?"

The tall soldier faced about as upon relentless pursuers. In his eyes there was a great appeal. "Leave me be, can't yeh? Leave me be fer a minnit."

The youth recoiled. "Why, Jim," he said, in a dazed way, " what 's the matter with you?"

The tall soldier turned and, lurching dangerously, went on. The youth and the tattered soldier followed, sneaking as if whipped, feeling unable to face the stricken man if he should again confront them. They began to have thoughts of a solemn ceremony. There was something rite-like in these movements of the doomed soldier. And there was a resemblance in him to a devotee of a mad religion, blood-sucking, muscle-wrenching, bone-crushing. They were awed and afraid. They hung back lest he have at command a dreadful weapon.

At last, they saw him stop and stand motionless. Hastening up, they perceived that his face wore an expression telling that he had at last found the place for which he had struggled. His spare figure was erect; his bloody hands were quietly at his side. He was waiting with patience for something that he had come to meet. He was at the rendezvous. They paused and stood, expectant.

There was a silence.

Finally, the chest of the doomed soldier began to heave with a strained motion. It increased in violence until it was as if an animal was within and was kicking and tumbling furiously to be free.

This spectacle of gradual strangulation made the youth writhe, and once as his friend rolled his eyes, he saw something in them that made him sink wailing to the ground. He raised his voice in a last supreme call.

"Jim—Jim—Jim——"

The tall soldier opened his lips and spoke. He made a gesture. "Leave me be—don't tech me—leave me be——"

There was another silence while he waited.

Suddenly, his form stiffened and straightened. Then it was shaken by a prolonged ague. He stared into space. To the two watchers there was a curious and profound dignity in the firm lines of his awful face.

He was invaded by a creeping strangeness that slowly enveloped him. For a moment the tremor of his legs caused him to dance a sort of hideous hornpipe. His arms beat wildly about his head in expression of implike enthusiasm.

His tall figure stretched itself to its full height. There was a slight rending sound. Then it began to swing forward, slow and straight, in the manner of a falling tree. A swift muscular contortion made the left shoulder strike the ground first.

The body seemed to bounce a little way from the earth. "God!" said the tattered soldier.

The youth had watched, spellbound, this ceremony at the place of meeting. His face had been twisted into an expression of every agony he had imagined for his friend.

He now sprang to his feet and, going closer, gazed upon the pastelike face. The mouth was open and the teeth showed in a laugh.

As the flap of the blue jacket fell away from the body, he could see that the side looked as if it had been chewed by wolves.

The youth turned, with sudden, livid rage, toward the battlefield. He shook his fist. He seemed about to deliver a philippic.

"Hell——"

The red sun was pasted in the sky like a wafer.

Chapter X

THE TATTERED MAN stood musing.

"Well, he was reg'lar jim-dandy fer nerve, wa'n't he," said he finally in a little awestruck voice. "A reg'lar jim-dandy." He thoughtfully poked one of the docile hands with his foot. "I wonner where he got 'is stren'th from? I never seen a man do like that before. It was a funny thing. Well, he was a reg'lar jim-dandy."

The youth desired to screech out his grief. He was stabbed, but his tongue lay dead in the tomb of his mouth. He threw himself again upon the ground and began to brood.

The tattered man stood musing.

"Look-a-here, pardner," he said, after a time. He regarded the corpse as he spoke. "He 's up an' gone, ain't 'e, an' we might as well begin t' look out fer ol' number one. This here thing is all over. He 's up an' gone, ain't 'e? An' he 's all right here. Nobody won't bother 'im. An' I must say I ain't enjoying any great health m'self these days."

The youth, awakened by the tattered soldier's tone, looked quickly up. He saw that he was swinging uncertainly on his legs and that his face had turned to a shade of blue.

"Good Lord!" he cried, "you ain't goin' t'—not you, too."

The tattered man waved his hand. "Nary die," he said. "All I want is some pea soup an' a good bed. Some pea soup," he repeated dreamfully.

The youth arose from the ground. "I wonder where he came from. I left him over there." He pointed. "And now I find 'im here. And he was coming from over there, too." He indicated a new direction. They both turned toward the body as if to ask of it a question.

"Well," at length spoke the tattered man, "there ain't no use in our stayin' here an' tryin' t' ask him anything."

The youth nodded an assent wearily. They both turned to gaze for a moment at the corpse.

The youth murmured something.

"Well, he was a jim-dandy, wa'n't 'e?" said the tattered man as if in response.

They turned their backs upon it and started away. For a

time they stole softly, treading with their toes. It remained laughing there in the grass.

"I'm commencin' t' feel pretty bad," said the tattered man, suddenly breaking one of his little silences. "I'm commencin' t' feel pretty damn' bad."

The youth groaned. "O Lord!" He wondered if he was to be the tortured witness of another grim encounter.

But his companion waved his hand reassuringly. "Oh, I'm not goin' t' die yit! There too much dependin' on me fer me t' die yit. No, sir! Nary die! I *can't*! Ye'd oughta see th' swad a' chil'ren I've got, an' all like that."

The youth glancing at his companion could see by the shadow of a smile that he was making some kind of fun.

As they plodded on the tattered soldier continued to talk. "Besides, if I died, I wouldn't die th' way that feller did. That was th' funniest thing. I'd jest flop down, I would. I never seen a feller die th' way that feller did.

"Yeh know Tom Jamison, he lives next door t' me up home. He's a nice feller, he is, an' we was allus good friends. Smart, too. Smart as a steel trap. Well, when we was a-fightin' this atternoon, all-of-a-sudden he begin t' rip up an' cuss an' beller at me. 'Yer shot, yeh blamed infernal!'—he swear horrible—he ses t' me. I put up m' hand t' m' head an' when I looked at m' fingers, I seen, sure 'nough, I was shot. I give a holler an' begin t' run, but b'fore I could git away another one hit me in th' arm an' whirl' me clean 'round. I got skeared when they was all a-shootin' b'hind me an' I run t' beat all, but I cotch it pretty bad. I've an idee I'd a' been fightin' yit, if t'was n't fer Tom Jamison."

Then he made a calm announcement: "There's two of 'em—little ones—but they 're beginnin' t' have fun with me now. I don't b'lieve I kin walk much furder."

They went slowly on in silence. "Yeh look pretty peek-ed yerself," said the tattered man at last. "I bet yeh 've got a worser one than yeh think. Ye'd better take keer of yer hurt. It don't do t' let sech things go. It might be inside mostly, an' them plays thunder. Where is it located?" But he continued his harangue without waiting for a reply. "I see a feller git hit plum in th' head when my reg'ment was a-standin' at ease onct. An' everybody yelled out to 'im: 'Hurt, John? Are yeh hurt much?' 'No,' ses he. He looked kinder surprised, an' he went on tellin' 'em how he felt. He sed he didn't feel nothin'. But, by dad, th' first thing that feller knowed he was dead. Yes, he was dead—stone dead. So, yeh wanta watch out. Yeh might have some queer kind 'a hurt yerself. Yeh can't never tell. Where is your'n located?"

The youth had been wriggling since the introduction of this topic. He now gave a cry of exasperation and made a furious motion with his hand. "Oh, don't bother me!" he said. He was enraged against the tattered man, and could have strangled him. His companions seemed ever to play intolerable parts. They were ever upraising the ghost of shame on the stick of their curiosity. He turned toward the tattered man as one at bay. "Now, don't bother me," he repeated with desperate menace.

"Well, Lord knows I don't wanta bother anybody," said the other. There was a little accent of despair in his voice as he replied, "Lord knows I 've gota 'nough m' own t' tend to."

The youth, who had been holding a bitter debate with himself and casting glances of hatred and contempt at the tattered man, here spoke in a hard voice. "Good-by," he said.

The tattered man looked at him in gaping amazement. "Why—why, pardner, where yeh goin'?" he asked unsteadily. The youth looking at him, could see that he, too, like that other one, was beginning to act dumb and animal-like. His thoughts seemed to be floundering about in his head. "Now—now—look—a—here, you Tom Jamison—now—I won't have this—this here won't do. Where—where yeh goin'?"

The youth pointed vaguely. "Over there," he replied.

"Well, now look—a—here—now," said the tattered man, rambling on in idiot fashion. His head was hanging forward and his words were slurred. "This thing won't do, now, Tom Jamison. It won't do. I know yeh, yeh pig-headed devil. Yeh wanta go trompin' off with a bad hurt. It ain't right—now— Tom Jamison—it ain't. Yeh wanta leave me take keer of yeh, Tom Jamison. It ain't—right—it ain't—fer yeh t' go—trompin' off—with a bad hurt—it ain't—ain't—ain't right—it ain't."

In reply the youth climbed a fence and started away. He could hear the tattered man bleating plaintively.

Once he faced about angrily. "What?"

"Look—a—here, now, Tom Jamison—now—it ain't——"

The youth went on. Turning at a distance he saw the tattered man wandering about helplessly in the field.

He now thought that he wished he was dead. He believed that he envied those men whose bodies lay strewn over the grass of the fields and on the fallen leaves of the forest.

The simple questions of the tattered man had been knife thrusts to him. They asserted a society that probes pitilessly at secrets until all is apparent. His late companion's chance persistency made him feel that he could not keep his crime concealed in his bosom. It was sure to be brought plain by one of those arrows which cloud the air and are constantly pricking, discovering, proclaiming those things which are willed to be forever hidden. He admitted that he could not defend himself against this agency. It was not within the power of vigilance.

Chapter XI

H E BECAME AWARE that the furnace roar of the battle was growing louder. Great brown clouds had floated to the still heights of air before him. The noise, too, was approaching. The woods filtered men and the fields became dotted.

As he rounded a hillock, he perceived that the roadway was now a crying mass of wagons, teams, and men. From the heaving tangle issued exhortations, commands, imprecations. Fear was sweeping it all along. The cracking whips bit and horses plunged and tugged. The white-topped wagons strained and stumbled in their exertions like fat sheep.

The youth felt comforted in a measure by this sight. They were all retreating. Perhaps, then, he was not so bad after all. He seated himself and watched the terror-stricken wagons. They fled like soft, ungainly animals. All the roarers and lashers served to help him to magnify the dangers and horrors of the engagement that he might try to prove to himself that the thing with which men could charge him was in truth a symmetrical act. There was an amount of pleasure to him in watching the wild march of this vindication.

Presently the calm head of a forward-going column of infantry appeared in the road. It came swiftly on. Avoiding the obstructions gave it the sinuous movement of a serpent. The men at the head butted mules with their musket stocks. They prodded teamsters indifferent to all howls. The men forced their way through parts of the dense mass by strength. The blunt head of the column pushed. The raving teamsters swore many strange oaths.

The commands to make way had the ring of a great importance in them. The men were going forward to the heart of the din. They were to confront the eager rush of the enemy. They felt the pride of their onward movement when the remainder of the army seemed trying to dribble down this road. They tumbled teams about with a fine feeling that it was no matter so long as their column got to the front in time. This importance made their faces grave and stern. And the backs of the officers were very rigid.

As the youth looked at them the black weight of his woe

returned to him. He felt that he was regarding a procession of chosen beings. The separation was as great to him as if they had marched with weapons of flame and banners of sunlight. He could never be like them. He could have wept in his longings.

He searched about in his mind for an adequate malediction for the indefinite cause, the thing upon which men turn the words of final blame. It—whatever it was—was responsible for him, he said. There lay the fault.

The haste of the column to reach the battle seemed to the forlorn young man to be something much finer than stout fighting. Heroes, he thought, could find excuses in that long seething lane. They could retire with perfect self-respect and make excuses to the stars.

He wondered what those men had eaten that they could be in such haste to force their way to grim chances of death. As he watched his envy grew until he thought that he wished to change lives with one of them. He would have liked to have used a tremendous force, he said, throw off himself and become a better. Swift pictures of himself, apart, yet in himself, came to him—a blue desperate figure leading lurid charges with one knee forward and a broken blade high—a blue, determined figure standing before a crimson and steel assault, getting calmly killed on a high place before the eyes of all. He thought of the magnificent pathos of his dead body.

These thoughts uplifted him. He felt the quiver of war desire. In his ears, he heard the ring of victory. He knew the frenzy of a rapid successful charge. The music of the trampling feet, the sharp voices, the clanking arms of the column near him made him soar on the red wings of war. For a few moments he was sublime.

He thought that he was about to start for the front. Indeed, he saw a picture of himself, dust-stained, haggard, panting, flying to the front at the proper moment to seize and throttle the dark, leering witch of calamity.

Then the difficulties of the thing began to drag at him. He hesitated, balancing awkwardly on one foot.

He had no rifle; he could not fight with his hands, said he resentfully to his plan. Well, rifles could be had for the picking. They were extraordinarily profuse.

Also, he continued, it would be a miracle if he found his regiment. Well, he could fight with any regiment.

He started forward slowly. He stepped as if he expected to tread upon some explosive thing. Doubts and he were struggling.

He would truly be a worm if any of his comrades should see him returning thus, the marks of his flight upon him. There was a reply that the intent fighters did not care for what happened rearward saving that no hostile bayonets appeared there. In the battle-blur his face would, in a way, be hidden, like the face of a cowled man.

But then he said that his tireless fate would bring forth, when the strife lulled for a moment, a man to ask of him an explanation. In imagination he felt the scrutiny of his companions as he painfully labored through some lies.

Eventually, his courage expended itself upon these objections. The debates drained him of his fire.

He was not cast down by this defeat of his plan, for, upon studying the affair carefully, he could not but admit that the objections were very formidable.

Furthermore, various ailments had begun to cry out. In their presence he could not persist in flying high with the wings of war; they rendered it almost impossible for him to see himself in a heroic light. He tumbled headlong.

He discovered that he had a scorching thirst. His face was so dry and grimy that he thought he could feel his skin crackle. Each bone of his body had an ache in it, and seemingly threatened to break with each movement. His feet were like two sores. Also, his body was calling for food. It was more powerful than a direct hunger. There was a dull, weight-like feeling in his stomach, and, when he tried to walk, his head swayed and he tottered. He could not see with distinctness. Small patches of green mist floated before his vision.

While he had been tossed by many emotions, he had not been aware of ailments. Now they beset him and made clamor. As he was at last compelled to pay attention to them, his capacity for self-hate was multiplied. In despair, he declared that he was not like those others. He now conceded it to be impossible that he should ever become a hero. He was a craven loon. Those pictures of glory were piteous things. He groaned from his heart and went staggering off.

A certain mothlike quality within him kept him in the vicinity of the battle. He had a great desire to see, and to get news. He wished to know who was winning.

He told himself that, despite his unprecedented suffering, he had never lost his greed for a victory, yet, he said, in a half-apologetic manner to his conscience, he could not but know that a defeat for the army this time might mean many favorable things for him. The blows of the enemy would splinter regiments into fragments. Thus, many men of courage, he considered, would be obliged to desert the colors and scurry like chickens. He would appear as one of them. They would be sullen brothers in distress, and he could then easily believe he had not run any farther or faster than they. And if he himself could believe in his virtuous perfection, he conceived that there would be small trouble in convincing all others.

He said, as if in excuse for this hope, that previously the army had encountered great defeats and in a few months had shaken off all blood and tradition of them, emerging as bright and valiant as a new one; thrusting out of sight the memory of disaster, and appearing with the valor and confidence of unconquered legions. The shrilling voices of the people at home would pipe dismally for a time, but various generals were usually compelled to listen to these ditties. He of course felt no compunctions for proposing a general as a sacrifice. He could not tell who the chosen for the barbs might be, so he could center no direct sympathy upon him. The people were afar and he did not conceive public opinion to be accurate at long range. It was quite probable they would hit the wrong man who, after he had recovered from his amazement would perhaps spend the rest of his days in writing replies to the songs of his alleged failure. It would be very unfortunate, no doubt, but in this case a general was of no consequence to the youth.

In a defeat there would be a roundabout vindication of himself. He thought it would prove, in a manner, that he had fled early because of his superior powers of perception. A serious prophet upon predicting a flood should be the first man to climb a tree. This would demonstrate that he was indeed a seer.

A moral vindication was regarded by the youth as a very important thing. Without salve, he could not, he thought, wear the sore badge of his dishonor through life. With his heart continually assuring him that he was despicable, he could not exist without making it, through his actions, apparent to all men.

If the army had gone gloriously on he would be lost. If the din meant that now his army's flags were tilted forward he was a condemned wretch. He would be compelled to doom himself to isolation. If the men were advancing, their indifferent feet were trampling upon his chances for a successful life.

As these thoughts went rapidly through his mind, he turned upon them and tried to thrust them away. He denounced himself as a villain. He said that he was the most unutterably selfish man in existence. His mind pictured the soldiers who would place their defiant bodies before the spear of the yelling battle fiend, and as he saw their dripping corpses on an imagined field, he said that he was their murderer.

Again he thought that he wished he was dead. He believed that he envied a corpse. Thinking of the slain, he achieved a great contempt for some of them, as if they were guilty for thus becoming lifeless. They might have been killed by lucky chances, he said, before they had had opportunities to flee or before they had been really tested. Yet they would receive laurels from tradition. He cried out bitterly that their crowns were stolen and their robes of glorious memories were shams. However, he still said that it was a great pity he was not as they.

A defeat of the army had suggested itself to him as a means of escape from the consequences of his fall. He considered, now, however, that it was useless to think of such a possibility. His education had been that success for that mighty blue machine was certain; that it would make victories as a contrivance turns out buttons. He presently discarded all his speculations in the other direction. He returned to the creed of soldiers.

When he perceived again that it was not possible for the

army to be defeated, he tried to bethink him of a fine tale which he could take back to his regiment, and with it turn the expected shafts of derision.

But, as he mortally feared these shafts, it became impossible for him to invent a tale he felt he could trust. He experimented with many schemes, but threw them aside one by one as flimsy. He was quick to see vulnerable places in them all.

Furthermore, he was much afraid that some arrow of scorn might lay him mentally low before he could raise his protecting tale.

He imagined the whole regiment saying: "Where 's Henry Fleming? He run, didn't 'e? Oh, my!" He recalled various persons who would be quite sure to leave him no peace about it. They would doubtless question him with sneers, and laugh at his stammering hesitation. In the next engagement they would try to keep watch of him to discover when he would run.

Wherever he went in camp, he would encounter insolent and lingeringly cruel stares. As he imagined himself passing near a crowd of comrades, he could hear some one say, "There he goes!"

Then, as if the heads were moved by one muscle, all the faces were turned toward him with wide, derisive grins. He seemed to hear some one make a humorous remark in a low tone. At it the others all crowed and cackled. He was a slang phrase.

Chapter XII

THE COLUMN that had butted stoutly at the obstacles in the roadway was barely out of the youth's sight before he saw dark waves of men come sweeping out of the woods and down through the fields. He knew at once that the steel fibers had been washed from their hearts. They were bursting from their coats and their equipments as from entanglements. They charged down upon him like terrified buffaloes.

Behind them blue smoke curled and clouded above the treetops, and through the thickets he could sometimes see a distant pink glare. The voices of the cannon were clamoring in interminable chorus.

The youth was horrorstricken. He stared in agony and amazement. He forgot that he was engaged in combating the universe. He threw aside his mental pamphlets on the philosophy of the retreated and rules for the guidance of the damned.

The fight was lost. The dragons were coming with invincible strides. The army, helpless in the matted thickets and blinded by the overhanging night, was going to be swallowed. War, the red animal, war, the blood-swollen god, would have bloated fill.

Within him something bade to cry out. He had the impulse to make a rallying speech, to sing a battle hymn, but he could only get his tongue to call into the air: "Why—why—what—what 's th' matter?"

Soon he was in the midst of them. They were leaping and scampering all about him. Their blanched faces shone in the dusk. They seemed, for the most part, to be very burly men. The youth turned from one to another of them as they galloped along. His incoherent questions were lost. They were heedless of his appeals. They did not seem to see him.

They sometimes gabbled insanely. One huge man was asking of the sky: "Say, where de plank road? Where de plank road!" It was as if he had lost a child. He wept in his pain and dismay.

Presently, men were running hither and thither in all ways. The artillery booming, forward, rearward, and on the flanks made jumble of ideas of direction. Landmarks had vanished into the gathered gloom. The youth began to imagine that he had got into the center of the tremendous quarrel, and he could perceive no way out of it. From the mouths of the fleeing men came a thousand wild questions, but no one made answers.

The youth, after rushing about and throwing interrogations at the heedless bands of retreating infantry, finally clutched a man by the arm. They swung around face to face.

"Why—why——" stammered the youth struggling with his balking tongue.

The man screamed: "Let go me! Let go me!" His face was livid and his eyes were rolling uncontrolled. He was heaving and panting. He still grasped his rifle, perhaps having forgotten to release his hold upon it. He tugged frantically, and the youth being compelled to lean forward was dragged several paces.

"Let go me! Let go me!"

"Why—why——" stuttered the youth.

"Well, then!" bawled the man in a lurid rage. He adroitly and fiercely swung his rifle. It crushed upon the youth's head. The man ran on.

The youth's fingers had turned to paste upon the other's arm. The energy was smitten from his muscles. He saw the flaming wings of lightning flash before his vision. There was a deafening rumble of thunder within his head.

Suddenly his legs seemed to die. He sank writhing to the ground. He tried to arise. In his efforts against the numbing pain he was like a man wrestling with a creature of the air.

There was a sinister struggle.

Sometimes he would achieve a position half erect, battle with the air for a moment, and then fall again, grabbing at the grass. His face was of a clammy pallor. Deep groans were wrenched from him.

At last, with a twisting movement, he got upon his hands and knees, and from thence, like a babe trying to walk, to his feet. Pressing his hands to his temples he went lurching over the grass.

He fought an intense battle with his body. His dulled senses wished him to swoon and he opposed them stub-

bornly, his mind portraying unknown dangers and mutila-
tions if he should fall upon the field. He went tall soldier
fashion. He imagined secluded spots where he could fall and
be unmolested. To search for one he strove against the tide of
his pain.

Once he put his hand to the top of his head and timidly
touched the wound. The scratching pain of the contact made
him draw a long breath through his clinched teeth. His fin-
gers were dabbled with blood. He regarded them with a fixed
stare.

Around him he could hear the grumble of jolted cannon as
the scurrying horses were lashed toward the front. Once, a
young officer on a besplashed charger nearly ran him down.
He turned and watched the mass of guns, men, and horses
sweeping in a wide curve toward a gap in a fence. The officer
was making excited motions with a gauntleted hand. The
guns followed the teams with an air of unwillingness, of
being dragged by the heels.

Some officers of the scattered infantry were cursing and
railing like fishwives. Their scolding voices could be heard
above the din. Into the unspeakable jumble in the roadway
rode a squadron of cavalry. The faded yellow of their facings
shone bravely. There was a mighty altercation.

The artillery were assembling as if for a conference.

The blue haze of evening was upon the field. The lines of
forest were long purple shadows. One cloud lay along the
western sky partly smothering the red.

As the youth left the scene behind him, he heard the guns
suddenly roar out. He imagined them shaking in black rage.
They belched and howled like brass devils guarding a gate.
The soft air was filled with the tremendous remonstrance.
With it came the shattering peal of opposing infantry. Turn-
ing to look behind him, he could see sheets of orange light
illumine the shadowy distance. There were subtle and sudden
lightnings in the far air. At times he thought he could see
heaving masses of men.

He hurried on in the dusk. The day had faded until he
could barely distinguish place for his feet. The purple dark-
ness was filled with men who lectured and jabbered. Some-
times he could see them gesticulating against the blue and

somber sky. There seemed to be a great ruck of men and munitions spread about in the forest and in the fields.

The little narrow roadway now lay lifeless. There were overturned wagons like sun-dried bowlders. The bed of the former torrent was choked with the bodies of horses and splintered parts of war machines.

It had come to pass that his wound pained him but little. He was afraid to move rapidly, however, for a dread of disturbing it. He held his head very still and took many precautions against stumbling. He was filled with anxiety, and his face was pinched and drawn in anticipation of the pain of any sudden mistake of his feet in the gloom.

His thoughts, as he walked, fixed intently upon his hurt. There was a cool, liquid feeling about it and he imagined blood moving slowly down under his hair. His head seemed swollen to a size that made him think his neck to be inadequate.

The new silence of his wound made much worriment. The little blistering voices of pain that had called out from his scalp were, he thought, definite in their expression of danger. By them he believed that he could measure his plight. But when they remained ominously silent he became frightened and imagined terrible fingers that clutched into his brain.

Amid it he began to reflect upon various incidents and conditions of the past. He bethought him of certain meals his mother had cooked at home, in which those dishes of which he was particularly fond had occupied prominent positions. He saw the spread table. The pine walls of the kitchen were glowing in the warm light from the stove. Too, he remembered how he and his companions used to go from the school-house to the bank of a shaded pool. He saw his clothes in disorderly array upon the grass of the bank. He felt the swash of the fragrant water upon his body. The leaves of the overhanging maple rustled with melody in the wind of youthful summer.

He was overcome presently by a dragging weariness. His head hung forward and his shoulders were stooped as if he were bearing a great bundle. His feet shuffled along the ground.

He held continuous arguments as to whether he should lie

down and sleep at some near spot, or force himself on until
he reached a certain haven. He often tried to dismiss the
question, but his body persisted in rebellion and his senses
nagged at him like pampered babies.

At last he heard a cheery voice near his shoulder: "Yeh
seem t' be in a pretty bad way, boy?"

The youth did not look up, but he assented with thick
tongue. "Uh!"

The owner of the cheery voice took him firmly by the arm.
"Well," he said, with a round laugh, "I'm goin' your way. Th'
hull gang is goin' your way. An' I guess I kin give yeh a lift."
They began to walk like a drunken man and his friend.

As they went along, the man questioned the youth and as-
sisted him with the replies like one manipulating the mind of
a child. Sometimes he interjected anecdotes. "What reg'ment
do yeh b'long teh? Eh? What 's that? Th' 304th N' York?
Why, what corps is that in? Oh, it is? Why, I thought they
wasn't engaged t'-day—they 're 'way over in th' center. Oh,
they was, eh? Well, pretty nearly everybody got their share 'a
fightin' t'-day. By dad, I give myself up fer dead any number
'a times. There was shootin' here an' shootin' there, an' hol-
lerin' here an' hollerin' there, in th' damn' darkness, until I
couldn't tell t' save m' soul which side I was on. Sometimes
I thought I was sure 'nough from Ohier, an' other times I
could 'a swore I was from th' bitter end of Florida. It was th'
most mixed up dern thing I ever see. An' these here hull
woods is a reg'lar mess. It 'll be a miracle if we find our reg'-
ments t'-night. Pretty soon, though, we 'll meet a-plenty of
guards an' provost-guards, an' one thing an' another. Ho!
there they go with an off'cer, I guess. Look at his hand a-
draggin'. He 's got all th' war he wants, I bet. He won't be
talkin' so big about his reputation an' all when they go t'
sawin' off his leg. Poor feller! My brother 's got whiskers jest
like that. How did yeh git 'way over here, anyhow? Your reg'-
ment is a long way from here, ain't it? Well, I guess we can
find it. Yeh know there was a boy killed in my comp'ny t'-day
that I thought th' world an' all of. Jack was a nice feller. By
ginger, it hurt like thunder t' see ol' Jack jest git knocked flat.
We was a-standin' purty peaceable fer a spell, 'though there
was men runnin' ev'ry way all 'round us, an' while we was a-

standin' like that, 'long come a big fat feller. He began t' peck at Jack's elbow, an' he ses: 'Say, where 's th' road t' th' river?' An' Jack, he never paid no attention, an' th' feller kept on a-peckin' at his elbow an' sayin': 'Say, where 's th' road t' th' river?' Jack was a-lookin' ahead all th' time tryin' t' see th' Johnnies comin' through th' woods, an' he never paid no attention t' this big fat feller fer a long time, but at last he turned 'round an' he ses: 'Ah, go t' hell an' find th' road t' th' river!' An' jest then a shot slapped him bang on th' side th' head. He was a sergeant, too. Them was his last words. Thunder, I wish we was sure 'a findin' our reg'ments t'-night. It 's goin' t' be long huntin'. But I guess we kin do it."

In the search which followed, the man of the cheery voice seemed to the youth to possess a wand of a magic kind. He threaded the mazes of the tangled forest with a strange fortune. In encounters with guards and patrols he displayed the keenness of a detective and the valor of a gamin. Obstacles fell before him and became of assistance. The youth, with his chin still on his breast, stood woodenly by while his companion beat ways and means out of sullen things.

The forest seemed a vast hive of men buzzing about in frantic circles, but the cheery man conducted the youth without mistakes, until at last he began to chuckle with glee and self-satisfaction. "Ah, there yeh are! See that fire?"

The youth nodded stupidly.

"Well, there 's where your reg'ment is. An' now, good-by, ol' boy, good luck t' yeh."

A warm and strong hand clasped the youth's languid fingers for an instant, and then he heard a cheerful and audacious whistling as the man strode away. As he who had so befriended him was thus passing out of his life, it suddenly occurred to the youth that he had not once seen his face.

Chapter XIII

THE YOUTH went slowly toward the fire indicated by his departed friend. As he reeled, he bethought him of the welcome his comrades would give him. He had a conviction that he would soon feel in his sore heart the barbed missiles of ridicule. He had no strength to invent a tale; he would be a soft target.

He made vague plans to go off into the deeper darkness and hide, but they were all destroyed by the voices of exhaustion and pain from his body. His ailments, clamoring, forced him to seek the place of food and rest, at whatever cost.

He swung unsteadily toward the fire. He could see the forms of men throwing black shadows in the red light, and as he went nearer it became known to him in some way that the ground was strewn with sleeping men.

Of a sudden he confronted a black and monstrous figure. A rifle barrel caught some glinting beams. "Halt! halt!" He was dismayed for a moment, but he presently thought that he recognized the nervous voice. As he stood tottering before the rifle barrel, he called out: "Why, hello, Wilson, you—you here?"

The rifle was lowered to a position of caution and the loud soldier came slowly forward. He peered into the youth's face. "That you, Henry?"

"Yes, it's—it's me."

"Well, well, ol' boy," said the other, "by ginger, I'm glad t' see yeh! I give yeh up fer a goner. I thought yeh was dead sure enough." There was husky emotion in his voice.

The youth found that now he could barely stand upon his feet. There was a sudden sinking of his forces. He thought he must hasten to produce his tale to protect him from the missiles already at the lips of his redoubtable comrades. So, staggering before the loud soldier, he began: "Yes, yes. I've—I've had an awful time. I've been all over. Way over on th' right. Ter'ble fightin' over there. I had an awful time. I got separated from th' reg'ment. Over on th' right, I got shot. In th' head. I never see sech fightin'. Awful time. I don't see how I could a' got separated from th' reg'ment. I got shot, too."

His friend had stepped forward quickly. "What? Got shot? Why didn't yeh say so first? Poor ol' boy, we must—hol' on a minnit; what am I doin'. I'll call Simpson."

Another figure at that moment loomed in the gloom. They could see that it was the corporal. "Who yeh talkin' to, Wilson?" he demanded. His voice was anger-toned. "Who yeh talkin' to? Yeh th' derndest sentinel—why—hello, Henry, you here? Why, I thought you was dead four hours ago! Great Jerusalem, they keep turnin' up every ten minutes or so! We thought we'd lost forty-two men by straight count, but if they keep on a-comin' this way, we'll git th' comp'ny all back by mornin' yit. Where was yeh?"

"Over on th' right. I got separated"—began the youth with considerable glibness.

But his friend had interrupted hastily. "Yes, an' he got shot in th' head an' he's in a fix, an' we must see t' him right away." He rested his rifle in the hollow of his left arm and his right around the youth's shoulder.

"Gee, it must hurt like thunder!" he said.

The youth leaned heavily upon his friend. "Yes, it hurts—hurts a good deal," he replied. There was a faltering in his voice.

"Oh," said the corporal. He linked his arm in the youth's and drew him forward. "Come on, Henry. I'll take keer 'a yeh."

As they went on together the loud private called out after them: "Put 'im t' sleep in my blanket, Simpson. An'—hol' on a minnit—here's my canteen. It's full 'a coffee. Look at his head by th' fire an' see how it looks. Maybe it's a pretty bad un. When I git relieved in a couple 'a minnits, I'll be over an' see t' him."

The youth's senses were so deadened that his friend's voice sounded from afar and he could scarcely feel the pressure of the corporal's arm. He submitted passively to the latter's directing strength. His head was in the old manner hanging forward upon his breast. His knees wobbled.

The corporal led him into the glare of the fire. "Now, Henry," he said, "let's have look at yer ol' head."

The youth sat down obediently and the corporal, laying aside his rifle, began to fumble in the bushy hair of his comrade. He was obliged to turn the other's head so that the full flush of the fire light would beam upon it. He puckered his mouth with a critical air. He drew back his lips and whistled through his teeth when his fingers came in contact with the splashed blood and the rare wound.

"Ah, here we are!" he said. He awkwardly made further investigations. "Jest as I thought," he added, presently. "Yeh've been grazed by a ball. It's raised a queer lump jest as if some feller had lammed yeh on th' head with a club. It stopped a-bleedin' long time ago. Th' most about it is that in th' mornin' yeh'll feel that a number ten hat wouldn't fit yeh. An' your head'll be all het up an' feel as dry as burnt pork. An' yeh may git a lot 'a other sicknesses, too, by mornin'. Yeh can't never tell. Still, I don't much think so. It's jest a damn' good belt on th' head, an' nothin' more. Now, you jest sit here an' don't move, while I go rout out th' relief. Then I'll send Wilson t' take keer 'a yeh."

The corporal went away. The youth remained on the ground like a parcel. He stared with a vacant look into the fire.

After a time he aroused, for some part, and the things about him began to take form. He saw that the ground in the deep shadows was cluttered with men, sprawling in every conceivable posture. Glancing narrowly into the more distant darkness, he caught occasional glimpses of visages that loomed pallid and ghostly, lit with a phosphorescent glow. These faces expressed in their lines the deep stupor of the tired soldiers. They made them appear like men drunk with wine. This bit of forest might have appeared to an ethereal wanderer as a scene of the result of some frightful debauch.

On the other side of the fire the youth observed an officer asleep, seated bolt upright, with his back against a tree. There was something perilous in his position. Badgered by dreams, perhaps, he swayed with little bounces and starts, like an old, toddy-stricken grandfather in a chimney corner. Dust and stains were upon his face. His lower jaw hung down as if lacking strength to assume its normal position. He was the picture of an exhausted soldier after a feast of war.

He had evidently gone to sleep with his sword in his arms. These two had slumbered in an embrace, but the weapon had been allowed in time to fall unheeded to the ground. The brass-mounted hilt lay in contact with some parts of the fire.

Within the gleam of rose and orange light from the burning sticks were other soldiers, snoring and heaving, or lying deathlike in slumber. A few pairs of legs were stuck forth, rigid and straight. The shoes displayed the mud or dust of marches and bits of rounded trousers, protruding from the blankets, showed rents and tears from hurried pitchings through the dense brambles.

The fire crackled musically. From it swelled light smoke. Overhead the foliage moved softly. The leaves, with their faces turned toward the blaze, were colored shifting hues of silver, often edged with red. Far off to the right, through a window in the forest could be seen a handful of stars lying, like glittering pebbles, on the black level of the night.

Occasionally, in this low-arched hall, a soldier would arouse and turn his body to a new position, the experience of his sleep having taught him of uneven and objectionable places upon the ground under him. Or, perhaps, he would lift himself to a sitting posture, blink at the fire for an unintelligent moment, throw a swift glance at his prostrate companion, and then cuddle down again with a grunt of sleepy content.

The youth sat in a forlorn heap until his friend the loud young soldier came, swinging two canteens by their light strings. "Well, now, Henry, ol' boy," said the latter, " we'll have yeh fixed up in jest about a minnit."

He had the bustling ways of an amateur nurse. He fussed around the fire and stirred the sticks to brilliant exertions. He made his patient drink largely from the canteen that contained the coffee. It was to the youth a delicious draught. He tilted his head afar back and held the canteen long to his lips. The cool mixture went caressingly down his blistered throat. Having finished, he sighed with comfortable delight.

The loud young soldier watched his comrade with an air of satisfaction. He later produced an extensive handkerchief from his pocket. He folded it into a manner of bandage and soused water from the other canteen upon the middle of it. This crude arrangement he bound over the youth's head, tying the ends in a queer knot at the back of the neck.

"There," he said, moving off and surveying his deed, "yeh look like th' devil, but I bet yeh feel better."

The youth contemplated his friend with grateful eyes. Upon his aching and swelling head the cold cloth was like a tender woman's hand.

"Yeh don't holler ner say nothin'," remarked his friend approvingly. "I know I'm a blacksmith at takin' keer 'a sick folks, an' yeh never squeaked. Yer a good un, Henry. Most 'a men would a' been in th' hospital long ago. A shot in th' head ain't foolin' business."

The youth made no reply, but began to fumble with the buttons of his jacket.

"Well, come, now," continued his friend, "come on. I must put yeh t' bed an' see that yeh git a good night's rest."

The other got carefully erect, and the loud young soldier led him among the sleeping forms lying in groups and rows. Presently he stooped and picked up his blankets. He spread the rubber one upon the ground and placed the woolen one about the youth's shoulders.

"There now," he said, "lie down an' git some sleep."

The youth, with his manner of doglike obedience, got carefully down like a crone stooping. He stretched out with a murmur of relief and comfort. The ground felt like the softest couch.

But of a sudden he ejaculated: "Hol' on a minnit! Where you goin' t' sleep?"

His friend waved his hand impatiently. "Right down there by yeh."

"Well, but hol' on a minnit," continued the youth. "What yeh goin' t' sleep in? I've got your——"

The loud young soldier snarled: "Shet up an' go on t' sleep. Don't be makin' a damn' fool 'a yerself," he said severely.

After the reproof the youth said no more. An exquisite drowsiness had spread through him. The warm comfort of the blanket enveloped him and made a gentle languor. His head fell forward on his crooked arm and his weighted lids went softly down over his eyes. Hearing a splatter of musketry from the distance, he wondered indifferently if those men sometimes slept. He gave a long sigh, snuggled down into his blanket, and in a moment was like his comrades.

Chapter XIV

WHEN THE YOUTH AWOKE it seemed to him that he had been asleep for a thousand years, and he felt sure that he opened his eyes upon an unexpected world. Gray mists were slowly shifting before the first efforts of the sun rays. An impending splendor could be seen in the eastern sky. An icy dew had chilled his face, and immediately upon arousing he curled farther down into his blanket. He stared for a while at the leaves overhead, moving in a heraldic wind of the day.

The distance was splintering and blaring with the noise of fighting. There was in the sound an expression of a deadly persistency, as if it had not began and was not to cease.

About him were the rows and groups of men that he had dimly seen the previous night. They were getting a last draught of sleep before the awakening. The gaunt, careworn features and dusty figures were made plain by this quaint light at the dawning, but it dressed the skin of the men in corpse-like hues and made the tangled limbs appear pulseless and dead. The youth started up with a little cry when his eyes first swept over this motionless mass of men, thick-spread upon the ground, pallid, and in strange postures. His disordered mind interpreted the hall of the forest as a charnel place. He believed for an instant that he was in the house of the dead, and he did not dare to move lest these corpses start up, squalling and squawking. In a second, however, he achieved his proper mind. He swore a complicated oath at himself. He saw that this somber picture was not a fact of the present, but a mere prophecy.

He heard then the noise of a fire crackling briskly in the cold air, and, turning his head, he saw his friend pottering busily about a small blaze. A few other figures moved in the fog, and he heard the hard cracking of axe blows.

Suddenly there was a hollow rumble of drums. A distant bugle sang faintly. Similar sounds, varying in strength, came from near and far over the forest. The bugles called to each other like brazen gamecocks. The near thunder of the regimental drums rolled.

The body of men in the woods rustled. There was a general

uplifting of heads. A murmuring of voices broke upon the air. In it there was much bass of grumbling oaths. Strange gods were addressed in condemnation of the early hours necessary to correct war. An officer's peremptory tenor rang out and quickened the stiffened movement of the men. The tangled limbs unraveled. The corpse-hued faces were hidden behind fists that twisted slowly in the eye sockets.

The youth sat up and gave vent to an enormous yawn. "Thunder!" he remarked petulantly. He rubbed his eyes, and then putting up his hand felt carefully of the bandage over his wound. His friend, perceiving him to be awake, came from the fire. "Well, Henry, ol' man, how do yeh feel this mornin'?" he demanded.

The youth yawned again. Then he puckered his mouth to a little pucker. His head, in truth, felt precisely like a melon, and there was an unpleasant sensation at his stomach.

"Oh, Lord, I feel pretty bad," he said.

"Thunder!" exclaimed the other. "I hoped ye'd feel all right this mornin'. Let's see th' bandage—I guess it's slipped." He began to tinker at the wound in rather a clumsy way until the youth exploded.

"Gosh-dern it!" he said in sharp irritation; "you're the hangdest man I ever saw! You wear muffs on your hands. Why in good thunderation can't you be more easy? I'd rather you'd stand off an' throw guns at it. Now, go slow, an' don't act as if you was nailing down carpet."

He glared with insolent command at his friend, but the latter answered soothingly. "Well, well, come now, an' git some grub," he said. "Then, maybe, yeh'll feel better."

At the fireside the loud young soldier watched over his comrade's wants with tenderness and care. He was very busy marshaling the little black vagabonds of tin cups and pouring into them the streaming, iron colored mixture from a small and sooty tin pail. He had some fresh meat, which he roasted hurriedly upon a stick. He sat down then and contemplated the youth's appetite with glee.

The youth took note of a remarkable change in his comrade since those days of camp life upon the river bank. He seemed no more to be continually regarding the proportions of his personal prowess. He was not furious at small words that pricked his conceits. He was no more a loud young soldier. There was about him now a fine reliance. He showed a quiet belief in his purposes and his abilities. And this inward confidence evidently enabled him to be indifferent to little words of other men aimed at him.

The youth reflected. He had been used to regarding his comrade as a blatant child with an audacity grown from his inexperience, thoughtless, headstrong, jealous, and filled with a tinsel courage. A swaggering babe accustomed to strut in his own dooryard. The youth wondered where had been born these new eyes; when his comrade had made the great discovery that there were many men who would refuse to be subjected by him. Apparently, the other had now climbed a peak of wisdom from which he could perceive himself as a very wee thing. And the youth saw that ever after it would be easier to live in his friend's neighborhood.

His comrade balanced his ebony coffee-cup on his knee. "Well, Henry," he said, "what d'yeh think th' chances are? D'yeh think we'll wallop 'em?"

The youth considered for a moment. "Day-b'fore-yesterday," he finally replied, with boldness, "you would 'a' bet you'd lick the hull kit-an'-boodle all by yourself."

His friend looked a trifle amazed. "Would I?" he asked. He pondered. "Well, perhaps I would," he decided at last. He stared humbly at the fire.

The youth was quite disconcerted at this surprising reception of his remarks. "Oh, no, you wouldn't either," he said, hastily trying to retrace.

But the other made a deprecating gesture. "Oh, yeh needn't mind, Henry," he said. "I believe I was a pretty big fool in those days." He spoke as after a lapse of years.

There was a little pause.

"All th' officers say we've got th' rebs in a pretty tight box," said the friend, clearing his throat in a commonplace way. "They all seem t' think we've got 'em jest where we want 'em."

"I don't know about that," the youth replied. "What I seen over on th' right makes me think it was th' other way about. From where I was, it looked as if we was gettin' a good poundin' yestirday."

"D'yeh think so?" inquired the friend. "I thought we handled 'em pretty rough yestirday."

"Not a bit," said the youth. "Why, lord, man, you didn't see nothing of the fight. Why!" Then a sudden thought came to him. "Oh! Jim Conklin's dead."

His friend started. "What? Is he? Jim Conklin?"

The youth spoke slowly. "Yes. He's dead. Shot in th' side."

"Yeh don't say so. Jim Conklin. . . . poor cuss!"

All about them were other small fires surrounded by men with their little black utensils. From one of these near came sudden sharp voices in a row. It appeared that two light-footed soldiers had been teasing a huge, bearded man, causing him to spill coffee upon his blue knees. The man had gone into a rage and had sworn comprehensively. Stung by his language, his tormentors had immediately bristled at him with a great show of resenting unjust oaths. Possibly there was going to be a fight.

The friend arose and went over to them, making pacific motions with his arms. "Oh, here, now, boys, what's th' use?" he said. "We'll be at th' rebs in less'n an hour. What's th' good fightin' 'mong ourselves?"

One of the light-footed soldiers turned upon him red-faced and violent. "Yeh needn't come around here with yer preachin'. I s'pose yeh don't approve 'a fightin' since Charley Morgan licked yeh; but I don't see what business this here is 'a yours or anybody else."

"Well, it ain't," said the friend mildly. "Still I hate t' see——"

There was a tangled argument.

"Well, he——," said the two, indicating their opponent with accusative forefingers.

The huge soldier was quite purple with rage. He pointed at the two soldiers with his great hand, extended clawlike. "Well, they——"

But during this argumentative time the desire to deal blows seemed to pass, although they said much to each other. Finally the friend returned to his old seat. In a short while the three antagonists could be seen together in an amiable bunch.

"Jimmie Rogers ses I'll have t' fight him after th' battle

t'-day," announced the friend as he again seated himself. "He ses he don't allow no interferin' in his business. I hate t' see th' boys fightin' 'mong themselves."

The youth laughed. "Yer changed a good bit. Yeh ain't at all like yeh was. I remember when you an' that Irish feller——" He stopped and laughed again.

"No, I didn't use t' be that way," said his friend thoughtfully. "That's true 'nough."

"Well, I didn't mean——" began the youth.

The friend made another deprecatory gesture. "Oh, yeh needn't mind, Henry."

There was another little pause.

"Th' reg'ment lost over half th' men yestirday," remarked the friend eventually. "I thought 'a course they was all dead, but, laws, they kep' a-comin' back last night until it seems, after all, we didn't lose but a few. They'd been scattered all over, wanderin' around in th' woods, fightin' with other reg'-ments, an' everything. Jest like you done."

"So?" said the youth.

Chapter XV

THE REGIMENT was standing at order arms at the side of a lane, waiting for the command to march, when suddenly the youth remembered the little packet enwrapped in a faded yellow envelope which the loud young soldier with lugubrious words had intrusted to him. It made him start. He uttered an exclamation and turned toward his comrade.

"Wilson!"

"What?"

His friend, at his side in the ranks, was thoughtfully staring down the road. From some cause his expression was at that moment very meek. The youth, regarding him with sidelong glances, felt impelled to change his purpose. "Oh, nothing," he said.

His friend turned his head in some surprise, "Why, what was yeh goin' t' say?"

"Oh, nothing," repeated the youth.

He resolved not to deal the little blow. It was sufficient that the fact made him glad. It was not necessary to knock his friend on the head with the misguided packet.

He had been possessed of much fear of his friend, for he saw how easily questionings could make holes in his feelings. Lately, he had assured himself that the altered comrade would not tantalize him with a persistent curiosity, but he felt certain that during the first period of leisure his friend would ask him to relate his adventures of the previous day.

He now rejoiced in the possession of a small weapon with which he could prostrate his comrade at the first signs of a cross-examination. He was master. It would now be he who could laugh and shoot the shafts of derision.

The friend had, in a weak hour, spoken with sobs of his own death. He had delivered a melancholy oration previous to his funeral, and had doubtless in the packet of letters, presented various keepsakes to relatives. But he had not died, and thus he had delivered himself into the hands of the youth.

The latter felt immensely superior to his friend, but he inclined to condescension. He adopted toward him an air of patronizing good humor.

His self-pride was now entirely restored. In the shade of its flourishing growth he stood with braced and self-confident legs, and since nothing could now be discovered he did not shrink from an encounter with the eyes of judges, and allowed no thoughts of his own to keep him from an attitude of manfulness. He had performed his mistakes in the dark, so he was still a man.

Indeed, when he remembered his fortunes of yesterday, and looked at them from a distance he began to see something fine there. He had license to be pompous and veteranlike.

His panting agonies of the past he put out of his sight.

In the present, he declared to himself that it was only the doomed and the damned who roared with sincerity at circumstance. Few but they ever did it. A man with a full stomach and the respect of his fellows had no business to scold about anything that he might think to be wrong in the ways of the universe, or even with the ways of society. Let the unfortunates rail; the others may play marbles.

He did not give a great deal of thought to these battles that lay directly before him. It was not essential that he should plan his ways in regard to them. He had been taught that many obligations of a life were easily avoided. The lessons of yesterday had been that retribution was a laggard and blind. With these facts before him he did not deem it necessary that he should become feverish over the possibilities of the ensuing twenty-four hours. He could leave much to chance. Besides, a faith in himself had secretly blossomed. There was a little flower of confidence growing within him. He was now a man of experience. He had been out among the dragons, he said, and he assured himself that they were not so hideous as he had imagined them. Also, they were inaccurate; they did not sting with precision. A stout heart often defied, and defying, escaped.

And, furthermore, how could they kill him who was the chosen of gods and doomed to greatness?

He remembered how some of the men had run from the battle. As he recalled their terror-struck faces he felt a scorn for them. They had surely been more fleet and more wild than was absolutely necessary. They were weak mortals. As for himself, he had fled with discretion and dignity.

He was aroused from this reverie by his friend, who, having hitched about nervously and blinked at the trees for a time, suddenly coughed in an introductory way, and spoke.

"Fleming!"

"What?"

The friend put his hand up to his mouth and coughed again. He fidgeted in his jacket.

"Well," he gulped, at last, "I guess yeh might as well give me back them letters." Dark, prickling blood had flushed into his cheeks and brow.

"All right, Wilson," said the youth. He loosened two buttons of his coat, thrust in his hand, and brought forth the packet. As he extended it to his friend the latter's face was turned from him.

He had been slow in the act of producing the packet because during it he had been trying to invent a remarkable comment upon the affair. He could conjure nothing of sufficient point. He was compelled to allow his friend to escape unmolested with his packet. And for this he took unto himself considerable credit. It was a generous thing.

His friend at his side seemed suffering great shame. As he contemplated him, the youth felt his heart grow more strong and stout. He had never been compelled to blush in such manner for his acts; he was an individual of extraordinary virtues.

He reflected, with condescending pity: "Too bad! Too bad! The poor devil, it makes him feel tough!"

After this incident, and as he reviewed the battle pictures he had seen, he felt quite competent to return home and make the hearts of the people glow with stories of war. He could see himself in a room of warm tints telling tales to listeners. He could exhibit laurels. They were insignificant; still, in a district where laurels were infrequent, they might shine.

He saw his gaping audience picturing him as the central figure in blazing scenes. And he imagined the consternation and the ejaculations of his mother and the young lady at the seminary as they drank his recitals. Their vague feminine formula for beloved ones doing brave deeds on the field of battle without risk of life would be destroyed.

Chapter XVI

A SPUTTERING OF MUSKETRY was always to be heard. Later, the cannon had entered the dispute. In the fog-filled air their voices made a thudding sound. The reverberations were continual. This part of the world led a strange, battleful existence.

The youth's regiment was marched to relieve a command that had lain long in some damp trenches. The men took positions behind a curving line of rifle pits that had been turned up, like a large furrow, along the line of woods. Before them was a level stretch, peopled with short, deformed stumps. From the woods beyond came the dull popping of the skirmishers and pickets, firing in the fog. From the right came the noise of a terrific fracas.

The men cuddled behind the small embankment and sat in easy attitudes awaiting their turn. Many had their backs to the firing. The youth's friend lay down, buried his face in his arms, and almost instantly, it seemed, he was in a deep sleep.

The youth leaned his breast against the brown dirt and peered over at the woods and up and down the line. Curtains of trees interfered with his ways of vision. He could see the low line of trenches but for a short distance. A few idle flags were perched on the dirt hills. Behind them were rows of dark bodies with a few heads sticking curiously over the top.

Always the noise of skirmishers came from the woods on the front and left, and the din on the right had grown to frightful proportions. The guns were roaring without an instant's pause for breath. It seemed that the cannon had come from all parts and were engaged in a stupendous wrangle. It became impossible to make a sentence heard.

The youth wished to launch a joke—a quotation from newspapers. He desired to say, "All quiet on the Rappahannock," but the guns refused to permit even a comment upon their uproar. He never successfully concluded the sentence. But at last the guns stopped, and among the men in the rifle pits rumors again flew, like birds, but they were now for the most part black creatures who flapped their wings drearily near to the ground and refused to rise on any wings of hope.

The men's faces grew doleful from the interpreting of omens. Tales of hesitation and uncertainty on the part of those high in place and responsibility came to their ears. Stories of disaster were borne into their minds with many proofs. This din of musketry on the right, growing like a released genie of sound, expressed and emphasized the army's plight.

The men were disheartened and began to mutter. They made gestures expressive of the sentence: "Ah, what more can we do?" And it could always be seen that they were bewildered by the alleged news and could not fully comprehend a defeat.

Before the gray mists had been totally obliterated by the sun rays, the regiment was marching in a spread column that was retiring carefully through the woods. The disordered, hurrying lines of the enemy could sometimes be seen down through the groves and little fields. They were yelling, shrill and exultant.

At this sight the youth forgot many personal matters and became greatly enraged. He exploded in loud sentences. "B'jiminey, we're generaled by a lot 'a lunkheads."

"More than one feller has said that t'-day," observed a man.

His friend, recently aroused, was still very drowsy. He looked behind him until his mind took in the meaning of the movement. Then he sighed. "Oh, well, I s'pose we got licked," he remarked sadly.

The youth had a thought that it would not be handsome for him to freely condemn other men. He made an attempt to restrain himself, but the words upon his tongue were too bitter. He presently began a long and intricate denunciation of the commander of the forces.

"Mebbe, it wa'n't all his fault—not all together. He did th' best he knowed. It's our luck t' git licked often," said his friend in a weary tone. He was trudging along with stooped shoulders and shifting eyes like a man who has been caned and kicked.

"Well, don't we fight like the devil? Don't we do all that men can?" demanded the youth loudly.

He was secretly dumfounded at this sentiment when it came from his lips. For a moment his face lost its valor and he looked guiltily about him. But no one questioned his right to deal in such words, and presently he recovered his air of courage. He went on to repeat a statement he had heard going from group to group at the camp that morning. "The brigadier said he never saw a new reg'ment fight the way we fought yestirday, didn't he? And we didn't do better than many another reg'ment, did we? Well, then, you can't say it's th' army's fault, can you?"

In his reply, the friend's voice was stern. " 'A course not," he said. "No man dare say we don't fight like th' devil. No man will ever dare say it. Th' boys fight like hell-roosters. But still—still, we don't have no luck."

"Well, then, if we fight like the devil an' don't ever whip, it must be the general's fault," said the youth grandly and decisively. "And I don't see any sense in fighting and fighting and fighting, yet always losing through some derned old lunkhead of a general."

A sarcastic man who was tramping at the youth's side, then spoke lazily. "Mebbe yeh think yeh fit th' hull battle yestirday, Fleming," he remarked.

The speech pierced the youth. Inwardly he was reduced to an abject pulp by these chance words. His legs quaked privately. He cast a frightened glance at the sarcastic man.

"Why, no," he hastened to say in a conciliating voice, "I don't think I fought the whole battle yesterday."

But the other seemed innocent of any deeper meaning. Apparently, he had no information. It was merely his habit. "Oh!" he replied in the same tone of calm derision.

The youth, nevertheless, felt a threat. His mind shrank from going near to the danger, and thereafter he was silent. The significance of the sarcastic man's words took from him all loud moods that would make him appear prominent. He became suddenly a modest person.

There was low-toned talk among the troops. The officers were impatient and snappy, their countenances clouded with the tales of misfortune. The troops, sifting through the forest, were sullen. In the youth's company once a man's laugh rang out. A dozen soldiers turned their faces quickly toward him and frowned with vague displeasure.

The noise of firing dogged their footsteps. Sometimes, it seemed to be driven a little way, but it always returned again with increased insolence. The men muttered and cursed, throwing black looks in its direction.

In a clear space the troops were at last halted. Regiments and brigades, broken and detached through their encounters with thickets, grew together again and lines were faced toward the pursuing bark of the enemy's infantry.

This noise, following like the yelpings of eager, metallic hounds, increased to a loud and joyous burst, and then, as the sun went serenely up the sky, throwing illuminating rays into the gloomy thickets, it broke forth into prolonged pealings. The woods began to crackle as if afire.

"Whoop-a-dadee," said a man, "here we are! Everybody fightin'. Blood an' destruction."

"I was willin' t' bet they'd attack as soon as th' sun got fairly up," savagely asserted the lieutenant who commanded the youth's company. He jerked without mercy at his little mustache. He strode to and fro with dark dignity in the rear of his men, who were lying down behind whatever protection they had collected.

A battery had trundled into position in the rear and was thoughtfully shelling the distance. The regiment, unmolested as yet, awaited the moment when the gray shadows of the woods before them should be slashed by the lines of flame. There was much growling and swearing.

"Good Gawd," the youth grumbled, "we're always being chased around like rats! It makes me sick. Nobody seems to know where we go or why we go. We just get fired around from pillar to post and get licked here and get licked there, and nobody knows what it's done for. It makes a man feel like a damn' kitten in a bag. Now, I'd like to know what the eternal thunders we was marched into these woods for anyhow, unless it was to give the rebs a regular pot shot at us. We came in here and got our legs all tangled up in these cussed briers, and then we begin to fight and the rebs had an easy time of it. Don't tell me it's just luck! I know better. It's this derned old——"

The friend seemed jaded, but he interrupted his comrade with a voice of calm confidence. "It'll turn out all right in th' end," he said.

"Oh, the devil it will! You always talk like a dog-hanged parson. Don't tell me! I know——"

At this time there was an interposition by the savage-minded lieutenant, who was obliged to vent some of his inward dissatisfaction upon his men. "You boys shut right up! There no need 'a your wastin' your breath in long-winded arguments about this an' that an' th' other. You've been jawin' like a lot 'a old hens. All you've got t' do is to fight, an' you'll get plenty 'a that t' do in about ten minutes. Less talkin' an' more fightin' is what's best for you boys. I never saw sech gabbling jackasses."

He paused, ready to pounce upon any man who might have the temerity to reply. No words being said, he resumed his dignified pacing.

"There's too much chin music an' too little fightin' in this war, anyhow," he said to them, turning his head for a final remark.

The day had grown more white, until the sun shed his full radiance upon the thronged forest. A sort of a gust of battle came sweeping toward that part of the line where lay the youth's regiment. The front shifted a trifle to meet it squarely. There was a wait. In this part of the field there passed slowly the intense moments that precede the tempest.

A single rifle flashed in a thicket before the regiment. In an instant it was joined by many others. There was a mighty song of clashes and crashes that went sweeping through the woods. The guns in the rear, aroused and enraged by shells that had been thrown burr-like at them, suddenly involved themselves in a hideous altercation with another band of guns. The battle roar settled to a rolling thunder, which was a single, long explosion.

In the regiment there was a peculiar kind of hesitation denoted in the attitudes of the men. They were worn, exhausted, having slept but little and labored much. They rolled their eyes toward the advancing battle as they stood awaiting the shock. Some shrank and flinched. They stood as men tied to stakes.

Chapter XVII

THIS ADVANCE OF THE ENEMY had seemed to the youth like a ruthless hunting. He began to fume with rage and exasperation. He beat his foot upon the ground, and scowled with hate at the swirling smoke that was approaching like a phantom flood. There was a maddening quality in this seeming resolution of the foe to give him no rest, to give him no time to sit down and think. Yesterday he had fought and had fled rapidly. There had been many adventures. For to-day he felt that he had earned opportunities for contemplative repose. He could have enjoyed portraying to uninitiated listeners various scenes at which he had been a witness or ably discussing the processes of war with other proved men. Too it was important that he should have time for physical recuperation. He was sore and stiff from his experiences. He had received his fill of all exertions, and he wished to rest.

But those other men seemed never to grow weary; they were fighting with their old speed. He had a wild hate for the relentless foe. Yesterday, when he had imagined the universe to be against him, he had hated it, little gods and big gods; to-day he hated the army of the foe with the same great hatred. He was not going to be badgered of his life, like a kitten chased by boys, he said. It was not well to drive men into final corners; at those moments they could all develop teeth and claws.

He leaned and spoke into his friend's ear. He menaced the woods with a gesture. "If they keep on chasing us, by Gawd, they'd better watch out. Can't stand *too* much."

The friend twisted his head and made a calm reply. "If they keep on a-chasin' us they'll drive us all inteh th' river."

The youth cried out savagely at this statement. He crouched behind a little tree, with his eyes burning hatefully and his teeth set in a curlike snarl. The awkward bandage was still about his head, and upon it, over his wound, there was a spot of dry blood. His hair was wondrously tousled, and some straggling, moving locks hung over the cloth of the bandage down toward his forehead. His jacket and shirt were open at the throat, and exposed his young bronzed neck. There could be seen spasmodic gulpings at his throat.

His fingers twined nervously about his rifle. He wished that it was an engine of annihilating power. He felt that he and his companions were being taunted and derided from sincere convictions that they were poor and puny. His knowledge of his inability to take vengeance for it made his rage into a dark and stormy specter, that possessed him and made him dream of abominable cruelties. The tormentors were flies sucking insolently at his blood, and he thought that he would have given his life for a revenge of seeing their faces in pitiful plights.

The winds of battle had swept all about the regiment, until the one rifle, instantly followed by others, flashed in its front. A moment later the regiment roared forth its sudden and valiant retort. A dense wall of smoke settled slowly down. It was furiously slit and slashed by the knifelike fire from the rifles.

To the youth the fighters resembled animals tossed for a death struggle into a dark pit. There was a sensation that he and his fellows, at bay, were pushing back, always pushing fierce onslaughts of creatures who were slippery. Their beams of crimson seemed to get no purchase upon the bodies of their foes; the latter seemed to evade them with ease, and come through, between, around, and about with unopposed skill.

When, in a dream, it occurred to the youth that his rifle was an impotent stick, he lost sense of everything but his hate, his desire to smash into pulp the glittering smile of victory which he could feel upon the faces of his enemies.

The blue smoke-swallowed line curled and writhed like a snake stepped upon. It swung its ends to and fro in an agony of fear and rage.

The youth was not conscious that he was erect upon his feet. He did not know the direction of the ground. Indeed, once he even lost the habit of balance and fell heavily. He was up again immediately. One thought went through the chaos of his brain at the time. He wondered if he had fallen because he had been shot. But the suspicion flew away at once. He did not think more of it.

He had taken up a first position behind the little tree, with a direct determination to hold it against the world. He had not deemed it possible that his army could that day succeed, and from this he felt the ability to fight harder. But the throng had surged in all ways, until he lost directions and locations, save that he knew where lay the enemy.

The flames bit him, and the hot smoke broiled his skin. His rifle barrel grew so hot that ordinarily he could not have borne it upon his palms; but he kept on stuffing cartridges into it, and pounding them with his clanking, bending ramrod. If he aimed at some changing form through the smoke, he pulled his trigger with a fierce grunt, as if he were dealing a blow of the fist with all his strength.

When the enemy seemed falling back before him and his fellows, he went instantly forward, like a dog who, seeing his foes lagging, turns and insists upon being pursued. And when he was compelled to retire again, he did it slowly, sullenly, taking steps of wrathful despair.

Once he, in his intent hate, was almost alone, and was firing, when all those near him had ceased. He was so engrossed in his occupation that he was not aware of a lull.

He was recalled by a hoarse laugh and a sentence that came to his ears in a voice of contempt and amazement. "Yeh infernal fool, don't yeh know enough t' quit when there ain't anything t' shoot at? Good Gawd!"

He turned then and, pausing with his rifle thrown half into position, looked at the blue line of his comrades. During this moment of leisure they seemed all to be engaged in staring with astonishment at him. They had become spectators. Turning to the front again he saw, under the lifted smoke, a deserted ground.

He looked bewildered for a moment. Then there appeared upon the glazed vacancy of his eyes a diamond point of intelligence. "Oh," he said, comprehending.

He returned to his comrades and threw himself upon the ground. He sprawled like a man who had been thrashed. His flesh seemed strangely on fire, and the sounds of the battle continued in his ears. He groped blindly for his canteen.

The lieutenant was crowing. He seemed drunk with fighting. He called out to the youth: "By heavens, if I had ten thousand wild cats like you I could tear th' stomach outa this war in less'n a week!" He puffed out his chest with large dignity as he said it.

Some of the men muttered and looked at the youth in awe-struck ways. It was plain that as he had gone on loading and firing and cursing without the proper intermission, they had found time to regard him. And they now looked upon him as a war devil.

The friend came staggering to him. There was some fright and dismay in his voice. "Are yeh all right, Fleming? Do yeh feel all right? There ain't nothin' th' matter with yeh, Henry, is there?"

"No," said the youth with difficulty. His throat seemed full of knobs and burrs.

These incidents made the youth ponder. It was revealed to him that he had been a barbarian, a beast. He had fought like a pagan who defends his religion. Regarding it, he saw that it was fine, wild, and, in some ways, easy. He had been a tremendous figure, no doubt. By this struggle he had overcome obstacles which he had admitted to be mountains. They had fallen like paper peaks, and he was now what he called a hero. And he had not been aware of the process. He had slept and, awakening, found himself a knight.

He lay and basked in the occasional stares of his comrades. Their faces were varied in degrees of blackness from the burned powder. Some were utterly smudged. They were reeking with perspiration, and their breaths came hard and wheezing. And from these soiled expanses they peered at him.

"Hot work! Hot work!" cried the lieutenant deliriously. He walked up and down, restless and eager. Sometimes his voice could be heard in a wild, incomprehensible laugh.

When he had a particularly profound thought upon the science of war he always unconsciously addressed himself to the youth.

There was some grim rejoicing by the men. "By thunder, I bet this army'll never see another new reg'ment like us!"

"You bet!"

"A dog, a woman, an' a walnut tree,
Th' more yeh beat 'em, th' better they be!

That's like us."

"Lost a piler men, they did. If an ol' woman swep' up th' woods she'd git a dustpanful."

"Yes, an' if she'll come around ag'in in 'bout an hour she'll git a pile more."

The forest still bore its burden of clamor. From off under the trees came the rolling clatter of the musketry. Each distant thicket seemed a strange porcupine with quills of flame. A cloud of dark smoke, as from smoldering ruins, went up toward the sun now bright and gay in the blue, enameled sky.

Chapter XVIII

THE RAGGED LINE had respite for some minutes, but during its pause the struggle in the forest became magnified until the trees seemed to quiver from the firing and the ground to shake from the rushing of the men. The voices of the cannon were mingled in a long and interminable row. It seemed difficult to live in such an atmosphere. The chests of the men strained for a bit of freshness, and their throats craved water.

There was one shot through the body, who raised a cry of bitter lamentation when came this lull. Perhaps he had been calling out during the fighting also, but at that time no one had heard him. But now the men turned at the woeful complaints of him upon the ground.

"Who is it? Who is it?"

"It's Jimmie Rogers. Jimmie Rogers."

When their eyes first encountered him there was a sudden halt, as if they feared to go near. He was thrashing about in the grass, twisting his shuddering body into many strange postures. He was screaming loudly. This instant's hesitation seemed to fill him with a tremendous, fantastic contempt, and he damned them in shrieked sentences.

The youth's friend had a geographical illusion concerning a stream, and he obtained permission to go for some water. Immediately canteens were showered upon him. "Fill mine, will yeh?" "Bring me some, too." "And me, too." He departed, ladened. The youth went with his friend, feeling a desire to throw his heated body into the stream and, soaking there, drink quarts.

They made a hurried search for the supposed stream, but did not find it. "No water here," said the youth. They turned without delay and began to retrace their steps.

From their position as they again faced toward the place of the fighting, they could of course comprehend a greater amount of the battle than when their visions had been blurred by the hurling smoke of the line. They could see dark stretches winding along the land, and on one cleared space there was a row of guns making gray clouds, which were

filled with large flashes of orange-colored flame. Over some
foliage they could see the roof of a house. One window,
glowing a deep murder red, shone squarely through the
leaves. From the edifice a tall leaning tower of smoke went
far into the sky.

Looking over their own troops, they saw mixed masses
slowly getting into regular form. The sunlight made twin-
kling points of the bright steel. To the rear there was a
glimpse of a distant roadway as it curved over a slope. It was
crowded with retreating infantry. From all the interwoven
forest arose the smoke and bluster of the battle. The air was
always occupied by a blaring.

Near where they stood shells were flip-flapping and hoot-
ing. Occasional bullets buzzed in the air and spanged into tree
trunks. Wounded men and other stragglers were slinking
through the woods.

Looking down an aisle of the grove, the youth and his
companion saw a jangling general and his staff almost ride
upon a wounded man, who was crawling on his hands and
knees. The general reined strongly at his charger's opened
and foamy mouth and guided it with dexterous horsemanship
past the man. The latter scrambled in wild and torturing
haste. His strength evidently failed him as he reached a place
of safety. One of his arms suddenly weakened, and he fell,
sliding over upon his back. He lay stretched out, breathing
gently.

A moment later the small, creaking cavalcade was directly
in front of the two soldiers. Another officer, riding with the
skillful abandon of a cowboy, galloped his horse to a position
directly before the general. The two unnoticed foot soldiers
made a little show of going on, but they lingered near in the
desire to overhear the conversation. Perhaps, they thought,
some great inner historical things would be said.

The general, whom the boys knew as the commander of
their division, looked at the other officer and spoke coolly, as
if he were criticising his clothes. "Th' enemy's formin' over
there for another charge," he said. "It'll be directed against
Whiterside, an' I fear they'll break through there unless we
work like thunder t' stop them."

The other swore at his restive horse, and then cleared his

throat. He made a gesture toward his cap. "It'll be hell t' pay stoppin' them," he said shortly.

"I presume so," remarked the general. Then he began to talk rapidly and in a lower tone. He frequently illustrated his words with a pointing finger. The two infantrymen could hear nothing until finally he asked: "What troops can you spare?"

The officer who rode like a cowboy reflected for an instant. "Well," he said, "I had to order in th' 12th to help th' 76th, an' I haven't really got any. But there's th' 304th. They fight like a lot 'a mule drivers. I can spare them best of any."

The youth and his friend exchanged glances of astonishment.

The general spoke sharply. "Get 'em ready, then. I'll watch developments from here, an' send you word when t' start them. It'll happen in five minutes."

As the other officer tossed his fingers toward his cap and wheeling his horse, started away, the general called out to him in a sober voice: "I don't believe many of your mule drivers will get back."

The other shouted something in reply. He smiled.

With scared faces, the youth and his companion hurried back to the line.

These happenings had occupied an incredibly short time, yet the youth felt that in them he had been made aged. New eyes were given to him. And the most startling thing was to learn suddenly that he was very insignificant. The officer spoke of the regiment as if he referred to a broom. Some part of the woods needed sweeping, perhaps, and he merely indicated a broom in a tone properly indifferent to its fate. It was war, no doubt, but it appeared strange.

As the two boys approached the line, the lieutenant perceived them and swelled with wrath. "Fleming—Wilson— how long does it take yeh to git water, anyhow—where yeh been to."

But his oration ceased as he saw their eyes, which were large with great tales. "We're goin' t' charge—we're goin' t' charge!" cried the youth's friend, hastening with his news.

"Charge?" said the lieutenant. "Charge? Well, b'Gawd!

Now, this is real fightin'." Over his soiled countenance there went a boastful smile. "Charge? Well, b'Gawd!"

A little group of soldiers surrounded the two youths. "Are we, sure 'nough? Well, I'll be derned! Charge? What fer? What at? Wilson, you're lyin'."

"I hope to die," said the youth, pitching his tones to the key of angry remonstrance. "Sure as shooting, I tell you."

And his friend spoke in re-enforcement. "Not by a blame sight, he ain't lyin'. We heard 'em talkin'."

They caught sight of two mounted figures a short distance from them. One was the colonel of the regiment and the other was the officer who had received orders from the commander of the division. They were gesticulating at each other. The soldier, pointing at them, interpreted the scene.

One man had a final objection: "How could yeh hear 'em talkin'?" But the men, for a large part, nodded, admitting that previously the two friends had spoken truth.

They settled back into reposeful attitudes with airs of having accepted the matter. And they mused upon it, with a hundred varieties of expression. It was an engrossing thing to think about. Many tightened their belts carefully and hitched at their trousers.

A moment later the officers began to bustle among the men, pushing them into a more compact mass and into a better alignment. They chased those that straggled and fumed at a few men who seemed to show by their attitudes that they had decided to remain at that spot. They were like critical shepherds struggling with sheep.

Presently, the regiment seemed to draw itself up and heave a deep breath. None of the men's faces were mirrors of large thoughts. The soldiers were bended and stooped like sprinters before a signal. Many pairs of glinting eyes peered from the grimy faces toward the curtains of the deeper woods. They seemed to be engaged in deep calculations of time and distance.

They were surrounded by the noises of the monstrous altercation between the two armies. The world was fully interested in other matters. Apparently, the regiment had its small affair to itself.

The youth, turning, shot a quick, inquiring glance at his

friend. The latter returned to him the same manner of look. They were the only ones who possessed an inner knowledge. "Mule drivers—hell t' pay—don't believe many will get back." It was an ironical secret. Still, they saw no hesitation in each other's faces, and they nodded a mute and unprotesting assent when a shaggy man near them said in a meek voice: "We'll git swallowed."

Chapter XIX

THE YOUTH STARED at the land in front of him. Its foliages now seemed to veil powers and horrors. He was unaware of the machinery of orders that started the charge, although from the corners of his eyes he saw an officer, who looked like a boy a-horseback, come galloping, waving his hat. Suddenly he felt a straining and heaving among the men. The line fell slowly forward like a toppling wall, and, with a convulsive gasp that was intended for a cheer, the regiment began its journey. The youth was pushed and jostled for a moment before he understood the movement at all, but directly he lunged ahead and began to run.

He fixed his eye upon a distant and prominent clump of trees where he had concluded the enemy were to be met, and he ran toward it as toward a goal. He had believed throughout that it was a mere question of getting over an unpleasant matter as quickly as possible, and he ran desperately, as if pursued for a murder. His face was drawn hard and tight with the stress of his endeavor. His eyes were fixed in a lurid glare. And with his soiled and disordered dress, his red and inflamed features surmounted by the dingy rag with its spot of blood, his wildly swinging rifle and banging accouterments, he looked to be an insane soldier.

As the regiment swung from its position out into a cleared space the woods and thickets before it awakened. Yellow flames leaped toward it from many directions. The forest made a tremendous objection.

The line lurched straight for a moment. Then the right wing swung forward; it in turn was surpassed by the left. Afterward the center careered to the front until the regiment was a wedge-shaped mass, but an instant later the opposition of the bushes, trees, and uneven places on the ground split the command and scattered it into detached clusters.

The youth, light-footed, was unconsciously in advance. His eyes still kept note of the clump of trees. From all places near it the clannish yell of the enemy could be heard. The little flames of rifles leaped from it. The song of the bullets was in the air and shells snarled among the treetops. One tumbled directly into the middle of a hurrying group and exploded in crimson fury. There was an instant's spectacle of a man, almost over it, throwing up his hands to shield his eyes.

Other men, punched by bullets, fell in grotesque agonies. The regiment left a coherent trail of bodies.

They had passed into a clearer atmosphere. There was an effect like a revelation in the new appearance of the landscape. Some men working madly at a battery were plain to them, and the opposing infantry's lines were defined by the gray walls and fringes of smoke.

It seemed to the youth that he saw everything. Each blade of the green grass was bold and clear. He thought that he was aware of every change in the thin, transparent vapor that floated idly in sheets. The brown or gray trunks of the trees showed each roughness of their surfaces. And the men of the regiment, with their starting eyes and sweating faces, running madly, or falling, as if thrown headlong, to queer, heaped-up corpses—all were comprehended. His mind took a mechanical but firm impression, so that afterward everything was pictured and explained to him, save why he himself was there.

But there was a frenzy made from this furious rush. The men, pitching forward insanely, had burst into cheerings, moblike and barbaric, but tuned in strange keys that can arouse the dullard and the stoic. It made a mad enthusiasm that, it seemed, would be incapable of checking itself before granite and brass. There was the delirium that encounters despair and death, and is heedless and blind to the odds. It is a temporary but sublime absence of selfishness. And because it was of this order was the reason, perhaps, why the youth wondered, afterward, what reasons he could have had for being there.

Presently the straining pace ate up the energies of the men. As if by agreement, the leaders began to slacken their speed. The volleys directed against them had had a seeming windlike effect. The regiment snorted and blew. Among some stolid trees it began to falter and hesitate. The men, staring intently, began to wait for some of the distant walls of smoke to move and disclose to them the scene. Since much of their strength and their breath had vanished, they returned to caution. They were become men again.

The youth had a vague belief that he had run miles, and he thought, in a way, that he was now in some new and unknown land.

The moment the regiment ceased its advance the protesting splutter of musketry became a steadied roar. Long and accurate fringes of smoke spread out. From the top of a small hill came level belchings of yellow flame that caused an inhuman whistling in the air.

The men, halted, had opportunity to see some of their comrades dropping with moans and shrieks. A few lay under foot, still or wailing. And now for an instant the men stood, their rifles slack in their hands, and watched the regiment dwindle. They appeared dazed and stupid. This spectacle seemed to paralyze them, overcome them with a fatal fascination. They stared woodenly at the sights, and, lowering their eyes, looked from face to face. It was a strange pause, and a strange silence.

Then, above the sounds of the outside commotion, arose the roar of the lieutenant. He strode suddenly forth, his infantile features black with rage.

"Come on, yeh fools!" he bellowed. "Come on! Yeh can't stay here. Yeh must come on." He said more, but much of it could not be understood.

He started rapidly forward, with his head turned toward the men. "Come on," he was shouting. The men stared with blank and yokel-like eyes at him. He was obliged to halt and retrace his steps. He stood then with his back to the enemy and delivered gigantic curses into the faces of the men. His body vibrated from the weight and force of his imprecations. And he could string oaths with the facility of a maiden who strings beads.

The friend of the youth aroused. Lurching suddenly forward and dropping to his knees, he fired an angry shot at the persistent woods. This action awakened the men. They huddled no more like sheep. They seemed suddenly to bethink them of their weapons, and at once commenced firing. Belabored by their officers, they began to move forward. The regiment, involved like a cart involved in mud and muddle, started unevenly with many jolts and jerks. The men stopped now every few paces to fire and load, and in this manner moved slowly on from trees to trees.

The flaming opposition in their front grew with their advance until it seemed that all forward ways were barred by the thin leaping tongues, and off to the right an ominous demonstration could sometimes be dimly discerned. The smoke lately generated was in confusing clouds that made it difficult for the regiment to proceed with intelligence. As he passed through each curling mass the youth wondered what would confront him on the farther side.

The command went painfully forward until an open space interposed between them and the lurid lines. Here, crouching and cowering behind some trees, the men clung with desperation, as if threatened by a wave. They looked wild-eyed, and as if amazed at this furious disturbance they had stirred. In the storm there was an ironical expression of their importance. The faces of the men, too, showed a lack of a certain feeling of responsibility for being there. It was as if they had been driven. It was the dominant animal failing to remember in the supreme moments the forceful causes of various superficial qualities. The whole affair seemed incomprehensible to many of them.

As they halted thus the lieutenant again began to bellow profanely. Regardless of the vindictive threats of the bullets, he went about coaxing, berating, and bedamning. His lips, that were habitually in a soft and childlike curve, were now writhed into unholy contortions. He swore by all possible deities.

Once he grabbed the youth by the arm. "Come on, yeh lunkhead!" he roared. "Come on! We'll all git killed if we stay here. We've on'y got t' go across that lot. An' then"—the remainder of his idea disappeared in a blue haze of curses.

The youth stretched forth his arm. "Cross there?" His mouth was puckered in doubt and awe.

"Certainly. Jest 'cross th' lot! We can't stay here," screamed the lieutenant. He poked his face close to the youth and waved his bandaged hand. "Come on!" Presently he grappled with him as if for a wrestling bout. It was as if he planned to drag the youth by the ear on to the assault.

The private felt a sudden unspeakable indignation against his officer. He wrenched fiercely and shook him off.

"Come on yerself, then," he yelled. There was a bitter challenge in his voice.

They galloped together down the regimental front. The friend scrambled after them. In front of the colors the three men began to bawl: "Come on! come on!" They danced and gyrated like tortured savages.

The flag, obedient to these appeals, bended its glittering form and swept toward them. The men wavered in indecision for a moment, and then with a long, wailful cry the dilapidated regiment surged forward and began its new journey.

Over the field went the scurrying mass. It was a handful of men splattered into the faces of the enemy. Toward it instantly sprang the yellow tongues. A vast quantity of blue smoke hung before them. A mighty banging made ears valueless.

The youth ran like a madman to reach the woods before a bullet could discover him. He ducked his head low, like a football player. In his haste his eyes almost closed, and the scene was a wild blur. Pulsating saliva stood at the corners of his mouth.

Within him, as he hurled himself forward, was born a love, a despairing fondness for this flag which was near him. It was a creation of beauty and invulnerability. It was a goddess, radiant, that bended its form with an imperious gesture to him. It was a woman, red and white, hating and loving, that called him with the voice of his hopes. Because no harm could come to it he endowed it with power. He kept near, as if it could be a saver of lives, and an imploring cry went from his mind.

In the mad scramble he was aware that the color sergeant flinched suddenly, as if struck by a bludgeon. He faltered, and then became motionless, save for his quivering knees.

He made a spring and a clutch at the pole. At the same instant his friend grabbed it from the other side. They jerked at it, stout and furious, but the color sergeant was dead, and the corpse would not relinquish its trust. For a moment there was a grim encounter. The dead man, swinging with bended back, seemed to be obstinately tugging, in ludicrous and awful ways, for the possession of the flag.

It was past in an instant of time. They wrenched the flag furiously from the dead man, and, as they turned again, the corpse swayed forward with bowed head. One arm swung high, and the curved hand fell with heavy protest on the friend's unheeding shoulder.

Chapter XX

WHEN THE TWO YOUTHS turned with the flag they saw that much of the regiment had crumbled away, and the dejected remnant was coming slowly back. The men, having hurled themselves in projectile fashion, had presently expended their forces. They slowly retreated, with their faces still toward the spluttering woods, and their hot rifles still replying to the din. Several officers were giving orders, their voices keyed to screams.

"Where in hell yeh goin'?" the lieutenant was asking in a sarcastic howl. And a red-bearded officer, whose voice of triple brass could plainly be heard, was commanding: "Shoot into 'em! Shoot into 'em, Gawd damn their souls!" There was a *melée* of screeches, in which the men were ordered to do conflicting and impossible things.

The youth and his friend had a small scuffle over the flag. "Give it t' me!" "No, let me keep it!" Each felt satisfied with the other's possession of it, but each felt bound to declare, by an offer to carry the emblem, his willingness to further risk himself. The youth roughly pushed his friend away.

The regiment fell back to the stolid trees. There it halted for a moment to blaze at some dark forms that had begun to steal upon its track. Presently it resumed its march again, curving among the tree trunks. By the time the depleted regiment had again reached the first open space they were receiving a fast and merciless fire. There seemed to be mobs all about them.

The greater part of the men, discouraged, their spirits worn by the turmoil, acted as if stunned. They accepted the pelting of the bullets with bowed and weary heads. It was of no purpose to strive against walls. It was of no use to batter themselves against granite. And from this consciousness that they had attempted to conquer an unconquerable thing there seemed to arise a feeling that they had been betrayed. They glowered with bent brows, but dangerously, upon some of the officers, more particularly upon the red-bearded one with the voice of triple brass.

However, the rear of the regiment was fringed with men,

who continued to shoot irritably at the advancing foes. They seemed resolved to make every trouble. The youthful lieutenant was perhaps the last man in the disordered mass. His forgotten back was toward the enemy. He had been shot in the arm. It hung straight and rigid. Occasionally he would cease to remember it, and be about to emphasize an oath with a sweeping gesture. The multiplied pain caused him to swear with incredible power.

The youth went along with slipping, uncertain feet. He kept watchful eyes rearward. A scowl of mortification and rage was upon his face. He had thought of a fine revenge upon the officer who had referred to him and his fellows as mule drivers. But he saw that it could not come to pass. His dreams had collapsed when the mule drivers, dwindling rapidly, had wavered and hesitated on the little clearing, and then had recoiled. And now the retreat of the mule drivers was a march of shame to him.

A dagger-pointed gaze from without his blackened face was held toward the enemy, but his greater hatred was riveted upon the man, who, not knowing him, had called him a mule driver.

When he knew that he and his comrades had failed to do anything in successful ways that might bring the little pangs of a kind of remorse upon the officer, the youth allowed the rage of the baffled to possess him. This cold officer upon a monument, who dropped epithets unconcernedly down, would be finer as a dead man, he thought. So grievous did he think it that he could never possess the secret right to taunt truly in answer.

He had pictured red letters of curious revenge. "We *are* mule drivers, are we?" And now he was compelled to throw them away.

He presently wrapped his heart in the cloak of his pride and kept the flag erect. He harangued his fellows, pushing against their chests with his free hand. To those he knew well he made frantic appeals, beseeching them by name. Between him and the lieutenant, scolding and near to losing his mind with rage, there was felt a subtle fellowship and equality. They supported each other in all manner of hoarse, howling protests.

But the regiment was a machine run down. The two men babbled at a forceless thing. The soldiers who had heart to go slowly were continually shaken in their resolves by a knowledge that comrades were slipping with speed back to the lines. It was difficult to think of reputation when others were thinking of skins. Wounded men were left crying on this black journey.

The smoke fringes and flames blustered always. The youth, peering once through a sudden rift in a cloud, saw a brown mass of troops, interwoven and magnified until they appeared to be thousands. A fierce-hued flag flashed before his vision.

Immediately, as if the uplifting of the smoke had been prearranged, the discovered troops burst into a rasping yell, and a hundred flames jetted toward the retreating band. A rolling gray cloud again interposed as the regiment doggedly replied. The youth had to depend again upon his misused ears, which were trembling and buzzing from the *melée* of musketry and yells.

The way seemed eternal. In the clouded haze men became panic-stricken with the thought that the regiment had lost its path, and was proceeding in a perilous direction. Once the men who headed the wild procession turned and came pushing back against their comrades, screaming that they were being fired upon from points which they had considered to be toward their own lines. At this cry a hysterical fear and dismay beset the troops. A soldier, who heretofore had been ambitious to make the regiment into a wise little band that would proceed calmly amid the huge-appearing difficulties, suddenly sank down and buried his face in his arms with an air of bowing to a doom. From another a shrill lamentation rang out filled with profane allusions to a general. Men ran hither and thither, seeking with their eyes roads of escape. With serene regularity, as if controlled by a schedule, bullets buffed into men.

The youth walked stolidly into the midst of the mob, and with his flag in his hands took a stand as if he expected an attempt to push him to the ground. He unconsciously assumed the attitude of the color bearer in the fight of the preceding day. He passed over his brow a hand that trembled.

His breath did not come freely. He was choking during this small wait for the crisis.

His friend came to him. "Well, Henry, I guess this is good-by-John."

"Oh, shut up, you damned fool!" replied the youth, and he would not look at the other.

The officers labored like politicians to beat the mass into a proper circle to face the menaces. The ground was uneven and torn. The men curled into depressions and fitted themselves snugly behind whatever would frustrate a bullet.

The youth noted with vague surprise that the lieutenant was standing mutely with his legs far apart and his sword held in the manner of a cane. The youth wondered what had happened to his vocal organs that he no more cursed.

There was something curious in this little intent pause of the lieutenant. He was like a babe which, having wept its fill, raises its eyes and fixes upon a distant toy. He was engrossed in this contemplation, and the soft under lip quivered from self-whispered words.

Some lazy and ignorant smoke curled slowly. The men, hiding from the bullets, waited anxiously for it to lift and disclose the plight of the regiment.

The silent ranks were suddenly thrilled by the eager voice of the youthful lieutenant bawling out: "Here they come! Right onto us, b'Gawd!" His further words were lost in a roar of wicked thunder from the men's rifles.

The youth's eyes had instantly turned in the direction indicated by the awakened and agitated lieutenant, and he had seen the haze of treachery disclosing a body of soldiers of the enemy. They were so near that he could see their features. There was a recognition as he looked at the types of faces. Also he perceived with dim amazement that their uniforms were rather gay in effect, being light gray, accented with a brilliant-hued facing. Too, the clothes seemed new.

These troops had apparently been going forward with caution, their rifles held in readiness, when the youthful lieutenant had discovered them and their movement had been interrupted by the volley from the blue regiment. From the moment's glimpse, it was derived that they had been unaware of the proximity of their dark-suited foes or had mistaken the direction. Almost instantly they were shut utterly from the youth's sight by the smoke from the energetic rifles of his companions. He strained his vision to learn the accomplishment of the volley, but the smoke hung before him.

The two bodies of troops exchanged blows in the manner of a pair of boxers. The fast angry firings went back and forth. The men in blue were intent with the despair of their circumstances and they seized upon the revenge to be had at close range. Their thunder swelled loud and valiant. Their curving front bristled with flashes and the place resounded with the clangor of their ramrods. The youth ducked and dodged for a time and achieved a few unsatisfactory views of the enemy. There appeared to be many of them and they were replying swiftly. They seemed moving toward the blue regiment, step by step. He seated himself gloomily on the ground with his flag between his knees.

As he noted the vicious, wolflike temper of his comrades he had a sweet thought that if the enemy was about to swallow the regimental broom as a large prisoner, it could at least have the consolation of going down with bristles forward.

But the blows of the antagonist began to grow more weak. Fewer bullets ripped the air, and finally, when the men slackened to learn of the fight, they could see only dark, floating smoke. The regiment lay still and gazed. Presently some chance whim came to the pestering blur, and it began to coil heavily away. The men saw a ground vacant of fighters. It would have been an empty stage if it were not for a few corpses that lay thrown and twisted into fantastic shapes upon the sward.

At sight of this tableau, many of the men in blue sprang from behind their covers and made an ungainly dance of joy. Their eyes burned and a hoarse cheer of elation broke from their dry lips.

It had begun to seem to them that events were trying to prove that they were impotent. These little battles had evidently endeavored to demonstrate that the men could not fight well. When on the verge of submission to these opinions, the small duel had showed them that the proportions were not impossible, and by it they had revenged themselves upon their misgivings and upon the foe.

The impetus of enthusiasm was theirs again. They gazed about them with looks of uplifted pride, feeling new trust in the grim, always confident weapons in their hands. And they were men.

Chapter XXI

P RESENTLY THEY KNEW that no firing threatened them. All ways seemed once more opened to them. The dusty blue lines of their friends were disclosed a short distance away. In the distance there were many colossal noises, but in all this part of the field there was a sudden stillness.

They perceived that they were free. The depleted band drew a long breath of relief and gathered itself into a bunch to complete its trip.

In this last length of journey the men began to show strange emotions. They hurried with nervous fear. Some who had been dark and unfaltering in the grimmest moments now could not conceal an anxiety that made them frantic. It was perhaps that they dreaded to be killed in insignificant ways after the times for proper military deaths had passed. Or, perhaps, they thought it would be too ironical to get killed at the portals of safety. With backward looks of perturbation, they hastened.

As they approached their own lines there was some sarcasm exhibited on the part of a gaunt and bronzed regiment that lay resting in the shade of trees. Questions were wafted to them.

"Where th' hell yeh been?"

"What yeh comin' back fer?"

"Why didn't yeh stay there?"

"Was it warm out there, sonny?"

"Goin' home now, boys?"

One shouted in taunting mimicry: "Oh, mother, come quick an' look at th' sojers!"

There was no reply from the bruised and battered regiment, save that one man made broadcast challenges to fist fights and the red-bearded officer walked rather near and glared in great swashbuckler style at a tall captain in the other regiment. But the lieutenant suppressed the man who wished to fist fight, and the tall captain, flushing at the little fanfare of the red-bearded one, was obliged to look intently at some trees.

The youth's tender flesh was deeply stung by these remarks.

From under his creased brows he glowered with hate at the mockers. He meditated upon a few revenges. Still, many in the regiment hung their heads in criminal fashion, so that it came to pass that the men trudged with sudden heaviness, as if they bore upon their bended shoulders the coffin of their honor. And the youthful lieutenant, recollecting himself, began to mutter softly in black curses.

They turned when they arrived at their old position to regard the ground over which they had charged.

The youth in this contemplation was smitten with a large astonishment. He discovered that the distances, as compared with the brilliant measurings of his mind, were trivial and ridiculous. The stolid trees, where much had taken place, seemed incredibly near. The time, too, now that he reflected, he saw to have been short. He wondered at the number of emotions and events that had been crowded into such little spaces. Elfin thoughts must have exaggerated and enlarged everything, he said.

It seemed, then, that there was bitter justice in the speeches of the gaunt and bronzed veterans. He veiled a glance of disdain at his fellows who strewed the ground, choking with dust, red from perspiration, misty-eyed, disheveled.

They were gulping at their canteens, fierce to wring every mite of water from them, and they polished at their swollen and watery features with coat sleeves and bunches of grass.

However, to the youth there was a considerable joy in musing upon his performances during the charge. He had had very little time previously in which to appreciate himself, so that there was now much satisfaction in quietly thinking of his actions. He recalled bits of color that in the flurry had stamped themselves unawares upon his engaged senses.

As the regiment lay heaving from its hot exertions the officer who had named them as mule drivers came galloping along the line. He had lost his cap. His tousled hair streamed wildly, and his face was dark with vexation and wrath. His temper was displayed with more clearness by the way in which he managed his horse. He jerked and wrenched savagely at his bridle, stopping the hard-breathing animal with a furious pull near the colonel of the regiment. He immediately exploded in reproaches which came unbidden to the ears of the men. They were suddenly alert, being always curious about black words between officers.

"Oh, thunder, MacChesnay, what an awful bull you made of this thing!" began the officer. He attempted low tones, but his indignation caused certain of the men to learn the sense of his words. "What an awful mess you made! Good Lord, man, you stopped about a hundred feet this side of a very pretty success! If your men had gone a hundred feet farther you would have made a great charge, but as it is—what a lot of mud diggers you've got anyway!"

The men, listening with bated breath, now turned their curious eyes upon the colonel. They had a ragamuffin interest in this affair.

The colonel was seen to straighten his form and put one hand forth in oratorical fashion. He wore an injured air; it was as if a deacon had been accused of stealing. The men were wiggling in an ecstasy of excitement.

But of a sudden the colonel's manner changed from that of a deacon to that of a Frenchman. He shrugged his shoulders. "Oh, well, general, we went as far as we could," he said calmly.

"As far as you could? Did you, b'Gawd?" snorted the other. "Well, that wasn't very far, was it?" he added, with a glance of cold contempt into the other's eyes. "Not very far, I think. You were intended to make a diversion in favor of Whiterside. How well you succeeded your own ears can now tell you." He wheeled his horse and rode stiffly away.

The colonel, bidden to hear the jarring noises of an engagement in the woods to the left, broke out in vague damnations.

The lieutenant, who had listened with an air of impotent rage to the interview, spoke suddenly in firm and undaunted tones. "I don't care what a man is—whether he is a general or what—if he says th' boys didn't put up a good fight out there he's a damned fool."

"Lieutenant," began the colonel, severely, "this is my own affair, and I'll trouble you——"

The lieutenant made an obedient gesture. "All right, colonel, all right," he said. He sat down with an air of being content with himself.

The news that the regiment had been reproached went along the line. For a time the men were bewildered by it. "Good thunder!" they ejaculated, staring at the vanishing form of the general. They conceived it to be a huge mistake.

Presently, however, they began to believe that in truth their efforts had been called light. The youth could see this conviction weigh upon the entire regiment until the men were like cuffed and cursed animals, but withal rebellious.

The friend, with a grievance in his eye, went to the youth. "I wonder what he does want," he said. "He must think we went out there an' played marbles! I never see sech a man!"

The youth developed a tranquil philosophy for these moments of irritation. "Oh, well," he rejoined, "he probably didn't see nothing of it at all and got mad as blazes, and concluded we were a lot of sheep, just because we didn't do what he wanted done. It's a pity old Grandpa Henderson got killed yestirday—he'd have known that we did our best and fought good. It's just our awful luck, that's what."

"I should say so," replied the friend. He seemed to be deeply wounded at an injustice. "I should say we did have awful luck! There's no fun in fightin' fer people when everything yeh do—no matter what—ain't done right. I have a notion t' stay behind next time an' let 'em take their ol' charge an' go t' th' devil with it."

The youth spoke soothingly to his comrade. "Well, we both did good. I'd like to see the fool what'd say we both didn't do as good as we could!"

"Of course we did," declared the friend stoutly. "An' I'd break th' feller's neck if he was as big as a church. But we're all right, anyhow, for I heard one feller say that we two fit th' best in th' reg'ment, an' they had a great argument 'bout it. Another feller, 'a course, he had t' up an' say it was a lie—he seen all what was goin' on an' he never seen us from th' beginnin' t' th' end. An' a lot more struck in an' ses it wasn't a lie—we did fight like thunder, an' they give us quite a send-off. But this is what I can't stand—these everlastin' ol' soldiers, titterin' an' laughin', an' then that general, he's crazy."

The youth exclaimed with sudden exasperation: "He's a lunkhead! He makes me mad. I wish he'd come along next time. We'd show 'im what——"

He ceased because several men had come hurrying up. Their faces expressed a bringing of great news.

"O Flem, yeh jest oughta heard!" cried one, eagerly.

"Heard what?" said the youth.

"Yeh jest oughta heard!" repeated the other, and he arranged himself to tell his tidings. The others made an excited circle. "Well, sir, th' colonel met your lieutenant right by us— it was damnedest thing I ever heard—an' he ses: 'Ahem! ahem!' he ses. 'Mr. Hasbrouck!' he ses, 'by th' way, who was that lad what carried th' flag?' he ses. There, Flemin', what d' yeh think 'a that? 'Who was th' lad what carried th' flag?' he ses, an' th' lieutenant, he speaks up right away: 'That's Flemin', an' he's a jimhickey,' he ses, right away. What? I say he did. 'A jimhickey,' he ses—those 'r his words. He did, too. I say he did. If you kin tell this story better than I kin, go ahead an' tell it. Well, then, keep yer mouth shet. Th' lieutenant, he ses: 'He's a jimhickey,' an' th' colonel, he ses: 'Ahem! ahem! he is, indeed, a very good man t' have, ahem! He kep' th' flag 'way t' th' front. I saw 'im. He's a good un,' ses th' colonel. 'You bet,' ses th' lieutenant, 'he an' a feller named Wilson was at th' head 'a th' charge, an' howlin' like Indians all th' time,' he ses. 'Head 'a th' charge all th' time,' he ses. 'A feller named Wilson,' he ses. There, Wilson, m'boy, put that in a letter an' send it hum t' yer mother, hay? 'A feller named Wilson,' he ses. An' th' colonel, he ses: 'Were they, indeed? Ahem! ahem! My sakes!' he ses. 'At th' head 'a th' reg'ment?' he ses. 'They were,' ses th' lieutenant. 'My sakes!' ses th' colonel. He ses: 'Well, well, well,' he ses, 'those two babies?' 'They were,' ses th' lieutenant. 'Well, well,' ses th' colonel, 'they deserve t' be major-generals,' he ses. 'They deserve t' be major-generals.' "

The youth and his friend had said: "Huh!" "Yer lyin', Thompson." "Oh, go t' blazes!" "He never sed it." "Oh, what a lie!" "Huh!" But despite these youthful scoffings and embarrassments, they knew that their faces were deeply flushing from thrills of pleasure. They exchanged a secret glance of joy and congratulation.

They speedily forgot many things. The past held no pictures of error and disappointment. They were very happy, and their hearts swelled with grateful affection for the colonel and the youthful lieutenant.

Chapter XXII

WHEN THE WOODS again began to pour forth the dark-hued masses of the enemy the youth felt serene self-confidence. He smiled briefly when he saw men dodge and duck at the long screechings of shells that were thrown in giant handfuls over them. He stood, erect and tranquil, watching the attack begin against a part of the line that made a blue curve along the side of an adjacent hill. His vision being unmolested by smoke from the rifles of his companions, he had opportunities to see parts of the hard fight. It was a relief to perceive at last from whence came some of these noises which had been roared into his ears.

Off a short way he saw two regiments fighting a little separate battle with two other regiments. It was in a cleared space, wearing a set-apart look. They were blazing as if upon a wager, giving and taking tremendous blows. The firings were incredibly fierce and rapid. These intent regiments apparently were oblivious of all larger purposes of war, and were slugging each other as if at a matched game.

In another direction he saw a magnificent brigade going with the evident intention of driving the enemy from a wood. They passed in out of sight and presently there was a most awe-inspiring racket in the wood. The noise was unspeakable. Having stirred this prodigious uproar, and, apparently, finding it too prodigious, the brigade, after a little time, came marching airily out again with its fine formation in nowise disturbed. There were no traces of speed in its movements. The brigade was jaunty and seemed to point a proud thumb at the yelling wood.

On a slope to the left there was a long row of guns, gruff and maddened, denouncing the enemy, who, down through the woods, were forming for another attack in the pitiless monotony of conflicts. The round red discharges from the guns made a crimson flare and a high, thick smoke. Occasional glimpses could be caught of groups of the toiling artillerymen. In the rear of this row of guns stood a house, calm and white, amid bursting shells. A congregation of horses, tied to a long railing, were tugging frenziedly at their bridles. Men were running hither and thither.

The detached battle between the four regiments lasted for some time. There chanced to be no interference, and they settled their dispute by themselves. They struck savagely and powerfully at each other for a period of minutes, and then the lighter-hued regiments faltered and drew back, leaving the dark-blue lines shouting. The youth could see the two flags shaking with laughter amid the smoke remnants.

Presently there was a stillness, pregnant with meaning. The blue lines shifted and changed a trifle and stared expectantly at the silent woods and fields before them. The hush was solemn and churchlike, save for a distant battery that, evidently unable to remain quiet, sent a faint rolling thunder over the ground. It irritated, like the noises of unimpressed boys. The men imagined that it would prevent their perched ears from hearing the first words of the new battle.

Of a sudden the guns on the slope roared out a message of warning. A spluttering sound had begun in the woods. It swelled with amazing speed to a profound clamor that involved the earth in noises. The splitting crashes swept along the lines until an interminable roar was developed. To those in the midst of it it became a din fitted to the universe. It was the whirring and thumping of gigantic machinery, complications among the smaller stars. The youth's ears were filled cups. They were incapable of hearing more.

On an incline over which a road wound he saw wild and desperate rushes of men perpetually backward and forward in riotous surges. These parts of the opposing armies were two long waves that pitched upon each other madly at dictated points. To and fro they swelled. Sometimes, one side by its yells and cheers would proclaim decisive blows, but a moment later the other side would be all yells and cheers. Once the youth saw a spray of light forms go in houndlike leaps toward the waving blue lines. There was much howling, and presently it went away with a vast mouthful of prisoners. Again, he saw a blue wave dash with such thunderous force against a gray obstruction that it seemed to clear the earth of it and leave nothing but trampled sod. And always in their swift and deadly rushes to and fro the men screamed and yelled like maniacs.

Particular pieces of fence or secure positions behind collections of trees were wrangled over, as gold thrones or pearl bedsteads. There were desperate lunges at these chosen spots seemingly every instant, and most of them were bandied like light toys between the contending forces. The youth could not tell from the battle flags flying like crimson foam in many directions which color of cloth was winning.

His emaciated regiment bustled forth with undiminished fierceness when its time came. When assaulted again by bullets, the men burst out in a barbaric cry of rage and pain. They bent their heads in aims of intent hatred behind the projected hammers of their guns. Their ramrods clanged loud with fury as their eager arms pounded the cartridges into the rifle barrels. The front of the regiment was a smoke-wall penetrated by the flashing points of yellow and red.

Wallowing in the fight, they were in an astonishingly short time resmudged. They surpassed in stain and dirt all their previous appearances. Moving to and fro with strained exertion, jabbering the while, they were, with their swaying bodies, black faces, and glowing eyes, like strange and ugly fiends jigging heavily in the smoke.

The lieutenant, returning from a tour after a bandage, produced from a hidden receptacle of his mind new and portentous oaths suited to the emergency. Strings of expletives he swung lashlike over the backs of his men, and it was evident that his previous efforts had in nowise impaired his resources.

The youth, still the bearer of the colors, did not feel his idleness. He was deeply absorbed as a spectator. The crash and swing of the great drama made him lean forward, intent-eyed, his face working in small contortions. Sometimes he prattled, words coming unconsciously from him in grotesque exclamations. He did not know that he breathed; that the flag hung silently over him, so absorbed was he.

A formidable line of the enemy came within dangerous range. They could be seen plainly—tall, gaunt men with excited faces running with long strides toward a wandering fence.

At sight of this danger the men suddenly ceased their cursing monotone. There was an instant of strained silence before they threw up their rifles and fired a plumping volley at the foes. There had been no order given; the men, upon recognizing the menace, had immediately let drive their flock of bullets without waiting for word of command.

But the enemy were quick to gain the protection of the wandering line of fence. They slid down behind it with remarkable celerity, and from this position they began briskly to slice up the blue men.

These latter braced their energies for a great struggle. Often, white clinched teeth shone from the dusky faces. Many heads surged to and fro, floating upon a pale sea of smoke. Those behind the fence frequently shouted and yelped in taunts and gibelike cries, but the regiment maintained a stressed silence. Perhaps, at this new assault the men recalled the fact that they had been named mud diggers, and it made their situation thrice bitter. They were breathlessly intent upon keeping the ground and thrusting away the rejoicing body of the enemy. They fought swiftly and with a despairing savageness denoted in their expressions.

The youth had resolved not to budge whatever should happen. Some arrows of scorn that had buried themselves in his heart had generated strange and unspeakable hatred. It was clear to him that his final and absolute revenge was to be achieved by his dead body lying, torn and gluttering, upon the field. This was to be a poignant retaliation upon the officer who had said "mule drivers," and later "mud diggers," for in all the wild graspings of his mind for a unit responsible for his sufferings and commotions he always seized upon the man who had dubbed him wrongly. And it was his idea, vaguely formulated, that his corpse would be for those eyes a great and salt reproach.

The regiment bled extravagantly. Grunting bundles of blue began to drop. The orderly sergeant of the youth's company was shot through the cheeks. Its supports being injured, his jaw hung afar down, disclosing in the wide cavern of his mouth a pulsing mass of blood and teeth. And with it all he made attempts to cry out. In his endeavor there was a dreadful earnestness, as if he conceived that one great shriek would make him well.

The youth saw him presently go rearward. His strength

seemed in nowise impaired. He ran swiftly, casting wild glances for succor.

Others fell down about the feet of their companions. Some of the wounded crawled out and away, but many lay still, their bodies twisted into impossible shapes.

The youth looked once for his friend. He saw a vehement young man, powder-smeared and frowzled, whom he knew to be him. The lieutenant, also, was unscathed in his position at the rear. He had continued to curse, but it was now with the air of a man who was using his last box of oaths.

For the fire of the regiment had begun to wane and drip. The robust voice, that had come strangely from the thin ranks, was growing rapidly weak.

Chapter XXIII

THE COLONEL came running along back of the line. There were other officers following him. "We must charge'm!" they shouted. "We must charge'm!" they cried with resentful voices, as if anticipating a rebellion against this plan by the men.

The youth, upon hearing the shouts, began to study the distance between him and the enemy. He made vague calculations. He saw that to be firm soldiers they must go forward. It would be death to stay in the present place, and with all the circumstances to go backward would exalt too many others. Their hope was to push the galling foes away from the fence.

He expected that his companions, weary and stiffened, would have to be driven to this assault, but as he turned toward them he perceived with a certain surprise that they were giving quick and unqualified expressions of assent. There was an ominous, clanging overture to the charge when the shafts of the bayonets rattled upon the rifle barrels. At the yelled words of command the soldiers sprang forward in eager leaps. There was new and unexpected force in the movement of the regiment. A knowledge of its faded and jaded condition made the charge appear like a paroxysm, a display of the strength that comes before a final feebleness. The men scampered in insane fever of haste, racing as if to achieve a sudden success before an exhilarating fluid should leave them. It was a blind and despairing rush by the collection of men in dusty and tattered blue, over a green sward and under a sapphire sky, toward a fence, dimly outlined in smoke, from behind which spluttered the fierce rifles of enemies.

The youth kept the bright colors to the front. He was waving his free arm in furious circles, the while shrieking mad calls and appeals, urging on those that did not need to be urged, for it seemed that the mob of blue men hurling themselves on the dangerous group of rifles were again grown suddenly wild with an enthusiasm of unselfishness. From the many firings starting toward them, it looked as if they would merely succeed in making a great sprinkling of corpses on the grass between their former position and the fence. But they were in a state of frenzy, perhaps because of forgotten vanities, and it made an exhibition of sublime recklessness. There was no obvious questioning, nor figurings, nor diagrams. There was, apparently, no considered loopholes. It appeared that the swift wings of their desires would have shattered against the iron gates of the impossible.

He himself felt the daring spirit of a savage, religion-mad. He was capable of profound sacrifices, a tremendous death. He had no time for dissections, but he knew that he thought of the bullets only as things that could prevent him from reaching the place of his endeavor. There were subtle flashings of joy within him that thus should be his mind.

He strained all his strength. His eyesight was shaken and dazzled by the tension of thought and muscle. He did not see anything excepting the mist of smoke gashed by the little knives of fire, but he knew that in it lay the aged fence of a vanished farmer protecting the snuggled bodies of the gray men.

As he ran a thought of the shock of contact gleamed in his mind. He expected a great concussion when the two bodies of troops crashed together. This became a part of his wild battle madness. He could feel the onward swing of the regiment about him and he conceived of a thunderous, crushing blow that would prostrate the resistance and spread consternation and amazement for miles. The flying regiment was going to have a catapultian effect. This dream made him run faster among his comrades, who were giving vent to hoarse and frantic cheers.

But presently he could see that many of the men in gray did not intend to abide the blow. The smoke, rolling, disclosed men who ran, their faces still turned. These grew to a crowd, who retired stubbornly. Individuals wheeled frequently to send a bullet at the blue wave.

But at one part of the line there was a grim and obdurate group that made no movement. They were settled firmly down behind posts and rails. A flag, ruffled and fierce, waved over them and their rifles dinned fiercely.

The blue whirl of men got very near, until it seemed that in truth there would be a close and frightful scuffle. There was an expressed disdain in the opposition of the little group, that changed the meaning of the cheers of the men in blue. They became yells of wrath, directed, personal. The cries of the two parties were now in sound an interchange of scathing insults.

They in blue showed their teeth; their eyes shone all white. They launched themselves as at the throats of those who stood resisting. The space between dwindled to an insignificant distance.

The youth had centered the gaze of his soul upon that other flag. Its possession would be high pride. It would express bloody minglings, near blows. He had a gigantic hatred for those who made great difficulties and complications. They caused it to be as a craved treasure of mythology, hung amid tasks and contrivances of danger.

He plunged like a mad horse at it. He was resolved it should not escape if wild blows and darings of blows could seize it. His own emblem, quivering and aflare, was winging toward the other. It seemed there would shortly be an encounter of strange beaks and claws, as of eagles.

The swirling body of blue men came to a sudden halt at close and disastrous range and roared a swift volley. The group in gray was split and broken by this fire, but its riddled body still fought. The men in blue yelled again and rushed in upon it.

The youth, in his leapings, saw, as through a mist, a picture of four or five men stretched upon the ground or writhing upon their knees with bowed heads as if they had been stricken by bolts from the sky. Tottering among them was the rival color bearer, whom the youth saw had been bitten vitally by the bullets of the last formidable volley. He perceived this man fighting a last struggle, the struggle of one whose legs are grasped by demons. It was a ghastly battle. Over his face was the bleach of death, but set upon it was the dark and hard lines of desperate purpose. With this terrible grin of resolution he hugged his precious flag to him and was stumbling and staggering in his design to go the way that led to safety for it.

But his wounds always made it seem that his feet were retarded, held, and he fought a grim fight, as with invisible ghouls fastened greedily upon his limbs. Those in advance of the scampering blue men, howling cheers, leaped at the fence. The despair of the lost was in his eyes as he glanced back at them.

The youth's friend went over the obstruction in a tumbling heap and sprang at the flag as a panther at prey. He pulled at it and, wrenching it free, swung up its red brilliancy with a mad cry of exultation even as the color bearer, gasping, lurched over in a final throe and, stiffening convulsively, turned his dead face to the ground. There was much blood upon the grass blades.

At the place of success there began more wild clamorings of cheers. The men gesticulated and bellowed in an ecstasy. When they spoke it was as if they considered their listener to be a mile away. What hats and caps were left to them they often slung high in the air.

At one part of the line four men had been swooped upon, and they now sat as prisoners. Some blue men were about them in an eager and curious circle. The soldiers had trapped strange birds, and there was an examination. A flurry of fast questions was in the air.

One of the prisoners was nursing a superficial wound in the foot. He cuddled it, baby-wise, but he looked up from it often to curse with an astonishing utter abandon straight at the noses of his captors. He consigned them to red regions; he called upon the pestilential wrath of strange gods. And with it all he was singularly free from recognition of the finer points of the conduct of prisoners of war. It was as if a clumsy clod had trod upon his toe and he conceived it to be his privilege, his duty, to use deep, resentful oaths.

Another, who was a boy in years, took his plight with great calmness and apparent good nature. He conversed with the men in blue, studying their faces with his bright and keen eyes. They spoke of battles and conditions. There was an acute interest in all their faces during this exchange of view points. It seemed a great satisfaction to hear voices from where all had been darkness and speculation.

The third captive sat with a morose countenance. He preserved a stoical and cold attitude. To all advances he made one reply without variation, "Ah, go t' hell!"

The last of the four was always silent and, for the most part, kept his face turned in unmolested directions. From the views the youth received he seemed to be in a state of absolute dejection. Shame was upon him, and with it profound regret that he was, perhaps, no more to be counted in the ranks of his fellows. The youth could detect no expression that would allow him to believe that the other was giving a thought to his narrowed future, the pictured dungeons, perhaps, and starvations and brutalities, liable to the imagination. All to be seen was shame for captivity and regret for the right to antagonize.

After the men had celebrated sufficiently they settled down behind the old rail fence, on the opposite side to the one from which their foes had been driven. A few shot perfunctorily at distant marks.

There was some long grass. The youth nestled in it and rested, making a convenient rail support the flag. His friend, jubilant and glorified, holding his treasure with vanity, came to him there. They sat side by side and congratulated each other.

Chapter XXIV

THE ROARINGS that had stretched in a long line of sound across the face of the forest began to grow intermittent and weaker. The stentorian speeches of the artillery continued in some distant encounter, but the crashes of the musketry had almost ceased. The youth and his friend of a sudden looked up, feeling a deadened form of distress at the waning of these noises, which had become a part of life. They could see changes going on among the troops. There were marchings this way and that way. A battery wheeled leisurely. On the crest of a small hill was the thick gleam of many departing muskets.

The youth arose. "Well, what now, I wonder?" he said. By his tone he seemed to be preparing to resent some new monstrosity in the way of dins and smashes. He shaded his eyes with his grimy hand and gazed over the field.

His friend also arose and stared. "I bet we're goin' t' git along out of this an' back over th' river," said he.

"Well, I swan!" said the youth.

They waited, watching. Within a little while the regiment received orders to retrace its way. The men got up grunting from the grass, regretting the soft repose. They jerked their stiffened legs, and stretched their arms over their heads. One man swore as he rubbed his eyes. They all groaned "O Lord!" They had as many objections to this change as they would have had to a proposal for a new battle.

They trampled slowly back over the field across which they had run in a mad scamper.

The regiment marched until it had joined its fellows. The reformed brigade, in column, aimed through a wood at the road. Directly they were in a mass of dust-covered troops, and were trudging along in a way parallel to the enemy's lines as these had been defined by the previous turmoil.

They passed within view of a stolid white house, and saw in front of it groups of their comrades lying in wait behind a neat breastwork. A row of guns were booming at a distant enemy. Shells thrown in reply were raising clouds of dust and splinters. Horsemen dashed along the line of intrenchments.

At this point of its march the division curved away from the field and went winding off in the direction of the river. When the significance of this movement had impressed itself upon the youth he turned his head and looked over his shoulder toward the trampled and *débris*-strewed ground. He breathed a breath of new satisfaction. He finally nudged his friend. "Well, it's all over," he said to him.

His friend gazed backward. "B'Gawd, it is," he assented. They mused.

For a time the youth was obliged to reflect in a puzzled and uncertain way. His mind was undergoing a subtle change. It took moments for it to cast off its battleful ways and resume its accustomed course of thought. Gradually his brain emerged from the clogged clouds, and at last he was enabled to more closely comprehend himself and circumstance.

He understood then that the existence of shot and counter-shot was in the past. He had dwelt in a land of strange, squalling upheavals and had come forth. He had been where there was red of blood and black of passion, and he was escaped. His first thoughts were given to rejoicings at this fact.

Later he began to study his deeds, his failures, and his achievements. Thus, fresh from scenes where many of his usual machines of reflection had been idle, from where he had proceeded sheeplike, he struggled to marshal all his acts.

At last they marched before him clearly. From this present view point he was enabled to look upon them in spectator fashion and to criticise them with some correctness, for his new condition had already defeated certain sympathies.

Regarding his procession of memory he felt gleeful and un-regretting, for in it his public deeds were paraded in great and shining prominence. Those performances which had been witnessed by his fellows marched now in wide purple and gold, having various deflections. They went gayly with music. It was pleasure to watch these things. He spent delightful minutes viewing the gilded images of memory.

He saw that he was good. He recalled with a thrill of joy the respectful comments of his fellows upon his conduct.

Nevertheless, the ghost of his flight from the first engagement appeared to him and danced. There were small shoutings in his brain about these matters. For a moment he blushed, and the light of his soul flickered with shame.

A specter of reproach came to him. There loomed the dogging memory of the tattered soldier—he who, gored by bullets and faint for blood, had fretted concerning an imagined wound in another; he who had loaned his last of strength and intellect for the tall soldier; he who, blind with weariness and pain, had been deserted in the field.

For an instant a wretched chill of sweat was upon him at the thought that he might be detected in the thing. As he stood persistently before his vision, he gave vent to a cry of sharp irritation and agony.

His friend turned. "What's the matter, Henry?" he demanded. The youth's reply was an outburst of crimson oaths.

As he marched along the little branch-hung roadway among his prattling companions this vision of cruelty brooded over him. It clung near him always and darkened his view of these deeds in purple and gold. Whichever way his thoughts turned they were followed by the somber phantom of the desertion in the fields. He looked stealthily at his companions, feeling sure that they must discern in his face evidences of this pursuit. But they were plodding in ragged array, discussing with quick tongues the accomplishments of the late battle.

"Oh, if a man should come up an' ask me, I'd say we got a dum good lickin'."

"Lickin'—in yer eye! We ain't licked, sonny. We're goin' down here aways, swing aroun', an' come in behint 'em."

"Oh, hush, with your comin' in behint 'em. I've seen all 'a that I wanta. Don't tell me about comin' in behint——"

"Bill Smithers, he ses he'd rather been in ten hundred battles than been in that heluva hospital. He ses they got shootin' in th' nighttime, an' shells dropped plum among 'em in th' hospital. He ses sech hollerin' he never see."

"Hasbrouck? He's th' best off'cer in this here reg'ment. He's a whale."

"Didn't I tell yeh we'd come aroun' in behint 'em? Didn't I tell yeh so? We——"

"Oh, shet yeh mouth!"

For a time this pursuing recollection of the tattered man

took all elation from the youth's veins. He saw his vivid error, and he was afraid that it would stand before him all his life. He took no share in the chatter of his comrades, nor did he look at them or know them, save when he felt sudden suspicion that they were seeing his thoughts and scrutinizing each detail of the scene with the tattered soldier.

Yet gradually he mustered force to put the sin at a distance. And at last his eyes seemed to open to some new ways. He found that he could look back upon the brass and bombast of his earlier gospels and see them truly. He was gleeful when he discovered that he now despised them.

With this conviction came a store of assurance. He felt a quiet manhood, nonassertive but of sturdy and strong blood. He knew that he would no more quail before his guides wherever they should point. He had been to touch the great death, and found that, after all, it was but the great death. He was a man.

So it came to pass that as he trudged from the place of blood and wrath his soul changed. He came from hot plowshares to prospects of clover tranquilly, and it was as if hot plowshares were not. Scars faded as flowers.

It rained. The procession of weary soldiers became a bedraggled train, despondent and muttering, marching with churning effort in a trough of liquid brown mud under a low, wretched sky. Yet the youth smiled, for he saw that the world was a world for him, though many discovered it to be made of oaths and walking sticks. He had rid himself of the red sickness of battle. The sultry nightmare was in the past. He had been an animal blistered and sweating in the heat and pain of war. He turned now with a lover's thirst to images of tranquil skies, fresh meadows, cool brooks—an existence of soft and eternal peace.

Over the river a golden ray of sun came through the hosts of leaden rain clouds.

THE END

GEORGE'S MOTHER

I

In the swirling rain that came at dusk the broad avenue glistened with that deep bluish tint which is so widely condemned when it is put into pictures. There were long rows of shops, whose fronts shone with full, golden light. Here and there, from druggists' windows, or from the red street-lamps that indicated the positions of fire-alarm boxes, a flare of uncertain, wavering crimson was thrown upon the wet pavements.

The lights made shadows, in which the buildings loomed with a new and tremendous massiveness, like castles and fortresses. There were endless processions of people, mighty hosts, with umbrellas waving, banner-like, over them. Horse-cars, aglitter with new paint, rumbled in steady array between the pillars that supported the elevated railroad. The whole street resounded with the tinkle of bells, the roar of iron-shod wheels on the cobbles, the ceaseless trample of the hundreds of feet. Above all, too, could be heard the loud screams of the tiny newsboys, who scurried in all directions. Upon the corners, standing in from the dripping eaves, were many loungers, descended from the world that used to prostrate itself before pageantry.

A brown young man went along the avenue. He held a tin lunch-pail under his arm in a manner that was evidently uncomfortable. He was puffing at a corn-cob pipe. His shoulders had a self-reliant poise, and the hang of his arms and the raised veins of his hands showed him to be a man who worked with his muscles.

As he passed a street-corner a man in old clothes gave a shout of surprise, and rushing impetuously forward, grasped his hand.

"Hello, Kelcey, ol' boy," cried the man in old clothes. "How's th' boy, anyhow? Where in thunder yeh been fer th' last seventeen years? I'll be hanged if you ain't th' last man I ever expected t' see."

The brown youth put his pail to the ground and grinned. "Well, if it ain't ol' Charley Jones," he said, ecstatically shaking hands. "How are yeh, anyhow? Where yeh been keepin' yerself? I ain't seen yeh fer a year!"

"Well, I should say so! Why, th' last time I saw you was up in Handyville!"

"Sure! On Sunday, we——"

"Sure! Out at Bill Sickles's place. Let's go get a drink!"

They made toward a little glass-fronted saloon that sat blinking jovially at the crowds. It engulfed them with a gleeful motion of its two widely smiling lips.

"What'll yeh take, Kelcey?"

"Oh, I guess I'll take a beer."

"Gimme little whiskey, John."

The two friends leaned against the bar and looked with enthusiasm upon each other.

"Well, well, I'm thunderin' glad t' see yeh," said Jones.

"Well, I guess," replied Kelcey. "Here's to yeh, ol' man."

"Let 'er go."

They lifted their glasses, glanced fervidly at each other, and drank.

"Yeh ain't changed much, on'y yeh've growed like th' devil," said Jones, reflectively, as he put down his glass. "I'd know yeh anywheres!"

"Certainly yeh would," said Kelcey. "An' I knew you, too, th' minute I saw yeh. Yer changed, though!"

"Yes," admitted Jones, with some complacency, "I s'pose I am." He regarded himself in the mirror that multiplied the bottles on the shelf back of the bar. He should have seen a grinning face with a rather pink nose. His derby was perched carelessly on the back part of his head. Two wisps of hair straggled down over his hollow temples. There was something very worldly and wise about him. Life did not seem to confuse him. Evidently he understood its complications. His hand thrust into his trousers' pocket, where he jingled keys, and his hat perched back on his head expressed a young man of vast knowledge. His extensive acquaintance with bartenders aided him materially in this habitual expression of wisdom.

Having finished he turned to the barkeeper. "John, has any of th' gang been in t'-night yet?"

"No—not yet," said the barkeeper. "Ol' Bleecker was

aroun' this afternoon about four. He said if I seen any of th'
boys t' tell 'em he'd be up t'-night if he could get away. I saw
Connor an' that other fellah goin' down th' avenyeh about an
hour ago. I guess they'll be back after awhile."

"This is th' hang-out fer a great gang," said Jones, turning
to Kelcey. "They're a great crowd, I tell yeh. We own th'
place when we get started. Come aroun' some night. Any
night, almost. T'-night, b' jiminy. They'll almost all be here,
an' I'd like t' interduce yeh. They're a great gang! Gre-e-at!"

"I'd like teh," said Kelcey.

"Well, come ahead, then," cried the other, cordially. "Yeh'd
like t' know 'em. It's an outa sight crowd. Come aroun' t'-
night!"

"I will if I can."

"Well, yeh ain't got anything t' do, have yeh?" demanded
Jones. "Well, come along, then. Yeh might just as well spend
yer time with a good crowd 'a fellahs. An' it's a great gang.
Great! Gre-e-at!"

"Well, I must make fer home now, anyhow," said Kelcey.
"It's late as blazes. What'll yeh take this time, ol' man?"

"Gimme little more whiskey, John!"

"Guess I'll take another beer!"

Jones emptied the whiskey into his large mouth and then
put the glass upon the bar. "Been in th' city long?" he asked.
"Um—well, three years is a good deal fer a slick man. Doin'
well? Oh, well, nobody's doin' well these days." He looked
down mournfully at his shabby clothes. "Father's dead, ain't
'ee? Yeh don't say so? Fell off a scaffoldin', didn't 'ee? I heard
it somewheres. Mother's livin', of course? I thought she was.
Fine ol' lady—fi-i-ne. Well, you're th' last of her boys. Was
five of yeh onct, wasn't there? I knew four m'self. Yes, five! I
thought so. An' all gone but you, hey? Well, you'll have t'
brace up an' be a comfort t' th' ol' mother. Well, well, well,
who would 'a thought that on'y you'd be left out 'a all that
mob 'a tow-headed kids. Well, well, well, it's a queer world,
ain't it?"

A contemplation of this thought made him sad. He sighed
and moodily watched the other sip beer.

"Well, well, it's a queer world—a damn queer world."

"Yes," said Kelcey, "I'm th' on'y one left!" There was an

accent of discomfort in his voice. He did not like this dwelling upon a sentiment that was connected with himself.

"How is th' ol' lady, anyhow?" continued Jones. "Th' last time I remember she was as spry as a little ol' cricket, an' was helpeltin' aroun' th' country lecturin' before W.C.T.U.'s an' one thing an' another."

"Oh, she's pretty well," said Kelcey.

"An' outa five boys you're th' on'y one she's got left? Well, well—have another drink before yeh go."

"Oh, I guess I've had enough."

A wounded expression came into Jones's eyes. "Oh, come on," he said.

"Well, I'll take another beer!"

"Gimme little more whiskey, John!"

When they had concluded this ceremony, Jones went with his friend to the door of the saloon. "Good-by, ol' man," he said, genially. His homely features shone with friendliness. "Come aroun', now, sure. T'-night! See? They're a great crowd. Gre-e-at!"

II

A MAN with a red, mottled face put forth his head from a window and cursed violently. He flung a bottle high across two backyards at a window of the opposite tenement. It broke against the bricks of the house and the fragments fell crackling upon the stones below. The man shook his fist.

A bare-armed woman, making an array of clothes on a line in one of the yards, glanced casually up at the man and listened to his words. Her eyes followed his to the other tenement. From a distant window, a youth with a pipe, yelled some comments upon the poor aim. Two children, being in the proper yard, picked up the bits of broken glass and began to fondle them as new toys.

From the window at which the man raged came the sound of an old voice, singing. It quavered and trembled out into the air as if a sound-spirit had a broken wing.

> "Should I be car-reed tew th' skies
> O-on flow'ry be-eds of ee-ease,
> While others fought tew win th' prize
> An' sailed through blood-ee seas."

The man in the opposite window was greatly enraged. He continued to swear.

A little old woman was the owner of the voice. In a fourth-story room of the red and black tenement she was trudging on a journey. In her arms she bore pots and pans, and sometimes a broom and dust-pan. She wielded them like weapons. Their weight seemed to have bended her back and crooked her arms until she walked with difficulty. Often she plunged her hands into water at a sink. She splashed about, the dwindled muscles working to and fro under the loose skin of her arms. She came from the sink, steaming and bedraggled as if she had crossed a flooded river.

There was the flurry of a battle in this room. Through the clouded dust or steam one could see the thin figure dealing mighty blows. Always her way seemed beset. Her broom was continually poised, lance-wise, at dust demons. There came clashings and clangings as she strove with her tireless foes.

It was a picture of indomitable courage. And as she went on her way her voice was often raised in a long cry, a strange war-chant, a shout of battle and defiance, that rose and fell in harsh screams, and exasperated the ears of the man with the red, mottled face.

> "Should I be car-reed tew th' skies
>   O-on flow'ry be-eds of ee-ease——"

Finally she halted for a moment. Going to the window she sat down and mopped her face with her apron. It was a lull, a moment of respite. Still it could be seen that she even then was planning skirmishes, charges, campaigns. She gazed thoughtfully about the room and noted the strength and position of her enemies. She was very alert.

At last, she turned to the mantel. "Five o'clock," she murmured, scrutinizing a little, swaggering, nickel-plated clock.

She looked out at chimneys growing thickly on the roofs. A man at work on one seemed like a bee. In the intricate yards below, vine-like lines had strange leaves of cloth. To her ears there came the howl of the man with the red, mottled face. He was engaged in a furious altercation with the youth who had called attention to his poor aim. They were like animals in a jungle.

In the distance an enormous brewery towered over the other buildings. Great gilt letters advertised a brand of beer. Thick smoke came from funnels and spread near it like vast and powerful wings. The structure seemed a great bird, flying. The letters of the sign made a chain of gold hanging from its neck. The little old woman looked at the brewery. It vaguely interested her, for a moment, as a stupendous affair, a machine of mighty strength.

Presently she sprang from her rest and began to buffet with her shrivelled arms. In a moment the battle was again in full swing. Terrific blows were given and received. There arose the clattering uproar of a new fight. The little intent warrior never hesitated nor faltered. She fought with a strong and relentless will. Beads and lines of perspiration stood upon her forehead.

Three blue plates were leaning in a row on the shelf back of the stove. The little old woman had seen it done somewhere. In front of them swaggered the round nickel-plated clock. Her son had stuck many cigarette pictures in the rim of a looking-glass that hung near. Occasional chromos were tacked upon the yellowed walls of the room. There was one in a gilt frame. It was quite an affair, in reds and greens. They all seemed like trophies.

It began to grow dark. A mist came winding. Rain plashed softly upon the window-sill. A lamp had been lighted in the opposite tenement; the strong orange glare revealed the man with a red, mottled face. He was seated by a table, smoking and reflecting.

The little old woman looked at the clock again. "Quarter 'a six."

She had paused for a moment, but she now hurled herself fiercely at the stove that lurked in the gloom, red-eyed, like a dragon. It hissed, and there was renewed clangor of blows. The little old woman dashed to and fro.

III

As it grew toward seven o'clock the little old woman became nervous. She often would drop into a chair and sit staring at the little clock.

"I wonder why he don't come," she continually repeated. There was a small, curious note of despair in her voice. As she sat thinking and staring at the clock the expressions of her face changed swiftly. All manner of emotions flickered in her eyes and about her lips. She was evidently perceiving in her imagination the journey of a loved person. She dreamed for him mishaps and obstacles. Something tremendous and irritating was hindering him from coming to her.

She had lighted an oil-lamp. It flooded the room with vivid yellow glare. The table, in its oil-cloth covering, had previously appeared like a bit of bare, brown desert. It now was a white garden, growing the fruits of her labor.

"Seven o'clock," she murmured, finally. She was aghast.

Then suddenly she heard a step upon the stair. She sprang up and began to bustle about the room. The little fearful emotions passed at once from her face. She seemed now to be ready to scold.

Young Kelcey entered the room. He gave a sigh of relief, and dropped his pail in a corner. He was evidently greatly wearied by a hard day of toil.

The little old woman hobbled over to him and raised her wrinkled lips. She seemed on the verge of tears and an outburst of reproaches.

"Hello!" he cried, in a voice of cheer. "Been gettin' anxious?"

"Yes," she said, hovering about him. "Where yeh been, George? What made yeh so late? I've been waitin' th' longest while. Don't throw your coat down there. Hang it up behind th' door."

The son put his coat on the proper hook, and then went to splatter water in a tin wash-basin at the sink.

"Well, yeh see, I met Jones—you remember Jones? Ol' Handyville fellah. An' we had t' stop an' talk over ol' times. Jones is quite a boy."

The little old woman's mouth set in a sudden straight line. "Oh, that Jones," she said. "I don't like him."

The youth interrupted a flurry of white towel to give a glance of irritation. "Well, now, what's th' use of talkin' that way?" he said to her. "What do yeh know 'bout 'im? Ever spoke to 'im in yer life?"

"Well, I don't know as I ever did since he grew up," replied the little old woman. "But I know he ain't th' kind 'a man I'd like t' have you go around with. He ain't a good man. I'm sure he ain't. He drinks."

Her son began to laugh. "Th' dickens he does?" He seemed amazed, but not shocked at this information.

She nodded her head with the air of one who discloses a dreadful thing. "I'm sure of it! Once I saw 'im comin' outa Simpson's Hotel, up in Handyville, an' he could hardly walk. He drinks! I'm sure he drinks!"

"Holy smoke!" said Kelcey.

They sat down at the table and began to wreck the little white garden. The youth leaned back in his chair, in the manner of a man who is paying for things. His mother bended alertly forward, apparently watching each mouthful. She perched on the edge of her chair, ready to spring to her feet and run to the closet or the stove for anything that he might need. She was as anxious as a young mother with a babe. In the careless and comfortable attitude of the son there was denoted a great deal of dignity.

"Yeh ain't eatin' much t'-night, George?"

"Well, I ain't very hungry, t' tell th' truth."

"Don't yeh like yer supper, dear? Yeh must eat somethin', chile. Yeh mustn't go without."

"Well, I'm eatin' somethin', ain't I?"

He wandered aimlessly through the meal. She sat over behind the little blackened coffee-pot and gazed affectionately upon him.

After a time she began to grow agitated. Her worn fingers were gripped. It could be seen that a great thought was within her. She was about to venture something. She had arrived at a supreme moment. "George," she said, suddenly, "come t' prayer-meetin' with me t'-night."

The young man dropped his fork. "Say, you must be crazy," he said, in amazement.

"Yes, dear," she continued, rapidly, in a small pleading voice, "I'd like t' have yeh go with me onct in a while. Yeh never go with me any more, dear, an' I'd like t' have yeh go. Yeh ain't been anywheres at all with me in th' longest while."

"Well," he said, " well, but what th' blazes——"

"Ah, come on," said the little old woman. She went to him and put her arms about his neck. She began to coax him with caresses.

The young man grinned. "Thunderation!" he said, " what would I do at a prayer-meetin'?"

The mother considered him to be consenting. She did a little antique caper.

"Well, yeh can come an' take care 'a yer mother," she cried, gleefully. "It's such a long walk every Thursday night alone, an' don't yeh s'pose that when I have such a big, fine, strappin' boy, I want 'im t' beau me aroun' some? Ah, I knew ye'd come."

He smiled for a moment, indulgent of her humor. But presently his face turned a shade of discomfort. "But—" he began, protesting.

"Ah, come on," she continually repeated.

He began to be vexed. He frowned into the air. A vision came to him of dreary blackness arranged in solemn rows. A mere dream of it was depressing.

"But—" he said again. He was obliged to make great search for an argument. Finally he concluded, "But what th' blazes would I do at prayer-meetin'?"

In his ears was the sound of a hymn, made by people who tilted their heads at a prescribed angle of devotion. It would be too apparent that they were all better than he. When he entered they would turn their heads and regard him with suspicion. This would be an enormous aggravation, since he was certain that he was as good as they.

"Well, now, y' see," he said, quite gently, "I don't wanta go, an' it wouldn't do me no good t' go if I didn't wanta go."

His mother's face swiftly changed. She breathed a huge sigh, the counterpart of ones he had heard upon like occasions. She put a tiny black bonnet on her head, and wrapped her figure in an old shawl. She cast a martyr-like glance upon her son and went mournfully away. She resembled a limited funeral procession.

The young man writhed under it to an extent. He kicked moodily at a table-leg. When the sound of her footfalls died away he felt distinctly relieved.

IV

THAT NIGHT, when Kelcey arrived at the little smiling saloon, he found his friend Jones standing before the bar engaged in a violent argument with a stout man.

"Oh, well," this latter person was saying, "you can make a lot of noise, Charlie, for a man that never says anything—let's have a drink!"

Jones was waving his arms and delivering splintering blows upon some distant theories. The stout man chuckled fatly and winked at the bartender.

The orator ceased for a moment to say, "Gimme little whiskey, John." At the same time he perceived young Kelcey. He sprang forward with a welcoming cry. "Hello, ol' man, didn't much think ye'd come." He led him to the stout man.

"Mr. Bleecker—my friend Mr. Kelcey!"

"How d'yeh do!"

"Mr. Kelcey, I'm happy to meet you, sir; have a drink."

They drew up in line and waited. The busy hands of the bartender made glasses clink. Mr. Bleecker, in a very polite way, broke the waiting silence.

"Never been here before, I believe, have you, Mr. Kelcey?"

The young man felt around for a high-bred reply. "Er—no—I've never had that—er—pleasure," he said.

After a time the strained and wary courtesy of their manners wore away. It became evident to Bleecker that his importance slightly dazzled the young man. He grew warmer. Obviously, the youth was one whose powers of perception were developed. Directly, then, he launched forth into a tale of by-gone days, when the world was better. He had known all the great men of that age. He reproduced his conversations with them. There were traces of pride and of mournfulness in his voice. He rejoiced at the glory of the world of dead spirits. He grieved at the youth and flippancy of the present one. He lived with his head in the clouds of the past, and he seemed obliged to talk of what he saw there.

Jones nudged Kelcey ecstatically in the ribs. "You've got th' ol' man started in great shape," he whispered.

Kelcey was proud that the prominent character of the place

talked at him, glancing into his eyes for appreciation of fine points.

Presently they left the bar, and going into a little rear room, took seats about a table. A gas-jet with a colored globe shed a crimson radiance. The polished wood of walls and furniture gleamed with faint rose-colored reflections. Upon the floor sawdust was thickly sprinkled.

Two other men presently came. By the time Bleecker had told three tales of the grand past, Kelcey was slightly acquainted with everybody.

He admired Bleecker immensely. He developed a brotherly feeling for the others, who were all gentle-spoken. He began to feel that he was passing the happiest evening of his life. His companions were so jovial and good-natured; and everything they did was marked by such courtesy.

For a time the two men who had come in late did not presume to address him directly. They would say: "Jones, won't your friend have so and so, or so and so?" And Bleecker would begin his orations: "Now, Mr. Kelcey, don't you think——"

Presently he began to believe that he was a most remarkably fine fellow, who had at last found his place in a crowd of most remarkably fine fellows.

Jones occasionally breathed comments into his ear.

"I tell yeh, Bleecker's an ol'-timer. He was a husky guy in his day, yeh can bet. He was one 'a th' best known men in N' York onct. Yeh ought to hear him tell about——"

Kelcey listened intently. He was profoundly interested in these intimate tales of men who had gleamed in the rays of old suns.

"That O'Connor's a damn fine fellah," interjected Jones once, referring to one of the others. "He's one 'a th' best fellahs I ever knowed. He's always on th' dead level. An' he's always jest th' same as yeh see 'im now—good-natured an' grinnin'."

Kelcey nodded. He could well believe it.

When he offered to buy drinks there came a loud volley of protests. "No, no, Mr. Kelcey," cried Bleecker, "no, no. To-night you are our guest. Some other time——"

"Here," said O'Connor, "it's my turn now."

He called and pounded for the bartender. He then sat with a coin in his hand warily eying the others. He was ready to frustrate them if they offered to pay.

After a time Jones began to develop qualities of great eloquence and wit. His companions laughed. "It's the whiskey talking now," said Bleecker.

He grew earnest and impassioned. He delivered speeches on various subjects. His lectures were to him very imposing. The force of his words thrilled him. Sometimes he was overcome.

The others agreed with him in all things. Bleecker grew almost tender, and considerately placed words here and there for his use. As Jones became fiercely energetic the others became more docile in agreeing. They soothed him with friendly interjections.

His mood changed directly. He began to sing popular airs with enthusiasm. He congratulated his companions upon being in his society. They were excited by his frenzy. They began to fraternize in jovial fashion. It was understood that they were true and tender spirits. They had come away from a grinding world filled with men who were harsh.

When one of them chose to divulge some place where the world had pierced him, there was a chorus of violent sympathy. They rejoiced at their temporary isolation and safety.

Once a man, completely drunk, stumbled along the floor of the saloon. He opened the door of the little room and made a show of entering. The men sprang instantly to their feet. They were ready to throttle any invader of their island. They elbowed each other in rivalry as to who should take upon himself the brunt of an encounter.

"Oh!" said the drunken individual, swaying on his legs and blinking at the party, "oh! thish private room?"

"That's what it is, Willie," said Jones. "An' you git outa here er we'll throw yeh out."

"That's what we will," said the others.

"Oh," said the drunken man. He blinked at them aggrievedly for an instant and then went away.

They sat down again. Kelcey felt, in a way, that he would have liked to display his fidelity to the others by whipping the intruder.

The bartender came often. "Gee, you fellahs er tanks," he said, in a jocular manner, as he gathered empty glasses and polished the table with his little towel.

Through the exertions of Jones the little room began to grow clamorous. The tobacco-smoke eddied about the forms of the men in ropes and wreaths. Near the ceiling there was a thick gray cloud.

Each man explained, in his way, that he was totally out of place in the before-mentioned world. They were possessed of various virtues which were unappreciated by those with whom they were commonly obliged to mingle; they were fitted for a tree-shaded land, where everything was peace. Now that five of them had congregated it gave them happiness to speak their inmost thoughts without fear of being misunderstood.

As he drank more beer Kelcey felt his breast expand with manly feeling. He knew that he was capable of sublime things. He wished that some day one of his present companions would come to him for relief. His mind pictured a little scene. In it he was magnificent in his friendship.

He looked upon the beaming faces and knew that if at that instant there should come a time for a great sacrifice he would blissfully make it. He would pass tranquilly into the unknown, or into bankruptcy, amid the ejaculations of his companions upon his many virtues.

They had no bickerings during the evening. If one chose to momentarily assert himself, the others instantly submitted.

They exchanged compliments. Once old Bleecker stared at Jones for a few moments. Suddenly he broke out: "Jones, you're one of the finest fellows I ever knew!" A flush of pleasure went over the other's face, and then he made a modest gesture, the protest of an humble man. "Don't flim-flam me, ol' boy," he said, with earnestness. But Bleecker roared that he was serious about it. The two men arose and shook hands emotionally. Jones bunted against the table and knocked off a glass.

Afterward a general hand-shaking was inaugurated. Brotherly sentiments flew about the room. There was an uproar of fraternal feeling.

Jones began to sing. He beat time with precision and

dignity. He gazed into the eyes of his companions, trying to call music from their souls. O'Connor joined in heartily, but with another tune. Off in a corner old Bleecker was making a speech.

The bartender came to the door. "Gee, you fellahs er making a row. It's time fer me t' shut up th' front th' place, an' you mugs better sit on yerselves. It's one o'clock."

They began to argue with him. Kelcey, however, sprang to his feet. "One o'clock," he said. "Holy smoke, I mus' be flyin'!"

There came protesting howls from Jones. Bleecker ceased his oration. "My dear boy—" he began. Kelcey searched for his hat. "I've gota go t' work at seven," he said.

The others watched him with discomfort in their eyes. "Well," said O'Connor, "if one goes we might as well all go." They sadly took their hats and filed out.

The cold air of the street filled Kelcey with vague surprise. It made his head feel hot. As for his legs, they were like willow-twigs.

A few yellow lights blinked. In front of an all-night restaurant a huge red electric lamp hung and sputtered. Horse-car bells jingled far down the street. Overhead a train thundered on the elevated road.

On the sidewalk the men took fervid leave. They clutched hands with extraordinary force and proclaimed, for the last time, ardent and admiring friendships.

When he arrived at his home Kelcey proceeded with caution. His mother had left a light burning low. He stumbled once in his voyage across the floor. As he paused to listen he heard the sound of little snores coming from her room.

He lay awake for a few moments and thought of the evening. He had a pleasurable consciousness that he had made a good impression upon those fine fellows. He felt that he had spent the most delightful evening of his life.

V

KELCEY WAS CROSS in the morning. His mother had been obliged to shake him a great deal, and it had seemed to him a most unjust thing. Also, when he, blinking his eyes, had entered the kitchen, she had said: "Yeh left th' lamp burnin' all night last night, George. How many times must I tell yeh never t' leave th' lamp burnin'?"

He ate the greater part of his breakfast in silence, moodily stirring his coffee and glaring at a remote corner of the room with eyes that felt as if they had been baked. When he moved his eyelids there was a sensation that they were cracking. In his mouth there was a singular taste. It seemed to him that he had been sucking the end of a wooden spoon. Moreover, his temper was rampant within him. It sought something to devour.

Finally he said, savagely: "Damn these early hours!"

His mother jumped as if he had flung a missile at her. "Why, George—" she began.

Kelcey broke in again. "Oh, I know all that—but this gettin' up in th' mornin' so early makes me sick. Jest when a man is gettin' his mornin' nap he's gota get up. I——"

"George, dear," said his mother, "yeh know how I hate yeh t' swear, dear. Now please don't." She looked beseechingly at him.

He made a swift gesture. "Well, I ain't swearin', am I?" he demanded. "I was on'y sayin' that this gettin'-up business gives me a pain, wasn't I?"

"Well, yeh know how swearin' hurts me," protested the little old woman. She seemed about to sob. She gazed off retrospectively. She apparently was recalling persons who had never been profane.

"I don't see where yeh ever caught this way a' swearin' out at everything," she continued, presently. "Fred, ner John, ner Willie never swore a bit. Ner Tom neither, except when he was real mad."

The son made another gesture. It was directed into the air, as if he saw there a phantom injustice. "Oh, good thunder," he said, with an accent of despair. Thereupon, he relapsed into a mood of silence. He sombrely regarded his plate.

This demeanor speedily reduced his mother to meekness. When she spoke again it was in a conciliatory voice. "George, dear, won't yeh bring some sugar home t'-night?" It could be seen that she was asking for a crown of gold.

Kelcey aroused from his semi-slumber. "Yes, if I kin remember it," he said.

The little old woman arose to stow her son's lunch into the pail. When he had finished his breakfast he stalked for a time about the room in a dignified way. He put on his coat and hat, and taking his lunch-pail went to the door. There he halted, and without turning his head, stiffly said: "Well, good-by!"

The little old woman saw that she had offended her son. She did not seek an explanation. She was accustomed to these phenomena. She made haste to surrender.

"Ain't yeh goin' t' kiss me good-by," she asked in a little woful voice.

The youth made a pretence of going on, deaf-heartedly. He wore the dignity of an injured monarch.

Then the little old woman called again in forsaken accents: "George—George—ain't yeh goin' t' kiss me good-by?" When he moved he found that she was hanging to his coat-tails.

He turned eventually with a murmur of a sort of tenderness. "Why, 'a course I am," he said. He kissed her. Withal there was an undertone of superiority in his voice, as if he were granting an astonishing suit. She looked at him with reproach and gratitude and affection.

She stood at the head of the stairs and watched his hand sliding along the rail as he went down. Occasionally she could see his arm and part of his shoulder. When he reached the first floor she called to him: "Good-by!"

The little old woman went back to her work in the kitchen with a frown of perplexity upon her brow. "I wonder what was th' matter with George this mornin'," she mused. "He didn't seem a bit like himself!"

As she trudged to and fro at her labor she began to speculate. She was much worried. She surmised in a vague way that he was a sufferer from a great internal disease. It was something no doubt that devoured the kidneys or quietly fed upon the lungs. Later, she imagined a woman, wicked and fair, who had fascinated him and was turning his life into a bitter thing. Her mind created many wondrous influences that were swooping like green dragons at him. They were changing him to a morose man, who suffered silently. She longed to discover them, that she might go bravely to the rescue of her heroic son. She knew that he, generous in his pain, would keep it from her. She racked her mind for knowledge.

However, when he came home at night he was extraordinarily blithe. He seemed to be a lad of ten. He capered all about the room. When she was bringing the coffee-pot from the stove to the table, he made show of waltzing with her so that she spilled some of the coffee. She was obliged to scold him.

All through the meal he made jokes. She occasionally was compelled to laugh, despite the fact that she believed that she should not laugh at her own son's jokes. She uttered reproofs at times, but he did not regard them.

"Golly," he said once, "I feel fine as silk. I didn't think I'd get over feelin' bad so quick. It—" He stopped abruptly.

During the evening he sat content. He smoked his pipe and read from an evening paper. She bustled about at her work. She seemed utterly happy with him there, lazily puffing out little clouds of smoke and giving frequent brilliant dissertations upon the news of the day. It seemed to her that she must be a model mother to have such a son, one who came home to her at night and sat contented, in a languor of the muscles after a good day's toil. She pondered upon the science of her management.

The week thereafter, too, she was joyous, for he stayed at home each night of it, and was sunny-tempered. She became convinced that she was a perfect mother, rearing a perfect son. There came often a love-light into her eyes. The wrinkled, yellow face frequently warmed into a smile of the kind that a maiden bestows upon him who to her is first and perhaps last.

VI

THE LITTLE OLD WOMAN habitually discouraged all out-bursts of youthful vanity upon the part of her son. She feared that he would get to think too much of himself, and she knew that nothing could do more harm. Great self-esteem was always passive, she thought, and if he grew to regard his qualities of mind as forming a dazzling constellation, he would tranquilly sit still and not do those wonders she expected of him. So she was constantly on the alert to suppress even a shadow of such a thing. As for him he ruminated with the savage, vengeful bitterness of a young man, and decided that she did not comprehend him.

But despite her precautions he often saw that she believed him to be the most marvellous young man on the earth. He had only to look at those two eyes that became lighted with a glow from her heart whenever he did some excessively brilliant thing. On these occasions he could see her glance triumphantly at a neighbor, or whoever happened to be present. He grew to plan for these glances. And then he took a vast satisfaction in detecting and appropriating them.

Nevertheless, he could not understand why, directly after a scene of this kind, his mother was liable to call to him to hang his coat on the hook under the mantel, her voice in a key of despair as if he were negligent and stupid in what was, after all, the only important thing in life.

"If yeh'll only get in the habit of doin' it, it'll be jest as easy as throwin' it down anywheres," she would say to him. "When yeh pitch it down anywheres, somebody's got t' pick it up, an' that'll most likely be your poor ol' mother. Yeh can hang it up yerself, if yeh'll on'y think." This was intolerable. He usually went then and hurled his coat savagely at the hook. The correctness of her position was maddening.

It seemed to him that anyone who had a son of his glowing attributes should overlook the fact that he seldom hung up his coat. It was impossible to explain this situation to his mother. She was unutterably narrow. He grew sullen.

There came a time, too, that, even in all his mother's tremendous admiration for him, he did not entirely agree with her. He was delighted that she liked his great wit. He spurred himself to new and flashing effort because of this appreciation. But for the greater part he could see that his mother took pride in him in quite a different way from that in which he took pride in himself. She rejoiced at qualities in him that indicated that he was going to become a white and looming king among men. From these she made pictures in which he appeared as a benign personage, blessed by the filled hands of the poor, one whose brain could hold massive thoughts and awe certain men about whom she had read. She was fêted as the mother of this enormous man. These dreams were her solace. She spoke of them to no one because she knew that, worded, they would be ridiculous. But she dwelt with them, and they shed a radiance of gold upon her long days, her sorry labor. Upon the dead altars of her life she had builded the little fires of hope for another.

He had a complete sympathy for as much as he understood of these thoughts of his mother. They were so wise that he admired her foresight. As for himself, however, most of his dreams were of a nearer time. He had many of the distant future when he would be a man with a cloak of coldness concealing his gentleness and his faults, and of whom the men and, more particularly, the women, would think with reverence. He agreed with his mother that at that time he would go through the obstacles to other men like a flung stone. And then he would have power and he would enjoy having his bounty and his wrath alike fall swiftly upon those below. They would be awed. And above all he would mystify them.

But then his nearer dreams were a multitude. He had begun to look at the great world revolving near to his nose. He had a vast curiosity concerning this city in whose complexities he was buried. It was an impenetrable mystery, this city. It was a blend of many enticing colors. He longed to comprehend it completely, that he might walk understandingly in its greatest marvels, its mightiest march of life, its sin. He dreamed of a comprehension whose pay was the admirable attitude of a man of knowledge. He remembered Jones. He could not help but admire a man who knew so many bartenders.

VII

AN INDEFINITE WOMAN was in all of Kelcey's dreams. As a matter of fact it was not he whom he pictured as wedding her. It was a vision of himself greater, finer, more terrible. It was himself as he expected to be. In scenes which he took mainly from pictures, this vision conducted a courtship, strutting, posing, and lying through a drama which was magnificent from glow of purple. In it he was icy, self-possessed; but she, the dream-girl, was consumed by wild, torrential passion. He went to the length of having her display it before the people. He saw them wonder at his tranquillity. It amazed them infinitely to see him remain cold before the glory of this peerless woman's love. She was to him as beseeching for affection as a pet animal, but still he controlled appearances and none knew of his deep abiding love. Some day, at the critical romantic time, he was going to divulge it. In these long dreams there were accessories of castle-like houses, wide lands, servants, horses, clothes.

They began somewhere in his childhood. When he ceased to see himself as a stern general pointing a sword at the nervous and abashed horizon, he became this sublime king of a vague woman's heart. Later when he had read some books, it all achieved clearer expression. He was told in them that there was a goddess in the world whose business it was to wait until he should exchange a glance with her. It became a creed, subtly powerful. It saved discomfort for him and for several women who flitted by him. He used her as a standard.

Often he saw the pathos of her long wait, but his faith did not falter. The world was obliged to turn gold in time. His life was to be fine and heroic, else he would not have been born. He believed that the common-place lot was the sentence, the doom of certain people who did not know how to feel. His blood was a tender current of life. He thought that the usual should fall to others whose nerves were of lead. Occasionally he wondered how fate was going to begin in making an enormous figure of him; but he had no doubt of the result. A chariot of pink clouds was coming for him. His faith was his reason for existence. Meanwhile he could dream of the indefinite woman and the fragrance of roses that came from her hair.

One day he met Maggie Johnson on the stairs. She had a pail of beer in one hand and a brown-paper parcel under her arm. She glanced at him. He discovered that it would wither his heart to see another man signally successful in the smiles of her. And the glance that she gave him was so indifferent and so unresponsive to the sudden vivid admiration in his own eyes that he immediately concluded that she was magnificent in two ways.

As she came to the landing, the light from a window passed in a silver gleam over the girlish roundness of her cheek. It was a thing that he remembered.

He was silent for the most part at supper that night. He was particularly unkind when he did speak. His mother, observing him apprehensively, tried in vain to picture the new terrible catastrophe. She eventually concluded that he did not like the beef-stew. She put more salt in it.

He saw Maggie quite frequently after the meeting upon the stairs. He reconstructed his dreams and placed her in the full glory of that sun. The dream-woman, the goddess, pitched from her pedestal, lay prostrate, unheeded, save when he brought her forth to call her insipid and childish in the presence of his new religion.

He was relatively happy sometimes when Maggie's mother would get drunk and make terrific uproars. He used then to sit in the dark and make scenes in which he rescued the girl from her hideous environment.

He laid clever plans by which he encountered her in the halls, at the door, on the street. When he succeeded in meeting her he was always overcome by the thought that the whole thing was obvious to her. He could feel the shame of it burn his face and neck. To prove to her that she was mistaken he would turn away his head or regard her with a granite stare.

After a time he became impatient of the distance between them. He saw looming princes who would aim to seize her. Hours of his leisure and certain hours of his labor he spent in contriving. The shade of this girl was with him continually. With her he built his grand dramas so that he trod in clouds, the matters of his daily life obscured and softened by a mist.

He saw that he need only break down the slight conventional barriers and she would soon discover his noble character. Sometimes he could see it all in his mind. It was very skilful. But then his courage flew away at the supreme moment. Perhaps the whole affair was humorous to her. Perhaps she was watching his mental contortions. She might laugh. He felt that he would then die or kill her. He could not approach the dread moment. He sank often from the threshold of knowledge. Directly after these occasions, it was his habit to avoid her to prove that she was a cipher to him.

He reflected that if he could only get a chance to rescue her from something, the whole tragedy would speedily unwind.

He met a young man in the halls one evening who said to him: "Say, me frien', where d' d' Johnson birds live in heh? I can't fin' me feet in dis bloomin' joint. I been battin' round heh fer a half-hour."

"Two flights up," said Kelcey stonily. He had felt a sudden quiver of his heart. The grandeur of the clothes, the fine worldly air, the experience, the self-reliance, the courage that shone in the countenance of this other young man made him suddenly sink to the depths of woe. He stood listening in the hall, flushing and ashamed of it, until he heard them coming down-stairs together. He slunk away then. It would have been a horror to him if she had discovered him there. She might have felt sorry for him.

They were going out to a show, perhaps. That pig of the world in his embroidered cloak was going to dazzle her with splendor. He mused upon how unrighteous it was for other men to dazzle women with splendor.

As he appreciated his handicap he swore with savage, vengeful bitterness. In his home his mother raised her voice in a high key of monotonous irritability. "Hang up yer coat, can't yeh, George?" she cried at him. "I can't go round after yeh all th' time. It's jest as easy t' hang it up as it is t' throw it down that way. Don't yeh ever git tired 'a hearin' me yell at yeh!"

"Yes," he exploded. In this word he put a profundity of sudden anger. He turned toward his mother a face, red, seamed, hard with hate and rage. They stared a moment in silence. Then she turned and staggered toward her room. Her hip struck violently against the corner of the table during this blind passage. A moment later the door closed.

Kelcey sank down in a chair with his legs thrust out straight and his hands deep in his trousers' pockets. His chin was forward upon his breast and his eyes stared before him. There swept over him all the self-pity that comes when the soul is turned back from a road.

VIII

DURING THE NEXT FEW DAYS Kelcey suffered from his first gloomy conviction that the earth was not grateful to him for his presence upon it. When sharp words were said to him, he interpreted them with what seemed to be a lately acquired insight. He could now perceive that the universe hated him. He sank to the most sublime depths of despair.

One evening of this period he met Jones. The latter rushed upon him with enthusiasm. "Why, yer jest th' man I wanted t' see! I was comin' round t' your place t'-night. Lucky I met yeh! Ol' Bleecker's goin' t' give a blow-out t'-morrah night. Anything yeh want t' drink! All th' boys 'll be there an' everything. He tol' me expressly that he wanted yeh t' be there. Great time! Great! Can yeh come?"

Kelcey grasped the other's hand with fervor. He felt now that there was some solacing friendship in space. "You bet I will, ol' man," he said, huskily. "I'd like nothin' better in th' world!"

As he walked home he thought that he was a very grim figure. He was about to taste the delicious revenge of a partial self-destruction. The universe would regret its position when it saw him drunk.

He was a little late in getting to Bleecker's lodging. He was delayed while his mother read aloud a letter from an old uncle, who wrote in one place: "God bless the boy! Bring him up to be the man his father was." Bleecker lived in an old three-storied house on a side-street. A Jewish tailor lived and worked in the front parlor, and old Bleecker lived in the back parlor. A German, whose family took care of the house, occupied the basement. Another German, with a wife and eight children, rented the dining-room. The two upper floors were inhabited by tailors, dressmakers, a pedler, and mysterious people who were seldom seen. The door of the little hall-bedroom, at the foot of the second flight, was always open, and in there could be seen two bended men who worked at mending opera-glasses. The German woman in the dining-room was not friends with the little dressmaker in the rear room of the third floor, and frequently they yelled the vilest names up and down between the balusters. Each part of the woodwork was scratched and rubbed by the contact of innumerable persons. In one wall there was a long slit with chipped edges, celebrating the time when a man had thrown a hatchet at his wife. In the lower hall there was an eternal woman, with a rag and a pail of suds, who knelt over the worn oil-cloth. Old Bleecker felt that he had quite respectable and high-class apartments. He was glad to invite his friends.

Bleecker met Kelcey in the hall. He wore a collar that was cleaner and higher than his usual one. It changed his appearance greatly. He was now formidably aristocratic. "How are yeh, ol' man?" he shouted. He grasped Kelcey's arm, and, babbling jovially, conducted him down the hall and into the ex-parlor.

A group of standing men made vast shadows in the yellow glare of the lamp. They turned their heads as the two entered. "Why, hello, Kelcey, ol' man," Jones exclaimed, coming rapidly forward. "Good fer you! Glad yeh come! Yeh know O'Connor, 'a course! An' Schmidt! an' Woods! Then there's Zeusentell! Mr. Zeusentell—my friend Mr. Kelcey! Shake hands—both good fellows, damnitall! Then here is—oh, gentlemen, my friend Mr. Kelcey! A good fellow, he is, too! I've known 'im since I was a kid! Come, have a drink!" Everybody was excessively amiable. Kelcey felt that he had social standing. The strangers were cautious and respectful.

"By all means," said old Bleecker. "Mr. Kelcey, have a drink! An' by th' way, gentlemen, while we're about it, let's all have a drink!" There was much laughter. Bleecker was so droll at times.

With mild and polite gesturing they marched up to the table. There were upon it a keg of beer, a long row of whiskey bottles, a little heap of corn-cob pipes, some bags of tobacco, a box of cigars, and a mighty collection of glasses, cups, and mugs. Old Bleecker had arranged them so deftly that they resembled a primitive bar. There was considerable scuffling for possession of the cracked cups. Jones politely but vehemently insisted upon drinking from the worst of the assortment. He was quietly opposed by others. Everybody showed that they were awed by Bleecker's lavish hospitality. Their demeanors expressed their admiration at the cost of this entertainment.

Kelcey took his second mug of beer away to a corner and sat down with it. He wished to socially reconnoitre. Over in a corner a man was telling a story, in which at intervals he grunted like a pig. A half dozen men were listening. Two or three others sat alone in isolated places. They looked expectantly bright, ready to burst out cordially if anyone should address them. The row of bottles made quaint shadows upon the table, and upon a side-wall the keg of beer created a portentous black figure that reared toward the ceiling, hovering over the room and its inmates with spectral stature. Tobacco-smoke lay in lazy cloud-banks overhead.

Jones and O'Connor stayed near the table, occasionally being affable in all directions. Kelcey saw old Bleecker go to them and heard him whisper: "Come, we must git th' thing started. Git th' thing started." Kelcey saw that the host was fearing that all were not having a good time. Jones conferred with O'Connor and then O'Connor went to the man named Zeusentell. O'Connor evidently proposed something. Zeusentell refused at once. O'Connor beseeched. Zeusentell remained implacable. At last O'Connor broke off his argument, and going to the centre of the room, held up his hand. "Gentlemen," he shouted loudly, "we will now have a recitation by Mr. Zeusentell, entitled 'Patrick Clancy's Pig'!" He then glanced triumphantly at Zeusentell and said: "Come on!" Zeusentell had been twisting and making pantomimic appeals. He said, in a reproachful whisper: "You son of a gun."

The men turned their heads to glance at Zeusentell for a moment and then burst into a sustained clamor. "Hurray! Let 'er go! Come—give it t' us! Spring it! Spring it! Let it come!" As Zeusentell made no advances, they appealed personally. "Come, ol' man, let 'er go! Whatter yeh 'fraid of? Let 'er go! Go ahn! Hurry up!"

Zeusentell was protesting with almost frantic modesty. O'Connor took him by the lapel and tried to drag him; but he leaned back, pulling at his coat and shaking his head. "No, no, I don't know it, I tell yeh! I can't! I don't know it! I tell yeh I don't know it! I've forgotten it, I tell yeh! No—no—no—no. Ah, say, lookahere, le' go me, can't yeh? What's th' matter with yeh? I tell yeh I don't know it!" The men applauded violently. O'Connor did not relent. A little battle was waged until all of a sudden Zeusentell was seen to grow wondrously solemn. A hush fell upon the men. He was about to begin. He paused in the middle of the floor and nervously adjusted his collar and cravat. The audience became grave. " 'Patrick Clancy's Pig,' " announced Zeusentell in a shrill, dry, unnatural tone. And then he began in rapid sing-song:

> "Patrick Clancy had a pig
> Th' pride uv all th' nation,
> The half uv him was half as big
> As half uv all creation——"

When he concluded the others looked at each other to convey their appreciation. They then wildly clapped their hands or tinkled their glasses. As Zeusentell went toward his seat a man leaned over and asked: "Can yeh tell me where I kin git that." He had made a great success. After an enormous pressure he was induced to recite two more tales. Old Bleecker finally led him forward and pledged him in a large drink. He declared that they were the best things he had ever heard.

The efforts of Zeusentell imparted a gayety to the company. The men having laughed together were better acquainted, and there was now a universal topic. Some of the party, too, began to be quite drunk.

The invaluable O'Connor brought forth a man who could play the mouth-organ. The latter, after wiping his instrument upon his coat-sleeve, played all the popular airs. The men's heads swayed to and fro in the clouded smoke. They grinned and beat time with their feet. A valor, barbaric and wild, began to show in their poses and in their faces, red and glistening from perspiration. The conversation resounded in a hoarse roar. The beer would not run rapidly enough for Jones, so he remained behind to tilt the keg. This caused the black shadow on the wall to retreat and advance, sinking mystically to loom forward again with sudden menace, a huge dark figure controlled, as by some unknown emotion. The glasses, mugs, and cups travelled swift and regular, catching orange reflections from the lamp-light. Two or three men were grown so careless that they were continually spilling their drinks. Old Bleecker, cackling with pleasure, seized time to glance triumphantly at Jones. His party was going to be a success.

IX

O F A SUDDEN Kelcey felt the buoyant thought that he
was having a good time. He was all at once an enthu-
siast, as if he were at a festival of a religion. He felt that there
was something fine and thrilling in this affair isolated from a
stern world, and from which the laughter arose like incense.
He knew that old sentiment of brotherly regard for those
about him. He began to converse tenderly with them. He was
not sure of his drift of thought, but he knew that he was
immensely sympathetic. He rejoiced at their faces, shining red
and wrinkled with smiles. He was capable of heroisms.

His pipe irritated him by going out frequently. He was too
busy in amiable conversations to attend to it. When he arose
to go for a match he discovered that his legs were a trifle
uncertain under him. They bended and did not precisely obey
his intent. At the table he lit a match and then, in laughing at
a joke made near him, forgot to apply it to the bowl of his
pipe. He succeeded with the next match after annoying trou-
ble. He swayed so that the match would appear first on one
side of the bowl and then on the other. At last he happily got
it directly over the tobacco. He had burned his fingers. He
inspected them, laughing vaguely.

Jones came and slapped him on the shoulder. "Well, ol'
man, let's take a drink fer ol' Handyville's sake!"

Kelcey was deeply affected. He looked at Jones with moist
eyes. "I'll go yeh," he said. With an air of profound mel-
ancholy, Jones poured out some whiskey. They drank rev-
erently. They exchanged a glistening look of tender
recollections and then went over to where Bleecker was tell-
ing a humorous story to a circle of giggling listeners. The
old man sat like a fat, jolly god. "—and just at that moment
th' old woman put her head out of th' window an' said:
'Mike, yez lezy divil, fer phwat do yez be slapin' in me new
geranium bid?' An' Mike woke up an' said: 'Domn a wash-
woman thot do niver wash her own bidclues. Here do I be
slapin' in nothin' but dhirt an' wades.' " The men slapped
their knees, roaring loudly. They begged him to tell an-
other. A clamor of comment arose concerning the anecdote,

so that when old Bleecker began a fresh one nobody was heeding.

It occurred to Jones to sing. Suddenly he burst forth with a ballad that had a rippling waltz movement, and seizing Kelcey, made a furious attempt to dance. They sprawled over a pair of outstretched legs and pitched headlong. Kelcey fell with a yellow crash. Blinding lights flashed before his vision. But he arose immediately, laughing. He did not feel at all hurt. The pain in his head was rather pleasant.

Old Bleecker, O'Connor, and Jones, who now limped and drew breath through his teeth, were about to lead him with much care and tenderness to the table for another drink, but he laughingly pushed them away and went unassisted. Bleecker told him: "Great Gawd, your head struck hard enough t' break a trunk."

He laughed again, and with a show of steadiness and courage he poured out an extravagant portion of whiskey. With cold muscles he put it to his lips and drank it. It chanced that this addition dazed him like a powerful blow. A moment later it affected him with blinding and numbing power. Suddenly unbalanced, he felt the room sway. His blurred sight could only distinguish a tumbled mass of shadow through which the beams from the light ran like swords of flame. The sound of the many voices was to him like the roar of a distant river. Still, he felt that if he could only annul the force of these million winding fingers that gripped his senses, he was capable of most brilliant and entertaining things.

He was at first of the conviction that his feelings were only temporary. He waited for them to pass away, but the mental and physical pause only caused a new reeling and swinging of the room. Chasms with inclined approaches were before him; peaks leaned toward him. And withal he was blind and numb with surprise. He understood vaguely in his stupefaction that it would disgrace him to fall down a chasm.

At last he perceived a shadow, a form, which he knew to be Jones. The adorable Jones, the supremely wise Jones, was walking in this strange land without fear or care, erect and tranquil. Kelcey murmured in admiration and affection, and fell toward his friend. Jones's voice sounded as from the shores of the unknown. "Come, come, ol' man, this will never do. Brace up." It appeared after all that Jones was not wholly wise. "Oh, I'm—all ri' Jones! I'm all ri'! I wan' shing song! Tha's all! I wan' shing song!"

Jones was stupid. "Come now, sit down an' shut up."

It made Kelcey burn with fury. "Jones, le' me alone, I tell yeh! Le' me alone! I wan' shing song er te' story! G'l'm'n, I lovsh girl live down my shtreet. Thash reason 'm drunk, 'tis! She——"

Jones seized him and dragged him toward a chair. He heard him laugh. He could not endure these insults from his friend. He felt a blazing desire to strangle his companion. He threw out his hand violently, but Jones grappled him close and he was no more than a dried leaf. He was amazed to find that Jones possessed the strength of twenty horses. He was forced skilfully to the floor.

As he lay, he reflected in great astonishment upon Jones's muscle. It was singular that he had never before discovered it. The whole incident had impressed him immensely. An idea struck him that he might denounce Jones for it. It would be a sage thing. There would be a thrilling and dramatic moment in which he would dazzle all the others. But at this moment he was assailed by a mighty desire to sleep. Sombre and soothing clouds of slumber were heavily upon him. He closed his eyes with a sigh that was yet like that of a babe.

When he awoke, there was still the battleful clamor of the revel. He half arose with a plan of participating, when O'Connor came and pushed him down again, throwing out his chin in affectionate remonstrance and saying, "Now, now," as to a child.

The change that had come over these men mystified Kelcey in a great degree. He had never seen anything so vastly stupid as their idea of his state. He resolved to prove to them that they were dealing with one whose mind was very clear. He kicked and squirmed in O'Connor's arms, until, with a final wrench, he scrambled to his feet and stood tottering in the middle of the room. He would let them see that he had a strangely lucid grasp of events. "G'l'm'n, I lovsh girl! I ain' drunker'n yeh all are! She——"

He felt them hurl him to a corner of the room and pile chairs and tables upon him until he was buried beneath a stupendous mountain. Far above, as up a mine's shaft, there were voices, lights, and vague figures. He was not hurt physically, but his feelings were unutterably injured. He, the brilliant, the good, the sympathetic had been thrust fiendishly from the party. They had had the comprehension of red lobsters. It was an unspeakable barbarism. Tears welled piteously from his eyes. He planned long diabolical explanations!

X

A T FIRST the gray lights of dawn came timidly into the room, remaining near the windows, afraid to approach certain sinister corners. Finally, mellow streams of sunshine poured in, undraping the shadows to disclose the putrefaction, making pitiless revelation. Kelcey awoke with a groan of undirected misery. He tossed his stiffened arms about his head for a moment and then leaning heavily upon his elbow stared blinking at his environment. The grim truthfulness of the day showed disaster and death. After the tumults of the previous night the interior of this room resembled a decaying battle-field. The air hung heavy and stifling with the odors of tobacco, men's breaths, and beer half filling forgotten glasses. There was ruck of broken tumblers, pipes, bottles, spilled tobacco, cigar stumps. The chairs and tables were pitched this way and that way, as after some terrible struggle. In the midst of it all lay old Bleecker stretched upon a couch in deepest sleep, as abandoned in attitude, as motionless, as ghastly as if it were a corpse that had been flung there.

A knowledge of the thing came gradually into Kelcey's eyes. He looked about him with an expression of utter woe, regret, and loathing. He was compelled to lie down again. A pain above his eyebrows was like that from an iron-clamp.

As he lay pondering, his bodily condition created for him a bitter philosophy, and he perceived all the futility of a red existence. He saw his life problems confronting him like granite giants and he was no longer erect to meet them. He had made a calamitous retrogression in his war. Spectres were to him now as large as clouds.

Inspired by the pitiless ache in his head, he was prepared to reform and live a white life. His stomach informed him that a good man was the only being who was wise. But his perception of his future was hopeless. He was aghast at the prospect of the old routine. It was impossible. He trembled before its exactions.

Turning toward the other way, he saw that the gold portals of vice no longer enticed him. He could not hear the strains of alluring music. The beckoning sirens of drink had been killed by this pain in his head. The desires of his life suddenly lay dead like mullein stalks. Upon reflection, he saw, therefore, that he was perfectly willing to be virtuous if somebody would come and make it easy for him.

When he stared over at old Bleecker, he felt a sudden contempt and dislike for him. He considered him to be a tottering old beast. It was disgusting to perceive aged men so weak in sin. He dreaded to see him awaken lest he should be required to be somewhat civil to him.

Kelcey wished for a drink of water. For some time he had dreamed of the liquid, deliciously cool. It was an abstract, uncontained thing that poured upon him and tumbled him, taking away his pain like a kind of surgery. He arose and staggered slowly toward a little sink in a corner of the room. He understood that any rapid movement might cause his head to split.

The little sink was filled with a chaos of broken glass and spilled liquids. A sight of it filled him with horror, but he rinsed a glass with scrupulous care, and filling it, took an enormous drink. The water was an intolerable disappointment. It was insipid and weak to his scorched throat and not at all cool. He put down the glass with a gesture of despair. His face became fixed in the stony and sullen expression of a man who waits for the recuperative power of morrows.

Old Bleecker awakened. He rolled over and groaned loudly. For awhile he thrashed about in a fury of displeasure at his bodily stiffness and pain. Kelcey watched him as he would have watched a death agony. "Good Gawd," said the old man, "beer an' whiskey make th' devil of a mix. Did yeh see th' fight?"

"No," said Kelcey, stolidly.

"Why, Zeusentell an' O'Connor had a great old mill. They were scrappin' all over th' place. I thought we were all goin' t' get pulled. Thompson, that fellah over in th' corner, though, he sat down on th' whole business. He was a dandy! He had t' poke Zeusentell! He was a bird! Lord, I wish I had a Manhattan!"

Kelcey remained in bitter silence while old Bleecker dressed. "Come an' get a cocktail," said the latter briskly. This was part of his aristocracy. He was the only man of them who knew much about cocktails. He perpetually referred to them. "It'll brace yeh right up! Come along! Say, you get full too soon. You oughter wait until later, me boy! You're too speedy!" Kelcey wondered vaguely where his companion had lost his zeal for polished sentences, his iridescent mannerisms.

"Come along," said Bleecker.

Kelcey made a movement of disdain for cocktails, but he followed the other to the street. At the corner they separated. Kelcey attempted a friendly parting smile and then went on up the street. He had to reflect to know that he was erect and using his own muscles in walking. He felt like a man of paper, blown by the winds. Withal, the dust of the avenue was galling to his throat, eyes, and nostrils, and the roar of traffic cracked his head. He was glad, however, to be alone, to be rid of old Bleecker. The sight of him had been as the contemplation of a disease.

His mother was not at home. In his little room he mechanically undressed and bathed his head, arms, and shoulders. When he crawled between the two white sheets he felt a first lifting of his misery. His pillow was soothingly soft. There was an effect that was like the music of tender voices.

When he awoke again his mother was bending over him giving vent to alternate cries of grief and joy. Her hands trembled so that they were useless to her. "Oh, George, George, where have yeh been? What has happened t' yeh? Oh, George, I've been so worried! I didn't sleep a wink all night."

Kelcey was instantly wide awake. With a moan of suffering he turned his face to the wall before he spoke. "Never mind, mother, I'm all right. Don't fret now! I was knocked down by a truck last night in th' street, an' they took me t' th' hospital; but it's all right now. I got out jest a little while ago. They told me I'd better go home an' rest up."

His mother screamed in pity, horror, joy, and self-reproach for something unknown. She frenziedly demanded the details. He sighed with unutterable weariness. "Oh—wait—wait— wait," he said shutting his eyes as from the merciless monotony of a pain. "Wait—wait—please wait. I can't talk now. I want t' rest."

His mother condemned herself with a little cry. She adjusted his pillow, her hands shaking with love and tenderness.

"There, there, don't mind, dearie! But yeh can't think how worried I was—an' crazy. I was near frantic. I went down t' th' shop, an' they said they hadn't seen anything 'a yeh there. The foreman was awful good t' me. He said he'd come up this afternoon t' see if yeh had come home yet. He tol' me not t' worry. Are yeh sure yer all right? Ain't there anythin' I kin git fer yeh? What did th' docter say?"

Kelcey's patience was worn. He gestured, and then spoke querulously. "Now—now—mother, it's all right, I tell yeh! All I need is a little rest an' I'll be as well as ever. But it makes it all th' worse if yeh stand there an' ask me questions an' make me think. Jest leave me alone fer a little while, an' I'll be as well as ever. Can't yeh do that?"

The little old woman puckered her lips funnily. "My, what an old bear th' boy is!" She kissed him blithely. Presently she went out, upon her face a bright and glad smile that must have been a reminiscence of some charming girlhood.

XI

A T ONE TIME Kelcey had a friend who was struck in the head by the pole of a truck and knocked senseless. He was taken to the hospital, from which he emerged in the morning an astonished man, with rather a dim recollection of the accident. He used to hold an old brier-wood pipe in his teeth in a manner peculiar to himself, and, with a brown derby hat tilted back on his head, recount his strange sensations. Kelcey had always remembered it as a bit of curious history. When his mother cross-examined him in regard to the accident, he told this story with barely a variation. Its truthfulness was incontestable.

At the shop he was welcomed on the following day with considerable enthusiasm. The foreman had told the story and there were already jokes created concerning it. Mike O'Donnell, whose wit was famous, had planned a humorous campaign, in which he made charges against Kelcey, which were, as a matter of fact, almost the exact truth. Upon hearing it, Kelcey looked at him suddenly from the corners of his eyes, but otherwise remained imperturbable. O'Donnell eventually despaired. "Yez can't goiy that kid! He tekes ut all loike mate an' dhrink." Kelcey often told the story, his pipe held in his teeth peculiarly, and his derby tilted back on his head.

He remained at home for several evenings, content to read the papers and talk with his mother. She began to look around for the tremendous reason for it. She suspected that his nearness to death in the recent accident had sobered his senses and made him think of high things. She mused upon it continually. When he sat moodily pondering she watched him. She said to herself that she saw the light breaking in upon his spirit. She felt that it was a very critical period of his existence. She resolved to use all her power and skill to turn his eyes toward the lights in the sky. Accordingly she addressed him one evening. "Come, go t' prayer-meetin' t'-night with me, will yeh, George?" It sounded more blunt than she intended.

He glanced at her in sudden surprise. "Huh?"

As she repeated her request, her voice quavered. She felt

that it was a supreme moment. "Come, go t' prayer-meetin' t'-night, won't yeh?"

He seemed amazed. "Oh, I don't know," he began. He was fumbling in his mind for a reason for refusing. "I don't wanta go. I'm tired as th' dickens!" His obedient shoulders sank down languidly. His head mildly drooped.

The little old woman, with a quick perception of her helplessness, felt a motherly rage at her son. It was intolerable that she could not impart motion to him in a chosen direction. The waves of her desires were puny against the rocks of his indolence. She had a great wish to beat him. "I don't know what I'm ever goin' t' do with yeh," she told him, in a choking voice. "Yeh won't do anything I ask yeh to. Yeh never pay th' least bit 'a attention t' what I say. Yeh don't mind me any more than yeh would a fly. Whatever am I goin' t' do with yeh?" She faced him in a battleful way, her eyes blazing with a sombre light of despairing rage.

He looked up at her ironically. "I don't know," he said, with calmness. "What are yeh?" He had traced her emotions and seen her fear of his rebellion. He thrust out his legs in the easy scorn of a rapier-bravo. "What are yeh?"

The little old woman began to weep. They were tears without a shame of grief. She allowed them to run unheeded down her cheeks. As she stared into space her son saw her regarding there the powers and influences that she had held in her younger life. She was in some way acknowledging to fate that she was now but withered grass, with no power but the power to feel the winds. He was smitten with a sudden shame. Besides, in the last few days he had gained quite a character for amiability. He saw something grand in relenting at this point. "Well," he said, trying to remove a sulky quality from his voice, " well, if yer bound t' have me go, I s'pose I'll have t' go."

His mother, with strange, immobile face, went to him and kissed him on the brow. "All right, George!" There was in her wet eyes an emotion which he could not fathom.

She put on her bonnet and shawl, and they went out together. She was unusually silent, and made him wonder why she did not appear gleeful at his coming. He was resentful because she did not display more appreciation of his sacrifice.

Several times he thought of halting and refusing to go farther, to see if that would not wring from her some acknowledgment.

In a dark street the little chapel sat humbly between two towering apartment-houses. A red street-lamp stood in front. It threw a marvellous reflection upon the wet pavements. It was like the death-stain of a spirit. Farther up the brilliant lights of an avenue made a span of gold across the black street. A roar of wheels and a clangor of bells came from this point, interwoven into a sound emblematic of the life of the city. It seemed somehow to affront this solemn and austere little edifice. It suggested an approaching barbaric invasion. The little church, pierced, would die with a fine, illimitable scorn for its slayers.

When Kelcey entered with his mother he felt a sudden quaking. His knees shook. It was an awesome place to him. There was a menace in the red padded carpet and the leather doors, studded with little brass tacks that penetrated his soul with their pitiless glances. As for his mother, she had acquired such a new air that he would have been afraid to address her. He felt completely alone and isolated at this formidable time.

There was a man in the vestibule who looked at them blandly. From within came the sound of singing. To Kelcey there was a million voices. He dreaded the terrible moment when the doors should swing back. He wished to recoil, but at that instant the bland man pushed the doors aside and he followed his mother up the centre aisle of the little chapel. To him there was a riot of lights that made him transparent. The multitudinous pairs of eyes that turned toward him were implacable in their cool valuations.

They had just ceased singing. He who conducted the meeting motioned that the services should wait until the new-comers found seats. The little old woman went slowly on toward the first rows. Occasionally she paused to scrutinize vacant places, but they did not seem to meet her requirements. Kelcey was in agony. He thought the moment of her decision would never come. In his unspeakable haste he walked a little faster than his mother. Once she paused to glance in her calculating way at some seats and he forged ahead. He halted abruptly and returned, but by that time she had resumed her thoughtful march up the aisle. He could have assassinated her. He felt that everybody must have seen his torture, during which his hands were to him like monstrous swollen hides. He was wild with a rage in which his lips turned slightly livid. He was capable of doing some furious, unholy thing.

When the little old woman at last took a seat, her son sat down beside her slowly and stiffly. He was opposing his strong desire to drop.

When from the mists of his shame and humiliation the scene came before his vision, he was surprised to find that all eyes were not fastened upon his face. The leader of the meeting seemed to be the only one who saw him. He stared gravely, solemnly, regretfully. He was a pale-faced, but plump young man in a black coat that buttoned to his chin. It was evident to Kelcey that his mother had spoken of him to the young clergyman, and that the latter was now impressing upon him the sorrow caused by the contemplation of his sin. Kelcey hated the man.

A man seated alone over in a corner began to sing. He closed his eyes and threw back his head. Others, scattered sparsely throughout the innumerable light-wood chairs, joined him as they caught the air. Kelcey heard his mother's frail, squeaking soprano. The chandelier in the centre was the only one lighted, and far at the end of the room one could discern the pulpit swathed in gloom, solemn and mystic as a bier. It was surrounded by vague shapes of darkness on which at times was the glint of brass, or of glass that shone like steel, until one could feel there the presence of the army of the unknown, possessors of the great eternal truths, and silent listeners at this ceremony. High up, the stained-glass windows loomed in leaden array like dull-hued banners, merely catching occasional splashes of dark wine-color from the lights. Kelcey fell to brooding concerning this indefinable presence which he felt in a church.

One by one people arose and told little tales of their religious faith. Some were tearful and others calm, emotionless, and convincing. Kelcey listened closely for a time. These people filled him with a great curiosity. He was not familiar with their types.

At last the young clergyman spoke at some length. Kelcey

was amazed, because, from the young man's appearance, he would not have suspected him of being so glib; but the speech had no effect on Kelcey, excepting to prove to him again that he was damned.

XII

KELCEY SOMETIMES WONDERED whether he liked beer. He had been obliged to cultivate a talent for imbibing it. He was born with an abhorrence which he had steadily battled until it had come to pass that he could drink from ten to twenty glasses of beer without the act of swallowing causing him to shiver. He understood that drink was an essential to joy, to the coveted position of a man of the world and of the streets. The saloons contained the mystery of a street for him. When he knew its saloons he comprehended the street. Drink and its surroundings were the eyes of a superb green dragon to him. He followed a fascinating glitter, and the glitter required no explanation.

Directly after old Bleecker's party he almost reformed. He was tired and worn from the tumult of it, and he saw it as one might see a skeleton emerged from a crimson cloak. He wished then to turn his face away. Gradually, however, he recovered his mental balance. Then he admitted again by his point of view that the thing was not so terrible. His headache had caused him to exaggerate. A drunk was not the blight which he had once remorsefully named it. On the contrary, it was a mere unpleasant incident. He resolved, however, to be more cautious.

When prayer-meeting night came again his mother approached him hopefully. She smiled like one whose request is already granted. "Well, will yeh go t' prayer-meetin' with me t'-night again?"

He turned toward her with eloquent suddenness, and then riveted his eyes upon a corner of the floor. "Well, I guess not," he said.

His mother tearfully tried to comprehend his state of mind. "What has come over yeh?" she said, tremblingly. "Yeh never used t' be this way, George. Yeh never used t' be so cross an' mean t' me——"

"Oh, I ain't cross an' mean t' yeh," he interpolated, exasperated and violent.

"Yes, yeh are, too! I ain't hardly had a decent word from yeh in ever so long. Yer as cross an' as mean as yeh can be. I don't know what t' make of it. It can't be—" There came a look in her eyes that told that she was going to shock and alarm him with her heaviest sentence—"it can't be that yeh've got t' drinkin'."

Kelcey grunted with disgust at the ridiculous thing. "Why, what an old goose yer gettin' t' be."

She was compelled to laugh a little, as a child laughs between tears at a hurt. She had not been serious. She was only trying to display to him how she regarded his horrifying mental state. "Oh, of course, I didn't mean that, but I think yeh act jest as bad as if yeh did drink. I wish yeh would do better, George!"

She had grown so much less frigid and stern in her censure that Kelcey seized the opportunity to try to make a joke of it. He laughed at her, but she shook her head and continued: "I do wish yeh would do better. I don't know what's t' become 'a yeh, George. Yeh don't mind what I say no more'n if I was th' wind in th' chimbly. Yeh don't care about nothin' 'cept goin' out nights. I can't ever get yeh t' prayer-meetin' ner church; yeh never go out with me anywheres unless yeh can't get out of it; yeh swear an' take on sometimes like everything, yeh never——"

He gestured wrathfully in interruption. "Say, lookahere, can't yeh think 'a something I do?"

She ended her oration then in the old way. "An' I don't know what's goin' t' become 'a yeh."

She put on her bonnet and shawl and then came and stood near him, expectantly. She imparted to her attitude a subtle threat of unchangeableness. He pretended to be engrossed in his newspaper. The little swaggering clock on the mantel became suddenly evident, ticking with loud monotony. Presently she said, firmly: "Well, are yeh comin'?"

He was reading.

"Well, are yeh comin'?"

He threw his paper down, angrily. "Oh, why don't yeh go on an' leave me alone?" he demanded in supreme impatience. "What do yeh wanta pester me fer? Yeh'd think there was robbers. Why can't yeh go alone er else stay home? You wanta go an' I don't wanta go, an' yeh keep all time tryin' t' drag me. Yeh know I don't wanta go." He concluded in a last defiant wounding of her. "What do I care 'bout those ol' bags-'a-wind anyhow? They gimme a pain!"

His mother turned her face and went from him. He sat staring with a mechanical frown. Presently he went and picked up his newspaper.

Jones told him that night that everybody had had such a good time at old Bleecker's party that they were going to form a club. They waited at the little smiling saloon, and then amid much enthusiasm all signed a membership-roll. Old Bleecker, late that night, was violently elected president. He made speeches of thanks and gratification during the remainder of the meeting. Kelcey went home rejoicing. He felt that at any rate he would have true friends. The dues were a dollar for each week.

He was deeply interested. For a number of evenings he fairly gobbled his supper in order that he might be off to the little smiling saloon to discuss the new organization. All the men were wildly enthusiastic. One night the saloon-keeper announced that he would donate half the rent of quite a large room over his saloon. It was an occasion for great cheering. Kelcey's legs were like whalebone when he tried to go upstairs upon his return home, and the edge of each step was moved curiously forward.

His mother's questions made him snarl. "Oh, nowheres!" At other times he would tell her: "Oh, t' see some friends 'a mine! Where d' yeh s'pose?"

Finally, some of the women of the tenement concluded that the little old mother had a wild son. They came to condole with her. They sat in the kitchen for hours. She told them of his wit, his cleverness, his kind heart.

XIII

AT A CERTAIN TIME Kelcey discovered that some young men who stood in the cinders between a brick wall and the pavement, and near the side-door of a corner saloon, knew more about life than other people. They used to lean there smoking and chewing, and comment upon events and persons. They knew the neighborhood extremely well. They debated upon small typical things that transpired before them until they had extracted all the information that existence contained. They sometimes inaugurated little fights with foreigners or well-dressed men. It was here that Sapristi Glielmi, the pedler, stabbed Pete Brady to death, for which he got a life-sentence. Each patron of the saloon was closely scrutinized as he entered the place. Sometimes they used to throng upon the heels of a man and in at the bar assert that he had asked them in to drink. When he objected, they would claim with one voice that it was too deep an insult and gather about to thrash him. When they had caught chance customers and absolute strangers, the barkeeper had remained in stolid neutrality, ready to serve one or seven, but two or three times they had encountered the wrong men. Finally, the proprietor had come out one morning and told them, in the fearless way of his class, that their pastime must cease. "It quits right here! See? Right here! Th' nex' time yeh try t' work it, I come with th' bung-starter, an' th' mugs I miss with it git pulled. See? It quits!" Infrequently, however, men did ask them in to drink.

The policeman of that beat grew dignified and shrewd whenever he approached this corner. Sometimes he stood with his hands behind his back and cautiously conversed with them. It was understood on both sides that it was a good thing to be civil.

In winter this band, a trifle diminished in numbers, huddled in their old coats and stamped little flat places in the snow, their faces turned always toward the changing life in the streets. In the summer they became more lively. Sometimes, then, they walked out to the curb to look up and down the street. Over in a trampled vacant lot, surrounded by high tenement-houses, there was a sort of a den among some bowlders. An old truck was made to form a shelter. The small hoodlums of that vicinity all avoided the spot. So many of them had been thrashed upon being caught near it. It was the summer-time lounging-place of the band from the corner.

They were all too clever to work. Some of them had worked, but these used their experiences as stores from which to draw tales. They were like veterans with their wars. One lad in particular used to recount how he whipped his employer, the proprietor of a large grain and feed establishment. He described his victim's features and form and clothes with minute exactness. He bragged of his wealth and social position. It had been a proud moment of the lad's life. He was like a savage who had killed a great chief.

Their feeling for contemporaneous life was one of contempt. Their philosophy taught that in a large part the whole thing was idle and a great bore. With fine scorn they sneered at the futility of it. Work was done by men who had not the courage to stand still and let the skies clap together if they willed.

The vast machinery of the popular law indicated to them that there were people in the world who wished to remain quiet. They awaited the moment when they could prove to them that a riotous upheaval, a cloud-burst of destruction would be a delicious thing. They thought of their fingers buried in the lives of these people. They longed dimly for a time when they could run through decorous streets with crash and roar of war, an army of revenge for pleasures long possessed by others, a wild sweeping compensation for their years without crystal and gilt, women and wine. This thought slumbered in them, as the image of Rome might have lain small in the hearts of the barbarians.

Kelcey respected these youths so much that he ordinarily used the other side of the street. He could not go near to them, because if a passer-by minded his own business he was a disdainful prig and had insulted them; if he showed that he was aware of them they were likely to resent his not minding his own business and prod him into a fight if the opportunity were good. Kelcey longed for their acquaintance and friendship, for with it came social safety and ease; they were respected so universally.

Once in another street Fidsey Corcoran was whipped by a short, heavy man. Fidsey picked himself up, and in the fury of defeat hurled pieces of brick at his opponent. The short man dodged with skill and then pursued Fidsey for over a block. Sometimes he got near enough to punch him. Fidsey raved in maniacal fury. The moment the short man would attempt to resume his own affairs, Fidsey would turn upon him again, tears and blood upon his face, with the lashed rage of a vanquished animal. The short man used to turn about, swear madly, and make little dashes. Fidsey always ran and then returned as pursuit ceased. The short man apparently wondered if this maniac was ever going to allow him to finish whipping him. He looked helplessly up and down the street. People were there who knew Fidsey, and they remonstrated with him; but he continued to confront the short man, gibbering like a wounded ape, using all the eloquence of the street in his wild oaths.

Finally the short man was exasperated to black fury. He decided to end the fight. With low snarls, ominous as death, he plunged at Fidsey.

Kelcey happened there then. He grasped the short man's shoulder. He cried out in the peculiar whine of the man who interferes. "Oh, hol' on! Yeh don't wanta hit 'im any more! Yeh've done enough to 'im now! Leave 'im be!"

The short man wrenched and tugged. He turned his face until his teeth were almost at Kelcey's cheek: "Le' go me! Le' go me, you——" The rest of his sentence was screamed curses.

Kelcey's face grew livid from fear, but he somehow managed to keep his grip. Fidsey, with but an instant's pause, plunged into the new fray.

They beat the short man. They forced him against a high board-fence where for a few seconds their blows sounded upon his head in swift thuds. A moment later Fidsey descried a running policeman. He made off, fleet as a shadow. Kelcey noted his going. He ran after him.

Three or four blocks away they halted. Fidsey said: "I'd 'a licked dat big stuff in 'bout a minute more," and wiped the blood from his eyes.

At the gang's corner, they asked: "Who soaked yeh,

Fidsey?" His description was burning. Everybody laughed. "Where is 'e now?" Later they began to question Kelcey. He recited a tale in which he allowed himself to appear prominent and redoubtable. They looked at him then as if they thought he might be quite a man.

Once when the little old woman was going out to buy something for her son's supper, she discovered him standing at the side-door of the saloon engaged intimately with Fidsey and the others. She slunk away, for she understood that it would be a terrible thing to confront him and his pride there with youths who were superior to mothers.

When he arrived home he threw down his hat with a weary sigh, as if he had worked long hours, but she attacked him before he had time to complete the falsehood. He listened to her harangue with a curled lip. In defence he merely made a gesture of supreme exasperation. She never understood the advanced things in life. He felt the hopelessness of ever making her comprehend. His mother was not modern.

XIV

THE LITTLE OLD WOMAN arose early and bustled in the preparation of breakfast. At times she looked anxiously at the clock. An hour before her son should leave for work she went to his room and called him in the usual tone of sharpness, "George! George!"

A sleepy growl came to her.

"Come, come it's time t' git up," she continued. "Come now, git right up!"

Later she went again to the door. "George, are yeh gittin' up?"

"Huh?"

"Are yeh gittin' up?"

"Yes, I'll git right up!" He had introduced a valor into his voice which she detected to be false. She went to his bedside and took him by the shoulder. "George—George—git up!"

From the mist-lands of sleep he began to protest incoherently. "Oh, le' me be, won' yeh? 'M sleepy!"

She continued to shake him. "Well, it's time t' git up. Come—come—come on, now."

Her voice, shrill with annoyance, pierced his ears in a slender, piping thread of sound. He turned over on the pillow to bury his head in his arms. When he expostulated, his tones came half-smothered. "Oh le' me be, can't yeh? There's plenty 'a time! Jest fer ten minutes! 'M sleepy!"

She was implacable. "No, yeh must git up now! Yeh ain't got more'n time enough t' eat yer breakfast an' git t' work."

Eventually he arose, sullen and grumbling. Later he came to his breakfast, blinking his dry eyelids, his stiffened features set in a mechanical scowl.

Each morning his mother went to his room, and fought a battle to arouse him. She was like a soldier. Despite his pleadings, his threats, she remained at her post, imperturbable and unyielding. These affairs assumed large proportions in his life. Sometimes he grew beside himself with a bland, unformulated wrath. The whole thing was a consummate imposition. He felt that he was being cheated of his sleep. It was an injustice to compel him to arise morning after morning with bitter regularity, before the sleep-gods had at all loosened their grasp. He hated that unknown force which directed his life.

One morning he swore a tangled mass of oaths, aimed into the air, as if the injustice poised there. His mother flinched at first; then her mouth set in the little straight line. She saw that the momentous occasion had come. It was the time of the critical battle. She turned upon him valorously. "Stop your swearin', George Kelcey. I won't have yeh talk so before me! I won't have it! Stop this minute! Not another word! Do yeh think I'll allow yeh t' swear b'fore me like that? Not another word! I won't have it! I declare I won't have it another minute!"

At first her projected words had slid from his mind as if striking against ice, but at last he heeded her. His face grew sour with passion and misery. He spoke in tones dark with dislike. "Th' 'ell yeh won't? Whatter yeh goin' t' do 'bout it?" Then, as if he considered that he had not been sufficiently impressive, he arose and slowly walked over to her. Having arrived at point-blank range he spoke again. "Whatter yeh goin' t' do 'bout it?" He regarded her then with an unaltering scowl, albeit his mien was as dark and cowering as that of a condemned criminal.

She threw out her hands in the gesture of an impotent one. He was acknowledged victor. He took his hat and slowly left her.

For three days they lived in silence. He brooded upon his mother's agony and felt a singular joy in it. As opportunity offered, he did little despicable things. He was going to make her abject. He was now uncontrolled, ungoverned; he wished to be an emperor. Her suffering was all a sort of compensation for his own dire pains.

She went about with a gray, impassive face. It was as if she had survived a massacre in which all that she loved had been torn from her by the brutality of savages.

One evening at six he entered and stood looking at his mother as she peeled potatoes. She had hearkened to his coming listlessly, without emotion, and at his entrance she did not raise her eyes.

"Well, I'm fired," he said, suddenly.

It seemed to be the final blow. Her body gave a convulsive movement in the chair. When she finally lifted her eyes, horror possessed her face. Her under jaw had fallen. "Fired? Outa work? Why—George?" He went over to the window and stood with his back to her. He could feel her gray stare upon him.

"Yep! Fired!"

At last she said, "Well—whatter yeh goin' t' do?"

He tapped the pane with his finger-nail. He answered in a tone made hoarse and unnatural by an assumption of gay carelessness, "Oh, nothin'!"

She began, then, her first weeping. "Oh—George—George—George——"

He looked at her scowling. "Ah, whatter yeh givin' us? Is this all I git when I come home f'm being fired? Anybody 'ud think it was my fault. I couldn't help it."

She continued to sob in a dull, shaking way. In the pose of her head there was an expression of her conviction that comprehension of her pain was impossible to the universe. He paused for a moment, and then, with his usual tactics, went out, slamming the door. A pale flood of sunlight, imperturbable at its vocation, streamed upon the little old woman, bowed with pain, forlorn in her chair.

XV

KELCEY WAS STANDING on the corner next day when three little boys came running. Two halted some distance away, and the other came forward. He halted before Kelcey, and spoke importantly.

"Hey, your ol' woman's sick."

"What?"

"Your ol' woman's sick."

"Git out!"

"She is, too!"

"Who tol' yeh?"

"Mis' Callahan. She said fer me t' run an' tell yeh. Dey want yeh."

A swift dread struck Kelcey. Like flashes of light little scenes from the past shot through his brain. He had thoughts of a vengeance from the clouds. As he glanced about him the familiar view assumed a meaning that was ominous and dark. There was prophecy of disaster in the street, the buildings, the sky, the people. Something tragic and terrible in the air was known to his nervous, quivering nostrils. He spoke to the little boy in a tone that quavered. "All right!"

Behind him he felt the sudden contemplative pause of his companions of the gang. They were watching him. As he went rapidly up the street he knew that they had come out to the middle of the walk and were staring after him. He was glad that they could not see his face, his trembling lips, his eyes wavering in fear. He stopped at the door of his home and stared at the panel as if he saw written thereon a word. A moment later he entered. His eye comprehended the room in a frightened glance.

His mother sat gazing out at the opposite walls and windows. She was leaning her head upon the back of the chair. Her face was overspread with a singular pallor, but the glance of her eyes was strong and the set of her lips was tranquil.

He felt an unspeakable thrill of thanksgiving at seeing her seated there calmly. "Why, mother, they said yeh was sick," he cried, going toward her impetuously. "What's th' matter?"

She smiled at him. "Oh, it ain't nothin'! I on'y got kinda

dizzy, that's all." Her voice was sober and had the ring of vitality in it.

He noted her common-place air. There was no alarm or pain in her tones, but the misgivings of the street, the pro-phetic twinges of his nerves made him still hesitate. "Well—are you sure it ain't? They scared me 'bout t' death."

"No, it ain't anything, on'y some sorta dizzy feelin'. I fell down b'hind th' stove. Missis Callahan, she came an' picked me up. I must 'a laid there fer quite a while. Th' docter said he guessed I'd be all right in a couple 'a hours. I don't feel nothin'!"

Kelcey heaved a great sigh of relief. "Lord, I was scared." He began to beam joyously, since he was escaped from his fright. "Why, I couldn't think what had happened," he told her.

"Well, it ain't nothin'," she said.

He stood about awkwardly, keeping his eyes fastened upon her in a sort of surprise, as if he had expected to discover that she had vanished. The reaction from his panic was a thrill of delicious contentment. He took a chair and sat down near her, but presently he jumped up to ask: "There ain't nothin' I can git fer yeh, is ther?" He looked at her eagerly. In his eyes shone love and joy. If it were not for the shame of it he would have called her endearing names.

"No, ther ain't nothin'," she answered. Presently she con-tinued, in a conversational way, "Yeh ain't found no work yit, have yeh?"

The shadow of his past fell upon him then and he became suddenly morose. At last he spoke in a sentence that was a vow, a declaration of change. "No, I ain't, but I'm goin' t' hunt fer it hard, you bet."

She understood from his tone that he was making peace with her. She smiled at him gladly. "Yer a good boy, George!" A radiance from the stars lit her face.

Presently she asked, "D' yeh think yer old boss would take yeh on ag'in if I went t' see him?"

"No," said Kelcey, at once. "It wouldn't do no good! They got all th' men they want. There ain't no room there. It wouldn't do no good." He ceased to beam for a moment as he thought of certain disclosures. "I'm goin' t' try to git work everywheres. I'm goin' t' make a wild break t' git a job, an' if there's one anywheres I'll git it."

She smiled at him again. "That's right, George!"

When it came supper-time he dragged her in her chair over to the table and then scurried to and fro to prepare a meal for her. She laughed gleefully at him. He was awkward and densely ignorant. He exaggerated his helplessness sometimes until she was obliged to lean back in her chair to laugh. Afterward they sat by the window. Her hand rested upon his hair.

XVI

W HEN KELCEY went to borrow money from old
Bleecker, Jones and the others, he discovered that he
was below them in social position. Old Bleecker said gloomily
that he did not see how he could loan money at that time.
When Jones asked him to have a drink, his tone was careless.
O'Connor recited at length some bewildering financial trou-
bles of his own. In them all he saw that something had been
reversed. They remained silent upon many occasions, when
they might have grunted in sympathy for him.

As he passed along the street near his home he perceived
Fidsey Corcoran and another of the gang. They made elo-
quent signs. "Are yeh wid us?"

He stopped and looked at them. "What's wrong with
yeh?"

"Are yeh wid us er not," demanded Fidsey. "New barkeep'!
Big can! We got it over in d' lot. Big can, I tell yeh." He drew
a picture in the air, so to speak, with his enthusiastic
fingers.

Kelcey turned dejectedly homeward. "Oh, I guess not, this
roun'."

"What's d' matter wi'che?" said Fidsey. "Yer gittin' t' be a
reg'lar willie! Come ahn, I tell yeh! Youse gits one smoke at
d' can b'cause yeh b'longs t' d' gang, an' yeh don't wanta give
it up widout er scrap! See? Some udder john'll git yer smoke.
Come ahn!"

When they arrived at the place among the bowlders in the
vacant lot, one of the band had a huge and battered tin-pail
tilted afar up. His throat worked convulsively. He was
watched keenly and anxiously by five or six others. Their eyes
followed carefully each fraction of distance that the pail was
lifted. They were very silent.

Fidsey burst out violently as he perceived what was in
progress. "Heh, Tim, yeh big sojer, le' go d' can! What 'a yeh
tink! Wese er in dis! Le' go dat!"

He who was drinking made several angry protesting con-
tortions of his throat. Then he put down the pail and
swore. "Who's a big sojer? I ain't gittin' more'n me own

smoke! Yer too bloomin' swift! Yeh'd tink yeh was d' on'y mug what owned dis can! Close yer face while I gits me smoke!"

He took breath for a moment and then returned the pail to its tilted position. Fidsey went to him and worried and clamored. He interfered so seriously with the action of drinking that the other was obliged to release the pail again for fear of choking.

Fidsey grabbed it and glanced swiftly at the contents. "Dere! Dat's what I was hollerin' at! Lookut d' beer! Not 'nough t' wet yer t'roat! Yehs can't have not'in' on d' level wid youse damn' tanks! Youse was a reg'lar resevoiy, Tim Connigan! Look what yeh lef' us! Ah, say, youse was a dandy! What 'a yeh tink we ah? Willies? Don' we want no smoke? Say, lookut dat can! It's drier'n hell! What 'a yeh tink?"

Tim glanced in at the beer. Then he said: "Well, d' mug what come b'fore me, he on'y lef' me dat much. Blue Billee, he done d' swallerin'! I on'y had a tas'e!"

Blue Billie, from his seat near, called out in wrathful protest: "Yeh lie, Tim. I never had more'n a mouf-ful!" An inspiration evidently came to him then, for his countenance suddenly brightened, and, arising, he went toward the pail. "I ain't had me reg'lar smoke yit! Guess I come in aheader Fidsey, don' I?"

Fidsey, with a sardonic smile, swung the pail behind him. "I guess nit! Not dis minnet! Youse hadger smoke. If yeh ain't, yeh don't git none. See?"

Blue Billie confronted Fidsey determinedly. "D' 'ell I don't!"

"Nit," said Fidsey.

Billie sat down again.

Fidsey drank his portion. Then he manœuvred skilfully before the crowd until Kelcey and the other youth took their shares. "Youse er a mob 'a tanks," he told the gang. "Nobody 'ud git not'in' if dey wasn't on t' yehs!"

Blue Billie's soul had been smouldering in hate against Fidsey. "Ah, shut up! Youse ain't gota take care 'a dose two mugs, dough. Youse hadger smoke, ain't yeh? Den yer tr'u. G' home!"

"Well, I hate t' see er bloke use 'imself fer a tank," said Fidsey. "But youse don't wanta go jollyin' 'round 'bout d' can, Blue, er youse'll git done."

"Who'll do me?" demanded Blue Billie, casting his eye about him.

"Kel' will," said Fidsey, bravely.

"D' 'ell he will?"

"Dat's what he will!"

Blue Billie made the gesture of a warrior. "He never saw d' day 'a his life dat he could do me little finger. If 'e says much t' me, I'll push 'is face all over d' lot."

Fidsey called to Kelcey. "Say, Kel, hear what dis mug is chewin'?"

Kelcey was apparently deep in other matters. His back was half-turned.

Blue Billie spoke to Fidsey in a battleful voice. "Did 'e ever say 'e could do me?"

Fidsey said: "Soitenly 'e did. Youse is dead easy, 'e says. He says he kin punch holes in you, Blue!"

"When did 'e say it?"

"Oh—any time. Youse is a cinch, Kel' says."

Blue Billie walked over to Kelcey. The others of the band followed him exchanging joyful glances.

"Did youse say yeh could do me?"

Kelcey slowly turned, but he kept his eyes upon the ground. He heard Fidsey darting among the others telling of his prowess, preparing them for the downfall of Blue Billie. He stood heavily on one foot and moved his hands nervously. Finally he said, in a low growl, "Well, what if I did?"

The sentence sent a happy thrill through the band. It was the formidable question. Blue Billie braced himself. Upon him came the responsibility of the next step. The gang fell back a little upon all sides. They looked expectantly at Blue Billie.

He walked forward with a deliberate step until his face was close to Kelcey.

"Well, if you did," he said, with a snarl between his teeth, "I'm goin' t' t'ump d' life outa yeh right heh!"

A little boy, wild of eye and puffing, came down the slope as from an explosion. He burst out in a rapid treble, "Is dat

Kelcey feller here? Say, yeh ol' woman's sick again. Dey want yeh! Yehs better run! She's awful sick!"

The gang turned with loud growls. "Ah, git outa here!" Fidsey threw a stone at the little boy and chased him a short distance, but he continued to clamor, "Youse better come, Kelcey feller! She's awful sick! She was hollerin'! Dey been lookin' fer yeh over'n hour!" In his eagerness he returned part way, regardless of Fidsey!

Kelcey had moved away from Blue Billie. He said: "I guess I'd better go!" They howled at him. "Well," he continued, "I can't—I don't wanta—I don't wanta leave me mother be—she—"

His words were drowned in the chorus of their derision. "Well, lookahere"—he would begin and at each time their cries and screams ascended. They dragged at Blue Billie. "Go fer 'im, Blue! Slug 'im! Go ahn!"

Kelcey went slowly away while they were urging Blue Billie to do a decisive thing. Billie stood fuming and blustering and explaining himself. When Kelcey had achieved a considerable distance from him, he stepped forward a few paces and hurled a terrible oath. Kelcey looked back darkly.

XVII

WHEN HE ENTERED the chamber of death, he was brooding over the recent encounter and devising extravagant revenges upon Blue Billie and the others.

The little old woman was stretched upon her bed. Her face and hands were of the hue of the blankets. Her hair, seemingly of a new and wondrous grayness, hung over her temples in whips and tangles. She was sickeningly motionless, save for her eyes, which rolled and swayed in maniacal glances.

A young doctor had just been administering medicine. "There," he said, with a great satisfaction, "I guess that'll do her good!" As he went briskly toward the door he met Kelcey. "Oh," he said. "Son?"

Kelcey had that in his throat which was like fur. When he forced his voice, the words came first low and then high as if they had broken through something. "Will she—will she——"

The doctor glanced back at the bed. She was watching them as she would have watched ghouls, and muttering. "Can't tell," he said. "She's wonderful woman! Got more vitality than you and I together! Can't tell! May—may not! Good-day! Back in two hours."

In the kitchen Mrs. Callahan was feverishly dusting the furniture, polishing this and that. She arranged everything in decorous rows. She was preparing for the coming of death. She looked at the floor as if she longed to scrub it.

The doctor paused to speak in an undertone to her, glancing at the bed. When he departed she labored with a renewed speed.

Kelcey approached his mother. From a little distance he called to her. "Mother—mother——" He proceeded with caution lest this mystic being upon the bed should clutch at him.

"Mother—mother—don't yeh know me?" He put forth apprehensive, shaking fingers and touched her hand.

There were two brilliant steel-colored points upon her eyeballs. She was staring off at something sinister.

Suddenly she turned to her son in a wild babbling appeal. "Help me! Help me! Oh, help me! I see them coming."

Kelcey called to her as to a distant place. "Mother! Mother!" She looked at him, and then there began within her a struggle to reach him with her mind. She fought with some implacable power whose fingers were in her brain. She called to Kelcey in stammering, incoherent cries for help.

Then she again looked away. "Ah, there they come! There they come! Ah, look—look—loo—" She arose to a sitting posture without the use of her arms.

Kelcey felt himself being choked. When her voice pealed forth in a scream he saw crimson curtains moving before his eyes. "Mother—oh, mother—there's nothin'—there's nothin'——"

She was at a kitchen-door with a dish-cloth in her hand. Within there had just been a clatter of crockery. Down through the trees of the orchard she could see a man in a field ploughing. "Bill—o-o-oh, Bill—have yeh seen Georgie? Is he out there with you? Georgie! Georgie! Come right here this minnet! Right—this—minnet!"

She began to talk to some people in the room. "I want t' know what yeh want here! I want yeh t' git out! I don't want yeh here! I don't feel good t'-day, an' I don't want yeh here! I don't feel good t'-day! I want yeh t' git out!" Her voice became peevish. "Go away! Go away! Go away!"

Kelcey lay in a chair. His nerveless arms allowed his fingers to sweep the floor. He became so that he could not hear the chatter from the bed, but he was always conscious of the ticking of the little clock out on the kitchen shelf.

When he aroused, the pale-faced but plump young clergyman was before him.

"My poor lad——" began this latter.

The little old woman lay still with her eyes closed. On the table at the head of the bed was a glass containing a water-like medicine. The reflected lights made a silver star on its side. The two men sat side by side, waiting. Out in the kitchen Mrs. Callahan had taken a chair by the stove and was waiting.

Kelcey began to stare at the wall-paper. The pattern was clusters of brown roses. He felt them like hideous crabs crawling upon his brain.

Through the door-way he saw the oil-cloth covering of the

table catching a glimmer from the warm afternoon sun. The window disclosed a fair, soft sky, like blue enamel, and a fringe of chimneys and roofs, resplendent here and there. An endless roar, the eternal trample of the marching city, came mingled with vague cries. At intervals the woman out by the stove moved restlessly and coughed.

Over the transom from the hall-way came two voices.

"Johnnie!"

"Wot!"

"You come right here t' me! I want yehs t' go t' d' store fer me!"

"Ah, ma, send Sally!"

"No, I will not! You come right here!"

"All right, in a minnet!"

"Johnnie!"

"In a minnet, I tell yeh!"

"Johnnie——" There was the sound of a heavy tread, and later a boy squealed. Suddenly the clergyman started to his feet. He rushed forward and peered. The little old woman was dead.

THE THIRD VIOLET

Chapter I

THE ENGINE bellowed its way up the slanting, winding valley. Grey crags, and trees with roots fastened cleverly to the steeps, looked down at the struggles of the black monster.

When the train finally released its passengers, they burst forth with the enthusiasm of escaping convicts. A great bustle ensued on the platform of the little mountain station. The idlers and philosophers from the village were present to examine the consignment of people from the city. These latter, loaded with bundles and children, thronged at the stage drivers. The stage drivers thronged at the people from the city.

Hawker, with his clothes case, his paint box, his easel, climbed awkwardly down the steps of the car. The easel swung uncontrolled and knocked against the head of a little boy who was disembarking backward with fine caution. "Hello, little man," said Hawker, "did it hurt?" The child regarded him in silence and with sudden interest as if Hawker had called his attention to a phenomenon. The young painter was politely waiting until the little boy should conclude his examination, but a voice behind him cried: "Roger, go on down." A nurse maid was conducting a little girl where she would probably be struck by the other end of the easel. The boy resumed his cautious descent.

The stage drivers made such great noise as a collection that as individuals their identities were lost. With a highly important air, as a man proud of being so busy, the baggageman of the train was thundering trunks at other employees on the platform. Hawker, prowling through the crowd, heard a voice near his shoulder say: "Do you know where is the stage for Hemlock Inn?" Hawker turned and found a young woman regarding him. A wave of astonishment whirled into his hair and he turned his eyes quickly for fear that she would think that he had looked at her. He said: "Yes—certainly—I think I can find it." At the same time he was crying to himself: "Wouldn't I like to paint her, though. What a glance— oh, murder. The—the—the distance in her eyes."

He went fiercely from one driver to another. That obdurate

stage for Hemlock Inn must appear at once. Finally he perceived a man who grinned expectantly at him. "Oh," said Hawker, "you drive the stage for Hemlock Inn." The man admitted it. Hawker said: "Here is the stage." The young woman smiled.

The driver inserted Hawker and his luggage far into the end of the vehicle. He sat there, crooked forward so that his eyes should see the first coming of the girl into the frame of light at the other end of the stage. Presently she appeared there. She was bringing the little boy, the little girl, the nurse maid, and another young woman who was at once to be known as the mother of the two children. The girl indicated the stage with a small gesture of triumph. When they were all seated uncomfortably in the huge covered vehicle, the little boy gave Hawker a glance of recognition. "It hurted then, but it's all right now," he informed him cheerfully.

"Did it?" replied Hawker. "I'm sorry."

"Oh, I didn't mind it much," continued the little boy, swinging his long red-leather leggins bravely to and fro. "I don't cry when I'm hurt, anyhow." He cast a meaning look at his tiny sister, whose soft lips set defensively.

The driver climbed into his seat and after a scrutiny of the group in the gloom of the stage, he chirped to his horses. They began a slow and thoughtful trotting. Dust streamed out behind the vehicle. In front, the green hills were still and serene in the evening air. A beam of gold struck them a-slant and on the sky was lemon and pink information of the sun's sinking. The driver knew many people along the road and from time to time he conversed with them in yells.

The two children were opposite Hawker. They sat very correctly mucilaged to their seats, but their large eyes were always upon Hawker, calmly valuing him.

"Do you think it nice to be in the country? I do," said the boy.

"I like it very well," answered Hawker.

"I shall go fishing and hunting and everything. Maybe I shall shot a bears."

"I hope you may."

"Did you ever shot a bears?"

"No."

"Well, I didn't, too, but maybe I will. Mister Hollanden, he said he'd look around for one. Where I live——"

"Roger," interrupted the mother from her seat at Hawker's side, "perhaps every one is not interested in your conversation." The boy seemed embarrassed at this interruption, for he leaned back in silence with an apologetic look at Hawker. Presently the stage began to climb the hills and the two children were obliged to take grip upon the cushions for fear of being precipitated upon the nurse maid.

Fate had arranged it so that Hawker could not observe the girl with the—the—the distance in her eyes without leaning forward and discovering to her his interest. Secretly and impiously he wriggled in his seat and as the bumping stage swung its passengers this way and that way, he obtained fleeting glances of a cheek, an arm or a shoulder.

The driver's conversation tone to his passengers was also a yell. "Train was an hour late t'night," he said, addressing the interior. "It'll be nine o'clock before we git t' th' inn an' it'll be perty dark travellin'."

Hawker waited decently, but at last he said: "Will it?"

"Yes. No moon." He turned to face Hawker and roared: "You're ol' Jim Hawker's son, hain't yeh?"

"Yes."

"I thort I'd seen yeh b'fore. Live in the city, now, don't yeh?"

"Yes."

"Want t' git off at th' cross-road?"

"Yes."

"Come up fer a little stay doorin' th' summer?"

"Yes."

"On'y charge yeh a quarter if yeh git off at cross-road. Useter charge 'em fifty cents, but I ses t' th' ol' man: ' 'Tain't no use. Goldern 'em, they'll walk ruther'n put up fifty cents.' Yep. On'y a quarter."

In the shadows, Hawker's expression seemed assassin-like. He glanced furtively down the stage. She was apparently deep in talk with the mother of the children.

Chapter II

WHEN HAWKER PUSHED at the old gate, it hesitated because of a broken hinge. A dog barked with loud ferocity and came headlong over the grass.

"Hello, Stanley, old man," cried Hawker. The ardor for battle was instantly smitten from the dog and his barking swallowed in a gurgle of delight. He was a large orange and white setter and he partly expressed his emotion by twisting his body into a fantastic curve and then dancing over the ground with his head and his tail very near to each other. He gave vent to little sobs in a wild attempt to vocally describe his gladness. "Well, 'e was a dreat dod," said Hawker, and the setter, overwhelmed, contorted himself wonderfully.

There were lights in the kitchen and at the first barking of the dog the door had been thrown open. Hawker saw his two sisters shading their eyes and peering down the yellow stream. Presently they shouted: "Here he is." They flung themselves out and upon him. "Why, Will—why, Will—" they panted. "We're awful glad to see you." In a whirlwind of ejaculation and unanswerable interrogation, they grappled the clothes case, the paint box, the easel, and dragged him toward the house.

He saw his old mother seated in a rocking chair by the table. She had laid aside her paper and was adjusting her glasses as she scanned the darkness. "Hello, mother," cried Hawker, as he entered. His eyes were bright. The old mother reached her arms to his neck. She murmured soft and half-articulate words. Meanwhile, the dog writhed from one to another. He raised his muzzle high to express his delight. He was always fully convinced that he was taking a principal part in this ceremony of welcome and that everybody was heeding him.

"Have you had your supper?" asked the old mother as soon as she recovered herself. The girls clamored sentences at him. "Pa's out in the barn, Will. What made you so late? He said maybe he'd go up to the cross-roads to see if he could see the stage. Maybe he's gone. What made you so late? And, oh, we got a new buggy."

The old mother repeated anxiously, "Have you had your supper?"

"No," said Hawker, "but——"

The three women sprang to their feet. "Well! We'll git you something right away." They bustled about the kitchen and dove from time to time into the cellar. They called to each other in happy voices.

Steps sounded on the line of stones that led from the door toward the barn and a shout came from the darkness. "Well, William, home again, hey?" Hawker's grey father came stamping genially into the room. "I thought maybe you got lost. I was comin' to hunt you," he said, grinning, as they stood with gripped hands. "What made you so late?"

While Hawker confronted the supper, the family sat about and contemplated him with shining eyes. His sisters noted his tie and propounded some questions concerning it. His mother watched to make sure that he should consume a notable quantity of the preserved cherries. "He used to be so fond of 'em when he was little," she said.

"Oh, Will," cried the younger sister, "do you remember Lil' Johnson? Yeh. She's married. Married las' June."

"Is the boy's room all ready, mother?" asked the father.

"We fixed it this mornin'," she said.

"And do you remember Jeff Decker?" shouted the elder sister. "Well, he's dead. Yep. Drowned pickerel fishin'—poor feller."

"Well, how are you getting along, William?" asked the father. "Sell many pictures?"

"An occasional one."

"Saw your illustrations in the May number of *Perkinson's*." The old man paused for a moment and then added quite weakly: "Pretty good."

"How's everything about the place?"

"Oh, just about the same—'bout the same. The colt run away with me last week, but didn't break nothin', though. I was scared because I had out the new buggy—we got a new buggy—but it didn't break nothin'. I'm goin' to sell the oxen in the fall. I don't want to winter 'em. And then in the spring I'll get a good hoss team. I rented th' back five-acre to John Westfall. I had more'n I could handle with only one hired hand. Times is pickin' up a little, but not much—not much."

"And we got a new school teacher," said one of the girls.

"Will, you never noticed my new rocker," said the old mother, pointing. "I set it right where I thought you'd see it and you never took no notice. Ain't it nice? Father bought it at Monticello for my birthday. I thought you'd notice it first thing."

When Hawker had retired for the night, he raised a sash and sat by the window smoking. The odor of the woods and the fields came sweetly to his nostrils. The crickets chanted their hymn of the night. On the black brow of the mountain he could see two long rows of twinkling dots which marked the position of Hemlock Inn.

Chapter III

Hawker had a writing friend named Hollanden. In New York, Hollanden had announced his resolution to spend the summer at Hemlock Inn. "I don't like to see the world progressing," he had said. "I shall go to Sullivan county for a time."

In the morning Hawker took his painting equipment and after maneuvering in the fields until he had proved to himself that he had no desire to go toward the inn, he went toward it. The time was only nine o'clock and he knew that he could not hope to see Hollanden before eleven, as it was only through rumor that Hollanden was aware that there was a sunrise and an early morning.

Hawker encamped in front of some fields of vivid yellow stubble on which trees made olive shadows and which was overhung by a china-blue sky and sundry little white clouds. He fiddled away perfunctorily at it. A spectator would have believed probably that he was sketching the pines on the hill where shone the red porches of Hemlock Inn.

Finally a white-flannel young man walked into the landscape. Hawker waved a brush. "Hi, Hollie, get out of the color-scheme." At this cry the white-flannel young man looked down at his feet apprehensively. Finally he came forward grinning. "Why, hello, Hawker, old boy. Glad to find you here." He perched on a boulder and began to study Hawker's canvas, and the vivid yellow stubble with the olive shadows. He wheeled his eyes from one to the other. "Say, Hawker," he said suddenly, " why don't you marry Miss Fanhall?"

Hawker had a brush in his mouth, but he took it quickly out and said: "Marry Miss Fanhall? Who the devil is Miss Fanhall?"

Hollanden clasped both hands about his knee and looked thoughtfully away. "Oh, she's a girl."

"She is?" said Hawker.

"Yes. She came to the inn last night with her sister-in-law and a small tribe of young Fanhalls. There's six of them, I think."

"Two," said Hawker. "A boy and a girl."

"How do you—oh, you must have come up with them. Of course. Why, then you saw her."

"Was that her?" asked Hawker, listlessly.

"Was that her?" cried Hollanden, with indignation. "Was that her?"

"Oh," said Hawker.

Hollanden mused again. "She's got lots of money," he said. "Loads of it. And I think she would be fool enough to have sympathy for you in your work. They are a tremendously wealthy crowd, although they treat it simply. It would be a good thing for you. I believe—yes, I am sure she could be fool enough to have sympathy for you in your work. And now if you weren't such a hopeless chump——"

"Oh, shut up, Hollie," said the painter.

For a time Hollanden did as he was bid, but at last he talked again. "Can't think why they came up here. Must be her sister-in-law's health. Something like that. She——"

"Great heavens," said Hawker, "you speak of nothing else."

"Well, you saw her, didn't you?" demanded Hollanden. "What can you expect, then, from a man of my sense? You— you old stick—you——"

"It was quite dark," protested the painter.

" 'Quite dark,' " repeated Hollanden in a wrathful voice. "What if it was?"

"Well, that is bound to make a difference in a man's opinion, you know."

"No, it isn't. It was light down at the railroad station, anyhow. If you had any sand—thunder, but I did get up early this morning. Say, do you play tennis?"

"After a fashion," said Hawker. "Why?"

"Oh, nothing," replied Hollanden, sadly. "Only they are wearing me out at the game. I had to get up and play before breakfast this morning with the Worcester girls, and there is a lot more mad players who will be down on me before long. It's a terrible thing to be a tennis player."

"Why, you used to put yourself out so little for people," remarked Hawker.

"Yes, but up there"—Hollanden jerked his thumb in the direction of the inn—"they think I'm so amiable."

"Well, I'll come up and help you out."

"Do," Hollanden laughed. "You and Miss Fanhall can team it against the littlest Worcester girl and me." He regarded the landscape and meditated. Hawker struggled for a grip on the thought of the stubble.

"That color of hair and eyes always knocks me ke-plunk," observed Hollanden, softly.

Hawker looked up irascibly. "What color hair and eyes?" he demanded. "I believe you're crazy."

" 'What color hair and eyes?' " repeated Hollanden, with a savage gesture. "You've got no more appreciation than a post."

"They are good enough for me," muttered Hawker, turning again to his work. He scowled first at the canvas and then at the stubble. "Seems to me you had best take care of yourself instead of planning for me," he said.

"Me!" cried Hollanden. "Me! Take care of myself! My boy, I've got a past of sorrow and gloom. I——"

"You're nothing but a kid," said Hawker, glaring at the other man.

"Oh, of course," said Hollanden, wagging his head with midnight wisdom. "Oh, of course."

"Well, Hollie," said Hawker, with sudden affability, "I didn't mean to be unpleasant, but then you are rather ridiculous, you know, sitting up there and howling about the color of hair and eyes."

"I'm not ridiculous."

"Yes, you are, you know, Hollie."

The writer waved his hand despairingly. "And you rode in the train with her and in the stage."

"I didn't see her in the train," said Hawker.

"Oh, then you saw her in the stage. Ha-ha, you old thief. I sat up here and you sat down there and lied." He jumped from his perch and belabored Hawker's shoulders.

"Stop that," said the painter.

"Oh, you old thief, you lied to me. You lied—— Hold on—bless my life, here she comes now."

Chapter IV

ONE DAY Hollanden said: "There are forty-two people at Hemlock Inn, I think. Fifteen are middle-aged ladies of the most aggressive respectability. They have come here for no discernible purpose save to get where they can see people and be displeased at them. They sit in a large group on that porch and take measurements of character as importantly as if they constituted the jury of heaven. When I arrived at Hemlock Inn I at once cast my eye searchingly about me. Perceiving this assemblage, I cried: 'There they are.' Barely waiting to change my clothes, I made for this formidable body and endeavored to conciliate it. Almost every day I sit down among them and lie like a machine. Privately I believe they should be hanged, but publicly I glisten with admiration. Do you know, there is one of 'em who I know has not moved from the inn in eight days, and this morning I said to her: 'These long walks in the clear mountain air are doing you a world of good.' And I keep continually saying: 'Your frankness is so charming.' Because of the great law of universal balance, I know that this illustrious corps will believe good of themselves with exactly the same readiness that they will believe ill of others. So I ply them with it. In consequence, the worst they ever say of me is: 'Isn't that Mr. Hollanden a peculiar man?' And you know, my boy, that's not so bad for a literary person." After some thought he added: "Good people, too. Good wives—good mothers—and everything of that kind, you know. But conservative, very conservative. Hate anything radical. Cannot endure it. Were that way themselves once, you know. They hit the mark, too, sometimes. Such general volleyings can't fail to hit everything. May the devil fly away with them."

Hawker regarded the group nervously, and at last propounded a great question. "Say, I wonder where they all are recruited. When you come to think that almost every summer hotel——"

"Certainly," said Hollanden. "Almost every summer hotel. I've studied the question and have nearly established the fact that almost every summer hotel is furnished with a full corps of——"

"To be sure," said Hawker. "And if you search for them in the winter, you can find barely a sign of them until you examine the boarding-houses and then you observe——"

"Certainly," said Hollanden. "Of course. By the way," he added, "you haven't got any obviously loose screws in your character, have you?"

"No," said Hawker, after consideration. "Only general poverty—that's all."

"Of course, of course," said Hollanden. "But that's bad. They'll get on to you—sure. Particularly since you come up here to see Miss Fanhall so much."

Hawker glinted his eyes at his friend. "You've got a deuced open way of speaking," he observed.

"Deuced open, is it?" cried Hollanden. "It isn't near so open as your devotion to Miss Fanhall, which is as plain as a red petticoat hung on a hedge."

Hawker's face gloomed and he said: "Well, it might be plain to you, you infernal cat, but that doesn't prove that all those old hens can see it."

"I tell you that if they look twice at you they can't fail to see it. And it's bad, too. Very bad. What's the matter with you? Haven't you ever been in love before?"

"None of your business," replied Hawker.

Hollanden thought upon this point for a time. "Well," he admitted finally, "that's true in a general way, but I hate to see you managing your affairs so stupidly."

Rage flamed into Hawker's face and he cried passionately: "I tell you it is none of your business." He suddenly confronted the other man.

Hollanden surveyed this outburst with a critical eye and then slapped his knee with emphasis. "You certainly have got it. A million times worse than I thought. Why, you—you—you're heels over head."

"What if I am?" said Hawker, with a gesture of defiance and despair.

Hollanden saw a dramatic situation in the distance and with a bright smile he studied it. "Say," he exclaimed, "suppose she should not go to the picnic to-morrow. She said this morning she did not know if she could go. Somebody was expected from New York, I think. Wouldn't it break you up, though! Eh?"

"You're so dev'lish clever," said Hawker with sullen irony.

Hollanden was still regarding the distant dramatic situation. "And rivals, too. The woods must be crowded with them. A girl like that, you know. And then, all that money. Say, your rivals must number enough to make a brigade of militia. Imagine them, swarming around. But then it doesn't matter so much," he went on cheerfully. "You've got a good play there. You must appreciate them to her—you understand—appreciate them kindly like a man in a watch-tower. You must laugh at them only about once a week and then very tolerantly, you understand—and kindly and—and appreciatively."

"You're a colossal ass, Hollie," said Hawker. "You——"

"Yes—yes—I know," replied the other peacefully. "A colossal ass. Of course." After looking into the distance again he murmured: "I'm worried about that picnic. I wish I knew she was going. By heavens, as a matter of fact, she must be made to go."

"What have you got to do with it?" cried the painter in another sudden outburst.

"There—there," said Hollanden, waving his hand. "You fool. Only a spectator, I assure you."

Hawker seemed overcome then with a deep dislike of himself. "Oh, well, you know, Hollie, this sort of thing——" He broke off and gazed at the trees. "This sort of thing—— It——"

"How?" asked Hollanden.

"Confound you for a meddling, gabbling idiot," cried Hawker suddenly.

Hollanden replied: "What did you do with that violet she dropped at the side of the tennis court yesterday?"

Chapter V

Mrs. fanhall, with the two children, the Worcester girls, and Hollanden, clambered down the rocky path. Miss Fanhall and Hawker had remained on top of the ledge. Hollanden showed much zeal in conducting his contingent to the foot of the falls. Through the trees they could see the cataract, a great shimmering white thing, booming and thundering until all the leaves gently shuddered.

"I wonder where Miss Fanhall and Mr. Hawker have gone," said the younger Miss Worcester. "I wonder where they've gone."

"Millicent," said Hollanden, looking at her fondly, "you always had such great thought for others."

"Well, I wonder where they've gone."

At the foot of the falls where the mist arose in silver clouds and the green water swept into the pool, Miss Worcester, the elder, seated on the moss, exclaimed: "Oh, Mr. Hollanden, what makes all literary men so peculiar?"

"And all that just because I said that I could have made better digestive organs than Providence if it is true that he made mine," replied Hollanden with reproach. "Here, Roger," he cried, as he dragged the child away from the brink. "Don't fall in there, or you won't be the full-back at Yale in 1907, as you have planned. I'm sure I don't know how to answer you, Miss Worcester. I've inquired of innumerable literary men and none of 'em know. I may say I have chased that problem for years. I might give you my personal history and see if that would throw any light on the subject." He looked about him with chin high until his glance had noted the two vague figures at the top of the cliff. "I might give you my personal history——"

Mrs. Fanhall looked at him curiously, and the elder Worcester girl cried: "Oh, do!"

After another scanning of the figures at the top of the cliff, Hollanden established himself in an oratorical pose on a great weather-beaten stone. "Well—you must understand—I started my career—my career, you understand—with a determination to be a prophet and, although I have ended in being

293

an acrobat, a trained bear of the magazines, and a juggler of comic paragraphs, there was once carven upon my lips a smile which made many people detest me, for it hung before them like a banshee whenever they tried to be satisfied with themselves. I was informed from time to time that I was making no great holes in the universal plan, and I came to know that one person in every two thousand of the people I saw had heard of me, and that four out of five of these had forgotten it. And then one in every two of those who remembered that they had heard of me regarded the fact that I wrote as a great impertinence. I admitted these things and in defense merely builded a maxim that stated that each wise man in this world is concealed amid some twenty thousand fools. If you have eyes for mathematics this conclusion should interest you. Meanwhile I created a gigantic dignity, and when men saw this dignity and heard that I was a literary man they respected me. I concluded that the simple campaign of existence for me was to delude the populace or as much of it as would look at me. I did. I do. And now I can make myself quite happy concocting sneers about it. Others may do as they please, but as for me," he concluded ferociously, "I shall never disclose to anybody that an acrobat, a trained bear of the magazines, a juggler of comic paragraphs is not a priceless pearl of art and philosophy."

"I don't believe a word of it is true," said Miss Worcester.

"What do you expect of autobiography?" demanded Hollanden with asperity.

"Well, anyhow, Hollie," exclaimed the younger sister. "You didn't explain a thing about how literary men came to be so peculiar, and that's what you started out to do, you know."

"Well," said Hollanden, crossly, "you must never expect a man to do what he starts to do, Millicent. And besides," he went on, with the gleam of a sudden idea in his eyes, "literary men are not peculiar, anyhow."

The elder Worcester girl looked angrily at him. "Indeed? Not you, of course, but the others?"

"They are all asses," said Hollanden, genially.

The elder Worcester girl reflected. "I believe you try to make us think and then just tangle us up purposely."

The younger Worcester girl reflected. "You are an absurd old thing, you know, Hollie."

Hollanden climbed offendedly from the great weather-beaten stone. "Well, I shall go and see that the men have not spilled the luncheon while breaking their necks over these rocks. Would you like to have it spread here, Mrs. Fanhall? Never mind consulting the girls. I assure you I shall spend a great deal of energy and temper in bullying them into doing just as they please. Why, when I was in Brussels——"

"Oh, come now, Hollie. You never were in Brussels, you know," said the younger Worcester girl.

"What of that, Millicent?" demanded Hollanden. "This is autobiography."

"Well, I don't care, Hollie. You tell such whoppers."

With a gesture of despair he again started away. Whereupon the Worcester girls shouted in chorus: "Oh, I say, Hollie, come back. Don't be angry. We didn't mean to tease you, Hollie—really, we didn't."

"Well, if you didn't," said Hollanden, " why did you——"

The elder Worcester girl was gazing fixedly at the top of the cliff. "Oh, there they are. I wonder why they don't come down?"

Chapter VI

STANLEY, THE SETTER, walked to the edge of the precipice and looking over at the falls, wagged his tail in friendly greeting. He was braced warily so that if this howling white animal should reach up a hand for him he could flee in time.

The girl stared dreamily at the red-stained crags that projected from the pines of the hill across the stream. Hawker lazily aimed bits of moss at the oblivious dog and missed him.

"It must be fine to have something to think of beyond just living," said the girl to the crags.

"I suppose you mean art?" said Hawker.

"Yes. Of course. It must be finer at any rate than the ordinary thing."

He mused for a time. "Yes. It is—it must be," he said. "But then—I'd rather just lie here."

The girl seemed aggrieved. "Oh, no, you wouldn't. You couldn't stop. It's dreadful to talk like that, isn't it. I always thought that painters were——"

"Of course. They should be. Maybe they are. I don't know. Sometimes I am. But not to-day."

"Well, I should think you ought to be so much more contented than just ordinary people. Now, I——"

"You," he cried—"you are not 'just ordinary people.' "

"Well, but when I try to recall what I have thought about in my life I can't remember, you know. That's what I mean."

"You shouldn't talk that way," he told her.

"But why do you insist that life should be so highly absorbing for me?"

"You have everything you wish for," he answered in a voice of deep gloom.

"Certainly not. I am a woman."

"But——"

"A woman to have everything she wishes for would have to be Providence. There are some things that are not in the world."

"Well, what are they?" he asked of her.

"That's just it," she said, nodding her head. "No one knows. That's what makes the trouble."

"Well, you are very unreasonable."

"What?"

"You are very unreasonable. If I were you—an heiress——"

The girl flushed and turned upon him angrily.

"Well!" He glowered back at her. "You are, you know. You can't deny it."

She looked at the red-stained crags. At last she said: "You seemed really contemptuous."

"Well, I assure you that I do not feel contemptuous. On the contrary, I am filled with admiration. Thank heaven, I am a man of the world. Whenever I meet heiresses, I always have the deepest admiration." As he said this, he wore a brave hang-dog expression. The girl surveyed him coldly from his chin to his eyebrows. "You have a handsome audacity, too."

He lay back in the long grass and contemplated the clouds.

"You should have been a Chinese soldier of fortune," she said.

He threw another little clod at Stanley and struck him on the head.

"You are the most scientifically unbearable person in the world," she said.

Stanley came back to see his master and to assure himself that the clump on the head was not intended as a sign of serious displeasure. Hawker took the dog's long ears and tried to tie them into a knot.

"And I don't see why you so delight in making people detest you," she continued.

Having failed to make a knot of the dog's ears, Hawker leaned back and surveyed his failure admiringly. "Well—I don't," he said.

"You do."

"No, I don't."

"Yes, you do. You just say the most terrible things as if you positively enjoyed saying them."

"Well, what did I say, now? What did I say?"

"Why, you said that you always had the most extraordinary admiration for heiresses whenever you met them."

"Well, what's wrong with that sentiment?" he said. "You can't find fault with that."

"It is utterly detestable."

"Not at all," he answered sullenly. "I consider it a tribute—a graceful tribute."

Miss Fanhall arose and went forward to the edge of the cliff. She became absorbed in the falls. Far below her, a bough of a hemlock drooped to the water and each swirling mad wave caught it and made it nod—nod—nod. Her back was half turned toward Hawker.

After a time Stanley, the dog, discovered some ants scurrying in the moss and he at once began to watch them and wag his tail.

"Isn't it curious," observed Hawker, "how an animal as large as a dog will sometimes be so entertained by the very smallest things?"

Stanley pawed gently at the moss and then thrust his head forward to see what the ants did under the circumstances.

"In the hunting season," continued Hawker, having waited a moment, "this dog knows nothing on earth but his master and the partridges. He is lost to all other sound and movement. He moves through the woods like a steel machine. And when he scents the bird—ah, it is beautiful. Shouldn't you like to see him then?"

Some of the ants had perhaps made war-like motions and Stanley was pretending that this was a reason for excitement. He reared a-back and made grumbling noises in his throat.

After another pause Hawker went on: "And now see the precious old fool. He is deeply interested in the movements of little ants and as childish and ridiculous over them as if they were highly important. There, you old blockhead, let them alone."

Stanley could not be induced to end his investigations and he told his master that the ants were the most thrilling and dramatic animals of his experience.

"Oh, by the way," said Hawker, at last, as his glance caught upon the crags across the river, "did you ever hear the legend of those rocks yonder? Over there where I am pointing. Where I'm pointing. Did you ever hear it? What? Yes? No? Well, I shall tell it you." He settled comfortably in the long grass.

Chapter VII

O NCE UPON A TIME, there was a beautiful Indian maiden, of course. And she was, of course, beloved by a youth from another tribe who was very handsome and stalwart and a mighty hunter, of course. But the maiden's father was, of course, a stern old chief, and when the question of his daughter's marriage came up, he, of course, declared that the maiden should be wedded only to a warrior of her tribe. And, of course, when the young man heard this he said that in such case he would, of course, fling himself headlong from that crag. The old chief was, of course, obdurate, and, of course, the youth did, of course, as he had said. And, of course, the maiden wept." After Hawker had waited for some time, he said with severity: "You seem to have no great appreciation of folk-lore."

The girl suddenly bended her head. "Listen," she said. "They're calling. Don't you hear Hollie's voice?"

They went to another place, and looking down over the shimmering tree-tops they saw Hollanden waving his arms. "It's luncheon," said Hawker. "Look how frantic he is."

The path required that Hawker should assist the girl very often. His eyes shone at her whenever he held forth his hand to help her down a blessed steep place. She seemed rather pensive. The route to luncheon was very long. Suddenly he took seat on an old tree and said: "Oh, I don't know why it is. Whenever I'm with you, I—I have no wits—nor good nature—nor anything. It's the worst luck."

He had left her standing on a boulder, where she was provisionally helpless. "Hurry," she said. "They're waiting for us."

Stanley, the setter, had been sliding down cautiously behind them. He now stood wagging his tail and waiting for the way to be cleared.

Hawker leaned his head on his hand and pondered dejectedly. "It's the worst luck."

"Hurry," she said. "They're waiting for us."

At luncheon the girl was for the most part silent. Hawker was superhumanly amiable. Somehow he gained the impression that they all quite fancied him, and it followed that being clever was very easy. Hollanden listened and approved him with a benign countenance.

There was a little boat fastened to the willows at the edge of the black pool. After the spread, Hollanden navigated various parties around to where they could hear the great hollow roar of the falls beating against the sheer rocks. Stanley swam after sticks at the request of little Roger.

Once Hollanden succeeded in making the others so engrossed in being amused that Hawker and Miss Fanhall were left alone staring at the white bubbles that floated solemnly on the black water. After Hawker had stared at them a sufficient time, he said: "Well, you are an heiress, you know."

In return she chose to smile radiantly. Turning toward him, she said: "If you will be good, now—always—perhaps I'll forgive you."

They drove home in the sombre shadows of the hills with Stanley padding along under the wagon. The Worcester girls tried to induce Hollanden to sing and in consequence there was quarreling until the blinking lights of the inn appeared above them as if a great lantern hung there.

Hollanden conveyed his friend some distance on the way home from the inn to the farm. "Good time at the picnic?" said the writer.

"Yes."

"Picnics are mainly places where the jam gets on the dead leaves and from thence to your trousers. But this was a good little picnic." He glanced at Hawker. "But you don't look as if you had such a swell time."

Hawker waved his hand tragically. "Yes—no. I don't know."

"What's wrong with you?" asked Hollanden.

"I tell you what it is, Hollie," said the painter, darkly, "whenever I'm with that girl I'm such a blockhead. I'm not so stupid, Hollie. You know I'm not. But when I'm with her I can't be clever to save my life."

Hollanden pulled contentedly at his pipe. "Maybe she don't notice it."

"Notice it!" muttered Hawker, scornfully. "Of course she notices it. In conversation with her I tell you I am as interesting as an iron dog." His voice changed as he cried: "I don't know why it is. I don't know why it is."

Blowing a huge cloud of smoke into the air, Hollanden studied it thoughtfully. "Hits some fellows that way," he said. "And of course it must be deuced annoying. Strange thing, but now under those circumstances I'm very glib. Very glib, I assure you."

"I don't care what you are," answered Hawker. "All those confounded affairs of yours—they were not——"

"No," said Hollanden, stolidly puffing. "Of course not. I understand that. But, look here, Billie," he added, with sudden brightness, "maybe you are not a blockhead, after all. You are on the inside, you know, and you can't see from there. Besides, you can't tell what a woman will think. You can't tell what a woman will think."

"No," said Hawker, grimly. "And you suppose that is my only chance."

"Oh, don't be such a chump," said Hollanden in a tone of vast exasperation.

They strode for some time in silence. The mystic pines swaying over the narrow road made talk sibilantly to the wind. Stanley the setter took it upon himself to discover some menacing presence in the woods. He walked on his toes and with his eyes glinting sideways. He swore half under his breath.

"And work, too," burst out Hawker at last. "I came up here this season to work and I haven't done a thing that ought not to be shot at."

"Don't you find that your love sets fire to your genius?" asked Hollanden gravely.

"No. I'm hanged if I do."

Hollanden sighed then with an air of relief. "I was afraid that a popular impression was true," he said. "But it's all right. You would rather sit still and moon, wouldn't you?"

"Moon—blast you. I couldn't moon to save my life."

"Oh, well, I didn't mean moon, exactly."

Chapter VIII

THE BLUE NIGHT of the lake was embroidered with black tree forms. Silver drops sprinkled from the lifted oars. Somewhere in the gloom of the shore there was a dog who from time to time raised his sad voice to the stars.

"But, still, the life of the studios——" began the girl.

Hawker scoffed. "There were six of us. Mainly we smoked. Sometimes we played hearts and at other times poker—on credit, you know—credit. And when we had the materials and got something to do, we worked. Did you ever see these beautiful red and green designs that surround the common tomato can?"

"Yes."

"Well," he said proudly, "I have made them. Whenever you come upon tomatoes remember that they might once have been encompassed in my design. When first I came back from Paris I began to paint, but nobody wanted me to paint. Later, I got into green corn and asparagus——"

"Truly?"

"Yes, indeed. It is true."

"But, still, the life of the studios——"

"There were six of us. Fate ordained that only one in the crowd could have money at one time. The other five lived off him and despised themselves. We despised ourselves five times as long as we had admiration."

"And was this just because you had no money?"

"It was because we had no money in New York," said Hawker.

"Well, after a while, something happened——"

"Oh, no, it didn't. Something impended always, but it never happened."

"In a case like that one's own people must be such a blessing. The sympathy——"

" 'One's own people,' " said Hawker.

"Yes," she said. "One's own people and more intimate friends. The appreciation——"

" 'The appreciation,' " said Hawker. "Yes, indeed."

He seemed so ill-tempered that she became silent. The boat

floated through the shadows of the trees and out to where the water was like a blue crystal. The dog on the shore threshed about in the reeds and waded in the shallows, mourning his unhappy state in an occasional cry. Hawker stood up and sternly shouted. Thereafter silence was among the reeds. The moon slipped sharply through the little clouds.

The girl said: "I liked that last picture of yours."

"What?"

"At the last exhibition, you know, you had that one with the cows—and things—in the snow—and—and a haystack."

"Yes," he said. "Of course. Did you like it really? I thought it about my best. And you really remembered it? Oh," he cried, "Hollanden, perhaps, recalled it to you."

"Why, no," she said. "I remembered it. Of course."

"Well, what made you remember it?" he demanded, as if he had cause to be indignant.

"Why—I just remembered it because—I liked it and because—well, the people with me said—said it was about the best thing in the exhibit and they talked about it a good deal. And then I remembered that Hollie had spoken of you and then I—I——"

"Never mind," he said. After a moment he added: "The confounded picture was no good anyhow."

The girl started. "What makes you speak so of it? It was good. Of course, I don't know—I can't talk about pictures, but," she said in distress, "everybody said it was fine."

"It wasn't any good," he persisted with dogged shakes of the head.

From off in the darkness they heard the sound of Hollanden's oars splashing in the water. Sometimes there was squealing by the Worcester girls and at other times loud arguments on points of navigation.

"Oh," said the girl, suddenly. "Mr. Oglethorpe is coming tomorrow."

"Mr. Oglethorpe?" said Hawker. "Is he?"

"Yes." She gazed off at the water. "He's an old friend of ours. He is always so good and Roger and little Helen simply adore him. He was my brother's chum in college and they were quite inseparable until Herbert's death. He always brings me violets. But I know you will like him."

"I shall expect to," said Hawker.

"I'm so glad he is coming. What time does that morning stage get here?"

"About eleven," said Hawker.

"He wrote that he would come then. I hope he won't disappoint us."

"Undoubtedly he will be here," said Hawker.

The wind swept from the ridge top where some great bare pines stood in the moonlight. A loon called in its strange unearthly note from the lake shore. As Hawker turned the boat toward the dock, the flashing rays from the moon fell upon the head of the girl in the rear seat and he rowed very slowly.

The girl was looking away somewhere with a mystic, shining glance. She leaned her chin in her hand. Hawker facing her, merely paddled sub-consciously. He seemed greatly impressed and expectant.

At last she spoke very slowly. "I wish I knew Mr. Oglethorpe was not going to disappoint us."

Hawker said: "Why, no, I imagine not."

"Well, he is a trifle uncertain in matters of time. The children—and all of us—will be anxious. I know you will like him."

Chapter IX

"E H?" SAID HOLLANDEN. "Oglethorpe? Oglethorpe? Why, he's that friend of the Fanhalls. Yes, of course, I know him. Deuced good fellow, too. What about him?"

"Oh, nothing, only he's coming here to-morrow," answered Hawker. "What kind of a fellow did you say he was?"

"Deuced good fellow. What are you so—— Say, by the nine mad blacksmiths of Donawhiroo, he's your rival. Why, of course. Glory, but I must be thick-headed to-night."

Hawker said: "Where's your tobacco?"

"Yonder in that jar. Got a pipe?"

"Yes. How do you know he's my rival?"

"Know it? Why, hasn't he been—— Say, this is getting thrilling." Hollanden sprang to his feet and, filling a pipe, flung himself into the chair and began to rock himself madly to and fro. He puffed clouds of smoke.

Hawker stood with his face in shadow. At last he said in tones of deep weariness: "Well, I think I'd better be going home and turning in."

"Hold on," Hollanden exclaimed, turning his eyes from a prolonged stare at the ceiling. "Don't go yet. Why, man, this is just the time when—— Say, who would ever think of Jem Oglethorpe's turning up to harry you. Just at this time, too."

"Oh," cried Hawker, suddenly filled with rage, "you remind me of an accursed duffer. Why can't you tell me something about the man instead of sitting there and gibbering those crazy things at the ceiling."

"By the piper——"

"Oh, shut up. Tell me something about Oglethorpe, can't you? I want to hear about him. Quit all that other business."

"Why, Jem Oglethorpe—he—why, say, he's one of the best fellows going. If he were only an ass! If he were only an ass, now, you could feel easy in your mind. But he isn't. No, indeed. Why, blast him, there isn't a man that knows him who doesn't like Jem Oglethorpe. Excepting the chumps."

The window of the little room was open and the voices of the pines could be heard as they sang of their long sorrow. Hawker pulled a chair close and stared out into the darkness.

The people on the porch of the inn were frequently calling: "Good night! Good night!"

Hawker said: "And of course he's got train loads of money."

"You bet he has. He can pave streets with it. Lordie, but this is a situation."

A heavy scowl settled upon Hawker's brow and he kicked at the dressing case. "Say, Hollie, look here, sometimes I think you regard me as a bug and like to see me wriggle. But——"

"Oh, don't be a fool," said Hollanden, glaring through the smoke. "Under the circumstances you are privileged to rave and ramp around like a wounded lunatic, but for heaven's sake don't swoop down on me like that. Especially when I'm—when I'm doing all I can for you."

"Doing all you can for me! Nobody asked you to. You talk as if I was an infant."

"There! That's right. Blaze up like a fire balloon just because I said that, will you? A man in your condition—why, confound you, you are an infant."

Hawker seemed again overwhelmed in a great dislike of himself. "Oh, well, of course, Hollie, it——" He waved his hand. "A man feels like—like——"

"Certainly he does," said Hollanden. "That's all right, old man."

"And, look now, Hollie, here's this Oglethorpe——"

"May the devil fly away with him."

"Well, here he is, coming along when I thought maybe—after awhile, you know—I might stand some show. And you are acquainted with him, so give me a line on him."

"Well, I would advise you to——"

"Blow your advice. I want to hear about Oglethorpe."

"Well, in the first place, he is a rattling good fellow, as I told you before, and this is what makes it so——"

"Oh, hang what it makes it. Go on."

"He is a rattling good fellow, and he has stacks of money. Of course in this case, his having money doesn't affect the situation much. Miss Fanhall——"

"Say, can you keep to the thread of the story, you infernal literary man?"

"Well, he's popular. He don't talk money—ever. And if he's wicked, he's not sufficiently proud of it to be perpetually describing his sins. And then he is not so hideously brilliant, either. That's great credit to a man in these days. And then he—well, take it altogether, I should say Jem Oglethorpe was a smashing good fellow."

"I wonder how long he is going to stay?" murmured Hawker.

During this conversation his pipe had often died out. It was out at this time. He lit another match. Hollanden had watched the fingers of his friend as the match was scratched. "You're nervous, Billie," he said.

Hawker straightened in his chair. "No, I'm not."

"I saw your fingers tremble when you lit that match."

"Oh, you lie."

Hollanden mused again. "He's popular with women, too," he said ultimately. "And often a woman will like a man and hunt his scalp just because she knows other women like him and want his scalp."

"Yes, but not——"

"Hold on. You were going to say that she was not like other women, weren't you?"

"Not exactly that, but——"

"Well, we will have all that understood."

After a period of silence, Hawker said: "I must be going."

As the painter walked toward the door, Hollanden cried to him: "Heavens! Of all pictures of a weary pilgrim." His voice was very compassionate.

Hawker wheeled and an oath spun through the smoke clouds.

Chapter X

WHERE'S MR. HAWKER this morning?" asked the younger Miss Worcester. "I thought he was coming up to play tennis."

"I don't know. Confound him, I don't see why he didn't come," said Hollanden, looking across the shining valley. He frowned questioningly at the landscape. "I wonder where in the mischief he is?"

The Worcester girls began also to stare at the great gleaming stretch of green and gold. "Didn't he tell you he was coming?" they demanded.

"He didn't say a word about it," answered Hollanden. "I supposed of course he was coming. We will have to postpone the melee."

Later he met Miss Fanhall. "You look as if you were going for a walk."

"I am," she said, swinging her parasol. "To meet the stage. Have you seen Mr. Hawker to-day?"

"No," he said. "He is not coming up this morning. He is in a great fret about that field of stubble and I suppose he is down there sketching the life out of it. These artists—they take such a fiendish interest in their work. I dare say we won't see much of him until he has finished it. Where did you say you were going to walk?"

"To meet the stage."

"Oh, well, I won't have to play tennis for an hour, and if you insist——"

"Of course."

As they strolled slowly in the shade of the trees, Hollanden began: "Isn't that Hawker an ill-bred old thing?"

"No. He is not." Then after a time she said: "Why?"

"Oh, he gets so absorbed in a beastly smudge of paint that I really suppose he cares nothing for anything else in the world. Men who are really artists—I don't believe they are capable of deep human affections. So much of them is occupied by art. There's not much left over, you see."

"I don't believe it at all," she exclaimed.

308

"You don't, eh?" cried Hollanden, scornfully. "Well, let me tell you, young woman, there is a great deal of truth in it. Now, there's Hawker, as good a fellow as ever lived, too, in a way, and yet he's an artist. Why, look how he treats—look how he treats that poor setter dog."

"Why, he's as kind to him as he can be," she declared.

"And I tell you he is not," cried Hollanden.

"He is, Hollie. You—you are unspeakable when you get in these moods."

"There—that's just you in an argument. I'm not in a mood at all. Now, look—the dog loves him with simple unquestioning devotion that fairly brings tears to one's eyes——"

"Yes," she said.

"And he—why, he's as cold and stern——"

"He isn't. He isn't, Hollie. You are awf'ly unfair."

"No, I'm not. I am simply a liberal observer. And Hawker with his people, too," he went on darkly. "You can't tell—you don't know anything about it—but I tell you that what I have seen proves my assertion that the artistic mind has no space left for the human affections. And as for the dog——"

"I thought you were his friend, Hollie?"

"Whose?"

"No. Not the dog's. And yet you—really, Hollie, there is something unnatural in you. You are so stupidly keen in looking at people that you do not possess common loyalty to your friends. It is because you are a writer, I suppose. That has to explain so many things. Some of your traits are very disagreeable."

"There—there," plaintively cried Hollanden. "This is only about the treatment of a dog, mind you. Goodness, what an oration."

"It wasn't about the treatment of a dog. It was about your treatment of your friends."

"Well," he said, sagely, "it only goes to show that there is nothing impersonal in the mind of a woman. I undertook to discuss broadly——"

"Oh, Hollie!"

"At any rate it was rather below you to do such scoffing at me."

"Well, I didn't mean—not all of it, Hollie."

"Well, I didn't mean what I said about the dog and all that, either."

"You didn't?" She turned toward him, large-eyed.

"No. Not a single word of it."

"Well, what did you say it for, then?" she demanded indignantly.

"I said it," answered Hollanden placidly, "just to tease you." He looked abstractedly up to the trees.

Presently she said slowly: "Just to tease me?"

At this time Hollanden wore an unmistakable air of having a desire to turn up his coat collar. "Oh, come now——" he began nervously.

"George Hollanden," said the voice at his shoulder. "You are not only disagreeable, but you are hopelessly ridiculous. I—I wish you would never speak to me again."

"Oh, come now, Grace, don't—don't—— Look! There's the stage coming, isn't it?"

"No, the stage is not coming. I wish—I wish you were at the bottom of the sea, George Hollanden. And—and Mr. Hawker, too. There!"

"Oh, bless my soul! And all about an infernal dog," wailed Hollanden. "Look! Honest, now, there's the stage. See it! See it!"

"It isn't there at all," she said.

Gradually he seemed to recover his courage. "What made you so tremendously angry? I don't see why."

After consideration, she said decisively: "Well, because."

"That's why I teased you," he rejoined.

"Well, because—because——"

"Go on," he told her finally. "You are doing very well." He waited patiently.

"Well," she said, "it is dreadful to defend somebody so—so excitedly and then have it turn out just a tease. I don't know what he would think."

"Who would think?"

"Why—he."

"What could he think? Now, what could he think? Why," said Hollanden, waxing eloquent, "he couldn't under any circumstances think—think anything at all. Now, could he?"

She made no reply.

"Could he?"

She was apparently reflecting.

"Under any circumstances," persisted Hollanden, "he couldn't think anything at all. Now, could he?"

"No," she said.

"Well, why are you angry at me, then?"

Chapter XI

"JOHN," said the old mother from the profound mufflings of the pillow and quilts.

"What?" said the old man. · He was tugging at his right boot and his tone was very irascible.

"I think William's changed a good deal."

"Well, what if he has?" replied the father in another burst of ill-temper. He was then tugging at his left boot.

"Yes, I'm afraid he's changed a good deal," said the muffled voice from the bed. "He's got a good many fine friends, now, John. Folks what put on a good many airs, and he don't care for his home like he did."

"Oh, well, I don't guess he's changed very much," said the old man, cheerfully. He was now free of both boots.

She raised herself on an elbow and looked out with a troubled face. "John, I think he likes that girl."

"What girl?" said he.

" 'What girl!' Why that awful handsome girl you see around—of course."

"Do you think he likes 'er?"

"I'm afraid so—I'm afraid so," murmured the mother, mournfully.

"Oh, well," said the old man without alarm, nor grief, nor pleasure in his tone.

He turned the lamp's wick very low and carried the lamp to the head of the stairs where he perched it on the step. When he returned he said: "She's mighty good-lookin'."

"Well, that ain't everything," she snapped. "How do we know she ain't proud and selfish, and—everything?"

"How do you know she is?" returned the old man.

"And she may just be leading him on."

"Do him good, then," said he with impregnable serenity. "Next time he'll know better."

"Well, I'm worried about it," she said, as she sank back on the pillow again. "I think William's changed a good deal. He don't seem to care about—us—like he did."

"Oh, go to sleep," said the father, drowsily.

She was silent for a time and then she said: "John!"

"What?"

"Do you think I better speak to him about that girl?"

"No."

She grew silent again, but at last she demanded: "Why not?"

" 'Cause it's none of your business. Go to sleep, will you." And presently he did, but the old mother lay blinking wide-eyed into the darkness.

In the morning Hawker did not appear at the early break-fast eaten when the blue glow of dawn shed its ghostly lights upon the valley. The old mother placed various dishes on the back part of the stove. At ten o'clock he came downstairs. His mother was sweeping busily in the parlor at the time, but she saw him and ran to the back part of the stove. She slid the various dishes onto the table. "Did you oversleep?" she asked.

"Yes. I don't feel very well this morning," he said. He pulled his chair close to the table and sat there staring.

She renewed her sweeping in the parlor. When she re-turned, he sat still staring undeviatingly at nothing.

"Why don't you eat your breakfast?" she said, anxiously.

"I tell you, mother, I don't feel very well this morning," he answered quite sharply.

"Well," she said meekly, "drink some coffee and you'll feel better."

Afterward he took his painting machinery and left the house. His younger sister was at the well. She looked at him with a little smile and a little sneer. "Going up to the inn this morning?" she said.

"I don't see how that concerns you, Mary?" he rejoined with dignity.

"Oh, my," she said airily.

"But since you are so interested I don't mind telling you that I'm not going up to the inn this morning."

His sister fixed him with her eye. "She ain't mad at you, is she, Will?"

"I don't know what you mean, Mary." He glared hatefully at her and strode away.

Stanley saw him going through the fields and leaped a fence jubilantly in pursuit. In a wood, the light sifted through the foliage and burned with a peculiar reddish lustre on the masses of dead leaves. He frowned at it for a while from different points. Presently he erected his easel and began to paint. After a time he threw down his brush and swore. Stanley, who had been solemnly staring at the scene as if he too was sketching it, looked up in surprise.

In wandering aimlessly through the fields and the forest, Hawker once found himself near the road to Hemlock Inn. He shied away from it quickly as if it were a great snake.

While most of the family were at supper, Mary, the younger sister, came charging breathlessly into the kitchen. "Ma—sister—" she cried. "I know why—why Will didn't go to the inn to-day. There's another fellow come. Another fellow."

"Who? Where? What do you mean?" exclaimed her mother and her sister.

"Why, another fellow up at the inn," she shouted, triumphant in her information. "Another fellow come up on the stage this morning. And she went out driving with him this afternoon."

"Well!" exclaimed her mother and her sister.

"Yep! And he's an awful good-looking fellow, too. And she—oh, my—she looked as if she thought the world and all of him."

"Well!" exclaimed her mother and her sister again.

"Sho!" said the old man. "You wimen leave William alone and quit your gabbling."

The three women made a combined assault upon him. "Well, we ain't a-hurting him, are we, Pa? You needn't be so snifty. I guess we ain't a-hurting him much."

"Well," said the old man. And to this argument he added: "Sho!"

They kept him out of the subsequent consultations.

Chapter XII

THE NEXT DAY, as little Roger was going toward the tennis court, a large orange and white setter ran effusively from around the corner of the inn and greeted him. Miss Fanhall, the Worcester girls, Hollanden and Oglethorpe faced to the front like soldiers. Hollanden cried: "Why, Billie Hawker must be coming." Hawker at that moment appeared, coming toward them with a smile which was not overconfident.

Little Roger went off to perform some festivities of his own on the brown carpet under a clump of pines. The dog to join him felt obliged to circle widely about the tennis court. He was much afraid of this tennis court with its tiny round things that sometimes hit him. When near it he usually slunk along at a little sheep-trot and with an eye of wariness upon it.

At her first opportunity the younger Worcester girl said: "You didn't come up yesterday, Mr. Hawker?"

Hollanden seemed to think that Miss Fanhall turned her head as if she wished to hear the explanation of the painter's absence, so he engaged her in swift and fierce conversation.

"No," said Hawker. "I was resolved to finish a sketch of a stubble field which I began a good many days ago. You see, I was going to do such a great lot of work this summer and I've done hardly a thing. I really ought to compel myself to do some, you know."

"There," said Hollanden, with a victorious nod. "Just what I told you."

"You didn't tell us anything of the kind," retorted the Worcester girls with one voice.

A middle-aged woman came upon the porch of the inn and after scanning for a moment the group at the tennis court, she hurriedly withdrew. Presently she appeared again accompanied by five more middle-aged women. "You see," she said to the others. "It is as I said. He has come back."

The five surveyed the group at the tennis court and then said: "So he has. I knew he would. Well, I declare. Did you ever." Their voices were pitched at low keys and they moved with care, but their smiles were broad and full of a strange glee.

"I wonder how he feels," said one in subtle ecstasy.

Another laughed. "You know how you would feel, my dear, if you were him and saw yourself suddenly cut out by a man who was so hopelessly superior to you. Why, Oglethorpe's a thousand times better looking. And then think of his wealth and social position."

One whispered dramatically: "They say he never came up here at all yesterday."

Another replied: "No more he did. That's what we've been talking about. Stayed down at the farm all day, poor fellow."

"Do you really think she cares for Oglethorpe?"

"Care for him? Why, of course she does. Why, when they came up the path yesterday morning I never saw a girl's face so bright. I asked my husband how much of the Chambers Street Bank stock Oglethorpe owned and he said that if Oglethorpe took his money out there wouldn't be enough left to buy a pie."

The youngest woman in the corps said: "Well, I don't care. I think it is too bad. I don't see anything so much in that Mr. Oglethorpe."

The others at once patronized her. "Oh, you don't, my dear. Well, let me tell you that bank stock waves in the air like a banner. You would see it if you were her."

"Well, she don't have to care for his money."

"Oh, no, of course she don't have to. But they are just the ones that do, my dear. They are just the ones that do."

"Well, it's a shame."

"Oh, of course. It's a shame."

The woman who had assembled the corps said to one at her side: "Oh, the commonest kind of people, my dear, the commonest kind. The father is a regular farmer, you know. He drives oxen. Such language! You can really hear him miles away bellowing at those oxen. And the girls are shy, half-wild things—oh, you have no idea. I saw one of them yesterday when we were out driving. She dodged as we came along, for I suppose she was ashamed of her frock, poor child. And the mother—well, I wish you could see her. A little old dried-up thing. We saw her carrying a pail of water from the well, and, oh, she bent and staggered dreadfully, poor thing."

"And the gate to their front yard, it has a broken hinge,

you know. Of course, that's an awful bad sign. When people let their front gate hang on one hinge, you know what that means."

After gazing again at the group at the court, the youngest member of the corps said: "Well, he's a good tennis player, anyhow."

The others smiled indulgently. "Oh, yes, my dear, he's a good tennis player."

Chapter XIII

ONE DAY Hollanden said in greeting to Hawker: "Well, he's gone."

"Who?" asked Hawker.

"Why, Oglethorpe, of course. Who did you think I meant?"

"How did I know?" said Hawker, angrily.

"Well," retorted Hollanden, "your chief interest was in his movements, I thought."

"Why, of course not, hang you. Why should I be interested in his movements?"

"Well, you weren't then. Does that suit you?"

After a period of silence Hawker asked: "What did he—what made him go?"

"Who?"

"Why—Oglethorpe."

"How was I to know you meant him? Well, he went because some important business affairs in New York demanded it, he said, but he is coming back again in a week. They had rather a late interview on the porch last evening."

"Indeed," said Hawker, stiffly.

"Yes, and he went away this morning looking particularly elated. Aren't you glad?"

"I don't see how it concerns me," said Hawker, with still greater stiffness.

In a walk to the lake that afternoon Hawker and Miss Fanhall found themselves side by side and silent. The girl contemplated the distant purple hills as if Hawker were not at her side and silent. Hawker frowned at the roadway. Stanley the setter scouted the fields in a genial gallop.

At last the girl turned to him. "Seems to me—" she said. "Seems to me you are dreadfully quiet this afternoon."

"I am thinking about my wretched field of stubble," he answered, still frowning.

Her parasol swung about until the girl was looking up at his inscrutable profile. "Is it then so important that you haven't time to talk to me?" she asked with an air of what might have been timidity.

A smile swept the scowl from his face. "No, indeed," he said, instantly. "Nothing is so important as that."

She seemed aggrieved then. "Hum—you didn't look so," she told him.

"Well, I didn't mean to look any other way," he said contritely. "You know what a bear I am sometimes. Hollanden says it is a fixed scowl from trying to see uproarious pinks, yellows and blues."

A little brook, a brawling, ruffianly little brook, swaggered from side to side down the glade, swirling in white leaps over the great dark rocks and shouting challenge to the hillsides. Hollanden and the Worcester girls had halted in a place of ferns and wet moss. Their voices could be heard quarreling above the clamor of the stream. Stanley the setter had soused himself in a pool and then gone and rolled in the dust of the road. He blissfully lolled there with his coat now resembling an old door mat.

"Don't you think Jem is a wonderfully good fellow," said the girl to the painter.

"Why, yes, of course," said Hawker.

"Well, he is," she retorted, suddenly defensive.

"Of course," he repeated loudly.

She said: "Well, I don't think you like him as well as I like him."

"Certainly not," said Hawker.

"You don't?" She looked at him in a kind of astonishment.

"Certainly not," said Hawker again and very irritably. "How in the wide world do you expect me to like him as well as you like him?"

"I don't mean as well——" she explained.

"Oh," said Hawker.

"But I mean you don't like him the way I do at all—the way I expected you to like him. I thought men of a certain pattern always fancied their kind of men wherever they met them, don't you know. And I was so sure you and Jem would be friends."

"Oh," cried Hawker. Presently he added: "But he isn't my kind of a man at all."

"He is. Jem is one of the best fellows in the world."

Again Hawker cried: "Oh!"

They paused and looked down at the brook. Stanley sprawled panting in the dust and watched them. Hawker leaned against a hemlock. He sighed and frowned and then finally coughed with great resolution. "I suppose, of course, that I am unjust to him. I care for you myself, you understand, and so it becomes——"

He paused for a moment because he heard a rustling of her skirts as if she had moved suddenly. Then he continued: "And so it becomes difficult for me to be fair to him. I am not able to see him with a true eye." He bitterly addressed the trees on the opposite side of the glen. "Oh, I care for you, of course. You might have expected it." He turned from the trees and strode toward the roadway. The uninformed and disreputable Stanley arose and wagged his tail.

As if the girl had cried out at a calamity, Hawker said again: "Well, you might have expected it."

Chapter XIV

A<small>T THE LAKE</small> Hollanden went pickerel fishing, lost his hook in a gaunt, grey stump, and earned much distinction by his skill in discovering words to express his emotion without resorting to the list ordinarily used in such cases. The younger Miss Worcester ruined a new pair of boots, and Stanley sat on the bank and howled the song of the forsaken. At the conclusion of the festivities, Hollanden said: "Billie, you ought to take the boat back."

"Why had I? You borrowed it."

"Well, I borrowed it, and it was a lot of trouble and now you ought to take it back."

Ultimately Hawker said: "Oh, let's both go."

On this journey Hawker made a long speech to his friend, and at the end of it he exclaimed: "And now do you think she cares so much for Oglethorpe? Why, she as good as told me that he was only a very great friend."

Hollanden wagged his head dubiously. "What a woman says doesn't amount to shucks. It's the way she says it—that's what counts. Besides," he cried in a brilliant afterthought, "she wouldn't tell you, anyhow, you fool."

"You're an encouraging brute," said Hawker with a rueful grin.

Later the Worcester girls seized upon Hollanden and piled him high with ferns and mosses. They dragged the long grey lichens from the chins of venerable pines and ran with them to Hollanden and dashed them into his arms. "Oh, hurry up, Hollie," they cried, because with his great load he frequently fell behind them in the march. He once positively refused to carry these things another step. Some distance further on the road he positively refused to carry this old truck another step. When almost to the inn he positively refused to carry this senseless rubbish another step. The Worcester girls had such vivid contempt for his expressed unwillingness that they neglected to tell him of any appreciation they might have had for his noble struggle.

As Hawker and Miss Fanhall proceeded slowly, they heard a voice ringing through the foliage. "Whoa! Haw! Git-ap!

Blast you! Haw! Haw, drat your hides! Will you haw? Git-ap! Gee! Whoa!"

Hawker said: "The others are a good ways ahead. Hadn't we better hurry a little."

The girl obediently mended her pace.

"Whoa! Haw! Git-ap!" shouted the voice in the distance. "Git over there, Red. Git over! Gee! Git-ap!" And these cries pursued the man and the maid.

At last Hawker said: "That's my father."

"Where?" she asked, looking bewildered.

"Back there. Driving those oxen."

The voice shouted: "Whoa! Git-ap! Gee! Red, git over there now, will you? I'll trim the skin off'n you in a minute. Whoa! Haw! Haw! Whoa! Git-ap!"

Hawker repeated: "Yes, that's my father."

"Oh, is it?" she said. "Let's wait for him."

"All right," said Hawker, sullenly.

Presently a team of oxen waddled into view around the curve of the road. They swung their heads slowly from side to side, bended under the yoke and looking out at the world with their great eyes in which was a mystic note of their humble, submissive, toilsome lives. An old wagon creaked after them and erect upon it was the tall and tattered figure of the farmer swinging his whip and yelling: "Whoa! Haw there! Git-ap!" The lash flicked and flew over the broad backs of the animals.

"Hello, father," said Hawker.

"Whoa—back—whoa! Why, hello, William, what you doing here?"

"Oh, just taking a walk. Miss Fanhall, this is my father. Father——"

"How d' you do!" The old man balanced himself with care and then raised his straw hat from his head with a quick gesture and with what was perhaps a slightly apologetic air, as if he feared that he was rather overdoing the ceremonial part.

The girl, later, became very intent upon the oxen. "Aren't they nice old things," she said as she stood looking into the faces of the team. "But what makes their eyes so very sad?"

"I dunno," said the old man.

She was apparently unable to resist a desire to pat the nose of the nearest ox and for that purpose she stretched forth a cautious hand. But the ox moved restlessly at the moment and the girl put her hand apprehensively behind herself and backed away. The old man on the wagon grinned. "They won't hurt you," he told her.

"They won't bite, will they?" she asked, casting a glance of inquiry at the old man, and then turning her eyes again upon the fascinating animals.

"No," said the old man, still grinning. "Just as gentle as kittens."

She approached them circuitously. "Sure?" she said.

"Sure," replied the old man. He climbed from the wagon and came to the heads of the oxen. With him as an ally, she finally succeeded in patting the nose of the nearest ox. "Aren't they solemn, kind old fellows. Don't you get to think a great deal of them?"

"Well, they're kind of aggravating beasts sometimes," he said. "But they're a good yoke—a good yoke. They can haul with anything in this region."

"It doesn't make them so terribly tired, does it?" she said, hopefully. "They are such strong animals."

"No-o-o," he said. "I dunno. I never thought much about it."

With their heads close together they became so absorbed in their conversation that they seemed to forget the painter. He sat on a log and watched them.

Ultimately the girl said: "Won't you give us a ride?"

"Sure," said the old man. "Come on and I'll help you up." He assisted her very painstakingly to the old board that usually served him as a seat and he clambered to a place beside her. "Come on, William," he called. The painter climbed into the wagon and stood behind his father, putting his hand on the old man's shoulder to preserve his balance.

"Which is the near ox?" asked the girl with a serious frown.

"Git-ap! Haw! That one there," said the old man.

"And this one is the off ox?"

"Yep."

"Well, suppose you sat here where I do? Would this one be the near ox and that one the off ox, then?"

"Nope. Be just same."

"Then the near ox isn't always the nearest one to a person, at all. That ox there is always the near ox?"

"Yep. Always. 'Cause when you drive 'em a-foot, you always walk on the left side."

"Well! I never knew that before."

After studying them in silence for a while, she said: "Do you think they are happy?"

"I dunno," said the old man. "I never thought." As the wagon creaked on they gravely discussed this problem, contemplating profoundly the backs of the animals. Hawker gazed in silence at the meditating two before him. Under the wagon Stanley the setter walked slowly, wagging his tail in placid contentment and ruminating upon his experiences.

At last the old man said cheerfully: "Shall I take you around by the inn?"

Hawker started and seemed to wince at the question. Perhaps he was about to interrupt, but the girl cried: "Oh, will you? Take us right to the door? Oh, that will be awf'ly good of you."

"Why—" began Hawker. "You don't want—you don't want to ride to the inn on an—on an ox wagon, do you?"

"Why, of course I do," she retorted, directing a withering glance at him.

"Well——" he protested.

"Let 'er be, William," interrupted the old man. "Let 'er do what she wants to. I guess everybody in th' world ain't even got an ox wagon to ride in. Have they?"

"No, indeed," she returned, while withering Hawker again.

"Gee! Gee! Whoa! Haw! Git-ap! Haw! Whoa! Back!"

After these two attacks, Hawker became silent.

"Gee! Gee! Gee there, blast—s'cuse me! Gee! Whoa! Git-ap!"

All the boarders of the inn were upon its porches waiting for the dinner gong. There was a surge toward the railing as a middle-aged woman passed the word along her middle-aged friends that Miss Fanhall, accompanied by Mr. Hawker, had arrived on the ox cart of Mr. Hawker's father.

"Whoa! Haw! Git-ap!" said the old man in more subdued tones. "Whoa there, Red! Whoa, now! Wh-o-a!"

Hawker helped the girl to alight and she paused for a

moment conversing with the old man about the oxen. Then she ran smiling up the steps to meet the Worcester girls.

"Oh, such a lovely time. Those dear old oxen—you should have been with us."

Chapter XV

"OH, MISS FANHALL."

"What is it, Mrs. Truscot?"

"That was a great prank of yours last night, my dear. We all enjoyed the joke so much."

" 'Prank'?"

"Yes, your riding on the ox cart with that old farmer and that young Mr. What's-his-name, you know. We all thought it delicious. Ah, my dear, after all—don't be offended—if we had your people's wealth and position we might do that sort of unconventional thing, too, but, ah, my dear, we can't, we can't. Isn't the young painter a charming man?"

Out on the porch Hollanden was haranguing his friends. He heard a step and glanced over his shoulder to see who was about to interrupt him. He suddenly ceased his oration and said: "Hello! What's the matter with Grace?" The heads turned promptly.

As the girl came toward them, it could be seen that her cheeks were very pink and her eyes were flashing general wrath and defiance.

The Worcester girls burst into eager interrogations. "Oh, nothing," she replied at first, but later she added in an undertone: "That wretched Mrs. Truscot——"

"What did she say?" whispered the younger Worcester girl.

"Why, she said—oh, nothing."

Both Hollanden and Hawker were industriously reflecting.

Later in the morning, Hawker said privately to the girl: "I know what Mrs. Truscot talked to you about."

She turned upon him belligerently. "You do?"

"Yes," he answered with meekness. "It was undoubtedly some reference to your ride upon the ox wagon."

She hesitated a moment and then said: "Well?"

With still greater meekness he said: "I am very sorry."

"Are you—indeed?" she inquired loftily. "Sorry for what? Sorry that I rode upon your father's ox wagon, or sorry that Mrs. Truscot was rude to me about it?"

"Well—in some ways it was my fault."

"Was it? I suppose you intend to apologize for your father's owning an ox wagon, don't you?"

"No, but——"

"Well, I am going to ride in the ox wagon whenever I choose. Your father, I know, will always be glad to have me. And if it so shocks you there is not the slightest necessity of your coming with us."

They glowered at each other and he said: "You have twisted the question with the usual ability of your sex."

She pondered as if seeking some particularly destructive retort. She ended by saying bluntly: "Did you know that we were going home next week?"

A flush came suddenly to his face. "No! Going home? Who? You?"

"Why, of course." And then with an indolent air she continued: "I meant to have told you before this, but somehow it quite escaped me."

He stammered: "Are—are you, honestly?"

She nodded. "Why, of course. Can't stay here forever, you know."

They were then silent for a long time.

At last Hawker said: "Do you remember what I told you yesterday?"

"No. What was it?"

He cried indignantly: "You know very well what I told you."

"I do not."

"No," he sneered. "Of course not. You never take the trouble to remember such things. Of course not. Of course not."

"You are a very ridiculous person," she vouchsafed after eyeing him coldly.

He arose abruptly. "I believe I am. By heavens, I believe I am," he cried in a fury.

She laughed. "You are more ridiculous now than I have yet seen you."

After a pause he said magnificently: "Well, Miss Fanhall, you will doubtless find Mr. Hollanden's conversation to have a much greater interest than that of such a ridiculous person."

Hollanden approached them with the blithesome step of an

untroubled man. "Hello, you two people, why don't you—oh—ahem. Hold on, Billie, where you going?"

"I——" began Hawker.

"Oh, Hollie," cried the girl impetuously, "do tell me how to do that slam-thing, you know. I've tried it so often, but I don't believe I hold my racquet right. And you do it so beautifully."

"Oh, that," said Hollanden. "It's not so very difficult. I'll show it you. You don't want to know this minute, do you?"

"Yes," she answered.

"Well, come over to the court, then. Come ahead, Billie."

"No," said Hawker, without looking at his friend. "I can't this morning, Hollie. I've got to go to work. Good-by." He comprehended them both in a swift bow and stalked away.

Hollanden turned quickly to the girl. "What was the matter with Billie? What was he grinding his teeth for? What was the matter with him?"

"Why, nothing—was there?" she asked in surprise.

"Why, he was grinding his teeth until he sounded like a stone crusher," said Hollanden in a severe tone. "What was the matter with him?"

"How should I know?" she retorted.

"You've been saying something to him."

"I! I didn't say a thing."

"Yes, you did."

"Hollie, don't be absurd."

Hollanden debated with himself for a time and then observed: "Oh, well, I always said he was an ugly-tempered fellow——"

The girl flashed him a little glance.

"And now I am sure of it. As ugly-tempered a fellow as ever lived."

"I believe you," said the girl. Then she added: "All men are. I declare I think you to be the most incomprehensible creatures. One never knows what to expect of you. And you explode and go into rages and make yourselves utterly detestable over the most trivial matters and at the most unexpected times. You are all mad, I think."

"I!" cried Hollanden wildly. "What in the mischief have I done?"

Chapter XVI

"LOOK HERE," said Hollanden at length, "I thought you were so wonderfully anxious to learn that stroke?"

"Well, I am," she said.

"Come on, then." As they walked toward the tennis court he seemed to be plunged in mournful thought. In his eyes was a singular expression which perhaps denoted the woe of the optimist pushed suddenly from his height. He sighed. "Oh, well, I suppose all women, even the best of them, are that way."

"What way?" she said.

"My dear child," he answered in a benevolent manner, "you have disappointed me because I have discovered that you resemble the rest of your sex."

"Ah?" she remarked, maintaining a non-committal attitude.

"Yes," continued Hollanden with a sad but kindly smile, "even you, Grace, were not above fooling with the affections of a poor country swain until he don't know his ear from the tooth he had pulled two years ago."

She laughed. "He would be furious if he heard you call him a country swain."

"Who would?" said Hollanden.

"Why the country swain, of course," she rejoined.

Hollanden seemed plunged in mournful reflection again. "Well, it's a shame, Grace, anyhow," he observed, wagging his head dolefully. "It's a howling, wicked shame."

"Hollie, you have no brains at all," she said, "despite your opinion."

"No," he replied, ironically. "Not a bit."

"Well, you haven't, you know, Hollie."

"At any rate," he said in an angry voice, "I have some comprehension and sympathy for the feelings of others."

"Have you?" she asked. "How do you mean, Hollie? Do you mean you have feeling for them in their various sorrows? Or do you mean that you understand their minds?"

Hollanden ponderously began: "There have been people who have not questioned my ability to——"

"Oh, then, you mean that you both feel for them in their

sorrows and comprehend the machinery of their minds. Well, let me tell you that in regard to the last thing, you are wrong. You know nothing of any one's mind. You know less about human nature than anybody I have met."

Hollanden looked at her in artless astonishment. He said: "Now, I wonder what made you say that?" This interrogation did not seem to be addressed to her, but was evidently a statement to himself of a problem. He meditated for some moments. Eventually he said: "I suppose you mean that I do not understand you?"

"Why do you suppose I mean that?"

"That's what a person usually means when he—or she—charges another with not understanding the entire world."

"Well, at any rate, it is not what I mean at all," she said. "I mean that you habitually blunder about other people's affairs in the belief, I imagine, that you are a great philanthropist, when you are only making an extraordinary exhibition of yourself."

"The dev——" began Hollanden. Afterward he said: "Now, I wonder what in blue thunder you mean this time?"

" 'Mean this time?' My meaning is very plain, Hollie. I supposed the words were clear enough."

"Yes," he said, thoughtfully, "your words were clear enough, but then you were of course referring back to some event or series of events in which I had the singular ill-fortune to displease you. Maybe you don't know yourself and spoke only from the emotion generated by the event or series of events in which, as I have said, I had the singular ill-fortune to displease you."

"How awf'ly clever," she said.

"But I can't recall the event or series of events at all," he continued, musing with a scholarly air and disregarding her mockery. "I can't remember a thing about it. To be sure, it might have been that time when——"

"I think it very stupid of you to hunt for a meaning when I believe I made everything so perfectly clear," she said, wrathfully.

"Well, you yourself might not be aware of what you really meant," he answered, sagely. "Women often do that sort of thing, you know. Women often speak from motives which, if brought face to face with them, they wouldn't be able to distinguish from any other thing which they had never before seen."

"Hollie, if there is a disgusting person in the world it is he who pretends to know so much concerning a woman's mind."

"Well, that's because they who know or pretend to know so much about a woman's mind are invariably satirical, you understand," said Hollanden, cheerfully.

A dog ran frantically across the lawn, his nose high in the air and his countenance expressing vast perturbation and alarm. "Why, Billie forgot to whistle for his dog when he started for home," said Hollanden. "Come here, old man. Well, 'e was a nice dog." The girl also gave invitation, but the setter would not heed them. He spun wildly about the lawn until he seemed to strike his master's trail and then with his nose near to the ground went down the road at an eager gallop. They stood and watched him.

"Stanley's a nice dog," said Hollanden.

"Indeed, he is," replied the girl fervently.

Presently Hollanden remarked: "Well, don't let's fight any more, particularly since we can't decide what we're fighting about. I can't discover the reason and you don't know it, so——"

"I do know it. I told you very plainly."

"Well, all right. Now, this is the way to work that slam. You give the ball a sort of a lift—see—underhanded and with your arm crooked and stiff. Here, you smash this other ball into the net. Hi! Look out! If you hit it that way you'll knock it over the hotel. Let the ball drop nearer to the ground. Oh, heavens, not on the ground. Well, it's hard to do it from the serve, anyhow. I'll go over to the other court and bat you some easy ones."

Afterward when they were going toward the inn, the girl suddenly began to laugh.

"What you giggling at?" said Hollanden.

"I was thinking how furious he would be if he heard you call him a country swain," she rejoined.

"Who?" asked Hollanden.

Chapter XVII

O GLETHORPE CONTENDED that the men who made the most money from books were the best authors. Hollanden contended that they were the worst. Oglethorpe said that such a question should be left to the people. Hollanden said that the people habitually made wrong decisions on questions that were left to them. "That is the most odiously aristocratic belief," said Oglethorpe.

"No," said Hollanden. "I like the people. But, considered generally, they are a collection of ingenuous blockheads."

"But they read your books," said Oglethorpe, grinning.

"That is through a mistake," replied Hollanden.

As the discussion grew in size it incited the close attention of the Worcester girls, but Miss Fanhall did not seem to hear it. Hawker, too, was staring into the darkness with a gloomy and preoccupied air.

"Are you sorry that this is your last evening at Hemlock Inn?" said the painter at last in a low tone.

"Why, yes—certainly," said the girl.

Under the sloping porch of the inn the vague orange light from the parlors drifted to the black wall of the night.

"I shall miss you," said the painter.

"Oh, I dare say," said the girl.

Hollanden was lecturing at length and wonderfully. In the mystic spaces of the night the pines could be heard in their weird monotone as they softly smote branch and branch as if moving in some solemn and sorrowful dance.

"This has been quite the most delightful summer of my experience," said the painter.

"I have found it very pleasant," said the girl.

From time to time Hawker glanced furtively at Oglethorpe, Hollanden and the Worcester girls. This glance expressed no desire for their well being.

"I shall miss you," he said to the girl again. His manner was rather desperate. She made no reply, and, after leaning toward her, he subsided with an air of defeat.

Eventually he remarked: "It will be very lonely here again. I dare say I shall return to New York myself in a few weeks."

"I hope you will call," she said.

"I shall be delighted," he answered, stiffly and with a dissatisfied look at her.

"Oh, Mr. Hawker," cried the younger Worcester girl, suddenly emerging from the cloud of argument which Hollanden and Oglethorpe kept in the air, "won't it be sad to lose Grace? Indeed, I don't know what we shall do. Sha'n't we miss her dreadfully?"

"Yes," said Hawker, "we shall, of course, miss her dreadfully."

"Yes, won't it be frightful?" said the elder Worcester girl. "I can't imagine what we will do without her. And Hollie is only going to spend ten more days. Oh, dear—mamma, I believe, will insist on staying the entire summer. It was papa's orders, you know, and I really think she is going to obey them. He said he wanted her to have one period of rest at any rate. She is such a busy woman in town, you know."

"Here," said Hollanden, wheeling to them suddenly, "you all look as if you were badgering Hawker, and he looks badgered. What are you saying to him?"

"Why," answered the younger Worcester girl, "we were only saying to him how lonely it would be without Grace."

"Oh!" said Hollanden.

As the evening grew old, the mother of the Worcester girls joined the group. This was a sign that the girls were not to long delay the vanishing time. She sat almost upon the edge of her chair, as if she expected to be called upon at any moment to arise and bow "good-night," and she repaid Hollanden's eloquent attentions with the placid and absent-minded smiles of the chaperone who waits.

Once the younger Worcester girl shrugged her shoulders and turned to say: "Mamma, you make me nervous." Her mother merely smiled in a still more placid and absent-minded manner.

Oglethorpe arose to drag his chair nearer to the railing, and when he stood the Worcester mother moved and looked around expectantly, but Oglethorpe took seat again. Hawker kept an anxious eye upon her.

Presently Miss Fanhall arose.

"Why, you are not going in already, are you?" said Hawker

and Hollanden and Oglethorpe. The Worcester mother moved toward the door, followed by her daughters, who were protesting in muffled tones. Hollanden pitched violently upon Oglethorpe. "Well, at any rate——" he said. He picked the thread of a past argument with great agility.

Hawker said to the girl: "I—I—I shall miss you dreadfully."

She turned to look at him and smiled. "Shall you?" she said in a low voice.

"Yes," he said. Thereafter he stood before her awkwardly and in silence. She scrutinized the boards of the floor. Suddenly she drew a violet from a cluster of them upon her gown and thrust it out to him as she turned toward the approaching Oglethorpe.

"Good-night, Mr. Hawker," said the latter. "I am very glad to have met you, I'm sure. Hope to see you in town. Goodnight."

He stood near when the girl said to Hawker: "Good-by. You have given us such a charming summer. We shall be delighted to see you in town. You must come some time when the children can see you, too. Good-by."

"Good-by," replied Hawker, eagerly and feverishly trying to interpret the inscrutable feminine face before him. "I shall come at my first opportunity."

"Good-by."

"Good-by."

Down at the farmhouse, in the black quiet of the night, a dog lay curled on the door mat. Of a sudden the tail of this dog began to thump-thump on the boards. It began as a lazy movement, but it passed into a state of gentle enthusiasm and then into one of curiously loud and joyful celebration. At last the gate clicked. The dog uncurled and went to the edge of the steps to greet his master. He gave adoring, tremulous welcome with his clear eyes shining in the darkness. "Well, Stan, old boy," said Hawker, stooping to stroke the dog's head. After his master had entered the house the dog went forward and sniffed at something that lay on the top step. Apparently it did not interest him greatly, for he returned in a moment to the door mat.

But he was again obliged to uncurl himself, for his master

came out of the house with a lighted lamp and made search of the door mat, the steps and the walk, swearing meanwhile in an undertone. The dog wagged his tail and sleepily watched this ceremony. When his master had again entered the house, the dog went forward and sniffed at the top step, but the thing that had lain there was gone.

Chapter XVIII

IT WAS EVIDENT at breakfast that Hawker's sisters had achieved information. "What's the matter with you this morning?" asked one. "You look as if you hadn't slep' well."

"There is nothing the matter with me," he rejoined, looking glumly at his plate.

"Well, you look kind of broke up."

"How I look is of no consequence. I tell you there is nothing the matter with me."

"Oh," said his sister. She exchanged meaning glances with the other feminine members of the family. Presently the other sister observed: "I heard she was going home to-day."

"Who?" said Hawker, with a challenge in his tone.

"Why, that New York girl. Miss What's-her-name," replied the sister, with an undaunted smile.

"Did you, indeed? Well, perhaps she is."

"Oh, you don't know for sure, I s'pose."

Hawker arose from the table and taking his hat went away.

"Mary!" said the mother in the sepulchral tone of belated but conscientious reproof.

"Well, I don't care. He needn't be so grand. I didn't go to tease him. I don't care."

"Well, you ought to care," said the old man suddenly. "There's no sense in you wimen folks pestering the boy all the time. Let him alone with his own business, can't you?"

"Well, ain't we leaving him alone?"

"No, you ain't. 'Cept when he ain't here. I don't wonder the boy grabs his hat and skips out when you git to going."

"Well, what did we say to him, now? Tell us what we said to him that was so dreadful."

"Aw, thunder an' lightnin'," cried the old man, with a sudden great snarl. They seemed to know by this ejaculation that he had emerged in an instant from that place where man endures, and they ended the discussion. The old man continued his breakfast.

During his walk that morning Hawker visited a certain cascade, a certain lake, and some roads, paths, groves, nooks. Later in the day he made a sketch, choosing an hour when

336

the atmosphere was of a dark blue, like powder smoke in the shade of trees, and the western sky was burning in strips of red. He painted with a wild face like a man who is killing.

After supper he and his father strolled under the apple boughs in the orchard and smoked. Once he gestured wearily. "Oh, I guess I'll go back to New York in a few days."

"Um," replied his father calmly. "All right, William."

Several days later Hawker accosted his father in the barn-yard. "I suppose you think sometimes I don't care so much about you and the folks and the old place any more. But I do."

"Um," said the old man. "When you goin'?"

"Where?" asked Hawker, flushing.

"Back to New York."

"Why——I hadn't thought much about—— Oh, next week, I guess."

"Well, do as you like, William. You know how glad me an' mother and the girls are to have you home with us whenever you can come. You know that. But you must do as you think best and if you ought to go back to New York, now, William, why—do as you think best."

"Well, my work——" said Hawker.

From time to time the mother made wondering speech to the sisters. "How much nicer William is now. He's just as good as he can be. There for a while he was so cross and out of sorts. I don't see what could have come over him. But now he's just as good as he can be."

Hollanden told him: "Come up to the inn more, you fool."

"I was up there yesterday."

"Yesterday! What of that? I've seen the time when the farm couldn't hold you for two hours during the day."

"Go to blazes."

"Millicent got a letter from Grace Fanhall the other day."

"That so?"

"Yes, she did. Grace wrote—— Say, does that shadow look pure purple to you?"

"Certainly it does or I wouldn't paint it so, duffer. What did she write?"

"Well, if that shadow is pure purple my eyes are liars. It looks a kind of a slate color to me. Lord, if what you fellows say in your pictures is true, the whole earth must be blazing and burning and glowing and——"

Hawker went into a rage. "Oh, you don't know anything about color, Hollie. For heaven's sake, shut up or I'll smash you with the easel."

"Well, I was going to tell you what Grace wrote in her letter. She said——"

"Go on."

"Gimme time, can't you? She said that town was stupid and that she wished she was back at Hemlock Inn."

"Oh! Is that all?"

" 'Is that all!' I wonder what you expected? Well, and she asked to be recalled to you."

"Yes? Thanks."

"And that's all. 'Gad, for such a devoted man as you were, your enthusiasm and interest is stupendous."

The father said to the mother: "Well, William's going back to New York next week."

"Is he? Why, he ain't said nothing to me about it."

"Well, he is, anyhow."

"I declare. What do you s'pose he's going back before September for, John?"

"How do I know?"

"Well, it's funny. John, I bet—I bet he's going back so's he can see that girl."

"He says it's his work."

Chapter XIX

WRINKLES HAD BEEN PEERING into the little dry goods box that acted as a cupboard. "There are only two eggs and half a loaf of bread left," he announced brutally.

"Heavens," said Warwickson from where he lay smoking on the bed. He spoke in a dismal voice. This tone, it is said, had earned him his popular name of Great Grief.

From different points of the compass Wrinkles looked at the little cupboard with a tremendous scowl, as if he intended thus to frighten the eggs into becoming more than two and the bread into becoming a loaf. "Plague take it," he exclaimed.

"Oh, shut up, Wrinkles," said Grief from the bed.

Wrinkles sat down with an air austere and virtuous. "Well, what are we going to do?" he demanded of the others.

Grief, after swearing, said: "There! That's right. Now, you're happy. The holy office of the inquisition. Blast your buttons, Wrinkles, you always try to keep us from starving peacefully. It is two hours before dinner, anyhow, and——"

"Well, but what are we going to do?" persisted Wrinkles.

Pennoyer with his head bended afar down had been busily scratching at a pen-and-ink drawing. He looked up from his board to utter a plaintive optimism. "The *Monthly Amazement* may pay me to-morrow. They ought to. I've waited over three months now. I'm going down there to-morrow and perhaps I'll get it."

His friends listened with airs of tolerance. "Oh, no doubt, Penny, old man." But at last Wrinkles giggled pityingly. Over on the bed Grief croaked deep down in his throat. Nothing was said for a long time thereafter.

The crash of the New York streets came faintly to this room. Occasionally one could hear the tramp of feet in the intricate corridors of the begrimed building which squatted, slumbering and old, between two exalted commercial structures that would have had to bend afar down to perceive it. The northward march of the city's progress had happened not to overturn this aged structure and it huddled there, lost and forgotten, while the cloud-veering towers strode on.

Meanwhile the first shadows of dusk came in at the blurred windows of the room. Pennoyer threw down his pen and tossed his drawing over on the wonderful heap of stuff that hid the table. "It's too dark to work." He lit a pipe and walked about stretching his shoulders like a man whose labor was valuable.

When the dusk came fully, the youths grew apparently sad. The solemnity of the gloom seemed to make them ponder. "Light the gas, Wrinkles," said Grief fretfully.

The flood of orange light showed clearly the dull walls lined with sketches, the tousled bed in one corner, the masses of boxes and trunks in another, a little dead stove and the wonderful table. Moreover, there were wine-colored draperies flung in some places and on a shelf, high up, there were plaster casts with dust in the creases. A long stove-pipe wandered off in the wrong direction and then turned impulsively toward a hole in the wall. There were some elaborate cobwebs on the ceiling.

"Well, let's eat," said Grief.

"Eat!" said Wrinkles with a jeer. "I told you there was only two eggs and a little bread left. How are we going to eat?"

Again brought face to face with this problem and at the hour for dinner, Pennoyer and Grief thought profoundly. "Thunder and turf," Grief finally announced as the result of his deliberations.

"Well, if Billie Hawker was only home——" began Pennoyer.

"But he isn't," objected Wrinkles. "And that settles that."

Grief and Pennoyer thought more. Ultimately Grief said: "Oh, well, let's eat what we've got." The others at once agreed to this suggestion, as if it had been in their minds.

Later there came a quick step in the passage and a confident little thunder upon the door. Wrinkles arranging the tin pail on the gas stove, Pennoyer engaged in slicing the bread and Great Grief affixing the rubber tube to the gas stove, yelled: "Come in."

The door opened and Miss Florinda O'Connor, the model, dashed into the room like a gale of obstreperous autumn leaves.

"Why, hello, Splutter," they cried.

"Oh, boys, I've come to dine with you."

It was like a squall striking a fleet of yachts.

Grief spoke first. "Yes, you have?" he said incredulously.

"Why, certainly I have. What's the matter?"

They grinned. "Well, old lady," responded Grief, "you've hit us at the wrong time. We are, in fact, all out of everything. No dinner—to mention—and, what's more, we haven't got a sou."

"What? Again?" cried Florinda.

"Yes, again. You'd better dine home to-night."

"But I'll—I'll stake you," said the girl eagerly. "Oh, you poor old idiots. It's a shame. Say, I'll stake you."

"Certainly not," said Pennoyer sternly.

"What are you talking about, Splutter?" demanded Wrinkles in an angry voice.

"No, that won't go down," said Grief in a resolute yet wistful tone.

Florinda divested herself of her hat, jacket and gloves and put them where she pleased. "Got coffee, haven't you? Well, I'm not going to stir a step. You're a fine lot of birds," she added bitterly. "You've all pulled me out of a whole lot of scrapes—oh, any number of times—and now you're broke, you go acting like a set of dudes."

Great Grief had fixed the coffee to boil on the gas stove, but he had to watch it closely, for the rubber tube was short and a chair was balanced on a trunk and two bundles of kindling were balanced on the chair and the gas stove was balanced on the kindling. Coffee-making was here accounted a feat.

Pennoyer dropped a piece of bread to the floor. "There! I'll have to go shy one."

Wrinkles sat playing serenades on his guitar and staring with a frown at the table as if he was applying some strange method of clearing it of its litter.

Florinda assaulted Great Grief. "Here! That's not the way to make coffee."

"What ain't?"

"Why, the way you're making it. You want to take——"
She explained some way to him which he couldn't understand.

"For heaven's sake, Wrinkles, tackle that table. Don't sit there like a music box," said Pennoyer, grappling the eggs and starting for the gas stove.

Later as they sat around the board, Wrinkles said with satisfaction: "Well, the coffee's good, anyhow."

"'Tis good," said Florinda. "But it isn't made right. I'll show you how, Penny. You first——"

"Oh, dry up, Splutter," said Grief. "Here, take an egg."

"I don't like eggs," said Florinda.

"Take an egg," said the three hosts menacingly.

"I tell you I don't like eggs."

"Take—an—egg," they said again.

"Oh, well," said Florinda, "I'll take one, then. But you needn't act like such a set of dudes. And, oh, maybe you didn't have much lunch. I had such a daisy lunch. Up at Pontiac's studio. He's got a lovely studio."

The three looked to be oppressed. Grief said sullenly: "I saw some of his things over in Stencil's gallery and they're rotten."

"Yes, rotten," said Pennoyer.

"Rotten," said Grief.

"Oh, well," retorted Florinda, "if a man has a swell studio and dresses—oh, sort of like a Willie, you know, you fellows sit here like owls in a cave and say rotten—rotten—rotten. You're away off. Pontiac's landscapes——"

"Landscapes be blowed. Put any of his work alongside of Billie Hawker's and see how it looks."

"Oh, well, Billie Hawker's," said Florinda. "Oh, well."

At the mention of Hawker's name, they had all turned to scan her face.

Chapter XX

"H E WROTE that he was coming home this week," said Pennoyer.

"Did he?" asked Florinda, indifferently.

"Yes. Aren't you glad?"

They were still watching her face.

"Yes, of course, I'm glad. Why shouldn't I be glad?" cried the girl with defiance.

They grinned.

"Oh, certainly. Billie Hawker is a good fellow, Splutter. You have a particular right to be glad."

"You people make me tired," Florinda retorted. "Billie Hawker doesn't give a rap about me and he never tried to make out that he did."

"No," said Grief. "But that isn't saying that you don't care a rap about Billie Hawker. Ah, Florinda."

It seemed that the girl's throat suffered a slight contraction. "Well, and what if I do?" she demanded finally.

"Have a cigarette?" answered Grief.

Florinda took a cigarette, lit it, and perching herself on a divan which was secretly a coal box, she smoked fiercely.

"What if I do?" she again demanded. "It's better than liking one of you dubs, anyhow."

"Oh, Splutter, you poor little outspoken kid," said Wrinkles in a sad voice.

Grief searched among the pipes until he found the best one. "Yes, Splutter, don't you know that when you are so frank you defy every law of your sex, and wild eyes will take your trail?"

"Oh, you talk through your hat," replied Florinda. "Billie don't care whether I like him or whether I don't. And if he should hear me now he wouldn't be glad or give a hang either way. I know that." The girl paused and looked at the row of plaster casts. "Still, you needn't be throwing it at me all the time."

"We didn't," said Wrinkles, indignantly. "You threw it at yourself."

343

"Well," continued Florinda. "It's better than liking one of you dubs, anyhow. He makes money and——"

"There," said Grief. "Now you've hit it. Bedad, you've reached a point in eulogy where if you move again you will have to go backwards."

"Of course I don't care anything about a fellow's having money——"

"No, indeed, you don't, Splutter," said Pennoyer.

"But then you know what I mean. A fellow isn't a man and doesn't stand up straight unless he has some money. And Billie Hawker makes enough so that you feel that nobody could walk over him, don't you know. And there isn't anything jay about him, either. He's a thoroughbred, don't you know?"

After reflection Pennoyer said: "It's pretty hard on the rest of us, Splutter."

"Well, of course, I like him, but—but——"

"What?" said Pennoyer.

"I don't know," said Florinda.

Purple Sanderson lived in this room, but he usually dined out. At a certain time in his life, before he came to be a great artist, he had learned the gas-fitter's trade and when his opinions were not identical with the opinions of the art managers of the greater number of New York publications he went to see a friend who was a plumber, and the opinions of this man he was thereafter said to respect. He frequented a very neat restaurant on Twenty-third street. It was known that on Saturday nights Wrinkles, Grief and Pennoyer frequently quarreled with him.

As Florinda ceased speaking Purple entered. "Hello, there, Splutter." As he was neatly hanging up his coat he said to the others: "Well, the rent will be due in four days."

"Will it?" asked Pennoyer, astounded.

"Certainly it will," responded Purple, with the air of a superior financial man.

"My soul," said Wrinkles.

"Oh, shut up, Purple," said Grief. "You make me weary, coming around here with your chin about rent. I was just getting happy."

"Well, how are we going to pay it? That's the point," said Sanderson.

Wrinkles sank deeper in his chair and played despondently on his guitar. Grief cast a look of rage at Sanderson and then stared at the wall. Pennoyer said: "Well, we might borrow it from Billie Hawker."

Florinda laughed then.

"Or," continued Pennoyer, hastily, "if those *Amazement* people pay me when they said they would, I'll have money."

"So you will," said Grief. "You will have money to burn. Did the *Amazement* people ever pay you when they said they would? You are wonderfully important all of a sudden, it seems to me. You talk like an artist."

Wrinkles, too, smiled at Pennoyer. "The *Eminent Magazine* people wanted Penny to hire models and make a try for them, too. It would only cost him a stack of blues. By the time he has invested all his money he hasn't got and the rent is three weeks overdue he will be able to tell the landlord to wait seven months until the Monday morning after the day of publication. Go ahead, Penny."

After a period of silence Sanderson, in an obstinate manner, said: "Well, what's to be done? The rent has got to be paid."

Wrinkles played more sad music. Grief frowned deeper. Pennoyer was evidently searching his mind for a plan.

Florinda took the cigarette from between her lips that she might grin with greater freedom.

"We might throw Purple out," said Grief with an inspired air. "That would stop all this discussion."

"You," said Sanderson, furiously. "You can't keep serious a minute. If you didn't have us to take care of you, you wouldn't even know when they threw you out in the street."

"Wouldn't I?" said Grief.

"Well, look here," interposed Florinda. "I'm going home unless you can be more interesting. I am dead sorry about the rent, but I can't help it and——"

"Here! Sit down! Hold on, Splutter," they shouted. Grief turned to Sanderson. "Purple, you shut up."

Florinda curled again on the divan and lit another cigarette. The talk waged about the names of other and more successful painters whose work they usually pronounced "Rotten."

Chapter XXI

PENNOYER COMING HOME one morning with two gigantic cakes to accompany the coffee at the breakfast in the den, saw a young man bounce from a horse-car. He gave a shout. "Hello there, Billie! Hello!"

"Hello, Penny," said Hawker. "What you doing out so early?" It was somewhat after nine o'clock.

"Out to get breakfast," said Pennoyer, waving the cakes. "Have a good time, old man?"

"Great."

"Do much work?"

"No. Not so much. How are all the people?"

"Oh, pretty good. Come in and see us eat breakfast," said Pennoyer, throwing open the door of the den. Wrinkles, in his shirt, was making coffee. Grief sat in a chair trying to loosen the grasp of sleep. "Why, Billie Hawker, b'ginger," they cried.

"How's the wolf, boys? At the door yet?"

" 'At the door yet?' He's half way up the back stairs and coming fast. He and the landlord will be here to-morrow. 'Mr. Landlord, allow me to present Mr. F. Wolf of Hunger, N.J. Mr. Wolf—Mr. Landlord.' "

"Bad as that?" said Hawker.

"You bet it is. Easy street is somewhere in heaven for all we know. Have some breakfast—coffee and cake, I mean."

"No, thanks, boys. Had breakfast."

Wrinkles added to the shirt, Grief aroused himself and Pennoyer brought the coffee. Cheerfully throwing some drawings from the table to the floor, they thus made room for the breakfast and grouped themselves with beaming smiles at the board.

"Well, Billie, come back to the old gang again, eh? How did the country seem? Do much work?"

"Not very much. A few things. How's everybody?"

"Splutter was in last night. Looking out of sight. Seemed glad to hear that you were coming back soon."

"Did she? Penny, did anybody call wanting me to do a ten-thousand-dollar portrait for them?"

"No. That frame-maker, though, was here with a bill. I told him——"

Afterward Hawker crossed the corridor and threw open the door of his own large studio. The great skylight, far above his head, shed its clear rays upon a scene which appeared to indicate that some one had very recently ceased work here and started for the country. A distant closet door was open and the interior showed the effects of a sudden pillage.

There was an unfinished "Girl in Apple Orchard" upon the tall Dutch easel and sketches and studies were thick upon the floor. Hawker took a pipe and filled it from his friend, the tan and gold jar. He cast himself into a chair and taking an envelope from his pocket, emptied two violets from it to the palm of his hand and stared long at them. Upon the walls of the studio, various labors of his life in heavy gilt frames contemplated him and the violets.

At last Pennoyer burst impetuously in upon him. "Hi, Billie, come over and—— What's the matter?"

Hawker had hastily placed the violets in the envelope and hurried it to his pocket. "Nothing," he answered.

"Why, I thought——" said Pennoyer. "I thought you looked rather rattled. Didn't you have—I thought I saw something in your hand."

"Nothing, I tell you," cried Hawker.

"Er—oh, I beg your pardon," said Pennoyer. "Why, I was going to tell you that Splutter is over in our place and she wants to see you."

"Wants to see me? What for?" demanded Hawker. "Why don't she come over here, then?"

"I'm sure I don't know," replied Pennoyer. "She sent me to call you."

"Well, do you think I'm going to—— Oh, well, I suppose she wants to be unpleasant and knows she loses a certain mental position if she comes over here, but if she meets me in your place she can be as infernally disagreeable as she—— That's it, I'll bet."

When they entered the den, Florinda was gazing from the window. Her back was toward the door.

At last she turned to them, holding herself very straight.

"Well, Billie Hawker," she said grimly. "You don't seem very glad to see a fellow."

"Why, heavens, did you think I was going to turn somersaults in the air?"

"Well, you didn't come out when you heard me pass your door," said Florinda with gloomy resentment.

Hawker appeared to be ruffled and vexed. "Oh, Great Scott," he said, making a gesture of despair.

Florinda returned to the window. In the ensuing conversation she took no part save when there was opportunity to harry some speech of Hawker's, which she did in short contemptuous sentences. Hawker made no reply save to glare in her direction. At last he said: "Well, I must go over and do some work." Florinda did not turn from the window. "Well, so long, boys," said Hawker. "I'll see you later."

As the door slammed Pennoyer apologetically said: "Billie is a trifle off his feed this morning."

"What about?" asked Grief.

"I don't know. But when I went to call him, he was sitting deep in his chair staring at some——" He looked at Florinda and became silent.

"Staring at what?" asked Florinda, turning then from the window.

Pennoyer seemed embarrassed. "Why, I don't know—nothing, I guess—I couldn't see very well—I was only fooling."

Florinda scanned his face suspiciously. "Staring at what?" she demanded imperatively.

"Nothing, I tell you," shouted Pennoyer.

Florinda looked at him and wavered and debated. Presently she said softly: "Ah, go on, Penny. Tell me."

"It wasn't anything at all, I say," cried Pennoyer stoutly. "I was only giving you a jolly. Sit down, Splutter, and hit a cigarette."

She obeyed, but she continued to cast the dubious eye at Pennoyer. Once she said to him privately: "Go on, Penny, tell me. I know it was something from the way you are acting."

"Oh, let up, Splutter, for heaven's sake."

"Tell me," beseeched Florinda.

"No."

"Tell me."

"No."

"Pl-e-a-se, tell me."

"No."

"Oh, go on."

"No."

"Ah, what makes you so mean, Penny. You know I'd tell you if it was the other way about."

"But it's none of my business, Splutter. I can't tell you something which is Billie Hawker's private affair. If I did I would be a chump."

"But I'll never say you told me. Go on."

"No."

"Pl-e-a-se, tell me."

"No."

Chapter XXII

WHEN FLORINDA HAD GONE, Grief said: "Well, what was it?" Wrinkles looked curiously from his drawing board.

Pennoyer lit his pipe and held it at the side of his mouth in the manner of a deliberate man. At last he said: "It was two violets."

"You don't say," ejaculated Wrinkles.

"Well, I'm hanged," cried Grief. "Holding them in his hand and moping over them, eh?"

"Yes," responded Pennoyer. "Rather that way."

"Well, I'm hanged," said both Grief and Wrinkles. They grinned in a pleased, urchin-like manner. "Say, who do you suppose she is? Somebody he met this summer, no doubt. Would you ever think old Billie would get into that sort of a thing. Well, I'll be gol-durned."

Ultimately Wrinkles said: "Well, it's his own business." This was spoken in a tone of duty.

"Of course, it's his own business," retorted Grief. "But who would ever think——" Again they grinned.

When Hawker entered the den some minutes later, he might have noticed something unusual in the general demeanor. "Say, Grief, will you loan me your—— What's up?" he asked.

For answer they grinned at each other and then grinned at him.

"You look like a lot of Chessy cats," he told them.

They grinned on.

Apparently feeling unable to deal with these phenomena, he went at last to the door. "Well, this is a fine exhibition," he said, standing with his hand on the knob and regarding them. "Won election bets? Some good old auntie just died? Found something new to pawn? No? Well, I can't stand this. You resemble those fish they discover at deep sea. Good-by."

As he opened the door, they cried out: "Hold on, Billie. Billie, look here. Say, who is she?"

"What?"

"Who is she?"

"Who is who?"

They laughed and nodded. "Why, you know. She. Don't you understand? She."

"You talk like a lot of crazy men," said Hawker. "I don't know what you mean."

"Oh, you don't, eh? You don't? Oh, no. How about those violets you were moping over this morning? Eh, old man? Oh, no, you don't know what we mean. Oh, no. How about those violets, eh? How about 'em?"

Hawker with flushed and wrathful face looked at Pennoyer. "Penny——" But Grief and Wrinkles roared an interruption. "Oh, ho, Mr. Hawker, so it's true, is it? It's true? You are a nice bird, you are. Well, you old rascal. Durn your picture."

Hawker, menacing them once with his eyes, went away. They sat cackling.

At noon when he met Wrinkles in the corridor he said: "Hey, Wrinkles, come here for a minute, will you? Say, old man, I—I——"

"What?" said Wrinkles.

"Well, you know, I—I—of course, every man is likely to make an accursed idiot of himself once in a while, and I——"

"And you what?" asked Wrinkles.

"Well, we are a kind of a band of hoodlums, you know, and I'm just enough idiot to feel that I don't care to hear—don't care to hear—well, her name used, you know."

"Bless your heart," replied Wrinkles. "We haven't used her name. We don't know her name. How could we use it?"

"Well, I know," said Hawker. "But you understand what I mean, Wrinkles."

"Yes, I understand what you mean," said Wrinkles with dignity. "I don't suppose you are any worse of a stuff than common. Still, I didn't know that we were such outlaws."

"Of course, I have overdone the thing," responded Hawker hastily. "But—you ought to understand how I mean it, Wrinkles."

After Wrinkles had thought for a time he said: "Well, I guess I do. All right. That goes."

Upon entering the den, Wrinkles said: "You fellows have got to quit guying Billie, do you hear?"

"We?" cried Grief. "We've got to quit? What do you do?"

"Well, I quit, too."

Pennoyer said: "Ah, ha, Billie has been jumping on you."

"No, he didn't," maintained Wrinkles. "But he let me know it was—well, rather a—rather a—sacred subject." Wrinkles blushed when the others snickered.

In the afternoon, as Hawker was going slowly down the stairs, he was almost impaled upon the feather of a hat which, upon the head of a lithe and rather slight girl, charged up at him through the gloom.

"Hello, Splutter," he cried. "You are in a hurry."

"That you, Billie?" said the girl peering, for the hallways of this old building remained always in a dungeon-like darkness.

"Yes, it is. Where are you going at such a headlong gait?"

"Up to see the boys. I've got a bottle of wine and some—some pickles, you know. I'm going to make them let me dine with them to-night. Coming back, Billie?"

"Why, no, I don't expect to."

He moved then accidentally in front of the light that sifted through the dull grey panes of a little window.

"Oh, cracky," cried the girl. "How fine you are, Billie. Going to a coronation?"

"No," said Hawker, looking seriously over his collar and down at his clothes. "Fact is—er—well, I've got to make a call."

"A call—bless us. And are you really going to wear those grey gloves you're holding there, Billie? Say, wait until you get around the corner. They won't stand 'em on this street."

"Oh, well," said Hawker, deprecating the gloves. "Oh, well."

The girl looked up at him. "Who you going to call on?"

"Oh," said Hawker. "A friend."

"Must be somebody most extraordinary. You look so dreadfully correct. Come back, Billie, won't you? Come back and dine with us?"

"Why I—I don't believe I can."

"Oh, come on. It's fun when we all dine together. Won't you, Billie?"

"Well, I——"

"Oh, don't be so stupid." The girl stamped her foot and flashed her eyes at him angrily.

"Well, I'll see—I will if I can—I can't tell——" He left her rather precipitately.

Hawker eventually appeared at a certain austere house where he rang the bell with quite nervous fingers.

But she was not at home. As he went down the steps, his eyes were as those of a man whose fortunes have tumbled upon him. As he walked down the street he wore in some subtle way, the air of a man who has been grievously wronged. When he rounded the corner, his lips were set strangely as if he were a man seeking revenge.

Chapter XXIII

IT'S JUST RIGHT," said Grief.

"It isn't quite cool enough," said Wrinkles.

"Well, I guess I know the proper temperature for claret."

"Well, I guess you don't. If it was buttermilk, now, you would know, but you can't tell anything about claret."

Florinda ultimately decided the question. "It isn't quite cool enough," she said, laying her hand on the bottle. "Put it on the window ledge, Grief."

"Hum! Splutter, I thought you knew more than——"

"Oh, shut up," interposed the busy Pennoyer from a remote corner. "Who is going after the potato salad? That's what I want to know. Who is going?"

"Wrinkles," said Grief.

"Grief," said Wrinkles.

"There," said Pennoyer, coming forward and scanning a late work with an eye of satisfaction. "There's the three glasses and the little tumbler and then, Grief, you will have to drink out of a mug."

"I'll be double-dyed black if I will!" cried Grief. "I wouldn't drink claret out of a mug to save my soul from being pinched."

"You duffer. You talk like a bloomin' British chump, on whom the sun never sets. What do you want?"

"Well, there's enough without that—what's the matter with you? Three glasses and the little tumbler."

"Yes, but if Billie Hawker comes——"

"Well, let him drink out of the mug, then. He——"

"No, he won't," said Florinda, suddenly. "I'll take the mug myself."

"All right, Splutter," rejoined Grief, meekly. "I'll keep the mug. But still, I don't see why Billie Hawker——"

"I shall take the mug," reiterated Florinda, firmly.

"But I don't see why——"

"Let her alone, Grief," said Wrinkles. "She has decided that it is heroic. You can't move her now."

"Well, who is going for the potato salad?" cried Pennoyer again. "That's what I want to know."

"Wrinkles," said Grief.

"Grief," said Wrinkles.

"Do you know," remarked Florinda, raising her head from where she had been toiling over the spaghetti, "I don't care so much for Billie Hawker as I did once." Her sleeves were rolled above the elbows of her wonderful arms and she turned from the stove and poised a fork as if she had been smitten at her task with this inspiration.

There was a short silence, and then Wrinkles said politely: "No?"

"No," continued Florinda. "I really don't believe I do." She suddenly started. "Listen! Isn't that him coming now?"

The dull trample of a step could be heard in some distant corridor, but it died slowly to silence.

"I thought that might be him," she said, turning to the spaghetti again.

"I hope the old Indian comes," said Pennoyer. "But I don't believe he will. Seems to me he must be going to see——"

"Who?" asked Florinda.

"Well, you know, Hollanden and he usually dine together when they are both in town."

Florinda looked at Pennoyer. "I know, Penny. You must have thought I was remarkably clever not to understand all your blundering. But I don't care so much. Really I don't."

"Of course not," assented Pennoyer.

"Really I don't."

"Of course not."

"Listen," exclaimed Grief, who was near the door. "There he comes now." Somebody approached, whistling an air from "Traviata," which rang loud and clear and low and muffled as the whistler wound among the intricate hallways. This air was as much a part of Hawker as his coat. The spaghetti had arrived at a critical stage. Florinda gave it her complete attention.

When Hawker opened the door he ceased whistling and said gruffly: "Hello!"

"Just the man," said Grief. "Go after the potato salad, will you, Billie? There's a good boy. Wrinkles has refused."

"He can't carry the salad with those gloves," interrupted Florinda, raising her eyes from her work and contemplating them with displeasure.

"Hang the gloves," cried Hawker, dragging them from his hands and hurling them at the divan. "What's the matter with you, Splutter?"

Pennoyer said: "My, what a temper you are in, Billie."

"I am," replied Hawker. "I feel like an Apache. Where do you get this accursed potato salad?"

"On Second avenue. You know where. At the old place."

"No, I don't," snapped Hawker.

"Why——"

"Here," said Florinda. "I'll go." She had already rolled down her sleeves and was arraying herself in her hat and jacket.

"No, you won't," said Hawker, filled with wrath. "I'll go myself."

"We can both go, Billie, if you are so bent," replied the girl in a conciliatory voice.

"Well, come on, then. What are you standing there for?"

When these two had departed, Wrinkles said: "Lordie! What's wrong with Billie?"

"He's been discussing art with some pot-boiler," said Grief, speaking as if this was the final condition of human misery.

"No, sir," said Pennoyer. "It's something connected with the now celebrated violets."

Out in the corridor Florinda said: "What—what makes you so ugly, Billie?"

"Why, I am not ugly, am I?"

"Yes, you are. Ugly as anything."

Probably he saw a grievance in her eyes, for he said: "Well, I don't want to be ugly." His tone seemed tender. The halls were intensely dark and the girl placed her hand on his arm. As they rounded a turn in the stairs a straying lock of her hair brushed against his temple. "Oh," said Florinda in a low voice.

"We'll get some more claret," observed Hawker, musingly. "And some cognac for the coffee. And some cigarettes. Do you think of anything more, Splutter?"

As they came from the shop of the illustrious purveyors of potato salad on Second avenue, Florinda cried anxiously: "Here, Billie, you let me carry that."

"What infernal nonsense," said Hawker, flushing. "Certainly not."

"Well," protested Florinda. "It might soil your gloves somehow."

"In heaven's name, what if it does? Say, young woman, do you think I am one of these cholly boys?"

"No, Billie, but then you know——"

"Well, if you don't take me for some kind of a Willie, give us peace on this blasted glove business!"

"I didn't mean——"

"Well, you've been intimating that I've got the only pair of grey gloves in the universe, but you are wrong. There are several pairs, and these need not be preserved as unique in history."

"They're not grey. They're——"

"They are grey. I suppose your distinguished ancestors in Ireland did not educate their families in the matter of gloves, and so you are not expected to——"

"Billie!"

"You are not expected to believe that people wear gloves excepting in cold weather, and then you expect to see mittens."

On the stairs in the darkness he suddenly exclaimed: "Here! Look out, or you'll fall." He reached for her arm, but she evaded him. Later he said again: "Look out, girl. What makes you stumble around so? Here! Give me the bottle of wine. I can carry it all right. There! Now, can you manage?"

Chapter XXIV

"Penny," said Grief, looking across the table at his friend, "if a man thinks a heap of two violets, how much would he think of a thousand violets?"

"Two into a thousand goes five hundred times, you fool," said Pennoyer. "I would answer your question if it were not upon a forbidden subject."

In the distance Wrinkles and Florinda were making Welsh rabbits.

"Hold your tongues," said Hawker. "Barbarians!"

"Grief," said Pennoyer, "if a man loves a woman better than the whole universe, how much does he love the whole universe?"

"Gawd knows," said Grief, piously. "Although it ill befits me to answer your question."

Wrinkles and Florinda came with the Welsh rabbits very triumphant. "There," said Florinda. "Soon as these are finished I must go home. It is after eleven o'clock. Pour the ale, Grief."

At a later time Purple Sanderson entered from the world. He hung up his hat and cast a look of proper financial dissatisfaction at the remnants of the feast. "Who has been——"

"Before you breathe, Purple, you graceless scum, let me tell you that we will stand no reference to the two violets here," said Pennoyer.

"What the——"

"Oh, that's all right, Purple," said Grief, "but you were going to say something about the two violets right then. Weren't you now, you old bat?"

Sanderson grinned expectantly. "What's the row?" said he.

"No row at all," they told him. "Just an agreement to keep you from chattering obstinately about the two violets."

"What two violets?"

"Have a rabbit, Purple," advised Wrinkles, "and never mind those maniacs."

"Well, what is this business about two violets?"

"Oh, it's just some dream. They gibber at anything."

"I think I know," said Florinda, nodding. "It is something that concerns Billie Hawker."

Grief and Pennoyer scoffed, and Wrinkles said: "You know nothing about it, Splutter. It doesn't concern Billie Hawker at all."

"Well, then, what is he looking sideways for?" cried Florinda.

Wrinkles reached for his guitar and played a serenade. "The silver moon is shining——"

"Dry up," said Pennoyer.

Then Florinda cried again: "What does he look sideways for?"

Pennoyer and Grief giggled at the imperturbable Hawker, who destroyed rabbit in silence.

"It's you, is it, Billie?" said Sanderson. "You are in this two-violet business."

"I don't know what they're talking about," replied Hawker.

"Don't you, honestly?" asked Florinda.

"Well, only a little."

"There!" said Florinda, nodding again. "I knew he was in it."

"He isn't in it at all," said Pennoyer and Grief.

Later, when the cigarettes had become exhausted, Hawker volunteered to go after a further supply, and as he arose a question seemed to come to the edge of Florinda's lips and pend there. The moment that the door was closed upon him she demanded: "What is that about the two violets?"

"Nothing at all," answered Pennoyer, apparently much aggrieved. He sat back with an air of being a fortress of reticence.

"Oh, go on, tell me. Penny, I think you are very mean. Grief, you tell me."

> "The silver moon is shining.
>   Oh, come my love to me.
>   My heart——"

"Be still, Wrinkles, will you. What was it, Grief? Oh, go ahead and tell me."

"What do you want to know for?" cried Grief, vastly exasperated. "You've got more blamed curiosity. It isn't anything at all, I keep saying to you."

"Well, I know it is," said Florinda, sullenly, "or you would tell me."

When Hawker brought the cigarettes, Florinda smoked one and then announced: "Well, I must go now."

"Who is going to take you home, Splutter?"

"Oh, any one," replied Florinda.

"I tell you what," said Grief. "We'll throw some poker hands, and the one who wins will have the distinguished honor of conveying Miss Splutter to her home and mother."

Pennoyer and Wrinkles speedily routed the dishes to one end of the table. Grief's fingers spun the halves of a pack of cards together with the pleased eagerness of a good player. The faces grew solemn with the gambling solemnity. "Now, you Indians," said Grief, dealing. "A draw, you understand, and then a show-down."

Florinda leaned forward in her chair until it was poised on two legs. The cards of Purple Sanderson and of Hawker were faced toward her. Sanderson was gravely regarding two pair—aces and queens. Hawker scanned a little pair of sevens. "They draw, don't they?" she said to Grief.

"Certainly," said Grief. "How many, Wrink?"

"Four," replied Wrinkles, plaintively.

"Gimme three," said Pennoyer.

"Gimme one," said Sanderson.

"Gimme three," said Hawker. When he picked up his hand again Florinda's chair was tilted perilously. She saw another seven added to the little pair. Sanderson's draw had not assisted him.

"Same to the dealer," said Grief. "What you got, Wrink?"

"Nothing," said Wrinkles, exhibiting it face upward on the table. "Good-by, Florinda."

"Well, I've got two small pair," ventured Pennoyer, hopefully. "Beat 'em?"

"No good," said Sanderson. "Two pair—aces up."

"No good," said Hawker. "Three sevens."

"Beats me," said Grief. "Billie, you are the fortunate man. Heaven guide you on Third avenue."

Florinda had gone to the window. "Who won?" she asked, wheeling about carelessly.

"Billie Hawker."

"What? Did he?" she said in surprise.

"Never mind, Splutter. I'll win sometime," said Pennoyer. "Me, too," cried Grief. "Good-night, old girl," said Wrinkles. They crowded in the doorway. "Hold onto Billie. Remember the two steps going up." Pennoyer called intelligently into the stygian blackness: "Can you see all right?"

Florinda lived in a flat with fire escapes written all over the face of it. The street in front was being repaired. It had been said by imbecile residents of the vicinity that the paving was never allowed to remain down for a sufficient time to be invalided by the tramping millions, but that it was kept perpetually stacked in little mountains through the unceasing vigilance of a virtuous and heroic city government which insisted that everything should be repaired. The alderman for the district had sometimes asked indignantly of his fellow-members why this street had not been repaired, and they, aroused, had at once ordered it to be repaired. Moreover, shopkeepers whose stables were adjacent placed trucks and other vehicles strategically in the darkness. Into this tangled midnight Hawker conducted Florinda. The great avenue behind them was no more than a level stream of yellow light, and the distant merry bells might have been on boats floating down it. Grim loneliness hung over the uncouth shapes in the street which was being repaired.

"Billie," said the girl suddenly, " what makes you so mean to me?"

A peaceful citizen emerged from behind a pile of debris, but he might not have been a peaceful citizen, so the girl clung to Hawker.

"Why, I'm not mean to you, am I?"

"Yes," she answered. As they stood on the steps of the flat of innumerable fire escapes, she slowly turned and looked up at him. Her face was of a strange pallor in this darkness and her eyes were as when the moon shines in a lake of the hills.

He returned her glance. "Florinda," he cried, as if enlightened, and gulping suddenly at something in his throat. The girl studied the steps and moved from side to side, as do the guilty ones in country schoolhouses. Then she went slowly into the flat.

There was a little red lamp hanging on a pile of stones to warn people that the street was being repaired.

Chapter XXV

"I'LL GET MY CHECK from the *Gamin* on Saturday," said Grief. "They bought that string of comics."

"Well, then, we'll arrange the present funds to last until Saturday noon," said Wrinkles. "That gives us quite a lot. We can have a table d'hote on Friday night."

However, the cashier of the *Gamin* office looked under his respectable brass wiring and said: "Very sorry, Mr.—er—Warwickson, but our payday is Monday. Come around any time after ten."

"Oh, it doesn't matter," said Grief.

When he plunged into the den his visage flamed with rage. "Don't get my check until Monday morning, any time after ten," he yelled, and flung a portfolio of mottled green into the danger zone of the casts.

"Thunder," said Pennoyer, sinking at once to a profound despair.

"Monday morning, any time after ten," murmured Wrinkles in astonishment and sorrow.

While Grief marched to and fro threatening the furniture, Pennoyer and Wrinkles allowed their under jaws to fall and remained as men smitten between the eyes by the god of calamity.

"Singular thing," muttered Pennoyer at last. "You get so frightfully hungry as soon as you learn that there are no more meals coming."

"Oh, well——" said Wrinkles. He took up his guitar.

> Oh, some folks say dat a niggah won' steal,
>   'Way down yondeh in d' cohn'fiel',
> But Ah caught two in my cohn'fiel',
>   'Way down yondeh in d' cohn'fiel'.

"Oh, let up," said Grief, as if unwilling to be moved from his despair.

"Oh, let up," said Pennoyer, as if he disliked the voice and the ballad.

In his studio Hawker sat braced nervously forward on a

little stool before his tall Dutch easel. Three sketches lay on the floor near him and he glared at them constantly while painting at the large canvas on the easel.

He seemed engaged in some kind of a duel. His hair dishevelled, his eyes gleaming, he was in a deadly scuffle. In the sketches was the landscape of heavy blue, as if seen through powder smoke, and all the skies burned red. There was in these notes a sinister quality of hopelessness, eloquent of a defeat, as if the scene represented the last hour on a field of disastrous battle. Hawker seemed attacking with this picture something fair and beautiful of his own life, a possession of his mind, and he did it fiercely, mercilessly, formidably. His arm moved with the energy of a strange wrath. He might have been thrusting with a sword.

There was a knock at the door. "Come in." Pennoyer entered sheepishly. "Well?" cried Hawker, with an echo of savagery in his voice. He turned from the canvas precisely as one might emerge from a fight. "Oh," he said, perceiving Pennoyer. The glow in his eyes slowly changed. "What is it, Penny?"

"Billie," said Pennoyer, "Grief was to get his check to-day, but they put him off until Monday, and so, you know—er—well——"

"Oh," said Hawker again.

When Pennoyer had gone, Hawker sat motionless before his work. He stared at the canvas in a meditation so profound that it was probably unconscious of itself.

The light from above his head slanted more and more toward the east.

Once he arose and lighted a pipe. He returned to the easel and stood staring with his hands in his pockets. He moved like one in a sleep. Suddenly the gleam shot into his eyes again. He dropped to the stool and grabbed a brush. At the end of a certain long tumultuous period he clinched his pipe more firmly in his teeth and puffed strongly. The thought might have occurred to him that it was not a-light, for he looked at it with a vague, questioning glance. There came another knock at the door. "Go to the devil," he shouted without turning his head.

Hollanden crossed the corridor then to the den.

"Hi, there, Hollie! Hello, boy! Just the fellow we want to see! Come in—sit down—hit a pipe. Say, who was the girl Billie Hawker went mad over this summer?"

"Blazes!" said Hollanden, recovering slowly from this onslaught. "Who—what—how did you Indians find it out?"

"Oh, we tumbled," they cried in delight. "We tumbled."

"There!" said Hollanden, reproaching himself. "And I thought you were such a lot of blockheads."

"Oh, we tumbled," they cried again, in their ecstasy. "But who is she? That's the point."

"Well, she was a girl."

"Yes. Go on."

"A New York girl."

"Yes."

"A perfectly stunning New York girl."

"Yes. Go ahead."

"A perfectly stunning New York girl of a very wealthy and rather old-fashioned family."

"Well, I'll be shot! You don't mean it? She is practically seated on top of the Matterhorn. Poor old Billie!"

"Not at all," said Hollanden, composedly.

It was a common habit of Purple Sanderson to call attention at night to the resemblance of the den to some little ward in a hospital. Upon this night, when Sanderson and Grief were buried in slumber, Pennoyer moved restlessly. "Wrink," he called softly into the darkness in the direction of the divan which was secretly a coal box.

"What?" said Wrinkles in a surly voice. His mind had evidently been caught at the threshold of sleep.

"Do you think Florinda cares much for Billie Hawker?"

Wrinkles fretted through some oaths. "How in thunder do I know?" The divan creaked as he turned his face to the wall.

"Well——" muttered Pennoyer.

Chapter XXVI

T HE HARMONY of summer sunlight on leaf and blade of green was not known to the two windows which looked forth at an obviously endless building of brown stone about which there was the poetry of a prison. Inside, great folds of lace swept down in orderly cascades, as water trained to fall mathematically. The colossal chandelier, gleaming like a Siamese headdress, caught the subtle flashes from unknown places.

Hawker heard a step and the soft swishing of a woman's dress. He turned toward the door swiftly with a certain dramatic impulsiveness. But when she entered the room he said: "How delighted I am to see you again."

She had said: "Why, Mr. Hawker, it was so charming in you to come."

It did not appear that Hawker's tongue could wag to his purpose. The girl seemed in her mind to be frantically shuffling her pack of social receipts and finding none of them made to meet this situation. Finally Hawker said that he thought "Hearts at War" was a very good play.

"Did you?" she said in surprise. "I thought it much like the others."

"Well, so did I," he cried hastily. "The same figures moving around in the mud of modern confusion. I really didn't intend to say that I liked it. Fact is—meeting you rather moved me out of my mental track."

"Mental track?" she said. "I didn't know clever people had mental tracks. I thought it was a privilege of the theologians."

"Who told you I was clever?" he demanded.

"Why—" she said, opening her eyes wider. "Nobody."

Hawker smiled and looked upon her with gratitude. "Of course! 'Nobody!' There couldn't be such an idiot. I am sure you should be astonished to learn that I believed such an imbecile existed. But——"

"Oh," she said.

"But I think you might have spoken less bluntly."

"Well," she said, after wavering for a time, "you are clever, aren't you?"

"Certainly," he answered reassuringly.

"Well, then?" she retorted with triumph in her tone. And this interrogation was apparently to her the final victorious argument.

At his discomfiture, Hawker grinned.

"You haven't asked news of Stanley," he said. "Why don't you ask news of Stanley?"

"Oh, and how was he?"

"The last I saw of him he stood down at the end of the pasture—the pasture, you know—wagging his tail in blissful anticipation of an invitation to come with me and when it finally dawned upon him that he was not to receive it, he turned and went back toward the house 'like a man suddenly stricken with age,' as the story-tellers eloquently say. Poor old dog."

"And you left him?" she said reproachfully. Then she asked: "Do you remember how he amused you playing with the ants at the falls?"

"No."

"Why, he did. He pawed at the moss and you sat there laughing. I remember distinctly."

"You remember distinctly? Why, I thought—well, your back was turned, you know. Your gaze was fixed upon something before you and you were utterly lost to the rest of the world. You could not have known if Stanley pawed the moss and I laughed. So, you see, you are mistaken. As a matter of fact, I utterly deny that Stanley pawed the moss or that I laughed or that any ants appeared at the falls at all."

"I have always said that you should have been a Chinese soldier of fortune," she observed, musingly. "Your daring and ingenuity would be prized by the Chinese."

"There are innumerable tobacco jars in China," he said, measuring the advantages. "Moreover, there is no perspective. You don't have to walk two miles to see a friend. No. He is always there near you, so that you can't move a chair without hitting your distant friend. You——"

"Did Hollie remain as attentive as ever to the Worcester girls?"

"Yes, of course. As attentive as ever. He dragged me into all manner of tennis games——"

"Why, I thought you loved to play tennis?"

"Oh, well——" said Hawker. "I did until you left."

"My sister has gone to the park with the children. I know she will be vexed when she finds that you have called."

Ultimately Hawker said: "Do you remember our ride behind my father's oxen?"

"No," she answered. "I had forgotten it completely. Did we ride behind your father's oxen?"

After a moment he said: "That remark would be prized by the Chinese. We did. And you most graciously professed to enjoy it, which earned my deep gratitude and admiration. For no one knows better than I," he added meekly, "that it is no great comfort or pleasure to ride behind my father's oxen."

She smiled retrospectively. "Do you remember how the people on the porch hurried to the railing?"

Chapter XXVII

NEAR THE DOOR, the stout proprietress sat entrenched behind the cash desk in a Parisian manner. She looked with practiced amiability at her guests, who dined noisily and with great fire, discussing momentous problems furiously, making wide maniacal gestures through the cigarette smoke. Meanwhile the little handful of waiters ran to and fro wildly. Imperious and importunate cries rang at them from all directions. "Gustave! Adolphe!" Their faces expressed a settled despair. They answered calls, commands, oaths, in a semi-distraction, fleeting among the tables as if pursued by some dodging animal. Their breaths came in gasps. If they had been convict laborers they could not have surveyed their positions with countenances of more unspeakable injury. Withal they carried incredible masses of dishes and threaded their ways with skill. They served people with such speed and violence that it often resembled a personal assault. They struck two blows at a table and left there a knife and a fork. Then came the viands in a volley. The clatter of this business was loud and bewilderingly rapid like the gallop of a thousand horses.

In a remote corner a band of mandolins and guitars played the long, sweeping, mad melody of a Spanish waltz. It seemed to go tingling to the hearts of many of the diners. Their eyes glittered with enthusiasm, with abandon, with deviltry. They swung their heads from side to side in rhythmic movement. High in air curled the smoke from the innumerable cigarettes. The long black claret bottles were in clusters upon the tables. At an end of the hall, two men with maudlin grins sang the waltz uproariously, but always a trifle belated.

An unsteady person leaning back in his chair to murmur swift compliments to a woman at another table, suddenly sprawled out upon the floor. He scrambled to his feet, and turning to the escort of the woman, heatedly blamed him for the accident. They exchanged a series of tense bitter insults, which spatted back and forth between them like pellets. People arose from their chairs and stretched their necks. The musicians stood in a body, their faces turned with expressions of keen excitement toward this quarrel, but their fingers still twinkling over their instruments, sending into the middle of this turmoil the passionate mad Spanish music. The proprietor of the place came in agitation and plunged headlong into the argument, where he thereafter appeared as a frantic creature, harried to the point of insanity, for they buried him at once in long vociferous threats, explanations, charges, every form of declamation known to their race. The music, the noise of the galloping horses, the voices of the brawlers gave the whole thing the quality of war.

There were two men in the cafe who seemed to be tranquil. Hollanden carefully stacked one lump of sugar upon another in the middle of his saucer and poured cognac over them. He touched a match to the cognac and the blue and yellow flames eddied in the saucer. "I wonder what those two fools are bellowing at?" he said, turning about irritably.

"Hanged if I know," muttered Hawker in reply. "This place makes me weary anyhow. Hear the blooming din."

"What's the matter?" said Hollanden. "You used to say this was the one natural, the one truly Bohemian resort in the city. You swore by it."

"Well, I don't like it so much any more."

"Ho," cried Hollanden. "You're getting correct—that's it exactly. You will become one of these intensely—— Look, Billie, the little one is going to punch him."

"No, he isn't. They never do," said Hawker, morosely. "Why did you bring me here to-night, Hollie?"

"I? I bring you? Good heavens, I came as a concession to you. What are you talking about? Hi, the little one is going to punch him—sure!"

He gave the scene his undivided attention for a moment. Then he turned again. "You will become correct. I know you will. I have been watching. You are about to achieve a respectability that will make a stone saint blush for himself. What's the matter with you? You act as if you thought falling in love with a girl was a most extraordinary circumstance. I wish they would put those people out. Of course, I know that you—— There! The little one has swiped at him at last."

After a time he resumed his oration. "Of course, I know that you are not reformed in the matter of this uproar and this remarkable consumption of bad wine. It is not that. It is a fact that there are indications that some other citizen was fortunate enough to possess your napkin before you, and moreover you are sure that you would hate to be caught by your correct friends with any such consomme in front of you as we had to-night. You have got an eye suddenly for all kinds of gilt. You are in the way of becoming a most unbearable person. Oh, look—the little one and the proprietor are having it now. You are in the way of becoming a most unbearable person. Presently many of your friends will not be fine enough. In heaven's name, why don't they throw him out? Are they going to howl and gesticulate there all night?"

"Well," said Hawker, "a man would be a fool if he did like this dinner."

"Certainly. But what an immaterial part in the glory of this joint is the dinner. Who cares about the dinner? No one comes here to eat—that's what you always claimed. Well, there, at last they are throwing him out. I hope he lands on his head. Really, you know, Billie, it is such a fine thing being in love that one is sure to be detestable to the rest of the world, and that is the reason they created a proverb to the other effect. You want to look out."

"You talk like a blasted old granny," said Hawker. "Haven't changed at all. This place is all right. Only——"

"You are gone," interrupted Hollanden in a sad voice. "It is very plain. You are gone."

Chapter XXVIII

THE PROPRIETOR of the place, having pushed to the street the little man who may have been the most vehement, came again and resumed the discussion with the remainder of the men of war. Many of these had volunteered, and they were very enduring.

"Yes, you are gone," said Hollanden, with the sobriety of graves in his voice. "You are gone! Hi," he cried, "there is Lucian Pontiac! Hi, Pontiac! Sit down here!"

A man with a tangle of hair and with that about his mouth which showed that he had spent many years in manufacturing a proper modesty with which to bear his greatness, came toward them smiling.

"Hello, Pontiac," said Hollanden. "Here's another great painter. Do you know Mr. Hawker? Mr. William Hawker— Mr. Pontiac."

"Mr. Hawker—delighted," said Pontiac. "Although I have not known you personally, I can assure you that I have long been a great admirer of your abilities."

The proprietor of the place and the men of war had at length agreed to come to an amicable understanding. They drank liquors, while each firmly but now silently upheld his dignity.

"Charming place," said Pontiac. "So thoroughly Parisian in spirit. And from time to time, Mr. Hawker, I use one of your models. Must say she has the best arm and wrist in the universe. Stunning figure—stunning."

"You mean Florinda?" said Hawker.

"Yes. That's the name. Very fine girl. Lunches with me from time to time and chatters so volubly. That's how I learned you posed her occasionally. If the models didn't gossip, we would never know what painters were addicted to profanity. Now that old Thorndike—he told me you swore like a drill-sergeant if the model winked a finger at the critical time. Very fine girl, Florinda. And honest, too. Honest as the devil. Very curious thing. Of course, honesty among the girl models is very common, very common—quite universal thing, you know—but then it always strikes me as being very curious, very curious. I've been much attracted by your girl, Florinda."

"My girl?" said Hawker.

"Well, she always speaks of you in a proprietory way, you know. And then she considers that she owes you some kind of obedience and allegiance and devotion. I remember last week I said to her: 'You can go now. Come again Friday.' But she said: 'I don't think I can come on Friday. Billie Hawker is home now, and he may want me then.' Said I: 'The devil take Billie Hawker. He hasn't engaged you for Friday, has he? Well, then, I engage you now.' But she shook her head. No, she couldn't come on Friday. Billie Hawker was home, and he might want her any day. 'Well, then,' said I, 'you have my permission to do as you please, since you are resolved upon it anyway. Go to your Billie Hawker.' Did you need her on Friday?"

"No," said Hawker.

"Well, then, the minx, I shall scold her. Stunning figure—stunning. It was only last week that old Charley Master said to me mournfully: 'There are no more good models. Great Scott, not a one.' 'You're 'way off, my boy,' I said. 'There is one good model.' And then I named your girl. I mean the girl who claims to be yours."

"Poor little beggar," said Hollanden.

"Who?" said Pontiac.

"Florinda," answered Hollanden. "I suppose——"

Pontiac interrupted. "Oh, of course, it is too bad. Everything is too bad. My dear sir, nothing is so much to be regretted as the universe. But this Florinda is such a sturdy young soul. The world is against her, but, bless your heart, she is equal to the battle. She is strong in the manner of a little child. Why, you don't know her. She——"

"I know her very well."

"Well, perhaps you do, but for my part I think you don't appreciate her formidable character. And stunning figure—stunning."

"Damn it," said Hawker to his coffee cup, which he had accidentally overturned.

"Well," resumed Pontiac, "she is a stunning model and I think, Mr. Hawker, you are to be envied."

"Eh?" said Hawker.

"I wish I could inspire my models with such obedience and devotion. Then I would not be obliged to rail at them for being late and have to badger them for not showing up at all. She has a beautiful figure—beautiful."

Chapter XXIX

WHEN HAWKER WENT again to the house of the great windows, he looked first at the colossal chandelier, and perceiving that it had not moved, he smiled in a certain friendly and familiar way.

"It must be a fine thing," said the girl, dreamily. "I always feel envious of that sort of life."

"What sort of life?"

"Why—I don't know exactly—but there must be a great deal of freedom about it. I went to a studio tea once, and——"

"A studio tea! Merciful heavens! Go on."

"Yes. A studio tea. Don't you like them? To be sure, we didn't know whether the man could paint very well, and I suppose you think it is an imposition for any one who is not a great painter to give a tea."

"Go on."

"Well, he had the dearest little Japanese servants, and some of the cups came from Algiers and some from Turkey and some from—— What's the matter?"

"Go on. I'm not interrupting you."

"Well, that's all. Excepting that everything was charming in color and I thought what a lazy, beautiful life the man must lead, lounging in such a studio, smoking monogrammed cigarettes and remarking how badly all the other men painted."

"Very fascinating. But——"

"Oh, you are going to ask if he could draw. I'm sure I don't know, but the tea that he gave was charming."

"I was on the verge of telling you something about artist life, but if you have seen a lot of draperies and drank from a cup of Algiers, you know all about it."

"You, then, were going to make it something very terrible and tell how young painters struggled and all that."

"No, not exactly. But listen. I suppose there is an aristocracy who, whether they paint well or paint ill, certainly do give charming teas, as you say, and all other kinds of charming affairs, too, but when I hear people talk as if that was the whole life it makes my hair rise, you know, because I am sure that as they get to know me better and better they will see

375

how I fall short of that kind of an existence, and I shall prob-
ably take a great tumble in their estimation. They might even
conclude that I cannot paint, which would be very unfair,
because I can paint, you know."

"Well, proceed to arrange my point of view so that you
sha'n't tumble in my estimation when I discover that you
don't lounge in a studio, smoke monogrammed cigarettes and
remark how badly the other men paint."

"That's it. That's precisely what I wish to do."

"Begin."

"Well, in the first place——"

"In the first place—what?"

"Well, I started to study when I was very poor, you under-
stand. Look here, I'm telling you these things because I want
you to know, somehow. It isn't that I'm not ashamed of it.
Well, I began very poor, and I—as a matter of fact—I—well,
I earned myself over half the money for my studying and the
other half I bullied and badgered and beat out of my poor
old dad. I worked pretty hard in Paris and I returned here
expecting to become a great painter at once. I didn't, though.
In fact, I had my worst moments then. It lasted for some
years. Of course, the faith and endurance of my father was by
this time worn to a shadow. This time when I needed him
the most. However, things got a little better and a little bet-
ter, until I found that by working quite hard I could make
what was to me a fair income. That's where I am now, too."

"Why are you so ashamed of this story?"

"The poverty."

"Poverty isn't anything to be ashamed of."

"Great heavens, have you the temerity to get off that old
nonsensical remark. Poverty is everything to be ashamed of.
Did you ever see a person not ashamed of his poverty? Cer-
tainly not. Of course when a man gets very rich he will brag
so loudly of the poverty of his youth that one would never
suppose that he was once ashamed of it. But he was."

"Well, anyhow, you shouldn't be ashamed of the story you
have just told me."

"Why not? Do you refuse to allow me the great right of
being like other men?"

"I think it was—brave, you know."

"Brave—nonsense. Those things are not brave. Impression to that effect created by the men who have been through the mill for the greater glory of the men who have been through the mill."

"I don't like to hear you talk that way. It sounds wicked, you know."

"Well, it certainly wasn't heroic. I can remember distinctly that there was not one heroic moment."

"No, but it was—it was——"

"It was what?"

"Well, somehow I like it, you know."

Chapter XXX

"THERE'S THREE of them," said Grief, in a hoarse whisper. "Four, I tell you!" said Wrinkles, in a low, excited tone.

"Four!" breathed Pennoyer, with decision.

They held fierce pantomimic argument. From the corridor came sounds of rustling dresses and rapid feminine conversation.

Grief had kept his ear to the panel of the door. His hand was stretched back warning the others to silence. Presently he turned his head and whispered: "Three!"

"Four!" whispered Pennoyer and Wrinkles.

"Hollie is there, too," whispered Grief. "Billie is unlocking the door. Now, they're going in. Hear them cry out, 'Oh, isn't it lovely!' Jinks!" He began a noiseless dance about the room. "Jinks, don't I wish I had a big studio and a little reputation. Wouldn't I have my swell friends come to see me and wouldn't I entertain 'em." He adopted a descriptive manner and with his forefinger indicated various spaces of the wall. "Here is a little thing I did in Brittany. Peasant woman in sabots. This brown spot here is the peasant woman and those two white things are the sabots. Peasant woman in sabots, don't you see? Women in Brittany, of course, all wear sabots, you understand. Convenience of the painters. I see you are looking at that little thing I did in Morocco. Ah, you admire it? Well, not so bad—not so bad. Arab smoking pipe squatting in doorway. This long streak here is the pipe. Clever, you say? Oh, thanks. You are too kind. Well, all Arabs do that, you know. Sole occupation. Convenience of the painters. Now, this little thing here I did in Venice. Grand canal, you know. Gondolier leaning on his oar. Convenience of the painters. Oh, yes, American subjects are well enough, but hard to find, you know, hard to find. Morocco, Venice, Brittany, Holland—all ablaze with color, you know—quaint form—all that. We are so hideously modern over here. And besides nobody has painted us much. How the devil can I paint America when nobody has done it before me? My dear sir, are you aware that that would be originality? Good

378

heavens! We are not aesthetic, you understand. Oh, yes, some good mind comes along and understands a thing and does it, and after that it is aesthetic—yes, of course, but then —well—— Now, here is a little Holland thing of mine— it——"

The others had evidently not been heeding him. "Shut up," said Wrinkles, suddenly. "Listen." Grief paused his harangue and they sat in silence, their lips apart, their eyes from time to time exchanging eloquent messages. A dulled melodious babble came from Hawker's studio.

At length Pennoyer murmured wistfully: "I would like to see her."

Wrinkles started noiselessly to his feet. "Well, I tell you she's a peach. I was going up the steps, you know, with a loaf of bread under my arm when I chanced to look up the street and saw Billie and Hollanden coming with four of them."

"Three," said Grief.

"Four! And I tell you I scattered. One of the two with Billie was a peach—a peach."

"Oh, lord," groaned the others, enviously. "Billie's in luck."

"How do you know," said Wrinkles. "Billie is a blamed good fellow, but that doesn't say she will care for him—more likely that she won't."

They sat again in silence, grinning and listening to the murmur of voices.

There came the sound of a step in the hallway. It ceased at a point opposite the door of Hawker's studio. Presently it was heard again. Florinda entered the den. "Hello," she cried. "Who is over in Billie's place. I was just going to knock——"

They motioned at her violently. "Sh," they whispered. Their countenances were very impressive.

"What's the matter with you fellows," asked Florinda, in her ordinary tone. Whereupon they made gestures of still greater wildness. "S-s-sh."

Florinda lowered her voice properly. "Who is over there?"

"Some swells," they whispered.

Florinda bended her head. Presently she gave a little start. "Who is over there?" Her voice became a tone of deep awe. "She?"

Wrinkles and Grief exchanged a swift glance. Pennoyer said gruffly: "Who do you mean?"

"Why," said Florinda, "you know. She. The—the girl that Billie likes."

Pennoyer hesitated for a moment, and then said wrathfully: "Of course she is! Who do you suppose?"

"Oh," said Florinda. She took a seat upon the divan, which was privately a coal box, and unbuttoned her jacket at the throat. "Is she—is she—very handsome, Wrink?"

Wrinkles replied stoutly: "No."

Grief said: "Let's make a sneak down the hall to the little unoccupied room at the front of the building and look from the window there. When they go out we can pipe 'em off."

"Come on," they exclaimed, accepting this plan with glee.

Wrinkles opened the door and seemed about to glide away, when he suddenly turned and shook his head. "It's dead wrong," he said, ashamed.

"Oh, go on," eagerly whispered the others. Presently they stole pattering down the corridor, grinning, exclaiming and cautioning each other.

At the window Pennoyer said: "Now, for heaven's sake, don't let them see you. Be careful, Grief, you'll tumble. Don't lean on me that way, Wrink. Think I'm a barn door? Here they come. Keep back. Don't let them see you."

"O-o-oh," said Grief. "Talk about a peach. Well, I should say so."

Florinda's fingers tore at Wrinkles' coat sleeve. "Wrink, Wrink, is that her? Is that her? On the left of Billie? Is that her, Wrink?"

"What? Yes. Stop pinching me. Yes, I tell you. That's her. Are you deaf?"

Chapter XXXI

IN THE EVENING Pennoyer conducted Florinda to the flat of many fire escapes. After a period of silent tramping through the great golden avenue and the street that was being repaired, she said: "Penny, you are very good to me."

"Why?" said Pennoyer.

"Oh, because you are. You—you are very good to me, Penny."

"Well, I guess I'm not killing myself."

"There isn't many fellows like you."

"No?"

"No. There isn't many fellows like you, Penny. I tell you most everything and you just listen and don't argue with me and tell me I'm a fool because you know that it—because you know that it can't be helped anyhow."

"Oh, nonsense, you kid. Almost anybody would be glad to——"

"Penny, do you think she is very beautiful?" Florinda's voice had a singular quality of awe in it.

"Well," replied Pennoyer, "I don't know."

"Yes, you do, Penny. Go ahead and tell me."

"Well——"

"Go ahead."

"Well, she is rather handsome, you know."

"Yes," said Florinda, dejectedly. "I suppose she is." After a time she cleared her throat and remarked indifferently: "I suppose Billie cares a lot for her?"

"Oh, I imagine that he does. In a way."

"Why, of course he does," insisted Florinda. "What do you mean by 'in a way'? You know very well that Billie thinks his eyes of her."

"No, I don't."

"Yes you do. You know you do. You are talking in that way just to brace me up. You know you are."

"No, I'm not."

"Penny," said Florinda, thankfully, "what makes you so good to me?"

381

"Oh, I guess I'm not so astonishingly good to you. Don't be silly."

"But you are good to me, Penny. You don't make fun of me the way—the way the other boys would. You are just as good as you can be. But you do think she is beautiful, don't you?"

"They wouldn't make fun of you," said Pennoyer.

"But do you think she is beautiful?"

"Look here, Splutter, let up on that, will you? You keep harping on one string all the time. Don't bother me."

"But, honest now, Penny, you do think she is beautiful?"

"Well, then, confound it—no. No. No."

"Oh, yes, you do, Penny. Go ahead now. Don't deny it just because you are talking to me. Own up now, Penny. You do think she is beautiful?"

"Well," said Pennoyer, in a dull roar of irritation, "do you?"

Florinda walked in silence, her eyes upon the yellow flashes which lights sent to the pavement. In the end she said: "Yes."

"Yes, what?" asked Pennoyer sharply.

"Yes, she—yes, she is—beautiful."

"Well, then?" cried Pennoyer, abruptly closing the discussion.

Florinda announced something as a fact. "Billie thinks his eyes of her."

"How do you know he does?"

"Don't scold at me, Penny. You—you——"

"I'm not scolding at you. There! What a goose you are, Splutter. Don't for heaven's sake go to whimpering on the street. I didn't say anything to make you feel that way. Come, pull yourself together."

"I'm not whimpering."

"No, of course not; but then you look as if you were on the edge of it. What a little idiot!"

Chapter XXXII

WHEN THE SNOW FELL upon the clashing life of the city, the exiled stones, beaten by myriad strange feet, were told of the dark silent forests where the flakes swept through the hemlocks and swished softly against the boulders.

In his studio Hawker smoked a pipe, clasping his knee with thoughtful interlocked fingers. He was gazing sourly at his finished picture. Once he started to his feet with a cry of vexation. Looking back over his shoulder, he swore an insult into the face of the picture. He paced to and fro smoking belligerently and from time to time eyeing it. The helpless thing remained upon the easel facing him.

Hollanden entered and stopped abruptly at sight of the great scowl. "What's wrong, now?" he said.

Hawker gestured at the picture. "That dunce of a thing. It makes me tired. It isn't worth a hang. Blame it!"

"What?" Hollanden strode forward and stood before the painting with legs apart in a properly critical manner. "What? Why, you said it was your best thing."

"Aw," said Hawker, waving his arms, "it's no good. I abominate it. I didn't get what I wanted, I tell you. I didn't get what I wanted. That?" he shouted, pointing thrust-way at it. "That? It's vile. Aw, it makes me weary."

"You're in a nice state," said Hollanden, turning to take a critical view of the painter. "What has got into you now. I swear—you are more kinds of a chump!"

Hawker crooned dismally. "I can't paint. I can't paint for a damn. I'm no good. What in thunder was I invented for, anyhow, Hollie?"

"You're a fool," said Hollanden. "I hope to die if I ever saw such a complete idiot. You give me a pain. Just because she don't——"

"It isn't that. She has nothing to do with it, although I know well enough—I know well enough——"

"What?"

"I know well enough she doesn't care a hang for me. It isn't that. It is because—it is because I can't paint. Look at

383

that thing over there. Remember the thought and energy I——
Damn the thing."

"Why, did you have a row with her?" asked Hollanden,
perplexed. "I didn't know——"

"No, of course, you didn't know," cried Hawker, sneering.
"Because I had no row. It isn't that, I tell you. But I know
well enough"—he shook his fist, vaguely—"that she don't
care an old tomato can for me. Why should she?" he de-
manded, with a curious defiance. "In the name of heaven,
why should she?"

"I don't know," said Hollanden. "I don't know, I'm sure.
But then, women have no social logic. This is the great bless-
ing of the world. There is only one thing which is superior
to the multiplicity of social forms, and that is a woman's
mind—a young woman's mind. Oh, of course, sometimes
they are logical, but let a woman be so once and she will
repent of it to the end of her days. The safety of the world's
balance lies in woman's illogical mind. I think——"

"Go to blazes," said Hawker. "I don't care what you think.
I am sure of one thing, and that is that she doesn't care a
hang for me."

"I think," Hollanden continued, "that society is doing very
well in its work of bravely lawing away at Nature, but there
is one immovable thing—a woman's illogical mind. That is
our safety. Thank heaven, it——"

"Go to blazes," said Hawker again.

Chapter XXXIII

As HAWKER AGAIN entered the room of the great windows he glanced in sidelong bitterness at the chandelier. When he was seated, he looked at it in open defiance and hatred.

Men in the street were shovelling at the snow. The noise of their instruments scraping on the stones came plainly to Hawker's ears in a harsh chorus, and this sound at this time was perhaps to him a miserere.

"I came to tell you," he began. "I came to tell you that perhaps I am going away."

"Going away?" she cried. "Where?"

"Well, I don't know—quite. You see I am rather indefinite as yet. I thought of going for the winter somewhere in the Southern States. I am decided merely this much, you know—I am going somewhere. But I don't know where. 'Way off, anyhow."

"We shall be very sorry to lose you," she remarked. "We——"

"And I thought," he continued, "that I would come and say 'adios' now for fear that I might leave very suddenly. I do that sometimes. I'm afraid you will forget me very soon, but I want to tell you that——"

"Why," said the girl in some surprise, "you speak as if you were going away for all time. You surely do not mean to utterly desert New York?"

"I think you misunderstand me," he said. "I give this important air to my farewell to you because to me it is a very important event. Perhaps you recollect that once I told you that I cared for you. Well, I still care for you and so I can only go away somewhere—some place 'way off—where—where—— See?"

"New York is a very large place," she observed.

"Yes, New York is a very large—— How good of you to remind me. But then you don't understand. You can't understand. I know I can find no place where I will cease to remember you, but then I can find some place where I can cease to remember in a way that I am myself. I shall never try to forget you. Those two violets, you know—one I found near

385

the tennis court and the other you gave me, you remember—
I shall take them with me."

"Here," said the girl, tugging at her gown for a moment.
"Here. Here's a third one." She thrust a violet toward him.

"If you were not so serenely insolent," said Hawker, "I
would think that you felt sorry for me. I don't wish you to
feel sorry for me. And I don't wish to be melodramatic. I
know it is all commonplace enough, and I didn't mean to act
like a tenor. Please don't pity me."

"I don't," she replied. She gave the violet a little fling.

Hawker lifted his head suddenly and glowered at her. "No,
you don't," he at last said slowly, "you don't. Moreover there
is no reason why you should take the trouble. But——"

He paused when the girl leaned and peered over the arm
of her chair precisely in the manner of a child at the brink of
a fountain. "There's my violet on the floor," she said. "You
treated it quite contemptuously, didn't you?"

"Yes."

Together they stared at the violet. Finally he stooped and
took it in his fingers. "I feel as if this third one was pelted at
me, but I shall keep it. You are rather a cruel person, but,
heaven guard us, that only fastens a man's love the more upon
a woman."

She laughed. "That is not a very good thing to tell a
woman."

"No," he said gravely, "it is not, but then I fancy that
somebody may have told you previously."

She stared at him and then said: "I think you are revenged
for my serene insolence."

"Great heavens, what an armor," he cried. "I suppose after
all, I did feel a trifle like a tenor when I first came here, but
you have chilled it all out of me. Let's talk upon indifferent
topics." But he started abruptly to his feet. "No," he said, "let
us not talk upon indifferent topics. I am not brave, I assure
you, and it—it might be too much for me." He held out his
hand. "Good-by."

"You are going?"

"Yes, I am going. Really I didn't think how it would bore
you for me to come around here and croak in this fashion."

"And you are not coming back for a long, long time?"

"Not for a long, long time." He mimicked her tone. "I have the three violets, now, you know, and you must remember that I took the third one even when you flung it at my head. That will remind you how submissive I was in my devotion. When you recall the two others, it will remind you of what a fool I was. Dare say you won't miss three violets."

"No," she said.

"Particularly the one you flung at my head. That violet was certainly freely-given."

"I didn't fling it at your head." She pondered for a time with her eyes upon the floor. Then she murmured: "No more freely-given than the one I gave you that night—that night at the inn."

"So very good of you to tell me so."

Her eyes were still upon the floor.

"Do you know," said Hawker, "it is very hard to go away and leave an impression in your mind that I am a fool. That is very hard. Now, you do think I am a fool, don't you?"

She remained silent. Once she lifted her eyes and gave him a swift look with much indignation in it.

"Now you are enraged. Well, what have I done?"

It seemed that some tumult was in her mind, for she cried out to him at last in sudden tearfulness: "Oh, do go. Go. Please. I want you to go."

Under this swift change, Hawker appeared as a man struck from the sky. He sprang to his feet, took two steps forward and spoke a word which was an explosion of delight and amazement. He said: "What?"

With heroic effort, she slowly raised her eyes until, a-light with anger, defiance, unhappiness, they met his eyes.

Later, she told him that he was perfectly ridiculous.

THE MONSTER

I

LITTLE JIM was, for the time, engine Number 36, and he was making the run between Syracuse and Rochester. He was fourteen minutes behind time, and the throttle was wide open. In consequence, when he swung around the curve at the flower-bed, a wheel of his cart destroyed a peony. Number 36 slowed down at once and looked guiltily at his father, who was mowing the lawn. The doctor had his back to this accident, and he continued to pace slowly to and fro, pushing the mower.

Jim dropped the tongue of the cart. He looked at his father and at the broken flower. Finally he went to the peony and tried to stand it on its pins, resuscitated, but the spine of it was hurt, and it would only hang limply from his hand. Jim could do no reparation. He looked again toward his father.

He went on to the lawn, very slowly, and kicking wretchedly at the turf. Presently his father came along with the whirring machine, while the sweet new grass blades spun from the knives. In a low voice, Jim said, "Pa!"

The doctor was shaving this lawn as if it were a priest's chin. All during the season he had worked at it in the coolness and peace of the evenings after supper. Even in the shadow of the cherry-trees the grass was strong and healthy. Jim raised his voice a trifle. "Pa!"

The doctor paused, and with the howl of the machine no longer occupying the sense, one could hear the robins in the cherry-trees arranging their affairs. Jim's hands were behind his back, and sometimes his fingers clasped and unclasped. Again he said, "Pa!" The child's fresh and rosy lip was lowered.

The doctor stared down at his son, thrusting his head forward and frowning attentively. "What is it, Jimmie?"

"Pa!" repeated the child at length. Then he raised his finger and pointed at the flower-bed. "There!"

"What?" said the doctor, frowning more. "What is it, Jim?"

After a period of silence, during which the child may have undergone a severe mental tumult, he raised his finger and repeated his former word—"There!" The father had respected this silence with perfect courtesy. Afterward his glance carefully followed the direction indicated by the child's finger, but he could see nothing which explained to him. "I don't understand what you mean, Jimmie," he said.

It seemed that the importance of the whole thing had taken away the boy's vocabulary. He could only reiterate, "There!"

The doctor mused upon the situation, but he could make nothing of it. At last he said, "Come, show me."

Together they crossed the lawn toward the flower-bed. At some yards from the broken peony Jimmie began to lag. "There!" The word came almost breathlessly.

"Where?" said the doctor.

Jimmie kicked at the grass. "There!" he replied.

The doctor was obliged to go forward alone. After some trouble he found the subject of the incident, the broken flower. Turning then, he saw the child lurking at the rear and scanning his countenance.

The father reflected. After a time he said, "Jimmie, come here." With an infinite modesty of demeanor the child came forward. "Jimmie, how did this happen?"

The child answered, "Now—I was playin' train—and—now—I runned over it."

"You were doing what?"

"I was playin' train."

The father reflected again. "Well, Jimmie," he said, slowly, "I guess you had better not play train any more to-day. Do you think you had better?"

"No, sir," said Jimmie.

During the delivery of the judgment the child had not faced his father, and afterward he went away, with his head lowered, shuffling his feet.

II

It was apparent from Jimmie's manner that he felt some kind of desire to efface himself. He went down to the stable. Henry Johnson, the negro who cared for the doctor's horses, was sponging the buggy. He grinned fraternally when he saw Jimmie coming. These two were pals. In regard to almost everything in life they seemed to have minds precisely alike.

Of course there were points of emphatic divergence. For instance, it was plain from Henry's talk that he was a very handsome negro, and he was known to be a light, a weight, and an eminence in the suburb of the town, where lived the larger number of the negroes, and obviously this glory was over Jimmie's horizon; but he vaguely appreciated it and paid deference to Henry for it mainly because Henry appreciated it and deferred to himself. However, on all points of conduct as related to the doctor, who was the moon, they were in complete but unexpressed understanding. Whenever Jimmie became the victim of an eclipse he went to the stable to solace himself with Henry's crimes. Henry, with the elasticity of his race, could usually provide a sin to place himself on a footing with the disgraced one. Perhaps he would remember that he had forgotten to put the hitching-strap in the back of the buggy on some recent occasion, and had been reprimanded by the doctor. Then these two would commune subtly and without words concerning their moon, holding themselves sympathetically as people who had committed similar treasons. On the other hand, Henry would sometimes choose to absolutely repudiate this idea, and when Jimmie appeared in his shame would bully him most virtuously, preaching with assurance the precepts of the doctor's creed, and pointing out to Jimmie all his abominations. Jimmie did not discover that this was odious in his comrade. He accepted it and lived in its shadow with humility, merely trying to conciliate the saintly Henry with acts of deference. Won by this attitude, Henry would sometimes allow the child to enjoy the felicity of squeezing the sponge over a buggy-wheel, even when Jimmie was still gory from unspeakable deeds.

Whenever Henry dwelt for a time in sackcloth, Jimmie did not patronize him at all. This was a justice of his age, his condition. He did not know. Besides, Henry could drive a horse, and Jimmie had a full sense of this sublimity. Henry personally conducted the moon during the splendid journeys through the country roads, where farms spread on all sides, with sheep, cows, and other marvels abounding.

"Hello, Jim!" said Henry, poising his sponge. Water was dripping from the buggy. Sometimes the horses in the stalls stamped thunderingly on the pine floor. There was an atmosphere of hay and of harness.

For a minute Jimmie refused to take an interest in anything. He was very downcast. He could not even feel the wonders of wagon-washing. Henry, while at his work, narrowly observed him.

"Your pop done wallop yer, didn't he?" he said at last.

"No," said Jimmie, defensively; "he didn't."

After this casual remark Henry continued his labor, with a scowl of occupation. Presently he said: "I done tol' yer many's th' time not to go a-foolin' an' a-projjeckin' with them flowers. Yer pop don' like it nohow." As a matter of fact, Henry had never mentioned flowers to the boy.

Jimmie preserved a gloomy silence, so Henry began to use seductive wiles in this affair of washing a wagon. It was not until he began to spin a wheel on the tree, and the sprinkling water flew everywhere, that the boy was visibly moved. He had been seated on the sill of the carriage-house door, but at the beginning of this ceremony he arose and circled toward the buggy, with an interest that slowly consumed the remembrance of a late disgrace.

Johnson could then display all the dignity of a man whose duty it was to protect Jimmie from a splashing. "Look out, boy! look out! You done gwi' spile yer pants. I raikon your mommer don't 'low this foolishness, she know it. I ain't gwi' have you round yere spilin' yer pants, an' have Mis' Trescott light on me pressen'ly. 'Deed I ain't."

He spoke with an air of great irritation, but he was not annoyed at all. This tone was merely a part of his importance. In reality he was always delighted to have the child there to witness the business of the stable. For one thing, Jimmie was invariably overcome with reverence when he was told how beautifully a harness was polished or a horse groomed. Henry explained each detail of this kind with unction, procuring great joy from the child's admiration.

III

After Johnson had taken his supper in the kitchen, he went to his loft in the carriage-house and dressed himself with much care. No belle of a court circle could bestow more mind on a toilet than did Johnson. On second thought, he was more like a priest arraying himself for some parade of the church. As he emerged from his room and sauntered down the carriage drive, no one would have suspected him of ever having washed a buggy.

It was not altogether a matter of the lavender trousers, nor yet the straw hat with its bright silk band. The change was somewhere far in the interior of Henry. But there was no cake-walk hyperbole in it. He was simply a quiet, well-bred gentleman of position, wealth, and other necessary achievements out for an evening stroll, and he had never washed a wagon in his life.

In the morning, when in his working-clothes, he had met a friend—"Hello, Pete!" "Hello, Henry!" Now, in his effulgence, he encountered this same friend. His bow was not at all haughty. If it expressed anything, it expressed consummate generosity—"Good-evenin', Misteh Washington." Pete, who was very dirty, being at work in a potato-patch, responded in a mixture of abasement and appreciation—"Good-evenin', Misteh Johnsing."

The shimmering blue of the electric arc-lamps was strong in the main street of the town. At numerous points it was conquered by the orange glare of the outnumbering gas-lights in the windows of shops. Through this radiant lane moved a crowd, which culminated in a throng before the post-office, awaiting the distribution of the evening mails. Occasionally there came into it a shrill electric street-car, the motor singing like a cageful of grasshoppers, and possessing a great gong that clanged forth both warnings and simple noise. At the little theatre, which was a varnish and red-plush miniature of one of the famous New York theatres, a company of strollers was to play *East Lynne*. The young men of the town were mainly gathered at the corners, in distinctive groups, which expressed various shades and lines of chumship, and had little to do with any social gradations. There they discussed everything with critical insight, passing the whole town in review as it swarmed in the street. When the gongs of the electric cars ceased for a moment to harry the ears, there could be heard the sound of the feet of the leisurely crowd on the blue-stone pavement, and it was like the peaceful evening lashing at the shore of a lake. At the foot of the hill, where two lines of maples sentinelled the way, an electric lamp glowed high among the embowering branches, and made most wonderful shadow-etchings on the road below it.

When Johnson appeared amid the throng a member of one of the profane groups at a corner instantly telegraphed news of this extraordinary arrival to his companions. They hailed him. "Hello, Henry! Going to walk for a cake to-night?"

"Ain't he smooth?"

"Why, you've got that cake right in your pocket, Henry!"

"Throw out your chest a little more."

Henry was not ruffled in any way by these quiet admonitions and compliments. In reply he laughed a supremely good-natured, chuckling laugh, which nevertheless expressed an underground complacency of superior metal.

Young Griscom, the lawyer, was just emerging from Reifsnyder's barber shop, rubbing his chin contentedly. On the steps he dropped his hand and looked with wide eyes into the crowd. Suddenly he bolted back into the shop. "Wow!" he cried to the parliament; "you ought to see the coon that's coming!"

Reifsnyder and his assistant instantly poised their razors high and turned toward the window. Two belathered heads reared from the chairs. The electric shine in the street caused an effect like water to them who looked through the glass from the yellow glamour of Reifsnyder's shop. In fact, the people without resembled the inhabitants of a great aquarium that here had a square pane in it. Presently into this frame swam the graceful form of Henry Johnson.

"Chee!" said Reifsnyder. He and his assistant with one accord threw their obligations to the winds, and leaving their lathered victims helpless, advanced to the window. "Ain't he a taisy?" said Reifsnyder, marvelling.

But the man in the first chair, with a grievance in his mind, had found a weapon. "Why, that's only Henry Johnson, you blamed idiots! Come on now, Reif, and shave me. What do you think I am—a mummy?"

Reifsnyder turned, in a great excitement. "I bait you any money that vas not Henry Johnson! Henry Johnson! Rats!"

The scorn put into this last word made it an explosion. "That man vas a Pullman-car porter or someding. How could that be Henry Johnson?" he demanded, turbulently. "You vas crazy."

The man in the first chair faced the barber in a storm of indignation. "Didn't I give him those lavender trousers?" he roared.

And young Griscom, who had remained attentively at the window, said: "Yes, I guess that was Henry. It looked like him."

"Oh, vell," said Reifsnyder, returning to his business, "if you think so! Oh, vell!" He implied that he was submitting for the sake of amiability.

Finally the man in the second chair, mumbling from a mouth made timid by adjacent lather, said: "That was Henry Johnson all right. Why, he always dresses like that when he wants to make a front! He's the biggest dude in town—anybody knows that."

"Chinger!" said Reifsnyder.

Henry was not at all oblivious of the wake of wondering ejaculation that streamed out behind him. On other occasions he had reaped this same joy, and he always had an eye for the demonstration. With a face beaming with happiness he turned away from the scene of his victories into a narrow side street, where the electric light still hung high, but only to exhibit a row of tumble-down houses leaning together like paralytics.

The saffron Miss Bella Farragut, in a calico frock, had been crouched on the front stoop, gossiping at long range, but she espied her approaching caller at a distance. She dashed around the corner of the house, galloping like a horse. Henry saw it all, but he preserved the polite demeanor of a guest when a waiter spills claret down his cuff. In this awkward situation he was simply perfect.

The duty of receiving Mr. Johnson fell upon Mrs. Farragut, because Bella, in another room, was scrambling wildly into her best gown. The fat old woman met him with a great ivory smile, sweeping back with the door, and bowing low. "Walk in, Misteh Johnson, walk in. How is you dis ebenin', Misteh Johnson—how is you?"

Henry's face showed like a reflector as he bowed and bowed, bending almost from his head to his ankles. "Good-evenin', Mis' Fa'gut; good-evenin'. How is you dis evenin'? Is all you' folks well, Mis' Fa'gut?"

After a great deal of kowtow, they were planted in two chairs opposite each other in the living-room. Here they exchanged the most tremendous civilities, until Miss Bella swept into the room, when there was more kowtow on all sides, and a smiling show of teeth that was like an illumination.

The cooking-stove was of course in this drawing-room, and on the fire was some kind of a long-winded stew. Mrs. Farragut was obliged to arise and attend to it from time to time. Also young Sim came in and went to bed on his pallet in the corner. But to all these domesticities the three maintained an absolute dumbness. They bowed and smiled and ignored and imitated until a late hour, and if they had been the occupants of the most gorgeous salon in the world they could not have been more like three monkeys.

After Henry had gone, Bella, who encouraged herself in the appropriation of phrases, said, "Oh, ma, isn't he divine?"

IV

A Saturday evening was a sign always for a larger crowd to parade the thoroughfare. In summer the band played until ten o'clock in the little park. Most of the young men of the town affected to be superior to this band, even to despise it; but in the still and fragrant evenings they invariably turned out in force, because the girls were sure to attend this concert, strolling slowly over the grass, linked closely in pairs, or preferably in threes, in the curious public dependence upon one another which was their inheritance. There was no particular social aspect to this gathering, save that group regarded group with interest, but mainly in silence. Perhaps one girl would nudge another girl and suddenly say, "Look! there goes Gertie Hodgson and her sister!" And they would appear to regard this as an event of importance.

On a particular evening a rather large company of young men were gathered on the sidewalk that edged the park. They remained thus beyond the borders of the festivities because of their dignity, which would not exactly allow them to appear in anything which was so much fun for the younger lads. These latter were careering madly through the crowd, precipitating minor accidents from time to time, but usually fleeing like mist swept by the wind before retribution could lay its hands upon them.

The band played a waltz which involved a gift of prominence to the bass horn, and one of the young men on the sidewalk said that the music reminded him of the new engines on the hill pumping water into the reservoir. A similarity of this kind was not inconceivable, but the young man did not say it because he disliked the band's playing. He said it because it was fashionable to say that manner of thing concerning the band. However, over in the stand, Billie Harris, who played the snare-drum, was always surrounded by a throng of boys, who adored his every whack.

After the mails from New York and Rochester had been finally distributed, the crowd from the post-office added to the mass already in the park. The wind waved the leaves of the maples, and, high in the air, the blue-burning globes of the arc lamps caused the wonderful traceries of leaf shadows on the ground. When the light fell upon the upturned face of a girl, it caused it to glow with a wonderful pallor. A policeman came suddenly from the darkness and chased a gang of obstreperous little boys. They hooted him from a distance. The leader of the band had some of the mannerisms of the great musicians, and during a period of silence the crowd smiled when they saw him raise his hand to his brow, stroke it sentimentally, and glance upward with a look of poetic anguish. In the shivering light, which gave to the park an effect like a great vaulted hall, the throng swarmed, with a gentle murmur of dresses switching the turf, and with a steady hum of voices.

Suddenly, without preliminary bars, there arose from afar the great hoarse roar of a factory whistle. It raised and swelled to a sinister note, and then it sang on the night wind one long call that held the crowd in the park immovable, speechless. The band-master had been about to vehemently let fall his hand to start the band on a thundering career through a popular march, but, smitten by this giant voice from the night, his hand dropped slowly to his knee, and, his mouth agape, he looked at his men in silence. The cry died away to a wail, and then to stillness. It released the muscles of the company of young men on the sidewalk, who had been like statues, posed eagerly, lithely, their ears turned. And then they wheeled upon each other simultaneously, and, in a single explosion, they shouted, "One!"

Again the sound swelled in the night and roared its long ominous cry, and as it died away the crowd of young men wheeled upon each other and, in chorus, yelled, "Two!"

There was a moment of breathless waiting. Then they bawled, "Second district!" In a flash the company of indolent and cynical young men had vanished like a snowball disrupted by dynamite.

V

Jake Rogers was the first man to reach the home of Tuscarora Hose Company Number Six. He had wrenched his key from his pocket as he tore down the street, and he jumped at the spring-lock like a demon. As the doors flew back before his hands he leaped and kicked the wedges from a pair of wheels, loosened a tongue from its clasp, and in the glare of the electric light which the town placed before each of its hose-houses the next comers beheld the spectacle of Jake Rogers bent like hickory in the manfulness of his pulling, and the heavy cart was moving slowly toward the doors. Four men joined him at the time, and as they swung with the cart out into the street, dark figures sped toward them from the ponderous shadows back of the electric lamps. Some set up the inevitable question, "What district?"

"Second," was replied to them in a compact howl. Tuscarora Hose Company Number Six swept on a perilous wheel into Niagara Avenue, and as the men, attached to the cart by the rope which had been paid out from the windlass under the tongue, pulled madly in their fervor and abandon, the gong under the axle clanged incitingly. And sometimes the same cry was heard, "What district?"

"Second."

On a grade Johnnie Thorpe fell, and exercising a singular muscular ability, rolled out in time from the track of the oncoming wheel, and arose, dishevelled and aggrieved, casting a look of mournful disenchantment upon the black crowd that poured after the machine. The cart seemed to be the apex of a dark wave that was whirling as if it had been a broken dam. Back of the lad were stretches of lawn, and in that direction front doors were banged by men who hoarsely shouted out into the clamorous avenue, "What district?"

At one of these houses a woman came to the door bearing a lamp, shielding her face from its rays with her hands. Across the cropped grass the avenue represented to her a kind of black torrent, upon which, nevertheless, fled numerous miraculous figures upon bicycles. She did not know that the towering light at the corner was continuing its nightly whine.

Suddenly a little boy somersaulted around the corner of the house as if he had been projected down a flight of stairs by a cataputian boot. He halted himself in front of the house by dint of a rather extraordinary evolution with his legs. "Oh, ma," he gasped, "can I go? Can I, ma?"

She straightened with the coldness of the exterior mother-judgment, although the hand that held the lamp trembled slightly. "No, Willie; you had better come to bed."

Instantly he began to buck and fume like a mustang. "Oh, ma," he cried, contorting himself—"oh, ma, can't I go? Please, ma, can't I go? Can't I go, ma?"

"It's half past nine now, Willie."

He ended by wailing out a compromise: "Well, just down to the corner, ma? Just down to the corner?"

From the avenue came the sound of rushing men who wildly shouted. Somebody had grappled the bell-rope in the Methodist church, and now over the town rang this solemn and terrible voice, speaking from the clouds. Moved from its peaceful business, this bell gained a new spirit in the portentous night, and it swung the heart to and fro, up and down, with each peal of it.

"Just down to the corner, ma?"

"Willie, it's half past nine now."

VI

The outlines of the house of Doctor Trescott had faded quietly into the evening, hiding a shape such as we call Queen

Anne against the pall of the blackened sky. The neighborhood was at this time so quiet, and seemed so devoid of obstructions, that Hannigan's dog thought it a good opportunity to prowl in forbidden precincts, and so came and pawed Trescott's lawn, growling, and considering himself a formidable beast. Later, Peter Washington strolled past the house and whistled, but there was no dim light shining from Henry's loft, and presently Peter went his way. The rays from the street, creeping in silvery waves over the grass, caused the row of shrubs along the drive to throw a clear, bold shade.

A wisp of smoke came from one of the windows at the end of the house and drifted quietly into the branches of a cherry-tree. Its companions followed it in slowly increasing numbers, and finally there was a current controlled by invisible banks which poured into the fruit-laden boughs of the cherry-tree. It was no more to be noted than if a troop of dim and silent gray monkeys had been climbing a grape-vine into the clouds.

After a moment the window brightened as if the four panes of it had been stained with blood, and a quick ear might have been led to imagine the fire-imps calling and calling, clan joining clan, gathering to the colors. From the street, however, the house maintained its dark quiet, insisting to a passer-by that it was the safe dwelling of people who chose to retire early to tranquil dreams. No one could have heard this low droning of the gathering clans.

Suddenly the panes of the red window tinkled and crashed to the ground, and at other windows there suddenly reared other flames, like bloody spectres at the apertures of a haunted house. This outbreak had been well planned, as if by professional revolutionists.

A man's voice suddenly shouted: "Fire! Fire! Fire!" Hannigan had flung his pipe frenziedly from him because his lungs demanded room. He tumbled down from his perch, swung over the fence, and ran shouting toward the front door of the Trescotts'. Then he hammered on the door, using his fists as if they were mallets. Mrs. Trescott instantly came to one of the windows on the second floor. Afterward she knew she had been about to say, "The doctor is not at home, but if you will leave your name, I will let him know as soon as he comes."

Hannigan's bawling was for a minute incoherent, but she understood that it was not about croup.

"What?" she said, raising the window swiftly.

"Your house is on fire! You're all ablaze! Move quick if—" His cries were resounding in the street as if it were a cave of echoes. Many feet pattered swiftly on the stones. There was one man who ran with an almost fabulous speed. He wore lavender trousers. A straw hat with a bright silk band was held half crumpled in his hand.

As Henry reached the front door, Hannigan had just broken the lock with a kick. A thick cloud of smoke poured over them, and Henry, ducking his head, rushed into it. From Hannigan's clamor he knew only one thing, but it turned him blue with horror. In the hall a lick of flame had found the cord that supported "Signing the Declaration." The engraving slumped suddenly down at one end, and then dropped to the floor, where it burst with the sound of a bomb. The fire was already roaring like a winter wind among the pines.

At the head of the stairs Mrs. Trescott was waving her arms as if they were two reeds. "Jimmie! Save Jimmie!" she screamed in Henry's face. He plunged past her and disappeared, taking the long-familiar routes among these upper chambers, where he had once held office as a sort of second assistant house-maid.

Hannigan had followed him up the stairs, and grappled the arm of the maniacal woman there. His face was black with rage. "You must come down," he bellowed.

She would only scream at him in reply: "Jimmie! Jimmie! Save Jimmie!" But he dragged her forth while she babbled at him.

As they swung out into the open air a man ran across the lawn, and seizing a shutter, pulled it from its hinges and flung it far out upon the grass. Then he frantically attacked the other shutters one by one. It was a kind of temporary insanity.

"Here, you," howled Hannigan, "hold Mrs. Trescott— And stop—"

The news had been telegraphed by a twist of the wrist of a neighbor who had gone to the fire-box at the corner, and the time when Hannigan and his charge struggled out of the house was the time when the whistle roared its hoarse night call, smiting the crowd in the park, causing the leader of the band, who was about to order the first triumphal clang of a military march, to let his hand drop slowly to his knee.

VII

Henry pawed awkwardly through the smoke in the upper halls. He had attempted to guide himself by the walls, but they were too hot. The paper was crimpling, and he expected at any moment to have a flame burst from under his hands.

"Jimmie!"

He did not call very loud, as if in fear that the humming flames below would overhear him.

"Jimmie! Oh, Jimmie!"

Stumbling and panting, he speedily reached the entrance to Jimmie's room and flung open the door. The little chamber had no smoke in it at all. It was faintly illumined by a beautiful rosy light reflected circuitously from the flames that were consuming the house. The boy had apparently just been aroused by the noise. He sat in his bed, his lips apart, his eyes wide, while upon his little white-robed figure played caressingly the light from the fire. As the door flew open he had before him this apparition of his pal, a terror-stricken negro, all tousled and with wool scorching, who leaped upon him and bore him up in a blanket as if the whole affair were a case of kidnapping by a dreadful robber chief. Without waiting to go through the usual short but complete process of wrinkling up his face, Jimmie let out a gorgeous bawl, which resembled the expression of a calf's deepest terror. As Johnson, bearing him, reeled into the smoke of the hall, he flung his arms about his neck and buried his face in the blanket. He called twice in muffled tones: "Mam-ma! Mam-ma!"

When Johnson came to the top of the stairs with his burden, he took a quick step backward. Through the smoke that rolled to him he could see that the lower hall was all ablaze. He cried out then in a howl that resembled Jimmie's former achievement. His legs gained a frightful faculty of bending sideways. Swinging about precariously on these reedy legs, he made his way back slowly, back along the upper hall. From the way of him then, he had given up almost all idea of escaping from the burning house, and with it the desire. He was submitting, submitting because of his fathers, bending his mind in a most perfect slavery to this conflagration.

He now clutched Jimmie as unconsciously as when, running toward the house, he had clutched the hat with the bright silk band.

Suddenly he remembered a little private staircase which led from a bedroom to an apartment which the doctor had fitted up as a laboratory and work-house, where he used some of his leisure, and also hours when he might have been sleeping, in devoting himself to experiments which came in the way of his study and interest.

When Johnson recalled this stairway the submission to the blaze departed instantly. He had been perfectly familiar with it, but his confusion had destroyed the memory of it.

In his sudden momentary apathy there had been little that resembled fear, but now, as a way of safety came to him, the old frantic terror caught him. He was no longer creature to the flames, and he was afraid of the battle with them. It was a singular and swift set of alternations in which he feared twice without submission, and submitted once without fear.

"Jimmie!" he wailed, as he staggered on his way. He wished this little inanimate body at his breast to participate in his tremblings. But the child had lain limp and still during these headlong charges and countercharges, and no sign came from him.

Johnson passed through two rooms and came to the head of the stairs. As he opened the door great billows of smoke poured out, but gripping Jimmie closer, he plunged down through them. All manner of odors assailed him during this flight. They seemed to be alive with envy, hatred, and malice. At the entrance to the laboratory he confronted a strange spectacle. The room was like a garden in the region where might be burning flowers. Flames of violet, crimson, green, blue, orange, and purple were blooming everywhere. There was one blaze that was precisely the hue of a delicate coral. In another place was a mass that lay merely in phosphorescent inaction like a pile of emeralds. But all these marvels were to be seen dimly through clouds of heaving, turning, deadly smoke.

Johnson halted for a moment on the threshold. He cried out again in the negro wail that had in it the sadness of the swamps. Then he rushed across the room. An orange-colored flame leaped like a panther at the lavender trousers. This animal bit deeply into Johnson. There was an explosion at one side, and suddenly before him there reared a delicate, trembling sapphire shape like a fairy lady. With a quiet smile she blocked his path and doomed him and Jimmie. Johnson shrieked, and then ducked in the manner of his race in fights. He aimed to pass under the left guard of the sapphire lady. But she was swifter than eagles, and her talons caught in him as he plunged past her. Bowing his head as if his neck had been struck, Johnson lurched forward, twisting this way and that way. He fell on his back. The still form in the blanket flung from his arms, rolled to the edge of the floor and beneath the window.

Johnson had fallen with his head at the base of an old-fashioned desk. There was a row of jars upon the top of this desk. For the most part, they were silent amid this rioting, but there was one which seemed to hold a scintillant and writhing serpent.

Suddenly the glass splintered, and a ruby-red snakelike thing poured its thick length out upon the top of the old desk. It coiled and hesitated, and then began to swim a languorous way down the mahogany slant. At the angle it waved its sizzling molten head to and fro over the closed eyes of the man beneath it. Then, in a moment, with mystic impulse, it moved again, and the red snake flowed directly down into Johnson's upturned face.

Afterward the trail of this creature seemed to reek, and amid flames and low explosions drops like red-hot jewels pattered softly down it at leisurely intervals.

VIII

Suddenly all roads led to Doctor Trescott's. The whole town flowed toward one point. Chippeway Hose Company Number One toiled desperately up Bridge Street Hill even as the

Tuscaroras came in an impetuous sweep down Niagara Avenue. Meanwhile the machine of the hook-and-ladder experts from across the creek was spinning on its way. The chief of the fire department had been playing poker in the rear room of Whiteley's cigar-store, but at the first breath of the alarm he sprang through the door like a man escaping with the kitty.

In Whilomville, on these occasions, there was always a number of people who instantly turned their attention to the bells in the churches and school-houses. The bells not only emphasized the alarm, but it was the habit to send these sounds rolling across the sky in a stirring brazen uproar until the flames were practically vanquished. There was also a kind of rivalry as to which bell should be made to produce the greatest din. Even the Valley Church, four miles away among the farms, had heard the voices of its brethren, and immediately added a quaint little yelp.

Doctor Trescott had been driving homeward, slowly smoking a cigar, and feeling glad that this last case was now in complete obedience to him, like a wild animal that he had subdued, when he heard the long whistle, and chirped to his horse under the unlicensed but perfectly distinct impression that a fire had broken out in Oakhurst, a new and rather high-flying suburb of the town which was at least two miles from his own home. But in the second blast and in the ensuing silence he read the designation of his own district. He was then only a few blocks from his house. He took out the whip and laid it lightly on the mare. Surprised and frightened at this extraordinary action, she leaped forward, and as the reins straightened like steel bands, the doctor leaned backward a trifle. When the mare whirled him up to the closed gate he was wondering whose house could be afire. The man who had rung the signal-box yelled something at him, but he already knew. He left the mare to her will.

In front of his door was a maniacal woman in a wrapper. "Ned!" she screamed at sight of him. "Jimmie! Save Jimmie!"

Trescott had grown hard and chill. "Where?" he said. "Where?"

Mrs. Trescott's voice began to bubble. "Up—up—up—" She pointed at the second-story windows.

Hannigan was already shouting: "Don't go in that way! You can't go in that way!"

Trescott ran around the corner of the house and disappeared from them. He knew from the view he had taken of the main hall that it would be impossible to ascend from there. His hopes were fastened now to the stairway which led from the laboratory. The door which opened from this room out upon the lawn was fastened with a bolt and lock, but he kicked close to the lock and then close to the bolt. The door with a loud crash flew back. The doctor recoiled from the roll of smoke, and then bending low, he stepped into the garden of burning flowers. On the floor his stinging eyes could make out a form in a smouldering blanket near the window. Then, as he carried his son toward the door, he saw that the whole lawn seemed now alive with men and boys, the leaders in the great charge that the whole town was making. They seized him and his burden, and overpowered him in wet blankets and water.

But Hannigan was howling: "Johnson is in there yet! Henry Johnson is in there yet! He went in after the kid! Johnson is in there yet!"

These cries penetrated to the sleepy senses of Trescott, and he struggled with his captors, swearing, unknown to him and to them, all the deep blasphemies of his medical-student days. He arose to his feet and went again toward the door of the laboratory. They endeavored to restrain him, although they were much affrighted at him.

But a young man who was a brakeman on the railway, and lived in one of the rear streets near the Trescotts, had gone into the laboratory and brought forth a thing which he laid on the grass.

IX

There were hoarse commands from in front of the house. "Turn on your water, Five!" "Let 'er go, One!" The gathering crowd swayed this way and that way. The flames, towering high, cast a wild red light on their faces. There came the clangor of a gong from along some adjacent street. The crowd exclaimed at it. "Here comes Number Three!" "That's Three a-comin'!" A panting and irregular mob dashed into view, dragging a hose-cart. A cry of exultation arose from the little boys. "Here's Three!" The lads welcomed Never-Die Hose Company Number Three as if it was composed of a chariot dragged by a band of gods. The perspiring citizens flung themselves into the fray. The boys danced in impish joy at the displays of prowess. They acclaimed the approach of Number Two. They welcomed Number Four with cheers. They were so deeply moved by this whole affair that they bitterly guyed the late appearance of the hook and ladder company, whose heavy apparatus had almost stalled them on the Bridge Street hill. The lads hated and feared a fire, of course. They did not particularly want to have anybody's house burn, but still it was fine to see the gathering of the companies, and amid a great noise to watch their heroes perform all manner of prodigies.

They were divided into parties over the worth of different companies, and supported their creeds with no small violence. For instance, in that part of the little city where Number Four had its home it would be most daring for a boy to contend the superiority of any other company. Likewise, in another quarter, when a strange boy was asked which fire company was the best in Whilomville, he was expected to answer "Number One." Feuds, which the boys forgot and remembered according to chance or the importance of some recent event, existed all through the town.

They did not care much for John Shipley, the chief of the department. It was true that he went to a fire with the speed of a falling angel, but when there he invariably lapsed into a certain still mood, which was almost a preoccupation, moving leisurely around the burning structure and surveying it, puffing meanwhile at a cigar. This quiet man, who even when life was in danger seldom raised his voice, was not much to their fancy. Now old Sykes Huntington, when he was chief, used to bellow continually like a bull and gesticulate in a sort of delirium. He was much finer as a spectacle than this Shipley, who viewed a fire with the same steadiness that he viewed a raise in a large jack-pot. The greater number of the boys could never understand why the members of these companies persisted in re-electing Shipley, although they often pretended to understand it, because "My father says" was a very formidable phrase in argument, and the fathers seemed almost unanimous in advocating Shipley.

At this time there was considerable discussion as to which company had gotten the first stream of water on the fire. Most of the boys claimed that Number Five owned that distinction, but there was a determined minority who contended for Number One. Boys who were the blood adherents of other companies were obliged to choose between the two on this occasion, and the talk waxed warm.

But a great rumor went among the crowds. It was told with hushed voices. Afterward a reverent silence fell even upon the boys. Jimmie Trescott and Henry Johnson had been burned to death, and Doctor Trescott himself had been most savagely hurt. The crowd did not even feel the police pushing at them. They raised their eyes, shining now with awe, toward the high flames.

The man who had information was at his best. In low tones he described the whole affair. "That was the kid's room—in the corner there. He had measles or somethin', and this coon—Johnson—was a-settin' up with 'im, and Johnson got sleepy or somethin' and upset the lamp, and the doctor he was down in his office, and he came running up, and they all got burned together till they dragged 'em out."

Another man, always preserved for the deliverance of the final judgment, was saying: "Oh, they'll die sure. Burned to flinders. No chance. Hull lot of 'em. Anybody can see." The crowd concentrated its gaze still more closely upon these flags of fire which waved joyfully against the black sky. The bells of the town were clashing unceasingly.

A little procession moved across the lawn and toward the street. There were three cots, borne by twelve of the firemen. The police moved sternly, but it needed no effort of theirs to open a lane for this slow cortège. The men who bore the cots were well known to the crowd, but in this solemn parade during the ringing of the bells and the shouting, and with the red glare upon the sky, they seemed utterly foreign, and Whilomville paid them a deep respect. Each man in this stretcher party had gained a reflected majesty. They were footmen to death, and the crowd made subtle obeisance to this august dignity derived from three prospective graves. One woman turned away with a shriek at sight of the covered body on the first stretcher, and people faced her suddenly in silent and mournful indignation. Otherwise there was barely a sound as these twelve important men with measured tread carried their burdens through the throng.

The little boys no longer discussed the merits of the different fire companies. For the greater part they had been routed. Only the more courageous viewed closely the three figures veiled in yellow blankets.

X

Old Judge Denning Hagenthorpe, who lived nearly opposite the Trescotts, had thrown his door wide open to receive the afflicted family. When it was publicly learned that the doctor and his son and the negro were still alive, it required a specially detailed policeman to prevent people from scaling the front porch and interviewing these sorely wounded. One old lady appeared with a miraculous poultice, and she quoted most damning scripture to the officer when he said that she could not pass him. Throughout the night some lads old enough to be given privileges or to compel them from their mothers remained vigilantly upon the kerb in anticipation of a death or some such event. The reporter of the *Morning Tribune* rode thither on his bicycle every hour until three o'clock.

Six of the ten doctors in Whilomville attended at Judge Hagenthorpe's house.

Almost at once they were able to know that Trescott's burns were not vitally important. The child would possibly be scarred badly, but his life was undoubtedly safe. As for the negro Henry Johnson, he could not live. His body was frightfully seared, but more than that, he now had no face. His face had simply been burned away.

Trescott was always asking news of the two other patients. In the morning he seemed fresh and strong, so they told him that Johnson was doomed. They then saw him stir on the bed, and sprang quickly to see if the bandages needed readjusting. In the sudden glance he threw from one to another he impressed them as being both leonine and impracticable.

The morning paper announced the death of Henry Johnson. It contained a long interview with Edward J. Hannigan, in which the latter described in full the performance of Johnson at the fire. There was also an editorial built from all the best words in the vocabulary of the staff. The town halted in its accustomed road of thought, and turned a reverent attention to the memory of this hostler. In the breasts of many people was the regret that they had not known enough to give him a hand and a lift when he was alive, and they judged themselves stupid and ungenerous for this failure.

The name of Henry Johnson became suddenly the title of a saint to the little boys. The one who thought of it first could, by quoting it in an argument, at once overthrow his antagonist, whether it applied to the subject or whether it did not.

> Nigger, nigger, never die,
> Black face and shiny eye.

Boys who had called this odious couplet in the rear of Johnson's march buried the fact at the bottom of their hearts.

Later in the day Miss Bella Farragut, of No. 7 Watermelon Alley, announced that she had been engaged to marry Mr. Henry Johnson.

XI

The old judge had a cane with an ivory head. He could never think at his best until he was leaning slightly on this stick and smoothing the white top with slow movements of his hands. It was also to him a kind of narcotic. If by any chance he mislaid it, he grew at once very irritable, and was likely to speak sharply to his sister, whose mental incapacity he had patiently endured for thirty years in the old mansion on Ontario Street. She was not at all aware of her brother's opinion of her endowments, and so it might be said that the judge had successfully dissembled for more than a quarter of a century, only risking the truth at the times when his cane was lost.

On a particular day the judge sat in his arm-chair on the porch. The sunshine sprinkled through the lilac-bushes and poured great coins on the boards. The sparrows disputed in the trees that lined the pavements. The judge mused deeply, while his hands gently caressed the ivory head of his cane.

Finally he arose and entered the house, his brow still furrowed in a thoughtful frown. His stick thumped solemnly in regular beats. On the second floor he entered a room where Doctor Trescott was working about the bedside of Henry Johnson. The bandages on the negro's head allowed only one thing to appear, an eye, which unwinkingly stared at the judge. The latter spoke to Trescott on the condition of the patient. Afterward he evidently had something further to say, but he seemed to be kept from it by the scrutiny of the unwinking eye, at which he furtively glanced from time to time.

When Jimmie Trescott was sufficiently recovered, his mother had taken him to pay a visit to his grandparents in Connecticut. The doctor had remained to take care of his patients, but as a matter of truth he spent most of his time at Judge Hagenthorpe's house, where lay Henry Johnson. Here he slept and ate almost every meal in the long nights and days of his vigil.

At dinner, and away from the magic of the unwinking eye, the judge said, suddenly, "Trescott, do you think it is—" As Trescott paused expectantly, the judge fingered his knife. He said, thoughtfully, "No one wants to advance such ideas, but somehow I think that that poor fellow ought to die."

There was in Trescott's face at once a look of recognition, as if in this tangent of the judge he saw an old problem. He merely sighed and answered, "Who knows?" The words were spoken in a deep tone that gave them an elusive kind of significance.

The judge retreated to the cold manner of the bench. "Perhaps we may not talk with propriety of this kind of action, but I am induced to say that you are performing a questionable charity in preserving this negro's life. As near as I can understand, he will hereafter be a monster, a perfect monster, and probably with an affected brain. No man can observe you as I have observed you and not know that it was a matter of conscience with you, but I am afraid, my friend, that it is one of the blunders of virtue." The judge had delivered his views with his habitual oratory. The last three words he spoke with a particular emphasis, as if the phrase was his discovery.

The doctor made a weary gesture. "He saved my boy's life."

"Yes," said the judge, swiftly—"yes, I know!"

"And what am I to do?" said Trescott, his eyes suddenly lighting like an outburst from smouldering peat. "What am I to do? He gave himself for—for Jimmie. What am I to do for him?"

The judge abased himself completely before these words. He lowered his eyes for a moment. He picked at his cucumbers.

Presently he braced himself straightly in his chair. "He will be your creation, you understand. He is purely your creation. Nature has very evidently given him up. He is dead. You are restoring him to life. You are making him, and he will be a monster, and with no mind."

"He will be what you like, judge," cried Trescott, in sudden, polite fury. "He will be anything, but, by God! he saved my boy."

The judge interrupted in a voice trembling with emotion: "Trescott! Trescott! Don't I know?"

Trescott had subsided to a sullen mood. "Yes, you know," he answered, acidly; "but you don't know all about your own boy being saved from death." This was a perfectly childish allusion to the judge's bachelorhood. Trescott knew that the remark was infantile, but he seemed to take desperate delight in it.

But it passed the judge completely. It was not his spot.

"I am puzzled," said he, in profound thought. "I don't know what to say."

Trescott had become repentant. "Don't think I don't appreciate what you say, judge. But—"

"Of course!" responded the judge, quickly. "Of course."

"It—" began Trescott.

"Of course," said the judge.

In silence they resumed their dinner.

"Well," said the judge, ultimately, "it is hard for a man to know what to do."

"It is," said the doctor, fervidly.

There was another silence. It was broken by the judge:

"Look here, Trescott; I don't want you to think—"

"No, certainly not," answered the doctor, earnestly.

"Well, I don't want you to think I would say anything to— It was only that I thought that I might be able to suggest to you that—perhaps—the affair was a little dubious."

With an appearance of suddenly disclosing his real mental perturbation, the doctor said: "Well, what would you do? Would you kill him?" he asked, abruptly and sternly.

"Trescott, you fool," said the old man, gently.

"Oh, well, I know, judge, but then—" He turned red, and spoke with new violence: "Say, he saved my boy—do you see? He saved my boy."

"You bet he did," cried the judge, with enthusiasm. "You bet he did." And they remained for a time gazing at each other, their faces illuminated with memories of a certain deed.

After another silence, the judge said, "It is hard for a man to know what to do."

XII

Late one evening Trescott, returning from a professional call, paused his buggy at the Hagenthorpe gate. He tied the mare to the old tin-covered post, and entered the house. Ultimately he appeared with a companion—a man who walked slowly and carefully, as if he were learning. He was wrapped to the heels in an old-fashioned ulster. They entered the buggy and drove away.

After a silence only broken by the swift and musical humming of the wheels on the smooth road, Trescott spoke. "Henry," he said, "I've got you a home here with old Alek Williams. You will have everything you want to eat and a good place to sleep, and I hope you will get along there all right. I will pay all your expenses, and come to see you as often as I can. If you don't get along, I want you to let me know as soon as possible, and then we will do what we can to make it better."

The dark figure at the doctor's side answered with a cheerful laugh. "These buggy wheels don' look like I washed 'em yestehday, docteh," he said.

Trescott hesitated for a moment, and then went on insistently, "I am taking you to Alek Williams, Henry, and I—"

The figure chuckled again. "No, 'deed! No seh! Alek Williams don' know a hoss! 'Deed he don't. He don' know a hoss from a pig." The laugh that followed was like the rattle of pebbles.

Trescott turned and looked sternly and coldly at the dim form in the gloom from the buggy-top. "Henry," he said, "I didn't say anything about horses. I was saying—"

"Hoss? Hoss?" said the quavering voice from these near shadows. "Hoss? 'Deed I don't know all erbout a hoss! 'Deed I don't." There was a satirical chuckle.

At the end of three miles the mare slackened and the doctor leaned forward, peering, while holding tight reins. The wheels of the buggy bumped often over out-cropping bowlders. A window shone forth, a simple square of topaz on a great black hill-side. Four dogs charged the buggy with ferocity, and when it did not promptly retreat, they circled courageously around the flanks, baying. A door opened near the window in the hill-side, and a man came and stood on a beach of yellow light.

"Yah! yah! You Roveh! You Susie! Come yah! Come yah this minit!"

Trescott called across the dark sea of grass, "Hello, Alek!"

"Hello!"

"Come down here and show me where to drive."

The man plunged from the beach into the surf, and Trescott could then only trace his course by the fervid and polite ejaculations of a host who was somewhere approaching. Presently Williams took the mare by the head, and uttering cries of welcome and scolding the swarming dogs, led the equipage toward the lights. When they halted at the door and Trescott was climbing out, Williams cried, "Will she stand, docteh?"

"She'll stand all right, but you better hold her for a minute. Now, Henry." The doctor turned and held both arms to the dark figure. It crawled to him painfully like a man going down a ladder. Williams took the mare away to be tied to a little tree, and when he returned he found them awaiting him in the gloom beyond the rays from the door.

He burst out then like a siphon pressed by a nervous thumb. "Hennery! Hennery, ma ol' frien'. Well, if I ain' glade. If I ain' glade!"

Trescott had taken the silent shape by the arm and led it forward into the full revelation of the light. "Well, now, Alek, you can take Henry and put him to bed, and in the morning I will—"

Near the end of this sentence old Williams had come front to front with Johnson. He gasped for a second, and then yelled the yell of a man stabbed in the heart.

For a fraction of a moment Trescott seemed to be looking for epithets. Then he roared: "You old black chump! You old black—Shut up! Shut up! Do you hear?"

Williams obeyed instantly in the matter of his screams, but he continued in a lowered voice: "Ma Lode amassy! Who'd ever think? Ma Lode amassy!"

Trescott spoke again in the manner of a commander of a battalion. "Alek!"

The old negro again surrendered, but to himself he repeated in a whisper, "Ma Lode!" He was aghast and trembling.

As these three points of widening shadows approached the golden doorway a hale old negress appeared there, bowing. "Good-evenin', docteh! Good-evenin'! Come in! come in!" She had evidently just retired from a tempestuous struggle to place the room in order, but she was now bowing rapidly. She made the effort of a person swimming.

"Don't trouble yourself, Mary," said Trescott, entering. "I've brought Henry for you to take care of, and all you've got to do is to carry out what I tell you." Learning that he was not followed, he faced the door, and said, "Come in, Henry."

Johnson entered. "Whee!" shrieked Mrs. Williams. She almost achieved a back somersault. Six young members of the tribe of Williams made simultaneous plunge for a position behind the stove, and formed a wailing heap.

XIII

"You know very well that you and your family lived usually on less than three dollars a week, and now that Doctor Trescott pays you five dollars a week for Johnson's board, you live like millionaires. You haven't done a stroke of work since

Johnson began to board with you—everybody knows that—
and so what are you kicking about?"

The judge sat in his chair on the porch, fondling his cane,
and gazing down at old Williams, who stood under the lilac-
bushes. "Yes, I know, jedge," said the negro, wagging his
head in a puzzled manner. " 'Tain't like as if I didn't 'preciate
what the docteh done, but—but—well, yeh see, jedge," he
added, gaining a new impetus, "it's—it's hard wuk. This ol'
man nev' did wuk so hard. Lode, no."

"Don't talk such nonsense, Alek," spoke the judge, sharply.
"You have never really worked in your life—anyhow enough
to support a family of sparrows, and now when you are in a
more prosperous condition than ever before, you come
around talking like an old fool."

The negro began to scratch his head. "Yeh see, jedge," he
said at last, "my ol' 'ooman she cain't 'ceive no lady callahs,
nohow."

"Hang lady callers!" said the judge, irascibly. "If you have
flour in the barrel and meat in the pot, your wife can get
along without receiving lady callers, can't she?"

"But they won't come ainyhow, jedge," replied Williams,
with an air of still deeper stupefaction. "Noner ma wife's
frien's ner noner ma frien's'll come near ma res'dence."

"Well, let them stay home if they are such silly people."

The old negro seemed to be seeking a way to elude this
argument, but evidently finding none, he was about to shuffle
meekly off. He halted, however. "Jedge," said he, "ma ol'
'ooman's near driv' abstracted."

"Your old woman is an idiot," responded the judge.

Williams came very close and peered solemnly through a
branch of lilac. "Jedge," he whispered, "the chillens."

"What about them?"

Dropping his voice to funereal depths, Williams said,
"They—they cain't eat."

"Can't eat!" scoffed the judge, loudly. "Can't eat! You must
think I am as big an old fool as you are. Can't eat—the little
rascals! What's to prevent them from eating?"

In answer, Williams said, with mournful emphasis, "Hen-
nery." Moved with a kind of satisfaction at his tragic use of

the name, he remained staring at the judge for a sign of its effect.

The judge made a gesture of irritation. "Come, now, you old scoundrel, don't beat around the bush any more. What are you up to? What do you want? Speak out like a man, and don't give me any more of this tiresome rigamarole."

"I ain't er-beatin' round 'bout nuffin, jedge," replied Williams, indignantly. "No, seh; I say whatter got to say right out. 'Deed I do."

"Well, say it, then."

"Jedge," began the negro, taking off his hat and switching his knee with it, "Lode knows I'd do jes 'bout as much fer five dollehs er week as ainy cul'd man, but—but this yere business is awful, jedge. I raikon ain't been no sleep in—in my house sence docteh done fetch 'im."

"Well, what do you propose to do about it?"

Williams lifted his eyes from the ground and gazed off through the trees. "Raikon I got good appetite, an' sleep jes like er dog, but he—he's done broke me all up. 'Tain't no good, nohow. I wake up in the night; I hear 'im, mebbe, er-whimperin' an' er-whimperin', an' I sneak an' I sneak until I try th' do' to see if he locked in. An' he keep me er-puzzlin' an' er-quakin' all night long. Don't know how 'll do in th' winter. Can't let 'im out where th' chillen is. He'll done freeze where he is now." Williams spoke these sentences as if he were talking to himself. After a silence of deep reflection he continued: "Folks go round sayin' he ain't Hennery Johnson at all. They say he's er devil!"

"What?" cried the judge.

"Yesseh," repeated Williams in tones of injury, as if his veracity had been challenged. "Yesseh. I'm er-tellin' it to yeh straight, jedge. Plenty cul'd people folks up my way say it is a devil."

"Well, you don't think so yourself, do you?"

"No. 'Tain't no devil. It's Hennery Johnson."

"Well, then, what is the matter with you? You don't care what a lot of foolish people say. Go on 'tending to your business, and pay no attention to such idle nonsense."

" 'Tis nonsense, jedge; but he *looks* like er devil."

"What do you care what he looks like?" demanded the judge.

"Ma rent is two dollehs and er half er month," said Williams, slowly.

"It might just as well be ten thousand dollars a month," responded the judge. "You never pay it, anyhow."

"Then, anoth' thing," continued Williams, in his reflective tone. "If he was all right in his haid I could stan' it; but, jedge, he's crazier 'n er loon. Then when he looks like er devil, an' done skears all ma frien's away, an' ma chillens cain't eat, an' ma ole 'ooman jes raisin' Cain all the time, an' ma rent two dollehs an' er half er month, an' him not right in his haid, it seems like five dollehs er week—"

The judge's stick came down sharply and suddenly upon the floor of the porch. "There," he said, "I thought that was what you were driving at."

Williams began swinging his head from side to side in the strange racial mannerism. "Now hol' on a minit, jedge," he said, defensively. " 'Tain't like as if I didn't 'preciate what the docteh done. 'Tain't that. Docteh Trescott is er kind man, an' 'tain't like as if I didn't 'preciate what he done; but—but—"

"But what? You are getting painful, Alek. Now tell me this: did you ever have five dollars a week regularly before in your life?"

Williams at once drew himself up with great dignity, but in the pause after that question he drooped gradually to another attitude. In the end he answered, heroically: "No, jedge, I ain't. An' 'tain't like as if I was er-sayin' five dollehs wasn't er lot er money fer a man like me. But, jedge, what er man oughter git fer this kinder wuk is er salary. Yesseh, jedge," he repeated, with a great impressive gesture; "fer this kinder wuk er man oughter git er Salary." He laid a terrible emphasis upon the final word.

The judge laughed. "I know Doctor Trescott's mind concerning this affair, Alek; and if you are dissatisfied with your boarder, he is quite ready to move him to some other place; so, if you care to leave word with me that you are tired of the arrangement and wish it changed, he will come and take Johnson away."

Williams scratched his head again in deep perplexity. "Five

dollehs is er big price fer bo'd, but 'tain't no big price fer the bo'd of er crazy man," he said, finally.

"What do you think you ought to get?" asked the judge.

"Well," answered Alek, in the manner of one deep in a balancing of the scales, "he looks like er devil, an' done skears e'rybody, an' ma chillens cain't eat, an' I cain't sleep, an' he ain't right in his haid, an'—"

"You told me all those things."

After scratching his wool, and beating his knee with his hat, and gazing off through the trees and down at the ground, Williams said, as he kicked nervously at the gravel, "Well, jedge, I think it is wuth—" He stuttered.

"Worth what?"

"Six dollehs," answered Williams, in a desperate outburst.

The judge lay back in his great arm-chair and went through all the motions of a man laughing heartily, but he made no sound save a slight cough. Williams had been watching him with apprehension.

"Well," said the judge, "do you call six dollars a salary?"

"No, seh," promptly responded Williams. " 'Tain't a salary. No, 'deed! 'Tain't a salary." He looked with some anger upon the man who questioned his intelligence in this way.

"Well, supposing your children can't eat?"

"I—"

"And supposing he looks like a devil? And supposing all those things continue? Would you be satisfied with six dollars a week?"

Recollections seemed to throng in Williams's mind at these interrogations, and he answered dubiously. "Of co'se a man who ain't right in his haid, an' looks like er devil— But six dollehs—" After these two attempts at a sentence Williams suddenly appeared as an orator, with a great shiny palm waving in the air. "I tell yeh, jedge, six dollehs is six dollehs, but if I git six dollehs for bo'ding Hennery Johnson, I uhns it! I uhns it!"

"I don't doubt that you earn six dollars for every week's work you do," said the judge.

"Well, if I bo'd Hennery Johnson fer six dollehs er week, I uhns it! I uhns it!" cried Williams, wildly.

XIV

Reifsnyder's assistant had gone to his supper, and the owner of the shop was trying to placate four men who wished to be shaved at once. Reifsnyder was very garrulous—a fact which made him rather remarkable among barbers, who, as a class, are austerely speechless, having been taught silence by the hammering reiteration of a tradition. It is the customers who talk in the ordinary event.

As Reifsnyder waved his razor down the cheek of a man in the chair, he turned often to cool the impatience of the others with pleasant talk, which they did not particularly heed.

"Oh, he should have let him die," said Bainbridge, a railway engineer, finally replying to one of the barber's orations. "Shut up, Reif, and go on with your business!"

Instead, Reifsnyder paused shaving entirely, and turned to front the speaker. "Let him die?" he demanded. "How vas that? How can you let a man die?"

"By letting him die, you chump," said the engineer. The others laughed a little, and Reifsnyder turned at once to his work, sullenly, as a man overwhelmed by the derision of numbers.

"How vas that?" he grumbled later. "How can you let a man die when he vas done so much for you?"

" 'When he vas done so much for you?' " repeated Bainbridge. "You better shave some people. How vas that? Maybe this ain't a barber shop?"

A man hitherto silent now said, "If I had been the doctor, I would have done the same thing."

"Of course," said Reifsnyder. "Any man vould do it. Any man that vas not like you, you—old—flint-hearted—fish." He had sought the final words with painful care, and he delivered the collection triumphantly at Bainbridge. The engineer laughed.

The man in the chair now lifted himself higher, while Reifsnyder began an elaborate ceremony of anointing and combing his hair. Now free to join comfortably in the talk, the man said: "They say he is the most terrible thing in the world. Young Johnnie Bernard—that drives the grocery wagon—

saw him up at Alek Williams's shanty, and he says he couldn't eat anything for two days."

"Chee!" said Reifsnyder.

"Well, what makes him so terrible?" asked another.

"Because he hasn't got any face," replied the barber and the engineer in duet.

"Hasn't got any face?" repeated the man. "How can he do without any face!"

> "He has no face in the front of his head,
>   In the place where his face ought to grow."

Bainbridge sang these lines pathetically as he arose and hung his hat on a hook. The man in the chair was about to abdicate in his favor. "Get a gait on you now," he said to Reifsnyder. "I go out at 7.31."

As the barber foamed the lather on the cheeks of the engineer he seemed to be thinking heavily. Then suddenly he burst out. "How would you like to be with no face?" he cried to the assemblage.

"Oh, if I had to have a face like yours—" answered one customer.

Bainbridge's voice came from a sea of lather. "You're kicking because if losing faces became popular, you'd have to go out of business."

"I don't think it will become so much popular," said Reifsnyder.

"Not if it's got to be taken off in the way his was taken off," said another man. "I'd rather keep mine, if you don't mind."

"I guess so!" cried the barber. "Just think!"

The shaving of Bainbridge had arrived at a time of comparative liberty for him. "I wonder what the doctor says to himself?" he observed. "He may be sorry he made him live."

"It was the only thing he could do," replied a man. The others seemed to agree with him.

"Supposing you were in his place," said one, "and Johnson had saved your kid. What would you do?"

"Certainly!"

"Of course! You would do anything on earth for him.

You'd take all the trouble in the world for him. And spend your last dollar on him. Well, then?"

"I wonder how it feels to be without any face?" said Reifsnyder, musingly.

The man who had previously spoken, feeling that he had expressed himself well, repeated the whole thing. "You would do anything on earth for him. You'd take all the trouble in the world for him. And spend your last dollar on him. Well, then?"

"No, but look," said Reifsnyder; "supposing you don't got a face!"

XV

As soon as Williams was hidden from the view of the old judge he began to gesture and talk to himself. An elation had evidently penetrated to his vitals, and caused him to dilate as if he had been filled with gas. He snapped his fingers in the air, and whistled fragments of triumphal music. At times, in his progress toward his shanty, he indulged in a shuffling movement that was really a dance. It was to be learned from the intermediate monologue that he had emerged from his trials laurelled and proud. He was the unconquerable Alexander Williams. Nothing could exceed the bold self-reliance of his manner. His kingly stride, his heroic song, the derisive flourish of his hands—all betokened a man who had successfully defied the world.

On his way he saw Zeke Paterson coming to town. They hailed each other at a distance of fifty yards.

"How do, Broth' Paterson?"

"How do, Broth' Williams?"

They were both deacons.

"Is you' folks well, Broth' Paterson?"

"Middlin', middlin'. How's you' folks, Broth' Williams?"

Neither of them had slowed his pace in the smallest degree. They had simply begun this talk when a considerable space separated them, continued it as they passed, and added polite questions as they drifted steadily apart. Williams's mind seemed to be a balloon. He had been so inflated that he had not noticed that Paterson had definitely shied into the dry ditch as they came to the point of ordinary contact.

Afterward, as he went a lonely way, he burst out again in song and pantomimic celebration of his estate. His feet moved in prancing steps.

When he came in sight of his cabin, the fields were bathed in a blue dusk, and the light in the window was pale. Cavorting and gesticulating, he gazed joyfully for some moments upon this light. Then suddenly another idea seemed to attack his mind, and he stopped, with an air of being suddenly dampened. In the end he approached his home as if it were the fortress of an enemy.

Some dogs disputed his advance for a loud moment, and then discovering their lord, slunk away embarrassed. His reproaches were addressed to them in muffled tones.

Arriving at the door, he pushed it open with the timidity of a new thief. He thrust his head cautiously sideways, and his eyes met the eyes of his wife, who sat by the table, the lamp-light defining a half of her face. " 'Sh!" he said, uselessly. His glance travelled swiftly to the inner door which shielded the one bed-chamber. The pickaninnies, strewn upon the floor of the living-room, were softly snoring. After a hearty meal they had promptly dispersed themselves about the place and gone to sleep. " 'Sh!" said Williams again to his motionless and silent wife. He had allowed only his head to appear. His wife, with one hand upon the edge of the table and the other at her knee, was regarding him with wide eyes and parted lips as if he were a spectre. She looked to be one who was living in terror, and even the familiar face at the door had thrilled her because it had come suddenly.

Williams broke the tense silence. "Is he all right?" he whispered, waving his eyes toward the inner door. Following his glance timorously, his wife nodded, and in a low tone answered,

"I raikon he's done gone t' sleep."

Williams then slunk noiselessly across his threshold.

He lifted a chair, and with infinite care placed it so that it faced the dreaded inner door. His wife moved slightly, so as to also squarely face it. A silence came upon them in which they seemed to be waiting for a calamity, pealing and deadly.

Williams finally coughed behind his hand. His wife started, and looked upon him in alarm. " 'Pears like he done gwine keep quiet ter-night," he breathed. They continually pointed their speech and their looks at the inner door, paying it the homage due to a corpse or a phantom. Another long stillness followed this sentence. Their eyes shone white and wide. A wagon rattled down the distant road. From their chairs they looked at the window, and the effect of the light in the cabin was a presentation of an intensely black and solemn night. The old woman adopted the attitude used always in church at funerals. At times she seemed to be upon the point of breaking out in prayer.

"He mighty quiet ter-night," whispered Williams. "Was he good ter-day?" For answer his wife raised her eyes to the ceiling in the supplication of Job. Williams moved restlessly. Finally he tiptoed to the door. He knelt slowly and without a sound, and placed his ear near the key-hole. Hearing a noise behind him, he turned quickly. His wife was staring at him aghast. She stood in front of the stove, and her arms were spread out in the natural movement to protect all her sleeping ducklings.

But Williams arose without having touched the door. "I raikon he er-sleep," he said, fingering his wool. He debated with himself for some time. During this interval his wife remained, a great fat statue of a mother shielding her children.

It was plain that his mind was swept suddenly by a wave of temerity. With a sounding step he moved toward the door. His fingers were almost upon the knob when he swiftly ducked and dodged away, clapping his hands to the back of his head. It was as if the portal had threatened him. There was a little tumult near the stove, where Mrs. Williams's desperate retreat had involved her feet with the prostrate children.

After the panic Williams bore traces of a feeling of shame. He returned to the charge. He firmly grasped the knob with his left hand, and with his other hand turned the key in the lock. He pushed the door, and as it swung portentously open he sprang nimbly to one side like the fearful slave liberating the lion. Near the stove a group had formed, the terror-stricken mother with her arms stretched, and the aroused children clinging frenziedly to her skirts.

The light streamed after the swinging door, and disclosed a room six feet one way and six feet the other way. It was small enough to enable the radiance to lay it plain. Williams peered warily around the corner made by the door-post.

Suddenly he advanced, retired, and advanced again with a howl. His palsied family had expected him to spring backward, and at his howl they heaped themselves wondrously. But Williams simply stood in the little room emitting his howls before an open window. "He's gone! He's gone! He's gone!" His eye and his hand had speedily proved the fact. He had even thrown open a little cupboard.

Presently he came flying out. He grabbed his hat, and hurled the outer door back upon its hinges. Then he tumbled headlong into the night. He was yelling: "Docteh Trescott! Docteh Trescott!" He ran wildly through the fields, and galloped in the direction of town. He continued to call to Trescott, as if the latter was within easy hearing. It was as if Trescott was poised in the contemplative sky over the running negro, and could heed this reaching voice—"Docteh Trescott!"

In the cabin, Mrs. Williams, supported by relays from the battalion of children, stood quaking watch until the truth of daylight came as a re-enforcement and made them arrogant, strutting, swashbuckler children, and a mother who proclaimed her illimitable courage.

XVI

Theresa Page was giving a party. It was the outcome of a long series of arguments addressed to her mother, which had been overheard in part by her father. He had at last said five words, "Oh, let her have it." The mother had then gladly capitulated.

Theresa had written nineteen invitations, and distributed them at recess to her schoolmates. Later her mother had composed five large cakes, and still later a vast amount of lemonade.

So the nine little girls and the ten little boys sat quite primly in the dining-room, while Theresa and her mother plied them with cake and lemonade, and also with ice-cream. This primness sat now quite strangely upon them. It was owing to the presence of Mrs. Page. Previously in the parlor alone with their games they had overturned a chair; the boys had let more or less of their hoodlum spirit shine forth. But when circumstances could be possibly magnified to warrant it, the girls made the boys victims of an insufferable pride, snubbing them mercilessly. So in the dining-room they resembled a class at Sunday-school, if it were not for the subterranean smiles, gestures, rebuffs, and poutings which stamped the affair as a children's party.

Two little girls of this subdued gathering were planted in a settle with their backs to the broad window. They were beaming lovingly upon each other with an effect of scorning the boys.

Hearing a noise behind her at the window, one little girl turned to face it. Instantly she screamed and sprang away, covering her face with her hands. "What was it? What was it?" cried every one in a roar. Some slight movement of the eyes of the weeping and shuddering child informed the company that she had been frightened by an appearance at the window. At once they all faced the imperturbable window, and for a moment there was a silence. An astute lad made an immediate census of the other lads. The prank of slipping out and looming spectrally at a window was too venerable. But the little boys were all present and astonished.

As they recovered their minds they uttered warlike cries, and through a side door sallied rapidly out against the terror. They vied with each other in daring.

None wished particularly to encounter a dragon in the darkness of the garden, but there could be no faltering when the fair ones in the dining-room were present. Calling to each other in stern voices, they went dragooning over the lawn, attacking the shadows with ferocity, but still with the caution of reasonable beings. They found, however, nothing new to the peace of the night. Of course there was a lad who told a great lie. He described a grim figure, bending low and slinking off along the fence. He gave a number of details, rendering his lie more splendid by a repetition of certain forms which he recalled from romances. For instance, he insisted that he had heard the creature emit a hollow laugh.

Inside the house the little girl who had raised the alarm was still shuddering and weeping. With the utmost difficulty was she brought to a state approximating calmness by Mrs. Page. Then she wanted to go home at once.

Page entered the house at this time. He had exiled himself until he concluded that this children's party was finished and gone. He was obliged to escort the little girl home because she screamed again when they opened the door and she saw the night.

She was not coherent even to her mother. Was it a man? She didn't know. It was simply a thing, a dreadful thing.

XVII

In Watermelon Alley the Farraguts were spending their evening as usual on the little rickety porch. Sometimes they howled gossip to other people on other rickety porches. The thin wail of a baby arose from a near house. A man had a terrific altercation with his wife, to which the alley paid no attention at all.

There appeared suddenly before the Farraguts a monster making a low and sweeping bow. There was an instant's pause, and then occurred something that resembled the effect of an upheaval of the earth's surface. The old woman hurled herself backward with a dreadful cry. Young Sim had been perched gracefully on a railing. At sight of the monster he simply fell over it to the ground. He made no sound, his eyes stuck out, his nerveless hands tried to grapple the rail to prevent a tumble, and then he vanished. Bella, blubbering, and with her hair suddenly and mysteriously dishevelled, was crawling on her hands and knees fearsomely up the steps.

Standing before this wreck of a family gathering, the monster continued to bow. It even raised a deprecatory claw. "Don' make no botheration 'bout me, Miss Fa'gut," it said, politely. "No, 'deed. I jes drap in ter ax if yer well this evenin', Miss Fa'gut. Don' make no botheration. No, 'deed. I gwine ax you to go to er daince with me, Miss Fa'gut. I ax you if I can have the magnifercent gratitude of you' company on that 'casion, Miss Fa'gut."

The girl cast a miserable glance behind her. She was still crawling away. On the ground beside the porch young Sim raised a strange bleat, which expressed both his fright and his lack of wind. Presently the monster, with a fashionable amble, ascended the steps after the girl.

She grovelled in a corner of the room as the creature took a chair. It seated itself very elegantly on the edge. It held an old cap in both hands. "Don' make no botheration, Miss Fa'gut. Don' make no botherations. No, 'deed. I jes drap in ter ax you if you won' do me the proud of acceptin' ma humble invitation to er daince, Miss Fa'gut."

She shielded her eyes with her arms and tried to crawl past it, but the genial monster blocked the way. "I jes drap in ter ax you 'bout er daince, Miss Fa'gut. I ax you if I kin have the magnifercent gratitude of you' company on that 'casion, Miss Fa'gut."

In a last outbreak of despair, the girl, shuddering and wailing, threw herself face downward on the floor, while the monster sat on the edge of the chair gabbling courteous invitations, and holding the old hat daintily to its stomach.

At the back of the house, Mrs. Farragut, who was of enormous weight, and who for eight years had done little more than sit in an arm-chair and describe her various ailments, had with speed and agility scaled a high board fence.

XVIII

The black mass in the middle of Trescott's property was hardly allowed to cool before the builders were at work on another house. It had sprung upward at a fabulous rate. It was like a magical composition born of the ashes. The doctor's office was the first part to be completed, and he had already moved in his new books and instruments and medicines.

Trescott sat before his desk when the chief of police arrived. "Well, we found him," said the latter.

"Did you?" cried the doctor. "Where?"

"Shambling around the streets at daylight this morning. I'll be blamed if I can figure on where he passed the night."

"Where is he now?"

"Oh, we jugged him. I didn't know what else to do with him. That's what I want you to tell me. Of course we can't keep him. No charge could be made, you know."

"I'll come down and get him."

The official grinned retrospectively. "Must say he had a fine career while he was out. First thing he did was to break up a children's party at Page's. Then he went to Watermelon Alley. Whoo! He stampeded the whole outfit. Men, women, and children running pell-mell, and yelling. They say one old woman broke her leg, or something, shinning over a fence. Then he went right out on the main street, and an Irish girl threw a fit, and there was a sort of a riot. He began to run, and a big crowd chased him, firing rocks. But he gave them the slip somehow down there by the foundry and in the railroad yard. We looked for him all night, but couldn't find him."

"Was he hurt any? Did anybody hit him with a stone?"

"Guess there isn't much of him to hurt any more, is there? Guess he's been hurt up to the limit. No. They never touched him. Of course nobody really wanted to hit him, but you know how a crowd gets. It's like—it's like—"

"Yes, I know."

For a moment the chief of the police looked reflectively at the floor. Then he spoke hesitatingly. "You know Jake Winter's little girl was the one that he scared at the party. She is pretty sick, they say."

"Is she? Why, they didn't call me. I always attend the Winter family."

"No? Didn't they?" asked the chief, slowly. "Well—you know—Winter is—well, Winter has gone clean crazy over this business. He wanted—he wanted to have you arrested."

"Have me arrested? The idiot! What in the name of wonder could he have me arrested for?"

"Of course. He is a fool. I told him to keep his trap shut. But then you know how he'll go all over town yapping about the thing. I thought I'd better tip you."

"Oh, he is of no consequence; but then, of course, I'm obliged to you, Sam."

"That's all right. Well, you'll be down to-night and take him out, eh? You'll get a good welcome from the jailer. He don't like his job for a cent. He says you can have your man whenever you want him. He's got no use for him."

"But what is this business of Winter's about having me arrested?"

"Oh, it's a lot of chin about your having no right to allow this—this—this man to be at large. But I told him to tend to his own business. Only I thought I'd better let you know. And I might as well say right now, doctor, that there is a good deal of talk about this thing. If I were you, I'd come to the jail pretty late at night, because there is likely to be a crowd around the door, and I'd bring a—er—mask, or some kind of a veil, anyhow."

XIX

Martha Goodwin was single, and well along into the thin years. She lived with her married sister in Whilomville. She performed nearly all the house-work in exchange for the priv-ilege of existence. Every one tacitly recognized her labor as a form of penance for the early end of her betrothed, who had died of small-pox, which he had not caught from her.

But despite the strenuous and unceasing workaday of her life, she was a woman of great mind. She had adamantine opinions upon the situation in Armenia, the condition of women in China, the flirtation between Mrs. Minster of Ni-agara Avenue and young Griscom, the conflict in the Bible class of the Baptist Sunday-school, the duty of the United States toward the Cuban insurgents, and many other colossal matters. Her fullest experience of violence was gained on an occasion when she had seen a hound clubbed, but in the plan which she had made for the reform of the world she advo-cated drastic measures. For instance, she contended that all the Turks should be pushed into the sea and drowned, and that Mrs. Minster and young Griscom should be hanged side by side on twin gallows. In fact, this woman of peace, who had seen only peace, argued constantly for a creed of illimit-able ferocity. She was invulnerable on these questions, be-cause eventually she overrode all opponents with a sniff. This sniff was an active force. It was to her antagonists like a bang over the head, and none was known to recover from this expression of exalted contempt. It left them windless and con-quered. They never again came forward as candidates for suppression. And Martha walked her kitchen with a stern brow, an invincible being like Napoleon.

Nevertheless her acquaintances, from the pain of their defeats, had been long in secret revolt. It was in no wise a conspiracy, because they did not care to state their open rebellion, but nevertheless it was understood that any woman who could not coincide with one of Martha's contentions was entitled to the support of others in the small circle. It amounted to an arrangement by which all were required to disbelieve any theory for which Martha fought. This, however, did not prevent them from speaking of her mind with profound respect.

Two people bore the brunt of her ability. Her sister Kate was visibly afraid of her, while Carrie Dungen sailed across from her kitchen to sit respectfully at Martha's feet and learn the business of the world. To be sure, afterward, under another sun, she always laughed at Martha and pretended to deride her ideas, but in the presence of the sovereign she always remained silent or admiring. Kate, the sister, was of no consequence at all. Her principal delusion was that she did all the work in the upstairs rooms of the house, while Martha did it downstairs. The truth was seen only by the husband, who treated Martha with a kindness that was half banter, half deference. Martha herself had no suspicion that she was the only pillar of the domestic edifice. The situation was without definitions. Martha made definitions, but she devoted them entirely to the Armenians and Griscom and the Chinese and other subjects. Her dreams, which in early days had been of love of meadows and the shade of trees, of the face of a man, were now involved otherwise, and they were companioned in the kitchen curiously, Cuba, the hot-water kettle, Armenia, the washing of the dishes, and the whole thing being jumbled. In regard to social misdemeanors, she who was simply the mausoleum of a dead passion was probably the most savage critic in town. This unknown woman, hidden in a kitchen as in a well, was sure to have a considerable effect of the one kind or the other in the life of the town. Every time it moved a yard, she had personally contributed an inch. She could hammer so stoutly upon the door of a proposition that it would break from its hinges and fall upon her, but at any rate it moved. She was an engine, and the fact that she did not know that she was an engine contributed largely to the effect. One reason that she was formidable was that she did not even imagine that she was formidable. She remained a weak, innocent, and pig-headed creature, who alone would defy the universe if she thought the universe merited this proceeding.

One day Carrie Dungen came across from her kitchen with speed. She had a great deal of grist. "Oh," she cried, "Henry Johnson got away from where they was keeping him, and came to town last night, and scared everybody almost to death."

Martha was shining a dish-pan, polishing madly. No reasonable person could see cause for this operation, because the pan already glistened like silver. "Well!" she ejaculated. She imparted to the word a deep meaning. "This, my prophecy, has come to pass." It was a habit.

The overplus of information was choking Carrie. Before she could go on she was obliged to struggle for a moment. "And, oh, little Sadie Winter is awful sick, and they say Jake Winter was around this morning trying to get Doctor Trescott arrested. And poor old Mrs. Farragut sprained her ankle in trying to climb a fence. And there's a crowd around the jail all the time. They put Henry in jail because they didn't know what else to do with him, I guess. They say he is perfectly terrible."

Martha finally released the dish-pan and confronted the headlong speaker. "Well!" she said again, poising a great brown rag. Kate had heard the excited new-comer, and drifted down from the novel in her room. She was a shivery little woman. Her shoulder-blades seemed to be two panes of ice, for she was constantly shrugging and shrugging. "Serves him right if he was to lose all his patients," she said suddenly, in blood-thirsty tones. She snipped her words out as if her lips were scissors.

"Well, he's likely to," shouted Carrie Dungen. "Don't a lot of people say that they won't have him any more? If you're sick and nervous, Doctor Trescott would scare the life out of you, wouldn't he? He would me. I'd keep thinking."

Martha, stalking to and fro, sometimes surveyed the two other women with a contemplative frown.

XX

After the return from Connecticut, little Jimmie was at first much afraid of the monster who lived in the room over the carriage-house. He could not identify it in any way. Gradually, however, his fear dwindled under the influence of a weird fascination. He sidled into closer and closer relations with it.

One time the monster was seated on a box behind the stable basking in the rays of the afternoon sun. A heavy crêpe veil was swathed about its head.

Little Jimmie and many companions came around the corner of the stable. They were all in what was popularly known as the baby class, and consequently escaped from school a half-hour before the other children. They halted abruptly at sight of the figure on the box. Jimmie waved his hand with the air of a proprietor.

"There he is," he said.

"O-o-o!" murmured all the little boys—"o-o-o!" They shrank back, and grouped according to courage or experience, as at the sound the monster slowly turned its head. Jimmie had remained in the van alone. "Don't be afraid! I won't let him hurt you," he said, delighted.

"Huh!" they replied, contemptuously. "We ain't afraid."

Jimmie seemed to reap all the joys of the owner and exhibitor of one of the world's marvels, while his audience remained at a distance—awed and entranced, fearful and envious.

One of them addressed Jimmie gloomily. "Bet you dassent walk right up to him." He was an older boy than Jimmie, and habitually oppressed him to a small degree. This new social elevation of the smaller lad probably seemed revolutionary to him.

"Huh!" said Jimmie, with deep scorn. "Dassent I? Dassent I, hey? Dassent I?"

The group was immensely excited. It turned its eyes upon the boy that Jimmie addressed. "No, you dassent," he said, stolidly, facing a moral defeat. He could see that Jimmie was resolved. "No, you dassent," he repeated, doggedly.

"Ho!" cried Jimmie. "You just watch!—you just watch!"

Amid a silence he turned and marched toward the monster.

But possibly the palpable wariness of his companions had an effect upon him that weighed more than his previous experience, for suddenly, when near to the monster, he halted dubiously. But his playmates immediately uttered a derisive shout, and it seemed to force him forward. He went to the monster and laid his hand delicately on its shoulder. "Hello, Henry," he said, in a voice that trembled a trifle. The monster was crooning a weird line of negro melody that was scarcely more than a thread of sound, and it paid no heed to the boy.

Jimmie strutted back to his companions. They acclaimed him and hooted his opponent. Amidst this clamor the larger boy with difficulty preserved a dignified attitude.

"I dassent, dassent I?" said Jimmie to him. "Now, you're so smart, let's see you do it!"

This challenge brought forth renewed taunts from the others. The larger boy puffed out his cheeks. "Well, I ain't afraid," he explained, sullenly. He had made a mistake in diplomacy, and now his small enemies were tumbling his prestige all about his ears. They crowed like roosters and bleated like lambs, and made many other noises which were supposed to bury him in ridicule and dishonor. "Well, I ain't afraid," he continued to explain through the din.

Jimmie, the hero of the mob, was pitiless. "You ain't afraid, hey?" he sneered. "If you ain't afraid, go do it, then."

"Well, I would if I wanted to," the other retorted. His eyes wore an expression of profound misery, but he preserved steadily other portions of a pot-valiant air. He suddenly faced one of his persecutors. "If you're so smart, why don't you go do it?" This persecutor sank promptly through the group to the rear. The incident gave the badgered one a breathing-spell, and for a moment even turned the derision in another direction. He took advantage of his interval. "I'll do it if anybody else will," he announced, swaggering to and fro.

Candidates for the adventure did not come forward. To defend themselves from this counter-charge, the other boys again set up their crowing and bleating. For a while they would hear nothing from him. Each time he opened his lips their chorus of noises made oratory impossible. But at last he was able to repeat that he would volunteer to dare as much in the affair as any other boy.

"Well, you go first," they shouted.

But Jimmie intervened to once more lead the populace against the large boy. "You're mighty brave, ain't you?" he said to him. "You dared me to do it, and I did—didn't I? Now who's afraid?" The others cheered this view loudly, and they instantly resumed the baiting of the large boy.

He shamefacedly scratched his left shin with his right foot. "Well, I ain't afraid." He cast an eye at the monster. "Well, I ain't afraid." With a glare of hatred at his squalling tormentors, he finally announced a grim intention. "Well, I'll do it, then, since you're so fresh. Now!"

The mob subsided as with a formidable countenance he turned toward the impassive figure on the box. The advance was also a regular progression from high daring to craven hesitation. At last, when some yards from the monster, the lad came to a full halt, as if he had encountered a stone wall. The observant little boys in the distance promptly hooted. Stung again by these cries, the lad sneaked two yards forward. He was crouched like a young cat ready for a backward spring. The crowd at the rear, beginning to respect this display, uttered some encouraging cries. Suddenly the lad gathered himself together, made a white and desperate rush forward, touched the monster's shoulder with a far-out-stretched finger, and sped away, while his laughter rang out wild, shrill, and exultant.

The crowd of boys reverenced him at once, and began to throng into his camp, and look at him, and be his admirers. Jimmie was discomfited for a moment, but he and the larger boy, without agreement or word of any kind, seemed to recognize a truce, and they swiftly combined and began to parade before the others.

"Why, it's just as easy as nothing," puffed the larger boy. "Ain't it, Jim?"

"Course," blew Jimmie. "Why, it's as e-e-easy."

They were people of another class. If they had been decorated for courage on twelve battle-fields, they could not have made the other boys more ashamed of the situation.

Meanwhile they condescended to explain the emotions of the excursion, expressing unqualified contempt for any one who could hang back. "Why, it ain't nothin'. He won't do nothin' to you," they told the others, in tones of exasperation.

One of the very smallest boys in the party showed signs of a wistful desire to distinguish himself, and they turned their attention to him, pushing at his shoulders while he swung away from them, and hesitated dreamily. He was eventually induced to make furtive expedition, but it was only for a few yards. Then he paused, motionless, gazing with open mouth. The vociferous entreaties of Jimmie and the large boy had no power over him.

Mrs. Hannigan had come out on her back porch with a pail of water. From this coign she had a view of the secluded portion of the Trescott grounds that was behind the stable. She perceived the group of boys, and the monster on the box. She shaded her eyes with her hand to benefit her vision. She screeched then as if she was being murdered. "Eddie! Eddie! You come home this minute!"

Her son querulously demanded, "Aw, what for?"

"You come home this minute. Do you hear?"

The other boys seemed to think this visitation upon one of their number required them to preserve for a time the hang-dog air of a collection of culprits, and they remained in guilty silence until the little Hannigan, wrathfully protesting, was pushed through the door of his home. Mrs. Hannigan cast a piercing glance over the group, stared with a bitter face at the Trescott house, as if this new and handsome edifice was insulting her, and then followed her son.

There was wavering in the party. An inroad by one mother always caused them to carefully sweep the horizon to see if there were more coming. "This is my yard," said Jimmie, proudly. "We don't have to go home."

The monster on the box had turned its black crêpe countenance toward the sky, and was waving its arms in time to a religious chant. "Look at him now," cried a little boy. They turned, and were transfixed by the solemnity and mystery of the indefinable gestures. The wail of the melody was mournful and slow. They drew back. It seemed to spellbind them with the power of a funeral. They were so absorbed that they did not hear the doctor's buggy drive up to the stable. Trescott got out, tied his horse, and approached the group. Jimmie saw him first, and at his look of dismay the others wheeled.

"What's all this, Jimmie?" asked Trescott, in surprise.

The lad advanced to the front of his companions, halted, and said nothing. Trescott's face gloomed slightly as he scanned the scene.

"What were you doing, Jimmie?"

"We was playin'," answered Jimmie, huskily.

"Playing at what?"

"Just playin'."

Trescott looked gravely at the other boys, and asked them to please go home. They proceeded to the street much in the manner of frustrated and revealed assassins. The crime of trespass on another boy's place was still a crime when they had only accepted the other boy's cordial invitation, and they were used to being sent out of all manner of gardens upon the sudden appearance of a father or a mother. Jimmie had wretchedly watched the departure of his companions. It involved the loss of his position as a lad who controlled the privileges of his father's grounds, but then he knew that in the beginning he had no right to ask so many boys to be his guests.

Once on the sidewalk, however, they speedily forgot their shame as trespassers, and the large boy launched forth in a description of his success in the late trial of courage. As they went rapidly up the street, the little boy who had made the furtive expedition cried out confidently from the rear, "Yes, and I went almost up to him, didn't I, Willie?"

The large boy crushed him in a few words. "Huh!" he scoffed. "You only went a little way. I went clear up to him."

The pace of the other boys was so manly that the tiny thing had to trot, and he remained at the rear, getting entangled in their legs in his attempts to reach the front rank and become of some importance, dodging this way and that way, and always piping out his little claim to glory.

XXI

"By-the-way, Grace," said Trescott, looking into the dining-room from his office door, "I wish you would send Jimmie to me before school-time."

When Jimmie came, he advanced so quietly that Trescott did not at first note him. "Oh," he said, wheeling from a cabinet, "here you are, young man."

"Yes, sir."

Trescott dropped into his chair and tapped the desk with a thoughtful finger. "Jimmie, what were you doing in the back garden yesterday—you and the other boys—to Henry?"

"We weren't doing anything, pa."

Trescott looked sternly into the raised eyes of his son. "Are you sure you were not annoying him in any way? Now what were you doing, exactly?"

"Why, we—why, we—now—Willie Dalzel said I dassent go right up to him, and I did; and then he did; and then— the other boys were 'fraid; and then—you comed."

Trescott groaned deeply. His countenance was so clouded in sorrow that the lad, bewildered by the mystery of it, burst suddenly forth in dismal lamentations. "There, there. Don't cry, Jim," said Trescott, going round the desk. "Only—" He sat in a great leather reading-chair, and took the boy on his knee. "Only I want to explain to you—"

After Jimmie had gone to school, and as Trescott was about to start on his round of morning calls, a message arrived from Doctor Moser. It set forth that the latter's sister was dying in the old homestead, twenty miles away up the valley, and asked Trescott to care for his patients for the day at least. There was also in the envelope a little history of each case and of what had already been done. Trescott replied to the messenger that he would gladly assent to the arrangement.

He noted that the first name on Moser's list was Winter, but this did not seem to strike him as an important fact. When its turn came, he rang the Winter bell. "Good-morning, Mrs. Winter," he said, cheerfully, as the door was opened. "Doctor Moser has been obliged to leave town to-day, and he has asked me to come in his stead. How is the little girl this morning?"

Mrs. Winter had regarded him in stony surprise. At last she said: "Come in! I'll see my husband." She bolted into the house. Trescott entered the hall, and turned to the left into the sitting-room.

Presently Winter shuffled through the door. His eyes flashed toward Trescott. He did not betray any desire to advance far into the room. "What do you want?" he said.

"What do I want? What do I want?" repeated Trescott, lifting his head suddenly. He had heard an utterly new challenge in the night of the jungle.

"Yes, that's what I want to know," snapped Winter. "What do you want?"

Trescott was silent for a moment. He consulted Moser's memoranda. "I see that your little girl's case is a trifle serious," he remarked. "I would advise you to call a physician soon. I will leave you a copy of Doctor Moser's record to give to any one you may call." He paused to transcribe the record on a page of his note-book. Tearing out the leaf, he extended it to Winter as he moved toward the door. The latter shrunk against the wall. His head was hanging as he reached for the paper. This caused him to grasp air, and so Trescott simply let the paper flutter to the feet of the other man.

"Good-morning," said Trescott from the hall. This placid retreat seemed to suddenly arouse Winter to ferocity. It was as if he had then recalled all the truths which he had formulated to hurl at Trescott. So he followed him into the hall, and down the hall to the door, and through the door to the porch, barking in fiery rage from a respectful distance. As Trescott imperturbably turned the mare's head down the road, Winter stood on the porch, still yelping. He was like a little dog.

XXII

"Have you heard the news?" cried Carrie Dungen, as she sped toward Martha's kitchen. "Have you heard the news?" Her eyes were shining with delight.

"No," answered Martha's sister Kate, bending forward eagerly. "What was it? What was it?"

Carrie appeared triumphantly in the open door. "Oh, there's been an awful scene between Doctor Trescott and Jake Winter. I never thought that Jake Winter had any pluck at all, but this morning he told the doctor just what he thought of him."

"Well, what did he think of him?" asked Martha.

"Oh, he called him everything. Mrs. Howarth heard it through her front blinds. It was terrible, she says. It's all over town now. Everybody knows it."

"Didn't the doctor answer back?"

"No! Mrs. Howarth—she says he never said a word. He just walked down to his buggy and got in, and drove off as co-o-o-l. But Jake gave him jinks, by all accounts."

"But what did he say?" cried Kate, shrill and excited. She was evidently at some kind of a feast.

"Oh, he told him that Sadie had never been well since that night Henry Johnson frightened her at Theresa Page's party, and he held him responsible, and how dared he cross his threshold—and—and—and—"

"And what?" said Martha.

"Did he swear at him?" said Kate, in fearsome glee.

"No—not much. He did swear at him a little, but not more than a man does anyhow when he is real mad, Mrs. Howarth says."

"O-oh!" breathed Kate. "And did he call him any names?"

Martha, at her work, had been for a time in deep thought. She now interrupted the others. "It don't seem as if Sadie Winter had been sick since that time Henry Johnson got loose. She's been to school almost the whole time since then, hasn't she?"

They combined upon her in immediate indignation. "School? School? I should say not. Don't think for a moment. School!"

Martha wheeled from the sink. She held an iron spoon, and it seemed as if she was going to attack them. "Sadie Winter has passed here many a morning since then carrying her school-bag. Where was she going? To a wedding?"

The others, long accustomed to a mental tyranny, speedily surrendered.

"Did she?" stammered Kate. "I never saw her."

Carrie Dungen made a weak gesture.

"If I had been Doctor Trescott," exclaimed Martha, loudly, "I'd have knocked that miserable Jake Winter's head off."

Kate and Carrie, exchanging glances, made an alliance in the air. "I don't see why you say that, Martha," replied Carrie, with considerable boldness, gaining support and sympathy from Kate's smile. "I don't see how anybody can be blamed for getting angry when their little girl gets almost scared to death and gets sick from it, and all that. Besides, everybody says—"

"Oh, I don't care what everybody says," said Martha.

"Well, you can't go against the whole town," answered Carrie, in sudden sharp defiance.

"No, Martha, you can't go against the whole town," piped Kate, following her leader rapidly.

" 'The whole town,' " cried Martha. "I'd like to know what you call 'the whole town.' Do you call these silly people who are scared of Henry Johnson 'the whole town'?"

"Why, Martha," said Carrie, in a reasoning tone, "you talk as if you wouldn't be scared of him!"

"No more would I," retorted Martha.

"O-oh, Martha, how you talk!" said Kate. "Why, the idea! Everybody's afraid of him."

Carrie was grinning. "You've never seen him, have you?" she asked, seductively.

"No," admitted Martha.

"Well, then, how do you know that you wouldn't be scared?"

Martha confronted her. "Have you ever seen him? No? Well, then, how do you know you *would* be scared?"

The allied forces broke out in chorus: "But, Martha, everybody says so. Everybody says so."

"Everybody says what?"

"Everybody that's seen him say they were frightened almost to death. 'Tisn't only women, but it's men too. It's awful."

Martha wagged her head solemnly. "I'd try not to be afraid of him."

"But supposing you could not help it?" said Kate.

"Yes, and look here," cried Carrie. "I'll tell you another thing. The Hannigans are going to move out of the house next door."

"On account of him?" demanded Martha.

Carrie nodded. "Mrs. Hannigan says so herself."

"Well, of all things!" ejaculated Martha. "Going to move, eh? You don't say so! Where they going to move to?"

"Down on Orchard Avenue."

"Well, of all things! Nice house?"

"I don't know about that. I haven't heard. But there's lots of nice houses on Orchard."

"Yes, but they're all taken," said Kate. "There isn't a vacant house on Orchard Avenue."

"Oh yes, there is," said Martha. "The old Hampstead house is vacant."

"Oh, of course," said Kate. "But then I don't believe Mrs. Hannigan would like it there. I wonder where they can be going to move to?"

"I'm sure I don't know," sighed Martha. "It must be to some place we don't know about."

"Well," said Carrie Dungen, after a general reflective silence, "it's easy enough to find out, anyhow."

"Who knows—around here?" asked Kate.

"Why, Mrs. Smith, and there she is in her garden," said Carrie, jumping to her feet. As she dashed out of the door, Kate and Martha crowded at the window. Carrie's voice rang out from near the steps. "Mrs. Smith! Mrs. Smith! Do you know where the Hannigans are going to move to?"

XXIII

The autumn smote the leaves and the trees of Whilomville were panoplied in crimson and yellow. The winds grew stronger, and in the melancholy purple of the nights the home shine of a window became a finer thing. The little boys, watching the sear and sorrowful leaves drifting down from the maples, dreamed of the near time when they could heap bushels in the streets and burn them during the abrupt evenings.

Three men walked down Niagara Avenue. As they approached Judge Hagenthorpe's house he came down his walk to meet them in the manner of one who has been waiting.

"Are you ready, judge?" one said.

"All ready," he answered.

The four then walked to Trescott's house. He received them in his office, where he had been reading. He seemed surprised at this visit of four very active and influential citizens, but he had nothing to say of it.

After they were all seated, Trescott looked expectantly from one face to another. There was a little silence. It was broken by John Twelve, the wholesale grocer, who was worth $400,000, and reported to be worth over a million.

"Well, doctor," he said, with a short laugh, "I suppose we might as well admit at once that we've come to interfere in something which is none of our business."

"Why, what is it?" asked Trescott, again looking from one face to another. He seemed to appeal particularly to Judge Hagenthorpe, but the old man had his chin lowered musingly to his cane, and would not look at him.

"It's about what nobody talks of—much," said Twelve. "It's about Henry Johnson."

Trescott squared himself in his chair. "Yes?" he said.

Having delivered himself of the title, Twelve seemed to become more easy. "Yes," he answered, blandly, "we wanted to talk to you about it."

"Yes?" said Trescott.

Twelve abruptly advanced on the main attack. "Now see here, Trescott, we like you, and we have come to talk right out about this business. It may be none of our affairs and all that, and as for me, I don't mind if you tell me so; but I am not going to keep quiet and see you ruin yourself. And that's how we all feel."

"I am not ruining myself," answered Trescott.

"No, maybe you are not exactly ruining yourself," said Twelve, slowly, "but you are doing yourself a great deal of harm. You have changed from being the leading doctor in town to about the last one. It is mainly because there are always a large number of people who are very thoughtless fools, of course, but then that doesn't change the condition."

A man who had not heretofore spoken said, solemnly, "It's the women."

"Well, what I want to say is this," resumed Twelve. "Even

if there are a lot of fools in the world, we can't see any reason why you should ruin yourself by opposing them. You can't teach them anything, you know."

"I am not trying to teach them anything." Trescott smiled wearily. "I—It is a matter of—well—"

"And there are a good many of us that admire you for it immensely," interrupted Twelve; "but that isn't going to change the minds of all those ninnies."

"It's the women," stated the advocate of this view again.

"Well, what I want to say is this," said Twelve. "We want you to get out of this trouble and strike your old gait again. You are simply killing your practice through your infernal pig-headedness. Now this thing is out of the ordinary, but there must be ways to—to beat the game somehow, you see. So we've talked it over—about a dozen of us—and, as I say, if you want to tell us to mind our own business, why, go ahead; but we've talked it over, and we've come to the conclusion that the only way to do is to get Johnson a place somewhere off up the valley, and—"

Trescott wearily gestured. "You don't know, my friend. Everybody is so afraid of him, they can't even give him good care. Nobody can attend to him as I do myself."

"But I have a little no-good farm up beyond Clarence Mountain that I was going to give to Henry," cried Twelve, aggrieved. "And if you—and if you—if you—through your house burning down, or anything—why, all the boys were prepared to take him right off your hands, and—and—"

Trescott arose and went to the window. He turned his back upon them. They sat waiting in silence. When he returned he kept his face in the shadow. "No, John Twelve," he said, "it can't be done."

There was another stillness. Suddenly a man stirred on his chair.

"Well, then, a public institution—" he began.

"No," said Trescott; "public institutions are all very good, but he is not going to one."

In the background of the group old Judge Hagenthorpe was thoughtfully smoothing the polished ivory head of his cane.

XXIV

Trescott loudly stamped the snow from his feet and shook the flakes from his shoulders. When he entered the house he went at once to the dining-room, and then to the sitting-room. Jimmie was there, reading painfully in a large book concerning giraffes and tigers and crocodiles.

"Where is your mother, Jimmie?" asked Trescott.

"I don't know, pa," answered the boy. "I think she is upstairs."

Trescott went to the foot of the stairs and called, but there came no answer. Seeing that the door of the little drawing-room was open, he entered. The room was bathed in the half-light that came from the four dull panes of mica in the front of the great stove. As his eyes grew used to the shadows he saw his wife curled in an arm-chair. He went to her. "Why, Grace," he said, "didn't you hear me calling you?"

She made no answer, and as he bent over the chair he heard her trying to smother a sob in the cushion.

"Grace!" he cried. "You're crying!"

She raised her face. "I've got a headache, a dreadful headache, Ned."

"A headache?" he repeated, in surprise and incredulity.

He pulled a chair close to hers. Later, as he cast his eye over the zone of light shed by the dull red panes, he saw that a low table had been drawn close to the stove, and that it was burdened with many small cups and plates of uncut tea-cake. He remembered that the day was Wednesday, and that his wife received on Wednesdays.

"Who was here to-day, Gracie?" he asked.

From his shoulder there came a mumble, "Mrs. Twelve."

"Was she—um," he said. "Why—didn't Anna Hagenthorpe come over?"

The mumble from his shoulder continued, "She wasn't well enough."

Glancing down at the cups, Trescott mechanically counted them. There were fifteen of them. "There, there," he said. "Don't cry, Grace. Don't cry."

The wind was whining around the house and the snow

beat aslant upon the windows. Sometimes the coal in the stove settled with a crumbling sound and the four panes of mica flushed a sudden new crimson. As he sat holding her head on his shoulder, Trescott found himself occasionally trying to count the cups. There were fifteen of them.

ASBURY PARK

Contents

Avon's School by the Sea

AVON-BY-THE-SEA, Aug. 3 (Special).—It has become an exceedingly popular notion of late years to found summer schools at seaside and mountain resorts, so that people in their thirst for knowledge might combine the cool breezes from hillside or ocean with useful instruction and entertainment. This idea has taken such root that dozens of summer schools are flourishing all over the country. It is a noticeable fact, too, that the students of our schools and colleges are not the ones that take all the advantages of the course in summer instruction, but the business and professional men and teachers themselves are present in large numbers. On the grounds of the Seaside Assembly here one may see—and learn a great lesson from the sight—a man with the sharp, keen eye of business, and, it may be, with gray hairs on his forehead, wending his way with his books to the Hall of Philosophy to take a lesson in French, or to Otis Hall to study art. It is a familiar scene anywhere to see the old man, who has battled with adversity, put his hand on a young man's head and say: "My boy, study hard; don't give up your books. How much more I might have been in the world if I had thought more of my Caesar's Commentaries and my geometry than I did of sleighride parties and corn huskings." But here the old man has a partial way out of his difficulties. Of course, many of his lost opportunities can never be regained, but if when he comes to a beautiful summer resort for his vacation he spends an hour a day taking a course in a language or in some study that concerns his business, he receives an immense benefit. The teachers here find that men and women in middle life make just as enthusiastic scholars as the young people who are satisfying their first cravings after knowledge.

In Madame Alberti's classes in physical culture, it is interesting to note the look of surprise on people's faces, many of them showing the marks of age, when they learn for the first time the proper way to pick up articles from the floor or the scientific method of taking a chair, or, as an old farmer said to a friend, when asked how he liked the lecture, "I'm going on sixty-six-year-old, an' I never knew how to shet a door or git out'n a wagon before."

The teachers and instructors here are all of recognized ability, and the lecturers that come here are men who stand at the head of their respective pursuits in science or art. On next Monday the session of the American Institute of Christian Philosophy opens. The Rev. Charles F. Deems, D.D., of New-York, the president, was here a few days ago, making the final arrangements for the opening. The learned members of the institute are already making their appearance with their baggage at the hotels and boarding houses. The guests claim that they can tell the members of the institute from afar by a certain wise, grave and reverend air that hangs over them from the top of their glossy silk hats to their equally glossy boots. A member gazes at the wild tossing of the waves with a calm air of understanding and philosophy that the poor youthful graduate from college, with only a silk sash and flannel suit to assert his knowledge with, can never hope to acquire. When he learns to row on the lake or river, to his philosophical mind he is only describing an arc from the rowlock as a centre, with a radius equal to the distance between the fulcrum or rowlock and the point of resistance, vulgarly known as the tip end of the oar. When he "catches a crab" and goes over backward, he gets up and, after rubbing the back of his head, he calmly returns anew to what he calls a demonstration of the principles of applied force. He watches the merry dancers at the hotel hops with an air that says: "Vanity, vanity, all is vanity." Yet he has no doubt in his own mind, from certain little geometric calculations of his own, that he could waltz in such a scientific manner, with such an application of the laws of motion, that the best dancers would, indeed, be surprised.

Professor L. C. Elson, of the Boston Conservatory of Music, gave two of the finest lectures here ever listened to on the Assembly grounds. He had with him several rolls of old music on parchment taken from monasteries in Europe more than 600 years ago, and now worth more than their weight in gold.

Among the noted teachers connected with the art department of the Seaside Assembly is Professor Conrad Diehl, of

New-York. His genial manner has already made him many friends here and his lectures are of intense interest to his enthusiastic pupils. He began his career in art as an apprentice to some of the Art-Industries in Illinois. From there he went to the Art School in Munich for a five-years' course. He returned to Chicago with a large picture of the play scene in "Hamlet," which he presented to the Chicago Art Association in 1865. The same year he went to Paris and entered Gérôme's atelier classes at the Ecole des Beaux Arts. It was there he painted his large picture from "Macbeth," with which he came to Chicago in 1867. He assumed charge of the classes of the Chicago Academy of Design, which he conducted with but a short intermission up to the time of the great fire. He saved his picture by cutting the canvas out of the frame. Then he went to St. Louis and established an art school. The donation of the "Macbeth" picture to the city as a nucleus of a public art gallery called into existence the St. Louis Art Society. It was in the public schools of St. Louis that he developed his "Grammar of Form Languages." After serving some time as the head of the art department of the Missouri State University, he came to New-York and became the co-laborer of John Ward Stimson in the New-York Institute for Artist Artisans.

Among other prominent people connected with the Assembly is Mr. Albert G. Thies, the well-known New-York tenor. Mr. Thies has been spending his summer here, and while so doing has become identified with the Assembly in a musical capacity. He has a voice of great compass and sweetness, with which he has several times charmed the guests of the hotels and the Assembly audiences. He has had adventures and escapades in foreign lands such as fall to the lot of but few singers. He was educated first as a pianist, and made a tour of the Continent, playing in London, Paris, Vienna, Dublin and so on. In studying voice-culture to improve his phrasing, he discovered that he had a splendid tenor voice. So he abandoned the piano, became a singer, and finally made a tour of the world. After his return to London his adventuresome spirit took him to Africa. There he became a friend of Chinese Gordon, and was thrown in connection with Henry M. Stanley in a number of ways. He played and sang before all the British magnates of Southern Africa, and finally had the pleasure of playing before royalty, in the person of the old Chief Cetewayo, styled "King" of the Zulus, but at that time a prisoner in the hands of the English. The old "King" was much pleased with Mr. Thies's performance, and had about made up his mind to give one of his wives to the musician. In fact, he brought the four then with him in for Mr. Thies's inspection. They were all over six feet four inches in height. The "King" seemed rather dazed at finding his elegant gift "declined with thanks." The American musician was in Southern Africa at the time of the smallpox plague, when 9,000 people were down with the disease, and 3,000 deaths occurred. He helped to nurse the sufferers and escaped unscathed. He returned to America, settled in New-York, and began a musical career in America which has been very successful.

Howells Discussed at Avon-by-the-Sea

AVON-BY-THE-SEA, Aug. 17 (Special).—At the Seaside Assembly the morning lecture was delivered by Professor Hamlin Garland, of Boston, on W. D. Howells, the novelist. He said: "No man stands for a more vital principle than does Mr. Howells. He stands for modern-spirit, sympathy and truth. He believes in the progress of ideals, the relative in art. His definition of idealism cannot be improved upon, 'the truthful treatment of material.' He does not insist upon any special material, but only that the novelist be true to himself and to things as he sees them. It is absurd to call him photographic. The photograph is false in perspective, in light and shade, in focus. When a photograph can depict atmosphere and sound, the comparison will have some meaning, and then it will not be used as a reproach. Mr. Howells' work has deepened in insight and widened in sympathy from the first. His canvas has grown large, and has thickened with figures. Between *Their Wedding Journey* and *A Hazard of New Fortunes* there is an immense distance. *A Modern Instance* is the greatest, most rigidly artistic novel ever written by an American, and ranks with the great novels of the world. *A Hazard of New Fortunes* is the greatest, sanest, truest study of a city in fiction. The test of the value of Mr. Howells' work will come fifty years from now, when his sheaf of novels will form the most accurate, sympathetic and artistic study of American society yet made by an American. Howells is a many-sided man, a humorist of astonishing delicacy and imagination, and he has written of late some powerful poems in a full, free style. He is by all odds the most American and vital of our literary men to-day. He stands for all that is progressive and humanitarian in our fiction, and his following increases each day. His success is very great, and it will last."

The evening lecture was delivered by James Clement Ambrose, of Chicago. His subject was "The Sham Family."

On the Boardwalk

ASBURY PARK, N.J., Aug. 13. — During the summer months the famous boardwalk at this resort takes a sudden leap into a prominence quite equal, it would seem, to that of any street, boulevard or plaza on the earth. Apparently the centre of the world of people, not of science nor art, is situated somewhere under the long line of electric lights which dangles over the great cosmopolitan thoroughfare. It is the world of the middle classes; add but princes and gamblers and it would be what the world calls the world.

In the evening it is a glare of light and a swirl of gayly attired women and well-dressed men. There is a terrific tooting by brass bands and a sort of roar of conversation that swells up continually from the throng. There are no clusters of "fakirs" adding their shrill cries to the clamor, nor none of the many noisy devices to catch the unwatched nickle. Only the crowds, the bands and the surf.

Occasionally philosophers ponder over the question why all these people come down to the beach evening after evening. There is the sea; but it is evident, at first glance, that no one ever looks at the sea or considers it in any way. The crowd at Asbury Park does not sit and gape at the sea. The Atlantic Ocean is a matter of very small consequence. No doubt occasional glances are thrown at it. Lovers on the beach are supposed sometimes to contemplate it, when the moon peeps over the horizon, but it is apparent that the ocean is a secondary matter and is merely tolerated. It could not be the music, of course, because thousands of people would not congregate to hear indifferent bands play.

But the people come to see the people. The huge wooden hotels empty themselves directly after dinner; the boarding-houses seem to turn upside down and shake out every boarder; the cottagers make ready for an evening stroll, and up in the business part of the town the merchants and clerks bestir themselves and finish their work, roll down their sleeves and put on their coats. Then all hie to the big boardwalk. For there is joy to the heart in a crowd. One is in life and of life then. Nothing escapes; the world is going on and one is there to perceive it.

The walk itself is a heavy plank structure varying from 50 to 100 feet in width, and extending along the entire ocean frontage of the town. It is built on heavy pilings whose tops are usually from four to ten feet above the beach. Rows of immovable wooden benches stretch along the edge of the walk, and landward a lawn comes flush with it. Next to this is a brick walk and then the driveway, Ocean-ave. Statues, allegorical and memorial, occupy positions on the lawn, with also many little pavilions and summer houses. During certain hours this great passage is fairly choked with humanity. The whole space— one mile long by 50 to 100 feet wide—is alive and swarming with pedestrians. Confusion never reigns only because the general pace is leisurely and every one "keeps moving."

Day excursion trains sometimes bring down as many as 15,000 people to enjoy a few cool hours by the sea. This momentarily gives the resort a population of about 45,000. And they all appear on the beach. When great public meetings are held on the beach and boardwalk, audiences of 10,000 persons gather frequently. It is said that 20,000 people watched the participants in the annual baby parade as the nurse maids trundled their charges down the walk.

The average summer guest here is a rather portly man, with a good watch-chain and a business suit of clothes, a wife and about three children. He stands in his two shoes with American self-reliance and, playing casually with his watch-chain, looks at the world with a clear eye. He submits to the arrogant prices of some of the hotel proprietors with a calm indifference; he will pay fancy prices for things with a great unconcern. However, deliberately and baldly attempt to beat him out of fifteen cents and he will put his hands in his pockets, spread his legs apart and wrangle, in a loud voice, until sundown. All day he lies in the sand or sits on a bench, reading papers and smoking cigars, while his blessed babies are dabbling around throwing sand down his back and emptying their little pails of sea-water in his boots. In the evening he puts on his best and takes his wife and the "girls" down to the boardwalk. He enjoys himself in a very mild way and dribbles out a lot of money under the impression that he is proceeding cheaply.

However, the long-famous "summer girl" takes precedence in point of interest. She has been enshrined in sentimental rhyme and satirical prose for so long that it is difficult for one to tell just what she is and what she isn't. If one is to believe the satirists, a man would better encase himself in a barrel, put dinner-plates down his trousers' legs and shake hands with her by means of a very long-handled pitchfork. If the rhymers are to be relied on, she is a maiden with a bonny blue eye and a tender smile and with a red heart palpitant under fields of white flannel. At any rate, she is here on the boardwalk in overwhelming force and the golden youths evidently believe the poets.

The amount of summer girl and golden youth business that goes on around this boardwalk is amazing. A young man comes here, mayhap, from a distant city. Everything is new to him and in consequence, he is a new young man. He is not the same steady and, perhaps, sensible lad who bended all winter over the ledger in the city office. There is a little more rose-tint and gilt-edge to him. He finds here on the beach, as he saunters forth in his somewhat false hues, a summer girl who just suits him. She exactly fits his new environment. When he returns to the ledger he lays down his coat of strange colors and visions fade. Allah il Allah.

But she, with her escort or escorts, makes life at summer resorts. She is a bit of interesting tinsel flashing near the sombre hued waves. She gives the zest to life on the great boardwalk. Without her the men would perish from weariness or fall to fighting. Men usually fall to fighting if they are left alone long enough, and the crowd on the boardwalk would be a mob without the smile of the summer girl. She absent, the bands would play charges and retreats and the soda-water fountains would run blood. Man is compelled by nature to be either a lover or a red-handed villain.

Great storms create havoc with the heavy planking of the walk nearly every fall. The huge beams are torn and twisted and smashed by the breakers in a regardless manner, making an annual bill of expense of $15,000. This bill for repairs is met by James A. Bradley. He is a millionaire, who bought the land upon which this resort is situated years ago for a nominal price. He still has great possessions here. A part of them is the ocean front. Everybody knows him and everybody calls him "Founder Bradley." He is a familiar figure at any hour of the day. He wears a white sun-umbrella with a green lining and has very fierce and passionate whiskers, whose rigidity is relieved by an occasional twinkle in his bright Irish eye. He walks habitually with bended back and thoughtful brow, continually in the depths of some great question of finance, involving, mayhap, a change in the lumber market or the price of nails. He is noted for his wealth, his whiskers and his eccentricities. He is a great seeker after the curious. When he perceives it he buys it. Then he takes it down to the beach and puts it on the boardwalk with a little sign over it, informing the traveller of its history, its value and its virtues.

On the boardwalk now are some old boats, an ancient ship's bell, a hand fire engine of antique design, an iron anchor, a marble bathtub and various articles of interest to everybody. It is his boardwalk, and if he wants to put 7,000 fire engines and bathtubs on it he will do so. It is his privilege. No man should object to everybody doing as he pleases with his own fire engines and bathtubs.

"Founder" Bradley has lots of sport with his ocean front and boardwalk. It amuses him and he likes it. It warms his heart to see the thousands of people tramping over his boards, helter-skeltering in his sand and diving into that ocean of the Lord's which is adjacent to the beach of James A. Bradley. He likes to edit signs and have them tacked up around. There is probably no man in the world that can beat "Founder" Bradley in writing signs. His work has an air of philosophic thought about it which is very taking to any one of a literary turn of mind. He usually starts off with an abstract truth, an axiom, not foreign nor irrelevant, but bearing somewhat upon a hidden meaning in the sign—"Keep off the grass," or something of that sort. Occasionally he waxes sarcastic; at other times, historical. He may devote four lines to telling the public what happened in 1869 and draw from that a one-line lesson as to what they may not do at that moment. He has made sign-painting a fine art, and he is a master. His work, sprinkled broadcast over the boardwalk, delights the critics and incidentally warns the unwary. Strangers need no guide-book nor policemen. They have signs confronting them at all points, under their feet, over their heads and before their noses. "Thou shalt not" do this, nor that, nor the other.

He also shows genius of an advanced type and the qualities of authorship in his work. He is no mere bungler nor trivial paint-slinger. He has those powers of condensation which are so much admired at this day. For instance: "Modesty of apparel is as becoming to a lady in a bathing suit as to a lady dressed in silks and satins." There are some very sweet thoughts in that declaration. It is really a beautiful expression of sentiment. It is modest and delicate. Its author merely insinuates. There is nothing to shake vibratory senses in such gentle phraseology. Supposing he had said: "Don't go in the water attired merely in a tranquil smile," or "Do not appear on the beach when only enwrapped in reverie." A thoughtless man might have been guilty of some such unnecessary uncouthness. But to "Founder" Bradley it would be impossible. He is not merely a man. He is an artist.

Parades and Entertainments

ASBURY PARK, N.J., Aug. 20 (Special).—The parade of the Junior Order of United American Mechanics here on Wednesday afternoon was a deeply impressive one to some persons. There were hundreds of the members of the order, and they wound through the streets to the music of enough brass bands to make furious discords. It probably was the most awkward, ungainly, uncut and uncarved procession that ever raised clouds of dust on sun-beaten streets. Nevertheless, the spectacle of an Asbury Park crowd confronting such an aggregation was an interesting sight to a few people.

Asbury Park creates nothing. It does not make; it merely amuses. There is a factory where nightshirts are manufactured, but it is some miles from town. This is a resort of wealth and leisure, of women and considerable wine. The throng along the line of march was composed of summer gowns, lace parasols, tennis trousers, straw hats and indifferent smiles. The procession was composed of men, bronzed, slope-shouldered, uncouth and begrimed with dust. Their clothes fitted them illy, for the most part, and they had no ideas of marching. They merely plodded along, not seeming quite to understand, stolid, unconcerned and, in a certain sense, dignified—a pace and a bearing emblematic of their lives. They smiled occasionally and from time to time greeted friends in the crowd on the sidewalk. Such an assemblage of the spraddle-legged men of the middle class, whose hands were bent and shoulders stooped from delving and constructing, had never appeared to an Asbury Park summer crowd, and the latter was vaguely amused.

The bona fide Asbury Parker is a man to whom a dollar, when held close to his eye, often shuts out any impression he may have had that other people possess rights. He is apt to consider that men and women, especially city men and women, were created to be mulcted by him. Hence the tan-colored, sun-beaten honesty in the faces of the members of the Junior Order of United American Mechanics is expected to have a very staggering effect upon them. The visitors were men who possessed principles.

A highly attractive feature of social entertainment at the Lake Avenue Hotel during the past week has been the informal piano recitals given by Miss Ella L. Flock, of Hackettstown, N.J., who is one of the guests of that house. Miss Flock won a gold medal for superiority in piano playing at the Centenary Collegiate Institute last spring by her fine performance of Beethoven's "Sonata Pathetique." She plays with singular power and grace of expression, and with the assured touch of a virtuoso.

Professor Milo Deyo and wife are spending the summer in the Park. Professor Deyo gave a delightful entertainment last week at the Lake Avenue Hotel, at which he played several of his original compositions.

The leader of the beach band has arranged Professor Deyo's very popular air de ballet "Enchantment," and this piece is now the greatest favorite of any that the band renders.

The Pace of Youth

I

STIMSON STOOD in a corner and glowered. He was a fierce man and had indomitable whiskers, albeit he was very small.

"That young tarrier," he whispered to himself. "He wants to quit makin' eyes at Lizzie. This is too much of a good thing. First thing you know, he'll get fired."

His brow creased in a frown, he strode over to the huge open doors and looked at a sign. "Stimson's Mammoth Merry-Go-Round," it read, and the glory of it was great. Stimson stood and contemplated the sign. It was an enormous affair; the letters were as large as men. The glow of it, the grandeur of it was very apparent to Stimson. At the end of his contemplation, he shook his head thoughtfully, determinedly. "No, no," he muttered. "This is too much of a good thing. First thing you know, he'll get fired."

A soft booming sound of surf, mingled with the cries of bathers, came from the beach. There was a vista of sand and sky and sea that drew to a mystic point far away in the northward. In the mighty angle, a girl in a red dress was crawling slowly like some kind of a spider on the fabric of nature. A few flags hung lazily above where the bathhouses were marshalled in compact squares. Upon the edge of the sea stood a ship with its shadowy sails painted dimly upon the sky, and high overhead in the still, sun-shot air a great hawk swung and circled slowly.

Within the merry-go-round there was a whirling circle of ornamental lions, giraffes, camels, ponies, goats, glittering with varnish and metal that caught swift reflections from windows high above them. With stiff wooden legs, they swept on in a never-ending race while a great orchestrion clamored in wild speed. The summer sunlight sprinkled its gold upon the garnet canopies carried by the tireless racers and upon all the devices of decoration that made Stimson's machine magnificent and famous. A host of laughing children bestrode the animals, bending forward like charging cavalrymen and shak-

465

ing reins and whooping in glee. At intervals they leaned out perilously to clutch at iron rings that were tendered to them by a long wooden arm. At the intense moment before the swift grab for the rings one could see their little nervous bodies quiver with eagerness; the laughter rang shrill and excited. Down in the long rows of benches, crowds of people sat watching the game, while occasionally a father might arise and go near to shout encouragement, cautionary commands, or applause at his flying offspring. Frequently mothers called out: "Be careful, Georgie!" The orchestrion bellowed and thundered on its platform, filling the ears with its long monotonous song. Over in a corner a man in a white apron and behind a counter roared above the tumult: "Pop corn! Pop corn!"

A young man stood upon a small, raised platform, erected in the manner of a pulpit and just without the line of the circling figures. It was his duty to manipulate the wooden arm and affix the rings. When all were gone into the hands of the triumphant children, he held forth a basket, into which they returned all save the coveted brass one, which meant another ride free and made the holder very illustrious. The young man stood all day upon his narrow platform, affixing rings or holding forth the basket. He was a sort of general squire in these lists of childhood. He was very busy.

And yet Stimson, the astute, had noticed that the young man frequently found time to twist about on his platform and smile at a girl who shyly sold tickets behind a silvered netting. This, indeed, was the great reason of Stimson's glowering. The young man upon the raised platform had no manner of license to smile at the girl behind the silvered netting. It was a most gigantic insolence. Stimson was amazed at it. "By jiminy," he said to himself again, "that fellow is smiling at my daughter." Even in this tone of great wrath it could be discerned that Stimson was filled with wonder that any youth should dare smile at the daughter in the presence of the august father.

Often the dark-eyed girl peered between the shining wires, and, upon being detected by the young man, she usually turned her head away quickly to prove to him that she was not interested. At other times, however, her eyes seemed filled with a tender fear lest he should fall from that exceedingly dangerous platform. As for the young man, it was plain that these glances filled him with valor, and he stood carelessly upon his perch, as if he deemed it of no consequence that he might fall from it. In all the complexities of his daily life and duties he found opportunity to gaze ardently at the vision behind the netting.

This silent courtship was conducted over the heads of the crowd who thronged about the bright machine. The swift, eloquent glances of the young man went noiselessly and unseen with their message. There had finally become established between the two in this manner a subtle understanding and companionship. They communicated accurately all that they felt. The boy told his love, his reverence, his hope in the changes of the future. The girl told him that she loved him, that she did not love him, that she did not know if she loved him, that she loved him. Sometimes a little sign saying "Cashier" in gold letters, and hanging upon the silvered netting, got directly in range and interfered with a tender message.

The love affair had not continued without anger, unhappiness, despair. The girl had once smiled brightly upon a youth who came to buy some tickets for his little sister, and the young man upon the platform observing this smile had been filled with gloomy rage. He stood like a dark statue of vengeance upon his pedestal and thrust out the basket to the children with a gesture that was full of scorn for their hollow happiness, for their insecure and temporary joy. For five hours he did not once look at the girl when she was looking at him. He was going to crush her with his indifference; he was going to demonstrate that he had never been serious. However, when he narrowly observed her in secret he discovered that she seemed more blythe than was usual with her. When he found that his apparent indifference had not crushed her he suffered greatly. She did not love him, he concluded. If she had loved him she would have been crushed. For two days he lived a miserable existence upon his high perch. He consoled himself by thinking of how unhappy he was, and by swift, furtive glances at the loved face. At any rate he was in her presence, and he could get a good view from his perch when there was no interference by the little sign: "Cashier."

But suddenly, swiftly, these clouds vanished and under the imperial blue sky of the restored confidence they dwelt in peace, a peace that was satisfaction, a peace that, like a babe, put its trust in the treachery of the future. This confidence endured until the next day, when she, for an unknown cause, suddenly refused to look at him. Mechanically, he continued his task, his brain dazed, a tortured victim of doubt, fear, suspicion. With his eyes he supplicated her to telegraph an explanation. She replied with a stony glance that froze his blood. There was a great difference in their respective reasons for becoming angry. His were always foolish, but apparent, plain as the moon. Hers were subtle, feminine, as incomprehensible as the stars, as mysterious as the shadows at night.

They fell and soared, and soared and fell in this manner until they knew that to live without each other would be a wandering in deserts. They had grown so intent upon the uncertainties, the variations, the guessings of their affair that the world had become but a huge immaterial background. In time of peace their smiles were soft and prayerful, caresses confided to the air. In time of war, their youthful hearts, capable of profound agony, were wrung by the intricate emotions of doubt. They were the victims of the dread angel of affectionate speculation that forces the brain endlessly on roads that lead nowhere.

At night, the problem of whether she loved him confronted the young man like a specter, looming as high as a hill and telling him not to delude himself. Upon the following day, this battle of the night displayed itself in the renewed fervor of his glances and in their increased number. Whenever he thought he could detect that she too was suffering, he felt a thrill of joy.

But there came a time when the young man looked back upon these contortions with contempt. He believed then that he had imagined his pain. This came about when the redoubtable Stimson marched forward to participate.

"This has got to stop," Stimson had said to himself, as he stood and watched them. They had grown careless of the light world that clattered about them; they were become so engrossed in their personal drama that the language of their eyes was almost as obvious as gestures. And Stimson, through his keenness, his wonderful, infallible penetration, suddenly came into possession of these obvious facts. "Well, of all the nerves," he said, regarding with a new interest the young man upon the perch.

He was a resolute man. He never hesitated to grapple with a crisis. He decided to overturn everything at once, for, although small, he was very fierce and impetuous. He resolved to crush this dreaming.

He strode over to the silvered netting. "Say, you want to quit your everlasting grinning at that idiot," he said, grimly.

The girl cast down her eyes and made a little heap of quarters into a stack. She was unable to withstand the terrible scrutiny of her small and fierce father.

Stimson turned from his daughter and went to a spot beneath the platform. He fixed his eyes upon the young man and said: "I've been speakin' to Lizzie. You better attend strictly to your own business or there'll be a new man here next week." It was as if he had blazed away with a shotgun. The young man reeled upon his perch. At last he in a measure regained his composure and managed to stammer: "A—all right, sir." He knew that denials would be futile with the terrible Stimson. He agitatedly began to rattle the rings in the basket and pretend that he was obliged to count them or inspect them in some way. He, too, was unable to face the great Stimson.

For a moment Stimson stood in fine satisfaction and gloated over the effect of his threat. "I've fixed them," he said complacently, and went out to smoke a cigar and revel in himself. Through his mind went the proud reflection that people who came in contact with his granite will usually ended in quick and abject submission.

II

One evening, a week after Stimson had indulged in the proud reflection that people who came in contact with his granite will usually ended in quick and abject submission, a young feminine friend of the girl behind the silvered netting came to her there and asked her to walk on the beach after

"Stimson's Mammoth Merry-Go-Round" was closed for the night. The girl assented with a nod.

The young man upon the perch holding the rings saw this nod and judged its meaning. Into his mind came an idea of defeating the watchfulness of the redoubtable Stimson.

When the merry-go-round was closed and the two girls started for the beach, he wandered off aimlessly in another direction, but he kept them in view, and as soon as he was assured that he had escaped the vigilance of Stimson, he followed them.

The electric lights on the beach made a broad band of tremoring light, extending parallel to the sea, and upon the wide walk there slowly paraded a great crowd intermingling, intertwining, sometimes colliding. In the darkness stretched the vast purple expanse of the ocean, and the deep indigo sky above was peopled with yellow stars. Occasionally out upon the water a whirling mass of froth suddenly flashed into view, like a great ghostly robe appearing, and then vanished, leaving the sea in its darkness, from whence came those bass tones of the water's unknown emotion. A wind, cool, reminiscent of the wave wastes, made the women hold their wraps about their throats and caused the men to grip the rims of their straw hats. It carried the noise of the band in the pavilion in gusts. Sometimes people unable to hear the music glanced up at the pavilion and were reassured upon beholding the distant leader still gesticulating and bobbing and the other members of the band with their lips glued to their instruments. High in the sky soared an unassuming moon, faintly silver.

For a time the young man was afraid to approach the two girls. He followed them at a distance and called himself a coward. At last, however, he saw them stop on the outer edge of the crowd and stand silently listening to the voices of the sea. When he came to where they stood, he was trembling in his agitation. They had not seen him.

"Lizzie," he began. "I——"

The girl wheeled instantly and put her hand to her throat. "Oh, Frank, how you frightened me," she said—inevitably.

"Well, you know I—I——" he stuttered.

But the other girl was one of those beings who are born to attend at tragedies. She had for love a reverence, an admiration that was greater the more that she contemplated the fact that she knew nothing of it. This couple with their emotions, awed her and made her humbly wish that she might be destined to be of some service to them. She was very homely.

When the young man faltered before them, she, in her sympathy, actually overestimated the crisis and felt that he might fall dying at their feet. Shyly, but with courage, she marched to the rescue. "Won't you come and walk on the beach with us," she said. The young man gave her a glance of deep gratitude which was not without the patronage which a man in his condition naturally feels for one who pities it. The three walked on.

Finally the being who was born to attend at this tragedy said that she wished to sit down and gaze at the sea, alone.

They politely urged her to walk on with them, but she was obstinate. She wished to gaze at the sea, alone. The young man swore to himself that he would be her friend until he died.

And so the two young lovers went on without her. They turned once to look at her.

"Jennie's awful nice," said the girl.

"You bet she is," replied the young man, ardently.

They were silent for a little time.

At last the girl said: "You were angry at me yesterday."

"No, I wasn't."

"Yes, you were, too. You wouldn't look at me once all day."

"No, I wasn't angry. I was only putting on."

Though she had, of course, known it, this confession seemed to make her very indignant. She flashed a resentful glance at him. "Oh, were you, indeed!" she said, with a great air.

For a few minutes she was so haughty with him that he loved her to madness. And directly this poem which stuck at his lips came forth lamely in fragments.

When they walked back toward the other girl and saw the patience of her attitude, their hearts swelled in a patronizing and secondary tenderness for her.

They were very happy. If they had been miserable they would have charged this fairy scene of the night with a criminal heartlessness, but as they were joyous, they vaguely wondered how the purple sea, the yellow stars, the changing crowd under the electric lights could be so phlegmatic and stolid.

They walked home by the lakeside way and out upon the water those gay paper lanterns, flashing, fleeting and careering, sang to them, sang a chorus of red and violet and green and gold, a song of mystic lands of the future.

One day when business paused during the dull, sultry afternoon, Stimson went up town. Upon his return he found that the popcorn man from his stand over in a corner was keeping an eye upon the cashier's cage, and that nobody at all was attending to the wooden arm and the iron rings.

He strode forward like a sergeant of grenadiers. "Where in thunder is Lizzie?" he demanded, a cloud of rage in his eyes.

The popcorn man, although associated long with Stimson, had never got over being dazed. "They've—they've—gone round to th'—th'—house," he said, with difficulty, as if he had just been stunned.

"Whose house?" snapped Stimson.

"Your—your house, I 'spose," said the popcorn man.

Stimson marched round to his home. Kingly denunciations surged, already formulated, to the tip of his tongue, and he bided the moment when his anger could fall upon the heads of that pair of children.

He found his wife convulsive and in tears.

"Where's Lizzie?"

And then she burst forth: "Oh—John—John—they've run away—I know they have. They drove by here not three minutes ago. They must have done it on purpose to bid me good-bye, for Lizzie waved her hand sad-like, and then, before I could get out to ask where they were going or what, Frank whipped up the horse."

Stimson gave vent to a dreadful roar. "Get my revolver—get a hack—get my revolver, d——, do you hear—what the devil——" His voice became incoherent.

He had always ordered his wife about as if she were a battalion of infantry, and despite her misery, the training of years forced her to spring mechanically to obey, but suddenly she turned to him a shrill appeal.

"Oh, John—not—the—revolver."

"Confound it, let go of me," he roared again and shook her from him.

He ran hatless upon the street. There was a multitude of hacks at the summer resort, but it was ages to him before he could find one. Then he charged it like a bull. "Up town," he yelled, as he tumbled into the rear seat. The hackman thought of severed arteries. His galloping horse distanced a large number of citizens who had been running to find what caused such contortions by the little hatless man.

It chanced as the bouncing hack went along near the lake, Stimson gazed across the calm, gray expanse and recognized a color in a bonnet and a poise of a head. A buggy was traveling along a highway that led to Sorington. Stimson bellowed: "There—there—there they are—in that buggy."

The hackman became inspired with the full knowledge of the situation. He struck a delirious blow with the whip. His mouth expanded in a grin of excitement and joy. It came to pass that this old vehicle, with its drowsy horse and its dusty-eyed and tranquil driver, seemed suddenly to awaken, to become animated and fleet. The horse ceased to ruminate on his state, his air of reflection vanished. He became intent upon his aged legs and spread them in quaint and ridiculous devices for speed. The driver, his eyes shining, sat critically in his seat. He watched each motion of this rattling machine down before him. He resembled an engineer. He used the whip with judgment and deliberation as the engineer would have used coal or oil. The horse clacked swiftly upon the macadam, the wheels hummed, the body of the vehicle wheezed and groaned.

Stimson, in the rear seat, was erect in that impassive attitude that comes sometimes to the furious man when he is obliged to leave the battle to others. Frequently, however, the tempest in his breast came to his face and he howled: "Go it—go it—you're gaining; pound 'im; thump the life out of 'im; hit 'im hard, you fool." His hand grasped the rod that supported the carriage top, and it was clinched so that the nails were faintly blue.

Ahead, that other carriage had been flying with speed, as from realization of the menace in the rear. It bowled away rapidly, drawn by the eager spirit of a young and modern

horse. Stimson could see the buggy-top bobbing, bobbing.
That little pane, like an eye, was a derision to him. Once he
leaned forward and bawled angry sentences. He began to feel
impotent; his whole expedition was the tottering of an old
man upon the trail of birds. A sense of age made him choke
again with wrath. That other vehicle, that was youth, with
youth's pace, it was swift-flying with the hope of dreams. He
began to comprehend those two children ahead of him, and
he knew a sudden and strange awe, because he understood
the power of their young blood, the power to fly strongly
into the future and feel and hope again, even at that time
when his bones must be laid in the earth.

The dust rose easily from the hot road and stifled the nos-
trils of Stimson. The highway vanished far away in a point
with a suggestion of intolerable length. The other vehicle was
becoming so small that Stimson could no longer see the de-
risive eye.

At last the hackman drew rein to his horse and turned to
look at Stimson. "No use, I guess," he said. Stimson made a
gesture of acquiescence, rage, despair. As the hackman turned
his dripping horse about, Stimson sank back with the aston-
ishment and grief of a man who has been defied by the uni-
verse. He had been in a great perspiration and now his bald
head felt cool and uncomfortable. He put up his hand with
the sudden recollection that he had forgotten his hat.

At last he made a gesture. It meant that at any rate he was
not responsible.

SULLIVAN COUNTY

Contents

The Last of the Mohicans

F EW OF THE OLD, gnarled and weather-beaten inhabitants of the pines and boulders of Sullivan County are great readers of books or students of literature. On the contrary, the man who subscribes for the county's weekly newspaper is the man who has attained sufficient position to enable him to leave his farm labors for literary pursuits. The historical traditions of the region have been handed down from generation to generation, at the firesides in the old homesteads. The aged grandsire recites legends to his grandson; and when the grandson's head is silvered he takes his corn-cob pipe from his mouth and transfixes his children and his children's children with stirring tales of hunter's exploit and Indian battle. Historians are wary of this form of procedure. Insignificant facts, told from mouth to mouth down the years, have been known to become of positively appalling importance by the time they have passed from behind the last corn-cob in the last chimney corner. Nevertheless, most of these fireside stories are verified by books written by learned men, who have dived into piles of mouldy documents and dusty chronicles to establish their facts.

This gives the great Sullivan County thunderbolt immense weight. And they hurl it at no less a head than that which once evolved from its inner recesses the famous Leatherstocking Tales. The old story-tellers of this district are continually shaking metaphorical fists at *The Last of the Mohicans* of J. Fenimore Cooper. Tell them that they are aiming their shafts at one of the standard novels of American literature and they scornfully sneer; endeavor to oppose them with the intricacies of Indian history and they shriek defiance. No consideration for the author, the literature or the readers can stay their hands, and they claim without reservation that the last of the Mohicans, the real and only authentic last of the Mohicans, was a demoralized, dilapidated inhabitant of Sullivan County.

The work in question is of course a visionary tale and the historical value of the plot is not a question of importance. But when the two heroes of Sullivan County and J. Fenimore Cooper, respectively, are compared, the pathos lies in the contrast, and the lover of the noble and fictional Uncas is overcome with great sadness. Even as Cooper claims that his Uncas was the last of the children of the Turtle, so do the sages of Sullivan County roar from out their rockbound fastnesses that their nondescript Indian was the last of the children of the Turtle. The pathos lies in the contrast between the noble savage of fiction and the sworn-to claimant of Sullivan County.

All know well the character of Cooper's hero, Uncas, that bronze god in a North American wilderness, that warrior with the eye of the eagle, the ear of the fox, the tread of the cat-like panther, and the tongue of the wise serpent of fable. Over his dead body a warrior cries:

"Why has thou left us, pride of the Wapanachki? Thy time has been like that of the sun when in the trees; thy glory brighter than his light at noonday. Thou art gone, youthful warrior, but a hundred Wyandots are clearing the briers from thy path to the world of spirits. Who that saw thee in battle would believe that thou couldst die? Who before thee has ever shown Uttawa the way into the fight? Thy feet were like the wings of eagles; thine arm heavier than falling branches from the pine; and thy voice like the Manitto when he speaks in the clouds. The tongue of Uttawa is weak and his heart exceedingly heavy. Pride of the Wapanachki, why hast thou left us?"

The last of the Mohicans supported by Sullivan County is a totally different character. They have forgotten his name. From their description of him he was no warrior who yearned after the blood of his enemies as the hart panteth for the water-brooks; on the contrary he developed a craving for the rum of the white men which rose superior to all other anxieties. He had the emblematic Turtle tatooed somewhere under his shirt-front. Arrayed in tattered, torn and ragged garments which some white man had thrown off, he wandered listlessly from village to village and from house to house, his only ambition being to beg, borrow or steal a drink. The settlers helped him because they knew his story. They knew of the long line of mighty sachems sleeping under the pines of the mountains. He was a veritable "poor Indian." He dragged through his wretched life in helpless misery. No one could be more alone in the world than he and when he died there was no one to call him pride of anything nor to inquire why he had left them.

Hunting Wild Hogs

I F THE WELL-WORN and faded ghost of many an old scout
or trapper of long ago could arise from beneath the de-
cayed shingle with awkward hunting-knife carvings where it
lies, it could doubtless create a thrill by reciting tales of the
panther's gleaming eyes and sharp claws. Mayhap, in a thou-
sand varieties of chimney-corner, old, gnarled and knotted
forty-niners curdle the blood and raise the hair of their listen-
ers with legends of the ferocious and haughty grizzly bear.
But it is certain that there are only three men in the United
States to-day who have proper right to thrill anybody, curdle
any blood, or raise any hair with tales of the hunting and
killing of the famous wild hogs of ancient and modern Eu-
rope upon the territory of the United States. The hog of com-
merce and domesticity has escaped from broken pens and
wrecked trains and lives in the wilds of Canada and Missis-
sippi, and also, it is claimed, in some parts of this State, but
they make no such sport as the long-haired, swift-running,
powerful animals from Europe. The latter are prominent in-
deed in mythology and history. They are said to be the most
wily and cunning of animals. They are very fleet of foot and
make great speed through exceedingly rough country. The
Sullivan County hunters say that when one of these animals
"strikes a line" for a certain point they will not stop for ob-
structions that would make a bear turn out. They say that
they have seen bunches of scrub-oaks as big as a man's wrist
broken and bent aside like reeds where one of the wild hogs
has charged through them. They turn out for no bush or little
tree, but bolt directly at it. In the fields they root holes with
their snouts that would flatter a plough.

Otto Plock, a wealthy New-York banker, has a country-seat
in the Neversink Valley. He imported a number of wild hogs
from Europe and turned them loose in his park. The shaggy
beasts must have added a picturesqueness to Mr. Plock's
grounds. But one morning they disappeared. They digged
under the fences with their strong snouts and scattered over
the country. They almost immediately began a series of night
expeditions against the farmers' corn and potato fields. It is

said that they did great damage. In a single night they would so root up a field with their powerful hoofs and snouts that it would be unrecognizable the next day. The farmers became agitated. They were aroused to action. They turned out in armed brigades. They spent certain sums for ammunition. In the corner stores they laid their plans, and individuals told what they were going to do. They then mustered their forces and attacked the surrounding hills. The wild hogs evaded the army with astonishing ease. The farmers then turned their attention to poison. They fixed up little meals and left them in open places but with no success. To one farm the hogs took a great liking. In its corn-fields they even tore down stalks by the dozen and heaped them in a fence-corner to sleep upon. A neighbor decided to make an investigation. He took a boy, a gun and a position behind a wall, and sat waiting one night for the appearance of the hogs. But he went to sleep. Then the boy, looking over the wall, discovered the wild hogs, not fifteen feet away. He cried out and the animals ran. The man groaned, grunted, stood up, rubbed his eyes, remembered about the hogs, and shot off his gun. The hogs went on. Later the skeleton of the wild boar was found on Shawangunk Mountain. The tusks were about eight inches in length.

The great liar appeared all over Orange and Sullivan Counties, and lots of wild hogs were seen. Children going to school were frightened home by wild hogs. Men coming home late at night saw wild hogs. It became a sort of fashion to see wild hogs and turn around and come back. But when the outraged farmers made such a terrific onslaught upon the stern and rock-bound land the wild hogs, it appears, withdrew to Sullivan County. This county may have been formed by a very reckless and distracted giant who, observing a tract of tipped-up and impossible ground, stood off and carelessly pelted trees and boulders at it. Not admiring the results of his labors he set off several earthquakes under it and tried to wreck it. He succeeded beyond his utmost expectations, undoubtedly. In the holes and crevices, valleys and hills, caves and swamps of this uneven country, the big game of the southern part of this State have made their last stand. Isolated wanderers are sometimes chased by everybody who owns a gun, and by every dog that has legs, in thickly-populated portions of other counties, but here is where the bear tears the bark from the pines devoid of the fear of hunters until he hears the help of the hounds on the ridges.

Here the wild hogs were in a country which just suited them. Its tangled forests, tumbled rocks and intricate swamps were for them admirable places of residence. Here they remained unmolested for a long time. The first man to kill one of them was Special County Judge William H. Crane, of Port Jervis. While on one of the Hartwood Park hunts, he was standing on a "runway" for deer. He suddenly heard a great scampering of feet and crackling of brush ahead and to the right of him. The next moment a small herd of what afterward proved to be the wild hogs dashed through the brush to his right. Turning quickly, he caught a glimpse of a brown body and fired. They carried home a wild hog weighing 200 pounds. The carcass was inspected, photographed and sketched. A magnificent skin, with stuffed head, now hangs in the club-house at Hartwood Park.

The last hog hunt resulted in untold glory and meat for the successful ones. Lew Boyd, the famous bear hunter, was the hero of the expedition. He is a six-foot-four-inch man, with broad shoulders, a good eye, and legs that have no superior for travel in a rough country. He chased one of the hogs in this hunt for over 200 miles, and the animal was shot by him on the seventh day of the chase. A party of hunters took the trail of two of the hogs and followed it for two days. They did not catch sight of the game. On the third day they met Lew Boyd. He joined them, and they followed the trails in the snow all day. Toward night, one by one, the party began to be discouraged and to drop out. Finally all had disappeared over the ridges but Boyd, who never disappears in such case, and Charles Stearns, of Oakland Valley. They plodded along together, endeavoring to get over a few miles more before sunset. As they were passing through a little gulch, Boyd, upon looking up the side of it, perceived both wild hogs in the bushes about 100 yards away. As he exclaimed to his companion, one of the hogs wheeled and tore through the bushes like a brown cyclone. Boyd whirled about and fired, but the animal did not stop. The other one came charging down the hill directly at the hunters. Stearns fired within forty yards, and that hog, too, then wheeled and scurried over the hill after her companion. The hunters followed as rapidly as possible. Some 400 yards from the scene of the shooting Boyd suddenly discovered that in their great haste they were following but one track. They turned back, and found where the two animals had separated. Following the new track they came to a dead hog in the brush. Stearns of course argued that this was his game. Boyd then went on after the other. Along the trail were great clots of blood from a wound in the throat. Yet the hog travelled with great speed, and Boyd was compelled to go home that night and leave his hog in the woods. The next day seven men turned out to assist in the search. The party trailed the wounded animal to White Cedar Swamp, a narrow, heavily-wooded marsh five miles in length. At the southern end Boyd placed three men on each side of the swamp. These, with two men to drive straight through, would form a very effective pocket. They were ordered to keep about seventy-five yards apart, and not to get behind or ahead, but to proceed slowly and all to keep their relative positions. In this manner Boyd was sure that he could get the hog. This was thought to be a sure mode of procedure, but the second man on the left pushed close to the first man on the same side and the hog passed out at railway speed between the second man and the third man.

They traced the animal to Beaver Dam Swamp and gave up the search for the night. In the morning they met near the place and Boyd placed his men about the swamp. There was a young man with a bulldog upon the scene, who said his dog would fight anything. Boyd told him, however, to hold the animal until the hunters were in their positions, but the young man succeeded with great difficulty in making the bulldog follow the track into the swamps some moments before he should have done so. As a result the hog escaped from the swamp, and Boyd sent the young man and his bulldog a safe distance to the rear. They followed the trail all the rest of that day. The hog's wound had ceased to bleed and it was making good time on its travels. The hunters could only count upon coming up with it once a day. At night it would make itself a bed by tearing down young trees and bushes and heaping them in a huge pile. Boyd says he has seen a quarter of an acre pretty well cleared of small growth to make one of these temporary couches. When once aroused the hog was good for a twenty-mile run over the rocks and fallen logs. The principal hunter had almost an entirely new lot of followers every day. Men would grow enthusiastic for twenty-four hours and join the hunt, and drop out next day to make room for some one else. Some were frozen away, some were wearied quickly and a number were scared away. Every night, except one or two, Boyd returned to his home from where he left the trail, always at least six miles away. In the morning he would walk back and resume it. On the fourth day the pursuers again were up with the hog, which had as before hidden itself in a swamp. Boyd placed his men and had the swamp beaten. Now, as above mentioned, some of these men thought the wild hog was a dangerous animal. In such cases men have great fancies for each other's society, and pairs of Boyd's men often feebly insisted upon being allowed to sit upon the same log. As the swamp was being beaten one of the hunters became lonesome and went over to see another hunter. The other hunter came half way to meet the first hunter. The hog left the swamp six feet from where the first hunter was told to stand. Boyd was angry. Three times had he laid careful plans and three times had a man who was in a hurry, a man with a bulldog and a man who was lonesome made all his efforts vain. He called the lonesome men and stated the case in forcible English, concluding with the remark: "Boys, if you are frightened, go home! Don't come into the woods and hunt an animal you are afraid of." The young men tilted their noses, shouldered their weapons and made large and defiant tracks in the snow over the hill.

The chase continued all that day and all the next. At the close of the fifth all the hunters gave up the hunt except Boyd. They told him they were rapidly freezing to death, they were worn to skin and bone, and they could not keep up any longer. Boyd called them several names, but they were firm. They departed after impressing upon him the fact that he was doomed to certain death from cold, exposure or fatigue if he did not give up the hunt. In reply he hitched up his trousers and started on his lonely quest.

The hog now showed the first signs of giving out. It did not stop any more to make those elaborate preparations for a night of repose, but simply crawled under a slanting rock or fallen tree as if it had no time to spare. The fifth night was spent by Boyd in Oakland. There they tried to dissuade him. They told him he would never catch it, and if he did it would kill him. An old German told him frightful tales of the animal's powers in battle. He told how horses and men went down before the terrible tusk of the boar of Europe and Bengal. He said that in his native land the wild hogs used often to rip the bark from the pines, rub the pitch into their bristles and then go and roll in a soft clay, which, baked upon their sides by the sun, would make them impervious to bullets. Boyd failed to be impressed. The sixth day was a long and cold one. An icy north wind swept over the ridges and through the gulleys, and the snow drifted heavily. Long icicles hung on Boyd's mustache and his face was frozen blue as he clambered over logs, fell down rocks and plunged through snowbanks, the while keeping both eyes upon the tracks of the hog, which were rapidly being obliterated by the snow. The close of the day brought him no success.

The next day he again took up the chase. The drifting snow made the task of keeping the trail a difficult one. Several times he found himself off the track and lost time looking it up. About noon he discovered fresh blood. This made him, of course, redouble his exertions. Late in the day he discovered a fox standing in the track of the hog, sniffing at the blood on the snow. He fired at the fox and hit it behind the ear. Immediately after the report there was a grunt in the bushes twenty yards away; the wild hog bounded from a clump of bushes and swiftly plunged through the woods. Instantly Boyd turned and fired. Then he started on a run in pursuit. A hundred yards further on he found the hog lying stone dead. Half an hour later it would have been too dark to have shot correctly. He left the dead hog and walked eight miles in the dark through the woods and drifts to his home. In the morning he drove his team upon old logging roads to within a mile or so of his game. Then he and a boy tied a stick in its jaws and dragged it over the snow to the horses. On the afternoon of the eighth day the carcass was hung up in his barn and the struggle was over. Assuming that only five of the wild hogs were in Mr. Plock's park and escaped, the Hartwood Park hunters have accounted for all of them but one. Judge Crane took a second shot in the direction of the fast-lessening noise, after he had fired at the spot of brown in the brush, and it is believed by Boyd that a second pig received a fatal wound from that shot. This of course would end the hunting of the wild hog in the United States.

The people of Sullivan County are wonderful yarn-spinners and they have some great additions to their list of tales. Doubtless for years to come those that know the story will tell to admiring listeners how "Lew" Boyd chased the wounded wild hog for 200 miles.

Four Men in a Cave

THE MOON rested for a moment in the top of a tall pine on a hill.

The little man was standing in front of the camp-fire making oration to his companions.

"We can tell a great tale when we get back to the city, if we investigate this thing," said he, in conclusion.

They were won.

The little man was determined to explore a cave, because its black mouth had gaped at him. The four men took lighted pine-knots and clambered over boulders down a hill. In a thicket on the mountain-side lay a little tilted hole. At its side they halted.

"Well?" said the little man.

They fought for last place and the little man was overwhelmed. He tried to struggle from under by crying that if the fat, pudgy man came after, he would be corked. But he finally administered a cursing over his shoulder and crawled into the hole. His companions gingerly followed.

A passage, the floor of damp clay and pebbles, the walls slimy, green-mossed and dripping, sloped downward. In the cave-atmosphere the torches became studies in red blaze and black smoke.

"Ho!" cried the little man, stifled and bedraggled, "let's go back." His companions were not brave. They were last. The next one to the little man pushed him on, so the little man said sulphurous words and cautiously continued his crawl.

Things that hung, seemed to be upon the wet, uneven ceiling, ready to drop upon the men's bare necks. Under their hands the clammy floor seemed alive and writhing. When the little man endeavored to stand erect the ceiling forced him down. Knobs and points came out and punched him. His clothes were wet and mud-covered, and his eyes, nearly blinded by smoke, tried to pierce the darkness always before his torch.

"Oh, I say, you fellows, let's go back!" cried he. At that moment he caught the gleam of trembling light in the blurred shadows before him.

"Ho!" he said, "here's another way out."

The passage turned abruptly. The little man put one hand around the corner but it touched nothing. He investigated and discovered that the little corridor took a sudden dip down a hill. At the bottom shone a yellow light.

The little man wriggled painfully about and descended feet in advance. The others followed his plan. All picked their way with anxious care. The traitorous rocks rolled from beneath the little man's feet and roared thunderously below him. Lesser stones, loosened by the men above him, hit him in the back. He gained a seemingly firm foothold and turning half about, swore redly at his companions for dolts and careless fools. The pudgy man sat, puffing and perspiring, high in the rear of the procession. The fumes and smoke from four pine-knots were in his blood. Cinders and sparks lay thick in his eyes and hair. The pause of the little man angered him.

"Go on, you fool," he shouted. "Poor, painted man, you are afraid!"

"Ho!" said the little man, "come down here and go on yourself, imbecile!"

The pudgy man vibrated with passion. He leaned downward. "Idiot——"

He was interrupted by one of his feet which flew out and crashed into the man in front of and below him. It is not well to quarrel upon a slippery incline, when the unknown is below. The fat man, having lost the support of one pillar-like foot, lurched forward. His body smote the next man, who hurtled into the next man. Then they all fell upon the cursing little man.

They slid in a body down over the slippery, slimy floor of the passage. The stone avenue must have wibble-wobbled with the rush of this ball of tangled men and strangled cries. The torches went out with the combined assault upon the little man. The adventurers whirled to the unknown in darkness. The little man felt that he was pitching to death, but even in his convolutions he bit and scratched at his companions, for he was satisfied that it was their fault. The swirling mass went some twenty feet and lit upon a level dry place in a strong, yellow light of candles. It dissolved and became eyes.

The four men lay in a heap upon the floor of a gray chamber. A small fire smouldered in a corner, the smoke disappearing in a crack. In another corner was a bed of faded hemlock boughs and two blankets. Cooking utensils and clothes lay about, with boxes and a barrel.

Of these things the four men took small cognizance. The pudgy man did not curse the little man, nor did the little man swear, in the abstract. Eight widened eyes were fixed upon the centre of the room of rocks.

A great gray stone, cut squarely, like an altar, sat in the middle of the floor. Over it burned three candles in swaying tin cups hung from the ceiling. Before it, with what seemed to be a small volume clasped in his yellow fingers, stood a man. He was an infinitely sallow person in the brown checked shirt of the ploughs and cows. The rest of his apparel was boots. A long gray beard dangled from his chin. He fixed glinting, fiery eyes upon the heap of men and remained motionless. Fascinated, their tongues cleaving, their blood cold, they arose to their feet. The gleaming glance of the recluse swept slowly over the group until it found the face of the little man. There it stayed and burned.

The little man shrivelled and crumpled as the dried leaf under the glass.

Finally the recluse slowly, deeply spoke. It was a true voice from a cave, cold, solemn and damp.

"It's your ante," he said.

"What?" said the little man.

The hermit tilted his beard and laughed a laugh that was either the chatter of a banshee in a storm or the rattle of pebbles in a tin box. His visitors' flesh seemed ready to drop from their bones.

They huddled together and cast fearful eyes over their shoulders. They whispered.

"A vampire!" said one.

"A ghoul!" said another.

"A Druid before the sacrifice," murmured another.

"The shade of an Aztec witch doctor," said the little man.

As they looked, the inscrutable's face underwent a change. It became a livid background for his eyes, which blazed at the little man like impassioned carbuncles. His voice arose to a howl of ferocity. "It's your ante!" With a panther-like motion, he drew a long, thin knife and advanced, stooping. Two cadaverous hounds came from nowhere and, scowling and growling, made desperate feints at the little man's legs. His quaking companions pushed him forward.

Tremblingly he put his hand to his pocket.

"How much?" he said, with a shivering look at the knife that glittered.

The carbuncles faded.

"Three dollars," said the hermit, in sepulchral tones which rang against the walls and among the passages, awakening long-dead spirits with voices. The shaking little man took a roll of bills from a pocket and placed "three ones" upon the altar-like stone. The recluse looked at the little volume with reverence in his eyes. It was a pack of playing cards.

Under the three swinging candles, upon the altar-like stone, the gray-beard and the agonized little man played at poker. The three other men crouched in a corner and stared with eyes that gleamed with terror. Before them sat the cadaverous hounds, licking their red lips. The candles burned low and began to flicker. The fire in the corner expired.

Finally the game came to a point where the little man laid down his hand and quavered: "I can't call you this time, sir. I'm dead broke."

"What?" shrieked the recluse. "Not call me? Villain! Dastard! Cur! I have four queens, miscreant!" His voice grew so mighty that it could not fit his throat. He choked, wrestling with his lungs, for a moment. Then the power of his body was concentrated in a word: "Go!"

He pointed a quivering, yellow finger at a wide crack in the rock. The little man threw himself at it with a howl. His erstwhile frozen companions felt their blood throb again. With great bounds they plunged after the little man. A minute of scrambling, falling and pushing brought them to open air. They climbed the distance to their camp in furious springs.

The sky in the east was a lurid yellow. In the west the footprints of departing night lay on the pine trees. In front of their replenished camp-fire sat John Willerkins, the guide.

"Hello!" he shouted at their approach. "Be you fellers ready to go deer huntin'?"

Without replying, they stopped and debated among themselves in whispers.

Finally the pudgy man came forward.

"John," he inquired, "do you know anything peculiar about this cave below here?"

"Yes," said Willerkins at once, "Tom Gardner."

"What?" said the pudgy man.

"Tom Gardner!"

"How's that?"

"Well, you see," said Willerkins slowly, as he took dignified pulls at his pipe, "Tom Gardner was onct a fambly man, who lived in these here parts on a nice leetle farm. He uster go away to the city orften, and one time he got a-gamblin' in one of them there dens. He wentter the dickens right quick then. At last he kum home one time and tol' his folks he had up and sold the farm and all he had in the worl'. His leetle wife, she died then. Tom, he went crazy, and soon after——"

The narrative was interrupted by the little man, who became possessed of devils.

"Iwouldn'tgiveacussifhehadleftme'noughmoneytogethome-onthedoggonedgrayhairedredpirate," he shrilled, in a seething sentence. The pudgy man gazed at the little man calmly and sneeringly.

"Oh well," he said, " we can tell a great tale when we get back to the city after having investigated this thing."

"Go to the devil!" replied the little man.

The Octopush

FOUR MEN once upon a time went into the wilderness seeking for pickerel. They proceeded to a pond which is different from all other sheets of water in the world excepting the remaining ponds in Sullivan County. A scrawny stone dam, clinging in apparent desperation to its foundation, wandered across a wild valley. In the beginning, the baffled waters had retreated to a forest. In consequence, the four men confronted a sheet of water from which there up-reared countless grey, haggard tree-trunks. Squat stumps, in multitudes, stretched long, lazy roots over the surface of the water. Floating logs and sticks bumped gently against the dam. All manner of weeds throttled the lilies and dragged them down. Great pine trees came from all sides to the pond's edge.

In their journey the four men encountered a creature with a voice from a tomb. His person was concealed behind an enormous straw hat. In graveyard accents, he demanded that he be hired to assist them in their quest. They agreed. From a recess of the bank he produced a blunt-ended boat, painted a very light blue, with yellow finishings, in accordance with Sullivan aesthetics. Two sculls whittled from docile pine boards lay under the seats. Pegs were driven into the boat's sides at convenient row-lock intervals. In deep, impressive tones, the disguised individual told the four men that, to his knowledge, the best way to catch pickerel was to " 'skidder' fur 'em from them there stumps." The four men clambered into the beautiful boat and the individual manoeuvered his craft until he had dealt out to four low-spreading stumps, four fishers. He thereupon repaired to a fifth stump where he tied his boat. Perching himself upon the stump-top, he valiantly grasped a mildewed corn-cob between his teeth, ladened with black, eloquent tobacco. At a distance it smote the senses of the four men.

The sun gleamed merrily upon the waters, the gaunt, towering tree-trunks and the stumps lying like spatters of wood which had dropped from the clouds. Troops of blue and silver darning-needles danced over the surface. Bees bustled about the weeds which grew in the shallow places. Butterflies flickered in the air. Down in the water, millions of fern branches quavered and hid mysteries. The four men sat still and 'skiddered.' The individual puffed tremendously. Ever and anon, one of the four would cry ecstatically or swear madly. His fellows, upon standing to gaze at him, would either find him holding a stout fish, or nervously struggling with a hook and line entangled in the hordes of vindictive weeds and sticks on the bottom. They had fortune, for the pickerel is a voracious fish. His only faults are in method. He has a habit of furiously charging the fleeting bit of glitter and then darting under a log or around a corner with it.

At noon, the individual corralled the entire outfit upon a stump where they lunched while he entertained them with anecdote. Afterward he redistributed them, each to his personal stump. They fished. He contemplated the scene and made observations which rang across the water to the four men in bass solos. Toward the close of the day, he grew evidently thoughtful, indulging in no more spasmodic philosophy. The four men fished intently until the sun had sunk down to some tree-tops and was peering at them like the face of an angry man over a hedge. Then one of the four stood up and shouted across to where the individual sat enthroned upon the stump.

"You had better take us ashore now." The other three repeated: "Yes, come take us ashore."

Whereupon the individual carefully took an erect position. Then, waving a great yellow-brown bottle and tottering, he gave vent to a sepulchral roar.

"You fellersh—hic—kin all go—hic—ter blazersh."

The sun slid down and threw a flare upon the silence, coloring it red. The man who had stood up drew a long, deep breath and sat down heavily. Stupefaction rested upon the four men.

Dusk came and fought a battle with the flare before their eyes. Tossing shadows and red beams mingled in combat. Then the stillness of evening lay upon the waters.

The individual began to curse in deep maudlin tones. "Dern fools," he said, "dern fools! Why don'tcher g'home?"

"He's full as a fiddler," said the little man on the third stump. The rest groaned. They sat facing the stump whereon the individual perched, beating them with mighty oaths. Occasionally he took a drink from the bottle. "Shay, you'm fine lot fellers," he bellowed, " why blazersh don'tcher g'home?"

The little man on the third stump pondered. He got up finally and made oration. He, in the beginning, elaborated the many good qualities which he alleged the individual possessed. Next he painted graphically the pitiful distress and woe of their plight. Then he described the reward due to the individual if he would relieve them, and ended with an earnest appeal to the humanity of the individual, alleging, again, his many virtues. The object of the address struggled to his feet, and in a voice of far-away thunder, said: "Dern fool, g'home." The little man sat down and swore crimson oaths.

A night wind began to roar and clouds bearing a load of rain appeared in the heavens and threatened their position. The four men shivered and turned up their coat collars. Suddenly it struck each that he was alone, separated from humanity by impassable gulfs. All those things which come forth at night began to make noises. Unseen animals scrambled and flopped among the weeds and sticks. Weird features masqueraded awfully in robes of shadow. Each man felt that he was compelled to sit on something that was damply alive. A legion of frogs in the grass by the shore and a host of toads in the trees chanted. The little man started up and shrieked that all creeping things were inside his stump. Then he tried to sit facing four ways, because dread objects were approaching at his back. The individual was drinking and hoarsely singing. At different times they labored with him. It availed them nought. "G'home, dern fools." Among themselves they broached various plans for escape. Each involved a contact with the black water, in which were things that wriggled. They shuddered and sat still.

A ghost-like mist came and hung upon the waters. The pond became a grave-yard. The grey tree-trunks and dark logs turned to monuments and crypts. Fire-flies were wisp-lights dancing over graves, and then, taking regular shapes, appeared like brass nails in crude caskets. The individual began to gibber. A gibber in a bass voice appals the stoutest heart. It is the declamation of a genie. The little man began to sob;

another groaned and the two remaining, being timid by nature, swore great lurid oaths which blazed against the sky.

Suddenly the individual sprang up and gave tongue to a yell which raised the hair on the four men's heads and caused the waters to ruffle. Chattering, he sprang into the boat and grasping an oar paddled frantically to the little man's stump. He tumbled out and cowered at the little man's feet, looking toward his stump with eyes that saw the unknown.

"Stump turned inter an octopush. I was a-settin' on his mouth," he howled.

The little man kicked him.

"Legs all commenced move, dern octopush!" moaned the shrunken individual.

The little man kicked him. But others cried out against him, so directly he left off. Climbing into the boat he went about collecting his companions. They then proceeded to the stump whereon the individual lay staring wild-eyed at his "octopush." They gathered his limp form into the boat and rowed ashore. "How far is it to the nearest house?" they demanded savagely of him. "Four miles," he replied in a voice of cave-damp. The four men cursed him and built a great fire of pine sticks. They sat by it all night and listened to the individual who dwelt in phantom shadows by the water's edge dismally crooning about an "octopush."

A Ghoul's Accountant

IN A WILDERNESS sunlight is noise. Darkness is a great, tremendous silence, accented by small and distant sounds. The music of the wind in the trees is songs of loneliness, hymns of abandonment, and lays of the absence of things congenial and alive.

Once a campfire lay dying in a fit of temper. A few weak flames struggled cholerically among the burned-out logs. Beneath, a mass of angry, red coals glowered and hated the world. Some hemlocks sighed and sung and a wind purred in the grass. The moon was looking through the locked branches at four imperturbable bundles of blankets which lay near the agonized campfire. The fire groaned in its last throes, but the bundles made no sign.

Off in the gloomy unknown a foot fell upon a twig. The laurel leaves shivered at the stealthy passing of danger. A moment later a man crept into the spot of dim light. His skin was fiercely red and his whiskers infinitely black. He gazed at the four passive bundles and smiled a smile that curled his lips and showed yellow, disordered teeth. The campfire threw up two lurid arms and, quivering, expired. The voices of the trees grew hoarse and frightened. The bundles were stolid.

The intruder stepped softly nearer and looked at the bundles. One was shorter than the others. He regarded it for some time motionless. The hemlocks quavered nervously and the grass shook. The intruder slid to the short bundle and touched it. Then he smiled. The bundle partially up-reared itself, and the head of a little man appeared.

"Lord!" he said. He found himself looking at the grin of a ghoul condemned to torment.

"Come," croaked the ghoul.

"What?" said the little man. He began to feel his flesh slide to and fro on his bones as he looked into this smile.

"Come," croaked the ghoul.

"What?" the little man whimpered. He grew gray and could not move his legs. The ghoul lifted a three-pronged pickerel-spear and flashed it near the little man's throat. He saw menace on its points. He struggled heavily to his feet.

He cast his eyes upon the remaining mummy-like bundles, but the ghoul confronted his face with the spear.

"Where?" shivered the little man.

The ghoul turned and pointed into the darkness. His countenance shone with lurid light of triumph.

"Go!" he croaked.

The little man blindly staggered in the direction indicated. The three bundles by the fire were still immovable. He tried to pierce the cloth with a glance, and opened his mouth to whoop, but the spear ever threatened his face.

The bundles were left far in the rear and the little man stumbled on alone with the ghoul. Tangled thickets tripped him, saplings buffeted him, and stones turned away from his feet. Blinded and badgered, he began to swear frenziedly. A foam drifted to his mouth, and his eyes glowed with a blue light.

"Go on!" thunderously croaked the ghoul.

The little man's blood turned to salt. His eyes began to decay and refused to do their office. He fell from gloom to gloom.

At last a house was before them. Through a yellow-papered window shone an uncertain light. The ghoul conducted his prisoner to the uneven threshold and kicked the decrepit door. It swung groaning back and he dragged the little man into a room.

A soiled oil-lamp gave a feeble light that turned the pine-board walls and furniture a dull orange. Before a table sat a wild, gray man. The ghoul threw his victim upon a chair and went and stood by the man. They regarded the little man with eyes that made wheels revolve in his soul.

He cast a dazed glance about the room and saw vaguely that it was dishevelled as from a terrific scuffle. Chairs lay shattered, and dishes in the cupboard were ground to pieces. Destruction had been present. There were moments of silence. The ghoul and the wild, gray man contemplated their victim. A throe of fear passed over him and he sank limp in his chair. His eyes swept feverishly over the faces of his tormentors.

At last the ghoul spoke.

"Well!" he said to the wild, gray man.

The other cleared his throat and stood up.

"Stranger," he said, suddenly, "how much is thirty-three bushels of pertaters at sixty-four an' a half a bushel?"

The ghoul leaned forward to catch the reply. The wild, gray man straightened his figure and listened. A fierce light shone on their faces. Their breaths came swiftly. The little man wriggled his legs in agony.

"Twenty-one, no, two, six and——"

"Quick!" hissed the ghoul, hoarsely.

"Twenty-one dollars and twenty-eight cents and a half," laboriously stuttered the little man.

The ghoul gave a tremendous howl.

"There, Tom Jones, dearn yer!" he yelled, " what did I tell yer! hey? Hain't I right? See? Didn't I tell yer that?"

The wild, gray man's body shook. He was delivered of a frightful roar. He sprang forward and kicked the little man out of the door.

The Black Dog

THERE WAS A CEASELESS rumble in the air as the heavy raindrops battered upon the laurel-thickets and the matted moss and haggard rocks beneath. Four water-soaked men made their difficult ways through the drenched forest. The little man stopped and shook an angry finger at where night was stealthily following them. "Cursed be fate and her children and her children's children! We are everlastingly lost!" he cried. The panting procession halted under some dripping, drooping hemlocks and swore in wrathful astonishment.

"It will rain for forty days and forty nights," said the pudgy man, moaningly, "and I feel like a wet loaf of bread, now. We shall never find our way out of this wilderness until I am made into a porridge."

In desperation, they started again to drag their listless bodies through the watery bushes. After a time, the clouds withdrew from above them and great winds came from concealment and went sweeping and swirling among the trees. Night also came very near and menaced the wanderers with darkness. The little man had determination in his legs. He scrambled among the thickets and made desperate attempts to find a path or road. As he climbed a hillock, he espied a small clearing upon which sat desolation and a venerable house, wept over by wind-waved pines.

"Ho," he cried, "here's a house."

His companions straggled painfully after him as he fought the thickets between him and the cabin. At their approach, the wind frenziedly opposed them and skirled madly in the trees. The little man boldly confronted the weird glances from the crannies of the cabin and rapped on the door. A score of timbers answered with groans and, within, something fell to the floor with a clang.

"Ho," said the little man. He stepped back a few paces.

Somebody in a distant part started and walked across the floor toward the door with an ominous step. A slate-colored man appeared. He was dressed in a ragged shirt and trousers, the latter stuffed into his boots. Large tears were falling from his eyes.

"How-d'-do, my friend?" said the little man, affably.

"My ol' uncle, Jim Crocker, he's sick ter death," replied the slate-colored person.

"Ho," said the little man. "Is that so?"

The latter's clothing clung desperately to him and water sogged in his boots. He stood patiently on one foot for a time.

"Can you put us up here until to-morrow?" he asked, finally.

"Yes," said the slate-colored man.

The party passed into a little unwashed room, inhabited by a stove, a stairway, a few precarious chairs and a misshapen table.

"I'll fry yer some po'k and make yer some coffee," said the slate-colored man to his guests.

"Go ahead, old boy," cried the little man cheerfully from where he sat on the table, smoking his pipe and dangling his legs.

"My ol' uncle, Jim Crocker, he's sick ter death," said the slate-colored man.

"Think he'll die?" asked the pudgy man, gently.

"No!"

"No?"

"He won't die! He's an ol' man, but he won't die, yit! The black dorg hain't been around yit!"

"The black dog?" said the little man, feebly. He struggled with himself for a moment.

"What's the black dog?" he asked at last.

"He's a sperrit," said the slate-colored man in a voice of sombre hue.

"Oh, he is? Well?"

"He hants these parts, he does, an' when people are goin' ter die, he comes an' sets an' howls."

"Ho," said the little man. He looked out of the window and saw night making a million shadows.

The little man moved his legs nervously.

"I don't believe in these things," said he, addressing the slate-colored man, who was scuffling with a side of pork.

"Wot things?" came incoherently from the combatant.

"Oh, these-er-phantoms and ghosts and what not. All rot, I say."

"That's because you have merely a stomach and no soul," grunted the pudgy man.

"Ho, old pudgkins!" replied the little man. His back curved with passion. A tempest of wrath was in the pudgy man's eye. The final epithet used by the little man was a carefully-studied insult, always brought forth at a crisis. They quarrelled.

"All right, pudgkins, bring on your phantom," cried the little man in conclusion.

His stout companion's wrath was too huge for words. The little man smiled triumphantly. He had staked his opponent's reputation.

The visitors sat silent. The slate-colored man moved about in a small personal atmosphere of gloom.

Suddenly, a strange cry came to their ears from somewhere. It was a low, trembling call which made the little man quake privately in his shoes. The slate-colored man bounded at the stairway, and disappeared with a flash of legs through a hole in the ceiling. The party below heard two voices in conversation, one belonging to the slate-colored man, and the other in the quavering tones of age. Directly the slate-colored man reappeared from above and said: "The ol' man is took bad for his supper."

He hurriedly prepared a mixture with hot water, salt and beef. Beef-tea, it might be called. He disappeared again. Once more the party below heard, vaguely, talking over their heads. The voice of age arose to a shriek.

"Open the window, fool! Do you think I can live in the smell of your soup?"

Mutterings by the slate-colored man and the creaking of a window were heard.

The slate-colored man stumbled down the stairs, and said with intense gloom, "The black dorg'll be along soon."

The little man started, and the pudgy man sneered at him. They ate a supper and then sat waiting. The pudgy man listened so palpably that the little man wished to kill him. The wood-fire became excited and sputtered frantically. Without, a thousand spirits of the winds had become entangled in the pine branches and were lowly pleading to be loosened. The slate-colored man tiptoed across the room and lit a timid candle. The men sat waiting.

The phantom dog lay cuddled to a round bundle, asleep down the roadway against the windward side of an old shanty. The spectre's master had moved to Pike County. But the dog lingered as a friend might linger at the tomb of a friend. His fur was like a suit of old clothes. His jowls hung and flopped, exposing his teeth. Yellow famine was in his eyes. The wind-rocked shanty groaned and muttered, but the dog slept. Suddenly, however, he got up and shambled to the roadway. He cast a long glance from his hungry, despairing eyes in the direction of the venerable house. The breeze came full to his nostrils. He threw back his head and gave a long, low howl and started intently up the road. Maybe he smelled a dead man.

The group around the fire in the venerable house were listening and waiting. The atmosphere of the room was tense. The slate-colored man's face was twitching and his drabbed hands were gripped together. The little man was continually looking behind his chair. Upon the countenance of the pudgy man appeared conceit for an approaching triumph over the little man, mingled with apprehension for his own safety. Five pipes glowed as rivals of the timid candle. Profound silence drooped heavily over them. Finally the slate-colored man spoke.

"My ol' uncle, Jim Crocker, he's sick ter death."

The four men started and then shrank back in their chairs.

"Damn it!" replied the little man, vaguely.

Again there was a long silence. Suddenly it was broken by a wild cry from the room above. It was a shriek that struck upon them with appalling swiftness, like a flash of lightning. The walls whirled and the floor rumbled. It brought the men together with a rush. They huddled in a heap and stared at the white terror in each other's faces. The slate-colored man grasped the candle and flared it above his head. "The black dorg," he howled, and plunged at the stairway. The maddened four men followed frantically, for it is better to be in the presence of the awful than only within hearing.

Their ears still quivering with the shriek, they bounded through the hole in the ceiling, and into the sick room.

With quilts drawn closely to his shrunken breast for a shield, his bony hand gripping the cover, an old man lay, with glazing eyes fixed on the open window. His throat gurgled and a froth appeared at his mouth.

From the outer darkness came a strange, unnatural wail, burdened with weight of death and each note filled with foreboding. It was the song of the spectral dog.

"God!" screamed the little man. He ran to the open window. He could see nothing at first save the pine-trees, engaged in a furious combat tossing back and forth and struggling. The moon was peeping cautiously over the rims of some black clouds. But the chant of the phantom guided the little man's eyes, and he at length perceived its shadowy form on the ground under the window. He fell away gasping at the sight. The pudgy man crouched in a corner, chattering insanely. The slate-colored man, in his fear, crooked his legs and looked like a hideous Chinese idol. The man upon the bed was turned to stone, save the froth, which pulsated.

In the final struggle, terror will fight the inevitable. The little man roared maniacal curses, and, rushing again to the window, began to throw various articles at the spectre.

A mug, a plate, a knife, a fork, all crashed or clanged on the ground, but the song of the spectre continued. The bowl of beef-tea followed. As it struck the ground the phantom ceased its cry.

The men in the chamber sank limply against the walls, with the unearthly wail still ringing in their ears and the fear unfaded from their eyes. They waited again.

The little man felt his nerves vibrate. Destruction was better than another wait. He grasped a candle and, going to the window, held it over his head and looked out.

"Ho!" he said.

His companions crawled to the window and peered out with him.

"He's eatin' the beef-tea," said the slate-colored man, faintly.

"The damn dog was hungry," said the pudgy man.

"There's your phantom," said the little man to the pudgy man.

On the bed, the old man lay dead. Without, the spectre was wagging its tail.

Killing His Bear

I N A FIELD of snow some green pines huddled together and sang in quavers as the wind whirled among the gullies and ridges. Icicles dangled from the trees' beards, and fine dusts of snow lay upon their brows. On the ridge-top a dismal choir of hemlocks crooned over one that had fallen. The dying sun created a dim purple and flame-colored tumult on the horizon's edge and then sank until level crimson beams struck the trees. As the red rays retreated, armies of shadows stole forward. A gray, ponderous stillness came heavily in the steps of the sun. A little man stood under the quavering pines. He was muffled to the nose in fur and wool, and a hideous cap was pulled tightly over his ears. His cold and impatient feet had stamped a small platform of hard snow beneath him. A black-barrelled rifle lay in the hollow of his arm. His eyes, watery from incessant glaring, swept over the snowfields in front of him. His body felt numb and bloodless, and soft curses came forth and froze on the icy wind. The shadows crept about his feet until he was merely a blurred blackness, with keen eyes.

Off over the ridges, through the tangled sounds of night, came the yell of a hound on the trail. It pierced the ears of the little man and made his blood swim in his veins. His eyes eagerly plunged at the wall of thickets across the stone field, but he moved not a finger or foot. Save his eyes, he was frozen to a statue. The cry of the hound grew louder and louder, then passed away to a faint yelp, then still louder. At first it had a strange vindictiveness and bloodthirstiness in it. Then it grew mournful as the wailing of a lost thing, as, perhaps, the dog gained on a fleeing bear. A hound, as he nears large game, has the griefs of the world on his shoulders and his baying tells of the approach of death. He is sorry he came.

The long yells thrilled the little man. His eyes gleamed and grew small and his body stiffened to intense alertness. The trees kept up their crooning, and the light in the west faded to a dull red splash, but the little man's fancy was fixed on the panting, foam-spattered hound, cantering with his hot nose to the ground in the rear of the bear, which runs as easily and as swiftly as a rabbit, through brush, timber and swale. Swift pictures of himself in a thousand attitudes under a thousand combinations of circumstances, killing a thousand bears, passed panoramically through him.

The yell of the hound grew until it smote the little man like a call to battle. He leaned forward, and the second finger of his right hand played a low, nervous pat-pat on the trigger of his rifle. The baying grew fierce and blood-curdling for a moment, then the dog seemed to turn directly toward the little man, and the notes again grew wailing and mournful. It was a hot trail.

The little man, with nerves tingling and blood throbbing, remained in the shadows, like a fantastic bronze figure, with jewelled eyes swaying sharply in its head. Occasionally he thought he could hear the branches of the bushes in front swish together. Then silence would come again.

The hound breasted the crest of the ridge, a third of a mile away, and suddenly his full-toned cry rolled over the tangled thickets to the little man. The bear must be very near. The little man kept so still and listened so tremendously that he could hear his blood surge in his veins. All at once he heard a swish-swish in the bushes. His rifle was at his shoulder and he sighted uncertainly along the front of the thicket. The swish of the bushes grew louder. In the rear the hound was mourning over a warm scent.

The thicket opened and a great bear, indistinct and vague in the shadows, bounded into the little man's view, and came terrifically across the open snowfield. The little man stood like an image. The bear did not "shamble" nor " wobble"; there was no awkwardness in his gait; he ran like a frightened kitten. It would be an endless chase for the lithe-limbed hound in the rear.

On he came, directly toward the little man. The animal heard only the crying behind him. He knew nothing of the thing with death in its hands standing motionless in the shadows before him.

Slowly the little man changed his aim until it rested where the head of the approaching shadowy mass must be. It was a wee motion, made with steady nerves and a soundless swaying of the rifle-barrel; but the bear heard, or saw, and knew.

The animal whirled swiftly and started in a new direction with an amazing burst of speed. Its side was toward the little man now. His rifle-barrel was searching swiftly over the dark shape. Under the fore-shoulder was the place. A chance to pierce the heart, sever an artery or pass through the lungs. The little man saw swirling fur over his gun-barrel. The earth faded to nothing. Only space and the game, the aim and the hunter. Mad emotions, powerful to rock worlds, hurled through the little man, but did not shake his tiniest nerve.

When the rifle cracked it shook his soul to a profound depth. Creation rocked and the bear stumbled.

The little man sprang forward with a roar. He scrambled hastily in the bear's track. The splash of red, now dim, threw a faint, timid beam on a kindred shade on the snow. The little man bounded in the air.

"Hit!" he yelled, and ran on. Some hundreds of yards forward he came to a dead bear with his nose in the snow. Blood was oozing slowly from a wound under the shoulder, and the snow about was sprinkled with blood. A mad froth lay in the animal's open mouth and his limbs were twisted from agony.

The little man yelled again and sprang forward, waving his hat as if he were leading the cheering of thousands. He ran up and kicked the ribs of the bear. Upon his face was the smile of the successful lover.

A Tent in Agony

FOUR MEN once came to a wet place in the roadless forest to fish. They pitched their tent fair upon the brow of a pine-clothed ridge of riven rocks whence a bowlder could be made to crash through the brush and whirl past the trees to the lake below. On fragrant hemlock boughs they slept the sleep of unsuccessful fishermen, for upon the lake alternately the sun made them lazy and the rain made them wet. Finally they ate the last bit of bacon and smoked and burned the last fearful and wonderful hoecake.

Immediately a little man volunteered to stay and hold the camp while the remaining three should go the Sullivan county miles to a farmhouse for supplies. They gazed at him dismally. "There's only one of you—the devil make a twin," they said in parting malediction, and disappeared down the hill in the known direction of a distant cabin. When it came night and the hemlocks began to sob they had not returned. The little man sat close to his companion, the campfire, and encouraged it with logs. He puffed fiercely at a heavy built brier, and regarded a thousand shadows which were about to assault him. Suddenly he heard the approach of the unknown, crackling the twigs and rustling the dead leaves. The little man arose slowly to his feet, his clothes refused to fit his back, his pipe dropped from his mouth, his knees smote each other. "Hah!" he bellowed hoarsely in menace. A growl replied and a bear paced into the light of the fire. The little man supported himself upon a sapling and regarded his visitor.

The bear was evidently a veteran and a fighter, for the black of his coat had become tawny with age. There was confidence in his gait and arrogance in his small, twinkling eye. He rolled back his lips and disclosed his white teeth. The fire magnified the red of his mouth. The little man had never before confronted the terrible and he could not wrest it from his breast. "Hah!" he roared. The bear interpreted this as the challenge of a gladiator. He approached warily. As he came near, the boots of fear were suddenly upon the little man's feet. He cried out and then darted around the campfire. "Ho!" said the bear to himself, "this thing won't fight—it runs. Well,

suppose I catch it." So upon his features there fixed the ani-
mal look of going—somewhere. He started intensely around
the campfire. The little man shrieked and ran furiously. Twice
around they went.

The hand of heaven sometimes falls heavily upon the righ-
teous. The bear gained.

In desperation the little man flew into the tent. The bear
stopped and sniffed at the entrance. He scented the scent of
many men. Finally he ventured in.

The little man crouched in a distant corner. The bear ad-
vanced, creeping, his blood burning, his hair erect, his jowls
dripping. The little man yelled and rustled clumsily under the
flap at the end of the tent. The bear snarled awfully and made
a jump and a grab at his disappearing game. The little man,
now without the tent, felt a tremendous paw grab his coat
tails. He squirmed and wriggled out of his coat, like a school-
boy in the hands of an avenger. The bear howled trium-
phantly and jerked the coat into the tent and took two bites,
a punch and a hug before he discovered his man was not in
it. Then he grew not very angry, for a bear on a spree is not
a black-haired pirate. He is merely a hoodlum. He lay down
on his back, took the coat on his four paws and began to play
uproariously with it. The most appalling, bloodcurdling
whoops and yells came to where the little man was crying in
a treetop and froze his blood. He moaned a little speech
meant for a prayer and clung convulsively to the bending
branches. He gazed with tearful wistfulness at where his com-
rade, the campfire, was giving dying flickers and crackles.
Finally, there was a roar from the tent which eclipsed all
roars; a snarl which it seemed would shake the stolid silence
of the mountain and cause it to shrug its granite shoulders.
The little man quaked and shrivelled to a grip and a pair of
eyes. In the glow of the embers he saw the white tent quiver
and fall with a crash. The bear's merry play had disturbed the
centre pole and brought a chaos of canvas about his head.

Now the little man became the witness of a mighty scene.
The tent began to flounder. It took flopping strides in the
direction of the lake. Marvellous sounds came from within—
rips and tears, and great groans and pants. The little man
went into giggling hysterics.

The entangled monster failed to extricate himself before he had frenziedly walloped the tent to the edge of the mountain. So it came to pass that three men, clambering up the hill with bundles and baskets, saw their tent approaching.

It seemed to them like a white-robed phantom pursued by hornets. Its moans riffled the hemlock twigs.

The three men dropped their bundles and scurried to one side, their eyes gleaming with fear. The canvas avalanche swept past them. They leaned, faint and dumb, against trees and listened, their blood stagnant. Below them it struck the base of a great pine tree, where it writhed and struggled. The three watched its convolutions a moment and then started terrifically for the top of the hill. As they disappeared, the bear cut loose with a mighty effort. He cast one dishevelled and agonized look at the white thing, and then started wildly for the inner recesses of the forest.

The three fear-stricken individuals ran to the rebuilt fire. The little man reposed by it calmly smoking. They sprang at him and overwhelmed him with interrogations. He contemplated darkness and took a long, pompous puff. "There's only one of me—and the devil made a twin," he said.

The Mesmeric Mountain

ON THE BROW of a pine-plumed hillock there sat a little man with his back against a tree. A venerable pipe hung from his mouth and smoke-wreaths curled slowly sky-ward. He was muttering to himself with his eyes fixed on an irregular black opening in the green wall of forest at the foot of the hill. Two vague wagon ruts led into the shadows. The little man took his pipe in his hands and addressed the listening pines.

"I wonder what the devil it leads to," said he.

A grey, fat rabbit came lazily from a thicket and sat in the opening. Softly stroking his stomach with his paw, he looked at the little man in a thoughtful manner. The little man threw a stone and the rabbit blinked and ran through the opening. Green, shadowy portals seemed to close behind him.

The little man started. "He's gone down that roadway," he said, with ecstatic mystery to the pines. He sat a long time and contemplated the door to the forest. Finally, he arose and, awakening his limbs, started away. But he stopped and looked back.

"I can't imagine what it leads to," muttered he. He trudged over the brown mats of pine needles to where, in a fringe of laurel, a tent was pitched and merry flames caroused about some logs. A pudgy man was fuming over a collection of tin dishes. He came forward and waved a plate furiously in the little man's face.

"I've washed the dishes for three days. What do you think I am——"

He ended a red oration with a roar: "Damned if I do it anymore."

The little man gazed dim-eyed away. "I've been wonderin' what it leads to."

"What?"

"That road out yonder. I've been wonderin' what it leads to. Maybe, some discovery or something," said the little man.

The pudgy man laughed. "You're an idiot. It leads to ol' Jim Boyd's over on the Lumberland Pike."

"Ho!" said the little man, "I don't believe that."

The pudgy man swore. "Fool, what does it lead to, then?"

"I don't know just what but I'm sure it leads to something great or something. It looks like it."

While the pudgy man was cursing, two more men came from obscurity with fish dangling from birch twigs. The pudgy man made an obviously herculean struggle and a meal was prepared. As he was drinking his cup of coffee, he suddenly spilled it and swore. The little man was wandering off.

"He's gone to look at that hole," cried the pudgy man.

The little man went to the edge of the pine-plumed hillock and, sitting down, began to make smoke and regard the door to the forest. There was stillness for an hour. Compact clouds hung unstirred in the sky. The pines stood motionless, and pondering.

Suddenly, the little man slapped his knee and bit his tongue. He stood up and determinedly filled his pipe, rolling his eye over the bowl to the door-way. Keeping his eyes fixed he slid dangerously to the foot of the hillock and walked down the wagon-ruts. A moment later, he passed from the noise of the sunshine to the gloom of the woods.

The green portals closed, shutting out live things. The little man trudged on alone.

Tall tangled grass grew in the road-way and the trees bended obstructing branches. The little man followed on over pine-clothed ridges and down through water-soaked swales. His shoes were cut by rocks of the mountains and he sank ankle-deep in mud and moss of swamps. A curve, just ahead, lured him miles.

Finally, as he wended the side of a ridge, the road disappeared from beneath his feet. He battled with hordes of ignorant bushes on his way to knolls and solitary trees which invited him. Once he came to a tall, bearded pine. He climbed it and perceived in the distance a peak. He uttered an ejaculation and fell out.

He scrambled to his feet and said: "That's Jones's Mountain, I guess. It's about six miles from our camp as the crow flies."

He changed his course away from the mountain and attacked the bushes again. He climbed over great logs, golden-brown in decay, and was opposed by thickets of dark green laurel. A brook slid through the ooze of a swamp, cedars and hemlocks hung their sprays to the edges of pools.

The little man began to stagger in his walk. After a time, he stopped and mopped his brow.

"My legs are about to shrivel up and drop off," he said. . . . "Still if I keep on in this direction, I am safe to strike the Lumberland Pike before sun-down."

He dived at a clump of tag-alders and emerging, confronted Jones's Mountain.

The wanderer sat down in a clear place and fixed his eyes on the summit. His mouth opened widely and his body swayed at times. The little man and the peak stared in silence.

A lazy lake lay asleep near the foot of the mountain. In its bed of water-grass some frogs leered at the sky and crooned. The sun sank in red silence and the shadows of the pines grew formidable. The expectant hush of evening, as if some thing were going to sing a hymn, fell upon the peak and the little man.

A leaping pickerel off on the water created a silver circle that was lost in black shadows. The little man shook himself and started to his feet, crying: "For the love of Mike, there's eyes in this mountain! I feel 'em! Eyes!"

He fell on his face.

When he looked again, he immediately sprang erect and ran.

"It's comin'!"

The mountain was approaching.

The little man scurried sobbing through the thick growth. He felt his brain turning to water. He vanquished brambles with mighty bounds.

But after a time, he came again to the foot of the mountain.

"God!" he howled, "it's been follerin' me!" He grovelled.

Casting his eyes upward made circles swirl in his blood.

"I'm shackled I guess," he moaned. As he felt the heel of the mountain about to crush his head, he sprang again to his feet. He grasped a handful of small stones and hurled them.

"Damn you!" he shrieked, loudly. The pebbles rang against the face of the mountain.

The little man then made an attack. He climbed with hands and feet, wildly. Brambles forced him back and stones slid from beneath his feet. The peak swayed and tottered and was ever about to smite with a granite arm. The summit was a blaze of red wrath.

But the little man at last reached the top. Immediately he swaggered with valor to the edge of the cliff. His hands were scornfully in his pockets.

He gazed at the western horizon edged sharply against a yellow sky. "Ho!" he said. "There's Boyd's house and the Lumberland Pike."

The mountain under his feet was motionless.

NEW YORK CITY,
1892 – 94

Contents

The Broken-Down Van

THE GAS LAMPS had just been lit and the two great red
furniture vans with impossible landscapes on their sides
rolled and plunged slowly along the street. Each was drawn
by four horses, and each almost touched the roaring elevated
road above. They were on the uptown track of the surface
road—indeed the street was so narrow that they must be on
one track or the other.

They tossed and pitched and proceeded slowly, and a horse
car with a red light came up behind. The car was red, and the
bullseye light was red, and the driver's hair was red. He blew
his whistle shrilly and slapped the horse's lines impatiently.
Then he whistled again. Then he pounded on the red dash
board with his car-hook till the red light trembled. Then a car
with a green light crept up behind the car with the red light;
and the green driver blew his whistle and pounded on his
dash board; and the conductor of the red car seized his strap
from his position on the rear platform and rung such a rat-
tling tattoo on the gong over the red driver's head that the
red driver became frantic and stood up on his toes and puffed
out his cheeks as if he were playing the trombone in a Ger-
man street-band and blew his whistle till an imaginative per-
son could see slivers flying from it, and pounded his red dash
board till the metal was dented in and the car-hook was bent.
And just as the driver of a newly-come car with a blue light
began to blow his whistle and pound his dash board and the
green conductor began to ring his bell like a demon which
drove the green driver mad and made him rise up and blow
and pound as no man ever blew or pounded before, which
made the red conductor lose the last vestige of control of
himself and caused him to bounce up and down on his bell
strap as he grasped it with both hands in a wild, maniacal
dance, which of course served to drive uncertain Reason from
her tottering throne in the red driver, who dropped his whis-
tle and his hook and began to yell, and ki-yi, and whoop
harder than the worst personal devil encountered by the stern-
est of Scotch Presbyterians ever yelled and ki-yied and
whooped on the darkest night after the good man had drunk

the most hot Scotch whiskey; just then the left-hand forward
wheel on the rear van fell off and the axle went down. The
van gave a mighty lurch and then swayed and rolled and
rocked and stopped; the red driver applied his brake with a
jerk and his horses turned out to keep from being crushed
between car and van; the other drivers applied their brakes
with a jerk and their horses turned out; the two cliff-dwelling
men on the shelf half-way up the front of the stranded van
began to shout loudly to their brother cliff-dwellers on the
forward van; a girl, six years old, with a pail of beer crossed
under the red car horses' necks; a boy, eight years old,
mounted the red car with the sporting extras of the evening
papers; a girl, ten years old, went in front of the van horses
with two pails of beer; an unclassified boy poked his finger in
the black grease in the hub of the right-hand hind van wheel
and began to print his name on the red landscape on the van's
side; a boy with a little head and big ears examined the white
rings on the martingales of the van leaders with a view of
stealing them in the confusion; a sixteen-year-old girl without
any hat and with a roll of half-finished vests under her arm
crossed the front platform of the green car. As she stepped up
on to the sidewalk a barber from a ten-cent shop said "Ah!
there!" and she answered "smarty!" with withering scorn and
went down a side street. A few drops of warm summer rain
began to fall.

Well, the van was wrecked and something had got to be
done. It was on the busiest car track on Manhattan Island.
The cliff-dwellers got down in some mysterious way—prob-
ably on a rope ladder. Their brethren drove their van down a
side street and came back to see what was the matter.

"The nut is off," said the captain of the wrecked van.

"Yes," said the first mate, "the nut is off."

"Hah," said the captain of the other van, "the nut is off."

"Yer right," said his first mate, "the nut is off."

The driver of the red car came up, hot and irritated. But he
had regained his reason. "The nut is off," he said.

The drivers of the green and of the blue car came along.
"The nut," they said in chorus, "is off."

The red, green and blue conductors came forward. They
examined the situation carefully as became men occupying a

higher position. Then they made this report through the chairman, the red conductor:

"The nut is gone."

"Yes," said the driver of the crippled van, who had spoken first, "yes, the damned nut is lost."

Then the driver of the other van swore, and the two assistants swore, and the three car drivers swore and the three car conductors used some polite but profane expressions. Then a strange man, an unknown man and an outsider, with his trousers held up by a trunk-strap, who stood at hand, swore harder than any of the rest. The others turned and looked at him inquiringly and savagely. The man wriggled nervously.

"You wanter tie it up," he said at last.

"Wot yo' goin' to tie it to, you cussed fool?" asked the assistant of the head van scornfully, "a berloon?"

"Ha, ha!" laughed the others.

"Some folks make me tired," said the second van driver.

"Go and lose yourself with the nut," said the red conductor, severely.

"That's it," said the others. "Git out, 'fore we t'row you out."

The officiously profane stranger slunk away.

The crisis always produces the man.

In this crisis the man was the first van driver.

"Bill," said the first van driver, "git some candles." Bill vanished.

A car with a white light, a car with a white and red light, a car with a white light and a green bar across it, a car with a blue light and a white circle around it, another car with a red bullseye light and one with a red flat light had come up and stopped. More were coming to extend the long line. The elevated trains thundered overhead, and made the street tremble. A dozen horse cars went down on the other track, and the drivers made derisive noises, rather than speaking derisive words at their brother van-bound drivers. Each delayed car was full of passengers, and they craned their necks and peppery old gentlemen inquired what the trouble was, and a happy individual who had been to Coney Island began to sing.

Trucks, mail-wagons and evening paper carts crowded past.

A jam was imminent. A Chatham Square cab fought its way along with a man inside wearing a diamond like an arc-light. A hundred people stopped on either sidewalk; ten per cent of them whistled "Boom-de-ay." A half dozen small boys managed to just miss being killed by passing teams. Four Jews looked out of four different pawnshops. Pullers-in for three clothing stores were alert. The ten-cent barber eyed a Division-st. girl who was a millinery puller-in and who was chewing gum with an earnest, almost fierce, motion of the jaw. The ever-forward flowing tide of the growlers flowed on. The men searched under the slanting rays of the electric light for the lost nut, back past a dozen cars; scattering drops of rain continued to fall and a hand-organ came up and began an overture.

Just then Bill rose up from somewhere with four candles. The leader lit them and each van man took one and they continued the search for the nut. The humorous driver on a blue car asked them why they didn't get a fire-fly; the equally playful driver of a white car advised them of the fact that the moon would be up in the course of two or three hours. Then a gust of wind came and blew out the candles. The hand-organ man played on. A dozen newsboys arrived with evening paper extras about the Presidential nomination. The passengers bought the extras and found that they contained nothing new. A man with a stock of suspenders on his arm began to look into the trade situation. He might have made a sale to the profane man with the trunk-strap but he had disappeared. The leader again asserted himself.

"Bill," he shouted, "you git a lager beer-keg." Bill was gone in an instant.

"Jim," continued the leader, in a loud voice, as if Jim were up at the sharp end of the mainmast and the leader was on the deck, "Jim, unhitch them hosses and take out the pole."

Jim started to obey orders. A policeman came and walked around the van, looked at the prostrated wheel, started to say something, concluded not to, made the hand-organ man move on, and then went to the edge of the sidewalk and began talking to the Division-st. girl with the gum, to the infinite disgust of the cheap barber. The trunk-strap man came out of a restaurant with a sign of "Breakfast, 13 cents; Dinner,

15 cents," where he had been hidden and slunk into the liquor store next door with a sign of "Hot spiced rum, 6 cents; Sherry with a Big Egg in it, 5 cents." At the door he almost stepped on a small boy with a pitcher of beer so big that he had to set it down and rest every half block.

Bill was now back with the keg. "Set it right there," said the leader. "Now you, Jim, sock that pole under the axle and we'll h'ist 'er up and put the keg under."

One of the horses began kicking the front of the van. "Here, there!" shouted the leader and the horse subsided. "Six or seven o' you fellers git under that pole," commanded the leader, and he was obeyed. "Now all together!" The axle slowly rose and Bill slipped under the chime of the keg. But it was not high enough to allow the wheel to go on. "Git a paving block," commanded the leader to Bill. Just then a truck loaded with great, noisy straps of iron tried to pass. The wheels followed the car track too long, the truck struck the rear of the van and the axle went down with a crash while the keg rolled away into the gutter. Even great leaders lose their self-control sometimes; Washington swore at the Battle of Long Island; so this van leader now swore. His language was plain and scandalous. The truckman offered to lick the van man till he couldn't walk. He stopped his horses to get down to do it. But the policeman left the girl and came and made the truckman give over his warlike movement, much to the disgust of the crowd. Then he punched the suspender man in the back with the end of his club and went back to the girl. But the second delay was too much for the driver of the green car, and he turned out his horses and threw his car from the track. It pitched like a skiff in the swell of a steamer. It staggered and rocked and as it went past the van plunged into the gutter and made the crowd stand back, but the horses strained themselves and finally brought it up and at last it blundered on to its track and rolled away at a furious rate with the faces of the passengers wreathed in smiles and the conductor looking proudly back. Two other cars followed the example of the green and went lumbering past on the stones.

"Tell them fellers we'll be out of their way now in a minute," said the leader to the red conductor. Bill had arrived with the paving block. "Up with 'er, now," called the leader.

The axle went up again and the keg with the stone on top of it went under. The leader seized the wheel himself and slipped it on. "Hitch on them hosses!" he commanded, and it was done. "Now, pull slow there, Bill," and Bill pulled slow. The great red car with the impossible landscape gave a preliminary rock and roll, the wheel which had made the trouble dropped down an inch or two from the keg and the van moved slowly forward. There was nothing to hold the wheel on and the leader walked close to it and watched it anxiously. But it stayed on to the corner, and around the corner, and into the side street. The red driver gave a triumphant ki-yi and his horses plunged forward in their collars eagerly. The other drivers gave glad ki-yis and the other horses plunged ahead. Twenty cars rolled past at a fast gait. "Now, youse fellys, move on!" said the policeman, and the crowd broke up. The cheap barber was talking to a girl with one black eye, but he retreated to his shop with the sign which promised "bay rum and a clean towel to every customer." Inside the liquor store the trunk-strap man was telling a man with his sleeves rolled up how two good men could have put their shoulders under the van and h'isted it up while a ten-year-old boy put on the wheel.

An Ominous Baby

A BABY WAS wandering in a strange country. He was a
tattered child with a frowsled wealth of yellow hair. His
dress, of a checked stuff, was soiled and showed the marks of
many conflicts like the chain-shirt of a warrior. His sun-
tanned knees shone above wrinkled stockings which he pulled
up occasionally with an impatient movement when they en-
tangled his feet. From a gaping shoe there appeared an array
of tiny toes.

He was toddling along an avenue between rows of stolid,
brown houses. He went slowly, with a look of absorbed in-
terest on his small, flushed face. His blue eyes stared curi-
ously. Carriages went with a musical rumble over the smooth
asphalt. A man with a chrysanthemum was going up steps.
Two nursery maids chatted as they walked slowly, while their
charges hobnobbed amiably between perambulators. A truck
wagon roared thunderously in the distance.

The child from the poor district made way along the brown
street filled with dull gray shadows. High up, near the roofs,
glancing sun-rays changed cornices to blazing gold and sil-
vered the fronts of windows. The wandering baby stopped
and stared at the two children laughing and playing in their
carriages among the heaps of rugs and cushions. He braced
his legs apart in an attitude of earnest attention. His lower
jaw fell and disclosed his small, even teeth. As they moved
on, he followed the carriages with awe in his face as if con-
templating a pageant. Once one of the babies, with twittering
laughter, shook a gorgeous rattle at him. He smiled jovially
in return.

Finally a nursery maid ceased conversation and, turning,
made a gesture of annoyance.

"Go 'way, little boy," she said to him. "Go 'way. You're all
dirty."

He gazed at her with infant tranquillity for a moment and
then went slowly off, dragging behind him a bit of rope he
had acquired in another street. He continued to investigate
the new scenes. The people and houses struck him with inter-
est as would flowers and trees. Passengers had to avoid the

small, absorbed figure in the middle of the sidewalk. They glanced at the intent baby face covered with scratches and dust as with scars and powder smoke.

After a time, the wanderer discovered upon the pavement, a pretty child in fine clothes playing with a toy. It was a tiny fire engine painted brilliantly in crimson and gold. The wheels rattled as its small owner dragged it uproariously about by means of a string. The babe with his bit of rope trailing behind him paused and regarded the child and the toy. For a long while he remained motionless, save for his eyes, which followed all movements of the glittering thing.

The owner paid no attention to the spectator but continued his joyous imitations of phases of the career of a fire engine. His gleeful baby laugh rang against the calm fronts of the houses. After a little, the wandering baby began quietly to sidle nearer. His bit of rope, now forgotten, dropped at his feet. He removed his eyes from the toy and glanced expectantly at the other child.

"Say," he breathed, softly.

The owner of the toy was running down the walk at top speed. His tongue was clanging like a bell and his legs were galloping. An iron post on the corner was all ablaze. He did not look around at the coaxing call from the small, tattered figure on the curb.

The wandering baby approached still nearer and, presently, spoke again. "Say," he murmured, "le' me play wif it?"

The other child interrupted some shrill tootings. He bended his head and spoke disdainfully over his shoulder.

"No," he said.

The wanderer retreated to the curb. He failed to notice the bit of rope, once treasured. His eyes followed as before the winding course of the engine, and his tender mouth twitched.

"Say," he ventured at last, "is dat yours?"

"Yes," said the other, tilting his round chin. He drew his property suddenly behind him as if it were menaced. "Yes," he repeated, "it's mine."

"Well, le' me play wif it?" said the wandering baby, with a trembling note of desire in his voice.

"No," cried the pretty child with determined lips. "It's mine! My ma-ma buyed it."

"Well, tan't I play wif it?" His voice was a sob. He stretched forth little, covetous hands.

"No," the pretty child continued to repeat. "No, it's mine."

"Well, I want to play wif it," wailed the other. A sudden, fierce frown mantled his baby face. He clenched his thin hands and advanced with a formidable gesture. He looked some wee battler in a war.

"It's mine! It's mine!" cried the pretty child, his voice in the treble of outraged rights.

"I want it," roared the wanderer.

"It's mine! It's mine!"

"I want it!"

"It's mine!"

The pretty child retreated to the fence, and there paused at bay. He protected his property with outstretched arms. The small vandal made a charge. There was a short scuffle at the fence. Each grasped the string to the toy and tugged. Their faces were wrinkled with baby rage, the verge of tears.

Finally, the child in tatters gave a supreme tug and wrenched the string from the other's hands. He set off rapidly down the street, bearing the toy in his arms. He was weeping with the air of a wronged one who has at last succeeded in achieving his rights. The other baby was squalling lustily. He seemed quite helpless. He wrung his chubby hands and railed.

After the small barbarian had got some distance away, he paused and regarded his booty. His little form curved with pride. A soft, gleeful smile loomed through the storm of tears. With great care, he prepared the toy for travelling. He stopped a moment on a corner and gazed at the pretty child whose small figure was quivering with sobs. As the latter began to show signs of beginning pursuit, the little vandal turned and vanished down a dark side street as into a swallowing cavern.

A Great Mistake

A N ITALIAN KEPT a fruit stand on a corner where he had good aim at the people who came down from the elevated station and at those who went along two thronged streets. He sat most of the day in a backless chair that was placed strategically.

There was a babe living hard by, up five flights of stairs, who regarded this Italian as a tremendous being. The babe had investigated this fruit stand. It had thrilled him as few things he had met with in his travels had thrilled him. The sweets of the world laid there in dazzling rows, tumbled in luxurious heaps. When he gazed at this Italian seated amid such splendid treasure, his lower lip hung low and his eyes raised to the vendor's face were filled with deep respect, worship, as if he saw omnipotence.

The babe came often to this corner. He hovered about the stand and watched each detail of the business. He was fascinated by the tranquility of the vendor, the majesty of power and possession. At times, he was so engrossed in his contemplation that people, hurrying, had to use care to avoid bumping him down.

He had never ventured very near to the stand. It was his habit to hang warily about the curb. Even there he resembled a babe who looks unbidden at a feast of gods.

One day, however, as the baby was thus staring, the vendor arose and going along the front of the stand, began to polish oranges with a red pocket-handkerchief. The breathless spectator moved across the sidewalk until his small face almost touched the vendor's sleeve. His fingers were gripped in a fold of his dress.

At last, the Italian finished with the oranges and returned to his chair. He drew a newspaper printed in his language from behind a bunch of bananas. He settled himself in a comfortable position and began to glare savagely at the print. The babe was left face to face with the massed joys of the world.

For a time he was a simple worshipper at this golden shrine. Then tumultuous desires began to shake him. His dreams were of conquest. His lips moved. Presently into his head there came a little plan.

He sidled nearer, throwing swift and cunning glances at the Italian. He strove to maintain his conventional manner, but the whole plot was written upon his countenance.

At last he had come near enough to touch the fruit. From the tattered skirt came slowly his small dirty hand. His eyes were still fixed upon the vendor. His features were set, save for the under lip, which had a faint fluttering movement. The hand went forward.

Elevated trains thundered to the station and the stairway poured people upon the sidewalks. There was a deep sea roar from feet and wheels going ceaselessly. None seemed to perceive the babe engaged in the great venture.

The Italian turned his paper. Sudden panic smote the babe. His hand dropped and he gave vent to a cry of dismay. He remained for a moment staring at the vendor. There was evidently a great debate in his mind. His infant intellect had defined the Italian. The latter was undoubtedly a man who would eat babes that provoked him. And the alarm in him when the vendor had turned his newspaper brought vividly before him the consequences if he were detected.

But at this moment, the vendor gave a blissful grunt and tilting his chair against a wall, closed his eyes. His paper dropped unheeded.

The babe ceased his scrutiny and again raised his hand. It was moved with supreme caution toward the fruit. The fingers were bent, claw-like, in the manner of great heart-shaking greed.

Once he stopped and chattered convulsively because the vendor moved in his sleep. The babe with his eyes still upon the Italian again put forth his hand and the rapacious fingers closed over a round bulb.

And it was written that the Italian should at this moment open his eyes. He glared at the babe a fierce question. Thereupon the babe thrust the round bulb behind him and with a face expressive of the deepest guilt, began a wild but elaborate series of gestures declaring his innocence.

The Italian howled. He sprang to his feet, and with three steps overtook the babe. He whirled him fiercely and took from the little fingers a lemon.

A Dark-Brown Dog

A CHILD WAS STANDING on a street-corner. He leaned with one shoulder against a high board-fence and swayed the other to and fro, the while kicking carelessly at the gravel.

Sunshine beat upon the cobbles, and a lazy summer wind raised yellow dust which trailed in clouds down the avenue. Clattering trucks moved with indistinctness through it. The child stood dreamily gazing.

After a time, a little dark-brown dog came trotting with an intent air down the sidewalk. A short rope was dragging from his neck. Occasionally he trod upon the end of it and stumbled.

He stopped opposite the child, and the two regarded each other. The dog hesitated for a moment, but presently he made some little advances with his tail. The child put out his hand and called him. In an apologetic manner the dog came close, and the two had an interchange of friendly pattings and waggles. The dog became more enthusiastic with each moment of the interview, until with his gleeful caperings he threatened to overturn the child. Whereupon the child lifted his hand and struck the dog a blow upon the head.

This thing seemed to overpower and astonish the little dark-brown dog, and wounded him to the heart. He sank down in despair at the child's feet. When the blow was repeated, together with an admonition in childish sentences, he turned over upon his back, and held his paws in a peculiar manner. At the same time with his ears and his eyes he offered a small prayer to the child.

He looked so comical on his back, and holding his paws peculiarly, that the child was greatly amused and gave him little taps repeatedly, to keep him so. But the little dark-brown dog took this chastisement in the most serious way, and no doubt considered that he had committed some grave crime, for he wriggled contritely and showed his repentance in every way that was in his power. He pleaded with the child and petitioned him, and offered more prayers.

At last the child grew weary of this amusement and turned

toward home. The dog was praying at the time. He lay on his back and turned his eyes upon the retreating form.

Presently he struggled to his feet and started after the child. The latter wandered in a perfunctory way toward his home, stopping at times to investigate various matters. During one of these pauses he discovered the little dark-brown dog who was following him with the air of a footpad.

The child beat his pursuer with a small stick he had found. The dog lay down and prayed until the child had finished, and resumed his journey. Then he scrambled erect and took up the pursuit again.

On the way to his home the child turned many times and beat the dog, proclaiming with childish gestures that he held him in contempt as an unimportant dog, with no value save for a moment. For being this quality of animal the dog apologized and eloquently expressed regret, but he continued stealthily to follow the child. His manner grew so very guilty that he slunk like an assassin.

When the child reached his door-step, the dog was industriously ambling a few yards in the rear. He became so agitated with shame when he again confronted the child that he forgot the dragging rope. He tripped upon it and fell forward.

The child sat down on the step and the two had another interview. During it the dog greatly exerted himself to please the child. He performed a few gambols with such abandon that the child suddenly saw him to be a valuable thing. He made a swift, avaricious charge and seized the rope.

He dragged his captive into a hall and up many long stairways in a dark tenement. The dog made willing efforts, but he could not hobble very skilfully up the stairs because he was very small and soft, and at last the pace of the engrossed child grew so energetic that the dog became panic-stricken. In his mind he was being dragged toward a grim unknown. His eyes grew wild with the terror of it. He began to wiggle his head frantically and to brace his legs.

The child redoubled his exertions. They had a battle on the stairs. The child was victorious because he was completely absorbed in his purpose, and because the dog was very small. He dragged his acquirement to the door of his home, and finally with triumph across the threshold.

No one was in. The child sat down on the floor and made overtures to the dog. These the dog instantly accepted. He beamed with affection upon his new friend. In a short time they were firm and abiding comrades.

When the child's family appeared, they made a great row. The dog was examined and commented upon and called names. Scorn was leveled at him from all eyes, so that he became much embarrassed and drooped like a scorched plant. But the child went sturdily to the center of the floor, and, at the top of his voice, championed the dog. It happened that he was roaring protestations, with his arms clasped about the dog's neck, when the father of the family came in from work.

The parent demanded to know what the blazes they were making the kid howl for. It was explained in many words that the infernal kid wanted to introduce a disreputable dog into the family.

A family council was held. On this depended the dog's fate, but he in no way heeded, being busily engaged in chewing the end of the child's dress.

The affair was quickly ended. The father of the family, it appears, was in a particularly savage temper that evening, and when he perceived that it would amaze and anger everybody if such a dog were allowed to remain, he decided that it should be so. The child, crying softly, took his friend off to a retired part of the room to hobnob with him, while the father quelled a fierce rebellion of his wife. So it came to pass that the dog was a member of the household.

He and the child were associated together at all times save when the child slept. The child became a guardian and a friend. If the large folk kicked the dog and threw things at him, the child made loud and violent objections. Once when the child had run, protesting loudly, with tears raining down his face and his arms outstretched, to protect his friend, he had been struck in the head with a very large saucepan from the hand of his father, enraged at some seeming lack of courtesy in the dog. Ever after, the family were careful how they threw things at the dog. Moreover, the latter grew very skilful in avoiding missiles and feet. In a small room containing a stove, a table, a bureau and some chairs, he would display strategic ability of a high order, dodging, feinting and scuttling about among the furniture. He could force three or four people armed with brooms, sticks and handfuls of coal, to use all their ingenuity to get in a blow. And even when they did, it was seldom that they could do him a serious injury or leave any imprint.

But when the child was present, these scenes did not occur. It came to be recognized that if the dog was molested, the child would burst into sobs, and as the child, when started, was very riotous and practically unquenchable, the dog had therein a safeguard.

However, the child could not always be near. At night, when he was asleep, his dark-brown friend would raise from some black corner a wild, wailful cry, a song of infinite lowliness and despair, that would go shuddering and sobbing among the buildings of the block and cause people to swear. At these times the singer would often be chased all over the kitchen and hit with a great variety of articles.

Sometimes, too, the child himself used to beat the dog, although it is not known that he ever had what could be truly called a just cause. The dog always accepted these thrashings with an air of admitted guilt. He was too much of a dog to try to look to be a martyr or to plot revenge. He received the blows with deep humility, and furthermore he forgave his friend the moment the child had finished, and was ready to caress the child's hand with his little red tongue.

When misfortune came upon the child, and his troubles overwhelmed him, he would often crawl under the table and lay his small distressed head on the dog's back. The dog was ever sympathetic. It is not to be supposed that at such times he took occasion to refer to the unjust beatings his friend, when provoked, had administered to him.

He did not achieve any notable degree of intimacy with the other members of the family. He had no confidence in them, and the fear that he would express at their casual approach often exasperated them exceedingly. They used to gain a certain satisfaction in underfeeding him, but finally his friend the child grew to watch the matter with some care, and when he forgot it, the dog was often successful in secret for himself.

So the dog prospered. He developed a large bark, which came wondrously from such a small rug of a dog. He ceased to howl persistently at night. Sometimes, indeed, in his sleep, he would utter little yells, as from pain, but that occurred, no doubt, when in his dreams he encountered huge flaming dogs who threatened him direfully.

His devotion to the child grew until it was a sublime thing. He wagged at his approach; he sank down in despair at his departure. He could detect the sound of the child's step among all the noises of the neighborhood. It was like a calling voice to him.

The scene of their companionship was a kingdom governed by this terrible potentate, the child; but neither criticism nor rebellion ever lived for an instant in the heart of the one subject. Down in the mystic, hidden fields of his little dog-soul bloomed flowers of love and fidelity and perfect faith.

The child was in the habit of going on many expeditions to observe strange things in the vicinity. On these occasions his friend usually jogged aimfully along behind. Perhaps, though, he went ahead. This necessitated his turning around every quarter-minute to make sure the child was coming. He was filled with a large idea of the importance of these journeys. He would carry himself with such an air! He was proud to be the retainer of so great a monarch.

One day, however, the father of the family got quite exceptionally drunk. He came home and held carnival with the cooking utensils, the furniture and his wife. He was in the midst of this recreation when the child, followed by the dark-brown dog, entered the room. They were returning from their voyages.

The child's practised eye instantly noted his father's state. He dived under the table, where experience had taught him was a rather safe place. The dog, lacking skill in such matters, was, of course, unaware of the true condition of affairs. He looked with interested eyes at his friend's sudden dive. He interpreted it to mean: Joyous gambol. He started to patter across the floor to join him. He was the picture of a little dark-brown dog en route to a friend.

The head of the family saw him at this moment. He gave a huge howl of joy, and knocked the dog down with a heavy coffee-pot. The dog, yelling in supreme astonishment and fear, writhed to his feet and ran for cover. The man kicked out with a ponderous foot. It caused the dog to swerve as if caught in a tide. A second blow of the coffee-pot laid him upon the floor.

Here the child, uttering loud cries, came valiantly forth like a knight. The father of the family paid no attention to these calls of the child, but advanced with glee upon the dog. Upon being knocked down twice in swift succession, the latter apparently gave up all hope of escape. He rolled over on his back and held his paws in a peculiar manner. At the same time with his eyes and his ears he offered up a small prayer.

But the father was in a mood for having fun, and it occurred to him that it would be a fine thing to throw the dog out of the window. So he reached down and grabbing the animal by a leg, lifted him, squirming, up. He swung him two or three times hilariously about his head, and then flung him with great accuracy through the window.

The soaring dog created a surprise in the block. A woman watering plants in an opposite window gave an involuntary shout and dropped a flower-pot. A man in another window leaned perilously out to watch the flight of the dog. A woman, who had been hanging out clothes in a yard, began to caper wildly. Her mouth was filled with clothes-pins, but her arms gave vent to a sort of exclamation. In appearance she was like a gagged prisoner. Children ran whooping.

The dark-brown body crashed in a heap on the roof of a shed five stories below. From thence it rolled to the pavement of an alleyway.

The child in the room far above burst into a long, dirgelike cry, and toddled hastily out of the room. It took him a long time to reach the alley, because his size compelled him to go downstairs backward, one step at a time, and holding with both hands to the step above.

When they came for him later, they found him seated by the body of his dark-brown friend.

An Experiment in Misery

IT WAS LATE at night, and a fine rain was swirling softly down, causing the pavements to glisten with hue of steel and blue and yellow in the rays of the innumerable lights. A youth was trudging slowly, without enthusiasm, with his hands buried deep in his trousers' pockets, toward the downtown places where beds can be hired for coppers. He was clothed in an aged and tattered suit, and his derby was a marvel of dust-covered crown and torn rim. He was going forth to eat as the wanderer may eat, and sleep as the homeless sleep. By the time he had reached City Hall Park he was so completely plastered with yells of "bum" and "hobo," and with various unholy epithets that small boys had applied to him at intervals, that he was in a state of the most profound dejection. The sifting rain saturated the old velvet collar of his overcoat, and as the wet cloth pressed against his neck, he felt that there no longer could be pleasure in life. He looked about him searching for an outcast of highest degree that the two might share miseries. But the lights threw a quivering glare over rows and circles of deserted benches that glistened damply, showing patches of wet sod behind them. It seemed that their usual freights had fled on this night to better things. There were only squads of well-dressed Brooklyn people who swarmed toward the Bridge.

The young man loitered about for a time and then went shuffling off down Park Row. In the sudden descent in style of the dress of the crowd he felt relief, and as if he were at last in his own country. He began to see tatters that matched his tatters. In Chatham Square there were aimless men strewn in front of saloons and lodging houses, standing sadly, patiently, reminding one vaguely of the attitudes of chickens in a storm. He aligned himself with these men, and turned slowly to occupy himself with the flowing life of the great street.

Through the mists of the cold and storming night, the cable cars went in silent procession, great affairs shining with red and brass, moving with formidable power, calm and irresistible, dangerful and gloomy, breaking silence only by the

538

loud fierce cry of the gong. Two rivers of people swarmed along the side-walks, spattered with black mud, which made each shoe leave a scar-like impression. Overhead elevated trains with a shrill grinding of the wheels stopped at the station, which upon its leg-like pillars seemed to resemble some monstrous kind of crab squatting over the street. The quick fat puffings of the engines could be heard. Down an alley there were sombre curtains of purple and black, on which street lamps dully glittered like embroidered flowers.

A saloon stood with a voracious air on a corner. A sign leaning against the front of the doorpost announced: "Free hot soup to-night." The swing doors snapping to and fro like ravenous lips, made gratified smacks as the saloon gorged itself with plump men, eating with astounding and endless appetite, smiling in some indescribable manner as the men came from all directions like sacrifices to a heathenish superstition.

Caught by the delectable sign, the young man allowed himself to be swallowed. A bartender placed a schooner of dark and portentous beer on the bar. Its monumental form upreared until the froth a-top was above the crown of the young man's brown derby.

"Soup over there, gents," said the bartender, affably. A little yellow man in rags and the youth grasped their schooners and went with speed toward a lunch counter, where a man with oily but imposing whiskers ladled genially from a kettle until he had furnished his two mendicants with a soup that was steaming hot and in which there were little floating suggestions of chicken. The young man, sipping his broth, felt the cordiality expressed by the warmth of the mixture, and he beamed at the man with oily but imposing whiskers, who was presiding like a priest behind an altar. "Have some more, gents?" he inquired of the two sorry figures before him. The little yellow man accepted with a swift gesture, but the youth shook his head and went out, following a man whose wondrous seediness promised that he would have a knowledge of cheap lodging houses.

On the side-walk he accosted the seedy man. "Say, do you know a cheap place t' sleep?"

The other hesitated for a time, gazing sideways. Finally he

nodded in the direction of up the street. "I sleep up there," he said, " when I've got th' price."

"How much?"

"Ten cents."

The young man shook his head dolefully. "That's too rich for me."

At that moment there approached the two a reeling man in strange garments. His head was a fuddle of bushy hair and whiskers from which his eyes peered with a guilty slant. In a close scrutiny it was possible to distinguish the cruel lines of a mouth, which looked as if its lips had just closed with satisfaction over some tender and piteous morsel. He appeared like an assassin steeped in crimes performed awkwardly.

But at this time his voice was tuned to the coaxing key of an affectionate puppy. He looked at the men with wheedling eyes and began to sing a little melody for charity.

"Say, gents, can't yeh give a poor feller a couple of cents t' git a bed. I got five an I gits anudder two I gits me a bed. Now, on th' square, gents, can't yeh jest gimme two cents t' git a bed. Now, yeh know how a respecter'ble gentlem'n feels when he's down on his luck an' I——"

The seedy man, staring with imperturbable countenance at a train which clattered overhead, interrupted in an expressionless voice: "Ah, go t' h——!"

But the youth spoke to the prayerful assassin in tones of astonishment and inquiry. "Say, you must be crazy! Why don't yeh strike somebody that looks as if they had money?"

The assassin, tottering about on his uncertain legs, and at intervals brushing imaginary obstacles from before his nose, entered into a long explanation of the psychology of the situation. It was so profound that it was unintelligible.

When he had exhausted the subject the young man said to him: "Let's see th' five cents."

The assassin wore an expression of drunken woe at this sentence, filled with suspicion of him. With a deeply pained air he began to fumble in his clothing, his red hands trembling. Presently he announced in a voice of bitter grief, as if he had been betrayed: "There's on'y four."

"Four," said the young man thoughtfully. "Well, look-a-here, I'm a stranger here, an' if ye'll steer me to your cheap joint I'll find the other three."

The assassin's countenance became instantly radiant with joy. His whiskers quivered with the wealth of his alleged emotions. He seized the young man's hand in a transport of delight and friendliness.

"B'gawd," he cried, "if ye'll do that, b'gawd, I'd say yeh was a damned good feller, I would, an' I'd remember yeh all m' life, I would, b'gawd, an' if I ever got a chance I'd return th' compliment"—he spoke with drunken dignity—"b'gawd, I'd treat yeh white, I would, an' I'd allus remember yeh——"

The young man drew back, looking at the assassin coldly. "Oh, that's all right," he said. "You show me th' joint—that's all you've got t' do."

The assassin, gesticulating gratitude, led the young man along a dark street. Finally he stopped before a little dusty door. He raised his hand impressively. "Look-a-here," he said, and there was a thrill of deep and ancient wisdom upon his face, "I've brought yeh here, an' that's my part, ain't it? If th' place don't suit yeh yeh needn't git mad at me, need yeh? There won't be no bad feelin', will there?"

"No," said the young man.

The assassin waved his arm tragically and led the march up the steep stairway. On the way the young man furnished the assassin with three pennies. At the top a man with benevolent spectacles looked at them through a hole in the board. He collected their money, wrote some names on a register, and speedily was leading the two men along a gloom shrouded corridor.

Shortly after the beginning of this journey the young man felt his liver turn white, for from the dark and secret places of the building there suddenly came to his nostrils strange and unspeakable odors that assailed him like malignant diseases with wings. They seemed to be from human bodies closely packed in dens; the exhalations from a hundred pairs of reeking lips; the fumes from a thousand bygone debauches; the expression of a thousand present miseries.

A man, naked save for a little snuff colored undershirt, was parading sleepily along the corridor. He rubbed his eyes, and, giving vent to a prodigious yawn, demanded to be told the time.

"Half past one."

The man yawned again. He opened a door, and for a moment his form was outlined against a black, opaque interior. To this door came the three men, and as it was again opened the unholy odors rushed out like released fiends, so that the young man was obliged to struggle as against an overpowering wind.

It was some time before the youth's eyes were good in the intense gloom within, but the man with benevolent spectacles led him skillfully, pausing but a moment to deposit the limp assassin upon a cot. He took the youth to a cot that lay tranquilly by the window, and, showing him a tall locker for clothes that stood near the head with the ominous air of a tombstone, left him.

The youth sat on his cot and peered about him. There was a gas jet in a distant part of the room that burned a small flickering orange hued flame. It caused vast masses of tumbled shadows in all parts of the place, save where, immediately about it, there was a little gray haze. As the young man's eyes became used to the darkness he could see upon the cots that thickly littered the floor the forms of men sprawled out, lying in death-like silence or heaving and snoring with tremendous effort, like stabbed fish.

The youth locked his derby and his shoes in the mummy case near him and then lay down with his old and familiar coat around his shoulders. A blanket he handled gingerly, drawing it over part of the coat. The cot was leather covered and cold as melting snow. The youth was obliged to shiver for some time on this affair, which was like a slab. Presently, however, his chill gave him peace, and during this period of leisure from it he turned his head to stare at his friend, the assassin, whom he could dimly discern where he lay sprawled on a cot in the abandon of a man filled with drink. He was snoring with incredible vigor. His wet hair and beard dimly glistened and his inflamed nose shone with subdued luster like a red light in a fog.

Within reach of the youth's hand was one who lay with yellow breast and shoulders bare to the cold drafts. One arm hung over the side of the cot and the fingers lay full length upon the wet cement floor of the room. Beneath the inky brows could be seen the eyes of the man exposed by the partly opened lids. To the youth it seemed that he and this corpse-like being were exchanging a prolonged stare and that the other threatened with his eyes. He drew back, watching his neighbor from the shadows of his blanket edge. The man did not move once through the night, but lay in this stillness as of death, like a body stretched out, expectant of the surgeon's knife.

And all through the room could be seen the tawny hues of naked flesh, limbs thrust into the darkness, projecting beyond the cots; up-reared knees; arms hanging, long and thin, over the cot edges. For the most part they were statuesque, carven, dead. With the curious lockers standing all about like tombstones there was a strange effect of a graveyard, where bodies were merely flung.

Yet occasionally could be seen limbs wildly tossing in fantastic, nightmare gestures, accompanied by guttural cries, grunts, oaths. And there was one fellow off in a gloomy corner, who in his dreams was oppressed by some frightful calamity, for of a sudden he began to utter long wails that went almost like yells from a hound, echoing wailfully and weird through this chill place of tombstones, where men lay like the dead.

The sound, in its high piercing beginnings that dwindled to final melancholy moans, expressed a red and grim tragedy of the unfathomable possibilities of the man's dreams. But to the youth these were not merely the shrieks of a vision pierced man. They were an utterance of the meaning of the room and its occupants. It was to him the protest of the wretch who feels the touch of the imperturbable granite wheels and who then cries with an impersonal eloquence, with a strength not from him, giving voice to the wail of a whole section, a class, a people. This, weaving into the young man's brain and mingling with his views of these vast and somber shadows that like mighty black fingers curled around the naked bodies, made the young man so that he did not sleep, but lay carving biographies for these men from his meager experience. At times the fellow in the corner howled in a writhing agony of his imaginations.

Finally a long lance point of gray light shot through the

dusty panes of the window. Without, the young man could see roofs drearily white in the dawning. The point of light yellowed and grew brighter, until the golden rays of the morning sun came in bravely and strong. They touched with radiant color the form of a small, fat man, who snored in stuttering fashion. His round and shiny bald head glowed suddenly with the valor of a decoration. He sat up, blinked at the sun, swore fretfully and pulled his blanket over the ornamental splendors of his head.

The youth contentedly watched this rout of the shadows before the bright spears of the sun and presently he slumbered. When he awoke he heard the voice of the assassin raised in valiant curses. Putting up his head he perceived his comrade seated on the side of the cot engaged in scratching his neck with long finger nails that rasped like files.

"Hully Jee dis is a new breed. They've got can openers on their feet," he continued in a violent tirade.

The young man hastily unlocked his closet and took out his shoes and hat. As he sat on the side of the cot, lacing his shoes, he glanced about and saw that daylight had made the room comparatively commonplace and uninteresting. The men, whose faces seemed stolid, serene or absent, were engaged in dressing, while a great crackle of bantering conversation arose.

A few were parading in unconcerned nakedness. Here and there were men of brawn, whose skins shone clear and ruddy. They took splendid poses, standing massively, like chiefs. When they had dressed in their ungainly garments there was an extraordinary change. They then showed bumps and deficiencies of all kinds.

There were others who exhibited many deformities. Shoulders were slanting, humped, pulled this way and pulled that way. And notable among these latter men was the little fat man who had refused to allow his head to be glorified. His pudgy form, builded like a pear, bustled to and fro, while he swore in fish-wife fashion. It appeared that some article of his apparel had vanished.

The young man, attired speedily, went to his friend, the assassin. At first the latter looked dazed at the sight of the youth. This face seemed to be appealing to him through the cloud wastes of his memory. He scratched his neck and reflected. At last he grinned, a broad smile gradually spreading until his countenance was a round illumination. "Hello, Willie," he cried, cheerily.

"Hello," said the young man. "Are yeh ready t' fly?"

"Sure." The assassin tied his shoe carefully with some twine and came ambling.

When he reached the street the young man experienced no sudden relief from unholy atmospheres. He had forgotten all about them, and had been breathing naturally and with no sensation of discomfort or distress.

He was thinking of these things as he walked along the street, when he was suddenly startled by feeling the assassin's hand, trembling with excitement, clutching his arm, and when the assassin spoke, his voice went into quavers from a supreme agitation.

"I'll be hully, bloomin' blowed, if there wasn't a feller with a nightshirt on up there in that joint!"

The youth was bewildered for a moment, but presently he turned to smile indulgently at the assassin's humor.

"Oh, you're a d—— liar," he merely said.

Whereupon the assassin began to gesture extravagantly and take oath by strange gods. He frantically placed himself at the mercy of remarkable fates if his tale were not true. "Yes, he did! I cross m' heart thousan' times!" he protested, and at the time his eyes were large with amazement, his mouth wrinkled in unnatural glee. "Yessir! A nightshirt! A hully white nightshirt!"

"You lie!"

"Nosir! I hope ter die b'fore I kin git anudder ball if there wasn't a jay wid a hully, bloomin' white nightshirt!"

His face was filled with the infinite wonder of it. "A hully white nightshirt," he continually repeated.

The young man saw the dark entrance to a basement restaurant. There was a sign which read, "No mystery about our hash," and there were other age stained and world battered legends which told him that the place was within his means. He stopped before it and spoke to the assassin. "I guess I'll git somethin' t' eat."

At this the assassin, for some reason, appeared to be quite

embarrassed. He gazed at the seductive front of the eating place for a moment. Then he started slowly up the street. "Well, goodby, Willie," he said, bravely.

For an instant the youth studied the departing figure. Then he called out, "Hol' on a minnet." As they came together he spoke in a certain fierce way, as if he feared that the other would think him to be weak. "Look-a-here, if yeh wanta git some breakfas' I'll lend yeh three cents t' do it with. But say, look-a-here, you've gota git out an' hustle. I ain't goin' t' support yeh, or I'll go broke b'fore night. I ain't no millionaire."

"I take me oath, Willie," said the assassin, earnestly, "th' on'y thing I really needs is a ball. Me t'roat feels like a fryin' pan. But as I can't git a ball, why, th' next bes' thing is breakfast, an' if yeh do that fer me, b'gawd, I'd say yeh was th' whitest lad I ever see."

They spent a few moments in dexterous exchanges of phrases, in which they each protested that the other was, as the assassin had originally said, a "respecter'ble gentlem'n." And they concluded with mutual assurances that they were the souls of intelligence and virtue. Then they went into the restaurant.

There was a long counter, dimly lighted from hidden sources. Two or three men in soiled white aprons rushed here and there.

The youth bought a bowl of coffee for two cents and a roll for one cent. The assassin purchased the same. The bowls were webbed with brown seams, and the tin spoons wore an air of having emerged from the first pyramid. Upon them were black, moss-like encrustations of age, and they were bent and scarred from the attacks of long forgotten teeth. But over their repast the wanderers waxed warm and mellow. The assassin grew affable as the hot mixture went soothingly down his parched throat, and the young man felt courage flow in his veins.

Memories began to throng in on the assassin, and he brought forth long tales, intricate, incoherent, delivered with a chattering swiftness as from an old woman. "——great job out'n Orange. Boss keep yeh hustlin', though, all time. I was there three days, and then I went an' ask'im t' lend me a dollar. 'G-g-go ter the devil,' he ses, an' I lose me job.

——"South no good. Damn niggers work for twenty-five an' thirty cents a day. Run white man out. Good grub, though. Easy livin'.

——"Yas; useter work little in Toledo, raftin' logs. Make two or three dollars er day in the spring. Lived high. Cold as ice, though, in the winter——

"I was raised in northern N'York. O-o-o-oh, yeh jest oughto live there. No beer ner whisky, though, way off in the woods. But all th' good hot grub yeh can eat. B'gawd, I hung around there long as I could till th' ol' man fired me. 'Git t'hell outa here, yeh wuthless skunk, git t'hell outa here an' go die,' he ses. 'You're a hell of a father,' I ses, 'you are,' an' I quit 'im."

As they were passing from the dim eating place they encountered an old man who was trying to steal forth with a tiny package of food, but a tall man with an indomitable mustache stood dragon fashion, barring the way of escape. They heard the old man raise a plaintive protest. "Ah, you always want to know what I take out, and you never see that I usually bring a package in here from my place of business."

As the wanderers trudged slowly along Park Row, the assassin began to expand and grow blithe. "B'gawd, we've been livin' like kings," he said, smacking appreciative lips.

"Look out or we'll have t' pay fer it t' night," said the youth, with gloomy warning.

But the assassin refused to turn his gaze toward the future. He went with a limping step, into which he injected a suggestion of lamb-like gambols. His mouth was wreathed in a red grin.

In the City Hall Park the two wanderers sat down in the little circle of benches sanctified by traditions of their class. They huddled in their old garments, slumbrously conscious of the march of the hours which for them had no meaning.

The people of the street hurrying hither and thither made a blend of black figures, changing, yet frieze-like. They walked in their good clothes as upon important missions, giving no gaze to the two wanderers seated upon the benches. They expressed to the young man his infinite distance from all that he valued. Social position, comfort, the pleasures of living, were unconquerable kingdoms. He felt a sudden awe.

And in the background a multitude of buildings, of pitiless hues and sternly high, were to him emblematic of a nation forcing its regal head into the clouds, throwing no downward glances; in the sublimity of its aspirations ignoring the wretches who may flounder at its feet. The roar of the city in his ear was to him the confusion of strange tongues, babbling heedlessly; it was the clink of coin, the voice of the city's hopes which were to him no hopes.

He confessed himself an outcast, and his eyes from under the lowered rim of his hat began to glance guiltily, wearing the criminal expression that comes with certain convictions.

An Experiment in Luxury

I F YOU ACCEPT this invitation you will have an opportunity to make another social study," said the old friend.

The youth laughed. "If they caught me making a study of them they'd attempt a murder. I would be pursued down Fifth avenue by the entire family."

"Well," persisted the old friend who could only see one thing at a time, "it would be very interesting. I have been told all my life that millionaires have no fun, and I know that the poor are always assured that the millionaire is a very unhappy person. They are informed that miseries swarm around all wealth, that all crowned heads are heavy with care, and——"

"But still——" began the youth.

"And, in the irritating, brutalizing, enslaving environment of their poverty, they are expected to solace themselves with these assurances," continued the old friend. He extended his gloved palm and began to tap it impressively with a finger of his other hand. His legs were spread apart in a fashion peculiar to his oratory. "I believe that it is mostly false. It is true that wealth does not release a man from many things from which he would gladly purchase release. Consequences cannot be bribed. I suppose that every man believes steadfastly that he has a private tragedy which makes him yearn for other existences. But it is impossible for me to believe that these things equalize themselves; that there are burrs under all rich cloaks and benefits in all ragged jackets, and the preaching of it seems wicked to me. There are those who have opportunities; there are those who are robbed of——"

"But look here," said the young man; "what has this got to do with my paying Jack a visit?"

"It has got a lot to do with it," said the old friend sharply. "As I said, there are those who have opportunities; there are those who are robbed——"

"Well, I won't have you say Jack ever robbed anybody of anything, because he's as honest a fellow as ever lived," interrupted the youth, with warmth. "I have known him for years, and he is a perfectly square fellow. He doesn't know about these infernal things. He isn't criminal because you say he is benefited by a condition which other men created."

"I didn't say he was," retorted the old friend. "Nobody is responsible for anything. I wish to Heaven somebody was, and then we could all jump on him. Look here, my boy, our modern civilization is——"

"Oh, the deuce!" said the young man.

The old friend then stood very erect and stern. "I can see by your frequent interruptions that you have not yet achieved sufficient pain in life. I hope one day to see you materially changed. You are yet——"

"There he is now," said the youth, suddenly. He indicated a young man who was passing. He went hurriedly toward him, pausing once to gesture adieu to his old friend.

The house was broad and brown and stolid like the face of a peasant. It had an inanity of expression, an absolute lack of artistic strength that was in itself powerful because it symbolized something. It stood, a homely pile of stone, rugged, grimly self reliant, asserting its quality as a fine thing when in reality the beholder usually wondered why so much money had been spent to obtain a complete negation. Then from another point of view it was important and mighty because it stood as a fetich, formidable because of traditions of worship.

When the great door was opened the youth imagined that the footman who held a hand on the knob looked at him with a quick, strange stare. There was nothing definite in it; it was all vague and elusive, but a suspicion was certainly denoted in some way. The youth felt that he, one of the outer barbarians, had been detected to be a barbarian by the guardian of the portal, he of the refined nose, he of the exquisite sense, he who must be more atrociously aristocratic than any that he serves. And the youth, detesting himself for it, found that he would rejoice to take a frightful revenge upon this lackey who, with a glance of his eyes, had called him a name. He would have liked to have been for a time a dreadful social perfection whose hand, waved lazily, would cause hordes of the idolatrous imperfect to be smitten in the eyes. And in the tumult of his imagination he did not think it strange that he should plan in his vision to come around to this house and with the power of his new social majesty, reduce this footman to ashes.

He had entered with an easy feeling of independence, but after this incident the splendor of the interior filled him with awe. He was a wanderer in a fairy land, and who felt that his presence marred certain effects. He was an invader with a shamed face, a man who had come to steal certain colors, forms, impressions that were not his. He had a dim thought that some one might come to tell him to begone.

His friend, unconscious of this swift drama of thought, was already upon the broad staircase. "Come on," he called. When the youth's foot struck from a thick rug and changed upon the tiled floor he was almost frightened.

There was cool abundance of gloom. High up stained glass caught the sunlight, and made it into marvelous hues that in places touched the dark walls. A broad bar of yellow gilded the leaves of lurking plants. A softened crimson glowed upon the head and shoulders of a bronze swordsman, who perpetually strained in a terrific lunge, his blade thrust at random into the shadow, piercing there an unknown something.

An immense fire place was at one end, and its furnishings gleamed until it resembled a curious door of a palace, and on the threshold, where one would have to pass a fire burned redly. From some remote place came the sound of a bird twittering busily. And from behind heavy portieres came a subdued noise of the chatter of three, twenty or a hundred women.

He could not relieve himself of this feeling of awe until he had reached his friend's room. There they lounged carelessly and smoked pipes. It was an amazingly comfortable room. It expressed to the visitor that he could do supremely as he chose, for it said plainly that in it the owner did supremely as he chose. The youth wondered if there had not been some domestic skirmishing to achieve so much beautiful disorder. There were various articles left about defiantly, as if the owner openly flaunted the feminine ideas of precision. The disarray of a table that stood prominently defined the entire room. A set of foils, a set of boxing gloves, a lot of illustrated papers, an inkstand and a hat lay entangled upon it. Here was surely a young man, who, when his menacing mother, sisters or ser-

vants knocked, would open a slit in the door like a Chinaman
in an opium joint, and tell them to leave him to his beloved
devices. And yet, withal, the effect was good, because the dis-
order was not necessary, and because there are some things
that when flung down, look to have been flung by an artist.
A baby can create an effect with a guitar. It would require
genius to deal with the piled up dishes in a Cherry street sink.

The youth's friend lay back upon the broad seat that fol-
lowed the curve of the window and smoked in blissful lazi-
ness. Without one could see the windowless wall of a house
overgrown with a green, luxuriant vine. There was a glimpse
of a side street. Below were the stables. At intervals a little
fox terrier ran into the court and barked tremendously.

The youth, also blissfully indolent, kept up his part of the
conversation on the recent college days, but continually he
was beset by a stream of sub-conscious reflection. He was
beginning to see a vast wonder in it that they two lay sleepily
chatting with no more apparent responsibility than rabbits,
when certainly there were men, equally fine perhaps, who
were being blackened and mashed in the churning life of the
lower places. And all this had merely happened; the great se-
cret hand had guided them here and had guided others there.
The eternal mystery of social condition exasperated him at
this time. He wondered if incomprehensible justice were the
sister of open wrong.

And, above all, why was he impressed, awed, overcome by
a mass of materials, a collection of the trophies of wealth,
when he knew that to him their dominant meaning was that
they represented a lavish expenditure? For what reason did
his nature so deeply respect all this? Perhaps his ancestors had
been peasants bowing heads to the heel of appalling pomp of
princes or rows of little men who stood to watch a king kill
a flower with his cane. There was one side of him that said
there were finer things in life, but the other side did homage.

Presently he began to feel that he was a better man than
many—entitled to a great pride. He stretched his legs like a
man in a garden, and he thought that he belonged to the
garden. Hues and forms had smothered certain of his com-
prehensions. There had been times in his life when little
voices called to him continually from the darkness; he heard

them now as an idle, half-smothered babble on the horizon edge. It was necessary that it should be so, too. There was the horizon, he said, and, of course, there should be a babble of pain on it. Thus it was written; it was a law, he thought. And, anyway, perhaps it was not so bad as those who babbled tried to tell.

In this way and with this suddenness he arrived at a stage. He was become a philosopher, a type of the wise man who can eat but three meals a day, conduct a large business and understand the purposes of infinite power. He felt valuable. He was sage and important.

There were influences, knowledges that made him aware that he was idle and foolish in his new state, but he inwardly reveled like a barbarian in his environment. It was delicious to feel so high and mighty, to feel that the unattainable could be purchased like a penny bun. For a time, at any rate, there was no impossible. He indulged in monarchical reflections.

As they were dressing for dinner his friend spoke to him in this wise: "Be sure not to get off anything that resembles an original thought before my mother. I want her to like you, and I know that when any one says a thing cleverly before her he ruins himself with her forever. Confine your talk to orthodox expressions. Be dreary and unspeakably common-place in the true sense of the word. Be damnable."

"It will be easy for me to do as you say," remarked the youth.

"As far as the old man goes," continued the other, "he's a blooming good fellow. He may appear like a sort of a crank if he happens to be in that mood, but he's all right when you come to know him. And besides he doesn't dare do that sort of thing with me, because I've got nerve enough to bully him. Oh, the old man is all right."

On their way down the youth lost the delightful mood that he had enjoyed in his friend's rooms. He dropped it like a hat on the stairs. The splendor of color and form swarmed upon him again. He bowed before the strength of this interior; it said a word to him which he believed he should despise, but instead he crouched. In the distance shone his enemy, the footman.

"There will be no people here to-night, so you may see the

usual evening row between my sister Mary and me, but don't be alarmed or uncomfortable, because it is quite an ordinary matter," said his friend, as they were about to enter a little drawing room that was well apart from the grander rooms.

The head of the family, the famous millionaire, sat on a low stool before the fire. He was deeply absorbed in the gambols of a kitten who was plainly trying to stand on her head that she might use all four paws in grappling with an evening paper with which her playmate was poking her ribs. The old man chuckled in complete glee. There was never such a case of abstraction, of want of care. The man of millions was in a far land where mechanics and bricklayers go, a mystic land of little, universal emotions, and he had been guided to it by the quaint gestures of a kitten's furry paws.

His wife, who stood near, was apparently not at all a dweller in thought lands. She was existing very much in the present. Evidently she had been wishing to consult with her husband on some tremendous domestic question, and she was in a state of rampant irritation, because he refused to acknowledge at this moment that she or any such thing as a tremendous domestic question was in existence. At intervals she made savage attempts to gain his attention.

As the youth saw her she was in a pose of absolute despair. And her eyes expressed that she appreciated all the tragedy of it. Ah, they said, hers was a life of terrible burden, of appalling responsibility; her pathway was beset with unsolved problems, her horizon was lined with tangled difficulties, while her husband—the man of millions—continued to play with the kitten. Her expression was an admission of heroism.

The youth saw that here at any rate was one denial of his oratorical old friend's statement. In the face of this woman there was no sign that life was sometimes a joy. It was impossible that there could be any pleasure in living for her. Her features were as lined and creased with care and worriment as those of an apple woman. It was as if the passing of each social obligation, of each binding form of her life had left its footprints, scarring her face.

Somewhere in her expression there was terrible pride, that kind of pride which, mistaking the form for the real thing, worships itself because of its devotion to the form.

In the lines of the mouth and the set of the chin could be seen the might of a grim old fighter. They denoted all the power of machination of a general, veteran of a hundred battles. The little scars at the corners of her eyes made a wondrously fierce effect, baleful, determined, without regard somehow to ruck of pain. Here was a savage, a barbarian, a spear woman of the Philistines, who fought battles to excel in what are thought to be the refined and worthy things in life; here was a type of Zulu chieftainess who scuffled and scrambled for place before the white altars of social excellence. And woe to the socially weaker who should try to barricade themselves against that dragon.

It was certain that she never rested in the shade of the trees. One could imagine the endless churning of that mind. And plans and other plans coming forth continuously, defeating a rival here, reducing a family there, bludgeoning a man here, a maid there. Woe and wild eyes followed like obedient sheep upon her trail.

Too, the youth thought he could see that here was the true abode of conservatism—in the mothers, in those whose ears displayed their diamonds instead of their diamonds displaying their ears, in the ancient and honorable controllers who sat in remote corners and pulled wires and respected themselves with a magnitude of respect that heaven seldom allows on earth. There lived tradition and superstition. They were perhaps ignorant of that which they worshiped, and, not comprehending it at all, it naturally followed that the fervor of their devotion could set the sky ablaze.

As he watched, he saw that the mesmeric power of a kitten's waving paws was good. He rejoiced in the spectacle of the little fuzzy cat trying to stand on its head, and by this simple antic defeating some intention of a great domestic Napoleon.

The three girls of the family were having a musical altercation over by the window. Then and later the youth thought them adorable. They were wonderful to him in their charming gowns. They had time and opportunity to create effects, to be beautiful. And it would have been a wonder to him if he had not found them charming, since making themselves so could but be their principal occupation.

Beauty requires certain justices, certain fair conditions. When in a field no man can say: "Here should spring up a flower; here one should not." With incomprehensible machinery and system, nature sends them forth in places both strange and proper, so that, somehow, as we see them each one is a surprise to us. But at times, at places, one can say: "Here no flower can flourish." The youth wondered then why he had been sometimes surprised at seeing women fade, shrivel, their bosoms flatten, their shoulders crook forward, in the heavy swelter and wrench of their toil. It must be difficult, he thought, for a woman to remain serene and uncomplaining when she contemplated the wonder and the strangeness of it.

The lights shed marvelous hues of softened rose upon the table. In the encircling shadows the butler moved with a mournful, deeply solemn air. Upon the table there was color of pleasure, of festivity, but this servant in the background went to and fro like a slow religious procession.

The youth felt considerable alarm when he found himself involved in conversation with his hostess. In the course of this talk he discovered the great truth that when one submits himself to a thoroughly conventional conversation he runs risks of being most amazingly stupid. He was glad that no one cared to overhear it.

The millionaire, deprived of his kitten, sat back in his chair and laughed at the replies of his son to the attacks of one of the girls. In the rather good wit of his offspring he took an intense delight, but he laughed more particularly at the words of the son.

Indicated in this light chatter about the dinner table there was an existence that was not at all what the youth had been taught to see. Theologians had for a long time told the poor man that riches did not bring happiness, and they had solemnly repeated this phrase until it had come to mean that misery was commensurate with dollars, that each wealthy man was inwardly a miserable wretch. And when a wail of despair or rage had come from the night of the slums they had stuffed this epigram down the throat of he who cried out and told him that he was a lucky fellow. They did this because they feared.

The youth, studying this family group, could not see that

they had great license to be pale and haggard. They were no doubt fairly good, being not strongly induced toward the by-paths. Various worlds turned open doors toward them. Wealth in a certain sense is liberty. If they were fairly virtuous he could not see why they should be so persistently pitied.

And no doubt they would dispense their dollars like little seeds upon the soil of the world if it were not for the fact that since the days of the ancient great political economist, the more exalted forms of virtue have grown to be utterly impracticable.

Mr. Binks' Day Off

WHEN BINKS was coming up town in a Broadway cable car one afternoon he caught some superficial glimpses of Madison square as he ducked his head to peek through between a young woman's bonnet and a young man's newspaper. The green of the little park vaguely astonished Binks. He had grown accustomed to a white and brown park; now, all at once, it was radiant green. The grass, the leaves, had come swiftly, silently, as if a great green light from the sky had shone suddenly upon the little desolate hued place.

The vision cheered the mind of Binks. It cried to him that nature was still supreme; he had begun to think the banking business to be the pivot on which the universe turned. Produced by this wealth of young green, faint faraway voices called to him. Certain subtle memories swept over him. The million leaves looked into his soul and said something sweet and pure in an unforgotten song, the melody of his past. Binks began to dream.

When he arrived at the little Harlem flat he sat down to dinner with an air of profound dejection, which Mrs. Binks promptly construed into an insult to her cooking, and to the time and thought she had expended in preparing the meal. She promptly resented it. "Well, what's the matter now?" she demanded. Apparently she had asked this question ten thousand times.

"Nothin'," said Binks, shortly, filled with gloom. He meant by this remark that his ailment was so subtle that her feminine mind would not be enlightened by any explanation.

The head of the family was in an ugly mood. The little Binkses suddenly paused in their uproar and became very wary children. They knew that it would be dangerous to do anything irrelevant to their father's bad temper. They studied his face with their large eyes, filled with childish seriousness and speculation. Meanwhile they ate with the most extraordinary caution. They handled their little forks with such care that there was barely a sound. At each slight movement of their father they looked apprehensively at him, expecting the explosion.

The meal continued amid a somber silence. At last, however, Binks spoke, clearing his throat of the indefinite rage that was in it and looking over at his wife. The little Binkses seemed to inwardly dodge, but he merely said: "I wish I could get away into the country for awhile!"

His wife bristled with that brave anger which agitates a woman when she sees fit to assume that her husband is weak spirited. "If I worked as hard as you do, if I slaved over those old books the way you do, I'd have a vacation once in awhile or I'd tear their old office down." Upon her face was a Roman determination. She was a personification of all manner of courages and rebellions and powers.

Binks felt the falsity of her emotion in a vague way, but at that time he only made a sullen gesture. Later, however, he cried out in a voice of sudden violence: "Look at Tommie's dress! Why the dickens don't you put a bib on that child?"

His wife glared over Tommie's head at her husband, as she leaned around in her chair to tie on the demanded bib. The two looked as hostile as warring redskins. In the wife's eyes there was an intense opposition and defiance, an assertion that she now considered the man she had married to be beneath her in intellect, industry, valor. There was in this glance a jeer at the failures of his life. And Binks, filled with an inexpressible rebellion at what was to him a lack of womanly perception and sympathy in her, replied with a look that called his wife a drag, an uncomprehending thing of vain ambitions, the weight of his existence.

The baby meanwhile began to weep because his mother, in her exasperation, had yanked him and hurt his neck. Her anger, groping for an outlet, had expressed itself in the nervous strength of her fingers. "Keep still, Tommie," she said to him. "I didn't hurt you. You needn't cry the minute anybody touches you!" He made a great struggle and repressed his loud sobs, but the tears continued to fall down his cheeks and his under lip quivered from a baby sense of injury, the anger of an impotent child who seems as he weeps to be planning revenges.

"I don't see why you don't keep that child from eternally crying," said Binks, as a final remark. He then arose and went away to smoke, leaving Mrs. Binks with the children and the dishevelled table.

Later that night, when the children were in bed, Binks said to his wife: "We ought to get away from the city for awhile at least this spring. I can stand it in the summer, but in the spring——" He made a motion with his hand that represented the new things that are born in the heart when spring comes into the eyes.

"It will cost something, Phil," said Mrs. Binks.

"That's true," said Binks. They both began to reflect, contemplating the shackles of their poverty. "And besides, I don't believe I could get off," said Binks after a time.

Nothing more was said of it that night. In fact, it was two or three days afterward that Binks came home and said: "Margaret, you get the children ready on Saturday noon and we'll all go out and spend Sunday with your Aunt Sarah!"

When he came home on Saturday his hat was far back on the back of his head from the speed he was in. Mrs. Binks was putting on her bonnet before the glass, turning about occasionally to admonish the little Binkses, who, in their new clothes, were wandering around, stiffly, and getting into all sorts of small difficulties. They had been ready since 11 o'clock. Mrs. Binks had been obliged to scold them continually, one after the other, and sometimes three at once.

"Hurry up," said Binks, immediately, "ain't got much time. Say, you ain't going to let Jim wear that hat, are you? Where's his best one? Good heavens, look at Margaret's dress! It's soiled already! Tommie, stop that, do you hear? Well, are you ready?"

Indeed, it was not until the Binkses had left the city far behind and were careering into New Jersey that they recovered their balances. Then something of the fresh quality of the country stole over them and cooled their nerves. Horse cars and ferry-boats were maddening to Binks when he was obliged to convoy a wife and three children. He appreciated the vast expanses of green, through which ran golden hued roads. The scene accented his leisure and his lack of responsibility.

Near the track a little river jostled over the stones. At times the cool thunder of its roar came faintly to the ear. The Ram-

apo Hills were in the background, faintly purple, and sur-
mounted with little peaks that shone with the luster of the
sun. Binks began to joke heavily with the children. The little
Binkses, for their part, asked the most superhuman questions
about details of the scenery. Mrs. Binks leaned contentedly
back in her seat and seemed to be at rest, which was a most
extraordinary thing.

When they got off the train at the little rural station they
created considerable interest. Two or three loungers began to
view them in a sort of concentrated excitement. They were
apparently fascinated by the Binkses and seemed to be indulg-
ing in all manner of wild and intense speculation. The agent,
as he walked into his station, kept his head turned. Across the
dusty street, wide at this place, a group of men upon the
porch of a battered grocery store shaded their eyes with their
hands. The Binkses felt dimly like a circus and were a trifle
bewildered by it. Binks gazed up and down, this way and
that; he tried to be unaware of the stare of the citizens.
Finally, he approached the loungers, who straightened their
forms suddenly and looked very expectant.

"Can you tell me where Miss Pattison lives?"

The loungers arose as one man. "It's th' third house up that
road there."

"It's a white house with green shutters!"

"There, that's it—yeh can see it through th' trees!" Binks
discerned that his wife's aunt was a well known personage,
and also that the coming of the Binkses was an event of vast
importance. When he marched off at the head of his flock, he
felt like a drum-major. His course was followed by the un-
wavering, intent eyes of the loungers.

The street was lined with two rows of austere and solemn
trees. In one way it was like parading between the plumes on
an immense hearse. These trees, lowly sighing in a breath-like
wind, oppressed one with a sense of melancholy and dreari-
ness. Back from the road, behind flower beds, controlled by
box-wood borders, the houses were asleep in the drowsy air.
Between them one could get views of the fields lying in a
splendor of gold and green. A monotonous humming song
of insects came from the regions of sunshine, and from some
hidden barnyard a hen suddenly burst forth in a sustained

cackle of alarm. The tranquillity of the scene contained a meaning of peace and virtue that was incredibly monotonous to the warriors from the metropolis. The sense of a city is battle. The Binkses were vaguely irritated and astonished at the placidity of this little town. This life spoke to them of no absorbing nor even interesting thing. There was something unbearable about it. "I should go crazy if I had to live here," said Mrs. Binks. A warrior in the flood-tide of his blood, going from the hot business of war to a place of utter quiet, might have felt that there was an insipidity in peace. And thus felt the Binkses from New York. They had always named the clash of the swords of commerce as sin, crime, but now they began to imagine something admirable in it. It was high wisdom. They put aside their favorite expressions: "The curse of gold," "A mad passion to get rich," "The rush for the spoils." In the light of their contempt for this stillness, the conflicts of the city were exalted. They were at any rate wondrously clever.

But what they did feel was the fragrance of the air, the radiance of the sunshine, the glory of the fields and the hills. With their ears still clogged by the tempest and fury of city uproars, they heard the song of the universal religion, the mighty and mystic hymn of nature, whose melody is in each landscape. It appealed to their elemental selves. It was as if the earth had called recreant and heedless children and the mother word, of vast might and significance, brought them to sudden meekness. It was the universal thing whose power no one escapes. When a man hears it he usually remains silent. He understands then the sacrilege of speech.

When they came to the third house, the white one, with the green blinds, they perceived a woman, in a plaid sun bonnet, walking slowly down a path. Around her was a riot of shrubbery and flowers. From the long and tangled grass of the lawn grew a number of cherry trees. Their dark green foliage was thickly sprinkled with bright red fruit. Some sparrows were scuffling among the branches. The little Binkses began to whoop at sight of the woman in the plaid sun bonnet.

"Hay-oh, Aunt Sarah, hay-oh!" they shouted.

The woman shaded her eyes with her hand. "Well, good

gracious, if it ain't Marg'ret Binks! An' Phil, too! Well, I am surprised!"

She came jovially to meet them. "Why, how are yeh all? I'm awful glad t' see yeh!"

The children, filled with great excitement, babbled questions and ejaculations while she greeted the others.

"Say, Aunt Sarah, gimme some cherries!"

"Look at th' man over there!"

"Look at th' flowers!"

"Gimme some flowers, Aunt Sarah!"

And little Tommie, red faced from the value of his information, bawled out: "Aunt Sah-wee, dey have horse tars where I live!" Later he shouted: "We come on a twain of steam tars!"

Aunt Sarah fairly bristled with the most enthusiastic hospitality. She beamed upon them like a sun. She made desperate attempts to gain possession of everybody's bundles that she might carry them to the house. There was a sort of a little fight over the baggage. The children clamored questions at her; she tried heroically to answer them. Tommie, at times, deluged her with news.

The curtains of the dining room were pulled down to keep out the flies. This made a deep, cool gloom in which corners of the old furniture caught wandering rays of light and shone with a mild luster. Everything was arranged with an unspeakable neatness that was the opposite of comfort. A branch of an apple tree moved by the gentle wind, brushed softly against the closed blinds.

"Take off yer things," said Aunt Sarah.

Binks and his wife remained talking to Aunt Sarah, but the children speedily swarmed out over the farm, raiding in countless directions. It was only a matter of seconds before Jimmie discovered the brook behind the barn. Little Margaret roamed among the flowers, bursting into little cries at sight of new blossoms, new glories. Tommie gazed at the cherry trees for a few moments in profound silence. Then he went and procured a pole. It was very heavy, relatively. He could hardly stagger under it, but with infinite toil he dragged it to the proper place and somehow managed to push it erect. Then with a deep earnestness of demeanor he began a little onslaught upon the trees. Very often his blow missed the entire tree and the pole thumped on the ground. This necessitated the most extraordinary labor. But then at other times he would get two or three cherries at one wild swing of his weapon.

Binks and his wife spent the larger part of the afternoon out under the apple trees at the side of the house. Binks lay down on his back, with his head in the long lush grass. Mrs. Binks moved lazily to and fro in a rocking chair that had been brought from the house. Aunt Sarah, sometimes appearing, was strenuous in an account of relatives, and the Binkses had only to listen. They were glad of it, for this warm, sleepy air, pulsating with the sounds of insects, had enchained them in a great indolence.

It was to this place that Jimmie ran after he had fallen into the brook and scrambled out again. Holding his arms out carefully from his dripping person, he was roaring tremendously. His new sailor suit was a sight. Little Margaret came often to describe the wonders of her journeys, and Tommie, after a frightful struggle with the cherry trees, toddled over and went to sleep in the midst of a long explanation of his operations. The breeze stirred the locks on his baby forehead. His breath came in long sighs of content. Presently he turned his head to cuddle deeper into the grass. One arm was thrown in childish abandon over his head. Mrs. Binks stopped rocking to gaze at him. Presently she bended and noiselessly brushed away a spear of grass that was troubling the baby's temple. When she straightened up she saw that Binks, too, was absorbed in a contemplation of Tommie. They looked at each other presently, exchanging a vague smile. Through the silence came the voice of a plowing farmer berating his horses in a distant field.

The peace of the hills and the fields came upon the Binkses. They allowed Jimmie to sit up in bed and eat cake while his clothes were drying. Uncle Daniel returned from a wagon journey and recited them a ponderous tale of a pig that he had sold to a man with a red beard. They had no difficulty in feeling much interest in the story.

Binks began to expand with enormous appreciations. He would not go into the house until they compelled him. And as soon as the evening meal was finished he dragged his wife forth on a trip to the top of the hill behind the house. There was a great view from there, Uncle Daniel said.

The path, gray with little stones in the dusk, extended above them like a pillar. The pines were beginning to croon in a mournful key, inspired by the evening winds. Mrs. Binks had great difficulty in climbing this upright road. Binks was obliged to assist her, which he did with a considerable care and tenderness. In it there was a sort of a reminiscence of their courtship. It was a repetition of old days. Both enjoyed it because of this fact, although they subtly gave each other to understand that they disdained this emotion as an altogether un-American thing, for she, as a woman, was proud, and he had great esteem for himself as a man.

At the summit they seated themselves upon a fallen tree, near the edge of a cliff. The evening silence was upon the earth below them. Far in the west the sun lay behind masses of corn colored clouds, tumbled and heaved into crags, peaks and canyons. On either hand stood the purple hills in motionless array. The valley lay wreathed in somber shadows. Slowly there went on the mystic process of the closing of the day. The corn colored clouds faded to yellow and finally to a faint luminous green, inexpressibly vague. The rim of the hills was then an edge of crimson. The mountains became a profound blue. From the night, approaching in the east, came a wind. The trees of the mountain raised plaintive voices, bending toward the faded splendors of the day.

This song of the trees arose in low, sighing melody into the still air. It was filled with an infinite sorrow—a sorrow for birth, slavery, death. It was a wail telling the griefs, the pains of all ages. It was the symbol of agonies. It celebrated all suffering. Each man finds in this sound the expression of his own grief. It is the universal voice raised in lamentations.

As the trees huddled and bended as if to hide from their eyes a certain sight the green tints became blue. A faint suggestion of yellow replaced the crimson. The sun was dead.

The Binkses had been silent. These songs of the trees awe. They had remained motionless during this ceremony, their eyes fixed upon the mighty and indefinable changes which spoke to them of the final thing—the inevitable end. Their

eyes had an impersonal expression. They were purified, chas-
tened by this sermon, this voice calling to them from the sky.
The hills had spoken and the trees had crooned their song.
Binks finally stretched forth his arm in a wondering gesture.

"I wonder why," he said; "I wonder why the dickens it—
why it—why——"

Tangled in his tongue was the unformulated question of
the centuries, but Mrs. Binks had stolen forth her arm and
linked it with his. Her head leaned softly against his shoulder.

The Art Students' League Building

S INCE THE Art Students' League moved to the fine new building on West 57th St., there remains nothing but the consolation of historical value for the old structure that extends from No. 143 to No. 147 East 23d St. This building with its commonplace front is as a matter of fact one of the landmarks of American art. The old place once rang with the voices of a crowd of art students who in those days past built their ideals of art-schools upon the most approved Parisian models and it is a fact generally unknown to the public that this staid puritanical old building once contained about all that was real in the Bohemian quality of New York. The exterior belies the interior in a tremendous degree. It is plastered with signs, and wears sedately the air of being what it is not. The interior however is a place of slumberous corridors rambling in puzzling turns and curves. The large studios rear their brown rafters over scenes of lonely quiet. Gradually the tinkers, the tailors, and the plumbers who have captured the ground floor are creeping toward those dim ateliers above them. One by one the besieged artists give up the struggle and the time is not far distant when the conquest of the tinkers, the tailors and the plumbers will be complete.

Nevertheless, as long as it stands, the old building will be to a great many artists of this country a place endeared to them by the memory of many an escapade of the old student days when the boys of the life class used to row gaily with the boys of the "preparatory antique" in the narrow halls. Every one was gay, joyous, and youthful in those blithe days and the very atmosphere of the old place cut the austere and decorous elements out of a man's heart and made him rejoice when he could divide his lunch of sandwiches with the model.

Who does not remember the incomparable "soap slides," of those days when the whole class in the hour of rest slid whooping across the floor one after another. The water and soap with which the brushes were washed used to make fine ice when splashed upon the floor and the hopes of America in art have taken many a wild career upon the slippery stretch.

And who does not remember the little man who attempted the voyage when seated in a tin-wash-basin and who came to grief and arose covered with soap and deluged the studio with profanity.

Once when the women's life class bought a new skeleton for the study of anatomy, they held a very swagger function in their class room and christened it "Mr. Jolton Bones" with great pomp and ceremony. Up in the boys' life class the news of the ceremony created great excitement. They were obliged to hold a rival function without delay. And the series of great pageants, ceremonials, celebrations and fetes which followed were replete with vivid color and gorgeous action. The Parisian custom, exhaustively recounted in "Trilby" of requiring each new member of a class to make a spread for his companions was faithfully followed. Usually it consisted of beer, crackers and brie cheese.

After the Art Students' League moved to Fifty-Seventh St., the life classes of the National Academy of Design school moved in for a time and occasionally the old building was alive with its old uproar and its old spirit. After their departure, the corridors settled down to dust and quiet. Infrequently of a night one could pass a studio door and hear the cheerful rattle of half of a dozen tongues, hear a guitar twinkling an accompaniment to a song, see a mass of pipe smoke cloud the air. But this too vanished and now one can only hear the commercial voices of the tinkers, the tailors and the plumbers.

In the top-most and remotest studio there is an old beam which bears this line from Emerson in half-obliterated chalk marks: "Congratulate yourselves if you have done something strange and extravagant and broken the monotony of a decorous age." It is a memory of the old days.

Stories Told by an Artist

A Tale About How "Great Grief" Got His Holiday Dinner

WRINKLES HAD BEEN PEERING into the little drygoods box that acted as a cupboard. "There is only two eggs and a half of a loaf of bread left," he announced brutally.

"Heavens!" said Warwickson from where he lay smoking on the bed. He spoke in his usual dismal voice. By it he had earned his popular name of Great Grief.

Wrinkles was a thrifty soul. A sight of an almost bare cupboard maddened him. Even when he was not hungry, the ghosts of his careful ancestors caused him to rebel against it. He sat down with a virtuous air. "Well, what are we going to do?" he demanded of the others. It is good to be the thrifty man in a crowd of unsuccessful artists, for then you can keep the others from starving peacefully. "What are we going to do?"

"Oh, shut up, Wrinkles," said Grief from the bed. "You make me think."

Little Pennoyer, with head bended afar down, had been busily scratching away at a pen and ink drawing. He looked up from his board to utter his plaintive optimism.

"The *Monthly Amazement* may pay me to-morrow. They ought to. I've waited over three months now. I'm going down there to-morrow, and perhaps I'll get it."

His friends listened to him tolerantly, but at last Wrinkles could not omit a scornful giggle. He was such an old man, almost twenty-eight, and he had seen so many little boys be brave. "Oh, no doubt, Penny, old man." Over on the bed, Grief croaked deep down in his throat. Nothing was said for a long time thereafter.

The crash of the New York streets came faintly. Occasionally one could hear the tramp of feet in the intricate corridors of this begrimed building that squatted, slumbering and aged between two exalted commercial structures that would have had to bend afar down to perceive it. The light snow beat pattering into the window corners and made vague and grey the vista of chimneys and roofs. Often, the wind scurried swiftly and raised a long cry.

Great Grief leaned upon his elbow. "See to the fire, will you, Wrinkles?"

Wrinkles pulled the coal box out from under the bed and threw open the stove door preparatory to shoveling some fuel. A red glare plunged at the first faint shadows of dusk. Little Pennoyer threw down his pen and tossed his drawing over on the wonderful heap of stuff that hid the table. "It's too dark to work." He lit his pipe and walked about, stretching his shoulders like a man whose labor was valuable.

When the dusk came it saddened these youths. The solemnity of darkness always caused them to ponder. "Light the gas, Wrinkles," said Grief.

The flood of orange light showed clearly the dull walls lined with sketches, the tousled bed in one corner, the mass of boxes and trunks in another, the little fierce stove and the wonderful table. Moreover, there were some wine colored draperies flung in some places, and on a shelf, high up, there was a plaster cast dark with dust in the creases. A long stove-pipe wandered off in the wrong direction and then twined impulsively toward a hole in the wall. There were some extensive cobwebs on the ceiling.

"Well, let's eat," said Grief.

Later there came a sad knock at the door. Wrinkles, arranging a tin pail on the stove, little Pennoyer busy at slicing the bread, and Great Grief, affixing the rubber tube to the gas stove, yelled: "Come in!"

The door opened and Corinson entered dejectedly. His overcoat was very new. Wrinkles flashed an envious glance at it, but almost immediately he cried: "Hello, Corrie, old boy!"

Corinson sat down and felt around among the pipes until he found a good one. Great Grief had fixed the coffee to boil on the gas stove, but he had to watch it closely, for the rubber tube was short, and a chair was balanced on a trunk and then the gas stove was balanced on the chair. Coffee making was a feat.

"Well," said Grief, with his back turned, "how goes it, Corrie? How's Art, hey?" He fastened a terrible emphasis upon the word.

"Crayon portraits," said Corinson.

"What?" They turned toward him with one movement, as if from a lever connection. Little Pennoyer dropped his knife.

"Crayon portraits," repeated Corinson. He smoked away in profound cynicism. "Fifteen dollars a week, or more, this time of year, you know." He smiled at them calmly like a man of courage.

Little Pennoyer picked up his knife again. "Well, I'll be blowed," said Wrinkles. Feeling it incumbent upon him to think, he dropped into a chair and began to play serenades on his guitar and watch to see when the water for the eggs would boil. It was a habitual pose.

Great Grief, however, seemed to observe something bitter in the affair. "When did you discover that you couldn't draw?" he said, stiffly.

"I haven't discovered it yet," replied Corinson, with a serene air. "I merely discovered that I would rather eat."

"Oh!" said Grief.

"Hand me the eggs, Grief," said Wrinkles. "The water's boiling."

Little Pennoyer burst into the conversation. "We'd ask you to dinner, Corrie, but there's only three of us and there's two eggs. I dropped a piece of bread on the floor, too. I'm shy one."

"That's all right, Penny," said the other, "don't trouble yourself. You artists should never be hospitable. I'm going, anyway. I've got to make a call. Well, good night, boys. I've got to make a call. Drop in and see me."

When the door closed upon him, Grief said: "The coffee's done. I hate that fellow. That overcoat cost thirty dollars, if it cost a red. His egotism is so tranquil. It isn't like yours, Wrinkles. He——"

The door opened again and Corinson thrust in his head. "Say, you fellows, you know it's Thanksgiving to-morrow."

"Well, what of it?" demanded Grief.

Little Pennoyer said: "Yes, I know it is, Corrie, I thought of it this morning."

"Well, come out and have a table d'hote with me to-morrow night. I'll blow you off in good style."

While Wrinkles played an exuberant air on his guitar, little

Pennoyer did part of a ballet. They cried ecstatically: "Will we? Well, I guess yes!"

When they were alone again Grief said: "I'm not going, anyhow. I hate that fellow."

"Oh, fiddle," said Wrinkles. "You're an infernal crank. And, besides, where's your dinner coming from to-morrow night if you don't go? Tell me that."

Little Pennoyer said: "Yes, that's so, Grief. Where's your dinner coming from if you don't go?"

Grief said: "Well, I hate him, anyhow."

As To Payment of the Rent

Little Pennoyer's four dollars could not last forever. When he received it he and Wrinkles and Great Grief went to a table d'hote. Afterward little Pennoyer discovered that only two dollars and a half remained. A small magazine away down town had accepted one out of the six drawings that he had taken them, and later had given him four dollars for it. Penny was so disheartened when he saw that his money was not going to last forever that, even with two dollars and a half in his pockets, he felt much worse then he had when he was penniless, for at that time he anticipated twenty-four. Wrinkles lectured upon "Finance."

Great Grief said nothing, for it was established that when he received six dollar checks from comic weeklies he dreamed of renting studios at seventy-five dollars per month, and was likely to go out and buy five dollars' worth of second hand curtains and plaster casts.

When he had money Penny always hated the cluttered den in the old building. He desired then to go out and breathe boastfully like a man. But he obeyed Wrinkles, the elder and the wise, and if you had visited that room about ten o'clock of a morning or about seven of an evening you would have thought that rye bread, frankfurters and potato salad from Second avenue were the only foods in the world.

Purple Sanderson lived there, too, but then he really ate. He had learned parts of the gasfitter's trade before he came to be such a great artist, and when his opinions disagreed with that of every art manager in New York he went to see a plumber, a friend of his, for whose opinion he had a great

deal of respect. In consequence he frequented a very neat res-
taurant on Twenty-third street and sometimes on Saturday
nights he openly scorned his companions.

Purple was a good fellow, Grief said, but one of his singu-
larly bad traits was that he always remembered everything.
One night, not long after little Pennoyer's great discovery,
Purple came in and as he was neatly hanging up his coat, said:
"Well, the rent will be due in four days."

"Will it?" demanded Penny, astounded. Penny was always
astounded when the rent came due. It seemed to him the
most extraordinary occurrence.

"Certainly it will," said Purple with the irritated air of a
superior financial man.

"My soul!" said Wrinkles.

Great Grief lay on the bed smoking a pipe and waiting for
fame. "Oh, go home, Purple. You resent something. It wasn't
me—it was the calendar."

"Try and be serious a moment, Grief."

"You're a fool, Purple."

Penny spoke from where he was at work. "Well, if those
Amazement people pay me when they said they would I'll
have money then."

"So you will, dear," said Grief, satirically. "You'll have
money to burn. Did the *Amazement* people ever pay you
when they said they would? You're wonderfully important all
of a sudden, it seems to me. You talk like an artist."

Wrinkles, too, smiled at little Pennoyer. "The *Established
Magazine* people wanted Penny to hire models and make a try
for them, too. It will only cost him a big blue chip. By the
time he has invested all the money he hasn't got and the rent
is two weeks overdue he will be able to tell the landlord to
wait seven months until the Monday morning after the day
of publication. Go ahead, Penny."

It was the habit to make game of little Pennoyer. He was
always having gorgeous opportunities, with no opportunity
to take advantage of his opportunities.

Penny smiled at them, his tiny, tiny smile of courage.

"You're a confident little cuss," observed Grief, irrelevantly.

"Well, the world has no objection to your being confident,
also, Grief," said Purple.

"Hasn't it?" said Grief. "Well, I want to know!"

Wrinkles could not be light spirited long. He was obliged to despair when occasion offered. At last he sank down in a chair and seized his guitar. "Well, what's to be done?" he said. He began to play mournfully.

"Throw Purple out," mumbled Grief from the bed.

"Are you fairly certain that you will have money then, Penny?" asked Purple.

Little Pennoyer looked apprehensive. "Well, I don't know," he said.

And then began that memorable discussion, great in four minds. The tobacco was of the "Long John" brand. It smelled like burning mummies.

How Pennoyer Disposed of His Sunday Dinner

Once Purple Sanderson went to his home in St. Lawrence county to enjoy some country air, and, incidentally, to explain his life failure to his people. Previously, Great Grief had given him odds that he would return sooner than he then planned, and everybody said that Grief had a good bet. It is not a glorious pastime, this explaining of life failures.

Later, Great Grief and Wrinkles went to Haverstraw to visit Grief's cousin and sketch. Little Pennoyer was disheartened, for it is bad to be imprisoned in brick and dust and cobbles when your ear can hear in the distance the harmony of the summer sunlight upon leaf and blade of green. Besides, he did not hear Wrinkles and Grief discoursing and quarreling in the den and Purple coming in at six o'clock with contempt.

On Friday afternoon he discovered that he only had fifty cents to last until Saturday morning, when he was to get his check from the *Gamin*. He was an artful little man by this time, however, and it is as true as the sky that when he walked toward the *Gamin* office on Saturday he had twenty cents remaining.

The cashier nodded his regrets. "Very sorry, Mr.—er— Pennoyer, but our pay day, you know, is on Monday. Come around any time after ten."

"Oh, it don't matter," said Penny. As he walked along on his return he reflected deeply how he could invest his twenty cents in food to last until Monday morning any time after ten. He bought two coffee cakes in a Third avenue bakery. They were very beautiful. Each had a hole in the center and a handsome scallop all around the edges.

Penny took great care of those cakes. At odd times he would rise from his work and go to see that no escape had been made. On Sunday he got up at noon and compressed breakfast and noon into one meal. Afterward he had almost three-quarters of a cake still left to him. He congratulated himself that with strategy he could make it endure until Monday morning, any time after ten.

At three in the afternoon there came a faint-hearted knock. "Come in," said Penny. The door opened and old Tim Connegan, who was trying to be a model, looked in apprehensively. "I beg pardon, sir," he said, at once.

"Come in, Tim, you old thief," said Penny. Tim entered, slowly and bashfully. "Sit down," said Penny. Tim sat down and began to rub his knees, for rheumatism had a mighty hold upon him.

Penny lit his pipe and crossed his legs. "Well, how goes it?"

Tim moved his square jaw upward and flashed Penny a little glance.

"Bad?" said Penny.

The old man raised his hand impressively. "I've been to every studio in the hull city and I never see such absences in my life. What with the seashore and the mountains, and this and that resort, I think all the models will be starved by fall. I found one man in up on Fifty-seventh street. He ses to me: 'Come around Tuesday—I may want yez and I may not.' That was last week. You know, I live down on the Bowery, Mr. Pennoyer, and when I got up there on Tuesday, he ses: 'Confound you, are you here again?' ses he. I went and sat down in the park, for I was too tired for the walk back. And there you are, Mr. Pennoyer. What with tramping around to look for men that are a thousand miles away, I'm near dead."

"It's hard," said Penny.

"It is, sir. I hope they'll come back soon. The summer is the death of us all, sir, it is. Sure, I never know where my next meal is coming until I get it. That's true."

"Had anything to-day?"

"Yes, sir—a little."

"How much?"

"Well, sir, a lady give me a cup of coffee this morning. It was good, too, I'm telling you."

Penny went to his cupboard. When he returned, he said: "Here's some cake."

Tim thrust forward his hands, palms erect. "Oh, now, Mr. Pennoyer, I couldn't. You——"

"Go ahead. What's the odds?"

"Oh, now——"

"Go ahead, you old bat."

Penny smoked.

When Tim was going out, he turned to grow eloquent again. "Well, I can't tell you how much I'm obliged to you, Mr. Pennoyer. You——"

"Don't mention it, old man."

Penny smoked.

The Men in the Storm

A T ABOUT THREE O'CLOCK of the February afternoon, the
blizzard began to swirl great clouds of snow along
the streets, sweeping it down from the roofs and up from the
pavements until the faces of pedestrians tingled and burned
as from a thousand needle-prickings. Those on the walks hud-
dled their necks closely in the collars of their coats and went
along stooping like a race of aged people. The drivers of ve-
hicles hurried their horses furiously on their way. They were
made more cruel by the exposure of their positions, aloft on
high seats. The street cars, bound up-town, went slowly, the
horses slipping and straining in the spongy brown mass that
lay between the rails. The drivers, muffled to the eyes, stood
erect and facing the wind, models of grim philosophy. Over-
head the trains rumbled and roared, and the dark structure of
the elevated railroad, stretching over the avenue, dripped little
streams and drops of water upon the mud and snow beneath it.

All the clatter of the street was softened by the masses that
lay upon the cobbles until, even to one who looked from a
window, it became important music, a melody of life made
necessary to the ear by the dreariness of the pitiless beat and
sweep of the storm. Occasionally one could see black figures
of men busily shovelling the white drifts from the walks. The
sounds from their labor created new recollections of rural ex-
periences which every man manages to have in a measure.
Later, the immense windows of the shops became aglow with
light, throwing great beams of orange and yellow upon the
pavement. They were infinitely cheerful, yet in a way they
accented the force and discomfort of the storm, and gave a
meaning to the pace of the people and the vehicles, scores of
pedestrians and drivers, wretched with cold faces, necks and
feet, speeding for scores of unknown doors and entrances,
scattering to an infinite variety of shelters, to places which the
imagination made warm with the familiar colors of home.

There was an absolute expression of hot dinners in the pace
of the people. If one dared to speculate upon the destination
of those who came trooping, he lost himself in a maze of
social calculations; he might fling a handful of sand and at-

tempt to follow the flight of each particular grain. But as to the suggestion of hot dinners, he was in firm lines of thought, for it was upon every hurrying face. It is a matter of tradition; it is from the tales of childhood. It comes forth with every storm.

However, in a certain part of a dark West-side street, there was a collection of men to whom these things were as if they were not. In this street was located a charitable house where for five cents the homeless of the city could get a bed at night and, in the morning, coffee and bread.

During the afternoon of the storm, the whirling snows acted as drivers, as men with whips, and at half-past three, the walk before the closed doors of the house was covered with wanderers of the street, waiting. For some distance on either side of the place they could be seen lurking in door-ways and behind projecting parts of buildings, gathering in close bunches in an effort to get warm. A covered wagon drawn up near the curb sheltered a dozen of them. Under the stairs that led to the elevated railway station, there were six or eight, their hands stuffed deep in their pockets, their shoul-ders stooped, jiggling their feet. Others always could be seen coming, a strange procession, some slouching along with the characteristic hopeless gait of professional strays, some com-ing with hesitating steps wearing the air of men to whom this sort of thing was new.

It was an afternoon of incredible length. The snow, blow-ing in twisting clouds, sought out the men in their meagre hiding-places and skilfully beat in among them, drenching their persons with showers of fine, stinging flakes. They crowded together, muttering, and fumbling in their pockets to get their red, inflamed wrists covered by the cloth.

Newcomers usually halted at one of the groups and ad-dressed a question, perhaps much as a matter of form, "Is it open yet?"

Those who had been waiting inclined to take the ques-tioner seriously and become contemptuous. "No; do yeh think we'd be standin' here?"

The gathering swelled in numbers steadily and persistently. One could always see them coming, trudging slowly through the storm.

Finally, the little snow plains in the street began to assume a leaden hue from the shadows of evening. The buildings up-reared gloomily save where various windows became brilliant figures of light that made shimmers and splashes of yellow on the snow. A street lamp on the curb struggled to illuminate, but it was reduced to impotent blindness by the swift gusts of sleet crusting its panes.

In this half-darkness, the men began to come from their shelter places and mass in front of the doors of charity. They were of all types, but the nationalities were mostly American, German and Irish. Many were strong, healthy, clear-skinned fellows with that stamp of countenance which is not fre-quently seen upon seekers after charity. There were men of undoubted patience, industry and temperance, who in time of ill-fortune, do not habitually turn to rail at the state of soci-ety, snarling at the arrogance of the rich and bemoaning the cowardice of the poor, but who at these times are apt to wear a sudden and singular meekness, as if they saw the world's progress marching from them and were trying to perceive where they had failed, what they had lacked, to be thus van-quished in the race. Then there were others of the shifting, Bowery lodging-house element who were used to paying ten cents for a place to sleep, but who now came here because it was cheaper.

But they were all mixed in one mass so thoroughly that one could not have discerned the different elements but for the fact that the laboring men, for the most part, remained silent and impassive in the blizzard, their eyes fixed on the windows of the house, statues of patience.

The sidewalk soon became completely blocked by the bod-ies of the men. They pressed close to one another like sheep in a winter's gale, keeping one another warm by the heat of their bodies. The snow came down upon this compressed group of men until, directly from above, it might have ap-peared like a heap of snow-covered merchandise, if it were not for the fact that the crowd swayed gently with a unani-mous, rhythmical motion. It was wonderful to see how the snow lay upon the heads and shoulders of these men, in little ridges an inch thick perhaps in places, the flakes steadily add-ing drop and drop, precisely as they fall upon the unresisting grass of the fields. The feet of the men were all wet and cold and the wish to warm them accounted for the slow, gentle, rhythmical motion. Occasionally some man whose ears or nose tingled acutely from the cold winds would wriggle down until his head was protected by the shoulders of his companions.

There was a continuous murmuring discussion as to the probability of the doors being speedily opened. They persistently lifted their eyes toward the windows. One could hear little combats of opinion.

"There's a light in th' winder!"

"Naw; it's a reflection f'm across th' way."

"Well, didn't I see 'em lite it?"

"You did?"

"I did!"

"Well, then, that settles it!"

As the time approached when they expected to be allowed to enter, the men crowded to the doors in an unspeakable crush, jamming and wedging in a way that it seemed would crack bones. They surged heavily against the building in a powerful wave of pushing shoulders. Once a rumor flitted among all the tossing heads.

"They can't open th' doors! Th' fellers er smack up ag'in 'em."

Then a dull roar of rage came from the men on the outskirts; but all the time they strained and pushed until it appeared to be impossible for those that they cried out against to do anything but be crushed to pulp.

"Ah, git away f'm th' door!"

"Git outa that!"

"Throw 'em out!"

"Kill 'em!"

"Say, fellers, now, what th' 'ell? Give 'em a chanct t' open th' door!"

"Yeh damned pigs, give 'em a chanct t' open th' door!"

Men in the outskirts of the crowd occasionally yelled when a boot-heel of one of frantic trampling feet crushed on their freezing extremities.

"Git off me feet, yeh clumsy tarrier!"

"Say, don't stand on me feet! Walk on th' ground!"

A man near the doors suddenly shouted: "O-o-oh! Le' me out—le' me out!" And another, a man of infinite valor, once twisted his head so as to half face those who were pushing behind him. "Quit yer shovin', yeh ——" and he delivered a volley of the most powerful and singular invective straight into the faces of the men behind him. It was as if he was hammering the noses of them with curses of triple brass. His face, red with rage, could be seen; upon it, an expression of sublime disregard of consequences. But nobody cared to reply to his imprecations; it was too cold. Many of them snickered and all continued to push.

In occasional pauses of the crowd's movement the men had opportunity to make jokes; usually grim things, and no doubt very uncouth. Nevertheless, they are notable—one does not expect to find the quality of humor in a heap of old clothes under a snowdrift.

The winds seemed to grow fiercer as time wore on. Some of the gusts of snow that came down on the close collection of heads cut like knives and needles, and the men huddled, and swore, not like dark assassins, but in a sort of an American fashion, grimly and desperately, it is true, but yet with a wondrous under-effect, indefinable and mystic, as if there was some kind of humor in this catastrophe, in this situation in a night of snow-laden winds.

Once, the window of the huge dry-goods shop across the street furnished material for a few moments of forgetfulness. In the brilliantly-lighted space appeared the figure of a man. He was rather stout and very well clothed. His whiskers were fashioned charmingly after those of the Prince of Wales. He stood in an attitude of magnificent reflection. He slowly stroked his moustache with a certain grandeur of manner, and looked down at the snow-encrusted mob. From below, there was denoted a supreme complacence in him. It seemed that the sight operated inversely, and enabled him to more clearly regard his own environment, delightful relatively.

One of the mob chanced to turn his head and perceive the figure in the window. "Hello, lookit 'is whiskers," he said genially.

Many of the men turned then, and a shout went up. They called to him in all strange keys. They addressed him in every manner, from familiar and cordial greetings to carefully-worded advice concerning changes in his personal appearance. The man presently fled, and the mob chuckled ferociously like ogres who had just devoured something.

They turned then to serious business. Often they addressed the stolid front of the house.

"Oh, let us in fer Gawd's sake!"

"Let us in or we'll all drop dead!"

"Say, what's th' use o' keepin' all us poor Indians out in th' cold?"

And always some one was saying, "Keep off me feet."

The crushing of the crowd grew terrific toward the last. The men, in keen pain from the blasts, began almost to fight. With the pitiless whirl of snow upon them, the battle for shelter was going to the strong. It became known that the basement door at the foot of a little steep flight of stairs was the one to be opened, and they jostled and heaved in this direction like laboring fiends. One could hear them panting and groaning in their fierce exertion.

Usually some one in the front ranks was protesting to those in the rear: "O—o—ow! Oh, say, now, fellers, let up, will yeh? Do yeh wanta kill somebody?"

A policeman arrived and went into the midst of them, scolding and berating, occasionally threatening, but using no force but that of his hands and shoulders against these men who were only struggling to get in out of the storm. His decisive tones rang out sharply: "Stop that pushin' back there! Come, boys, don't push! Stop that! Here, you, quit yer shovin'! Cheese that!"

When the door below was opened, a thick stream of men forced a way down the stairs, which were of an extraordinary narrowness and seemed only wide enough for one at a time. Yet they somehow went down almost three abreast. It was a difficult and painful operation. The crowd was like a turbulent water forcing itself through one tiny outlet. The men in the rear, excited by the success of the others, made frantic exertions, for it seemed that this large band would more than fill the quarters and that many would be left upon the pavements. It would be disastrous to be of the last, and accordingly men with the snow biting their faces, writhed and twisted with their might. One expected that from the tremendous pressure, the narrow passage to the basement door would be so choked and clogged with human limbs and bodies that movement would be impossible. Once indeed the crowd was forced to stop, and a cry went along that a man had been injured at the foot of the stairs. But presently the slow movement began again, and the policeman fought at the top of the flight to ease the pressure on those who were going down.

A reddish light from a window fell upon the faces of the men when they, in turn, arrived at the last three steps and were about to enter. One could then note a change of expression that had come over their features. As they thus stood upon the threshold of their hopes, they looked suddenly content and complacent. The fire had passed from their eyes and the snarl had vanished from their lips. The very force of the crowd in the rear, which had previously vexed them, was regarded from another point of view, for it now made it inevitable that they should go through the little doors into the place that was cheery and warm with light.

The tossing crowd on the sidewalk grew smaller and smaller. The snow beat with merciless persistence upon the bowed heads of those who waited. The wind drove it up from the pavements in frantic forms of winding white, and it seethed in circles about the huddled forms, passing in, one by one, three by three, out of the storm.

Coney Island's Failing Days

D OWN HERE at your Coney Island, toward the end of the season, I am made to feel very sad," said the stranger to me. "The great mournfulness that settles upon a summer resort at this time always depresses me exceedingly. The mammoth empty buildings, planned by extraordinarily optimistic architects, remind me in an unpleasant manner of my youthful dreams. In those days of visions I erected huge castles for the reception of my friends and admirers, and discovered later that I could have entertained them more comfortably in a small two story frame structure. There is a mighty pathos in these gaunt and hollow buildings, impassively and stolidly suffering from an enormous hunger for the public. And the unchangeable, ever imperturbable sea pursues its quaint devices blithely at the feet of these mournful wooden animals, gabbling and frolicking, with no thought for absent man nor maid!"

As the stranger spoke, he gazed with considerable scorn at the emotions of the sea; and the breeze from the far Navesink hills gently stirred the tangled, philosophic hair upon his forehead. Presently he went on: "The buildings are in effect more sad than the men, but I assure you that some of the men look very sad. I watched a talented and persuasive individual who was operating in front of a tintype gallery, and he had only the most marvelously infrequent opportunities to display his oratory and finesse. The occasional stragglers always managed to free themselves before he could drag them into the gallery and take their pictures. In the long intervals he gazed about him with a bewildered air, as if he felt his world dropping from under his feet. Once I saw him spy a promising youth afar off. He lurked with muscles at a tension, and then at the proper moment he swooped. 'Look-a-here,' he said, with tears of enthusiasm in his eyes, 'the best picture in the world! An' on'y four fer a quarter. On'y jest try it, an' you'll go away perfectly satisfied!'

" 'I'll go away perfectly satisfied without trying it,' replied the promising youth, and he did. The tintype man wanted to dash his samples to the ground and whip the promising youth. He controlled himself, however, and went to watch the approach of two women and a little boy who were nothing more than three dots, away down the board walk.

"At one place I heard the voice of a popcorn man raised in a dreadful note, as if he were chanting a death hymn. It made me shiver as I felt all the tragedy of the collapsed popcorn market. I began to see that it was an insult to the pain and suffering of these men to go near to them without buying anything. I took new and devious routes sometimes.

"As for the railroad guards and station men, they were so tolerant of the presence of passengers that I felt it to be an indication of their sense of relief from the summer's battle. They did not seem so greatly irritated by patrons of the railroad as I have seen them at other times. And in all the beer gardens the waiters had opportunity to indulge that delight in each other's society and conversation which forms so important a part in a waiter's idea of happiness. Sometimes the people in a sparsely occupied place will fare more strange than those in a crowded one. At one time I waited twenty minutes for a bottle of the worst beer in Christendom while my waiter told a charmingly naive story to a group of his compatriots. I protested sotto voce at the time that such beer might at least have the merit of being brought quickly.

"The restaurants, however, I think to be quite delicious, being in a large part thoroughly disreputable and always provided with huge piles of red boiled crabs. These huge piles of provision around on the floor and on the oyster counters always give me the opinion that I am dining on the freshest food in the world, and I appreciate the sensation. If need be, it also allows a man to revel in dreams of unlimited quantity.

"I found countless restaurants where I could get things almost to my taste, and, as I ate, watch the grand, eternal motion of the sea and have the waiter come up and put the pepper castor on the menu card to keep the salt breeze from interfering with my order for dinner.

"And yet I have an occasional objection to the sea when dining in sight of it; for a man with a really artistic dining sense always feels important as a duke when he is indulging in his favorite pastime, and, as the sea always makes me feel that I am a trivial object, I cannot dine with absolute comfort in its presence. The conflict of the two perceptions disturbs me. This is why I have grown to prefer the restaurants down among the narrow board streets. I tell you this because I think an explanation is due to you."

As we walked away from the beach and around one of those huge buildings whose pathos had so aroused the stranger's interest, we came into view of two acres of merry-go-rounds, circular swings, roller coasters, observation wheels and the like. The stranger paused and regarded them.

"Do you know," he said, "I am deeply fascinated by all these toys. For, of course, you perceive that they are really enlarged toys. They reinforce me in my old opinion that humanity only needs to be provided for ten minutes with a few whirligigs and things of the sort, and it can forget at least four centuries of misery. I rejoice in these whirligigs," continued the stranger, eloquently, "and as I watch here and there a person going around and around or up and down, or over and over, I say to myself that whirligigs must be made in heaven.

"It is a mystery to me why some man does not provide a large number of wooden rocking horses and let the people sit and dreamfully rock themselves into temporary forgetfulness. There could be intense quiet enforced by special policemen, who, however, should allow subdued conversation on the part of the patrons of the establishment. Deaf mutes should patrol to and fro selling slumberous drinks. These things are none of them insane. They are particularly rational. A man needs a little nerve quiver, and he gets it by being flopped around in the air like a tailless kite. He needs the introduction of a reposeful element, and he procures it upon a swing that makes him feel like thirty-five emotional actresses all trying to swoon upon one rug. There are some people who stand apart and deride these machines. If you could procure a dark night for them and the total absence of their friends they would smile, many of them. I assure you that I myself would indulge in these forms of intoxication if I were not a very great philosopher."

We strolled to the music hall district, where the sky lines of the rows of buildings are wondrously near to each other, and the crowded little thoroughfares resemble the eternal "Street

Scene in Cairo." There was an endless strumming and tooting and shrill piping in clamor and chaos, while at all times there were interspersed the sharp cracking sounds from the shooting galleries and the coaxing calls of innumerable fakirs. At the stand where one can throw at wooden cats and negro heads and be in danger of winning cigars, a self reliant youth bought a whole armful of base balls, and missed with each one. Everybody grinned. A heavily built man openly jeered. "You couldn't hit a church!" "Couldn't I?" retorted the young man, bitterly. Near them three bad men were engaged in an intense conversation. The fragment of a sentence suddenly dominated the noises. "He's got money to burn." The sun, meanwhile, was muffled in the clouds back of Staten Island and the Narrows. Softened tones of sapphire and carmine touched slantingly the sides of the buildings. A view of the sea, to be caught between two of the houses, showed it to be of a pale, shimmering green. The lamps began to be lighted, and shed a strong orange radiance. In one restaurant the only occupants were a little music hall singer and a youth. She was laughing and chatting in a light hearted way not peculiar to music hall girls. The youth looked as if he desired to be at some other place. He was singularly wretched and uncomfortable. The stranger said he judged from appearances that the little music hall girl must think a great deal of that one youth. His sympathies seemed to be for the music hall girl. Finally there was a sea of salt meadow, with a black train shooting across it.

"I have made a discovery in one of these concert halls," said the stranger, as we retraced our way. "It is an old gray haired woman, who occupies proudly the position of chief pianiste. I like to go and sit and wonder by what mighty process of fighting and drinking she achieved her position. To see her, you would think she was leading an orchestra of seventy pieces, although she alone composes it. It is great reflection to watch that gray head. At those moments I am willing to concede that I must be relatively happy, and that is a great admission from a philosopher of my attainments.

"How seriously all these men out in front of the dens take their vocations. They regard people with a voracious air, as if they contemplated any moment making a rush and a grab and mercilessly compelling a great expenditure. This scant and feeble crowd must madden them. When I first came to this part of the town I was astonished and delighted, for it was the nearest approach to a den of wolves that I had encountered since leaving the West. Oh, no, of course the Coney Island of to-day is not the Coney Island of the ancient days. I believe you were about to impale me upon that sentence, were you not?"

We walked along for some time in silence until the stranger went to buy a frankfurter. As he returned, he said: "When a man is respectable he is fettered to certain wheels, and when the chariot of fashion moves, he is dragged along at the rear. For his agony, he can console himself with the law that if a certain thing has not yet been respectable, he need only wait a sufficient time and it will eventually be so. The only disadvantage is that he is obliged to wait until other people wish to do it, and he is likely to lose his own craving. Now I have a great passion for eating frankfurters on the street, and if I were respectable I would be obliged to wait until the year 3365, when men will be able to hold their positions in society only by consuming immense quantities of frankfurters on the street. And by that time I would have undoubtedly developed some new pastime. But I am not respectable. I am a philosopher. I eat frankfurters on the street with the same equanimity that you might employ toward a cigarette.

"See those three young men enjoying themselves. With what rakish, daredevil airs they smoke those cigars. Do you know, the spectacle of three modern young men enjoying themselves is something that I find vastly interesting and instructive. I see revealed more clearly the purposes of the inexorable universe which plans to amuse us occasionally to keep us from the rebellion of suicide. And I see how simply and drolly it accomplishes its end. The insertion of a mild quantity of the egotism of sin into the minds of these young men causes them to wildly enjoy themselves. It is necessary to encourage them, you see, at this early day. After all, it is only great philosophers who have the wisdom to be utterly miserable."

As we walked toward the station the stranger stopped often to observe types which interested him. He did it with an unconscious calm insolence as if the people were bugs. Once a bug threatened to beat him. "What 'cher lookin' at?" he asked of him. "My friend," said the stranger, "if any one displays real interest in you in this world, you should take it as an occasion for serious study and reflection. You should be supremely amazed to find that a man can be interested in anybody but himself!" The belligerent seemed quite abashed. He explained to a friend: "He ain't right! What? I dunno. Something 'bout 'study' er something! He's got wheels in his head!"

On the train the cold night wind blew transversely across the reeling cars, and in the dim light of the lamps one could see the close rows of heads swaying and jolting with the motion. From directly in front of us peanut shells fell to the floor amid a regular and interminable crackling. A stout man, who slept with his head forward upon his breast, crunched them often beneath his uneasy feet. From some unknown place a drunken voice was raised in song.

"This return of the people to their battles always has a stupendous effect upon me," said the stranger. "The gayety which arises upon these Sunday night occasions is different from all other gayeties. There is an unspeakable air of recklessness and bravado and grief about it. This train load is going toward that inevitable, overhanging, devastating Monday. That singer there to-morrow will be a truckman, perhaps, and swearing ingeniously at his horses and other truckmen. He feels the approach of this implacable Monday. Two hours ago he was engulfed in whirligigs and beer and had forgotten that there were Mondays. Now he is confronting it, and as he can't battle it, he scorns it. You can hear the undercurrent of it in that song, which is really as grievous as the cry of a child. If he had no vanity—well, it is fortunate for the world that we are not all great thinkers."

We sat on the lower deck of the Bay Ridge boat and watched the marvelous lights of New York looming through the purple mist. The little Italian band situated up one stairway, through two doors and around three corners from us, sounded in beautiful, faint and slumberous rhythm. The breeze fluttered again in the stranger's locks. We could hear the splash of the waves against the bow. The sleepy lights looked at us with hue of red and green and orange. Overhead some dust colored clouds scudded across the deep indigo sky. "Thunderation," said the stranger, "if I did not know of so many yesterdays and have such full knowledge of to-mor-rows, I should be perfectly happy at this moment, and that would create a sensation among philosophers all over the world."

In a Park Row Restaurant

"WHENEVER I COME into a place of this sort I am reminded of the Battle of Gettysburg," remarked the stranger. To make me hear him he had to raise his voice considerably, for we were seated in one of the Park Row restaurants during the noon-hour rush. "I think that if a squadron of Napoleon's dragoons charged into this place they would be trampled under foot before they could get a biscuit. They were great soldiers, no doubt, but they would at once perceive that there were many things about sweep and dash and fire of war of which they were totally ignorant.

"I come in here for the excitement. You know, when I was Sheriff, long ago, of one of the gayest counties of Nevada, I lived a life that was full of thrills, for the citizens could not quite comprehend the uses of a sheriff, and did not like to see him busy himself in other people's affairs continually. One man originated a popular philosophy, in which he asserted that if a man required pastime, it was really better to shoot the sheriff than any other person, for then it would be quite impossible for the sheriff to organize a posse and pursue the assassin. The period which followed the promulgation of this theory gave me habits which I fear I can never outwear. I require fever and exhilaration in life, and when I come in here it carries me back to the old days."

I was obliged to put my head far forward, or I could never have heard the stranger's remarks. Crowds of men were swarming in from streets and invading the comfort of seated men in order that they might hang their hats and overcoats upon the long rows of hooks that lined the sides of the room. The finding of vacant chairs became a serious business. Men dashed to and fro in swift searches. Some of those already seated were eating with terrible speed or else casting impatient or tempestuous glances at the waiters.

Meanwhile the waiters dashed about the room as if a monster pursued them and they sought escape wildly through the walls. It was like the scattering and scampering of a lot of water bugs, when one splashes the surface of the brook with a pebble. Withal, they carried incredible masses of dishes and

591

threaded their swift ways with rare skill. Perspiration stood upon their foreheads, and their breaths came strainedly. They served customers with such speed and violence that it often resembled a personal assault. The crumbs from the previous diner were swept off with one fierce motion of a napkin. A waiter struck two blows at the table and left there a knife and a fork. And then came the viands in a volley, thumped down in haste, causing men to look sharp to see if their trousers were safe.

There was in the air an endless clatter of dishes, loud and bewilderingly rapid, like the gallop of a thousand horses. From afar back, at the places of communication to the kitchen, there came the sound of a continual roaring altercation, hoarse and vehement, like the cries of the officers of a regiment under attack. A mist of steam fluttered where the waiters crowded and jostled about the huge copper coffee urns. Over in one corner a man who toiled there like a foundryman was continually assailed by sharp cries. "Brown th' wheat!" An endless string of men were already filing past the cashier, and, even in these moments, this latter was a marvel of self possession and deftness. As the spring doors clashed to and fro, one heard the interminable thunder of the street, and through the window, partially obscured by displayed vegetables and roasts and pies, could be seen the great avenue, a picture in gray tones, save where a bit of green park gleamed, the foreground occupied by this great typical turmoil of car and cab, truck and mail van, wedging their way through an opposing army of the same kind and surrounded on all sides by the mobs of hurrying people.

"A man might come in here with a very creditable stomach and lose his head and get indigestion," resumed the stranger, thoughtfully. "It is astonishing how fast a man can eat when he tries. This air is surcharged with appetites. I have seen very orderly, slow moving men become possessed with the spirit of this rush, lose control of themselves and all at once begin to dine like madmen. It is impossible not to feel the effect of this impetuous atmosphere.

"When consommé grows popular in these places all breweries will have to begin turning out soups. I am reminded of the introduction of canned soup into my town in the West.

When the boys found that they could not get full on it they wanted to lynch the proprietor of the supply store for selling an inferior article, but a drummer who happened to be in town explained to them that it was a temperance drink.

"It is plain that if the waiters here could only be put upon a raised platform and provided with repeating rifles that would shoot corn-muffins, butter cakes, Irish stews or any delicacy of the season, the strain of this strife would be greatly lessened. As long as the waiters were competent marksmen, the meals here would be conducted with great expedition. The only difficulty would be when for instance a waiter made an error and gave an Irish stew to the wrong man. The latter would have considerable difficulty in passing it along to the right one. Of course the system would cause awkward blunders for a time. You can imagine an important gentleman in a white waist-coat getting up to procure the bill-of-fare from an adjacent table and by chance intercepting a hamburger-steak bound for a man down by the door. The man down by the door would refuse to pay for a steak that had never come into his possession.

"In some such manner thousands of people could be accommodated in restaurants that at present during the noon hour can feed only a few hundred. Of course eloquent pickets would have to be stationed in the distance to intercept any unsuspecting gentleman from the West who might consider the gunnery of the waiters in a personal way and resent what would look to them like an assault. I remember that my old friend Jim Wilkinson, the ex-sheriff of Tin Can, Nevada, got very drunk one night and wandered into the business end of the bowling alley there. Of course he thought that they were shooting at him and in reply he killed three of the best bowlers in Tin Can."

The Fire

WE WERE WALKING on one of the shadowy side streets, west of Sixth avenue. The midnight silence and darkness was upon it save where at the point of intersection with the great avenue, there was a broad span of yellow light. From there came the steady monotonous jingle of streetcar bells and the weary clatter of hoofs on the cobbles. While the houses in this street turned black and mystically silent with the night, the avenue continued its eternal movement and life, a great vein that never slept nor paused. The gorgeous orange-hued lamps of a saloon flared plainly, and the figures of some loungers could be seen as they stood on the corner. Passing to and fro, the tiny black figures of people made an ornamental border on this fabric of yellow light.

The stranger was imparting to me some grim midnight reflections upon existence, and in the heavy shadows and in the great stillness pierced only by the dull thunder of the avenue, they were very impressive.

Suddenly the muffled cry of a woman came from one of those dark, impassive houses near us. There was the sound of the splinter and crash of broken glass, falling to the pavement. "What's that," gasped the stranger. The scream contained that ominous quality, that weird timbre which denotes fear of imminent death.

A policeman, huge and panting, ran past us with glitter of buttons and shield in the darkness. He flung himself upon the fire-alarm box at the corner where the lamp shed a flicker of carmine tints upon the pavement. "Come on," shouted the stranger. He dragged me excitedly down the street. We came upon an old four story structure, with a long sign of a bakery over the basement windows, and the region about the quaint front door plastered with other signs. It was one of those ancient dwellings which the churning process of the city had changed into a hive of little industries.

At this time some dull grey smoke, faintly luminous in the night, writhed out from the tops of the second story windows, and from the basement there glared a deep and terrible hue of red, the color of satanic wrath, the color of murder. "Look! Look!" shouted the stranger.

It was extraordinary how the street awakened. It seemed but an instant before the pavements were studded with people. They swarmed from all directions, and from the dark mass arose countless exclamations, eager and swift.

"Where is it? Where is it?"

"No. 135."

"It's that old bakery."

"Is everybody out?"

"Look—gee—say, lookut 'er burn, would yeh?"

The windows of almost every house became crowded with people, clothed and partially clothed, many having rushed from their beds. Here were many women, and as their eyes fastened upon that terrible growing mass of red light one could hear their little cries, quavering with fear and dread. The smoke oozed in greater clouds from the spaces between the sashes of the windows, and urged by the fervor of the heat within, ascended in more rapid streaks and curves.

Upon the sidewalk there had been a woman who was fumbling mechanically with the buttons at the neck of her dress. Her features were lined in anguish; she seemed to be frantically searching her memory—her memory, that poor feeble contrivance that had deserted her at the first of the crisis, at the momentous time. She really struggled and tore hideously at some frightful mental wall that upreared between her and her senses, her very instincts. The policeman, running back from the fire-alarm box, grabbed her, intending to haul her away from danger of falling things. Then something came to her like a bolt from the sky. The creature turned all grey, like an ape. A loud shriek rang out that made the spectators bend their bodies, twisting as if they were receiving sword thrusts.

"My baby! My baby! My baby!"

The policeman simply turned and plunged into the house. As the woman tossed her arms in maniacal gestures about her head, it could then be seen that she waved in one hand a little bamboo easel, of the kind which people sometimes place in corners of their parlors. It appeared that she had with great difficulty saved it from the flames. Its cost should have been about 30 cents.

A long groaning sigh came from the crowd in the street, and from all the thronged windows. It was full of distress and pity, and a sort of cynical scorn for their impotency. Occasionally the woman screamed again. Another policeman was fending her off from the house, which she wished to enter in the frenzy of her motherhood, regardless of the flames. These people of the neighborhood, aroused from their beds, looked at the spectacle in a half-dazed fashion at times, as if they were contemplating the ravings of a red beast in a cage. The flames grew as if fanned by tempests, a sweeping, inexorable appetite of a thing, shining, with fierce, pitiless brilliancy, gleaming in the eyes of the crowd that were upturned to it in an ecstasy of awe, fear and, too, half barbaric admiration. They felt the human helplessness that comes when nature breaks forth in passion, overturning the obstacles, emerging at a leap from the position of a slave to that of a master, a giant. There became audible a humming noise, the buzzing of curious machinery. It was the voices of the demons of the flame. The house, in manifest heroic indifference to the fury that raged in its entrails, maintained a stolid and imperturbable exterior, looming black and immovable against the turmoil of crimson.

Eager questions were flying to and fro in the street.

"Say, did a copper go in there?"

"Yeh! He come out again, though."

"He did not! He's in there yet!"

"Well, didn't I see 'im?"

"How long ago was the alarm sent in?"

" 'Bout a minute."

A woman leaned perilously from a window of a nearby apartment house and spoke querulously into the shadowy, jostling crowd beneath her, "Jack!"

And the voice of an unknown man in an unknown place answered her gruffly and short in the tones of a certain kind of downtrodden husband who rebels upon occasion, "What?"

"Will you come up here," cried the woman, shrilly irritable. "Supposin' this house should get afire——" It came to pass that during the progress of the conflagration these two held a terse and bitter domestic combat, infinitely commonplace in language and mental maneuvers.

The blaze had increased with a frightful vehemence and swiftness. Unconsciously, at times, the crowd dully moaned, their eyes fascinated by this exhibition of the strength of nature, their master after all, that ate them and their devices at will whenever it chose to fling down their little restrictions. The flames changed in color from crimson to lurid orange as glass was shattered by the heat, and fell crackling to the pavement. The baker, whose shop had been in the basement, was running about, weeping. A policeman had fought interminably to keep the crowd away from the front of the structure.

"Thunderation!" yelled the stranger, clutching my arm in a frenzy of excitement, "did you ever see anything burn so? Why, it's like an explosion. It's only been a matter of seconds since it started."

In the street, men had already begun to turn toward each other in that indefinite regret and sorrow, as if they were not quite sure of the reason of their mourning.

"Well, she's a goner!"

"Sure—went up like a box of matches!"

"Great Scott, lookut 'er burn!"

Some individual among them furnished the inevitable grumble. "Well, these——" It was a half-coherent growling at conditions, men, fate, law.

Then, from the direction of the avenue there suddenly came a tempestuous roar, a clattering, rolling rush and thunder, as from the headlong sweep of a battery of artillery. Wild and shrill, like a clangorous noise of war, arose the voice of a gong.

One could see a sort of a delirium of excitement, of ardorous affection, go in a wave of emotion over this New York crowd, usually so stoical. Men looked at each other. "Quick work, eh?" They crushed back upon the pavements, leaving the street almost clear. All eyes were turned toward the corner, where the lights of the avenue glowed.

The roar grew and grew until it was as the sound of an army, charging. That policeman's hurried fingers sending the alarm from the box at the corner had aroused a tornado, a storm of horses, machinery, men. And now they were coming in clamor and riot of hoofs and wheels, while over all rang the piercing cry of the gong, tocsin-like, a noise of barbaric fights.

It thrilled the blood, this thunder. The stranger jerked his shoulders nervously and kept up a swift muttering. "Hear 'em come!" he said, breathlessly.

Then in an instant a fire patrol wagon, as if apparitional, flashed into view at the corner. The lights of the avenue gleamed for an instant upon the red and brass of the wagon, the helmets of the crew and the glossy sides of the galloping horses. Then it swung into the dark street and thundered down upon its journey, with but a half-view of a driver making his reins to be steel ribbons over the backs of his horses, mad from the fervor of their business.

The stranger's hand tightened convulsively upon my arm. His enthusiasm was like the ardor of one who looks upon the pageantry of battles. "Ah, look at 'em! Look at 'em! Ain't that great? Why it hasn't been any time at all since the alarm was sent in, and now look!" As this clanging, rolling thing, drawn swiftly by the beautiful might of the horses, clamored through the street, one could feel the cheers, wild and valorous, at the very lips of these people habitually so calm, cynical, impassive. The crew tumbled from their wagon and ran toward the house. A hoarse shout arose high above the medley of noises.

Other roars, other clangings, were to be heard from all directions. It was extraordinary, the loud rumblings of wheels and the pealings of gongs aroused by a movement of the policeman's fingers.

Of a sudden, three white horses dashed down the street with their engine, a magnificent thing of silver-like glitter, that sent a storm of red sparks high into the air and smote the heart with the wail of its whistle.

A hosecart swept around the corner and into the narrow lane, whose close walls made the reverberations like the crash of infantry volleys. There was shine of lanterns, of helmets, of rubber coats, of the bright, strong trappings of the horses. The driver had been confronted by a dreadful little problem in street cars and elevated railway pillars just as he was about to turn into the street, but there had been no pause, no hesitation. A clever dodge, a shrill grinding of the wheels in the street-car tracks, a miss of this and an escape of that by a beautifully narrow margin, and the hosecart went on its head-long way. When the gleam-white and gold of the cart stopped in the shadowy street, it was but a moment before a stream of water, of a cold steel color, was plunging through a window into the yellow glare, into this house which was now a den of fire wolves, lashing, carousing, leaping, straining. A wet snake-like hose trailed underfoot to where the steamer was making the air pulsate with its swift vibrations.

From another direction had come another thunder that developed into a crash of sounds, as a hook-and-ladder truck, with long and graceful curves, spun around the other corner, with the horses running with steady leaps toward the place of the battle. It was always obvious that these men who drove were drivers in blood and fibre, charioteers incarnate.

When the ladders were placed against the side of the house, firemen went slowly up them, dragging their hose. They became outlined like black beetles against the red and yellow expanses of flames. A vast cloud of smoke, sprinkled thickly with sparks, went coiling heavily toward the black sky. Touched by the shine of the blaze, the smoke sometimes glowed dull red, the color of bricks. A crowd that, it seemed, had sprung from the cobbles, born at the sound of the wheels rushing through the night, thickly thronged the walks, pushed here and there by the policemen who scolded them roundly, evidently in an eternal state of injured surprise at their persistent desire to get a view of things.

As we walked to the corner we looked back and watched the red glimmer from the fire shine on the dark surging crowd over which towered at times the helmets of police. A billow of smoke swept away from the structure. Occasionally, burned out sparks, like fragments of dark tissue, fluttered in the air. At the corner a steamer was throbbing, churning, shaking in its power as if overcome with rage. A fireman was walking tranquilly about it scrutinizing the mechanism. He wore a blasé air. They all, in fact, seemed to look at fires with the calm, unexcited vision of veterans. It was only the populace with their new nerves, it seemed, who could feel the thrill and dash of these attacks, these furious charges made in the dead of night, at high noon, at any time, upon the common enemy, the loosened flame.

When Man Falls, a Crowd Gathers

A MAN AND A BOY were trudging slowly along an East-Side street. It was nearly six o'clock in the evening and this street, which led to one of the East River ferries, was crowded with laborers, shop men and shop women, hurrying to their dinners. The store windows were a-glare.

The man and the boy conversed in Italian, mumbling the soft syllables and making little quick egotistical gestures. They walked with the lumbering peasant's gait, slowly, and blinking their black eyes at the passing show of the street.

Suddenly the man wavered on his limbs and glared bewildered and helpless as if some blinding light had flashed before his vision; then he swayed like a drunken man and fell. The boy grasped his companion's arm frantically and made an attempt to support him so that the limp form slid to the sidewalk with an easy motion as a body sinks in the sea. The boy screamed.

Instantly, from all directions people turned their gaze upon the prone figure. In a moment there was a dodging, pushing, peering group about the man. A volley of questions, replies, speculations flew to and fro above all the bobbing heads.

"What's th' matter? What's th' matter?"

"Oh, a jag, I guess!"

"Nit; he's got a fit!"

"What's th' matter? What's th' matter?"

Two streams of people coming from different directions met at this point to form a crowd. Others came from across the street.

Down under their feet, almost lost under this throng, lay the man, hidden in the shadows caused by their forms which in fact barely allowed a particle of light to pass between them. Those in the foremost rank bended down, shouldering each other, eager, anxious to see everything. Others behind them crowded savagely for a place like starving men fighting for bread. Always, the question could be heard flying in the air. "What's the matter?" Some, near to the body and perhaps feeling the danger of being forced over upon it, twisted their heads and protested violently to those unheeding ones who were scuffling in the rear. "Say, quit yer shovin', can't yeh? What d' yeh want, anyhow? Quit!"

A man back in the crowd suddenly said: "Say, young feller, you're a peach wid dose feet o' yours. Keep off me!"

Another voice said: "Well, dat's all right——"

The boy who had been walking with the man who fell was standing helplessly, a terrified look in his eyes. He held the man's hand. Sometimes he gave it a little jerk that was at once an appeal, a reproach, a caution. And, withal, it was a timid calling to the limp and passive figure as if he half expected to arouse it from its coma with a pleading touch of his fingers. Occasionally, he looked about him with swift glances of indefinite hope, as if assistance might come from the clouds. The men near him questioned him, but he did not seem to understand. He answered them "Yes" or "No," blindly, with no apparent comprehension of their language. They frequently jostled him until he was obliged to put his hand upon the breast of the body to maintain his balance.

Those that were nearest to the man upon the side-walk at first saw his body go through a singular contortion. It was as if an invisible hand had reached up from the earth and had seized him by the hair. He seemed dragged slowly, relentlessly backward, while his body stiffened convulsively, his hands clenched, and his arms swung rigidly upward. A slight froth was upon his chin. Through his pallid half-closed lids could be seen the steel-colored gleam of his eyes that were turned toward all the bending, swaying faces and in the inanimate thing upon the pave yet burned threateningly, dangerously, shining with a mystic light, as a corpse might glare at those live ones who seemed about to trample it under foot.

As for the men near, they hung back, appearing as if they expected it to spring erect and clutch at them. Their eyes however were held in a spell of fascination. They seemed scarcely to breathe. They were contemplating a depth into which a human being had sunk and the marvel of this mystery of life or death held them chained. Occasionally from the rear, a man came thrusting his way impetuously, satisfied that there was a horror to be seen and apparently insane to get a view of it. Less curious persons swore at these men when they trod upon their toes.

The loaded street-cars jingled past this scene in endless parade. Occasionally, from where the elevated railroad crossed the street there came a rhythmical roar, suddenly begun and suddenly ended. Over the heads of the crowd hung an immovable canvas sign. "Regular dinner twenty cents."

After the first spasm of curiosity had passed away, there were those in the crowd who began to consider ways to help. A voice called: "Rub his wrists." The boy and some one on the other side of the man began to rub his wrists and slap his palms, but still the body lay inert, rigid. When a hand was dropped the arm fell like a stick. A tall German suddenly appeared and resolutely began to push the crowd back. "Get back there—get back," he continually repeated as he pushed them. He had psychological authority over this throng; they obeyed him. He and another knelt by the man in the darkness and loosened his shirt at the throat. Once they struck a match and held it close to the man's face. This livid visage suddenly appearing under their feet in the light of the match's yellow glare, made the throng shudder. Half articulate exclamations could be heard. There were men who nearly created a battle in the madness of their desire to see the thing.

Meanwhile others with magnificent passions for abstract statistical information were questioning the boy. "What's his name?" "Where does he live?"

Then a policeman appeared. The first part of the little play had gone on without his assistance but now he came swiftly, his helmet towering above the multitude of black derbys and shading that confident, self-reliant police face. He charged the crowd as if he were a squadron of Irish lancers. The people fairly withered before this onslaught. He shouted: "Come, make way there! Make way!" He was evidently a man whose life was half-pestered out of him by the inhabitants of the city who were sufficiently unreasonable and stupid as to insist on being in the streets. His was the rage of a placid cow, who wishes to lead a life of tranquillity, but who is eternally besieged by flies that hover in clouds.

When he arrived at the centre of the crowd he first demanded threateningly: "Well, what's th' matter here?" And then when he saw that human bit of wreckage at the bottom of the sea of men he said to it: "Come, git up outa that! Git outa here!"

Whereupon hands were raised in the crowd and a volley of decorated information was blazed at the officer.

"Ah, he's got a fit! Can't yeh see!"

"He's got a fit!"

"He's sick!"

"What th' ell yeh doin'? Leave 'm be!"

The policeman menaced with a glance the crowd from whose safe interior the defiant voices had emerged.

A doctor had come. He and the policeman bended down at the man's side. Occasionally the officer upreared to create room. The crowd fell away before his threats, his admonitions, his sarcastic questions and before the sweep of those two huge buckskin gloves.

At last, the peering ones saw the man on the side-walk begin to breathe heavily, with the strain of overtaxed machinery, as if he had just come to the surface from some deep water. He uttered a low cry in his foreign tongue. It was a babyish squeal or like the sad wail of a little storm-tossed kitten. As this cry went forth to all those eager ears the jostling and crowding recommenced until the doctor was obliged to yell warningly a dozen times. The policeman had gone to send an ambulance call.

When a man struck another match and in its meagre light the doctor felt the skull of the prostrate one to discover if any wound or fracture had been caused by his fall to the stone side-walk, the crowd pressed and crushed again. It was as if they fully anticipated a sight of blood in the gleam of the match and they scrambled and dodged for positions. The policeman returned and fought with them. The doctor looked up frequently to scold at them and to sharply demand more space.

At last out of the golden haze made by the lamps far up the street, there came the sound of a gong beaten rapidly, impatiently. A monstrous truck loaded to the sky with barrels scurried to one side with marvelous agility. And then the black ambulance with its red light, its galloping horse, its dull gleam of lettering and bright shine of gong clattered into view. A young man, as imperturbable always as if he were going to a picnic, sat thoughtfully upon the rear seat.

When they picked up the limp body, from which came little moans and howls, the crowd almost turned into a mob, a silent mob, each member of which struggled for one thing. Afterward some resumed their ways with an air of relief, as if they themselves had been in pain and were at last recovered. Others still continued to stare at the ambulance on its banging, clanging return journey until it vanished into the golden haze. It was as if they had been cheated. Their eyes expressed discontent at this curtain which had been rung down in the midst of the drama. And this impenetrable fabric suddenly intervening between a suffering creature and their curiosity, seemed to appear to them as an injustice.

In the Depths of a Coal Mine

THE BREAKERS SQUATTED upon the hillsides and in the valley like enormous preying monsters eating of the sunshine, the grass, the green leaves. The smoke from their nostrils had ravaged the air of coolness and fragrance. All that remained of the vegetation looked dark, miserable, half-strangled. Along the summit-line of the mountain, a few unhappy trees were etched upon the clouds. Overhead stretched a sky of imperial blue, incredibly far away from the sombre land.

We approached the colliery over paths of coal-dust that wound among the switches. The breaker loomed above us, a huge and towering frame of blackened wood. It ended in a little curious peak and upon its sides there was a profusion of windows appearing at strange and unexpected points. Through occasional doors one could see the flash of whirring machinery. Men with wondrously blackened faces and garments came forth from it. The sole glitter upon their persons was at their hats where the little tin lamps were carried. They went stolidly along, some swinging lunch-pails carelessly, but the marks upon them of their forbidding and mystic calling fascinated our new eyes until they passed from sight. They were symbols of a grim, strange war that was being waged in the sunless depths of the earth.

Around the huge central building clustered other and lower ones, sheds, engine-houses, machine-shops, offices. Railroad tracks extended in web-like ways. Upon them stood files of begrimed coal-cars. Other huge structures similar to the one near us up-reared their uncouth heads upon the hills of the surrounding country. From each, a mighty hill of culm extended. Upon these tremendous heaps of waste from the mines, mules and cars appeared like toys. Down in the valley, upon the railroads, long trains crawled painfully southward where a low-hanging grey cloud with a few projecting spires and chimneys indicated a town.

Car after car came from a shed beneath which lay hidden the mouth of the shaft. They were dragged creaking up an inclined cable-road to the top of the breaker.

At the top of the breaker, laborers were dumping the coal

into chutes. The huge lumps slid slowly on their journey down through the building from which they were to emerge in classified fragments. Great teeth on revolving cylinders caught them and chewed them. At places, there were grates that bid each size go into its proper chute. The dust lay inches deep on every motionless thing and clouds of it made the air dark as from a violent tempest. A mighty gnashing sound filled the ears. With terrible appetite this huge and hideous monster sat imperturbably munching coal, grinding its mammoth jaws with unearthly and monotonous uproar.

In a large room sat the little slate-pickers. The floor slanted at an angle of forty-five degrees, and the coal having been masticated by the great teeth was streaming sluggishly in long iron troughs. The boys sat straddling these troughs and as the mass moved slowly, they grabbed deftly at the pieces of slate therein. There were five or six of them, one above another, over each trough. The coal is expected to be fairly pure after it passes the final boy. The howling machinery was above them. High up, dim figures moved about in the dust clouds.

These little men were a terrifically dirty band. They resembled the New York gamins in some ways but they laughed more and when they laughed their faces were a wonder and a terror. They had an air of supreme independence and seemed proud of their kind of villainy. They swore long oaths with skill.

Through their ragged shirts we could get occasional glimpses of shoulders black as stoves. They looked precisely like imps as they scrambled to get a view of us. Work ceased while they tried to ascertain if we were willing to give away any tobacco. The man who perhaps believes that he controls them came and harangued the crowd. He talked to the air.

The slate-pickers, all through this region, are yet at the spanking period. One continually wonders about their mothers and if there are any school-houses. But as for them, they are not concerned. When they get time off, they go out on the culm-heap and play base-ball, or fight with boys from other breakers, or among themselves, according to the opportunities. And before them always is the hope of one day getting to be door-boys down in the mines and, later, mule-boys. And yet later laborers and helpers. Finally when they have grown to be great big men they may become miners, real miners, and go down and get "squeezed," or perhaps escape to a shattered old man's estate with a mere "miner's asthma." They are very ambitious.

Meanwhile, they live in a place of infernal dins. The crash and thunder of the machinery is like the roar of an immense cataract. The room shrieks and blares and bellows. Clouds of dust blur the air until the windows shine pallidly, afar off. All the structure is a-tremble from the heavy sweep and circle of the ponderous mechanism. Down in the midst of it, sit these tiny urchins, where they earn fifty-five cents a day each. They breathe this atmosphere until their lungs grow heavy and sick with it. They have this clamor in their ears until it is wonderful that they have any hoodlum valor remaining. But they are uncowed; they continue to swagger. And at the top of the breaker laborers can always be seen dumping the roaring coal down the wide, voracious maw of the creature.

Over in front of a little tool house, a man, smoking a pipe, sat on a bench. "Yes," he said, "I'll take yeh down, if yeh like." He led us by little cinder paths to the shed over the shaft of the mine. A gigantic fan-wheel, near by, was twirling swiftly. It created cool air for the miners, who on the lowest vein of this mine were some eleven hundred and fifty feet below the surface. As we stood silently waiting for the elevator, we had opportunity to gaze at the mouth of the shaft. The walls were of granite blocks, slimy, moss-grown, dripping with water. Below was a curtain of ink-like blackness. It was like the opening of an old well, sinister from tales of crime.

The black greasy cables began to run swiftly. We stood staring at them and wondering. Then of a sudden, the elevator appeared and stopped with a crash. It was a plain wooden platform. Upon two sides iron bars ran up to support a stout metal roof. The men upon it, as it came into view, were like apparitions from the centre of the earth.

A moment later, we marched aboard, armed with little lights, feeble and gasping in the daylight. There was an instant's creak of machinery and then the landscape that had been framed for us by the door-posts of the shed, disappeared in a flash. We were dropping with extraordinary swiftness straight into the earth. It was a plunge, a fall. The flames of the little lamps fluttered and flew and struggled like tied birds to release themselves from the wicks. "Hang on," bawled our guide above the tumult.

The dead black walls slid swiftly by. They were a swirling dark chaos on which the mind tried vainly to locate some coherent thing, some intelligible spot. One could only hold fast to the iron bars and listen to the roar of this implacable descent. When the faculty of balance is lost, the mind becomes a confusion. The will fought a great battle to comprehend something during this fall, but one might as well have been tumbling among the stars. The only thing was to await revelation.

It was a journey that held a threat of endlessness.

Then suddenly the dropping platform slackened its speed. It began to descend slowly and with caution. At last, with a crash and a jar, it stopped. Before us stretched an inscrutable darkness, a soundless place of tangible loneliness. Into the nostrils came a subtly strong odor of powder-smoke, oil, wet earth. The alarmed lungs began to lengthen their respirations.

Our guide strode abruptly into the gloom. His lamp flared shades of yellow and orange upon the walls of a tunnel that led away from the foot of the shaft. Little points of coal caught the light and shone like diamonds. Before us, there was always the curtain of an impenetrable night. We walked on with no sound save the crunch of our feet upon the coal-dust of the floor. The sense of an abiding danger in the roof was always upon our foreheads. It expressed to us all the unmeasured, deadly tons above us. It was a superlative might that regarded with the supreme calmness of almighty power the little men at its mercy. Sometimes we were obliged to bend low to avoid it. Always our hands rebelled vaguely from touching it, refusing to affront this gigantic mass.

All at once, far ahead, shone a little flame, blurred and difficult of location. It was a tiny indefinite thing, like a wisp-light. We seemed to be looking at it through a great fog. Presently, there were two of them. They began to move to and fro and dance before us.

After a time we came upon two men crouching where the roof of the passage came near to meeting the floor. If the picture could have been brought to where it would have had the opposition and the contrast of the glorious summer-time earth, it would have been a grim and ghastly thing. The garments of the men were no more sable than their faces and when they turned their heads to regard our tramping party, their eye-balls and teeth shone white as bleached bones. It was like the grinning of two skulls there in the shadows. The tiny lamps on their hats made a trembling light that left weirdly shrouded the movements of their limbs and bodies. We might have been confronting terrible spectres.

But they said "Hello, Jim" to our conductor. Their mouths expanded in smiles—wide and startling smiles.

In a moment they turned again to their work. When the lights of our party reinforced their two lamps, we could see that one was busily drilling into the coal with a long thin bar. The low roof ominously pressed his shoulders as he bended at his toil. The other knelt behind him on the loose lumps of coal.

He who worked at the drill engaged in conversation with our guide. He looked back over his shoulder, continuing to poke away. "When are yeh goin' t' measure this up, Jim?" he demanded. "Do yeh wanta git me killed?"

"Well, I'd measure it up t'-day, on'y I ain't got me tape," replied the other.

"Well, when will yeh? Yeh wanta hurry up," said the miner. "I don't wanta git killed."

"Oh, I'll be down on Monday."

"Humph!"

They engaged in a sort of an altercation in which they made jests.

"You'll be carried out o' there feet first before long."

"Will I?"

Yet one had to look closely to understand that they were not about to spring at each other's throats. The vague illumination created all the effect of the snarling of two wolves.

We came upon other little low-roofed chambers each containing two men, a "miner" who makes the blasts and his "laborer" who loads the coal upon the cars and assists the miner generally. And at each place there was this same effect of strangely satanic smiles and eye-balls wild and glittering in the pale glow of the lamps.

Sometimes, the scenes in their weird strength were absolutely infernal. Once when we were traversing a silent tunnel in another mine, we came suddenly upon a wide place where some miners were lying down in a group. As they up-reared to gaze at us, it resembled a resurrection. They slowly uprose with ghoul-like movements, mysterious figures robed in enormous shadows. The swift flashes of the steel-gleaming eyes were upon our faces.

At another time, when my companion, struggling against difficulties, was trying to get a sketch of the mule "Molly Maguire," a large group of miners gathered about us, intent upon the pencil of the artist. "Molly," indifferent to the demands of art, changed her position after a moment and calmly settled into a new one. The men all laughed and this laugh created the most astonishing and supernatural effect. In an instant, the gloom was filled with luminous smiles. Shining forth all about us were eyes, glittering as with cold blue flame. "Whoa, Molly," the men began to shout. Five or six of them clutched "Molly" by her tail, her head, her legs. They were going to hold her motionless until the portrait was finished. "He's a good feller," they had said of the artist, and it would be a small thing to hold a mule for him. Upon the roof were vague dancing reflections of red and yellow.

From this tunnel of our first mine we went with our guide to the foot of the main shaft. Here we were in the most important passage of a mine, the main gangway. The wonder of these avenues is the noise—the crash and clatter of machinery as the elevator speeds up-ward with the loaded cars and drops thunderingly with the empty ones. The place resounds with the shouts of mule-boys and there can always be heard the noise of approaching coal-cars, beginning in mild rumbles and then swelling down upon one in a tempest of sound. In the air is the slow painful throb of the pumps working at the water which collects in the depths. There is booming and banging and crashing until one wonders why the tremendous walls are not wrenched by the force of this uproar. And up and down the tunnel, there is a riot of lights, little orange points flickering and flashing. Miners stride in swift and sombre procession. But the meaning of it all is in the deep bass rattle of a blast in some hidden part of the mine. It is war. It is the most savage part of all in the endless battle between man and nature. These miners are grimly in the van. They have carried the war into places where nature has the strength of a million giants. Sometimes their enemy becomes exasperated and snuffs out ten, twenty, thirty lives. Usually she remains calm, and takes one at a time with method and precision. She need not hurry. She possesses eternity. After a blast, the smoke, faintly luminous, silvery, floats silently through the adjacent tunnels.

In our first mine we speedily lost all ideas of time, direction, distance. The whole thing was an extraordinary, black puzzle. We were impelled to admire the guide because he knew all the tangled passages. He led us through little tunnels three and four feet wide and with roofs that sometimes made us crawl. At other times we were in avenues twenty feet wide, where double rows of tracks extended. There were stretches of great darkness, majestic silences. The three hundred miners were distributed into all sorts of crevices and corners of the labyrinth, toiling in this city of endless night. At different points one could hear the roar of traffic about the foot of the main shaft, to which flowed all the commerce of the place.

We were made aware of distances later by our guide, who would occasionally stop to tell us our position by naming a point of the familiar geography of the surface. "Do yeh remember that rolling-mill yeh passed coming up? Well, you're right under it." "You're under th' depot now." The length of these distances struck us with amazement when we reached the surface. Near Scranton one can really proceed for miles, in the black streets of the mines.

Over in a wide and lightless room we found the mule-stables. There we discovered a number of these animals standing with an air of calmness and self-possession that was somehow amazing to find in a mine. A little dark urchin came and belabored his mule "China" until he stood broadside to us that we might admire his innumerable fine qualities. The stable was like a dungeon. The mules were arranged in solemn rows. They turned their heads toward our lamps. The glare made their eyes shine wondrously, like lenses. They resembled enormous rats.

About the room stood bales of hay and straw. The commonplace air worn by the long-eared slaves made it all infinitely usual. One had to wait to see the tragedy of it. It was not until we had grown familiar with the life and the traditions of the mines that we were capable of understanding the story told by these beasts standing in calm array, with spread legs.

It is a common affair for mules to be imprisoned for years in the limitless night of the mines. Our acquaintance, "China," had been four years buried. Upon the surface there had been the march of the seasons; the white splendor of snows had changed again and again to the glories of green springs. Four times had the earth been ablaze with the decorations of brilliant autumns. But "China" and his friends had remained in these dungeons from which daylight, if one could get a view up a shaft, would appear a tiny circle, a silver star aglow in a sable sky.

Usually when brought to the surface, these animals tremble at the earth, radiant in the sunshine. Later, they go almost mad with fantastic joy. The full splendor of the heavens, the grass, the trees, the breezes breaks upon them suddenly. They caper and career with extravagant mulish glee. Once a miner told me of a mule that had spent some delirious months upon the surface after years of labor in the mines. Finally the time came when he was to be taken back into the depths. They attempted to take him through a tunnel in the hillside. But the memory of a black existence was upon him; he knew that gaping mouth that threatened to swallow him. He had all the strength of mind for which his race is famous. No cudgellings could induce him. The men held conventions and discussed plans to budge that mule. The celebrated quality of obstinacy in him won him liberty to gambol clumsily about on the surface.

After being long in the mines, the mules are apt to duck and dodge at the close glare of lamps, but some of them have been known to have piteous fears of being left in the dead darkness. They seem then, somehow, like little children. We met a boy once who said that sometimes the only way he could get his resolute team to move was to run ahead of them with the light. Afraid of the darkness, they would trot hurriedly after him and so take the train of heavy cars to a desired place.

To those who have known the sun-light there may come the fragrant dream. Perhaps this is what they brood over when they stand solemnly in rows with slowly flapping ears. A recollection may appear to them, a recollection of pastures of a lost paradise. Perhaps they despair and thirst for this bloom that lies in an unknown direction and at impossible distances.

We were appalled occasionally at the quantity of mud we encountered in our wanderings through some of the tunnels. The feet of men and mules had churned it usually into a dull-brown clinging mass. In very wet mines all sorts of gruesome fungi grow upon the wooden props that support the uncertain-looking ceiling. The walls are dripping and dank. Upon them too there frequently grows a moss-like fungus, white as a druid's beard, that thrives in these deep dens but shrivels and dies at contact with the sun-light.

Great and mystically dreadful is the earth from a mine's depth. Man is in the implacable grasp of nature. It has only to tighten slightly and he is crushed like a bug. His loudest shriek of agony would be as impotent as his final moan to bring help from that fair land that lies, like Heaven, over his head. There is an insidious silent enemy in the gas. If the huge fan-wheel on the top of the earth should stop for a brief period, there is certain death and a panic more terrible than any occurring where the sun has shone ensues down under the tons of rock. If a man may escape the gas, the floods, the "squeezes" of falling rock, the cars shooting through little tunnels, the precarious elevators, the hundred perils, there usually comes to him an attack of "miner's asthma" that slowly racks and shakes him into the grave. Meanwhile he gets three dollars per day, and his laborer one dollar and a quarter.

In the chamber at the foot of the shaft, as we were departing, a group of the men were resting. They lay about in careless poses. When we climbed aboard the elevator, we had a moment in which to turn and regard them. Then suddenly the study in black faces and crimson and orange lights vanished. We were on our swift way to the surface. Far above us in the engine-room, the engineer sat with his hand on a lever and his eye on the little model of the shaft wherein a miniature elevator was making the ascent even as our elevator was making it. In fact, the same mighty engines give power to both, and their positions are relatively the same always. I had forgotten about the new world that I was to behold in a moment. My mind was occupied with a mental picture of this faraway engineer, who sat in his high chair by his levers, a statue of responsibility and fidelity, cool-brained, clear-eyed, steady of hand. His arms guided the flight of this platform in its mad and unseen ascent. It was always out of his sight, yet the huge thing obeyed him as a horse its master. When one gets upon the elevator down one of those tremendous holes, one thinks naturally of the engineer.

Of a sudden the fleeting walls became flecked with light. It increased to a downpour of sunbeams. The high sun was afloat in a splendor of spotless blue. The distant hills were arrayed in purple and stood like monarchs. A glory of gold was upon the near-by earth. The cool fresh air was wine.

Of that sinister struggle far below there came no sound, no suggestion save the loaded cars that emerged one after another in eternal procession and were sent creaking up the incline that their contents might be fed into the mouth of the breaker, imperturbably cruel and insatiate, black emblem of greed, and of the gods of this labor.

Howells Fears the Realists Must Wait

WILLIAM DEAN HOWELLS leaned his cheek upon the two outstretched fingers of his right hand and gazed thoughtfully at the window—the panes black from the night without, although studded once or twice with little electric stars far up on the west side of the Park. He was looking at something which his memory had just brought to him.

"I have a little scheme," he at last said slowly. "I saw a young girl out in a little Ohio town once—she was the daughter of the carpet-woman there—that is to say, her mother made rag-carpets and rugs for the villagers. And this girl had the most wonderful instinct in manner and dress. Her people were of the lowest of the low in a way and yet this girl was a lady. It used to completely amaze me—to think how this girl could grow there in that squalor. She was as chic as chic could be and yet the money spent and the education was nothing—nothing at all. Where she procured her fine taste you could not imagine. It was deeply interesting to me. It over-turned so many of my rooted social dogmas. It was the impossible, appearing suddenly. And then there was another in Cambridge—a wonderful type. I have come upon them occasionally here and there. I intend to write something of the kind if I can. I have thought of a good title, too, I think—a name of a flower—'The Ragged Lady.' "

"I suppose that is a long ways off," said the other man reflectively. "I am anxious to hear what you say in 'The Story of a Play.' Do you raise your voice towards reforming the abuses that are popularly supposed to hide in the manager's office for use upon the struggling artistic playwright and others? Do you recite the manager's divine misapprehension of art?"

"No, I do not," said Mr. Howells.

"Why?" said the other man.

"Well, in the first place, the manager is a man of business. He preserves himself. I suppose he judges not against art but between art and art. He looks at art through the crowds."

"I don't like reformatory novels anyhow," said the other man.

"And in the second place," continued Mr. Howells, "it does no good to go at things hammer and tongs in this obvious way. I believe that every novel should have an intention. A man should mean something when he writes. Ah, this writing merely to amuse people—why, it seems to me altogether vulgar. A man may as well blacken his face and go out and dance on the street for pennies. The author is a sort of trained bear, if you accept certain standards. If literary men are to be the public fools, let us at any rate have it clearly understood, so that those of us who feel differently can take measures. But on the other hand a novel should never preach and berate and storm. It does no good. As a matter of fact a book of that kind is ineffably tiresome. People don't like to have their lives half cudgeled out in that manner, especially in these days, when a man, likely enough, only reaches for a book when he wishes to be fanned, so to speak, after the heat of the daily struggle. When a writer desires to preach in an obvious way, he should announce his intention—let him cry out then that he is in the pulpit. But it is the business of the novel——"

"Ah," said the other man.

"It is the business of the novel to picture the daily life in the most exact terms possible with an absolute and clear sense of proportion. That is the important matter—the proportion. As a usual thing, I think, people have absolutely no sense of proportion. Their noses are tight against life, you see. They perceive mountains where there are no mountains, but frequently a great peak appears no larger than a rat-trap. An artist sees a dog down the street—well, his eye instantly relates the dog to its surroundings. The dog is proportioned to the buildings and the trees. Whereas many people can conceive of that dog's tail resting upon a hill-top."

"You have often said that the novel is a perspective," observed the other man.

"A perspective—certainly. It is a perspective made for the benefit of people who have no true use of their eyes. The novel, in its real meaning, adjusts the proportions. It preserves the balances. It is in this way that lessons are to be taught and reforms to be won. When people are introduced to each other, they will see the resemblances, and won't want to fight so badly."

"I suppose that when a man tries to write 'what the people want'—when he tries to reflect the popular desire, it is a bad quarter of an hour for the laws of proportion."

"Do you recall any of the hosts of stories that began in love and end a little further on. Those stories used to represent life to the people and I believe they do now to a large class. Life began when the hero saw a certain girl, and it ended abruptly when he married her. Love and courtship was not an incident, a part of life—it was the whole of it. All else was of no value. Men of that religion must have felt very stupid when they were engaged at anything but courtship. Do you see the false proportion? Do you see the dog with his tail upon the hill-top? Somebody touched the universal heart with the fascinating theme—the relation of man to maid—and, for many years, it was as if no other relation could be recognized in fiction. Here and there an author raised his voice, but not loudly. I like to see the novelists treating some of the other important things in life—the relation of mother and son, of husband and wife, in fact all these things that we live in continually. The other can be but fragmentary."

"I suppose there must be two or three new literary people just back of the horizon somewheres," said the other man. "Books upon these lines that you speak of are what might be called unpopular. Do you think them to be a profitable investment?"

"From my point of view it is the right—it is sure to be a profitable investment. After that it is a question of perseverance—courage. A writer of skill cannot be defeated because he remains true to his conscience. It is a long serious conflict sometimes, but he must win, if he does not falter. Lowell said to me one time: 'After all, the barriers are very thin. They are paper. If a man has his conscience and one or two friends who can help him it becomes very simple at last.'"

"Mr. Howells," said the other man suddenly, "have you observed a change in the literary pulse of the country within the last four months. Last winter, for instance, it seemed that realism was almost about to capture things, but then recently I have thought that I saw coming a sort of a counter-wave, a flood of the other—a reaction, in fact. Trivial, temporary, perhaps, but a reaction, certainly."

Mr. Howells dropped his hand in a gesture of emphatic assent. "What you say is true. I have seen it coming. . . . I suppose we shall have to wait."

AMERICAN CIVIL WAR

Contents

A Mystery of Heroism:
A Detail of an American Battle

THE DARK UNIFORMS of the men were so coated with dust from the incessant wrestling of the two armies that the regiment almost seemed a part of the clay bank which shielded them from the shells. On the top of the hill a battery was arguing in tremendous roars with some other guns and to the eye of the infantry, the artillerymen, the guns, the caissons, the horses, were distinctly outlined upon the blue sky. When a piece was fired a red streak as round as a log flashed low in the heavens, like a monstrous bolt of lightning. The men of the battery wore white duck trousers, which somehow emphasized their legs, and when they ran and crowded in little groups at the bidding of the shouting officers, it was more impressive than usual to the infantry.

Fred Collins of A Company was saying: "Thunder, I wisht I had a drink. Ain't there any water round here?" Then somebody yelled: "There goes th' bugler!"

As the eyes of half of the regiment swept in one machine-like movement there was an instant's picture of a horse in a great convulsive leap of a death wound and a rider leaning back with a crooked arm and spread fingers before his face. On the ground was the crimson terror of an exploding shell, with fibres of flame that seemed like lances. A glittering bugle swung clear of the rider's back as fell headlong the horse and the man. In the air was an odor as from a conflagration.

Sometimes they of the infantry looked down at a fair little meadow which spread at their feet. Its long, green grass was rippling gently in a breeze. Beyond it was the grey form of a house half torn to pieces by shells and by the busy axes of soldiers who had pursued firewood. The line of an old fence was now dimly marked by long weeds and by an occasional post. A shell had blown the well-house to fragments. Little lines of grey smoke ribboning upward from some embers indicated the place where had stood the barn.

From beyond a curtain of green woods there came the sound of some stupendous scuffle as if two animals of the size of islands were fighting. At a distance there were occasional appearances of swift-moving men, horses, batteries, flags, and, with the crashing of infantry volleys were heard, often, wild and frenzied cheers. In the midst of it all, Smith and Ferguson, two privates of A Company, were engaged in a heated discussion, which involved the greatest questions of the national existence.

The battery on the hill presently engaged in a frightful duel. The white legs of the gunners scampered this way and that way and the officers redoubled their shouts. The guns, with their demeanors of stolidity and courage, were typical of something infinitely self-possessed in this clamor of death that swirled around the hill.

One of a "swing" team was suddenly smitten quivering to the ground and his maddened brethren dragged his torn body in their struggle to escape from this turmoil and danger. A young soldier astride one of the leaders swore and fumed in his saddle and furiously jerked at the bridle. An officer screamed out an order so violently that his voice broke and ended the sentence in a falsetto shriek.

The leading company of the infantry regiment was somewhat exposed and the colonel ordered it moved more fully under the shelter of the hill. There was the clank of steel against steel.

A lieutenant of the battery rode down and passed them, holding his right arm carefully in his left hand. And it was as if this arm was not at all a part of him, but belonged to another man. His sober and reflective charger went slowly. The officer's face was grimy and perspiring and his uniform was tousled as if he had been in direct grapple with an enemy. He smiled grimly when the men stared at him. He turned his horse toward the meadow.

Collins of A Company said: "I wisht I had a drink. I bet there's water in that there ol' well yonder!"

"Yes; but how you goin' to git it?"

For the little meadow which intervened was now suffering a terrible onslaught of shells. Its green and beautiful calm had vanished utterly. Brown earth was being flung in monstrous handfuls. And there was a massacre of the young blades of grass. They were being torn, burned, obliterated. Some curious fortune of the battle had made this gentle little meadow the object of the red hate of the shells and each one as it exploded seemed like an imprecation in the face of a maiden.

The wounded officer who was riding across this expanse said to himself: "Why, they couldn't shoot any harder if the whole army was massed here!"

A shell struck the grey ruins of the house and as, after the roar, the shattered wall fell in fragments, there was a noise which resembled the flapping of shutters during a wild gale of winter. Indeed the infantry paused in the shelter of the bank, appeared as men standing upon a shore contemplating a madness of the sea. The angel of calamity had under its glance the battery upon the hill. Fewer white-legged men labored about the guns. A shell had smitten one of the pieces and after the flare, the smoke, the dust, the wrath of this blow was gone, it was possible to see white legs stretched horizontally upon the ground. And at that interval to the rear, where it is the business of battery horses to stand with their noses to the fight awaiting the command to drag their guns out of the destruction or into it or wheresoever these incomprehensible humans demanded with whip and spur—in this line of passive and dumb spectators, whose fluttering hearts yet would not let them forget the iron laws of man's control of them—in this rank of brute-soldiers there had been relentless and hideous carnage. From the ruck of bleeding and prostrate horses, the men of the infantry could see one animal raising its stricken body with its fore-legs and turning its nose with mystic and profound eloquence toward the sky.

Some comrades joked Collins about his thirst. "Well, if yeh want a drink so bad, why don't yeh go git it?"

"Well, I will in a minnet if yeh don't shut up."

A lieutenant of artillery floundered his horse straight down the hill with as great concern as if it were level ground. As he galloped past the colonel of the infantry, he threw up his hand in swift salute. "We've got to get out of that," he roared angrily. He was a black-bearded officer, and his eyes, which resembled beads, sparkled like those of an insane man. His jumping horse sped along the column of infantry.

The fat major standing carelessly with his sword held horizontally behind him and with his legs far apart, looked after the receding horseman and laughed. "He wants to get back with orders pretty quick or there'll be no batt'ry left," he observed.

The wise young captain of the second company hazarded to the lieutenant colonel that the enemy's infantry would probably soon attack the hill, and the lieutenant colonel snubbed him.

A private in one of the rear companies looked out over the meadow and then turned to a companion and said: "Look there, Jim." It was the wounded officer from the battery, who some time before had started to ride across the meadow, supporting his right arm carefully with his left hand. This man had encountered a shell apparently at a time when no one perceived him and he could now be seen lying face downward with a stirruped foot stretched across the body of his dead horse. A leg of the charger extended slantingly upward precisely as stiff as a stake. Around this motionless pair the shells still howled.

There was a quarrel in A Company. Collins was shaking his fist in the faces of some laughing comrades. "Dern yeh! I ain't afraid t' go. If yeh say much, I will go!"

"Of course, yeh will! Yeh'll run through that there medder, won't yeh?"

Collins said, in a terrible voice: "You see, now!" At this ominous threat his comrades broke into renewed jeers.

Collins gave them a dark scowl and went to find his captain. The latter was conversing with the colonel of the regiment.

"Captain," said Collins, saluting and standing at attention. In those days all trousers bagged at the knees. "Captain, I want t' git permission to go git some water from that there well over yonder!"

The colonel and the captain swung about simultaneously and stared across the meadow. The captain laughed. "You must be pretty thirsty, Collins?"

"Yes, sir; I am."

"Well—ah," said the captain. After a moment he asked: "Can't you wait?"

"No, sir."

The colonel was watching Collins's face. "Look here, my

lad," he said, in a pious sort of a voice. "Look here, my lad."
Collins was not a lad. "Don't you think that's taking pretty
big risks for a little drink of water?"

"I dunno," said Collins, uncomfortably. Some of the re-
sentment toward his companions, which perhaps had forced
him into this affair, was beginning to fade. "I dunno wether
'tis."

The colonel and the captain contemplated him for a time.

"Well," said the captain finally.

"Well," said the colonel, "if you want to go, why go."

Collins saluted. "Much obliged t' yeh."

As he moved away the colonel called after him. "Take some
of the other boys' canteens with you an' hurry back now."

"Yes, sir. I will."

The colonel and the captain looked at each other then, for
it had suddenly occurred that they could not for the life of
them tell whether Collins wanted to go or whether he did
not.

They turned to regard Collins and as they perceived him
surrounded by gesticulating comrades the colonel said: "Well,
by thunder! I guess he's going."

Collins appeared as a man dreaming. In the midst of the
questions, the advice, the warnings, all the excited talk of his
company mates, he maintained a curious silence.

They were very busy in preparing him for his ordeal. When
they inspected him carefully it was somewhat like the exami-
nation that grooms give a horse before a race; and they were
amazed, staggered by the whole affair. Their astonishment
found vent in strange repetitions.

"Are yeh sure a-goin'?" they demanded again and again.

"Certainly I am," cried Collins, at last furiously.

He strode sullenly away from them. He was swinging five
or six canteens by their cords. It seemed that his cap would
not remain firmly on his head, and often he reached and
pulled it down over his brow.

There was a general movement in the compact column.
The long animal-like thing moved slightly. Its four hundred
eyes were turned upon the figure of Collins.

"Well, sir, if that ain't th' derndest thing. I never thought
Fred Collins had the blood in him for that kind of business."

"What's he goin' to do, anyhow?"

"He's goin' to that well there after water."

"We ain't dyin' of thirst, are we? That's foolishness."

"Well, somebody put him up to it an' he's doin' it."

"Say, he must be a desperate cuss."

When Collins faced the meadow and walked away from the regiment he was vaguely conscious that a chasm, the deep valley of all prides, was suddenly between him and his comrades. It was provisional, but the provision was that he return as a victor. He had blindly been led by quaint emotions and laid himself under an obligation to walk squarely up to the face of death.

But he was not sure that he wished to make a retraction even if he could do so without shame. As a matter of truth he was sure of very little. He was mainly surprised.

It seemed to him supernaturally strange that he had allowed his mind to maneuver his body into such a situation. He understood that it might be called dramatically great.

However, he had no full appreciation of anything excepting that he was actually conscious of being dazed. He could feel his dulled mind groping after the form and color of this incident.

Too, he wondered why he did not feel some keen agony of fear cutting his sense like a knife. He wondered at this because human expression had said loudly for centuries that men should feel afraid of certain things and that all men who did not feel this fear were phenomena, heroes.

He was then a hero. He suffered that disappointment which we would all have if we discovered that we were ourselves capable of those deeds which we most admire in history and legend. This, then, was a hero. After all, heroes were not much.

No, it could not be true. He was not a hero. Heroes had no shames in their lives and, as for him, he remembered borrowing fifteen dollars from a friend and promising to pay it back the next day, and then avoiding that friend for ten months. When at home his mother had aroused him for the early labor of his life on the farm, it had often been his fashion to be irritable, childish, diabolical, and his mother had died since he had come to the war.

He saw that in this matter of the well, the canteens, the shells, he was an intruder in the land of fine deeds.

He was now about thirty paces from his comrades. The regiment had just turned its many faces toward him.

From the forest of terrific noises there suddenly emerged a little uneven line of men. They fired fiercely and rapidly at distant foliage on which appeared little puffs of white smoke. The spatter of skirmish firing was added to the thunder of the guns on the hill. The little line of men ran forward. A color-sergeant fell flat with his flag as if he had slipped on ice. There was hoarse cheering from this distant field.

Collins suddenly felt that two demon fingers were pressed into his ears. He could see nothing but flying arrows, flaming red. He lurched from the shock of this explosion, but he made a mad rush for the house, which he viewed as a man submerged to the neck in a boiling surf might view the shore. In the air, little pieces of shell howled and the earthquake explosions drove him insane with the menace of their roar. As he ran the canteens knocked together with a rhythmical tinkling.

As he neared the house each detail of the scene became vivid to him. He was aware of some bricks of the vanished chimney lying on the sod. There was a door which hung by one hinge.

Rifle bullets called forth by the insistent skirmishers came from the far-off bank of foliage. They mingled with the shells and the pieces of shells until the air was torn in all directions by hootings, yells, howls. The sky was full of fiends who directed all their wild rage at his head.

When he came to the well he flung himself face downward and peered into its darkness. There were furtive silver glintings some feet from the surface. He grabbed one of the canteens and, unfastening its cap, swung it down by the cord. The water flowed slowly in with an indolent gurgle.

And now as he lay with his face turned away he was suddenly smitten with the terror. It came upon his heart like the grasp of claws. All the power faded from his muscles. For an instant he was no more than a dead man.

The canteen filled with a maddening slowness in the manner of all bottles. Presently he recovered his strength and addressed a screaming oath to it. He leaned over until it seemed as if he intended to try to push water into it with his hands. His eyes as he gazed down into the well shone like two pieces of metal and in their expression was a great appeal and a great curse. The stupid water derided him.

There was the blaring thunder of a shell. Crimson light shone through the swift-boiling smoke and made a pink reflection on part of the wall of the well. Collins jerked out his arm and canteen with the same motion that a man would use in withdrawing his head from a furnace.

He scrambled erect and glared and hesitated. On the ground near him lay the old well bucket, with a length of rusty chain. He lowered it swiftly into the well. The bucket struck the water and then turning lazily over, sank. When, with hand reaching tremblingly over hand, he hauled it out, it knocked often against the walls of the well and spilled some of its contents.

In running with a filled bucket, a man can adopt but one kind of gait. So through this terrible field over which screamed practical angels of death Collins ran in the manner of a farmer chased out of a dairy by a bull.

His face went staring white with anticipation—anticipation of a blow that would whirl him around and down. He would fall as he had seen other men fall, the life knocked out of them so suddenly that their knees were no more quick to touch the ground than their heads. He saw the long blue line of the regiment, but his comrades were standing looking at him from the edge of an impossible star. He was aware of some deep wheel ruts and hoof prints in the sod beneath his feet.

The artillery officer who had fallen in this meadow had been making groans in the teeth of the tempest of sound. These futile cries, wrenched from him by his agony, were heard only by shells, bullets. When wild-eyed Collins came running, this officer raised himself. His face contorted and blanched from pain, he was about to utter some great beseeching cry. But suddenly his face straightened and he called: "Say, young man, give me a drink of water, will you?"

Collins had no room amid his emotions for surprise. He was mad from the threats of destruction.

"I can't," he screamed, and in this reply was a full description of his quaking apprehension. His cap was gone and his hair was riotous. His clothes made it appear that he had been dragged over the ground by the heels. He ran on.

The officer's head sank down and one elbow crooked. His foot in its brass-bound stirrup still stretched over the body of his horse and the other leg was under the steed.

But Collins turned. He came dashing back. His face had now turned grey and in his eyes was all terror. "Here it is! Here it is!"

The officer was as a man gone in drink. His arm bended like a twig. His head drooped as if his neck was of willow. He was sinking to the ground, to lie face downward.

Collins grabbed him by the shoulder. "Here it is. Here's your drink. Turn over! Turn over, man, for God's sake!"

With Collins hauling at his shoulder, the officer twisted his body and fell with his face turned toward that region where lived the unspeakable noises of the swirling missiles. There was the faintest shadow of a smile on his lips as he looked at Collins. He gave a sigh, a little primitive breath like that from a child.

Collins tried to hold the bucket steadily, but his shaking hands caused the water to splash all over the face of the dying man. Then he jerked it away and ran on.

The regiment gave him a welcoming roar. The grimed faces were wrinkled in laughter.

His captain waved the bucket away. "Give it to the men!"

The two genial, sky-larking young lieutenants were the first to gain possession of it. They played over it in their fashion.

When one tried to drink the other teasingly knocked his elbow. "Don't, Billie! You'll make me spill it," said the one. The other laughed.

Suddenly there was an oath, the thud of wood on the ground, and a swift murmur of astonishment from the ranks. The two lieutenants glared at each other. The bucket lay on the ground empty.

A Grey Sleeve

I

IT LOOKS as if it might rain this afternoon," remarked the lieutenant of artillery.

"So it does," the infantry captain assented. He glanced casually at the sky. When his eyes had lowered to the green-shadowed landscape before him, he said fretfully: "I wish those fellows out yonder would quit pelting at us. They've been at it since noon."

At the edge of a grove of maples, across wide fields, there occasionally appeared little puffs of smoke of a dull hue in this gloom of sky which expressed an impending rain. The long wave of blue and steel in the field moved uneasily at the eternal barking of the far-away sharpshooters, and the men, leaning upon their rifles, stared at the grove of maples. Once a private turned to borrow some tobacco from a comrade in the rear rank, but, with his hand still stretched out, he continued to twist his head and glance at the distant trees. He was afraid the enemy would shoot him at a time when he was not looking.

Suddenly the artillery officer said: "See what's coming!"

Along the rear of the brigade of infantry a column of cavalry was sweeping at a hard gallop. A lieutenant riding some yards to the right of the column bawled furiously at the four troopers just at the rear of the colors. They had lost distance and made a little gap, but at the shouts of the lieutenant they urged their horses forward. The bugler, careering along behind the captain of the troop, fought and tugged like a wrestler to keep his frantic animal from bolting far ahead of the column.

On the springy turf the innumerable hoofs thundered in a swift storm of sound. In the brown faces of the troopers their eyes were set like bits of flashing steel.

The long line of the infantry regiments standing at ease underwent a sudden movement at the rush of the passing squadron. The foot soldiers turned their heads to gaze at the torrent of horses and men.

The yellow folds of the flag fluttered back in silken shuddering waves, as if it were a reluctant thing. Occasionally a giant spring of a charger would rear the firm and steady figure of a soldier suddenly head and shoulders above his comrades. Over the noise of the scudding hoofs could be heard the creaking of leather trappings, the jingle and clank of steel and the tense low-toned commands or appeals of the men to their horses. And the horses were mad with the headlong sweep of this movement. Powerful underjaws bended back and straightened so that the bits were clamped as rigidly as vises upon the teeth, and glistening necks arched in desperate resistance to the hands at the bridles. Swinging their heads in rage at the granite laws of their lives which bended even their angers and their ardors to chosen directions and chosen paces, their flight was as a flight of harnessed demons.

The captain's bay kept its pace at the head of the squadron with the lithe bounds of a thoroughbred, and this horse was proud as a chief at the roaring trample of his fellows behind him. The captain's glance was calmly upon the grove of maples from whence the sharpshooters of the enemy had been picking at the blue line. He seemed to be reflecting. He stolidly rose and fell with the plunges of his horse in all the indifference of a deacon's figure seated plumply in church. And it occurred to many of the watching infantry to wonder why this officer could remain imperturbable and reflective when his squadron was thundering and swarming behind him like the rushing of a flood.

The column swung in a saber-curve toward a break in a fence and dashed into a roadway. Once a little plank bridge was encountered, and the sound of the hoofs upon it was like the long roll of many drums. An old captain in the infantry turned to his first lieutenant and made a remark which was a compound of bitter disparagement of cavalry in general and soldierly admiration of this particular troop.

Suddenly the bugle sounded and the column halted with a jolting upheaval amid sharp, brief cries. A moment later the men had tumbled from their horses and carbines in hand were running in a swarm toward the grove of maples. In the road, one of every four of the troopers was standing with braced legs and pulling and hauling at the bridles of four frenzied horses.

The captain was running awkwardly in his boots. He held his saber low so that the point often threatened to catch in the turf. His yellow hair ruffled out from under his faded cap. "Go in hard now," he roared in a voice of hoarse fury. His face was violently red.

The troopers threw themselves upon the grove like wolves upon a great animal. Along the whole front of the wood there was the dry crackling of musketry, with bitter, swift flashes and smoke that writhed like stung phantoms. The troopers yelled shrilly and spanged bullets low into the foliage.

For a moment, when near the woods, the line almost halted. The men struggled and fought for a time like swimmers encountering a powerful current. Then with a supreme effort they went on again. They dashed madly at the grove, whose foliage from the high light of the field was as inscrutable as a wall.

Then suddenly each detail of the calm trees became apparent and with a few more frantic leaps the men were in the cool gloom of the woods. There was a heavy odor as from burnt paper. Wisps of grey smoke wound upward. The men halted and, grimy, perspiring and puffing, they searched the recesses of the woods with eager, fierce glances. Figures could be seen flitting afar off. A dozen carbines rattled at them in an angry volley.

During this pause the captain strode along the line, his face lit with a broad smile of contentment. "When he sends this crowd to do anything, I guess he'll find we do it pretty sharp," he said to the grinning lieutenant.

"Say, they didn't stand that rush a minute, did they?" said the subaltern. Both officers were profoundly dusty in their uniforms, and their faces were soiled like those of two urchins.

Out in the grass behind them were three tumbled and silent forms.

Presently the line moved forward again. The men went from tree to tree like hunters stalking game. Some at the left of the line fired occasionally and those at the right gazed curiously in that direction. The men still breathed heavily from their scramble across the field.

Of a sudden a trooper halted and said: "Hello! there's a

house!" Everyone paused. The men turned to look at their leader.

The captain stretched his neck and swung his head from side to side. "By George, it is a house!" he said.

Through the wealth of leaves there vaguely loomed the form of a large, white house. These troopers, brown-faced from many days of campaigning, each feature of them telling of their placid confidence and courage, were stopped abruptly by the appearance of this house. There was some subtle suggestion—some tale of an unknown thing which watched them from they knew not what part of it.

A rail fence girted a wide lawn of tangled grass. Seven pines stood along a driveway which led from two distant posts of a vanished gate. The blue-clothed troopers moved forward until they stood at the fence peering over it.

The captain put one hand on the top rail and seemed to be about to climb the fence when suddenly he hesitated and said in a low voice: "Watson, what do you think of it?"

The lieutenant stared at the house. "Derned if I know!" he replied.

The captain pondered. It happened that the whole company had turned a gaze of profound awe and doubt upon this edifice which confronted them. The men were very silent.

At last the captain swore and said: "We are certainly a pack of fools. Derned old deserted house halting a company of Union cavalry and making us gape like babies."

"Yes, but there's something—something——" insisted the subaltern in a half stammer.

"Well, if there's 'something—something' in there, I'll get it out," said the captain. "Send Sharpe clean around to the other side with about twelve men, so we will sure bag your 'something—something,' and I'll take a few of the boys and find out what's in the damned old thing."

He chose the nearest eight men for his "storming party," as the lieutenant called it. After he had waited some minutes for the others to get into position, he said "come ahead" to his eight men and climbed the fence.

The brighter light of the tangled lawn made him suddenly feel tremendously apparent and he wondered if there could be some mystic thing in the house which was regarding this approach. His men trudged silently at his back. They stared at the windows and lost themselves in deep speculations as to the probability of there being, perhaps, eyes behind the blinds—malignant eyes, piercing eyes.

Suddenly a corporal in the party gave vent to a startled exclamation, and half threw his carbine into position. The captain turned quickly and the corporal said: "I saw an arm move the blinds. An arm with a grey sleeve!"

"Don't be a fool, Jones, now," said the captain sharply.

"I swear t'——" began the corporal, but the captain silenced him.

When they arrived at the front of the house the troopers paused, while the captain went softly up the front steps. He stood before the large front door and studied it. Some crickets chirped in the long grass and the nearest pine could be heard in its endless sighs. One of the privates moved uneasily and his foot crunched the gravel. Suddenly the captain swore angrily and kicked the door with a loud crash. It flew open.

II

The bright lights of the day flashed into the old house when the captain angrily kicked open the door. He was aware of a wide hallway carpeted with matting and extending deep into the dwelling. There was also an old walnut hat rack and a little marble-topped table with a vase and two books upon it. Further back was a great venerable fireplace containing dreary ashes.

But directly in front of the captain was a young girl. The flying open of the door had obviously been an utter astonishment to her and she remained transfixed there in the middle of the floor, staring at the captain with wide eyes.

She was like a child caught at the time of a raid upon the cake. She wavered to and fro upon her feet and held her hands behind her. There were two little points of terror in her eyes as she gazed up at the young captain in dusty blue, with his reddish, bronze complexion, his yellow hair, his bright saber held threateningly.

These two remained motionless and silent, simply staring at each other for some moments.

The captain felt his rage fade out of him and leave his mind limp. He had been violently angry, because this house had made him feel hesitant, wary. He did not like to be wary. He liked to feel confident, sure. So he had kicked the door open and had been prepared to march in like a soldier of wrath.

But now he began, for one thing, to wonder if his uniform was so dusty and old in appearance. Moreover, he had a feeling that his face was covered with a compound of dust, grime and perspiration. He took a step forward and said: "I didn't mean to frighten you." But his voice was coarse from his battle-howling. It seemed to him to have hempen fibers in it.

The girl's breath came in little, quick gasps, and she looked at him as she would have looked at a serpent.

"I didn't mean to frighten you," he said again.

The girl, still with her hands behind her, began to back away.

"Is there anyone else in the house?" he went on, while slowly following her. "I don't wish to disturb you, but we had a fight with some rebel skirmishers in the woods, and I thought maybe some of them might have come in here. In fact, I was pretty sure of it. Are there any of them here?"

The girl looked at him and said: "No!" He wondered why extreme agitation made the eyes of some women so limpid and bright.

"Who is here besides yourself?"

By this time his pursuit had driven her to the end of the hall, and she remained there with her back to the wall and her hands still behind her. When she answered this question she did not look at him, but down at the floor. She cleared her voice and then said: "There is no one here."

"No one?"

She lifted her eyes to him in that appeal that the human being must make even to falling trees, crashing bowlders, the sea in a storm, and said: "No, no, there is no one here." He could plainly see her tremble.

Of a sudden he bethought him that she had always kept her hands behind her. As he recalled her air when first discovered, he remembered she appeared precisely as a child detected at one of the crimes of childhood. Moreover, she had always backed away from him. He thought now that she was concealing something which was an evidence of the presence of the enemy in the house.

"What are you holding behind you?" he said suddenly.

She gave a little quick moan as if some grim hand had throttled her.

"What are you holding behind you?"

"Oh, nothing—please. I am not holding anything behind me; indeed I'm not."

"Very well. Hold your hands out in front of you, then."

"Oh, indeed, I'm not holding anything behind me. Indeed, I'm not."

"Well," he began. Then he paused, and remained for a moment dubious. Finally, he laughed. "Well, I shall have my men search the house, anyhow. I'm sorry to trouble you, but I feel sure that there is some one here whom we want." He turned to the corporal, who, with the other men, was gaping quietly in at the door, and said: "Jones, go through the house."

As for himself, he remained planted in front of the girl, for she evidently did not dare to move and allow him to see what she held so carefully behind her back. So she was his prisoner.

The men rummaged around on the ground floor of the house. Sometimes the captain called to them, "Try that closet," "Is there any cellar?" But they found no one, and at last they went trooping toward the stairs which led to the second floor.

But at this movement on the part of the men the girl uttered a cry, a cry of such fright and appeal that the men paused. "Oh, don't go up there! Please don't go up there!—ple-ease! There is no one there! Indeed—indeed there is not! Oh, ple-ease!"

"Go on, Jones," said the captain, calmly.

The obedient corporal made a preliminary step, and the girl bounded toward the stairs with another cry.

As she passed him, the captain caught sight of that which she had concealed behind her back, and which she had forgotten in this supreme moment. It was a pistol.

She ran to the first step, and standing there, faced the men, one hand extended with perpendicular palm, and the other holding the pistol at her side. "Oh, please, don't go up there. Nobody is there—indeed, there is not. P-l-e-a-s-e." Then suddenly she sank swiftly down upon the step, and, huddling forlornly, began to weep in the agony and with the convulsive tremors of an infant. The pistol fell from her fingers and rattled down to the floor.

The astonished troopers looked at their astonished captain. There was a short silence.

Finally, the captain stooped and picked up the pistol. It was a heavy weapon of the army pattern. He ascertained that it was empty.

He leaned toward the shaking girl, and said gently: "Will you tell me what you were going to do with this pistol?"

He had to repeat the question a number of times, but at last a muffled voice said, "Nothing."

"Nothing!" He insisted quietly upon a further answer. At the tender tones of the captain's voice, the phlegmatic corporal turned and winked gravely at the man next to him.

"Won't you tell me?"

The girl shook her head.

"Please tell me?"

The silent privates were moving their feet uneasily and wondering how long they were to wait.

The captain said, "Please won't you tell me?"

Then this girl's voice began in stricken tones half-coherent, and amid violent sobbing: "It was grandpa's. He—he—he said he was going to shoot anybody who came in here—he didn't care if there were thousands of 'em. And—and I know he would, and I was afraid they'd kill him. And so—and—so I stole away his pistol—and I was going to hide it when you—you—you kicked open the door."

The men straightened up and looked at each other. The girl began to weep again.

The captain mopped his brow. He peered down at the girl. He mopped his brow again. Suddenly he said: "Ah, don't cry like that."

He moved restlessly and looked down at his boots. He mopped his brow again.

Then he gripped the corporal by the arm and dragged him some yards back from the others. "Jones," he said, in an intensely earnest voice, " will you tell me what in the devil I am going to do?"

The corporal's countenance became illuminated with satisfaction at being thus requested to advise his superior officer. He adopted an air of great thought and finally said: "Well, of course, the feller with the grey sleeve must be upstairs, and we must get past the girl and up there somehow. Suppose I take her by the arm and lead her——"

"What!" interrupted the captain from between his clinched teeth. As he turned away from the corporal, he said fiercely over his shoulder: "You touch that girl and I'll split your skull!"

III

The corporal looked after his captain with an expression of mingled amazement, grief and philosophy. He seemed to be saying to himself that there unfortunately were times, after all, when one could not rely upon the most reliable of men. When he returned to the group he found the captain bending over the girl and saying: "Why is it that you don't want us to search upstairs?"

The girl's head was buried in her crossed arms. Locks of her hair had escaped from their fastenings and these fell upon her shoulder.

"Won't you tell me?"

The corporal here winked again at the man next to him.

"Because—" the girl moaned. "Because—there isn't anybody up there."

The captain at last said timidly: "Well, I'm afraid—I'm afraid we'll have to——"

The girl sprang to her feet again and implored him with her hands. She looked deep into his eyes with her glance which was at this time like that of the fawn when it says to the hunter: "Have mercy upon me."

These two stood regarding each other. The captain's foot was on the bottom step, but he seemed to be shrinking. He wore an air of being deeply wretched and ashamed. There was a silence.

Suddenly the corporal said in a quick, low tone: "Look out, captain!"

All turned their eyes swiftly toward the head of the stairs. There had appeared there a youth in a grey uniform. He stood looking coolly down at them. No word was said by the troopers. The girl gave vent to a little wail of desolation. "Oh, Harry!"

He began slowly to descend the stairs. His right arm was in a white sling and there were some fresh blood stains upon the cloth. His face was rigid and deathly pale, but his eyes flashed like lights. The girl was again moaning in an utterly dreary fashion as the youth came slowly down toward the silent men in blue.

Six steps from the bottom of the flight he halted and said: "I reckon it's me you're looking for."

The troopers had crowded forward a trifle and, posed in lithe, nervous attitudes, were watching him like cats. The captain remained unmoved. At the youth's question he merely nodded his head and said: "Yes."

The young man in grey looked down at the girl and then, in the same even tone which now, however, seemed to vibrate with suppressed fury, he said: "And is that any reason why you should insult my sister?"

At this sentence the girl intervened, desperately, between the young man in grey and the officer in blue. "Oh, don't, Harry, don't! He was good to me! He was good to me, Harry—indeed, he was."

The youth came on in his quiet, erect fashion until the girl could have touched either of the men with her hand, for the captain still remained with his foot upon the first step. She continually repeated: "Oh, Harry! Oh, Harry!"

The youth in grey maneuvered to glare into the captain's face first over one shoulder of the girl and then over the other. In a voice that rang like metal, he said: "You are armed and unwounded, while I have no weapons and am wounded, but——"

The captain had stepped back and sheathed his saber. The eyes of these two men were gleaming fire, but otherwise the captain's countenance was imperturbable. He said: "You are mistaken. You have no reason to——"

"You lie!"

All save the captain and the youth in grey started in an electric movement. These two words crackled in the air like shattered glass. There was a breathless silence.

The captain cleared his throat. His look at the youth contained a quality of singular and terrible ferocity, but he said in his stolid tone: "I don't suppose you mean what you say now."

Upon his arm he had felt the pressure of some unconscious little fingers. The girl was leaning against the wall as if she no longer knew how to keep her balance, but those fingers—he held his arm very still. She murmured: "Oh, Harry, don't! He was good to me! Indeed he was!"

The corporal had come forward until he in a measure confronted the youth in grey, for he saw those fingers upon the captain's arm and he knew that sometimes very strong men were not able to move hand nor foot under such conditions.

The youth had suddenly seemed to become weak. He breathed heavily and hung to the railing. He was glaring at the captain, and apparently summoning all his will power to combat his weakness. The corporal addressed him with profound straightforwardness: "Don't you be a derned fool!" The youth turned toward him so fiercely that the corporal threw up a knee and an elbow like a boy who expects to be cuffed.

The girl pleaded with the captain. "You won't hurt him? Will you? He don't know what he's saying. He's wounded, you know. Please don't mind him!"

"I won't touch him," said the captain with rather extraordinary earnestness. "Don't you worry about it at all. I won't touch him!"

Then he looked at her and the girl suddenly withdrew her fingers from his arm.

The corporal contemplated the top of the stairs and remarked without surprise: "There's another of 'em coming!"

An old man was clambering down the stairs with much speed. He waved a cane wildly. "Get out of my house, you thieves! Get out! I won't have you cross my threshold! Get out!" He mumbled and wagged his head in an old man's fury. It was plainly his intention to assault them.

And so it occurred that a young girl became engaged in protecting a stalwart captain, fully armed, and with eight grim troopers at his back, from the attack of an old man with a walking stick.

A blush passed over the temples and brow of the captain and he looked particularly savage and weary. Despite the girl's efforts he suddenly faced the old man.

"Look here," he said distinctly. "We came in because we had been fighting in the woods yonder and we concluded that some of the enemy were in this house, especially when we saw a grey sleeve at the window. But this young man is wounded and I have nothing to say to him. I will even take it for granted that there are no others like him upstairs. We will go away, leaving your damned old house just as we found it. And we are no more thieves and rascals than you are."

The old man simply roared: "I haven't got a cow nor a pig nor a chicken on the place. Your soldiers have stolen everything they could carry away. They have torn down half my fences for firewood. This afternoon some of your accursed bullets even broke my window panes!"

The girl had been faltering: "Grandpa! Oh, grandpa!"

The captain looked at the girl. She returned his glance from the shadow of the old man's shoulder. After studying her face a moment, he said: "Well, we will go now." He strode toward the door and his men clanked docilely after him.

At this time there was the sound of harsh cries and rushing footsteps from without. The door flew open and a whirlwind composed of blue-coated troopers came in with a swoop. It was headed by the lieutenant. "Oh, here you are," he cried, catching his breath. "We thought——hi! look at the girl!"

The captain said intensely: "Shut up, you fool!"

The men settled to a halt with a clash and bang. There could be heard the dulled sound of many hoofs outside of the house.

"Did you order up the horses?" inquired the captain.

"Yes, we thought——"

"Well, then, let's get out of here," interrupted the captain, morosely.

The men began to filter out into the open air. The youth in grey had been hanging dismally to the railing of the stairway. He now was climbing slowly up to the second floor. The old man was addressing himself directly to the serene corporal.

"Not a chicken on the place," he cried.

"Well, I didn't take your chickens, did I?"

"No, maybe you didn't, but——"

The captain crossed the hall and stood before the girl in rather a culprit's fashion. "You are not angry at me, are you?" he asked timidly.

"No," she said. She hesitated a moment and then suddenly held out her hand. "You were good to me—and I'm—much obliged."

The captain took her hand and then he blushed, for he found himself unable to formulate a sentence that applied in any way to the situation.

She did not seem to need that hand for a time.

He loosened his grasp presently, for he was ashamed to hold it so long without saying anything clever. At last with an air of charging an intrenched brigade, he contrived to say: "I would rather do anything than frighten you or trouble you."

His brow was warmly perspiring. He had a sense of being hideous in his dusty uniform and with his grimy face.

She said: "Oh, I'm so glad it was you instead of somebody who might have—might have hurt brother Harry and grandpa!"

He told her: "I wouldn't have hurt 'em for anything!"

There was a little silence.

"Well, good-bye," he said at last.

"Good-bye!"

He walked toward the door past the old man who was scolding at the vanishing figure of the corporal. The captain looked back. She had remained there watching him.

At the bugle's order, the troopers standing beside their horses swung briskly into the saddle. The lieutenant said to the first sergeant:

"Williams, did they ever meet before?"

"Hanged if I know."

"Well, say——"

The captain saw a curtain move at one of the windows. He

cantered from his position at the head of the column and steered his horse between two flower beds.

"Well, good-bye!"

The squadron trampled slowly past.

"Good-bye."

They shook hands.

He evidently had something enormously important to say to her, but it seems that he could not manage it. He struggled heroically. The bay charger with his great mystically solemn eyes looked around the corner of his shoulder at the girl.

The captain studied a pine tree. The girl inspected the grass beneath the window. The captain said hoarsely: "I don't suppose—I don't suppose—I'll ever see you again!"

She looked at him affrightedly and shrank back from the window. He seemed to have woefully expected a reception of this kind for his question. He gave her instantly a glance of appeal.

She said: "Why, no, I don't suppose we will."

"Never?"

"Why, no—'tain't possible. You—you are a—Yankee!"

"Oh, I know it, but——" Eventually he continued: "Well, some day, you know, when there's no more fighting, we might——" He observed that she had again withdrawn suddenly into the shadow so he said: "Well, good-bye!"

When he held her fingers she bowed her head and he saw a pink blush steal over the curves of her cheek and neck.

"Am I never going to see you again?"

She made no reply.

"Never!" he repeated.

After a long time he bended over to hear a faint reply: "Sometimes—when there are no troops in the neighborhood—grandpa don't mind if I—walk over as far as that old oak tree yonder—in the afternoons."

It appeared that the captain's grip was very strong, for she uttered an exclamation and looked at her fingers as if she expected to find them mere fragments. He rode away.

The bay horse leaped a flower bed. They were almost to the drive when the girl uttered a panic-stricken cry.

The captain wheeled his horse violently and upon this return journey went straight through a flower bed.

The girl had clasped her hands. She beseeched him wildly with her eyes. "Oh, please, don't believe it. I never walk to the old oak tree. Indeed, I don't. I never—never—never walk there."

The bridle drooped on the bay charger's neck. The captain's figure seemed limp. With an expression of profound dejection and gloom he stared off at where the leaden sky met the dark green line of the woods. The long-impending rain began to fall with a mournful patter, drop and drop. There was a silence.

At last a low voice said: "Well—I might—sometimes I might—perhaps—but only once in a great while—I might walk to the old tree—in the afternoons."

The Little Regiment

I

THE FOG MADE the clothes of the column of men in the roadway seem of a luminous quality. It imparted to the heavy infantry overcoats a new color, a kind of blue which was so pale that a regiment might have been merely a long, low shadow in the mist. However, a muttering, one part grumble, three parts joke, hovered in the air above the thick ranks, and blended in an undertoned roar, which was the voice of the column.

The town on the southern shore of the little river loomed spectrally, a faint etching upon the grey cloud-masses which were shifting with oily languor. A long row of guns upon the northern bank had been pitiless in their hatred, but a little battered belfry could be dimly seen still pointing with invincible resolution toward the heavens.

The enclouded air vibrated with noises made by hidden colossal things. The infantry tramplings, the heavy rumbling of the artillery, made the earth speak of gigantic preparation. Guns on distant heights thundered from time to time with sudden nervous roar, as if unable to endure in silence a knowledge of hostile troops massing, other guns going to position. These sounds, near and remote, defined an immense battle-ground, described the tremendous width of the stage of the prospective drama. The voice of the guns, slightly casual, unexcited in their challenges and warnings, could not destroy the unutterable eloquence of the word in the air, a meaning of impending struggle which made the breath halt at the lips.

The column in the roadway was ankle-deep in mud. The men swore piously at the rain which drizzled upon them, compelling them to stand always very erect in fear of the drops that would sweep in under their coat-collars. The fog was as cold as wet clothes. The men stuffed their hands deep in their pockets and huddled their muskets in their arms. The machinery of orders had rooted these soldiers deeply into the mud precisely as almighty nature roots mullein stalks.

They listened and speculated when a tumult of fighting

came from the dim town across the river. When the noise lulled for a time, they resumed their descriptions of the mud and graphically exaggerated the number of hours they had been kept waiting. The general commanding their division rode along the ranks, and they cheered admiringly, affectionately, crying out to him gleeful prophecies of the coming battle. Each man scanned him with a peculiarly keen personal interest, and afterward spoke of him with unquestioning devotion and confidence, narrating anecdotes which were mainly untrue.

When the jokers lifted the shrill voices which invariably belonged to them, flinging witticisms at their comrades, a loud laugh would sweep from rank to rank, and soldiers who had not heard would lean forward and demand repetition. When were borne past them some wounded men with grey and blood-smeared faces, and eyes that rolled in that helpless beseeching for assistance from the sky which comes with supreme pain, the soldiers in the mud watched intently, and from time to time asked of the bearers an account of the affair. Frequently they bragged of their corps, their division, their brigade, their regiment. Anon, they referred to the mud and the cold drizzle. Upon this threshold of a wild scene of death they, in short, defied the proportion of events with that splendor of heedlessness which belongs only to veterans.

"Like a lot of wooden soldiers," swore Billie Dempster, moving his feet in the thick mass, and casting a vindictive glance indefinitely; "standing in the mud for a hundred years."

"Oh, shut up!" murmured his brother Dan. The manner of his words implied that this fraternal voice near him was an indescribable bore.

"Why should I shut up?" demanded Billie.

"Because you're a fool," cried Dan, taking no time to debate it; "the biggest fool in the regiment."

There was but one man between them, and he was habituated. These insults from brother to brother had swept across his chest, flown past his face, many times during two long campaigns. Upon this occasion he simply grinned first at one, then at the other.

The way of these brothers was not an unknown topic in

regimental gossip. They had enlisted simultaneously, with each sneering loudly at the other for doing it. They left their little town and went forward with the flag, exchanging protestations of undying suspicion. In the camp life they so openly despised each other that when entertaining quarrels were lacking, their companions often contrived situations calculated to bring forth display of this fraternal dislike.

Both were large-limbed, strong young men, and often fought with friends in camp unless one was near to interfere with the other. This latter happened rather frequently, because Dan, preposterously willing for any manner of combat, had a very great horror of seeing Billie in a fight; and Billie, almost odiously ready himself, simply refused to see Dan stripped to his shirt and with his fists aloft. This sat queerly upon them, and made them the objects of plots.

When Dan would jump through a ring of eager soldiers and drag forth his raving brother by the arm, a thing often predicted would almost come to pass. When Billie performed the same office for Dan, the prediction would again miss fulfilment by an inch. But indeed they never fought together, although they were perpetually upon the verge.

They expressed longing for such conflict. As a matter of truth, they had at one time made full arrangement for it, but even with the encouragement and interest of half of the regiment they somehow failed to achieve collision.

If Dan became a victim of police duty, no jeering was so destructive to the feelings as Billie's comment. If Billie got a call to appear at the headquarters, none would so genially prophesy his complete undoing as Dan. Small misfortunes to one were, in truth, invariably greeted with hilarity by the other, who seemed to see in them great reënforcement of his opinion.

As soldiers, they expressed each for each a scorn intense and blasting. After a certain battle, Billie was promoted to corporal. When Dan was told of it, he seemed smitten dumb with astonishment and patriotic indignation. He stared in silence, while the dark blood rushed to Billie's forehead, and he shifted his weight from foot to foot. Dan at last found his tongue, and said: "Well, I'm derned!" If he had heard that an army mule had been appointed to the post of corps commander, his tone could not have had more derision in it. Afterward, he adopted a fervid insubordination, an almost religious reluctance to obey the new corporal's orders, which came near to developing the desired strife.

It is here finally to be recorded also that Dan, most ferociously profane in speech, very rarely swore in the presence of his brother; and that Billie, whose oaths came from his lips with the grace of falling pebbles, was seldom known to express himself in this manner when near his brother Dan.

At last the afternoon contained a suggestion of evening. Metallic cries rang suddenly from end to end of the column. They inspired at once a quick, business-like adjustment. The long thing stirred in the mud. The men had hushed and were looking across the river. A moment later the shadowy mass of pale-blue figures was moving steadily toward the stream. There could be heard from the town a clash of swift fighting and cheering. The noise of the shooting coming through the heavy air had its sharpness taken from it, and sounded in thuds.

There was a halt upon the bank above the pontoons. When the column went winding down the incline, and streamed out upon the bridge, the fog had faded to a great degree, and in the clearer dusk the guns on a distant ridge were enabled to perceive the crossing. The long whirling outcries of the shells came into the air above the men. An occasional solid shot struck the surface of the river and dashed into view a sudden vertical jet. The distance was subtly illuminated by the lightning from the deep-booming guns. One by one the batteries on the northern shore aroused, the innumerable guns bellowed in angry oration at the distant ridge. The rolling thunder crashed and reverberated as a wild surf sounds on a still night, and to this music the column marched across the pontoons.

The waters of the grim river curled away in a smile from the ends of the great boats, and slid swiftly beneath the planking. The dark, riddled walls of the town upreared before the troops, and from a region hidden by these hammered and tumbled houses came incessantly the yells and firings of a prolonged and close skirmish.

When Dan had called his brother a fool, his voice had been

so decisive, so brightly assured, that many men had laughed, considering it to be great humor under the circumstances. The incident happened to rankle deep in Billie. It was not any strange thing that his brother had called him a fool. In fact, he often called him a fool with exactly the same amount of cheerful and prompt conviction, and before large audiences, too. Billie wondered in his own mind why he took such profound offence in this case; but, at any rate, as he slid down the bank and on to the bridge with his regiment, he was searching his knowledge for something that would pierce Dan's blithesome spirit. But he could contrive nothing at this time, and his impotency made the glance which he was once able to give his brother still more malignant.

The guns far and near were roaring a fearful and grand introduction for this column which was marching upon the stage of death. Billie felt it, but only in a numb way. His heart was cased in that curious dissonant metal which covers a man's emotions at such times. The terrible voices from the hills told him that in this wide conflict his life was an insignificant fact, and that his death would be an insignificant fact. They portended the whirlwind to which he would be as necessary as a waved butterfly's wing. The solemnity, the sadness of it came near enough to make him wonder why he was neither solemn nor sad. When his mind vaguely adjusted events according to their importance to him, it appeared that the uppermost thing was the fact that upon the eve of battle, and before many comrades, his brother had called him a fool.

Dan was in a particularly happy mood. "Hurray! Look at 'em shoot," he said, when the long witches' croon of the shells came into the air. It enraged Billie when he felt the little thorn in him, and saw at the same time that his brother had completely forgotten.

The column went from the bridge into more mud. At this southern end there was a chaos of hoarse directions and commands. Darkness was coming upon the earth, and regiments were being hurried up the slippery bank. As Billie floundered in the black mud, amid the swearing, sliddering crowd, he suddenly resolved that, in the absence of other means of hurting Dan, he would avoid looking at him, refrain from speaking to him, pay absolutely no heed to his existence; and this done skilfully would, he imagined, soon reduce his brother to a poignant sensitiveness.

At the top of the bank the column again halted and re-arranged itself, as a man after a climb rearranges his clothing. Presently the great steel-backed brigade, an infinitely graceful thing in the rhythm and ease of its veteran movement, swung up a little narrow, slanting street.

Evening had come so swiftly that the fighting on the remote borders of the town was indicated by thin flashes of flame. Some building was on fire, and its reflection upon the clouds was an oval of delicate pink.

II

All demeanor of rural serenity had been wrenched violently from the little town by the guns and by the waves of men which had surged through it. The hand of war laid upon this village had in an instant changed it to a thing of remnants. It resembled the place of a monstrous shaking of the earth itself. The windows, now mere unsightly holes, made the tumbled and blackened dwellings seem skeletons. Doors lay splintered to fragments. Chimneys had flung their bricks everywhere. The artillery fire had not neglected the rows of gentle shade-trees which had lined the streets. Branches and heavy trunks cluttered the mud in driftwood tangles, while a few shattered forms had contrived to remain dejectedly, mournfully up-right. They expressed an innocence, a helplessness, which per-force created a pity for their happening into this cauldron of battle. Furthermore, there was under foot a vast collection of odd things reminiscent of the charge, the fight, the retreat. There were boxes and barrels filled with earth, behind which riflemen had lain snugly, and in these little trenches were the dead in blue with the dead in grey, the poses eloquent of the struggles for possession of the town until the history of the whole conflict was written plainly in the streets.

And yet the spirit of this little city, its quaint individuality, poised in the air above the ruins, defying the guns, the sweep-ing volleys; holding in contempt those avaricious blazes which had attacked many dwellings. The hard earthen side-walks proclaimed the games that had been played there during long lazy days, in the careful shadows of the trees. "General Merchandise," in faint letters upon a long board, had to be read with a slanted glance, for the board dangled by one end; but the porch of the old store was a palpable legend of wide-hatted men, smoking.

This subtle essence, this soul of the life that had been, brushed like invisible wings the thoughts of the men in the swift columns that came up from the river.

In the darkness a loud and endless humming arose from the great blue clouds bivouacked in the streets. From time to time a sharp spatter of firing from far picket lines entered this bass chorus. The smell from the smouldering ruins floated on the cold night breeze.

Dan, seated ruefully upon the doorstep of a shot-pierced house, was proclaiming the campaign badly managed. Orders had been issued forbidding camp-fires.

Suddenly he ceased his oration, and scanning the group of his comrades, said: "Where's Billie? Do you know?"

"Gone on picket."

"Get out! Has he?" said Dan. "No business to go on picket. Why don't some of them other corporals take their turn?"

A bearded private was smoking his pipe of confiscated tobacco, seated comfortably upon a horse-hair trunk which he had dragged from the house. He observed: "*Was* his turn."

"No such thing," cried Dan. He and the man on the horse-hair trunk held discussion, in which Dan stoutly maintained that if his brother had been sent on picket it was an injustice. He ceased his argument when another soldier, upon whose arms could faintly be seen the two stripes of a corporal, entered the circle. "Humph," said Dan, " where you been?"

The corporal made no answer. Presently Dan said: "Billie, where you been?"

His brother did not seem to hear these inquiries. He glanced at the house which towered above them, and remarked casually to the man on the horse-hair trunk: "Funny, ain't it? After the pelting this town got, you'd think there wouldn't be one brick left on another."

"Oh," said Dan, glowering at his brother's back. "Getting mighty smart, ain't you?"

The absence of camp-fires allowed the evening to make apparent its quality of faint silver light in which the blue clothes of the throng became black, and the faces became white expanses, void of expression. There was considerable excitement a short distance from the group around the doorstep. A soldier had chanced upon a hoop-skirt, and arrayed in it he was performing a dance amid the applause of his companions. Billie and a greater part of the men immediately poured over there to witness the exhibition.

"What's the matter with Billie?" demanded Dan of the man upon the horse-hair trunk.

"How do I know?" rejoined the other in mild resentment. He arose and walked away. When he returned he said briefly, in a weather-wise tone, that it would rain during the night.

Dan took a seat upon one end of the horse-hair trunk. He was facing the crowd around the dancer, which in its hilarity swung this way and that way. At times he imagined that he could recognize his brother's face.

He and the man on the other end of the trunk thoughtfully talked of the army's position. To their minds, infantry and artillery were in a most precarious jumble in the streets of the town; but they did not grow nervous over it, for they were used to having the army appear in a precarious jumble to their minds. They had learned to accept such puzzling situations as a consequence of their position in the ranks, and were now usually in possession of a simple but perfectly immovable faith that somebody understood the jumble. Even if they had been convinced that the army was a headless monster, they would merely have nodded with the veteran's singular cynicism. It was none of their business as soldiers. Their duty was to grab sleep and food when occasion permitted, and cheerfully fight wherever their feet were planted, until more orders came. This was a task sufficiently absorbing.

They spoke of other corps, and this talk being confidential, their voices dropped to tones of awe. "The Ninth"—"The First"—"The Fifth"—"The Sixth"—"The Third"—the simple numerals rang with eloquence, each having a meaning which was to float through many years as no intangible arithmetical mist, but as pregnant with individuality as the names of cities.

Of their own corps they spoke with a deep veneration, an

idolatry, a supreme confidence which apparently would not blanch to see it matched against everything.

It was as if their respect for other corps was due partly to a wonder that organizations not blessed with their own famous numeral could take such an interest in war. They could prove that their division was the best in the corps, and that their brigade was the best in the division. And their regiment—it was plain that no fortune of life was equal to the chance which caused a man to be born, so to speak, into this command, the proud keystone of the defending arch.

At times Dan covered with insults the character of a vague unnamed general to whose petulance and busy-body spirit he ascribed the order which made hot coffee impossible.

Dan said that victory was certain in the coming battle. The other man seemed rather dubious. He remarked upon the fortified line of hills which had impressed him even from the other side of the river. "Shucks," said Dan. "Why, we——" He pictured a splendid overflowing of these hills by the sea of men in blue. During the period of this conversation Dan's glance searched the merry throng about the dancer. Above the babble of voices in the street a far-away thunder could sometimes be heard—evidently from the very edge of the horizon—the boom-boom of restless guns.

III

Ultimately the night deepened to the tone of black velvet. The outlines of the fireless camp were like the faint drawings upon ancient tapestry. The glint of a rifle, the shine of a button might have been of threads of silver and gold sewn upon the fabric of the night. There was little presented to the vision, but to a sense more subtle there was discernible in the atmosphere something like a pulse; a mystic beating which would have told a stranger of the presence of a giant thing—the slumbering mass of regiments and batteries.

With fires forbidden, the floor of a dry old kitchen was thought to be a good exchange for the cold earth of December, even if a shell had exploded in it and knocked it so out of shape that when a man lay curled in his blanket his last waking thought was likely to be of the wall that bellied out above him as if strongly anxious to topple upon the score of soldiers.

Billie looked at the bricks ever about to descend in a shower upon his face, listened to the industrious pickets plying their rifles on the border of the town, imagined some measure of the din of the coming battle, thought of Dan and Dan's chagrin, and, rolling over in his blanket, went to sleep with satisfaction.

At an unknown hour he was aroused by the creaking of boards. Lifting himself upon his elbow, he saw a sergeant prowling among the sleeping forms. The sergeant carried a candle in an old brass candlestick. He would have resembled some old farmer on an unusual midnight tour if it were not for the significance of his gleaming buttons and striped sleeves.

Billie blinked stupidly at the light until his mind returned from the journeys of slumber. The sergeant stooped among the unconscious soldiers, holding the candle close, and peering into each face.

"Hello, Haines," said Billie. "Relief?"

"Hello, Billie," said the sergeant. "Special duty."

"Dan got to go?"

"Jameson, Hunter, McCormack, D. Dempster. Yes. Where is he?"

"Over there by the winder," said Billie, gesturing. "What is it for, Haines?"

"You don't think I know, do you?" demanded the sergeant. He began to pipe sharply but cheerily at men upon the floor. "Come, Mac, get up here. Here's a special for you. Wake up, Jameson. Come along, Dannie, me boy."

Each man at once took this call to duty as a personal affront. They pulled themselves out of their blankets, rubbed their eyes, and swore at whoever was responsible. "Them's orders," cried the sergeant. "Come! Get out of here." An undetailed head with dishevelled hair thrust out from a blanket, and a sleepy voice said: "Shut up, Haines, and go home."

When the detail clanked out of the kitchen, all but one of the remaining men seemed to be again asleep. Billie, leaning on his elbow, was gazing into darkness. When the footsteps died to silence, he curled himself into his blanket.

At the first cool lavender lights of daybreak he aroused again and scanned his recumbent companions. Seeing a wakeful one he asked: "Is Dan back yet?"

The man said: "Hain't seen 'im."

Billie put both hands behind his head and scowled into the air. "Can't see the use of these cussed details in the nighttime," he muttered in his most unreasonable tones. "Darn nuisances. Why can't they——" He grumbled at length and graphically.

When Dan entered with the squad, however, Billie was convincingly asleep.

IV

The regiment trotted in double time along the street, and the colonel seemed to quarrel over the right of way with many artillery officers. Batteries were waiting in the mud, and the men of them, exasperated by the bustle of this ambitious infantry, shook their fists from saddle and caisson, exchanging all manner of taunts and jests. The slanted guns continued to look reflectively at the ground.

On the outskirts of the crumbled town a fringe of blue figures were firing into the fog. The regiment swung out into skirmish lines, and the fringe of blue figures departed, turning their backs and going joyfully around the flank.

The bullets began a low moan off toward a ridge which loomed faintly in the heavy mist. When the swift crescendo had reached its climax, the missiles zipped just overhead, as if piercing an invisible curtain. A battery on the hill was crashing with such tumult that it was as if the guns had quarrelled and had fallen pell-mell and snarling upon each other. The shells howled on their journey toward the town. From short-range distance there came a spatter of musketry, sweeping along an invisible line and making faint sheets of orange light.

Some in the new skirmish lines were beginning to fire at various shadows discerned in the vapor, forms of men suddenly revealed by some humor of the laggard masses of clouds. The crackle of musketry began to dominate the purring of the hostile bullets. Dan, in the front rank, held his rifle poised, and looked into the fog keenly, coldly, with the air of a sportsman. His nerves were so steady that it was as if they had been drawn from his body, leaving him merely a muscular machine; but his numb heart was somehow beating to the pealing march of the fight.

The waving skirmish line went backward and forward, ran this way and that way. Men got lost in the fog, and men were found again. Once they got too close to the formidable ridge, and the thing burst out as if repulsing a general attack. Once another blue regiment was apprehended on the very edge of firing into them. Once a friendly battery began an elaborate and scientific process of extermination. Always as busy as brokers, the men slid here and there over the plain, fighting their foes, escaping from their friends, leaving a history of many movements in the wet yellow turf, damning the atmosphere, blazing away every time they could identify the enemy.

In one mystic changing of the fog, as if the fingers of spirits were drawing aside these draperies, a small group of the grey skirmishers, silent, statuesque, were suddenly disclosed to Dan and those about him. So vivid and near were they that there was something uncanny in the revelation.

There might have been a second of mutual staring. Then each rifle in each group was at the shoulder. As Dan's glance flashed along the barrel of his weapon, the figure of a man suddenly loomed as if the musket had been a telescope. The short black beard, the slouch hat, the pose of the man as he sighted to shoot, made a quick picture in Dan's mind. The same moment, it would seem, he pulled his own trigger, and the man, smitten, lurched forward, while his exploding rifle made a slanting crimson streak in the air, and the slouch hat fell before the body. The billows of the fog, governed by singular impulses, rolled between.

"You got that feller sure enough," said a comrade to Dan. Dan looked at him absent-mindedly.

V

When the next morning calmly displayed another fog, the men of the regiment exchanged eloquent comments; but they did not abuse it at length, because the streets of the town now contained enough galloping aides to make three troops of cavalry, and they knew that they had come to the verge of the great fight.

Dan conversed with the man who had once possessed a horse-hair trunk; but they did not mention the line of hills which had furnished them in more careless moments with an agreeable topic. They avoided it now as condemned men do the subject of death, and yet the thought of it stayed in their eyes as they looked at each other and talked gravely of other things.

The expectant regiment heaved a long sigh of relief when the sharp call, "Fall in!" repeated indefinitely, arose in the streets. It was inevitable that a bloody battle was to be fought, and they wanted to get it off their minds. They were, however, doomed again to spend a long period planted firmly in the mud. They craned their necks and wondered where some of the other regiments were going.

At last the mists rolled carelessly away. Nature made at this time all provisions to enable foes to see each other, and immediately the roar of guns resounded from every hill. The endless crackling of the skirmishers swelled to rolling crashes of musketry. Shells screamed with panther-like noises at the houses. Dan looked at the man of the horse-hair trunk, and the man said: "Well, here she comes!"

The tenor voices of young officers and the deep and hoarse voices of the older ones rang in the streets. These cries pricked like spurs. The masses of men vibrated from the suddenness with which they were plunged into the situation of troops about to fight. That the orders were long-expected did not concern the emotion.

Simultaneous movement was imparted to all these thick bodies of men and horses that lay in the town. Regiment after regiment swung rapidly into the streets that faced the sinister ridge.

This exodus was theatrical. The little sober-hued village had been like the cloak which disguises the king of drama. It was now put aside, and an army, splendid thing of steel and blue, stood forth in the sun-light.

Even the soldiers in the heavy columns drew deep breaths at the sight, more majestic than they had dreamed. The heights of the enemy's position were crowded with men who resembled people come to witness some mighty pageant. But as the column moved steadily to their positions, the guns, matter-of-fact warriors, doubled their number, and shells burst with red thrilling tumult on the crowded plain. One came into the ranks of the regiment, and after the smoke and the wrath of it had faded, leaving motionless figures, every one stormed according to the limits of his vocabulary, for veterans detest being killed when they are not busy.

The regiment sometimes looked sideways at its brigade companions composed of men who had never been in battle; but no frozen blood could withstand the heat of the splendor of this army before the eyes on the plain, these lines so long that the flanks were little streaks, this mass of men of one intention. The recruits carried themselves heedlessly. At the rear was an idle battery, and three artillerymen in a foolish row on a caisson nudged each other and grinned at the recruits. "You'll catch it pretty soon," they called out. They were impersonally gleeful, as if they themselves were not also likely to catch it pretty soon. But with this picture of an army in their hearts, the new men perhaps felt the devotion which the drops may feel for the wave; they were of its power and glory; they smiled jauntily at the foolish row of gunners, and told them to go to blazes.

The column trotted across some little bridges and spread quickly into lines of battle. Before them was a bit of plain, and back of the plain was the ridge. There was no time left for considerations. The men were staring at the plain, mightily wondering how it would feel to be out there, when a brigade in advance yelled and charged. The hill was all grey smoke and fire-points.

That fierce elation in the terrors of war, catching a man's heart and making it burn with such ardor that he becomes capable of dying, flashed in the faces of the men like colored lights, and made them resemble leashed animals, eager, ferocious, daunting at nothing. The line was really in its first leap before the wild, hoarse crying of the orders.

The greed for close quarters which is the emotion of a bayonet charge came then into the minds of the men and developed until it was a madness. The field, with its faded grass of a Southern winter, seemed miles in width to this fury.

High, slow-moving masses of smoke, with an odor of burning cotton, engulfed the line until the men might have been swimmers. Before them the ridge, the shore of this grey sea, was outlined, crossed, and re-crossed by sheets of flame. The howl of the battle arose to the noise of innumerable wind-demons.

The line, galloping, scrambling, plunging like a herd of wounded horses, went over a field that was sown with corpses, the records of other charges.

Directly in front of the black-faced, whooping Dan, carousing in this onward sweep like a new kind of fiend, a wounded man appeared, raising his shattered body, and staring at this rush of men down upon him. It seemed to occur to him that he was to be trampled; he made a desperate, piteous effort to escape; then finally huddled in a waiting heap. Dan and the soldier near him widened the interval between them without looking down, without appearing to heed the wounded man. This little clump of blue seemed to reel past them as bowlders reel past a train.

Bursting through a smoke-wave, the scampering, unformed bunches came upon the wreck of the brigade that had preceded them, a floundering mass stopped afar from the hill by the swirling volleys.

It was as if a necromancer had suddenly shown them a picture of the fate which awaited them; but the line with a muscular spasm hurled itself over this wreckage and onward, until men were stumbling amid the relics of other assaults, the point where the fire from the ridge consumed.

The men, panting, perspiring, with crazed faces, tried to push against it; but it was as if they had come to a wall. The wave halted, shuddered in an agony from the quick struggle of its two desires, then toppled and broke into a fragmentary thing which has no name.

Veterans could now at last be distinguished from recruits. The new regiments were instantly gone, lost, scattered, as if they never had been. But the sweeping failure of the charge, the battle, could not make the veterans forget their business. With a last throe, the band of maniacs drew itself up and blazed a volley at the hill, insignificant to those iron intrenchments, but nevertheless expressing that singular final despair which enables men to coolly defy the walls of a city of death.

After this episode the men renamed their command. They called it the Little Regiment.

VI

"I seen Dan shoot a feller yesterday. Yes, sir. I'm sure it was him that done it. And maybe he thinks about that feller now, and wonders if *he* tumbled down just about the same way. Them things come up in a man's mind."

Bivouac fires upon the side-walks, in the streets, in the yards, threw high their wavering reflections, which examined, like slim, red fingers, the dingy, scarred walls and the piles of tumbled brick. The droning of voices again arose from great blue crowds.

The odor of frying bacon, the fragrance from countless little coffee-pails floated among the ruins. The rifles, stacked in the shadows, emitted flashes of steely light. Wherever a flag lay horizontally from one stack to another was the bed of an eagle which had led men into the mystic smoke.

The men about a particular fire were engaged in holding in check their jovial spirits. They moved whispering around the blaze, although they looked at it with a certain fine contentment, like laborers after a day's hard work.

There was one who sat apart. They did not address him save in tones suddenly changed. They did not regard him directly, but always in little sidelong glances.

At last a soldier from a distant fire came into this circle of light. He studied for a time the man who sat apart. Then he hesitatingly stepped closer and said: "Got any news, Dan?"

"No," said Dan.

The new-comer shifted his feet. He looked at the fire, at the sky, at the other men, at Dan. His face expressed a curious despair; his tongue was plainly in rebellion. Finally, however, he contrived to say: "Well, there's some chance yet, Dan. Lots of the wounded are still lying out there, you know. There's some chance yet."

"Yes," said Dan.

The soldier shifted his feet again, and looked miserably into the air. After another struggle he said: "Well, there's some chance yet, Dan." He moved hastily away.

One of the men of the squad, perhaps encouraged by this example, now approached the still figure. "No news yet, hey?" he said, after coughing behind his hand.

"No," said Dan.

"Well," said the man, "I've been thinking of how he was fretting about you the night you went on special duty. You recollect? Well, sir, I was surprised. He couldn't say enough about it. I swan, I don't believe he slep' a wink after you left, but just lay awake cussing special duty and worrying. I was surprised. But there he lay cussing. He——"

Dan made a curious sound, as if a stone had wedged in his throat. He said: "Shut up, will you?"

Afterward the men would not allow this moody contemplation of the fire to be interrupted.

"Oh, let him alone, can't you?"

"Come away from there, Casey!"

"Say, can't you leave him be?"

They moved with reverence about the immovable figure, with its countenance of mask-like invulnerability.

VII

After the red round eye of the sun had stared long at the little plain and its burden, darkness, a sable mercy, came heavily upon it, and the wan hands of the dead were no longer seen in strange frozen gestures.

The heights in front of the plain shone with tiny camp-fires, and from the town in the rear, small shimmerings ascended from the blazes of the bivouac. The plain was a black expanse upon which, from time to time, dots of light, lanterns, floated slowly here and there. These fields were long steeped in grim mystery.

Suddenly, upon one dark spot, there was a resurrection. A strange thing had been groaning there, prostrate. Then it suddenly dragged itself to a sitting posture, and became a man.

The man stared stupidly for a moment at the lights on the

hill, then turned and contemplated the faint coloring over the town. For some moments he remained thus, staring with dull eyes, his face unemotional, wooden.

Finally he looked around him at the corpses dimly to be seen. No change flashed into his face upon viewing these men. They seemed to suggest merely that his information concerning himself was not too complete. He ran his fingers over his arms and chest, bearing always the air of an idiot upon a bench at an almshouse door.

Finding no wound in his arms nor in his chest, he raised his hand to his head, and the fingers came away with some dark liquid upon them. Holding these fingers close to his eyes, he scanned them in the same stupid fashion, while his body gently swayed.

The soldier rolled his eyes again toward the town. When he arose, his clothing peeled from the frozen ground like wet paper. Hearing the sound of it, he seemed to see reason for deliberation. He paused and looked at the ground, then at his trousers, then at the ground.

Finally he went slowly off toward the faint reflection, holding his hands palm outward before him, and walking in the manner of a blind man.

VIII

The immovable Dan again sat unaddressed in the midst of comrades, who did not joke aloud. The dampness of the usual morning fog seemed to make the little camp-fires furious.

Suddenly a cry arose in the streets, a shout of amazement and delight. The men making breakfast at the fire looked up quickly. They broke forth in clamorous exclamation: "Well! Of all things! Dan! Dan! Look who's coming! Oh, Dan!"

Dan the silent raised his eyes and saw a man, with a bandage of the size of a helmet about his head, receiving a furious demonstration from the company. He was shaking hands and explaining and haranguing to a high degree.

Dan started. His skin of bronze flushed to his temples. He seemed about to leap from the ground, but then suddenly he sank back, and resumed his impassive gazing.

The men were in a flurry. They looked from one to the

other. "Dan! Look! See who's coming!" some cried again. "Dan! Look!"

He scowled at last, and moved his shoulders sullenly. "Well, don't I know it?"

But they could not be convinced that his eyes were in service. "Dan! Why can't you look? See who's coming!"

He made a gesture then of irritation and rage. "Damn it! Don't I know it?"

The man with a bandage of the size of a helmet moved forward, always shaking hands and explaining. At times his glance wandered to Dan, who sat with his eyes riveted.

After a series of shiftings, it occurred naturally that the man with the bandage was very near to the man who saw the flames. He paused, and there was a little silence. Finally he said: "Hello, Dan."

"Hello, Billie."

The Veteran

OUT OF THE LOW WINDOW could be seen three hickory trees placed irregularly in a meadow that was resplendent in spring-time green. Further away, the old dismal belfry of the village church loomed over the pines. A horse meditating in the shade of one of the hickories lazily swished his tail. The warm sunshine made an oblong of vivid yellow on the floor of the grocery.

"Could you see the whites of their eyes?" said the man who was seated on a soap-box.

"Nothing of the kind," replied old Henry warmly. "Just a lot of flitting figures, and I let go at where they 'peared to be the thickest. Bang!"

"Mr. Fleming," said the grocer. His deferential voice expressed somehow the old man's exact social weight. "Mr. Fleming, you never was frightened much in them battles, was you?"

The veteran looked down and grinned. Observing his manner the entire group tittered. "Well, I guess I was," he answered finally. "Pretty well scared, sometimes. Why, in my first battle I thought the sky was falling down. I thought the world was coming to an end. You bet I was scared."

Every one laughed. Perhaps it seemed strange and rather wonderful to them that a man should admit the thing, and in the tone of their laughter there was probably more admiration than if old Fleming had declared that he had always been a lion. Moreover, they knew that he had ranked as an orderly sergeant, and so their opinion of his heroism was fixed. None, to be sure, knew how an orderly sergeant ranked, but then it was understood to be somewhere just shy of a major-general's stars. So when old Henry admitted that he had been frightened there was a laugh.

"The trouble was," said the old man, "I thought they were all shooting at me. Yes, sir. I thought every man in the other army was aiming at me in particular and only me. And it seemed so darned unreasonable, you know. I wanted to explain to 'em what an almighty good fellow I was, because I thought then they might quit all trying to hit me. But I couldn't explain, and they kept on being unreasonable—blim!—blam!—bang! So I run!"

Two little triangles of wrinkles appeared at the corners of his eyes. Evidently he appreciated some comedy in this recital. Down near his feet, however, little Jim, his grandson, was visibly horror-stricken. His hands were clasped nervously, and his eyes were wide with astonishment at this terrible scandal, his most magnificent grandfather telling such a thing.

"That was at Chancellorsville. Of course, afterward I got kind of used to it. A man does. Lots of men, though, seem to feel all right from the start. I did, as soon as I 'got on to it,' as they say now, but at first I was pretty flustered. Now, there was young Jim Conklin, old Si Conklin's son—that used to keep the tannery—you none of you recollect him—well, he went into it from the start just as if he was born to it. But with me it was different. I had to get used to it."

When little Jim walked with his grandfather he was in the habit of skipping along on the stone pavement in front of the three stores and the hotel of the town and betting that he could avoid the cracks. But upon this day he walked soberly, with his hand gripping two of his grandfather's fingers. Sometimes he kicked abstractedly at dandelions that curved over the walk. Any one could see that he was much troubled.

"There's Sickles's colt over in the medder, Jimmie," said the old man. "Don't you wish you owned one like him?"

"Um," said the boy, with a strange lack of interest. He continued his reflections. Then finally he ventured: "Grandpa—now—was that true what you was telling those men?"

"What?" asked the grandfather. "What was I telling them?"

"Oh, about your running."

"Why, yes, that was true enough, Jimmie. It was my first fight, and there was an awful lot of noise, you know."

Jimmie seemed dazed that this idol, of its own will, should so totter. His stout boyish idealism was injured.

Presently the grandfather said: "Sickles's colt is going for a drink. Don't you wish you owned Sickles's colt, Jimmie?"

The boy merely answered: "He ain't as nice as our'n." He lapsed then to another moody silence.

One of the hired men, a Swede, desired to drive to the

county seat for purposes of his own. The old man loaned a horse and an unwashed buggy. It appeared later that one of the purposes of the Swede was to get drunk.

After quelling some boisterous frolic of the farm-hands and boys in the garret, the old man had that night gone peacefully to sleep when he was aroused by clamoring at the kitchen door. He grabbed his trousers, and they waved out behind as he dashed forward. He could hear the voice of the Swede, screaming and blubbering. He pushed the wooden button, and, as the door flew open, the Swede, a maniac, stumbled inward, chattering, weeping, still screaming. "De barn fire! Fire! Fire! De barn fire! Fire! Fire! Fire!"

There was a swift and indescribable change in the old man. His face ceased instantly to be a face; it became a mask, a grey thing, with horror written about the mouth and eyes. He hoarsely shouted at the foot of the little rickety stairs, and immediately, it seemed, there came down an avalanche of men. No one knew that during this time the old lady had been standing in her night-clothes at the bed room door yelling: "What's th' matter? What's th' matter? What's th' matter?"

When they dashed toward the barn it presented to their eyes its usual appearance, solemn, rather mystic in the black night. The Swede's lantern was overturned at a point some yards in front of the barn doors. It contained a wild little conflagration of its own, and even in their excitement some of those who ran felt a gentle secondary vibration of the thrifty part of their minds at sight of this overturned lantern. Under ordinary circumstances it would have been a calamity.

But the cattle in the barn were trampling, trampling, trampling, and above this noise could be heard a humming like the song of innumerable bees. The old man hurled aside the great doors, and a yellow flame leaped out at one corner and sped and wavered frantically up the old grey wall. It was glad, terrible, this single flame, like the wild banner of deadly and triumphant foes.

The motley crowd from the garret had come with all the pails of the farm. They flung themselves upon the well. It was a leisurely old machine, long dwelling in indolence. It was in the habit of giving out water with a sort of reluctance. The men stormed at it, cursed it, but it continued to allow the buckets to be filled only after the wheezy windlass had howled many protests at the mad-handed men.

With his opened knife in his hand old Fleming himself had gone headlong into the barn, where the stifling smoke swirled with the air-currents, and where could be heard in its fulness the terrible chorus of the flames, laden with tones of hate and death, a hymn of wonderful ferocity.

He flung a blanket over an old mare's head, cut the halter close to the manger, led the mare to the door, and fairly kicked her out to safety. He returned with the same blanket and rescued one of the work-horses. He took five horses out, and then came out himself with his clothes bravely on fire. He had no whiskers, and very little hair on his head. They soused five pailfuls of water on him. His eldest son made a clean miss with the sixth pailful because the old man had turned and was running down the decline and around to the basement of the barn where were the stanchions of the cows. Some one noticed at the time that he ran very lamely, as if one of the frenzied horses had smashed his hip.

The cows, with their heads held in the heavy stanchions, had thrown themselves, strangled themselves, tangled themselves; done everything which the ingenuity of their exuberant fear could suggest to them.

Here as at the well the same thing happened to every man save one. Their hands went mad. They became incapable of everything save the power to rush into dangerous situations.

The old man released the cow nearest the door, and she, blind drunk with terror, crashed into the Swede. The Swede had been running to and fro babbling. He carried an empty milk-pail, to which he clung with an unconscious fierce enthusiasm. He shrieked like one lost as he went under the cow's hoofs, and the milk-pail, rolling across the floor, made a flash of silver in the gloom.

Old Fleming took a fork, beat off the cow, and dragged the paralyzed Swede to the open air. When they had rescued all the cows save one, which had so fastened herself that she could not be moved an inch, they returned to the front of the barn and stood sadly, breathing like men who had reached the final point of human effort.

Many people had come running. Someone had even gone to the church, and now, from the distance, rang the tocsin note of the old bell. There was a long flare of crimson on the sky which made remote people speculate as to the where-abouts of the fire.

The long flames sang their drumming chorus in voices of the heaviest bass. The wind whirled clouds of smoke and cin-ders into the faces of the spectators. The form of the old barn was outlined in black amid these masses of orange-hued flames.

And then came this Swede again, crying as one who is the weapon of the sinister fates. "De colts! De colts! You have forgot de colts!"

Old Fleming staggered. It was true; they had forgotten the two colts in the box-stalls at the back of the barn. "Boys," he said, "I must try to get 'em out." They clamored about him then, afraid for him, afraid of what they should see. Then they talked wildly each to each. "Why, it's sure death!" "He would never get out!" "Why, it's suicide for a man to go in there!" Old Fleming stared absent-mindedly at the open doors. "The poor little things," he said. He rushed into the barn.

When the roof fell in, a great funnel of smoke swarmed toward the sky, as if the old man's mighty spirit, released from its body—a little bottle—had swelled like the genie of fable. The smoke was tinted rose-hue from the flames, and perhaps the unutterable midnights of the universe will have no power to daunt the color of this soul.

An Episode of War

THE LIEUTENANT'S RUBBER BLANKET lay on the ground, and upon it he had poured the company's supply of coffee. Corporals and other representatives of the grimy and hot-throated men who lined the breastwork had come for each squad's portion.

The lieutenant was frowning and serious at this task of division. His lips pursed as he drew with his sword various crevices in the heap until brown squares of coffee, astoundingly equal in size, appeared on the blanket. He was on the verge of a great triumph in mathematics and the corporals were thronging forward, each to reap a little square, when suddenly the lieutenant cried out and looked quickly at a man near him as if he suspected it was a case of personal assault. The others cried out also when they saw blood upon the lieutenant's sleeve.

He had winced like a man stung, swayed dangerously, and then straightened. The sound of his hoarse breathing was plainly audible. He looked sadly, mystically, over the breastwork at the green face of a wood where now were many little puffs of white smoke. During this moment, the men about him gazed statue-like and silent, astonished and awed by this catastrophe which had happened when catastrophes were not expected—when they had leisure to observe it.

As the lieutenant stared at the wood, they too swung their heads so that for another moment all hands, still silent, contemplated the distant forest as if their minds were fixed upon the mystery of a bullet's journey.

The officer had, of course, been compelled to take his sword at once into his left hand. He did not hold it by the hilt. He gripped it at the middle of the blade, awkwardly. Turning his eyes from the hostile wood, he looked at the sword as he held it there, and seemed puzzled as to what to do with it, where to put it. In short this weapon had of a sudden become a strange thing to him. He looked at it in a kind of stupefaction, as if he had been miraculously endowed with a trident, a sceptre, or a spade.

Finally, he tried to sheath it. To sheath a sword held by the left hand, at the middle of the blade, in a scabbard hung at the left hip, is a feat worthy of a sawdust ring. This wounded officer engaged in a desperate struggle with the sword and the wobbling scabbard, and during the time of it, he breathed like a wrestler.

But at this instant the men, the spectators, awoke from their stone-like poses and crowded forward sympathetically. The orderly-sergeant took the sword and tenderly placed it in the scabbard. At the time, he leaned nervously backward, and did not allow even his finger to brush the body of the lieutenant. A wound gives strange dignity to him who bears it. Well men shy from this new and terrible majesty. It is as if the wounded man's hand is upon the curtain which hangs before the revelations of all existence, the meaning of ants, potentates, wars, cities, sunshine, snow, a feather dropped from a bird's wing, and the power of it sheds radiance upon a bloody form, and makes the other men understand sometimes that they are little. His comrades look at him with large eyes thoughtfully. Moreover, they fear vaguely that the weight of a finger upon him might send him headlong, precipitate the tragedy, hurl him at once into the dim grey unknown. And so the orderly-sergeant while sheathing the sword leaned nervously backward.

There were others who proffered assistance. One timidly presented his shoulder and asked the lieutenant if he cared to lean upon it, but the latter waved them away mournfully. He wore the look of one who knows he is the victim of a terrible disease and understands his helplessness. He again stared over the breastwork at the forest, and then turning went slowly rearward. He held his right wrist tenderly in his left hand, as if the wounded arm was made of very brittle glass.

And the men in silence stared at the wood, then at the departing lieutenant—then at the wood, then at the lieutenant.

As the wounded officer passed from the line of battle, he was enabled to see many things which as a participant in the fight were unknown to him. He saw a general on a black horse gazing over the lines of blue infantry at the green woods which veiled his problems. An aide galloped furiously, dragged his horse suddenly to a halt, saluted, and presented a paper. It was, for a wonder, precisely like an historical painting.

To the rear of the general and his staff, a group, composed of a bugler, two or three orderlies, and the bearer of the corps standard, all upon maniacal horses, were working like slaves to hold their ground, preserve their respectful interval, while the shells bloomed in the air about them, and caused their chargers to make furious quivering leaps.

A battery, a tumultuous and shining mass, was swirling toward the right. The wild thud of hoofs, the cries of the riders shouting blame and praise, menace and encouragement, and, last, the roar of the wheels, the slant of the glistening guns, brought the lieutenant to an intent pause. The battery swept in curves that stirred the heart; it made halts as dramatic as the crash of a wave on the rocks, and when it fled onward, this aggregation of wheels, levers, motors, had a beautiful unity, as if it were a missile. The sound of it was a war-chorus that reached into the depths of man's emotion.

The lieutenant, still holding his arm as if it were of glass, stood watching this battery until all detail of it was lost, save the figures of the riders, which rose and fell and waved lashes over the black mass.

Later he turned his eyes toward the battle where the shooting sometimes crackled like bush-fires, sometimes sputtered with exasperating irregularity, and sometimes reverberated like the thunder. He saw the smoke rolling upward and saw crowds of men who ran and cheered, or stood and blazed away at the inscrutable distance.

He came upon some stragglers and they told him how to find the field hospital. They described its exact location. In fact these men, no longer having part in the battle, knew more of it than others. They told the performance of every corps, every division, the opinion of every general. The lieutenant, carrying his wounded arm rearward, looked upon them with wonder.

At the roadside a brigade was making coffee and buzzing with talk like a girls' boarding-school. Several officers came out to him and inquired concerning things of which he knew nothing. One, seeing his arm, began to scold. "Why, man, that's no way to do. You want to fix that thing." He appropriated the lieutenant and the lieutenant's wound. He cut the sleeve and laid bare the arm, every nerve of which softly fluttered under his touch. He bound his handkerchief over the wound, scolding away in the meantime. His tone allowed one to think that he was in the habit of being wounded every day. The lieutenant hung his head, feeling, in this presence, that he did not know how to be correctly wounded.

The low white tents of the hospital were grouped around an old school-house. There was here a singular commotion. In the foreground two ambulances interlocked wheels in the deep mud. The drivers were tossing the blame of it back and forth, gesticulating and berating, while from the ambulances, both crammed with wounded, there came an occasional groan. An interminable crowd of bandaged men were coming and going. Great numbers sat under the trees nursing heads or arms or legs. There was a dispute of some kind raging on the steps of the school-house. Sitting with his back against a tree a man with a face as grey as a new army blanket was serenely smoking a corn-cob pipe. The lieutenant wished to rush forward and inform him that he was dying.

A busy surgeon was passing near the lieutenant. "Good morning," he said with a friendly smile. Then he caught sight of the lieutenant's arm and his face at once changed. "Well, let's have a look at it." He seemed possessed suddenly of a great contempt for the lieutenant. This wound evidently placed the latter on a very low social plane. The doctor cried out impatiently. What mutton-head had tied it up that way anyhow. The lieutenant answered: "Oh, a man."

When the wound was disclosed the doctor fingered it disdainfully. "Humph," he said. "You come along with me and I'll 'tend to you." His voice contained the same scorn as if he were saying: "You will have to go to jail."

The lieutenant had been very meek but now his face flushed, and he looked into the doctor's eyes. "I guess I won't have it amputated," he said.

"Nonsense, man! nonsense! nonsense!" cried the doctor. "Come along, now. I won't amputate it. Come along. Don't be a baby."

"Let go of me," said the lieutenant, holding back wrathfully. His glance fixed upon the door of the old school-house, as sinister to him as the portals of death.

And this is the story of how the lieutenant lost his arm. When he reached home his sisters, his mother, his wife, sobbed for a long time at the sight of the flat sleeve. "Oh, well," he said, standing shamefaced amid these tears, "I don't suppose it matters so much as all that."

THE WEST AND MEXICO

Contents

An Excursion Ticket

B ILLIE ATKINS is a traveler. He has seen the cold blue
gleam of the Northern lakes, the tangled green thickets
of Florida and the white peaks of the Rockies. All this has he
seen and much more, for he has been a tramp for sixteen
years.

One winter evening when the "sitting room" of a lodging
house just off the Bowery was thronged with loungers Billie
came in, mellow with drink and in the eloquent stage. He
chose to charm them with a description of a journey from
Denver to Omaha. They all listened with appreciation, for
when Billie is quite drunk he tells a tale with indescribable
gestures and humorous emotions that makes one feel that,
after all, the buffets of fate are rather more comic than other-
wise.

It seems that when Billie was in Denver last winter it sud-
denly occurred to him that he wished to be in Omaha. He
did not deem it necessary to explain this fancy: he merely
announced that he happened to be in Denver last winter and
that then it occurred to him that he wished to be in Omaha.
Apparently these ideas come to his class like bolts of compel-
ling lightning. After that swift thought, it was impossible for
Denver to contain him; he must away to Omaha. When the
night express on the Union Pacific pulled out Billie "made a
great sneak" behind some freight cars and climbed onto the
"blind" end of the baggage car.

It was a very dark night and Billie congratulated himself
that he had not been discovered. He huddled to a little heap
on the car platform and thought, with a woman's longing, of
Omaha.

However, it was not long before an icy stream of water
struck Billie a startling blow in the face, and as he raised his
eyes he saw in the red glare from the engine a very jocular
fireman crouching on the coal and holding the nozzle of a
small hose in his hand. And at frequent intervals during the
night this jocular fireman would climb up on the coal and
play the hose on Billie. The drenched tramp changed his po-

sition and curled himself up into a little ball and swore graphically, all to no purpose. The fireman persisted with his hose and when he thought that Billie was getting too comfortable he came back to the rear of the tender and doused him with a pailful of very cold water.

But Billie stuck to his position. For one reason, the express went too fast for him to get safely off, and for another reason he wished to go to Omaha.

The train rushed into the cold gray of dawn on the prairies. The biting chill of the morning made Billie shake in his wet clothes. He adjusted himself on the edge of the rocking car platform where he could catch the first rays of the sun. And it was this change of position that got him into certain difficulties. At about eight o'clock the express went roaring through a little village. Billie, sunning himself on the edge of the steps, espied three old farmers seated on the porch of the village store. They grinned at him and waved their arms.

"I taut they was jest givin' me er jolly," said Billie, "so I waved me hand at 'em an' gives 'em er laugh, an' th' train went on. But it turned out they wasn't motionin' t' me at all, but was all th' while givin' er tip t' th' brakey that I was on th' blind. An' 'fore I knew it th' brakey came over th' top, or aroun' th' side, or somehow, an' I was a-gittin' kicked in th' neck.

" 'Gitoffahere! gitoffahere!'

"I was dead escared b'cause th' train was goin' hell bentin'.

" 'Gitoffahere! gitoffahere!'

" 'Oh, please, mister,' I sez, 'I can't git off—th' train's goin' too fast.'

"But he kept on kickin' me fer a while til finally he got tired an' stopped th' train b'cause I could a-never got off th' way she was runnin'. By this time th' passengers in all th' cars got onto it that they was puttin' er bum off th' blind, an' when I got down off th' step, I see every winder in th' train was fuller heads, an' they gimme er great laugh until I had t' turn me back an' walk off."

As it happened, the nearest station to where Billie then found himself was eighteen miles distant. He dried his clothes as best he could and then swore along the tracks for a mile or two. But it was weary business—tramping along in the vast vacancy of the plains. Billie got tired and lay down to wait for a freight train. After a time one came and as the long string of boxcars thundered past him, he made another "great sneak" and a carefully calculated run and grab. He got safely on the little step and then he began to do what he called "ridin' th' ladder." That is to say, he clung to the little iron ladder that is fastened to the end of each car. He remained hanging there while the long train crept slowly over the plains.

He did not dare to show himself above the top of the car for fear of the brakeman. He considered himself safe down between the ends of the jolting cars, but once, as he chanced to look toward the sky, he saw a burly brakeman leaning on the brakewheel and regarding him.

"Come up here," said the brakeman.

Billie climbed painfully to the top of the car.

"Got any money?" said the brakeman.

"No," replied Billie.

"Well, then, gitoffahere," said the brakeman, and Billie received another installment of kicks. He went down the ladder and puckered his mouth and drew in his breath, preparatory to getting off the car, but the train had arrived at a small grade and Billie became frightened. The little wheels were all a-humming and the cars lurched like boats on the sea.

"Oh, please, mister," said Billie, "I can't git off. It's a-goin' too fast."

The brakeman swore and began the interesting operation of treading, with his brass toed boots, on Billie's fingers. Billie hung hard. He cast glances of despair at the rapid fleeting ground and shifted his grip often. But presently the brakeman's heels came down with extraordinary force and Billie involuntarily released his hold.

He fell in a heap and rolled over and over. His face and body were scratched and bruised, and on the top of his head there was a contusion that fitted like a new derby. His clothes had been rags, but they were now exaggerated out of all semblance of clothes. He sat up and looked at the departing train. "Gawd-dernit," he said, "I'll never git t' Omaha at this rate."

Presently Billie developed a most superhuman hunger. He saw the houses of a village some distance away, and he made for them, resolved to have something to eat if it cost a life. But still he knew he would be arrested if he appeared on the streets of any well organized, respectable town in the trousers he was then obliged to wear. He was in a quandary until by good fortune he perceived a pair of brown overalls hanging on a line in the rear of an isolated house.

He "made a great sneak on 'em." This sort of thing requires patience, but not more than an hour later, he bore off a large square of cloth which he had torn from one leg of the overalls. At another house he knocked at the door and when a woman came he stood very carefully facing her and requested a needle and thread. She gave them to him, and he waited until she had shut the door before he turned and went away.

He retired then into a thick growing patch of sunflowers on the outskirts of the town and started in to sew the piece of overall to his trousers. He had not been engaged long at his task before "two hundred kids" accumulated in front of the sunflower patch and began to throw stones at him. For some time the sky was darkened by a shower of missiles of all sizes. Occasionally Billie, without his trousers, would make little forays, yelling savage threats. These would compel the boys to retire some distance, but they always returned again with renewed ardor. Billie thought he would never get his trousers mended.

But this adventure was the cause of his again meeting Black John Randolph, who Billie said was "th' whitest pardner" he ever had. While he was engaged in conflict with the horde of boys a negro came running down the road and began to belabor them with a boot blacking kit. The boys ran off, and Billie saw with delight that his rescuer was Black John Randolph, whom he had known in Memphis.

Billie, unmolested, sewed his trousers. Then he told Black John that he was hungry, and the two swooped down on the town. Black John shined shoes until dark. He shined for all the available citizens of the place. Billie stood around and watched. The earnings were sixty cents. They spent it all for gingerbread, for it seems that Billie had developed a sudden marvelous longing for gingerbread.

Having feasted, Billie decided to make another attempt for Omaha. He and Black John went to the railroad yard and there they discovered an east-bound freight car that was empty save for one tramp and seven cans of peaches. They parleyed with the tramp and induced him to give up his claim on two-thirds of the car. They settled very comfortably, and that night Billie was again on his way to Omaha. The three of them lived for twenty-four hours on canned peaches, and would have been happy ever after no doubt if it had not happened that their freight car was presently switched off to a side line, and sent careering off in the wrong direction.

When Billie discovered this he gave a whoop and fell out of the car, for he was very particular about walking, and he did not wish to be dragged far from the main line. He trudged back to it, and there discovered a lumber car that contained about forty tramps.

This force managed to overawe the trainmen for a time and compel a free ride for a few miles, but presently the engine was stopped, and the trainmen formed in war array and advanced with clubs.

Billie had had experience in such matters. He "made a sneak." He repaired to a coal car and cuddled among the coal. He buried his body completely, and of his head only his nose and his eyes could have been seen.

The trainmen spread the tramps out over the prairie in a wide fleeing circle, as when a stone is hurled into a placid creek. They remained cursing in their beards, and the train went on.

Billie, snug in his bed, smiled without disarranging the coal that covered his mouth, and thought of Omaha.

But in an hour or two he got impatient, and upreared his head to look at the scenery. An eagle eyed brakeman espied him.

"Got any money?"

"No."

"Well, then, gitoffahere."

Billie got off. The brakeman continued to throw coal at him until the train had hauled him beyond range.

"Hully mack'rel," said Billie, "I'll never git t' Omaha."

He was quite discouraged. He lay down on a bank beside the track to think, and while there he went to sleep. When he awoke a freight train was thundering past him. Still half asleep, he made a dash and a grab. He was up the ladder and on top of the car before he had recovered all of his faculties. A brakeman charged on him.

"Got any money?"

"No, but, please, mister, won't yeh please let me stay on yer train fer a little ways? I'm awful tired, an' I wanta git t' Omaha."

The brakeman reflected. Then he searched Billie's pockets, and finding half a plug of tobacco, took possession of it. He decided to let Billie ride for a time.

Billie perched on top of the car and admired the changing scenery while the train went twenty miles. Then the brakeman induced him to get off, considering no doubt that a twenty mile ride was sufficient in exchange for a half plug of tobacco.

The rest of the trip is incoherent, like the detailed accounts of great battles. Billie boarded trains and got thrown off on his head, on his left shoulder, on his right shoulder, on his hands and knees. He struck the ground slanting, straight from above and full sideways. His clothes were shredded and torn like the sails of a gale blown brig. His skin was tattooed with bloody lines, crosses, triangles, and all the devices known to geometry. But he wouldn't walk, and he was bound to reach Omaha. So he let the trainmen use him as a projectile with which to bombard the picturesque Western landscape.

And eventually he reached Omaha. One night, when it was snowing and cold winds whistled among the city's chimneys, he arrived in a coal car. He was filled with glee that he had reached the place of his endeavor. He could not repress his pride when he thought of the conquered miles. He went forth from the coal car with a blithe step.

The police would not let him stand on a corner nor sit down anywhere. They drove him about for two or three hours, until he happened to think of the railroad station. He went there, and was just getting into a nice doze by the warm red stove in the waiting room, when an official of some kind took him by the collar, and leading him calmly to the door, kicked him out into the snow. After that he was ejected from four saloons in rapid succession.

"Hully mack'rel!" he said, as he stood in the snow and quavered and trembled.

Until three o'clock in the morning various industrious policemen kept him moving from place to place as if he were pawn in a game of chess, until finally Billie became desperate and approached an officer in this fashion:

"Say, mister, won't yeh please arrest me? I wanta go t' jail so's I kin sleep."

"What?"

"I say, won't yer please arrest me? I wanta go to t' jail so's I kin sleep."

The policeman studied Billie for a moment. Then he made an impatient gesture.

"Oh, can't yeh arrest yerself? The jail's a long ways from here, an' I don't wanta take yeh way up there."

"Sure—I kin," said Billie. "Where is it?"

The policeman gave him directions, and Billie started for the jail.

He had considerable difficulty in finding it. He was often obliged to accost people in the street.

"Please, mister, can yeh tell me where the jail is?"

At last he found it, and after a short parley, they admitted him. They gave him permission to sleep on a sort of an iron slab swung by four chains from the ceiling. Billie sank down upon this couch and arrayed his meager rags about his form. Before he was completely in the arms of the slumber god, however, he made a remark expressive of a new desire, a sudden born longing. "Hully mack'rel. I mus' start back fer Denver in th' mornin'."

Nebraska's Bitter Fight for Life

EDDYVILLE, DAWSON CO., NEB., Feb. 22.—The vast prairies in this section of Nebraska contain a people who are engaged in a bitter and deadly fight for existence. Some of the reports telegraphed to the East have made it appear that the entire State of Nebraska is a desert. In reality the situation is serious, but it does not include the whole State. However, people feel that thirty counties in pain and destitution is sufficient.

The blot that is laid upon the map of the State begins in the north beyond Custer county. It is there about fifty miles wide. It slowly widens then in a southward direction until when it crosses the Platte River it is over a hundred miles wide. The country to the north and to the west of this blot is one of the finest grazing grounds in the world and the cattlemen there are not suffering. Valentine is in this portion which is exempt. To the eastward, the blot shades off until one finds moderate crops.

In June, 1894, the bounteous prolific prairies of this portion of Nebraska were a-shine with the young and tender green of growing corn. Round and fat cattle filled the barnyards of the farmers. The trees that were congregated about the little homesteads were of the vivid and brave hue of healthy and vigorous vegetation. The towns were alive with the commerce of an industrious and hopeful community. These mighty brown fields stretching for miles under the imperial blue sky of Nebraska had made a promise to the farmer. It was to compensate him for his great labor, his patience, his sacrifices. Under the cool, blue dome the winds gently rustled the arrays of waist-high stalks.

Then, on one day about the first of July there came a menace from the southward. The sun had been growing prophetically more fierce day by day, and in July there began these winds from the south, mild at first and subtle like the breaths of the panting countries of the tropics. The corn in the fields underwent a preliminary quiver from this breeze burdened with an omen of death. In the following days it

688

became stronger, more threatening. The farmers turned anxious eyes toward their fields where the corn was beginning to rustle with a dry and crackling sound which went up from the prairie like cries.

Then from the southern horizon came the scream of a wind hot as an oven's fury. Its valor was great in the presence of the sun. It came when the burning disc appeared in the east and it weakened when the blood-red, molten mass vanished in the west. From day to day, it raged like a pestilence. The leaves of the corn and of the trees turned yellow and sapless like leather. For a time they stood the blasts in the agony of a futile resistance. The farmers helpless, with no weapon against this terrible and inscrutable wrath of nature, were spectators at the strangling of their hopes, their ambitions, all that they could look to from their labor. It was as if upon the massive altar of the earth, their homes and their families were being offered in sacrifice to the wrath of some blind and pitiless deity.

The country died. In the rage of the wind, the trees struggled, gasped through each curled and scorched leaf, then, at last, ceased to exist, and there remained only the bowed and bare skeletons of trees. The corn shivering as from fever, bent and swayed abjectly for a time, then one by one the yellow and tinder-like stalks, twisted and pulled by the rage of the hot breath, died in the fields and the vast and sometimes beautiful green prairies were brown and naked.

In a few weeks this prosperous and garden-like country was brought to a condition of despair, but still this furnace-wind swept along the dead land, whirling great clouds of dust, straws, blades of grass. A farmer, gazing from a window was confronted by a swirling tempest of dust that intervened between his vision and his scorched fields. The soil of the roads turned to powder in this tempest, and men traveling against the winds found all the difficulties of some hideous and unnatural snow storm. At nightfall the winds always vanished and the sky which had glistened like a steel shield became of a soft blue, as the purple shadows of a merciful night advanced from the west.

These farmers now found themselves existing in a virtual desert. The earth from which they had wrested each morsel which they had put into their mouths had now abandoned them. Nature made light of her obligation under the toil of these men. This vast tract was now a fit place for the nomads of Sahara.

And yet, for the most part, there was no wavering, no absence of faith in the ultimate success of the beautiful soil. Some few despaired at once and went to make new homes in the north, in the south, in the east, in the west. But the greater proportion of the people of this stricken district were men who loved their homes, their farms, their neighborhoods, their counties. They had become rooted in this soil, which so seldom failed them in compensation for their untiring and persistent toil. They could not move all the complexities of their social life and their laboring life. The magic of home held them from traveling toward the promise of other lands. And upon these people there came the weight of the strange and unspeakable punishment of nature. They are a fearless folk, completely American. Their absolute types are now sitting about New England dinner tables. They summoned their strength for a long war with cold and hunger. Prosperity was at the distance of a new crop of 1895. It was to be from August to August. Between these months loomed the great white barrier of the winter of 1894–95. It was a supreme battle to which to look forward. It required the profound and dogged courage of the American peoples who have come into the West to carve farms, railroads, towns, cities, in the heart of a world fortified by enormous distances.

The weakest were, of course, the first to cry out at the pain of it. Farmers, morally certain of the success of the crop, had already gone into debt for groceries and supplies. The hot winds left these men without crops and without credit. They were instantly confronted with want. They stood for a time reluctant. Then family by family they drove away to other States where there might be people who would give their great muscular hands opportunity to earn food for their wives and little children.

Then came the struggle of the ones who stood fast. They were soon driven to bay by nature, now the pitiless enemy. They were sturdy and dauntless. When the cry for help came from their lips it was to be the groan from between the clenched teeth. Men began to offer to work at the rate of twenty-five cents a day, but, presently, in the towns no one had work for them, and, after a time, barely anyone had twenty-five cents a day which they dared invest in labor. Life in the little towns halted. The wide roads, which had once been so busy, became the dry veins of the dead land.

Meanwhile, the chill and tempest of the inevitable winter had gathered in the north and swept down upon the devastated country. The prairies turned bleak and desolate.

The wind was a direct counter-part of the summer. It came down like wolves of ice. And then was the time that from this district came that first wail, half impotent rage, half despair. The men went to feed the starving cattle in their tiny allowances in clothes that enabled the wind to turn their bodies red and then blue with cold. The women shivered in the houses where fuel was as scarce as flour, and where flour was sometimes as scarce as diamonds.

The cry for aid was heard everywhere. The people of a dozen States responded in a lavish way and almost at once. A relief commission was appointed by Governor Holcomb at Lincoln to receive the supplies and distribute them to the people in want. The railroad companies granted transportation to the cars that came in loaded with coal and flour from Iowa and Minnesota, fruit from California, groceries and clothing from New York and Ohio, and almost everything possible from Georgia and Louisiana. The relief commission became involved in a mighty tangle. It was obliged to contend with enormous difficulties.

Sometimes a car arrives in Lincoln practically in pawn. It has accumulated the freight charges of perhaps half a dozen railroads. The commission then corresponds and corresponds with railroads to get the charges remitted. It is usually the fault of the people sending the car who can arrange for free and quick transportation by telegraphing the commission in Lincoln a list of what their car, or cars, contain. The commission will then arrange all transportation.

A facetious freight agent in the East labelled one carload of food: "Outfit for emigrants." This car reached the people who needed it only after the most extraordinary delays and after many mistakes and explanations and re-explanations. Meanwhile, a certain minority began to make war upon the commission at the expense of the honest and needy majority. Men resorted to all manner of tricks in order to seduce the commission into giving them supplies which they did not need. Also various unscrupulous persons received donations of provisions from the East and then sold them to the people at a very low rate it is true, but certainly at the most obvious of profits. The commission detected one man selling a donated carload of coal at the price of forty cents per ton. They discovered another man who had collected some two thousand dollars from charitable folk in other States, and of this sum he really gave to the people about eight hundred dollars. The commission was obliged to make long wars upon all these men who wished to practice upon the misery of the farmers.

As is mentioned above, this stricken district does not include in any manner the entire State of Nebraska, but, nevertheless, certain counties that are not in the drought portion had no apparent hesitation about vociferously shouting for relief. When the State Legislature appropriated one hundred and fifty thousand dollars to help the starving districts, one or two counties in the east at once sent delegations to the capital to apply for a part of it. They said, ingenuously, that it was the State's money and they wanted their share of it.

To one town in the northern part of the State there was sent from the East a carload of coal. The citizens simply apportioned it on the basis of so much per capita. They appointed a committee to transport the coal from the car to each man's residence. It was the fortune of this committee finally to get into the office of a citizen who was fairly prosperous.

"Where do yeh want yer coal put?" they said, with a clever and sly wink.

"What coal?"

"Why, our coal! Your coal! The coal what was sent here."

"Git out 'a here! If you put any coal in my cellar I'll kill some of yeh."

They argued for a long time. They did not dare to leave anyone out of the conspiracy. He could then tell of it. Having failed with him, they went to his wife and tried to get her to allow them to put the coal in the cellar. In this also they were not successful.

These are a part of the difficulties with which the commission fights. Its obligation is to direct all supplies from the generous and pitying inhabitants of other States into the correct paths to reach the suffering. To do this over a territory covering many hundreds of square miles, and which is but meagrely connected by railroads, is not an easy task.

L. P. Ludden, the secretary and general manager of the commission, works early and late and always. In his office at Lincoln he can be seen at any time when people are usually awake working over the correspondence of the bureau. He is confronted each mail by a heap of letters that is as high as a warehouse. He told the writer of this article that he had not seen his children for three weeks, save when they were asleep. He always looked into their room when he arrived home late at night and always before he left early in the morning.

But he is the most unpopular man in the State of Nebraska. He is honest, conscientious and loyal; he is hard-working and has great executive ability. He struggles heroically with the thugs who wish to filch supplies, and with the virtuous but misguided philanthropists who write to learn of the folks that received their fifty cents and who expect a full record of this event.

From a hundred towns whose citizens are in despair for their families, arises a cry against Ludden. From a hundred towns whose citizens do not need relief and in consequence do not get it, there arises a cry against Ludden. The little newspapers print the uncompromising sentence: "Ludden must go!" Delegations call upon the governor and tell him that the situation would be mitigated if they could only have relief from Ludden. Members of the legislature prodded by their rural constituents, arise and demand an explanation of the presence in office of Ludden. And yet this man with the square jaw and the straight set lips hangs on in the indomitable manner of a man of the soil. He remains in front of the tales concerning him; merely turns them into his bureau and an explanation comes out by the regular machinery of his system, to which he has imparted his personal quality of inevitableness. Once, grown tired of the abuse, he asked of the

governor leave to resign, but the governor said that it would
be impossible now to appoint a new man without some great
and disastrous halt of the machinery. Ludden returned to his
post and to the abuse.

But in this vast area of desolated land there has been no
benefit derived from the intrigues and scufflings at Lincoln
which is two hundred miles away from the scene of the suf-
fering. This town of Eddyville is in the heart of the stricken
territory. The thermometer at this time registers eighteen de-
grees below zero. The temperature of the room which is the
writer's bedchamber is precisely one and a half degrees below
zero. Over the wide white expanses of prairie, the icy winds
from the north shriek, whirling high sheets of snow and en-
veloping the house in white clouds of it. The tempest forces
fine stinging flakes between the rattling sashes of the window
that fronts the storm. The air has remained gloomy the entire
day. From other windows can be seen the snowflakes fleeing
into the south, traversing as level a line as bullets, speeding
like the wind. The people in the sod houses are much more
comfortable than those who live in frame dwellings. Many of
these latter are high upon ridges of the prairie and the fingers
of the storm clutch madly at them. The sod houses huddle
close to the ground and their thick walls restrain the heat of
the scant wood-fire from escaping.

Eddyville is a typical town of the drought district. Ap-
proaching it over the prairie, one sees a row of little houses,
blocked upon the sky. Most of them are one storied. Some of
the stores have little square false-fronts. The buildings strag-
gle at irregular intervals along the street and a little board
sidewalk connects them. On all sides stretches the wind-swept
prairie.

This town was once a live little place. From behind the low
hillocks, the farmers came jogging behind their sturdy teams.
The keepers of the three or four stores did a thriving trade.
But at this time the village lies as inanimate as a corpse. In
the rears of the stores, a few men perhaps, sit listlessly by the
stoves. The people of the farms remain close in-doors during
this storm. They have not enough warm clothing to venture
into the terrible blasts. One can drive past house after house
without seeing signs of life unless it be a weak curl of smoke

scudding away from a chimney. Occasionally, too, one finds a deserted homestead, a desolate and unhappy thing upon the desolate and unhappy prairie.

And for miles around this town lie the countless acres of the drought-pestered district.

Some distance from here a man was obliged to leave his wife and baby and go into the eastern part of the State to make a frenzied search for work that might be capable of furnishing them with food. The woman lived alone with her baby until the provisions were gone. She had received a despairing letter from her husband. He was still unable to get work. Everybody was searching for it; none had it to give. Meanwhile he had ventured a prodigious distance from home.

The nearest neighbor was three miles away. She put her baby in its little ramshackle carriage and traveled the three miles. The family there shared with her as long as they could—two or three days. Then she went on to the next house. There, too, with the quality of mercy which comes with incredible suffering, they shared with her. From house to house she went pushing her baby-carriage. She received a meal here, three meals here, a meal and a bed here. The baby was a weak and puny child.

During this swirling storm, the horses huddle abjectly and stolidly in the fields, their backs humped and turned toward the eye of the wind, their heads near the ground, their manes blowing over their eyes. Ice crusts their soft noses. The writer asked a farmer this morning: "How will your horses get through the winter?"

"I don't know," he replied, calmly. "I ain't got nothing to give 'em. I got to turn 'em out and let 'em russle for theirselves. Of course if they get enough to live on, all right, an' if they don't they'll have to starve."

"And suppose there are a few more big storms like this one?"

"Well, I don't suppose there'll be a horse left round here by ploughin' time then. The people ain't got nothin' to feed 'em upon in the spring. A horse'll russle for himself in the snow, an' then when th' spring rains comes, he'll go all to pieces unless he gets good nursin' and feedin'. But we won't have nothin' to give 'em."

Horses are, as a usual thing, cheaper in this country than good saddles, but at this time, there is a fair proportion of men who would willingly give away their favorite horses if they could thus insure the animals warm barns and plenty of feed.

But the people cannot afford to think now of these minor affections of their hearts.

The writer rode forty-five miles through the country, recently. The air turned the driver a dark shade, until he resembled some kind of a purple Indian from Brazil, and the team became completely coated with snow and ice, as if their little brown bodies were in quaint ulsters. They became dull and stupid in the storm. Under the driver's flogging they barely stirred, holding their heads dejectedly, with an expression of unutterable patient weariness. Six men were met upon the road. They strode along silently with patches of ice upon their beards. The fields were for the most part swept bare of snow, and there appeared then the short stumps of the corn, where the hot winds of the summer had gnawed the stalks away.

Yet this is not in any sense a type of a Nebraska storm. It is phenomenal. It is typical only of the misfortunes of this part of the State. It is commensurate with other things, that this tempest should come at precisely the time when it will be remarkable if certain of the people endure it.

Eddyville received a consignment of aid recently. There were eighty sacks of flour and a dozen boxes of clothing. For miles about the little village the farmers came with their old wagons and their ill-fed horses. Some of them blushed when they went before the local committee to sign their names and get the charity. They were strong, fine, sturdy men, not bended like the Eastern farmer but erect and agile. Their faces occasionally expressed the subtle inner tragedy which relief of food and clothing at this time can do but little to lighten. The street was again lively, but there was an elemental mournfulness in the little crowd. They spoke of the weather a great deal.

Two days afterward the building where the remainder of the relief stores had been put away, burned to the ground.

A farmer in Lincoln county recently said: "No, I didn't get no aid. I hadter drive twenty-five miles t' git my flour, an' then drive back agin an' I didn't think th' team would stand it, they been poor-fed so long. Besides I'd hadter put up a dollar to keep th' team over night an' I didn't have none. I hain't had no aid!"

"How did you get along?"

"Don't git along, stranger. Who the hell told you I did get along?"

In the meantime, the business men in the eastern part of the State, particularly in the splendid cities of Omaha and Lincoln, are beginning to feel the great depression resulting from extraordinary accounts which have plastered the entire State as a place of woe. Visitors to the country have looked from car-windows to see the famine-stricken bodies of the farmers lying in the fields and have trod lightly in the streets of Omaha to keep from crushing the bodies of babes. But the point should be emphasized that the grievous condition is confined to a comparatively narrow section of the western part of the State.

Governor Holcomb said to the writer: "It is true that there is much misery in the State, but there is not the universal privation which has been declared. Crop failure was unknown until 1890 when the farmers lost much of their labor, but at that time, and in 1893, when a partial loss was experienced, the eastern half of the State was able to take care of the western half where the failure was pronounced.

"This year has been so complete a failure as to reduce many to extreme poverty, but I do not think that there are more than twenty per cent at present in need. Great irrigation enterprises that are now being inaugurated will, no doubt, eliminate the cause of failure in large districts of the western part of the State. The grain that is produced and stock that is raised in this State put it in the front rank of the great agricultural commonwealths. I have no doubt that in a year or two her barns will be overflowing. I see nothing in the present situation nor in the history of the State as I have observed it for sixteen years that ought to discourage those who contemplate coming here to make homes. In the western part of the State, a vast amount of unwise speculation has caused great losses, but that part of the country cannot be excelled for grazing, and irrigation will, no doubt, render it safe and profitable for agriculture. In the greater part of the State, the people are suffering no more than a large percentage of the agricultural districts of other States. It has been brought about as much by the general national depression as by local causes."

It is probable that a few years will see the farms in the great Platte River valley watered by irrigation, but districts that have not an affluence of water will depend upon wind-mills. The wells in this State never fail during a drought. They furnish an abundance of cool and good water. Some farmers plan to build little storage reservoirs upon the hillocks of the prairie. They are made by simply throwing up banks of earth, and then allowing cattle to trample the interiors until a hard and water-tight bottom is formed. In this manner a farmer will be in a degree independent of the most terrible droughts.

Taking the years in groups of five the rainfall was at its lowest from 1885 to 1890 when the general average was 22.34 inches. The general average for 1891, 1892 and 1893 was 23.85 inches. But 1894 now enters the contest with a record of but 13.10 inches. People are now shouting that Nebraska is to become arid. In past years when rainfalls were enormous they shouted that Nebraska was to become a great pond.

The final quality of these farmers who have remained in this portion of the State is their faith in the ultimate victory of the land and their industry. They have a determination to wait until nature, with her mystic processes, restores to them the prosperity and bounty of former years. "If a man stays right by this country, he'll come out all right in the end."

Almost any man in the district will cease speaking of his woes to recite the beauties of the times when the great rolling prairies are green and golden with the splendor of young corn, the streams are silver in the light of the sun, and when from the wide roads and the little homesteads there arises the soundless essence of a hymn from the happy and prosperous people.

But then there now is looming the eventual catastrophe that would surely depopulate the country. These besieged farmers are battling with their condition with an eye to the rest and success of next August. But if they can procure no money with which to buy seed when spring comes around, the calamity that ensues is an eternal one, as far as they and their farms here are concerned. They have no resort then but to load their families in wagons behind their hungry horses and set out to conquer these great distances, which like walls shut them from the charitable care of other and more fortunate communities.

In the meantime, they depend upon their endurance, their capacity to help each other, and their steadfast and unyielding courage.

Seen at Hot Springs

HOT SPRINGS, ARK., March 3.—This town arises to defeat a certain favorite theory of all truly great philosophers. They have long ago proven that spring is the time when human emotion emerges from a covering of cynical darkness and becomes at once blithe and true. They have decided that the great green outburst of nature in the spring is essential to the senses before that mighty forgetfulness, that vast irresponsibility of feeling can come upon a man and allow him to enjoy himself.

The Hot Springs crowd, however, display this exuberance in the dead of winter. It has precisely the same quality as the gaiety of the Atlantic Coast resorts in the dead of summer. There is then proven that the human emotions are not at all guided by the calendar. It is merely a question of latitude. The other theory would confine a man to only one wild exuberant outbreak of feeling per year. It was invented in England.

As soon as the train reaches the great pine belt of Arkansas one becomes aware of the intoxication in the resinous air. It is heavy, fragrant with the odor from the vast pine tracts and its subtle influence contains a prophecy of the spirit of the little city afar in the hills. Tawny roads, the soil precisely the hue of a lion's mane, wander through the groves. Nearer the town a stream of water that looks like a million glasses of lemon phosphate brawls over the rocks.

And then at last, at the railway station, comes that incoherent mass of stage drivers and baggagemen which badgers all resorts, roaring and gesticulating, as unintelligible always as a row of Homeric experts, while behind them upon the sky are painted the calm turrets of the innumerable hotels and, still further back, the green ridges and peaks of the hills. Not all travellers venture to storm that typical array of hackmen; some make a slinking detour and, coming out suddenly from behind the station, sail away with an air of half relief, half guilt. At any rate, the stranger must circumnavigate these howling dervishes before he can gain his first glance of the vivid yellow sun-light, the green groves and the buildings of the springs.

When a man decides that he has seen the whole of the town he has only seen half of it. The other section is behind a great hill that with imperial insolence projects into the valley. The main street was once the bed of a mountain stream. It winds persistently around the base of this hill until it succeeds in joining the two sections. The dispossessed river now flows through a tunnel. Electric cars with whirring and clanging noises bowl along with modern indifference upon this grave of a torrent of the hills.

The motive of this main street is purely cosmopolitan. It undoubtedly typifies the United States better than does any existing thoroughfare, for it resembles the North and the South, the East and the West. For a moment a row of little wooden stores will look exactly like a portion of a small prairie village, but, later, one is confronted by a group of austere business blocks that are completely Eastern in expression. The street is bright at times with gaudy gypsy coloring; it is grey in places with dull and Puritanical hues. It is wealthy and poor; it is impertinent and courteous. It apparently comprehends all men and all moods and has little to say of itself. It is satisfied to exist without being defined nor classified.

And upon the pavement the crowd displays the reason of the street's knowledge of localities. There will be mingled an accent from the South, a hat and pair of boots from the West, a hurry and important engagement from the North, and a fine gown from the East.

An advantage of this condition is that no man need feel strange here. He may assure himself that there are men of his kind present. If, however, he is mistaken and there are no men of his kind in Hot Springs, he can conclude that he is a natural phenomenon and doomed to the curiosity of all peoples.

In Broadway perhaps people would run after a Turk to stare at his large extravagant trousers. Here it is doubtful if he would excite them at all. They would expect a Turk; they would comprehend that there were Turks and why there were Turks; they would accept the Turk with a mere raise of the eyebrows. This street thoroughly understands geography, and its experience of men is great. The instructors have been New York swells, Texas cattlemen, Denver mining kings, Chicago business men, and commercial travellers from the universe. This profound education has destroyed its curiosity and created a sort of a wide sympathy, not tender, but tolerant.

It is this absence of localism and the bigotry of classes which imparts to the entire town a peculiarly interesting flavor. There has been too general a contribution to admit two identical patterns. They were all different. And from these the town and the people were builded. Some of the hotels are enormous and like palaces. Some are like farm houses. Some are as small and plain as pine shanties. This superior education has impressed upon the town the fact that pocketbooks differentiate as do the distances to stars.

The bath houses for the most part stand in one row. They are close together and resemble mansions. They seem to be the abodes of peculiarly subdued and home-loving millionaires. The medicinal water is distributed under the supervision of the United States government, which in fact has reserved all the land save that valley in which the town lies. The water is first collected from all the springs into a principal reservoir. From thence it is again pumped through pipes to the bath houses. The government itself operates a free bath house, where 900 people bathe daily. The private ones charge a fee, which ranges from 20 to 60 cents.

Crowds swarm to these baths. A man becomes a creature of three conditions. He is about to take a bath—he is taking a bath—he has taken a bath. Invalids hobble slowly from their hotels, assisted perhaps by a pair of attendants. Soldiers from the U. S. Army and Navy Hospital trudge along assisting their rheumatic limbs with canes. All day there is a general and widespread march upon the baths.

In the quiet and intensely hot interiors of these buildings men involved in enormous bath-robes lounge in great rocking chairs. In other rooms the negro attendants scramble at the bidding of the bathers. Through the high windows the sunlight enters and pierces the curling masses of vapor which rise slowly in the heavy air.

There is naturally an Indian legend attached to these springs. In short, the Kanawagas were a great tribe with many hunters and warriors among them. They swung ponderous clubs with which they handily brained the ambitious but weaker warriors of other tribes. But at last a terrible scourge broke forth, and they who had strode so proudly under the trees, crawled piteously on the pine-needles and called in beseeching voices toward the yellow sunset. After festivals, rites, avowals, sacrifices, the Spirit of the Wind heard the low clamor of his Indians and suddenly vapors began to emerge from the waters of what had been a cool mountain spring. The pool had turned hot. The wise men debated. At last, a courageous and inquisitive red man bathed. He liked it; others bathed. The scourge fled.

The servants at Hot Springs are usually that class of colored boys who come from the far South. They are very black and have good-humored, rolling eyes. They are not so sublime as Pullman-car porters. They have not that profound dignity, that impressive aspect of exhaustive learning, that inspiring independence, which the public admires in the other class. They are good-natured and not blessed with the sophistication that one can see at a distance. As waiters, they bend and slide and amble with consummate willingness. Sometimes they move at a little jig-trot.

And, in conclusion, there is a certain fervor, a certain intenseness about life in Hot Springs that reminds philosophers of the times when the Monmouth Park Racing Association and Phil Daly vied with each other in making Long Branch a beloved and celebrated city. It is not obvious, it is for the most part invisible, soundless. And yet it is to be discovered.

The traveller for the hat firm in Ogallala, Neb., remarked that a terrible storm had raged through the country during the second week in February. He surmised that it was the worst blizzard for many years. In New Orleans, the hackmen raised their fare to ten dollars, he had heard.

The youthful stranger with the blonde and innocent hair, agreed with these remarks.

"Well," said the traveller for the hat firm, at last, "let's get a drink of that What-you-may-call-it Spring water, and then go and listen to the orchestra at the Arlington."

In the saloon, a man was leaning against the bar. As the traveller and the youthful stranger entered, this man said to the bar-tender: "I'll shake you for the drinks?"

"Same old game," said the traveller. "Always trying to beat the bar-tender, eh?"

"Well, I'll shake you for the drinks? How's that suit you?" said the man, ruffling his whiskers.

"All right," said the traveller for the hat firm in Ogallala, Neb. "I tell you what I'll do—I'll shake you for a dollar even."

"All right," said the man.

The traveller won. "Well, I tell you. I'll give you a chance to get your money back. I'll shake you for two bones."

The traveller won. "I'll shake you for four bones."

The traveller won.

"Got change for a five? I want a dollar back," said the man.

"No," said the traveller. "But I've got another five. I'll shake you for the two fives."

When the traveller for the hat firm in Ogallala, Neb., had won fifty dollars from the man with ruffled whiskers, the latter said: "Excuse me for a moment, please. You wait here for me, please. You're a winner."

As the man vanished, the traveller for the hat firm in Ogallala, Neb., turned to the youthful stranger with the blonde and innocent hair, in an outburst of gleeful victory. "Well, that was easy," he cried ecstatically. "Fifty dollars in 'bout four minutes. Here—you take half and I'll take half, and we'll go blow it." He tendered five five-dollars to the youthful stranger with the blonde and innocent hair. The bar-tender was sleepily regardant. At the end of the bar was lounging a man with no drink in front of him.

The youthful stranger said: "Oh, you might as well keep it. I don't need it. I——"

"But, look here," exclaimed the traveller for the hat firm in Ogallala, Neb., "you might as well take it. I'd expect you to do the same if you won. It ain't anything among sporting men. You take half and I'll take half, and we'll go blow it. You're as welcome as sunrise, my dear fellow. Take it along—it's nothing. What are you kickin' about?" He spoke in tones of supreme anguish, at this harsh treatment from a friend.

"No," said the youthful stranger with the blonde and innocent hair, to the traveller for the hat firm in Ogallala, Neb.,

"I guess I'll stroll back up-town. I want to write a letter to my mother."

In the back room of the saloon, the man with the ruffled beard was silently picking hieroglyphics out of his whiskers.

Galveston, Texas, in 1895

IT IS THE FORTUNE of travellers to take note of differences and publish them to their friends. It is the differences that are supposed to be valuable. The travellers seek them bravely, and cudgel their wits to find means to unearth them. But in this search they are confronted continually by the resemblances and the intrusion of commonplace and most obvious similarity into a field that is being ploughed in the romantic fashion is what causes an occasional resort to the imagination.

The winter found a cowboy in south-western Nebraska who had just ended a journey from Kansas City, and he swore bitterly as he remembered how little boys in Kansas City followed him about in order to contemplate his wide-brimmed hat. His vivid description of this incident would have been instructive to many Eastern readers. The fact that little boys in Kansas City could be profoundly interested in the sight of a wide-hatted cowboy would amaze a certain proportion of the populace. Where then can one expect cowboys if not in Kansas City? As a matter of truth, however, a steam boiler with four legs and a tail, galloping down the main street of the town, would create no more enthusiasm there than a real cow-puncher. For years the farmers have been driving the cattlemen back, back toward the mountains and into Kansas, and Nebraska has come to an almost universal condition of yellow trolly-cars with clanging gongs and whirring wheels, and conductors who don't give a curse for the public. And travellers tumbling over each other in their haste to trumpet the radical differences between Eastern and Western life have created a generally wrong opinion. No one has yet dared to declare that if a man drew three trays in Syracuse, N.Y., in many a Western city the man would be blessed with a full house. The declaration has no commercial value. There is a distinct fascination in being aware that in some parts of the world there are purple pigs, and children who are born with china mugs dangling where their ears should be. It is this fact which makes men sometimes grab tradition in wonder; color and attach contemporaneous date-lines to it. It is this fact which has kept the sweeping march of the West from being chronicled in any particularly true manner.

In a word, it is the passion for differences which has prevented a general knowledge of the resemblances.

If a man comes to Galveston resolved to discover every curious thing possible, and to display every point where Galveston differed from other parts of the universe, he would have the usual difficulty in shutting his eyes to the similarities. Galveston is often original, full of distinctive characters. But it is not like a town in the moon. There are, of course, a thousand details of street color and life which are thoroughly typical of any American city. The square brick business blocks, the mazes of telegraph wires, the trolly-cars clamoring up and down the streets, the passing crowd, the slight fringe of reflective and reposeful men on the curb, all disappoint the traveller, and he goes out in the sand somewhere and digs in order to learn if all Galveston clams are not schooner-rigged.

Accounts of these variations are quaint and interesting reading, to be sure, but then, after all, there are the great and elemental facts of American life. The cities differ as peas—in complexion, in size, in temperature—but the fundamental part, the composition, remains.

There has been a wide education in distinctions. It might be furtively suggested that the American people did not thoroughly know their mighty kinship, their universal emotions, their identical view-points upon many matters about which little is said. Of course, when the foreign element is injected very strongly, a town becomes strange, unfathomable, wearing a sort of guilty air which puzzles the American eye. There begins then a great diversity, and peas become turnips, and the differences are profound. With them, however, this prelude has nothing to do. It is a mere attempt to impress a reader with the importance of remembering that an illustration of Galveston streets can easily be obtained in Maine. Also, that the Gulf of Mexico could be mistaken for the Atlantic Ocean, and that its name is not printed upon it in tall red letters, notwithstanding the legend which has been supported by the geographies.

There are but three lifts in the buildings of Galveston. This is not because the people are skilled climbers; it is because the buildings are for the most part not high.

A certain Colonel Menard bought this end of the island of Galveston from the Republic of Texas in 1838 for fifty thousand dollars. He had a premonition of the value of wide streets for the city of his dreams, and he established a minimum width of seventy feet. The widest of the avenues is one hundred and fifty feet. The fact that this is not extraordinary for 1898 does not prevent it from being marvellous as municipal forethought in 1838.

In 1874 the United States Government decided to erect stone jetties at the entrance to the harbor of Galveston in order to deepen the water on the outer and inner bars, whose shallowness compelled deep-water ships to remain outside and use lighters to transfer their cargoes to the wharves of the city. Work on the jetties was in progress when I was in Galveston in 1895—in fact, two long, low black fingers of stone stretched into the Gulf. There are men still living who had confidence in the Governmental decision of 1874, and these men now point with pride to the jetties and say that the United States Government is nothing if not inevitable.

The soundings at mean low tide were thirteen feet on the inner bar and about twelve feet on the outer bar. At present there is twenty-three feet of water where once was the inner bar, and as the jetties have crept toward the sea they have achieved eighteen feet of water in the channel of the outer bar at mean low tide. The plan is to gain a depth of thirty feet. The cost is to be about seven million dollars.

Undoubtedly in 1874 the people of Galveston celebrated the decision of the Government with great applause, and prepared to welcome mammoth steamers at the wharves during the next spring. It was in 1889, however, that matters took conclusive form. In 1895 the prayer of Galveston materialised.

In 1889, Iowa, Nebraska, Missouri, Kansas, California, Arkansas, Texas, Wyoming, and New Mexico began a serious pursuit of Congress. Certain products of these States and Territories could not be exported with profit, owing to the high rate for transportation to Eastern ports. They demanded a harbor on the coast of Texas with a depth and area sufficient for great sea-crossing steamers. The board of army engineers which was appointed by Congress decided on Galveston as the point. The plan was to obtain by means of artificial constructions a volume and velocity of tidal flow that would maintain a navigable channel. The jetties are seven thousand feet apart, in order to allow ample room for the escape of the enormous flow of water from the inner bar.

Galveston has always been substantial and undeviating in its amount of business. Soon after the war it attained a commercial solidity, and its progress has been steady but quite slow. The citizens now, however, are lying in wait for a real Western boom. Those products of the West which have been walled in by the railroad transportation rates to Eastern ports are now expected to pass through Galveston. An air of hope pervades the countenance of each business man. The city, however, exported 1,500,000 bales of cotton last season, and the Chamber of Commerce has already celebrated the fact.

A train approaches the Island of Galveston by means of a long steel bridge across a bay, which glitters like burnished metal in the winter-time sunlight. The vast number of white two-storied frame houses in the outskirts remind one of New England, if it were not that the island is level as a floor. Later, in the commercial part of the town, appear the conventional business houses and the trolly-cars. Far up the cross-streets is the faint upheaval of the surf of the breeze-blown Gulf, and in the other direction the cotton steamers are arrayed with a fresco upon their black sides of dusky chuckling stevedores handling the huge bales amid a continual and foreign conversation, in which all the subtle and incomprehensible gossip of their social relations goes from mouth to mouth, the bales leaving little tufts of cotton all over their clothing.

Galveston has a rather extraordinary number of very wealthy people. Along the finely-paved drives their residences can be seen, modern for the most part and poor in architecture. Occasionally, however, one comes upon a typical Southern mansion, its galleries giving it a solemn shade and its whole air one of fine and enduring dignity. The palms standing in the grounds of these houses seem to pause at this time of year, and patiently abide the coming of the hot breath of summer. They still remain of a steadfast green and their color is a wine.

Underfoot the grass is of a yellow hue, here and there patched with a faint impending verdancy. The famous snow-storm here this winter played havoc with the color of the veg-etation, and one can now observe the gradual recovery of the trees, the shrubbery, the grass. In this vivid sunlight their vi-tality becomes enormous.

This storm also had a great effect upon the minds of the citizens. They would not have been more astonished if it had rained suspender buttons. The writer read descriptions of this storm in the newspapers of the date. Since his arrival here he has listened to 574 accounts of it.

Galveston has the aspect of a seaport. New York is not a seaport; a seaport is, however, a certain detail of New York. But in Galveston the docks, the ships, the sailors, are a large element in the life of the town. Also, one can sometimes find here that marvellous type the American sailor. American sea-men are not numerous enough to ever depreciate in value. A town that can produce a copy of the American sailor should encase him in bronze and unveil him on the Fourth of July. A veteran of the waves explained to the writer the reason that American youths do not go to sea. He said it was because saddles are too expensive. The writer congratulated the vet-eran of the waves upon his lucid explanation of this great question.

Galveston has its own summer resorts. In the heat of the season, life becomes sluggish in the streets. Men move about with an extraordinary caution as if they expected to be shot as they approached each corner.

At the beach, however, there is a large hotel which over-flows with humanity, and in front is, perhaps, the most com-fortable structure in the way of bath-houses known to the race. Many of the rooms are ranged about the foot of a large dome. A gallery connects them, but the principal floor to this structure is the sea itself, to which a flight of steps leads. Gal-veston's 35,000 people divide among themselves in summer a reliable wind from the Gulf.

There is a distinctly cosmopolitan character to Galveston's people. There are men from everywhere. The city does not represent Texas. It is unmistakably American, but in a general manner. Certain Texas differentiations are not observable in this city.

Withal, the people have the Southern frankness, the honesty which enables them to meet a stranger without deep suspicion, and they are the masters of a hospitality which is instructive to cynics.

Stephen Crane in Texas

S AN ANTONIO, TEX., January 6, 1889. "Ah," they said, "you
are going to San Anton? I wish I was. There's a town
for you."

From all manner of people, business men, consumptive
men, curious men and wealthy men, there came an exhibition
of a profound affection for San Antonio. It seemed to sym-
bolize for them the poetry of life in Texas.

There is an eloquent description of the city which makes it
consist of three old ruins and a row of Mexicans sitting in the
sun. The author, of course, visited San Antonio in the year
1101. While this is undoubtedly a masterly literary effect, one
can feel glad that after all we don't steer our ships according
to these literary effects.

At first the city presents a totally modern aspect to the as-
tonished visitor. The principal streets are lanes between rows
of handsome business blocks, and upon them proceeds with
important uproar the terrible and almighty trolley car. The
prevailing type of citizen is not seated in the sun; on the con-
trary he is making his way with the speed and intentness of
one who competes in a community that is commercially in
earnest. And the victorious derby hat of the North spreads its
wings in the holy place of legends.

This is the dominant quality. This is the principal color of
San Antonio. Later one begins to see that these edifices of
stone and brick and iron are reared on ashes, upon the ambi-
tions of a race. It expresses again the victory of the North.
The serene Anglo-Saxon erects business blocks upon the
dreams of the transient monks; he strings telegraph wires
across the face of their sky of hope; and over the energy, the
efforts, the accomplishments of these pious fathers of the
early church passes the wheel, the hoof, the heel.

Here, and there, however, one finds in the main part of the
town, little old buildings, yellow with age, solemn and severe
in outline, that have escaped by a miracle or by a historical
importance, the whirl of the modern life. In the Mexican
quarter there remains, too, much of the old character, but
despite the tenderness which San Antonio feels for these

monuments, the unprotected mass of them must get trampled into shapeless dust which lies always behind the march of this terrible century. The feet of the years will go through many old roofs.

Trolley cars are merciless animals. They gorge themselves with relics. They make really coherent history look like an omelet. If a trolley car had trolleyed around Jericho, the city would not have fallen; it would have exploded.

Centuries ago the white and gold banner of Spain came up out of the sea and the Indians, mere dots of black on the vast Texan plain, saw a moving glitter of silver warriors on the horizon's edge. There came then the long battle of soldier and priest, side by side, against these stubborn barbaric hordes, who wished to retain both their gods and their lands. Sword and crozier made frenzied circles in the air. The soldiers varied their fights with the Indians by fighting the French, and both the Indians and the French occasionally polished their armor for them with great neatness and skill.

During interval of peace and interval of war, toiled the pious monks, erecting missions, digging ditches, making farms and cudgeling their Indians in and out of the church. Sometimes, when the venerable fathers ran short of Indians to convert, the soldiers went on expeditions and returned dragging in a few score. The settlement prospered. Upon the gently rolling plains, the mission churches with their yellow stone towers outlined upon the sky, called with their bells at evening a multitude of friars and meek Indians and gleaming soldiers to service in the shadows before the flaming candles, the solemn shrine, the slow-pacing, chanting priests. And wicked and hopeless Indians, hearing these bells, scudded off into the blue twilight of the prairie.

The ruins of these missions are now besieged in the valley south of the city by indomitable thickets of mesquite. They rear their battered heads, their soundless towers, over dead forms, the graves of monks; and of the Spanish soldiers not one so much as flourishes a dagger.

Time has torn at these pale yellow structures and over-turned walls and towers here and there, defaced this and obliterated that. Relic hunters with their singular rapacity have dragged down little saints from their niches and pulled important stones from arches. They have performed offices of destruction of which the wind and the rain of the innumerable years was not capable. They are part of the general scheme of attack by nature.

The wind blows because it is the wind, the rain beats because it is the rain, the relic hunters hunt because they are relic hunters. Who can fathom the ways of nature? She thrusts her spear in the eye of Tradition and her agents feed on his locks. A little guide-book published here contains one of these "Good friend, forbear——" orations. But still this desperate massacre of the beautiful carvings goes on and it would take the ghosts of the monks with the ghosts of scourges, the phantoms of soldiers with the phantoms of swords, a scowling, spectral party, to stop the destruction. In the meantime, these portentous monuments to the toil, the profound convictions of the fathers, remain stolid and unyielding, with the bravery of stone, until it appears like the last stand of an army. Many years will charge them before the courage will abate which was injected into the mortar by the skillful monks.

It is something of a habit among the newspaper men and others who write here to say: "Well, there's a good market for Alamo stuff, now." Or perhaps they say: "Too bad! Alamo stuff isn't going very strong, now." Literary aspirants of the locality as soon as they finish writing about Her Eyes, begin on the Alamo. Statistics show that 69,710 writers of the state of Texas have begun at the Alamo.

Notwithstanding this fact, the Alamo remains the greatest memorial to courage which civilization has allowed to stand. The quaint and curious little building fronts on one of the most populous plazas of the city and because of Travis, Crockett, Bowie and their comrades, it maintains dignity amid the taller modern structures which front it. It is the tomb of the fiery emotions of Texans who refused to admit that numbers and Mexicans were arguments. Whether the swirl of life, the crowd upon the streets, pauses to look or not, the spirit that lives in this building, its air of contemplative silence, is as eloquent as an old battle flag.

The first Americans to visit San Antonio arrived in irons. This was the year 1800. There were eleven of them. They had fought one hundred and fifty Spanish soldiers on the eastern frontier and, by one of those incomprehensible chances which so often decides the color of battles, they had lost the fight. Afterward, Americans began to filter down through Louisiana until in 1834 there were enough of them to openly disagree with the young federal government in the City of Mexico, although there was not really any great number of them. Santa Anna didn't give a tin whistle for the people of Texas. He assured himself that he was capable of managing the republic of Mexico, and after coming to this decision he said to himself that that part of it which formed the state of Texas had better remain quiet with the others. In writing of what followed, a Mexican sergeant says: "The Texans fought like devils."

There was a culmination at the old Mission of the Alamo in 1836. This structure then consisted of a rectangular stone parapet 190 feet long and about 120 feet wide, with the existing Church of the Alamo in the southeast corner. Colonel William B. Travis, David Crockett and Colonel Bowie, whose monument is a knife with a peculiar blade, were in this enclosure with a garrison of something like one hundred and fifty men when they heard that Santa Anna was marching against them with an army of 4,000. The Texans shut themselves in the mission, and when Santa Anna demanded their surrender they fired a cannon and inaugurated the most appalling conflict of the continent.

Once Colonel Travis called his men together during a lull of the battle and said to them: "Our fate is sealed. * * * Our friends were evidently not informed of our perilous situation in time to save us. Doubtless they would have been here by this time if they had expected any considerable force of the enemy. * * * Then we must die."

He pointed out to them the three ways of being killed— surrendering to the enemy and being executed, making a rush through the enemy's lines and getting shot before they could inflict much damage, or of staying in the Alamo and holding out to the last, making themselves into a huge and terrible porcupine to be swallowed by the Mexican god of war. All the men save one adopted the last plan with their colonel.

This minority was a man named Rose. "I'm not prepared

to die, and shall not do so if I can avoid it." He was some
kind of a dogged philosopher. Perhaps he said: "What's the
use?" There is a strange inverted courage in the manner in
which he faced his companions with this sudden and short
refusal in the midst of a general exhibition of supreme brav-
ery. "No," he said. He bade them adieu and climbed the wall.
Upon its top he turned to look down at the upturned faces
of his silent comrades.

After the battle there were 521 dead Mexicans mingled with
the corpses of the Texans.

The Mexicans form a certain large part of the population
of San Antonio. Modern inventions have driven them toward
the suburbs, but they are still seen upon the main streets in
the ratio of one to eight and in their distant quarter of course
they swarm. A small percentage have reached positions of
business eminence.

The men wear for the most part wide-brimmed hats with
peaked crowns, and under these shelters appear their brown
faces and the inevitable cigarettes. The remainder of their ap-
parel has become rather Americanized, but the hat of ro-
mance is still superior. Many of the young girls are pretty,
and all of the old ones are ugly. These latter squat like clay
images, and the lines upon their faces and especially about the
eyes, make it appear as if they were always staring into the
eye of a blinding sun.

Upon one of the plazas, Mexican vendors with open-air
stands sell food that tastes exactly like pounded fire-brick
from hades—chili con carne, tamales, enchiladas, chili verde,
frijoles. In the soft atmosphere of the southern night, the
cheap glass bottles upon the stands shine like crystal and the
lamps glow with a tender radiance. A hum of conversation
ascends from the strolling visitors who are at their social
shrine.

The prairie about San Antonio is wrinkled into long low
hills, like immense waves, and upon them spreads a wilder-
ness of the persistent mesquite, a bush that grows in defiance
of everything. Some forty years ago the mesquite first assailed
the prairies about the city, and now from various high points
it can be seen to extend to the joining of earth and sky. The
individual bushes do not grow close together, and roads and

bridle paths cut through the dwarf forest in all directions. A certain class of Mexicans dwell in hovels amid the mesquite.

In the Mexican quarter of the town the gambling houses are crowded nightly, and before the serene dealers lie little stacks of silver dollars. A Mexican may not be able to raise enough money to buy beef tea for his dying grandmother, but he can always stake himself for a game of monte.

Upon a hillock of the prairie in the outskirts of the city is situated the government military post, Fort Sam Houston. There are four beautiful yellow and blue squadrons of cavalry, two beautiful red and blue batteries of light artillery and six beautiful white and blue companies of infantry. Officers' row resembles a collection of Newport cottages. There are magnificent lawns and gardens. The presence of so many officers of the line besides the gorgeous members of the staff of the commanding general, imparts a certain brilliant quality to San Antonio society. The drills upon the wide parade ground make a citizen proud.

Stephen Crane in Mexico (II)

CITY OF MEXICO, July 14.—The train rolled out of the Americanisms of San Antonio—the coal and lumber yards, the lines of freight cars, the innumerable tracks and black cinder paths—and into the southern expanses of mesquite.

In the smoking compartment, the capitalist from Chicago said to the archaeologist from Boston: "Well, here we go." The archaeologist smiled with placid joy.

The brown wilderness of mesquite drifted steadily and for hours past the car-windows. Occasionally a little ranch appeared half-buried in the bushes.

In the door-yard of one some little calicoed babies were playing and in the door-way itself a woman stood leaning her head against the post of it and regarding the train listlessly. Pale, worn, dejected, in her old and soiled gown, she was of a type to be seen North, East, South, West.

"That'll be one of our best glimpses of American civilization," observed the archaeologist then.

Cactus plants spread their broad pulpy leaves on the soil of reddish brown in the shade of the mesquite bushes. A thin silvery vapor appeared at the horizon.

"Say, I met my first Mexican, day before yesterday," said the capitalist. "Coming over from New Orleans. He was a peach. He could really talk more of the English language than any man I've ever heard. He talked like a mill-wheel. He had the happy social faculty of making everybody intent upon his conversation. You couldn't help it, you know. He put every sentence in the form of a question. 'San Anton' fine town—uh? F-i-n-n-e—uh? Gude beesness there—uh? Yes gude place for beesness—uh?' We all had to keep saying 'yes,' or 'certainly' or 'you bet your life,' at intervals of about three seconds."

"I went to school with some Cubans up North when I was a boy," said the archaeologist, "and they taught me to swear in Spanish. I'm all right in that. I can——"

"Don't you understand the conversational part at all?" demanded the capitalist.

"No," replied the archaeologist.

"Got friends in the City of Mexico?"

"No!"

"Well, by jiminy, you're going to have a daisy time!"

"Why, do you speak the language?"

"No!"

"Got any friends in the city?"

"No."

"Thunder."

These mutual acknowledgements riveted the two men to-gether. In this invasion, in which they were both facing the unknown, an acquaintance was a prize.

As the train went on over the astonishing brown sea of mesquite, there began to appear little prophecies of Mexico. A Mexican woman, perhaps, crouched in the door of a hut, her bare arms folded, her knees almost touching her chin, her head leaned against the door-post. Or perhaps a dusky sheep-herder in peaked sombrero and clothes the color of tan-bark, standing beside the track, his inscrutable visage turned toward the train. A cloud of white dust rising above the dull-colored bushes denoted the position of his flock. Over this lonely wilderness vast silence hung, a speckless sky, ignorant of bird or cloud.

"Look at this," said the capitalist.

"Look at that," said the archaeologist.

These premonitory signs threw them into fever of antici-pation. "Say, how much longer before we get to Laredo?" The conductor grinned. He recognized some usual, some typ-ical aspect in this impatience. "Oh, a long time yet."

But then finally when the whole prairie had turned a faint preparatory shadow-blue, some one told them: "See those low hills off yonder? Well, they're beyond the Rio Grande."

"Get out—are they?"

A sheep-herder with his flock raising pale dust-clouds over the lonely mesquite could no longer interest them. Their eyes were fastened on the low hills beyond the Rio Grande.

"There it is! There's the river!"

"Ah, no, it ain't!"

"I say it is."

Ultimately the train manœuvered through some low hills

and into sight of low-roofed houses across stretches of sand. Presently it stopped at a long wooden station. A score of Mexican urchins were congregated to see the arrival. Some twenty yards away stood a train composed of an engine, a mail and baggage car, a Pullman and three day coaches marked first, second and third class in Spanish. "There she is, my boy," said the capitalist. "There's the Aztec Limited. There's the train that's going to take us to the land of flowers and visions and all that."

There was a general charge upon the ticket office to get American money changed to Mexican money. It was a beautiful game. Two Mexican dollars were given for every American dollar. The passengers bid good-bye to their portraits of the national bird, with exultant smiles. They examined with interest the new bills which were quite gay with red and purple and green. As for the silver dollar, the face of it intended to represent a cap of liberty with rays of glory shooting from it, but it looked to be on the contrary a picture of an exploding bomb. The capitalist from Chicago jingled his coin with glee. "Doubled my money!"

"All aboard," said the conductor for the last time. Thereafter he said: "Vamanos." The train swung around the curve and toward the river. A soldier in blue fatigue uniform from the adjacent barracks, a portly German regardant at the entrance to his saloon, an elaborate and beautiful Anglo-Saxon oath from the top of a lumber pile, a vision of red and white and blue at the top of a distant staff, and the train was upon the high bridge that connects one nation with another.

Laredo appeared like a city veritably built upon sand. Little plats of vivid green grass appeared incredible upon this apparent waste. They looked like the grass mats of the theatrical stage. An old stone belfry arose above the low roofs. The river, shallow and quite narrow, flowed between wide banks of sand which seemed to express the stream's former records.

In Nuevo Laredo, there was a throng upon the platform— Mexican women, muffled in old shawls, and men, wrapped closely in dark-hued serapes. Over the heads of the men towered the peaked sombreros of fame. It was a preliminary picture painted in dark colors.

There was also a man in tan shoes and trousers of violent

English check. When a gentleman of Spanish descent is important, he springs his knee-joint forward to its limit with each step. This gentleman was springing his knee-joints as if they were of no consequence, as if he had a new pair at his service.

"You have only hand baggage," said the conductor. "You won't have to get out."

Presently, the gentleman in tan shoes entered the car, springing his knee-joints frightfully. He caused the porter to let down all the upper berths while he fumbled among the blankets and mattresses. The archaeologist and the capitalist had their valises already open and the gentleman paused in his knee-springing flight and gently peered in them. "All right," he said approvingly and pasted upon each of them a label which bore some formidable Mexican legend. Then he knee-springed himself away.

The train again invaded a wilderness of mesquite. It was amazing. The travellers had somehow expected a radical change the moment they were well across the Rio Grande. On the contrary, southern Texas was being repeated. They leaned close to the pane and stared into the mystic south. In the rear, however, Texas was represented by a long narrow line of blue hills, built up from the plain like a step.

Infrequently horsemen, shepherds, hovels appeared in the mesquite. Once, upon a small hillock a graveyard came into view and over each grave was a black cross. These somber emblems, lined against the pale sky, were given an inexpressibly mournful and fantastic horror from their color, new in this lonely land of brown bushes. The track swung to the westward and extended as straight as a rapier blade toward the rose-colored sky from whence the sun had vanished. The shadows of the mesquite deepened.

Presently the train paused at a village. Enough light remained to bring clearly into view some square yellow huts from whose rectangular doors there poured masses of crimson rays from the household fires. In these shimmering glows, dark and sinister shadows moved. The archaeologist and the capitalist were quite alone at this time in the sleeping-car and there was room for their enthusiasm, their ejaculations. Once they saw a black outline of a man upon one of these red can-

vasses. His legs were crossed, his arms were folded in his se-
rape, his hat resembled a charlotte russe. He leaned negli-
gently against the door-post. This figure justified to them all
their preconceptions. He was more than a painting. He was
the proving of certain romances, songs, narratives. He re-
newed their faith. They scrutinized him until the train moved
away.

They wanted mountains. They clamored for mountains.
"How soon, conductor, will we see any mountains?" The
conductor indicated a long shadow in the pallor of the after-
glow. Faint, delicate, it resembled the light rain-clouds of a
faraway shower.

The train, rattling rhythmically, continued toward the far
horizon. The deep mystery of night upon the mesquite prairie
settled upon it like a warning to halt. The windows presented
black expanses. At the little stations, calling voices could be
heard from the profound gloom. Cloaked figures moved in
the glimmer of lanterns.

The two travellers, hungry for color, form, action, strove
to penetrate with their glances these black curtains of dark-
ness which intervened between them and the new and strange
life. At last, however, the capitalist settled down in the smok-
ing compartment and recounted at length the extraordinary
attributes of his children in Chicago.

Before they retired they went out to the platform and
gazed into the south where the mountain range, still outlined
against the soft sky, had grown portentously large. To those
upon the train, the black prairie seemed to heave like a sea and
these mountains rose out of it like islands. In the west, a great
star shone forth. "It is as large as a cheese," said the capitalist.

The archaeologist asserted the next morning that he had
awakened at midnight and contemplated Monterey. It ap-
peared, he said, as a high wall and a distant row of lights.
When the capitalist awoke, the train was proceeding through
a great wide valley which was radiant in the morning sun-
shine. Mountain ranges, wrinkled, crumpled, bare of every-
thing save sage-brush, loomed on either side. Their little
peaks were yellow in the light and their sides were of the
faintest carmine tint, heavily interspersed with shadows. The
wide, flat plain itself was grown thickly with sage-brush, but

date palms were sufficiently numerous to make it look at times like a bed of some monstrous asparagus.

At every station a gorgeous little crowd had gathered to receive the train. Some were merely curious and others had various designs on the traveller—to beg from him or to sell to him. Indian women walked along the line of cars and held baskets of fruit toward the windows. Their broad, stolid faces were suddenly lit with a new commercial glow at the arrival of this trainful of victims. The men remained motionless and reposeful in their serapes. Back from the stations one could see the groups of white, flat-roofed adobe houses. From where a white road stretched over the desert toward the mountains, there usually arose a high, shining cloud of dust from the hoofs of some caballero's charger.

As this train conquered more and more miles toward its sunny destination, a regular progression in color could be noted. At Nuevo Laredo the prevailing tones in the dress of the people were brown, black and grey. Later an occasional purple or crimson serape was interpolated. And later still, the purple, the crimson and the other vivid hues became the typical colors, and even the trousers of dark cloth were replaced by dusty white cotton ones. A horseman in a red serape and a tall sombrero of maroon or pearl or yellow was vivid as an individual, but a dozen or two of them reposeful in the shade of some desert railway station made a chromatic delirium. In Mexico the atmosphere seldom softens anything. It devotes its energy to making high lights, bringing everything forward, making colors fairly volcanic.

The bare feet of the women pattered to and fro along the row of car windows. Their cajoling voices were always soft and musical. The fierce sun of the desert beat down upon their baskets, wherein the fruit and food was exposed to each feverish ray.

From time to time across this lonely sunbeaten expanse, from which a storm of fine, dry dust ascended upon any provocation at all, the train passed walls made of comparatively small stones which extended for miles over the plain and then ascended the distant mountains in an undeviating line. They expressed the most incredible and apparently stupid labor. To see a stone wall beginning high and wide and extending to the horizon in a thin, monotonous thread, makes one think of the innumerable hands that toiled at the stones to divide one extent of sage-brush from another. Occasionally the low roof of a hacienda could be seen, surrounded by outbuildings and buried in trees. These walls marked the boundary of each hacienda's domain.

"Certain times of year," said the conductor, "there is nothing for the Indian peons to do, and as the rancheros have to feed 'em and keep 'em anyhow, you know, why they set 'em to building these stone walls."

The archaeologist and the capitalist gazed with a new interest at the groups of dusty-footed peons at the little stations. The clusters of adobe huts wherein some of them dwelt resembled the pictures of Palestine tombs. Withal, they smiled amiably, contentedly, their white teeth gleaming.

When the train roared past the stone monument that marked the Tropic of Cancer, the two travellers leaned out dangerously.

"Look at that, would you?"

"Well, I'm hanged!"

They stared at it with awed glances. "Well, well, so that's it, is it?" When the southern face of the monument was presented, they saw the legend, "Zona Torrida."

"Thunder, ain't this great."

Finally, the valley grew narrower. The track wound near the bases of hills. Through occasional passes could be seen other ranges, leaden-hued, in the distance. The sage-bushes became scarce and the cactus began to grow with a greater courage. The young green of other and unknown plants became visible. Greyish dust in swirling masses marked the passage of the train.

At San Luis Potosi, the two travellers disembarked and again assailed one of those American restaurants which are located at convenient points. Roast chicken, tender steaks, chops, eggs, biscuit, pickles, cheese, pie, coffee, and just outside in blaring sunshine there was dust and Mexicans and a heathen chatter—a sort of an atmosphere of chili con carne, tortillas, tamales. The two travellers approached this table with a religious air as if they had encountered a shrine.

All the afternoon the cactus continued to improve in sizes.

It now appeared that the natives made a sort of a picket fence of one variety and shade trees from another. The brown faces of Indian women and babes peered from these masses of prickly green.

At Atotonilco, a church with red-tiled towers appeared surrounded by poplar trees that resembled hearse plumes, and in the stream that flowed near there was a multitude of heads with long black hair. A vast variety of feminine garments decorated the bushes that skirted the creek. A baby, brown as a water-jar and of the shape of an alderman, paraded the bank in utter indifference or ignorance or defiance.

At various times old beggars, grey and bent, tottered painfully with outstretched hats begging for centavos in voices that expressed the last degree of chill despair. Their clothing hung in the most supernatural tatters. It seemed miraculous that such fragments could stay upon human bodies. With some unerring inexplainable instinct they steered for the capitalist. He swore and blushed each time. "They take me for an easy thing," he said wrathfully. "No—I won't—get out— go away." The unmolested archaeologist laughed.

The churches north of Monterey had been for the most part small and meek structures surmounted by thin wooden crosses. They were now more impressive, with double towers of stone and in the midst of gardens and dependent buildings. Once the archaeologist espied a grey and solemn ruin of a chapel. The old walls and belfry appeared in the midst of a thicket of regardless cactus. He at once recited to the capitalist the entire history of Cortez and the Aztecs.

At night-fall, the train paused at a station where the entire village had come down to see it and gossip. There appeared to be no great lighting of streets. Two or three little lamps burned at the station and a soldier, or a policeman, carried a lantern which feebly illuminated his club and the bright steel of his revolver. In the profound gloom, the girls walked arm and arm, three or four abreast, and giggled. Bands of hoodlums scouted the darkness. One could hear their shrill cat-calls. Some pedlers came with flaring torches and tried to sell things.

In the early morning hours, the two travellers scrambled from their berths to discover that the train was high in air. It had begun its great climb of the mountains. Below and on the left, a vast plain of green and yellow fields was spread out like a checkered cloth. Here and there were tiny white villages, churches, haciendas. And beyond this plain arose the peak of Nevado de Toluca for 15,000 feet. Its eastern face was sun-smitten with gold and its snowy sides were shadowed with rose. The color of gold made it appear that this peak was staring with a high serene eternal glance into the East at the approach of the endless suns. And no one feels like talking in the presence of these mountains that stand like gods on the world, for fear that they might hear. Slowly the train wound around the face of the cliff.

When you come to this country, do not confuse the Mexican cakes with pieces of iron ore. They are not pieces of iron ore. They are cakes.

At a mountain station to which the train had climbed in some wonderful fashion, the travellers breakfasted upon cakes and coffee. The conductor, tall, strong, as clear-headed and as clear-eyed, as thoroughly a type of the American railroad man as if he were in charge of the Pennsylvania Limited, sat at the head of the table and harangued the attendant peon. The capitalist took a bite of cake and said "Gawd!"

This little plateau was covered with yellow grass which extended to the bases of the hills that were on all sides. These hills were grown thickly with pines, fragrant, gently waving in the cool breeze. Upon the station platform a cavalry officer, under a grey sombrero heavily ladened with silver braid, conversed with a swarthy trooper. Over the little plain, a native in a red blanket was driving a number of small donkeys who were each carrying an enormous load of fresh hay.

The conductor again yelled out a password to a Chinese lodge and the train renewed its attack upon these extraordinary ridges which intervened between it and its victory. The passengers prepared themselves. Every car window was hung full of heads that were for the most part surmounted by huge sombreros. A man with such a large roll of matting strapped to his back that he looked like a perambulating sentry-box, leaned upon his staff in the roadway and stared at the two engines. Puffing, panting, heaving, they strained like thoroughbred animals, with every steel muscle of their bodies and slowly the train was hauled up this tilted track.

In and out among the hills it went, higher and higher. Often two steel rails were visible far below on the other side of a ravine. It seemed incredible that ten minutes before, the train had been at that place.

In the depths of the valley, a brook brawled over the rocks. A man in dusty white garments lay asleep in the shade of a pine.

At last the whistle gave a triumphant howl. The summit—10,000 feet above the sea—was reached. A winding slide, a sort of tremendous toboggan affair began. Around and around among the hills glided the train. Little flat white villages displayed themselves in the valleys. The maguey plant, from which the Mexicans make their celebrated tanglefoot, flourished its lance-point leaves in long rows. The hills were checkered to their summits with brown fields. The train swinging steadily down the mountains crossed one stream thirteen times on bridges dizzily high.

Suddenly two white peaks, afar off, raised above the horizon, peering over the ridge. The capitalist nearly fell off the train. Popocatepetl and Ixtaccihuatl, the two giant mountains, clothed in snow that was like wool, were marked upon the sky. A glimpse was had of a vast green plain. In this distance, the castle of Chapultepec resembled a low thunder cloud.

Presently the train was among long white walls, green lawns, high shade trees. The passengers began their preparations for disembarking as the train manœuvered through the switches. At last there came a depot heavily fringed with people, an omnibus, a dozen cabs and a soldier in a uniform that fitted him like a bird cage. White dust arose high toward the blue sky. In some tall grass on the other side of the track, a little cricket suddenly chirped. The two travellers with shining eyes climbed out of the car. "A-a-ah," they said in a prolonged sigh of delight. The city of the Aztecs was in their power.

The Mexican Lower Classes

ABOVE ALL THINGS, the stranger finds the occupations of foreign peoples to be trivial and inconsequent. The average mind utterly fails to comprehend the new point of view and that such and such a man should be satisfied to carry bundles or mayhap sit and ponder in the sun all his life in this faraway country seems an abnormally stupid thing. The visitor feels scorn. He swells with a knowledge of his geographical experience. "How futile are the lives of these people," he remarks, "and what incredible ignorance that they should not be aware of their futility." This is the arrogance of the man who has not yet solved himself and discovered his own actual futility.

Yet, indeed, it requires wisdom to see a brown woman in one garment crouched listlessly in the door of a low adobe hut while a naked brown baby sprawls on his stomach in the dust of the roadway—it requires wisdom to see this thing and to see it a million times and yet to say: "Yes, this is important to the scheme of nature. This is part of her economy. It would not be well if it had never been."

It perhaps might be said—if any one dared—that the most worthless literature of the world has been that which has been written by the men of one nation concerning the men of another.

It seems that a man must not devote himself for a time to attempts at psychological perception. He can be sure of two things, form and color. Let him then see all he can but let him not sit in literary judgment on this or that manner of the people. Instinctively he will feel that there are similarities but he will encounter many little gestures, tones, tranquilities, rages, for which his blood, adjusted to another temperature, can possess no interpreting power. The strangers will be indifferent where he expected passion; they will be passionate where he expected calm. These subtle variations will fill him with contempt.

At first it seemed to me the most extraordinary thing that the lower classes of Indians in this country should insist upon existence at all. Their squalor, their ignorance seemed so absolute that death—no matter what it has in store—would appear as freedom, joy.

The people of the slums of our own cities fill a man with awe. That vast army with its countless faces immovably cynical, that vast army that silently confronts eternal defeat, it makes one afraid. One listens for the first thunder of the rebellion, the moment when this silence shall be broken by a roar of war. Meanwhile one fears this class, their numbers, their wickedness, their might—even their laughter. There is a vast national respect for them. They have it in their power to become terrible. And their silence suggests everything.

They are becoming more and more capable of defining their condition and this increase of knowledge evinces itself in the deepening of those savage and scornful lines which extend from near the nostrils to the corners of the mouth. It is very distressing to observe this growing appreciation of the situation.

I am not venturing to say that this appreciation does not exist in the lower classes of Mexico. No, I am merely going to say that I cannot perceive any evidence of it. I take this last position in order to preserve certain handsome theories which I advanced in the fore part of the article.

It is so human to be envious that of course even these Indians have envied everything from the stars of the sky to the birds, but you cannot ascertain that they feel at all the modern desperate rage at the accident of birth. Of course the Indian can imagine himself a king but he does not apparently feel that there is an injustice in the fact that he was not born a king any more than there is in his not being born a giraffe.

As far as I can perceive him, he is singularly meek and submissive. He has not enough information to be unhappy over his state. Nobody seeks to provide him with it. He is born, he works, he worships, he dies, all on less money than would buy a thoroughbred Newfoundland dog and who dares to enlighten him? Who dares cry out to him that there are plums, plums, plums in the world which belong to him? For my part, I think the apostle would take a formidable responsibility. I would remember that there really was no comfort in the plums after all as far as I had seen them and I would esteem no orations concerning the glitter of plums.

A man is at liberty to be virtuous in almost any position of life. The virtue of the rich is not so superior to the virtue of the poor that we can say that the rich have a great advantage. These Indians are by far the most poverty-stricken class with which I have met but they are not morally the lowest by any means. Indeed, as far as the mere form of religion goes, they are one of the highest. They are exceedingly devout, worshipping with a blind faith that counts a great deal among the theorists.

But according to my view this is not the measure of them. I measure their morality by what evidences of peace and contentment I can detect in the average countenance.

If a man is not given a fair opportunity to be virtuous, if his environment chokes his moral aspirations, I say that he has got the one important cause of complaint and rebellion against society. Of course it is always possible to be a martyr but then we do not wish to be martyrs. Martyrdom offers no inducements to the average mind. We prefer to be treated with justice and then martyrdom is not required. I never could appreciate those grey old gentlemen of history. Why did not they run? I would have run like mad and still respected myself and my religion.

I have said then that a man has the right to rebel if he is not given a fair opportunity to be virtuous. Inversely then, if he possesses this fair opportunity, he cannot rebel, he has no complaint. I am of the opinion that poverty of itself is no cause. It is something above and beyond. For example, there is Collis P. Huntington and William D. Rockefeller—as virtuous as these gentlemen are, I would not say that their virtue is any ways superior to mine for instance. Their opportunities are no greater. They can give more, deny themselves more in quantity but not relatively. We can each give all that we possess and there I am at once their equal.

I do not think however that they would be capable of sacrifices that would be possible to me. So then I envy them nothing. Far from having a grievance against them, I feel that they will confront an ultimate crisis that I, through my opportunities, may altogether avoid. There is in fact no advantage of importance which I can perceive them possessing over me.

It is for these reasons that I refuse to commit judgment upon these lower classes of Mexico. I even refuse to pity them. It is true that at night many of them sleep in heaps in door-ways, and spend their days squatting upon the pavements. It is true that their clothing is scant and thin. All manner of things of this kind is true but yet their faces have almost always a certain smoothness, a certain lack of pain, a serene faith. I can feel the superiority of their contentment.

One Dash—Horses

RICHARDSON PULLED UP his horse and looked back over the trail where the crimson serape of his servant flamed amid the dusk of the mesquite. The hills in the west were carved into peaks, and were painted the most profound blue. Above them, the sky was of that marvelous tone of green— like still, sun-shot water—which people denounce in pictures.

José was muffled deep in his blanket, and his great toppling sombrero was drawn low over his brow. He shadowed his master along the dimming trail in the fashion of an assassin. A cold wind of the impending night swept over the wilderness of mesquite.

"Man," said Richardson in lame Mexican as the servant drew near, "I want eat! I want sleep! Understand—no? Quickly! Understand?" "Si, señor," said José, nodding. He stretched one arm out of his blanket and pointed a yellow finger into the gloom. "Over there, small village! Si, señor."

They rode forward again. Once the American's horse shied and breathed quiveringly at something which he saw or imagined in the darkness, and the rider drew a steady, patient rein, and leaned over to speak tenderly as if he were addressing a frightened woman. The sky had faded to white over the mountains and the plain was a vast, pointless ocean of black.

Suddenly some low houses appeared squatting amid the bushes. The horsemen rode into a hollow until the houses rose against the sombre sundown sky, and then up a small hillock, causing these habitations to sink like boats in the sea of shadow.

A beam of red firelight fell across the trail. Richardson sat sleepily on his horse while the servant quarreled with somebody—a mere voice in the gloom—over the price of bed and board. The houses about him were for the most part like tombs in their whiteness and silence, but there were scudding black figures that seemed interested in his arrival.

José came at last to the horses' heads, and the American slid stiffly from his seat. He muttered a greeting, as with his spurred feet he clicked into the adobe house that confronted him. The

732

brown stolid face of a woman shone in the light of the fire. He seated himself on the earthen floor and blinked drowsily at the blaze. He was aware that the woman was clinking earthenware and hieing here and everywhere in the maneuvers of the housewife. From a dark corner of the room there came the sound of two or three snores twining together.

The woman handed him a bowl of tortillas. She was a submissive creature, timid and large-eyed. She gazed at his enormous silver spurs, his large and impressive revolver, with the interest and admiration of the highly privileged cat of the adage. When he ate, she seemed transfixed off there in the gloom, her white teeth shining.

José entered, staggering under two Mexican saddles, large enough for building sites. Richardson decided to smoke a cigarette, and then changed his mind. It would be much finer to go to sleep. His blanket hung over his left shoulder, furled into a long pipe of cloth, according to a Mexican fashion. By doffing his sombrero, unfastening his spurs and his revolver belt, he made himself ready for the slow blissful twist into the blanket. Like a cautious man he lay close to the wall, and all his property was very near his hand.

The mesquite brush burned long. José threw two gigantic wings of shadow as he flapped his blanket about him—first across his chest under his arms, and then around his neck and across his chest again—this time over his arms, with the end tossed on his right shoulder. A Mexican thus snugly enveloped can nevertheless free his fighting arm in a beautifully brisk way, merely shrugging his shoulder as he grabs for the weapon at his belt. (They always wear their serapes in this manner.)

The firelight smothered the rays which, streaming from a moon as large as a drum head, were struggling at the open door. Richardson heard from the plain the fine, rhythmical trample of the hoofs of hurried horses. He went to sleep wondering who rode so fast and so late. And in the deep silence the pale rays of the moon must have prevailed against the red spears of the fire until the room was slowly flooded to its middle with a rectangle of silver light.

Richardson was awakened by the sound of a guitar. It was badly played—in this land of Mexico, from which the romance of the instrument ascends to us like a perfume. The guitar was groaning and whining like a badgered soul. A noise of scuffling feet accompanied the music. Sometimes laughter arose, and often the voices of men saying bitter things to each other, but always the guitar cried on, the treble sounding as if some one were beating iron, and the bass humming like bees. "Damn it—they're having a dance," muttered Richardson, fretfully. He heard two men quarreling in short, sharp words, like pistol shots; they were calling each other worse names than common people know in other countries. He wondered why the noise was so loud. Raising his head from his saddle pillow, he saw, with the help of the valiant moonbeams, a blanket hanging flat against the wall at the further end of the room. Being of the opinion that it concealed a door, and remembering that Mexican drink made men very drunk, he pulled his revolver closer to him and prepared for sudden disaster.

Richardson was dreaming of his far and beloved North.

"Well, I would kill him, then!"

"No, you must not!"

"Yes, I will kill him! Listen! I will ask this American beast for his beautiful pistol and spurs and money and saddle, and if he will not give them—you will see!"

"But these Americans—they are a strange people. Look out, señor."

Then twenty voices took part in the discussion. They rose in quavering shrillness, as from men badly drunk. Richardson felt the skin draw tight around his mouth, and his knee-joints turned to bread. He slowly came to a sitting posture, glaring at the motionless blanket at the far end of the room. This stiff and mechanical movement, accomplished entirely by the muscles of the waist, must have looked like the rising of a corpse in the wan moonlight, which gave everything a hue of the grave.

My friend, take my advice and never be executed by a hangman who doesn't talk the English language. It, or anything that resembles it, is the most difficult of deaths. The tumultuous emotions of Richardson's terror destroyed that slow and careful process of thought by means of which he understood Mexican. Then he used his instinctive comprehension of the first and universal language, which is tone. Still it is disheartening not to be able to understand the detail of threats against the blood of your body.

Suddenly the clamor of voices ceased. There was a silence—a silence of decision. The blanket was flung aside, and the red light of a torch flared into the room. It was held high by a fat, round-faced Mexican, whose little snake-like mustache was as black as his eyes, and whose eyes were black as jet. He was insane with the wild rage of a man whose liquor is dully burning at his brain. Five or six of his fellows crowded after him. The guitar, which had been thrummed doggedly during the time of the high words, now suddenly stopped. They contemplated each other. Richardson sat very straight and still, his right hand lost in the folds of his blanket. The Mexicans jostled in the light of the torch, their eyes blinking and glittering.

The fat one posed in the manner of a grandee. Presently his hand dropped to his belt, and from his lips there spun an epithet—a hideous word which often foreshadows knife-blows, a word peculiarly of Mexico, where people have to dig deep to find an insult that has not lost its savor. The American did not move. He was staring at the fat Mexican with a strange fixedness of gaze, not fearful, not dauntless, not anything that could be interpreted. He simply stared.

The fat Mexican must have been disconcerted, for he continued to pose as a grandee, with more and more sublimity, until it would have been easy for him to have fallen over backward. His companions were swaying in a very drunken manner. They still blinked their little beady eyes at Richardson. Ah, well, sirs, here was a mystery. At the approach of their menacing company, why did not this American cry out and turn pale, or run, or pray them mercy? The animal merely sat still, and stared, and waited for them to begin. Well, evidently he was a great fighter; or perhaps he was an idiot. Indeed, this was an embarrassing situation, for who was going forward to discover whether he was a great fighter or an idiot?

To Richardson, whose nerves were tingling and twitching like live wires and whose heart jolted inside him, this pause was a long horror; and for these men who could so frighten him there began to swell in him a fierce hatred—a hatred that made him long to be capable of fighting all of them, a hatred that made him capable of fighting all of them. A 44-caliber revolver can make a hole large enough for little boys to shoot marbles through, and there was a certain fat Mexican with a mustache like a snake who came extremely near to have eaten his last tamale merely because he frightened a man too much.

José had slept the first part of the night in his fashion, his body hunched into a heap, his legs crooked, his head touching his knees. Shadows had obscured him from the sight of the invaders. At this point he arose, and began to prowl quakingly over toward Richardson, as if he meant to hide behind him.

Of a sudden the fat Mexican gave a howl of glee. José had come within the torch's circle of light. With roars of ferocity the whole group of Mexicans pounced on the American's servant. He shrank shuddering away from them, beseeching by every device of word and gesture. They pushed him this way and that. They beat him with their fists. They stung him with their curses. As he groveled on his knees, the fat Mexican took him by the throat and said: "I am going to kill you!" And continually they turned their eyes to see if they were to succeed in causing the initial demonstration by the American. Richardson looked on impassively. Under the blanket, however, his fingers were clinched as rigidly as iron upon the handle of his revolver.

Here suddenly two brilliant clashing chords from the guitar were heard, and a woman's voice, full of laughter and confidence, cried from without: "Hello! Hello! Where are you?" The lurching company of Mexicans instantly paused and looked at the ground. One said, as he stood with his legs wide apart in order to balance himself: "It is the girls. They have come!" He screamed in answer to the question of the woman: "Here!" And without waiting he started on a pilgrimage toward the blanket-covered door. One could now hear a number of female voices giggling and chattering.

Two other Mexicans said: "Yes, it is the girls! Yes!" They also started quietly away. Even the fat Mexican's ferocity seemed to be affected. He looked uncertainly at the still-immovable American. Two of his friends grasped him gayly: "Come, the girls are here! Come!" He cast another glower at

Richardson. "But this—," he began. Laughing, his comrades hustled him toward the door. On its threshold and holding back the blanket with one hand, he turned his yellow face with a last challenging glare toward the American. José, bewailing his state in little sobs of utter despair and woe, crept to Richardson and huddled near his knee. Then the cries of the Mexicans meeting the girls were heard, and the guitar burst out in joyous humming.

The moon clouded, and but a faint square of light fell through the open main door of the house. The coals of the fire were silent save for occasional sputters. Richardson did not change his position. He remained staring at the blanket which hid the strategic door in the far end. At his knees José was arguing, in a low, aggrieved tone, with the saints. Without the Mexicans laughed and danced, and—it would appear from the sound—drank more.

In the stillness and night Richardson sat wondering if some serpent-like Mexican was sliding toward him in the darkness, and if the first thing he knew of it would be the deadly sting of the knife. "Sssh," he whispered, to José. He drew his revolver from under the blanket and held it on his leg. The blanket over the door fascinated him. It was a vague form, black and unmoving. Through the opening it shielded was to come, probably, threats, death. Sometimes he thought he saw it move. As grim white sheets, the black and silver of coffins, all the panoply of death, affect us because of that which they hide, so this blanket, dangling before a hole in an adobe wall, was to Richardson a horrible emblem, and a horrible thing in itself. In his present mood Richardson could not have been brought to touch it with his finger.

The celebrating Mexicans occasionally howled in song. The guitarist played with speed and enthusiasm. Richardson longed to run. But in this vibrating and threatening gloom his terror convinced him that a move on his part would be a signal for the pounce of death. José, crouching abjectly, occasionally mumbled. Slowly and ponderous as stars the minutes went.

Suddenly Richardson thrilled and started. His breath, for a moment, left him. In sleep his nerveless fingers had allowed his revolver to fall and clang upon the hard floor. He grabbed it up hastily, and his glance swept apprehensively over the room. A chill blue light of dawn was in the place. Every outline was slowly growing; detail was following detail. The dread blanket did not move. The riotous company had gone or become silent. Richardson felt in his blood the effect of this cold dawn. The candor of breaking day brought his nerve. He touched José. "Come," he said. His servant lifted his lined yellow face, and comprehended. Richardson buckled on his spurs and strode up; José obediently lifted the two great saddles. Richardson held two bridles and a blanket on his left arm; in his right hand he held his revolver. They sneaked toward the door.

The man who said that spurs jingled was insane. Spurs have a mellow clash—clash—clash. Walking in spurs—notably Mexican spurs—you remind yourself vaguely of a telegraphic lineman. Richardson was inexpressibly shocked when he came to walk. He sounded to himself like a pair of cymbals. He would have known of this if he had reflected; but then he was escaping, not reflecting. He made a gesture of despair, and from under the two saddles José tried to make one of hopeless horror. Richardson stooped, and with shaking fingers unfastened the spurs. Taking them in his left hand, he picked up his revolver and they slunk on toward the door. On the threshold Richardson looked back. In a corner, he saw, watching him with large eyes, the Indian man and woman who had been his hosts. Throughout the night they had made no sign, and now they neither spoke nor moved. Yet Richardson thought he detected meek satisfaction at his departure.

The street was still and deserted. In the eastern sky there was a lemon-colored patch. José had picketed the horses at the side of the house. As the two men came around the corner, Richardson's animal set up a whinny of welcome. The little horse had evidently heard them coming. He stood facing them, his ears cocked forward, his eyes bright with welcome.

Richardson made a frantic gesture, but the horse in his happiness at the appearance of his friends whinnied with enthusiasm. The American felt at this time that he could have strangled his well-beloved steed. Upon the threshold of safety, he was being betrayed by his horse, his friend. He felt the same hate for the horse that he would have felt for a dragon. And yet, as he glanced wildly about him, he could see nothing stirring in the street, nor at the doors of the tomb-like houses.

José had his own saddle girth and both bridles buckled in a moment. He curled the picket ropes with a few sweeps of his arm. The fingers of Richardson, however, were shaking so that he could hardly buckle the girth. His hands were invisible mittens. He was wondering, calculating, hoping about his horse. He knew the little animal's willingness and courage under all circumstances up to this time, but then—here it was different. Who could tell if some wretched instance of equine perversity was not about to develop. Maybe the little fellow would not feel like smoking over the plain at express speed this morning, and so he would rebel and kick and be wicked. Maybe he would be without feeling of interest, and run listlessly. All men who have had to hurry in the saddle know what it is to be on a horse who does not understand the dramatic situation. Riding a lame sheep is bliss to it. Richardson, fumbling furiously at the girth, thought of these things.

Presently he had it fastened. He swung into the saddle, and as he did so his horse made a mad jump forward. The spurs of José scratched and tore the flanks of his great black animal, and side by side the two horses raced down the village street. The American heard his horse breathe a quivering sigh of excitement. Those four feet skimmed. They were as light as fairy puff balls. The houses of the village glided past in a moment, and the great, clear, silent plain appeared like a pale blue sea of mist and wet bushes. Above the mountains the colors of the sunlight were like the first tones, the opening chords of the mighty hymn of the morning.

The American looked down at his horse. He felt in his heart the first thrill of confidence. The little animal, unurged and quite tranquil, moving his ears this way and that way with an air of interest in the scenery, was nevertheless bounding into the eye of the breaking day with the speed of a frightened antelope. Richardson, looking down, saw the long, fine reach of forelimb, as steady as steel machinery. As the ground reeled past, the long, dried grasses hissed, and cactus plants were dull blurs. A wind whirled the horse's mane over his rider's bridle hand.

José's profile was lined against the pale sky. It was as that of a man who swims alone in an ocean. His eyes glinted like metal, fastened on some unknown point ahead of him, some fabulous place of safety. Occasionally his mouth puckered in a little unheard cry; and his legs, bended back, worked spasmodically as his spurred heels sliced the flanks of his charger.

Richardson consulted the gloom in the west for signs of a hard-riding, yelling cavalcade. He knew that whereas his friends the enemy had not attacked him when he had sat still and with apparent calmness confronted them, they would certainly take furiously after him now that he had run from them—now that he had confessed to them that he was the weaker. Their valor would grow like weeds in the spring, and upon discovering his escape they would ride forth dauntless warriors. Sometimes he was sure he saw them. Sometimes he was sure he heard them. Continually looking backward over his shoulder, he studied the purple expanses where the night was marching away. José rolled and shuddered in his saddle, persistently disturbing the stride of the black horse, fretting and worrying him until the white foam flew, and the great shoulders shone like satin from the sweat.

At last, Richardson drew his horse carefully down to a walk. José wished to rush insanely on, but the American spoke to him sternly. As the two paced forward side by side, Richardson's little horse thrust over his soft nose and inquired into the black's condition.

Riding with José was like riding with a corpse. His face resembled a cast in lead. Sometimes he swung forward and almost pitched from his seat. Richardson was too frightened himself to do anything but hate this man for his fear. Finally, he issued a mandate which nearly caused José's eyes to slide out of his head and fall to the ground like two coins. "Ride behind me—about fifty paces."

"Señor——" stuttered the servant. "Go," cried the American, furiously. He glared at the other and laid his hand on his revolver. José looked at his master wildly. He made a piteous gesture. Then slowly he fell back, watching the hard face of the American for a sign of mercy. Richardson had resolved in his rage that at any rate he was going to use the eyes and ears of extreme fear to detect the approach of danger; and so he established his servant as a sort of an outpost.

As they proceeded he was obliged to watch sharply to see that the servant did not slink forward and join him. When José made beseeching circles in the air with his arm he replied by menacingly gripping his revolver. José had a revolver, too; nevertheless it was very clear in his mind that the revolver was distinctly an American weapon. He had been educated in the Rio Grande country.

Richardson lost the trail once. He was recalled to it by the loud sobs of his servant.

Then at last José came clattering forward, gesticulating and wailing. The little horse sprang to the shoulder of the black. They were off.

Richardson, again looking backward, could see a slanting flare of dust on the whitening plain. He thought that he could detect small moving figures in it.

José's moans and cries amounted to a university course in theology. They broke continually from his quivering lips. His spurs were as motors. They forced the black horse over the plain in great headlong leaps. But under Richardson there was a little insignificant rat-colored beast who was running apparently with almost as much effort as it requires for a bronze statue to stand still. As a matter of truth, the ground seemed merely something to be touched from time to time with hoofs that were as light as blown leaves. Occasionally Richardson lay back and pulled stoutly at his bridle to keep from abandoning his servant. José harried at his horse's mouth, flopped around in the saddle and made his two heels beat like flails. The black ran like a horse in despair.

Crimson serapes in the distance resembled drops of blood on the great cloth of plain. Richardson began to dream of all possible chances. Although quite a humane man, he did not once think of his servant. José being a Mexican, it was natural that he should be killed in Mexico; but for himself, a New Yorker—— He remembered all the tales of such races for life, and he thought them badly written.

The great black horse was growing indifferent. The jabs of José's spurs no longer caused him to bound forward in wild leaps of pain. José had at last succeeded in teaching him that spurring was to be expected, speed or no speed, and now he took the pain of it dully and stolidly, as an animal who finds that doing his best gains him no respite. José was turned into a raving maniac. He bellowed and screamed, working his arms and his heels like one in a fit. He resembled a man on a sinking ship, who appeals to the ship. Richardson, too, cried madly to the black horse. The spirit of the horse responded to these calls, and quivering and breathing heavily he made a great effort, a sort of a final rush, not for himself apparently, but because he understood that his life's sacrifice, perhaps, had been invoked by these two men who cried to him in the universal tongue. Richardson had no sense of appreciation at this time—he was too frightened—but often now he remembers a certain black horse.

From the rear could be heard a yelling, and once a shot was fired—in the air, evidently. Richardson moaned as he looked back. He kept his hand on his revolver. He tried to imagine the brief tumult of his capture—the flurry of dust from the hoofs of horses pulled suddenly to their haunches, the shrill, biting curses of the men, the ring of the shots, his own last contortion. He wondered, too, if he could not somehow manage to pelt that fat Mexican, just to cure his abominable egotism.

It was José, the terror-stricken, who at last discovered safety. Suddenly he gave a howl of delight and astonished his horse into a new burst of speed. They were on a little ridge at the time, and the American at the top of it saw his servant gallop down the slope and into the arms, so to speak, of a small column of horsemen in gray and silver clothes. In the dim light of the early morning they were as vague as shadows, but Richardson knew them at once for a detachment of rurales, that crack cavalry corps of the Mexican army which polices the plain so zealously, being of themselves the law and the arm of it—a fierce and swift-moving body that knows little of prevention but much of vengeance. They drew up suddenly, and the rows of great silver-trimmed sombreros bobbed in surprise.

Richardson saw José throw himself from his horse and begin to jabber at the leader of the party. When he arrived he found that his servant had already outlined the entire situation, and was then engaged in describing him, Richardson, as an American señor of vast wealth who was the friend of almost every governmental potentate within two hundred miles. This seemed to profoundly impress the officer. He bowed gravely to Richardson and smiled significantly at his men, who unslung their carbines.

The little ridge hid the pursuers from view, but the rapid thud of their horses' feet could be heard. Occasionally they yelled and called to each other. Then at last they swept over the brow of the hill, a wild mob of almost fifty drunken horsemen. When they discerned the pale-uniformed rurales, they were sailing down the slope at top speed.

If toboggans half way down a hill should suddenly make up their minds to turn around and go back, there would be an effect somewhat like that now produced by the drunken horsemen. Richardson saw the rurales serenely swing their carbines forward, and, peculiar-minded person that he was, felt his heart leap into his throat at the prospective volley. But the officer rode forward alone.

It appeared that the man who owned the best horse in this astonished company was the fat Mexican with the snaky mustache, and, in consequence, this gentleman was quite a distance in the van. He tried to pull up, wheel his horse and scuttle back over the hill as some of his companions had done, but the officer called to him in a voice harsh with rage. "—!" howled the officer. "This señor is my friend, the friend of my friends. Do you dare pursue him, —? —! —! —! —!" These lines represent terrible names, all different, used by the officer.

The fat Mexican simply groveled on his horse's neck. His face was green; it could be seen that he expected death. The officer stormed with magnificent intensity: "—! —! —!" Finally he sprang from his saddle, and, running to the fat Mexican's side, yelled: "Go—" and kicked the horse in the belly with all his might. The animal gave a mighty leap into the air, and the fat Mexican, with one wretched glance at the contemplative rurales, aimed his steed for the top of the ridge. Richardson again gulped in expectation of a volley, for—it is said—this is one of the favorite methods of the rurales for disposing of objectionable people. The fat, green Mexican also evidently thought that he was to be killed while on the run, from the miserable look he cast at the troops. Nevertheless, he was allowed to vanish in a cloud of yellow dust at the ridge-top.

José was exultant, defiant, and, oh, bristling with courage. The black horse was drooping sadly, his nose to the ground. Richardson's little animal, with his ears bent forward, was staring at the horses of the rurales as if in an intense study. Richardson longed for speech, but he could only bend forward and pat the shining, silken shoulders. The little horse turned his head and looked back gravely.

The Wise Men: A Detail of American Life in Mexico

THEY WERE YOUTHS of subtle mind. They were very wicked according to report, and yet they managed to have it reflect credit upon them. They often had the well-informed and the great talkers of the American colony engaged in reciting their misdeeds, and facts relating to their sins were usually told with a flourish of awe and fine admiration.

One was from San Francisco and one was from New York, but they resembled each other in appearance. This is an idiosyncrasy of geography.

They were never apart in the City of Mexico, at any rate, excepting perhaps when one had retired to his hotel for a respite, and then the other was usually camped down at the office sending up servants with clamorous messages. "Oh, get up and come on down."

They were two lads—they were called the Kids—and far from their mothers. Occasionally some wise man pitied them, but he usually was alone in his wisdom. The other folk frankly were transfixed at the splendor of the audacity and endurance of these Kids. "When do those two boys ever sleep?" murmured a man as he viewed them entering a café about eight o'clock one morning. Their smooth infantile faces looked bright and fresh enough, at any rate. "Jim told me he saw them still at it about four-thirty this morning."

"Sleep!" ejaculated a companion in a glowing voice. "They never sleep! They go to bed once in every two weeks." His boast of it seemed almost a personal pride.

"They'll end with a crash, though, if they keep it up at this pace," said a gloomy voice from behind a newspaper.

The Café Colorado has a front of white and gold, in which is set larger plate-glass windows than are commonly to be found in Mexico. Two little wings of willow flip-flapping incessantly serve as doors. Under them small stray dogs go furtively into the café, and are shied into the street again by the waiters. On the sidewalk there is always a decorative effect in loungers, ranging from the newly-arrived and superior tourist to the old veteran of the silver mines bronzed by violent suns. They contemplate with various shades of interest the show of the street—the red, purple, dusty white, glaring forth against the walls in the furious sunshine.

One afternoon the Kids strolled into the Café Colorado. A half-dozen of the men who sat smoking and reading with a sort of Parisian effect at the little tables which lined two sides of the room, looked up and bowed smiling, and although this coming of the Kids was anything but an unusual event, at least a dozen men wheeled in their seats to stare after them. Three waiters polished tables, and moved chairs noisily, and appeared to be eager. Distinctly these Kids were of importance.

Behind the distant bar, the tall form of old Pop himself awaited them smiling with broad geniality. "Well, my boys, how are you?" he cried in a voice of profound solicitude. He allowed five or six of his customers to languish in the care of Mexican bar-tenders, while he himself gave his eloquent attention to the Kids, lending all the dignity of a great event to their arrival. "How are the boys to-day, eh?"

"You're a smooth old guy," said one, eyeing him. "Are you giving us this welcome so we won't notice it when you push your worst whisky at us?"

Pop turned in appeal from one Kid to the other Kid. "There, now, hear that, will you?" He assumed an oratorical pose. "Why, my boys, you always get the best—the very best—that this house has got."

"Yes, we do!" The Kids laughed. "Well, bring it out, anyhow, and if it's the same you sold us last night, we'll grab your cash register and run."

Pop whirled a bottle along the bar and then gazed at it with a rapt expression. "Fine as silk," he murmured. "Now just taste that, and if it isn't the finest whisky you ever put in your face, why I'm a liar, that's all."

The Kids surveyed him with scorn, and poured out their allowances. Then they stood for a time insulting Pop about his whisky. "Usually it tastes exactly like new parlor furniture," said the San Francisco Kid. "Well, here goes, and you want to look out for your cash register."

"Your health, gentlemen," said Pop with a grand air, and as he wiped his bristling grey moustache he wagged his head with reference to the cash register question. "I could catch you before you got very far."

"Why, are you a runner?" said one derisively.

"You just bank on me, my boy," said Pop, with deep emphasis. "I'm a flier."

The Kids set down their glasses suddenly and looked at him. "You must be," they said. Pop was tall and graceful and magnificent in manner, but he did not display those qualities of form which mean speed in the animal. His hair was grey; his face was round and fat from much living. The buttons of his glittering white vest formed a fine curve, so that if the concave surface of a piece of barrel-hoop had been laid against Pop it would have touched each button. "You must be," observed the Kids again.

"Well, you can laugh all you like, but—no jolly now, boys, I tell you I'm a winner. Why, I bet you I can skin anything in this town on a square go. When I kept my place in Eagle Pass there wasn't anybody who could touch me. One of these sure things came down from San Anton'. Oh, he was a runner he was. One of these people with wings. Well, I skinned 'im. What? Certainly I did. Never touched me."

The Kids had been regarding him in grave silence, but at this moment they grinned, and said quite in chorus: "Oh, you old liar!"

Pop's voice took on a whining tone of earnestness. "Boys, I'm telling it to you straight. I'm a flier."

One of the Kids had had a dreamy cloud in his eye and he cried out suddenly. "Say, what a joke to play this on Freddie."

The other jumped ecstatically. "Oh, wouldn't it be, though. Say he wouldn't do a thing but howl! He'd go crazy."

They looked at Pop as if they longed to be certain that he was, after all, a runner. "Say, now, Pop, on the level," said one of them wistfully, "can you run?"

"Boys," swore Pop, "I'm a peach! On the dead level, I'm a peach."

"By golly, I believe the old Indian can run," said one to the other, as if they were alone in conference.

"That's what I can," cried Pop.

The Kids said: "Well, so long, old man." They went to a table and sat down. They ordered a salad. They were always ordering salads. This was because one Kid had a wild passion for salads, and the other didn't care much. So at any hour of the day or night they might be seen ordering a salad. When this one came they went into a sort of executive session. It was a very long consultation. Some of the men noted it; they said there was deviltry afoot. Occasionally the Kids laughed in supreme enjoyment of something unknown. The low rumble of wheels came from the street. Often could be heard the parrot-like cries of distant vendors. The sunlight streamed through the green curtains, and made some little amber-colored flitterings on the marble floor. High up among the severe decorations of the ceiling—reminiscent of the days when the great building was a palace—a small white butterfly was wending through the cool air spaces. The long billiard hall stretched back to a vague gloom. The balls were always clicking, and one could see endless elbows crooking. Beggars slunk through the wicker doors, and were ejected by the nearest waiter. At last the Kids called Pop to them.

"Sit down, Pop. Have a drink." They scanned him carefully. "Say now, Pop, on your solemn oath, can you run?"

"Boys," said Pop piously, and raising his hand, "I can run like a rabbit."

"On your oath?"

"On my oath."

"Can you beat Freddie?"

Pop appeared to look at the matter from all sides. "Well, boys, I'll tell you. No man is cock-sure of anything in this world, and I don't want to say that I can best any man, but I've seen Freddie run, and I'm ready to swear I can beat 'im. In a hundred yards I'd just about skin 'im neat—you understand—just about neat. Freddie is a good average runner, but I—you understand—I'm just—a little—bit—better." The Kids had been listening with the utmost attention. Pop spoke the latter part slowly and meaningly. They thought he intended them to see his great confidence.

One said: "Pop, if you throw us in this thing, we'll come here and drink for two weeks without paying. We'll back you and work a josh on Freddie! But oh!—if you throw us!"

To this menace Pop cried: "Boys, I'll make the run of my life! On my oath!"

The salad having vanished, the Kids arose. "All right, now," they warned him. "If you play us for duffers, we'll get square. Don't you forget it."

"Boys, I'll give you a race for your money. Bank on that. I may lose—understand, I may lose—no man can help meeting a better man. But I think I can skin 'im, and I'll give you a run for your money, you bet."

"All right, then. But, look here," they told him, "you keep your face closed. Nobody but us gets in on this. Understand?"

"Not a soul," Pop declared. They left him, gesturing a last warning from the wicker doors.

In the street they saw Benson, his cane gripped in the middle, strolling among the white-clothed jabbering natives on the shady side. They semaphored to him eagerly, their faces ashine with a plot. He came across cautiously, like a man who ventures into dangerous company.

"We're going to get up a race. Pop and Fred. Pop swears he can skin 'im. This is a tip. Keep it dark, now. Say, won't Freddie be hot!"

Benson looked as if he had been compelled to endure these exhibitions of insanity for a century. "Oh, you fellows are off. Pop can't beat Freddie. He's an old bat. Why, it's impossible. Pop can't beat Freddie."

"Can't he? Want to bet he can't?" said the Kids. "There now, let's see—you're talking so large."

"Well, you——"

"Oh, bet. Bet or else close your trap. That's the way."

"How do you know you can pull off the race. Seen Freddie?"

"No, but——"

"Well, see him then. Can't bet now with no race arranged. I'll bet with you all right—all right. I'll give you fellows a tip though—you're a pair of asses. Pop can't run any faster than a brick school-house."

The Kids scowled at him and defiantly said: "Can't he?" They left him and went to the Casa Verde. Freddie, beautiful in his white jacket, was holding one of his innumerable conversations across the bar. He smiled when he saw them. "Where you boys been?" he demanded, in a paternal tone. Almost all the proprietors of American cafés in the city used to adopt a paternal tone when they spoke to the Kids.

"Oh, been 'round," they replied.

"Have a drink?" said the proprietor of the Casa Verde, forgetting his other social obligations. During the course of this ceremony one of the Kids remarked: "Freddie, Pop says he can beat you running."

"Does he?" observed Freddie without excitement. He was used to various snares of the Kids.

"That's what. He says he can leave you at the wire and not see you again."

"Well, he lies," replied Freddie placidly.

"And I'll bet you a bottle of wine that he can do it, too."

"Rats!" said Freddie.

"Oh, that's all right," pursued a Kid. "You can throw bluffs all you like, but he can lose you in a hundred yard dash, you bet."

Freddie drank his whisky, and then settled his elbows on the bar. "Say, now, what do you boys keep coming in here with some pipe-story all the time for? You can't josh me. Do you think you can scare me about Pop? Why, I know I can beat 'im. He's an old man. He can't run with me. Certainly not. Why, you fellows are just jollying me."

"Are we though?" said the Kids. "You daresn't bet the bottle of wine."

"Oh, of course I can bet you a bottle of wine," said Freddie disdainfully. "Nobody cares about a bottle of wine, but——"

"Well, make it five then," advised one of the Kids.

Freddie hunched his shoulders. "Why, certainly I will. Make it ten if you like, but——"

"We do," they said.

"Ten, is it? All right; that goes." A look of weariness came over Freddie's face. "But you boys are foolish. I tell you Pop is an old man. How can you expect him to run? Of course, I'm no great runner, but then I'm young and healthy and—and a pretty smooth runner, too. Pop is old and fat, and then he doesn't do a thing but tank all day. It's a cinch."

The Kids looked at him and laughed rapturously. They

waved their fingers at him. "Ah, there!" they cried. They meant they had made a victim of him.

But Freddie continued to expostulate. "I tell you he couldn't win—an old man like him. You're crazy. Of course, I know you don't care about ten bottles of wine, but, then— to make such bets as that. You're twisted."

"Are we, though?" cried the Kids in mockery. They had precipitated Freddie into a long and thoughtful treatise on every possible chance of the thing as he saw it. They disputed with him from time to time, and jeered at him. He labored on through his argument. Their childish faces were bright with glee.

In the midst of it Wilburson entered. Wilburson worked; not too much, though. He had hold of the Mexican end of a great importing house of New York, and as he was a junior partner he worked. But not too much, though. "What's the howl?" he said.

The Kids giggled. "We've got Freddie rattled."

"Why," said Freddie, turning to him, "these two Indians are trying to tell me that Pop can beat me running."

"Like the devil," said Wilburson, incredulously.

"Well, can't he?" demanded a Kid.

"Why, certainly not," said Wilburson, dismissing every possibility of it with a gesture. "That old bat? Certainly not. I'll bet fifty dollars that Freddie——"

"Take you," said a Kid.

"What?" said Wilburson, "that Freddie won't beat Pop?"

The Kid that had spoken now nodded his head.

"That Freddie won't beat Pop?" repeated Wilburson.

"Yes. It's a go?"

"Why, certainly," retorted Wilburson. "Fifty? All right."

"Bet you five bottles on the side," ventured the other Kid.

"Why, certainly," exploded Wilburson wrathfully. "You fellows must take me for something easy. I'll take all those kind of bets I can get. Cer—tain—ly."

They settled the details. The course was to be paced off on the asphalt of one of the adjacent side-streets, and then, at about eleven o'clock in the evening, the match would be run. Usually in Mexico the streets of a city grow lonely and dark but a little time after nine o'clock. There are occasional lurking figures, perhaps, but no crowds, lights, noise. The course would doubtless be undisturbed. As for the policemen in the vicinity, they—well, they were conditionally amiable.

The Kids went to see Pop; they told him of the arrangements, and then in deep tones they said: "Oh, Pop, if you throw us!"

Pop appeared to be a trifle shaken by the weight of responsibility thrust upon him, but he spoke out bravely. "Boys, I'll pinch that race. Now you watch me. I'll pinch it."

The Kids went then on some business of their own, for they were not seen again until evening. When they returned to the neighborhood of the Café Colorado the usual evening stream of carriages was whirling along the *calle*. The wheels hummed on the asphalt, and the coachmen towered in their great sombreros. On the sidewalk a gazing crowd sauntered, the better class self-satisfied and proud, in their derby hats and cutaway coats, the lower classes muffling their dark faces in their blankets, slipping along in leather sandals. An electric light sputtered and fumed over the throng. The afternoon shower had left the pave wet and glittering. The air was still laden with the odor of rain on flowers, grass, leaves.

In the Café Colorado a cosmopolitan crowd ate, drank, played billiards, gossiped, or read in the glaring yellow light. When the Kids entered a large circle of men that had been gesticulating near the bar greeted them with a roar.

"Here they are now!"

"Oh, you pair of peaches!"

"Say, got any more money to bet with?"

The Kids smiled complacently. Old Colonel Hammigan, grinning, pushed his way to them. "Say, boys, we'll all have a drink on you now because you won't have any money after eleven o'clock. You'll be going down the back stairs in your stocking feet."

Although the Kids remained unnaturally serene and quiet, argument in the Café Colorado became tumultuous. Here and there a man who did not intend to bet ventured meekly that perchance Pop might win, and the others swarmed upon him in a whirlwind of angry denial and ridicule.

Pop, enthroned behind the bar, looked over at this storm with a shadow of anxiety upon his face. This widespread flouting affected him, but the Kids looked blissfully satisfied with the tumult they had stirred.

Blanco, honest man, ever worrying for his friends, came to them. "Say, you fellows, you aren't betting too much? This thing looks kind of shaky, don't it?"

The faces of the Kids grew sober, and after consideration one said: "No, I guess we've got a good thing, Blanco. Pop is going to surprise them, I think."

"Well, don't——"

"All right, old boy. We'll watch out."

From time to time the Kids had much business with certain orange, red, blue, purple, and green bills. They were making little memoranda on the back of visiting cards. Pop watched them closely, the shadow still upon his face. Once he called to them, and when they came he leaned over the bar and said intensely: "Say, boys, remember, now—I might lose this race. Nobody can ever say for sure, and if I do, why——"

"Oh, that's all right, Pop," said the Kids, reassuringly. "Don't mind it. Do your derndest and let it go at that."

When they had left him, however, they went to a corner to consult. "Say, this is getting interesting. Are you in deep?" asked one anxiously of his friend.

"Yes, pretty deep," said the other stolidly. "Are you?"

"Deep as the devil," replied the other in the same tone.

They looked at each other stonily and went back to the crowd. Benson had just entered the café. He approached them with a gloating smile of victory. "Well, where's all that money you were going to bet?"

"Right here," said the Kids, thrusting into their vest pockets.

At eleven o'clock a curious thing was learned. When Pop and Freddie, the Kids and all, came to the little side street, it was thick with people. It seems that the news of this great race had spread like the wind among the Americans, and they had come to witness the event. In the darkness the crowd moved, gesticulating and mumbling in argument.

The principals, the Kids, and those with them, surveyed this scene with some dismay. "Say—here's a go." Even then a policeman might be seen approaching, the light from his little lantern flickering on his white cap, gloves, brass buttons, and on the butt of the old-fashioned Colt's revolver which hung at his belt. He addressed Freddie in swift Mexican. Freddie listened, nodding from time to time. Finally Freddie turned to the others to translate. "He says he'll get into trouble if he allows this race when all this crowd is here."

There was a murmur of discontent. The policeman looked at them with an expression of anxiety on his broad brown face.

"Oh, come on. We'll go hold it on some other fellow's beat," said one of the Kids. The group moved slowly away debating. Suddenly the other Kid cried: "I know! The Paseo!"

"By jiminy," said Freddie, "just the thing. We'll get a cab and go out to the Paseo. S-s-sh! Keep it quiet; we don't want all this mob."

Later they tumbled into a cab—Pop, Freddie, the Kids, old Colonel Hammigan and Benson. They whispered to the men who had wagered: "The Paseo." The cab whirled away up the black street. There was occasional grunts and groans, cries of "Oh, get off me feet," and of "Quit! you're killing me." Six people do not have fun in one cab. The principals spoke to each other with the respect and friendliness which comes to good men at such times. Once a Kid put his head out of the window and looked backward. He pulled it in again and cried: "Great Scott! Look at that, would you!" The others struggled to do as they were bid, and afterward shouted: "Holy smoke! Well, I'll be blowed! Thunder and turf!"

Galloping after them came innumerable other cabs, their lights twinkling, streaming in a great procession through the night. "The street is full of them," ejaculated the old colonel.

The Paseo de la Reforma is the famous drive of the City of Mexico, leading to the Castle of Chapultepec, which last ought to be well known in the United States.

It is a broad fine avenue of macadam with a much greater quality of dignity than anything of the kind we possess in our own land. It seems of the Old World, where to the beauty of the thing itself is added the solemnity of tradition and history, the knowledge that feet in buskins trod the same stones, that cavalcades of steel thundered there before the coming of carriages.

When the Americans tumbled out of their cabs the giant bronzes of Aztec and Spaniard loomed dimly above them like towers. The four rows of poplar trees rustled weirdly off there in the darkness. Pop took out his watch and struck a match. "Well, hurry up this thing. It's almost midnight."

The other cabs came swarming, the drivers lashing their horses, for these Americans, who did all manner of strange things, nevertheless always paid well for it. There was a mighty hubbub then in the darkness. Five or six men began to pace off the distance and quarrel. Others knotted their handkerchiefs together to make a tape. Men were swearing over bets, fussing and fuming about the odds. Benson came to the Kids swaggering. "You're a pair of asses." The cabs waited in a solid block down the avenue. Above the crowd the tall statues hid their visages in the night.

At last a voice floated through the darkness. "Are you ready there?" Everybody yelled excitedly. The men at the tape pulled it out straight. "Hold it higher, Jim, you fool!" A silence fell then upon the throng. Men bended down trying to pierce the darkness with their eyes. From out at the starting point came muffled voices. The crowd swayed and jostled.

The racers did not come. The crowd began to fret, its nerves burning. "Oh, hurry up," shrilled some one.

The voice called again: "Ready there?" Everybody replied: "Yes, all ready. Hurry up!"

There was more muffled discussion at the starting point. In the crowd a man began to make a proposition. "I'll bet twenty——" but the throng interrupted with a howl. "Here they come!" The thickly packed body of men swung as if the ground had moved. The men at the tape shouldered madly at their fellows, bawling: "Keep back! Keep back!"

From the profound gloom came the noise of feet pattering furiously. Vague forms flashed into view for an instant. A hoarse roar broke from the crowd. Men bended and swayed and fought. The Kids back near the tape exchanged another stolid look. A white form shone forth. It grew like a spectre. Always could be heard the wild patter. A barbaric scream broke from the crowd. "By Gawd, it's Pop! Pop! Pop's ahead!"

The old man spun toward the tape like a madman, his chin

thrown back, his grey hair flying. His legs moved like maniac machinery. And as he shot forward a howl as from forty cages of wild animals went toward the imperturbable chieftains in bronze. The crowd flung themselves forward. "Oh, you old Indian! You savage! You cuss, you! Dern my buttons, did you ever see such running?"

"Ain't he a peach! Well!"

"Say, this beats anything!"

"Where's the Kids? H-e-y, Kids!"

"Look at 'im, would you? Did you ever think?" These cries flew in the air blended in a vast shout of astonishment and laughter.

For an instant the whole great tragedy was in view. Freddie, desperate, his teeth shining, his face contorted, whirling along in deadly effort, was twenty feet behind the tall form of old Pop, who, dressed only in his—only in his underclothes—gained with each stride. One grand insane moment, and then Pop had hurled himself against the tape—victor!

Freddie, falling into the arms of some men, struggled with his breath, and at last managed to stammer: "Say, can't—can't that old—old man run!"

Pop, puffing and heaving, could only gasp: "Where's my shoes? Who's got my shoes?" Later Freddie scrambled panting through the crowd, and held out his hand. "Good man, Pop!" And then he looked up and down the tall, stout form. "Hell! who would think you could run like that."

The Kids were surrounded by a crowd, laughing tempestuously.

"How did you know he could run?"

"Why didn't you give me a line on him?"

"Say—great snakes!—you fellows had a nerve to bet on Pop."

"Why, I was cock-sure he couldn't win."

"Oh, you fellows must have seen him run before."

"Who would ever think it?"

Benson came by, filling the midnight air with curses. They turned to jeer him. "What's the matter, Benson?"

"Somebody pinched my handkerchief. I tied it up in that string. Damn it."

The Kids laughed blithely. "Why, hollo, Benson!" they said.

There was a great rush for cabs. Shouting, laughing, wondering, the crowd hustled into their conveyances, and the drivers flogged their horses toward the city again.

"Won't Freddie be crazy! Say, he'll be guyed about this for years."

"But who would ever think that old tank could run so?"

One cab had to wait while Pop and Freddie resumed various parts of their clothing.

As they drove home, Freddie said: "Well, Pop, you beat me."

Pop said: "That's all right, old man."

The Kids, grinning, said: "How much did you lose, Benson?"

Benson said defiantly: "Oh, not so much. How much did you win?"

"Oh, not so much."

Old Colonel Hammigan, squeezed down in a corner, had apparently been reviewing the event in his mind, for he suddenly remarked: "Well, I'm damned!"

They were late in reaching the Café Colorado, but when they did, the bottles were on the bar as thick as pickets on a fence.

The Five White Mice

F REDDIE WAS MIXING a cocktail. His hand with the long spoon was whirling swiftly and the ice in the glass hummed and rattled like a cheap watch. Over by the window, a gambler, a millionaire, a railway conductor and the agent of a vast American syndicate were playing seven-up. Freddie surveyed them with the ironical glance of a man who is mixing a cocktail.

From time to time a swarthy Mexican waiter came with his tray from the rooms at the rear and called his orders across the bar. The sounds of the indolent stir of the city, awakening from its siesta, floated over the screens which barred the sun and the inquisitive eye. From the faraway kitchen could be heard the roar of the old French chef, driving, herding and abusing his Mexican helpers.

A string of men came suddenly in from the street. They stormed up to the bar. There were impatient shouts. "Come, now, Freddie, don't stand there like a portrait of yourself. Wiggle!" Drinks of many kinds and colors, amber, green, mahogany, strong and mild, began to swarm upon the bar with all the attendants of lemon, sugar, mint and ice. Freddie, with Mexican support, worked like a sailor in the provision of them, sometimes talking with that scorn for drink and admiration for those who drink which is the attribute of a good bar-keeper.

At last a man was afflicted with a stroke of dice-shaking. A herculean discussion was waging and he was deeply engaged in it but at the same time he lazily flirted the dice. Occasionally he made great combinations. "Look at that, would you?" he cried proudly. The others paid little heed. Then violently the craving took them. It went along the line like an epidemic and involved them all. In a moment they had arranged a carnival of dice-shaking with money penalties and liquid prizes. They clamorously made it a point of honor with Freddie that he too should play and take his chance of sometimes providing this large group with free refreshment. With bended heads like foot-ball players they surged over the tinkling dice, jostling, cheering and bitterly arguing. One of the quiet com-

758

pany playing seven-up at the corner table said profanely that
the row reminded him of a bowling contest at a picnic.

After the regular shower, many carriages rolled over the
smooth *calle* and sent a musical thunder through the Casa
Verde. The shop-windows became aglow with light and the
walks were crowded with youths, callow and ogling, dressed
vainly according to supposititious fashions. The policemen
had muffled themselves in their gnome-like cloaks and placed
their lanterns as obstacles for the carriages in the middle of
the street. The City of Mexico gave forth the deep mellow
organ-tones of its evening resurrection.

But still the group at the bar of the Casa Verde were shak-
ing dice. They had passed beyond shaking for drinks for the
crowd, for Mexican dollars, for dinner, for the wine at dinner.
They had even gone to the trouble of separating the cigars
and cigarettes from the dinner's bill and causing a distinct
man to be responsible for them. Finally they were aghast.
Nothing remained within sight of their minds which even re-
motely suggested further gambling. There was a pause for
deep consideration.

"Well——"

"Well——"

A man called out in the exuberance of creation. "I know!
Let's shake for a box tonight at the circus! A box at the cir-
cus!" The group was profoundly edified. "That's it! That's it!
Come on now! Box at the circus!" A dominating voice cried:
"Three dashes—high man out!" An American, tall and with
a face of copper red from the rays that flash among the Sierra
Madres and burn on the cactus deserts, took the little leathern
cup and spun the dice out upon the polished wood. A fasci-
nated assemblage hung upon the bar-rail. Three kings turned
their pink faces upward. The tall man flourished the cup, bur-
lesquing, and flung the two other dice. From them he ulti-
mately extracted one more pink king. "There," he said.
"Now, let's see! Four kings!" He began to swagger in a sort
of provisional way.

The next man took the cup and blew softly in the top of it.
Poising it in his hand, he then surveyed the company with a
stony eye and paused. They knew perfectly well that he was
applying the magic of deliberation and ostentatious indiffer-

ence but they could not wait in tranquility during the performances of all these rites. They began to call out impatiently. "Come now—hurry up." At last the man with a gesture that was singularly impressive, threw the dice. The others set up a howl of joy. "Not a pair!" There was another solemn pause. The men moved restlessly. "Come, now, go ahead!" In the end the man, induced and abused, achieved something that was nothing in the presence of four kings. The tall man climbed on the foot-rail and leaned hazardously forward. "Four kings! My four kings are good to go out," he bellowed into the middle of the mob and although in a moment he did pass into the radiant region of exemption he continued to bawl advice and scorn.

The mirrors and oiled woods of the Casa Verde were now dancing with blue flashes from a great buzzing electric lamp. A host of quiet members of the Anglo-Saxon colony had come in for their pre-dinner cocktails. An amiable person was exhibiting to some tourists this popular American saloon. It was a very sober and respectable time of day. Freddie reproved courageously the dice-shaking brawlers and, in return, he received the choicest advice in a tumult of seven combined vocabularies. He laughed; he had been compelled to retire from the game but he was keeping an interested, if furtive, eye upon it.

Down at the end of the line, there was a youth at whom everybody railed for his flaming ill-luck. At each disaster, Freddie swore from behind the bar in a sort of affectionate contempt. "Why this Kid has had no luck for two days. Did you ever see such throwin'."

The contest narrowed eventually to the New York Kid and an individual who swung about placidly on legs that moved in nefarious circles. He had a grin that resembled a bit of carving. He was obliged to lean down and blink rapidly to ascertain the facts of his venture but fate presented him with five queens. His smile did not change but he puffed gently like a man who has been running.

The others, having emerged scatheless from this part of the conflict, waxed hilarious with the Kid. They smote him on either shoulder. "We've got you stuck for it, Kid! You can't beat that game! Five queens!"

Up to this time, the Kid had displayed only the temper of the gambler but the cheerful hoots of the players supplemented now by a ring of guying non-combatants caused him to feel profoundly that it would be fine to beat the five queens. He addressed a gambler's slogan to the interior of the cup.

> "Oh, five white mice of chance,
> Shirts of wool and corduroy pants,
> Gold and wine, women and sin,
> All for you if you let me come in—
> Into the house of chance."

Flashing the dice sardonically out upon the bar, he displayed three aces. From two dice in the next throw, he achieved one more ace. For his last throw, he rattled the single dice for a long time. He already had four aces; if he accomplished another one, the five queens were vanquished and the box at the circus came from the drunken man's pocket. All of the Kid's movements were slow and elaborate. For his last throw he planted the cup bottom-up on the bar with the one dice hidden under it. Then he turned and faced the crowd with the air of a conjuror or a cheat. "Oh, maybe it's an ace," he said in boastful calm. "Maybe it's an ace." Instantly he was presiding over a little drama in which every man was absorbed. The Kid leaned with his back against the bar-rail and with his elbows upon it. "Maybe it's an ace," he repeated.

A jeering voice in the background said: "Yes, maybe it is, Kid!"

The Kid's eyes searched for a moment among the men. "I'll bet fifty dollars it is an ace," he said.

Another voice asked: "American money?"

"Yes," answered the Kid.

"Oh!" There was a genial laugh at this discomfiture. However no one came forward at the Kid's challenge and presently he turned to the cup. "Now, I'll show you." With the manner of a mayor unveiling a statue, he lifted the cup. There was revealed naught but a ten-spot. In the roar which arose could be heard each man ridiculing the cowardice of his neighbor and above all the din rang the voice of Freddie berating everyone. "Why, there isn't one liver to every five men in the outfit. That was the greatest cold bluff I ever saw worked. He wouldn't know how to cheat with dice if he wanted to. Don't know the first thing about it. I could hardly keep from laughin' when I seen him drillin' you around. Why, I tell you, I had that fifty dollars right in my pocket if I wanted to be a chump. You're an easy lot——"

Nevertheless the group who had won in the circus-box game did not relinquish their triumph. They burst like a storm about the head of the Kid, swinging at him with their fists. " 'Five white mice'!" they quoted choking. " 'Five white mice'!"

"Oh, they are not so bad," said the Kid.

Afterward it often occurred that a man would suddenly jeer a finger at the Kid and derisively say: " 'Five white mice'."

On the route from the dinner to the circus, others of the party often asked the Kid if he had really intended to make his appeal to mice. They suggested other animals—rabbits, dogs, hedge-hogs, snakes, opossums. To this banter the Kid replied with a serious expression of his belief in the fidelity and wisdom of the five white mice. He presented a most eloquent case, decorated with fine language and insults, in which he proved that if one was going to believe in anything at all, one might as well choose the five white mice. His companions however at once and unanimously pointed out to him that his recent exploit did not place him in the light of a convincing advocate.

The Kid discerned two figures in the street. They were making imperious signs at him. He waited for them to approach, for he recognized one as the other Kid—the 'Frisco Kid—there were two Kids. With the 'Frisco Kid was Benson. They arrived almost breathless. "Where you been?" cried the 'Frisco Kid. It was an arrangement that upon a meeting the one that could first ask this question was entitled to use a tone of limitless injury. "What you been doing? Where you going? Come on with us. Benson and I have got a little scheme."

The New York Kid pulled his arm from the grapple of the other. "I can't. I've got to take these sutlers to the circus.

They stuck me for it shaking dice at Freddie's. I can't, I tell you."

The two did not at first attend to his remarks. "Come on! We've got a little scheme."

"I can't. They stuck me. I've got to take'm to the circus."

At this time it did not suit the men with the scheme to recognize these objections as important. "Oh, take'm some other time. Well, can't you take'm some other time? Let 'em go. Damn the circus. Get cold feet. What did you get stuck for? Get cold feet."

But despite their fighting, the New York Kid broke away from them. "I can't, I tell you. They stuck me." As he left them, they yelled with rage. "Well, meet us, now, do you hear? In the Casa Verde as soon as the circus quits! Hear?" They threw maledictions after him.

In the City of Mexico, a man goes to the circus without descending in any way to infant amusements because the Circo Teatro Orrin is one of the best in the world and too easily surpasses anything of the kind in the United States where it is merely a matter of a number of rings, if possible, and a great professional agreement to lie to the public. More-over the American clown who in the Mexican arena prances and gabbles is the clown to whom writers refer as the delight of their childhood and lament that he is dead. At this circus the Kid was not debased by the sight of mournful prisoner elephants and caged animals forlorn and sickly. He sat in his box until late and laughed and swore when past laughing at the comic, foolish, wise clown.

When he returned to the Casa Verde there was no display of the 'Frisco Kid and Benson. Freddie was leaning upon the bar listening to four men terribly discuss a question that was not plain. There was a card-game in the corner, of course. Sounds of revelry pealed from the rear rooms.

When the Kid asked Freddie if he had seen his friend and Benson, Freddie looked bored. "Oh, yes, they were in here just a minute ago but I don't know where they went. They've got their skates on. Where've they been? Came in here rolling across the floor like two little gilt gods. They wobbled around for a time and then 'Frisco wanted me to send six bottles of wine around to Benson's rooms, but I didn't have anybody to send this time of night and so they got mad and went out. Where did they get their loads?"

In the first deep gloom of the street, the Kid paused a moment debating. But presently he heard quavering voices. "Oh, Kid! Kid! Comere!" Peering, he recognized two vague figures against the opposite wall. He crossed the street and they said: "Hellokid."

"Say, where did you get it?" he demanded sternly. "You Indians better go home. What did you want to get scragged for?" His face was luminous with virtue.

As they swung to and fro, they made angry denials. "We ain' load'! We ain' load'. Big chump. Comonangetadrink." The sober youth turned then to his friend. "Hadn't you better go home, Kid? Come on, it's late. You'd better break away."

The 'Frisco Kid wagged his head decisively. "Got take Benson home first. He'll be wallowing 'round in a minute. Don't mind me. I'm all right."

"Cer'ly, he's all right," said Benson arousing from deep thought. "He's all right. But better take'm home, though. That's ri-right. He's load'. But he's all right. No need go home any more'n you. But better take'm home. He's load'." He looked at his companion with compassion. "Kid, you're load'."

The sober Kid spoke abruptly to his friend from San Francisco. "Kid, pull yourself together, now. Don't fool. We've got to brace this ass of a Benson all the way home. Get hold of his other arm."

The 'Frisco Kid immediately obeyed his comrade without a word or a glower. He seized Benson and came to attention like a soldier. Later, indeed, he meekly ventured: "Can't we take cab?" But when the New York Kid snapped out that there were no convenient cabs he subsided to an impassive silence. He seemed to be reflecting upon his state without astonishment, dismay or any particular emotion. He submitted himself woodenly to the direction of his friend.

Benson had protested when they had grasped his arms. "Washa doing?" he said in a new and guttural voice. "Washa doing? I ain' load'. Comonangetadrink. I——"

"Oh, come along, you idiot," said the New York Kid. The 'Frisco Kid merely presented the mien of a stoic to the appeal of Benson and in silence dragged away at one of his arms. Benson's feet came from that particular spot on the pavement with the reluctance of roots and also with the ultimate suddenness of roots. The three of them lurched out into the street in the abandon of tumbling chimneys. Benson was meanwhile noisily challenging the others to produce any reasons for his being taken home. His toes clashed into the kerb when they reached the other side of the *calle* and for a moment the Kids hauled him along with the points of his shoes scraping musically on the pavement. He balked formidably as they were about to pass the Casa Verde. "No! No! Leshavanothdrink! Anothdrink! Onemore!"

But the 'Frisco Kid obeyed the voice of his partner in a manner that was blind but absolute and they scummed Benson on past the door. Locked together the three swung into a dark street. The sober Kid's flank was continually careering ahead of the other wing. He harshly admonished the 'Frisco child and the latter promptly improved in the same manner of unthinking complete obedience. Benson began to recite the tale of a love affair, a tale that didn't even have a middle. Occasionally the New York Kid swore. They toppled on their way like three comedians playing at it on the stage.

At midnight a little Mexican street burrowing among the walls of the city is as dark as a whale's throat at deep sea. Upon this occasion heavy clouds hung over the capital and the sky was a pall. The projecting balconies could make no shadows.

"Shay," said Benson breaking away from his escort suddenly, "what want gome for? I ain' load'. You got reg'lar spool-fact'ry in your head—you N' York Kid there. Thish oth' Kid, he's mos' proper, mos' proper shober. He's drunk but—but he's shober."

"Ah, shut up, Benson," said the New York Kid. "Come along now. We can't stay here all night." Benson refused to be corralled but spread his legs and twirled like a dervish, meanwhile under the evident impression that he was conducting himself most handsomely. It was not long before he gained the opinion that he was laughing at the others. "Eight purple dogsh—dogs! Eight purple dogs. Thas what Kid'll see in the morn'. Look ou' for 'em. They——"

As Benson, describing the canine phenomena, swung wildly across the sidewalk, it chanced that three other pedestrians were passing in shadowy rank. Benson's shoulder jostled one of them.

A Mexican wheeled upon the instant. His hand flashed to his hip. There was a moment of silence during which Benson's voice was not heard raised in apology. Then an indescribable comment, one burning word, came from between the Mexican's teeth.

Benson, rolling about in a semi-detached manner, stared vacantly at the Mexican who thrust his lean yellow face forward while his fingers played nervously at his hip. The New York Kid could not follow Spanish well but he understood when the Mexican breathed softly: "Does the señor want fight?"

Benson simply gazed in gentle surprise. The woman next to him at dinner had said something inventive. His tailor had presented his bill. Something had occurred which was mildly out of the ordinary and his surcharged brain refused to cope with it. He displayed only the agitation of a smoker temporarily without a light.

The New York Kid had almost instantly grasped Benson's arm and was about to jerk him away when the other Kid who up to this time had been an automaton suddenly projected himself forward, thrust the rubber Benson aside and said: "Yes!"

There was no sound nor light in the world. The wall at the left happened to be of the common prison-like construction—no door, no window, no opening at all. Humanity was enclosed and asleep. Into the mouth of the sober Kid came a wretched bitter taste as if it had filled with blood. He was transfixed as if he was already seeing the lightning ripples on the knife-blade.

But the Mexican's hand did not move at that time. His face went still further forward and he whispered: "So?" The sober Kid saw this face as if he and it were alone in space—a yellow mask smiling in eager cruelty, in satisfaction, and above all it was lit with sinister decision. As for the features they were reminiscent of an unplaced, a forgotten type which really resembled with precision those of a man who had shaved him three times in Boston in 1888. But the expression burned his mind as sealing-wax burns the palm and fascinated, stupefied, he actually watched the progress of the man's thought toward the point where a knife would be wrenched from its sheath. The emotion, a sort of mechanical fury, a breeze made by electric fans, a rage made by vanity, smote the dark countenance in wave after wave.

Then the New York Kid took a sudden step forward. His hand was also at his hip. He was gripping there a revolver of robust size. He recalled that upon its black handle was stamped a hunting scene in which a sportsman in fine leggings and a peaked cap was taking aim at a stag less than one eighth of an inch away.

His pace forward caused instant movement of the Mexicans. One immediately took two steps to face him squarely. There was a general adjustment, pair and pair. This opponent of the New York Kid was a tall man and quite stout. His sombrero was drawn low over his eyes. His serape was flung on his left shoulder. His back was bended in the supposed manner of a Spanish grandee. This concave gentleman cut a fine and terrible figure. The lad, moved by the spirits of his modest and perpendicular ancestors, had time to feel his blood roar at sight of the pose.

He was aware that the third Mexican was over on the left fronting Benson and he was aware that Benson was leaning against the wall sleepily and peacefully eyeing the convention. So it happened that these six men stood, side fronting side, five of them with their right hands at their hips and with their bodies lifted nervously while the central pair exchanged a crescendo of provocations. The meaning of their words rose and rose. They were travelling in a straight line toward collision.

The New York Kid contemplated his Spanish grandee. He drew his revolver upward until the hammer was surely free of the holster. He waited immovable and watchful while the garrulous 'Frisco Kid expended two and a half lexicons on the middle Mexican.

The Eastern lad suddenly decided that he was going to be killed. His mind leaped forward and studied the aftermath. The story would be a marvel of brevity when first it reached the far New York home, written in a careful hand on a bit of cheap paper topped and footed and backed by the printed fortifications of the cable company. But they are often as stones flung into mirrors, these bits of paper upon which are laconically written all the most terrible chronicles of the times. He witnessed the uprising of his mother and sister and the invincible calm of his hard-mouthed old father who would probably shut himself in his library and smoke alone. Then his father would come and they would bring him here and say: "This is the place." Then, very likely, each would remove his hat. They would stand quietly with their hats in their hands for a decent minute. He pitied his old financing father, unyielding and millioned, a man who commonly spoke twenty-two words a year to his beloved son. The Kid understood it at this time. If his fate was not impregnable, he might have turned out to be a man and have been liked by his father.

The other Kid would mourn his death. He would be preternaturally correct for some weeks and recite the tale without swearing. But it would not bore him. For the sake of his dead comrade he would be glad to be preternaturally correct and to recite the tale without swearing.

These views were perfectly stereopticon, flashing in and away from his thought with an inconceivable rapidity until after all they were simply one quick dismal impression. And now here is the unreal real: into this Kid's nostrils, at the expectant moment of slaughter, had come the scent of new-mown hay, a fragrance from a field of prostrate grass, a fragrance which contained the sunshine, the bees, the peace of meadows and the wonder of a distant crooning stream. It had no right to be supreme but it was supreme and he breathed it as he waited for pain and a sight of the unknown.

But in the same instant, it may be, his thought flew to the 'Frisco Kid and it came upon him like a flicker of lightning that the 'Frisco Kid was not going to be there to perform, for instance, the extraordinary office of respectable mourner. The other Kid's head was muddled, his hand was unsteady, his agility was gone. This other Kid was facing the determined and most ferocious gentleman of the enemy. The New York Kid became convinced that his friend was lost. There was going to be a screaming murder. He was so certain of it that he wanted to shield his eyes from sight of the leaping arm and the knife. It was sickening, utterly sickening. The New York Kid might have been taking his first sea-voyage. A combination of honorable manhood and inability prevented him from running away.

He suddenly knew that it was possible to draw his own revolver and by a swift manoeuver face down all three Mexicans. If he was quick enough he would probably be victor. If any hitch occurred in the draw he would undoubtedly be dead with his friends. It was a new game; he had never been obliged to face a situation of this kind in the Beacon Club in New York. In this test, the lungs of the Kid still continued to perform their duty.

> "Oh, five white mice of chance,
>   Shirts of wool and corduroy pants,
>   Gold and wine, women and sin,
>   All for you if you let me come in—
>   Into the house of chance."

He thought of the weight and size of his revolver and dismay pierced him. He feared that in his hands it would be as unwieldy as a sewing-machine for this quick work. He imagined, too, that some singular providence might cause him to lose his grip as he raised his weapon. Or it might get fatally entangled in the tails of his coat. Some of the eels of despair lay wet and cold against his back.

But at the supreme moment the revolver came forth as if it were greased and it arose like a feather. This somnolent machine, after months of repose, was finally looking at the breasts of men.

Perhaps in this one series of movements, the Kid had unconsciously used nervous force sufficient to raise a bale of hay. Before he comprehended it he was standing behind his revolver glaring over the barrel at the Mexicans menacing first one and then another. His finger was tremoring on the trigger. The revolver gleamed in the darkness with a fine silver light.

The fulsome grandee sprang backward with a low cry. The

man who had been facing the 'Frisco Kid took a quick step away. The beautiful array of Mexicans was suddenly disorganized.

The cry and the backward steps revealed something of great importance to the New York Kid. He had never dreamed that he did not have a complete monopoly of all possible trepidations. The cry of the grandee was that of a man who suddenly sees a poisonous snake. Thus the Kid was able to understand swiftly that they were all human beings. They were unanimous in not wishing for too bloody combat. There was a sudden expression of the equality. He had vaguely believed that they were not going to evince much consideration for his dramatic development as an active factor. They even might be exasperated into an onslaught by it. Instead, they had respected his movement with a respect as great even as an ejaculation of fear and backward steps. Upon the instant he pounced forward and began to swear, unreeling great English oaths as thick as ropes and lashing the faces of the Mexicans with them. He was bursting with rage because these men had not previously confided to him that they were vulnerable. The whole thing had been an absurd imposition. He had been seduced into respectful alarm by the concave attitude of the grandee. And after all there had been an equality of emotion, an equality: he was furious. He wanted to take the serape of the grandee and swaddle him in it.

The Mexicans slunk back, their eyes burning wistfully. The Kid took aim first at one and then at another. After they had achieved a certain distance they paused and drew up in a rank. They then resumed some of their old splendor of manner. A voice hailed him in a tone of cynical bravado as if it had come from between high lips of smiling mockery. "Well, señor, it is finished?"

The Kid scowled into the darkness, his revolver drooping at his side. After a moment he answered: "I am willing." He found it strange that he should be able to speak after this silence of years.

"Good night, señor."

"Good night."

When he turned to look at the 'Frisco Kid he found him in his original position, his hand upon his hip. He was blinking in perplexity at the point from whence the Mexicans had vanished.

"Well," said the sober Kid crossly, "are you ready to go home now?"

The 'Frisco Kid said: "Where they gone?" His voice was undisturbed but inquisitive.

Benson suddenly propelled himself from his dreamful position against the wall. "Frishco Kid's all right. He's drunk's fool and he's all right. But you New York Kid, you're shober." He passed into a state of profound investigation. "Kid shober 'cause didn't go with us. Didn't go with us 'cause went to damn circus. Went to damn circus 'cause lose shakin' dice. Lose shakin' dice 'cause—what make lose shakin' dice, Kid?"

The New York Kid eyed the senile youth. "I don't know. The five white mice, maybe."

Benson puzzled so over this reply that he had to be held erect by his friends. Finally the 'Frisco Kid said: "Let's go home."

Nothing had happened.

A Man and Some Others

I

DARK MESQUIT SPREAD from horizon to horizon. There was no house or horseman from which a mind could evolve a city or a crowd. The world was declared to be a desert and unpeopled. Sometimes, however, on days when no heat-mist arose, a blue shape, dim, of the substance of a specter's veil, appeared in the southwest, and a pondering sheepherder might remember that there were mountains.

In the silence of these plains the sudden and childish banging of a tin pan could have made an iron-nerved man leap into the air. The sky was ever flawless; the manœuvering of clouds was an unknown pageant; but at times a sheep-herder could see, miles away, the long, white streamers of dust rising from the feet of another's flock, and the interest became intense.

Bill was arduously cooking his dinner, bending over the fire, and toiling like a blacksmith. A movement, a flash of strange color, perhaps, off in the bushes, caused him suddenly to turn his head. Presently he arose, and, shading his eyes with his hand, stood motionless and gazing. He perceived at last a Mexican sheep-herder winding through the brush toward his camp.

"Hello!" shouted Bill.

The Mexican made no answer, but came steadily forward until he was within some twenty yards. There he paused, and, folding his arms, drew himself up in the manner affected by the villain in the play. His serape muffled the lower part of his face, and his great sombrero shaded his brow. Being unexpected and also silent, he had something of the quality of an apparition; moreover, it was clearly his intention to be mysterious and devilish.

The American's pipe, sticking carelessly in the corner of his mouth, was twisted until the wrong side was uppermost, and he held his frying-pan poised in the air. He surveyed with evident surprise this apparition in the mesquit. "Hello, José!" he said; " what's the matter?"

The Mexican spoke with the solemnity of funeral tollings:

"Beel, you mus' geet off range. We want you geet off range. We no like. Un'erstan'? We no like."

"What you talking about?" said Bill. "No like what?"

"We no like you here. Un'erstan'? Too mooch. You mus' geet out. We no like. Un'erstan'?"

"Understand? No; I don't know what the blazes you're gittin' at." Bill's eyes wavered in bewilderment, and his jaw fell. "I must git out? I must git off the range? What you givin' us?"

The Mexican unfolded his serape with his small yellow hand. Upon his face was then to be seen a smile that was gently, almost caressingly murderous. "Beel," he said, "geet out!"

Bill's arm dropped until the frying-pan was at his knee. Finally he turned again toward the fire. "Go on, you dog-gone little yaller rat!" he said over his shoulder. "You fellers can't chase me off this range. I got as much right here as anybody."

"Beel," answered the other in a vibrant tone, thrusting his head forward and moving one foot, "you geet out or we keel you."

"Who will?" said Bill.

"I—and the others." The Mexican tapped his breast gracefully.

Bill reflected for a time, and then he said: "You ain't got no manner of license to warn me off'n this range, and I won't move a rod. Understand? I've got rights, and I suppose if I don't see 'em through, no one is likely to give me a good hand and help me lick you fellers, since I'm the only white man in half a day's ride. Now, look; if you fellers try to rush this camp, I'm goin' to plug about fifty per cent of the gentlemen present, sure. I'm goin' in for trouble, an' I'll git a lot of you. 'Nuther thing: if I was a fine valuable caballero like you, I'd stay in the rear till the shootin' was done, because I'm goin' to make a particular p'int of shootin' you through the chest." He grinned affably, and made a gesture of dismissal.

As for the Mexican, he waved his hands in a consummate expression of indifference. "Oh, all right," he said. Then, in a tone of deep menace and glee, he added: "We will keel you eef you no geet. They have decide'."

"They have, have they?" said Bill. "Well, you tell them to go to the devil!"

II

Bill had been a mine-owner in Wyoming, a great man, an aristocrat, one who possessed unlimited credit in the saloons down the gulch. He had the social weight that could interrupt a lynching or advise a bad man of the particular merits of a remote geographical point. However, the fates exploded the toy balloon with which they had amused Bill, and on the evening of the same day he was a professional gambler with ill fortune dealing him unspeakable irritation in the shape of three big cards whenever another fellow stood pat. It is well here to inform the world that Bill considered his calamities of life all dwarfs in comparison with the excitement of one particular evening, when three kings came to him with criminal regularity against a man who always filled a straight. Later he became a cow-boy, more weirdly abandoned than if he had never been an aristocrat. By this time all that remained of his former splendor was his pride, or his vanity, which was one thing which need not have remained. He killed the foreman of the ranch over an inconsequent matter as to which of them was a liar, and the midnight train carried him eastward. He became a brakeman on the Union Pacific, and really gained high honors in the hobo war that for many years has devastated the beautiful railroads of our country. A creature of ill fortune himself, he practised all the ordinary cruelties upon these other creatures of ill fortune. He was of so fierce a mien that tramps usually surrendered at once whatever coin or tobacco they had in their possession; and if afterward he kicked them from the train, it was only because this was a recognized treachery of the war upon the hoboes. In a famous battle fought in Nebraska in 1879, he would have achieved a lasting distinction if it had not been for a deserter from the United States army. He was at the head of a heroic and sweeping charge, which really broke the power of the hoboes in that county for three months; he had already worsted four tramps with his own coupling-stick, when a stone thrown by the ex-third baseman of F Troop's nine laid him flat on the prairie, and later enforced a stay in the hospital in Omaha. After his recovery he engaged with other railroads, and shuffled cars in countless yards. An order to strike came upon him in Michigan, and afterward the vengeance of the railroad pursued him until he assumed a name. This mask is like the darkness in which the burglar chooses to move. It destroys many of the healthy fears. It is a small thing, but it eats that which we call our conscience. The conductor of No. 419 stood in the caboose within two feet of Bill's nose, and called him a liar. Bill requested him to use a milder term. He had not bored the foreman of Tin Can Ranch with any such request, but had killed him with expedition. The conductor seemed to insist, and so Bill let the matter drop.

He became the bouncer of a saloon on the Bowery in New York. Here most of his fights were as successful as had been his brushes with the hoboes in the West. He gained the complete admiration of the four clean bartenders who stood behind the great and glittering bar. He was an honored man. He nearly killed Bad Hennessy, who, as a matter of fact, had more reputation than ability, and his fame moved up the Bowery and down the Bowery.

But let a man adopt fighting as his business, and the thought grows constantly within him that it is his business to fight. These phrases became mixed in Bill's mind precisely as they are here mixed; and let a man get this idea in his mind, and defeat begins to move toward him over the unknown ways of circumstances. One summer night three sailors from the U.S.S. *Seattle* sat in the saloon drinking and attending to other people's affairs in an amiable fashion. Bill was a proud man since he had thrashed so many citizens, and it suddenly occurred to him that the loud talk of the sailors was very offensive. So he swaggered upon their attention, and warned them that the saloon was the flowery abode of peace and gentle silence. They glanced at him in surprise, and without a moment's pause consigned him to a worse place than any stoker of them knew. Whereupon he flung one of them through the side door before the others could prevent it. On the sidewalk there was a short struggle, with many hoarse epithets in the air, and then Bill slid into the saloon again. A frown of false rage was upon his brow, and he strutted like a savage king. He took a long yellow night-stick from behind the lunch-counter, and started importantly toward the main doors to see that the incensed seamen did not again enter.

The ways of sailormen are without speech, and, together in the street, the three sailors exchanged no word, but they moved at once. Landsmen would have required two years of discussion to gain such unanimity. In silence, and immediately, they seized a long piece of scantling that lay handily. With one forward to guide the battering-ram, and with two behind him to furnish the power, they made a beautiful curve, and came down like the Assyrians on the front door of that saloon.

Strange and still strange are the laws of fate. Bill, with his kingly frown and his long night-stick, appeared at precisely that moment in the doorway. He stood like a statue of victory; his pride was at its zenith; and in the same second this atrocious piece of scantling punched him in the bulwarks of his stomach, and he vanished like a mist. Opinions differed as to where the end of the scantling landed him, but it was ultimately clear that it landed him in southwestern Texas, where he became a sheep-herder.

The sailors charged three times upon the plate-glass front of the saloon, and when they had finished, it looked as if it had been the victim of a rural fire company's success in saving it from the flames. As the proprietor of the place surveyed the ruins, he remarked that Bill was a very zealous guardian of property. As the ambulance surgeon surveyed Bill, he remarked that the wound was really an excavation.

III

As his Mexican friend tripped blithely away, Bill turned with a thoughtful face to his frying-pan and his fire. After dinner he drew his revolver from its scarred old holster, and examined every part of it. It was the revolver that had dealt death to the foreman, and it had also been in free fights in which it had dealt death to several or none. Bill loved it because its allegiance was more than that of man, horse, or dog. It questioned neither social nor moral position; it obeyed alike the saint and the assassin. It was the claw of the eagle,

the tooth of the lion, the poison of the snake; and when he
swept it from its holster, this minion smote where he listed,
even to the battering of a far penny. Wherefore it was his
dearest possession, and was not to be exchanged in south-
western Texas for a handful of rubies, nor even the shame and
homage of the conductor of No. 419.

During the afternoon he moved through his monotony of
work and leisure with the same air of deep meditation. The
smoke of his supper-time fire was curling across the shadowy
sea of mesquit when the instinct of the plainsman warned him
that the stillness, the desolation, was again invaded. He saw a
motionless horseman in black outline against the pallid sky.
The silhouette displayed serape and sombrero, and even the
Mexican spurs as large as pies. When this black figure began to
move toward the camp, Bill's hand dropped to his revolver.

The horseman approached until Bill was enabled to see
pronounced American features, and a skin too red to grow on
a Mexican face. Bill released his grip on his revolver.

"Hello!" called the horseman.

"Hello!" answered Bill.

The horseman cantered forward. "Good evening," he said,
as he again drew rein.

"Good evenin'," answered Bill, without committing himself
by too much courtesy.

For a moment the two men scanned each other in a way
that is not ill-mannered on the plains, where one is in danger
of meeting horse-thieves or tourists.

Bill saw a type which did not belong in the mesquit. The
young fellow had invested in some Mexican trappings of an
expensive kind. Bill's eyes searched the outfit for some sign of
craft, but there was none. Even with his local regalia, it was
clear that the young man was of a far, black Northern city.
He had discarded the enormous stirrups of his Mexican sad-
dle; he used the small English stirrup, and his feet were thrust
forward until the steel tightly gripped his ankles. As Bill's eyes
traveled over the stranger, they lighted suddenly upon the
stirrups and the thrust feet, and immediately he smiled in a
friendly way. No dark purpose could dwell in the innocent
heart of a man who rode thus on the plains.

As for the stranger, he saw a tattered individual with a tangle of hair and beard, and with a complexion turned brick-color from the sun and whisky. He saw a pair of eyes that at first looked at him as the wolf looks at the wolf, and then became childlike, almost timid, in their glance. Here was evidently a man who had often stormed the iron walls of the city of success, and who now sometimes valued himself as the rabbit values his prowess.

The stranger smiled genially, and sprang from his horse. "Well, sir, I suppose you will let me camp here with you to-night?"

"Eh?" said Bill.

"I suppose you will let me camp here with you to-night?"

Bill for a time seemed too astonished for words. "Well,"—he answered, scowling in inhospitable annoyance—" well, I don't believe this here is a good place to camp to-night, mister."

The stranger turned quickly from his saddle-girth.

"What?" he said in surprise. "You don't want me here? You don't want me to camp here?"

Bill's feet scuffled awkwardly, and he looked steadily at a cactus-plant. "Well, you see, mister," he said, "I'd like your company well enough, but—you see, some of these here greasers are goin' to chase me off the range to-night; and while I might like a man's company all right, I couldn't let him in for no such game when he ain't got nothin' to do with the trouble."

"Going to chase you off the range?" cried the stranger.

"Well, they said they were goin' to do it," said Bill.

"And—great heavens! will they kill you, do you think?"

"Don't know. Can't tell till afterwards. You see, they take some feller that's alone like me, and then they rush his camp when he ain't quite ready for 'em, and ginerally plug 'im with a sawed-off shot-gun load before he has a chance to git at 'em. They lay around and wait for their chance, and it comes soon enough. Of course a feller alone like me has got to let up watching some time. Maybe they ketch 'im asleep. Maybe the feller gits tired waiting, and goes out in broad day, and kills two or three just to make the whole crowd pile on him and settle the thing. I heard of a case like that once. It's awful hard on a man's mind—to git a gang after him."

"And so they're going to rush your camp to-night?" cried the stranger. "How do you know? Who told you?"

"Feller come and told me."

"And what are you going to do? Fight?"

"Don't see nothin' else to do," answered Bill, gloomily, still staring at the cactus-plant.

There was a silence. Finally the stranger burst out in an amazed cry. "Well, I never heard of such a thing in my life! How many of them are there?"

"Eight," answered Bill. "And now look-a-here; you ain't got no manner of business foolin' around here just now, and you might better lope off before dark. I don't ask no help in this here row. I know your happening along here just now don't give me no call on you, and you better hit the trail."

"Well, why in the name of wonder don't you go get the sheriff?" cried the stranger.

"Oh, h——!" said Bill.

IV

Long, smoldering clouds spread in the western sky, and to the east silver mists lay on the purple gloom of the wilderness.

Finally, when the great moon climbed the heavens and cast its ghastly radiance upon the bushes, it made a new and more brilliant crimson of the camp-fire, where the flames capered merrily through its mesquit branches, filling the silence with the fire chorus, an ancient melody which surely bears a message of the inconsequence of individual tragedy—a message that is in the boom of the sea, the sliver of the wind through the grass-blades, the silken clash of hemlock boughs.

No figures moved in the rosy space of the camp, and the search of the moonbeams failed to disclose a living thing in the bushes. There was no owl-faced clock to chant the weariness of the long silence that brooded upon the plain.

The dew gave the darkness under the mesquit a velvet quality that made air seem nearer to water, and no eye could have seen through it the black things that moved like monster lizards toward the camp. The branches, the leaves, that are fain to cry out when death approaches in the wilds, were frustrated by these uncanny bodies gliding with the finesse of the escaping serpent. They crept forward to the last point where assuredly no frantic attempt of the fire could discover them, and there they paused to locate the prey. A romance relates the tale of the black cell hidden deep in the earth, where, upon entering, one sees only the little eyes of snakes fixing him in menaces. If a man could have approached a certain spot in the bushes, he would not have found it romantically necessary to have his hair rise. There would have been a sufficient expression of horror in the feeling of the death-hand at the nape of his neck and in his rubber knee-joints.

Two of these bodies finally moved toward each other until for each there grew out of the darkness a face placidly smiling with tender dreams of assassination. "The fool is asleep by the fire, God be praised!" The lips of the other widened in a grin of affectionate appreciation of the fool and his plight. There was some signaling in the gloom, and then began a series of subtle rustlings, interjected often with pauses, during which no sound arose but the sound of faint breathing.

A bush stood like a rock in the stream of firelight, sending its long shadow backward. With painful caution the little company traveled along this shadow, and finally arrived at the rear of the bush. Through its branches they surveyed for a moment of comfortable satisfaction a form in a gray blanket extended on the ground near the fire. The smile of joyful anticipation fled quickly, to give place to a quiet air of business. Two men lifted shot-guns with much of the barrels gone, and sighting these weapons through the branches, pulled trigger together.

The noise of the explosions roared over the lonely mesquit as if these guns wished to inform the entire world; and as the gray smoke fled, the dodging company back of the bush saw the blanketed form twitching. Whereupon they burst out in chorus in a laugh, and arose as merry as a lot of banqueters. They gleefully gestured congratulations, and strode bravely into the light of the fire.

Then suddenly a new laugh rang from some unknown spot in the darkness. It was a fearsome laugh of ridicule, hatred, ferocity. It might have been demoniac. It smote them motionless in their gleeful prowl, as the stern voice from the sky smites the legendary malefactor. They might have been a weird group in wax, the light of the dying fire on their yellow faces, and shining athwart their eyes turned toward the darkness whence might come the unknown and the terrible.

The thing in the gray blanket no longer twitched; but if the knives in their hands had been thrust toward it, each knife was now drawn back, and its owner's elbow was thrown upward, as if he expected death from the clouds.

This laugh had so chained their reason that for a moment they had no wit to flee. They were prisoners to their terror. Then suddenly the belated decision arrived, and with bubbling cries they turned to run; but at that instant there was a long flash of red in the darkness, and with the report one of the men shouted a bitter shout, spun once, and tumbled headlong. The thick bushes failed to impede the rout of the others.

The silence returned to the wilderness. The tired flames faintly illumined the blanketed thing and the flung corse of the marauder, and sang the fire chorus, the ancient melody which bears the message of the inconsequence of human tragedy.

V

"Now you are worse off than ever," said the young man, dry-voiced and awed.

"No, I ain't," said Bill, rebelliously. "I'm one ahead."

After reflection, the stranger remarked, "Well, there's seven more."

They were cautiously and slowly approaching the camp. The sun was flaring its first warming rays over the gray wilderness. Upreared twigs, prominent branches, shone with golden light, while the shadows under the mesquit were heavily blue.

Suddenly the stranger uttered a frightened cry. He had arrived at a point whence he had, through openings in the thicket, a clear view of a dead face.

"Gosh!" said Bill, who at the next instant had seen the thing; "I thought at first it was that there José. That would have been queer, after what I told 'im yesterday."

They continued their way, the stranger wincing in his walk, and Bill exhibiting considerable curiosity.

The yellow beams of the new sun were touching the grim hues of the dead Mexican's face, and creating there an inhuman effect, which made his countenance more like a mask of dulled brass. One hand, grown curiously thinner, had been flung out regardlessly to a cactus bush.

Bill walked forward and stood looking respectfully at the body. "I know that feller; his name is Miguel. He——"

The stranger's nerves might have been in that condition when there is no backbone to the body, only a long groove. "Good heavens!" he exclaimed, much agitated; "don't speak that way!"

"What way?" said Bill. "I only said his name was Miguel."

After a pause the stranger said:

"Oh, I know; but——" He waved his hand. "Lower your voice, or something. I don't know. This part of the business rattles me, don't you see?"

"Oh, all right," replied Bill, bowing to the other's mysterious mood. But in a moment he burst out violently and loud in the most extraordinary profanity, the oaths winging from him as the sparks go from the funnel.

He had been examining the contents of the bundled gray blanket, and he had brought forth, among other things, his frying-pan. It was now only a rim with a handle; the Mexican volley had centered upon it. A Mexican shot-gun of the abbreviated description is ordinarily loaded with flat-irons, stove-lids, lead pipe, old horseshoes, sections of chain, window weights, railroad sleepers and spikes, dumb-bells, and any other junk which may be at hand. When one of these loads encounters a man vitally, it is likely to make an impression upon him, and a cooking-utensil may be supposed to subside before such an assault of curiosities.

Bill held high his desecrated frying-pan, turning it this way and that way. He swore until he happened to note the absence of the stranger. A moment later he saw him leading his horse from the bushes. In silence and sullenly the young man went about saddling the animal. Bill said, "Well, goin' to pull out?"

The stranger's hands fumbled uncertainly at the throatlatch. Once he exclaimed irritably, blaming the buckle for the trembling of his fingers. Once he turned to look at the dead face with the light of the morning sun upon it. At last he cried, "Oh, I know the whole thing was all square enough— couldn't be squarer—but—somehow or other, that man there takes the heart out of me." He turned his troubled face for another look. "He seems to be all the time calling me a— he makes me feel like a murderer."

"But," said Bill, puzzling, "you didn't shoot him, mister; I shot him."

"I know; but I feel that way, somehow. I can't get rid of it."

Bill considered for a time; then he said diffidently, "Mister, you're a' eddycated man, ain't you?"

"What?"

"You're what they call a'—a' eddycated man, ain't you?"

The young man, perplexed, evidently had a question upon his lips, when there was a roar of guns, bright flashes, and in the air such hooting and whistling as would come from a swift flock of steam-boilers. The stranger's horse gave a mighty, convulsive spring, snorting wildly in its sudden anguish, fell upon its knees, scrambled afoot again, and was away in the uncanny death run known to men who have seen the finish of brave horses.

"This comes from discussin' things," cried Bill, angrily.

He had thrown himself flat on the ground facing the thicket whence had come the firing. He could see the smoke winding over the bush-tops. He lifted his revolver, and the weapon came slowly up from the ground and poised like the glittering crest of a snake. Somewhere on his face there was a kind of smile, cynical, wicked, deadly, of a ferocity which at the same time had brought a deep flush to his face, and had caused two upright lines to glow in his eyes.

"Hello, José!" he called, amiable for satire's sake. "Got your old blunderbusses loaded up again yet?"

The stillness had returned to the plain. The sun's brilliant rays swept over the sea of mesquit, painting the far mists of the west with faint rosy light, and high in the air some great bird fled toward the south.

"You come out here," called Bill, again addressing the landscape, "and I'll give you some shootin' lessons. That ain't the way to shoot." Receiving no reply, he began to invent epithets and yell them at the thicket. He was something of a master of insult, and, moreover, he dived into his memory to bring forth imprecations tarnished with age, unused since fluent Bowery days. The occupation amused him, and sometimes he laughed so that it was uncomfortable for his chest to be against the ground.

Finally the stranger, prostrate near him, said wearily, "Oh, they've gone."

"Don't you believe it," replied Bill, sobering swiftly. "They're there yet—every man of 'em."

"How do you know?"

"Because I do. They won't shake us so soon. Don't put your head up, or they'll get you, sure."

Bill's eyes, meanwhile, had not wavered from their scrutiny of the thicket in front. "They're there, all right; don't you forget it. Now you listen." So he called out: "José! Ojo, José! Speak up, *hombre*! I want have talk. Speak up, you yaller cuss, you!"

Whereupon a mocking voice from off in the bushes said, "Señor?"

"There," said Bill to his ally; "didn't I tell you? The whole batch." Again he lifted his voice. "José—look—ain't you gittin' kinder tired? You better go home, you fellers, and git some rest."

The answer was a sudden furious chatter of Spanish, eloquent with hatred, calling down upon Bill all the calamities which life holds. It was as if some one had suddenly enraged a cageful of wildcats. The spirits of all the revenges which they had imagined were loosened at this time, and filled the air.

"They're in a holler," said Bill, chuckling, "or there'd be shootin'."

Presently he began to grow angry. His hidden enemies called him nine kinds of coward, a man who could fight only in the dark, a baby who would run from the shadows of such noble Mexican gentlemen, a dog that sneaked. They described the affair of the previous night, and informed him of the base advantage he had taken of their friend. In fact, they in all sincerity endowed him with every quality which he no less earnestly believed them to possess. One could have seen the phrases bite him as he lay there on the ground fingering his revolver.

VI

It is sometimes taught that men do the furious and desperate thing from an emotion that is as even and placid as the thoughts of a village clergyman on Sunday afternoon. Usually, however, it is to be believed that a panther is at the time born in the heart, and that the subject does not resemble a man picking mulberries.

"B' G——!" said Bill, speaking as from a throat filled with dust, "I'll go after 'em in a minute."

"Don't you budge an inch!" cried the stranger, sternly. "Don't you budge!"

"Well," said Bill, glaring at the bushes—" well——"

"Put your head down!" suddenly screamed the stranger, in white alarm. As the guns roared, Bill uttered a loud grunt, and for a moment leaned panting on his elbow, while his arm shook like a twig. Then he upreared like a great and bloody spirit of vengeance, his face lighted with the blaze of his last passion. The Mexicans came swiftly and in silence.

The lightning action of the next few moments was of the fabric of dreams to the stranger. The muscular struggle may not be real to the drowning man. His mind may be fixed on the far, straight shadows back of the stars, and the terror of them. And so the fight, and his part in it, had to the stranger only the quality of a picture half drawn. The rush of feet, the spatter of shots, the cries, the swollen faces seen like masks on the smoke, resembled a happening of the night.

And yet afterward certain lines, forms, lived out so strongly from the incoherence that they were always in his memory.

He killed a man, and the thought went swiftly by him, like the feather on the gale, that it was easy to kill a man.

Moreover, he suddenly felt for Bill, this grimy sheepherder, some deep form of idolatry. Bill was dying, and the dignity of last defeat, the superiority of him who stands in his grave, was in the pose of the lost sheep-herder.

*   *   *

The stranger sat on the ground idly mopping the sweat and powder-stain from his brow. He wore the gentle idiot smile of an aged beggar as he watched three Mexicans limping and staggering in the distance. He noted at this time that one who still possessed a serape had from it none of the grandeur of the cloaked Spaniard, but that against the sky the silhouette resembled a cornucopia of childhood's Christmas.

They turned to look at him, and he lifted his weary arm to menace them with his revolver. They stood for a moment banded together, and hooted curses at him.

Finally he arose, and, walking some paces, stooped to loosen Bill's gray hands from a throat. Swaying as if slightly drunk, he stood looking down into the still face.

Struck suddenly with a thought, he went about with dulled eyes on the ground, until he plucked his gaudy blanket from where it lay dirty from trampling feet. He dusted it carefully, and then returned and laid it over Bill's form. There he again stood motionless, his mouth just agape and the same stupid glance in his eyes, when all at once he made a gesture of fright and looked wildly about him.

He had almost reached the thicket when he stopped, smitten with alarm. A body contorted, with one arm stiff in the air, lay in his path. Slowly and warily he moved around it, and in a moment the bushes, nodding and whispering, their leaf-faces turned toward the scene behind him, swung and swung again into stillness and the peace of the wilderness.

The Bride Comes to Yellow Sky
I

THE GREAT PULLMAN was whirling onward with such dignity of motion that a glance from the window seemed simply to prove that the plains of Texas were pouring eastward. Vast flats of green grass, dull-hued spaces of mesquite and cactus, little groups of frame houses, woods of light and tender trees, all were sweeping into the east, sweeping over the horizon, a precipice.

A newly married pair had boarded this coach at San Antonio. The man's face was reddened from many days in the wind and sun, and a direct result of his new black clothes was that his brick-colored hands were constantly performing in a most conscious fashion. From time to time he looked down respectfully at his attire. He sat with a hand on each knee, like a man waiting in a barber's shop. The glances he devoted to other passengers were furtive and shy.

The bride was not pretty, nor was she very young. She wore a dress of blue cashmere, with small reservations of velvet here and there and with steel buttons abounding. She continually twisted her head to regard her puff sleeves, very stiff, straight, and high. They embarrassed her. It was quite apparent that she had cooked, and that she expected to cook, dutifully. The blushes caused by the careless scrutiny of some passengers as she had entered the car were strange to see upon this plain, under-class countenance, which was drawn in placid, almost emotionless lines.

They were evidently very happy. "Ever been in a parlor-car before?" he asked, smiling with delight.

"No," she answered. "I never was. It's fine, ain't it?"

"Great! And then after a while we'll go forward to the diner and get a big lay-out. Finest meal in the world. Charge a dollar."

"Oh, do they?" cried the bride. "Charge a dollar? Why, that's too much—for us—ain't it, Jack?"

"Not this trip, anyhow," he answered bravely. "We're going to go the whole thing."

Later, he explained to her about the trains. "You see, it's a thousand miles from one end of Texas to the other, and this train runs right across it and never stops but four times." He had the pride of an owner. He pointed out to her the dazzling fittings of the coach, and in truth her eyes opened wider as she contemplated the sea-green figured velvet, the shining brass, silver, and glass, the wood that gleamed as darkly brilliant as the surface of a pool of oil. At one end a bronze figure sturdily held a support for a separated chamber, and at convenient places on the ceiling were frescoes in olive and silver.

To the minds of the pair, their surroundings reflected the glory of their marriage that morning in San Antonio. This was the environment of their new estate, and the man's face in particular beamed with an elation that made him appear ridiculous to the negro porter. This individual at times surveyed them from afar with an amused and superior grin. On other occasions he bullied them with skill in ways that did not make it exactly plain to them that they were being bullied. He subtly used all the manners of the most unconquerable kind of snobbery. He oppressed them, but of this oppression they had small knowledge, and they speedily forgot that infrequently a number of travelers covered them with stares of derisive enjoyment. Historically there was supposed to be something infinitely humorous in their situation.

"We are due in Yellow Sky at 3.42," he said, looking tenderly into her eyes.

"Oh, are we?" she said, as if she had not been aware of it. To evince surprise at her husband's statement was part of her wifely amiability. She took from a pocket a little silver watch, and as she held it before her and stared at it with a frown of attention, the new husband's face shone.

"I bought it in San Anton' from a friend of mine," he told her gleefully.

"It's seventeen minutes past twelve," she said, looking up at him with a kind of shy and clumsy coquetry. A passenger, noting this play, grew excessively sardonic, and winked at himself in one of the numerous mirrors.

At last they went to the dining-car. Two rows of negro waiters in glowing white suits surveyed their entrance with the interest and also the equanimity of men who had been forewarned. The pair fell to the lot of a waiter who happened to feel pleasure in steering them through their meal. He viewed them with the manner of a fatherly pilot, his countenance radiant with benevolence. The patronage entwined with the ordinary deference was not plain to them. And yet as they returned to their coach they showed in their faces a sense of escape.

To the left, miles down a long purple slope, was a little ribbon of mist where moved the keening Rio Grande. The train was approaching it at an angle, and the apex was Yellow Sky. Presently it was apparent that as the distance from Yellow Sky grew shorter, the husband became commensurately restless. His brick-red hands were more insistent in their prominence. Occasionally he was even rather absent-minded and far-away when the bride leaned forward and addressed him.

As a matter of truth, Jack Potter was beginning to find the shadow of a deed weigh upon him like a leaden slab. He, the town marshal of Yellow Sky, a man known, liked, and feared in his corner, a prominent person, had gone to San Antonio to meet a girl he believed he loved, and there, after the usual prayers, had actually induced her to marry him, without consulting Yellow Sky for any part of the transaction. He was now bringing his bride before an innocent and unsuspecting community.

Of course, people in Yellow Sky married as it pleased them in accordance with a general custom; but such was Potter's thought of his duty to his friends, or of their idea of his duty, or of an unspoken form which does not control men in these matters, that he felt he was heinous. He had committed an extraordinary crime. Face to face with this girl in San Antonio, and spurred by his sharp impulse, he had gone headlong over all the social hedges. At San Antonio he was like a man hidden in the dark. A knife to sever any friendly duty, any form, was easy to his hand in that remote city. But the hour of Yellow Sky, the hour of daylight, was approaching.

He knew full well that his marriage was an important thing to his town. It could only be exceeded by the burning of the new hotel. His friends would not forgive him. Frequently he had reflected on the advisability of telling them by telegraph, but a new cowardice had been upon him. He feared to do it. And now the train was hurrying him toward a scene of amazement, glee, reproach. He glanced out of the window at the line of haze swinging slowly in toward the train.

Yellow Sky had a kind of brass band which played painfully to the delight of the populace. He laughed without heart as he thought of it. If the citizens could dream of his prospective arrival with his bride, they would parade the band at the station and escort them, amid cheers and laughing congratulations, to his adobe home.

He resolved that he would use all the devices of speed and plains-craft in making the journey from the station to his house. Once within that safe citadel, he could issue some sort of a vocal bulletin, and then not go among the citizens until they had time to wear off a little of their enthusiasm.

The bride looked anxiously at him. "What's worrying you, Jack?"

He laughed again. "I'm not worrying, girl. I'm only thinking of Yellow Sky."

She flushed in comprehension.

A sense of mutual guilt invaded their minds and developed a finer tenderness. They looked at each other with eyes softly aglow. But Potter often laughed the same nervous laugh. The flush upon the bride's face seemed quite permanent.

The traitor to the feelings of Yellow Sky narrowly watched the speeding landscape. "We're nearly there," he said.

Presently the porter came and announced the proximity of Potter's home. He held a brush in his hand and, with all his airy superiority gone, he brushed Potter's new clothes as the latter slowly turned this way and that way. Potter fumbled out a coin and gave it to the porter as he had seen others do. It was a heavy and muscle-bound business, as that of a man shoeing his first horse.

The porter took their bag, and as the train began to slow they moved forward to the hooded platform of the car. Presently the two engines and their long string of coaches rushed into the station of Yellow Sky.

"They have to take water here," said Potter, from a constricted throat and in mournful cadence as one announcing death. Before the train stopped his eye had swept the length

of the platform, and he was glad and astonished to see there
was none upon it but the station-agent, who, with a slightly
hurried and anxious air, was walking toward the water-tanks.
When the train had halted, the porter alighted first and placed
in position a little temporary step.

"Come on, girl," said Potter hoarsely. As he helped her
down they each laughed on a false note. He took the bag
from the negro, and bade his wife cling to his arm. As they
slunk rapidly away, his hang-dog glance perceived that they
were unloading the two trunks, and also that the station-
agent far ahead near the baggage-car had turned and was run-
ning toward him, making gestures. He laughed, and groaned
as he laughed, when he noted the first effect of his marital
bliss upon Yellow Sky. He gripped his wife's arm firmly to his
side, and they fled. Behind them the porter stood chuckling
fatuously.

II

The California Express on the Southern Railway was due
at Yellow Sky in twenty-one minutes. There were six men at
the bar of the Weary Gentleman saloon. One was a drummer
who talked a great deal and rapidly; three were Texans who
did not care to talk at that time; and two were Mexican
sheep-herders who did not talk as a general practice in the
Weary Gentleman saloon. The bar-keeper's dog lay on the
board-walk that crossed in front of the door. His head was
on his paws, and he glanced drowsily here and there with the
constant vigilance of a dog that is kicked on occasion. Across
the sandy street were some vivid green grass plots, so won-
derful in appearance amid the sands that burned near them in
a blazing sun that they caused a doubt in the mind. They
exactly resembled the grass mats used to represent lawns on
the stage. At the cooler end of the railway station a man with-
out a coat sat in a tilted chair and smoked his pipe. The fresh-
cut bank of the Rio Grande circled near the town, and there
could be seen beyond it a great plum-colored plain of mes-
quite.

Save for the busy drummer and his companions in the
saloon, Yellow Sky was dozing. The new-comer leaned grace-

fully upon the bar, and recited many tales with the confidence of a bard who has come upon a new field.

"——and at the moment that the old man fell down stairs with the bureau in his arms, the old woman was coming up with two scuttles of coal, and, of course——"

The drummer's tale was interrupted by a young man who suddenly appeared in the open door. He cried: "Scratchy Wilson's drunk, and has turned loose with both hands." The two Mexicans at once set down their glasses and faded out of the rear entrance of the saloon.

The drummer, innocent and jocular, answered: "All right, old man. S'pose he has. Come in and have a drink, anyhow."

But the information had made such an obvious cleft in every skull in the room that the drummer was obliged to see its importance. All had become instantly morose. "Say," said he, mystified, " what is this?" His three companions made the introductory gesture of eloquent speech, but the young man at the door forestalled them.

"It means, my friend," he answered, as he came into the saloon, "that for the next two hours this town won't be a health resort."

The bar-keeper went to the door and locked and barred it. Reaching out of the window, he pulled in heavy wooden shutters and barred them. Immediately a solemn, chapel-like gloom was upon the place. The drummer was looking from one to another.

"But say," he cried, " what is this, anyhow? You don't mean there is going to be a gun-fight?"

"Don't know whether there'll be a fight or not," answered one man grimly. "But there'll be some shootin'—some good shootin'."

The young man who had warned them waved his hand. "Oh, there'll be a fight fast enough, if anyone wants it. Anybody can get a fight out there in the street. There's a fight just waiting."

The drummer seemed to be swayed between the interest of a foreigner and a perception of personal danger.

"What did you say his name was?" he asked.

"Scratchy Wilson," they answered in chorus.

"And will he kill anybody? What are you going to do?

Does this happen often? Does he rampage around like this once a week or so? Can he break in that door?"

"No, he can't break down that door," replied the bar-keeper. "He's tried it three times. But when he comes you'd better lay down on the floor, stranger. He's dead sure to shoot at it, and a bullet may come through."

Thereafter the drummer kept a strict eye upon the door. The time had not yet been called for him to hug the floor, but as a minor precaution he sidled near to the wall. "Will he kill anybody?" he said again.

The men laughed low and scornfully at the question.

"He's out to shoot, and he's out for trouble. Don't see any good in experimentin' with him."

"But what do you do in a case like this? What do you do?"

A man responded: "Why, he and Jack Potter——"

But, in chorus, the other men interrupted: "Jack Potter's in San Anton'."

"Well, who is he? What's he got to do with it?"

"Oh, he's the town marshal. He goes out and fights Scratchy when he gets on one of these tears."

"Wow," said the drummer, mopping his brow. "Nice job he's got."

The voices had toned away to mere whisperings. The drummer wished to ask further questions which were born of an increasing anxiety and bewilderment; but when he attempted them, the men merely looked at him in irritation and motioned him to remain silent. A tense waiting hush was upon them. In the deep shadows of the room their eyes shone as they listened for sounds from the street. One man made three gestures at the bar-keeper, and the latter, moving like a ghost, handed him a glass and a bottle. The man poured a full glass of whisky, and set down the bottle noiselessly. He gulped the whisky in a swallow, and turned again toward the door in immovable silence. The drummer saw that the bar-keeper, without a sound, had taken a Winchester from beneath the bar. Later he saw this individual beckoning to him, so he tiptoed across the room.

"You better come with me back of the bar."

"No, thanks," said the drummer, perspiring. "I'd rather be where I can make a break for the back door."

Whereupon the man of bottles made a kindly but peremptory gesture. The drummer obeyed it, and finding himself seated on a box with his head below the level of the bar, balm was laid upon his soul at sight of various zinc and copper fittings that bore a resemblance to armor-plate. The bar-keeper took a seat comfortably upon an adjacent box.

"You see," he whispered, "this here Scratchy Wilson is a wonder with a gun—a perfect wonder—and when he goes on the war trail, we hunt our holes—naturally. He's about the last one of the old gang that used to hang out along the river here. He's a terror when he's drunk. When he's sober he's all right—kind of simple—wouldn't hurt a fly—nicest fellow in town. But when he's drunk—whoo!"

There were periods of stillness. "I wish Jack Potter was back from San Anton'," said the bar-keeper. "He shot Wilson up once—in the leg—and he would sail in and pull out the kinks in this thing."

Presently they heard from a distance the sound of a shot, followed by three wild yowls. It instantly removed a bond from the men in the darkened saloon. There was a shuffling of feet. They looked at each other. "Here he comes," they said.

III

A man in a maroon-colored flannel shirt, which had been purchased for purposes of decoration and made, principally, by some Jewish women on the east side of New York, rounded a corner and walked into the middle of the main street of Yellow Sky. In either hand the man held a long, heavy blue-black revolver. Often he yelled, and these cries rang through a semblance of a deserted village, shrilly flying over the roofs in a volume that seemed to have no relation to the ordinary vocal strength of a man. It was as if the surrounding stillness formed the arch of a tomb over him. These cries of ferocious challenge rang against walls of silence. And his boots had red tops with gilded imprints, of the kind beloved in winter by little sledding boys on the hillsides of New England.

The man's face flamed in a rage begot of whisky. His eyes,

rolling and yet keen for ambush, hunted the still door-ways and windows. He walked with the creeping movement of the midnight cat. As it occurred to him, he roared menacing information. The long revolvers in his hands were as easy as straws; they were moved with an electric swiftness. The little fingers of each hand played sometimes in a musician's way. Plain from the low collar of the shirt, the cords of his neck straightened and sank, straightened and sank, as passion moved him. The only sounds were his terrible invitations. The calm adobes preserved their demeanor at the passing of this small thing in the middle of the street.

There was no offer of fight; no offer of fight. The man called to the sky. There were no attractions. He bellowed and fumed and swayed his revolvers here and everywhere.

The dog of the bar-keeper of the Weary Gentleman saloon had not appreciated the advance of events. He yet lay dozing in front of his master's door. At sight of the dog, the man paused and raised his revolver humorously. At sight of the man, the dog sprang up and walked diagonally away, with a sullen head and growling. The man yelled, and the dog broke into a gallop. As it was about to enter an alley, there was a loud noise, a whistling, and something spat the ground directly before it. The dog screamed, and, wheeling in terror, galloped headlong in a new direction. Again there was a noise, a whistling, and sand was kicked viciously before it. Fear-stricken, the dog turned and flurried like an animal in a pen. The man stood laughing, his weapons at his hips.

Ultimately the man was attracted by the closed door of the Weary Gentleman saloon. He went to it, and hammering with a revolver, demanded drink.

The door remaining imperturbable, he picked a bit of paper from the walk and nailed it to the framework with a knife. He then turned his back contemptuously upon this popular resort, and walking to the opposite side of the street, and spinning there on his heel quickly and lithely, fired at the bit of paper. He missed it by a half inch. He swore at himself, and went away. Later, he comfortably fusilladed the windows of his most intimate friend. The man was playing with this town. It was a toy for him.

But still there was no offer of fight. The name of Jack Potter, his ancient antagonist, entered his mind, and he concluded that it would be a glad thing if he should go to Potter's house and by bombardment induce him to come out and fight. He moved in the direction of his desire, chanting Apache scalp-music.

When he arrived at it, Potter's house presented the same still, calm front as had the other adobes. Taking up a strategic position, the man howled a challenge. But this house regarded him as might a great stone god. It gave no sign. After a decent wait, the man howled further challenges, mingling with them wonderful epithets.

Presently there came the spectacle of a man churning himself into deepest rage over the immobility of a house. He fumed at it as the winter wind attacks a prairie cabin in the North. To the distance there should have gone the sound of a tumult like the fighting of two hundred Mexicans. As necessity bade him, he paused for breath or to reload his revolvers.

IV

Potter and his bride walked sheepishly and with speed. Sometimes they laughed together shamefacedly and low.

"Next corner, dear," he said finally.

They put forth the efforts of a pair walking bowed against a strong wind. Potter was about to raise a finger to point the first appearance of the new home when, as they circled the corner, they came face to face with a man in a maroon-colored shirt who was feverishly pushing cartridges into a large revolver. Upon the instant the man dropped this revolver to the ground, and, like lightning, whipped another from its holster. The second weapon was aimed at the bridegroom's chest.

There was a silence. Potter's mouth seemed to be merely a grave for his tongue. He exhibited an instinct to at once loosen his arm from the woman's grip, and he dropped the bag to the sand. As for the bride, her face had gone as yellow as old cloth. She was a slave to hideous rites gazing at the apparitional snake.

The two men faced each other at a distance of three paces.

He of the revolver smiled with a new and quiet ferocity. "Tried to sneak up on me," he said. "Tried to sneak up on me!" His eyes grew more baleful. As Potter made a slight movement, the man thrust his revolver venomously forward. "No, don't you do it, Jack Potter. Don't you move a finger toward a gun just yet. Don't you move an eyelash. The time has come for me to settle with you, and I'm goin' to do it my own way and loaf along with no interferin'. So if you don't want a gun bent on you, just mind what I tell you."

Potter looked at his enemy. "I ain't got a gun on me, Scratchy," he said. "Honest, I ain't." He was stiffening and steadying, but yet somewhere at the back of his mind a vision of the Pullman floated, the sea-green figured velvet, the shining brass, silver, and glass, the wood that gleamed as darkly brilliant as the surface of a pool of oil—all the glory of the marriage, the environment of the new estate. "You know I fight when it comes to fighting, Scratchy Wilson, but I ain't got a gun on me. You'll have to do all the shootin' yourself."

His enemy's face went livid. He stepped forward and lashed his weapon to and fro before Potter's chest. "Don't you tell me you ain't got no gun on you, you whelp. Don't tell me no lie like that. There ain't a man in Texas ever seen you without no gun. Don't take me for no kid." His eyes blazed with light, and his throat worked like a pump.

"I ain't takin' you for no kid," answered Potter. His heels had not moved an inch backward. "I'm takin' you for a —— fool. I tell you I ain't got a gun, and I ain't. If you're goin' to shoot me up, you better begin now. You'll never get a chance like this again."

So much enforced reasoning had told on Wilson's rage. He was calmer. "If you ain't got a gun, why ain't you got a gun?" he sneered. "Been to Sunday-school?"

"I ain't got a gun because I've just come from San Anton' with my wife. I'm married," said Potter. "And if I'd thought there was going to be any galoots like you prowling around when I brought my wife home, I'd had a gun, and don't you forget it."

"Married!" said Scratchy, not at all comprehending.

"Yes, married. I'm married," said Potter distinctly.

"Married?" said Scratchy. Seemingly for the first time he

saw the drooping drowning woman at the other man's side. "No!" he said. He was like a creature allowed a glimpse of another world. He moved a pace backward, and his arm with the revolver dropped to his side. "Is this—is this the lady?" he asked.

"Yes, this is the lady," answered Potter.

There was another period of silence.

"Well," said Wilson at last, slowly, "I s'pose it's all off now."

"It's all off if you say so, Scratchy. You know I didn't make the trouble." Potter lifted his valise.

"Well, I 'low it's off, Jack," said Wilson. He was looking at the ground. "Married!" He was not a student of chivalry; it was merely that in the presence of this foreign condition he was a simple child of the earlier plains. He picked up his starboard revolver, and placing both weapons in their holsters, he went away. His feet made funnel-shaped tracks in the heavy sand.

The Blue Hotel

I

THE PALACE HOTEL at Fort Romper was painted a light blue, a shade that is on the legs of a kind of heron, causing the bird to declare its position against any background. The Palace Hotel, then, was always screaming and howling in a way that made the dazzling winter landscape of Nebraska seem only a gray swampish hush. It stood alone on the prairie, and when the snow was falling the town two hundred yards away was not visible. But when the traveler alighted at the railway station he was obliged to pass the Palace Hotel before he could come upon the company of low clap-board houses which composed Fort Romper, and it was not to be thought that any traveler could pass the Palace Hotel without looking at it. Pat Scully, the proprietor, had proved himself a master of strategy when he chose his paints. It is true that on clear days, when the great trans-continental expresses, long lines of swaying Pullmans, swept through Fort Romper, passengers were overcome at the sight, and the cult that knows the brown-reds and the subdivisions of the dark greens of the East expressed shame, pity, horror, in a laugh. But to the citizens of this prairie town, and to the people who would naturally stop there, Pat Scully had performed a feat. With this opulence and splendor, these creeds, classes, egotisms, that streamed through Romper on the rails day after day, they had no color in common.

As if the displayed delights of such a blue hotel were not sufficiently enticing, it was Scully's habit to go every morning and evening to meet the leisurely trains that stopped at Romper and work his seductions upon any man that he might see wavering, gripsack in hand.

One morning, when a snow-crusted engine dragged its long string of freight cars and its one passenger coach to the station, Scully performed the marvel of catching three men. One was a shaky and quick-eyed Swede, with a great shining cheap valise; one was a tall bronzed cowboy, who was on his way to a ranch near the Dakota line; one was a little silent man from the East, who didn't look it, and didn't announce

799

it. Scully practically made them prisoners. He was so nimble and merry and kindly that each probably felt it would be the height of brutality to try to escape. They trudged off over the creaking board sidewalks in the wake of the eager little Irishman. He wore a heavy fur cap squeezed tightly down on his head. It caused his two red ears to stick out stiffly, as if they were made of tin.

At last, Scully, elaborately, with boisterous hospitality, conducted them through the portals of the blue hotel. The room which they entered was small. It seemed to be merely a proper temple for an enormous stove, which, in the center, was humming with god-like violence. At various points on its surface the iron had become luminous and glowed yellow from the heat. Beside the stove Scully's son Johnnie was playing High-Five with an old farmer who had whiskers both gray and sandy. They were quarreling. Frequently the old farmer turned his face toward a box of sawdust—colored brown from tobacco juice—that was behind the stove, and spat with an air of great impatience and irritation. With a loud flourish of words Scully destroyed the game of cards, and bustled his son upstairs with part of the baggage of the new guests. He himself conducted them to three basins of the coldest water in the world. The cowboy and the Easterner burnished themselves fiery red with this water, until it seemed to be some kind of a metal polish. The Swede, however, merely dipped his fingers gingerly and with trepidation. It was notable that throughout this series of small ceremonies the three travelers were made to feel that Scully was very benevolent. He was conferring great favors upon them. He handed the towel from one to the other with an air of philanthropic impulse.

Afterward they went to the first room, and, sitting about the stove, listened to Scully's officious clamor at his daughters, who were preparing the midday meal. They reflected in the silence of experienced men who tread carefully amid new people. Nevertheless, the old farmer, stationary, invincible in his chair near the warmest part of the stove, turned his face from the sawdust box frequently and addressed a glowing commonplace to the strangers. Usually he was answered in short but adequate sentences by either the cowboy or the

Easterner. The Swede said nothing. He seemed to be occupied in making furtive estimates of each man in the room. One might have thought that he had the sense of silly suspicion which comes to guilt. He resembled a badly frightened man.

Later, at dinner, he spoke a little, addressing his conversation entirely to Scully. He volunteered that he had come from New York, where for ten years he had worked as a tailor. These facts seemed to strike Scully as fascinating, and afterward he volunteered that he had lived at Romper for fourteen years. The Swede asked about the crops and the price of labor. He seemed barely to listen to Scully's extended replies. His eyes continued to rove from man to man.

Finally, with a laugh and a wink, he said that some of these Western communities were very dangerous; and after his statement he straightened his legs under the table, tilted his head, and laughed again, loudly. It was plain that the demonstration had no meaning to the others. They looked at him wondering and in silence.

II

As the men trooped heavily back into the front room, the two little windows presented views of a turmoiling sea of snow. The huge arms of the wind were making attempts— mighty, circular, futile—to embrace the flakes as they sped. A gate-post like a still man with a blanched face stood aghast amid this profligate fury. In a hearty voice Scully announced the presence of a blizzard. The guests of the blue hotel, lighting their pipes, assented with grunts of lazy masculine contentment. No island of the sea could be exempt in the degree of this little room with its humming stove. Johnnie, son of Scully, in a tone which defined his opinion of his ability as a card-player, challenged the old farmer of both gray and sandy whiskers to a game of High-Five. The farmer agreed with a contemptuous and bitter scoff. They sat close to the stove, and squared their knees under a wide board. The cowboy and the Easterner watched the game with interest. The Swede remained near the window, aloof, but with a countenance that showed signs of an inexplicable excitement.

The play of Johnnie and the gray-beard was suddenly ended by another quarrel. The old man arose while casting a look of heated scorn at his adversary. He slowly buttoned his coat, and then stalked with fabulous dignity from the room. In the discreet silence of all other men the Swede laughed. His laughter rang somehow childish. Men by this time had begun to look at him askance, as if they wished to inquire what ailed him.

A new game was formed jocosely. The cowboy volunteered to become the partner of Johnnie, and they all then turned to ask the Swede to throw in his lot with the little Easterner. He asked some questions about the game, and learning that it wore many names, and that he had played it when it was under an alias, he accepted the invitation. He strode toward the men nervously, as if he expected to be assaulted. Finally, seated, he gazed from face to face and laughed shrilly. This laugh was so strange that the Easterner looked up quickly, the cowboy sat intent and with his mouth open, and Johnnie paused, holding the cards with still fingers.

Afterward there was a short silence. Then Johnnie said: "Well, let's get at it. Come on now!" They pulled their chairs forward until their knees were bunched under the board. They began to play, and their interest in the game caused the others to forget the manner of the Swede.

The cowboy was a board-whacker. Each time that he held superior cards he whanged them, one by one, with exceeding force, down upon the improvised table, and took the tricks with a glowing air of prowess and pride that sent thrills of indignation into the hearts of his opponents. A game with a board-whacker in it is sure to become intense. The countenances of the Easterner and the Swede were miserable whenever the cowboy thundered down his aces and kings, while Johnnie, his eyes gleaming with joy, chuckled and chuckled.

Because of the absorbing play none considered the strange ways of the Swede. They paid strict heed to the game. Finally, during a lull caused by a new deal, the Swede suddenly addressed Johnnie: "I suppose there have been a good many men killed in this room." The jaws of the others dropped and they looked at him.

"What in hell are you talking about?" said Johnnie.

The Swede laughed again his blatant laugh, full of a kind of false courage and defiance. "Oh, you know what I mean all right," he answered.

"I'm a liar if I do!" Johnnie protested. The card was halted, and the men stared at the Swede. Johnnie evidently felt that as the son of the proprietor he should make a direct inquiry. "Now, what might you be drivin' at, mister?" he asked. The Swede winked at him. It was a wink full of cunning. His fingers shook on the edge of the board. "Oh, maybe you think I have been to nowheres. Maybe you think I'm a tenderfoot?"

"I don't know nothin' about you," answered Johnnie, "and I don't give a damn where you've been. All I got to say is that I don't know what you're driving at. There hain't never been nobody killed in this room."

The cowboy, who had been steadily gazing at the Swede, then spoke. "What's wrong with you, mister?"

Apparently it seemed to the Swede that he was formidably menaced. He shivered and turned white near the corners of his mouth. He sent an appealing glance in the direction of the little Easterner. During these moments he did not forget to wear his air of advanced pot-valor. "They say they don't know what I mean," he remarked mockingly to the Easterner.

The latter answered after prolonged and cautious reflection. "I don't understand you," he said, impassively.

The Swede made a movement then which announced that he thought he had encountered treachery from the only quarter where he had expected sympathy if not help. "Oh, I see you are all against me. I see——"

The cowboy was in a state of deep stupefaction. "Say," he cried, as he tumbled the deck violently down upon the board. "Say, what are you gittin' at, hey?"

The Swede sprang up with the celerity of a man escaping from a snake on the floor. "I don't want to fight!" he shouted. "I don't want to fight!"

The cowboy stretched his long legs indolently and deliberately. His hands were in his pockets. He spat into the sawdust box. "Well, who the hell thought you did?" he inquired.

The Swede backed rapidly toward a corner of the room. His hands were out protectingly in front of his chest, but he was making an obvious struggle to control his fright. "Gentlemen," he quavered, "I suppose I am going to be killed before I can leave this house! I suppose I am going to be killed before I can leave this house!" In his eyes was the dying swan look. Through the windows could be seen the snow turning blue in the shadow of dusk. The wind tore at the house and some loose thing beat regularly against the clap-boards like a spirit tapping.

A door opened, and Scully himself entered. He paused in surprise as he noted the tragic attitude of the Swede. Then he said: "What's the matter here?"

The Swede answered him swiftly and eagerly: "These men are going to kill me."

"Kill you!" ejaculated Scully. "Kill you! What are you talkin'?"

The Swede made the gesture of a martyr.

Scully wheeled sternly upon his son. "What is this, Johnnie?"

The lad had grown sullen. "Damned if I know," he answered. "I can't make no sense to it." He began to shuffle the cards, fluttering them together with an angry snap. "He says a good many men have been killed in this room, or something like that. And he says he's goin' to be killed here too. I don't know what ails him. He's crazy, I shouldn't wonder."

Scully then looked for explanation to the cowboy, but the cowboy simply shrugged his shoulders.

"Kill you?" said Scully again to the Swede. "Kill you? Man, you're off your nut."

"Oh, I know," burst out the Swede. "I know what will happen. Yes, I'm crazy—yes. Yes, of course, I'm crazy—yes. But I know one thing——" There was a sort of sweat of misery and terror upon his face. "I know I won't get out of here alive."

The cowboy drew a deep breath, as if his mind was passing into the last stages of dissolution. "Well, I'm dog-goned," he whispered to himself.

Scully wheeled suddenly and faced his son. "You've been troublin' this man!"

Johnnie's voice was loud with its burden of grievance. "Why, good Gawd, I ain't done nothin' to 'im."

The Swede broke in. "Gentlemen, do not disturb yourselves. I will leave this house. I will go 'way because——" He accused them dramatically with his glance. "Because I do not want to be killed."

Scully was furious with his son. "Will you tell me what is the matter, you young divil? What's the matter, anyhow? Speak out!"

"Blame it," cried Johnnie in despair, "don't I tell you I don't know. He—he says we want to kill him, and that's all I know. I can't tell what ails him."

The Swede continued to repeat: "Never mind, Mr. Scully, never mind. I will leave this house. I will go away, because I do not wish to be killed. Yes, of course, I am crazy—yes. But I know one thing! I will go away. I will leave this house. Never mind, Mr. Scully, never mind. I will go away."

"You will not go 'way," said Scully. "You will not go 'way until I hear the reason of this business. If anybody has troubled you I will take care of him. This is my house. You are under my roof, and I will not allow any peaceable man to be troubled here." He cast a terrible eye upon Johnnie, the cowboy, and the Easterner.

"Never mind, Mr. Scully, never mind. I will go 'way. I do not wish to be killed." The Swede moved toward the door, which opened upon the stairs. It was evidently his intention to go at once for his baggage.

"No, no," shouted Scully peremptorily; but the white-faced man slid by him and disappeared. "Now," said Scully severely, "what does this mane?"

Johnnie and the cowboy cried together: "Why, we didn't do nothin' to 'im!"

Scully's eyes were cold. "No," he said, "you didn't?"

Johnnie swore a deep oath. "Why, this is the wildest loon I ever see. We didn't do nothin' at all. We were jest sittin' here playin' cards and he——"

The father suddenly spoke to the Easterner. "Mr. Blanc," he asked, "what has these boys been doin'?"

The Easterner reflected again. "I didn't see anything wrong at all," he said at last slowly.

Scully began to howl. "But what does it mane?" He stared ferociously at his son. "I have a mind to lather you for this, me boy."

Johnnie was frantic. "Well, what have I done?" he bawled at his father.

III

"I think you are tongue-tied," said Scully finally to his son, the cowboy and the Easterner, and at the end of this scornful sentence he left the room.

Upstairs the Swede was swiftly fastening the straps of his great valise. Once his back happened to be half-turned toward the door, and hearing a noise there, he wheeled and sprang up, uttering a loud cry. Scully's wrinkled visage showed grimly in the light of the small lamp he carried. This yellow effulgence, streaming upward, colored only his prominent features, and left his eyes, for instance, in mysterious shadow. He resembled a murderer.

"Man, man!" he exclaimed, "have you gone daffy?"

"Oh, no! Oh, no!" rejoined the other. "There are people in this world who know pretty nearly as much as you do—understand?"

For a moment they stood gazing at each other. Upon the Swede's deathly pale cheeks were two spots brightly crimson and sharply edged, as if they had been carefully painted. Scully placed the light on the table and sat himself on the edge of the bed. He spoke ruminatively. "By cracky, I never heard of such a thing in my life. It's a complete muddle. I can't for the soul of me think how you ever got this idea into your head." Presently he lifted his eyes and asked: "And did you sure think they were going to kill you?"

The Swede scanned the old man as if he wished to see into his mind. "I did," he said at last. He obviously suspected that this answer might precipitate an outbreak. As he pulled on a strap his whole arm shook, the elbow wavering like a bit of paper.

Scully banged his hand impressively on the foot-board of the bed. "Why, man, we're goin' to have a line of ilictric street-cars in this town next spring."

" 'A line of electric street-cars,' " repeated the Swede stupidly.

"And," said Scully, "there's a new railroad goin' to be built down from Broken Arm to here. Not to mintion the four churches and the smashin' big brick school-house. Then there's the big factory, too. Why, in two years Romper'll be a met-tro-*pol*-is."

Having finished the preparation of his baggage, the Swede straightened himself. "Mr. Scully," he said with sudden hardihood, "how much do I owe you?"

"You don't owe me anythin'," said the old man angrily.

"Yes, I do," retorted the Swede. He took seventy-five cents from his pocket and tendered it to Scully; but the latter snapped his fingers in disdainful refusal. However, it happened that they both stood gazing in a strange fashion at three silver pieces on the Swede's open palm.

"I'll not take your money," said Scully at last. "Not after what's been goin' on here." Then a plan seemed to strike him. "Here," he cried, picking up his lamp and moving toward the door. "Here! Come with me a minute."

"No," said the Swede in overwhelming alarm.

"Yes," urged the old man. "Come on! I want you to come and see a picter—just across the hall—in my room."

The Swede must have concluded that his hour was come. His jaw dropped and his teeth showed like a dead man's. He ultimately followed Scully across the corridor, but he had the step of one hung in chains.

Scully flashed the light high on the wall of his own chamber. There was revealed a ridiculous photograph of a little girl. She was leaning against a balustrade of gorgeous decoration, and the formidable bang to her hair was prominent. The figure was as graceful as an upright sled-stake, and, withal, it was of the hue of lead. "There," said Scully tenderly. "That's the picter of my little girl that died. Her name was Carrie. She had the purtiest hair you ever saw! I was that fond of her, she——"

Turning then he saw that the Swede was not contemplating the picture at all, but, instead, was keeping keen watch on the gloom in the rear.

"Look, man!" shouted Scully heartily. "That's the picter of

my little gal that died. Her name was Carrie. And then here's the picter of my oldest boy, Michael. He's a lawyer in Lincoln an' doin' well. I gave that boy a grand eddycation, and I'm glad for it now. He's a fine boy. Look at 'im now. Ain't he bold as blazes, him there in Lincoln, an honored an' respicted gintleman. An honored an' respicted gintleman," concluded Scully with a flourish. And so saying, he smote the Swede jovially on the back.

The Swede faintly smiled.

"Now," said the old man, "there's only one more thing." He dropped suddenly to the floor and thrust his head beneath the bed. The Swede could hear his muffled voice. "I'd keep it under me piller if it wasn't for that boy Johnnie. Then there's the old woman—— Where is it now? I never put it twice in the same place. Ah, now come out with you!"

Presently he backed clumsily from under the bed, dragging with him an old coat rolled into a bundle. "I've fetched him," he muttered. Kneeling on the floor he unrolled the coat and extracted from its heart a large yellow-brown whisky bottle.

His first maneuver was to hold the bottle up to the light. Reassured, apparently, that nobody had been tampering with it, he thrust it with a generous movement toward the Swede.

The weak-kneed Swede was about to eagerly clutch this element of strength, but he suddenly jerked his hand away and cast a look of horror upon Scully.

"Drink," said the old man affectionately. He had arisen to his feet, and now stood facing the Swede.

There was a silence. Then again Scully said: "Drink!"

The Swede laughed wildly. He grabbed the bottle, put it to his mouth, and as his lips curled absurdly around the opening and his throat worked, he kept his glance burning with hatred upon the old man's face.

IV

After the departure of Scully the three men, with the cardboard still upon their knees, preserved for a long time an astounded silence. Then Johnnie said: "That's the dod-dangest Swede I ever see."

"He ain't no Swede," said the cowboy scornfully.

"Well, what is he then?" cried Johnnie. "What is he then?"

"It's my opinion," replied the cowboy deliberately, "he's some kind of a Dutchman." It was a venerable custom of the country to entitle as Swedes all light-haired men who spoke with a heavy tongue. In consequence the idea of the cowboy was not without its daring. "Yes, sir," he repeated. "It's my opinion this feller is some kind of a Dutchman."

"Well, he says he's a Swede, anyhow," muttered Johnnie sulkily. He turned to the Easterner: "What do you think, Mr. Blanc?"

"Oh, I don't know," replied the Easterner.

"Well, what do you think makes him act that way?" asked the cowboy.

"Why, he's frightened!" The Easterner knocked his pipe against a rim of the stove. "He's clear frightened out of his boots."

"What at?" cried Johnnie and cowboy together.

The Easterner reflected over his answer.

"What at?" cried the others again.

"Oh, I don't know, but it seems to me this man has been reading dime-novels, and he thinks he's right out in the middle of it—the shootin' and stabbin' and all."

"But," said the cowboy, deeply scandalized, "this ain't Wyoming, ner none of them places. This is Nebrasker."

"Yes," added Johnnie, "an' why don't he wait till he gits *out West*?"

The traveled Easterner laughed. "It isn't different there even—not in these days. But he thinks he's right in the middle of hell."

Johnnie and the cowboy mused long.

"It's awful funny," remarked Johnnie at last.

"Yes," said the cowboy. "This is a queer game. I hope we don't git snowed in, because then we'd have to stand this here man bein' around with us all the time. That wouldn't be no good."

"I wish pop would throw him out," said Johnnie.

Presently they heard a loud stamping on the stairs, accompanied by ringing jokes in the voice of old Scully, and laughter, evidently from the Swede. The men around the stove stared vacantly at each other. "Gosh," said the cowboy. The door flew open, and old Scully, flushed and anecdotal, came into the room. He was jabbering at the Swede, who followed him, laughing bravely. It was the entry of two roysterers from a banquet hall.

"Come now," said Scully sharply to the three seated men, "move up and give us a chance at the stove." The cowboy and the Easterner obediently sidled their chairs to make room for the newcomers. Johnnie, however, simply arranged himself in a more indolent attitude, and then remained motionless.

"Come! Git over, there," said Scully.

"Plenty of room on the other side of the stove," said Johnnie.

"Do you think we want to sit in the draught?" roared the father.

But the Swede here interposed with a grandeur of confidence. "No, no. Let the boy sit where he likes," he cried in a bullying voice to the father.

"All right! All right!" said Scully deferentially. The cowboy and the Easterner exchanged glances of wonder.

The five chairs were formed in a crescent about one side of the stove. The Swede began to talk; he talked arrogantly, profanely, angrily. Johnnie, the cowboy and the Easterner maintained a morose silence, while old Scully appeared to be receptive and eager, breaking in constantly with sympathetic ejaculations.

Finally the Swede announced that he was thirsty. He moved in his chair, and said that he would go for a drink of water.

"I'll git it for you," cried Scully at once.

"No," said the Swede contemptuously. "I'll get it for myself." He arose and stalked with the air of an owner off into the executive parts of the hotel.

As soon as the Swede was out of hearing Scully sprang to his feet and whispered intensely to the others. "Upstairs he thought I was tryin' to poison 'im."

"Say," said Johnnie, "this makes me sick. Why don't you throw 'im out in the snow?"

"Why, he's all right now," declared Scully. "It was only that he was from the East and he thought this was a tough place. That's all. He's all right now."

The cowboy looked with admiration upon the Easterner. "You were straight," he said. "You were on to that there Dutchman."

"Well," said Johnnie to his father, "he may be all right now, but I don't see it. Other time he was scared, and now he's too fresh."

Scully's speech was always a combination of Irish brogue and idiom, Western twang and idiom, and scraps of curiously formal diction taken from the story-books and newspapers. He now hurled a strange mass of language at the head of his son. "What do I keep? What do I keep? What do I keep?" he demanded in a voice of thunder. He slapped his knee impressively, to indicate that he himself was going to make reply, and that all should heed. "I keep a hotel," he shouted. "A hotel, do you mind? A guest under my roof has sacred privileges. He is to be intimidated by none. Not one word shall he hear that would prijudice him in favor of goin' away. I'll not have it. There's no place in this here town where they can say they iver took in a guest of mine because he was afraid to stay here." He wheeled suddenly upon the cowboy and the Easterner. "Am I right?"

"Yes, Mr. Scully," said the cowboy, "I think you're right."

"Yes, Mr. Scully," said the Easterner, "I think you're right."

V

At six-o'clock supper, the Swede fizzed like a fire-wheel. He sometimes seemed on the point of bursting into riotous song, and in all his madness he was encouraged by old Scully. The Easterner was incased in reserve; the cowboy sat in wide-mouthed amazement, forgetting to eat, while Johnnie wrath-ily demolished great plates of food. The daughters of the house when they were obliged to replenish the biscuits approached as warily as Indians, and, having succeeded in their purposes, fled with ill-concealed trepidation. The Swede domineered the whole feast, and he gave it the appearance of a cruel bacchanal. He seemed to have grown suddenly taller; he gazed, brutally disdainful, into every face. His voice rang through the room. Once when he jabbed out harpoon-fashion with his fork to pinion a biscuit the weapon nearly impaled the hand of the Easterner which had been stretched quietly out for the same biscuit.

After supper, as the men filed toward the other room, the Swede smote Scully ruthlessly on the shoulder. "Well, old boy, that was a good square meal." Johnnie looked hopefully at his father; he knew that shoulder was tender from an old fall; and indeed it appeared for a moment as if Scully was going to flame out over the matter, but in the end he smiled a sickly smile and remained silent. The others understood from his manner that he was admitting his responsibility for the Swede's new viewpoint.

Johnnie, however, addressed his parent in an aside. "Why don't you license somebody to kick you downstairs?" Scully scowled darkly by way of reply.

When they were gathered about the stove, the Swede insisted on another game of High-Five. Scully gently deprecated the plan at first, but the Swede turned a wolfish glare upon him. The old man subsided, and the Swede canvassed the others. In his tone there was always a great threat. The cowboy and the Easterner both remarked indifferently that they would play. Scully said that he would presently have to go to meet the 6.58 train, and so the Swede turned menacingly upon Johnnie. For a moment their glances crossed like blades, and then Johnnie smiled and said: "Yes, I'll play."

They formed a square with the little board on their knees. The Easterner and the Swede were again partners. As the play went on, it was noticeable that the cowboy was not board-whacking as usual. Meanwhile, Scully, near the lamp, had put on his spectacles and, with an appearance curiously like an old priest, was reading a newspaper. In time he went out to meet the 6.58 train, and, despite his precautions, a gust of polar wind whirled into the room as he opened the door. Besides scattering the cards, it chilled the players to the marrow. The Swede cursed frightfully. When Scully returned, his entrance disturbed a cozy and friendly scene. The Swede again cursed. But presently they were once more intent, their heads bent forward and their hands moving swiftly. The Swede had adopted the fashion of board-whacking.

Scully took up his paper and for a long time remained immersed in matters which were extraordinarily remote from him. The lamp burned badly, and once he stopped to adjust the wick. The newspaper as he turned from page to page rustled with a slow and comfortable sound. Then suddenly he heard three terrible words: "You are cheatin'!"

Such scenes often prove that there can be little of dramatic import in environment. Any room can present a tragic front; any room can be comic. This little den was now hideous as a torture-chamber. The new faces of the men themselves had changed it upon the instant. The Swede held a huge fist in front of Johnnie's face, while the latter looked steadily over it into the blazing orbs of his accuser. The Easterner had grown pallid; the cowboy's jaw had dropped in that expression of bovine amazement which was one of his important mannerisms. After the three words, the first sound in the room was made by Scully's paper as it floated forgotten to his feet. His spectacles had also fallen from his nose, but by a clutch he had saved them in air. His hand, grasping the spectacles, now remained poised awkwardly and near his shoulder. He stared at the card-players.

Probably the silence was while a second elapsed. Then, if the floor had been suddenly twitched out from under the men they could not have moved quicker. The five had projected themselves headlong toward a common point. It happened that Johnnie in rising to hurl himself upon the Swede had stumbled slightly because of his curiously instinctive care for the cards and the board. The loss of the moment allowed time for the arrival of Scully, and also allowed the cowboy time to give the Swede a great push which sent him staggering back. The men found tongue together, and hoarse shouts of rage, appeal or fear burst from every throat. The cowboy pushed and jostled feverishly at the Swede, and the Easterner and Scully clung wildly to Johnnie; but, through the smoky air, above the swaying bodies of the peace-compellers, the eyes of the two warriors ever sought each other in glances of challenge that were at once hot and steely.

Of course the board had been overturned, and now the whole company of cards was scattered over the floor, where the boots of the men trampled the fat and painted kings and queens as they gazed with their silly eyes at the war that was waging above them.

Scully's voice was dominating the yells. "Stop now! Stop, I say! Stop, now——"

Johnnie, as he struggled to burst through the rank formed by Scully and the Easterner, was crying: "Well, he says I cheated! He says I cheated! I won't allow no man to say I cheated! If he says I cheated, he's a—— ——!"

The cowboy was telling the Swede: "Quit, now! Quit, d'ye hear——"

The screams of the Swede never ceased. "He did cheat! I saw him! I saw him——"

As for the Easterner, he was importuning in a voice that was not heeded. "Wait a moment, can't you? Oh, wait a moment. What's the good of a fight over a game of cards? Wait a moment——"

In this tumult no complete sentences were clear. "Cheat"—"Quit"—"He says"—These fragments pierced the uproar and rang out sharply. It was remarkable that whereas Scully undoubtedly made the most noise, he was the least heard of any of the riotous band.

Then suddenly there was a great cessation. It was as if each man had paused for breath, and although the room was still lighted with the anger of men, it could be seen that there was no danger of immediate conflict, and at once Johnnie, shouldering his way forward, almost succeeded in confronting the Swede. "What did you say I cheated for? What did you say I cheated for? I don't cheat and I won't let no man say I do!"

The Swede said: "I saw you! I saw you!"

"Well," cried Johnnie, "I'll fight any man what says I cheat!"

"No, you won't," said the cowboy. "Not here."

"Ah, be still, can't you?" said Scully, coming between them.

The quiet was sufficient to allow the Easterner's voice to be heard. He was repeating: "Oh, wait a moment, can't you? What's the good of a fight over a game of cards? Wait a moment."

Johnnie, his red face appearing above his father's shoulder, hailed the Swede again. "Did you say I cheated?"

The Swede showed his teeth. "Yes."

"Then," said Johnnie, "we must fight."

"Yes, fight," roared the Swede. He was like a demoniac. "Yes, fight! I'll show you what kind of a man I am! I'll show you who you want to fight! Maybe you think I can't fight! Maybe you think I can't! I'll show you, you skin, you card-sharp! Yes, you cheated! You cheated! You cheated!"

"Well, let's git at it, then, mister," said Johnnie coolly.

The cowboy's brow was beaded with sweat from his efforts in intercepting all sorts of raids. He turned in despair to Scully. "What are you goin' to do now?"

A change had come over the Celtic visage of the old man. He now seemed all eagerness; his eyes glowed.

"We'll let them fight," he answered stalwartly. "I can't put up with it any longer. I've stood this damned Swede till I'm sick. We'll let them fight."

VI

The men prepared to go out of doors. The Easterner was so nervous that he had great difficulty in getting his arms into the sleeves of his new leather-coat. As the cowboy drew his fur-cap down over his ears his hands trembled. In fact, Johnnie and old Scully were the only ones who displayed no agitation. These preliminaries were conducted without words.

Scully threw open the door. "Well, come on," he said. Instantly a terrific wind caused the flame of the lamp to struggle at its wick, while a puff of black smoke sprang from the chimney-top. The stove was in mid-current of the blast, and its voice swelled to equal the roar of the storm. Some of the scarred and bedabbled cards were caught up from the floor and dashed helplessly against the further wall. The men lowered their heads and plunged into the tempest as into a sea.

No snow was falling, but great whirls and clouds of flakes, swept up from the ground by the frantic winds, were streaming southward with the speed of bullets. The covered land was blue with the sheen of an unearthly satin, and there was no other hue save where at the low black railway station— which seemed incredibly distant—one light gleamed like a tiny jewel. As the men floundered into a thigh-deep drift, it was known that the Swede was bawling out something.

Scully went to him, put a hand on his shoulder and projected an ear. "What's that you say?" he shouted.

"I say," bawled the Swede again, "I won't stand much show against this gang. I know you'll all pitch on me."

Scully smote him reproachfully on the arm. "Tut, man," he yelled. The wind tore the words from Scully's lips and scattered them far a-lee.

"You are all a gang of——" boomed the Swede, but the storm also seized the remainder of this sentence.

Immediately turning their backs upon the wind, the men had swung around a corner to the sheltered side of the hotel. It was the function of the little house to preserve here, amid this great devastation of snow, an irregular V-shape of heavily-incrusted grass, which crackled beneath the feet. One could imagine the great drifts piled against the windward side. When the party reached the comparative peace of this spot it was found that the Swede was still bellowing.

"Oh, I know what kind of a thing this is! I know you'll all pitch on me. I can't lick you all!"

Scully turned upon him panther-fashion. "You'll not have to whip all of us. You'll have to whip my son Johnnie. An' the man what troubles you durin' that time will have me to dale with."

The arrangements were swiftly made. The two men faced each other, obedient to the harsh commands of Scully, whose face, in the subtly luminous gloom, could be seen set in the austere impersonal lines that are pictured on the countenances of the Roman veterans. The Easterner's teeth were chattering, and he was hopping up and down like a mechanical toy. The cowboy stood rock-like.

The contestants had not stripped off any clothing. Each was in his ordinary attire. Their fists were up, and they eyed each other in a calm that had the elements of leonine cruelty in it.

During this pause, the Easterner's mind, like a film, took lasting impressions of three men—the iron-nerved master of the ceremony; the Swede, pale, motionless, terrible; and Johnnie, serene yet ferocious, brutish yet heroic. The entire prelude had in it a tragedy greater than the tragedy of action, and this aspect was accentuated by the long mellow cry of the blizzard, as it sped the tumbling and wailing flakes into the black abyss of the south.

"Now!" said Scully.

The two combatants leaped forward and crashed together like bullocks. There was heard the cushioned sound of blows, and of a curse squeezing out from between the tight teeth of one.

As for the spectators, the Easterner's pent-up breath exploded from him with a pop of relief, absolute relief from the tension of the preliminaries. The cowboy bounded into the air with a yowl. Scully was immovable as from supreme amazement and fear at the fury of the fight which he himself had permitted and arranged.

For a time the encounter in the darkness was such a perplexity of flying arms that it presented no more detail than would a swiftly-revolving wheel. Occasionally a face, as if illumined by a flash of light, would shine out, ghastly and marked with pink spots. A moment later, the men might have been known as shadows, if it were not for the involuntary utterance of oaths that came from them in whispers.

Suddenly a holocaust of warlike desire caught the cowboy, and he bolted forward with the speed of a broncho. "Go it, Johnnie; go it! Kill him! Kill him!"

Scully confronted him. "Kape back," he said; and by his glance the cowboy could tell that this man was Johnnie's father.

To the Easterner there was a monotony of unchangeable fighting that was an abomination. This confused mingling was eternal to his sense, which was concentrated in a longing for the end, the priceless end. Once the fighters lurched near him, and as he scrambled hastily backward, he heard them breathe like men on the rack.

"Kill him, Johnnie! Kill him! Kill him! Kill him!" The cowboy's face was contorted like one of those agony-masks in museums.

"Keep still," said Scully icily.

Then there was a sudden loud grunt, incomplete, cut-short, and Johnnie's body swung away from the Swede and fell with sickening heaviness to the grass. The cowboy was barely in time to prevent the mad Swede from flinging himself upon his prone adversary. "No, you don't," said the cowboy, interposing an arm. "Wait a second."

Scully was at his son's side. "Johnnie! Johnnie, me boy?" His voice had a quality of melancholy tenderness. "Johnnie? Can you go on with it?" He looked anxiously down into the bloody pulpy face of his son.

There was a moment of silence, and then Johnnie answered in his ordinary voice: "Yes, I—it—yes."

Assisted by his father he struggled to his feet. "Wait a bit now till you git your wind," said the old man.

A few paces away the cowboy was lecturing the Swede. "No, you don't! Wait a second!"

The Easterner was plucking at Scully's sleeve. "Oh, this is enough," he pleaded. "This is enough! Let it go as it stands. This is enough!"

"Bill," said Scully, "git out of the road." The cowboy stepped aside. "Now." The combatants were actuated by a new caution as they advanced toward collision. They glared at each other, and then the Swede aimed a lightning blow that carried with it his entire weight. Johnnie was evidently half-stupid from weakness, but he miraculously dodged, and his fist sent the over-balanced Swede sprawling.

The cowboy, Scully and the Easterner burst into a cheer that was like a chorus of triumphant soldiery, but before its conclusion the Swede had scuffled agilely to his feet and come in berserk abandon at his foe. There was another perplexity of flying arms, and Johnnie's body again swung away and fell, even as a bundle might fall from a roof. The Swede instantly staggered to a little wind-waved tree and leaned upon it, breathing like an engine, while his savage and flame-lit eyes roamed from face to face as the men bent over Johnnie. There was a splendor of isolation in his situation at this time which the Easterner felt once when, lifting his eyes from the man on the ground, he beheld that mysterious and lonely figure, waiting.

"Are you any good yet, Johnnie?" asked Scully in a broken voice.

The son gasped and opened his eyes languidly. After a moment he answered: "No—I ain't—any good—any—more."

Then, from shame and bodily ill, he began to weep, the tears furrowing down through the blood-stains on his face. "He was too—too—too heavy for me."

Scully straightened and addressed the waiting figure. "Stranger," he said, evenly, "it's all up with our side." Then his voice changed into that vibrant huskiness which is commonly the tone of the most simple and deadly announcements. "Johnnie is whipped."

Without replying, the victor moved off on the route to the front door of the hotel.

The cowboy was formulating new and unspellable blasphemies. The Easterner was startled to find that they were out in a wind that seemed to come direct from the shadowed arctic floes. He heard again the wail of the snow as it was flung to its grave in the south. He knew now that all this time the cold had been sinking into him deeper and deeper, and he wondered that he had not perished. He felt indifferent to the condition of the vanquished man.

"Johnnie, can you walk?" asked Scully.

"Did I hurt—hurt him any?" asked the son.

"Can you walk, boy? Can you walk?"

Johnnie's voice was suddenly strong. There was a robust impatience in it. "I asked you whether I hurt him any!"

"Yes, yes, Johnnie," answered the cowboy consolingly; "he's hurt a good deal."

They raised him from the ground, and as soon as he was on his feet he went tottering off, rebuffing all attempts at assistance. When the party rounded the corner they were fairly blinded by the pelting of the snow. It burned their faces like fire. The cowboy carried Johnnie through the drift to the door. As they entered some cards again rose from the floor and beat against the wall.

The Easterner rushed to the stove. He was so profoundly chilled that he almost dared to embrace the glowing iron. The Swede was not in the room. Johnnie sank into a chair, and folding his arms on his knees, buried his face in them. Scully, warming one foot and then the other at a rim of the stove, muttered to himself with Celtic mournfulness. The cowboy had removed his fur-cap, and with a dazed and rueful air he was now running one hand through his tousled locks. From overhead they could hear the creaking of boards, as the Swede tramped here and there in his room.

The sad quiet was broken by the sudden flinging open of a door that led toward the kitchen. It was instantly followed by an inrush of women. They precipitated themselves upon Johnnie amid a chorus of lamentation. Before they carried their prey off to the kitchen, there to be bathed and harangued with that mixture of sympathy and abuse which is a feat of their sex, the mother straightened herself and fixed old Scully with an eye of stern reproach. "Shame be upon you, Patrick Scully!" she cried. "Your own son, too. Shame be upon you!"

"There, now! Be quiet, now!" said the old man weakly.

"Shame be upon you, Patrick Scully!" The girls, rallying to this slogan, sniffed disdainfully in the direction of those trembling accomplices, the cowboy and the Easterner. Presently they bore Johnnie away, and left the three men to dismal reflection.

VII

"I'd like to fight this here Dutchman myself," said the cowboy, breaking a long silence.

Scully wagged his head sadly. "No, that wouldn't do. It wouldn't be right. It wouldn't be right."

"Well, why wouldn't it?" argued the cowboy. "I don't see no harm in it."

"No," answered Scully with mournful heroism. "It wouldn't be right. It was Johnnie's fight, and now we mustn't whip the man just because he whipped Johnnie."

"Yes, that's true enough," said the cowboy; "but—he better not get fresh with me, because I couldn't stand no more of it."

"You'll not say a word to him," commanded Scully, and even then they heard the tread of the Swede on the stairs. His entrance was made theatric. He swept the door back with a bang and swaggered to the middle of the room. No one looked at him. "Well," he cried, insolently, at Scully, "I s'pose you'll tell me now how much I owe you?"

The old man remained stolid. "You don't owe me nothin'."

"Huh!" said the Swede, "huh! Don't owe 'im nothin'."

The cowboy addressed the Swede. "Stranger, I don't see how you come to be so gay around here."

Old Scully was instantly alert. "Stop!" he shouted, holding his hand forth, fingers upward. "Bill, you shut up!"

The cowboy spat carelessly into the sawdust box. "I didn't say a word, did I?" he asked.

"Mr. Scully," called the Swede, "how much do I owe you?" It was seen that he was attired for departure, and that he had his valise in his hand.

"You don't owe me nothin'," repeated Scully in his same imperturbable way.

"Huh!" said the Swede. "I guess you're right. I guess if it was any way at all, you'd owe me somethin'. That's what I guess." He turned to the cowboy. " 'Kill him! Kill him! Kill him!' " he mimicked, and then guffawed victoriously. " 'Kill him!' " He was convulsed with ironical humor.

But he might have been jeering the dead. The three men were immovable and silent, staring with glassy eyes at the stove.

The Swede opened the door and passed into the storm, giving one derisive glance backward at the still group.

As soon as the door was closed, Scully and the cowboy leaped to their feet and began to curse. They trampled to and fro, waving their arms and smashing into the air with their fists. "Oh, but that was a hard minute!" wailed Scully. "That was a hard minute! Him there leerin' and scoffin'! One bang at his nose was worth forty dollars to me that minute! How did you stand it, Bill?"

"How did I stand it?" cried the cowboy in a quivering voice. "How did I stand it? Oh!"

The old man burst into sudden brogue. "I'd loike to take that Swade," he wailed, "and hould 'im down on a shtone flure and bate 'im to a jelly wid a shtick!"

The cowboy groaned in sympathy. "I'd like to git him by the neck and ha-ammer him"—he brought his hand down on a chair with a noise like a pistol-shot—"hammer that there Dutchman until he couldn't tell himself from a dead coyote!"

"I'd bate 'im until he——"

"I'd show *him* some things——"

And then together they raised a yearning fanatic cry. "Oh-o-oh! if we only could——"

"Yes!"

"Yes!"

"And then I'd——"

"O-o-oh!"

VIII

The Swede, tightly gripping his valise, tacked across the face of the storm as if he carried sails. He was following a line of little naked gasping trees, which he knew must mark the way of the road. His face, fresh from the pounding of John-nie's fists, felt more pleasure than pain in the wind and the driving snow. A number of square shapes loomed upon him finally, and he knew them as the houses of the main body of the town. He found a street and made travel along it, leaning heavily upon the wind whenever, at a corner, a terrific blast caught him.

He might have been in a deserted village. We picture the world as thick with conquering and elate humanity, but here, with the bugles of the tempest pealing, it was hard to imagine a peopled earth. One viewed the existence of man then as a marvel, and conceded a glamour of wonder to these lice which were caused to cling to a whirling, fire-smote, ice-locked, disease-stricken, space-lost bulb. The conceit of man was explained by this storm to be the very engine of life. One was a coxcomb not to die in it. However, the Swede found a saloon.

In front of it an indomitable red light was burning, and the snow-flakes were made blood-color as they flew through the circumscribed territory of the lamp's shining. The Swede pushed open the door of the saloon and entered. A sanded expanse was before him, and at the end of it four men sat about a table drinking. Down one side of the room extended a radiant bar, and its guardian was leaning upon his elbows listening to the talk of the men at the table. The Swede dropped his valise upon the floor, and, smiling fraternally upon the barkeeper, said: "Gimme some whisky, will you?"

The man placed a bottle, a whisky-glass, and a glass of ice-thick water upon the bar. The Swede poured himself an abnormal portion of whisky and drank it in three gulps. "Pretty bad night," remarked the bartender indifferently. He was making the pretension of blindness, which is usually a distinction of his class; but it could have been seen that he was furtively studying the half-erased blood-stains on the face of the Swede. "Bad night," he said again.

"Oh, it's good enough for me," replied the Swede, hardily, as he poured himself some more whisky. The barkeeper took his coin and maneuvered it through its reception by the highly-nickeled cash-machine. A bell rang; a card labeled "20 cts." had appeared.

"No," continued the Swede, "this isn't too bad weather. It's good enough for me."

"So?" murmured the barkeeper languidly.

The copious drams made the Swede's eyes swim, and he breathed a trifle heavier. "Yes, I like this weather. I like it. It suits me." It was apparently his design to impart a deep significance to these words.

"So?" murmured the bartender again. He turned to gaze dreamily at the scroll-like birds and bird-like scrolls which had been drawn with soap upon the mirrors back of the bar.

"Well, I guess I'll take another drink," said the Swede presently. "Have something?"

"No, thanks; I'm not drinkin'," answered the bartender. Afterward he asked: "How did you hurt your face?"

The Swede immediately began to boast loudly. "Why, in a fight. I thumped the soul out of a man down here at Scully's hotel."

The interest of the four men at the table was at last aroused.

"Who was it?" said one.

"Johnnie Scully," blustered the Swede. "Son of the man what runs it. He will be pretty near dead for some weeks, I can tell you. I made a nice thing of him, I did. He couldn't get up. They carried him in the house. Have a drink?"

Instantly the men in some subtle way incased themselves in reserve. "No, thanks," said one. The group was of curious formation. Two were prominent local business men; one was the district-attorney; and one was a professional gambler of the kind known as "square." But a scrutiny of the group would not have enabled an observer to pick the gambler from the men of more reputable pursuits. He was, in fact, a man so delicate in manner, when among people of fair class, and so judicious in his choice of victims, that in the strictly masculine part of the town's life he had come to be explicitly trusted and admired. People called him a thoroughbred. The fear and contempt with which his craft was regarded was undoubtedly the reason that his quiet dignity shone conspicuous above the quiet dignity of men who might be merely hatters, billiard-markers or grocery clerks. Beyond an occasional unwary traveler, who came by rail, this gambler was supposed to prey solely upon reckless and senile farmers, who, when flush with good crops, drove into town in all the pride and confidence of an absolutely invulnerable stupidity. Hearing at times in circuitous fashion of the despoilment of such a farmer, the important men of Romper invariably laughed in contempt of the victim, and if they thought of the wolf at all, it was with a kind of pride at the knowledge that he would never dare think of attacking their wisdom and courage. Besides, it was popular that this gambler had a real wife and two real children in a neat cottage in a suburb, where he led an exemplary home life, and when any one even suggested a discrepancy in his character, the crowd immediately vociferated descriptions of this virtuous family circle. Then men who led exemplary home lives, and men who did not lead exemplary home lives, all subsided in a bunch, remarking that there was nothing more to be said.

However, when a restriction was placed upon him—as, for instance, when a strong clique of members of the new Pollywog Club refused to permit him, even as a spectator, to appear in the rooms of the organization—the candor and gentleness with which he accepted the judgment disarmed many of his foes and made his friends more desperately partisan. He invariably distinguished between himself and a respectable Romper man so quickly and frankly that his manner actually appeared to be a continual broadcast compliment.

And one must not forget to declare the fundamental fact of

his entire position in Romper. It is irrefutable that in all affairs outside of his business, in all matters that occur eternally and commonly between man and man, this thieving card-player was so generous, so just, so moral, that, in a contest, he could have put to flight the consciences of nine-tenths of the citizens of Romper.

And so it happened that he was seated in this saloon with the two prominent local merchants and the district-attorney.

The Swede continued to drink raw whisky, meanwhile babbling at the barkeeper and trying to induce him to indulge in potations. "Come on. Have a drink. Come on. What—no? Well, have a little one then. By gawd, I've whipped a man tonight, and I want to celebrate. I whipped him good, too. Gentlemen," the Swede cried to the men at the table, "have a drink?"

"Ssh!" said the barkeeper.

The group at the table, although furtively attentive, had been pretending to be deep in talk, but now a man lifted his eyes toward the Swede and said shortly: "Thanks. We don't want any more."

At this reply the Swede ruffled out his chest like a rooster. "Well," he exploded, "it seems I can't get anybody to drink with me in this town. Seems so, don't it? Well!"

"Ssh!" said the barkeeper.

"Say," snarled the Swede, "don't you try to shut me up. I won't have it. I'm a gentleman, and I want people to drink with me. And I want 'em to drink with me now. *Now*—do you understand?" He rapped the bar with his knuckles.

Years of experience had calloused the bartender. He merely grew sulky. "I hear you," he answered.

"Well," cried the Swede, "listen hard then. See those men over there? Well, they're going to drink with me, and don't you forget it. Now you watch."

"Hi!" yelled the barkeeper, "this won't do!"

"Why won't it?" demanded the Swede. He stalked over to the table, and by chance laid his hand upon the shoulder of the gambler. "How about this?" he asked, wrathfully. "I asked you to drink with me."

The gambler simply twisted his head and spoke over his shoulder. "My friend, I don't know you."

"Oh, hell!" answered the Swede, "come and have a drink."

"Now, my boy," advised the gambler kindly, "take your hand off my shoulder and go 'way and mind your own business." He was a little slim man, and it seemed strange to hear him use this tone of heroic patronage to the burly Swede. The other men at the table said nothing.

"What? You won't drink with me, you little dude! I'll make you then! I'll make you!" The Swede had grasped the gambler frenziedly at the throat, and was dragging him from his chair. The other men sprang up. The barkeeper dashed around the corner of his bar. There was a great tumult, and then was seen a long blade in the hand of the gambler. It shot forward, and a human body, this citadel of virtue, wisdom, power, was pierced as easily as if it had been a melon. The Swede fell with a cry of supreme astonishment.

The prominent merchants and the district-attorney must have at once tumbled out of the place backward. The bartender found himself hanging limply to the arm of a chair and gazing into the eyes of a murderer.

"Henry," said the latter, as he wiped his knife on one of the towels that hung beneath the bar-rail, "you tell 'em where to find me. I'll be home, waiting for 'em." Then he vanished. A moment afterward the barkeeper was in the street dinning through the storm for help, and, moreover, companionship.

The corpse of the Swede, alone in the saloon, had its eyes fixed upon a dreadful legend that dwelt a-top of the cash-machine. "This registers the amount of your purchase."

IX

Months later, the cowboy was frying pork over the stove of a little ranch near the Dakota line, when there was a quick thud of hoofs outside, and, presently, the Easterner entered with the letters and the papers.

"Well," said the Easterner at once, "the chap that killed the Swede has got three years. Wasn't much, was it?"

"He has? Three years?" The cowboy poised his pan of pork, while he ruminated upon the news. "Three years. That ain't much."

"No. It was a light sentence," replied the Easterner as he unbuckled his spurs. "Seems there was a good deal of sympathy for him in Romper."

"If the bartender had been any good," observed the cowboy thoughtfully, "he would have gone in and cracked that there Dutchman on the head with a bottle in the beginnin' of it and stopped all this here murderin'."

"Yes, a thousand things might have happened," said the Easterner tartly.

The cowboy returned his pan of pork to the fire, but his philosophy continued. "It's funny, ain't it? If he hadn't said Johnnie was cheatin' he'd be alive this minute. He was an awful fool. Game played for fun, too. Not for money. I believe he was crazy."

"I feel sorry for that gambler," said the Easterner.

"Oh, so do I," said the cowboy. "He don't deserve none of it for killin' who he did."

"The Swede might not have been killed if everything had been square."

"Might not have been killed?" exclaimed the cowboy. "Everythin' square? Why, when he said that Johnnie was cheatin' and acted like such a jackass? And then in the saloon he fairly walked up to git hurt?" With these arguments the cowboy browbeat the Easterner and reduced him to rage.

"You're a fool!" cried the Easterner viciously. "You're a bigger jackass than the Swede by a million majority. Now let me tell you one thing. Let me tell you something. Listen! Johnnie *was* cheating!"

" 'Johnnie,' " said the cowboy blankly. There was a minute of silence, and then he said robustly: "Why, no. The game was only for fun."

"Fun or not," said the Easterner, "Johnnie was cheating. I saw him. I know it. I saw him. And I refused to stand up and be a man. I let the Swede fight it out alone. And you—you were simply puffing around the place and wanting to fight. And then old Scully himself! We are all in it! This poor gambler isn't even a noun. He is kind of an adverb. Every sin is the result of a collaboration. We, five of us, have collaborated in the murder of this Swede. Usually there are from a dozen to forty women really involved in every murder, but in this case it seems to be only five men—you, I, Johnnie, old Scully, and that fool of an unfortunate gambler came merely as a culmination, the apex of a human movement, and gets all the punishment."

The cowboy, injured and rebellious, cried out blindly into this fog of mysterious theory. "Well, I didn't do anythin', did I?"

Twelve O'Clock

"Where were you at twelve o'clock, noon, on the 9th of
June, 1875?"—*Question on intelligent cross-examination.*

I

"EXCUSE *ME*," said Ben Roddle with graphic gestures to a
group of citizens in Nantucket's store. "Excuse *me*.
When them fellers in leather pants an' six-shooters ride in, I
go home an' set in th' cellar. That's what I do. When you see
me pirooting through the streets at th' same time an' occasion
as them punchers, you kin put me down fer bein' crazy. Ex-
cuse *me*."

"Why, Ben," drawled old Nantucket, "you ain't never really
seen 'em turned loose. Why, I kin remember—in th' old
days—when——"

"Oh, damn yer old days!" retorted Roddle. Fixing Nan-
tucket with the eye of scorn and contempt, he said: "I sup-
pose you'll be sayin' in a minute that in th' old days you used
to kill Injuns, won't you?"

There was some laughter, and Roddle was left free to ex-
pand his ideas on the periodic visits of cowboys to the town.
"Mason Rickets, he had ten big punkins a-sittin' in front of
his store, an' them fellers from the Upside-down-F ranch shot
'em up—shot 'em all up—an' Rickets lyin' on his belly in th'
store a-callin' fer 'em to quit it. An' what did they do! Why,
they *laughed* at 'im!—just *laughed* at 'im! That don't do a
town no good. Now, how would an eastern capiterlist"—(it
was the town's humor to be always gassing of phantom inves-
tors who were likely to come any moment and pay a thousand
prices for everything)—"how would an eastern capiterlist like
that? Why, you couldn't see 'im fer th' dust on his trail. Then
he'd tell all his friends that 'their town may be all right, but
ther's too much loose-handed shootin' fer my money.' An'
he'd be right, too. Them rich fellers, they don't make no bad
breaks with their money. They watch it all th' time b'cause
they know blame well there ain't hardly room fer their feet
fer th' pikers an' tin-horns an' thimble-riggers what are layin'

fer 'em. I tell you, one puncher racin' his cow-pony hell-bent-fer-election down Main Street an' yellin' an' shootin' an' nothin' at all done about it, would scare away a whole herd of capiterlists. An' it ain't right. It oughter be stopped."

A pessimistic voice asked: "How you goin' to stop it, Ben?"

"Organize," replied Roddle pompously. "Organize: that's the only way to make these fellers lay down. I——"

From the street sounded a quick scudding of pony hoofs, and a party of cowboys swept past the door. One man, however, was seen to draw rein and dismount. He came clanking into the store. "Mornin', gentlemen," he said, civilly.

"Mornin'," they answered in subdued voices.

He stepped to the counter and said, "Give me a paper of fine cut, please." The group of citizens contemplated him in silence. He certainly did not look threatening. He appeared to be a young man of twenty-five years, with a tan from wind and sun, with a remarkably clear eye from perhaps a period of enforced temperance, a quiet young man who wanted to buy some tobacco. A six-shooter swung low on his hip, but at the moment it looked more decorative than warlike; it seemed merely a part of his odd gala dress—his sombrero with its band of rattlesnake skin, his great flaming neckerchief, his belt of embroidered Mexican leather, his high-heeled boots, his huge spurs. And, above all, his hair had been watered and brushed until it lay as close to his head as the fur lays to a wet cat. Paying for his tobacco, he withdrew.

Ben Roddle resumed his harangue. "Well, there you are! Looks like a calm man now, but in less'n half an hour he'll be as drunk as three bucks an' a squaw, an' then . . . . excuse *me*!"

II

On this day the men of two outfits had come into town, but Ben Roddle's ominous words were not justified at once. The punchers spent most of the morning in an attack on whiskey which was too earnest to be noisy.

At five minutes of eleven, a tall, lank, brick-colored cowboy strode over to Placer's Hotel. Placer's Hotel was a notable place. It was the best hotel within two hundred miles. Its office was filled with arm-chairs and brown papier-maché receptacles. At one end of the room was a wooden counter painted a bright pink, and on this morning a man was behind the counter writing in a ledger. He was the proprietor of the hotel, but his customary humor was so sullen that all strangers immediately wondered why in life he had chosen to play the part of mine host. Near his left hand, double doors opened into the dining-room, which in warm weather was always kept darkened in order to discourage the flies, which was not compassed at all.

Placer, writing in his ledger, did not look up when the tall cowboy entered.

"Mornin', mister," said the latter. "I've come to see if you kin grub-stake th' hull crowd of us fer dinner t'day."

Placer did not then raise his eyes, but with a certain churlishness, as if it annoyed him that his hotel was patronized, he asked: "How many?"

"Oh, about thirty," replied the cowboy. "An' we want th' best dinner you kin raise an' scrape. Everything th' best. We don't care what it costs s'long as we git a good square meal. We'll pay a dollar a head: by God, we will! We won't kick on nothin' in the bill if you do it up fine. If you ain't got it in th' house, russle th' hull town fer it. That's our gait. So you just tear loose, an' we'll——"

At this moment the machinery of a cuckoo-clock on the wall began to whirr, little doors flew open, and a wooden bird appeared and cried, "Cuckoo!" And this was repeated until eleven o'clock had been announced, while the cowboy, stupefied, glassy-eyed, stood with his red throat gulping. At the end he wheeled upon Placer and demanded: *"What in hell is that?"*

Placer revealed by his manner that he had been asked this question too many times. "It's a clock," he answered shortly.

"I know it's a clock," gasped the cowboy; "but what *kind* of a clock?"

"A cuckoo-clock. Can't you see?"

The cowboy, recovering his self-possession by a violent effort, suddenly went shouting into the street. "Boys! Say, boys! Com' 'ere a minute!"

His comrades, comfortably inhabiting a near-by saloon,

heard his stentorian calls, but they merely said to one an-
other: "What's th' matter with Jake?—he's off his nut again."

But Jake burst in upon them with violence. "Boys," he
yelled, "come over to th' hotel! They got a clock with a bird
inside it, an' when it's eleven o'clock or anything like that, th'
bird comes out an' says, '*toot*-toot, *toot*-toot!' that way, as
many times as whatever time of day it is. It's immense! Come
on over!"

The roars of laughter which greeted his proclamation were
of two qualities; some men laughing because they knew all
about cuckoo-clocks, and other men laughing because they
had concluded that the eccentric Jake had been victimized by
some wise child of civilization.

Old Man Crumford, a venerable ruffian who probably had
been born in a corral, was particularly offensive with his loud
guffaws of contempt. "Bird a-comin' out of a clock an' a-
tellin' ye th' time! Haw-haw-haw!" He swallowed his whis-
key. "A bird! a-tellin' ye th' time! Haw-haw! Jake, you ben up
agin some new drink. You ben drinkin' lonely an' got up agin
some snake-medicine licker. A bird a-tellin' ye th' time! Haw-
haw!"

The shrill voice of one of the younger cowboys piped from
the background. "Brace up, Jake. Don't let 'em laugh at ye.
Bring 'em that salt cod-fish of yourn what kin pick out th' ace."

"Oh, he's only kiddin' us. Don't pay no 'tention to 'im. He
thinks he's smart."

A cowboy whose mother had a cuckoo-clock in her house
in Philadelphia spoke with solemnity. "Jake's a liar. There's
no such clock in the world. What? a bird inside a clock to tell
the time? Change your drink, Jake."

Jake was furious, but his fury took a very icy form. He bent
a withering glance upon the last speaker. "I don't mean a *live*
bird," he said, with terrible dignity. "It's a wooden bird,
an'——"

"A wooden bird!" shouted Old Man Crumford. "Wooden
bird a-tellin' ye th' time! Haw-haw!"

But Jake still paid his frigid attention to the Philadelphian.
"An' if yer sober enough to walk, it ain't such a blame long
ways from here to th' hotel, an' I'll bet my pile agin yours if
you only got two bits."

"I don't want your money, Jake," said the Philadelphian. "Somebody's been stringin' you—that's all. I wouldn't take your money." He cleverly appeared to pity the other's innocence.

"You couldn't *git* my money," cried Jake, in sudden hot anger. "You couldn't git it. Now—since yer so fresh—let's see how much you got." He clattered some large gold pieces noisily upon the bar.

The Philadelphian shrugged his shoulders and walked away. Jake was triumphant. "Any more bluffers 'round here?" he demanded. "Any more? Any more bluffers? Where's all these here hot sports? Let 'em step up. Here's my money— come an' git it."

But they had ended by being afraid. To some of them his tale was absurd, but still one must be circumspect when a man throws forty-five dollars in gold upon the bar and bids the world come and win it. The general feeling was expressed by Old Man Crumford, when with deference he asked: "Well, this here bird, Jake—what kinder lookin' bird is it?"

"It's a little brown thing," said Jake briefly. Apparently he almost disdained to answer.

"Well—how does it work?" asked the old man meekly.

"Why in blazes don't you go an' look at it?" yelled Jake. "Want me to paint it in iles fer you? Go an' look!"

III

Placer was writing in his ledger. He heard a great trample of feet and clink of spurs on the porch, and there entered quietly the band of cowboys, some of them swaying a trifle, and these last being the most painfully decorous of all. Jake was in advance. He waved his hand toward the clock. "There she is," he said laconically. The cowboys drew up and stared. There was some giggling, but a serious voice said half-audibly, "I don't see no bird."

Jake politely addressed the landlord. "Mister, I've fetched these here friends of mine in here to see yer clock——"

Placer looked up suddenly. "Well, they can see it, can't they?" he asked in sarcasm. Jake, abashed, retreated to his fellows.

There was a period of silence. From time to time the men shifted their feet. Finally, Old Man Crumford leaned toward Jake, and in a penetrating whisper demanded, "Where's th' bird?" Some frolicsome spirits on the outskirts began to call "Bird! Bird!" as men at a political meeting call for a particular speaker.

Jake removed his big hat and nervously mopped his brow.

The young cowboy with the shrill voice again spoke from the skirts of the crowd. "Jake, is ther' sure-'nough a bird in that thing?"

"Yes. Didn't I tell you once?"

"Then," said the shrill-voiced man, in a tone of conviction, "it ain't a clock at all. It's a bird-cage."

"I tell you it's a clock," cried the maddened Jake, but his retort could hardly be heard above the howls of glee and derision which greeted the words of him of the shrill voice.

Old Man Crumford was again rampant. "Wooden bird a-tellin' ye th' time! Haw-haw!"

Amid the confusion Jake went again to Placer. He spoke almost in supplication. "Say, mister, what time does this here thing go off agin?"

Placer lifted his head, looked at the clock, and said: "Noon."

There was a stir near the door, and Big Watson of the Square-X outfit, and at this time very drunk indeed, came shouldering his way through the crowd and cursing everybody. The men gave him much room, for he was notorious as a quarrelsome person when drunk. He paused in front of Jake, and spoke as through a wet blanket. "What's all this —— monkeyin' about?"

Jake was already wild at being made a butt for everybody, and he did not give backward. "None a' your damn business, Watson."

"Huh?" growled Watson, with the surprise of a challenged bull.

"I said," repeated Jake distinctly, "it's none a' your damn business."

Watson whipped his revolver half out of its holster. "I'll make it m' business, then, you ——"

But Jake had backed a step away, and was holding his left-hand palm outward toward Watson, while in his right he held his six-shooter, its muzzle pointing at the floor. He was shouting in a frenzy,—"No—don't you try it, Watson! Don't you dare try it, or, by Gawd, I'll kill you, sure—*sure!*"

He was aware of a torment of cries about him from fearful men; from men who protested, from men who cried out because they cried out. But he kept his eyes on Watson, and those two glared murder at each other, neither seeming to breathe, fixed like statues.

A loud new voice suddenly rang out: "Hol' on a minute!" All spectators who had not stampeded turned quickly, and saw Placer standing behind his bright pink counter, with an aimed revolver in each hand.

"Cheese it!" he said. "I won't have no fightin' here. If you want to fight, git out in the street."

Big Watson laughed, and, speeding up his six-shooter like a flash of blue light, he shot Placer through the throat—shot the man as he stood behind his absurd pink counter with his two aimed revolvers in his incompetent hands. With a yell of rage and despair, Jake smote Watson on the pate with his heavy weapon, and knocked him sprawling and bloody. Somewhere a woman shrieked like windy, midnight death. Placer fell behind the counter, and down upon him came his ledger and his inkstand, so that one could not have told blood from ink.

The cowboys did not seem to hear, see, or feel, until they saw numbers of citizens with Winchesters running wildly upon them. Old Man Crumford threw high a passionate hand. "Don't shoot! We'll not fight ye fer 'im."

Nevertheless two or three shots rang, and a cowboy who had been about to gallop off suddenly slumped over on his pony's neck, where he held for a moment like an old sack, and then slid to the ground, while his pony, with flapping rein, fled to the prairie.

"In God's name, don't shoot!" trumpeted Old Man Crumford. "We'll not fight ye fer 'im!"

"It's murder," bawled Ben Roddle.

In the chaotic street it seemed for a moment as if everybody would kill everybody. "Where's the man what done it?" These hot cries seemed to declare a war which would result in an

absolute annihilation of one side. But the cowboys were sing-
ing out against it. They would fight for nothing—yes—they
often fought for nothing—but they would not fight for this
dark something.

At last, when a flimsy truce had been made between the
inflamed men, all parties went to the hotel. Placer, in some
dying whim, had made his way out from behind the pink
counter, and, leaving a horrible trail, had travelled to the
centre of the room, where he had pitched headlong over the
body of Big Watson.

The men lifted the corpse and laid it at the side.

"Who done it?" asked a white, stern man.

A cowboy pointed at Big Watson. "That's him," he said
huskily.

There was a curious grim silence, and then suddenly, in the
death-chamber, there sounded the loud whirring of the
clock's works, little doors flew open, a tiny wooden bird ap-
peared and cried "Cuckoo"—twelve times.

Moonlight on the Snow

I

THE TOWN of War Post had an evil name for three hundred miles in every direction. It radiated like the shine from some stupendous light. The citizens of the place had been for years grotesquely proud of their fame as a collection of hard-shooting gentlemen who invariably "got" the men who came up against them. When a citizen went abroad in the land he said, "I'm f'm War Post." And it was as if he had said, "I am the devil himself."

But ultimately it became known to War Post that the serene-browed angel of peace was in the vicinity. The angel was full of projects for taking comparatively useless bits of prairie and sawing them up into town lots, and making chaste and beautiful maps of his handiwork which shook the souls of people who had never been in the West. He commonly traveled here and there in a light wagon, from the tail-board of which he made orations which soared into the empyrean regions of true hydrogen gas. Towns far and near listened to his voice and followed him singing, until in all that territory you couldn't throw a stone at a jack-rabbit without hitting the site of a projected mammoth hotel; estimated cost, fifteen thousand dollars. The stern and lonely buttes were given titles like grim veterans awarded tawdry patents of nobility—Cedar Mountain, Red Cliffs, Lookout Peak. And from the East came both the sane and the insane with hope, with courage, with hoarded savings, with cold decks, with Bibles, with knives in boots, with humility and fear, with bland impudence. Most came with their own money; some came with money gained during a moment of inattention on the part of somebody in the East. And high in the air was the serene-browed angel of peace, with his endless gabble and his pretty maps. It was curious to walk out of an evening to the edge of a vast silent sea of prairie, and to reflect that the angel had parceled this infinity into building lots.

But no change had come to War Post. War Post sat with her reputation for bloodshed pressed proudly to her bosom and saw her mean neighbors leap into being as cities. She saw

drunken old reprobates selling acres of red-hot dust and be-
coming wealthy men of affairs, who congratulated themselves
on their shrewdness in holding land which, before the boom,
they would have sold for enough to buy a treat all 'round in
the Straight Flush Saloon—only nobody would have given
it.

War Post saw dollars rolling into the coffers of a lot of
contemptible men who couldn't shoot straight. She was
amazed and indignant. She saw her standard of excellence,
her creed, her reason for being great, all tumbling about her
ears, and after the preliminary gasps she sat down to think it
out.

The first man to voice a conclusion was Bob Hether, the
popular barkeeper in Stevenson's Crystal Palace. "It's this
here gun-fighter business," he said, leaning on his bar, and,
with the gentle, serious eyes of a child, surveying a group of
prominent citizens who had come in to drink at the expense
of Tom Larpent, a gambler. They solemnly nodded assent.
They stood in silence, holding their glasses and thinking.

Larpent was a chief factor in the life of the town. His gam-
bling-house was the biggest institution in War Post. More-
over, he had been educated somewhere, and his slow speech
had a certain mordant quality which was apt to puzzle War
Post, and men heeded him for the reason that they were not
always certain as to what he was saying. "Yes, Bob," he
drawled, "I think you are right. The value of human life has
to be established before there can be theatres, water-works,
street cars, women and babies."

The other men were rather aghast at this cryptic speech,
but somebody managed to snigger appreciatively and the ten-
sion was eased.

Smith Hanham, who whirled roulette for Larpent, then
gave his opinion.

"Well, when all this here coin is floatin' 'round, it 'pears to
me we orter git our hooks on some of it. Them little tin-
horns over at Crowdger's Corners are up to their necks in it,
an' we ain't yit seen a centavo. Not a centavetto. That ain't
right. It's all well enough to sit 'round takin' money away
from innercent cow-punchers s'long's ther's nothin' better;
but when these here speculators come 'long flashin' rolls as

big as water-buckets, it's up to us to whirl in an' git some of it."

This became the view of the town, and, since the main stip-ulation was virtue, War Post resolved to be virtuous. A great meeting was held, at which it was decreed that no man should kill another man under penalty of being at once hanged by the populace. All the influential citizens were present, and as-serted their determination to deal out a swift punishment which would take no note of an acquaintance or friendship with the guilty man. Bob Hether made a loud, long speech, in which he declared that he for one would help hang his "own brother" if his "own brother" transgressed this law which now, for the good of the community, must be forever held sacred. Everybody was enthusiastic save a few Mexicans, who did not quite understand; but as they were more than likely to be the victims of any affray in which they were en-gaged, their silence was not considered ominous.

At half-past ten on the next morning Larpent shot and killed a man who had accused him of cheating at a game. Larpent had then taken a chair by the window.

II

Larpent grew tired of sitting in the chair by the window. He went to his bedroom, which opened off the gambling hall. On the table was a bottle of rye whiskey, of a brand which he specially and secretly imported from the East. He took a long drink; he changed his coat after laving his hands and brushing his hair. He sat down to read, his hand falling familiarly upon an old copy of Scott's "Fair Maid of Perth."

In time he heard the slow trample of many men coming up the stairs. The sound certainly did not indicate haste; in fact, it declared all kinds of hesitation. The crowd poured into the gambling hall; there was low talk; a silence; more low talk. Ultimately somebody rapped diffidently on the door of the bedroom. "Come in," said Larpent. The door swung back and disclosed War Post with a delegation of its best men in the front, and at the rear men who stood on their toes and craned their necks. There was no noise. Larpent looked up casually into the eyes of Bob Hether. "So you've come up to the scratch all right, eh, Bobbie?" he asked kindly. "I was wondering if you would weaken on the blood-curdling speech you made yesterday."

Hether first turned deadly pale and then flushed beet red. His six-shooter was in his hand, and it appeared for a moment as if his weak fingers would drop it to the floor. "Oh, never mind," said Larpent in the same tone of kindly patronage. "The community must and shall hold this law forever sacred; and your own brother lives in Connecticut, doesn't he?" He laid down his book and arose. He unbuckled his revolver belt and tossed it on the bed. A look of impatience had come suddenly upon his face. "Well, you don't want me to be master of ceremonies at my own hanging, do you? Why don't somebody say something or do something? You stand around like a lot of bottles. Where's your tree, for instance? You know there isn't a tree between here and the river. Damned little jack-rabbit town hasn't even got a tree for its hanging. Hello, Coats, you live in Crowdger's Corners, don't you? Well, you keep out of this thing, then. The Corners has had its boom, and this is a speculation in real estate which is the business solely of the citizens of War Post."

The behavior of the crowd became extraordinary. Men began to back away; eye did not meet eye; they were victims of an inexplicable influence; it was as if they had heard sinister laughter from a gloom. "I know," said Larpent considerately, "that this isn't as if you were going to hang a comparative stranger. In a sense, this is an intimate affair. I know full well you could go out and jerk a comparative stranger into kingdom come and make a sort of festal occasion of it. But when it comes to performing the same office for an old friend, even the ferocious Bobbie Hether stands around on one leg like a damned white-livered coward. In short, my milk-fed patriots, you seem fat-headed enough to believe that I am going to hang myself if you wait long enough; but unfortunately I am going to allow you to conduct your own real-estate speculations. It seems to me there should be enough men here who understand the value of corner lots in a safe and godly town, and hence should be anxious to hurry this business."

The icy tones had ceased, and the crowd breathed a great sigh, as if it had been freed of a physical pain. But still no one seemed to know where to reach for the scruff of this weird situation. Finally there was some jostling on the outskirts of the crowd, and some men were seen to be pushing old Billie Simpson forward amid some protests. Simpson was, on occasion, the voice of the town. Somewhere in his past he had been a Baptist preacher. He had fallen far, very far, and the only remnant of his former dignity was a fatal facility of speech when half drunk. War Post used him on those state occasions when it became bitten with a desire to "do the thing up in style." So the citizens pushed the blear-eyed old ruffian forward until he stood hemming and hawing in front of Larpent. It was evident at once that he was brutally sober, and hence wholly unfitted for whatever task had been planned for him. A dozen times he croaked like a frog, meanwhile wiping the back of his hand rapidly across his mouth. At last he managed to stammer, "Mister Larpent——"

In some indescribable manner Larpent made his attitude of respectful attention to be grossly contemptuous and insulting. "Yes, Mister Simpson?"

"Er—now—Mister Larpent," began the old man hoarsely, " we wanted to know——" Then obviously feeling that there was a detail which he had forgotten, he turned to the crowd and whispered, "Where is it?" Many men precipitately cleared themselves out of the way, and down this lane Larpent had an unobstructed view of the body of the man he had slain. Old Simpson again began to croak like a frog, "Mister Larpent."

"Yes, Mister Simpson."

"Do you—er—do you—admit——"

"Oh, certainly," said the gambler good-humoredly. "There can be no doubt of it, Mister Simpson, although, with your well-known ability to fog things, you may later possibly prove that you did it yourself. I shot him because he was too officious. Not quite enough men are shot on that account, Mister Simpson. As one fitted in every way by nature to be consummately officious, I hope you will agree with me, Mister Simpson."

Men were plucking old Simpson by the sleeve and giving him directions. One could hear him say, "What?" "Yes." "All right." "What?" "All right." In the end he turned hurriedly upon Larpent and blurted out, "Well, I guess we're goin' to hang you."

Larpent bowed. "I had a suspicion that you would," he said in a pleasant voice. "There has been an air of determination about the entire proceeding, Mister Simpson."

There was an awkward moment. "Well—well—well, come ahead——"

Larpent courteously relieved a general embarrassment. "Why, of course. We must be moving. Clergy first, Mister Simpson. I'll take my old friend, Bobbie Hether, on my right hand, and we'll march soberly to the business, thus lending a certain dignity to this outing of real-estate speculators."

"Tom," quavered Bob Hether, "for Gawd's sake, keep your mout' shut."

"He invokes the deity," remarked Larpent placidly. "But, no; my last few minutes I am resolved to devote to inquiries as to the welfare of my friends. Now, you, for instance, my dear Bobbie, present to-day the lamentable appearance of a rattlesnake that has been four times killed and then left in the sun to rot. It is the effect of friendship upon a highly delicate system. You suffer? It is cruel. Never mind; you will feel better presently."

III

War Post had always risen superior to her lack of a tree by making use of a fixed wooden crane which appeared over a second-story window on the front of Pigrim's general store. This crane had a long tackle always ready for hoisting merchandise to the store's loft. Larpent, coming in the midst of a slow-moving throng, cocked a bright bird-like eye at this crane.

"Mm—yes," he said.

Men began to work frantically. They called each to each in voices strenuous but low. They were in a panic to have the thing finished. Larpent's cold ironical survey drove them mad, and it entered the minds of some that it would be felicitous to hang him before he could talk more. But he occupied the time in pleasant discourse. "I see that Smith Hanham is not here. Perhaps some undue tenderness of sentiment keeps him away. Such feelings are entirely unnecessary. Don't you think so, Bobbie? Note the feverish industry with which the renegade parson works at the rope. You will never be hung, Simpson. You will be shot for fooling too near a petticoat which doesn't belong to you—the same old habit which got you flung out of the Church, you red-eyed old satyr. Ah, the Cross Trail stage coach approaches. What a situation!" The crowd turned uneasily to follow his glance, and saw, truly enough, the dusty rickety old vehicle coming at the gallop of four lean horses. Ike Boston was driving the coach, and far away he had seen and defined the throng in front of Pilgrim's store. First calling out excited information to his passengers, who were all inside, he began to lash his horses and yell. As a result he rattled wildly up to the scene just as they were arranging the rope around Larpent's neck.

"Whoa!" said he to his horses.

The inhabitants of War Post peered at the windows of the coach and saw therein six pale, horror-stricken faces. The men at the rope stood hesitating. Larpent smiled blandly. There was a silence. At last a broken voice cried from the coach: "Driver! Driver! What is it? What is it?"

Ike Boston spat between the wheel horses and mumbled that he s'posed anybody could see, less'n they were blind. The door of the coach opened and out stepped a beautiful young lady. She was followed by two little girls hand clasped in hand, and a white-haired old gentleman with a venerable and peaceful face. And the rough West stood in naked immorality before the eyes of the gentle East. The leather-faced men of War Post had never imagined such perfection of feminine charm, such radiance; and as the illumined eyes of the girl wandered doubtfully, fearfully, toward the man with the rope around his neck, a certain majority of the practiced ruffians tried to look as if they were having nothing to do with the proceedings.

"Oh," she said, in a low voice, " what are you going to do?"

At first none made reply; but ultimately a hero managed to break the harrowing stillness by stammering out, "Nothin'!" And then, as if aghast at his own prominence, he shied behind the shoulders of a big neighbor.

"Oh, I know," she said, "but it's wicked. Don't you see how wicked it is? Papa, do say something to them."

The clear, deliberate tones of Tom Larpent suddenly made every one stiffen. During the early part of the interruption he had seated himself upon the steps of Pigrim's store, in which position he had maintained a slightly bored air. He now was standing with the rope around his neck and bowing. He looked handsome and distinguished and—a devil. A devil as cold as moonlight upon the ice. "You are quite right, miss. They are going to hang me, but I can give you my word that the affair is perfectly regular. I killed a man this morning, and you see these people here who look like a fine collection of premier scoundrels are really engaged in forcing a real-estate boom. In short, they are speculators, land barons, and not the children of infamy which you no doubt took them for at first."

"O—oh!" she said, and shuddered.

Her father now spoke haughtily. "What has this man done? Why do you hang him without a trial, even if you have fair proofs?"

The crowd had been afraid to speak to the young lady, but a dozen voices answered her father. "Why, he admits it." "Didn't ye hear?" "There ain't no doubt about it." "No!" "He *sez* he did."

The old man looked at the smiling gambler. "Do you admit that you committed murder?"

Larpent answered slowly. "For the first question in a temporary acquaintance that is a fairly strong beginning. Do you wish me to speak as man to man, or to one who has some kind of official authority to meddle in a thing that is none of his affair?"

"I—ah—I," stuttered the other. "Ah—man to man."

"Then," said Larpent, "I have to inform you that this morning, at about 10:30, a man was shot and killed in my gambling house. He was engaged in the exciting business of trying to grab some money out of which he claimed I had swindled him. The details are not interesting."

The old gentleman waved his arm in a gesture of terror and despair and tottered toward the coach; the young lady fainted; the two little girls wailed. Larpent sat on the steps with the rope around his neck.

IV

The chief function of War Post was to prey upon the bands of cowboys who, when they had been paid, rode gayly into town to look for sin. To this end there were in War Post many thugs and thieves. There was treachery and obscenity and merciless greed in every direction. Even Mexico was levied upon to furnish a kind of ruffian which appears infrequently in the northern races. War Post was not good; it was not tender; it was not chivalrous; but——

But——

There was a quality to the situation in front of Pigrim's store which made War Post wish to stampede. There were the two children, their angelic faces turned toward the sky, weeping in the last anguish of fear; there was the beautiful form of the young lady prostrate in the dust of the road, with her trembling father bending over her; on the steps sat Larpent, waiting, with a derisive smile, while from time to time he turned his head in the rope to make a forked-tongued remark as to the character and bearing of some acquaintance. All the simplicity of a mere lynching was gone from this thing. Through some bewildering inner power of its own it had carried out of the hands of its inaugurators and was marching along like a great drama and they were only spectators. To them it was ungovernable; they could do no more than stand on one foot and wonder.

Some were heartily sick of everything and wished to run away. Some were so interested in the new aspect that they had forgotten why they had originally come to the front of Pigrim's store. These were the poets. A large practical class wished to establish at once the identity of the new comers. Who were they? Where did they come from? Where were they going to? It was truthfully argued that they were the parson for the new church at Crowdger's Corners, with his family.

And a fourth class—a dark-browed, muttering class— wished to go at once to the root of all disturbance by killing Ike Boston for trundling up his old omnibus and dumping out upon their ordinary lynching party such a load of tears and inexperience and sentimental argument. In low tones they addressed vitriolic reproaches.

"But how'd I know?" he protested, almost with tears. "How'd I know ther'd be all this here kick up?"

But Larpent suddenly created a great stir. He stood up, and his face was inspired with a new, strong resolution. "Look here, boys," he said decisively, "you hang me to-morrow. Or, anyhow, later on to-day. We can't keep frightening the young lady and these two poor babies out of their wits. Ease off on the rope, Simpson, you blackguard! Frightening women and children is your game, but I'm not going to stand it. Ike Boston, take your passengers on to Crowdger's Corners, and tell the young lady that, owing to her influence, the boys changed their minds about making me swing. Somebody lift the rope where it's caught under my ear, will you? Boys, when you want me you'll find me in the Crystal Palace."

His tone was so authoritative that some obeyed him at once involuntarily; but, as a matter of fact, his plan met with general approval. War Post heaved a great sigh of relief. Why had nobody thought earlier of so easy a way out of all these here tears?

V

Larpent went to the Crystal Palace, where he took his comfort like a gentleman, conversing with his friends and drinking. At nightfall two men rode into town, flung their bridles over a convenient post and clanked into the Crystal Palace. War Post knew them in a glance. Talk ceased and there was a watchful squaring back.

The foremost was Jack Potter, a famous town marshal of Yellow Sky, but now sheriff of the county; the other was Scratchy Wilson, once a no less famous desperado. They were both two-handed men of terrific prowess and courage, but War Post could hardly believe her eyes at view of this daring invasion. It was unprecedented.

Potter went straight to the bar, behind which frowned Bobbie Hether.

"You know a man by the name of Larpent?"

"Supposin' I do?" said Bobbie sourly.

"Well, I want him. Is he in the saloon?"

"Maybe he is an' maybe he isn't," said Bobbie.

Potter went back among the glinting eyes of the citizens. "Gentlemen, I want a man named Larpent. Is he here?"

War Post was sullen, but Larpent answered lazily for himself. "Why, you must mean me. My name is Larpent. What do you want?"

"I've got a warrant for your arrest."

There was a movement all over the room as if a puff of wind had come. The swing of a hand would have brought on a murderous mêlée. But after an instant the rigidity was broken by Larpent's laughter.

"Why, you're sold, sheriff!" he cried. "I've got a previous engagement. The boys are going to hang me to-night."

If Potter was surprised he betrayed nothing.

"The boys won't hang you to-night, Larpent," he said calmly, "because I'm goin' to take you in to Yellow Sky."

Larpent was looking at the warrant. "Only grand larceny," he observed. "But still, you know, I've promised these people to appear at their performance."

"You're goin' in with me," said the impassive sheriff.

"You bet he is, sheriff!" cried an enthusiastic voice, and it belonged to Bobbie Hether. The barkeeper moved down inside his rail, and, inspired like a prophet, he began a harangue to the citizens of War Post. "Now, look here, boys, that's jest what we want, ain't it? Here we were goin' to hang Tom Larpent jest for the reputation of the town, like. 'Long comes Sheriff Potter, the reg-u-lerly cons-ti-tuted officer of the law, an' he says, 'No; the man's mine.' Now, we want to make the reputation of the town as a law-abidin' place, so what do we say to Sheriff Potter? We says, 'A-a-ll right, sheriff; you're reg'lar; we ain't; he's your man.' But supposin' we go to fightin' over it? Then what becomes of the reputation of the town which we was goin' to swing Tom Larpent for?"

The immediate opposition to these views came from a source which a stranger might have difficulty in imagining. Men's foreheads grew thick with lines of obstinacy and disapproval. They were perfectly willing to hang Larpent yesterday, to-day, or to-morrow as a detail in a set of circumstances at War Post; but when some outsider from the alien town of Yellow Sky came into the sacred precincts of War Post and proclaimed the intention of extracting a citizen for cause, any citizen for any cause, the stomach of War Post was fed with a clan's blood, and her children gathered under one invisible banner, prepared to fight as few people in few ages were enabled to fight for their—points of view. There was a guttural murmuring.

"No; hold on!" screamed Bobbie, flinging up his hands. "He'll come clear all right. Tom," he appealed wildly to Larpent, "you never committed no —— —— low-down grand larceny?"

"No," said Larpent coldly.

"But how was it? Can't you tell us how it was?"

Larpent answered with plain reluctance. He waved his hand to indicate that it was all of little consequence. "Well, he was a tenderfoot, and he played poker with me, and he couldn't play quite good enough. But he thought he could; he could play extremely well, he thought. So he lost his money. I thought he'd squeal."

"Boys," begged Bobbie, "let the sheriff take him."

Some answered at once, "Yes!" Others continued to mutter. The sheriff had held his hand because, like all quiet and honest men, he did not wish to perturb any progress toward a peaceful solution; but now he decided to take the scene by the nose and make it obey him.

"Gentlemen," he said formally, "this man is comin' with me. Larpent, get up and come along."

This might have been the beginning, but it was practically the end. The two opinions in the minds of War Post fought in the air and, like a snow-squall, discouraged all action. Amid general confusion Jack Potter and Scratchy Wilson moved to the door with their prisoner. The last thing seen by the men in the Crystal Palace was the bronze countenance of Jack Potter as he backed from the place.

A man filled with belated thought suddenly cried out, "Well, they'll hang him fer this here shootin' game, anyhow."

Bobbie Hether looked disdain upon the speaker.

"Will they! An' where'll they get their witnesses? From here, do y' think? No; not a single one. All he's up against is a case of grand larceny; and—even supposin' he done it— what in hell does grand larceny amount to?"

NEW YORK CITY, 1896

Contents

Opium's Varied Dreams

OPIUM SMOKING in this country is believed to be more particularly a pastime of the Chinese, but in truth the greater number of the smokers are white men and white women. Chinatown furnishes the pipe, lamp and yen-hock, but let a man once possess a "layout" and a common American drug store furnishes him with the opium, and afterward China is discernible only in the traditions that cling to the habit.

There are 25,000 opium-smokers in the city of New York alone. At one time there were two great colonies, one in the Tenderloin, one of course in Chinatown. This was before the hammer of reform struck them. Now the two colonies are splintered into something less than 25,000 fragments. The smokers are disorganized, but they still exist.

The Tenderloin district of New York fell an early victim to opium. That part of the population which is known as the sporting class adopted the habit quickly. Cheap actors, race track touts, gamblers and the different kinds of confidence men took to it generally. Opium raised its yellow banner over the Tenderloin, attaining the dignity of a common vice.

Splendid "joints" were not uncommon then in New York. There was one on Forty-second street which would have been palatial if it were not for the bad taste of the decorations. An occasional man from Fifth avenue or Madison avenue would there have his private "layout," an elegant equipment of silver, ivory, gold. The bunks which lined all sides of the two rooms were nightly crowded and some of the people owned names which are not altogether unknown to the public. This place was raided because of sensational stories in the newspapers and the little wicket no longer opens to allow the anxious "fiend" to enter.

Upon the appearance of reform, opium retired to private flats. Here it now reigns and it will undoubtedly be an extremely long century before the police can root it from these little strongholds. Once, Billie Rostetter got drunk on whisky and emptied three scuttles of coal down the dumb-waiter shaft. This made a noise and Billie naturally was arrested. But opium is silent. These smokers do not rave. They lay and dream, or talk in low tones. The opium vice does not betray itself by heaving coal down dumb-waiter shafts.

People who declare themselves able to pick out opium-smokers on the street are usually deluded. An opium-smoker may look like a deacon or a deacon may look like an opium-smoker. One case is as probable as the other. The "fiends" can easily conceal their vice. They get up from the "layout," adjust their cravats, straighten their coat-tails and march off like ordinary people, and the best kind of an expert would not be willing to bet that they were or were not addicted to the habit.

It would be very hard to say just exactly what constitutes a "habit." With the fiends it is an elastic word. Ask a smoker if he has a habit and he will deny it. Ask him if some one who smokes the same amount has a habit and he will gracefully admit it. Perhaps the ordinary smoker consumes 25 cents worth of opium each day. There are others who smoke $1 worth. This is rather extraordinary and in this case at least it is safe to say that it is a "habit." The $1 smokers usually indulge in "high hats," which is the term for a large pill. The ordinary smoker is satisfied with "pin-heads." "Pin-heads" are about the size of a French pea.

"Habit-smokers" have a contempt for the "sensation-smoker." This latter is a person who has been won by the false glamour which surrounds the vice and who goes about really pretending that he has a ravenous hunger for the pipe. There are more "sensation-smokers" than one would imagine.

It is said to take one year of devotion to the pipe before one can contract a habit. As far as the writer's observation goes, he should say that it does not take any such long time. Sometimes an individual who has only smoked a few months will speak of nothing but pipe and when they "talk pipe" persistently it is a pretty sure sign that the drug has fastened its grip upon them so that at any rate they are not able to easily stop its use.

When a man arises from his first trial of the pipe, the nausea that clutches him is something that can give cards and spades and big casino to seasickness. If he had swallowed a live chimney-sweep he could not feel more like dying. The room and everything in it whirls like the inside of an electric light plant. There appears a thirst, a great thirst, and this thirst is so sinister and so misleading that if the novice drank spirits to satisfy it he would presently be much worse. The one thing that will make him feel again that life may be a joy is a cup of strong black coffee.

If there is a sentiment in the pipe for him he returns to it after this first unpleasant trial. Gradually, the power of the drug sinks into his heart. It absorbs his thought. He begins to lie with more and more grace to cover the shortcomings and little failures of his life. And then finally he may become a full-fledged "pipe fiend," a man with a "yen-yen."

A "yen-yen," be it known, is the hunger, the craving. It comes to a "fiend" when he separates himself from his pipe and takes him by the heart strings. If indeed he will not buck through a brick wall to get to the pipe, he at least will become the most disagreeable, sour-tempered person on earth until he finds a way to satisfy his craving.

When the victim arrives at the point where his soul calls for the drug, he usually learns to cook. The operation of rolling the pill and cooking it over the little lamp is a delicate task and it takes time to learn it. When a man can cook for himself and buys his own "layout," he is gone, probably. He has placed upon his shoulders an elephant which he may carry to the edge of forever. The Chinese have a preparation which they call a cure, but the first difficulty is to get the hop-fiend to take the preparation, and the second difficulty is to cure anything with this cure.

A "hop-fiend" will defend opium with eloquence and energy. He very seldom drinks spirits and so he gains an opportunity to make the most ferocious parallels between the effects of rum and the effects of opium. Ask him to free his mind and he will probably say: "Opium does not deprive you of your senses. It does not make a madman of you. But drink does! See? Who ever heard of a man committing murder when full of hop? Get him full of whisky and he might kill his father. I don't see why people kick so about opium smoking. If they knew anything about it they wouldn't talk that way. Let anybody drink rum who cares to, but as for me I would rather be what I am."

As before mentioned, there were at one time gorgeous opium dens in New York, but at the present time there is probably not one with any pretense to splendid decoration. The Chinamen will smoke in a cellar, bare, squalid, occupied by an odor that will float wooden chips. The police took the adornments from the vice and left nothing but the pipe itself. Yet the pipe is sufficient for its slant-eyed lover.

When prepared for smoking purposes, opium is a heavy liquid much like molasses. Ordinarily it is sold in hollow li-shi nuts or in little round tins resembling the old percussion cap-boxes. The pipe is a curious affair, particularly notable for the way in which it does not resemble the drawings of it that appear in print. The stem is of thick bamboo, the mouthpiece usually of ivory. The bowl crops out suddenly about four inches from the end of the stem. It is a heavy affair of clay or stone. The cavity is a mere hole, of the diameter of a lead pencil, drilled through the centre. The "yen-hock" is a sort of sharpened darning-needle. With it the cook takes the opium from the box. He twirls it dexterously with his thumb and forefinger until enough of the gummy substance adheres to the sharp point. Then he holds it over the tiny flame of the lamp which burns only peanut oil or sweet oil. The pill now exactly resembles boiling molasses. The clever fingers of the cook twirl it above the flame. Lying on his side comfortably, he takes the pipe in his left hand and transfers the cooked pill from the yen-hock to the bowl of the pipe where he again molds it with the yen-hock until it is a little button-like thing with a hole in the centre fitting squarely over the hole in the bowl. Dropping the yen-hock, the cook now uses two hands for the pipe. He extends the mouthpiece toward the one whose turn it is to smoke and as this latter leans forward in readiness, the cook draws the bowl toward the flame until the heat sets the pill to boiling. Whereupon, the smoker takes a long, deep draw at the pipe, the pill splutters and fries and a moment later the smoker sinks back tranquilly. An odor, heavy, aromatic, agreeable and yet disagreeable, hangs in the air and makes its way with peculiar powers of penetration. The group about the layout talk in low voices and watch the cook deftly molding another pill. The little flame casts a strong yellow light on their faces as they cuddle about the layout. As the pipe passes and passes around the circle, the voices drop to a mere indolent cooing, and the eyes that so lazily watch the cook at his work glisten and glisten from the influence of the drug until they resemble flashing bits of silver.

There is a similarity in coloring and composition in a group of men about a midnight camp-fire in a forest and a group of smokers about the layout tray with its tiny light. Everything, of course, is on a smaller scale with the smoking. The flame is only an inch and a half perhaps in height and the smokers huddle closely in order that every person may smoke undisturbed. But there is something in the abandon of the poses, the wealth of light on the faces and the strong mystery of shadow at the backs of the people that bring the two scenes into some kind of artistic brotherhood. And just as the lazy eyes about a camp-fire fasten themselves dreamfully upon the blaze of logs so do the lazy eyes about an opium layout fasten themselves upon the little yellow flame.

There is but one pipe, one lamp and one cook to each smoking layout. Pictures of nine or ten persons sitting in arm-chairs and smoking various kinds of curiously carved tobacco pipes probably serve well enough, but when they are named "Interior of an Opium Den" and that sort of thing, it is absurd. Opium could not be smoked like tobacco. A pill is good for one long draw. After that the cook molds another. A smoker would just as soon choose a gallows as an arm-chair for smoking purposes. He likes to curl down on a mattress placed on the floor in the quietest corner of a Tenderloin flat, and smoke there with no light but the tiny yellow spear from the layout lamp.

It is a curious fact that it is rather the custom to purchase for a layout tray one of those innocent black tin affairs which are supposed to be placed before baby as he takes his high chair for dinner.

If a beginner expects to have dreams of an earth dotted with white porcelain towers and a sky of green silk, he will, from all accounts, be much mistaken. "The Opium Smoker's Dream" seems to be mostly a mistake. The influence of "dope" is evidently a fine languor, a complete mental rest. The problems of life no longer appear. Existence is peace. The virtues of a man's friends, for instance, loom beautifully against his own sudden perfection. The universe is re-adjusted. Wrong departs, injustice vanishes; there is nothing but a quiet, a soothing harmony of all things—until the next morning.

And who should invade this momentary land of rest, this dream country, if not the people of the Tenderloin, they who are at once supersensitive and hopeless, the people who think more upon death and the mysteries of life, the chances of the hereafter, than any other class, educated or uneducated. Opium holds out to them its lie, and they embrace it eagerly, expecting to find a definition of peace, but they awake to find the formidable labors of life grown more formidable. And if the pipe should happen to ruin their lives they cling the more closely to it because then it stands between them and thought.

New York's Bicycle Speedway

THE BOWERY HAS HAD its day as a famous New York street. It is now a mere tradition. Broadway will long hold its place as the chief vein of the city's life. No process of expansion can ever leave it abandoned to the cheap clothing dealers and dime museum robbers. It is too strategic in position. But lately the Western Boulevard which slants from the Columbus monument at the southwest corner of Central Park to the river has vaulted to a startling prominence and is now one of the sights of New York. This is caused by the bicycle. Once the Boulevard was a quiet avenue whose particular distinctions were its shade trees and its third foot-walk which extended in Parisian fashion down the middle of the street. Also it was noted for its billboards and its huge and slumberous apartment hotels. Now, however, it is the great thoroughfare for bicycles. On these gorgeous spring days they appear in thousands. All mankind is a-wheel apparently and a person on nothing but legs feels like a strange animal. A mighty army of wheels streams from the brick wilderness below Central Park and speeds over the asphalt. In the cool of the evening it returns with swaying and flashing of myriad lamps.

The bicycle crowd has completely subjugated the street. The glittering wheels dominate it from end to end. The cafes and dining rooms of the apartment hotels are occupied mainly by people in bicycle clothes. Even the billboards have surrendered. They advertise wheels and lamps and tires and patent saddles with all the flaming vehemence of circus art. Even when they do condescend to still advertise a patent medicine, you are sure to confront a lithograph of a young person in bloomers who is saying in large type: "Yes, George, I find that Willowrum always refreshes me after these long rides."

Down at the Circle where stands the patient Columbus, the stores are crowded with bicycle goods. There are innumerable repair shops. Everything is bicycle. In the afternoon the parade begins. The great discoverer, erect on his tall grey shaft, must feel his stone head whirl when the battalions come swinging and shining around the curve.

It is interesting to note the way in which the blasphemous and terrible truck-drivers of the lower part of the city will hunt a bicyclist. A truck-driver, of course, believes that a wheelman is a pest. The average man could not feel more annoyance if nature had suddenly invented some new kind of mosquito. And so the truck-driver resolves in his dreadful way to make life as troublous and thrilling for the wheelman as he possibly can. The wheelman suffers under a great handicap. He is struggling over the most uneven cobbles which bless a metropolis. Twenty horses threaten him and forty wheels miss his shoulder by an inch. In his ears there is a hideous din. It surrounds him, envelopes him.

Add to this trouble, then, a truckman with a fiend's desire to see dead wheelmen. The situation affords deep excitement for everyone concerned.

But when a truck-driver comes to the Boulevard the beautiful balance of the universe is apparent. The teamster sits mute, motionless, casting sidelong glances at the wheels which spin by him. He still contrives to exhibit a sort of a sombre defiance, but he has no oath nor gesture nor wily scheme to drive a three-ton wagon over the prostrate body of some unhappy cyclist. On the Boulevard this roaring lion from down town is so subdued, so isolated that he brings tears to the sympathetic eye.

There is a new game on the Boulevard. It is the game of Bicycle Cop and Scorcher. When the scorcher scorches beyond the patience of the law, the bicycle policeman, if in sight, takes after him. Usually the scorcher has a blissful confidence in his ability to scorch and thinks it much easier to just ride away from the policeman than to go to court and pay a fine. So they go flying up the Boulevard with the whole mob of wheelmen and wheelwomen, eager to see the race, sweeping after them. But the bicycle police are mighty hard riders and it takes a flier to escape them. The affair usually ends in calamity for the scorcher, but in the meantime fifty or sixty cyclists have had a period of delirious joy.

Bicycle Cop and Scorcher is a good game, but after all it is not as good as the game that was played in the old days when the suggestion of a corps of bicycle police in neat knickerbockers would have scandalized Mulberry street. This was the game of Fat Policeman on Foot Trying to Stop a Spurt. A huge, unwieldy officer rushing out into the street and wildly trying to head off and grab some rider who was spinning along in just one silver flash was a sight that caused the populace to turn out in a body. If some madman started at a fierce gait from the Columbus monument, he could have the consciousness that at frequent and exciting intervals, red-faced policemen would gallop out at him and frenziedly clutch at his coat-tails. And owing to a curious dispensation, the majority of the policemen along the Boulevard were very stout and could swear most graphically in from two to five languages.

But they changed all that. The un-police-like bicycle police are wonderfully clever and the vivid excitement of other days is gone. Even the scorcher seems to feel depressed and narrowly looks over the nearest officer before he starts on his frantic career.

The girl in bloomers is, of course, upon her native heath when she steers her steel steed into the Boulevard. One becomes conscious of a bewildering variety in bloomers. There are some that fit and some that do not fit. There are some that were not made to fit and there are some that couldn't fit anyhow. As a matter of fact the bloomer costume is now in one of the primary stages of its evolution. Let us hope so at any rate. Of course every decent citizen concedes that women shall wear what they please and it is supposed that he covenants with himself not to grin and nudge his neighbor when anything particularly amazing passes him on the street but resolves to simply and industriously mind his own affairs. Still the situation no doubt harrows him greatly. No man was ever found to defend bloomers. His farthest statement, as an individual, is to advocate them for all women he does not know and cares nothing about. Most women become radical enough to say: "Why shouldn't I wear 'em, if I choose." Still, a second look at the Boulevard convinces one that the world is slowly, solemnly, inevitably coming to bloomers. We are about to enter an age of bloomers and the bicycle, that machine which has gained an economic position of the most tremendous importance, is going to be responsible for more than the bruises on the departed fat policemen of the Boulevard.

An Eloquence of Grief

THE WINDOWS were high and saintly, of the shape that is found in churches. From time to time a policeman at the door spoke sharply to some incoming person. "Take your hat off!" He displayed in his voice the horror of a priest when the sanctity of a chapel is defied or forgotten. The court-room was crowded with people who sloped back comfortably in their chairs, regarding with undeviating glances the procession and its attendant and guardian policemen that moved slowly inside the spear-topped railing. All persons connected with a case went close to the magistrate's desk before a word was spoken in the matter, and then their voices were toned to the ordinary talking strength. The crowd in the court-room could not hear a sentence; they could merely see shifting figures, men that gestured quietly, women that sometimes raised an eager eloquent arm. They could not always see the judge, although they were able to estimate his location by the tall stands surmounted by white globes that were at either hand of him. And so those who had come for curiosity's sweet sake wore an air of being in wait for a cry of anguish, some loud painful protestation that would bring the proper thrill to their jaded, world-weary nerves—wires that refused to vibrate for ordinary affairs.

Inside the railing the court officers shuffled the various groups with speed and skill; and behind the desk the magistrate patiently toiled his way through mazes of wonderful testimony.

In a corner of this space, devoted to those who had business before the judge, an officer in plain clothes stood with a girl that wept constantly. None seemed to notice the girl and there was no reason why she should be noticed if the curious in the body of the court-room were not interested in the devastation which tears bring upon some complexions. Her tears seemed to burn like acid and they left fierce pink marks on her face. Occasionally the girl looked across the room where two well-dressed young women and a man stood waiting with the serenity of people who are not concerned as to the interior fittings of a jail.

The business of the court progressed and presently the girl, the officer and the well-dressed contingent stood before the judge. Thereupon two lawyers engaged in some preliminary fire-wheels which were endured, generally, in silence. The girl, it appeared, was accused of stealing fifty dollars' worth of silk clothing from the room of one of the well-dressed women. She had been a servant in the house.

In a clear way and with none of the ferocity that an accuser often exhibits in a police-court, calmly and moderately, the two young women gave their testimony. Behind them stood their escort, always mute. His part, evidently, was to furnish the dignity, and he furnished it heavily, almost massively.

When they had finished, the girl told her part. She had full, almost Afric, lips, and they had turned quite white. The lawyer for the others asked some questions, which he did—be it said, in passing—with the air of a man throwing flower-pots at a stone house.

It was a short case and soon finished. At the end of it the judge said that, considering the evidence, he would have to commit the girl for trial. Instantly the quick-eyed court officer began to clear the way for the next case. The well-dressed women and their escort turned one way and the girl turned another, toward a door with an austere arch leading into a stone-paved passage. Then it was that a great cry rang through the court-room, the cry of this girl who believed that she was lost.

The loungers, many of them, underwent a spasmodic movement as if they had been knived. The court officers rallied quickly. The girl fell back opportunely for the arms of one of them, and her wild heels clicked twice on the floor. "I am innocent! Oh, I am innocent!"

People pity those who need none, and the guilty sob alone; but innocent or guilty, this girl's scream described such a profound depth of woe—it was so graphic of grief, that it slit with a dagger's sweep the curtain of common-place, and disclosed the gloom-shrouded spectre that sat in the young girl's heart so plainly, in so universal a tone of the mind, that a man heard expressed some far-off midnight terror of his own thought.

The cries died away down the stone-paved passage. A

patrolman leaned one arm composedly on the railing, and down below him stood an aged, almost toothless wanderer, tottering and grinning.

"Plase, yer honer," said the old man as the time arrived for him to speak, "if ye'll lave me go this time, I've niver been dhrunk befoor, sir."

A court officer lifted his hand to hide a smile.

Adventures of a Novelist

T<small>HIS IS A PLAIN TALE</small> of two chorus girls, a woman of the streets and a reluctant laggard witness. The tale properly begins in a resort on Broadway, where the two chorus girls and the reluctant witness sat the entire evening. They were on the verge of departing their several ways when a young woman approached one of the chorus girls, with outstretched hand.

"Why, how do you do?" she said. "I haven't seen you for a long time."

The chorus girl recognized some acquaintance of the past, and the young woman then took a seat and joined the party. Finally they left the table in this resort, and the quartet walked down Broadway together. At the corner of Thirty-first street one of the chorus girls said that she wished to take a car immediately for home, and so the reluctant witness left one of the chorus girls and the young woman on the corner of Thirty-first street while he placed the other chorus girl aboard an uptown cable car. The two girls who waited on the corner were deep in conversation.

The reluctant witness was returning leisurely to them. In the semi-conscious manner in which people note details which do not appear at the time important, he saw two men passing along Broadway. They passed swiftly, like men who are going home. They paid attention to none, and none at the corner of Thirty-first street and Broadway paid attention to them.

The two girls were still deep in conversation. They were standing at the curb facing the street. The two men passed unseen—in all human probability—by the two girls. The reluctant witness continued his leisurely way. He was within four feet of these two girls when suddenly and silently a man appeared from nowhere in particular and grabbed them both.

The astonishment of the reluctant witness was so great for the ensuing seconds that he was hardly aware of what transpired during that time, save that both girls screamed. Then he heard this man, who was now evidently an officer, say to them: "Come to the station house. You are under arrest for soliciting two men."

With one voice the unknown woman, the chorus girl and the reluctant witness cried out: "What two men?"

The officer said: "Those two men who have just passed."

And here began the wildest and most hysterical sobbing of the two girls, accompanied by spasmodic attempts to pull their arms away from the grip of the policeman. The chorus girl seemed nearly insane with fright and fury. Finally she screamed:

"Well, he's my husband." And with her finger she indicated the reluctant witness. The witness at once replied to the swift, questioning glance of the officer, "Yes; I am."

If it was necessary to avow a marriage to save a girl who is not a prostitute from being arrested as a prostitute, it must be done, though the man suffer eternally. And then the officer forgot immediately—without a second's hesitation, he forgot that a moment previously he had arrested this girl for soliciting, and so, dropping her arm, released her.

"But," said he, "I have got this other one." He was as picturesque as a wolf.

"Why arrest her, either?" said the reluctant witness.

"For soliciting those two men."

"But she didn't solicit those two men."

"Say," said the officer, turning, "do you know this woman?"

The chorus girl had it in mind to lie then for the purpose of saving this woman easily and simply from the palpable wrong she seemed to be about to experience. "Yes; I know her"—"I have seen her two or three times"—"Yes; I have met her before——" But the reluctant witness said at once that he knew nothing whatever of the girl.

"Well," said the officer, "she's a common prostitute."

There was a short silence then, but the reluctant witness presently said: "Are you arresting her as a common prostitute? She has been perfectly respectable since she has been with us. She hasn't done anything wrong since she has been in our company."

"I am arresting her for soliciting those two men," answered the officer, "and if you people don't want to get pinched, too, you had better not be seen with her."

Then began a parade to the station house—the officer and his prisoner ahead and two simpletons following.

At the station house the officer said to the sergeant behind the desk that he had seen the woman come from the resort on Broadway alone, and on the way to the corner of Thirty-first street solicit two men, and that immediately afterward she had met a man and a woman—meaning the chorus girl and the reluctant witness—on the said corner, and was in conversation with them when he arrested her. He did not mention to the sergeant at this time the arrest and release of the chorus girl.

At the conclusion of the officer's story the sergeant said, shortly: "Take her back." This did not mean to take the woman back to the corner of Thirty-first street and Broadway. It meant to take her back to the cells, and she was accordingly led away.

The chorus girl had undoubtedly intended to be an intrepid champion; had avowedly come to the station house for that purpose, but her entire time had been devoted to sobbing in the wildest form of hysteria. The reluctant witness was obliged to devote his entire time to an attempt to keep her from making an uproar of some kind. This paroxysm of terror, of indignation, and the extreme mental anguish caused by her unconventional and strange situation, was so violent that the reluctant witness could not take time from her to give any testimony to the sergeant.

After the woman was sent to the cell the reluctant witness reflected a moment in silence; then he said:

"Well, we might as well go."

On the way out of Thirtieth street the chorus girl continued to sob. "If you don't go to court and speak for that girl you are no man!" she cried. The arrested woman had, by the way, screamed out a request to appear in her behalf before the Magistrate.

"By George! I cannot," said the reluctant witness. "I can't afford to do that sort of thing. I—I——"

After he had left this girl safely, he continued to reflect: "Now this arrest I firmly believe to be wrong. This girl may be a courtesan, for anything that I know at all to the contrary. The sergeant at the station house seemed to know her as well as he knew the Madison square tower. She is then, in all probability, a courtesan. She is arrested, however, for soliciting those two men. If I have ever had a conviction in my life, I am convinced that she did not solicit those two men. Now, if these affairs occur from time to time, they must be witnessed occasionally by men of character. Do these reputable citizens interfere? No, they go home and thank God that they can still attend piously to their own affairs. Suppose I were a clerk and I interfered in this sort of a case. When it became known to my employers they would say to me: 'We are sorry, but we cannot have men in our employ who stay out until 2:30 in the morning in the company of chorus girls.'

"Suppose, for instance, I had a wife and seven children in Harlem. As soon as my wife read the papers she would say: 'Ha! You told me you had a business engagement! Half-past two in the morning with questionable company!'

"Suppose, for instance, I were engaged to the beautiful Countess of Kalamazoo. If she were to hear it, she would write: 'All is over between us. My future husband cannot rescue prostitutes at 2:30 in the morning.'

"These, then, must be three small general illustrations of why men of character say nothing if they happen to witness some possible affair of this sort, and perhaps these illustrations could be multiplied to infinity. I possess nothing so tangible as a clerkship, as a wife and seven children in Harlem, as an engagement to the beautiful Countess of Kalamazoo; but all that I value may be chanced in this affair. Shall I take this risk for the benefit of a girl of the streets?

"But this girl, be she prostitute or whatever, was at this time manifestly in my escort, and—Heaven save the blasphemous philosophy—a wrong done to a prostitute must be as purely a wrong as a wrong done to a queen," said the reluctant witness—this blockhead.

"Moreover, I believe that this officer has dishonored his obligation as a public servant. Have I a duty as a citizen, or do citizens have duty, as a citizen, or do citizens have no duties? Is it a mere myth that there was at one time a man who possessed a consciousness of civic responsibility, or has it become a distinction of our municipal civilization that men of this character shall be licensed to depredate in such a manner upon those who are completely at their mercy?"

He returned to the sergeant at the police station, and, after asking if he could send anything to the girl to make her more comfortable for the night, he told the sergeant the story of the arrest, as he knew it.

"Well," said the sergeant, "that may be all true. I don't defend the officer. I do not say that he was right, or that he was wrong, but it seems to me that I have seen you somewhere before and know you vaguely as a man of good repute; so why interfere in this thing? As for this girl, I know her to be a common prostitute. That's why I sent her back."

"But she was not arrested as a common prostitute. She was arrested for soliciting two men, and I know that she didn't solicit the two men."

"Well," said the sergeant, "that, too, may all be true, but I give you the plain advice of a man who has been behind this desk for years, and knows how these things go, and I advise you simply to stay home. If you monkey with this case, you are pretty sure to come out with mud all over you."

"I suppose so," said the reluctant witness. "I haven't a doubt of it. But I don't see how I can, in honesty, stay away from court in the morning."

"Well, do it anyhow," said the sergeant.

"But I don't see how I can do it."

The sergeant was bored. "Oh, I tell you, the girl is nothing but a common prostitute," he said, wearily.

The reluctant witness on reaching his room set the alarm clock for the proper hour.

In the court at 8:30 he met a reporter acquaintance. "Go home," said the reporter, when he had heard the story. "Go home; your own participation in the affair doesn't look very respectable. Go home."

"But it is a wrong," said the reluctant witness.

"Oh, it is only a temporary wrong," said the reporter. The definition of a temporary wrong did not appear at that time to the reluctant witness, but the reporter was too much in earnest to consider terms. "Go home," said he.

Thus—if the girl was wronged—it is to be seen that all circumstances, all forces, all opinions, all men were combined to militate against her. Apparently the united wisdom of the world declared that no man should do anything but throw his sense of justice to the winds in an affair of this description. "Let a man have a conscience for the daytime," said wisdom. "Let him have a conscience for the daytime, but it is idiocy for a man to have a conscience at 2:30 in the morning, in the case of an arrested prostitute."

The officer who had made the arrest told a story of the occurrence. The girl at the bar told a story of the occurrence. And the girl's story as to this affair was, to the reluctant witness, perfectly true. Nevertheless, her word could not be accounted of any value. It was impossible that any one in the courtroom could suppose that she was telling the truth, save the reluctant witness and the reporter to whom he had told the tale.

The reluctant witness recited what he believed to be a true accounting, and the Magistrate discharged the prisoner.

The reluctant witness has told this story merely because it is a story which the public of New York should know for once.

FLORIDA

Contents

Stephen Crane's Own Story

JACKSONVILLE, FLA., JAN. 6.—It was the afternoon of New Year's. The *Commodore* lay at her dock in Jacksonville and negro stevedores processioned steadily toward her with box after box of ammunition and bundle after bundle of rifles. Her hatch, like the mouth of a monster, engulfed them. It might have been the feeding time of some legendary creature of the sea. It was in broad daylight and the crowd of gleeful Cubans on the pier did not forbear to sing the strange patriotic ballads of their island.

Everything was perfectly open. The *Commodore* was cleared with a cargo of arms and munitions for Cuba. There was none of that extreme modesty about the proceeding which had marked previous departures of the famous tug. She loaded up as placidly as if she were going to carry oranges to New York, instead of Remingtons to Cuba. Down the river, furthermore, the revenue cutter *Boutwell*, the old isosceles triangle that protects United States interests in the St. Johns, lay at anchor, with no sign of excitement aboard her.

On the decks of the *Commodore* there were exchanges of farewells in two languages. Many of the men who were to sail upon her had many intimates in the old Southern town, and we who had left our friends in the remote North received our first touch of melancholy on witnessing these strenuous and earnest good-bys.

It seems, however, that there was more difficulty at the custom house. The officers of the ship and the Cuban leaders were detained there until a mournful twilight settled upon the St. Johns, and through a heavy fog the lights of Jacksonville blinked dimly.

Then at last the *Commodore* swung clear of the dock, amid a tumult of good-bys. As she turned her bow toward the distant sea the Cubans ashore cheered and cheered. In response the *Commodore* gave three long blasts of her whistle, which even to this time impressed me with their sadness. Somehow they sounded as wails.

Then at last we began to feel like filibusters. I don't suppose that the most stolid brain could contrive to believe that there is not a mere trifle of danger in filibustering, and so as we watched the lights of Jacksonville swing past us and heard the regular thump, thump, thump of the engines we did considerable reflecting.

But I am sure that there was no hifalutin emotions visible upon any of the faces which fronted the speeding shore. In fact, from cook's boy to captain, we were all enveloped in a gentle satisfaction and cheerfulness.

But less than two miles from Jacksonville this atrocious fog caused the pilot to ram the bow of the *Commodore* hard upon the mud, and in this ignominious position we were compelled to stay until daybreak.

It was to all of us more than a physical calamity. We were now no longer filibusters. We were men on a ship stuck in the mud. A certain mental somersault was made once more necessary. But word had been sent to Jacksonville to the captain of the revenue cutter *Boutwell*, and Captain Kilgore turned out promptly and generously fired up his old triangle and came at full speed to our assistance. She dragged us out of the mud and again we headed for the mouth of the river. The revenue cutter pounded along a half mile astern of us, to make sure that we did not take on board at some place along the river men for the Cuban army.

This was the early morning of New Year's Day, and the fine golden Southern sunlight fell full upon the river. It flashed over the ancient *Boutwell* until her white sides gleamed like pearl and her rigging was spun into little threads of gold. Cheers greeted the old *Commodore* from passing ships and from the shore. It was a cheerful, almost merry, beginning to our voyage.

At Mayport, however, we changed our river pilot for a man who could take her to open sea, and again the *Commodore* was beached. The *Boutwell* was fussing around us in her venerable way, and, upon seeing our predicament, she came again to assist us, but this time with engines reversed the *Commodore* dragged herself away from the grip of the sand and again the *Commodore* headed for the open sea.

The captain of the revenue cutter grew curious. He hailed the *Commodore*: "Are you fellows going to sea to-day?"

Captain Murphy of the *Commodore* called back: "Yes, sir."

And then as the whistle of the *Commodore* saluted him Captain Kilgore doffed his cap and said: "Well, gentlemen, I hope you have a pleasant cruise," and this was our last words from shore.

When the *Commodore* came to the enormous rollers that flee over the bar, a certain light-heartedness departed from the throats of the ship's company. The *Commodore* began to turn handsprings, and by the time she had gotten fairly to sea and turned into the eye of the roaring breeze that was blowing from the southeast there was an almost general opinion on board the vessel that a life on the rolling wave was not the finest thing in the world. On deck amidships lay five or six Cubans, limp, forlorn and infinitely depressed. In the bunks below lay more Cubans, also limp, forlorn and infinitely depressed. In the captain's quarters, back of the pilot house, the Cuban leaders were stretched out in postures of complete contentment to this terrestrial realm of their stomachs.

The *Commodore* was heavily laden and in this strong sea she rolled like a rubber ball. She appeared to be a gallant sea boat and bravely flung off the waves that swarmed over her bow. At this time the first mate was at the wheel, and I remember how proud he was of the ship as she dashed the white foaming waters aside and arose to the swells like a duck.

"Ain't she a daisy?" said he. But she certainly did do a remarkable lot of pitching and presently even some American seamen were made ill by the long wallowing motion of the ship. A squall confronted us dead ahead and in the impressive twilight of this New Year's Day the *Commodore* steamed sturdily toward a darkened part of the horizon. The State of Florida is very large when you look at it from an airship, but it is as narrow as a sheet of paper when you look at it sideways. The coast was merely a faint streak.

As darkness came upon the waters the *Commodore*'s wake was a broad, flaming path of blue and silver phosphorescence, and as her stout bow lunged at the great black waves she threw flashing, roaring cascades to either side. And all that was to be heard was the rhythmical and mighty pounding of the engines.

Being an inexperienced filibuster, the writer had undergone considerable mental excitement since the starting of the ship, and consequently he had not yet been to sleep, and so I went to the first mate's bunk to indulge myself in all the physical delights of holding one's self in bed. Every time the ship lurched I expected to be fired through a bulkhead, and it was neither amusing nor instructive to see in the dim light a certain accursed valise aiming itself at the top of my stomach with every lurch of the ship.

The cook was asleep on a bench in the galley. He was of a portly and noble exterior, and by means of a checker board he had himself wedged on this bench in such a manner that the motion of the ship would be unable to dislodge him. He awoke as I entered the galley, and, feeling moved, he delivered himself of some dolorous sentiments. "God," he said, in the course of his observations, "I don't feel right about this ship somehow. It strikes me that something is going to happen to us. I don't know what it is, but the old ship is going to get it in the neck, I think."

"Well, how about the men on board of her?" said I. "Are any of us going to get out, prophet?"

"Yes," said the cook, "sometimes I have these damned feelings come over me, and they are always right, and it seems to me somehow that you and I will both get out and meet again somewhere, down at Coney Island, perhaps, or some place like that."

Finding it impossible to sleep, I went back to the pilot house. An old seaman named Tom Smith, from Charleston, was then at the wheel. In the darkness I could not see Tom's face, except at those times when he leaned forward to scan the compass and the dim light from the box came upon his weather-beaten features.

"Well, Tom," said I, "how do you like filibustering?"

He said: "I think I am about through with it. I've been in a number of these expeditions, and the pay is good, but I think if I ever get back safe this time I will cut it."

I sat down in the corner of the pilot house and went almost to sleep. In the meantime the captain came on duty and he was standing near me when the chief engineer rushed up the stairs and cried hurriedly to the captain that there was something wrong in the engine room. He and the captain departed swiftly. I was drowsing there in my corner when the captain returned, and, going to the door of the little room directly back of the pilot house, cried to the Cuban leader:

"Say, can't you get those fellows to work? I can't talk their language and I can't get them started. Come on and get them going."

The Cuban leader turned to me then and said: "Go help in the fire-room. They are going to bail with buckets."

The engine room, by the way, represented a scene at this time taken from the middle kitchen of hades. In the first place, it was insufferably warm, and the lights burned faintly in a way to cause mystic and grewsome shadows. There was a quantity of soapish sea water swirling and sweeping and swishing among machinery that roared and banged and clattered and steamed, and in the second place, it was a devil of a ways down below.

Here I first came to know a certain young oiler named Billy Higgins. He was sloshing around this inferno filling buckets with water and passing them to a chain of men that extended up to the ship's side. Afterward we got orders to change our point of attack on the water and to operate through a little door on the windward side of the ship that led into the engine room.

During this time there was much talk of pumps out of order and many other statements of a mechanical kind, which I did not altogether comprehend, but understood to mean that there was a general and sudden ruin in the engine room.

There was no particular agitation at this time, and even later there was never a panic on board the *Commodore*. The party of men who worked with Higgins and me at this time were all Cubans, and we were under the direction of the Cuban leaders. Presently we were ordered again to the afterhold, and there was some hesitation about going into the abominable fire-room again, but Higgins dashed down the companionway with a bucket.

The heat and hard work in the fire-room affected me and I was obliged to come on deck again. Going forward I heard as I went talk of lowering the boats. Near the corner of the galley the mate was talking with a man.

"Why don't you send up a rocket?" said this unknown

person. And the mate replied: "What the hell do we want to send up a rocket for? The ship is all right."

Returning with a little rubber and cloth overcoat, I saw the first boat about to be lowered. A certain man was the first person in this first boat, and they were handing him in a valise about as large as a hotel. I had not entirely recovered from my astonishment and pleasure in witnessing this noble deed, when I saw another valise go to him. This valise was not perhaps so large as a hotel, but it was a big valise anyhow. Afterward there went to him something which looked to me like an overcoat.

Seeing the chief engineer leaning out of his little window, I remarked to him: "What do you think of that blank, blank, blank?"

"Oh, he's a bird," said the old chief.

It was now that was heard the order to get away the lifeboat, which was stowed on top of the deckhouse. The deckhouse was a mighty slippery place, and with each roll of the ship the men there thought themselves likely to take headers into the deadly black sea. Higgins was on top of the deckhouse, and, with the first mate and two colored stokers, we wrestled with that boat, which I am willing to swear weighed as much as a Broadway cable car. She might have been spiked to the deck. We could have pushed a little brick schoolhouse along a corduroy road as easily as we could have moved this boat. But the first mate got a tackle to her from a leaward davit, and on the deck below the captain corralled enough men to make an impression upon the boat. We were ordered to cease hauling then, and in this lull the cook of the ship came to me and said: "What are you going to do?"

I told him of my plans, and he said: "Well, my God, that's what I am going to do."

Now the whistle of the *Commodore* had been turned loose, and if there ever was a voice of despair and death it was in the voice of this whistle. It had gained a new tone. It was as if its throat was already choked by the water, and this cry on the sea at night, with a wind blowing the spray over the ship, and the waves roaring over the bow, and swirling white along the decks, was to each of us probably a song of man's end.

It was now that the first mate showed a sign of losing his

grip. To us who were trying in all stages of competence and experience to launch the lifeboat he raged in all terms of fiery satire and hammer-like abuse. But the boat moved at last and swung down toward the water.

Afterward when I went aft I saw the captain standing with his arm in a sling, holding on to a stay with his one good hand and directing the launching of the boat. He gave me a five-gallon jug of water to hold, and asked me what I was going to do. I told him what I thought was about the proper thing, and he told me then that the cook had the same idea, and ordered me to go forward and be ready to launch the ten-foot dingy. I remember very well that he turned then to swear at a colored stoker who was prowling around, done up in life preservers until he looked like a feather bed.

I went forward with my five-gallon jug of water, and when the captain came we launched the dingy, and they put me over the side to fend her off from the ship with an oar.

They handed me down the water jug, and then the cook came into the boat, and we sat there in the darkness, wondering why, by all our hopes of future happiness, the captain was so long in coming over the side and ordering us away from the doomed ship.

The captain was waiting for the other boat to go. Finally he hailed in the darkness: "Are you all right, Mr. Graines?"

The first mate answered: "All right, sir."

"Shove off then," cried the captain. The captain was just about to swing over the rail when a dark form came forward and a voice said: "Captain, I go with you."

The captain answered: "Yes, Billy; get in."

It was Billy Higgins, the oiler. Billy dropped into the boat and a moment later the captain followed, bringing with him an end of about forty yards of lead line. The other end was attached to the rail of the ship. As we swung back to leaward the captain said: "Boys, we will stay right near the ship till she goes down."

This cheerful information, of course, filled us all with glee. The line kept us headed properly into the wind and as we rode over the monstrous roarers we saw upon each rise the swaying lights of the dying *Commodore*.

When came the gray shade of dawn, the form of the *Com-*

modore grew slowly clear to us as our little ten-foot boat rose over each swell. She was floating with such an air of buoyancy that we laughed when we had time, and said: "What a guy it would be on those other fellows if she didn't sink at all."

But later we saw men aboard of her, and later still they began to hail us. I had forgotten to mention that previously we had loosened the end of the lead line and dropped much further to leeward. The men on board were a mystery to us, of course, as we had seen all the boats leave the ship. We rowed back to the ship, but did not approach too near, because we were four men in a ten-foot boat, and we knew that the touch of a hand on our gunwale would assuredly swamp us.

The first mate cried out from the ship that the third boat had foundered alongside. He cried that they had made rafts and wished us to tow them. The captain said: "All right."

Their rafts were floating astern.

"Jump in," cried the captain, but here was a singular and most harrowing hesitation. There were five white men and two negroes. This scene in the gray light of morning impressed one as would a view into some place where ghosts move slowly. These seven men on the stern of the sinking *Commodore* were silent. Save the words of the mate to the captain there was no talk. Here was death, but here also was a most singular and indefinable kind of fortitude.

Four men, I remember, clambered over the railing and stood there watching the cold, steely sheen of the sweeping waves.

"Jump," cried the captain again. The old chief engineer first obeyed the order. He landed on the outside raft and the captain told him how to grip the raft, and he obeyed as promptly and as docilely as a scholar in riding school.

A stoker followed him, and then the first mate threw his hands over his head and plunged into the sea. He had no life belt, and for my part, even when he did this horrible thing, I somehow felt that I could see in the expression of his hands, and in the very toss of his head, as he leaped thus to death, that it was rage, rage, rage unspeakable that was in his heart at the time.

And then I saw Tom Smith, the man who was going to

quit filibustering after this expedition, jump to a raft and turn his face toward us. On board the *Commodore* three men strode, still in silence and with their faces turned toward us. One man had his arms folded and was leaning against the deckhouse. His feet were crossed, so that the toe of his left foot pointed downward. There they stood gazing at us, and neither from the deck nor from the rafts was a voice raised. Still was there this silence.

The colored stoker on the first raft threw us a line and we began to tow. Of course, we perfectly understood the absolute impossibility of any such thing; our dingy was within six inches of the water's edge, there was an enormous sea running, and I knew that under the circumstances a tugboat would have no light task in moving these rafts. But we tried it, and would have continued to try it indefinitely, but that something critical came to pass. I was at an oar and so faced the rafts. The cook controlled the line. Suddenly the boat began to go backward, and then we saw this negro on the first raft pulling on the line hand over hand and drawing us to him.

He had turned into a demon. He was wild, wild as a tiger. He was crouched on this raft and ready to spring. Every muscle of him seemed to be turned into an elastic spring. His eyes were almost white. His face was the face of a lost man reaching upward, and we knew that the weight of his hand on our gunwale doomed us. The cook let go of the line.

We rowed around to see if we could not get a line from the chief engineer, and all this time, mind you, there were no shrieks, no groans, but silence, silence and silence, and then the *Commodore* sank. She lurched to windward, then swung afar back, righted and dove into the sea, and the rafts were suddenly swallowed by this frightful maw of the ocean. And then by the men on the ten-foot dingy were words said that were still not words, something far beyond words.

The lighthouse of Mosquito Inlet stuck up above the horizon like the point of a pin. We turned our dingy toward the shore. The history of life in an open boat for thirty hours would no doubt be very instructive for the young, but none is to be told here now. For my part I would prefer to tell the story at once, because from it would shine the splendid manhood of Captain Edward Murphy and of William Higgins, the oiler, but let it suffice at this time to say that when we were swamped in the surf and making the best of our way toward the shore the captain gave orders amid the wildness of the breakers as clearly as if he had been on the quarterdeck of a battleship.

John Kitchell of Daytona came running down the beach, and as he ran the air was filled with clothes. If he had pulled a single lever and undressed, even as the fire horses harness, he could not to me seem to have stripped with more speed. He dashed into the water and grabbed the cook. Then he went after the captain, but the captain sent him to me, and then it was that we saw Billy Higgins lying with his forehead on sand that was clear of the water, and he was dead.

The Open Boat

A tale intended to be after the fact. Being the experience of four
men from the sunk steamer Commodore

I

NONE OF THEM knew the color of the sky. Their eyes
glanced level, and were fastened upon the waves that
swept toward them. These waves were of the hue of slate,
save for the tops, which were of foaming white, and all of
the men knew the colors of the sea. The horizon narrowed
and widened, and dipped and rose, and at all times its edge
was jagged with waves that seemed thrust up in points like
rocks.

Many a man ought to have a bath-tub larger than the boat
which here rode upon the sea. These waves were most wrong-
fully and barbarously abrupt and tall, and each froth-top was
a problem in small boat navigation.

The cook squatted in the bottom and looked with both
eyes at the six inches of gunwale which separated him from
the ocean. His sleeves were rolled over his fat forearms, and
the two flaps of his unbuttoned vest dangled as he bent to
bail out the boat. Often he said: "Gawd! That was a narrow
clip." As he remarked it he invariably gazed eastward over the
broken sea.

The oiler, steering with one of the two oars in the boat,
sometimes raised himself suddenly to keep clear of water that
swirled in over the stern. It was a thin little oar and it seemed
often ready to snap.

The correspondent, pulling at the other oar, watched the
waves and wondered why he was there.

The injured captain, lying in the bow, was at this time bur-
ied in that profound dejection and indifference which comes,
temporarily at least, to even the bravest and most enduring
when, willy nilly, the firm fails, the army loses, the ship goes
down. The mind of the master of a vessel is rooted deep in
the timbers of her, though he command for a day or a decade,
and this captain had on him the stern impression of a scene
in the grays of dawn of seven turned faces, and later a stump

of a top-mast with a white ball on it that slashed to and fro
at the waves, went low and lower, and down. Thereafter there
was something strange in his voice. Although steady, it was
deep with mourning, and of a quality beyond oration or
tears.

"Keep'er a little more south, Billie," said he.

" 'A little more south,' sir," said the oiler in the stern.

A seat in this boat was not unlike a seat upon a bucking
broncho, and, by the same token, a broncho is not much
smaller. The craft pranced and reared, and plunged like an
animal. As each wave came, and she rose for it, she seemed
like a horse making at a fence outrageously high. The manner
of her scramble over these walls of water is a mystic thing,
and, moreover, at the top of them were ordinarily these prob-
lems in white water, the foam racing down from the summit
of each wave, requiring a new leap, and a leap from the air.
Then, after scornfully bumping a crest, she would slide, and
race, and splash down a long incline and arrive bobbing and
nodding in front of the next menace.

A singular disadvantage of the sea lies in the fact that after
successfully surmounting one wave you discover that there is
another behind it just as important and just as nervously anx-
ious to do something effective in the way of swamping boats.
In a ten-foot dingey one can get an idea of the resources of
the sea in the line of waves that is not probable to the average
experience, which is never at sea in a dingey. As each slaty
wall of water approached, it shut all else from the view of the
men in the boat, and it was not difficult to imagine that this
particular wave was the final outburst of the ocean, the last
effort of the grim water. There was a terrible grace in the
move of the waves, and they came in silence, save for the
snarling of the crests.

In the wan light, the faces of the men must have been
gray. Their eyes must have glinted in strange ways as they
gazed steadily astern. Viewed from a balcony, the whole
thing would doubtlessly have been weirdly picturesque. But
the men in the boat had no time to see it, and if they had
had leisure there were other things to occupy their minds.
The sun swung steadily up the sky, and they knew it was
broad day because the color of the sea changed from slate to

emerald-green, streaked with amber lights, and the foam was like tumbling snow. The process of the breaking day was unknown to them. They were aware only of this effect upon the color of the waves that rolled toward them.

In disjointed sentences the cook and the correspondent argued as to the difference between a life-saving station and a house of refuge. The cook had said: "There's a house of refuge just north of the Mosquito Inlet Light, and as soon as they see us, they'll come off in their boat and pick us up."

"As soon as who see us?" said the correspondent.

"The crew," said the cook.

"Houses of refuge don't have crews," said the correspondent. "As I understand them, they are only places where clothes and grub are stored for the benefit of shipwrecked people. They don't carry crews."

"Oh, yes, they do," said the cook.

"No, they don't," said the correspondent.

"Well, we're not there yet, anyhow," said the oiler, in the stern.

"Well," said the cook, "perhaps it's not a house of refuge that I'm thinking of as being near Mosquito Inlet Light. Perhaps it's a life-saving station."

"We're not there yet," said the oiler, in the stern.

II

As the boat bounced from the top of each wave, the wind tore through the hair of the hatless men, and as the craft plopped her stern down again the spray slashed past them. The crest of each of these waves was a hill, from the top of which the men surveyed, for a moment, a broad tumultuous expanse, shining and wind-riven. It was probably splendid. It was probably glorious, this play of the free sea, wild with lights of emerald and white and amber.

"Bully good thing it's an on-shore wind," said the cook. "If not, where would we be? Wouldn't have a show."

"That's right," said the correspondent.

The busy oiler nodded his assent.

Then the captain, in the bow, chuckled in a way that expressed humor, contempt, tragedy, all in one. "Do you think we've got much of a show, now, boys?" said he.

Whereupon the three were silent, save for a trifle of hemming and hawing. To express any particular optimism at this time they felt to be childish and stupid, but they all doubtless possessed this sense of the situation in their mind. A young man thinks doggedly at such times. On the other hand, the ethics of their condition was decidedly against any open suggestion of hopelessness. So they were silent.

"Oh, well," said the captain, soothing his children, " we'll get ashore all right."

But there was that in his tone which made them think, so the oiler quoth: "Yes! If this wind holds!"

The cook was bailing. "Yes! If we don't catch hell in the surf."

Canton flannel gulls flew near and far. Sometimes they sat down on the sea, near patches of brown sea-weed that rolled over the waves with a movement like carpets on a line in a gale. The birds sat comfortably in groups, and they were envied by some in the dingey, for the wrath of the sea was no more to them than it was to a covey of prairie chickens a thousand miles inland. Often they came very close and stared at the men with black bead-like eyes. At these times they were uncanny and sinister in their unblinking scrutiny, and the men hooted angrily at them, telling them to be gone. One came, and evidently decided to alight on the top of the captain's head. The bird flew parallel to the boat and did not circle, but made short sidelong jumps in the air in chicken-fashion. His black eyes were wistfully fixed upon the captain's head. "Ugly brute," said the oiler to the bird. "You look as if you were made with a jack-knife." The cook and the correspondent swore darkly at the creature. The captain naturally wished to knock it away with the end of the heavy painter, but he did not dare do it, because anything resembling an emphatic gesture would have capsized this freighted boat, and so with his open hand, the captain gently and carefully waved the gull away. After it had been discouraged from the pursuit the captain breathed easier on account of his hair, and others breathed easier because the bird struck their minds at this time as being somehow grewsome and ominous.

In the meantime the oiler and the correspondent rowed. And also they rowed.

They sat together in the same seat, and each rowed an oar. Then the oiler took both oars; then the correspondent took both oars; then the oiler; then the correspondent. They rowed and they rowed. The very ticklish part of the business was when the time came for the reclining one in the stern to take his turn at the oars. By the very last star of truth, it is easier to steal eggs from under a hen than it was to change seats in the dingey. First the man in the stern slid his hand along the thwart and moved with care, as if he were of Sèvres. Then the man in the rowing seat slid his hand along the other thwart. It was all done with the most extraordinary care. As the two sidled past each other, the whole party kept watchful eyes on the coming wave, and the captain cried: "Look out now! Steady there!"

The brown mats of sea-weed that appeared from time to time were like islands, bits of earth. They were travelling, apparently, neither one way nor the other. They were, to all intents, stationary. They informed the men in the boat that it was making progress slowly toward the land.

The captain, rearing cautiously in the bow, after the dingey soared on a great swell, said that he had seen the light-house at Mosquito Inlet. Presently the cook remarked that he had seen it. The correspondent was at the oars, then, and for some reason he too wished to look at the light-house, but his back was toward the far shore and the waves were important, and for some time he could not seize an opportunity to turn his head. But at last there came a wave more gentle than the others, and when at the crest of it he swiftly scoured the western horizon.

"See it?" said the captain.

"No," said the correspondent, slowly, "I didn't see anything."

"Look again," said the captain. He pointed. "It's exactly in that direction."

At the top of another wave, the correspondent did as he was bid, and this time his eyes chanced on a small still thing on the edge of the swaying horizon. It was precisely like the point of a pin. It took an anxious eye to find a light-house so tiny.

"Think we'll make it, Captain?"

"If this wind holds and the boat don't swamp, we can't do much else," said the captain.

The little boat, lifted by each towering sea, and splashed viciously by the crests, made progress that in the absence of sea-weed was not apparent to those in her. She seemed just a wee thing wallowing, miraculously, top-up, at the mercy of five oceans. Occasionally, a great spread of water, like white flames, swarmed into her.

"Bail her, cook," said the captain, serenely.

"All right, Captain," said the cheerful cook.

III

It would be difficult to describe the subtle brotherhood of men that was here established on the seas. No one said that it was so. No one mentioned it. But it dwelt in the boat, and each man felt it warm him. They were a captain, an oiler, a cook, and a correspondent, and they were friends, friends in a more curiously iron-bound degree than may be common. The hurt captain, lying against the water-jar in the bow, spoke always in a low voice and calmly, but he could never command a more ready and swiftly obedient crew than the motley three of the dingey. It was more than a mere recognition of what was best for the common safety. There was surely in it a quality that was personal and heartfelt. And after this devotion to the commander of the boat there was this comradeship that the correspondent, for instance, who had been taught to be cynical of men, knew even at the time was the best experience of his life. But no one said that it was so. No one mentioned it.

"I wish we had a sail," remarked the captain. "We might try my overcoat on the end of an oar and give you two boys a chance to rest." So the cook and the correspondent held the mast and spread wide the overcoat. The oiler steered, and the little boat made good way with her new rig. Sometimes the oiler had to scull sharply to keep a sea from breaking into the boat, but otherwise sailing was a success.

Meanwhile the light-house had been growing slowly larger. It had now almost assumed color, and appeared like a little gray shadow on the sky. The man at the oars could not be prevented from turning his head rather often to try for a glimpse of this little gray shadow.

At last, from the top of each wave the men in the tossing boat could see land. Even as the light-house was an upright shadow on the sky, this land seemed but a long black shadow on the sea. It certainly was thinner than paper. "We must be about opposite New Smyrna," said the cook, who had coasted this shore often in schooners. "Captain, by the way, I believe they abandoned that life-saving station there about a year ago."

"Did they?" said the captain.

The wind slowly died away. The cook and the correspondent were not now obliged to slave in order to hold high the oar. But the waves continued their old impetuous swooping at the dingey, and the little craft, no longer under way, struggled woundily over them. The oiler or the correspondent took the oars again.

Shipwrecks are *apropos* of nothing. If men could only train for them and have them occur when the men had reached pink condition, there would be less drowning at sea. Of the four in the dingey none had slept any time worth mentioning for two days and two nights previous to embarking in the dingey, and in the excitement of clambering about the deck of a foundering ship they had also forgotten to eat heartily.

For these reasons, and for others, neither the oiler nor the correspondent was fond of rowing at this time. The correspondent wondered ingenuously how in the name of all that was sane could there be people who thought it amusing to row a boat. It was not an amusement; it was a diabolical punishment, and even a genius of mental aberrations could never conclude that it was anything but a horror to the muscles and a crime against the back. He mentioned to the boat in general how the amusement of rowing struck him, and the weary-faced oiler smiled in full sympathy. Previously to the foundering, by the way, the oiler had worked double-watch in the engine-room of the ship.

"Take her easy, now, boys," said the captain. "Don't spend yourselves. If we have to run a surf you'll need all your strength, because we'll sure have to swim for it. Take your time."

Slowly the land arose from the sea. From a black line it became a line of black and a line of white—trees and sand. Finally, the captain said that he could make out a house on the shore. "That's the house of refuge, sure," said the cook. "They'll see us before long, and come out after us."

The distant light-house reared high. "The keeper ought to be able to make us out now, if he's looking through a glass," said the captain. "He'll notify the life-saving people."

"None of those other boats could have got ashore to give word of the wreck," said the oiler, in a low voice. "Else the life-boat would be out hunting us."

Slowly and beautifully the land loomed out of the sea. The wind came again. It had veered from the northeast to the southeast. Finally, a new sound struck the ears of the men in the boat. It was the low thunder of the surf on the shore. "We'll never be able to make the light-house now," said the captain. "Swing her head a little more north, Billie."

" 'A little more north,' sir," said the oiler.

Whereupon the little boat turned her nose once more down the wind, and all but the oarsman watched the shore grow. Under the influence of this expansion doubt and direful apprehension was leaving the minds of the men. The management of the boat was still most absorbing, but it could not prevent a quiet cheerfulness. In an hour, perhaps, they would be ashore.

Their back-bones had become thoroughly used to balancing in the boat and they now rode this wild colt of a dingey like circus men. The correspondent thought that he had been drenched to the skin, but happening to feel in the top pocket of his coat, he found therein eight cigars. Four of them were soaked with sea-water; four were perfectly scatheless. After a search, somebody produced three dry matches, and thereupon the four waifs rode impudently in their little boat, and with an assurance of an impending rescue shining in their eyes, puffed at the big cigars and judged well and ill of all men. Everybody took a drink of water.

IV

"Cook," remarked the captain, "there don't seem to be any signs of life about your house of refuge."

"No," replied the cook. "Funny they don't see us!"

A broad stretch of lowly coast lay before the eyes of the men. It was of dunes topped with dark vegetation. The roar of the surf was plain, and sometimes they could see the white lip of a wave as it spun up the beach. A tiny house was blocked out black upon the sky. Southward, the slim lighthouse lifted its little gray length.

Tide, wind, and waves were swinging the dingey northward. "Funny they don't see us," said the men.

The surf's roar was here dulled, but its tone was, nevertheless, thunderous and mighty. As the boat swam over the great rollers, the men sat listening to this roar. "We'll swamp sure," said everybody.

It is fair to say here that there was not a life-saving station within twenty miles in either direction, but the men did not know this fact and in consequence they made dark and opprobrious remarks concerning the eyesight of the nation's lifesavers. Four scowling men sat in the dingey and surpassed records in the invention of epithets.

"Funny they don't see us."

The light-heartedness of a former time had completely faded. To their sharpened minds it was easy to conjure pictures of all kinds of incompetency and blindness and, indeed, cowardice. There was the shore of the populous land, and it was bitter and bitter to them that from it came no sign.

"Well," said the captain, ultimately, "I suppose we'll have to make a try for ourselves. If we stay out here too long, we'll none of us have strength left to swim after the boat swamps."

And so the oiler, who was at the oars, turned the boat straight for the shore. There was a sudden tightening of muscles. There was some thinking.

"If we don't all get ashore—" said the captain. "If we don't all get ashore, I suppose you fellows know where to send news of my finish?"

They then briefly exchanged some addresses and admonitions. As for the reflections of the men, there was a great deal of rage in them. Perchance they might be formulated thus: "If I am going to be drowned—if I am going to be drowned— if I am going to be drowned, why, in the name of the seven mad gods who rule the sea, was I allowed to come thus far and contemplate sand and trees? Was I brought here merely to have my nose dragged away as I was about to nibble the sacred cheese of life? It is preposterous. If this old ninny-woman, Fate, cannot do better than this, she should be deprived of the management of men's fortunes. She is an old hen who knows not her intention. If she has decided to drown me, why did she not do it in the beginning and save me all this trouble. The whole affair is absurd. . . . But, no, she cannot mean to drown me. She dare not drown me. She cannot drown me. Not after all this work." Afterward the man might have had an impulse to shake his fist at the clouds. "Just you drown me, now, and then hear what I call you!"

The billows that came at this time were more formidable. They seemed always just about to break and roll over the little boat in a turmoil of foam. There was a preparatory and long growl in the speech of them. No mind unused to the sea would have concluded that the dingey could ascend these sheer heights in time. The shore was still afar. The oiler was a wily surfman. "Boys," he said, swiftly, "she won't live three minutes more and we're too far out to swim. Shall I take her to sea again, Captain?"

"Yes! Go ahead!" said the captain.

This oiler, by a series of quick miracles, and fast and steady oarsmanship, turned the boat in the middle of the surf and took her safely to sea again.

There was a considerable silence as the boat bumped over the furrowed sea to deeper water. Then somebody in gloom spoke. "Well, anyhow, they must have seen us from the shore by now."

The gulls went in slanting flight up the wind toward the gray desolate east. A squall, marked by dingy clouds, and clouds brick-red, like smoke from a burning building, appeared from the southeast.

"What do you think of those life-saving people? Ain't they peaches?"

"Funny they haven't seen us."

"Maybe they think we're out here for sport! Maybe they think we're fishin'. Maybe they think we're damned fools."

It was a long afternoon. A changed tide tried to force them southward, but wind and wave said northward. Far ahead, where coast-line, sea, and sky formed their mighty angle, there were little dots which seemed to indicate a city on the shore.

"St. Augustine?"

The captain shook his head. "Too near Mosquito Inlet."

And the oiler rowed, and then the correspondent rowed. Then the oiler rowed. It was a weary business. The human back can become the seat of more aches and pains than are registered in books for the composite anatomy of a regiment. It is a limited area, but it can become the theatre of innumerable muscular conflicts, tangles, wrenches, knots, and other comforts.

"Did you ever like to row, Billie?" asked the correspondent.

"No," said the oiler. "Hang it."

When one exchanged the rowing-seat for a place in the bottom of the boat, he suffered a bodily depression that caused him to be careless of everything save an obligation to wiggle one finger. There was cold sea-water swashing to and fro in the boat, and he lay in it. His head, pillowed on a thwart, was within an inch of the swirl of a wave crest, and sometimes a particularly obstreperous sea came in-board and drenched him once more. But these matters did not annoy him. It is almost certain that if the boat had capsized he would have tumbled comfortably out upon the ocean as if he felt sure that it was a great soft mattress.

"Look! There's a man on the shore!"

"Where?"

"There! See 'im? See 'im?"

"Yes, sure! He's walking along."

"Now he's stopped. Look! He's facing us!"

"He's waving at us!"

"So he is! By thunder!"

"Ah, now, we're all right! Now we're all right! There'll be a boat out here for us in half an hour."

"He's going on. He's running. He's going up to that house there."

The remote beach seemed lower than the sea, and it required a searching glance to discern the little black figure. The captain saw a floating stick and they rowed to it. A bath-towel was by some weird chance in the boat, and, tying this on the stick, the captain waved it. The oarsman did not dare turn his head, so he was obliged to ask questions.

"What's he doing now?"

"He's standing still again. He's looking, I think. . . . There he goes again. Toward the house. . . . Now he's stopped again."

"Is he waving at us?"

"No, not now! he was, though."

"Look! There comes another man!"

"He's running."

"Look at him go, would you."

"Why, he's on a bicycle. Now he's met the other man. They're both waving at us. Look!"

"There comes something up the beach."

"What the devil is that thing?"

"Why, it looks like a boat."

"Why, certainly it's a boat."

"No, it's on wheels."

"Yes, so it is. Well, that must be the life-boat. They drag them along shore on a wagon."

"That's the life-boat, sure."

"No, by——, it's—it's an omnibus."

"I tell you it's a life-boat."

"It is not! It's an omnibus. I can see it plain. See? One of those big hotel omnibuses."

"By thunder, you're right. It's an omnibus, sure as fate. What do you suppose they are doing with an omnibus? Maybe they are going around collecting the life-crew, hey?"

"That's it, likely. Look! There's a fellow waving a little black flag. He's standing on the steps of the omnibus. There come those other two fellows. Now they're all talking together. Look at the fellow with the flag. Maybe he ain't waving it!"

"That ain't a flag, is it? That's his coat. Why, certainly, that's his coat."

"So it is. It's his coat. He's taken it off and is waving it around his head. But would you look at him swing it!"

"Oh, say, there isn't any life-saving station there. That's just a winter resort hotel omnibus that has brought over some of the boarders to see us drown."

"What's that idiot with the coat mean? What's he signaling, anyhow?"

"It looks as if he were trying to tell us to go north. There must be a life-saving station up there."

"No! He thinks we're fishing. Just giving us a merry hand. See? Ah, there, Willie."

"Well, I wish I could make something out of those signals. What do you suppose he means?"

"He don't mean anything. He's just playing."

"Well, if he'd just signal us to try the surf again, or to go to sea and wait, or go north, or go south, or go to hell—there would be some reason in it. But look at him. He just stands there and keeps his coat revolving like a wheel. The ass!"

"There come more people."

"Now there's quite a mob. Look! Isn't that a boat?"

"Where? Oh, I see where you mean. No, that's no boat."

"That fellow is still waving his coat."

"He must think we like to see him do that. Why don't he quit it. It don't mean anything."

"I don't know. I think he is trying to make us go north. It must be that there's a life-saving station there somewhere."

"Say, he ain't tired yet. Look at 'im wave."

"Wonder how long he can keep that up. He's been revolving his coat ever since he caught sight of us. He's an idiot. Why aren't they getting men to bring a boat out. A fishing boat—one of those big yawls—could come out here all right. Why don't he do something?"

"Oh, it's all right, now."

"They'll have a boat out here for us in less than no time, now that they've seen us."

A faint yellow tone came into the sky over the low land. The shadows on the sea slowly deepened. The wind bore coldness with it, and the men began to shiver.

"Holy smoke!" said one, allowing his voice to express his impious mood, "if we keep on monkeying out here! If we've got to flounder out here all night!"

"Oh, we'll never have to stay here all night! Don't you worry. They've seen us now, and it won't be long before they'll come chasing out after us."

The shore grew dusky. The man waving a coat blended gradually into this gloom, and it swallowed in the same manner the omnibus and the group of people. The spray, when it dashed uproariously over the side, made the voyagers shrink and swear like men who were being branded.

"I'd like to catch the chump who waved the coat. I feel like soaking him one, just for luck."

"Why? What did he do?"

"Oh, nothing, but then he seemed so damned cheerful."

In the meantime the oiler rowed, and then the correspondent rowed, and then the oiler rowed. Gray-faced and bowed forward, they mechanically, turn by turn, plied the leaden oars. The form of the light-house had vanished from the southern horizon, but finally a pale star appeared, just lifting from the sea. The streaked saffron in the west passed before the all-merging darkness, and the sea to the east was black. The land had vanished, and was expressed only by the low and drear thunder of the surf.

"If I am going to be drowned—if I am going to be drowned—if I am going to be drowned, why, in the name of the seven mad gods who rule the sea, was I allowed to come thus far and contemplate sand and trees? Was I brought here merely to have my nose dragged away as I was about to nibble the sacred cheese of life?"

The patient captain, drooped over the water-jar, was sometimes obliged to speak to the oarsman.

"Keep her head up! Keep her head up!"

" 'Keep her head up,' sir." The voices were weary and low.

This was surely a quiet evening. All save the oarsman lay heavily and listlessly in the boat's bottom. As for him, his eyes were just capable of noting the tall black waves that swept forward in a most sinister silence, save for an occasional subdued growl of a crest.

The cook's head was on a thwart, and he looked without interest at the water under his nose. He was deep in other scenes. Finally he spoke. "Billie," he murmured, dreamfully, "what kind of pie do you like best?"

V

"Pie," said the oiler and the correspondent, agitatedly. "Don't talk about those things, blast you!"

"Well," said the cook, "I was just thinking about ham sandwiches, and——"

A night on the sea in an open boat is a long night. As darkness settled finally, the shine of the light, lifting from the sea in the south, changed to full gold. On the northern horizon a new light appeared, a small bluish gleam on the edge of the waters. These two lights were the furniture of the world. Otherwise there was nothing but waves.

Two men huddled in the stern, and distances were so magnificent in the dingey that the rower was enabled to keep his feet partly warmed by thrusting them under his companions. Their legs indeed extended far under the rowing-seat until they touched the feet of the captain forward. Sometimes, despite the efforts of the tired oarsman, a wave came piling into the boat, an icy wave of the night, and the chilling water soaked them anew. They would twist their bodies for a moment and groan, and sleep the dead sleep once more, while the water in the boat gurgled about them as the craft rocked.

The plan of the oiler and the correspondent was for one to row until he lost the ability, and then arouse the other from his sea-water couch in the bottom of the boat.

The oiler plied the oars until his head drooped forward, and the overpowering sleep blinded him. And he rowed yet afterward. Then he touched a man in the bottom of the boat, and called his name. "Will you spell me for a little while?" he said, meekly.

"Sure, Billie," said the correspondent, awakening and dragging himself to a sitting position. They exchanged places carefully, and the oiler, cuddling down in the sea-water at the cook's side, seemed to go to sleep instantly.

The particular violence of the sea had ceased. The waves came without snarling. The obligation of the man at the oars was to keep the boat headed so that the tilt of the rollers would not capsize her, and to preserve her from filling when the crests rushed past. The black waves were silent and hard to be seen in the darkness. Often one was almost upon the boat before the oarsman was aware.

In a low voice the correspondent addressed the captain. He was not sure that the captain was awake, although this iron man seemed to be always awake. "Captain, shall I keep her making for that light north, sir?"

The same steady voice answered him. "Yes. Keep it about two points off the port bow."

The cook had tied a life-belt around himself in order to get even the warmth which this clumsy cork contrivance could donate, and he seemed almost stove-like when a rower, whose teeth invariably chattered wildly as soon as he ceased his labor, dropped down to sleep.

The correspondent, as he rowed, looked down at the two men sleeping under foot. The cook's arm was around the oiler's shoulders, and, with their fragmentary clothing and haggard faces, they were the babes of the sea, a grotesque rendering of the old babes in the wood.

Later he must have grown stupid at his work, for suddenly there was a growling of water, and a crest came with a roar and a swash into the boat, and it was a wonder that it did not set the cook afloat in his life-belt. The cook continued to sleep, but the oiler sat up, blinking his eyes and shaking with the new cold.

"Oh, I'm awful sorry, Billie," said the correspondent, contritely.

"That's all right, old boy," said the oiler, and lay down again and was asleep.

Presently it seemed that even the captain dozed, and the correspondent thought that he was the one man afloat on all the oceans. The wind had a voice as it came over the waves, and it was sadder than the end.

There was a long, loud swishing astern of the boat, and a

gleaming trail of phosphorescence, like blue flame, was fur-
rowed on the black waters. It might have been made by a
monstrous knife.

Then there came a stillness, while the correspondent
breathed with the open mouth and looked at the sea.

Suddenly there was another swish and another long flash
of bluish light, and this time it was alongside the boat, and
might almost have been reached with an oar. The correspon-
dent saw an enormous fin speed like a shadow through the
water, hurling the crystalline spray and leaving the long glow-
ing trail.

The correspondent looked over his shoulder at the captain.
His face was hidden, and he seemed to be asleep. He looked
at the babes of the sea. They certainly were asleep. So, being
bereft of sympathy, he leaned a little way to one side and
swore softly into the sea.

But the thing did not then leave the vicinity of the boat.
Ahead or astern, on one side or the other, at intervals long or
short, fled the long sparkling streak, and there was to be
heard the whiroo of the dark fin. The speed and power of the
thing was greatly to be admired. It cut the water like a gigan-
tic and keen projectile.

The presence of this biding thing did not affect the man
with the same horror that it would if he had been a picnicker.
He simply looked at the sea dully and swore in an undertone.

Nevertheless, it is true that he did not wish to be alone
with the thing. He wished one of his companions to awaken
by chance and keep him company with it. But the captain
hung motionless over the water-jar and the oiler and the cook
in the bottom of the boat were plunged in slumber.

VI

"If I am going to be drowned—if I am going to be
drowned—if I am going to be drowned, why, in the name
of the seven mad gods who rule the sea, was I allowed to
come thus far and contemplate sand and trees?"

During this dismal night, it may be remarked that a man
would conclude that it was really the intention of the seven
mad gods to drown him, despite the abominable injustice of

it. For it was certainly an abominable injustice to drown a
man who had worked so hard, so hard. The man felt it would
be a crime most unnatural. Other people had drowned at sea
since galleys swarmed with painted sails, but still——

When it occurs to a man that nature does not regard him
as important, and that she feels she would not maim the uni-
verse by disposing of him, he at first wishes to throw bricks
at the temple, and he hates deeply the fact that there are no
bricks and no temples. Any visible expression of nature would
surely be pelleted with his jeers.

Then, if there be no tangible thing to hoot he feels, per-
haps, the desire to confront a personification and indulge in
pleas, bowed to one knee, and with hands supplicant, saying:
"Yes, but I love myself."

A high cold star on a winter's night is the word he feels
that she says to him. Thereafter he knows the pathos of his
situation.

The men in the dingey had not discussed these matters, but
each had, no doubt, reflected upon them in silence and ac-
cording to his mind. There was seldom any expression upon
their faces save the general one of complete weariness. Speech
was devoted to the business of the boat.

To chime the notes of his emotion, a verse mysteriously
entered the correspondent's head. He had even forgotten that
he had forgotten this verse, but it suddenly was in his mind.

> A soldier of the Legion lay dying in Algiers,
> There was lack of woman's nursing, there was dearth
>   of woman's tears;
> But a comrade stood beside him, and he took that
>   comrade's hand,
> And he said: "I never more shall see my own, my
>   native land."

In his childhood, the correspondent had been made ac-
quainted with the fact that a soldier of the Legion lay dying
in Algiers, but he had never regarded it as important. Myriads
of his school-fellows had informed him of the soldier's plight,
but the dinning had naturally ended by making him perfectly
indifferent. He had never considered it his affair that a soldier

of the Legion lay dying in Algiers, nor had it appeared to him as a matter for sorrow. It was less to him than the breaking of a pencil's point.

Now, however, it quaintly came to him as a human, living thing. It was no longer merely a picture of a few throes in the breast of a poet, meanwhile drinking tea and warming his feet at the grate; it was an actuality—stern, mournful, and fine.

The correspondent plainly saw the soldier. He lay on the sand with his feet out straight and still. While his pale left hand was upon his chest in an attempt to thwart the going of his life, the blood came between his fingers. In the far Algerian distance, a city of low square forms was set against a sky that was faint with the last sunset hues. The correspondent, plying the oars and dreaming of the slow and slower movements of the lips of the soldier, was moved by a profound and perfectly impersonal comprehension. He was sorry for the soldier of the Legion who lay dying in Algiers.

The thing which had followed the boat and waited had evidently grown bored at the delay. There was no longer to be heard the slash of the cut-water, and there was no longer the flame of the long trail. The light in the north still glimmered, but it was apparently no nearer to the boat. Sometimes the boom of the surf rang in the correspondent's ears, and he turned the craft seaward then and rowed harder. Southward, some one had evidently built a watch-fire on the beach. It was too low and too far to be seen, but it made a shimmering, roseate reflection upon the bluff back of it, and this could be discerned from the boat. The wind came stronger, and sometimes a wave suddenly raged out like a mountain-cat and there was to be seen the sheen and sparkle of a broken crest.

The captain, in the bow, moved on his water-jar and sat erect. "Pretty long night," he observed to the correspondent. He looked at the shore. "Those life-saving people take their time."

"Did you see that shark playing around?"

"Yes, I saw him. He was a big fellow, all right."

"Wish I had known you were awake."

Later the correspondent spoke into the bottom of the boat. "Billie!" There was a slow and gradual disentanglement. "Billie, will you spell me?"

"Sure," said the oiler.

As soon as the correspondent touched the cold comfortable sea-water in the bottom of the boat, and had huddled close to the cook's life-belt he was deep in sleep, despite the fact that his teeth played all the popular airs. This sleep was so good to him that it was but a moment before he heard a voice call his name in a tone that demonstrated the last stages of exhaustion. "Will you spell me?"

"Sure, Billie."

The light in the north had mysteriously vanished, but the correspondent took his course from the wide-awake captain.

Later in the night they took the boat farther out to sea, and the captain directed the cook to take one oar at the stern and keep the boat facing the seas. He was to call out if he should hear the thunder of the surf. This plan enabled the oiler and the correspondent to get respite together. "We'll give those boys a chance to get into shape again," said the captain. They curled down and, after a few preliminary chatterings and trembles, slept once more the dead sleep. Neither knew they had bequeathed to the cook the company of another shark, or perhaps the same shark.

As the boat caroused on the waves, spray occasionally bumped over the side and gave them a fresh soaking, but this had no power to break their repose. The ominous slash of the wind and the water affected them as it would have affected mummies.

"Boys," said the cook, with the notes of every reluctance in his voice, "she's drifted in pretty close. I guess one of you had better take her to sea again." The correspondent, aroused, heard the crash of the toppled crests.

As he was rowing, the captain gave him some whiskey and water, and this steadied the chills out of him. "If I ever get ashore and anybody shows me even a photograph of an oar——"

At last there was a short conversation.

"Billie. . . . Billie, will you spell me?"

"Sure," said the oiler.

VII

When the correspondent again opened his eyes, the sea and the sky were each of the gray hue of the dawning. Later, carmine and gold was painted upon the waters. The morning appeared finally, in its splendor, with a sky of pure blue, and the sunlight flamed on the tips of the waves.

On the distant dunes were set many little black cottages, and a tall white wind-mill reared above them. No man, nor dog, nor bicycle appeared on the beach. The cottages might have formed a deserted village.

The voyagers scanned the shore. A conference was held in the boat. "Well," said the captain, "if no help is coming, we might better try a run through the surf right away. If we stay out here much longer we will be too weak to do anything for ourselves at all." The others silently acquiesced in this reasoning. The boat was headed for the beach. The correspondent wondered if none ever ascended the tall wind-tower, and if then they never looked seaward. This tower was a giant, standing with its back to the plight of the ants. It represented in a degree, to the correspondent, the serenity of nature amid the struggles of the individual—nature in the wind, and nature in the vision of men. She did not seem cruel to him then, nor beneficent, nor treacherous, nor wise. But she was indifferent, flatly indifferent. It is, perhaps, plausible that a man in this situation, impressed with the unconcern of the universe, should see the innumerable flaws of his life and have them taste wickedly in his mind and wish for another chance. A distinction between right and wrong seems absurdly clear to him, then, in this new ignorance of the grave-edge, and he understands that if he were given another opportunity he would mend his conduct and his words, and be better and brighter during an introduction, or at a tea.

"Now, boys," said the captain, "she is going to swamp sure. All we can do is to work her in as far as possible, and then when she swamps, pile out and scramble for the beach. Keep cool now, and don't jump until she swamps sure."

The oiler took the oars. Over his shoulders he scanned the surf. "Captain," he said, "I think I'd better bring her about, and keep her head-on to the seas and back her in."

"All right, Billie," said the captain. "Back her in." The oiler swung the boat then and, seated in the stern, the cook and the correspondent were obliged to look over their shoulders to contemplate the lonely and indifferent shore.

The monstrous inshore rollers heaved the boat high until the men were again enabled to see the white sheets of water scudding up the slanted beach. "We won't get in very close," said the captain. Each time a man could wrest his attention from the rollers, he turned his glance toward the shore, and in the expression of the eyes during this contemplation there was a singular quality. The correspondent, observing the others, knew that they were not afraid, but the full meaning of their glances was shrouded.

As for himself, he was too tired to grapple fundamentally with the fact. He tried to coerce his mind into thinking of it, but the mind was dominated at this time by the muscles, and the muscles said they did not care. It merely occurred to him that if he should drown it would be a shame.

There were no hurried words, no pallor, no plain agitation. The men simply looked at the shore. "Now, remember to get well clear of the boat when you jump," said the captain.

Seaward the crest of a roller suddenly fell with a thunderous crash, and the long white comber came roaring down upon the boat.

"Steady now," said the captain. The men were silent. They turned their eyes from the shore to the comber and waited. The boat slid up the incline, leaped at the furious top, bounced over it, and swung down the long back of the wave. Some water had been shipped and the cook bailed it out.

But the next crest crashed also. The tumbling boiling flood of white water caught the boat and whirled it almost perpendicular. Water swarmed in from all sides. The correspondent had his hands on the gunwale at this time, and when the water entered at that place he swiftly withdrew his fingers, as if he objected to wetting them.

The little boat, drunken with this weight of water, reeled and snuggled deeper into the sea.

"Bail her out, cook! Bail her out," said the captain.

"All right, Captain," said the cook.

"Now, boys, the next one will do for us, sure," said the oiler. "Mind to jump clear of the boat."

The third wave moved forward, huge, furious, implacable. It fairly swallowed the dingey, and almost simultaneously the men tumbled into the sea. A piece of life-belt had lain in the bottom of the boat, and as the correspondent went overboard he held this to his chest with his left hand.

The January water was icy, and he reflected immediately that it was colder than he had expected to find it off the coast of Florida. This appeared to his dazed mind as a fact important enough to be noted at the time. The coldness of the water was sad; it was tragic. This fact was somehow so mixed and confused with his opinion of his own situation that it seemed almost a proper reason for tears. The water was cold.

When he came to the surface he was conscious of little but the noisy water. Afterward he saw his companions in the sea. The oiler was ahead in the race. He was swimming strongly and rapidly. Off to the correspondent's left, the cook's great white and corked back bulged out of the water, and in the rear the captain was hanging with his one good hand to the keel of the overturned dingey.

There is a certain immovable quality to a shore, and the correspondent wondered at it amid the confusion of the sea.

It seemed also very attractive, but the correspondent knew that it was a long journey, and he paddled leisurely. The piece of life-preserver lay under him, and sometimes he whirled down the incline of a wave as if he were on a hand-sled.

But finally he arrived at a place in the sea where travel was beset with difficulty. He did not pause swimming to inquire what manner of current had caught him, but there his progress ceased. The shore was set before him like a bit of scenery on a stage, and he looked at it and understood with his eyes each detail of it.

As the cook passed, much farther to the left, the captain was calling to him, "Turn over on your back, cook! Turn over on your back and use the oar."

"All right, sir." The cook turned on his back, and, paddling with an oar, went ahead as if he were a canoe.

Presently the boat also passed to the left of the correspondent with the captain clinging with one hand to the keel. He would have appeared like a man raising himself to look over a board fence, if it were not for the extraordinary gymnastics of the boat. The correspondent marvelled that the captain could still hold to it.

They passed on, nearer to shore—the oiler, the cook, the captain—and following them went the water-jar, bouncing gayly over the seas.

The correspondent remained in the grip of this strange new enemy—a current. The shore, with its white slope of sand and its green bluff, topped with little silent cottages, was spread like a picture before him. It was very near to him then, but he was impressed as one who in a gallery looks at a scene from Brittany or Holland.

He thought: "I am going to drown? Can it be possible? Can it be possible? Can it be possible?" Perhaps an individual must consider his own death to be the final phenomenon of nature.

But later a wave perhaps whirled him out of this small deadly current, for he found suddenly that he could again make progress toward the shore. Later still, he was aware that the captain, clinging with one hand to the keel of the dingey, had his face turned away from the shore and toward him, and was calling his name. "Come to the boat! Come to the boat!"

In his struggle to reach the captain and the boat, he reflected that when one gets properly wearied, drowning must really be a comfortable arrangement, a cessation of hostilities accompanied by a large degree of relief, and he was glad of it, for the main thing in his mind for some moments had been horror of the temporary agony. He did not wish to be hurt.

Presently he saw a man running along the shore. He was undressing with most remarkable speed. Coat, trousers, shirt, everything flew magically off him.

"Come to the boat," called the captain.

"All right, Captain." As the correspondent paddled, he saw the captain let himself down to bottom and leave the boat. Then the correspondent performed his one little marvel of the voyage. A large wave caught him and flung him with ease and supreme speed completely over the boat and far beyond it. It struck him even then as an event in gymnastics, and a true miracle of the sea. An overturned boat in the surf is not a plaything to a swimming man.

The correspondent arrived in water that reached only to his waist, but his condition did not enable him to stand for more than a moment. Each wave knocked him into a heap, and the under-tow pulled at him.

Then he saw the man who had been running and undressing, and undressing and running, come bounding into the water. He dragged ashore the cook, and then waded toward the captain, but the captain waved him away, and sent him to the correspondent. He was naked, naked as a tree in winter, but a halo was about his head, and he shone like a saint. He gave a strong pull, and a long drag, and a bully heave at the correspondent's hand. The correspondent, schooled in the minor formulæ, said: "Thanks, old man." But suddenly the man cried: "What's that?" He pointed a swift finger. The correspondent said: "Go."

In the shallows, face downward, lay the oiler. His forehead touched sand that was periodically, between each wave, clear of the sea.

The correspondent did not know all that transpired afterward. When he achieved safe ground he fell, striking the sand with each particular part of his body. It was as if he had dropped from a roof, but the thud was grateful to him.

It seems that instantly the beach was populated with men with blankets, clothes, and flasks, and women with coffeepots and all the remedies sacred to their minds. The welcome of the land to the men from the sea was warm and generous, but a still and dripping shape was carried slowly up the beach, and the land's welcome for it could only be the different and sinister hospitality of the grave.

When it came night, the white waves paced to and fro in the moonlight, and the wind brought the sound of the great sea's voice to the men on shore, and they felt that they could then be interpreters.

Flanagan and His
Short Filibustering Adventure

I

I HAVE GOT twenty men at me back who will fight to the death," said the warrior to the old filibuster.

"And they can be blowed, for all me," replied the old filibuster. "Common as sparrows. Cheap as cigarettes. Show me twenty men with steel clamps on their mouths, with holes in their heads where memory ought to be, and I want 'em. But twenty brave men merely? I'd rather have twenty brave onions."

Thereupon the warrior removed sadly, feeling that no salaams were paid to valor in these days of mechanical excellence.

Valor, in truth, is no bad thing to have when filibustering, but many medals are to be won by the man who knows not the meaning of pow-wow, before or afterward. Twenty brave men with tongues hung lightly may make trouble rise from the ground like smoke from grass because of their subsequent fiery pride, whereas twenty cow-eyed villains who accept unrighteous and far-compelling kicks as they do the rain of heaven may halo the ultimate history of an expedition with gold and plentifully bedeck their names, winning forty years of gratitude from patriots, simply by remaining silent. As for the cause, it may be only that they have no friends or other credulous furniture.

If it were not for the curse of the swinging tongue it is surely to be said that the filibustering industry, flourishing now in the United States, would be pie. Under correct conditions, it is merely a matter of dealing with some little detectives whose skill at search is rated by those who pay them at a value of twelve or twenty dollars each week. It is nearly axiomatic that normally a twelve-dollar-per-week detective cannot defeat a one-hundred-thousand-dollar filibustering excursion. Against the criminal the detective represents the commonwealth; but in this other case he represents his desire to show cause why his salary should be paid. He represents himself merely, and he counts no more than a grocer's clerk.

But the pride of the successful filibuster often smites him and his cause like an ax, and men who have not confided in their mothers go prone with him. It can make the dome of the Capitol tremble and incite the Senators to overturning benches. It can increase the salaries of detectives who could not detect the location of a pain in the chest. It is a wonderful thing, this pride.

Filibustering was once such a simple game. It was managed blandly by gentle captains and smooth and undisturbed gentlemen who at other times dealt in the law, soap, medicine, and bananas. It was a great pity that the little cote of doves in Washington was obliged to rustle officially, and naval men were kept from their berths at night, and sundry customhouse people got wiggings, all because the returned adventurer pow-wowed in his pride. A yellow and red banner would have been long since smothered in a shame of defeat if a contract to filibuster had been let to some admirable organization like one of our trusts.

And yet the game is not obsolete. It is still played by the wise and the silent, men whose names are not display-typed and blathered from one end of the country to the other.

There is in mind now a man who knew one side of a fence from the other side when he looked sharply. They were hunting for captains then to command the first vessels of what has since become a famous little fleet. One was recommended to this man, and he said: "Send him down to my office and I'll look him over." He was an attorney, and he liked to lean back in his chair, twirl a paper-knife, and let the other fellow talk.

The seafaring man came and stood and appeared confounded. The attorney asked the terrible first question of the filibuster to the applicant. He said: "Why do you want to go?"

The captain reflected, changed his attitude three times, and decided ultimately that he didn't know. He seemed greatly ashamed. The attorney, looking at him, saw that he had eyes that resembled a lambkin's eyes.

"Glory?" said the attorney at last.

"No-o," said the captain.

"Pay?"

"No-o. Not that, so much."

"Think they'll give you a land grant when they win out?"

"No. Never thought."

"No glory. No immense pay. No land grant. What are you going for, then?"

"Well, I don't know," said the captain, with his glance on the floor and shifting his position again. "I don't know. I guess it's just for fun, mostly." The attorney asked him out to have a drink.

When he stood on the bridge of his outgoing steamer, the attorney saw him again. His shore meekness and uncertainty were gone. He was clear-eyed and strong, aroused like a mastiff at night. He took his cigar out of his mouth and yelled some sudden language at the deck.

This steamer had about her a quality of unholy mediæval disrepair which is usually accounted the principal prerogative of the United States revenue marine. There is many a seaworthy ice-house if she was a good ship. She swashed through the seas as genially as an old wooden clock, burying her head under waves that came only like children at play, and on board it cost a ducking to go from anywhere to anywhere.

The captain had commanded vessels that shore people thought were liners, but when a man gets the ant of desire-to-see-what-it's-like stirring in his heart, he will wallow out to sea in a pail. The thing surpasses a man's love for his sweetheart. The great tank-steamer *Thunder Voice* had long been Flanagan's sweetheart, but he was far happier off Hatteras, watching this wretched little portmanteau boom down the slant of a wave.

The crew scraped acquaintance one with another gradually. Each man came ultimately to ask his neighbor what particular turn of ill-fortune or inherited deviltry caused him to try this voyage. When one frank, bold man saw another frank, bold man aboard, he smiled, and they became friends. There was not a mind on board the ship that was not fastened to the dangers of the coast of Cuba and taking wonder at this prospect and delight in it. Still, in jovial moments they termed each other accursed idiots.

At first there was some trouble in the engine-room, where there were many steel animals, for the most part painted red and in other places very shiny, bewildering, complex, incomprehensible to anyone who don't care, usually thumping, thumping, thumping with the monotony of a snore.

It seems that this engine was as whimsical as a gas-meter. The chief engineer was a fine old fellow with a grey moustache, but the engine told him that it didn't intend to budge until it felt better. He came to the bridge and said: "The blamed old thing has laid down on us, sir."

"Who was on duty?" roared the captain.

"The second, sir."

"Why didn't he call you?"

"Don't know, sir." Later the stokers had occasion to thank the stars that they were not second engineers.

The *Foundling* was soundly thrashed by the waves for loitering while the captain and the engineers fought the obstinate machinery. During this wait on the sea, the first gloom came to the faces of the company. The ocean is wide, and a ship is a small place for the feet, and an ill ship is worriment. Even when she was again under way, the gloom was still upon the crew. From time to time men went to the engine-room doors and, looking down, wanted to ask questions of the chief engineer, who slowly prowled to and fro and watched with careful eye his red-painted mysteries. No man wished to have a companion know that he was anxious, and so questions were caught at the lips. Perhaps none commented save the first mate, who remarked to the captain: "Wonder what the bally old thing will do, sir, when we're chased by a Spanish cruiser?"

The captain merely grinned. Later he looked over the side and said to himself with scorn: "Sixteen knots! Sixteen knots! Sixteen hinges on the inner gates of Hades! Sixteen knots! Seven is her gait, and nine if you crack her up to it."

There may never be a captain whose crew can't sniff his misgivings. They scent it as a herd scents the menace far through the trees and over the ridges. A captain that does not know that he is on a foundering ship sometimes can take his men to tea and buttered toast twelve minutes before the disaster; but let him fret for a moment in the loneliness of his cabin, and in no time it affects the liver of a distant and sensitive seaman. Even as Flanagan reflected on the *Foundling*, viewing her as a filibuster, word arrived that a winter of discontent had come to the stoke-room.

The captain knew that it requires sky to give a man courage. He sent for a stoker and talked to him on the bridge. The man, standing under the sky, instantly and shamefacedly denied all knowledge of the business. Nevertheless a jaw had presently to be broken by a fist because the *Foundling* could only steam nine knots and because the stoke-room has no sky, no wind, no bright horizon.

When the *Foundling* was somewhere off Savannah a blow came from the northeast, and the steamer, headed southeast, rolled like a boiling potato. The first mate was a fine officer, and so a wave crashed him into the deck-house and broke his arm. The cook was a good cook, and so the heave of the ship flung him heels over head with a pot of boiling water and caused him to lose interest in everything save his legs. "By the piper," said Flanagan to himself, "this filibustering is no trick with cards."

Later there was more trouble in the stoke-room. All the stokers participated save the one with a broken jaw, who had become discouraged. The captain had an excellent chest development. When he went aft, roaring, it was plain that a man could beat carpets with a voice like that one.

II

One night the *Foundling* was off the southern coast of Florida and running at half speed toward the shore. The captain was on the bridge. "Four flashes at intervals of one minute," he said to himself, gazing steadfastly toward the beach. Suddenly a yellow eye opened in the black face of the night and looked at the *Foundling* and closed again. The captain studied his watch and the shore. Three times more the eye opened and looked at the *Foundling* and closed again. The captain called to the vague figures on the deck below him. "Answer it." The flash of a light from the bow of the steamer displayed for a moment in golden color the crests of the in-riding waves.

The *Foundling* lay to and waited. The long swells rolled her gracefully, and her two stub masts reaching into the darkness swung with the solemnity of batons timing a dirge. When the ship had left Boston she had been as encrusted with ice as a Dakota stage-driver's beard; but now the gentle wind of Florida softly swayed the lock on the forehead of the coatless Flanagan, and he lit a new cigar without troubling to make a shield of his hands.

Finally a dark boat came plashing over the waves. As it came very near, the captain leaned forward and perceived that the men in her rowed like seamstresses, and at the same time a voice hailed him in bad English. "It's a dead sure connection," said he to himself.

At sea, to load two hundred thousand rounds of rifle am-munition, seven hundred and fifty rifles, two rapid-fire field guns with a hundred shells, forty bundles of machetes, and a hundred pounds of dynamite, from yawls and by men who are not born stevedores, and in a heavy ground swell and with the searchlight of a United States cruiser sometimes flashing like lightning in the sky to the southward, is no business for a Sunday-school class. When at last the *Foundling* was steam-ing for the open over the grey sea at dawn, there was not a man of the forty come aboard from the Florida shore, nor of the fifteen sailed from Boston, who was not glad, standing with his hair matted to his forehead with sweat, smiling at the broad wake of the *Foundling* and the dim streak on the horizon which was Florida.

But there is a point of the compass in these waters which men call the northeast. When the strong winds come from that direction they kick up a turmoil that is not good for a *Foundling* stuffed with coal and war-stores. In the gale which came, this ship was no more than a drunken soldier.

The Cuban leader, standing on the bridge with the captain, was presently informed that of his men thirty-nine out of a possible thirty-nine were seasick. And in truth they were sea-sick. There are degrees in this complaint, but that matter was waived between them. They were all sick to the limits. They strewed the deck in every posture of human anguish; and when the *Foundling* ducked and water came sluicing down from the bows, they let it sluice. They were satisfied if they could keep their heads clear of the wash; and if they could not keep their heads clear of the wash, they didn't care. Presently the *Foundling* swung her course to the southeast, and the waves pounded her broadside. The patriots were all ordered below decks, and there they howled and measured their misery one against another. All day the *Foundling* plopped and floundered over a blazing bright meadow of an ocean whereon the white foam was like flowers.

The captain on the bridge mused and studied the bare horizon. "Hell!" said he to himself, and the word was more in amazement than in indignation or sorrow. "Thirty-nine seasick passengers, the mate with a broken arm, a stoker with a broken jaw, the cook with a pair of scalded legs, and an engine likely to be taken with all these diseases, if not more. If I get back to a home port with a spoke of the wheel gripped in my hands, it'll be fair luck."

There is a kind of corn whisky bred in Florida which the natives declare is potent in the proportion of seven fights to a drink. Some of the Cuban volunteers had had the forethought to bring a small quantity of this whisky aboard with them, and being now in the fire-room and seasick, and feeling that they would not care to drink liquor for two or three years to come, they gracefully tendered their portions to the stokers. The stokers accepted these gifts without avidity, but with a certain earnestness of manner.

As they were stokers and toiling, the whirl of emotion was delayed, but it arrived ultimately and with emphasis. One stoker called another stoker a weird name, and the latter, righteously inflamed at it, smote his mate with an iron shovel, and the man fell headlong over a heap of coal which crashed gently while piece after piece rattled down upon the deck.

A third stoker was providentially enraged at the scene, and assailed the second stoker. They fought for some moments, while the seasick Cubans sprawled on the deck watched with languid rolling glances the ferocity of this scuffle. One was so indifferent to the strategic importance of the space he occupied that he was kicked in the shins.

When the second engineer came to separate the comba-

tants, he was sincere in his efforts, and he came near to disa-
bling them for life.

The captain said, "I'll go down there and——" But the
leader of the Cubans restrained him. "No, no," he cried, "you
must not. We must treat them like children, very gently, all
the time, you see, or else when we get back to a United States
port they will—what you call—spring? Yes—spring the
whole business. We must—jolly them. You see?"

"You mean," said the captain thoughtfully, "they are likely
to get mad and give the expedition dead away when we reach
port again unless we blarney them now?"

"Yes, yes," cried the Cuban leader, "unless we are so very
gentle with them they will make many troubles afterward for
us in the newspapers and then in court."

"Well, but I won't have my crew——" began the captain.

"But you must," interrupted the Cuban. "You must. It is
the only thing. You are like the captain of a pirate ship. You
see? Only you can't throw them overboard like him. You see?"

"Hum," said the captain, "this here filibustering business
has got a lot to it when you come to look it over."

He called the fighting stokers to the bridge, and the three
came meek and considerably battered. He was lecturing them
soundly but sensibly, when he suddenly tripped a sentence
and cried: "Here! Where's that other fellow? How does it
come he wasn't in the fight?"

The row of stokers cried at once eagerly: "He's hurt, sir.
He's got a broken jaw, sir."

"So he has. So he has," murmured the captain, much
embarrassed.

And because of all these affairs the *Foundling* steamed to-
ward Cuba with its crew in a sling, if one may be allowed to
speak in that way.

III

At night the *Foundling* approached the coast like a thief.
Her lights were muffled so that from the deck the sea shone
with its own radiance, like the faint shimmer of some kinds
of silk. The men on deck spoke in whispers, and even down
in the fire-room the hidden stokers working before the blood-

red furnace doors used no words and walked tip-toe. The stars were out in the blue-velvet sky, and their light with the soft shine of the sea caused the coast to appear black as the side of a coffin. The surf boomed in low thunder on the distant beach.

The *Foundling*'s engines ceased their thumping for a time. She glided quietly forward until a bell chimed faintly in the engine-room. Then she paused with a flourish of phosphorescent waters.

"Give the signal," said the captain. Three times a flash of light went from the bow. There was a moment of waiting. Then an eye like the one on the coast of Florida opened and closed, opened and closed, opened and closed. The Cubans, grouped in a great shadow on deck, burst into a low chatter of delight. A hiss from their leader silenced them.

"Well?" said the captain.

"All right," said the leader.

At the giving of the word it was not apparent that anyone on board of the *Foundling* had ever been seasick. The boats were lowered swiftly, too swiftly. Boxes of cartridges were dragged from the hold and passed over the side with a rapidity that made men in the boats exclaim against it. They were being bombarded. When a boat headed for shore its rowers pulled like madmen. The captain paced slowly to and fro on the bridge. In the engine-room the engineers stood at their station, and in the stoke-hole the firemen fidgeted silently around the furnace doors.

On the bridge Flanagan reflected. "Oh, I don't know," he observed, "this filibustering business isn't so bad. Pretty soon I'll be off to sea again with nothing to do but some big lying when I get into port."

In one of the boats returning from shore came twelve Cuban officers, the greater number of them convalescing from wounds, while two or three of them had been ordered to America on commissions from the insurgents. The captain welcomed them, and assured them of a speedy and safe voyage.

Presently he went again to the bridge and scanned the horizon. The sea was lonely like the spaces amid the suns. The captain grinned and softly smote his chest. "It's dead easy," said he.

It was near the end of the cargo, and the men were breathing like spent horses, although their elation grew with each moment, when suddenly a voice spoke from the sky. It was not a loud voice, but the quality of it brought every man on deck to full stop and motionless, as if they had all been changed to wax. "Captain," said the man at the masthead, "there's a light to the west'ard, sir. Think it's a steamer, sir."

There was a still moment until the captain called: "Well, keep your eye on it now." Speaking to the deck, he said: "Go ahead with your unloading."

The second engineer went to the galley to borrow a tin cup. "Hear the news, second?" asked the cook. "Steamer coming up from the west'ard."

"Gee!" said the second engineer. In the engine-room he said to the chief: "Steamer coming up to the west'ard, sir." The chief engineer began to test various little machines with which his domain was decorated. Finally he addressed the stoke-room. "Boys, I want you to look sharp now. There's a steamer coming up to the west'ard."

"All right, sir," said the stoke-room.

From time to time the captain hailed the masthead. "How is she now?"

"Seems to be coming down on us pretty fast, sir."

The Cuban leader came anxiously to the captain. "Do you think we can save all the cargo? It is rather delicate business. No?"

"Go ahead," said Flanagan. "Fire away. I'll wait for you."

There continued the hurried shuffling of feet on deck and the low cries of the men unloading the cargo. In the engine-room the chief and his assistant were staring at the gong. In the stoke-room the firemen breathed through their teeth. A shovel slipped from where it leaned against the side and banged on the floor. The stokers started and looked around quickly.

Climbing to the rail and holding on to a stay, the captain gazed westward. A light had raised out of the deep. After watching this light for a time he called to the Cuban leader,

"Well, as soon as you're ready now, we might as well be skipping out."

. Finally the Cuban leader told him: "Well, this is the last load. As soon as the boats come back you can be off."

"Shan't wait for all the boats," said the captain. "That fellow is too close." As the second boat came aboard, the *Foundling* turned, and like a black shadow stole seaward to cross the bows of the oncoming steamer. "Waited about ten minutes too long," said the captain to himself.

Suddenly the light in the west vanished. "Hum," said Flanagan, "he's up to some meanness." Everyone outside of the engine-rooms was set on watch. The *Foundling*, going at full speed into the northeast, slashed a wonderful trail of blue silver on the dark bosom of the sea.

A man on deck cried out hurriedly, "There she is, sir." Many eyes searched the western gloom, and one after another the glances of the men found a tiny black shadow on the deep with a line of white beneath it. "He couldn't be heading better if he had a line to us," said Flanagan.

There was a thin flash of red in the darkness. It was long and keen like a crimson rapier. A short, sharp report sounded, and then a shot whined swiftly in the air and blipped into the sea. The captain had been about to take a bite of plug tobacco at the beginning of this incident, and his arm was raised. He remained like a frozen figure while the shot whined, and then, as it blipped into the sea, his hand went to his mouth and he bit the plug. He looked wide-eyed at the shadow with its line of white.

The senior Cuban officer came hurriedly to the bridge. "It is no good to surrender," he cried; "they would only shoot or hang all of us."

There was another thin red flash and a report. A loud whirring noise passed over the ship.

"I'm not going to surrender," said the captain, hanging with both hands to the rail. He appeared like a man whose traditions of peace are clinched in his heart. He was as astonished as if his hat had turned into a dog. Presently he wheeled quickly and said: "What kind of a gun is that?"

"It is a one-pounder," cried the Cuban officer. "The boat is one of those little gunboats made from a yacht. You see?"

"Well, if it's only a yawl, he'll sink us in five more minutes," said Flanagan. For a moment he looked helplessly off at the horizon. His under jaw hung low. But, a moment later, something touched him like a stiletto point of inspiration. He leaped to the pilot-house and roared at the man at the wheel. The *Foundling* sheered suddenly to starboard, made a clumsy turn, and Flanagan was bellowing through the tube to the engine-room before anybody discovered that the old basket was heading straight for the Spanish gunboat. The ship lunged forward like a draught-horse on the gallop.

This strange manœuver by the *Foundling* first dealt consternation on board. Men instinctively crouched on the instant, and then swore their supreme oath, which was unheard by their own ears.

Later, the manœuver of the *Foundling* dealt consternation on board of the gunboat. She had been going victoriously forward, dim-eyed from the fury of her pursuit. Then this tall threatening shape had suddenly loomed over her like a giant apparition.

The people on board the *Foundling* heard panic shouts, hoarse orders. The little gunboat was paralyzed with astonishment.

Suddenly Flanagan yelled with rage and sprang for the wheel. The helmsman had turned his eyes away. As the captain whirled the wheel far to starboard he heard a crunch as the *Foundling*, lifted on a wave, smashed her shoulder against the gunboat, and he saw shooting past a little launch sort of a thing with men on her that ran this way and that way. The Cuban officers, joined by the cook and a seaman, emptied their revolvers into the surprised terror of the seas.

There was naturally no pursuit. Under comfortable speed the *Foundling* stood to the northward.

The captain went to his berth chuckling. "There, by God," he said. "There, now!"

IV

When Flanagan came again on deck, the first mate, his arm in a sling, walked the bridge. Flanagan was smiling a wide smile. The bridge of the *Foundling* was dipping afar and then afar. With each lunge of the little steamer the water seethed and boomed alongside and the spray dashed high and swiftly.

"Well," said Flanagan, inflating himself, " we've had a great deal of a time, and we've come through it all right, and thank heaven it is all over."

The sky in the northeast was of a dull brick-red in tone, shaded here and there by black masses that billowed out in some fashion from the flat heavens.

"Look there," said the mate.

"Hum," said the captain. "Looks like a blow, don't it?"

Later the surface of the water rippled and flickered in the preliminary wind. The sea had become the color of lead. The swashing sound of the waves on the sides of the *Foundling* was now provided with some manner of ominous significance. The men's shouts were hoarse.

A squall struck the *Foundling* on her starboard quarter, and she leaned under the force of it as if she were never to return to the even keel. "I'll be glad when we get in," said the mate. "I'm going to quit then. I've got enough."

"Hell!" said the beaming Flanagan.

The steamer crawled on into the northwest. The white water sweeping out from her deadened the chug-chug-chug of the tired old engines.

Once, when the boat careened, she laid her shoulder flat on the sea and rested in that manner. The mate, looking down the bridge, which slanted more than a coal-chute, whistled softly to himself. Slowly, heavily, the *Foundling* arose to meet another sea.

At night waves thundered mightily on the bows of the steamer, and water lit with the beautiful phosphorescent glamour went boiling and howling along the deck.

By good fortune the chief engineer crawled safely, but utterly drenched, to the galley for coffee. "Well, how goes it, chief?" said the cook, standing with his fat arms folded in order to prove that he could balance himself under any condition.

The engineer shook his head dejectedly. "This old biscuit-box will never see port again. Why, she'll fall to pieces."

Finally at night the captain said: "Launch the boats." The Cubans hovered about him. "Is the ship going to sink?" The captain addressed them politely. "Gentlemen, we are in trouble, but all I ask of you is that you do just what I tell you, and no harm will come to anybody."

The mate directed the lowering of the first boat, and the men performed this task with all decency, like people at the side of a grave.

A young oiler came to the captain. "The chief sends word, sir, that the water is almost up to the fires."

"Keep at it as long as you can."

"Keep at it as long as we can, sir."

Flanagan took the senior Cuban officer to the rail, and, as the steamer sheered high on a great sea, showed him a yellow dot on the horizon. It was smaller than a needle when its point is toward you.

"There," said the captain. The wind-driven spray was lashing his face. "That's Jupiter Light on the Florida coast. Put your men in the boat we've just launched, and the mate will take you to that light."

Afterward Flanagan turned to the chief engineer. "We can never beach her," said the old man. "The stokers have got to quit in a minute." Tears were in his eyes.

The *Foundling* was a wounded thing. She lay on the water with gasping engines, and each wave resembled her death blow.

Now the way of a good ship on the sea is finer than sword-play. But this is when she is alive. If a time comes that the ship dies, then her way is the way of a floating old glove, and she has that much vim, spirit, buoyancy. At this time many men on the *Foundling* suddenly came to know that they were clinging to a corpse.

The captain went to the stoke-room, and what he saw as he swung down the companion suddenly turned him hesitant and dumb. He had served the sea for many years, but this fire-room said something to him which he had not heard in his other voyages. Water was swirling to and fro with the roll of the ship, fuming greasily around half-strangled machinery that still attempted to perform its duty. Steam arose from the water, and through its clouds shone the red glare of the dying fires. As for the stokers, death might have been with silence in this room. One lay in his berth, his hands under his head, staring moodily at the wall. One sat near the foot of the companion, his face hidden in his arms. One leaned against the side, and gazed at the snarling water as it rose and its mad eddies among the machinery. In the unholy red light and grey mist of this stifling dim inferno they were strange figures with their silence and their immobility. The wretched *Foundling* groaned deeply as she lifted, and groaned deeply as she sank into the trough, while hurried waves then thundered over her with the noise of landslides. The terrified machinery was making gestures.

But Flanagan took control of himself suddenly, and then he stirred the fire-room. The stillness had been so unearthly that he was not altogether inapprehensive of strange and grim deeds when he charged into them, but precisely as they had submitted to the sea so they submitted to Flanagan. For a moment they rolled their eyes like hurt cows, but they obeyed the Voice. The situation simply required a Voice.

When the captain returned to the deck the hue of this fire-room was in his mind, and then he understood doom and its weight and complexion.

When finally the *Foundling* sank she shifted and settled as calmly as an animal curls down in the bush grass. Away over the waves two bobbing boats paused to witness this quiet death. It was a slow manœuver, altogether without the pageantry of uproar, but it flashed pallor into the faces of all men who saw it, and they groaned when they said: "There she goes!" Suddenly the captain whirled and knocked his head on the gunwale. He sobbed for a time, and then he sobbed and swore also.

There was a dance at the Imperial Inn. During the evening some irresponsible young men came from the beach bringing the statement that several boatloads of people had been perceived off shore. It was a charming dance, and none cared to take time to believe this tale. The fountain in the courtyard plashed softly, and couple after couple paraded through the aisles of palms where lamps with red shades threw a rose light upon the gleaming leaves. High on some balcony a mockingbird called into the evening. The band played its waltzes slumberously, and its music to the people among the palms came faintly and like the melodies in dreams.

Sometimes a woman said: "Oh, it is not really true, is it, that there was a wreck out at sea?"

A man usually said: "No, of course not."

At last, however, a youth came violently from the beach. He was triumphant in manner. "They're out there," he cried. "A whole boatload!" He received eager attention, and he told all that he supposed. His news destroyed the dance. After a time the band was playing beautifully to space. The guests had donned wraps and hurried to the beach. One little girl cried: "Oh, mamma, may I go too?" Being refused permission, she pouted.

As they came from the shelter of the great hotel, the wind was blowing swiftly from the sea, and at intervals a breaker shone livid. The women shuddered, and their bending companions seized opportunity to draw the cloaks closer. The sand of the beach was wet, and dainty slippers made imprints in it clear and deep.

"Oh, dear," said a girl, "supposin' they were out there drowning while we were dancing!"

"Oh, nonsense!" said her younger brother; "that don't happen."

"Well, it might, you know, Roger. How can you tell?"

A man who was not her brother gazed at her then with profound admiration. Later she complained of the damp sand, and drawing back her skirts, looked ruefully at her little feet.

A mother's son was venturing too near to the water in his interest and excitement. Occasionally she cautioned and reproached him from the background.

Save for the white glare of the breakers, the sea was a great wind-crossed void. From the throng of charming women floated the perfume of many flowers. Later there floated to them a body with a calm face of an Irish type. The expedition of the *Foundling* will never be historic.

GREECE

Contents

Greek War Correspondents

ATHENS, GREECE, MAY 1.—The advantage of international complication is the fact that it develops war correspondents. There are now exactly one hundred and thirty-one correspondents sitting in Constantinople, Athens and on the frontier. They seriously interfere with the movements of the two armies. They cloud the air and officers have to sweep the sky with brooms before they can gain a chance for their field glasses. The only creature that has not been thrown off its natural balance by this invasion is the bold flea of Greece. Even this could not disturb the calm industry of the Grecian flea. These animals operate with drills which they work by foot treadles, and afterward one feels as if one had been attacked by a fleet of red-hot stove lids. The fleas were superior to the correspondent. They continued to lead their untroubled life of work and they reaped about all the vengeance which Greece was able to get as a nation.

The earl of Perth Amboy, N.J., arrived here lately to represent a New York newspaper. He discovered at once that the Parthenon is too little, that it is far smaller than the American Tract Society building in New York. Then he looked over the Eastern question and said that it was absurd and departed in a cloud of dust upon which a stereopticon threw fresh details of the increase in circulation of his journal. He left Athens dripping with perspiration and blind and dazed with amazement. The diplomatic corps was particularly prostrated. Upon being informed that he was likely to return, the citizens are considering a plan to set fire to the city and retreat to the hills.

But this American whirlwind is a bottle of beer and a plate of crackers to the English correspondent who understands the Eastern question. Of course, one can't throw a stick into any part of Athens without hitting three men who understand the Eastern question, but the English correspondent has an iron-clad and immovable way of understanding a question which reminds one unmistakably of a god. He is perfectly simple and ingenuous about it. Apparently this ability to understand the Eastern question is given him because he is a British subject. He does not state this fact, but upon looking him over, one can see no other reason for his believing that he understands the Eastern question. He appropriates a knowledge of the Eastern question as blandly as his government appropriates an island or a tribe of negroes. The child-like air with which he recognizes his absolute infallibility is something very fascinating to those here who feel that the comprehension of the Eastern question is a mouse that sleeps in the mind of the empire of Russia, and if there is a man who knows aught of that mystic thing, he is a man with no tongue.

A consular officer who has devoted a number of years to the study of the peoples of the East and the conditions here was obliged by an obligation of social amiability to listen to a prolonged elucidation of the problems of the East by a London correspondent. The consular officer was not greatly bored, because by this time consular officers are inured to those phenomena. Finally when the London correspondent arrived at some phase of the situation to which the official had devoted study and time, the official indifferently gave his opinion. There was silence for a moment while the correspondent looked proudly at the official. Then the correspondent said: "On that subject I talk with men whose opinions I respect." He turned his back on the official.

His allusion to men whose opinions he would respect caused considerable excitement here and the first report of it was not credited. It was believed to be a rumor set afloat by the extremists. Finally public opinion decided that he must talk in his sleep.

But if the London correspondent here has an iron-clad and immovable sense of the divinity of his intelligence there are also in Athens American correspondents of the type who write to their journals: "I am the only correspondent up to the present time who has been able to penetrate to the fastnesses of Larissa. During the terrible journey across the desert that surrounds this city I was three times prostrated by the heat and had five horses die under me. My dragoman, Murphy, had his ears frost-bitten."

Seriously, people in official circles who are posted in all matters of news say there has not been a report sent from

Greece of this whoopetty-whoop description that is not terrifying in its assininity. The pity of it is that then the simple-minded people of Europe laugh at the poor correspondents instead of at the men who are really responsible for this sort of crime.

One expects foreigners to have a universal trust in the intelligence of the American people in the face of these splendid exhibitions.

There was a correspondent here who asked an interview of the king and because certain people took trouble for him he was granted it. He gave the interview to some of the Greek newspapers, also, and then by a singular juxtaposition of circumstances he left town. An aid-de-camp was sent to gather the editors of these newspapers and then an official spent a long time laboriously dictating the most sweeping denials. In delicate situations like an Eastern imbroglio an absurd interview is more than an annoyance. Later the correspondent cabled to his acquaintances in Athens to apply to the king for a decoration for him.

It would be deadly wrong not to speak now of the men who in affairs of this kind do their duty simply and faithfully and with no uproar. There is, for instance, an American correspondent here who has crossed Armenia in the midst of the troubles, who has lived in Crete with the insurgents and been in all the bombardments and fights there and who is now going to Arta in the hope of joining the wild band of volunteers who are about to raid into the troop-covered provinces of Turkey. In fact, he has as fine a record as a man can get out of such a situation. But, of course, no one knows him nor cares about it. He has no reputation at all relatively. His pay must naturally be in the same ratio.

To-day the king refused him an interview mainly because the wild ass of the desert who wanted a decoration had made the king wary of correspondents.

Crane at Velestino

ATHENS, MAY 10—(By Courier from Volo.)—When this war is done Velestino will be famed as its greatest battle.

The Greeks began with a reverse at Larissa, and the world expected the swiftest possible conclusion, but Velestino has proved that Greek soldiers when well led can cope successfully with Turks, even though outnumbered. This battle has proved them good fighters, long fighters, stayers. It must have surprised the world after Larissa.

I know all Greece rejoiced, and this battle's effect upon the Greek soldiers is like champagne. It made them perfectly happy. To be sure, the army retreated from Velestino, but it was no fault of this army. The commander bit his fingers and cursed when the order came to retreat. He knew that his army had victory within its grasp. For three days he had been holding the Turks beautifully in check, killing them as fast as they fell upon him. In the middle of intoxication of victory came the orders to fall back. Why? Reverses or something of the sort in other places may have been the reason, if there was a reason.

Smolenski knew, of course, that his retreat sacrificed Volo, and he raged like a soldier and a general. But, like a soldier and a general, he obeyed orders and the Turks occupied Velestino. And this after a three days' successful fight. The troops were jubilant, the commander confident—and then the Crown Prince ordered a retreat. My notion is that the Turks must have turned the far left of the Greeks. Probably by now New York knows more than Volo on this point. Anyhow, the Turks could never have turned the Greek right, and we who saw the worst of it feel doubts concerning the violence of the combat on the left.

The orders of retreat have crushed every man of this command. How the soldiers talked! Nobody wanted to fall back, save the few who would have fallen back anyhow. The Greeks understood the vastly superior number of the Turks, but they had whipped the vastly superior number of Turks three days and wanted to do it again.

Some other correspondents saw more of the battle than I did. I was rather laid up and had hurried on from Pharsala when I learned of the strong attack on Velestino. I knew that the taking of Velestino practically uncovered the base of the army at Volo, and so did not spare myself. But I only arrived at noon of the second day. I had seen skirmishes and small fights, but this was my first big battle.

The roll of musketry was tremendous. From a distance it was like tearing a cloth; nearer, it sounded like rain on a tin roof and close up it was just a long crash after crash. It was a beautiful sound—beautiful as I had never dreamed. It was more impressive than the roar of Niagara and finer than thunder or avalanche—because it had the wonder of human tragedy in it. It was the most beautiful sound of my experience, barring no symphony. The crash of it was ideal.

This is one point of view. Another might be taken from the men who died there.

The slaughter of the Turks was enormous. The fire of the Greeks was so fierce that the Turkish soldiers while charging shielded their eyes with their hands. Eight charges the Turks made on this day, and they were repulsed every time. The desperate Turkish cavalry even attacked their enemy on a steep, rocky hill. The insane, wicked squadrons were practically annihilated. Scattered fragments slid slowly back, leaving the plain black with wounded and dead men and horses. From a distance it was like a game. There was no blood, no expression, no horror to be seen.

All the assaults of the Turks this day resulted disastrously to them. The Greek troops fought with the steadiness of salaried bookkeepers, never tired, never complaining. It was a magnificent exhibition. The Greeks fought all the time with the artillery fire on them even in a musketry lull, but nobody minded anything. The Turks were in great numbers and fought according to the precepts of their religion. But the Greeks were never daunted and whipped them well. Sometimes it was fighting among gaunt hills, sometimes fighting on green plains; but always the Greeks held their position.

When night came shells burst infrequently, lighting the darkness. By the red flashes I saw the wounded taken to Volo.

There was very little outcry among them. They were mostly silent.

In the gray early morning the musketry fire began again. It rattled from hill to hill, batteries awoke and soon the whole play was resumed.

The Turkish guns were superior to those of the Greeks, who had mostly mountain howitzers. The Turkish artillery consisted principally of regulation field pieces, and I learned to curse the German officers who directed their fire. I think these officers are the normal results of German civilization, which teaches that a man should first of all be a soldier; ultimately he becomes simply a soldier, not a man at all. I consider these German officers hired assassins. One has strong feelings under such circumstances as these.

I watched for a long time the blue-clad Greek infantry march into position across a small plain. War takes a long time. The swiftness of chronological order of battle is not correct. A man has time to get shaved, or to lunch or to take a bath often in battles the descriptions of which read like a whirlwind. While I watched the Turks changed their attack from the Greek right on the plain to the Greek left on the rocky hill. Then the fighting became obscured from view.

The Greeks lay in trenches, snugly flattened against the dirt, firing carefully, while the Turks loomed close before them. Every ridge was fringed with smoke. I saw soldiers in the trench ease off and take a drink from their canteens, twist their cartridge belts to put the empty links behind them, or turn around to say something to a comrade. Then they went at it again.

I noticed one lieutenant standing up in the rear of a trench rolling a cigarette, his legs wide apart. In this careless attitude a shot went through his neck. His servant came from the trench and knelt weeping over the body, regardless of the battle. The men had to drag him in by the legs.

The reserves coming up passed a wayside shrine. The men paused to cross themselves and pray. A shell struck the shrine and demolished it. The men in the rear of the column were obliged to pray to the spot where the shrine had been.

An officer of a battery sent a man to the rear after another pair of field glasses, the first pair having been smashed by a

musket ball. The man brought a bottle of wine, having mis-
understood. Meanwhile the Turks were forming on a little
green hill 1,200 yards off. The officer was furious over the
man's mistake, but he never let go of that bottle of wine.

A member of the Foreign Legion came from the left,
wounded in the head. He was bandaged with magnificent
clumsiness with about nine yards of linen. I noticed a little
silk English flag embroidered on his sleeve. He was very sad
and said the battle was over. Most wounded men conclude
that the battle is over.

News came from the left that the Turks had tried to turn
the flank and failed. I saw no correspondents and supposed
them all to be in the thick of the fray.

The Turks formed on the right and moved slowly across
the plain and the battery of howitzers opened on them. I saw
troops moving to the rear to prevent a possible flank attack
in the direction of Volo.

The fight on the plain to the right began. Masses of Turk-
ish troops like shadows slowly moved toward the Greek
trenches indicated by gray lines of smoke. Shots began to rake
the trenches on the hill and to also rake the battery to the
rear. I hoped the Greeks on the plain would hurry and drive
the Turks from their position. They did it gallantly in a short,
ferocious infantry fight. The bit of woods where the fight oc-
curred seemed on fire. There was a great rattling and banging
and then the Turks went out defeated. There was general re-
joicing all along the Greek lines, the officers walked proudly,
the men in the trenches grinned. Then, mind you, just at this
time, late in the afternoon, after another successful day, came
the order to retreat.

Smolenski had apparently received the brunt of the fight-
ing. Yet the centre and left near Karadjah and at Pharsala had
again retired. No one could explain it. We were not aware of
the situation they faced, but it seemed an extraordinary order.

They say Smolenski wept.

I went down to see the retreat. A curious thing was that
the Turks seemed to understand the order as quickly as we
did. They moved up batteries with startling rapidity for the
Turks. Your correspondent got well shelled on his way.

The retreat was not disorderly, but wrathful and sullen. A

regiment of Ephzones, the kilted men, 2,000 strong, came down to cover the retreat and in the twilight, brightened by Turkish shells, the Greeks slowly withdrew. An order to advance and get whipped scares no soldiers, but an order to retreat scares a good many. No retreat can be as orderly as an advance. But this was distinctly a decent retreat. The troops moved at the usual time and kept well together.

A train came, the last Greek train to run on this road for a long time. It received a heavy fire. I wanted to see the engineer, but could not. There are few better men than this engineer even in the Greek army. A complication of a railroad accident and bombardment is a bad disease. All the way down on the train a man covered with bloody bandages talked to me in wild Greek.

I send this from Volo and before you print it the Turks will be here.

Stephen Crane Tells of War's Horrors

ATHENS, MAY 22 (On Board the *St. Marina*, Which Left Chalkis, Greece, May 18.)—We are carrying the wounded away from Domokos. There are eight hundred bullet-torn men aboard, some of them dead. This steamer was formerly used for transporting sheep, but it was taken by the Government for ambulance purposes. It is not a nice place for a well man, but war takes the finical quality out of its victims, and the soldiers do not complain. The ship is not large enough for its dreadful freight. But the men must be moved, and so 800 bleeding soldiers are jammed together in an insufferably hot hole, the light in which is so faint that we cannot distinguish the living from the dead.

Above the vibration of the machinery and the churning of the waves we have listened all night to the cries and groans of those who stopped the Turkish bullets in the trenches. Those who died, and there were not a few, could not be removed, and the corpses lay among the living men, shot through arm, chest, leg or jaw. The soldiers endured it with composure, I thought. Their indifference will never cease to be a marvel to me.

Near the hatch where I can see them is a man shot through the mouth. The bullet passed through both cheeks. He is asleep with his head pillowed on the bosom of a dead comrade. He had been awake for days, doubtless, marching on bread and water, to be finally wounded at Domokos and taken aboard this steamer. He is too weary to mind either his wound or his awful pillow. There is a breeze on the gulf and the ship is rolling, heaving one wounded man against the other.

Some of the wounded were taken off at Chalkis; the others will be taken to Athens, because there is not room for them in the Chalkis hospitals. Already we have traveled a night and a day under these cheerful circumstances that war brings to some of those who engage in it.

When we with our suffering freight arrived at Piraeus they were selling the newspaper extra, and people were shouting "Hurrah, hurrah for war!" And while they shouted a seemingly endless procession of stretchers proceeded from the ship, the still figures upon them.

I have seen Greek officers watch without a murmur women and children flocking away from their homes, fearing the Turks. And I saw these turn away. I heard even an English doctor groan deep in his chest when his eyes surveyed the ship's cargo. Words are not adequate to describe it. Yet the wounded soldiers themselves retained that marvelous composure, indifference, or whatever else you choose to call it.

There is just enough moaning and wailing to make a distinct chorus above the creaking of the deck timbers over that low hole where the lamps are smoking.

This is Wednesday, I think. We are at Stylidia. All day there have been clouds of dust upon the highroad over which Smolenski's division is retreating toward Thermopylae. The movement completely uncovers this place, and the Turks are advancing from Halmyros.

What I saw at Volo is repeated here. Every one is terror-stricken. The *Journal*'s dispatch boat, at Bay St. Marina, where the field hospital is located, was requested by the chief surgeon to go to Stylidia and save the last of the medicines of the field hospital. The dispatch boat took a schooner in tow and went to Stylidia, carrying an extra crew from the Greek warship. While the medicines were being put aboard I went ashore, where the last few women and children crowded the quay.

One long line of dust marked the road across the green plain where Smolenski marched away. And the people stared at this and then at the great mountains in back of the town, whence the Turks were coming. All the household goods of the city were piled on the pier. The town was completely empty, except for two battalions of Smolenski's rear guard, who slept in the streets, worn out, after a twenty hours' march. We loaded the steamer and schooner with women and children and household goods. The anchor was raised by two man-of-war's men, three fugitives and one Greek Red Cross nurse.

As we steamed away Smolenski's rear guard also left Stylidia. The beautiful little town, with its streets shaded by May trees and lemons and its ripening gardens, seemed to be putting on its best air, as to bid farewell to its citizens and to receive the Turks. The people on board are not looking at their city. They are asking if the Turks have reached Lamia and whether Thermopylae is safe.

With our departure Stylidia became as silent as a city of the dead. Its next inhabitants will be the Turkish soldiers. The steamer and schooner carried 183 people to safety, where the warships rode at anchor opposite Thermopylae. The women and children were drenched when we landed them in the small boats. There was a strong wind, and it was difficult, but our crew and the sailors from the warships worked like Trojans from the shore and back again. There were about thirty women with babies in their arms among the fugitives. The poor babies wailed and the mothers groaned. There were a lot of little girls, however, who sat quietly, not understanding what was the matter.

The refugees generally seemed dazed. The old women particularly. Uprooted from the spot they had lived so long, they kept their red eyes turned toward the shore as they sat on their rough bundles of clothes and blankets. Among the property we carried away was a goat and a calf, both protesting loudly. Our deck looked like an emigrant quarter of an Atlantic liner, except for the sick soldiers. The *Journal* steamer then went to St. Marina and landed the hospital stores.

Lieutenant-Colonel Caracolas came aboard there, much disturbed because some bread had been left at Stylidia. He was at the head of the commissary department of Smolenski's division. He asked us if we would try to get the bread. We agreed and found another schooner. We told the captain we were going to take him to Stylidia and he flatly refused to go. There was no time for argument; our extra bluejackets, seven in number, promptly stormed the schooner and took it by assault. I guess the captain of the schooner is talking of the outrage yet. The bluejackets got us a hawser, raised the anchor and we towed the protesting schooner back to Stylidia, with the captain on the bow, gesticulating violently throughout the voyage. Incidentally, we never found the bread.

Stylidia, now utterly deserted, was as dismal as a graveyard at midnight.

We steamed back to St. Marina and found Dr. Belline, chief

surgeon of the Greek army. He was worried about the safety of the hospital at St. Marina, but no orders had been issued for its removal. The obvious thing to do was to get orders from Thermopylae headquarters, and we carried the doctor across the gulf. He got the orders promptly and we took him back to St. Marina and took aboard the wounded men and Red Cross nurses of the hospital. The last boat had left the shore when a soldier came and said something to the interpreter, who shook his head negatively. The soldier turned quietly away.

On board the steamer your correspondent idly asked the interpreter what the soldier had said, and he answered that the soldier had asked for transportation to Chalkis on the ground that he was sick. The interpreter thought the man too well to go on a boat containing wounded men.

We sent ashore and after some trouble found the soldier. He was ill with fever, was shot through the calf of the leg and his knees were raw from kneeling in the trenches. We added him to our list of wounded and then steamed away for Chalkis.

There is more of this sort of thing in war than glory and heroic death, flags, banners, shouting and victory.

Death and the Child

I

THE PEASANTS who were streaming down the mountain trail had in their sharp terror evidently lost their ability to count. The cattle and the huge round bundles seemed to suffice to the minds of the crowd if there were now two in each case where there had been three. This brown stream poured on with a constant wastage of goods and beasts. A goat fell behind to scout the dried grass, and its owner, howling, flogging his donkeys, passed far ahead. A colt, suddenly frightened, made a stumbling charge up the hill-side. The expenditure was always profligate and always unnamed, unnoted. It was as if fear was a river, and this horde had simply been caught in the torrent, man tumbling over beast, beast over man, as helpless in it as the logs that fall and shoulder grindingly through the gorges of a lumber country. It was a freshet that might sear the face of the tall quiet mountain; it might draw a livid line across the land, this downpour of fear with a thousand homes adrift in the current—men, women, babes, animals. From it there arose a constant babble of tongues, shrill, broken, and sometimes choking as from men drowning. Many made gestures, painting their agonies on the air with fingers that twirled swiftly.

The blue bay with its pointed ships, and the white town lay below them, distant, flat, serene. There was upon this vista a peace that a bird knows when high in air it surveys the world, a great calm thing rolling noiselessly toward the end of the mystery. Here on the height one felt the existence of the universe scornfully defining the pain in ten thousand minds. The sky was an arch of stolid sapphire. Even to the mountains raising their mighty shapes from the valley, this headlong rush of the fugitives was too minute. The sea, the sky, and the hills combined in their grandeur to term this misery inconsequent. Then, too, it sometimes happened that a face seen as it passed on the flood reflected curiously the spirit of them all, and still more. One saw then a woman of the opinion of the vaults above the clouds. When a child cried it cried always because of some adjacent misfortune, some discomfort of a pack-saddle or rudeness of an encircling arm. In the dismal melody of this flight there were often sounding chords of apathy. Into these preoccupied countenances one felt that needles could be thrust without purchasing a scream. The trail wound here and there as the sheep had willed in the making of it.

Although this throng seemed to prove that the whole of humanity was fleeing in one direction—with every tie severed that binds us to the soil—a young man was walking rapidly up the mountain, hastening to a side of the path from time to time to avoid some particularly wide rush of people and cattle. He looked at everything in agitation and pity. Frequently he called admonitions to maniacal fugitives, and at other moments he exchanged strange stares with the imperturbable ones. They seemed to him to wear merely the expressions of so many boulders rolling down the hill. He exhibited wonder and awe with his pitying glances.

Turning once toward the rear, he saw a man in the uniform of a lieutenant of infantry marching the same way. He waited then, subconsciously elate at a prospect of being able to make into words the emotion which heretofore had only been expressed in the flash of eyes and sensitive movements of his flexible mouth. He spoke to the officer in rapid French, waving his arms wildly, and often pointing with a dramatic finger. "Ah, this is too cruel, too cruel, too cruel. Is it not? I did not think it would be as bad as this. I did not think—God's mercy—I did not think at all. And yet I am a Greek. Or at least my father was a Greek. I did not come here to fight. I am really a correspondent, you see? I was to write for an Italian paper. I have been educated in Italy. I have spent nearly all my life in Italy. At the schools and universities. I knew nothing of war! I was a student—a student. I came here merely because my father was a Greek, and for his sake I thought of Greece—I loved Greece. But I did not dream——"

He paused, breathing heavily. His eyes glistened from that soft overflow which comes on occasion to the glance of a young woman. Eager, passionate, profoundly moved, his first words while facing the procession of fugitives had been an active definition of his own dimension, his personal relation to men, geography, life. Throughout he had preserved the fiery dignity of a tragedian.

The officer's manner at once deferred to this outburst. "Yes," he said, polite but mournful, "these poor people! These poor people! I do not know what is to become of these poor people."

The young man declaimed again. "I had no dream—I had no dream that it would be like this! This is too cruel! Too cruel! Now I want to be a soldier. Now I want to fight. Now I want to do battle for the land of my father." He made a sweeping gesture into the northwest.

The officer was also a young man, but he was very bronzed and steady. Above his high military collar of crimson cloth with one silver star upon it, appeared a profile stern, quiet, and confident, respecting fate, fearing only opinion. His clothes were covered with dust; the only bright spot was the flame of the crimson collar. At the violent cries of his companion he smiled as if to himself, meanwhile keeping his eyes fixed in a glance ahead.

From a land toward which their faces were bent came a continuous boom of artillery fire. It was sounding in regular measures like the beating of a colossal clock—a clock that was counting the seconds in the lives of the stars, and men had time to die between the ticks. Solemn, oracular, inexorable, the great seconds tolled over the hills as if God fronted this dial rimmed by the horizon. The soldier and the correspondent found themselves silent. The latter in particular was sunk in a great mournfulness, as if he had resolved willy-nilly to swing to the bottom of the abyss where dwell secrets of this kind, and had learned beforehand that all to be met there was cruelty and hopelessness. A strap of his bright new leather leggings came unfastened, and he bowed over it slowly, impressively, as one bending over the grave of a child.

Then suddenly, the reverberations mingled until one could not separate an explosion from another, and into the hubbub came the drawling sound of a leisurely musketry fire. Instantly, for some reason of cadence, the noise was irritating, silly, infantile. This uproar was childish. It forced the nerves to object, to protest against this racket which was as idle as the din of a lad with a drum.

The lieutenant lifted his finger and pointed. He spoke in vexed tones, as if he held the other man personally responsible for the noise. "Well, there!" he said. "If you wish for war you now have an opportunity magnificent."

The correspondent raised himself upon his toes. He tapped his chest with gloomy pride. "Yes! There is war! There is the war I wish to enter. I fling myself in. I am a Greek, a Greek, you understand. I wish to fight for my country. You know the way. Lead me. I offer myself." Struck with a sudden thought, he brought a case from his pocket, and extracting a card handed it to the officer with a bow. "My name is Peza," he said simply.

A strange smile passed over the soldier's face. There was pity and pride—the vanity of experience—and contempt in it. "Very well," he said, returning the bow. "If my company is in the middle of the fight I shall be glad for the honor of your companionship. If my company is not in the middle of the fight, I will make other arrangements for you."

Peza bowed once more, very stiffly, and correctly spoke his thanks. On the edge of what he took to be a great venture toward death, he discovered that he was annoyed at something in the lieutenant's tone. Things immediately assumed new and extraordinary proportions. The battle, the great carnival of woe, was sunk at once to an equation with a vexation by a stranger. He wanted to ask the lieutenant what was his meaning. He bowed again majestically; the lieutenant bowed. They flung a shadow of manners, of capering tinsel ceremony across a land that groaned, and it satisfied something within themselves completely.

In the meantime the river of fleeing villagers had changed to simply a last dropping of belated creatures, who fled past stammering and flinging their hands high. The two men had come to the top of the great hill. Before them was a green plain as level as an inland sea. It swept northward, and merged finally into a length of silvery mist. Upon the near part of this plain, and upon two grey treeless mountains at the sides of it, were little black lines from which floated slanting sheets of smoke. It was not a battle to the nerves. One could survey it with equanimity, as if it were a tea-table; but upon Peza's mind it struck a loud clanging blow. It was war.

Edified, aghast, triumphant, he paused suddenly, his lips apart. He remembered the pageants of carnage that had marched through the dreams of his childhood. Love he knew that he had confronted, alone, isolated, wondering, an individual, an atom taking the hand of a titanic principle. But like the faintest breeze on his forehead, he felt here the vibration from the hearts of forty thousand men.

The lieutenant's nostrils were moving. "I must go at once," he said. "I must go at once."

"I will go with you wherever you go," shouted Peza loudly.

A primitive track wound down the side of the mountain, and in their rush they bounded from here to there, choosing risks which in the ordinary caution of man would surely have seemed of remarkable danger. The ardor of the correspondent surpassed the full energy of the soldier. Several times he turned and shouted: "Come on! Come on!"

At the foot of the path they came to a wide road which extended toward the battle in a yellow and straight line. Some men were trudging wearily to the rear. They were without rifles; their clumsy uniforms were dirty and all awry. They turned eyes dully aglow with fever upon the pair striding toward the battle. Others were bandaged with the triangular kerchief upon which one could still see through blood-stains the little explanatory pictures illustrating the ways to bind various wounds. "Fig. 1."—"Fig. 2."—"Fig. 7." Mingled with the pacing soldiers were peasants, indifferent, capable of smiling, gibbering about the battle, which was to them an ulterior drama. A man was leading a string of three donkeys to the rear, and at intervals he was accosted by wounded or fevered soldiers, from whom he defended his animals with ape-like cries and mad gesticulation. After much chattering they usually subsided gloomily, and allowed him to go with his sleek little beasts unburdened. Finally he encountered a soldier who walked slowly with the assistance of a staff. His head was bound with a wide bandage, grimy from blood and mud. He made application to the peasant, and immediately they were involved in a hideous Levantine discussion. The peasant whined and clamored, sometimes spitting like a kitten. The wounded soldier jawed on thunderously, his great hands stretched in claw-like graspings over the peasant's head. Once he raised his staff and made threat with it. Then suddenly the row was at an end. The other sick men saw their comrade mount the leading donkey and at once begin to drum with his heels. None attempted to gain the backs of the remaining animals. They gazed after him dully. Finally they saw the caravan outlined for a moment against the sky. The soldier was still waving his arms passionately, having it out with the peasant.

Peza was alive with despair for these men who looked at him with such doleful, quiet eyes. "Ah, my God!" he cried to the lieutenant, "these poor souls! These poor souls!"

The officer faced about angrily. "If you are coming with me there is no time for this." Peza obeyed instantly and with a sudden meekness. In the moment some portion of egotism left him, and he modestly wondered if the universe took cognizance of him to an important degree. This theatre for slaughter, built by the inscrutable needs of the earth, was an enormous affair, and he reflected that the accidental destruction of an individual, Peza by name, would perhaps be nothing at all.

With the lieutenant, he was soon walking along behind a series of little crescent-shaped trenches, in which were soldiers tranquilly interested, gossiping with the hum of a tea-party. Although these men were not at this time under fire, he concluded that they were fabulously brave. Else they would not be so comfortable, so at home in their sticky brown trenches. They were certain to be heavily attacked before the day was old. The universities had not taught him to understand this attitude. At the passing of the young man in very nice tweed, with his new leggings, his new white helmet, his new field-glass case, his new revolver holster, the soiled soldiers turned with the same curiosity which a being in strange garb meets at the corners of streets. He might as well have been promenading a populous avenue. The soldiers volubly discussed his identity.

To Peza there was something awful in the absolute familiarity of each tone, expression, gesture. These men, menaced with battle, displayed the curiosity of the café. Then, on the verge of his great encounter toward death, he found himself extremely embarrassed, composing his face with difficulty, wondering what to do with his hands, like a gawk at a levee.

He felt ridiculous, and also he felt awed, aghast, at these men who could turn their faces from the ominous front and debate his clothes, his business. There was an element which was new born into his theory of war. He was not averse to the brisk pace at which the lieutenant moved along the line.

The roar of fighting was always in Peza's ears. It came from some short hills ahead and to the left. The road curved suddenly and entered a wood. The trees stretched their luxuriant and graceful branches over grassy slopes. A breeze made all this verdure gently rustle and speak in long silken sighs. Absorbed in listening to the hurricane racket from the front, he still remembered that these trees were growing, the grass-blades were extending according to their process. He inhaled a deep breath of moisture and fragrance from the grove, a wet odor which expressed all the opulent fecundity of unmoved nature, marching on with her million plans for multiple life, multiple death.

Further on they came to a place where the Turkish shells were landing. There was a long hurtling sound in the air, and then one had sight of a shell. To Peza it was of the conical missiles which friendly officers had displayed to him on board warships. Curiously enough, too, this first shell smacked of the foundry, of men with smudged faces, of the blare of furnace fires. It brought machinery immediately into his mind. He thought that if he was killed there at that time it would be as romantic, to the old standards, as death by a bit of falling iron in a factory.

II

A child was playing on a mountain, and disregarding a battle that was waging on the plain. Behind him was the little cobbled hut of his fled parents. It was now occupied by a pearl-colored cow that stared out from the darkness, thoughtful and tender-eyed. The child ran to and fro, fumbling with sticks and making great machinations with pebbles. By a striking exercise of artistic license the sticks were ponies, cows, and dogs, and the pebbles were sheep. He was managing large agricultural and herding affairs. He was too intent on them to pay much heed to the fight four miles away, which at that distance resembled in sound the beating of surf upon rocks. However, there were occasions when some louder outbreak of that thunder stirred him from his serious occupation, and he turned then a questioning eye upon the battle, a small stick poised in his hand, interrupted in the act of sending his dog after his sheep. His tranquillity in regard to the death on the plain was as invincible as that of the mountain on which he stood.

It was evident that fear had swept the parents away from their home in a manner that could make them forget this child, the first-born. Nevertheless, the hut was cleaned bare. The cow had committed no impropriety in billeting herself at the domicile of her masters. This smoke-colored and odorous interior contained nothing as large as a humming-bird. Terror had operated on these runaway people in its sinister fashion, elevating details to enormous heights, causing a man to remember a button while he forgot a coat, overpowering every one with recollections of a broken coffee-cup, deluging them with fears for the safety of an old pipe, and causing them to forget their first-born. Meanwhile the child played soberly with his trinkets.

He was solitary; engrossed in his own pursuits, it was seldom that he lifted his head to inquire of the world why it made so much noise. The stick in his hand was much larger to him than was an army corps of the distance. It was too childish for the mind of the child. He was dealing with sticks.

The battle lines writhed at times in the agony of a sea-creature on the sands. These tentacles flung and waved in a supreme excitement of pain, and the struggles of the great outlined body brought it nearer and nearer to the child. Once he looked at the plain and saw some men running wildly across a field. He had seen people chasing obdurate beasts in such fashion, and it struck him immediately that it was a manly thing which he would incorporate in his game. Consequently he raced furiously at his stone sheep, flourishing a cudgel, crying the shepherd calls. He paused frequently to get a cue of manner from the soldiers fighting on the plain. He reproduced, to a degree, any movements which he accounted rational to his theory of sheep-herding, the business of men, the traditional and exalted living of his father.

III

It was as if Peza was a corpse walking on the bottom of the sea, and finding there fields of grain, groves, weeds, the faces of men, voices. War, a strange employment of the race, presented to him a scene crowded with familiar objects which wore the livery of their commonness placidly, undauntedly. He was smitten with keen astonishment; a spread of green grass lit with the flames of poppies was too old for the company of this new ogre. If he had been devoting the full lens of his mind to this phase, he would have known he was amazed that the trees, the flowers, the grass, all tender and peaceful nature had not taken to heels at once upon the outbreak of battle. He venerated the immovable poppies.

The road seemed to lead into the apex of an angle formed by the two defensive lines of the Greeks. There was a straggle of wounded men and of gunless and jaded men. These latter did not seem to be frightened. They remained very cool, walking with unhurried steps and busy in gossip. Peza tried to define them. Perhaps during the fight they had reached the limit of their mental storage, their capacity for excitement, for tragedy, and had then simply come away. Peza remembered his visit to a certain place of pictures, where he had found himself amid heavenly skies and diabolic midnights—the sunshine beating red upon desert sands, nude bodies flung to the shore in the green moon-glow, ghastly and starving men clawing at a wall in darkness, a girl at her bath with screened rays falling upon her pearly shoulders, a dance, a funeral, a review, an execution, all the strength of argus-eyed art; and he had whirled and whirled amid this universe with cries of woe and joy, sin and beauty, piercing his ears until he had been obliged to simply come away. He remembered that as he had emerged he had lit a cigarette with unction and advanced promptly to a café. A great hollow quiet seemed to be upon the earth.

This was a different case, but in his thoughts he conceded

the same causes to many of these gunless wanderers. They too may have dreamed at lightning speed until the capacity for it was overwhelmed. As he watched them he again saw himself walking toward the café, puffing upon his cigarette. As if to reinforce his theory, a soldier stopped him with an eager but polite inquiry for a match. He watched the man light his little roll of tobacco and paper and begin to smoke ravenously.

Peza no longer was torn with sorrow at the sight of wounded men. Evidently he found that pity had a numerical limit, and when this was passed the emotion became another thing. Now, as he viewed them, he merely felt himself very lucky, and beseeched the continuance of his superior fortune. At the passing of these slouched and stained figures he now heard a reiteration of warning. A part of himself was appealing through the medium of these grim shapes. It was plucking at his sleeve and pointing, telling him to beware, and so it had come to pass that he cared for the implacable misery of these soldiers only as he would have cared for the harms of broken dolls. His whole vision was focussed upon his own chance.

The lieutenant suddenly halted. "Look," he said. "I find that my duty is in another direction. I must go another way. But if you wish to fight you have only to go forward, and any officer of the fighting line will give you opportunity." He raised his cap ceremoniously; Peza raised his new white helmet. The stranger to battles uttered thanks to his chaperon, the one who had presented him. They bowed punctiliously, staring at each other with civil eyes.

The lieutenant moved quietly away through a field. In an instant it flashed upon Peza's mind that this desertion was perfidious. He had been subjected to a criminal discourtesy. The officer had fetched him into the middle of the thing, and then left him to wander helplessly toward death. At one time he was upon the point of shouting at the officer.

In the vale there was an effect as if one was then beneath the battle. It was going on above somewhere. Alone, unguided, Peza felt like a man groping in a cellar. He reflected, too, that one should always see the beginning of a fight. It was too difficult to thus approach it when the affair was in full swing. The trees hid all movements of troops from him, and he thought he might be walking out to the very spot which chance had provided for the reception of a fool. He asked eager questions of passing soldiers. Some paid no heed to him; others shook their heads mournfully. They knew nothing save that war was hard work. If they talked at all it was in testimony of having fought well, savagely. They did not know if the army was going to advance, hold its ground, or retreat; they were weary.

A long pointed shell flashed through the air and struck near the base of a tree with a fierce upheaval, compounded of earth and flames. Looking back, Peza could see the shattered tree quivering from head to foot. Its whole being underwent a convulsive tremor which was an exhibition of pain and, furthermore, deep amazement. As he advanced through the vale the shells continued to hiss and hurtle in long low flights, and the bullets purred in the air. The missiles were flying into the breast of an astounded nature. The landscape, bewildered, agonized, was suffering a rain of infamous shots, and Peza imagined a million eyes gazing at him with the gaze of startled antelopes.

There was a resolute crashing of musketry from the tall hill on the left, and from directly in front there was a mingled din of artillery and musketry firing. Peza felt that his pride was playing a great trick in forcing him forward in this manner under conditions of strangeness, isolation, and ignorance. But he recalled the manner of the lieutenant, the smile on the hilltop among the flying peasants. Peza blushed and pulled the peak of his helmet down on his forehead. He strode onward firmly. Nevertheless, he hated the lieutenant, and he resolved that on some future occasion he would take much trouble to arrange a stinging social revenge upon that grinning jackanapes. It did not occur to him until later that he was now going to battle mainly because at a previous time a certain man had smiled.

IV

The road moved around the base of a little hill, and on this hill a battery of mountain guns was leisurely shelling something unseen. In the lee of the height the mules, contented under their heavy saddles, were quietly browsing the long grass. Peza ascended the hill by a slanting path. He felt his heart beat swiftly; once at the top of the hill he would be obliged to look this phenomenon in the face. He hurried, with a mysterious idea of preventing by this strategy the battle from making his appearance a signal for some tremendous renewal. This vague thought seemed logical at the time. Certainly this living thing had knowledge of his coming. He endowed it with the intelligence of a barbaric deity. And so he hurried; he wished to surprise war, this terrible emperor, when it was only growling on its throne. The ferocious and horrible sovereign was not to be allowed to make the arrival a pretext for some fit of smoky rage and blood. In this half-lull, Peza had distinctly the sense of stealing upon the battle unawares.

The soldiers watching the mules did not seem to be impressed by anything august. Two of them sat side by side and talked comfortably; another lay flat upon his back staring dreamily at the sky; another cursed a mule for certain refractions. Despite their uniforms, their bandoleers and rifles, they were dwelling in the peace of hostlers. However, the long shells were whooping from time to time over the brow of the hill, and swirling in almost straight lines toward the vale of trees, flowers, and grass. Peza, hearing and seeing the shells, and seeing the pensive guardians of the mules, felt reassured. They were accepting the condition of war as easily as an old sailor accepts the chair behind the counter of a tobacco-shop. Or it was merely that the farm-boy had gone to sea, and he had adjusted himself to the circumstances immediately, and with only the usual first misadventures in conduct. Peza was proud and ashamed that he was not of them, these stupid peasants, who, throughout the world, hold potentates on their thrones, make statesmen illustrious, provide generals with lasting victories, all with ignorance, indifference, or half-witted hatred, moving the world with the strength of their arms and getting their heads knocked together in the name of God, the king, or the Stock Exchange—immortal, dreaming, hopeless asses who surrender their reason to the care of a shining puppet, and persuade some toy to carry their lives in his purse. Peza mentally abased himself before them, and wished to stir them with furious kicks.

As his eyes ranged above the rim of the plateau, he saw a group of artillery officers talking busily. They turned at once and regarded his ascent. A moment later a row of infantry soldiers in a trench beyond the little guns all faced him. Peza bowed to the officers. He understood at the time that he had made a good and cool bow, and he wondered at it, for his breath was coming in gasps; he was stifling from sheer excitement. He felt like a tipsy man trying to conceal his muscular uncertainty from the people in the street. But the officers did not display any knowledge. They bowed. Behind them Peza saw the plain, glittering green, with three lines of black marked upon it heavily. The front of the first of these lines was frothy with smoke. To the left of this hill was a craggy mountain, from which came a continual dull rattle of musketry. Its summit was ringed with the white smoke. The black lines on the plain slowly moved. The shells that came from there passed overhead with the sound of great birds frantically flapping their wings. Peza thought of the first sight of the sea during a storm. He seemed to feel against his face the wind that races over the tops of cold and tumultuous billows.

He heard a voice afar off. "Sir, what would you?" He turned, and saw the dapper captain of the battery standing beside him. Only a moment had elapsed. "Pardon me, sir," said Peza, bowing again. The officer was evidently reserving his bows; he scanned the new-comer attentively. "Are you a correspondent?" he asked. Peza produced a card. "Yes, I came as a correspondent," he replied, "but now, sir, I have other thoughts. I wish to help. You see? I wish to help."

"What do you mean?" said the captain. "Are you a Greek? Do you wish to fight?"

"Yes, I am a Greek. I wish to fight." Peza's voice surprised him by coming from his lips in even and deliberate tones. He thought with gratification that he was behaving rather well. Another shell travelling from some unknown point on the plain whirled close and furiously in the air, pursuing an apparently horizontal course, as if it were never going to touch the earth. The dark shape swished across the sky.

"Ah," cried the captain, now smiling, "I am not sure that we will be able to accommodate you with a fierce affair here just at this time, but——" He walked gaily to and fro behind the guns with Peza, pointing out to him the lines of the Greeks, and describing his opinion of the general plan of defence. He wore the air of an amiable host. Other officers questioned Peza in regard to the politics of the war. The king, the ministry, Germany, England, Russia, all these huge words were continually upon their tongues. "And the people in Athens? Were they——" Amid this vivacious babble Peza, seated upon an ammunition box, kept his glance high, watching the appearance of shell after shell. These officers were like men who had been lost for days in the forest. They were thirsty for any scrap of news. Nevertheless, one of them would occasionally dispute their informant courteously. What would Servia have to say to that? No, no, France and Russia could never allow it. Peza was elated. The shells killed no one; war was not so bad. He was simply having coffee in the smoking-room of some embassy where reverberate the names of nations.

A rumor had passed along the motley line of privates in the trench. The new arrival with the clean white helmet was a famous English cavalry officer come to assist the army with his counsel. They stared at the figure of him, surrounded by officers. Peza, gaining sense of the glances and whispers, felt that his coming was an event.

Later, he resolved that he could with temerity do something finer. He contemplated the mountain where the Greek infantry was engaged, and announced leisurely to the captain of the battery that he thought presently of going in that direction and getting into the fight. He re-affirmed the sentiments of a patriot. The captain seemed surprised. "Oh, there will be fighting here at this knoll in a few minutes," he said orientally. "That will be sufficient? You had better stay with us. Besides, I have been ordered to resume fire." The officers all tried to dissuade him from departing. It was really not worth the trouble. The battery would begin again directly. Then it would be amusing for him.

Peza felt that he was wandering with his protestations of high patriotism through a desert of sensible men. These officers gave no heed to his exalted declarations. They seemed too jaded. They were fighting the men who were fighting them. Palaver of the particular kind had subsided before their intense preoccupation in war as a craft. Moreover, many men had talked in that manner, and only talked.

Peza believed at first that they were treating him delicately. They were considerate of his inexperience. War had turned out to be such a gentle business that Peza concluded he could scorn this idea. He bade them a heroic farewell despite their objections.

However, when he reflected upon their ways afterward, he saw dimly that they were actuated principally by some universal childish desire for a spectator of their fine things. They were going into action, and they wished to be seen at war, precise and fearless.

V

Climbing slowly to the high infantry position, Peza was amazed to meet a soldier whose jaw had been half shot away, and who was being helped down the sheep track by two tearful comrades. The man's breast was drenched with blood, and from a cloth which he held to the wound drops were splashing wildly upon the stones of the path. He gazed at Peza for a moment. It was a mystic gaze, which Peza withstood with difficulty. He was exchanging looks with a spectre; all aspect of the man was somehow gone from this victim. As Peza went on, one of the unwounded soldiers loudly shouted to him to return and assist in this tragic march. But even Peza's fingers revolted; he was afraid of the spectre; he would not have dared to touch it. He was surely craven in the movement of refusal he made to them. He scrambled hastily on up the path. He was running away.

At the top of the hill he came immediately upon a part of the line that was in action. Another battery of mountain guns was here firing at the streaks of black on the plain. There were trenches filled with men lining parts of the crest, and near the base were other trenches, all crashing away mightily. The plain stretched as far as the eye could see, and from where silver mist ended this emerald ocean of grass, a great ridge of snow-topped mountains poised against a fleckless blue sky. Two knolls, green and yellow with grain, sat on the prairie confronting the dark hills of the Greek position. Between them were the lines of the enemy. A row of trees, a village, a stretch of road, showed faintly on this great canvas, this tremendous picture; but men, the Turkish battalions, were emphasized startlingly upon it. The ranks of troops between the knolls and the Greek position were as black as ink. The first line, of course, was muffled in smoke, but at the rear of it battalions crawled up and to and fro plainer than beetles on a plate. Peza had never understood that masses of men were so declarative, so unmistakable, as if nature makes every arrangement to give information of the coming and the presence of destruction, the end, oblivion. The firing was full, complete, a roar of cataracts, and this pealing of connected volleys was adjusted to the grandeur of the far-off range of snowy mountains. Peza, breathless, pale, felt that he had been set upon a pillar and was surveying mankind, the world. In the meantime dust had got in his eye. He took his handkerchief and mechanically administered to it.

An officer with a double stripe of purple on his trousers paced in the rear of the battery of howitzers. He waved a little cane. Sometimes he paused in his promenade to study the field through his glasses. "A fine scene, sir," he cried airily, upon the approach of Peza. It was like a blow in the chest to the wide-eyed volunteer. It revealed to him a point of view. "Yes, sir, it is a fine scene," he answered. They spoke in French. "I am happy to be able to entertain monsieur with a little fine practice," continued the officer. "I am firing upon that mass of troops you see there a little to the right. They are probably forming for another attack." Peza smiled; here again appeared manners, manners erect by the side of death.

The right-flank gun of the battery thundered; there was a belch of fire and smoke; the shell flung swiftly and afar was known only to the ear in which rang a broadening hooting wake of sound. The howitzer had thrown itself backward convulsively, and lay with its wheels moving in the air as a squad of men rushed toward it. And later, it seemed as if each little gun had made the supreme effort of its being in each particular shot. They roared with voices far too loud, and the thunderous effort caused a gun to bound as in a dying convulsion. And then occasionally one was hurled with wheels in air. These shuddering howitzers presented an appearance of so many cowards always longing to bolt to the rear, but being implacably held up to their business by this throng of soldiers, who ran in squads to drag them up again to their obligation. The guns were herded and cajoled and bullied interminably. One by one, in relentless program, they were dragged forward to contribute a profound vibration of steel and wood, a flash and a roar, to the important happiness of man.

The adjacent infantry celebrated a good shot with smiles and an outburst of gleeful talk.

"Look, sir," cried an officer once to Peza. Thin smoke was drifting lazily before Peza, and, dodging impatiently, he brought his eyes to bear upon that part of the plain indicated by the officer's finger. The enemy's infantry was advancing to attack. From the black lines had come forth an inky mass, which was shaped much like a human tongue. It advanced slowly, casually, without apparent spirit, but with an insolent confidence that was like a proclamation of the inevitable.

The impetuous part was all played by the defensive side. Officers called, men plucked each other by the sleeve; there were shouts, motions; all eyes were turned upon the inky mass which was flowing toward the base of the hills, heavily, languorously, as oily and thick as one of the streams that ooze through a swamp.

Peza was chattering a question at every one. In the way, pushed aside, or in the way again, he continued to repeat it. "Can they take the position? Can they take the position? Can they take the position?" He was apparently addressing an assemblage of deaf men. Every eye was busy watching every hand. The soldiers did not even seem to see the interesting stranger in the white helmet who was crying out so feverishly.

Finally, however, the hurried captain of the battery espied him and heeded his question. "No, sir! No, sir! It is impossible," he shouted angrily. His manner seemed to denote that if he had had sufficient time he would have completely insulted Peza. The latter swallowed the crumb of news without regard to the coating of scorn, and, waving his hand in adieu, he began to run along the crest of the hill toward the part of the Greek line against which the attack was directed.

VI

Peza, as he ran along the crest of the mountain, believed that his action was receiving the wrathful attention of the hosts of the foe. To him then it was incredible foolhardiness thus to call to himself the stares of thousands of hateful eyes. He was like a lad induced by playmates to commit some indiscretion in a cathedral. He was abashed; perhaps he even blushed as he ran. It seemed to him that the whole solemn ceremony of war had paused during this commission. So he scrambled wildly over the rocks in his haste to end the embarrassing ordeal. When he came among the crowning rifle-pits filled with eager soldiers he wanted to yell with joy. None noticed him save a young officer of infantry, who said: "Sir, what do you want?" It was obvious that people had devoted some attention to their own affairs.

Peza asserted, in Greek, that he wished above everything to battle for the fatherland. The officer nodded; with a smile he pointed to some dead men covered with blankets, from which were thrust upturned dusty shoes.

"Yes, I know, I know," cried Peza. He thought the officer was poetically alluding to the danger.

"No," said the officer at once. "I mean cartridges—a bandoleer. Take a bandoleer from one of them."

Peza went cautiously toward a body. He moved a hand toward the corner of a blanket. There he hesitated, stuck, as if his arm had turned to plaster. Hearing a rustle behind him, he spun quickly. Three soldiers of the close rank in the trench were regarding him. The officer came again and tapped him on the shoulder. "Have you any tobacco?" Peza looked at him in bewilderment. His hand was still extended toward the blanket which covered the dead soldier. "Yes," he said, "I have some tobacco." He gave the officer his pouch. As if in compensation, the other directed a soldier to strip the bandoleer from the corpse. Peza, having crossed the long cartridge-belt on his breast, felt that the dead man had flung his two arms around him.

A soldier with a polite nod and smile gave Peza a rifle, a relic of another dead man. Thus, he felt, besides the clutch of a corpse about his neck, that the rifle was as unhumanly horrible as a snake that lives in a tomb. He heard at his ear something that was in effect like the voices of those two dead men, their low voices speaking to him of bloody death, mutilation. The bandoleer gripped him tighter; he wished to raise his hands to his throat like a man who is choking. The rifle was clammy; upon his palms he felt the movement of the sluggish currents of a serpent's life; it was crawling and frightful.

All about him were these peasants, with their interested countenances, gibbering of the fight. From time to time a soldier cried out in semi-humorous lamentations descriptive of his thirst. One bearded man sat munching a great bit of hard bread. Fat, greasy, squat, he was like an idol made of tallow. Peza felt dimly that there was a distinction between this man and a young student who could write sonnets and play the piano quite well. This old blockhead was coolly gnawing at the bread, while he, Peza, was being throttled by a dead man's arms.

He looked behind him, and saw that a head by some chance had been uncovered from its blanket. Two liquid-like eyes were staring into his face. The head was turned a little sideways as if to get better opportunity for the scrutiny. Peza could feel himself blanch; he was being drawn and drawn by these dead men slowly, firmly down as to some mystic chamber under the earth where they could walk, dreadful figures, swollen and blood-marked. He was bidden; they had commanded him; he was going, going, going.

When the man in the new white helmet bolted for the rear, many of the soldiers in the trench thought that he had been struck. But those who had been nearest to him knew better. Otherwise they would have heard the silken, sliding, tender noise of the bullet and the thud of its impact. They bawled after him curses, and also outbursts of self-congratulation and vanity. Despite the prominence of the cowardly part, they were enabled to see in this exhibition a fine comment upon their own fortitude. The other soldiers thought that Peza had been wounded somewhere in the neck, because as he ran he was tearing madly at the bandoleer, the dead man's arms. The

soldier with the bread paused in his eating and cynically re-
marked upon the speed of the runaway.

An officer's voice was suddenly heard calling out the cal-
culation of the distance to the enemy, the readjustment of the
sights. There was a stirring rattle along the line. The men
turned their eyes to the front. Other trenches beneath them
to the right were already heavily in action. The smoke was
lifting toward the blue sky. The soldier with the bread placed
it carefully on a bit of paper beside him as he turned to kneel
in the trench.

VII

In the late afternoon, the child ceased his play on the
mountain with his flocks and his dogs. Part of the battle had
whirled very near to the base of his hill, and the noise was
great. Sometimes he could see fantastic smoky shapes which
resembled the curious figures in foam which one sees on the
slant of a rough sea. The plain, indeed, was etched in white
circles and whirligigs like the slope of a colossal wave. The
child took seat on a stone and contemplated the fight. He was
beginning to be astonished; he had never before seen cattle
herded with such uproar. Lines of flame flashed out here and
there. It was mystery.

Finally, without any preliminary indication, he began to
weep. If the men struggling on the plain had had time and
greater vision, they could have seen this strange tiny figure
seated on a boulder, surveying them while the tears streamed.
It was as simple as some powerful symbol.

As the magic clear light of day amid the mountains
dimmed the distances, and the plain shone as a pallid blue
cloth marked by the red threads of the firing, the child arose
and moved off to the unwelcoming door of his home. He
called softly for his mother, and complained of his hunger in
the familiar formulæ. The pearl-colored cow, grinding her
jaws thoughtfully, stared at him with her large eyes. The
peaceful gloom of evening was slowly draping the hills.

The child heard a rattle of loose stones on the hill-side, and
facing the sound, saw a moment later a man drag himself up
to the crest of the hill and fall panting. Forgetting his mother

and his hunger, filled with calm interest, the child walked forward and stood over the heaving form. His eyes, too, were now large and inscrutably wise and sad, like those of the animal in the house.

After a silence, he spoke inquiringly. "Are you a man?"

Peza rolled over quickly and gazed up into the fearless cherubic countenance. He did not attempt to reply. He breathed as if life was about to leave his body. He was covered with dust; his face had been cut in some way, and his cheek was ribboned with blood. All the spick of his former appearance had vanished in a general dishevelment, in which he resembled a creature that had been flung to and fro, up and down, by cliffs and prairies during an earthquake. He rolled his eye glassily at the child.

They remained thus until the child repeated his words. "Are you a man?"

Peza gasped in the manner of a fish. Palsied, windless, and abject, he confronted the primitive courage, the sovereign child, the brother of the mountains, the sky and the sea, and he knew that the definition of his misery could be written on a wee grass-blade.

ENGLAND AND IRELAND, 1897

Minor Excursions

Contents

London Impressions

I

LONDON AT FIRST consisted of a porter with the most charming manners in the world and a cabman with a supreme intelligence, both observing my profound ignorance without contempt or humor of any kind observable in their manners. It was in a great resounding vault of a place where there were many people who had come home, and I was displeased because they knew the detail of the business, whereas I was confronting the inscrutable. This made them appear very stony-hearted to the sufferings of one of whose existence, to be sure, they were entirely unaware, and I remember taking great pleasure in disliking them heartily for it. I was in an agony of mind over my baggage or my luggage, or my—perhaps it is well to shy around this terrible international question, but I remember that when I was a lad I was told that there was a whole nation that said luggage instead of baggage, and my boyish mind was filled at the time with incredulity and scorn. In the present case it was a thing that I understood to involve the most hideous confessions of imbecility on my part, because I had evidently to go out to some obscure point and espy it and claim it and take trouble for it, and I would rather have had my pockets filled with bread and cheese and had no baggage at all.

Mind you this was not at all an homage that I was paying to London. I was paying homage to a new game. A man properly lazy does not like new experiences until they become old ones. Moreover I have been taught that a man, any man, who has a thousand times more points of information on a certain thing than have I, will bully me because of it, and pour his advantages upon my bowed head until I am drenched with his superiority. It was in my education to concede some license of the kind in this case, but the holy father of a porter and the saintly cabman occupied the middle distance imperturbably, and did not come down from their hills to clout me with knowledge. From this fact I experienced a criminal elation. I lost view of the idea that if I had been brow-beaten by porters and cabmen from one end of the

United States to the other end, I should warmly like it be-
cause in numbers they are superior to me, and collectively
they can have a great deal of fun out of a matter that would
merely afford me the glee of the latent butcher.

This London, composed of a porter and a cabman, stood
to me subtly as a benefactor. I had scanned the drama and
found that I did not believe that the mood of the men ema-
nated unduly from the feature that there was probably more
shillings to the square inch of me than there were shillings to
the square inch of them. Nor yet was it any manner of pal-
pable warm-heartedness or other natural virtue. But it was a
perfect artificial virtue; it was drill—plain, simple drill. And
now was I glad of their drilling, and vividly approved of it
because I saw that it was good for me. Whether it was good
or bad for the porter and the cabman I could not know; but
that point, mark you, came within the pale of my respectable
rumination.

I am sure that it would have been more correct for me to
have alighted upon St. Paul's and described no emotion until
I was overcome by the Thames Embankment and the Houses
of Parliament, but as a matter of fact I did not see them for
some days, and at this time they did not concern me at all. I
was born in London at a railroad station, and my new vision
encompassed a porter and a cabman. They deeply absorbed
me in new phenomena, and I did not then care to see the
Thames Embankment nor the Houses of Parliament. I consid-
ered the porter and the cabman to be more important.

II

The cab finally rolled out of the gas-lit vault into a vast
expanse of gloom. This changed to the shadowy lines of a
street that was like a passage in a monstrous cave. The lamps
winking here and there resembled the little gleams at the caps
of the miners. They were not very competent illuminations at
best, merely being little pale flares of gas that at their most
heroic periods could only display one fact concerning this
tunnel—the fact of general direction. But at any rate I should
have liked to have observed the dejection of a search-light
if it had been called upon to attempt to bore through this

atmosphere. In it each man sat in his own little cylinder of vision, so to speak. It was not so small as a sentry-box nor so large as a circus-tent, but the walls were opaque, and what was passing beyond the dimensions of his cylinder no man knew.

It was evident that the paving was very greasy, but all the cabs that passed through my cylinder were going at a round trot, while the wheels, shod in rubber, whirred merely like bicycles. The hoofs of the animals themselves did not make that wild clatter which I knew so well. New York, in fact, roars always like ten thousand devils. We have ingenious and simple ways of making a din in New York that cause the stranger to conclude that each citizen is obliged by statute to provide himself with a pair of cymbals and a drum. If anything by chance can be turned into a noise it is promptly turned. We are engaged in the development of a human creature with very large, sturdy and doubly-fortified ears.

It was not too late at night, but this London moved with the decorum and caution of an undertaker. There was a silence and yet there was no silence. There was a low drone, perhaps, a humming contributed inevitably by closely gathered thousands, and yet on second thoughts it was to me a silence. I had perched my ears for the note of London, the sound made simply by the existence of five million people in one place. I had imagined something deep, vastly deep, a bass from a mythical organ; but I found, as far as I was concerned, only a silence.

New York in numbers is a mighty city, and all day and all night it cries its loud, fierce, aspiring cry, a noise of men beating upon barrels, a noise of men beating upon tin, a terrific racket that assails the abject skies. No one of us seemed to question this row as a certain consequence of three or four million people living together and scuffling for coin with more agility, perhaps, but otherwise in the usual way. However, after this easy silence of London, which in numbers is a mightier city, I began to feel that there was a seduction in this idea of necessity. Our noise in New York was not a consequence of our rapidity at all. It was a consequence of our bad pavements.

Any brigade of artillery in Europe that would love to assemble its batteries and then go on a gallop over the land, thundering and thundering, would give up the idea of thunder at once if it could hear Tim Mulligan drive a beer wagon along one of the side streets of cobbled New York.

III

Finally, a great thing came to pass. The cab-horse, proceeding at a sharp trot, found himself suddenly at the top of an incline where through the rain the pavement shone like an expanse of ice. It looked to me as if there was going to be a tumble. In an accident of such kind a hansom becomes really a cannon in which a man finds that he has paid shillings for the privilege of serving as a projectile. I was making a rapid calculation of the arc that I would describe in my flight, when the horse met his crisis with a masterly device that I could not have imagined. He tranquilly braced his four feet like a bundle of stakes, and then, with a gentle gaiety of demeanor, he slid swiftly and gracefully to the bottom of the hill as if he had been a toboggan. When the incline ended he caught his gait again with great dexterity, and went pattering off through another tunnel.

I at once looked upon myself as being singularly blessed by this sight. This horse had evidently originated this sytem of skating as a diversion or, more probably, as a precaution against the slippery pavement; and he was, of course, the inventor and sole proprietor—two terms that are not always in conjunction. It surely was not to be supposed that there could be two skaters like him in the world. He deserved to be known and publicly praised for this accomplishment. It was worthy of many records and exhibitions. But when the cab arrived at a place where some dipping streets met, and the flaming front of a music-hall temporarily widened my cylinder, behold, there were many cabs, and as the moment of necessity came, the horses were all skaters. They were gliding in all directions. It might have been a rink. A great omnibus was hailed by a hand from under an umbrella on the sidewalk, and the dignified horses bidden to halt from their trot did not waste time in wild and unseemly spasms. They, too, braced their legs and slid gravely to the end of their momentum.

It was not the feat, but it was the word, which had at this time the power to conjure memories of skating parties on moonlit lakes, with laughter ringing over the ice, and a great red bonfire on the shore among the hemlocks.

Ballydehob

THE ILLIMITABLE INVENTIVE INCAPACITY of the excursion companies has made many circular paths throughout Ireland, and on these well-pounded roads the guardians of the touring public may be seen drilling the little travellers in squads. To rise in rebellion, to face the superior clerk in his bureau, to endure his smile of pity and derision, and finally to wring freedom from him, is as difficult in some parts of Ireland as it is in all parts of Switzerland. To see the tourists chained in gangs and taken to see the Lakes of Killarney is a sad spectacle, because these people believe that they are learning Ireland, even as men believe that they are studying America when they contemplate the Niagara Falls.

But afterwards, if one escapes, one can go forth, unguided, untaught and alone, and look at Ireland. The joys of the pigmarket, the delirium of a little tap-room filled with brogue, the fierce excitement of viewing the Royal Irish Constabulary fishing for trout, the whole quaint and primitive machinery of the peasant-life, its melancholy, its sunshine, its humor—all this is then the property of the man who breaks like a Texan steer out of the pens and corrals of the tourist agencies. For what syndicate of maiden ladies—it is these who masquerade as tourist agencies—what syndicate of maiden ladies knows of the existence, for instance, of Ballydehob?

One has a sense of disclosure at writing the name of Ballydehob. It was really a valuable secret. There is in Ballydehob not one thing that is commonly pointed out to the stranger as a thing worthy of a half-tone reproduction in a book. There is no cascade, no peak, no lake, no guide with a fund of useless information, no gamins practised in the seduction of tourists. It is not an exhibit, an entry for a prize, like a heap of melons or a cow. It is simply an Irish village wherein live some three hundred Irish and four constables.

If one or two prayer-towers spindled above Ballydehob it would be a perfect Turkish village. The red tiles and red bricks of England do not appear at all. The houses are low, with soiled white walls. The doors open abruptly upon dark old rooms. Here and there in the street is some crude cob-bling done with round stones taken from the bed of a brook. At times there is a great deal of mud. Chickens depredate warily about the doorsteps, and intent pigs emerge for plunder from the alleys. It is unavoidable to admit that many people would consider Ballydehob quite too grimy.

Nobody lives here that has money. The average English tradesman with his back-breaking respect for this class, his reflex contempt for that class, his reverence for the tin gods, could here be a commercial lord and bully the people in one or two ways, until they were thrown back upon the defence which is always near them, the ability to cut his skin into strips with a wit that would be a foreign tongue to him. For amid his wrongs and his rights and his failures, his colossal failures, the Irishman retains this delicate blade for his enemies, for his friends, for himself, the ancestral dagger of fast sharp speaking from fast sharp seeing—an inheritance which could move the world. And the Royal Irish Constabulary fished for trout in the adjacent streams.

Mrs. Kearney keeps the hotel. In Ireland male inn-keepers die young. Apparently they succumb to conviviality when it is presented to them in the guise of a business duty. Naturally honest temperate men, their consciences are lulled to false security by this idea of hard drinking being necessary to the successful keeping of a public-house. It is very terrible.

But they invariably leave behind them capable widows, women who do not recognize conviviality as a business obligation. And so all through Ireland one finds these brisk widows, keeping hotels with a precision that is almost military.

In Kearney's there is always a wonderful collection of old women, bent figures shrouded in shawls who reach up scrawny fingers to take their little purchases from Mary Agnes, who presides sometimes at the bar, but more often at the shop that fronts it in the same room. In the gloom of a late afternoon these old women are as mystic as the swinging, chanting witches on a dark stage when the thunder-drum rolls and the lightning flashes by schedule. When a grey rain sweeps through the narrow street of Ballydehob, and makes heavy shadows in Kearney's taproom, these old creatures, with their high, mournful voices, and the mystery of their shawls, their moans and aged mutterings when they are obliged to take a step, raise the dead superstitions from the bottom of a man's mind.

"My boy," remarked my London friend cheerfully, "these might have furnished sons to be Aldermen or Congressmen in the great city of New York."

"Aldermen or Congressmen of the great city of New York always take care of their mothers," I answered meekly.

On a barrel, over in a corner, sat a yellow-bearded Irish farmer in tattered clothes who wished to exchange views on the Armenian massacres. He had much information and a number of theories in regard to them. He also advanced the opinion that the chief political aim of Russia, at present, is in the direction of China, and that it behoved other Powers to keep an eye on her. He thought the revolutionists in Cuba would never accept autonomy at the hands of Spain. His pipe glowed comfortably from his corner; waving the tuppenny glass of stout in the air, he discoursed on the business of the remote ends of the earth with the glibness of a fourth secretary of Legation. Here was a little farmer, digging betimes in a forlorn patch of wet ground, a man to whom a sudden two shillings would appeal as a miracle, a ragged, unkempt peasant, whose mind roamed the world like the soul of a lost diplomat. This unschooled man believed that the earth was a sphere inhabited by men that are alike in the essentials, different in the manners, the little manners, which are accounted of such great importance by the emaciated. He was to a degree capable of knowing that he lived on a sphere and not on the apex of a triangle.

And yet, when the talk had turned another corner, he confidently assured the assembled company that a hair from a horse's tail when thrown in a brook would turn shortly to an eel.

The Royal Irish Constabulary

THE NEWSPAPERS called it a Veritable Arsenal. There was a description of how the sergeant of Constabulary had bent an ear to receive whispered information of the concealed arms, and had then marched his men swiftly and by night to surround a certain house. The search elicited a double-barrelled breech-loading shot-gun, some empty shells, powder, shot, and a loading-machine. The point of it was that some of the Irish papers called it a Veritable Arsenal, and appeared to congratulate the Government upon having strangled another unhappy rebellion in its nest. They floundered and misnamed and misreasoned, and made a spectacle of the great modern craft of journalism until the affair of this poor poacher was too absurd to be pitable, and Englishmen over their coffee next morning must have almost believed that the prompt action of the Constabulary had quelled a rising. Thus it is that the Irish fight the Irish.

One cannot look Ireland straight in the face without seeing a great many constables. The country is dotted with little garrisons. It must have been said a thousand times that there is an absolute military occupation. The fact is too plain.

The constable himself becomes a figure interesting in its isolation. He has in most cases a social position which is somewhat analogous to that of a Turk in Thessaly. But then, in the same way, the Turk has the Turkish army. He can have battalions as companions and make the acquaintance of brigades. The constable has the Constabulary, it is true; but to be cooped with three or four others in a small white-washed iron-bound house on some bleak country side is not an exact parallel to the Thessalian situation. It looks to be a life that is infinitely lonely, ascetic, and barren. Two keepers of a lighthouse at a bitter end of land in a remote sea will, if they are properly let alone, make a murder in time. Five constables imprisoned 'mid a folk that will not turn a face toward them, five constables planted in a populated silence, may develop an acute and vivid economy, dwell in scowling dislike. A religious asylum in a snow-buried mountain pass will breed conspiring monks. A separated people will beget an egotism that is almost titanic. A world floating distinctly in space will call itself the only world. The progression is perfect.

But the constables take the second degree. They are next to the lighthouse keepers. The national custom of meeting stranger and friend alike on the road with a cheery greeting like "God save you" is too kindly and human a habit not to be missed. But all through the South of Ireland one sees the peasant turn his eyes pretentiously to the side of the road at the passing of the constable. It seemed to be generally understood that to note the presence of a constable was to make a conventional error. None looked, nodded, or gave sign. There was a line drawn so sternly that it reared like a fence. Of course, any policing force in any part of the world can gather at its heels a riff-raff of people, fawning always on a hand licensed to strike that would be larger than the army of the Potomac, but of these one ordinarily sees little. The mass of the Irish strictly obey the stern tenet. One hears often of the ostracism or other punishment that befell some girl who was caught flirting with a constable.

Naturally the constable retreats to his pride. He is commonly a soldierly-looking chap, straight, lean, long-strided, well set-up. His little saucer of a forage cap sits obediently on his ear, as it does for the British soldier. He swings a little cane. He takes his medicine with a calm and hard face, and evidently stares full into every eye. But it is singular to find in the situation of the Royal Irish Constabulary the quality of pathos.

It is not known if these places in the South of Ireland are called disturbed districts. Over them hangs the peace of Surrey, but the word disturbance has an elastic arrangement by which it can be made to cover anything. All of the villages visited garrisoned from four to ten men. They lived comfortably in their white houses, strolled in pairs over the country roads, picked blackberries, and fished for trout. If at some time there came a crisis, one man was more than enough to surround it. The remaining nine add dignity to the scene. The crises chiefly consisted of occasional drunken men who were unable to understand the local geography on Saturday nights.

The note continually struck was that each group of constables lived on a little social island, and there was no boat to take them off. There has been no such marooning since the days of the pirates. The sequestration must be complete when a man with a dinky little cap on his ear is not allowed to talk to the girls.

But they fish for trout. Isaac Walton is the father of the Royal Irish Constabulary. They could be seen on any fine day whipping the streams from source to mouth. There was one venerable sergeant who made a rod less than a yard long. With a line of about the same length attached to this rod, he haunted the gorse-hung banks of the little streams in the hills. An eight-inch ribbon of water lined with masses of heather and gorse will be accounted contemptible by a fisherman with an ordinary rod. But it was the pleasure of the sergeant to lay on his stomach at the side of such a stream and carefully, inch by inch, scout his hook through the pools. He probably caught more trout than any three men in the county Cork. He fished more than any twelve men in the county Cork. Some people had never seen him in any other posture but that of crowding forward on his stomach to peer into a pool. They did not believe the rumor that he sometimes stood or walked like a human.

A Fishing Village

THE BROOK CURVED DOWN over the rocks, innocent and white, until it faced a little strand of smooth gravel and flat stones. It turned then to the left, and thereafter its guilty current was tinged with the pink of diluted blood. Boulders standing neck-deep in the water were rimmed with red; they wore bloody collars whose tops marked the supreme instant of some tragic movement of the stream. In the pale green shallows of the bay's edge, the outward flow from the criminal little brook was as eloquently marked as if a long crimson carpet had been laid upon the waters. The scene of the carnage was the strand of smooth gravel and flat stones, and the fruit of the carnage was cleaned mackerel.

Far to the south, where the slate of the sea and the grey of the sky wove together, could be seen Fastnet Rock, a mere button on the moving, shimmering cloth, while a liner, no larger than a needle, spun a thread of smoke aslant. The gulls swept screaming along the dull line of the other shore of Roaring Water Bay, and, near the mouth of the brook, circled among the fishing boats that lay at anchor, their brown leathery sails idle and straight. The wheeling, shrieking, tumultuous birds stared with their hideous unblinking eyes at the Capers—men from Cape Clear—who prowled to and fro on the decks amid shouts and the creak of tackle. Shoreward, a little shrivelled man, overcome by a profound melancholy, fished hopelessly from the end of the pier. Back of him, on a hillside, sat a white village, nestled among more trees than is common in this part of southern Ireland.

A dinghy sculled by a youth in a blue jersey wobbled rapidly past the pier-head and stopped at the foot of the moss-green dank stone steps, where the waves were making slow but regular leaps to mount higher, and then falling back gurgling, choking, and waving the long dark seaweeds. The melancholy fisherman walked over to the top of the steps. The young man was fastening the painter of his boat in an iron ring. In the dinghy were three round baskets heaped high with mackerel. They glittered like masses of new silver coin at times and then other lights of faint carmine and peacock blue would chase across the sides of the fish in a radiance that was finer than silver.

The melancholy fisherman looked at this wealth. He shook his head mournfully. "Aw, now, Denny. This would not be a very good kill."

The young man snorted indignantly at his fellow towns-man. "This will be th' bist kill th' year, Mickey. Go along now."

The melancholy old man became immersed in a deeper gloom. "Shure I have been in th' way of seein' miny a grand day whin th' fish was runnin' sthrong in these wathers, but there will be no more big kills here. No more. No more." At the last his voice was only a dismal croak.

"Come along outa that now, Mickey," cried the youth impatiently. "Come away wid you."

"All gone now! A—ll go—o—ne now!" The old man wagged his grey head, and, standing over the baskets of fishes, groaned as Mordecai groaned for his people.

" 'Tis you would be cryin' out, Mickey, whativer," said the youth with scorn. He was giving his baskets into the hands of five incompetent but jovial little boys to carry to a waiting donkey cart.

"An' why should I not?" said the old man sternly. "Me—in want——"

As the youth swung his boat swiftly out toward an anchored smack, he made answer in a softer tone. "Shure, if yez got for th' askin', 'tis you, Mickey, that would niver be in want." The melancholy old man returned to his line. And the only moral in this incident is that the young man is the type that America procures from Ireland, and the old man is one of the home types, bent, pallid, hungry, disheartened, with a vision that magnifies with a microscopic glance any fly-wing of misfortune and heroically and conscientiously invents disasters for the future. Usually the thing that remains to one of this last type is a sympathy as quick and acute for others as is his pity for himself.

The donkey with his cartload of gleaming fish, and escorted by the whooping and laughing boys, galloped along the quay and up a street of the village until he was turned off at the gravelly strand, at the point where the color of the brook was changing. Here twenty people of both sexes and all ages were preparing the fish for the market. The mackerel, beautiful as fire-etched salvers, first were passed to a long table, around which worked as many women as could have elbow room. Each one could clean a fish with two motions of the knife. Then the washers, men who stood over the troughs filled with running water from the brook, soused the fish until the outlet became a sinister element that in an instant changed the brook from a happy thing of the gorse and heather of the hills to an evil stream, sullen and reddened. After being washed, the fish were carried to a group of girls with knives, who made the cuts that enabled each fish to flatten out in the manner known of the breakfast table. And after the girls came the men and boys, who rubbed each fish thoroughly with great handfuls of coarse salt, which was whiter than snow, and shone in the daylight from a multitude of gleaming points, diamond-like. Last came the packers, drilled in the art of getting neither too few nor too many mackerel into a barrel, sprinkling constantly prodigal layers of the brilliant salt. There were many intermediate corps of boys and girls carrying fish from point to point, and sometimes building them in stacks convenient to the hands of the more important laborers.

A vast tree hung its branches over the place. The leaves made a shadow that was religious in its effect, as if the spot was a chapel consecrated to labor. There was a hush upon the devotees. The women at the large table worked intently, steadfastly, with bowed heads. Their old petticoats were tucked high, showing the coarse men's brogans which they wore—and the visible ankles were proportioned to the brogans as the diameter of a straw is to that of a half-crown. The national red underpetticoat was a fundamental part of the scene.

Just over the wall, in the sloping street, could be seen the bejerseyed Capers, brawny, and with shocks of yellow beard. They paced slowly to and fro amid the geese and the children. They, too, spoke little, even to each other; they smoked short pipes in saturnine dignity and silence. It was the fish. They who go with nets upon the reeling sea grow still with the mystery and solemnity of the trade. It was Brittany; the first respectable catch of the year had changed this garrulous Irish hamlet into a hamlet of Brittany.

The Capers were waiting for a high tide. It had seemed for a long time that, for the south of Ireland, the mackerel had fled in company with the potato; but here at any rate was a temporary success, and the occasion was momentous. A strolling Caper took his pipe and pointed with the stem out upon the bay. There was little wind, but an ambitious skipper had raised his anchor, and the craft, her strained brown sails idly swinging, was drifting away on the first oily turn of the tide.

On the tip of the pier the figure of the melancholy old man was portrayed upon the polished water. He was still dangling his line, hopelessly. He gazed down into the misty water. Once he stirred and murmured, "Bad luck to thim." Otherwise, he seemed to remain motionless for hours. One by one the fishing-boats floated away. The brook changed its color, and, in the dusk, showed a tumble of pearly white among the rocks.

A cold night wind, sweeping transversely across the pier, awakened perhaps the rheumatism in the old man's bones. He arose, and, mumbling and grumbling, began to wind his line. The waves were lashing the stones. He moved off toward the intense darkness of the village streets.

Harold Frederic

THE PERSONALITY of Mr. Harold Frederic is probably the one least discussed of the better American novelists. The goings and comings, the manners and the countenances of our leading men of letters are commonly limned with glee and some precision by the popular journals. Frederic has escaped much of it through the fact that his duties of correspondence have obliged him to live the last fifteen years in London, and so has been beyond the range of our inferior artillery. It is probably not very graceful to appear now in the guise of an advanced patrol ultimately potting at a man who has enjoyed the finer kind of peace for fifteen years; and if it were impossible to use these paragraphs to write about the books, the potting of the man would not be done.

One approaches certain sections of the American colony in London with a stealthy footfall. In England, there is sometimes a cousinly outdoing of the English in those matters which are particularly unimportant. A certain sympathetic and singing chord of the mind induces one to advance upon the field with caution. It was my fault to conclude beforehand that, since Frederic had lived intimately so long in England, he would present some kind of austere and impressive variation on one of our national types, and I was secretly not quite prepared to subscribe to the change. It was a bit of mistaken speculation. There was a tall, heavy man, moustached and straight-glanced, seated in a leather chair in the smoking-room of a club, telling a story to a circle of intent people with all the skill of one trained in an American newspaper school. At a distance he might have been even then the editor of the Albany *Journal*.

The sane man does not live amid another people without seeking to adopt whatever he recognizes as better; without seeking to choose from the new material some advantage, even if it be only a trick of grilling oysters. Accordingly, Frederic was to be to me a cosmopolitan figure, representing many ways of many peoples; and, behold, he was still the familiar figure, with no gilding, no varnish, a great reminiscent panorama of the Mohawk Valley!

It was in Central New York that Frederic was born, and it is there he passed his childish days and his young manhood. He enjoys greatly to tell how he gained his first opinions of the alphabet from a strenuous and enduring study of the letters on an empty soap-box. At an early age he was induced by his parents to arise at 5:30 A.M., and distribute supplies of milk among the worthy populace.

In his clubs, details of this story are well known. He pitilessly describes the gray shine of the dawn that makes the snow appear the hue of lead, and, moreover, his boyish pain at the task of throwing the stiff harness over the sleepy horse, and then the long and circuitous sledding among the customers of the milk route. There is no pretense in these accounts; many self-made men portray their early hardships in a spirit of purest vanity. "And now look!" But there is none of this in Frederic. He simply feels a most absorbed interest in that part of his career which made him so closely acquainted with the voluminous life of rural America. His boyhood extended through that time when the North was sending its thousands to the war, and the lists of dead and wounded were returning in due course. The great country back of the line of fight— the waiting women, the lightless windows, the tables set for three instead of five—was a land elate or forlorn, triumphant or despairing, always strained, eager, listening, tragic in attitude, trembling and quivering like a vast mass of nerves from the shock of the far away conflicts in the South. Those were supreme years, and yet for the great palpitating regions it seems that the mind of this lad was the only sensitive plate exposed to the sunlight of '61–'65. The book, *In the Sixties*, which contains "The Copperhead," "Marsena," "The War Widow," "The Eve of the Fourth," and "My Aunt Susan," breathes the spirit of a Titanic conflict as felt and endured at the homes. One would think that such a book would have taken the American people by storm, but it is true that an earlier edition of *The Copperhead* sold less than a thousand copies in America. We have sometimes a way of wildly celebrating the shadow of a mullein-stalk against the wall of a woodshed, and remaining intensely ignorant of the vital things that are ours. I believe that at about the time of the appearance of these stories, the critics were making a great deal of noise in an attempt to stake the novelists down to the soil and make them write the impressive common life of the United States. This virtuous struggle to prevent the novelists from going ballooning off over some land of dreams and candy-palaces was distinguished by the fact that, contemporaneously, there was Frederic doing his locality, doing his Mohawk Valley, with the strong trained hand of a great craftsman, and the critics were making such a din over the attempt to have a certain kind of thing done, that they did not recognize its presence. All this goes to show that there are some painful elements in the art of creating an American literature by what may be called the rattlety-bang method. The important figures, the greater men, rise silently, unspurred, undriven. To be sure, they may come in for magnificent cudgelings later, but their approach is noiseless, invincible, and they are upon us like ghosts before the critics have time to begin their clatter.

But there is something dismally unfortunate in the passing of *Seth's Brother's Wife*, *In the Valley*, the historical novel, and *The Lawton Girl*. Of course, they all had their success in measure, but here was a chance and a reason for every American to congratulate himself. Another thing had been done. For instance, *In the Valley* is easily the best historical novel that our country has borne. Perhaps it is the only good one. *Seth's Brother's Wife* and *The Lawton Girl* are rimmed with fine portrayals. There are writing men who, in some stories, dash over three miles at a headlong pace, and in an adjacent story move like a boat being sailed over ploughed fields; but in Frederic one feels at once the perfect evenness of craft, the undeviating worth of the workmanship. The excellence is always sustained, and these books form, with *In the Sixties*, a row of big American novels. But if we knew it we made no emphatic sign, and it was not until the appearance of *The Damnation of Theron Ware* that the book audiences really said: "Here is a writer!" If I make my moan too strong over this phase of the matter, I have only the excuse that I believe the *In the Sixties* stories to form a most notable achievement in writing times in America. Abner Beech, the indomitable and ferocious farmer, with his impregnable disloyalty or conscience, or whatever; Aunt Susan always at her loom making rag-carpets which, as the war deepened, took on two eloquent colors—the blue of old army overcoats and the black of woman's mourning; the guileless Marsena and the simple tragedy of his death—these characters represent to me living people, as if the book breathed.

It is natural that since Frederic has lived so long in England, his pen should turn toward English life. One does not look upon this fact with unmixed joy. It is mournful to lose his work even for a time. It is for this reason that I have made myself disagreeable upon several occasions by my expressed views of *March Hares*. It is a worthy book, but one has a sense of desertion. We cannot afford a loss of this kind. But, at any rate, he has grasped English life with a precision of hand that is only equaled by the precision with which he grasped Irish life, and his new book will shine out for English eyes in a way with which they are not too familiar. It is a strong and striking delineation, free, bold, and straight.

In the mean time he is a prodigious laborer. Knowing the man and his methods, one can conceive him doing anything, unless it be writing a poor book, and, mind you, this is an important point.

Concerning the English "Academy"

AT LEAST ONCE in every three years in London some jour-
nal or clique is sure to turn up with a plan, more or less
disguised, for an English Academy founded on the manner of
the French Academy. Some of these attempts have been al-
most shamelessly financial, and others have been shamelessly
made for advertisement, so much so, that even if England
wanted an Academy of Art and Letters, she would be pre-
vented by the criminal impudence of the projectors. More-
over, Anglo-Saxon people usually object to the labelling of
one artist as being officially guaranteed superior to another.
It would surely mean at first a dreadful game of throat-cutting
and sand-bagging, from which would not emerge enough
children of light to form a coroner's jury, let alone an Acad-
emy of Art and Letters. It seems to be a general idea that the
arena should remain as a cleared place in which no distinc-
tions are recognized, where every man falls to and grabs what
wool he may. Even a description of the present situation does
not sound attractive.

But still the English powers are toying with the matter.
Many men of importance have sent for publication lists of
forty intellects which to their minds would form the proper
Academy. In each of these lists we have the sublime spectacle
of the writer leaving his own name out. This display of
wholesale generosity might have brought the London public
to tears had it not appeared later that there might be an ex-
change of contracts. "You put me in your list, and I'll put you
in mine."

Recently, a well-known critical journal, the London *Acad-
emy*, unanimously elected itself to the position of mentor, and
offered a prize of one hundred guineas to the book of signal
merit published in the year of 1897, and a prize of fifty guineas
for the next best book. Failures in projects of this kind dot
contemporaneous history, and they have always been accom-
panied by howls of execration from men who did not win a
prize, and from men who thought they knew who should
have won a prize. It was quite a daring thing on the part of
the *Academy* people. They had to steer their craft through the

988

inch-wide channel between ridicule and equally terrible indictments for unfairness and falsity. To thoughtful people herein lay the interest.

And now one comes to the result. Usually these affairs are absurd, but one must hasten to admit that the decision of *Academy* is at least perfectly sane. They have succeeded in delivering an opinion to which none can strongly object. It is too respectable. The *Academy* emerges in the most graceful fashion from the mists of its precarious venture. Not a single formidable voice will be raised in protest, and in this fact is victory.

The first prize of one hundred guineas was given to Mr. Stephen Phillips for his volume of *Poems*. The prize of fifty guineas was awarded to Mr. W. E. Henley for his *Essay on the Life, Genius and Achievement of Burns*, which is contained in the fourth volume of the Centenary edition of Burns. The *Academy* remarks: "It is not likely that the choice will please every one, but the most patient consideration of the whole matter convinces us that we have done well."

And that is precisely what they have done. Here is a task which few have been able to perform decently, mainly, perhaps, because few decent people have ever attempted it, but the *Academy* has carried it through, and the result is, in the artistic sense, respectable, inexorably respectable.

The novelists did not appear in great force in the discussions which were waged in the columns of the journal previous to the decisions. Many people suggested that the prizes should be given to Mr. Henry James for his *What Maisie Knew*, and to Mr. Joseph Conrad for his *The Nigger of the "Narcissus"*—a rendering which would have made a genial beginning for an English Academy of letters, since Mr. James is an American and Mr. Conrad was born in Poland. However, these two were the only novelists who figured prominently. They were not puny adversaries. Mr. James's book is alive with all the art which is at the command of that great workman, and as for the new man, Conrad, his novel is a marvel of fine descriptive writing. It is unquestionably the best story of the sea written by a man now alive, and as a matter of fact, one would have to make an extensive search among the tombs before he who has done better could be found. As for the ruck of writers who make the sea their literary domain, Conrad seems in effect simply to warn them off the premises, and tell them to remain silent. He comes nearer to an ownership of the mysterious life on the ocean than anybody who has written in this century.

Mr. Conrad was stoutly pressed for the prize, but the editors of the *Academy* judged the book to be "too slight and episodic," although they considered it "a remarkable imaginative feat marked by striking literary power." If one wanted to pause and quibble, one would instantly protest against their use of the word episodic, which as a critical epithet is absolutely and flagrantly worthless.

Mr. Rudyard Kipling's *Captains Courageous* was disqualified on grounds which are not, apparently, within the limits of the *Academy*'s declared purpose. The paper says: "Mr. Kipling has himself fixed his standard too high for *Captains Courageous* to be satisfying." If a man is to be measured according to his books of previous years, then the *Academy* has no right to the use of the name "1897." This is not, then, a question of the best book in 1897. This is, rather, a question as to whether some man in 1897 has written a book which is better than all other books in 1897, and also better than a book which he himself had written in 1849 or whenever you like. Apply this theory still further, and you find that the decision of the *Academy* amounts to a declaration that Mr. Henley's essay on Burns is the best thing ever from the pen of that gifted man—a declaration that will at least not gain a general assent.

The *Academy* also says: "Mr. William Watson's *Hope of the World* causes us to glance back to what he has done, rather than to look forward to what he may do."

Well, there you are. When a man or a paper elects to don a wig and sit on a bench to hear a case of art in all solemn finality, the world is not prepared to be dazzled by the wisdom of the decision. One can only hope for an artistically respectable result. The result in this case was artistically respectable. The *Academy* would have justified the entire complacence of its readers if it had not been thoughtless enough to give two columns of its reasons. The decisions themselves would have stood criticism with honor, even distinction, but the printed reasons often bewilder one with the agility with which the *Academy* apparently disregards the laws which the *Academy* has made. Perhaps they are too episodic. At any rate, they contain statements that are at variance with the original plan—at least in some eyes—and the affair was not, therefore, the success of esteem that it might have been.

CUBA

Contents

Stephen Crane at the Front for the World

SIBONEY, JUNE 24.—And this is the end of the third day since the landing of the troops. Yesterday was a day of insurgent fighting and rumors of insurgent fighting. The Cubans were supposed to be fighting somewhere in the hills with the regiment of Santiago de Cuba, which had been quite cut off from its native city. No American soldiery were implicated in any way in the battle. But to-day is different. The mounted infantry—the First Volunteer Cavalry—Teddie's Terrors—Wood's Weary Walkers—have had their first engagement. It was a bitter hard first fight for new troops, but no man can ever question the gallantry of this regiment.

As we landed from a despatch boat we saw the last troop of the mounted infantry wending slowly over the top of a huge hill. Three of us promptly posted after them upon hearing the statement that they had gone out with the avowed intention of finding the Spaniards and mixing it up with them.

They were far ahead of us by the time we reached the top of the mountain, but we swung rapidly on the path through the dense Cuban thickets and in time met and passed the hospital corps, a vacant, unloaded hospital corps, going ahead on mules. Then there was another long lonely march through the dry woods, which seemed almost upon the point of crackling into a blaze under the rays of the furious Cuban sun. We met nothing but blankets, shelter-tents, coats and other impedimenta, which the panting Rough Riders had flung behind them on their swift march.

In time we came in touch with a few stragglers, men down with heat, prone and breathing heavily, and then we struck the rear of the column. We were now about four miles out, with no troops nearer than that by the road.

I know nothing about war, of course, and pretend nothing, but I have been enabled from time to time to see brush fighting, and I want to say here plainly that the behavior of these Rough Riders while marching through the woods shook me with terror as I have never before been shaken.

It must now be perfectly understood throughout the length and breadth of the United States that the Spaniards have learned a great deal from the Cubans, and they are going to use against us the tactics which the Cubans have used so successfully against them. The marines at Guantanamo have learned it. The Indian-fighting regulars know it anyhow, but this regiment of volunteers knew nothing but their own superb courage. They wound along this narrow winding path, babbling joyously, arguing, recounting, laughing; making more noise than a train going through a tunnel.

Any one could tell from the conformation of the country when we were liable to strike the enemy's outposts, but the clatter of tongues did not then cease. Also, those of us who knew heard going from hillock to hillock the beautiful coo of the Cuban wood-dove—ah, the wood-dove! the Spanish-guerilla wood-dove which had presaged the death of gallant marines.

For my part, I declare that I was frightened almost into convulsions. Incidentally I mentioned the cooing of the doves to some of the men, but they said decisively that the Spaniards did not use this signal. I don't know how they knew.

Well, after we had advanced well into the zone of the enemy's fire—mark that—well into the zone of Spanish fire—a loud order came along the line: "There's a Spanish outpost just ahead and the men must stop talking."

"Stop talkin', can't ye, —— it," bawled a sergeant.

"Ah, say, can't ye stop talkin'?" howled another.

I was frightened before a shot was fired; frightened because I thought this silly brave force was wandering placidly into a great deal of trouble. They did. The firing began. Four little volleys were fired by members of a troop deployed to the right. Then the Mauser began to pop—the familiar Mauser pop. A captain announced that this distinct Mauser sound was our own Krag-Jorgensen. O misery!

Then the woods became aglow with fighting. Our people advanced, deployed, reinforced, fought, fell—in the bushes, in the tall grass, under the lone palms—before a foe not even half seen. Mauser bullets came from three sides. Mauser bullets—not Krag-Jorgensen—although men began to cry that they were being fired into by their own people—whined in almost all directions. Three troops went forward in skirmish order and in five minutes they called for reinforcements. They were under a cruel fire; half of the men hardly knew whence it came; but their conduct, by any soldierly standard, was magnificent.

Most persons with a fancy for military things suspect the value of an announcedly picked regiment. Better gather a simple collection of clerks from anywhere. But in this case the usual view changes. This regiment is as fine a body of men as were ever accumulated for war.

There was nothing to be seen but men straggling through the underbrush and firing at some part of the landscape. This was the scenic effect. Of course men said that they saw five hundred, one thousand, three thousand, fifteen thousand Spaniards, but—poof—in bush country of this kind it is almost impossible for one to see more than fifty men at a time. According to my opinion there were never more than five hundred men in the Spanish firing line. There might have been aplenty in touch with their centre and flanks, but as to the firing there were never more than five hundred men engaged. This is certain.

The Rough Riders advanced steadily and confidently under the Mauser bullets. They spread across some open ground—tall grass and palms—and there they began to fall, smothering and threshing down in the grass, marking man-shaped places among those luxuriant blades. The action lasted about one-half hour. Then the Spaniards fled. They had never had men fight them in this manner and they fled. The business was too serious.

Then the heroic rumor arose, soared, screamed above the bush. Everybody was wounded. Everybody was dead. There was nobody. Gradually there was somebody. There was the wounded, the important wounded. And the dead.

Meanwhile a soldier passing near me said: "There's a correspondent up there all shot to hell."

He guided me to where Edward Marshall lay, shot through the body. The following conversation ensued:

"Hello, Crane!"

"Hello, Marshall! In hard luck, old man?"

"Yes, I'm done for."

"Nonsense! You're all right, old boy. What can I do for you?"

"Well, you might file my despatches. I don't mean file 'em ahead of your own, old man—but just file 'em if you find it handy."

I immediately decided that he was doomed. No man could be so sublime in detail concerning the trade of journalism and not die. There was the solemnity of a funeral song in these absurd and fine sentences about despatches. Six soldiers gathered him up on a tent and moved slowly off.

"Hello!" shouted a stern and menacing person, "who are you? And what are you doing here? Quick!"

"I am a correspondent, and we are merely carrying back another correspondent who we think is mortally wounded. Do you care?"

The Rough Rider, somewhat abashed, announced that he did not care.

And now the wounded soldiers began to crawl, walk and be carried back to where, in the middle of the path, the surgeons had established a little field hospital.

"Say, doctor, this ain't much of a wound. I reckon I can go now back to my troop," said Arizona.

"Thanks, awfully, doctor. Awfully kind of you. I dare say I shall be all right in a moment," said New York.

This hospital was a spectacle of heroism. The doctors, gentle and calm, moved among the men without the common-senseless bullying of the ordinary ward. It was a sort of fraternal game. They were all in it, and of it, helping each other.

In the meantime three troops of the Ninth Cavalry were swinging through the woods, and a mile behind them the Seventy-first New York was moving forward eagerly to the rescue. But the day was done. The Rough Riders had bitten it off and chewed it up—chewed it up splendidly.

Stephen Crane's Vivid Story of the Battle of San Juan

IN FRONT OF SANTIAGO, JULY 4, via Old Point Comfort, Va., July 13.—The action at San Juan on July 1 was, particularly speaking, a soldiers' battle. It was like Inkerman, where the English fought half leaderless all day in a fog. Only the Cuban forest was worse than any fog.

No doubt when history begins to grind out her story we will find that many a thundering, fine, grand order was given for that day's work; but after all there will be no harm in contending that the fighting line, the men and their regimental officers, took the hill chiefly because they knew they could take it, some having no orders and others disobeying whatever orders they had.

In civil life the newspapers would have called it a grand, popular movement. It will never be forgotten as long as America has a military history.

A line of intrenched hills held by men armed with a weapon like the Mauser is not to be taken by a front attack of infantry unless the trenches have first been heavily shaken by artillery fire. Any theorist will say that it is impossible, and prove it to be impossible. But it was done, and we owe the success to the splendid gallantry of the American private soldier.

As near as one can learn headquarters expected little or no fighting on the 1st. Lawton's division was to go by the Caney road, chase the Spaniards out of that interesting village, and then, wheeling half to the left, march down to join the other divisions in some kind of attack on San Juan at daybreak on the 2d.

But somebody had been entirely misinformed as to the strength and disposition of the Spanish forces at Caney, and instead of taking Lawton six minutes to capture the town it took him nearly all day, as well it might.

The other divisions lying under fire, waiting for Lawton, grew annoyed at a delay which was, of course, not explained to them, and suddenly arose and took the formidable hills of

San Juan. It was impatience suddenly exalted to one of the sublime passions.

Lawton was well out toward Caney soon after daybreak, and by 7 o'clock we could hear the boom of Capron's guns in support of the infantry. The remaining divisions—Kent's and Wheeler's—were trudging slowly along the muddy trail through the forest.

When the first gun was fired a grim murmur passed along the lean column. "They're off!" somebody said.

The marching was of necessity very slow and even then the narrow road was often blocked. The men, weighted with their packs, cartridge belts and rifles, forded many streams, climbed hills, slid down banks and forced their way through thickets.

Suddenly there was a roar of guns just ahead and a little to the left. This was Grimes's battery going into action on the hill which is called El Paso. Then, all in a moment, the quiet column moving forward was opposed by men carrying terrible burdens. Wounded Cubans were being carried to the rear. Most of them were horribly mangled.

The second brigade of dismounted American cavalry had been in support of the battery, its position being directly to the rear. Some Cubans had joined there. The Spanish shrapnel fired at the battery was often cut too long, and passing over burst amid the supports and the Cubans.

The loss of the battery, the cavalry and the Cubans from this fire was forty men in killed and wounded, the First regular cavalry probably suffering most grievously. Presently there was a lull in the artillery fire, and down through spaces in the trees we could see the infantry still plodding with its packs steadily toward the front.

The artillerymen were greatly excited. Some showed with glee fragments of Spanish shells which had come dangerously near their heads. They had gone through their ordeal and were talking over it lightly.

In the meantime Lawton's division, some three miles away, was making plenty of noise. Caney is just at the base of a high willow-green, crinkled mountain, and Lawton was making his way over little knolls which might be termed foothills. We could see the great white clouds of smoke from Capron's guns and hear their roar punctuating the incessant drumming of the infantry. It was plain even then that Lawton was having considerably more of a fete than anybody had supposed previously.

At about 2,500 yards in front of Grimes's position on El Paso arose the gentle green hills of San Juan, dotted not too plentifully with trees—hills that resembled the sloping orchards of Orange County in summer. Here and there were houses built evidently as summer villas, but now loopholed and barricaded. They had heavy roofs of red tiles and were shaped much like Japanese, or, better, Javanese houses. Here and there, too, along the crests of these curving hillocks were ashen streaks, the rifle-pits of the Spaniards.

At the principal position of the enemy were a flag, a redoubt, a blockhouse and some sort of pagoda, in the shade of which Spanish officers were wont to promenade during lulls and negligently gossip about the battle. There was one man in a summer-resort straw hat. He did a deal of sauntering in the coolest manner possible, walking out in the clear sunshine and gazing languidly in our direction. He seemed to be carrying a little cane.

At 11.25 our artillery reopened on the central blockhouse and intrenchments. The Spanish fire had been remarkably fine, but it was our turn now. Grimes had his ranges to a nicety. After the great "shout of the gun" came the broad, windy, diminishing noise of the flung shell; then a fainter boom and a cloud of red debris out of the blockhouse or up from the ground near the trenches.

The Spanish infantry in the trenches fired a little volley immediately after every one of the American shells. It puzzled many to decide at what they could be firing, but it was finally resolved that they were firing just to show us that they were still there and were not afraid.

It must have been about 2 o'clock when the enemy's battery again retorted.

The cruel thing about this artillery duel was that our battery had nothing but old-fashioned powder, and its position was always as clearly defined as if it had been the Chicago fire. There is no secrecy about a battery that uses that kind of powder. The great billowy white smoke can be seen for miles.

On the other hand, the Spaniards were using the best smokeless. There is no use groaning over what was to be, but——!

However, fate elected that the Spanish shooting should be very bad. Only two-thirds of their shells exploded in this second affair. They all whistled high, and those that exploded raked the ground long since evacuated by the supports and the timbers. No one was hurt.

From El Paso to San Juan there is a broad expanse of dense forest, spotted infrequently with vividly green fields. It is traversed by a single narrow road which leads straight between the two positions, fording two little streams. Along this road had gone our infantry and also the military balloon. Why it was ever taken to such a position nobody knows, but there it was—huge, fat, yellow, quivering—being dragged straight into a zone of fire that would surely ruin it.

There were two officers in the car for the greater part of the way, and there surely were never two men who valued their lives less. But they both escaped unhurt, while the balloon sank down, torn to death by the bullets that were volleyed at it by the nervous Spaniards, who suspected dynamite. It was never brought out of the woods where it recklessly met its fate.

In these woods, unknown to some, including the Spaniards, was formulated the gorgeous plan of taking an impregnable position.

One saw a thin line of black figures moving across a field. They disappeared in the forest. The enemy was keeping up a terrific fire. Then suddenly somebody yelled: "By God, there go our boys up the hill!"

There is many a good American who would give an arm to get the thrill of patriotic insanity that coursed through us when we heard that yell.

Yes, they were going up the hill, up the hill. It was the best moment of anybody's life. An officer said to me afterward: "If we had been in that position and the Spaniards had come at us, we would have piled them up so high the last man couldn't have climbed over." But up went the regiments with no music save that ceaseless, fierce crashing of rifles.

The foreign attachés were shocked. "It is very gallant, but very foolish," said one sternly.

"Why, they can't take it, you know. Never in the world," cried another, much agitated. "It is slaughter, absolute slaughter."

The little Japanese shrugged his shoulders. He was one who said nothing.

The road from El Paso to San Juan was now a terrible road. It should have a tragic fame like the sunken road at Waterloo. Why we did not later hang some of the gentry who contributed from the trees to the terror of this road is not known.

The wounded were stringing back from the front, hundreds of them. Some walked unaided, an arm or a shoulder having been dressed at a field station. They stopped often enough to answer the universal hail "How is it going?" Others hobbled or clung to a friend's shoulders. Their slit trousers exposed red bandages. A few were shot horribly in the face and were led, bleeding and blind, by their mates.

And then there were the slow pacing stretcher-bearers with the dying or the insensible, the badly wounded, still figures with blood often drying brick color on their hot bandages.

Prostrate at the roadside were many others who had made their way thus far and were waiting for strength. Everywhere moved the sure-handed, invaluable Red Cross men.

Over this scene was a sort of haze of bullets. They were of two kinds. First, the Spanish lines were firing just a trifle high. Their bullets swept over our firing lines and poured into this devoted roadway, the single exit, even as it had been the single approach. The second fire was from guerillas concealed in the trees and in the thickets along the trail. They had come in under the very wings of our strong advance, taken good positions on either side of the road and were peppering our line of communication whenever they got a good target, no matter, apparently, what the target might be.

Red Cross men, wounded men, sick men, correspondents and attachés were all one to the guerilla. The move of sending an irregular force around the flanks of the enemy as he is making his front attack is so legitimate that some of us could not believe at first that the men hidden in the forest were really blazing away at the non-combatants or the wounded. Viewed simply as a bit of tactics, the scheme was admirable. But there is no doubt now that they intentionally fired at anybody they thought they could kill.

You can't mistake an ambulance driver when he is driving his ambulance. You can't mistake a wounded man when he is lying down and being bandaged. And when you see a field hospital you don't mistake it for a squadron of cavalry or a brigade of infantry.

After the guerillas had successfully rewounded some prostrate men in a hospital and killed an ambulance driver off his seat as he was taking his silent, suffering charges to the base, there were any number of humane and gentle hearted men in the army who were extremely anxious to see any guerillas that were caught hanged to the trees in which they were found. Our greatest punishment, after all, is to feed them until they are in danger of bursting.

As we went along the road we suddenly heard a cry behind us. "Oh, come quick! Come quick!" We turned and saw a young soldier spinning around frantically and grabbing at his leg. Evidently he had been going to the stream to fill his canteen, but a guerilla had barred him from that drink. Two Red Cross men rushed for him.

At the last ford, in the shelter of the muddy bank, lay a dismal band, forty men on their backs with doctors working at them and bullets singing in flocks over their heads. They rolled their eyes quietly at us. There was no groaning. They exhibited that profound patience which has been the marvel of every one.

After the ford was passed the woods cleared. The road passed through lines of barbed wire. There were, in fact, barbed wire fences running in almost every direction.

The mule train, galloping like a troop of cavalry, dashed up with a reinforcement of ammunition, every mule on the jump, the cowboys swinging their whips. They were under a fairly strong fire, but up they went.

One does not expect gallantry in a pack train, but incidentally it may be said that this charge, led by the bell mare, was one of the sights of the day.

At a place where the road cut through the crest of the ridge Borrowe and some of his men were working over his dynamite gun. After the fifth discharge something had got jammed. There was never such devotion to an inanimate thing as these men give to their dynamite gun. They will quarrel for her, starve for her, lose sleep for her and fight for her to the last ditch.

In the army there has always been two opinions of the dynamite gun. Some have said it was a most terrific engine of destruction, while others have called it a toy. With the bullets winging their long flights not very high overhead, Borrowe and his crowd at sight of us began their little hymn of praise, the chief note of which was one of almost pathetic insistence. If they ever get that gun into action again, they will make her hum.

The discomfited Spaniards, recovering from their panic, opened from their second line a most furious fire. It was first directed against one part of our line and then against another, as if they were feeling for our weakest point, fumbling around after the throat of the army.

Somebody on the left caught it for a time and then suddenly the enemy apparently devoted their entire attention to the position occupied by the Rough Riders. Some shrapnel, with fuses cut too long, passed over and burst from 100 to 200 yards to the rear. They acted precisely like things with strings to them. When the string was jerked, bang! went the hurtling explosive. But the infantry fire was very heavy, albeit high.

The American reply was in measured volleys. Part of a regiment would remain on the firing line while the other companies rested near by under the brow of the hill. Parties were sent after the packs. The commands knew with what other organizations they were in touch on the two flanks. Otherwise they knew nothing, save that they were going to hold their ground. They said so.

From our line could be seen a long, gray Spanish intrenchment, from 400 to 1,000 yards away, according to what part of our line one measured from. From it floated no smoke and no men appeared there, but it was making a noise like a million champagne corks.

Back of their intrenchments, perhaps another thousand yards, was a long building of masonry tinted pink. It flew many Red Cross flags and near it were other smaller structures also flying Red Cross flags. In fact, the enemy's third line of defense seemed to be composed of hospitals.

The city itself slanted down toward the bay, just a glimpse of silver. In the clear, white sunshine the houses of the suburbs, the hospitals and the long gray trenches were so vivid that they seemed far closer than they were.

To the rear, over the ground that the army had taken, a breeze was gently stirring the long grass and ruffling the surface of a pool that lay in a sort of meadow. The army took its glory calmly. Having nothing else to do, the army sat down and looked tranquilly at the scenery. There was not that exuberance of enthusiasm which surrounds the vicinity of a candidate for the Assembly.

The army was dusty, dishevelled, its hair matted to its forehead with sweat, its shirts glued to its back with the same, and indescribably dirty, thirsty, hungry, and a-weary from its bundles and its marches and its fights. It sat down on the conquered crest and felt satisfied.

"Well, hell! here we are."

News began to pass along the line. Lawton had taken Caney after a long fight and had lost heavily. The siege pieces were being unloaded at Siboney. Pando had succeeded in reinforcing Santiago that very morning with 8,400 men, 6,000 men, 4,500 men. Pando had not succeeded. And so on.

At dusk a comparative stillness settled upon the ridge. The shooting subsided to little nervous outbursts. In the trenches taken by our troops lay dead Spaniards.

The road to the rear increased its terrors in the darkness. The wounded men, stumbling along in the mud, a miasmic mist from the swampish ground filling their nostrils, heard often in the air the whiplash sound of a bullet that was meant for them by the lurking guerillas. A mile, two miles, two miles and a half to the rear, great populous hospitals had been formed.

The long lines of the hill began to intrench under cover of night, each regiment for itself, still, however, keeping in touch on the flanks. Each regiment dug in the ground that it had taken by its own valor. Some commands had two or three shovels, an axe or two, maybe a pick. Other regiments dug with their bayonets and shovelled out the dirt with their meat ration cans.

Darkness swallowed Santiago and the new intrenchments. The large tropic stars illumined the sky. On the safe side of the ridge our men had built some little red fires, no larger than hats, at which they cooked what food they possessed. There was no sound save to the rear, where throughout the night our pickets could be faintly heard exchanging shots with the guerillas.

On the very moment, it seemed, of the break of day, bang! the fight was on again. The firing broke out from one end of the prodigious V-shaped formation to the other. Our artillery took new advanced positions, but they were driven away by the swirling Mauser fire.

When the day was in full bloom Lawton's division, having marched all night, appeared in the road. The long, long column wound around the base of the ridge and disappeared among the woods and knolls on the right of Wheeler's line. The army was now concentrated in a splendid position.

It becomes necessary to speak of the men's opinion of the Cubans. To put it shortly, both officers and privates have the most lively contempt for the Cubans. They despise them. They came down here expecting to fight side by side with an ally, but this ally has done little but stay in the rear and eat army rations, manifesting an indifference to the cause of Cuban liberty which could not be exceeded by some one who had never heard of it.

In the great charge up the hills of San Juan the American soldiers who, for their part, sprinkled a thousand bodies in the grass, were not able to see a single Cuban assisting in what might easily turn out to be the decisive battle for Cuban freedom.

At Caney a company of Cubans came into action on the left flank of one of the American regiments just before the place was taken. Later they engaged a blockhouse at 2,000 yards and fired away all their ammunition. They sent back to the American commander for more, but they got only a snort of indignation.

As a matter of fact, the Cuban soldier, ignorant as only such isolation as has been his can make him, does not appreciate the ethics of the situation.

This great American army he views as he views the sky, the sea, the air; it is a natural and most happy phenomenon. He will go to sleep while this flood drowns the Spaniards.

The American soldier, however, thinks of himself often as a disinterested benefactor, and he would like the Cubans to play up to the ideal now and then. His attitude is mighty human. He does not really want to be thanked, and yet the total absence of anything like gratitude makes him furious. He is furious, too, because the Cubans apparently consider themselves under no obligation to take part in an engagement; because the Cubans will stay at the rear and collect haversacks, blankets, coats and shelter tents dropped by our troops.

The average Cuban here will not speak to an American unless to beg. He forgets his morning, afternoon or evening salutation unless he is reminded. If he takes a dislike to you he talks about you before your face, using a derisive undertone.

If he asks you a favor and you can't grant it his face grows sour in the expression of a man who has been deprived of an inalienable right. Then at all times he gibbers. Talk, talk, talk, talk. Heaven knows what it is all about; but certainly four Cubans can talk enough for four regiments.

The truth probably is that the food, raiment and security furnished by the Americans have completely demoralized the insurgents. When the force under Gomez came to Guantanamo to assist the marines they were a most efficient body of men. They guided the marines to the enemy and fought with them shoulder to shoulder, not very skilfully in the matter of shooting, but still with courage and determination.

After this action there ensued at Guantanamo a long peace. The Cubans built themselves a permanent camp and they began to eat, eat much, and to sleep long, day and night, until now, behold, there is no more useless body of men anywhere! A trifle less than half of them are on Dr. Edgar's sick list, and the others are practically insubordinate. So much food seems to act upon them like a drug.

Here with the army the demoralization has occurred on a big scale. It is dangerous, too, for the Cuban. If he stupidly, drowsily remains out of these fights, what weight is his voice to have later in the final adjustments? The officers and men of the army, if their feeling remains the same, will not be happy to see him have any at all. The situation needs a Gomez. It is more serious than these bestarred machete bearers know how to appreciate, and it is the worst thing for the cause of an independent Cuba that could possibly exist.

At San Juan the 2d of July was a smaller edition of the 1st. The men deepened their intrenchments, shot, slept and ate. On the 1st every man had been put into the fighting line. There was not a reserve as big as your hat. If the enemy broke through any part of the line there was nothing to stop them short of Siboney. On the 2d, however, some time after the arrival of Lawton, the Ninth Massachusetts and the Thirty-fourth Michigan came up.

Along the road from El Paso they had to pass some pretty grim sights. And there were some pretty grim odors, but the men were steady enough. "How far are they off?" they asked of a passing regular. "Oh, not far; but it's all right. We think they may run out of ammunition in the course of a week or ten days."

The volunteers laughed. But the pitiful thing about this advance was to see in the hands of the boys those terrible old rifles that smoke like brush fires and give the regimental line away to the enemy as plainly as an illuminated sign.

I remember that on the first day men of the Seventy-first who had lost their command would try to join one of the regular regiments, but the regulars would have none of them. "Get out of here with that d—— gun!" the regulars would say. During the battle just one shot from a Springfield would call a volley, for the Spaniards then knew just where to shoot. It was very hard on the Seventy-first New York and the Second Massachusetts.

At Caney about two hundred prisoners were taken. Two big squads of them were soldiers of the regular Spanish infantry in the usual blue-and-white pajamas. The others were the rummiest-looking set of men one could possibly imagine. They were native-born Cubans, reconcentrados, traitors, guerillas of the kind that bushwhacked us so unmercifully. Some were doddering old men, shaking with the palsy of their many years. Some were slim, dirty, bad-eyed boys. They were all of a lower class than one could find in any United States jail.

At first they had all expected to be butchered. In fact, to encourage them to fight, their officers had told them that if they gave in they need expect no mercy from the dreadful Americans.

Our great, good, motherly old country has nothing in her heart but mercy, and nothing in her pockets but beef, hard-tack and coffee for all of them—lemon-colored refugee from Santiago, wild-eyed prisoner from the trenches, Spanish guerilla from out the thickets, half-naked insurgent from the mountains—all of them.

In the church at Caney lie fifty-two Spanish wounded, attended by our surgeons. For a temporary affair, inaugurated in a moment, it is as good a hospital as ever raised its flag after a day of blood, and our surgeons and our Red Cross assistants were giving the best of their trained intelligence to the cure of the hurts of these men even while, on the road from San Juan to El Paso, the guerillas were shooting at our wounded.

Regulars Get No Glory

SIBONEY, JULY 9.—Of course people all over the United States are dying to hear the names of the men who are conspicuous for bravery in Shafter's army. But as a matter of fact nobody with the army is particularly conspicuous for bravery. The bravery of an individual here is not a quality which causes him to be pointed out by his admiring fellows; he is, rather, submerged in the general mass. Now, cowardice—that would make a man conspicuous. He would then be pointed out often enough, but—mere bravery—that is no distinction in the Fifth Corps of the United States Army.

The main fact that has developed in this Santiago campaign is that the soldier of the regular army is the best man standing on two feet on God's green earth. This fact is put forth with no pretense whatever of interesting the American public in it. The public doesn't seem to care very much for the regular soldier.

The public wants to learn of the gallantry of Reginald Marmaduke Maurice Montmorenci Sturtevant, and for goodness sake how the poor old chappy endures that dreadful hard-tack and bacon. Whereas, the name of the regular soldier is probably Michael Nolan and his life-sized portrait was not in the papers in celebration of his enlistment.

Just plain Private Nolan, blast him—he is of no consequence. He will get his name in the paper—oh, yes, when he is "killed." Or when he is "wounded." Or when he is "missing." If some good Spaniard shoots him through he will achieve a temporary notoriety, figuring in the lists for one brief moment in which he will appear to the casual reader mainly as part of a total, a unit in the interesting sum of men slain.

In fact, the disposition to leave out entirely all lists of killed and wounded regulars is quite a rational one since nobody cares to read them, anyhow, and their omission would allow room for oil paintings of various really important persons, limned as they were in the very act of being at the front, proud young men riding upon horses, the horses being still in Tampa and the proud young men being at Santiago, but still proud young men riding upon horses.

The ungodly Nolan, the sweating, swearing, overloaded, hungry, thirsty, sleepless Nolan, tearing his breeches on the barbed wire entanglements, wallowing through the muddy fords, pursuing his way through the stiletto-pointed thickets, climbing the fire-crowned hill—Nolan gets shot. One Nolan of this regiment or that regiment, a private, great chums in time of peace with a man by the name of Hennessy, him that had a fight with Snyder. Nearest relative is a sister, chambermaid in a hotel in Omaha. Hennessy, old fool, is going around looking glum, buried in taciturn silence, a silence that lasts two hours and eight minutes; touching tribute to Nolan.

There is a half-bred fox terrier in barracks at Reno. Who the deuce gets the dog now? Must by rights go to Hennessy. Brief argument during which Corporal Jenkins interpolates the thoughtful remark that they haven't had anything to eat that day. End of Nolan.

The three shining points about the American regular are his illimitable patience under anything which he may be called upon to endure, his superlative marksmanship and his ability in action to go ahead and win without any example or leading or jawing or trumpeting whatsoever. He knows his business, he does.

He goes into battle as if he had been fighting every day for three hundred years. If there is heavy firing ahead he does not even ask a question about it. He doesn't even ask whether the Americans are winning or losing. He agitates himself over no extraneous points. He attends exclusively to himself. In the Turk or the Cossack this is a combination of fatalism and woodenheadedness. It need not be said that these qualities are lacking in the regular.

After the battle, at leisure—if he gets any—the regular's talk is likely to be a complete essay on practical field operations. He will be full of views about the management of such and such a brigade, the practice of this or that battery, and be admiring or scornful in regard to the operations on the right flank. He will be a tireless critic, bolstering his opinions with technical information procured heaven only knows where. In fact, he will alarm you. You may say: "This man gabbles too much for to be a soldier."

Then suddenly the regular becomes impenetrable, enigmatic. It is a question of Orders. When he hears the appointed voice raised in giving an Order, he is a changed being. When an Order comes he has no more to say; he simply displays as fine a form of unquestioning obedience as there is to be seen anywhere. It is his sacred thing, his fetish, his religion. Nothing now can stop him but a bullet.

In speaking of Reginald Marmaduke Maurice Montmorenci Sturtevant and his life-sized portraits, it must not be supposed that the unfortunate youth admires that sort of thing. He is a man and a soldier, although not so good either as man or soldier as Michael Nolan. But he is in this game honestly and sincerely; he is playing it gallantly; and, if from time to time he is made to look ridiculous, it is not his fault at all. It is the fault of the public.

We are as a people a great collection of the most arrant kids about anything that concerns war, and if we can get a chance to perform absurdly we usually seize it. It will probably take us three more months to learn that the society reporter, invaluable as he may be in times of peace, has no function during the blood and smoke of battle.

I know of one newspaper whose continual cabled instructions to its men in Cuba were composed of interrogations as to the doings and appearance of various unhappy society young men who were decently and quietly doing their duty along o' Nolan and the others. The correspondents of this paper, being already impregnated with soldierly feeling, finally arose and said they'd be blamed if they would stand it.

And shame, deep shame, on those who, because somebody once led a cotillon, can seem to forget Nolan—Private Nolan of the regulars—shot through, his half-bred terrier being masterless at Reno and his sister being chambermaid in a hotel in Omaha; Nolan, no longer sweating, swearing, overloaded, hungry, thirsty, sleepless, but merely a corpse, attired in about forty cents' worth of clothes. Here's three volleys and taps to one Nolan, of this regiment or that regiment, and maybe some day, in a fairer, squarer land, he'll get his picture in the paper, too.

The Price of the Harness

I

TWENTY-FIVE MEN were making a road out of a path up the hillside. The light batteries in the rear were impatient to advance, but first must be done all that digging and smoothing which gains no incrusted medals from war. The men worked like gardeners, and a road was growing from the old pack-animal trail. Trees arched from a field of guinea-grass which resembled young wild corn. The day was still and dry. The men working were dressed in the consistent blue of United States regulars. They looked indifferent, almost stolid, despite the heat and the labor. There was little talking. From time to time a government pack-train, led by a sleek-sided tender bell-mare, came from one way or the other way, and the men stood aside as the strong, hard, black-and-tan animals crowded eagerly after their curious little feminine leader.

A volunteer staff officer appeared, and, sitting on his horse in the middle of the work, asked the sergeant in command some questions which were apparently not relevant to any military business. Men straggling along on various duties almost invariably spun some kind of a joke as they passed.

A corporal and four men were guarding boxes of spare ammunition at the top of the hill, and one of the number often went to the foot of the hill swinging canteens.

The day wore down to the Cuban dusk in which the shadows are all grim and of ghastly shape. The men began to lift their eyes from the shovels and picks, and glance in the direction of their camp. The sun threw his last lance through the foliage. The steep mountain range on the right turned blue and as without detail as a curtain. The tiny ruby of light ahead meant that the ammunition guard were cooking their supper. From somewhere in the world came a single rifle-shot. Figures appeared, dim in the shadow of the trees. A murmur, a sigh of quiet relief, arose from the working party. Later, they swung up the hill in an unformed formation, being always like soldiers, and unable even to carry a spade save like United States regular soldiers. As they passed through some fields, the bland white light of the end of the day feebly touched each hard bronze profile.

"Wonder if we'll git anythin' to eat," said Watkins, in a low voice.

"Should think so," said Nolan, in the same tone. They betrayed no impatience; they seemed to feel a kind of awe of the situation.

The sergeant turned. One could see the cool grey eye flashing under the brim of the campaign hat. "What in hell you fellers kickin' about?" he asked. They made no reply, understanding that they were being suppressed.

As they moved on, a murmur arose from the tall grass on each hand. It was the noise from the bivouac of ten thousand men, although one saw practically nothing from the low-cut roadway. The sergeant led his party up a wet clay bank and into a trampled field. Here were scattered tiny white shelter-tents, and in the darkness they were luminous like the rearing stones in a graveyard. A few fires burned blood-red, and the shadowy figures of men moved with no more expression of detail than there is in the swaying of foliage on a windy night.

The working party felt their way to where their tents were pitched. A man suddenly cursed; he had mislaid something and he knew he was not going to find it that night. Watkins spoke again with the monotony of a clock. "Wonder if we'll git anythin' to eat."

Martin, with eyes turned pensively to the stars, began a treatise. "Them Spaniards——"

"Oh, quit it," cried Nolan. "What th' piper do you know about th' Spaniards, you fat-headed Dutchman? Better think of your belly, you blunderin' swine, an' what you're goin' to put in it, grass or dirt."

A laugh, a sort of a deep growl, arose from the prostrate men. In the mean time the sergeant had reappeared and was standing over them. "No rations to-night," he said gruffly, and turning on his heel walked away.

This announcement was received in silence. But Watkins had flung himself face downward, and putting his lips close to a tuft of grass, he formulated oaths. Martin arose and going to his shelter, crawled in sulkily. After a long interval Nolan said aloud, "Hell!" Grierson, enlisted for the war, raised a querulous voice. "Well, I wonder when we *will* git fed?"

From the ground about him came a low chuckle full of ironical comment upon Grierson's lack of certain qualities which the other men felt themselves to possess.

II

In the cold light of dawn the men were on their knees, packing, strapping and buckling. The comic toy hamlet of shelter-tents had been wiped out as if by a cyclone. Through the trees could be seen the crimson of a light battery's blankets, and the wheels creaked like the sound of a musketry fight. Nolan, well gripped by his shelter-tent, his blanket and his cartridge belt, and bearing his rifle, advanced upon a small group of men who were hastily finishing a can of coffee.

"Say, give us a drink, will yeh?" he asked wistfully. He was as sad-eyed as an orphan beggar.

Every man in the group turned to look him straight in the face. He had asked for the principal ruby out of each one's crown. There was grim silence. Then one said, "What fer?" Nolan cast his glance to the ground and went away abashed.

But he espied Watkins and Martin surrounding Grierson, who had gained three pieces of hard-tack by mere force of his audacious inexperience. Grierson was fending his comrades off tearfully. "Now, don't be damn pigs," he cried. "Hold on a minute." Here Nolan asserted a claim. Grierson groaned. Kneeling piously, he divided the hard-tack with minute care into four portions. The men, who had had their heads together like players watching a wheel of fortune, arose suddenly, each chewing. Nolan interpolated a drink of water and sighed contentedly.

The whole forest seemed to be moving. From the field on the other side of the road a column of men in blue was slowly pouring; the battery had creaked on ahead; from the rear came a hum of advancing regiments. Then from a mile away rang the noise of a shot, then another shot; in a moment the rifles there were drumming, drumming, drumming. The artillery boomed out suddenly. A day of battle was begun.

The men made no exclamations. They rolled their eyes in

the direction of the sound, and then swept with a calm glance the forests and the hills which surrounded them, implacably mysterious forests and hills which lent to every rifle-shot the ominous quality which belongs to secret assassination. The whole scene would have spoken to the private soldiers of ambushes, sudden flank attacks, terrible disasters if it were not for those cool gentlemen with shoulder-straps and swords who, the private soldiers knew, were of another world and omnipotent for the business.

The battalion moved out into the mud and began a leisurely march in the damp shade of the trees. The advance of two batteries had churned the black soil into a formidable paste. The brown leggings of the men, stained with the mud of other days, took on a deeper color. Perspiration broke gently out on the reddish faces. With his heavy roll of blanket and the half of a shelter-tent crossing his right shoulder and under his left arm, each man presented the appearance of being clasped from behind, wrestler fashion, by a pair of thick white arms. There was something distinctive in the way they carried their rifles. There was the grace of an old hunter somewhere in it, the grace of a man whose rifle has become absolutely a part of himself. Furthermore, almost every blue shirt-sleeve was rolled to the elbow, disclosing fore-arms of almost incredible brawn. The rifles seemed light, almost fragile, in the hands that were at the end of these arms, never fat but always with rolling muscles and veins that seemed on the point of bursting. And another thing was the silence and the marvelous impassivity of the faces as the column made its slow way toward where the whole forest spluttered and fluttered with battle.

Opportunely, the battalion was halted astraddle of a stream, and before it again moved most of the men had filled their canteens. The firing increased. Ahead and to the left a battery was booming at methodical intervals, while the infantry racket was that continual drumming which, after all, often sounds like rain on a roof. Directly ahead one could hear the deep voices of field-pieces.

Some wounded Cubans were carried by in litters improvised from hammocks swung on poles. One had a ghastly cut in the throat, probably from a fragment of shell, and his head was turned as if Providence particularly wished to display this wide and lapping gash to the long column that was winding toward the front. And another Cuban, shot through the groin, kept up a continual wail as he swung from the tread of his bearers. "Ay—ee! Ay—ee! Madre mia! Madre mia!" He sang this bitter ballad into the ears of at least three thousand men as they slowly made way for his bearers on the narrow wood-path. These wounded insurgents were, then, to a large part of the advancing army, the visible messengers of blood-shed, death, and the men regarded them with thoughtful awe. This doleful sobbing cry, "Madre mia," was a tangible conse-quent misery of all that firing on in front into which the men knew they were soon to be plunged. Some of them wished to inquire of the bearers the details of what had happened, but they could not speak Spanish, and so it was as if fate had intentionally sealed the lips of all in order that even meager information might not leak out concerning this mystery— battle. On the other hand, many unversed private soldiers looked upon the unfortunate as men who had seen thousands maimed and bleeding, and absolutely could not conjure up any further interest in such scenes.

A young staff officer passed on horseback. The vocal Cuban was always wailing, but the officer wheeled past the bearers without heeding anything. And yet he never before had seen such a sight. His case was different from that of the private soldiers. He heeded nothing because he was busy, immensely busy and hurried with a multitude of reasons and desires for doing his duty perfectly. His whole life had been a mere pe-riod of preliminary reflection for this situation, and he had no clear idea of anything save his obligation as an officer. A man of this kind might be stupid; it is conceivable that in remote cases certain bumps on his head might be composed entirely of wood; but those traditions of fidelity and courage which have been handed to him from generation to generation, and which he has tenaciously preserved despite the persecution of legislators and the indifference of his country, make it incred-ible that in battle he should ever fail to give his best blood and his best thought for his general, for his men and for him-self. And so this young officer in the shapeless hat and the torn and dirty shirt failed to heed the wails of the wounded man, even as the pilgrim fails to heed the world as he raises his illumined face toward his purpose—rightly or wrongly his purpose—his sky of the ideal of duty; and the wonderful part of it is that he is guided by an ideal which he has himself created, and has alone protected from attack. The young man was merely an officer in the United States regular army.

The column swung across a shallow ford and took a road which passed the right flank of one of the American batteries. On a hill it was booming and belching great clouds of white smoke. The infantry looked up with interest. Arrayed below the hill and behind the battery were the horses and limbers, the riders checking their pawing mounts, and behind each rider a red blanket flamed against the fervent green of the bushes. As the infantry moved along the road, some of the battery horses turned at the noise of the trampling feet and surveyed the men with eyes deep as wells, serene, mournful, generous eyes, lit heart-breakingly with something that was akin to a philosophy, a religion of self-sacrifice—oh, gallant, gallant horses!

"I know a feller in that battery," said Nolan musingly. "A driver."

"Damn sight rather be a gunner," said Martin.

"Why would ye?" said Nolan opposingly.

"Well, I'd take my chances as a gunner b'fore I'd sit 'way up in th' air on a raw-boned plug an' git shot at."

"Aw——" began Nolan.

"They've had some losses t'-day all right," interrupted Grierson.

"Horses?" asked Watkins.

"Horses an' men too," said Grierson.

"How d'yeh know?"

"A feller told me there by the ford."

They kept only a part of their minds bearing on this discussion because they could already hear high in the air the wire-string note of the enemy's bullets.

III

The road taken by this battalion as it followed other battalions is something less than a mile long in its journey across a heavily wooded plain. It is greatly changed now; in fact it was metamorphosed in two days; but at that time it was a mere track through dense shrubbery from which rose great digni- fied arching trees. It was, in fact, a path through a jungle.

The battalion had no sooner left the battery in rear than bullets began to drive overhead. They made several different sounds, but as they were mainly high shots it was usual for them to make the faint note of a vibrant string touched elu- sively, half dreamily.

The military balloon, a fat, wavering yellow thing, was leading the advance like some new conception of war-god. Its bloated mass shone above the trees, and served incidentally to indicate to the men at the rear that comrades were in advance. The track itself exhibited for all its visible length a closely knit procession of soldiers in blue with breasts crossed by white shelter-tents. The first ominous order of battle came down the line. "Use the cut-off. Don't use the magazine until you're ordered." Non-commissioned officers repeated the command gruffly. A sound of clicking locks rattled along the column. All men knew that the time had come.

The front had burst out with a roar like a brush fire. The balloon was dying, dying a gigantic and public death before the eyes of two armies. It quivered, sank, faded into the trees amid the flurry of a battle that was suddenly and tremen- dously like a storm.

The American battery thundered behind the men with a shock that seemed likely to tear the backs of their heads off. The Spanish shrapnel fled on a line to their left, swirling and swishing in supernatural velocity. The noise of the rifle bullets broke in their faces like the noise of so many lamp chimneys or sped overhead in swift cruel spitting. And at the front the battle-sound, as if it were simply music, was beginning to swell and swell until the volleys rolled like a surf.

The officers shouted hoarsely. "Come on, men! Hurry up, boys! Come on, now! Hurry up!" The soldiers, running heav- ily in their accouterments, dashed forward. A baggage guard was swiftly detailed; the men tore their rolls from their shoul- ders as if the things were afire. The battalion, stripped for action, again dashed forward.

"Come on, men! Come on!" To them the battle was as yet merely a road through the woods crowded with troops who lowered their heads anxiously as the bullets fled high. But a moment later the column wheeled abruptly to the left and entered a field of tall green grass. The line scattered to a skirmish formation. In front was a series of knolls treed sparsely like orchards, and although no enemy was visible, these knolls were all popping and spitting with rifle-fire. In some places there were to be seen long grey lines of dirt intrenchments. The American shells were kicking up reddish clouds of dust from the brow of one of the knolls where stood a pagoda-like house. It was not much like a battle with men; it was a battle with a bit of charming scenery, enigmatically potent for death.

Nolan knew that Martin had suddenly fallen. "What——" he began.

"They've hit me," said Martin.

"Jesus!" said Nolan.

Martin lay on the ground, clutching his left fore-arm just below the elbow with all the strength of his right hand. His lips were pursed ruefully. He did not seem to know what to do. He continued to stare at his arm.

Then suddenly the bullets drove at them low and hard. The men flung themselves face down in the grass. Nolan lost all thought of his friend. Oddly enough, he felt somewhat like a man hiding under a bed, and he was just as sure that he could not raise his head high without being shot as a man hiding under a bed is sure that he cannot raise his head without bumping it.

A lieutenant was seated in the grass just behind him. He was in the careless and yet rigid pose of a man balancing a loaded plate on his knee at a picnic. He was talking in soothing paternal tones.

"Now don't get rattled. We're all right here. Just as safe as being in church. . . . They're all going high. Don't mind them. . . . Don't mind them. . . . They're all going high. We've got them rattled and they can't shoot straight. Don't mind them."

The sun burned down steadily from a pale sky upon the

crackling woods and knolls and fields. From the roar of musketry it might have been that the celestial heat was frying this part of the world.

Nolan snuggled close to the grass. He watched a grey line of intrenchments, above which floated the veriest gossamer of smoke. A flag lolled on a staff behind it. The men in the trench volleyed whenever an American shell exploded near them. It was some kind of infantile defiance. Frequently a bullet came from the woods directly behind Nolan and his comrades. They thought at the time that these bullets were from the rifle of some incompetent soldier of their own side.

There was no cheering. The men would have looked about them wondering where the army was if it were not that the crash of the fighting for the distance of a mile denoted plainly enough where that army was.

Officially, the battalion had not yet fired a shot; there had been merely some irresponsible popping by men on the extreme left flank. But it was known that the lieutenant-colonel who had been in command was dead, shot through the heart, and that the captains were thinned down to two. At the rear went on a long tragedy in which men, bent and hasty, hurried to shelter with other men, helpless, dazed and bloody. Nolan knew of it all from the hoarse and affrighted voices which he heard as he lay flattened in the grass. There came to him a sense of exultation. Here, then, was one of those dread and lurid situations which in a nation's history stand out in crimson letters, becoming tales of blood to stir generation after generation. And he was in it and unharmed. If he lived through the battle, he would be a hero of the desperate fight at —— and here he wondered for a second what fate would be pleased to bestow as a name for this battle.

But it is quite sure that hardly another man in the battalion was engaged in any thoughts concerning the historic. On the contrary, they deemed it ill that they were being badly cut up on a most unimportant occasion. It would have benefited the conduct of whoever were weak if they had known that they were engaged in a battle that would be famous forever.

IV

Martin had picked himself up from where the bullet had knocked him and addressed the lieutenant. "I'm hit, sir," he said.

The lieutenant was very busy. "All right, all right," he said, heeding the man just enough to learn where he was wounded. "Go over that way. You ought to see a dressing-station under those trees."

Martin found himself dizzy and sick. The sensation in his arm was distinctly galvanic. The feeling was so strange that he could wonder at times if a wound was really what ailed him. Once, in this dazed way, he examined his arm; he saw the hole. Yes, he was shot; that was it. And more than in any other way it affected him with a profound sadness.

As directed by the lieutenant, he went to the clump of trees, but he found no dressing-station there. He found only a dead soldier lying with his face buried in his arms and with his shoulders humped high as if he was convulsively sobbing. Martin decided to make his way to the road, deeming that he thus would better his chances of getting to a surgeon. But he suddenly found his way blocked by a fence of barbed wire. Such was his mental condition that he brought up at a rigid halt before this fence and stared stupidly at it. It did not seem to him possible that this obstacle could be defeated by any means. The fence was there and it stopped his progress. He could not go in that direction.

But as he turned he espied that procession of wounded men, strange pilgrims, which had already worn a path in the tall grass. They were passing through a gap in the fence. Martin joined them. The bullets were flying over them in sheets, but many of them bore themselves as men who had now exacted from fate a singular immunity. Generally there were no outcries, no kicking, no talk at all. They too, like Martin, seemed buried in a vague but profound melancholy.

But there was one who cried out loudly. A man shot in the head was being carried arduously by four comrades, and he continually yelled one word that was terrible in its primitive strength. "Bread! Bread! Bread!" Following him and his bearers were a limping crowd of men less cruelly wounded, who kept their eyes always fixed on him, as if they gained from his extreme agony some balm for their own sufferings.

"Bread! Give me bread!"

Martin plucked a man by the sleeve. The man had been shot in the foot and was making his way with the help of a curved, incompetent stick. It is an axiom of war that wounded men can never find straight sticks.

"What's the matter with that feller?" asked Martin.

"Nutty," said the man.

"Why is he?"

"Shot in th' head," answered the other impatiently.

The wail of the sufferer arose in the field amid the swift rasp of bullets and the boom and shatter of shrapnel. "Bread! Bread! Oh, God, can't you give me bread? Bread!" The bearers of him were suffering exquisite agony, and often exchanged glances which exhibited their despair of ever getting free of this tragedy. It seemed endless.

"Bread! Bread! Bread!"

But despite the fact that there was always in the way of this crowd a wistful melancholy, one must know that there were plenty of men who laughed, laughed at their wounds whimsically, quaintly inventing odd humors concerning bicycles and cabs, extracting from this shedding of their blood a wonderful amount of material for cheerful badinage, and with their faces twisted from pain as they stepped, they often joked like music-hall stars. And perhaps this was the most tearful part of all.

They trudged along a road until they reached a ford. Here under the eave of the bank lay a dismal company. In the mud and in the damp shade of some bushes were a half-hundred pale-faced men prostrate. Two or three surgeons were working there. Also there was a chaplain, grim-mouthed, resolute, his surtout discarded. Overhead always was that incessant maddening wail of bullets.

Martin was standing gazing drowsily at the scene when a surgeon grabbed him. "Here, what's the matter with you?" Martin was daunted. He wondered what he had done that the surgeon should be so angry with him.

"In the arm," he muttered, half shamefacedly.

After the surgeon had hastily and irritably bandaged the

injured member he glared at Martin and said, "You can walk all right, can't you?"

"Yes, sir," said Martin.

"Well, now, you just make tracks down that road."

"Yes, sir." Martin went meekly off. The doctor had seemed exasperated almost to the point of madness.

The road was at this time swept with the fire of a body of Spanish sharpshooters who had come cunningly around the flanks of the American army, and were now hidden in the dense foliage that lined both sides of the road. They were shooting at everything. The road was as crowded as a street in a city, and at an absurdly short range they emptied their rifles at the passing people. They were aided always by the over-sweep from the regular Spanish line of battle.

Martin was sleepy from his wound. He saw tragedy follow tragedy, but they created in him no feeling of horror.

A man with a red cross on his arm was leaning against a great tree. Suddenly he tumbled to the ground and writhed for a moment in the way of a child oppressed with colic. A comrade immediately began to bustle importantly. "Here," he called to Martin, "help me carry this man, will you?"

Martin looked at him with dull scorn. "I'll be damned if I do," he said. "Can't carry myself, let alone somebody else."

This answer, which rings now so inhuman, pitiless, did not affect the other man. "Well, all right," he said. "Here comes some other fellers." The wounded man had now turned blue-grey; his eyes were closed; his body shook in a gentle, persistent chill.

Occasionally Martin came upon dead horses, their limbs sticking out and up like stakes. One beast, mortally shot, was besieged by three or four men who were trying to push it into the bushes where it could live its brief time of anguish without thrashing to death any of the wounded men in the gloomy procession.

The mule train, with extra ammunition, charged toward the front, still led by the tinkling bell-mare.

An ambulance was stuck momentarily in the mud, and above the crack of battle one could hear the familiar objurgations of the driver as he whirled his lash.

Two privates were having a hard time with a wounded captain whom they were supporting to the rear. He was half cursing, half wailing out the information that he not only would not go another step toward the rear, but was certainly going to return at once to the front. They begged, pleaded at great length as they continually headed him off. They were not unlike two nurses with an exceptionally bad and head-strong little duke.

The wounded soldiers paused to look impassively upon this struggle. They were always like men who could not be aroused by anything further.

The visible hospital was mainly straggling thickets inter-sected with narrow paths, the ground being covered with men. Martin saw a busy person with a book and a pencil, but he did not approach him to become officially a member of the hospital. All he desired was rest and immunity from nag-ging. He took seat painfully under a bush and leaned his back upon the trunk. There he remained thinking, his face wooden.

V

"My Gawd," said Nolan, squirming on his belly in the grass, "I can't stand this much longer."

Then suddenly every rifle in the firing line seemed to go off of its own accord. It was the result of an order, but few men had heard the order; in the main they had fired because they heard others fire, and their sense was so quick that the volley did not sound too ragged. These marksmen had been lying for nearly an hour in stony silence, their sights adjusted, their fingers fondling their rifles, their eyes staring at the intrench-ments of the enemy. The battalion had suffered heavy losses, and these losses had been hard to bear, for a soldier always reasons that men lost during a period of inaction are men badly lost.

The line now sounded like a great machine set to running frantically in the open air, the bright sunshine of a green field. To the prut of the magazine rifles was added the under-chorus of the clicking mechanism, steady and swift as if the hand of one operator was controlling it all. It reminds one always of a loom, a great grand steel loom, clinking, clanking, plunking, plinking, to weave a woof of thin red threads, the cloth of death. By the men's shoulders under their eager hands dropped continually the yellow empty shells, spinning into the crushed grass blades to remain there and mark for the belated eye the line of a battalion's fight.

All impatience, all rebellious feeling, had passed out of the men as soon as they had been allowed to use their weapons against the enemy. They now were absorbed in this business of hitting something, and all the long training at the rifle ranges, all the pride of the marksman which had been so long alive in them, made them forget for the time everything but shooting. They were as deliberate and exact as so many watchmakers.

A new sense of safety was rightfully upon them. They knew that those mysterious men in the high far trenches in front were having the bullets sping in their faces with relentless and remarkable precision; they knew, in fact, that they were now doing the thing which they had been trained endlessly to do, and they knew they were doing it well. Nolan, for instance, was overjoyed. "Plug 'em," he said. "Plug 'em." He laid his face to his rifle as if it were his mistress. He was aiming under the shadow of a certain portico of a fortified house; there he could faintly see a long black line which he knew to be a loophole cut for riflemen, and he knew that every shot of his was going there under the portico, mayhap through the loop- hole to the brain of another man like himself. He loaded the awkward magazine of his rifle again and again. He was so intent that he did not know of new orders until he saw the men about him scrambling to their feet and running forward, crouching low as they ran.

He heard a shout. "Come on, boys! We can't be last! We're going up! We're going up!" He sprang to his feet and, stoop- ing, ran with the others. Something fine, soft, gentle, touched his heart as he ran. He had loved the regiment, the army, because the regiment, the army, was his life. He had no other outlook; and now these men, his comrades, were performing his dream-scenes for him. They were doing as he had or- dained in his visions. It is curious that in this charge he con- sidered himself as rather unworthy. Although he himself was in the assault with the rest of them, it seemed to him that his comrades were dazzlingly courageous. His part, to his mind, was merely that of a man who was going along with the crowd.

He saw Grierson biting madly with his pincers at a barbed-wire fence. They were half-way up the beautiful sylvan slope; there was no enemy to be seen, and yet the landscape rained bullets. Somebody punched him violently in the stomach. He thought dully to lie down and rest, but instead he fell with a crash.

The sparse line of men in blue shirts and dirty slouch hats swept on up the hill. He decided to shut his eyes for a moment because he felt very dreamy and peaceful. It seemed only a minute before he heard a voice say, "There he is." Grierson and Watkins had come to look for him. He searched their faces at once and keenly, for he had a thought that the line might be driven down the hill and leave him in Spanish hands. But he saw that everything was secure and he prepared no questions.

"Nolan," said Grierson clumsily, "do you know me?"

The man on the ground smiled softly. "Of course I know you, you chowder-faced monkey. Why wouldn't I know you?"

Watkins knelt beside him. "Where did they plug you, boy?"

Nolan was somewhat dubious. "It ain't much, I don't think, but it's somewheres there." He laid a finger on the pit of his stomach. They lifted his shirt and then privately they exchanged a glance of horror.

"Does it hurt, Jimmie?" said Grierson, hoarsely.

"No," said Nolan, "it don't hurt any, but I feel sort of dead-to-the-world and numb all over. I don't think it's very bad."

"Oh, it's all right," said Watkins.

"What I need is a drink," said Nolan, grinning at them. "I'm chilly—lyin' on this damp ground."

"It ain't very damp, Jimmie," said Grierson.

"Well, it is damp," said Nolan, with sudden irritability. "I can feel it. I'm wet, I tell you—wet through—just from lyin' here."

They answered hastily. "Yes, that's so, Jimmie. It *is* damp. That's so."

"Just put your hand under my back and see how wet the ground is," he said.

"No," they answered. "That's all right, Jimmie. We know it's wet."

"Well, put your hand under and see," he cried, stubbornly.

"Oh, never mind, Jimmie."

"No," he said in a temper. "See for yourself." Grierson seemed to be afraid of Nolan's agitation, and so he slipped a hand under the prostrate man, and presently withdrew it covered with blood. "Yes," he said, hiding his hand carefully from Nolan's eyes, "you were right, Jimmie."

"Of course I was," said Nolan, contentedly closing his eyes. "This hillside holds water like a swamp." After a moment he said: "Guess I ought to know. I'm flat here on it, and you fellers are standing up."

He did not know he was dying. He thought he was holding an argument on the condition of the turf.

VI

"Cover his face," said Grierson in a low and husky voice, afterward.

"What'll I cover it with?" said Watkins.

They looked at themselves. They stood in their shirts, trousers, leggings, shoes; they had nothing.

"Oh," said Grierson, "here's his hat." He brought it and laid it on the face of the dead man. They stood for a time. It was apparent that they thought it essential and decent to say or do something. Finally Watkins said in a broken voice, "Aw, it's a damn shame." They moved slowly off toward the firing line.

In the blue gloom of evening, in one of the fever tents, the two rows of still figures became hideous, charnel. The languid movement of a hand was surrounded with spectral mystery, and the occasional painful twisting of a body under a blanket was terrifying, as if dead men were moving in their graves under the sod. A heavy odor of sickness and medicine hung in the air.

"What regiment are you in?" said a feeble voice.

"Twenty-ninth Infantry," answered another voice.

"Twenty-ninth! Why, the man on the other side of me is in the Twenty-ninth."

"He is? . . . Hey there, partner, are you in the Twenty-ninth?"

A third voice merely answered wearily: "Martin of C Company."

"What? Jack, is that you?"

"It's part of me. . . . Who are you?"

"Grierson, you fat-head. I thought you were wounded."

There was the noise of a man gulping a great drink of water, and at its conclusion Martin said, "I am."

"Well, what you doin' in the fever place, then?"

Martin replied with drowsy impatience. "Got the fever too."

"Gee!" said Grierson.

Thereafter there was silence in the fever tent save for the noise made by a man over in a corner, a kind of man always found in an American crowd, a heroic, implacable comedian and patriot, of a humor that has bitterness and ferocity and love in it, and he was wringing from the situation a grim meaning by singing the Star-Spangled Banner with all the ardor which could be procured from his fever-stricken body.

"Billie," called Martin in a low voice, "where's Jimmie Nolan?"

"He's dead," said Grierson.

A triangle of raw gold light shone on a side of the tent. Somewhere in the valley an engine's bell was ringing, and it sounded of peace and home as if it hung on a cow's neck.

"An' where's Ike Watkins?"

"Well, he ain't dead, but he got shot through the lungs. They say he ain't got much show."

Through the clouded odors of sickness and medicine rang the dauntless voice of the man in the corner:

". . . Long may it wave. . . ."

The Clan of No-Name

Unwind my riddle.
Cruel as hawks the hours fly,
Wounded men seldom come home to die,
The hard waves see an arm flung high,
Scorn hits strong because of a lie,
Yet there exists a mystic tie.
Unwind my riddle.

I

S HE WAS OUT in the garden. Her mother came to her rap-
idly. "Margharita! Margharita, Mr. Smith is here!
Come!" Her mother was fat and commercially excited. Mr.
Smith was a matter of some importance to all Tampa people,
and since he was really in love with Margharita he was dis-
tinctly of more importance to this particular household.

Palm trees tossed their sprays over the fence toward the
rutted sand of the street. A little foolish fish-pond in the
centre of the garden emitted a sound of red-fins flipping, flip-
ping. "No, mamma," said the girl, "let Mr. Smith wait. I like
the garden in the moonlight."

Her mother threw herself into that state of virtuous aston-
ishment which is the weapon of her kind. "Margharita!"

The girl evidently considered herself to be a privileged
belle, for she answered quite carelessly: "Oh, let him wait."

The mother threw abroad her arms with a semblance of
great high-minded suffering and withdrew. Margharita
walked alone in the moonlit garden. Also an electric light
threw its shivering gleam over part of her parade.

There was peace for a time. Then suddenly through the
faint brown palings was stuck an envelope, white and square.
Margharita approached this envelope with an indifferent
stride. She hummed a silly air, she bore herself casually, but
there was something that made her grasp it hard, a peculiar
muscular exhibition, not discernible to indifferent eyes. She
did not clutch it, but she took it—simply took it in a way
that meant everything, and to measure it by vision it was a
picture of the most complete disregard.

She stood straight for a moment. Then she drew from her bosom a photograph and thrust it through the palings. She walked rapidly into the house.

II

A man in garb of blue and white—something relating to what we call bed-ticking—was seated in a curious little cupola on the top of a Spanish blockhouse. The blockhouse sided a white military road that curved away from the man's sight into a blur of trees. On all sides of him were fields of tall grass studded with palms and lined with fences of barbed wire. The sun beat aslant through the trees and the man sped his eyes deep into the dark tropical shadows that seemed velvet with coolness. These tranquil vistas resembled painted scenery in a theatre, and, moreover, a hot, heavy silence lay upon the land.

The soldier in the watching place leaned an unclean Mauser rifle in a corner and, reaching down, took a glowing coal on a bit of palm bark handed up to him by a comrade. The men below were mainly asleep. The sergeant in command drowsed near the open door, the arm above his head showing his long keen-angled chevrons attached carelessly with safety-pins. The sentry lit his cigarette and puffed languorously.

Suddenly he heard from the air around him the querulous, deadly-swift spit of rifle bullets and an instant later the pop-pety-pop of a small volley sounded in his face close, as if it were fired only ten feet away. Involuntarily he threw back his head quickly as if he were protecting his nose from a falling tile. He screamed an alarm and fell into the blockhouse. In the gloom of it men with their breaths coming sharply between their teeth were tumbling wildly for positions at the loop-holes. The door had been slammed, but the sergeant lay just within, propped up as when he drowsed, but now with blood flowing steadily over the hand that he pressed flatly to his chest. His face was in stark yellow agony. He chokingly repeated: "Fuego! Por Dios, hombres!"

The men's ill-conditioned weapons were jammed through the loop-holes and they began to fire from all four sides of the blockhouse from the simple data apparently that the enemy were in the vicinity. The fumes of burnt powder grew stronger and stronger in the little square fortress. The rattling of the magazine locks was incessant, and the interior might have been that of a gloomy manufactory if it were not for the sergeant down under the feet of the men, coughing out: "Por Dios, hombres! Por Dios! Fuego!"

III

A string of five Cubans in linen that had turned earthy brown in color slid through the woods at a pace that was neither a walk nor a run. It was a kind of a rack. In fact the whole manner of the men as they thus moved bore a rather comic resemblance to the American pacing horse. But they had come many miles since sun-up over mountainous and half-marked paths, and were plainly still fresh. The men were all practicos—guides. They made no sound in their swift travel, but moved their half-shod feet with the skill of cats. The woods lay around them in a deep silence such as one might find at the bottom of a lake.

Suddenly the leading practico raised his hand. The others pulled up short and dropped the butts of their weapons calmly and noiselessly to the ground. The leader whistled a low note, and immediately another practico appeared from the bushes. He moved close to the leader without a word, and then they spoke in whispers.

"There are twenty men and a sergeant in the blockhouse."

"And the road?"

"One company of cavalry passed to the east this morning at seven o'clock. They were escorting four carts. An hour later one horseman rode swiftly to the westward. About noon ten infantry soldiers with a corporal were taken from the big fort and put in the first blockhouse to the east of the fort. There were already twelve men there. We saw a Spanish column moving off toward Mariel."

"No more?"

"No more."

"Good. But the cavalry?"

"It is all right. They were going a long march."

"The expedition is half a league behind. Go and tell the General."

The scout disappeared. The five other men lifted their guns and resumed their rapid and noiseless progress. A moment later no sound broke the stillness save the thump of a mango as it dropped lazily from its tree to the grass. So strange had been the apparition of these men, their dress had been so allied in color to the soil, their passing had so little disturbed the solemn rumination of the forest, and their going had been so like a spectral dissolution, that a witness could have wondered if he dreamed.

IV

A small expedition had landed with arms from the United States and had now come out of the hills and to the edge of a wood. Before them was a long-grassed rolling prairie marked with palms. A half-mile away was the military road and they could see the top of a blockhouse. The insurgent scouts were moving somewhere off in the grass. The General sat comfortably under a tree, while his staff of three young officers stood about him chatting. Their linen clothing was notable from being distinctly whiter than those of the men who, one hundred and fifty in number, lay on the ground in a long brown fringe, ragged—indeed, bare in many places— but singularly reposeful, unworried, veteran-like.

The General, however, was thoughtful. He pulled continually at his little thin mustache. As far as the heavily patrolled and guarded military road was concerned, the insurgents had been in the habit of dashing across it in small bodies whenever they pleased, but to safely scoot over it with a valuable convoy of arms was decidedly a more important thing. So the General awaited the return of his practicos with anxiety. The still pampas betrayed no sign of their existence.

The General gave some orders and an officer counted off twenty men to go with him and delay any attempt of the troop of cavalry to return from the eastward. It was not an easy task, but it was a familiar task—checking the advance of a greatly superior force by a very hard fire from concealment. A few rifles had often bayed a strong column for sufficient length of time for all strategic purposes. The twenty men pulled themselves together tranquilly. They looked quite indifferent. Indeed, they had the supremely casual manner of old soldiers, hardened to battle as a condition of existence.

Thirty men were then told off whose function it was to worry and rag at the blockhouse and check any advance from the westward. A hundred men carrying precious burdens— besides their own equipment—were to pass in as much of a rush as possible between these two wings, cross the road and skip for the hills, their retreat being covered by a combination of the two firing parties. It was a trick that needed both luck and neat arrangement. Spanish columns were for ever prowling through this province in all directions and at all times. Insurgent bands—the lightest of light infantry—were kept on the jump even when they were not incommoded by fifty boxes, each one large enough for the coffin of a little man and heavier than if the little man were in it, and fifty small but formidable boxes of ammunition.

The carriers stood to their boxes and the firing parties leaned on their rifles. The General arose and strolled to and fro, his hands behind him. Two of his staff were jesting at the third, a young man with a face less bronzed and with very new accoutrements. On the strap of his cartouche were a gold star and a silver star placed in a horizontal line, denoting that he was a second lieutenant. He seemed very happy; he laughed at all their jests although his eye roved continually over the sunny grass-lands where was going to happen his first fight. One of his stars was bright, like his hopes; the other was pale, like death.

Two practicos came racking out of the grass. They spoke rapidly to the General; he turned and nodded to his officers. The two firing parties filed out and diverged toward their positions. The General watched them through his glasses. It was strange to note how soon they were dim to the unaided eye. The little patches of brown in the green grass did not look like men at all.

Practicos continually ambled up to the General. Finally he turned and made a sign to the bearers. The first twenty men in line picked up their boxes, and this movement rapidly spread to the tail of the line. The weighted procession moved painfully out upon the sunny prairie. The General, marching at the head of it, glanced continually back as if he were compelled to drag behind him some ponderous iron chain. Besides the obvious mental worry, his face bore an expression of intense physical strain, and he even bent his shoulders, unconsciously tugging at the chain to hurry it through this enemy-crowded valley.

V

The fight was opened by eight men who, snuggling in the grass within three hundred yards of the blockhouse, suddenly blazed away at the bed-ticking figure in the cupola and at the open door where they could see vague outlines. Then they laughed and yelled insulting language, for they knew that as far as the Spaniards were concerned the surprise was as much as having a diamond bracelet turn to soap. It was this volley that smote the sergeant and caused the man in the cupola to scream and tumble from his perch.

The eight men, as well as all other insurgents within fair range, had chosen good positions for lying close, and for a time they let the blockhouse rage, although the soldiers therein could occasionally hear above the clamor of their weapons shrill and almost wolfish calls coming from men whose lips were laid against the ground. But it is not in the nature of them of Spanish blood and armed with rifles to long endure the sight of anything so tangible as an enemy's blockhouse without shooting at it—other conditions being partly favorable. Presently the steaming soldiers in the little fort could hear the sping and shiver of bullets striking the wood that guarded their bodies.

A perfectly white smoke floated up over each firing Cuban, the penalty of the Remington rifle, but about the blockhouse there was only the lightest gossamer of blue. The blockhouse stood always for some big, clumsy and rather incompetent animal, while the insurgents, scattered on two sides of it, were little enterprising creatures of another species, too wise to come too near, but joyously ragging at its easiest flanks and dirling the lead into its sides in a way to make it fume and spit and rave like the tomcat when the glad, free-band foxhound pups catch him in the lane.

The men, outlying in the grass, chuckled deliriously at the fury of the Spanish fire. They howled opprobrium to encourage the Spaniards to fire more ill-used, incapable bullets. Whenever an insurgent was about to fire he ordinarily prefixed the affair with a speech. "Do you want something to eat? Yes? All right." Bang! "Eat that." The more common expressions of the incredibly foul Spanish tongue were trifles light as air in this badinage which was shrieked out from the grass during the spin of bullets and the dull rattle of the shooting.

But at some time there came a series of sounds from the east that began in a few disconnected pruts and ended as if an amateur was trying to play the long roll upon a muffled drum. Those of the insurgents in the blockhouse attacking party who had neighbors in the grass turned and looked at them seriously. They knew what the new sound meant. It meant that the twenty men who had gone to the eastward were now engaged. A column of some kind was approaching from that direction and they knew by the clatter that it was a solemn occasion.

In the first place, they were now on the wrong side of the road. They were obliged to cross it to rejoin the main body, provided, of course, that the main body succeeded itself in crossing it. To accomplish this the party at the blockhouse would have to move to the eastward until out of sight or good range of the maddened little fort. But judging from the heaviness of the firing the party of twenty who protected the east were almost sure to be driven immediately back. Hence travel in that direction would become exceedingly hazardous. Hence a man looked seriously at his neighbor. It might easily be that in a moment they were to become an isolated force and wofully on the wrong side of the road.

Any retreat to the westward was absurd, since primarily they would have to widely circle the blockhouse, and more than that they could hear even now in that direction Spanish bugle calling to Spanish bugle, far and near, until one would think that every man in Cuba was a trumpeter and had come forth to parade his talent.

VI

The insurgent General stood in the middle of the road gnawing his lips. Occasionally he stamped a foot and beat his hands passionately together. The carriers were streaming past him, patient, sweating fellows, bowed under their burdens, but they could not move fast enough for him when others of his men were engaged both to the east and to the west, and he, too, knew from the sound that those to the east were in a sore way. Moreover, he could hear that accursed bugling, bugling, bugling in the west.

He turned suddenly to the new lieutenant who stood behind him, pale and quiet. "Did you ever think a hundred men were so many?" he cried, incensed to the point of beating them. Then he said longingly: "Oh, for a half an hour! Or even twenty minutes!"

A practico racked violently up from the east. It is characteristic of these men that, although they take a certain roadster gait and hold it for ever, they cannot really run, sprint, race. "Captain Rodriguez is attacked by two hundred men, señor, and the cavalry is behind them. He wishes to know——"

The General was furious. He pointed. "Go! Tell Rodriguez to hold his place for twenty minutes, even if he leaves every man dead."

The practico shambled hastily off.

The last of the carriers were swarming across the road. The rifle-drumming in the east was swelling out and out, evidently coming slowly nearer. The General bit his nails. He wheeled suddenly upon the young lieutenant. "Go to Bas at the blockhouse. Tell him to hold the devil himself for ten minutes and then bring his men out of that place."

The long line of bearers was crawling like a dun worm toward the safety of the foot-hills. High bullets sang a faint song over the aide as he saluted. The bugles had in the west ceased, and that was more ominous than bugling. It meant that the Spanish troops were about to march, or perhaps that they had marched.

The young lieutenant ran along the road until he came to the bend which marked the range of sight from the blockhouse. He drew his machete, his stunning new machete, and

hacked feverishly at the barbed wire fence which lined the
north side of the road at that point. The first wire was ob-
durate, because it was too high for his stroke, but two more
cut like candy, and he stepped over the remaining one, tear-
ing his trousers in passing on the lively serpentine ends of the
severed wires. Once out in the field and bullets seemed to
know him and call for him and speak their wish to kill him.
But he ran on because it was his duty, and because he would
be shamed before men if he did not do his duty, and because
he was desolate out there all alone in the fields with death.

A man running in this manner from the rear was in im-
mensely greater danger than those who lay snug and closer.
But he did not know it. He thought because he was five
hundred—four hundred and fifty—four hundred yards away
from the enemy and others were only three hundred yards
away that they were in far more peril. He ran to join them
because of his opinion. He did not care to do it, but he
thought that was what men of his kind would do in such a
case. There was a standard and he must follow it, obey it,
because it was a monarch, the Prince of Conduct.

A bewildered and alarmed face raised itself from the grass
and a voice cried to him: "Drop, Manolo! Drop! Drop!" He
recognized Bas and flung himself to the earth beside him.

"Why," he said, panting, " what's the matter?"

"Matter?" said Bas. "You are one of the most desperate and
careless officers I know. When I saw you coming I wouldn't
have given a peseta for your life."

"Oh, no," said the young aide. Then he repeated his orders
rapidly. But he was hugely delighted. He knew Bas well. Bas
was a pupil of Maceo. Bas invariably led his men. He never
was a mere spectator of their battle; he was known for it
throughout the western end of the island. The new officer
had early achieved a part of his ambition—to be called a
brave man by established brave men.

"Well, if we get away from here quickly it will be better for
us," said Bas bitterly. "I've lost six men killed and more
wounded. Rodriguez can't hold his position there, and in a
little time more than a thousand men will come from the
other direction."

He hissed a low call, and later the young aide saw some of

the men sneaking off with the wounded, lugging them on their backs as porters carry sacks. The fire from the blockhouse had become a-weary, and as the insurgent fire also slackened, Bas and the young lieutenant lay in the weeds listening to the approach of the eastern fight which was sliding toward them like a door to shut them off.

Bas groaned. "I leave my dead. Look there." He swung his hand in a gesture and the lieutenant looking saw a corpse. He was not stricken as he expected. There was very little blood; it was a mere thing.

"Time to travel," said Bas suddenly. His imperative hissing brought his men near him. There were a few hurried questions and answers; then, characteristically, the men turned in the grass, lifted their rifles, and fired a last volley into the blockhouse, accompanying it with their shrill cries. Scrambling low to the ground, they were off in a winding line for safety. Breathing hard, the lieutenant stumbled his way forward. Behind him he could hear the men calling each to each: "Segue! Segue! Segue! Go on! Get out! Git!" Everybody understood that the peril of crossing the road was compounding from minute to minute.

VII

When they reached the gap through which the expedition had passed, they fled out upon the road like scared wild-fowl tracking along a sea-beach. A cloud of blue figures far up this dignified shaded avenue fired at once. The men already had begun to laugh as they shied one by one across the road. "Segue! Segue!" The hard part for the nerves had been the lack of information of the amount of danger. Now that they could see it, they accounted it all the more lightly for their previous anxiety.

Over in the other field Bas and the young lieutenant found Rodriguez, his machete in one hand, his revolver in the other, smoky, dirty, sweating. He shrugged his shoulders when he saw them and pointed disconsolately to the brown thread of carriers moving toward the foot-hills. His own men were crouched in line just in front of him, blazing like a prairie fire.

Now began the fight of a scant rear-guard to hold back the

pressing Spaniards until the carriers could reach the top of the ridge, a mile away. This ridge, by the way, was more steep than any roof; it conformed more to the sides of a French war-ship. Trees grew vertically from it, however, and a man burdened only with his rifle usually pulled himself wheezingly up in a sort of ladder-climbing process, grabbing the slim trunks above him. How the loaded carriers were to conquer it in a hurry, no one knew. Rodriguez shrugged his shoulders as one who would say with philosophy, smiles, tears, courage: "Isn't this a mess!"

At an order the men scattered back for four hundred yards with the rapidity and mystery of a handful of pebbles flung in the night. They left one behind, who cried out, but it was now a game in which some were sure to be left behind to cry out.

The Spaniards deployed on the road, and for twenty minutes remained there, pouring into the field such a fire from their magazines as was hardly heard at Gettysburg. As a matter of truth the insurgents were at this time doing very little shooting, being chary of ammunition. But it is possible for the soldier to confuse himself with his own noise, and undoubtedly the Spanish troops thought throughout their din that they were being fiercely engaged. Moreover, a firing-line—particularly at night or when opposed to a hidden foe—is nothing less than an emotional chord, a chord of a harp that sings because a puff of air arrives or when a bit of down touches it. This is always true of new troops or stupid troops, and these troops were rather stupid troops. But the way in which they mowed the verdure in the distance was a sight for a farmer.

Presently the insurgents slunk back to another position, where they fired enough shots to stir again the Spaniards into an opinion that they were in a heavy fight. But such a misconception could only endure for a number of minutes. Presently it was plain that the Spaniards were about to advance, and, moreover, word was brought to Rodriguez that a small band of guerillas were already making an attempt to worm around the right flank. Rodriguez cursed despairingly; he sent both Bas and the young lieutenant to that end of the line to hold the men to their work as long as possible.

In reality the men barely needed the presence of their offi-
cers. The kind of fighting left practically everything to the
discretion of the individual, and they arrived at concert of
action mainly because of the equality of experience in the wis-
doms of bushwhacking.

The yells of the guerillas could plainly be heard, and the
insurgents answered in kind. The young lieutenant found des-
perate work on the right flank. The men were raving mad
with it, babbling, tearful, almost frothing at the mouth. Two
terrible bloody creatures passed him, creeping on all fours,
and one in a whimper was calling upon God, his mother, and
a saint. The guerillas, as effectually concealed as the insur-
gents, were driving their bullets low through the smoke at
sight of a flame, a movement of the grass or sight of a patch
of dirty brown coat. They were no column-o'-four soldiers;
they were as slinky and snaky and quick as so many Indians.
They were, moreover, native Cubans, and because of their
treachery to the one-star flag they never by any chance re-
ceived quarter if they fell into the hands of the insurgents.
Nor, if the case was reversed, did they ever give quarter. It
was life and life, death and death; there was no middle
ground, no compromise. If a man's crowd was rapidly retreat-
ing and he was tumbled over by a slight hit, he should curse
the sacred graves that the wound was not through the precise
centre of his heart. The machete is a fine broad blade, but it
is not so nice as a drilled hole in the chest; no man wants his
death-bed to be a shambles. The men fighting on the insur-
gent right knew that if they fell they were lost.

On the extreme right the young lieutenant found five men
in a little saucer-like hollow. Two were dead, one was
wounded and staring blankly at the sky, and two were emp-
tying hot rifles furiously. Some of the guerillas had snaked
into positions only a hundred yards away.

The young man rolled in among the men in the saucer. He
could hear the barking of the guerillas and the screams of the
two insurgents. The rifles were popping and spitting in his
face, it seemed, while the whole land was alive with a noise
of rolling and drumming. Men could have gone drunken in
all this flashing and flying and snarling and din, but at this
time he was very deliberate. He knew that he was thrusting

himself into a trap whose door, once closed, opened only when the black hand knocked, and every part of him seemed to be in panic-stricken revolt. But something controlled him; something moved him inexorably in one direction; he perfectly understood, but he was only sad, sad with a serene dignity, with the countenance of a mournful young prince. He was of a kind—that seemed to be it—and the men of his kind, on peak or plain, from the dark northern ice-fields to the hot wet jungles, through all wine and want, through all lies and unfamiliar truth, dark or light, the men of his kind were governed by their gods, and each man knew the law and yet could not give tongue to it; but it was the law, and if the spirits of the men of his kind were all sitting in critical judgment upon him even then in the sky, he could not have bettered his conduct; he needs must obey the law, and always with the law there is only one way. But from peak and plain, from dark northern ice-fields and hot wet jungles, through wine and want, through all lies and unfamiliar truth, dark or light, he heard breathed to him the approval and the benediction of his brethren.

He stooped and gently took a dead man's rifle and some cartridges. The battle was hurrying, hurrying, hurrying, but he was in no haste. His glance caught the staring eye of the wounded soldier, and he smiled at him quietly. The man—simple doomed peasant—was not of his kind, but the law on fidelity was clear.

He thrust a cartridge into the Remington and crept up beside the two unhurt men. Even as he did so, three or four bullets cut so close to him that all his flesh tingled. He fired carefully into the smoke. The guerillas were certainly not now more than fifty yards away.

He raised him coolly for his second shot, and almost instantly it was as if some giant had struck him in the chest with a beam. It whirled him in a great spasm back into the saucer. As he put his two hands to his breast, he could hear the guerillas screeching exultantly, every throat vomiting forth all the infamy of a language prolific in the phrasing of infamy.

One of the other men came rolling slowly down the slope, while his rifle followed him, and striking another rifle, clanged out. Almost immediately the survivor howled and fled wildly. A whole volley missed him, and then one or more shots caught him as a bird is caught on the wing.

The young lieutenant's body seemed galvanized from head to foot. He concluded that he was not hurt very badly, but when he tried to move he found that he could not lift his hands from his breast. He had turned to lead. He had had a plan of taking a photograph from his pocket and looking at it.

There was a stir in the grass at the edge of the saucer, and a man appeared there looking where lay the four insurgents. His negro face was not an eminently ferocious one in its lines, but now it was lit with an illimitable blood-greed. He and the young lieutenant exchanged a singular glance; then he came stepping eagerly down. The young lieutenant closed his eyes, for he did not want to see the flash of the machete.

VIII

The Spanish Colonel was in a rage, and yet immensely proud—immensely proud, and yet in a rage of disappointment. There had been a fight, and the insurgents had retreated leaving their dead, but still a valuable expedition had broken through his lines and escaped to the mountains. As a matter of truth, he was not sure whether to be wholly delighted or wholly angry, for well he knew that the importance lay not so much in the truthful account of the action as it did in the heroic prose of the official report, and in the fight itself lay material for a purple splendid poem. The insurgents had run away—no one could deny it; it was plain even to whatever privates had fired with their eyes shut. This was worth a loud blow and splutter. However, when all was said and done, he could not help but reflect that if he had captured this expedition, he would have been a brigadier-general, if not more.

He was a short, heavy man with a beard, who walked in a manner common to all elderly Spanish officers and to many young ones. That is to say, he walked as if his spine was a stick and a little longer than his body; as if he suffered from some disease of the backbone which allowed him but scant use of his legs. He toddled along the road, gesticulating disdainfully and muttering, "Ca! Ca! Ca!"

He berated some soldiers for an immaterial thing, and as he approached the men stepped precipitately back as if he were a fire-engine. They were most of them young fellows, who displayed when under orders the manner of so many faithful dogs. At present they were black, tongue-hanging, thirsty boys, bathed in the nervous weariness of the after-battle time.

Whatever he may truly have been in character, the Colonel closely resembled a gluttonous and libidinous old pig, filled from head to foot with the pollution of a sinful life. "Ca!" he snarled as he toddled. "Ca! Ca!" The soldiers saluted as they backed to the side of the road. The air was full of the odor of burnt rags. Over on the prairie guerillas and regulars were rummaging the grass. A few unimportant shots sounded from near the base of the hills.

A guerilla, glad with plunder, came to a Spanish captain. He held in his hand a photograph. "Mira, señor. I took this from the body of an officer whom I killed machete to machete."

The captain shot from the corner of his eye a cynical glance at the guerilla, a glance which commented upon the last part of the statement. "M-m-m," he said. He took the photograph and gazed with a slow faint smile, the smile of a man who knows bloodshed and homes and love, at the face of a girl. He turned the photograph presently, and on the back of it was written: "One lesson in English I will give you—this: I love you, Margharita." The photograph had been taken in Tampa.

The officer was silent for a half-minute, while his face still wore the slow faint smile. "Pobrecito," he murmured finally with a philosophic sigh which was brother to a shrug. Without deigning a word to the guerilla he thrust the photograph in his pocket and walked away.

High over the green earth, in the dizzy blue heights, some great birds were slowly circling with down-turned beaks.

IX

Margharita was in the garden. The blue electric rays shone through the plumes of the palm and shivered in feathery images on the walk. In the little foolish fish-pond some stalwart fish was apparently bullying the others, for often there sounded a frantic splashing.

Her mother came to her rapidly. "Margharita, Mr. Smith is here! Come!"

"Oh, is he?" cried the girl. She followed her mother to the house. She swept into the little parlor with a grand air, the egotism of a savage. Smith had heard the whirl of her skirts in the hall, and his heart, as usual, thumped hard enough to make him gasp. Every time he called he would sit waiting, with the dull fear in his breast that her mother would enter and indifferently announce that she had gone up to heaven or off to New York with one of his dream-rivals, and he would never see her again in this wide world. And he would conjure up tricks to then escape from the house without any one observing his face break up into furrows. It was part of his love to believe in the absolute treachery of his adored one. So whenever he heard the whirl of her skirts in the hall he felt that he had again leased happiness from a dark fate.

She was rosily beaming and all in white. "Why, Mr. Smith!" she exclaimed, as if he was the last man in the world she expected to see.

"Good evenin'," he said, shaking hands nervously. He was always awkward and unlike himself at the beginning of one of these calls. It took him some time to get into form.

She posed her figure in operatic style on a chair before him and immediately galloped off a mile of questions, information of herself, gossip and general outcries, which left him no obligation but to look beamingly intelligent and from time to time say: "Yes?" His personal joy, however, was to stare at her beauty.

When she stopped and wandered as if uncertain which way to talk, there was a minute of silence which each of them had been educated to feel was very incorrect—very incorrect indeed. Polite people always babbled at each other like two brooks.

He knew that the responsibility was upon him, and although his mind was mainly upon the form of the proposal of marriage which he intended to make later, it was necessary that he should maintain his reputation as a well-bred man by saying something at once. It flashed upon him to ask: "Won't you please play?" But the time for the piano ruse was not yet; it was too early. So he said the first thing that came into his head: "Too bad about young Manolo Prat being killed over there in Cuba, wasn't it?"

"Wasn't it a pity?" she answered.

"They say his mother is heartbroken," he continued. "They're afraid she's goin' to die."

"And wasn't it queer that we didn't hear about it for almost two months?"

"Well, it's no use tryin' to git quick news from there."

Presently they advanced to matters more personal, and she used upon him a series of star-like glances which rumpled him at once to squalid slavery. He gloated upon her, afraid, afraid, yet more avaricious than a thousand misers. She fully comprehended; she laughed and taunted him with her eyes. She impressed upon him that she was like a will-o'-the-wisp, beautiful beyond compare, but impossible, almost impossible, but at least very difficult; then again, suddenly, impossible—impossible—impossible. He was glum; he would never dare propose to this radiance; it was like asking to be Pope.

A moment later there chimed into the room something that he knew to be a more tender note. The girl became dreamy as she looked at him; her voice lowered to a delicious intimacy of tone. He leaned forward; he was about to outpour his bully-ragged soul in fine words, when—presto —she was the most casual person he had ever laid eyes upon, and was asking him about the route of the proposed trolley line.

But nothing short of a fire could stop him now. He grabbed her hand. "Margharita," he murmured gutturally, "I want you to marry me!"

She glared at him in the most perfect lie of astonishment. "What do you say?"

He arose, and she thereupon arose also and fled back a step. He could only stammer out her name. And thus they stood, defying the principles of the dramatic art.

"I love you," he said at last.

"How—how do I know you really, truly love me?" she said, raising her eyes timorously to his face, and this timorous glance, this one timorous glance, made him the superior person in an instant. He went forward as confident as a grenadier, and, taking both her hands, kissed her.

That night she took a stained photograph from her dressing-table, and, holding it over the candle, burned it to nothing, her red lips meanwhile parted with the intentness of her occupation. On the back of the photograph was written: "One lesson in English I will give you—this: I love you."

For the word is clear only to the kind who on peak or plain, from dark northern ice-fields to the hot wet jungles, through all wine and want, through lies and unfamiliar truth, dark or light, are governed by the unknown gods, and though each man knows the law no man may give tongue to it.

Marines Signaling Under Fire
at Guantanamo

T HEY WERE four Guantanamo marines, officially known for the time as signalmen, and it was their duty to lie in the trenches of Camp McCalla, that faced the water, and, by day, signal the *Marblehead* with a flag and, by night, signal the *Marblehead* with lanterns. It was my good fortune—at that time I considered it my bad fortune, indeed—to be with them on two of the nights when a wild storm of fighting was pealing about the hill; and, of all the actions of the war, none were so hard on the nerves, none strained courage so near the panic point, as those swift nights in Camp McCalla. With a thousand rifles rattling; with the field-guns booming in your ears; with the diabolic Colt automatics clacking; with the roar of the *Marblehead* coming from the bay, and, last, with Mauser bullets sneering always in the air a few inches over one's head, and with this enduring from dusk to dawn, it is extremely doubtful if any one who was there will be able to forget it easily. The noise; the impenetrable darkness; the knowledge from the sound of the bullets that the enemy was on three sides of the camp; the infrequent bloody stumbling and death of some man with whom, perhaps, one had messed two hours previous; the weariness of the body, and the more terrible weariness of the mind, at the endlessness of the thing, made it wonderful that at least some of the men did not come out of it with their nerves hopelessly in shreds.

But, as this interesting ceremony proceeded in the darkness, it was necessary for the signal squad to coolly take and send messages. Captain McCalla always participated in the defense of the camp by raking the woods on two of its sides with the guns of the *Marblehead*. Moreover, he was the senior officer present, and he wanted to know what was happening. All night long the crews of the ships in the bay would stare sleeplessly into the blackness toward the roaring hill.

The signal squad had an old cracker-box placed on top of the trench. When not signaling, they hid the lanterns in this box; but as soon as an order to send a message was received, it became necessary for one of the men to stand up and expose the lights. And then—oh, my eye—how the guerillas hidden in the gulf of night would turn loose at those yellow gleams!

Signaling in this way is done by letting one lantern remain stationary—on top of the cracker-box, in this case—and moving the other over it to the left and right and so on in the regular gestures of the wig-wagging code. It is a very simple system of night communication, but one can see that it presents rare possibilities when used in front of an enemy who, a few hundred yards away, is overjoyed at sighting so definite a mark.

How, in the name of wonders, those four men at Camp McCalla were not riddled from head to foot and sent home more as repositories of Spanish ammunition than as marines is beyond all comprehension. To make a confession—when one of these men stood up to wave his lantern, I, lying in the trench, invariably rolled a little to the right or left, in order that, when he was shot, he would not fall on me. But the squad came off scathless, despite the best efforts of the most formidable corps in the Spanish army—the Escuadra de Guantanamo. That it was the most formidable corps in the Spanish army of occupation has been told me by many Spanish officers and also by General Menocal and other insurgent officers. General Menocal was Garcia's chief-of-staff when the latter was operating busily in Santiago province. The regiment was composed solely of *practicos*, or guides, who knew every shrub and tree on the ground over which they moved.

Whenever the adjutant, Lieutenant Draper, came plunging along through the darkness with an order—such as: "Ask the *Marblehead* to please shell the woods to the left"—my heart would come into my mouth, for I knew then that one of my pals was going to stand up behind the lanterns and have all Spain shoot at him.

The answer was always upon the instant: "Yes, sir." Then the bullets began to snap, snap, snap, at his head while all the woods began to crackle like burning straw. I could lie near and watch the face of the signalman, illumed as it was by the yellow shine of lantern light, and the absence of excitement, fright, or any emotion at all, on his countenance, was something to astonish all theories out of one's mind. The face was in every instance merely that of a man intent upon his business, the business of wig-wagging into the gulf of night where a light on the *Marblehead* was seen to move slowly.

These times on the hill resembled, in some days, those terrible scenes on the stage—scenes of intense gloom, blinding lightning, with a cloaked devil or assassin or other appropriate character muttering deeply amid the awful roll of the thunder-drums. It was theatric beyond words; one felt like a leaf in this booming chaos, this prolonged tragedy of the night. Amid it all one could see from time to time the yellow light on the face of a preoccupied signalman.

Possibly no man who was there ever before understood the true eloquence of the breaking of the day. We would lie staring into the east, fairly ravenous for the dawn. Utterly worn to rags, with our nerves standing on end like so many bristles, we lay and watched the east—the unspeakably obdurate and slow east. It was a wonder that the eyes of some of us did not turn to glass balls from the fixity of our gaze.

Then there would come into the sky a patch of faint blue light. It was like a piece of moonshine. Some would say it was the beginning of daybreak; others would declare it was nothing of the kind. Men would get very disgusted with each other in these low-toned arguments held in the trenches. For my part, this development in the eastern sky destroyed many of my ideas and theories concerning the dawning of the day; but then I had never before had occasion to give it such solemn attention.

This patch widened and whitened in about the speed of a man's accomplishment if he should be in the way of painting Madison Square Garden with a camel's hair brush. The guerillas always set out to whoop it up about this time, because they knew the occasion was approaching when it would be expedient for them to elope. I, at least, always grew furious with this wretched sunrise. I thought I could have walked around the world in the time required for the old thing to get up above the horizon.

One midnight, when an important message was to be sent to the *Marblehead*, Colonel Huntington came himself to the signal place with Adjutant Draper and Captain McCauley, the quartermaster. When the man stood up to signal, the colonel stood beside him. At sight of the lights, the Spaniards performed as usual. They drove enough bullets into that immediate vicinity to kill all the marines in the corps.

Lieutenant Draper was agitated for his chief. "Colonel, won't you step down, sir?"

"Why, I guess not," said the grey old veteran in his slow, sad, always-gentle way. "I'm in no more danger than the man."

"But, sir—" began the adjutant.

"Oh, it's all right, Draper."

So the colonel and the private stood side to side and took the heavy fire without either moving a muscle.

Day was always obliged to come at last, punctuated by a final exchange of scattering shots. And the light shone on the marines, the dumb guns, the flag. Grimy yellow face looked into grimy yellow face, and grinned with weary satisfaction. Coffee!

Usually it was impossible for many of the men to sleep at once. It always took me, for instance, some hours to get my nerves combed down. But then it was great joy to lie in the trench with the four signalmen, and understand thoroughly that that night was fully over at last, and that, although the future might have in store other bad nights, that one could never escape from the prison-house which we call the past.

At the wild little fight at Cusco there were some splendid exhibitions of wig-wagging under fire. Action began when an advanced detachment of marines under Lieutenant Lucas with the Cuban guides had reached the summit of a ridge overlooking a small valley where there was a house, a well, and a thicket of some kind of shrub with great broad, oily leaves. This thicket, which was perhaps an acre in extent, contained the guerillas. The valley was open to the sea. The distance from the top of the ridge to the thicket was barely two hundred yards.

The *Dolphin* had sailed up the coast in line with the marine advance, ready with her guns to assist in any action. Captain Elliott, who commanded the two hundred marines in this fight, suddenly called out for a signalman. He wanted a man to tell the *Dolphin* to open fire on the house and the thicket. It was a blazing, bitter hot day on top of the ridge with its shriveled chaparral and its straight, tall cactus plants. The sky was bare and blue, and hurt like brass. In two minutes the prostrate marines were red and sweating like so many hull-buried stokers in the tropics.

Captain Elliott called out:

"Where's a signalman? Who's a signalman here?"

A red-headed "mick"—I think his name was Clancy—at any rate, it will do to call him Clancy—twisted his head from where he lay on his stomach pumping his Lee, and, saluting, said that he was a signalman.

There was no regulation flag with the expedition, so Clancy was obliged to tie his blue polka-dot neckerchief on the end of his rifle. It did not make a very good flag. At first Clancy moved a ways down the safe side of the ridge and wig-wagged there very busily. But what with the flag being so poor for the purpose, and the background of ridge being so dark, those on the *Dolphin* did not see it. So Clancy had to return to the top of the ridge and outline himself and his flag against the sky.

The usual thing happened. As soon as the Spaniards caught sight of this silhouette, they let go like mad at it. To make things more comfortable for Clancy, the situation demanded that he face the sea and turn his back to the Spanish bullets. This was a hard game, mark you—to stand with the small of your back to volley firing. Clancy thought so. Everybody thought so. We all cleared out of his neighborhood. If he wanted sole possession of any particular spot on that hill, he could have it for all we would interfere with him.

It cannot be denied that Clancy was in a hurry. I watched him. He was so occupied with the bullets that snarled close to his ears that he was obliged to repeat the letters of his message softly to himself. It seemed an intolerable time before the *Dolphin* answered the little signal. Meanwhile, we gazed at him, marveling every second that he had not yet pitched headlong. He swore at times.

Finally the *Dolphin* replied to his frantic gesticulation, and he delivered his message. As his part of the transaction was quite finished—whoop!—he dropped like a brick into the firing line and began to shoot; began to get "hunky" with all those people who had been plugging at him. The blue polka-dot neckerchief still fluttered from the barrel of his rifle. I am quite certain that he let it remain there until the end of the fight.

The shells of the *Dolphin* began to plow up the thicket, kicking the bushes, stones, and soil into the air as if somebody was blasting there.

Meanwhile, this force of two hundred marines and fifty Cubans and the force of—probably—six companies of Spanish guerillas were making such an awful din that the distant Camp McCalla was all alive with excitement. Colonel Huntington sent out strong parties to critical points on the road to facilitate, if necessary, a safe retreat, and also sent forty men under Lieutenant Magill to come up on the left flank of the two companies in action under Captain Elliott. Lieutenant Magill and his men had crowned a hill which covered entirely the flank of the fighting companies, but when the *Dolphin* opened fire, it happened that Magill was in the line of the shots. It became necessary to stop the *Dolphin* at once. Captain Elliott was not near Clancy at this time, and he called hurriedly for another signalman.

Sergeant Quick arose, and announced that he was a signalman. He produced from somewhere a blue polka-dot neckerchief as large as a quilt. He tied it on a long, crooked stick. Then he went to the top of the ridge, and turning his back to the Spanish fire, began to signal to the *Dolphin*. Again we gave a man sole possession of a particular part of the ridge. We didn't want it. He could have it and welcome. If the young sergeant had had the smallpox, the cholera, and the yellow fever, we could not have slid out with more celerity.

As men have said often, it seemed as if there was in this war a God of Battles who held His mighty hand before the Americans. As I looked at Sergeant Quick wig-wagging there against the sky, I would not have given a tin tobacco-tag for his life. Escape for him seemed impossible. It seemed absurd to hope that he would not be hit; I only hoped that he would be hit just a little, little, in the arm, the shoulder, or the leg.

I watched his face, and it was as grave and serene as that of a man writing in his own library. He was the very embodiment of tranquillity in occupation. He stood there amid the animal-like babble of the Cubans, the crack of rifles, and the whistling snarl of the bullets, and wig-wagged whatever he had to wig-wag without heeding anything but his business. There was not a single trace of nervousness or haste.

To say the least, a fight at close range is absorbing as a spectacle. No man wants to take his eyes from it until that time comes when he makes up his mind to run away. To deliberately stand up and turn your back to a battle is in itself hard work. To deliberately stand up and turn your back to a battle and hear immediate evidences of the boundless enthusiasm with which a large company of the enemy shoot at you from an adjacent thicket is, to my mind at least, a very great feat. One need not dwell upon the detail of keeping the mind carefully upon a slow spelling of an important code message.

I saw Quick betray only one sign of emotion. As he swung his clumsy flag to and fro, an end of it once caught on a cactus pillar, and he looked sharply over his shoulder to see what had it. He gave the flag an impatient jerk. He looked annoyed.

"God Rest Ye, Merry Gentlemen"

LITTLE NELL, sometimes called the Blessed Damosel, was a war correspondent for the *New York Eclipse*, and at sea on the dispatch-boats he wore pyjamas, and on shore he wore what fate allowed him, which clothing was in the main unsuitable to the climate. He had been cruising in the Carribean on a small tug, awash always, habitable never, wildly looking for Cervera's fleet, although what he was going to do with four armored cruisers and two destroyers in the event of his really finding them had not been explained by the managing editor. The cabled instructions read: "Take tug. Go find Cervera's fleet." If his unfortunate nine-knot craft should happen to find these great twenty-knot ships, with their two spiteful and faster attendants, Little Nell had wondered how he was going to lose them again. He had marveled both publicly and in secret on the uncompromising asininity of managing editors at odd moments, but he had wasted little time. The *Jefferson G. Johnson* was already coaled, so he passed the word to his skipper, bought some canned meats, cigars and beer, and soon the *Johnson* sailed on her mission, tooting her whistle in graceful farewell to some friends of hers in the bay.

So the *Johnson* crawled giddily to one wave height after another, and fell, aslant, into one valley after another for a longer period than was good for the hearts of the men, because the *Johnson* was merely a harbor tug, with no architectural intention of parading the high seas, and the crew had never seen the decks all white water like a mere sunken reef. As for the cook, he blasphemed hopelessly hour in and hour out, meanwhile pursuing the equipment of his trade frantically from side to side of the galley. Little Nell dealt with a great deal of grumbling, but he knew it was not the real, evil grumbling. It was merely the unhappy words of men who wished expression of comradeship for their wet, forlorn, half-starved lives, to which, they explained, they were not accustomed, and for which, they explained, they were not properly paid. Little Nell condoled and condoled without difficulty. He laid words of gentle sympathy before them, and smothered his own misery behind the face of a reporter of the *New York Eclipse*. They tossed themselves in their cockleshell even as far as Martinique; they knew many races and many flags, but they did not find Cervera's fleet. If they had found that elusive squadron this timid story would never have been written; there would probably have been a lyric. The *Johnson* limped one morning into the Mole St. Nicholas, and there Little Nell received this dispatch: "Can't understand your inaction. What are you doing with the boat? Report immediately. Fleet transports already left Tampa. Expected destination near Santiago. Proceed there immediately. Place yourself under orders. ROGERS, *Eclipse*."

One day, steaming along the high luminous blue coast of Santiago province, they fetched into view the fleets, a knot of masts and funnels, looking incredibly inshore, as if they were glued to the mountains. Then mast left mast, and funnel left funnel, slowly, slowly, and the shore remained still, but the fleets seemed to move out toward the eager *Johnson*. At the speed of nine knots an hour the scene separated into its parts. On an easily rolling sea, under a crystal sky, black-hulled transports—erstwhile packets—lay waiting, while grey cruisers and gunboats lay near shore, shelling the beach and some woods. From their grey sides came thin red flashes, belches of white smoke, and then over the waters sounded boom— boom—boom-boom. The crew of the *Jefferson G. Johnson* forgave Little Nell all the suffering of a previous fortnight.

To the westward, about the mouth of Santiago harbor, sat a row of castellated grey battle-ships, their eyes turned another way, waiting.

The *Johnson* swung past a transport whose decks and rigging were a-swarm with black figures as if a tribe of bees had alighted upon a log. She swung past a cruiser indignant at being left out of the game, her deck thick with white-clothed tars watching the play of their luckier brethren. The cold blue lifting seas tilted the big ships easily, slowly, and heaved the little ones in the usual sinful way, as if very little babes had surreptitiously mounted sixteen-hand trotting hunters. The *Johnson* leered and tumbled her way through the community of ships. The bombardment ceased, and some of the troopships edged in near the land. Soon boats black with men and towed by launches were almost lost to view in the scintillant mystery of light which appeared where the sea met the land. A disembarkation had begun. The *Johnson* sped on at her nine knots, and Little Nell chafed exceedingly, gloating upon the shore through his glasses, anon glancing irritably over the side to note the efforts of the excited tug. Then at last they were in a sort of a cove, with troopships, newspaper boats and cruisers on all sides of them, and over the water came a great hum of human voices, punctuated frequently by the clang of engine-room gongs as the steamers manœuvred to avoid jostling.

In reality it was the great moment—the moment for which men, ships, islands and continents had been waiting for months—but somehow it did not look it. It was very calm; a certain strip of high green rocky shore was being rapidly populated from boat after boat; that was all. Like many pre-conceived moments, it refused to be supreme.

But nothing lessened Little Nell's frenzy. He knew that the army was landing—he could see it; and little did he care if the great moment did not look its part—it was his virtue as a correspondent to recognize the great moment in any disguise. The *Johnson* lowered a boat for him and he dropped into it swiftly, forgetting everything. However, the mate, a bearded philanthropist, flung after him a mackintosh and a bottle of whisky. Little Nell's face was turned toward those other boats filled with men, all eyes upon the placid, gentle, noiseless shore. Little Nell saw many soldiers seated stiffly beside upright rifle barrels, their blue breasts crossed with white shelter-tent and blanket-rolls. Launches screeched; jack-tars pushed or pulled with their boathooks; a beach was alive with working soldiers, some of them stark naked. Little Nell's boat touched the shore amid a babble of tongues, dominated at that time by a single stern voice which was repeating: "Fall in, B Company!"

He took his mackintosh and his bottle of whisky and invaded Cuba. It was a trifle bewildering. Companies of those same men in blue and brown were being rapidly formed and marched off across a little open space—near a pool—near some palm trees—near a house—into the hills. At one side a mulatto in dirty linen and an old straw hat was hospitably using a machete to cut open some green cocoanuts for a group of idle invaders. At the other side—up a bank—a blockhouse was burning furiously, while near it some railway sheds were smouldering, with a little Rogers engine standing amid the ruins, grey, almost white with ashes until it resembled a ghost. Little Nell dodged the encrimsoned blockhouse and proceeded to where he saw a little village street lined with flimsy wooden cottages. Some ragged Cuban cavalrymen were tranquilly tending their horses in a shed which had not yet grown cold of the Spanish occupation. Three American soldiers were trying to explain to a Cuban that they wished to buy drinks. A native rode by, clubbing his pony, as always. The sky was blue; the sea talked with a gravelly accent at the feet of some rocks; upon its bosom the ships sat quiet as gulls. There was no mention, directly, of invasion, invasion for war, save in the roar of the flames at the blockhouse; but none even heeded this conflagration, excepting to note that it threw out a great heat. It was warm, very warm. It was really hard for Little Nell to keep from thinking of his own affairs, his debts, other misfortunes, loves, prospects of happiness. Nobody was in a flurry; the Cubans were not tearfully grateful; the American troops were visibly glad of being released from those ill transports, and the men often asked with interest: "Where's the Spaniards?"

And yet it must have been a great moment! . . . It was a _great_ moment! . . . It seemed made to prove that the emphatic time of history is not the emphatic time of the common man, who throughout the changing of nations feels an itch on his shin, a pain in his head, hunger, thirst, a lack of sleep, the influence of his memory of past firesides, glasses of beer, girls, theatres, ideals, religions, parents, faces, hurts, joys.

Little Nell was hailed from a comfortable veranda, and, looking up, saw Walkley of the _Eclipse_, stretched in a yellow-and-green hammock, smoking his pipe with an air of having always lived in that house, in that village. "Oh, dear Little Nell, how glad I am to see your angel face again. There—don't try to hide it! I can see it. Did you bring a corkscrew, too? You're superseded as master of the slaves. Did you know it? And by Rogers, too! Rogers is a Sadducee, a cadaver and a pelican, appointed to the post of chief correspondent, no doubt, because of his rare gift of incapacity. Never mind."

"Where is he now?" asked Little Nell, taking seat on the steps.

"He is down interfering with the landing of the troops," answered Walkley, swinging a leg. "I hope you have the *Johnson* well stocked with food as well as with cigars, cigarettes and tobaccos, ales, wines and liquors. We shall need them. There is already famine in the house of Walkley. I have discovered that the system of transportation for our gallant soldiery does not strike in me the admiration which I have often felt when viewing the management of an ordinary bun-shop. A-hunger, stifling, jammed together amid odors and everybody irritable—ye gods, how irritable! And so I——Look! Look!"

The *Jefferson G. Johnson*, well known to them at an incredible distance, could be seen striding the broad sea, the smoke belching from her funnel, headed for Jamaica. "The Army Lands in Cuba!" shrieked Walkley. "Shafter's Army Lands near Santiago! Special type! Half the front page! Oh, the Sadducee! The cadaver! The pelican!"

Little Nell was dumb with astonishment and fear. Walkley, however, was at least not dumb. "That's the pelican! That's Mr. Rogers making his first impression upon the situation. He has engraved himself upon us. We are tattooed with him. There will be a fight to-morrow sure, and we will cover it even as you found Cervera's fleet. No food, no horses, no money. I am transport-lame; you are sea-weak. We will never see our salaries again. Whereby Rogers is a fool."

"Anybody else here?" asked Little Nell wearily.

"Only young Point." Point was an artist on the *Eclipse*. "But he has nothing. Pity there wasn't an almshouse here in this God-forsaken country. Here comes Point now." A sad-faced little man came along carrying much luggage. "Hello, Point, lithographer *and* genius; have you food—food? Well, then, you had better return yourself to Tampa by wire. You are no good here. Only one more little mouth to feed."

Point seated himself near Little Nell. "I haven't had anything to eat since daybreak," he said gloomily, "and I don't care much, for I am simply dog-tired!"

"Don't tell *me* you are dog-tired, my talented friend," cried Walkley from his hammock. "Think of me. And now, what's to be done?"

They stared for a time disconsolately at where, over the rim of the sea, trailed black smoke from the *Johnson*. From the landing-place below and to the right came the howls of a man who was superintending the disembarkation of some mules. The burning blockhouse still rendered its hollow roar. Suddenly the man-crowded landing set up its cheer, and the steamers all whistled long and raucously. Tiny black figures were raising an American flag over a blockhouse on the top of a great hill.

"That's mighty fine Sunday stuff," said Little Nell. "Well, I'll go and get the order in which the regiments landed, and who was first ashore, and all that. Then I'll go and try to find General Lawton's headquarters. His division has got the advance, I think."

"And, lo! I will write a burning description of the raising of the flag," said Walkley, "while the brilliant Point buskies for food. And makes damn sure he gets it," he added fiercely.

Little Nell thereupon wandered over the face of the earth, threading out the story of the landing of the regiments. He only found about fifty men who had been the first American soldier to set foot on Cuba, and of these he took the most probable. The army was going forward in detail as soon as the pieces were landed. There was a house something like a crude country tavern; the soldiers in it were looking over their rifles and talking; there was a well of water, quite hot; more palm trees—an inscrutable background.

When he arrived again at Walkley's mansion he found the veranda crowded with correspondents in khaki, duck, dungaree and flannel. They wore riding-breeches, but that was mainly forethought. They could see now that Fate intended them to walk. Some were writing copy while Walkley discoursed from his hammock. Rhodes—doomed to be shot in action some days later—was trying to borrow a canteen from men who had canteens and from men who had none. Young Point, wan, utterly worn out, was asleep on the floor. Walkley pointed to him. "That is how he appears after his foraging journey, during which he ran all Cuba through a sieve. Oh, yes. A can of corn and half a bottle of lime juice."

"Say, does anybody know the name of the commander of the Twenty-sixth Infantry?"

"Who commands the first brigade of Kent's division?"

"What was the name of the chap that raised the flag?"

"What time is it?"

And a woful man was wandering here and there with a cold pipe, saying plaintively: "Who's got a match? Anybody here got a match?"

Little Nell's left boot hurt him at the heel, and so he removed it, taking great care and whistling through his teeth. The heated dust was upon them all, making everybody feel that bathing was unknown and shattering their tempers. Young Point developed a snore which brought grim sarcasm from all quarters. Always, below, hummed the traffic of the landing-place.

When night came Little Nell thought best not to go to bed until late, because he recognized the mackintosh as but a feeble comfort. The evening was a glory. A breeze came from the sea, fanning spurts of flame out of the ashes and charred remains of the sheds, while overhead lay a splendid summer-night sky aflash with great tranquil stars. In the street of the village were two or three fires, frequently and suddenly reddening with their glare the figures of low-voiced men who moved here and there. The lights of the transports blinked on the murmuring plain in front of the village, and far to the westward Little Nell could sometimes note a subtle indication of a playing searchlight which alone marked the presence of the invisible battle-ships half-mooned about the entrance of Santiago harbor, waiting—waiting—waiting.

When Little Nell returned to the veranda he stumbled along a man-strewn place until he came to the spot where he had left his mackintosh; but he found it gone. His curses mingled then with those of the men upon whose bodies he had trodden. Two English correspondents, lying awake to smoke a last pipe, reared and looked at him lazily. "What's wrong, old chap?" murmured one. "Eh? Lost it, eh? Well, look here; come here and take a bit of my blanket. It's a jolly big one.

Oh, no trouble at all, man. . . . There you are. Got enough? Comfy? . . . Good-night."

A sleepy voice arose in the darkness. "If this hammock breaks I shall hit at least ten of those Indians down there. Never mind. This is war!"

The men slept. Once the sound of three or four shots rang across the windy night, and one head uprose swiftly from the veranda, two eyes looked dazedly at nothing, and the head as swiftly sank. Again a sleepy voice was heard. "Usual thing; nervous sentries." The men slept. Before dawn a pulseless, penetrating chill came into the air, and the correspondents awakened shivering into a blue world. Some of the fires still smouldered. Walkley and Little Nell kicked vigorously into Point's framework. "Come on, Brilliance! Wake up, Talent! Don't be sogering. It's too cold to sleep, but it's not too cold to hustle." Point sat up dolefully. Upon his face was a childish expression. "Where we going to get breakfast?" he asked sulkily.

"There's no breakfast for you, you hound. Get up and hustle." Accordingly they hustled. With exceeding difficulty they learned that nothing emotional had happened during the night save the killing of two Cubans who were so secure in ignorance that they could not understand the challenge of two American sentries. Then Walkley ran a gamut of commanding officers, and Little Nell pumped privates for their impressions of Cuba. When his indignation at the absence of breakfast allowed him, Point made sketches. At the full break of day the *Adolphus*, an *Eclipse* dispatch-boat, sent a boat ashore with Tailor and Shackles in it, and Walkley departed tearlessly for Jamaica, soon after he had bestowed upon his friends much canned goods and blankets.

"Well, we've got our stuff off," said Little Nell. "Now Point and I must breakfast."

Shackles for some reason carried a great hunting-knife, and with it Little Nell opened a can of beans. "Fall to," he said amiably to Point.

There were some hard biscuits. Afterward they—the four of them—marched off on the route of the troops. They were well loaded with luggage, particularly young Point, who had somehow made great gathering of unnecessary things. Hills covered with verdure soon enclosed them. They heard that the army had advanced some nine miles with no fighting. Evidences of the rapid advance were here and there; coats, gauntlets, blanket-rolls on the ground. Mule trains came herding back along the narrow trail to the sound of a little tinkling bell. Cubans were appropriating the tunics and blanket-rolls.

The four correspondents hurried onward. The surety of impending battle weighed upon them always, but there were a score of minor things more intimate. Little Nell's left heel had chafed until it must have been quite raw, and every moment he wished to take seat by the roadside and console himself from pain. Shackles and Point disliked each other extremely, and often they foolishly quarreled over something or over nothing. The blanket-rolls and packages for the hand oppressed everybody. It was like being burned out of a boarding-house and having to carry one's trunk eight miles to the nearest neighbor. Moreover, Point, since he had stupidly overloaded, with great wisdom placed various cameras and other trifles in the hands of his three less burdened and more sensible friends. This made them fume and gnash, but in complete silence, since he was hideously youthful and innocent and unaware. They all wished to rebel, but none of them saw their way clear because—they did not understand, but somehow it seemed a barbarous project—no one wanted to say anything—cursed him privately for a little ass, but—said nothing. For instance, Little Nell wished to remark: "Point, you are not a thoroughbred in a half of a way. You are an inconsiderate, thoughtless little swine." But in truth he said: "Point, when you started out you looked like a Christmas tree. If we keep on robbing you of your bundles there soon won't be anything left for the children." Point asked dubiously: "What do you mean?" Little Nell merely laughed with deceptive good nature.

They were always very thirsty. There was always a howl for the half bottle of lime juice. Five or six drops from it were simply heavenly in the warm water from the canteens. Point seemed to try to keep the lime juice in his possession in order that he might get more benefit of it. Before the war was ended the others found themselves declaring vehemently that they loathed Point, and yet when men asked them for reasons they grew quite inarticulate. The reasons seemed then so small, so childish, as the reasons of a lot of women. And yet at the time his offences loomed enormous.

The surety of impending battle still weighed upon them. Then it came that Shackles turned seriously ill. Suddenly he dropped his own and much of Point's traps upon the trail, wriggled out of his blanket-roll, flung it away, and took seat heavily at the roadside. They saw with surprise that his face was pale as death and yet streaming with sweat.

"Boys," he said in his ordinary voice, "I'm clean played out. I can't go another step. You fellows go on and leave me to come as soon as I am able."

"Oh, no, that wouldn't do at all," said Little Nell and Tailor together. Point moved over to a soft place and dropped amid whatever traps he was himself carrying.

"Don't know whether—it's—ancestral or merely from the—sun—but I've got a stroke," said Shackles, and gently slumped over to a prostrate position before either Little Nell or Tailor could reach him. Thereafter Shackles was parental; it was Little Nell and Tailor who were really suffering from a stroke—either ancestral or from the sun.

"Put my blanket-roll under my head, Nell, me son," he said gently. "There, now. That is very nice. It is delicious. Why, I'm all right, only—only tired." He closed his eyes and something like an easy slumber came over him. Once he opened his eyes. "Don't trouble about me," he remarked. But the two fussed about him, nervous, worried, discussing this plan and that plan.

It was Point who first made a business-like statement. Seated carelessly and indifferently upon his soft place, he finally blurted out: "Say. Look here. Some of us have got to go on. We can't all stay here. Some of us have got to go on."

It was quite true. The *Eclipse* could take no account of strokes. In the end Point and Tailor went on, leaving Little Nell to bring on Shackles as soon as possible. The latter two spent many hours in the grass by the roadside. They made numerous abrupt acquaintances with passing staff officers, privates, muleteers, many stopping to inquire the wherefore of the death-faced figure on the ground. Favors were done, often and often, by peer and peasant—small things—of no consequence and yet warming.

It was dark when Shackles and Little Nell had come slowly to where they could hear the murmur of the army's bivouac.

"Shack," gasped Little Nell to the man leaning forlornly upon him, "I guess we'd better bunk down here where we stand."

"All right, old boy. Anything you say," replied Shackles, in the bass and hollow voice which arrives with such condition.

They crawled into some bushes and distributed their belongings upon the ground. Little Nell spread out the blankets and generally played housemaid. Then they lay down, supperless, being too weary to eat. The men slept.

At dawn Little Nell awakened and looked wildly for Shackles, whose empty blanket was pressed flat like a wet newspaper on the ground. But at nearly the same moment Shackles appeared elate.

"Come on," he cried; "I've rustled an invitation for breakfast."

Little Nell came on with celerity. "Where? Who?" he said.

"Oh, some officers," replied Shackles airily. If he had been ill the previous day he showed it now only in some curious kind of deference he paid to Little Nell.

Shackles conducted his comrade, and soon they arrived at where a captain and his one subaltern arose courteously from where they were squatting near a fire of little sticks. They wore the wide white trouser-stripes of infantry officers, and upon the shoulders of their blue campaign shirts were the little marks of their rank, but otherwise there was little beyond their manners to render them different from the men who were busy with breakfast near them.

The captain was old, grizzled—a common type of captain in the tiny American army—overjoyed at the active service, confident of his business, and yet breathing out in some way a note of pathos. The war was come too late. Age was grappling him, and honors were only for his widow and his children—merely a better life insurance policy. He had spent his life policing Indians with much labor, cold and heat, but with no glory for him nor for his fellows. All he could do now was to die at the head of his men. If he had youthfully dreamed of a general's stars, they were now impossible to him, and he knew it. He was too old to leap so far; his sole honor was a new invitation to face death. And yet, with his ambitions lying half-strangled, he was going to take his men into any sort of holocaust because his traditions were of gentlemen and soldiers, and because . . . he loved it for itself . . . the thing itself . . . the whirl, the unknown. If he had been degraded at that moment to be a pot-wrestler, no power could have starved him from going through the campaign as a spectator. Why, the army! It was in each drop of his blood.

The lieutenant was very young. Perhaps he had been hurried out of West Point at the last moment, upon a shortage of officers appearing. To him all was opportunity. He was, in fact, in great luck. Instead of going off in 1898 to grill for an indefinite period on some God-forgotten heap of red-hot sand in New Mexico, he was here in Cuba—on real business—with his regiment. When the big engagement came he was sure to emerge from it either horizontally or at the head of a company, and what more could a boy ask? He was a very modest lad, and talked nothing of his frame of mind, but an expression of blissful contentment was ever upon his face. He really accounted himself the most fortunate boy of his time. And he felt almost certain that he would do well. . . . It was necessary to do well. . . . He would do well.

And yet in many ways these two were alike—the grizzled captain with his gently mournful countenance—"Too late"—and the elate young second lieutenant, his commission hardly dry. Here again it was the influence of the army. After all they were both children of the army.

It is possible to spring into the future here and chronicle what happened later. The captain, after thirty-five years of waiting for his chance, took his Mauser bullet through the brain at the foot of San Juan Hill in the very beginning of the battle, and the boy arrived on the crest panting, sweating, but unscratched, and not sure whether he commanded one company or a whole battalion. Thus Fate dealt to the hosts of Shackles and Little Nell.

The breakfast was of canned tomatoes stewed with hard bread, more hard bread, and coffee. It was very good fare, almost royal. Shackles and Little Nell were absurdly grateful as they felt the hot bitter coffee tingle in them. But they departed joyfully before the sun was fairly up, and passed into Siboney. They never saw the captain again.

The beach at Siboney was furious with traffic, even as had been the beach at Daiquiri. Launches shouted, jack-tars prodded with their boathooks, and load of men followed load of men. Straight, parade-like, on the shore stood a trumpeter playing familiar calls to the troop-horses who swam toward him eagerly through the salt seas. Crowding closely into the cove were transports of all sizes and ages. To the left and to the right of the little landing-beach green hills shot upward like the wings in a theatre. They were scarred here and there with blockhouses and rifle-pits. Up one hill a regiment was crawling, seemingly inch by inch. Shackles and Little Nell walked among palms and scrubby bushes, near pools, over spaces of sand holding little monuments of biscuit boxes, ammunition boxes and supplies of all kinds. Some regiment was just collecting itself from the ships, and the men made great patches of blue on the brown sand.

Shackles asked a question of a man accidentally. "Where's that regiment going to?" He pointed to the force that was crawling up the hill. The man grinned and said: "They're goin' to look for a fight."

"Looking for a fight," said Shackles and Little Nell together. They stared into each other's eyes. Then they set off for the foot of the hill. The hill was long and toilsome. Below them spread wider and wider a vista of ships quiet on a grey sea; a busy, black disembarkation-place; tall, still, green hills; a village of well-separated cottages; palms; a bit of road; soldiers marching. They passed vacant Spanish trenches; little twelve-foot blockhouses. Soon they were on a fine upland near the sea. The path, under ordinary conditions, must have been a beautiful wooded way. It wound in the shade of thickets of fine trees, then through rank growths of bushes with revealed and fantastic roots, then through a grassy space which had all the beauty of a neglected orchard. But always from under their feet scuttled noisy land-crabs, demons to the nerves, which in some ways possessed a semblance of moonlike faces upon their blue or red bodies, and these faces were turned with expressions of deepest horror upon Shackles and Little Nell as they sped to overtake the pugnacious regiment.

The route was paved with coats, hats, tent and blanket-rolls, ration-tins, haversacks—everything but ammunition belts, rifles and canteens.

They heard a dull noise of voices in front of them—men talking too loud for the etiquette of the forest—and presently they came upon two or three soldiers lying by the roadside, flame-faced, utterly spent from the hurried march in the heat. One man came limping back along the path. He looked to them anxiously for sympathy and comprehension. "Hurt m' knee. I swear I couldn't keep up with th' boys. I had to leave 'm. Wasn't that tough luck?" His collar rolled away from a red muscular neck, and his bare forearms were better than stanchions. Yet he was almost babyishly tearful in his attempt to make the two correspondents feel that he had not turned back because he was afraid. They gave him scant courtesy, tinctured with one drop of sympathetic yet cynical understanding. Soon they overtook the hospital squad—men addressing chaste language to some pack-mules—a talkative sergeant—two amiable cool-eyed young surgeons. Soon they were amid the rear troops of the dismounted volunteer cavalry regiment which was moving to attack. The men strode easily along, arguing one to another on ulterior matters. If they were going into battle they either did not know it or they concealed it well. They were more like men going into a bar at one o'clock in the morning. Their laughter rang through the Cuban woods. And in the meantime soft, mellow, sweet, sang the voice of the Cuban wood dove . . . the Spanish guerilla calling to his mate . . . forest music . . . on the flanks . . . deep back on both flanks . . . the adorable wood dove, singing only of love . . . some of the advancing Americans said it was beautiful . . . it *was* beautiful . . . the Spanish guerilla calling to his mate. . . . What could be more beautiful?

Shackles and Little Nell rushed precariously through waist-high bushes until they reached the centre of the single-filed regiment. The firing then broke out in front. All the woods set up a hot sputtering; the bullets sped along the path and across it from both sides. The thickets presented nothing but dense masses of light green foliage, out of which these swift steel things were born supernaturally.

It was a volunteer regiment going into its first action, against an enemy of unknown force, in a country where the vegetation was thicker than fur on a cat. There might have been a dreadful mess; but in military matters the only way to deal with a situation of this kind is to take it frankly by the throat and squeeze it to death. Shackles and Little Nell felt the thrill of the orders. "Come ahead, men! Keep right ahead, men! Come on!" The volunteer cavalry regiment, with all the willingness in the world, went ahead into the angle of a V-shaped Spanish formation.

It seemed that every leaf had turned into a soda-bottle and was popping its cork. Some of the explosions seemed to be against the men's very faces; others against the backs of their necks. "Now, men, keep goin' ahead. Keep on goin'." The forward troops were already engaged. They, at least, had something at which to shoot. . . . "Now, Captain, if you're ready." . . . "Stop that swearing there." . . . "Got a match?" . . . "Steady now, men."

A gate appeared in a barbed-wire fence. Within were billowy fields of long grass, dotted with palms and luxuriant mango trees. It was Elysian, a place for lovers, fair as Eden in its radiance of sun, under its blue sky. One might have expected to see white-robed figures walking slowly in the shadows. . . . A dead man, with a bloody face, lay twisted in a curious contortion at the waist. . . . Some one was shot in the leg—his pins knocked cleanly from under him. . . . "Keep goin', men." . . . The air roared, and the ground fled reelingly under their feet. . . . Light, shadow, trees, grass. . . . Bullets spat from every side. Once they were in a thicket, and the men, blanched and bewildered, turned one way and then another, not knowing which way to turn. "Keep goin', men." Soon they were in the sunlight again. They could see the long scant line which was being drained man by man—one might say drop by drop. The musketry rolled forth in great full measure from the magazine carbines. "Keep goin', men." . . . "Christ, I'm shot!" . . . "They're flankin' us, sir." . . . "We're bein' fired into by our own crowd, sir." . . . "Keep goin', men." A low ridge before them was a bottling establishment blowing up in detail. From the right—it seemed at that time to be the far right—they could hear steady, crashing volleys—the United States regulars in action.

Then suddenly—to use a phrase of the street—the whole bottom of the thing fell out. It was suddenly and mysteriously ended. The Spaniards had run away and some of the regulars were chasing them. It was a victory.

When the wounded men dropped in the tall grass they quite disappeared, as if they had sunk in water. Little Nell and Shackles were walking along through the fields, disputing.

"Well, damn it, man," cried Shackles, "we *must* get a list of the killed and wounded."

"That is not nearly so important," quoth Little Nell academically, "as to get the first account to New York of the first action of the army in Cuba."

They came upon Tailor lying with a bared torso and a small red hole through his left lung. He was calm, but evidently out of temper. "Good God, Tailor," they cried, dropping to their knees like two pagans, "are you hurt, old boy?"

"Hurt?" he said gently. "No, 'tis not so deep as a well nor so wide as a church door; but 'tis enough, d' you see? You understand, do you? Idiots."

Then he became very official. "Shackles, feel and see what's under my leg. It's a small stone or a burr or something. Don't be clumsy, now. Be careful. Be careful." Then he said angrily, "Oh, you didn't find it at all. Damn it!"

In reality there was nothing there, and so Shackles could not have removed it. "Sorry, old boy," he said meekly.

"Well, you may observe that I can't stay here more than a year," said Tailor with some oratory, "and the hospital people have their own work in hand. It behooves you, Nell, to fly to Siboney, arrest a dispatch-boat, get a cot and some other things, and some minions to carry me. If I get once down to the base I'm all right, but if I stay here I'm dead. Meantime Shackles can stay here and try to look as if he liked it."

There was no disobeying the man. Lying there with a little red hole in his left lung, he dominated them through his help-lessness and through their fear that if they angered him he would move and—bleed.

"Well?" said Little Nell.

"Yes," said Shackles, nodding.

Little Nell departed. "That blanket you lent me," Tailor called after him, "is back there somewhere with Point."

Little Nell noted that many of the men who were wandering among the wounded seemed so spent with the toil and excitement of their first action that they could hardly drag one leg after the other. He found himself suddenly in the same condition. His face, his neck, even his mouth, felt dry as sun-baked bricks, and his legs were foreign to him. But he swung desperately into his five-mile task. On the way he passed many things—bleeding men carried by comrades—others making their way grimly with encrimsoned arms—then the little settlement of the hospital squad—men on the ground everywhere, many in the path—one young captain dying with great gasps, his body pale blue, and glistening, like the inside of a rabbit's skin. But the voice of the Cuban wood dove, soft, mellow, sweet, singing only of love, was no longer heard from the wealth of foliage.

Presently the hurrying correspondent met another regiment coming to assist—a line of a thousand men in single file through the jungle. "Well, how is it going, old man?" "How is it coming on?" "Are we doin' 'em?" Then after an interval came other regiments moving out. He had to take to the bush to let these long lines pass him, and he was delayed and had to flounder amid brambles. But at last, like a successful pilgrim, he arrived at the brow of the great hill overlooking Siboney. His practiced eye scanned the fine broad brow of the sea with its clustering ships, but he saw thereon no *Eclipse* dispatch-boats. He zig-zagged heavily down the hill and arrived finally amid the dust and outcries of the base. He seemed to ask a thousand men if they had seen an *Eclipse* boat on the water or an *Eclipse* correspondent on the shore. They all answered "No."

He was like a poverty-stricken and unknown suppliant at a foreign court. Even his plea got only ill hearings. He had expected the news of the serious wounding of Tailor to appal the other correspondents, but they took it quite calmly. It was as if their sense of an impending great battle between two large armies had quite got them out of focus for these minor tragedies. Tailor was hurt—yes? They looked at Little Nell, dazed. How curious that Tailor should be almost the first; how *very* curious; yes. But as far as arousing them to any enthusiasm of active pity, it seemed impossible. He was lying up there in the grass, was he? Too bad, too bad, too bad!

Little Nell went alone and lay down in the sand with his back against a rock. Tailor was prostrate up there in the grass. Never mind. Nothing was to be done. The whole situation was too colossal. Then into his zone came Walkley the invincible.

"Walkley," yelled Little Nell. Walkley came quickly and Little Nell lay weakly against his rock and talked. In thirty seconds Walkley understood everything, had hurled a drink of whisky into Little Nell, had admonished him to lie quiet, and had gone to organize and manipulate. When he returned he was a trifle dubious and backward. Behind him was a singular squad of volunteers from the *Adolphus* carrying among them a wire-woven bed.

"Look here, Nell," said Walkley in bashful accents, "I've collected a battalion here which is willing to go bring Tailor, but—they say—you—can't you show them where he is?"

"Yes," said Little Nell, arising.

When the party arrived back at Siboney and deposited Tailor in the best place, Walkley had found a house and stocked it with canned soups. Therein Shackles and Little Nell revelled for a time and then rolled on the floor in their blankets. Little Nell tossed a great deal. "Oh, I'm so tired. Good God, I'm tired. I'm—tired."

In the morning a voice aroused them. It was a swollen, important circus voice, saying: "Where is Mr. Nell? I wish to see him immediately."

"Here I am, Rogers," cried Little Nell.

"Oh, Nell," said Rogers, "here's a dispatch to me which I thought you had better read."

Little Nell took the dispatch. It was: "Tell Nell can't understand his inaction. Tell him come home first steamer from Port Antonio, Jamaica.—*Eclipse*."

The Revenge of the Adolphus

I

"STAND BY."

Shackles had come down from the bridge of the *Adolphus* and flung this command at three fellow-correspondents who in the galley were busy with pencils trying to write something exciting and interesting from four days quiet cruising. They looked up casually. "What for?" They did not intend to arouse for nothing. Ever since Shackles had heard the men of the navy directing each other to stand by for this thing and that thing, he had used the two words as his pet phrase and was continually telling his friends to stand by. Sometimes its portentous and emphatic reiteration became highly exasperating and men were apt to retort sharply. "Well, I *am* standing by, ain't I?" On this occasion they detected that he was serious. "Well, what for?" they repeated. In his answer Shackles was reproachful as well as impressive. "Stand by? Stand by for a Spanish gunboat. A Spanish gunboat in chase! Stand by for *two* Spanish gunboats—*both* of them in chase!"

The others looked at him for a brief space and were almost certain that they saw truth written upon his countenance. Whereupon they tumbled out of the galley and galloped up to the bridge. The cook with a mere inkling of tragedy was now out on deck bawling, "What's the matter? What's the matter? What's the matter?" Aft, the grimy head of a stoker was thrust suddenly up through the deck, so to speak. The eyes flashed in a quick look astern and then the head vanished. The correspondents were scrambling on the bridge. "Where's my opry glasses, damn it? Here—let me take a look. Are they Spaniards, Captain? Are you sure?"

The skipper of the *Adolphus* was at the wheel. The pilot-house was so arranged that he could not see astern without hanging forth from one of the side windows, but apparently he had made early investigation. He did not reply at once. At sea, he never replied at once to questions. At the very first Shackles had discovered the merits of this deliberate manner and had taken delight in it. He invariably detailed his talk with the captain to the other correspondents. "Look here. I've just been to see the skipper. I said: 'I would like to put into Cape Haytien.' Then he took a little think. Finally he said: 'All right.' Then I said: 'I suppose we'll need to take on more coal there?' He took another little think. Finally he said: 'Yes.' I said: 'Ever ran into that port before?' He took another little think. Finally he said: 'Yes.' I said: 'Have a cigar?' He took another little think. See? There's where I fooled 'im———"

While the correspondents spun the hurried questions at him, the captain of the *Adolphus* stood with his brown hands on the wheel and his cold glance aligned straight over the bow of his ship.

"Are they Spanish gunboats, Captain? Are they, Captain?"

After a profound pause, he said: "Yes." The four correspondents hastily and in perfect time presented their backs to him and fastened their gaze on the pursuing foe. They saw a dull grey curve of sea going to the feet of the high green and blue coastline of northeastern Cuba, and on this sea were two miniature ships with clouds of iron-colored smoke pouring from their funnels.

One of the correspondents strolled elaborately to the pilot-house. "Aw—Captain," he drawled, "do you think they can catch us?"

The captain's glance was still aligned over the bow of his ship. Ultimately he answered: "I don't know."

From the top of the little *Adolphus*'s stack, thick dark smoke swept level for a few yards and then went rolling to leeward in great hot obscuring clouds. From time to time the grimy head was thrust through the deck, the eyes took the quick look astern and then the head vanished. The cook was trying to get somebody to listen to him. "Well, you know, damn it all, it won't be no fun to be ketched by them Spaniards. Be-Gawd, it *won't*. Look here, what do you think they'll do to us, hey? Say, I don't like this, you know. I'm damned if I do." The sea, cut by the hurried bow of the *Adolphus*, flung its waters astern in the formation of a wide angle and the lines of the angle ruffled and hissed as they fled, while the thumping screw tormented the water at the stern. The frame of the steamer underwent regular convulsions as in the strenuous sobbing of a child.

The mate was standing near the pilot-house. Without looking at him, the captain spoke his name. "Ed!"

"Yes, sir," cried the mate with alacrity.

The captain reflected for a moment. Then he said: "Are they gainin' on us?"

The mate took another anxious survey of the race. "No—o—yes, I think they are—a little."

After a pause the captain said: "Tell the chief to shake her up more."

The mate, glad of an occupation in these tense minutes, flew down to the engine-room door. "Skipper says shake 'er up more!" he bawled. The head of the chief engineer appeared, a grizzly head now wet with oil and sweat. "What?" he shouted angrily. It was as if he had been propelling the ship with his own arms. Now he was told that his best was not good enough. "What? Shake 'er up more? Why she can't carry another pound, I tell you! Not another ounce! We——" Suddenly he ran forward and climbed to the bridge. "Captain," he cried in the loud harsh voice of one who lived usually amid the thunder of machinery, "she can't do it, sir! Be-Gawd, she can't! She's turning over now faster than she ever did in her life and we'll all blow to hell——"

The low-toned, impassive voice of the captain suddenly checked the chief's clamor. "I'll blow her up," he said, "but I won't git ketched if I kin help it." Even then the listening correspondents found a second in which to marvel that the captain had actually explained his point of view to another human being.

The engineer stood blank. Then suddenly he cried: "All right, sir!" He threw a hurried look of despair at the correspondents, the deck of the *Adolphus*, the pursuing enemy, Cuba, the sky and the sea; he vanished in the direction of his post.

A correspondent was suddenly regifted with the power of prolonged speech. "Well, you see, the game is up, damn it. See? We can't get out of it. The skipper will blow up the whole bunch before he'll let his ship be taken, and the Spaniards are gaining. Well, that's what comes from going to war in an eight-knot tub." He bitterly accused himself, the others, and the dark, sightless, indifferent world.

This certainty of coming evil affected each one differently. One was made garrulous; one kept absent-mindedly snapping his fingers and gazing at the sea; another stepped nervously to and fro, looking everywhere as if for employment for his mind. As for Shackles he was silent and smiling, but it was a new smile that caused the lines about his mouth to betray quivering weakness. And each man looked at the others to discover their degree of fear and did his best to conceal his own, holding his crackling nerves with all his strength.

As the *Adolphus* rushed on, the sun suddenly emerged from behind grey clouds and its rays dealt titanic blows so that in a few minutes the sea was a glowing blue plain with the golden shine dancing at the tips of the waves. The coast of Cuba glowed with light. The pursuers displayed detail after detail in the new atmosphere. The voice of the cook was heard in high vexation. "Am I to git dinner as usual? How do I know? Nobody tells me what to do! Am I to git dinner as usual?"

The mate answered ferociously. "Of course you are! What do you s'pose? Ain't you the cook, you damn fool?"

The cook retorted in a mutinous scream. "Well, how would I know? If this ship is goin' to blow up——"

II

The captain called from the pilot-house. "Mr. Shackles! Oh, Mr. Shackles!" The correspondent moved hastily to a window. "What is it, Captain?" The skipper of the *Adolphus* raised a battered finger and pointed over the bows. "See 'er?" he asked, laconic but quietly jubilant. Another steamer was smoking at full speed over the sun-lit seas. A great billow of pure white was on her bows. "Great Scott!" cried Shackles. "Another Spaniard?"

"No," said the captain, "that there is a United States cruiser!"

"What?" Shackles was dumfounded into muscular paralysis. "No! Are you *sure*?"

The captain nodded. "Sure. Take the glass. See her ensign? Two funnels, two masts with fighting tops. She ought to be the *Chancellorville*."

Shackles choked. "Well, I'm blowed!"

"Ed!" said the captain.

"Yessir!"

"Tell the chief there is no hurry."

Shackles suddenly bethought him of his companions. He dashed to them and was full of quick scorn of their gloomy faces. "Hi, brace up there! Are you blind? Can't you see her?"

"See what?"

"Why, the *Chancellorville*, you blind mice!" roared Shackles. "See 'er? See 'er? See 'er?"

The others sprang, saw, and collapsed. Shackles was a madman for the purpose of distributing the news. "Cook!" he shrieked. "Don't you see 'er, cook? Good Gawd, man, don't you see 'er?" He ran to the lower deck and howled his information everywhere. Suddenly the whole ship smiled. Men clapped each other on the shoulder and joyously shouted. The captain thrust his head from the pilot-house to look back at the Spanish ships. Then he looked at the American cruiser. "Now, we'll see," he said grimly and vindictively to the mate. "Guess somebody else will do some runnin'." The mate chuckled.

The two gunboats were still headed hard for the *Adolphus* and she kept on her way. The American cruiser was coming swiftly. "It's the *Chancellorville*!" cried Shackles. "I know her! We'll see a fight at sea, my boys! A fight at sea!" The enthusiastic correspondents pranced in Indian revels.

The *Chancellorville*—2000 tons—18.6 knots—10 five-inch guns—came on tempestuously, sheering the water high with her sharp bow. From her funnels the smoke raced away in driven sheets. She loomed with extraordinary rapidity like a ship bulging and growing out of the sea. She swept by the *Adolphus* so close that one could have thrown a walnut on board. She was a glistening grey apparition with a blood-red water-line, with brown gun-muzzles and white-clothed motionless jack-tars; and in her rush she was silent, deadly silent. Probably there entered the mind of every man on board of the *Adolphus* a feeling of almost idolatry for this living thing, stern but, to their thought, incomparably beautiful. They would have cheered but that each man seemed to feel that a cheer would be too puny a tribute.

It was at first as if she did not see the *Adolphus*. She was going to pass without heeding this little vagabond of the high-seas. But suddenly a megaphone gaped over the rail of her bridge and a voice was heard measuredly, calmly intoning. "Halloa—there! Keep—well—to—the—north'ard—and—out of my—way—and I'll—go—in—and—see—what—those—people—want——" Then nothing was heard but the swirl of water. In a moment the *Adolphus* was looking at a high grey stern. On the quarter-deck sailors were poised about the breach of the after-pivot-gun.

The correspondents were revelling. "Captain," yelled Shackles, "we can't miss this! We must see it!" But the skipper had already flung over the wheel. "Sure," he answered almost at once. "We can't miss it."

The cook was arrogantly, grossly triumphant. His voice rang along the deck. "There, now! How will the Spinachers like that? Now, it's *our* turn! We've been doin' the runnin' away but now we'll do the chasin'!" Apparently feeling some twinge of nerves from the former strain, he suddenly demanded: "Say, who's got any whisky? I'm near dead for a drink."

When the *Adolphus* came about, she laid her course for a position to the northward of a coming battle, but the situation suddenly became complicated. When the Spanish ships discovered the identity of the ship that was steaming toward them, they did not hesitate over their plan of action. With one accord they turned and ran for port. Laughter arose from the *Adolphus*. The captain broke his orders, and, instead of keeping to the northward, he headed in the wake of the impetuous *Chancellorville*. The correspondents crowded on the bow.

The Spaniards when their broadsides became visible were seen to be ships of no importance, mere little gunboats for work in the shallows at the back of the reefs, and it was certainly discreet to refuse encounter with the five-inch guns of the *Chancellorville*. But the joyful *Adolphus* took no account of this discretion. The pursuit of the Spaniards had been so ferocious that the quick change to heels-over-head flight filled that corner of the mind which is devoted to the spirit of revenge. It was this that moved Shackles to yell taunts futilely at the far-away ships. "Well, how do you like it, eh? How do you like it?" The *Adolphus* was drinking compensation for her previous agony.

The mountains of the shore now shadowed high into the sky and the square white houses of a town could be seen near a vague cleft which seemed to mark the entrance to a port. The gunboats were now near to it.

Suddenly white smoke streamed from the bow of the *Chancellorville* and developed swiftly into a great bulb which drifted in fragments down the wind. Presently the deep-throated boom of the gun came to the ears on board the *Adolphus*. The shot kicked up a high jet of water into the air astern of the last gunboat. The black smoke from the funnels of the cruiser made her look like a collier on fire, and in her desperation she tried many more long shots, but presently the *Adolphus*, murmuring disappointment, saw the *Chancellorville* sheer from the chase.

In time they came up with her and she was an indignant ship. Gloom and wrath was on the forecastle and wrath and gloom was on the quarter-deck. A sad voice from the bridge said: "Just missed 'em." Shackles gained permission to board the cruiser, and in the cabin, he talked to Commander Surrey, tall, bald-headed and angry. "Shoals," said the captain of the *Chancellorville*. "I can't go any nearer and those gunboats could steam along a stone sidewalk if only it was wet." Then his bright eyes became brighter. "I tell you what! The *Chicken*, the *Holy Moses* and the *Mongolian* are on station off Nuevitas. If you will do me a favor—why, to-morrow I will give those people a game!"

III

The *Chancellorville* lay all night watching off the port of the two gunboats and, soon after daylight, the lookout descried three smokes to the westward and they were later made out to be the *Chicken*, the *Holy Moses* and the *Adolphus*, the latter tagging hurriedly after the United States vessels.

The *Chicken* had been a harbor tug but she was now the U.S.S. *Chicken*, by your leave. She carried a six-pounder for-ward and a six-pounder aft and her main point was her conspicuous vulnerability. The *Holy Moses* had been the private yacht of a Philadelphia millionaire. She carried six six-pounders and her main point was the chaste beauty of the officers' quarters.

On the bridge of the *Chancellorville* Commander Surrey surveyed his squadron with considerable satisfaction. Presently he signalled to the lieutenant who commanded the *Holy Moses* and to the boatswain who commanded the *Chicken* to come aboard the cruiser. This was all very well for the captain of the yacht, but it was not so easy for the captain of the tugboat who had two heavy lifeboats swung fifteen feet above the water. He had been accustomed to talking with senior officers from his own pilot-house through the intercession of the blessed megaphone. However he got a lifeboat over-side and was pulled to the *Chancellorville* by three men—which cut his crew almost into halves.

In the cabin of the *Chancellorville* Surrey disclosed to his two captains his desires concerning the Spanish gunboats and they were glad of being ordered down from the Nuevitas station where life was very dull. He also announced that there was a shore battery containing, he believed, four field guns—three-point-twos. His draught—he spoke of it as *his* draught—would enable him to go in close enough to engage the battery at moderate range, but he pointed out that the main parts of the attempt to destroy the Spanish gunboats must be left to the *Holy Moses* and the *Chicken*. His business, he thought, could only be to keep the air so singing about the ears of the battery that the men at the guns would be unable to take an interest in the dash of the smaller American craft into the bay.

The officers spoke in their turns. The captain of the *Chicken* announced that he saw no difficulties. The squadron would follow the senior officer's ship in line ahead, the senior officer's ship would engage the batteries as soon as possible, she would turn to starboard when the depth of water forced her to do so and the *Holy Moses* and the *Chicken* would run past her into the bay and fight the Spanish ships wherever they were to be found. The captain of the *Holy Moses* after some moments of dignified thought said that he had no suggestions to make that would better this plan.

Surrey pressed an electric bell; a marine orderly appeared; he was sent with a message. The message brought the executive officer and the navigating officer of the *Chancellorville* to the cabin and the five men nosed over a chart.

In the end Surrey declared that he had made up his mind and the juniors remained in expectant silence for three minutes while he stared at the bulkhead. Then he said that the plan of the *Chicken*'s captain seemed to him correct in the main. He would make one change. It was that he should first steam in and engage the battery and the other vessels should remain in their present positions until he signalled them to run into the bay. If the squadron steamed ahead in line, the battery could, if it chose, divide its fire between the S.O.P.'s ship and the vessels constituting the more important attack. He had no doubt, he said, that he could soon silence the battery by tumbling the earthworks on to the guns and driving away the men even if he did not succeed in hitting the pieces. Of course he had no doubt of being able to silence the battery in twenty minutes. Then he would signal for the *Holy Moses* and the *Chicken* to make their rush, and of course he would support them with his fire as much as conditions enabled him. He arose then indicating that the conference was at an end. The boatswain, who captained the *Chicken*, looked uncomfortable for a moment and then withdrew. He was not used to this cabin. In the few moments more the four men remained in the cabin, the talk changed its character completely. It was now unofficial, and the sharp badinage concealed furtive affections, academy friendships, the feelings of old-time shipmates, hiding everything under a veil of jokes. "Well, good luck to you, old boy! Don't get that valuable packet of yours sunk under you. Think how it would weaken the navy. Would you mind buying me three pairs of pyjamas in the town yonder? If your engines get disabled, tote her under your arm. You can do it. Good-bye, old man, don't forget to come out all right——"

When the captains of the *Holy Moses* and the *Chicken* came upon deck they strode it with a new step. They were proud men. The marine on duty above their boats looked at them curiously and with awe. He detected something which meant action, conflict. The boats' crews saw it also. As they pulled

their steady stroke they studied fleetingly the face of the offi-
cer in the stern-sheets. In both cases they perceived a glad
man and yet a man filled with a profound consideration of
the future.

IV

"Beat to quarters!"

Bugles and drums stirred the decks of the *Chancellorville*.
There was the noise of rushing feet, a clanging of scuttle-
plates, a rattling of ammunition hoists, followed directly by
the sinister, deep note of locking breech-plugs. As the cruiser
turned her bow toward the shore, she happened to steam near
the *Adolphus*. The usual calm voice hailed the despatch-boat.
"Keep—that—gauze under-shirt of yours—well—out of
the—line of fire."

"Ay, ay, sir!"

The cruiser then moved slowly toward the shore, watched
by every eye in the smaller American vessels. She was delib-
erate and steady, and this was reasonable even to the impa-
tience of the other craft because the wooded shore was likely
to suddenly develop new factors. Slowly she swung to star-
board, smoke belched over her and the roar of a gun came
along the water.

The battery was indicated by a long thin streak of yellow
earth. The first shot went high, ploughing the chaparral on
the hillside. The *Chancellorville* wore an air for a moment of
being deep in meditation. She flung another shell, which
landed squarely on the earthwork, making a great dun cloud.
Before the smoke had settled, there was a crimson flash from
the battery. To the watchers at sea, it was smaller than a nee-
dle. The shot made a geyser of crystal water, four hundred
yards from the *Chancellorville*.

The cruiser, having made up her mind, suddenly went at
the battery hammer and tongs. She moved to and fro casually,
but the thunder of her guns was swift and angry. Sometimes
she was quite hidden in her own smoke, but with exceeding
regularity the earth of the battery spurted into the air. The
Spanish shells for the most part went high and wide of the
cruiser, jetting the water far away.

Once a Spanish gunner took a festive side-show chance at the waiting group of the three nondescripts. It went like a flash over the *Adolphus*, singing a wistful metallic note. Whereupon the *Adolphus* broke hurriedly for the open sea, and men on the *Holy Moses* and the *Chicken* laughed hoarsely and cruelly. The correspondents had been standing excitedly on top of the pilot-house, but at the passing of the shell they promptly eliminated themselves by dropping with a thud to the deck below. The cook again was giving tongue. "Oh, say, this won't do! I'm damned if it will! We ain't no armored cruiser, you know. If one of them shells hits us—well, we finish right there. 'Tain't like as if it was our *business*, foolin' 'round within the range of them guns. There's no sense in it. Them other fellows don't seem to mind it, but it's their *business*. If it's your *business*, you go ahead and do it, but if it ain't, you—look at that, would you?"

The *Chancellorville* had set up a spread of flags, and the *Holy Moses* and the *Chicken* were steaming in.

V

They on the *Chancellorville* sometimes could see into the bay, and they perceived the enemy's gunboats moving out as if to give battle. Surrey feared that this impulse would not endure or that it was some mere pretence for the edification of the townspeople and the garrison, so he hastily signalled the *Holy Moses* and the *Chicken* to go in. Thankful for small favors, they came on tumultuously. The battery had ceased firing. As the two auxiliaries passed under the stern of the cruiser, the megaphone hailed them. "You—will—see—the—en—em—y—soon—as—you—round—the—point. A—fine—chance. Good—luck."

As a matter of fact, the Spanish gunboats had not been informed of the presence of the *Holy Moses* and the *Chicken* off the bar, and they were just blustering down the bay over the protective shoals to make it appear that they scorned the *Chancellorville*. But suddenly from around the point there burst into view a steam yacht, closely followed by a harbor tug. The gunboats took one swift look at this horrible sight and fled screaming.

Lieutenant Reigate, commanding the *Holy Moses*, had under his feet a craft that was capable of some speed, although before a solemn tribunal one would have to admit that she conscientiously belied almost everything that the contractors had said of her originally. Boatswain Pent, commanding the *Chicken*, was in possession of an utterly different kind. The *Holy Moses* was an antelope; the *Chicken* was a man who could carry a piano on his back. In this race Pent had the mortification of seeing his vessel outstripped badly.

The entrance of the two American craft had had a curious effect upon the shores of the bay. Apparently everyone had slept in the assurance that the *Chancellorville* could not cross the bar, and that the *Chancellorville* was the only hostile ship. Consequently, the appearance of the *Holy Moses* and the *Chicken* created a curious and complex emotion. Reigate on the bridge of the *Holy Moses* laughed when he heard the bugles shrilling and saw through his glasses the wee figures of men running hither and thither on the shore. It was the panic of the china when the bull entered the shop. The whole bay was bright with sun. Every detail of the shore was plain. From a brown hut abeam of the *Holy Moses* some little men ran out waving their arms and turning their tiny faces to look at the enemy. Directly ahead, some four miles, appeared the scattered white houses of a town with a wharf and some schooners in front of it. The gunboats were making for the town. There was a stone fort on the hill overshadowing, but Reigate conjectured that there was no artillery in it.

There was a sense of something intimate and impudent in the minds of the Americans. It was like climbing over a wall and fighting a man in his own garden. It was not that they could be in any wise shaken in their resolve; it was simply that the overwhelmingly Spanish aspect of things made them feel like gruff intruders. Like many of the emotions of war time, this emotion had nothing at all to do with war.

Reigate's only commissioned subordinate called up from the bow gun. "May I open fire, sir? I think I can fetch that last one."

"Yes." Immediately the six-pounder crashed, and in the air was the spinning-wire noise of the flying shot. It struck so close to the last gunboat that it appeared that the spray went aboard. The swift-handed men at the gun spoke of it. "Gave 'm a bath that time, anyhow. First one they've ever had. Dry 'em off this time, Jim." The young ensign said: "Steady." And so the *Holy Moses* raced in, firing, until the whole town, fort, water-front and shipping was as plain as if it had been done on paper by a mechanical draftsman. The gunboats were trying to hide in the bosom of the town. One was frantically tying up to the wharf and the other was anchoring within a hundred yards of the shore. The Spanish infantry, of course, had dug trenches along the beach, and suddenly the air over the *Holy Moses* sung with bullets. The shore-line thrummed with musketry. Also some antique shells screamed.

VI

The *Chicken* was doing her best. Pent's posture at the wheel seemed to indicate that her best was about thirty-four knots. In his eagerness he was braced as if he alone was taking in a 10,000-ton battleship through Hell Gate.

But the *Chicken* was not too far in the rear and Pent could see clearly that he was to have no minor part to play. Some of the antique shells had struck the *Holy Moses* and he could see the escaped steam shooting up from her. She lay close inshore and was lashing out with four six-pounders as if this was the last opportunity she would have to fire them. She had made the Spanish gunboats very sick. A solitary gun on the one moored to the wharf was from time to time firing wildly; otherwise the gunboats were silent. But the beach in front of the town was a line of fire. The *Chicken* headed for the *Holy Moses* and, as soon as possible, the six-pounder in her bow began to crack at the gunboat moored to the wharf.

In the meantime the *Chancellorville* prowled off the bar, listening to the firing, anxious, acutely anxious, and feeling her impotency in every inch of her smart steel frame. And in the meantime the *Adolphus* squatted on the waves and brazenly waited for news. One could thoughtfully count the seconds and reckon that in this second and that second a man had died—if one chose. But no one did it. Undoubtedly the spirit was that the flag should come away with honor, honor complete, perfect, leaving no loose unfinished end over which the Spaniards could erect a monument of satisfaction, glorifi-cation. The distant guns boomed to the ears of the silent blue-jackets at their stations on the cruiser.

The *Chicken* steamed up to the *Holy Moses* and took into her nostrils the odor of steam, gunpowder and burnt things. Rifle bullets simply streamed over them both. In the merest flash of time, Pent took into his remembrance the body of a dead quartermaster on the bridge of his consort. The two megaphones uplifted together, but Pent's eager voice cried out first.

"Are you injured, sir?"

"No, not completely. My engines can get me out after—after we have sunk those gunboats." The voice had been ut-terly conventional but it changed to sharpness. "Go in and sink that gunboat at anchor."

As the *Chicken* rounded the *Holy Moses* and started inshore, a man called to him from the depths of finished disgust. "They're takin' to their boats, sir." Pent looked and saw the men of the anchored gunboat lower their boats and pull like mad for shore.

The *Chicken*, assisted by the *Holy Moses*, began a methodi-cal killing of the anchored gunboat. The Spanish infantry on shore fired frenziedly at the *Chicken*. Pent, giving the wheel to a waiting sailor, stepped out to a point where he could see the men at the guns. One bullet spanged past him and into the pilot-house. He ducked his head into the window. "That hit you, Murry?" he inquired with interest.

"No, sir," cheerfully responded the man at the wheel.

Pent became very busy superintending the fire of his absurd battery. The anchored gunboat simply would not sink. It evinced that unnatural stubbornness which is sometimes dis-played by inanimate objects. The gunboat at the wharf had sunk as if she had been scuttled but this riddled thing at an-chor would not even take fire. Pent began to grow flurried—privately. He could not stay there for ever. Why didn't the damned gunboat admit its destruction. Why——

He was at the forward gun when one of his engine-room force came to him and after saluting, said serenely: "The men at the after-gun are all down, sir."

It was one of those curious lifts which an enlisted man,

without in any way knowing it, can give his officer. The impudent tranquillity of the man at once set Pent to rights and the stoker departed admiring the extraordinary coolness of his captain.

The next few moments contained little but heat, an odor, applied mechanics and an expectation of death. Pent developed a fervid and amazed appreciation of the men, his men, men he knew very well, but strange men. What explained them? He was doing his best because he was captain of the *Chicken* and he lived or died by the *Chicken*. But what could move these men to watch his eye in bright anticipation of his orders and then obey them with enthusiastic rapidity? What caused them to speak of the action as some kind of joke— particularly when they knew he could overhear them? What manner of men? And he anointed them secretly with his fullest affection.

Perhaps Pent did not think all this during the battle. Perhaps he thought it so soon after the battle that his full mind became confused as to the time. At any rate, it stands as an expression of his feeling.

The enemy had gotten a field-gun down to the shore and with it they began to throw three-inch shells at the *Chicken*. In this war it was usual that the down-trodden Spaniards in their ignorance should use smokeless powder while the Americans, by the power of the consistent everlasting three-ply, wire-woven, double back-action imbecility of a hay-seed government, used powder which on sea and on land cried their position to heaven, and, accordingly, good men got killed without reason. At first Pent could not locate the field-gun at all, but as soon as he found it, he ran aft with one man and brought the after six-pounder again into action. He paid little heed to the old gun-crew. One was lying on his face apparently dead; another was prone with a wound in the chest, while the third sat with his back to the deck-house holding a smitten arm. This last one called out huskily, "Give 'm hell, sir."

The minutes of the battle were either days, years, or they were flashes of a second. Once Pent looking up was astonished to see three shell holes in the *Chicken*'s funnel—made surreptitiously, so to speak. . . . "If we don't silence that field-gun she'll sink us, boys." . . . The eyes of the man sitting with his back against the deck-house were looking from out his ghastly face at the new gun-crew. He spoke with the supreme laziness of a wounded man. "Give 'm hell." . . . Pent felt a sudden twist of his shoulder. He was wounded—slightly. . . . The anchored gunboat was in flames.

VII

Pent took his little blood-stained tow-boat out to the *Holy Moses*. The yacht was already under way for the bay entrance. As they were passing out of range the Spaniards heroically redoubled their fire—which is their custom. Pent, moving busily about the decks, stopped suddenly at the door of the engine-room. His face was set and his eyes were steely. He spoke to one of the men. "During the action I saw you firing at the enemy with a rifle. I told you once to stop, and then I saw you at it again. Pegging away with a rifle is no part of your business. I want you to understand that you are in trouble." The humbled man did not raise his eyes from the deck. Presently the *Holy Moses* displayed an anxiety for the *Chicken*'s health.

"One killed and four wounded, sir."

"Have you enough men left to work your ship?"

After deliberation, Pent answered: "No, sir."

"Shall I send you assistance?"

"No, sir. I can get to sea all right."

As they neared the point they were edified by the sudden appearance of a serio-comic ally. The *Chancellorville* at last had been unable to stand the strain, and had sent in her launch with an ensign, five seamen and a number of marksmen marines. She swept hot-foot around the point, bent on terrible slaughter; the one-pounder of her bow presented a formidable appearance. The *Holy Moses* and the *Chicken* laughed until they brought indignation to the brow of the young ensign. But he forgot it when with some of his men he boarded the *Chicken* to do what was possible for the wounded. The nearest surgeon was aboard the *Chancellorville*. There was absolute silence on board the cruiser as the *Holy Moses* steamed up to report. The blue-jackets listened with all their ears. The commander of the yacht spoke slowly into his megaphone: "We have—destroyed—the two—gunboats—sir." There was a burst of confused cheering on the forecastle of the *Chancellorville*, but an officer's cry quelled it.

"Very—good. Will—you—come aboard?"

Correspondents were already on the deck of the cruiser, and although for a time they learned only that the navy can preserve a classic silence, they in the end received the story which is here told. Before the last of the wounded were hoisted aboard the cruiser the *Adolphus* was on her way to Key West. When she arrived at that port of desolation Shackles fled to file the telegrams and the other correspondents fled to the hotel for clothes, good clothes, clean clothes; and food, good food, much food; and drink, much drink, any kind of drink.

Days afterward, when the officers of the noble squadron received the newspapers containing an account of their performance, they looked at each other somewhat dejectedly: "Heroic assault—grand daring of Boatswain Pent—superb accuracy of the *Holy Moses'* fire—gallant tars of the *Chicken*—their names should be remembered as long as America stands—terrible losses of the enemy——"

When the Secretary of the Navy ultimately read the report of Commander Surrey, S.O.P., he had to prick himself with a dagger in order to remember that anything at all out of the ordinary had occurred.

Virtue in War

I

GATES HAD LEFT the regular army in 1890, those parts of him which had not been frozen having been well fried. He took with him nothing but an oaken constitution and a knowledge of the plains and the best wishes of his fellow-officers. The Standard Oil Company differs from the United States Government in that it understands the value of the loyal and intelligent services of good men and is almost certain to reward them at the expense of incapable men. This curious practice emanates from no beneficent emotion of the Standard Oil Company, on whose feelings you could not make a scar with a hammer and chisel. It is simply that the Standard Oil Company knows more than the United States Government and makes use of virtue whenever virtue is to its advantage. In 1890 Gates really felt in his bones that, if he lived a rigorously correct life and several score of his class-mates and intimate friends died off, he would get command of a troop of horse by the time he was unfitted by age to be an active cavalry leader. He left the service of the United States and entered the service of the Standard Oil Company. In the course of time he knew that, if he lived a rigorously correct life, his position and income would develop strictly in parallel with the worth of his wisdom and experience and he would not have to walk on the corpses of his friends.

But he was not happier. Part of his heart was in a barracks, and it was not enough to discourse of the old regiment over the port and cigars to ears which were polite enough to betray a languid ignorance. Finally came the year 1898, and Gates dropped the Standard Oil Company as if it were hot. He hit the steel trail to Washington and there fought the first serious action of the war. Like most Americans, he had a native State, and one morning he found himself major in a volunteer infantry regiment whose voice had a peculiar sharp twang to it which he could remember from childhood. The colonel welcomed the West Pointer with loud cries of joy; the lieutenant-colonel looked at him with the pebbly eye of distrust; and the senior major, having had up to this time the best battalion in the regiment, strongly disapproved of him. There were only two majors, so the lieutenant-colonel commanded the first battalion, which gave him an occupation. Lieutenant-colonels under the new rules do not always have occupations. Gates got the third battalion—four companies commanded by intelligent officers who could gauge the opinions of their men at two thousand yards and govern themselves accordingly. The battalion was immensely interested in the new major. It thought it ought to develop views about him. It thought it was its blankety-blank business to find out immediately if it liked him personally. In the company streets the talk was nothing else. Among the non-commissioned officers there were eleven old soldiers of the regular army, and they knew—and cared—that Gates had held commission in the "Sixteenth Cavalry"—as *Harper's Weekly* says. Over this fact they rejoiced and were glad, and they stood by to jump lively when he took command. He would know his work and he would know *their* work, and then in battle there would be killed only what men were absolutely necessary and the sick list would be comparatively free of fools.

The commander of the second battalion had been called by an Atlanta paper, "Major Rickets C. Carmony, the commander of the second battalion of the 307th——, is when at home one of the biggest wholesale hardware dealers in his State. Last evening he had ice cream, at his own expense, served out at the regular mess of the battalion, and after dinner the men gathered about his tent where three hearty cheers for the popular major were given." Carmony had bought twelve copies of this newspaper and mailed them home to his friends.

In Gates's battalion there were more kicks than ice cream, and there was no ice cream at all. Indignation ran high at the rapid manner in which he proceeded to make soldiers of them. Some of his officers hinted finally that the men wouldn't stand it. They were saying that they had enlisted to fight for their country—yes, but they weren't going to be bullied day in and day out by a perfect stranger. They were patriots, they were, and just as good men as ever stepped— just as good as Gates or anybody like him. But, gradually, despite itself, the battalion progressed. The men were not altogether conscious of it. They evolved rather blindly. Presently there were fights with Carmony's crowd as to which was the better battalion at drills, and at last there was no argument. It was generally admitted that Gates commanded the crack battalion. The men, believing that the beginning and the end of all soldiering was in these drills of precision, were somewhat reconciled to their major when they began to understand more of what he was trying to do for them, but they were still fiery untamed patriots of lofty pride and they resented his manner toward them. It was abrupt and sharp.

The time came when everybody knew that the Fifth Army Corps was the corps designated for the first active service in Cuba. The officers and men of the 307th observed with despair that their regiment was not in the Fifth Army Corps. The colonel was a strategist. He understood everything in a flash. Without a moment's hesitation he obtained leave and mounted the night express for Washington. There he drove Senators and Congressmen in span, tandem and four-in-hand. With the telegraph he stirred so deeply the governor, the people and the newspapers of his State that whenever on a quiet night the President put his head out of the White House he could hear the distant vast commonwealth humming with indignation. And as it is well known that the Chief Executive listens to the voice of the people, the 307th was transferred to the Fifth Army Corps. It was sent at once to Tampa, where it was brigaded with two dusty regiments of regulars, who looked at it calmly and said nothing. The brigade commander happened to be no less a person than Gates's old colonel in the "Sixteenth Cavalry"—as *Harper's Weekly* says—and Gates was cheered. The old man's rather solemn look brightened when he saw Gates in the 307th. There was a great deal of battering and pounding and banging for the 307th at Tampa, but the men stood it more in wonder than in anger. The two regular regiments carried them along when they could, and when they couldn't waited impatiently for them to come up. Undoubtedly the regulars wished the volunteers were in garrison at Sitka, but they said practically nothing. They minded their own regiments. The colonel was an invaluable man in a telegraph office. When came the scramble for transports the colonel retired to a telegraph office and talked so ably to

Washington that the authorities pushed a number of corps aside and made way for the 307th, as if on it depended everything. The regiment got one of the best transports, and after a series of delays and some starts, and an equal number of returns, they finally sailed for Cuba.

II

Now Gates had a singular adventure on the second morning after his arrival at Atlanta to take his post as a major in the 307th.

He was in his tent, writing, when suddenly the flap was flung away and a tall young private stepped inside.

"Well, Maje," said the newcomer genially, "how goes it?"

The major's head flashed up, but he spoke without heat.

"Come to attention and salute."

"Huh!" said the private.

"Come to attention and salute."

The private looked at him in resentful amazement, and then inquired:

"Ye ain't mad, are ye? Ain't nothin' to get huffy about, is there?"

"I—— Come to attention and salute."

"Well," drawled the private, as he stared, "seein' as ye are so darn perticular, I don't care if I do—if it'll make yer meals set on yer stomick any better."

Drawing a long breath and grinning ironically, he lazily pulled his heels together and saluted with a flourish.

"There," he said, with a return to his earlier genial manner. "How's that suit ye, Maje?"

There was a silence which to an impartial observer would have seemed pregnant with dynamite and bloody death. Then the major cleared his throat and coldly said:

"And now, what is your business?"

"Who—me?" asked the private. "Oh, I just sorter dropped in." With a deeper meaning he added: "Sorter dropped in in a friendly way, thinkin' ye was mebbe a different kind of a feller from what ye be."

The inference was clearly marked.

It was now Gates's turn to stare, and stare he unfeignedly did.

"Go back to your quarters," he said at length.

The volunteer became very angry.

"Oh, ye needn't be so up-in-th'-air, need ye? Don't know's I'm dead anxious to inflict my company on yer since I've had a good look at ye. There may be men in this here battalion what's had just as much edjewcation as you have, and I'm damned if they ain't got better *manners*. Good mornin'," he said, with dignity; and, passing out of the tent, he flung the flap back in place with an air of slamming it as if it had been a door. He made his way back to his company street, striding high. He was furious. He met a large crowd of his comrades.

"What's the matter, Lige?" asked one, who noted his temper.

"Oh, nothin'," answered Lige, with terrible feeling. "Nothin'. I jest been lookin' over the new major—that's all."

"What's he like?" asked another.

"Like?" cried Lige. "He's like nothin'. He ain't out'n the same kittle as us. No. Gawd made him all by himself— sep'rate. He's a speshul produc', he is, an' he won't have no truck with jest common— *men*, like you be."

He made a venomous gesture which included them all.

"Did he set on ye?" asked a soldier.

"Set on me? No," replied Lige, with contempt. "I set on *him*. I sized 'm up in a minute. 'Oh, I don't know,' I says, as I was comin' out; 'guess you ain't the only man in the world,' I says."

For a time Lige Wigram was quite a hero. He endlessly repeated the tale of his adventure, and men admired him for so soon taking the conceit out of the new officer. Lige was proud to think of himself as a plain and simple patriot who had refused to endure any high-soaring nonsense.

But he came to believe that he had not disturbed the singular composure of the major, and this concreted his hatred. He hated Gates, not as a soldier sometimes hates an officer, a hatred half of fear. Lige hated as man to man. And he was enraged to see that so far from gaining any hatred in return, he seemed incapable of making Gates have any thought of him save as a unit in a body of three hundred men. Lige might just as well have gone and grimaced at the obelisk in Central Park.

When the battalion became the best in the regiment he had no part in the pride of the companies. He was sorry when men began to speak well of Gates. He was really a very consistent hater.

III

The transport occupied by the 307th was commanded by some sort of a Scandinavian, who was afraid of the shadows of his own topmasts. He would have run his steamer away from a floating Gainsborough hat, and, in fact, he ran her away from less on some occasions. The officers, wishing to arrive with the other transports, sometimes remonstrated, and to them he talked of his owners. Every officer in the convoying warships loathed him, for in case any hostile vessel should appear they did not see how they were going to protect this rabbit, who would probably manage during a fight to be in about a hundred places on the broad, broad sea, and all of them offensive to the navy's plan. When he was not talking of his owners he was remarking to the officers of the regiment that a steamer really was not like a valise, and that he was unable to take his ship under his arm and climb trees with it. He further said that "them naval fellows" were not near so smart as they thought they were.

From an indigo sea arose the lonely shore of Cuba. Ultimately, the fleet was near Santiago, and most of the transports were bidden to wait a minute while the leaders found out their minds. The skipper to whom the 307th were prisoners waited for thirty hours half way between Jamaica and Cuba. He explained that the Spanish fleet might emerge from Santiago Harbor at any time, and he did not propose to be caught. His owners—— Whereupon the colonel arose as one having nine hundred men at his back, and he passed up to the bridge and he spake with the captain. He explained indirectly that each individual of his nine hundred men had decided to be the first American soldier to land for this campaign, and that in order to accomplish the marvel it was necessary for the transport to be nearer than forty-five miles from the Cuban coast. If the skipper would only land the regiment the colonel would consent to his then taking his interesting old ship and going to h—— with it. And the skipper spake with the colonel. He pointed out that as far as he officially was concerned, the United States Government did not exist. He was responsible solely to his owners. The colonel pondered these sayings. He perceived that the skipper meant that he was running his ship as he deemed best, in consideration of the capital invested by his owners, and that he was not at all concerned with the feelings of a certain American military expedition to Cuba. He was a free son of the sea—he was a sovereign citizen of the republic of the waves. He was like Lige.

However, the skipper ultimately incurred the danger of taking his ship under the terrible guns of the *New York*, *Iowa*, *Oregon*, *Massachusetts*, *Indiana*, *Brooklyn*, *Texas* and a score of cruisers and gunboats. It was a brave act for the captain of a United States transport, and he was visibly nervous until he could again get to sea, where he offered praises that the accursed 307th was no longer sitting on his head. For almost a week he rambled at his cheerful will over the adjacent high seas, having in his hold a great quantity of military stores as successfully secreted as if they had been buried in a copper box in the corner-stone of a new public building in Boston. He had had his master's certificate for twenty-one years, and those people couldn't tell a marlin-spike from the starboard side of the ship.

The 307th was landed in Cuba, but to their disgust they found that about ten thousand regulars were ahead of them. They got immediate orders to move out from the base on the road to Santiago. Gates was interested to note that the only delay was caused by the fact that many men of the other battalions strayed off sight-seeing. In time the long regiment wound slowly among hills that shut them from sight of the sea.

For the men to admire, there were palm-trees, little brown huts, passive, uninterested Cuban soldiers much worn from carrying American rations inside and outside. The weather was not oppressively warm, and the journey was said to be only about seven miles. There were no rumors save that there had been one short fight and the army had advanced to within sight of Santiago. Having a peculiar faculty for the derision of the romantic, the 307th began to laugh. Actually there was not *anything* in the world which turned out to be as books describe it. Here they had landed from the transport expecting to be at once flung into line of battle and sent on some kind of furious charge, and now they were trudging along a quiet trail lined with somnolent trees and grass. The whole business so far struck them as being a highly tedious burlesque.

After a time they came to where the camps of regular regiments marked the sides of the road—little villages of tents no higher than a man's waist. The colonel found his brigade commander and the 307th was sent off into a field of long grass, where the men grew suddenly solemn with the importance of getting their supper.

In the early evening some regulars told one of Gates's companies that at daybreak this division would move to an attack upon something.

"How d'you know?" said the company, deeply awed.

"Heard it."

"Well, what are we to attack?"

"Dunno."

The 307th was not at all afraid, but each man began to imagine the morrow. The regulars seemed to have as much interest in the morrow as they did in the last Christmas. It was none of their affair, apparently.

"Look here," said Lige Wigram to a man in the 17th Regular Infantry, " whereabouts are we goin' ter-morrow an' who do we run up against—do ye know?"

The 17th soldier replied truculently: "If I ketch th' —— —— —— what stole my terbaccer, I'll whirl in an' break every —— —— bone in his body."

Gates's friends in the regular regiments asked him numerous questions as to the reliability of his organization. Would the 307th stand the racket? They were certainly not contemptuous; they simply did not seem to consider it important whether the 307th would or whether it would not.

"Well," said Gates, "they won't run the length of a tent-peg if they can gain any idea of what they're fighting; they won't bunch if they've about six acres of open ground to move in; they won't get rattled at all if they see you fellows taking it easy; and they'll fight like the devil as long as they thoroughly, completely, absolutely, satisfactorily, exhaustively understand what the business is. They're lawyers. All excepting my battalion."

IV

Lige awakened into a world obscured by blue fog. Somebody was gently shaking him. "Git up; we're going to move." The regiment was buckling up itself. From the trail came the loud creak of a light battery moving ahead. The tones of all men were low; the faces of the officers were composed, serious. The regiment found itself moving along behind the battery before it had time to ask itself more than a hundred questions. The trail wound through a dense tall jungle, dark, heavy with dew.

The battle broke with a snap—far ahead. Presently Lige heard from the air above him a faint low note as if somebody were blowing softly in the mouth of a bottle. It was a stray bullet which had wandered a mile to tell him that war was before him. He nearly broke his neck looking upward. "Did ye hear that?" But the men were fretting to get out of this gloomy jungle. They wanted to see something. The faint rup-rup-rrrrup-rup on in the front told them that the fight had begun; death was abroad, and so the mystery of this wilderness excited them. This wilderness was portentously still and dark.

They passed the battery aligned on a hill above the trail, and they had not gone far when the gruff guns began to roar and they could hear the rocket-like swish of the flying shells. Presently everybody must have called out for the assistance of the 307th. Aides and couriers came flying back to them.

"Is this the 307th? Hurry up your men, please, Colonel. You're needed more every minute."

Oh, they were, were they? Then the regulars were not going to do *all* the fighting? The old 307th was bitterly proud or proudly bitter. They left their blanket-rolls under the guard of God and pushed on, which is one of the reasons why the Cubans of that part of the country were, later, so well equipped. There began to appear fields, hot, golden-green in the sun. On some palm-dotted knolls before them they could see little lines of black dots—the American advance. A few men fell, struck down by other men who, perhaps half a mile away, were aiming at somebody else. The loss was wholly in Carmony's battalion, which immediately bunched and backed away, coming with a shock against Gates's advance company. This shock sent a tremor through all of Gates's battalion until men in the very last files cried out nervously, "Well, what in hell is up now?" There came an order to deploy and advance. An occasional hoarse yell from the regulars could be heard. The deploying made Gates's heart bleed for the colonel. The old man stood there directing the movement, straight, fearless, sombrely defiant of—everything. Carmony's four companies were like four herds. And all the time the bullets from no living man knows where kept pecking at them and pecking at them. Gates, the excellent Gates, the highly educated and strictly military Gates, grew rankly insubordinate. He knew that the regiment was suffering from nothing but the deadly range and oversweep of the modern rifle, of which many proud and confident nations know nothing save that they have killed savages with it, which is the least of all informations.

Gates rushed upon Carmony.

"—— —— it, man, if you can't get your people to deploy, for —— sake give me a chance! I'm stuck in the woods!"

Carmony gave nothing, but Gates took all he could get and his battalion deployed and advanced like men. The old colonel almost burst into tears, and he cast one quick glance of gratitude at Gates, which the younger officer wore on his heart like a secret decoration.

There was a wild scramble up hill, down dale, through thorny thickets. Death smote them with a kind of slow rhythm, leisurely taking a man now here, now there, but the cat-spit sound of the bullets was always. A large number of the men of Carmony's battalion came on with Gates. They were willing to do anything, anything. They had no real fault, unless it was that early conclusion that any brave high-minded youth was necessarily a good soldier immediately, from the beginning. In them had been born a swift feeling that the unpopular Gates knew everything, and they followed the trained soldier.

If they followed him, he certainly took them into it. As they swung heavily up one steep hill, like so many wind-blown horses, they came suddenly out into the real advance. Little blue groups of men were making frantic rushes forward and then flopping down on their bellies to fire volleys while other groups made rushes. Ahead they could see a heavy house-like fort which was inadequate to explain from whence came the myriad bullets. The remainder of the scene was landscape. Pale men, yellow men, blue men came out of this landscape quiet and sad-eyed with wounds. Often they were grimly facetious. There is nothing in the American regular so amazing as his conduct when he is wounded—his apologetic limp, his deprecatory arm-sling, his embarrassed and ashamed shot-hole through the lungs. The men of the 307th looked at calm creatures who had divers punctures and they were made better. These men told them that it was only necessary to keep a-going. They of the 307th lay on their bellies, red, sweating and panting, and heeded the voice of the elder brother.

Gates walked back of his line, very white of face, but hard and stern past anything his men knew of him. After they had violently adjured him to lie down and he had given weak backs a cold, stiff touch, the 307th charged by rushes. The hatless colonel made frenzied speech, but the man of the time was Gates. The men seemed to feel that this was his business. Some of the regular officers said afterward that the advance of the 307th was very respectable indeed. They were rather surprised, they said. At least five of the crack regiments of the regular army were in this division, and the 307th could win no more than a feeling of kindly appreciation.

Yes, it was very good, very good indeed, but did you notice what was being done at the same moment by the 12th, the 17th, the 7th, the 8th, the 25th, the——

Gates felt that his charge was being a success. He was carrying out a successful function. Two captains fell bang on the grass and a lieutenant slumped quietly down with a death wound. Many men sprawled suddenly. Gates was keeping his men almost even with the regulars, who were charging on his flanks. Suddenly he thought that he must have come close to the fort and that a Spaniard had tumbled a great stone block down upon his leg. Twelve hands reached out to help him, but he cried:

"No—d—— your souls—go on—go on!"

He closed his eyes for a moment, and it really was only for a moment. When he opened them he found himself alone with Lige Wigram, who lay on the ground near him.

"Maje," said Lige, "yer a good man. I've been a-follerin' ye all day an' I want to say yer a good man."

The major turned a coldly scornful eye upon the private.

"Where are you wounded? Can you walk? Well, if you can, go to the rear and leave me alone. I'm bleeding to death, and you bother me."

Lige, despite the pain in his wounded shoulder, grew indignant.

"Well," he mumbled, "you and me have been on th' outs fer a long time, an' I only wanted to tell ye that what I seen of ye t'day has made me feel mighty diff'ent."

"Go to the rear—if you can walk," said the major.

"Now, Maje, look here. A little thing like that——"

"Go to the rear."

Lige gulped with sobs.

"Maje, I know I didn't understand ye at first, but ruther'n let a little thing like that come between us, I'd—I'd——"

"Go to the rear."

In this reiteration Lige discovered a resemblance to that first old offensive phrase, "Come to attention and salute." He pondered over the resemblance and he saw that nothing had changed. The man bleeding to death was the same man to whom he had once paid a friendly visit with unfriendly results. He thought now that he perceived a certain hopeless gulf, a gulf which is real or unreal, according to circumstances. Sometimes all men are equal; occasionally they are not. If Gates had ever criticized Lige's manipulation of a hay fork on the farm at home, Lige would have furiously disdained his hate or blame. He saw now that he must not openly approve the major's conduct in war. The major's pride was in his business, and his, Lige's, congratulations, were beyond all enduring.

The place where they were lying suddenly fell under a new heavy rain of bullets. They sputtered about the men, making the noise of large grasshoppers.

"Major!" cried Lige. "Major Gates! It won't do for ye to be left here, sir. Ye'll be killed."

"But you can't help it, lad. You take care of yourself."

"I'm damned if I do," said the private vehemently. "If I can't git *you* out, I'll stay and wait."

The officer gazed at his man with that same icy, contemptuous gaze.

"I'm—I'm a dead man anyhow. You go to the rear, do you hear?"

"No."

The dying major drew his revolver, cocked it and aimed it unsteadily at Lige's head.

"Will you obey orders?"

"No."

"One?"

"No."

"Two?"

"No."

Gates weakly dropped his revolver.

"Go to the devil, then. You're no soldier, but——" He tried to add something. "But——" He heaved a long moan. "But—you—you—oh, I'm so-o-o tired."

V

After the battle, three correspondents happened to meet on the trail. They were hot, dusty, weary, hungry and thirsty, and they repaired to the shade of a mango tree and sprawled luxuriously. Among them they mustered twoscore friends who on that day had gone to the far shore of the hereafter, but their senses were no longer resonant. Shackles was babbling plaintively about mint-juleps, and the others were bidding him to have done.

"By-the-way," said one at last, "it's too bad about poor old Gates of the 307th. He bled to death. His men were crazy.

They were blubbering and cursing around there like wild peo-
ple. It seems that when they got back there to look for him
they found him just about gone, and another wounded man
was trying to stop the flow with his hat! His hat, mind you.
Poor old Gatesie!"

"Oh, no, Shackles!" said the third man of the party. "Oh,
no; you're wrong. The best mint-juleps in the world are made
right in New York, Philadelphia or Boston. That Kentucky
idea is only a tradition."

A wounded man approached them. He had been shot
through the shoulder and his shirt had been diagonally cut
away, leaving much bare skin. Over the bullet's point of entry
there was a kind of a white spider, shaped from pieces of
adhesive plaster. Over the point of departure there was a
bloody bulb of cotton strapped to the flesh by other pieces of
adhesive plaster. His eyes were dreamy, wistful, sad. "Say,
gents, have any of ye got a bottle?" he asked.

A correspondent raised himself suddenly and looked with
bright eyes at the soldier.

"Well, you have got a nerve!" he said, grinning. "Have we
got a bottle, eh! Who in h—— do you think we are? If we
had a bottle of good licker, do you suppose we could let the
whole army drink out of it? You have too much faith in the
generosity of men, my friend!"

The soldier stared, ox-like, and finally said, "Huh?"

"I say," continued the correspondent, somewhat more
loudly, "that if we had had a bottle we would have probably
finished it ourselves by this time."

"But," said the other, dazed, "I *meant* an empty bottle. I
didn't mean no *full* bottle."

The correspondent was humorously irascible.

"An empty bottle! You must be crazy! Who ever heard of
a man looking for an empty bottle? It isn't sense! I've seen a
million men looking for full bottles, but you're the first man
I ever saw who insisted on the bottle's being empty. What in
the world do you want it for?"

"Well, ye see, mister," explained Lige, slowly, "our major
he was killed this mornin' an' we're jes' goin' to bury him, an'
I thought I'd jest take a look 'round an' see if I couldn't borry
an empty bottle, an' then I'd take an' write his name an' reg'-

ment on a paper an' put it in th' bottle an' bury it with him, so's when they come fer to dig him up sometime an' take him home, there sure wouldn't be no mistake."

"Oh!"

The Second Generation

I

CASPAR CADOGAN RESOLVED to go to the tropic wars and do something. The air was blue and gold with the pomp of soldiering, and in every ear rang the music of military glory. Caspar's father was a United States Senator from the great State of Skowmulligan, where the war fever ran very high. Chill is the blood of many of the sons of millionaires, but Caspar took the fever and posted to Washington. His father had never denied him anything, and this time all that Caspar wanted was a little captaincy in the army—just a simple little captaincy.

The old man had just been entertaining a delegation of respectable bunco-steerers from Skowmulligan who had come to him on a matter which is none of the public's business. Bottles of whisky and boxes of cigars were still on the table in the sumptuous private parlor. The Senator had said: "Well, gentlemen, I'll do what I can for you." By this sentence he meant whatever he meant.

Then he turned to his eager son. "Well, Caspar?" The youth poured out his modest desires. It was not altogether his fault. Life had taught him a generous faith in his own abilities. If any one had told him that he was simply an ordinary damned fool he would have opened his eyes wide at the person's lack of judgment. All his life people had admired him.

The Skowmulligan war-horse looked with quick disapproval into the eyes of his son. "Well, Caspar," he said slowly, "I am of the opinion that they've got all the golf experts and tennis champions and cotillion leaders and piano tuners and billiard markers they really need as officers. Now, if you were a soldier——"

"I know," said the young man with a gesture, "but I'm not exactly a fool, I hope, and I think if I get a chance I can do something. I'd like to try. I would, indeed."

The Senator drank a neat whisky and lit a cigar. He assumed an attitude of ponderous reflection. "Y-yes, but this country is full of young men who are not fools. Full of 'em."

Caspar fidgeted in the desire to answer that while he admitted the profusion of young men who were not fools, he felt that he himself possessed interesting and peculiar qualifications which would allow him to make his mark in any field of effort which he seriously challenged. But he did not make this graceful statement, for he sometimes detected something ironic in his father's temperament. The Skowmulligan war-horse had not thought of expressing an opinion of his own ability since the year 1865, when he was young, like Caspar.

"Well, well," said the Senator finally, "I'll see about it. I'll see about it." The young man was obliged to await the end of his father's characteristic method of thought. The war-horse never gave a quick answer, and if people tried to hurry him they seemed able to arouse in him only a feeling of irritation against making a decision at all. His mind moved like the wind, but practice had placed a Mexican bit in the mouth of his judgment. This old man of light quick thought had taught himself to move like an ox cart. Caspar said, "Yes, sir." He withdrew to his club, where, to the affectionate inquiries of some envious friends, he replied: "The old man is letting the idea soak."

The mind of the war-horse was decided far sooner than Caspar expected. In Washington a large number of well-bred handsome young men were receiving appointments as lieutenants, as captains, and occasionally as majors. They were a strong, healthy, clear-eyed educated collection. They were a prime lot. A German field-marshal would have beamed with joy if he could have had them—to send to school. Anywhere in the world they would have made a grand show as material, but, intrinsically, they were not lieutenants, captains and majors. They were fine men. Individual to individual, American manhood overmatches the best in Europe; but manhood is only an essential part of a lieutenant, a captain or a major. But at any rate, it had all the logic of going to sea in a bathing-machine.

The Senator found himself reasoning that Caspar was as good as any of them, and better than many. Presently he was bleating here and there that his boy should have a chance. "The boy's all right, I tell you, Henery. He's wild to go, and I don't see why they shouldn't give him a show. He's got plenty of nerve, and he's keen as a whip-lash. I'm going to get him an appointment, and if you can do anything to help it along I wish you would." Then he betook himself to the White House and the War Department and made a stir. People think that administrations are always slavishly, abominably anxious to please the machine. They are not; they wish the machine sunk in red fire, for by the power of ten thousand past words, looks, gestures, writings, the machine comes along and takes the administration by the nose and twists it, and the administration dare not even yell. The huge force which carries an election to success looks reproachfully at the administration and says, "Give me a penny!" That is a very small amount with which to reward a colossus.

The Skowmulligan war-horse got his penny and took it to his hotel where Caspar was moodily reading war rumors. "Well, my boy, here you are." Caspar was a captain and commissary on the staff of Brigadier-General Reilly, commander of the Second Brigade of the First Division of the Thirtieth Army Corps. "I had to work for it," said the Senator grimly. "They talked to me as if they thought you were some sort of empty-headed idiot. None of 'em seemed to know you personally. They just sort of took it for granted. Finally I got pretty hot in the collar." He paused a moment; his heavy grooved face set hard; his blue eyes shone. He clapped a hand down upon the handle of his chair. "Caspar, I've got you into this thing, and I believe you'll do all right, and I'm not saying this because I distrust either your sense or your grit. But I want you to understand you've *got to make a go of it*. I'm not going to talk any twaddle about your country and your country's flag. You understand all about that. But now you're a soldier, and there'll be this to do and that to do, and fightin' to do, and you've got to do *every damned one of 'em* right up to the handle. I don't know how much of a shindy this thing is goin' to be, but any shindy is enough to show how much there is in a man. You've got your appointment, and that's all I can do for you; but I'll thrash you with my own hands if, when the army gets back, the other fellows say my son is 'nothin' but a good-lookin' dude.' "

He ceased, breathing heavily. Caspar looked bravely and frankly at his father, and answered in a voice which was not very tremulous. "I'll do my best. This is my chance. I'll do my best with it."

The Senator had a marvelous ability of transition from one manner to another. Suddenly he seemed very kind. "Well, that's all right, then. I guess you'll get along all right with Reilly. I know him well, and he'll see you through. I helped him along once. And now about this commissary business. As I understand it, a commissary is a sort of caterer in a big way—that is, he looks out for a good many more things than a caterer has to bother his head about. Reilly's brigade has probably from two to three thousand men in it, and in regard to certain things you've got to look out for every man of 'em every day. I know perfectly well you couldn't successfully run a boarding-house in Ocean Grove. How you goin' to manage for all these soldiers, hey? Thought about it?"

"No," said Caspar, injured. "I didn't want to be a commissary. I wanted to be a captain in the line."

"They wouldn't hear of it. They said you would have to take a staff appointment where people could look after you."

"Well, let them look after me," cried Caspar resentfully; "but when there's any fighting to be done I guess I won't necessarily be the last man."

"That's it," responded the Senator. "That's the spirit." They both thought that the problem of war would eliminate to an equation of actual battle.

Ultimately Caspar departed into the South to an encampment in salty grass under pine trees. Here lay an army corps twenty thousand strong. Caspar passed into the dusty sunshine of it, and for many weeks he was lost to view.

II

"Of course I don't know a damned thing about it," said Caspar frankly and modestly to a circle of his fellow staff officers. He was referring to the duties of his office.

Their faces became expressionless; they looked at him with eyes in which he could fathom nothing. After a pause one politely said: "Don't you?" It was the inevitable two words of convention.

"Why," cried Caspar, "I didn't know what a commissary

officer was until I *was* one. My old guv'nor told me. He'd looked it up in a book somewhere, I suppose; but *I* didn't know."

"Didn't you?"

The young man's face glowed with sudden humor. "Do you know, the word was intimately associated in my mind with camels. Funny, eh? I think it came from reading that rhyme of Kipling's about the commissariat camel."

"Did it?"

"Yes. Funny, isn't it? Camels!"

The brigade was ultimately landed at Siboney as part of an army to attack Santiago. The scene at the landing sometimes resembled the inspiriting daily drama at the approach to the Brooklyn Bridge. There was a great bustle, during which the wise man kept his property gripped in his hands lest it might march off into the wilderness in the pocket of one of the striding regiments. Truthfully, Caspar should have had frantic occupation, but men saw him wandering fecklessly here and there crying: "Has any one seen my saddle-bags? Why, if I lose 'em I'm ruined. I've got everything packed away in 'em. Everything!"

They looked at him gloomily and without attention. "No," they said. It was to intimate that they would not give three whoops in Hades if he had lost his nose, his teeth and his self-respect. Reilly's brigade collected itself from the boats and went off, each regiment's soul burning with anger because some other regiment was in advance of it. Moving along through the scrub and under the palms, men talked mostly of things that did not pertain to the business in hand.

General Reilly finally planted his headquarters in some tall grass under a mango tree. "Where's Cadogan?" he said suddenly as he took off his hat and smoothed the wet grey hair from his brow. Nobody knew. "I saw him looking for his saddle-bags down at the landing," said an officer dubiously. "Bother him," said the general contemptuously. "Let him stay there."

Three venerable regimental commanders came, saluted stiffly and sat in the grass. There was a pow-wow, during which Reilly explained much that the division-commander had told him. The venerable colonels nodded; they understood. Everything was smooth and clear to their minds. But still, the colonel of the Forty-fourth Regular Infantry murmured about the commissariat. His men—— And then he launched forth in a sentiment concerning the privations of his men in which you were confronted with his feeling that his men—his men were the only creatures of importance in the universe, which feeling was entirely correct for him. Reilly grunted. He did what most commanders did. He set the competent line to doing the work of the incompetent part of the staff.

In time Caspar came trudging along the road merrily swinging his saddle-bags. "Well, General," he cried as he saluted, "I found 'em." "Did you?" said Reilly. Later an officer rushed to him tragically. "General, Cadogan is off there in the bushes eatin' potted ham and crackers all by himself." The officer was sent back into the bushes for Caspar, and the general sent Caspar with an order. Then Reilly and the three venerable colonels, grinning, partook of potted ham and crackers. "Tashe a' right," said Reilly with his mouth full. "Dorsey, see if 'e got some'n else."

"Mush be selfish young pig," said one of the colonels, with his mouth full. "Who's he, General?"

"Son—Sen'tor Cad'gan—ol' frien' mine—damn 'im."

Caspar wrote a letter:

"*Dear Father:*   I am sitting under a tree using the flattest part of my canteen for a desk. Even as I write the division ahead of us is moving forward and we don't know what moment the storm of battle may break out. I don't know what the plans are. General Reilly knows, but he is so good as to give me very little of his confidence. In fact, I might be part of a forlorn hope from all to the contrary I've heard from him. I understood you to say in Washington that you at one time had been of some service to him, but if that is true I can assure you he has completely forgotten it. At times his manner to me is little short of being offensive, but of course I understand that it is only the way of a crusty old soldier who has been made boorish and bearish by a long life among the Indians. I dare say I shall manage it all right without a row.

"When you hear that we have captured Santiago, please send me by first steamer a box of provisions and clothing, particularly sardines, pickles, and light-weight underwear. The other men on the staff are nice quiet chaps, but they seem a bit crude. There has been no fighting yet save the skirmish by Young's brigade. Reilly was furious because we couldn't get in it. I met General Peel yesterday. He was very nice. He said he knew you well when he was in Congress. Young Jack May is on Peel's staff. I knew him well in college. We spent an hour talking over old times. Give my love to all at home."

The march was leisurely. Reilly and his staff strolled out to the head of the long sinuous column and entered the sultry gloom of the forest. Some less fortunate regiments had to wait among the trees at the side of the trail, and as Reilly's brigade passed them, officer called to officer, classmate to classmate, in which rang a note of everything from West Point to Alaska. They were going into an action in which they, the officers, would lose over a hundred in killed and wounded—officers alone—and these greetings, in which many nicknames occurred, were in many cases farewells such as one pictures being given with ostentation, solemnity, fervor. "There goes Gory Widgeon! Hello, Gory! Where you starting for? Hey, Gory!"

Caspar communed with himself and decided that he was not frightened. He was eager and alert; he thought that now his obligation to his country, or himself, was to be faced, and he was mad to prove to old Reilly and the others that after all he was a very capable soldier.

III

Old Reilly was stumping along the line of his brigade and mumbling like a man with a mouthful of grass. The fire from the enemy's position was incredible in its swift fury, and Reilly's brigade was getting its share of a very bad ordeal. The old man's face was of the color of a tomato, and in his rage he mouthed and sputtered strangely. As he pranced along his thin line, scornfully erect, voices arose from the grass beseeching him to take care of himself. At his heels scrambled a bugler with pallid skin and clinched teeth, a chalky, trembling youth, who kept his eye on old Reilly's back and followed it.

The old gentleman was quite mad. Apparently he thought the whole thing a dreadful mess, but now that his brigade was irrevocably in it he was full-tilting here and everywhere to establish some irreproachable, immaculate kind of behavior on the part of every man jack in his brigade. The intentions of the three venerable colonels were the same. They stood behind their lines, quiet, stern, courteous old fellows, admonishing their regiments to be very pretty in the face of such a hail of magazine-rifle and machine-gun fire as has never in this world been confronted save by beardless savages when the white man has found occasion to take his burden to some new place.

And the regiments were pretty. The men lay on their little stomachs and got peppered according to the law, and said nothing as the good blood pumped out into the grass; and even if a solitary rookie tried to get a decent reason to move to some haven of rational men, the cold voice of an officer made him look criminal with a shame that was a credit to his regimental education. Behind Reilly's command was a bullet-torn jungle through which it could not move as a brigade; ahead of it were Spanish trenches on hills. Reilly considered that he was in a fix, no doubt, but he said this only to himself. Suddenly he saw on the right a little point of blue-shirted men already half-way up the hill. It was some pathetic fragment of the Sixth United States Infantry. Chagrined, shocked, horrified, Reilly bellowed to his bugler, and the chalk-faced youth unlocked his teeth and sounded the charges by rushes. The men formed hastily and grimly, and rushed. Apparently there awaited them only the fate of respectable soldiers. But they went because—of the opinions of others, perhaps. They went because—no low-down, loud-mouthed, pie-faced lot of jail-birds such as the Twenty-Seventh Infantry could do anything that they could not do better. They went because Reilly ordered it. They went because they went.

And yet not a man of them to this day has made a public speech explaining precisely how he did the whole thing and detailing with what initiative and ability he comprehended and defeated a situation which he did not comprehend at all.

Reilly never saw the top of the hill. He was heroically striving to keep up with his men when a bullet ripped quietly through his left lung, and he fell back into the arms of the bugler, who received him as he would have received a Christmas present. The three venerable colonels inherited the brigade in swift succession. The senior commanded for about fifty seconds, at the end of which he was mortally shot. Before they could get the news to the next in rank he, too, was shot. The junior colonel ultimately arrived with a lean and puffing little brigade at the top of the hill. The men lay down and fired volleys at whatever was practicable.

In and out of the ditch-like trenches lay the Spanish dead, lemon-faced corpses dressed in shabby blue and white ticking. Some were huddled down comfortably like sleeping children; one had died in the attitude of a man flung back in a dentist's chair; one sat in the trench with its chin sunk despondently to its breast; few preserved a record of the agitation of battle. With the greater number it was as if death had touched them so gently, so lightly, that they had not known of it. Death had come to them rather in the form of an opiate than of a bloody blow.

But the arrived men in the blue shirts had no thought of the sallow corpses. They were eagerly exchanging a hail of shots with the Spanish second line, whose ash-colored entrenchments barred the way to a city white amid trees. In the pauses the men talked.

"We done the best. Old E Company got there. Why, one time the hull of B Company was *behind* us. Hell!"

"Jones, he was the first man up. I saw 'im."

"*Which* Jones?"

"Did you see ol' Two-bars runnin' like a land-crab? Made good time, too. He hit only in the high places. He's all right."

"The lootenant is all right, too. He was a good ten yards ahead of the best of us. I hated him at the post, but for this here active service there's none of 'em can touch him."

"This is mighty different from being at the post."

"Well, we done it, an' it wasn't b'cause *I* thought it could be done. When we started, I ses to m'self: 'Well, here goes a lot a' damned fools.' "

" 'Tain't over yet."

"Oh, they'll never git us back from here. If they start to chase us back from here we'll pile 'em up so high the last ones can't climb over. We've come this far, an' we'll stay here. I ain't done pantin'."

"Anything is better than packin' through that jungle an' gettin' blistered from front, rear, an' both flanks. I'd rather tackle another hill than go trailin' in them woods, so thick you can't tell whether you are one man or a division of cav'lry."

"Where's that young kitchen-soldier, Cadogan, or whatever his name is? Ain't seen him to-day."

"Well, *I* seen him. He was right in with it. He got shot, too, about half up the hill, in the leg. I seen it. He's all right. Don't worry about him. He's all right."

"I seen 'im, too. He done his stunt. As soon as I can git this piece of barbed-wire entanglement out a' me throat I'll give 'm a cheer."

"He ain't shot at all, b'cause there he stands, there. See 'im?"

Rearward, the grassy slope was populous with little groups of men searching for the wounded. Reilly's brigade began to dig with its bayonets and shovel with its meat-ration cans.

IV

Senator Cadogan paced to and fro in his private parlor and smoked small brown weak cigars. These little wisps seemed utterly inadequate to console such a ponderous satrap.

It was the evening of the 1st of July, 1898, and the Senator was immensely excited, as could be seen from the superlatively calm way in which he called out to his private secretary, who was in an adjoining room. The voice was serene, gentle, affectionate, low. "Baker, I wish you'd go over again to the War Department and see if they've heard anything about Caspar."

A very bright-eyed hatchet-faced young man appeared in a doorway, pen still in hand. He was hiding a nettle-like irritation behind all the finished audacity of a smirk, sharp, lying, trustworthy young politician. "I've just got back from there, sir," he suggested.

The Skowmulligan war-horse lifted his eyes and looked for a short second into the eyes of his private secretary. It was not a glare or an eagle glance; it was something beyond the practice of an actor; it was simply meaning. The clever private secretary grabbed his hat and was at once enthusiastically away. "All right, sir," he cried. "I'll find out."

The War Department was ablaze with light, and messengers were running. With the assurance of a retainer of an old house, Baker made his way through much small-calibre vociferation. There was rumor of a big victory; there was rumor of a big defeat. In the corridors various watchdogs arose from their arm-chairs and asked him of his business in tones of uncertainty which in no wise compared with their previous habitual deference to the private secretary of the war-horse of Skowmulligan.

Ultimately Baker arrived in a room where some kind of a head clerk sat writing feverishly at a roll-top desk. Baker asked a question, and the head clerk mumbled profanely without lifting his head. Apparently he said: "How in the blankety-blank blazes do I know?"

The private secretary let his jaw fall. Surely some new spirit had come suddenly upon the heart of Washington—a spirit which Baker understood to be almost defiantly indifferent to the wishes of Senator Cadogan, a spirit which was not even courteously oily. What could it mean? Baker's fox-like mind sprang wildly to a conception of overturned factions, changed friends, new combinations. The assurance which had come from experience of a broad political situation suddenly left him, and he would not have been amazed if some one had told him that Senator Cadogan now controlled only six votes in the State of Skowmulligan. "Well," he stammered in his bewilderment, " well—there isn't any news of the old man's son, hey?" Again the head clerk replied blasphemously.

Eventually Baker retreated in disorder from the presence of this head clerk, having learned that the latter did not give a —— —— if Caspar Cadogan was sailing through Hades on an ice yacht.

Baker stormed other and more formidable officials. In fact, he struck as high as he dared. They one and all flung him short hard words, even as men pelt an annoying cur with pebbles. He emerged from the brilliant light, from the groups of men with anxious puzzled faces, and as he walked back to the hotel he did not know if his name was Baker or Cholmondeley.

However, as he walked up the stairs to the Senator's rooms he contrived to concentrate his intellect upon a manner of speaking.

The war-horse was still pacing his parlor and smoking. He paused at Baker's entrance. "Well?"

"Mr. Cadogan," said the private secretary coolly, "they told me at the Department that they did not give a gawd damn whether your son was alive or dead."

The Senator looked at Baker and smiled gently. "What's that, my boy?" he asked in a soft and considerate voice.

"They said——" gulped Baker with a certain tenacity. "They said that they didn't give a gawd damn whether your son was alive or dead."

There was a silence for the space of three seconds. Baker stood like an image; he had no machinery for balancing the issues of this kind of a situation, and he seemed to feel that if he stood as still as a stone frog he would escape the ravages of a terrible Senatorial wrath which was about to break forth in a hurricane speech which would snap off trees and sweep away barns.

"Well," drawled the Senator lazily, "who did you see, Baker?"

The private secretary resumed a certain usual manner of breathing. He told the names of the men whom he had seen.

"Ye-e-es," remarked the Senator. He took another little brown cigar and held it with a thumb and first finger, staring at it with the calm and steady scrutiny of a scientist investigating a new thing. "So they don't care whether Caspar is alive or dead, eh? Well . . . maybe they don't. . . . That's all right. . . . However . . . I think I'll just look in on 'em and state my views."

When the Senator had gone, the private secretary ran to the window and leaned afar out. Pennsylvania Avenue was gleaming silver blue in the light of many arc-lamps; the cable trains groaned along to the clangor of gongs; from the window the walks presented a hardly diversified aspect of shirt-waists and straw hats. Sometimes a newsboy screeched.

Baker watched the tall heavy figure of the Senator moving out to intercept a cable train. "Great Scott!" cried the private secretary to himself, "there'll be three distinct kinds of grand, plain practical fireworks. The old man is going for 'em. I wouldn't be in Lascum's boots. Ye gods, what a row there'll be."

In due time the Senator was closeted with some kind of deputy third-assistant battery-horse in the offices of the War Department. The official obviously had been told off to make a supreme effort to pacify Cadogan, and he certainly was acting according to his instructions. He was almost in tears; he spread out his hands in supplication, and his voice whined and wheedled. "Why, really, you know, Senator, we can only beg you to look at the circumstances. Two scant divisions at the top of that hill; over a thousand men killed and wounded; the line so thin that any strong attack would smash our army to flinders. The Spaniards have probably received re-enforcements under Pando; Shafter seems to be too ill to be actively in command of our troops; Lawton can't get up with his division before to-morrow. We are actually expecting . . . no, I won't say expecting . . . but we would not be surprised . . . nobody in the Department would be surprised if before daybreak we were compelled to give to the country the news of a disaster which would be the worst blow the national pride has ever suffered. Don't you see? Can't you see our position, Senator?"

The Senator, with a pale but composed face, contemplated the official with eyes that gleamed in a way not usual with the big self-controlled politician.

"I'll tell you frankly, sir," continued the other. "I'll tell you frankly, that at this moment we don't know whether we are a-foot or a-horseback. Everything is in the air. We don't know whether we have won a glorious victory or simply got ourselves in a devil of a fix."

The Senator coughed. "I suppose my boy is with the two divisions at the top of that hill? He's with Reilly."

"Yes; Reilly's brigade is up there."

"And when do you suppose the War Department can tell me if he is all right? I want to know."

"My dear Senator—frankly, I don't know. Again I beg you to think of our position. The army in a muddle; its general thinking that he must fall back, and yet not sure that he *can* fall back without losing the army. Why, we're worrying about the lives of sixteen thousand men and the self-respect of the nation, Senator."

"I see," observed the Senator, nodding his head slowly. "And naturally the welfare of one man's son doesn't—how do they say it?—doesn't cut any ice."

V

And in Cuba it rained. In a few days Reilly's brigade discovered that by their successful charge they had gained the inestimable privilege of sitting in a wet trench and slowly but surely starving to death. Men's tempers crumbled like dry bread. The soldiers who so cheerfully, quietly and decently had captured positions which the foreign experts had said were impregnable, now in turn underwent an attack which was furious as well as insidious. The heat of the sun alternated with rains which boomed and roared in their falling like mountain cataracts. It seemed as if men took the fever through sheer lack of other occupation. During the days of battle none had had time to get even a tropic headache, but no sooner was that brisk period over than men began to shiver and shudder by squads and platoons. Rations were scarce enough to make a little fat strip of bacon seem of the size of a corner lot, and coffee grains were pearls. There would have been godless quarreling over fragments if it were not that with these fevers came a great listlessness, so that men were almost content to die, if death required no exertion.

It was an occasion which distinctly separated the sheep from the goats. The goats were few enough, but their qualities glared out like crimson spots.

One morning Jameson and Ripley, two captains in the Forty-fourth Foot, lay under a flimsy shelter of sticks and palm branches. Their dreamy dull eyes contemplated the men in the trench which went to left and right. To them came Caspar Cadogan, moaning. "By gawd," he said, as he flung himself wearily on the ground, "I can't stand much more of this, you know. It's killing me." A bristly beard sprouted through the grime on his face; his eyelids were crimson; an indescribably dirty shirt fell away from his roughened neck; and at the same time various lines of evil and greed were deepened on his face, until he practically stood forth as a revelation, a confession. "I can't stand it. By gawd, I can't."

Stanford, a lieutenant under Jameson, came stumbling along toward them. He was a lad of the class of '98 at West Point. It could be seen that he was flaming with fever. He rolled a calm eye at them. "Have you any water, sir?" he said to his captain. Jameson got upon his feet and helped Stanford to lay his shaking length under the shelter. "No, boy," he answered gloomily. "Not a drop. You got any, Rip?"

"No," answered Ripley, looking with anxiety upon the young officer. "Not a drop."

"You, Cadogan?"

Here Caspar hesitated oddly for a second, and then in a tone of deep regret made answer: "No, Captain; not a mouthful."

Jameson moved off weakly. "You lay quietly, Stanford, and I'll see what I can russle."

Presently Caspar felt that Ripley was steadily regarding him. He returned the look with one of half-guilty questioning. "God forgive you, Cadogan," said Ripley, "but you are a damned beast. Your canteen is full of water."

Even then the apathy in their veins prevented the scene from becoming as sharp as the words sound. Caspar sputtered like a child, and at length merely said: "No, it isn't." Stanford lifted his head to shoot a keen proud glance at Caspar, and then turned away his face.

"You lie," said Ripley. "I can tell the sound of a full canteen as far as I can hear it."

"Well, if it is, I—I must have forgotten it."

"You lie; no man in this army just now forgets whether his canteen is full or empty. Hand it over."

Fever is the physical counterpart of shame, and when a man

has had the one he accepts the other with an ease which would revolt his healthy self. However, Caspar made a desperate struggle to preserve the forms. He arose and taking the string from his shoulder, passed the canteen to Ripley. But after all there was a whine in his voice, and the assumption of dignity was really a farce. "I think I had better go, Captain. You can have the water if you want it, I'm sure. But—but I fail to see—I fail to see what reason you have for insulting me."

"Do you?" said Ripley stolidly. "That's all right."

Caspar stood for a terrible moment. He simply did not have the strength to turn his back on this—this affair. It seemed to him that he must stand forever and face it. But when he found the audacity to look again at Ripley he saw the latter was not at all concerned with the situation. Ripley, too, had the fever. The fever changes all laws of proportion. Caspar went away.

"Here, youngster; here's your drink."

Stanford made a weak gesture. "I wouldn't touch a drop from his damned canteen if it was the last water in the world," he murmured in his high boyish voice.

"Don't you be a young jackass," quoth Ripley tenderly.

The boy stole a glance at the canteen. He felt the propriety of arising and hurling it after Caspar, but—he, too, had the fever.

"Don't you be a young jackass," said Ripley again.

VI

Senator Cadogan was happy. His son had returned from Cuba, and the 8.30 train that evening would bring him to the station nearest to the stone and red shingle villa which the senator and his family occupied on the shores of Long Island Sound. The Senator's steam yacht lay some hundred yards from the beach. She had just returned from a trip to Montauk Point, where the Senator had made a gallant attempt to gain his son from the transport on which he was coming from Cuba. He had fought a brave sea-fight with sundry petty little doctors and ship's officers, who had raked him with broadsides describing the laws of quarantine and had used inelegant speech to a United States Senator as he stood on the bridge of his own steam yacht. These men had grimly asked him to tell exactly how much better was Caspar than any other returning soldier.

But the Senator had not given them a long fight. In fact, the truth came to him quickly, and with almost a blush he had ordered the yacht back to her anchorage off the villa. As a matter of fact, the trip to Montauk Point had been undertaken largely from impulse. Long ago the Senator had decided that when his boy returned the greeting should have something Spartan in it. He would make a welcome such as most soldiers get. There should be no flowers and carriages when the other poor fellows got none. He should consider Caspar as a soldier. That was the way to treat a man. But, in the end, a sharp acid of anxiety had worked upon the iron old man, until he had ordered the yacht to take him out and make a fool of him. The result filled him with a chagrin which caused him to delegate to the mother and sisters the entire business of succoring Caspar at Montauk Point Camp. He had remained at home conducting the huge correspondence of an active national politician and waiting for this son whom he so loved and whom he so wished to be a man of a certain strong taciturn shrewd ideal. The recent yacht voyage he now looked upon as a kind of confession of his weakness, and he was resolved that no more signs should escape him.

But yet his boy had been down there against the enemy and among the fevers. There had been grave perils, and his boy must have faced them. And he could not prevent himself from dreaming through the poetry of fine actions, in which visions his son's face shone out manly and generous. During these periods the people about him, accustomed as they were to his silence and calm in time of stress, considered that affairs in Skowmulligan might be most critical. In no other way could they account for this exaggerated phlegm.

On the night of Caspar's return he did not go to dinner, but had a tray sent to his library, where he remained writing. At last he heard the spin of the dog-cart's wheels on the gravel of the drive, and a moment later there penetrated to him the sound of joyful feminine cries. He lit another cigar; he knew that it was now his part to bide with dignity the moment when his son should shake off that other welcome and come to him. He could still hear them; in their exuberance they seemed to be capering like school-children. He was impatient, but this impatience took the form of a polar stolidity.

Presently there were quick steps and a jubilant knock at his door. "Come in," he said. In came Caspar, thin, yellow and in soiled khaki. "They almost tore me to pieces," he cried, laughing. "They danced around like wild things." Then as they shook hands he dutifully said, "How are you, sir?"

"How are you, my boy?" answered the Senator casually but kindly.

"Better than I might expect, sir," cried Caspar cheerfully. "We had a pretty hard time, you know."

"You look as if they'd given you a hard run," observed the father in a tone of slight interest.

Caspar was eager to tell. "Yes, sir," he said rapidly. "We did, indeed. Why, it was awful. We—any of us—were lucky to get out of it alive. It wasn't so much the Spaniards, you know. The army took care of them all right. It was the fever and the—you know, we couldn't get anything to eat. And the mismanagement. Why, it was frightful."

"Yes, I've heard," said the Senator. A certain wistful look came into his eyes, but he did not allow it to become prominent. Indeed, he suppressed it. "And you, Caspar? I suppose you did your duty?"

Caspar answered with becoming modesty. "Well, I didn't do more than anybody else, I don't suppose, but—well, I got along all right, I guess."

"And this great charge up San Juan Hill?" asked the father slowly. "Were you in that?"

"Well—yes; I was in it," replied the son.

The Senator brightened a trifle. "You were, eh? In the front of it? or just sort of going along?"

"Well—I don't know. I couldn't tell exactly. Sometimes I was in front of a lot of them, and sometimes I was—just sort of going along."

This time the Senator emphatically brightened. "That's all right, then. And of course—of *course* you performed your commissary duties correctly?"

The question seemed to make Caspar uncommunicative and sulky. "I did when there was anything to do," he answered. "But the whole thing was on the most unbusiness-like basis you can imagine. And they wouldn't tell you anything. Nobody would take time to instruct you in your duties, and of course if you didn't know a thing then your superior officer would swoop down on you and ask you why in hell such and such a thing wasn't done in such and such a way. Of course I did the best I could."

The Senator's countenance had again become sombrely indifferent. "I see. But you weren't directly rebuked for incapacity, were you? No; of course you weren't. But—I mean—did any of your superior officers suggest that you were 'no good,' or anything of that sort? I mean—did you come off with a clean slate?"

Caspar took a small time to digest his father's meaning. "Oh, yes, sir," he cried at the end of his reflection. "The commissary was in such a hopeless mess anyhow that nobody thought of doing anything but curse Washington."

"Of course," rejoined the Senator harshly. "But supposing that you had been a competent and well-trained commissary officer? What then?"

Again the son took time for consideration, and in the end deliberately replied: "Well, if I had been a competent and well-trained commissary I would have sat there and eaten up my heart and cursed Washington."

"Well, then, that's all right. And now about this charge up San Juan? Did any of the generals speak to you afterward and say that you had done well? Didn't any of them see you?"

"Why, n-n-no, I don't suppose they did . . . any more than I did them. You see, this charge was a big thing and covered lots of ground, and I hardly saw anybody excepting a lot of the men."

"Well, but didn't any of the men see you? Weren't you ahead some of the time, leading them on and waving your sword?"

Caspar burst into laughter. "Why, no. I had all I could do to scramble along and try to keep up. And I didn't want to go up at all."

"Why?" demanded the Senator.

"Because—because the Spaniards were shooting so much. And you could see men falling—and the bullets rushed around you in—by the bushel. And then at last it seemed that if we once drove them away from the top of the hill there would be less danger. So we all went up."

The Senator chuckled over this description. "And you didn't flinch at all?"

"Well," rejoined Caspar humorously, "I won't say I wasn't frightened."

"No, of course not. But then you did not let anybody know it?"

"Of course not."

"You understand, naturally, that I am bothering you with all these questions because I desire to hear how my only son behaved in the crisis. I don't want to worry you with it. But if you went through the San Juan charge with credit I'll have you made a major."

"Well," said Caspar, "I wouldn't say I went through that charge with credit. I went through it all good enough, but the enlisted men around went through in the same way."

"But weren't you encouraging them and leading them on by your example?"

Caspar smirked. He began to see a point. "Well, sir," he said with a charming hesitation. "Aw—er—I—well, I dare say I was doing my share of it."

The perfect form of the reply delighted the father. He could not endure blatancy; his admiration was to be won only by a bashful hero. Now he beat his hand impulsively down upon the table. "That's what I wanted to know. That's it exactly. I'll have you made a major next week. You've found your proper field at last. You stick to the army, Caspar, and I'll back you up. That's the thing. In a few years it will be a great career. The United States is pretty sure to have an army of about a hundred and fifty thousand men. And starting in when you did and with me to back you up—why, we'll make you a general in seven or eight years. That's the ticket. You stay in the army." The Senator's face was flushed with enthusiasm, and he looked eagerly and confidently at his son.

But Caspar had pulled a long face. "The army?" he said. "Stay in the army?"

The Senator continued to outline quite rapturously his idea of the future. "The army, evidently, is just the place for you. You know as well as I do that you have not been a howling success, exactly, in anything else which you have tried. But now the army just suits you. It is the kind of career which especially suits you. Well, then, go in, and go at it hard. Go in to win. Go at it."

"But——" began Caspar.

The Senator interrupted swiftly. "Oh, don't worry about that part of it. I'll take care of all that. You won't get jailed in some Arizona adobe for the rest of your natural life. There won't be much more of that, anyhow; and besides, as I say, I'll look after all that end of it. The chance is splendid. A young, healthy and intelligent man, with the start you've already got, and with my backing, can do anything—anything! There will be a lot of active service—oh, yes, I'm sure of it—and everybody who——"

"But," said Caspar, wan, desperate, heroic, "father, I don't care to stay in the army."

The Senator lifted his eyes and his face darkened. "What?" he said. "What's that?" He looked at Caspar.

The son became tightened and wizened like an old miser trying to withhold gold. He replied with a sort of idiot obstinacy, "I don't care to stay in the army."

The Senator's jaw clinched down, and he was dangerous. But, after all, there was something mournful somewhere. "Why, what do you mean?" he asked gruffly.

"Why, I couldn't get along, you know. The—the——"

"The what?" demanded the father, suddenly uplifted with thunderous anger. "The what?"

Caspar's pain found a sort of outlet in mere irresponsible talk. "Well, you know—the other men, you know. I couldn't get along with them, you know. They're peculiar, somehow; odd; I didn't understand them, and they didn't understand me. We—we didn't hitch, somehow. They're a queer lot. They've got funny ideas. I don't know how to explain it exactly, but—somehow—I don't like 'em. That's all there is to it. They're good fellows enough, I know, but——"

"Oh, well, Caspar," interrupted the Senator. Then he

seemed to weigh a great fact in his mind. "I guess——" He paused again in profound consideration. "I guess——" He lit a small brown cigar. "I guess you are no damn good."

This Majestic Lie
I

IN THE TWILIGHT a great crowd was streaming up the Prado in Havana. The people had been down to the shore to laugh and twiddle their fingers at the American blockading fleet—mere colorless shapes on the edge of the sea. Gorgeous challenges had been issued to the far-away ships by little children and women while the men laughed. Havana was happy, for it was known that the illustrious sailor Don Patricio Montojo had with his fleet met the decaying ships of one Dewey and smitten them into stuffing for a baby's pillow. Of course the American sailors were drunk at the time, but the American sailors were always drunk. Newsboys galloped among the crowd crying *La Lucha* and *La Marina*. The papers said: "This is as we foretold. How could it be otherwise when the cowardly Yankees met our brave sailors?" But the tongues of the exuberant people ran more at large. One man said in a loud voice: "How unfortunate it is that we still have to buy meat in Havana when so much pork is floating in Manila Bay!" Amid the consequent laughter another man retorted: "Oh, never mind! That pork in Manila is rotten. It always was rotten." Still another man said: "But, little friend, it would make good manure for our fields if only we had it." And still another man said: "Ah, wait until our soldiers get with the wives of the Americans and there will be many little Yankees to serve hot on our tables. The men of the *Maine* simply made our appetites good. Never mind the pork in Manila. There will be plenty." Women laughed; children laughed because their mothers laughed; everybody laughed. And—a word with you—these people were cackling and chuckling and insulting their own dead, their own dead men of Spain, for if the poor green corpses floated then in Manila Bay they were not American corpses.

The newsboys came charging with an extra. The inhabitants of Philadelphia had fled to the forests because of a Spanish bombardment and also Boston was besieged by the Apaches who had totally invested the town. The Apache artillery had proven singularly effective and an American garrison had been unable to face it. In Chicago millionaires were giving away their palaces for two or three loaves of bread. These despatches were from Madrid and every word was truth, but they added little to the enthusiasm because the crowd—God help mankind—was greatly occupied with visions of Yankee pork floating in Manila Bay. This will be thought to be embittered writing. Very well; the writer admits its untruthfulness in one particular. It is untruthful in that it fails to reproduce one-hundredth part of the grossness and indecency of popular expression in Havana up to the time when the people knew they were beaten.

There were no lights on the Prado or in other streets because of a military order. In the slow-moving crowd there was a young man and an old woman. Suddenly the young man laughed a strange metallic laugh and spoke in English, not cautiously. "That's damned hard to listen to."

The woman spoke quickly. "Hush, you little idiot. Do you want to be walkin' across that grass-plot in Cabanas with your arms tied behind you?" Then she murmured sadly: "Johnnie, I wonder if that's true—what they say about Manila?"

"I don't know," said Johnnie, "but I think they're lying."

As they crossed the Plaza they could see that the Café Tacon was crowded with Spanish officers in blue and white pyjama uniforms. Wine and brandy was being wildly consumed in honor of the victory at Manila. "Let's hear what they say," said Johnnie to his companion, and they moved across the street and in under the *portales*. The owner of the Café Tacon was standing on a table making a speech amid cheers. He was advocating the crucifixion of such Americans as fell into Spanish hands and—it was all very sweet and white and tender, but above all, it was chivalrous, because it is well known that the Spaniards are a chivalrous people. It has been remarked both by the English newspapers and by the bulls that are bred for the red death. And secretly the corpses in Manila Bay mocked this jubilee—the mocking, mocking corpses in Manila Bay.

To be blunt, Johnnie was an American spy. Once he had been the manager of a sugar plantation in Pinar del Rio, and during the insurrection it had been his distinguished function to pay tribute of money, food and forage alike to Spanish columns and insurgent bands. He was performing this straddle with benefit to his crops and with mildew to his conscience when Spain and the United States agreed to skirmish, both in the name of honor. It then became a military necessity that he should change his base. Whatever of the province that was still alive was sorry to see him go for he had been a very dexterous man and food and wine had been in his house even when a man with a mango could gain the envy of an entire Spanish battalion. Without doubt he had been a mere trimmer, but it was because of his crop and he always wrote the word thus: C R O P. In those days a man of peace and commerce was in a position parallel to the watchmaker who essayed a task in the midst of a drunken brawl with oaths, bottles and bullets flying about his intent bowed head. So many of them—or all of them—were trimmers, and to any armed force they fervently said: "God assist you." And behold, the trimmers dwelt safely in a tumultuous land and without effort save that their little machines for trimming ran night and day. So many a plantation became covered with a maze of lies as if thick-webbing spiders had run from stalk to stalk in the cane. So sometimes a planter incurred an equal hatred from both sides and when in trouble there was no camp to which he could flee save, straight in air—the camp of the heavenly host.

If Johnnie had not had a crop he would have been plainly on the side of the insurgents, but his crop staked him down to the soil at a point where the Spaniards could always be sure of finding him—him or his crop—it is the same thing. But when war came between Spain and the United States he could no longer be the cleverest trimmer in Pinar del Rio. And he retreated upon Key West losing much of his baggage train, not because of panic but because of wisdom. In Key West he was no longer the manager of a big Cuban plantation; he was a little tan-faced refugee without much money. Mainly he listened; there was nought else to do. In the first place he was a young man of extremely slow speech and in the Key West Hotel tongues ran like pin-wheels. If he had projected his methodic way of thought and speech upon this hurricane he would have been as effective as the man who tries to smoke against the gale. This truth did not impress him. Really he was impressed with the fact that although he knew much of Cuba, he could not talk so rapidly and wisely of it as many war-correspondents who had not yet seen the island. Usually he brooded in silence over a bottle of beer and the loss of his crop. He received no sympathy, although there was a plentitude of tender souls. War's first step is to make expectation so high that all present things are fogged and darkened in a tense wonder of the future. None cared about the collapse of Johnnie's plantation when all were thinking of the probable collapse of cities and fleets.

In the meantime battle-ships, monitors, cruisers, gunboats and torpedo craft arrived, departed, arrived, departed. Rumors rang about the ears of warships hurriedly coaling. Rumors sang about the ears of warships leisurely coming to anchor. This happened and that happened and if the news arrived at Key West as a mouse, it was often enough cabled north as an elephant. The correspondents at Key West were perfectly capable of adjusting their perspective, but many of the editors in the United States were like deaf men at whom one has to roar. A few quiet words of information was not enough for them; one had to bawl into their ears a whirlwind tale of heroism, blood, death, victory or defeat—at any rate, a tragedy. The papers should have sent play-wrights to the first part of the war. Play-wrights are allowed to lower the curtain from time to time and say to the crowd: "Mark, ye, now! Three or four months are supposed to elapse." But the poor devils at Key West were obliged to keep the curtain up all the time. "This isn't a continuous performance." "Yes, it is; it's *got* to be a continuous performance. The welfare of the paper demands it. The people want news." Very well; continuous performance. It is strange how men of sense can go aslant at the bidding of other men of sense and combine to contribute to a general mess of exaggeration and bombast. But we did; and in the midst of the furor I remember the still figure of Johnnie, the planter, the ex-trimmer. He looked dazed.

This was in May.

We all liked him. From time to time some of us heard in his words the vibrant of a thoughtful experience. But it could not be well heard; it was only like the sound of a bell from under the floor. We were too busy with our own clatter. He was taciturn and competent while we solved the war in a babble of tongues. Soon we went about our peaceful paths saying ironically one to another: "War is hell." Meanwhile, managing editors fought us tooth and nail and we all were sent boxes of medals inscribed: "Incompetency." We became furious with ourselves. Why couldn't we send hair-raising despatches? Why couldn't we inflame the wires? All the ijjits did. If a first-class armored cruiser which had once been a towboat fired a six-pounder shot from her forward thirteen-inch gun turret the world heard of it, you bet. We were not idle men. We had come to report the war and we did it. Our good names and our salaries depended upon it and we were urged by our managing-editors to remember that the American people were a collection of super-nervous idiots who would immediately have convulsions if we did not throw them some news—any news. It was not true, at all. The American people were anxious for things decisive to happen; they were not anxious to be lulled to satisfaction with a drug. But we lulled them. We told them this and we told them that, and I warrant you our screaming sounded like the noise of a lot of sea-birds settling for the night among the black crags.

In the meantime, Johnnie stared and meditated. In his unhurried, unstartled manner he was singularly like another man who was flying the pennant as commander-in-chief of the North Atlantic Squadron. Johnnie was a refugee; the admiral was an admiral. And yet they were much akin, these two. Their brother was the Strategy Board—the only capable political institution of the war. At Key West the naval officers spoke of their business and were devoted to it and were bound to succeed in it, but when the flag-ship was in port the only two people who were independent and sane were the admiral and Johnnie. The rest of us were lulling the public with drugs.

There was much discussion of the new batteries at Havana. Johnnie was a typical American. In Europe a typical American is a man with a hard eye, chin-whiskers and a habit of speaking through his nose. Johnnie was a young man of great energy, ready to accomplish a colossal thing for the basic reason that he was ignorant of its magnitude. In fact he attacked all obstacles in life in a spirit of contempt, seeing them smaller than they were until he had actually surmounted them—when he was likely to be immensely pleased with himself. Somewhere in him there was a sentimental tenderness, but it was like a light seen afar at night; it came, went, appeared again in a new place, flickered, flared, went out, left you in a void and angry. And if his sentimental tenderness was a light, the darkness in which it puzzled you was his irony of soul. This irony was directed first at himself; then at you; then at the nation and the flag; then at God. It was a midnight in which you searched for the little elusive ashamed spark of tender sentiment. Sometimes you thought this was all pretext, the manner and the way of fear of the wit of others; sometimes you thought he was a hardened savage; usually you did not think but waited in the cheerful certainty that in time the little flare of light would appear in the gloom.

Johnnie decided that he would go and spy upon the fortifications of Havana. If any one wished to know of those batteries it was the admiral of the squadron, but the admiral of the squadron knew much. I feel sure that he knew the size and position of every gun. To be sure, new guns might be mounted at any time, but they would not be big guns, and doubtless he lacked in his cabin less information than would be worth a man's life. Still, Johnnie decided to be a spy. He would go and look. We of the newspapers pinned him fast to the tail of our kite and he was taken to see the admiral. I judge that the admiral did not display much interest in the plan. But at any rate it seems that he touched Johnnie smartly enough with a brush to make him, officially, a spy. Then Johnnie bowed and left the cabin. There was no other machinery. If Johnnie was to end his life and leave a little book about it no one cared—least of all Johnnie and the admiral. When he came aboard the tug he displayed his usual stalwart and rather selfish zest for fried eggs. It was all some kind of an ordinary matter. It was done every day. It was the business of packing pork, sewing shoes, binding hay. It was commonplace. No one could adjust it, get it in proportion, until—afterward. On a dark night they heaved him into a small boat and rowed him to the beach.

And one day he appeared at the door of a little lodging-house in Havana kept by Martha Clancy, born in Ireland, bred in New York, fifteen years married to a Spanish captain, and now a widow, keeping Cuban lodgers who had no money with which to pay her. She opened the door only a little way and looked down over her spectacles at him.

"Good-mornin', Martha," he said.

She looked a moment in silence. Then she made an indescribable gesture of weariness. "Come in," she said. He stepped inside. "And in God's name couldn't you keep your neck out of this rope? And so you had to come here, did you—to Havana? Upon my soul, Johnnie, my son, you are the biggest fool on two legs."

He moved past her into the court-yard and took his old chair at the table—between the winding stairway and the door—near the orange tree. "Why am I?" he demanded stoutly. She made no reply until she had taken seat in her rocking-chair and puffed several times upon a cigarette. Then through the smoke she said meditatively: "Everybody knows ye are a damned little mambi." Sometimes she spoke with an Irish accent.

He laughed. "I'm no more of a mambi than *you* are, anyhow."

"I'm no mambi. But your name is poison to half the Spaniards in Havana. That you know. And if you were once safe in Cayo Hueso, 'tis nobody but a born fool who would come blunderin' into Havana again. Have ye had your dinner?"

"What have you got?" he asked before committing himself.

She arose and spoke without confidence as she moved toward the cupboard. "There's some codfish salad."

"*What?*" said he.

"Codfish salad."

"*Codfish what?*"

"Codfish salad. Ain't it good enough for ye? Maybe this is Delmonico's—no? Maybe ye never heard that the Yankees have us blockaded, hey? Maybe ye think food can be picked in the streets here now, hey? I'll tell ye one thing, my son, if you stay here long you'll see the want of it and so you had best not throw it over your shoulder."

The spy settled determinedly in his chair and delivered himself of his final decision. "That may all be true, but I'm *damned* if I eat codfish salad."

Old Martha was a picture of quaint despair. "You'll not?"
"No!"

"Then," she sighed piously, "may the Lord have mercy on ye, Johnnie, for you'll never do here. 'Tis not the time for you. You're due after the blockade. Will you do me the favor of translating why you won't eat codfish salad, you skinny little insurrecto?"

"Codfish salad!" he said with a deep sneer. "Who ever heard of it!"

Outside, on the jumbled pavement of the street, an occasional two-wheel cart passed with deafening thunder, making one think of the overturning of houses. Down from the pale sky over the patio came a heavy odor of Havana itself, a smell of old straw. The wild cries of vendors could be heard at intervals.

"You'll not?"
"No."
"And why not?"
"Codfish salad? Not by a blame sight!"

"Well—all right then. You are more of a pig-headed young imbecile than even I thought from seeing you come into Havana here where half the town knows you and the poorest Spaniard would give a gold piece to see you go into Cabanas and forget to come out. Did I tell you my son Alfred is sick? Yes, poor little fellow, he lies up in the room you used to have. The fever. And did you see Woodham in Key West? Heaven save us, what quick time he made in getting out. I hear Figtree and Button are working in the cable office over there—no? And when is the war going to end? Are the Yankees going to try to take Havana? It will be a hard job, Johnnie! The Spaniards say it is impossible. Everybody is laughing at the Yankees. I hate to go into the street and hear them. Is General Lee going to lead the army? What's become of Springer? I see you've got a new pair of shoes."

In the evening there was a sudden loud knock at the outer door. Martha looked at Johnnie and Johnnie looked at Martha. He was still sitting in the patio, smoking. She took the lamp and set it on a table in the little parlor. This parlor connected the street-door with the patio, and so Johnnie would be protected from the sight of the people who knocked by the broad illuminated tract. Martha moved in pensive fashion upon the latch. "Who's there?" she asked casually.

"The police!" There it was, an old melodramatic incident from the stage, from the romances. One could scarce believe it. It had all the dignity of a classic resurrection. "The police!" One sneers at its probability; it is too venerable. But so it happened.

"Who?" said Martha.

"The police!"

"What do you want here?"

"Open the door and we'll tell you."

Martha drew back the ordinary huge bolts of a Havana house and opened the door a trifle. "Tell me what you want and begone quickly," she said, "for my little boy is ill of the fever——"

She could see four or five dim figures, and now one of these suddenly placed a foot well within the door so that she might not close it. "We have come for Johnnie. We must search your house."

"Johnnie? Johnnie? Who is Johnnie?" said Martha in her best manner.

The police inspector grinned with the light upon his face. "Don't you know Señor Johnnie from Pinar del Rio?" he asked.

"Before the war—yes. But now—where is he—he must be in Key West?"

"He is in your house."

"He? In my house? Do me the favor to think that I have some intelligence. Would I be likely to be harboring a Yankee in these times? You must think I have no more head than an Orden Publico. And I'll not have you search my house, for there is no one here save my son—who is maybe dying of the fever—and the doctor. The doctor is with him because now is the crisis, and any one little thing may kill or cure my boy, and you will do me the favor to consider what may happen if I allow five or six heavy-footed policemen to go tramping all over my house. You may think——"

"Stop it," said the chief police officer at last. He was laughing and weary and angry.

Martha checked her flow of Spanish. "There," she thought, "I've done my best. He ought to fall in with it." But as the police entered she began on them again. "You will search the house whether I like it or no. Very well; but if anything happens to my boy? It is a nice way of conduct, anyhow—coming into the house of a widow at night and talking much about this Yankee and——"

"For God's sake, señora, hold your tongue. We——"

"Oh, yes, the señora can for God's sake very well hold her tongue, but that wouldn't assist you men into the street where you belong. Take care; if my sick boy suffers from this prowling! No, you'll find nothing in that wardrobe. And do you think he would be under the table? Don't overturn all that linen. Look you, when you go upstairs tread lightly."

Leaving a man on guard at the street door and another in the patio, the chief policeman and the remainder of his men ascended to the gallery from which opened three sleeping-rooms. They were followed by Martha adjuring them to make no noise. The first room was empty; the second room was empty; as they approached the door of the third room Martha whispered supplications. "Now, in the name of God, don't disturb my boy." The inspector motioned his men to pause and then he pushed open the door. Only one weak candle was burning in the room and its yellow light fell upon the bed whereon was stretched the figure of a little curly-headed boy in a white nightie. He was asleep, but his face was pink with fever and his lips were murmuring some half-coherent childish nonsense. At the head of the bed stood the motionless figure of a man. His back was to the door, but upon hearing a noise he held up a solemn hand. There was an odor of medicine. Out on the balcony, Martha apparently was weeping.

The inspector hesitated for a moment; then he noiselessly entered the room and with his yellow cane prodded under the bed, in the cupboard and behind the window-curtains. Nothing came of it. He shrugged his shoulders and went out to the balcony. He was smiling sheepishly. Evidently he knew that he had been beaten. "Very good, señora," he said. "You are clever; some day I shall be clever, too." He shook his finger at her. He was threatening her but he affected to be playful. "Then—beware! Beware!"

Martha replied blandly. "My late husband, El Capitan Señor Don Patricio de Castellon y Valladolid, was a cavalier of Spain and if he was alive to-night he would now be cutting the ears from the heads of you and your miserable men who smell frightfully of cognac."

"Por Dios!" muttered the inspector as followed by his band he made his way down the spiral staircase. "It is a tongue! One vast tongue!" At the street-door they made ironical bows; they departed; they were angry men.

Johnnie came down when he heard Martha bolting the door behind the police. She brought back the lamp to the table in the patio and stood beside it, thinking. Johnnie dropped into his old chair. The expression on the spy's face was curious; it pictured glee, anxiety, self-complacency; above all it pictured self-complacency. Martha said nothing; she was still by the lamp, musing.

The long silence was suddenly broken by a tremendous guffaw from Johnnie. "Did you ever see sich a lot of fools!" He leaned his head far back and roared victorious merriment.

Martha was almost dancing in her apprehension. "Hush! Be quiet, you little demon! Hush! Do me the favor to allow them to get to the corner before you bellow like a walrus. Be quiet."

The spy ceased his laughter and spoke in indignation. "Why?" he demanded. "Ain't I got a right to laugh?"

"Not with a noise like a cow fallin' into a cucumber-frame," she answered sharply. "Do me the favor——" Then she seemed overwhelmed with a sense of the general hopelessness of Johnnie's character. She began to wag her head. "Oh, but you are the boy for gettin' yourself into the tiger's cage without even so much as the thought of a pocket-knife in your thick head. You would be a genius of the first water if you only had a little sense. And now you're here, what are you going to do?"

He grinned at her. "I'm goin' to hold an inspection of the land and sea defences of the city of Havana."

Martha's spectacles dropped low on her nose and, looking over the rims of them in grave meditation, she said: "If you can't put up with codfish salad you had better make short work of your inspection of the land and sea defences of the city of Havana. You are likely to starve in the meantime. A man who is particular about his food has come to the wrong town if he is in Havana now."

"No, but——" asked Johnnie seriously. "Haven't you any bread?"

"*Bread!*"

"Well, coffee then? Coffee alone will do."

"*Coffee!*"

Johnnie arose deliberately and took his hat. Martha eyed him. "And where do you think you are goin'?" she asked cuttingly.

Still deliberate, Johnnie moved in the direction of the street-door. "I'm goin' where I can get something to eat."

Martha sank into a chair with a moan which was a finished opinion—almost a definition—of Johnnie's behavior in life. "And where will you go?" she asked faintly.

"Oh, I don't know," he rejoined. "Some café. Guess I'll go to the Café Aguacate. They feed you well there. I remember——"

"*You* remember? *They* remember! They know you as well as if you were the sign over the door."

"Oh, they won't give me away," said Johnnie with stalwart confidence.

"Gi-give you away? Give you a-away?" stammered Martha.

The spy made no answer but went to the door, unbarred it and passed into the street. Martha caught her breath and ran after him and came face to face with him as he turned to shut the door. "Johnnie, if ye come back, bring a loaf of bread. I'm dyin' for one good honest bite in a slice of bread."

She heard his peculiar derisive laugh as she bolted the door. She returned to her chair in the patio. "Well, there," she said with affection, admiration and contempt. "There he goes! The most hard-headed little ignoramus in twenty nations! What does he care? Nothin'! And why is it? Pure bred-in-the-bone ignorance. Just because he can't stand codfish salad he goes out to a café! A café where they know him as if they had made him! . . . Well . . . . I won't see him again, probably. . . . But if he comes back, I hope he brings some bread. I'm near dead for it."

II

Johnnie strolled carelessly through dark narrow streets. Near every corner were two Orden Publicos—a kind of soldier-police—quiet in the shadow of some doorway, their Remingtons ready, their eyes shining. Johnnie walked past as if he owned them, and their eyes followed him with a sort of a lazy mechanical suspicion which was militant in none of its moods.

Johnnie was suffering from a desire to be splendidly imprudent. He wanted to make the situation gasp and thrill and tremble. From time to time he tried to conceive the idea of his being caught, but to save his eyes he could not imagine it. Such an event was impossible to his peculiar breed of fatalism which could not have conceded death until he had mouldered seven years.

He arrived at the Café Aguacate and found it much changed. The thick wooden shutters were up to keep light from shining into the street. Inside there were only a few Spanish officers. Johnnie walked to the private rooms at the rear. He found an empty one and pressed the electric button. When he had passed through the main part of the café no one had noted him. The first to recognize him was the waiter who answered the bell. This worthy man turned to stone before the presence of Johnnie.

"Buenos noche, Francisco," said the spy, enjoying himself. "I have hunger. Bring me bread, butter, eggs and coffee." There was a silence; the waiter did not move; Johnnie smiled casually at him.

The man's throat moved; then like one suddenly re-endowed with life, he bolted from the room. After a long time he returned with the proprietor of the place. In the wicked eye of the latter there gleamed the light of a plan. He did not respond to Johnnie's genial greeting, but at once proceeded to develop his position. "Johnnie," he said, "bread is very dear in Havana. It is very dear."

"Is it?" said Johnnie looking keenly at the speaker. He understood at once that here was some sort of an attack upon him.

"Yes," answered the proprietor of the Café Aguacate slowly and softly. "It is very dear. I think to-night one small bit of bread will cost you one centene—in advance." A centene approximates five dollars in gold.

The spy's face did not change. He appeared to reflect. "And how much for the butter?" he asked at last.

The proprietor gestured. "There is no butter. Do you think we can have everything with those Yankee pigs sitting out there on their ships?"

"And how much for the coffee?" asked Johnnie musingly.

Again the two men surveyed each other during a period of silence. Then the proprietor said gently: "I think your coffee will cost you about two centenes."

"And the eggs?"

"Eggs are very dear. I think eggs would cost you about three centenes for each one."

The new looked at the old; the North Atlantic looked at the Mediterranean; the wooden nutmeg looked at the olive. Johnnie slowly took six centenes from his pocket and laid them on the table. "That's for bread, coffee and *one* egg. I don't think I could eat more than one egg to-night. I'm not so hungry as I was."

The proprietor held a perpendicular finger and tapped the table with it. "Oh, señor," he said politely, "I think you would like two eggs."

Johnnie saw the finger. He understood it. "Ye-e-es," he drawled. "I would like two eggs." He placed three more centenes on the table.

"And a little thing for the waiter? I am sure his services will be excellent, invaluable."

"Ye-e-es, for the waiter." Another centene was laid on the table.

The proprietor bowed and preceded the waiter out of the room. There was a mirror on the wall and, springing to his feet, the spy thrust his face close to the honest glass. "Well, I'm damned!" he ejaculated. "Is this me or is this the Honorable D. Hayseed Whiskers of Kansas? Who am I, anyhow? Fifty dollars in gold! . . . Say, these people are clever. They know their business, they do. Bread, coffee and two eggs and not even sure of getting it! Fifty dol—— Never mind; wait until the war is over. Fifty dollars gold!" He sat for a long time; nothing happened. "Eh," he said at last, "that's the game." As the front door of the café closed upon him he heard the proprietor and one of the waiters burst into derisive laughter.

Martha was waiting for him. "And here ye are, safe back," she said with delight as she let him enter. "And did ye bring the bread? Did ye bring the bread?"

But she saw that he was raging like a lunatic. His face was red and swollen with temper; his eyes shot forth gleams. Presently he stood before her in the patio where the light fell on him. "Don't speak to me," he choked out waving his arms. "Don't speak to me! *Damn* your bread! I went to the Café Aguacate! Oh, yes, I went there! Of course, I did! And do you know what they did to me? No! Oh, they didn't do anything to me at all! Not a thing! Fifty dollars! Ten gold pieces!"

"May the saints guard us," cried Martha. "And what was that for?"

"Because they wanted them more than I did," snarled Johnnie. "Don't you see the game. I go into the Café Aguacate. The owner of the place says to himself, 'Hello! Here's that Yankee what they call Johnnie. He's got no right here in Havana. Guess I'll peach on him to the police. They'll put him in Cabanas as a spy.' Then he does a little more thinking, and finally he says, 'No; I guess I won't peach on him just this minute. First, I'll take a small flyer myself.' So in he comes and looks me right in the eye and says, 'Excuse me but it will be a centene for the bread, two centenes for the coffee, and eggs are at three centenes each. Besides there will be a small matter of another gold-piece for the waiter.' I think this over. I think it over hard. . . . He's clever anyhow. . . . When this cruel war is over I'll be after him. . . . I'm a nice secret agent of the United States government, I am. I come here to be too clever for all the Spanish police, and the first thing I do is get buncoed by a rotten little thimble-rigger in a café. Oh, yes, I'm all right."

"May the saints guard us!" cried Martha again. "I'm old

enough to be your mother, or maybe, your grandmother, and I've seen a lot; but it's many a year since I laid eyes on such a ign'rant and wrong-headed little red Indian as ye are! Why didn't ye take my advice and stay here in the house with decency and comfort. But he must be all for doing everything high and mighty. The Café Aguacate, if ye please. No plain food for His Highness. He turns up his nose at codfish sal——"

"Thunder and lightnin', are you going to ram that thing down my throat every two minutes, are you?" And in truth she could see that one more reference to that illustrious viand would break the back of Johnnie's gentle disposition as one breaks a twig on the knee. She shifted with Celtic ease. "Did ye bring the bread?" she asked.

He gazed at her for a moment and suddenly laughed. "I forgot to mention," he informed her impressively, "that they did not take the trouble to give me either the bread, the coffee or the eggs."

"The powers!" cried Martha.

"But it's all right. I stopped at a shop." From his pockets, he brought a small loaf, some kind of German sausage and a flask of Jamaica rum. "About all I could get. And they didn't want to sell them either. They expect presently they can exchange a box of sardines for a grand piano."

" 'We are not blockaded by the Yankee war-ships; we are blockaded by our grocers,' " said Martha, quoting the epidemic Havana saying. But she did not delay long from the little loaf. She cut a slice from it and sat eagerly munching. Johnnie seemed more interested in the Jamaica rum. He looked up from his second glass, however, because he heard a peculiar sound. The old woman was weeping. "Hey, what's this?" he demanded in distress, but with the manner of a man who thinks gruffness is the only thing that will make people feel better and cease. "What's this anyhow? What are you cryin' for?"

"It's the bread," sobbed Martha. "It's the—the br-e-a-d-d-d."

"Huh? What's the matter with it?"

"It's so good, so g-good." The rain of tears did not prevent her from continuing her unusual report. "Oh, it's so good!

This is the first in weeks. I didn't know bread could be so l-like heaven."

"Here," said Johnnie seriously. "Take a little mouthful of this rum. It will do you good."

"No; I only want the bub-bub-bread."

"Well, take the bread, too. . . . There you are. Now you feel better. . . . By jiminy, when I think of that Café Aguacate man! Fifty dollars gold! And then not to get anything either. Say, after the war I'm going there and I'm just going to raze that place to the ground. You see! I'll make him think he can charge ME fifteen dollars for an egg. . . . And then not give me the egg!"

III

Johnnie's subsequent activity in Havana could truthfully be related in part to a certain temporary price of eggs. It is interesting to note how close that famous event got to his eye so that, according to the law of perspective, it was as big as the Capitol at Washington, where centres the spirit of his nation. Around him he felt a similar and ferocious expression of life which informed him too plainly that if he was caught he was doomed. Neither the garrison nor the citizens of Havana would tolerate any nonsense in regard to him if he was caught. He would have the steel screw against his neck in short order. And what was the main thing to bear him up against the desire to run away before his work was done? A certain temporary price of eggs! It not only hid the Capitol at Washington; it obscured the dangers in Havana.

Something was learned of the Santa Clara battery because one morning an old lady in black accompanied by a young man—evidently her son—visited a house which was to rent on the height, in rear of the battery. The portero was too lazy and sleepy to show them over the premises, but he granted them permission to investigate for themselves. They spent most of their time on the flat parapeted roof of the house. At length they came down and said that the place did not suit them. The portero went to sleep again.

Johnnie was never discouraged by the thought that his operations would be of small benefit to the admiral com-

manding the fleet in adjacent waters and to the general com-
manding the army which was not going to attack Havana
from the land side. At that time it was all the world's opinion
that the army from Tampa would presently appear on the Cu-
ban beach at some convenient point to the east or west of
Havana. It turned out, of course, that the condition of the
defences of Havana was of not the sligthest military impor-
tance to the United States since the city was never attacked
either by land or sea. But Johnnie could not foresee this. He
continued to take his fancy risk, continued his majestic lie,
with satisfaction, sometimes with delight, and with pride.
And in the psychologic distance was old Martha dancing with
fear and shouting: "Oh, Johnnie, me son, what a born fool
ye are!"

Sometimes she would address him thus: "And when ye
learn all this, how are ye goin' to get out with it?" She was
contemptuous.

He would reply, as serious as a Cossack in his fatalism.
"Oh, I'll get out some way."

His manœuvres in the vicinity of Regla and Guanabacoa
were of a brilliant character. He haunted the sunny long grass
in the manner of a jack-rabbit. Sometimes he slept under a
palm, dreaming of the American advance fighting its way
along the military road to the foot of the Spanish defences.
Even when awake he often dreamed it and thought of the all-
day crash and hot roar of an assault. Without consulting
Washington, he had decided that Havana should be attacked
from the south-east. An advance from the west could be con-
tested right up to the bar of the Hotel Inglaterra, but when
the first ridge in the south-east would be taken the whole city
with most of its defences would lie under the American siege
guns. And the approach to this position was as reasonable as
is any approach toward the muzzles of magazine rifles. John-
nie viewed the grassy fields always as a prospective battle-
ground, and one can see him lying there, filling the landscape
with visions of slow-crawling black infantry columns, gallop-
ing batteries of artillery, streaks of faint blue smoke marking
the modern firing lines, clouds of dust, a vision of ten thou-
sand tragedies. And his ears heard the noises——

But he was no idle shepherd boy with a head haunted by

sombre and glorious fancies. On the contrary, he was much occupied with practical matters. Some months after the close of the war, he asked me: "Were you ever fired at from very near?" I explained some experiences which I had stupidly esteemed as having been rather near. "But did you ever have 'm fire a volley on you from close—very close—say thirty feet?"

Highly scandalized I answered, "No; in that case, I would not be the crowning feature of the Smithsonian Institute."

"Well," he said, "it's a funny effect. You feel as if every hair on your head had been snatched out by the roots." Questioned further he said: "I walked right up on a Spanish outpost at daybreak once, and about twenty men let go at me. Thought I was a Cuban army, I suppose."

"What did you do?"

"I run."

"Did they hit you, at all?"

"Naw."

It had been arranged that some light ship of the squadron should rendezvous with him at a certain lonely spot on the coast on a certain day and hour and pick him up. He was to wave something white. His shirt was not white, but he waved it whenever he could see the signal-tops of a war-ship. It was a very tattered banner. After a ten-mile scramble through almost pathless thickets, he had very little on him which respectable men would call a shirt, and the less one says about his trousers the better. This naked savage then walked all day up and down a small bit of beach waving a brown rag. At night he slept in the sand. At full daybreak he began to wave his rag; at noon he was waving his rag; at nightfall he donned his rag and strove to think of it as a shirt. Thus passed two days and nothing had happened. Then he retraced a twenty-five mile way to the house of old Martha. At first she took him to be one of Havana's terrible beggars and cried, "And do you come here for alms? Look out that I do not beg of you." The one unchanged thing was his laugh of pure mockery. When she heard it she dragged him through the door. He paid no heed to her ejaculations but went straight to where he had hidden some gold. As he was untying a bit of string from the neck of a small bag, he said, "How is little Alfred?" "Recovered, thank Heaven." He handed Martha a piece of gold. "Take this and buy what you can on the corner. I'm hungry." Martha departed with expedition. Upon her return she was beaming. She had foraged a thin chicken, a bunch of radishes and two bottles of wine. Johnnie had finished the radishes and one bottle of wine when the chicken was still a long way from the table. He called stoutly for more, and so Martha passed again into the street with another gold piece. She bought more radishes, more wine and some cheese. They had a grand feast, with Johnnie audibly wondering until a late hour why he had waved his rag in vain.

There was no end to his suspense, no end to his work. He knew everything. He was an animate guide-book. After he knew a thing once, he verified it in several different ways in order to make sure. He fitted himself for a useful career, like a young man in a college—with the difference that the shadow of the garrote fell ever upon his way, and that he was occasionally shot at, and that he could not get enough to eat, and that his existence was apparently forgotten, and that he contracted the fever. But——

One cannot think of the terms in which to describe a futility so vast, so colossal. He had builded a little boat, and the sea had receded and left him and his boat a thousand miles inland on the top of a mountain. The war-fate had left Havana out of its plan and thus isolated Johnnie and his several pounds of useful information. The war-fate left Havana to become the somewhat indignant victim of a peaceful occupation at the close of the conflict, and Johnnie's data was worth as much as a carpenter's lien on the North Pole. He had suffered and labored for about as complete a bit of absolute nothing as one could invent. If the company which owned the sugar plantation had not generously continued his salary during the war he would not have been able to pay his expenses on the amount allowed him by the government, which, by the way, was a more complete bit of absolute nothing than one could possibly invent.

IV

I met Johnnie in Havana in October, 1898. If I remember rightly the U.S.S. *Resolute* and the U.S.S. *Scorpion* were in the harbor, but beyond these two terrible engines of destruction there was not as yet any of the more stern signs of the American success. Many Americans were to be seen in the streets of Havana where they were not in any way molested. Among them was Johnnie in white duck and a straw hat, cool, complacent and with eyes rather more steady than ever. I addressed him upon the subject of his supreme failure, but I could not perturb his philosophy. In reply he simply asked me to dinner. "Come to the Café Aguacate at half-past seven to-night," he said. "I haven't been there in a long time. We shall see if they cook as well as ever." I turned up promptly and found Johnnie in a private room smoking a cigar in the presence of a waiter who was blue in the gills. "I've ordered the dinner," he said cheerfully. "Now I want to see if you won't be surprised how well they can do here in Havana." I was surprised. I was dumfounded. Rarely in the history of the world have two rational men sat down to such a dinner. It must have taxed the ability and endurance of the entire working force of the establishment to provide it. The variety of dishes was of course related to the markets of Havana, but the abundance and general profligacy was related only to Johnnie's imagination. Neither of us had an appetite. Our fancies fled in confusion before this puzzling luxury. I looked at Johnnie as if he were a native of Thibet. I had thought him to be a most simple man, and here I found him revelling in food like a fat old senator of Rome's decadence. And if the dinner itself put me to open-eyed amazement, the names of the wines finished everything. Apparently Johnnie had had but one standard, and that was the cost. If a wine had been very expensive, he had ordered it. I began to think him probably a maniac. At any rate, I was sure that we were both fools. Seeing my fixed stare, he spoke with affected languor: "I wish peacocks' brains and melted pearls were to be had here in Havana. We'd have 'em." Then he grinned. As a mere skirmisher I said: "In New York we think we dine well; but really this, you know—well—Havana——"

Johnnie waved his hand pompously. "Oh, I know."

Directly after coffee Johnnie excused himself for a moment and left the room. When he returned he said briskly, "Well, are you ready to go?" As soon as we were in a cab and safely out of hearing of the Café Aguacate Johnnie lay back and laughed long and joyously.

But I was very serious. "Look here, Johnnie," I said to him solemnly, "when you invite me to dine with you don't you ever do *that* again. And I'll tell you one thing—when you dine with me you will probably get the ordinary table d'hôte." I was an older man.

"Oh, that's all right," he cried. And then he too grew serious. "Well, as far as I am concerned—as far as I am concerned," he said, "the war is now over."

WHILOMVILLE

Contents

His New Mittens

I

LITTLE HORACE was walking home from school, brilliantly decorated by a pair of new red mittens. A number of boys were snow-balling gleefully in a field. They hailed him. "Come on, Horace. We're having a battle."

Horace was sad. "No," he said, "I can't. I've got to go home." At noon his mother had admonished him. "Now, Horace, you come straight home as soon as school is out. Do you hear? And don't you get them nice new mittens all wet, either. Do you hear?" Also his aunt had said: "I declare, Emily, it's a shame the way you allow that child to ruin his things." She had meant mittens. To his mother, Horace had dutifully replied: "Yes'm." But he now loitered in the vicinity of the group of uproarious boys, who were yelling like hawks as the white balls flew.

Some of them immediately analyzed this extraordinary hesitancy. "Hah!" they paused to scoff, "afraid of your new mittens, ain't you?" Some smaller boys, who were not yet so wise in discerning motives, applauded this attack with unreasonable vehemence. "A-fray-ed of his mit-tens! A-fray-ed of his mit-tens!" They sang these lines to cruel and monotonous music which is as old perhaps as American childhood and which it is the privilege of the emancipated adult to completely forget. "A-fray-ed of his mit-tens!"

Horace cast a tortured glance toward his playmates, and then dropped his eyes to the snow at his feet. Presently he turned to the trunk of one of the great maple trees that lined the kerb. He made a pretense of closely examining the rough and virile bark. To his mind this familiar street of Whilomville seemed to grow dark in the thick shadow of shame. The trees and the houses were now palled in purple.

"A-fray-ed of his mit-tens!" The terrible music had in it a meaning from the moonlit war-drums of chanting cannibals.

At last Horace, with supreme effort, raised his head. " 'Tain't them I care about," he said gruffly. "I've got to go home. That's all."

Whereupon each boy held his left forefinger as if it were a pencil and began to sharpen it derisively with his right forefinger. They came closer, and sang like a trained chorus, "A-fray-ed of his mittens!"

When he raised his voice to deny the charge it was simply lost in the screams of the mob. He was alone fronting all the traditions of boyhood held before him by inexorable representatives. To such a low state had he fallen that one lad, a mere baby, outflanked him and then struck him in the cheek with a heavy snow-ball. The act was acclaimed with loud jeers. Horace turned to dart at his assailant, but there was an immediate demonstration on the other flank, and he found himself obliged to keep his face toward the hilarious crew of tormentors. The baby retreated in safety to the rear of the crowd, where he was received with fulsome compliments upon his daring. Horace retreated slowly up the walk. He continually tried to make them heed him, but the only sound was the chant, "A-fray-ed of his mit-tens!" In this desperate withdrawal the beset and haggard boy suffered more than is the common lot of man.

Being a boy himself, he did not understand boys at all. He had of course the dismal conviction that they were going to dog him to his grave. But near the corner of the field they suddenly seemed to forget all about it. Indeed, they possessed only the malevolence of so many flitter-headed sparrows. The interest had swung capriciously to some other matter. In a moment they were off in the field again, carousing amid the snow. Some authoritative boy had probably said, "Aw, come on."

As the pursuit ceased, Horace ceased his retreat. He spent some time in what was evidently an attempt to adjust his self-respect, and then began to wander furtively down toward the group. He, too, had undergone an important change. Perhaps his sharp agony was only as durable as the malevolence of the others. In this boyish life obedience to some unformulated creed of manners was enforced with capricious but merciless rigor. However, they were, after all, his comrades, his friends.

They did not heed his return. They were engaged in an altercation. It had evidently been planned that this battle was between Indians and soldiers. The smaller and weaker boys had been induced to appear as Indians in the initial skirmish, but they were now very sick of it, and were reluctantly but steadfastly affirming their desire for a change of caste. The larger boys had all won great distinction, devastating Indians materially, and they wished the war to go on as planned. They explained vociferously that it was proper for the soldiers always to thrash the Indians. The little boys did not pretend to deny the truth of this argument; they confined themselves to the simple statement that, in that case, they wished to be soldiers. Each little boy willingly appealed to the others to remain Indians, but as for himself he reiterated his desire to enlist as a soldier. The larger boys were in despair over this dearth of enthusiasm in the small Indians. They alternately wheedled and bullied, but they could not persuade the little boys, who were really suffering dreadful humiliation rather than submit to another onslaught of soldiers. They were called all the baby names that had the power of stinging deep into their pride, but they remained firm.

Then a formidable lad, a leader of reputation, one who could whip many boys that wore long trousers, suddenly blew out his cheeks and shouted, "Well, all right then. I'll be an Indian myself. Now." The little boys greeted with cheers this addition to their wearied ranks, and seemed then content. But matters were not mended in the least, because all of the personal following of the formidable lad, with the addition of every outsider, spontaneously forsook the flag and declared themselves Indians. There were now no soldiers. The Indians had carried everything unanimously. The formidable lad used his influence, but his influence could not shake the loyalty of his friends, who refused to fight under any colors but his colors.

Plainly there was nothing for it but to coerce the little ones. The formidable lad again became a soldier, and then graciously permitted to join him all the real fighting strength of the crowd, leaving behind a most forlorn band of little Indians. Then the soldiers attacked the Indians, exhorting them to opposition at the same time.

The Indians at first adopted a policy of hurried surrender, but this had no success as none of the surrenders were accepted. They then turned to flee, bawling out protests. The ferocious soldiers pursued them amid shouts. The battle widened, developing all manner of marvelous detail.

Horace had turned toward home several times, but as a matter of fact this scene held him in a spell. It was fascinating beyond anything which the grown man understands. He had always in the back of his head a sense of guilt, even a sense of impending punishment for disobedience, but they could not weigh with the delirium of this snow battle.

II

One of the raiding soldiers, espying Horace, called out in passing, "A-fray-ed of his mit-tens!" Horace flinched at this renewal, and the other lad paused to taunt him again. Horace scooped some snow, molded it into a ball, and flung it at the other. "Ho," cried the boy, "you're an Indian, are you? Hey, fellers, here's an Indian that ain't been killed yet." He and Horace engaged in a duel in which both were in such haste to mold snow-balls that they had little time for aiming.

Horace once struck his opponent squarely in the chest. "Hey," he shouted, "you're dead. You can't fight any more, Pete. I killed you. You're dead."

The other boy flushed red, but he continued frantically to make ammunition. "You never touched me," he retorted glowering. "You never touched me. Where, now?" he added defiantly. "Where'd you hit me?"

"On the coat! Right on your breast. You can't fight any more. You're dead."

"You never!"

"I did, too. Hey, fellers, ain't he dead? I hit 'im square."

"He never!"

Nobody had seen the affair, but some of the boys took sides in absolute accordance with their friendship for one of the concerned parties. Horace's opponent went about contending, "He never touched me. He never came near me. He never came near me."

The formidable leader now came forward and accosted Horace. "What was you? An Indian? Well, then, you're dead—that's all. He hit you. I saw him."

"Me?" shrieked Horace. "He never came within a mile of me——"

At that moment he heard his name called in a certain familiar tune of two notes, with the last note shrill and prolonged. He looked toward the sidewalk and saw his mother standing there in her widow's weeds, with two brown paper parcels under her arm. A silence had fallen upon all the boys. Horace moved slowly toward his mother. She did not seem to note his approach; she was gazing austerely off through the naked branches of the maples where two crimson sunset bars lay on the deep blue sky.

At a distance of ten paces Horace made a desperate venture. "Oh, ma," he whined, "can't I stay out for a while?"

"No," she answered solemnly, "you come with me." Horace knew that profile; it was the inexorable profile. But he continued to plead, because it was not beyond his mind that a great show of suffering now might diminish his suffering later.

He did not dare to look back at his playmates. It was already a public scandal that he could not stay out as late as other boys and he could imagine his standing now that he had been again dragged off by his mother in sight of the whole world. He was a profoundly miserable human being.

Aunt Martha opened the door for them. Light streamed about her straight skirt. "Oh," she said, "so you found him on the road, eh? Well, I declare! It was about time!"

Horace slunk into the kitchen. The stove, spraddling out on its four iron legs, was gently humming. Aunt Martha had evidently just lighted the lamp, for she went to it and began to twist the wick experimentally.

"Now," said the mother, "let's see them mittens."

Horace's chin sank. The aspiration of the criminal, the passionate desire for an asylum from retribution, from justice, was aflame in his heart. "I—I—don't—don't know where they are," he gasped finally as he passed his hands over his pockets.

"Horace," intoned his mother, "you are telling me a story!"

" 'Tain't a story," he answered just above his breath. He looked like a sheep-stealer.

His mother held him by the arm, and began to search his

pockets. Almost at once she was able to bring forth a pair of very wet mittens. "Well, I declare!" cried Aunt Martha. The two women went close to the lamp and minutely examined the mittens, turning them over and over. Afterward, when Horace looked up, his mother's sad-lined, homely face was turned toward him. He burst into tears.

His mother drew a chair near the stove. "Just you sit there now, until I tell you to git off." He sidled meekly into the chair. His mother and his aunt went briskly about the business of preparing supper. They did not display a knowledge of his existence; they carried an effect of oblivion so far that they even did not speak to each other. Presently, they went into the dining and living room; Horace could hear the dishes rattling. His Aunt Martha brought a plate of food, placed it on a chair near him, and went away without a word.

Horace instantly decided that he would not touch a morsel of the food. He had often used this ruse in dealing with his mother. He did not know why it brought her to terms, but certainly it sometimes did.

The mother looked up when the aunt returned to the other room. "Is he eatin' his supper?" she asked.

The maiden aunt, fortified in ignorance, gazed with pity and contempt upon this interest. "Well, now, Emily, how do I know?" she queried. "Was I goin' to stand over 'im? Of all the worryin' you do about that child! It's a shame the way you're bringing up that child."

"Well, he ought to eat something. It won't do fer him to go without eatin'," the mother retorted weakly.

Aunt Martha, profoundly scorning the policy of concession which these words meant, uttered a long contemptuous sigh.

III

Alone in the kitchen, Horace stared with sombre eyes at the plate of food. For a long time he betrayed no sign of yielding. His mood was adamantine. He was resolved not to sell his vengeance for bread, cold ham, and a pickle, and yet it must be known that the sight of them affected him powerfully. The pickle in particular was notable for its seductive charm. He surveyed it darkly.

But at last unable to longer endure his state, his attitude in the presence of the pickle, he put out an inquisitive finger and touched it, and it was cool and green and plump. Then a full conception of the cruel woe of his situation swept upon him suddenly and his eyes filled with tears which began to move down his cheeks. He sniffled. His heart was black with hatred. He painted in his mind scenes of deadly retribution. His mother would be taught that he was not one to endure persecution meekly, without raising an arm in his defense. And so his dreams were of a slaughter of feelings, and near the end of them his mother was pictured as coming, bowed with pain, to his feet. Weeping, she implored his charity. Would he forgive her? No; his once tender heart had been turned to stone by her injustice. He could not forgive her. She must pay the inexorable penalty.

The first item in this horrible plan was the refusal of the food. This he knew by experience would work havoc in his mother's heart. And so he grimly waited.

But suddenly it occurred to him that the first part of his revenge was in danger of failing. The thought struck him that his mother might not capitulate in the usual way. According to his recollection, the time was more than due when she should come in, worried, sadly affectionate, and ask him if he was ill. It had then been his custom to hint in a resigned voice that he was the victim of secret disease, but that he preferred to suffer in silence and alone. If she was obdurate in her anxiety, he always asked her in a gloomy, low voice to go away and leave him to suffer in silence and alone in the darkness without food. He had known this manœuvering to result even in pie.

But what was the meaning of the long pause and the stillness? Had his old and valued ruse betrayed him? As the truth sank into his mind, he supremely loathed life, the world, his mother. Her heart was beating back the besiegers; he was a defeated child.

He wept for a time before deciding upon the final stroke. He would run away. In a remote corner of the world he would become some sort of bloody-handed person driven to a life of crime by the barbarity of his mother. She should never know his fate. He would torture her for years with doubts and doubts and drive her implacably to a repentant grave. Nor would his Aunt Martha escape. Some day, a century hence, when his mother was dead, he would write to his Aunt Martha and point out her part in the blighting of his life. For one blow against him now he would in time deal back a thousand; aye, ten thousand.

He arose and took his coat and cap. As he moved stealthily toward the door he cast a glance backward at the pickle. He was tempted to take it, but he knew if he left the plate inviolate his mother would feel even worse.

A blue snow was falling. People bowed forward were moving briskly along the walks. The electric lamps hummed amid showers of flakes. As Horace emerged from the kitchen a shrill squall drove the flakes around the corner of the house. He cowered away from it, and its violence illumed his mind vaguely in new directions. He deliberated upon a choice of remote corners of the globe. He found that he had no plans which were definite enough in a geographical way, but without much loss of time he decided upon California. He moved briskly as far as his mother's front gate on the road to California. He was off at last. His success was a trifle dreadful; his throat choked.

But at the gate he paused. He did not know if his journey to California would be shorter if he went down Niagara Avenue or off through Hogan Street. As the storm was very cold and the point was very important, he decided to withdraw for reflection to the wood-shed. He entered the dark shanty and took seat upon the old chopping-block upon which he was supposed to perform for a few minutes every afternoon when he returned from school. The wind screamed and shouted at the loose boards, and there was a rift of snow on the floor to leeward of a crack.

Here the idea of starting for California on such a night departed from his mind, leaving him ruminating miserably upon his martyrdom. He saw nothing for it but to sleep all night in the wood-shed and start for California in the morning bright and early. Thinking of his bed, he kicked over the floor and found that the innumerable chips were all frozen tightly, bedded in ice.

Later he viewed with joy some signs of excitement in the

house. The flare of a lamp moved rapidly from window to window. Then the kitchen door slammed loudly and a shawled figure sped toward the gate. At last he was making them feel his power. The shivering child's face was lit with saturnine glee as in the darkness of the wood-shed he gloated over the evidences of consternation in his home. The shawled figure had been his Aunt Martha dashing with the alarm to the neighbors.

The cold of the wood-shed was tormenting him. He endured only because of the terror he was causing. But then it occurred to him that, if they instituted a search for him they would probably examine the wood-shed. He knew that it would not be manful to be caught so soon. He was not positive now that he was going to remain away forever, but at any rate he was bound to inflict some more damage before allowing himself to be captured. If he merely succeeded in making his mother angry, she would thrash him on sight. He must prolong the time in order to be safe. If he held out properly, he was sure of a welcome of love, even though he should drip with crimes.

Evidently the storm had increased, for when he went out it swung him violently with its rough and merciless strength. Panting, stung, half-blinded with the driving flakes, he was now a waif, exiled, friendless, and poor. With a bursting heart, he thought of his home and his mother. To his forlorn vision they were as far away as Heaven.

IV

Horace was undergoing changes of feeling so rapidly that he was merely moved hither and then thither like a kite. He was now aghast at the merciless ferocity of his mother. It was she who had thrust him into this wild storm, and she was perfectly indifferent to his fate, perfectly indifferent. The forlorn wanderer could no longer weep. The strong sobs caught at his throat, making his breath come in short quick snuffles. All in him was conquered save the enigmatical childish ideal of form, manner. This principle still held out, and it was the only thing between him and submission. When he surrendered, he must surrender in a way that deferred to the undefined code. He longed simply to go to the kitchen and stumble in, but his unfathomable sense of fitness forbade him.

Presently he found himself at the head of Niagara Avenue, staring through the snow into the blazing windows of Stickney's butcher-shop. Stickney was the family butcher, not so much because of a superiority to other Whilomville butchers as because he lived next door and had been an intimate friend of the father of Horace. Rows of glowing pigs hung head downward back of the tables which bore huge pieces of red beef. Clumps of attenuated turkeys were suspended here and there. Stickney, hale and smiling, was bantering with a woman in a cloak, who, with a monster basket on her arm, was dickering for eight cents' worth of something. Horace watched them through a crusted pane. When the woman came out and passed him, he went toward the door. He touched the latch with his finger, but withdrew again suddenly to the sidewalk. Inside Stickney was whistling cheerily and assorting his knives.

Finally Horace went desperately forward, opened the door, and entered the shop. His head hung low. Stickney stopped whistling. "Hello, young man," he cried, " what brings you here?"

Horace halted, but said nothing. He swung one foot to and fro over the saw-dust floor.

Stickney had placed his two fat hands palms downward and wide apart on the table, in the attitude of a butcher facing a customer, but now he straightened.

"Here," he said, " what's wrong? What's wrong, kid?"

"Nothin'," answered Horace huskily. He labored for a moment with something in his throat, and afterward added, "O'ny—I've—I've run away, and——"

"Run away!" shouted Stickney. "Run away from what? Who?"

"From—home," answered Horace. "I don't like it there any more. I—" He had arranged an oration to win the sympathy of the butcher; he had prepared a table setting forth the merits of his case in the most logical fashion, but it was as if the wind had been knocked out of his mind. "I've run away. I——"

Stickney reached an enormous hand over the array of beef

and firmly grappled the emigrant. Then he swung himself to Horace's side. His face was stretched with laughter, and he playfully shook his prisoner. "Come—come—come. What dashed nonsense is this? Run away, hey? Run away?" Whereupon the child's long-tried spirit found vent in howls.

"Come, come," said Stickney busily. "Never mind, now, never mind. You just come along with me. It'll be all right. I'll fix it. Never you mind."

Five minutes later the butcher, with a great ulster over his apron, was leading the boy homeward.

At the very threshold Horace raised his last flag of pride. "No—no," he sobbed. "I don't want to. I don't want to go in there." He braced his foot against the step, and made a very respectable resistance.

"Now, Horace," cried the butcher. He thrust open the door with a bang. "Hello there!" Across the dark kitchen the door to the living room opened and Aunt Martha appeared. "You've found him!" she screamed.

"We've come to make a call," roared the butcher.

At the entrance to the living room a silence fell upon them all. Upon a couch Horace saw his mother lying limp, pale as death, her eyes gleaming with pain. There was an electric pause before she swung a waxen hand toward Horace. "My child," she murmured tremulously. Whereupon the sinister person addressed, with a prolonged wail of grief and joy, ran to her with speed. "Ma—ma! Ma—ma! Oh, ma—ma!" She was not able to speak in a known tongue as she folded him in her weak arms.

Aunt Martha turned defiantly upon the butcher because her face betrayed her. She was crying. She made a gesture half military, half feminine. "Won't you have a glass of our root-beer, Mr. Stickney? We make it ourselves."

Lynx-Hunting

J IMMIE LOUNGED about the dining room and watched his mother with large serious eyes. Suddenly he said: "Ma— now—can I borrow Pa's gun?"

She was overcome with the feminine horror which is able to mistake preliminary words for the full accomplishment of the dread thing. "Why, Jimmie!" she cried. "Of al-l wonders! Your father's gun! No indeed you can't!"

He was fairly well-crushed but he managed to mutter sullenly: "Well, Willie Dalzel, he's got a gun." In reality his heart had previously been beating with such tumult—he had himself been so impressed with the daring and sin of his request—that he was glad all was over now and his mother could do very little further harm to his sensibilities. He had been influenced into the venture by the larger boys.

"Huh," the Dalzel urchin had said, "your father's got a gun, hasn't he? Well why don't you bring that?"

Puffing himself, Jimmie had replied: "Well, I can if I want to." It was a black lie but really the Dalzel boy was too outrageous with his eternal bill-posting about the gun which a beaming uncle had entrusted to him. Its possession made him superior in manfulness to most boys in the neighborhood— or at least they enviously conceded him such position—but he was so over-bearing and stuffed the fact of his treasure so relentlessly down their throats that on this occasion the miserable Jimmie had lied as naturally as most animals swim.

Willie Dalzel had not been checkmated for he had instantly retorted: "Why don't you get it, then?"

"Well, I can if I want to."

"Well, get it then."

"Well, I can if I want to."

Thereupon Jimmie had paced away with great airs of surety as far as the door of his home where his manner changed to one of tremulous misgiving as it came upon him to address his mother in the dining room. There had happened that which had happened.

When Jimmie returned to his two distinguished companions he was blown out with a singular pomposity. He spoke these noble words: "Oh, well. I guess I don't want to take the gun out to-day."

They had been watching him with gleaming ferret eyes and they detected his falsity at once. They challenged him with shouted jibes but it was not in the rules for the conduct of boys that one should admit anything whatsoever and so Jimmie, backed into an ethical corner, lied as stupidly, as desperately, as hopelessly as ever lone savage fights when surrounded at last in his jungle.

Such accusations were never known to come to any point for the reason that the number and kind of denials always equaled or exceeded the number of accusations and no boy was ever brought really to book for these misdeeds.

In the end they went off together, Willie Dalzel with his gun being a trifle in advance and discoursing upon his various works. They passed along a maple-lined avenue, a highway common to boys bound for that freeland of hills and woods in which they lived in some part their romance of the moment—whether it was of Indians, miners, smugglers, soldiers or outlaws. The paths were their paths and much was known to them of the secrets of the dark-green hemlock thickets, the wastes of sweet-fern and huckleberry, the cliffs of gaunt blue-stone with the sumach burning red at their feet. Each boy had, I am sure, a conviction that some day the wilderness was to give forth to them a marvelous secret. They felt that the hills and the forest knew much and they heard a voice of it in the silence. It was vague, thrilling, fearful and altogether fabulous. The grown folk seemed to regard these wastes merely as so much distance between one place and another place or as rabbit cover, or as a district to be judged according to the value of the timber; but to the boys it spoke some great inspiriting word which they knew even as those who pace the shore know the enigmatic speech of the surf.

In the meantime, they lived there, in season, lives of ringing adventure—by dint of imagination.

The boys left the avenue, skirted hastily through some private grounds, climbed a fence and entered the thickets. It happened that at school the previous day Willie Dalzel had been forced to read and acquire in some part a solemn description of a lynx. The meagre information thrust upon him had caused him grimaces of suffering but now he said suddenly: "I'm goin' to shoot a lynx."

The other boys admired this statement but they were silent for a time. Finally Jimmie said meekly: "What's a lynx?" He had endured his ignorance as long as he was able.

The Dalzel boy mocked him. "Why, don't you know what a lynx is? A lynx? Why, a lynx is an animal somethin' like a cat, an' it's got great big green eyes and it sits on the limb of a tree an' jus' glares at you. It's a pretty bad animal, I tell you. Why, when I—"

"Huh," said the third boy; "where'd you ever see a lynx?"

"Oh, I've seen 'em. Plenty of 'em. I bet you'd be scared if you seen one once."

Jimmie and the other boy each demanded: "How do you know I would?"

They penetrated deeper into the woods. They climbed a rocky zig-zag path which led them at times where with their hands they could almost touch the tops of giant pines. The grey cliffs sprang sheer toward the sky. Willie Dalzel babbled about his impossible lynx and they stalked the mountain side like chamois-hunters although no noise of bird or beast broke the stillness of the hills. Below them, Whilomville was spread out somewhat like the cheap green and black lithograph of the time—"A Bird's Eye View of Whilomville, N.Y."

In the end, the boys reached the top of the mountain and scouted off among wild and desolate ridges. They were burning with the desire to slay large animals. They thought continually of elephants, lions, tigers, crocodiles. They discoursed upon their immaculate conduct in case such monsters confronted them and they all lied carefully about their courage.

The breeze was heavy with the smell of sweet-fern. The pines and hemlocks sighed as they waved their branches. In the hollows the leaves of the laurels were lacquered where the sun-light found them. No matter the weather, it would be impossible to long continue an expedition of this kind without a fire and presently they built one, snapping down for fuel the brittle under-branches of the pines. About this fire they were willed to conduct a sort of a play, the Dalzel boy taking the part of a bandit chief and the other boys being his trusty lieutenants. They stalked to and fro, long-strided, stern yet devil-may-care, three terrible little figures.

Jimmie had an uncle who made game of him whenever he caught him in this kind of play and often quoted derisively the following classic: "Once aboard the lugger, Bill, and the girl is mine. Now to burn the chateau and destroy all evidence of our crime. But, hark'e, Bill, no wiolence." Wheeling abruptly, he addressed these dramatic words to his comrades. They were impressed; they decided at once to be smugglers and in the most ribald fashion they talked about carrying off young women.

At last they continued their march through the woods. The smuggling motif was now grafted fantastically upon the original lynx idea which Willie Dalzel refused to abandon at any price.

Once they came upon an innocent bird who happened to be looking another way at the time. After a great deal of manoeuvring and big words, Willie Dalzel reared his fowling-piece and blew this poor thing into a mere rag of wet feathers. Of which he was proud.

Afterward the other big boy had a turn at another bird. Then it was plainly Jimmie's chance. The two others had of course some thought of cheating him out of this chance but, of a truth, he was timid to explode such a thunderous weapon and, as soon as they detected this fear, they simply over-bore him and made it clearly understood that if he refused to shoot he would lose his caste, his scalp-lock, his girdle, his honor.

They had reached the old death-colored snake-fence which marked the limits of the upper pasture of the Fleming farm. Under some hickory trees the path ran parallel to the fence. Behold, a small priestly chip-munk came to a rail and folding his hands on his abdomen addressed them in his own tongue. It was Jimmie's shot. Adjured by the others, he took the gun. His face was stiff with apprehension. The Dalzel boy was giving forth fine words. "Go ahead. Aw, don't be afraid. It's nothin' to do. Why, I've done it a million times. Don't shut both your eyes, now. Jus' keep one open and shut the other one. He'll get away if you don't watch out. Now you're all right. Why don't you let 'er go? Go ahead."

Jimmie with his legs braced apart was in the centre of the

path. His back was greatly bent owing to the mechanics of supporting the heavy gun. His companions were screeching in the rear. There was a wait.

Then he pulled trigger. To him, there was a frightful roar, his cheek and his shoulder took a stunning blow, his face felt a hot flush of fire and, opening his two eyes, he found that he was still alive. He was not too dazed to instantly adopt a becoming egotism. It had been the first shot of his life.

But directly after the well-mannered celebration of this victory, a certain cow which had been grazing in the line of fire was seen to break wildly across the pasture bellowing and bucking. The three smugglers and lynx-hunters looked at each other out of blanched faces. Jimmie had hit the cow. The first evidence of his comprehension of this fact was in the celerity with which he returned the discharged gun to Willie Dalzel.

They turned to flee; the land was black, as if it had been over-shadowed suddenly with thick storm-clouds; and even as they fled in their horror, a gigantic Swedish farm-hand came from the heavens and fell upon them, shrieking in eerie triumph. In a twinkle they were clouted prostrate. The Swede was elate and ferocious in a foreign and fulsome way. He continued to beat them and yell.

From the ground, they raised their dismal appeal. "Oh, please, mister, we didn't do it. He did it. I didn't do it. We didn't do it. We didn't mean to do it. Oh, please, mister."

In these moments of childish terror, little lads go half-blind and it is possible that few moments of their after-life made them suffer as they did when the Swede flung them over the fence and marched them toward the farm-house. They begged like cowards on the scaffold and each one was for himself. "Oh, please let me go, mister. I didn't do it, mister. He did it. Oh, p-l-ease let me go, mister."

The boyish view belongs to boys alone and if this tall and knotted laborer was needlessly without charity, none of the three lads questioned it. Usually when they were punished they decided that they deserved it and the more they were punished the more they were convinced that they were criminals of a most subterranean type. As to the hitting of the cow being a pure accident and therefore not of necessity a criminal matter, such reading never entered their heads. When things happened and they were caught, they commonly paid dire consequences and they were accustomed to measure the probabilities of woe utterly by the damage done and not in any way by the culpability. The shooting of a cow was plainly heinous and undoubtedly their dungeons would be knee-deep in water.

"He did it, mister!" This was a general outcry. Jimmie used it as often as did the others. As for them, it is certain that they had no direct thought of betraying their comrade for their own salvation. They thought themselves guilty because they were caught; when boys were not caught they might possibly be innocent. But captured boys were guilty. When they cried out that Jimmie was the culprit, it was, principally, a simple expression of terror.

Old Henry Fleming, the owner of the farm, strode across the pasture toward them. He had in his hand a most cruel whip. This whip he flourished. At his approach the boys suffered the agonies of the fire-regions. And yet anybody with half an eye could see that the whip in his hand was a mere accident and that he was a kind old man when he cared.

When he had come near he spoke crisply. "What you boys ben doin' to my cow?" The tone had deep threat in it. They all answered by saying that none of them had shot the cow. Their denials were tearful and clamorous and they crawled knee by knee. The vision of it was like three martyrs being dragged toward the stake. Old Fleming stood there, grim, tight-lipped. After a time, he said: "Which boy done it?"

There was some confusion and then Jimmie spake. "I done it, mister."

Fleming looked at him. Then he asked: "Well, what did you shoot 'er fer?"

Jimmie thought, hesitated, decided, faltered, and then formulated this: "I thought she was a lynx."

Old Fleming and his Swede at once lay down in the grass and laughed themselves helpless.

The Angel-Child

I

ALTHOUGH WHILOMVILLE was in no sense a summer resort, the advent of the warm season meant much to it for then came visitors from the city—people of considerable confidence—alighting upon their country cousins. Moreover, many citizens who could afford to do so escaped at this time to the seaside. The town, with the commercial life quite taken out of it, drawled and drowsed through long months during which nothing was worse than the white dust which arose behind every vehicle at blinding noon and nothing was finer than the cool sheen of the hose-sprays over the cropped lawns under the many maples in the twilight.

One summer, the Trescotts had a visitation. Mrs. Trescott owned a cousin who was a painter of high degree. I had almost said that he was of national reputation but—come to think of it—it is better to say that almost everybody in the United States who knew about art and its travail, knew about him. He had picked out a wife and naturally, looking at him, one wondered how he had done it. She was quick, beautiful, imperious while he was quiet, slow and misty. She was a veritable queen of health while he apparently was of a most brittle constitution. When he played tennis—particularly—he looked every minute as if he were going to break.

They lived in New York in awesome apartments wherein Japan and Persia and, indeed, all the world, confounded the observer. At the end, was a cathedral-like studio. They had one child. Perhaps it would be better to say that they had one CHILD. It was a girl. When she came to Whilomville with her parents it was patent that she had an inexhaustible store of white frocks and that her voice was high and commanding. These things the town knew quickly. Other things it was doomed to discover by a process.

Her effect upon the children of the Trescott neighborhood was singular. They at first feared, then admired, then embraced; in two days she was a Begum. All day long her voice could be heard directing, drilling, and compelling those free-born children, and to say that they felt oppression would be wrong, for they really fought for records of loyal obedience.

All went well until one day was her birthday.

On the morning of this day she walked out into the Trescott garden and said to her father confidently: "Papa, give me some money because this is my birthday."

He looked dreamily up from his easel. "Your birthday?" he murmured. Her envisioned father was never energetic enough to be irritable unless some one broke through into that place where he lived with the desires of his life. But neither wife nor child ever heeded or even understood the temperamental values and so some part of him had grown hardened to their inroads. "Money?" he said. "Here." He handed her a five-dollar bill. It was that he did not at all understand the nature of a five-dollar bill. He was deaf to it. He had it; he gave it; that was all.

She sallied forth to a waiting people—Jimmie Trescott, Dan Earl, Ella Earl, the Margate twins, the three Phelps children and others. "I've got some pennies now," she cried waving the bill, "and I am going to buy some candy." They were deeply stirred by this announcement. Most children are penniless three hundred days in the year and to another possessing five pennies they pay deference. To little Cora, waving a bright green note, these children paid heathenish homage. In some disorder they thronged after her to a small shop on Bridge Street hill. First of all, came ice-cream. Seated in the comic little back parlor, they clamored shrilly over plates of various flavors and the shop-keeper marveled that cream could vanish so quickly down throats that seemed wide open, always, for the making of excited screams.

These children represented the families of most excellent people. They were all born in whatever purple there was to be had in the vicinity of Whilomville. The Margate twins, for example, were out-and-out prize-winners. With their long golden curls and their countenances of similar vacuity, they shone upon the front bench of all Sunday-School functions, hand in hand, while their uplifted mother felt about her the envy of a hundred other parents, and less heavenly children scoffed from near the door.

Then there was little Dan Earl, probably the nicest boy in

the world, gentle, fine-grained, obedient to the point where he obeyed anybody. Jimmie Trescott himself was indeed the only child who was at all versed in villainy, but in these particular days he was on his very good behavior. As a matter of fact, he was in love. The beauty of his regal little cousin had stolen his manly heart.

Yes, they were all most excellent children, but loosened upon this candy-shop with five dollars, they resembled, in a tiny way, drunken revelling soldiers within the walls of a stormed city. Upon the heels of ice-cream and cake came chocolate mice, butter-scotch, "ever-lastings," chocolate cigars, taffy-on-a-stick, taffy-on-a-slate-pencil, and many semi-transparent devices resembling lions, tigers, elephants, horses, cats, dogs, cows, sheep, tables, chairs, engines (both railway and for the fighting of fire), soldiers, fine ladies, odd-looking men, clocks, watches, revolvers, rabbits and bedsteads. A cent was the price of a single wonder.

Some of the children, going quite daft, soon had thought to make fight over the spoils but their queen ruled with an iron grip. Her first inspiration was to satisfy her own fancies but as soon as that was done, she mingled prodigality with a fine justice, dividing, balancing, bestowing and sometimes taking away from somebody even that which he had.

It was an orgy. In thirty-five minutes those respectable children looked as if they had been dragged at the tail of a chariot. The sacred Margate twins, blinking and grunting, wished to take seat upon the floor and even the most durable Jimmie Trescott found occasion to lean against the counter, wearing at the time a solemn and abstracted air as if he expected something to happen to him shortly.

Of course, their belief had been in an unlimited capacity but they found there was an end. The shop-keeper handed the queen her change.

"Two-seventy-three from five leaves two-twenty-seven, Miss Cora," he said looking upon her with admiration.

She turned swiftly to her clan. "O-oh," she cried in amazement. "Look how much I have left!" They gazed at the coins in her palm. They knew then that it was not their capacities which were endless; it was the five dollars.

The queen led the way to the street. "We must think up

some way of spending more money," she said frowning. They stood in silence awaiting her further speech.

Suddenly she clapped her hands and screamed with delight. "Come on," she cried, "I know what let's do!" Now, behold, she had discovered the red and white pole in front of the shop of one William Neeltje, a barber by trade.

It becomes necessary to say a few words concerning Neeltje. He was new to the town. He had come and opened a dusty little shop on dusty Bridge Street hill and although the neighborhood knew from the courier winds that his diet was mainly cabbage, they were satisfied with that meagre data. Of course, Reifsnyder came to investigate him for the local Barbers' Union, but he found in him only sweetness and light, with a willingness to charge any price at all for a shave or a hair-cut. In fact the advent of Neeltje would have made barely a ripple upon the placid bosom of Whilomville if it were not that his name was Neeltje.

At first the people looked at his signboard out of the eye-corner and wondered lazily why anyone should bear the name of Neeltje, but as time went on, men spoke to other men saying, "How do you pronounce the name of that barber up there on Bridge Street hill?" And, then, before anyone could prevent it, the best minds of the town were splintering their lances against William Neeltje's signboard. If a man had a mental superior, he guided him seductively to this name and watched with glee his wrecking. The clergy of the town even entered the lists. There was one among them who had taken a collegiate prize in Syriac, as well as in several less opaque languages, and the other clergymen—at one of their weekly meetings—sought to betray him into this ambush. He pronounced the name correctly but that mattered little since none of them knew whether he did or did not; and so they took triumph according to their ignorance. Under these arduous circumstances it was certain that the town should look for a nickname and at this time the nickname was in process of formation. So William Neeltje lived on with his secret, smiling foolishly toward the world.

"Come on," cried little Cora. "Let's all get our hair cut! That's what let's do. Let's all get our hair cut! Come on! Come on! Come on!" The others were carried off their feet by the fury of this assault. To get their hair cut! What joy! Little did they know if this were fun; they only knew that their small leader said it was fun. Chocolate-stained but confident, the band marched into William Neeltje's barber-shop.

"We want to get our hair cut," said little Cora haughtily.

Neeltje, in his shirt sleeves, stood looking at them with his half-idiot smile.

"Hurry, now," commanded the queen. A dray horse toiled step by step, step by step, up Bridge Street hill; a far woman's voice arose; there could be heard the ceaseless hammers of shingling carpenters; all was summer peace. "Come on, now! Who's goin' first? Come on, Ella, you go first. Gettin' our hair cut! Oh, what fun!"

Little Ella Earl would not however be first in the chair. She was drawn toward it by a singular fascination but at the same time she was afraid of it and so she hung back, saying: "No! You go first! No! You go first!" The question was precipitated by the twins and one of the Phelps children. They made simultaneous rush for the chair and screamed and kicked, each pair preventing the third child. The queen entered this melee and decided in favor of the Phelps boy. He ascended the chair; thereat an awed silence fell upon the band. And always William Neeltje smiled fatuously.

He tucked a cloth in the neck of the Phelps boy and taking scissors began to cut his hair. The group of children came closer and closer. Even the queen was deeply moved. "Does it hurt any?" she asked in a wee voice.

"Naw," said the Phelps boy with dignity. "Anyhow, I've had m' hair cut afore."

When he appeared to them looking very soldierly with his cropped little head, there was a tumult over the chair. The Margate twins howled; Jimmie Trescott was kicking them on the shins. It was a fight.

But the twins could not prevail, being the smallest of all the children. The queen herself took the chair and ordered Neeltje as if he were a lady's-maid. To the floor there fell proud ringlets blazing even there in their humiliation with a full fine bronze light. Then Jimmie Trescott; then Ella Earl (two long ash-colored plaits); then a Phelps girl; then another Phelps girl; and so on from head to head. The ceremony received unexpected check when the turn came to Dan Earl. This lad, usually docile to any rein, had suddenly grown mulishly obstinate. No, he would not; he would not. He himself did not seem to know why he refused to have his hair cut, but despite the shrill derision of the company, he remained obdurate. Anyhow the twins, long held in check and now feverishly eager, were already struggling for the chair.

And so to the floor at last came the golden Margate curls, the heart-treasure and glory of a mother, three aunts and some feminine cousins.

All having been finished, the children, highly elate, thronged out into the street. They crowed and cackled with pride and joy, anon turning to scorn the cowardly Dan Earl.

Ella Earl was an exception. She had been pensive for some time and now the shorn little maiden began vaguely to weep. In the door of his shop William Neeltje stood watching them, upon his face a grin of almost inhuman idiocy.

II

It now becomes the duty of the unfortunate writer to exhibit these children to their fond parents. "Come on, Jimmie," cried little Cora, "let's go show mamma." And they hurried off, these happy children, to show mamma.

The Trescotts and their guests were assembled, indolently awaiting the luncheon bell. Jimmie and the angel-child burst in upon them. "Oh, mamma," shrieked little Cora, "see how fine I am! I've had my hair cut! Isn't it splendid! And Jimmie too."

The wretched mother took one sight, emitted one yell and fell into a chair. Mrs. Trescott let fall a large lady's-journal and made a nerveless mechanical clutch at it. The painter gripped the arms of his chair and leaned forward staring until his eyes were like two little clock-faces. Doctor Trescott did not move or speak.

To the children the next moments were chaotic. There was a loudly wailing mother and a pale-faced aghast mother; a stammering father and a grim and terrible father. The angel-child did not understand anything of it save the voice of calamity and in a moment all her little imperialism went to the winds. She ran sobbing to her mother. "Oh, ma-ma! Ma-ma! Ma-ma!"

The desolate Jimmie heard out of this inexplicable situation a voice which he knew well, a sort of a colonel's voice, and he obeyed like any good soldier. "Jimmie!"

He stepped three paces to the front. "Yessir."

"How did this—how did this happen?" said Trescott.

Now Jimmie could have explained how had happened anything which had happened but he did not know what had happened, so he said: "I—I—nothin'."

"And, oh, look at her frock," said Mrs. Trescott brokenly.

The words turned the mind of the mother of the angel-child. She looked up, her eyes blazing. " 'Frock'!" she repeated. " 'Frock'! What do I care for her 'frock'? 'Frock'!" she choked out again from the depths of her bitterness. Then she arose suddenly and whirled tragically upon her husband. "Look!" she declaimed. "All—her lovely—hair—all her lovely hair—gone—gone!" The painter was apparently in a fit; his jaw was set, his eyes were glazed, his body was stiff and straight. "All gone—all—her lovely hair—all gone—my poor little darlin'—my—poor—little—darlin'!" And the angel-child added her heart-broken voice to her mother's wail as they fled into each other's arms.

In the meantime, Trescott was patiently unravelling some skeins of Jimmie's tangled intellect. "And then you went to this barber's on the hill. Yes. And where did you get the money? Yes. I see. And who besides you and Cora had their hair cut? The Margate twi— Oh, lord!"

Over at the Margate place, old Eldridge Margate, the grandfather of the twins, was in the back garden picking peas and smoking ruminatively to himself. Suddenly he heard from the house great noises. Doors slammed; women rushed up stairs and down stairs calling to each other in voices of agony. And full and mellow upon the still air arose the roar of the twins in pain.

Old Eldridge stepped out of the pea patch and moved toward the house, puzzled, staring, not yet having decided that it was his duty to rush forward. Then, around the corner of the house shot his daughter Mollie, her face pale with excitement.

"What's the matter?" he cried.

"Oh, father," she gasped, "the children! They—"

Then around the corner of the house came the twins, howling at the top of their power, their faces flowing with tears. They were still hand in hand, the ruling passion being strong even in this suffering. At sight of them old Eldridge took his pipe hastily out of his mouth. "Good god!" he said.

And now what befell one William Neeltje, a barber by trade? And what was said by angry parents of the mother of such an angel-child? And what was the fate of the angel-child herself?

There was surely a tempest. With the exception of the Margate twins, the boys could well be eliminated from the affair. Of course it didn't matter if their hair was cut. Also the two little Phelps girls had had very short hair anyhow and their parents were not too greatly incensed. In the case of Ella Earl it was mainly the pathos of the little girl's own grieving, but her mother played a most generous part and called upon Mrs. Trescott and condoled with the mother of the angel-child over their equivalent losses. But the Margate contingent! They simply screeched.

Trescott, composed and cool-blooded, was in the middle of a giddy whirl. He was not going to allow the mobbing of his wife's cousins nor was he going to pretend that the spoliation of the Margate twins was a virtuous and beautiful act. He was elected, gratuitously, to the position of buffer.

But, curiously enough, the one who achieved the bulk of the misery was old Eldridge Margate who had been picking peas at the time. The feminine Margates stormed his position as individuals, in pairs, in teams and en masse. In two days they may have aged him seven years. He must destroy the utter Neeltje. He must midnightly massacre the angel-child and her mother. He must dip his arms in blood to the elbows.

Trescott took the first opportunity to express to him his concern over the affair but when the subject of the disaster was mentioned, old Eldridge, to the doctor's great surprise, actually chuckled long and deeply. "Oh, well, lookahere," said he. "I never was so much in love with them there damn curls.

The curls was purty—yes—but then I'd a darn sight rather see boys look more like boys than like two little wax figgers. An', ye know, the little cusses like it 'emselves. *They* never took no stock in all this washin' an' combin' an' fixin' an' goin' to church an' paradin' an' showin' off. They stood it because they was told to. That's all. Of course this here Neel-te-gee, er-whatever-his-name-is, is a plumb dumb ijit but I don't see what's to be done, now that the kids is full-well cropped. I might go and burn his shop over his head but that wouldn't bring no hair back onto the kids. They're even kickin' on sashes now an' that's all right 'cause what fer does a boy want a sash?"

Whereupon Trescott perceived that the old man wore his brains above his shoulders and Trescott departed from him, rejoicing greatly that it was only women who could not know that there was finality to most disasters and that when a thing was fully done, no amount of door-slamming, rushing up stairs and down stairs, calls, lamentations, tears could bring back a single hair to the heads of twins.

But the rains came and the winds blew in the most biblical way when a certain fact came to light in the Trescott household. Little Cora, corroborated by Jimmie, innocently remarked that five dollars had been given her by her father on her birthday and with this money the evil had been wrought. Trescott had known it but he—thoughtful man—had said nothing. For her part the mother of the angel-child had, up to that moment, never reflected that the consummation of the wickedness must have cost a small sum of money. But now it was all clear to her. He was the guilty one—he! "My angel-child!"

The scene which ensued was inspiriting. A few days later, loungers at the railway station saw a lady leading a shorn and still undaunted lamb. Attached to them was a husband and father who was plainly bewildered but still more plainly vexed, as if he would be saying: "Damn 'em! Why can't they leave me alone!"

The Lover and the Tell-Tale

WHEN THE ANGEL-CHILD returned with her parents to New York the fond heart of Jimmie Trescott felt its bruise greatly. For two days he simply moped, becoming a stranger to all former joys. When his old comrades yelled invitation as they swept off on some interesting quest, he replied with mournful gestures of disillusion.

He thought often of writing to her but of course the shame of it made him pause. Write a letter to a girl? The mere enormity of the idea caused him shudders. Persons of his quality never wrote letters to girls. Such was the occupation of mollycoddles and snivellers. He knew that if his acquaintances and friends found in him evidences of such weakness and general milkiness, they would fling themselves upon him like so many wolves and bait him beyond the borders of sanity.

However, one day at school in that time of the morning session when children of his age were allowed fifteen minutes of play in the school-grounds, he did not as usual rush forth ferociously to his games. Commonly he was of the worst hoodlums, preying upon his weaker brethren with all the cruel disregard of a grown man. On this particular morning he stayed in the school-room and with his tongue stuck from the corner of his mouth, and his head twisting in a painful way, he wrote to little Cora, pouring out to her all the poetry of his hungry soul as follows: "My dear Cora I love thee with all my hart oh come bac again, bac, bac gain for I love thee best of all oh come bac again When the spring come again we'l fly and we'l fly like a brid."

As for the last word he knew under normal circumstances perfectly well how to spell "bird" but in this case he had transposed two of the letters through excitement, supreme agitation.

Nor had this letter been composed without fear and furtive glancing. There was always a number of children who for the time cared more for the quiet of the school-room than for the tempest of the play-ground and there was always that dismal company who were being forcibly deprived of their recess— who were being "kept in." More than one curious eye was

turned upon the desperate and lawless Jimmie Trescott sud-
denly taken to ways of peace and as he felt these eyes he
flushed guiltily, with felonious glances from side to side.

It happened that a certain vigilant little girl had a seat di-
rectly across the aisle from Jimmie's seat and she had re-
mained in the room during the intermission because of her
interest in some absurd domestic details concerning her desk.
Parenthetically it might be stated that she was in the habit of
imagining this desk to be a house and at this time with an
important little frown, indicative of a proper matron, she was
engaged in dramatising her ideas of a household.

But this small Rose Goldege happened to be of a family
which numbered few males. It was in fact one of those curi-
ous middle-class families that hold much of their ground, re-
tain most of their position, after all their visible means of
support have been dropped in the grave. It contained now
only a collection of women who existed submissively, de-
fiantly, securely, mysteriously, in a pretentious and often ex-
asperating virtue. It was often too triumphantly clear that
they were free of bad habits. However, bad habits is a term
here used in a commoner meaning because it is certainly true
that the principal and indeed solitary joy which entered their
lonely lives was the joy of talking wickedly and busily about
their neighbors. It was all done without dream of its being of
the vulgarity of the alleys. Indeed it was simply a constitu-
tional but not incredible chastity and honesty expressing itself
in its ordinary superior way of the whirling circles of life and
the vehemence of the criticism was not lessened by a further
infusion of an acid of worldly defeat, worldly suffering and
worldly hopelessness.

Out of this family-circle had sprung the typical little girl
who discovered Jimmie Trescott agonizingly writing a letter
to his sweetheart. Of course all the children were the most
abandoned gossips but she was peculiarly adapted to the pur-
pose of making Jimmie miserable over this particular point. It
was her life to sit of evenings about the stove and hearken to
her mother and a lot of spinsters talk of many things. During
these evenings she was never licensed to utter an opinion ei-
ther one way or the other way. She was then simply a very
little girl sitting open-eyed in the gloom and listening to

many things which she often interpreted wrongly. They on their part kept up a kind of a smug-faced pretense of concealing from her information in detail of the wide-spread crime, which in effect may have been more elaborately dangerous than no pretense at all. Thus all her home teaching fitted her to at once recognize in Jimmie Trescott's manner that he was concealing something that would properly interest the world. She set up a scream. "Oh! Oh! Oh! Jimmie Trescott's writing to his girl! Oh! Oh!"

Jimmie cast a miserable glance upon her—a glance in which hatred mingled with despair. Through the open window, he could hear the boisterous cries of his friends—his hoodlum friends—who would no more understand the utter poetry of his position than they would understand an ancient tribal sign language. His face was set in a truer expression of horror than any of the romances describe upon the features of a man flung into a moat, a man shot in the breast with an arrow, a man cleft in the neck with a battle axe. He was suppedaneous of the fullest power of childish pain. His one course was to rush upon her and attempt by an impossible means of strangulation to keep her important news from the public.

The teacher, a thoughtful young woman at her desk upon the platform, saw a little scuffle which informed her that two of her scholars were larking. She called out sharply. The command penetrated to the middle of an early world struggle. In Jimmie's age there was no particular scruple in the minds of the male sex against laying warrior hands upon their weaker sisters. But of course this voice from the throne hindered Jimmie in what might have been a berserk attack.

Even the little girl was retarded by the voice but without being unlawful, she managed to soon shy through the door and out upon the play-ground, yelling: "Oh! Jimmie Trescott's been writing to his girl!"

The unhappy Jimmie was following as closely as he was allowed by his knowledge of the decencies to be preserved under the eye of the teacher.

Jimmie himself was mainly responsible for the scene which ensued on the play-ground. It is possible that the little girl might have run shrieking his infamy without exciting more than a general but unmilitant interest. These barbarians were excited only by the actual appearance of human woe; in that event, they cheered and danced. Jimmie made the strategic mistake of pursuing little Rose and thus exposed his thin skin to the whole school. He had in his cowering mind a vision of a hundred children turning from their play under the maple trees and speeding toward him over the gravel with sudden wild taunts. Upon him drove a yelping demoniac mob to which his words were futile. He saw in this mob boys that he dimly knew and his deadly enemies, and his retainers and his most intimate friends. The virulence of his deadly enemy was no greater than the virulence of his intimate friend. From the outskirts the little informer could be heard still screaming the news like a toy parrot with clockwork inside of it. It broke up all sorts of games not so much because of the mere fact of the letter-writing as because the children knew that some suf- ferer was at the last point and like little blood-fanged wolves they thronged to the scene of his destruction. They galloped about him shrilly chanting insults. He turned from one to another only to meet with howls. He was baited.

Then, in one instant, he changed all this with a blow. Bang! The most pitiless of the boys near him received a punch fairly and skilfully which made him bellow out like a walrus, and then Jimmie laid desperately into the whole world, striking out frenziedly in all directions. Boys who could handily whip him and knew it backed away from this onslaught. Here was intention—serious intention. They themselves were not in frenzy and their cooler judgment re- spected Jimmie's efforts when he ran amok. They saw that it really was none of their affair. In the meantime the wretched little girl who had caused the bloody riot was away by the fence weeping because boys were fighting.

Jimmie several times hit the wrong boy. That is to say, he several times hit a wrong boy hard enough to arouse also in him a spirit of wrath. Jimmie wore a little shirt-waist. It was passing now rapidly into oblivion. He was sobbing and there was one blood-stain upon his cheek. The school-ground sounded like a pine tree when a hundred crows roost in it at night.

Then upon the situation there pealed a brazen bell. It was a bell that these children obeyed even as older nations obey the formal law which is printed in calf-skin. It smote them into some sort of inaction; even Jimmie was influenced by its potency although as a finale he kicked out lustily into the legs of an intimate friend who had been one of the foremost in the torture.

When they came to form into line for the march into the school-room it was curious that Jimmie had many admirers. It was not his prowess; it was the soul he had infused into his gymnastics; and he, still panting, looked about him with a stern and challenging glare.

And yet when the long tramping line had entered the school-room his status had again changed. The other children then began to regard him as a boy in disrepair and boys in disrepair were always accosted ominously from the throne. Jimmie's march toward his seat was a feat. It was composed partly of a most slinking attempt to dodge the perception of the teacher and partly of pure braggadocio erected for the benefit of his observant fellow-men.

The teacher looked carefully down at him. "Jimmie Trescott," she said.

"Yes'm," he answered with a business-like briskness which really spelled out falsity in all its letters.

"Come up to the desk."

He arose mid the awe of the entire school-room. When he arrived, she said: "Jimmie, you've been fighting."

"Yes'm," he answered. This was not so much an admission of the fact as it was a concessional answer to anything she might say.

"Who have you been fighting?" she asked.

"I dunno, 'm."

Whereupon the empress blazed out in wrath. "You don't know who you've been fighting?"

Jimmie looked at her gloomily. "No, 'm."

She seemed about to disintegrate to mere flaming faggots of anger. "You don't know who you've been fighting?" she demanded, blazing. "Well—you stay in after school until you find out."

As he returned to his place all the children knew by his vanquished air that sorrow had fallen upon the house of Trescott. When he took his seat he saw gloating upon him the satanic black eyes of the little Goldege girl.

"Showin' Off"

JIMMIE TRESCOTT'S new velocipede had the largest front wheel of any velocipede in Whilomville. When it first arrived from New York, he wished to sacrifice school, food and sleep to it. Evidently he wished to become a sort of a perpetual velocipede-rider. But the powers of the family laid a number of judicious embargoes upon him and he was prevented from becoming a fanatic. Of course this caused him to retain a fondness for the three-wheeled thing much longer than if he had been allowed to debauch himself for a span of days. But in the end, it was an immaterial machine to him. For long periods he left it idle in the stable.

One day he loitered from school toward home by a very circuitous route. He was accompanied by only one of his retainers. The object of this detour was the wooing of a little girl in a red hood. He had been in love with her for some three weeks. His desk was near her desk at school but he had never spoken to her. He had been afraid to take such a radical step. It was not customary to speak to girls. Even boys who had school-going sisters seldom addressed them during that part of a day which was devoted to education.

The reasons for this conduct were very plain. First, the more robust boys considered talking with girls an unmanly occupation; second, the greater part of the boys were afraid; third, they had no idea of what to say because they esteemed the proper sentences should be supernaturally incisive and eloquent. In consequence, a small contingent of blue-eyed weaklings were the sole intimates of the frail sex and for it they were boisterously and disdainfully called "girl-boys."

But this situation did not prevent serious and ardent wooing. For instance, Jimmie and the little girl who wore the red hood must have exchanged glances at least two hundred times in every school-hour and this exchange of glances accomplished everything. In them, the two children renewed their curious inarticulate vows.

Jimmie had developed a devotion to school which was the admiration of his father and mother. In the mornings he was so impatient to have it made known to him that no misfortune had befallen his romance during the night that he was actually detected at times feverishly listening for the "first bell." Doctor Trescott was exceedingly complacent of the change and, as for Mrs. Trescott, she had ecstatic visions of a white-haired Jimmie leading the nations in knowledge, comprehending all from bugs to comets. It was merely the doing of the little girl in the red hood.

When Jimmie made up his mind to follow his sweetheart home from school, the project seemed such an arbitrary and shameless innovation that he hastily lied to himself about it. No; he was not following Abbie. He was merely making his way homeward through the new and rather longer route of Bryant Street and Oakland Park. It had nothing at all to do with a girl. It was a mere eccentric notion.

"Come on," said Jimmie gruffly to his retainer. "Let's go home this way."

"What fer?" demanded the retainer.

"Oh, b'cause."

"Huh?"

"Oh, it's more fun—goin' this way."

The retainer was bored and loth but that mattered very little. He did not know how to disobey his chief. Together they followed the trail of red-hooded Abbie and another small girl. These latter at once understood the object of the chase and looking back giggling they pretended to quicken their pace. But they were always looking back. Jimmie now began his courtship in earnest. The first thing to do was to prove his strength in battle. This was transacted by means of the retainer. He took that devoted boy and flung him heavily to the ground, meanwhile mouthing a preposterous ferocity.

The retainer accepted this incomprehensible behavior with a sort of bland resignation. After his over-throw, he raised himself, coolly brushed some dust and dead leaves from his clothes, and then seemed to forget the incident.

"I can jump further'n you can," said Jimmie in a loud voice.

"I know it," responded the retainer simply.

But this would not do. There must be a contest.

"Come on," shouted Jimmie imperiously. "Let's see you jump."

The retainer selected a footing on the kerb, balanced and calculated a moment, and jumped without enthusiasm. Jimmie's leap of course was longer.

"There!" he cried blowing out his lips. "I beat you, didn't I? Easy. I beat you." He made a great hub-bub as if the affair was unprecedented.

"Yes," admitted the retainer emotionless.

Later, Jimmie forced his retainer to run a race with him, held more jumping matches, flung him twice to earth and generally behaved as if a retainer was indestructible. If the retainer had been in the plot, it is conceivable that he would have endured this treatment with mere whispered half-laughing protests. But he was not in the plot at all and so he became enigmatic. One can not often sound the profound well in which lie the meanings of boyhood.

Following the two little girls, Jimmie eventually passed into that suburb of Whilomville which is called Oakland Park. At his heels came a badly-battered retainer. Oakland Park was a somewhat strange country to the boys. They were dubious of the manners and customs and of course they would have to meet the local chieftains who might look askance upon this invasion.

Jimmie's girl departed into her home with a last backward glance that almost blinded the thrilling boy. On this pretext and that pretext, he kept his retainer in play before the house. He had hopes that she would emerge as soon as she had deposited her school-bag.

A boy came along the walk. Jimmie knew him at school. He was Tommie Semple, one of the weaklings who made friends with the fair sex. "Hello, Tom," said Jimmie. "You live 'round here?"

"Yeh," said Tom with composed pride. At school, he was afraid of Jimmie but he did not evince any of this fear as he strolled well inside his own frontiers. Jimmie and his retainer had not expected this boy to display the manners of a minor chief and they contemplated him attentively. There was a silence. Finally Jimmie said: "I can put you down." He moved forward briskly. "Can't I?" he demanded.

The challenged boy backed away. "I know you can," he declared frankly and promptly.

The little girl in the red hood had come out with a hoop. She looked at Jimmie with an air of insolent surprise in the fact that he still existed and began to trundle her hoop off toward some other little girls who were shrilly playing near a nurse-maid and a perambulator. Jimmie adroitly shifted his position until he too was playing near the perambulator, pretentiously making mince-meat out of his retainer and Tommie Semple.

Of course, little Abbie had defined the meaning of Jimmie's appearance in Oakland Park. Despite this nonchalance and grand air of accident, nothing could have been more plain. Whereupon she of course became insufferably vain in manner and whenever Jimmie came near her she tossed her head and turned away her face and daintily swished her skirts as if he were contagion itself. But Jimmie was happy. His soul was satisfied with the mere presence of the beloved object so long as he could feel that she furtively gazed upon him from time to time and noted his extraordinary prowess which he was proving upon the persons of his retainer and Tommie Semple. And he was making an impression. There could be no doubt of it. He had many times caught her eye fixed admiringly upon him as he mauled the retainer. Indeed all the little girls gave attention to his deeds and he was the hero of the hour.

Presently a boy on a velocipede was seen to be tooling down toward them. "Who's this comin'?" said Jimmie bluntly to the Semple boy.

"That's Horace Glenn," said Tommie, "an' he's got a new velocipede an' he can ride it like anything."

"Can you lick him?" asked Jimmie.

"I don't—I never fought with 'im," answered the other. He bravely tried to appear as a man of respectable achievement but with Horace coming toward them the risk was too great. However he brightly added: "*Maybe* I could."

The advent of Horace on his new velocipede created a sensation which he haughtily accepted as a familiar thing. Only Jimmie and his retainer remained silent and impassive. Horace eyed the two invaders.

"Hello, Jimmie."

"Hello, Horace."

After the typical silence, Jimmie said pompously: "I got a velocipede."

"Have you?" asked Horace anxiously. He did not wish anybody in the world but himself to possess a velocipede.

"Yes," sang Jimmie. "An' it's a bigger one than that, too! A good deal bigger! An' it's a better one, too!"

"Huh," retorted Horace sceptically.

"Ain't I, Clarence? Ain't I? Ain't I got one bigger'n that?"

The retainer answered with alacrity. "Yes, he has! A good deal bigger! An' it's a dindy, too!"

This corroboration rather disconcerted Horace but he continued to scoff at any statement that Jimmie also owned a velocipede. As for the contention that this supposed velocipede could be larger than his own, he simply wouldn't hear of it.

Jimmie had been a very gallant figure before the coming of Horace but the new velocipede had relegated him to a squalid secondary position. So he affected to look with contempt upon it. Voluminously he bragged of the velocipede in the stable at home. He painted its virtues and beauty in loud and extravagant words, flaming words. And the retainer stood by, glibly endorsing everything.

The little company heeded him and he passed on vociferously from extravagance to utter impossibility. Horace was very sick of it. His defense was reduced to a mere mechanical grumbling. "Don't believe you got one 't all. Don't believe you got one 't all."

Jimmie turned upon him suddenly. "How fast can you go? How fast can you go?" he demanded. "Let's see. I bet you can't go fast."

Horace lifted his spirits and answered with proper defiance. "Can't I?" he mocked. "Can't I?"

"No, you can't," said Jimmie. "You can't go fast."

Horace cried: "Well, you see me now! I'll show you! I'll show you if I can't go fast!" Taking a firm seat on his vermilion machine, he pedalled furiously up the walk, turned, and pedalled back again. "There, now!" he shouted triumphantly. "Ain't that fast? There, now!" There was a low murmur of appreciation from the little girls. Jimmie saw with pain that even his divinity was smiling upon his rival. "There! Ain't that fast? Ain't that fast?" He strove to pin Jimmie down to an admission. He was exuberant with victory.

Notwithstanding a feeling of discomfiture, Jimmie did not lose a moment of time. "Why," he yelled, "that ain't goin' fast 't all! That ain't goin' fast 't all! Why, I can go almost *twice* as fast as that! Almost *twice* as fast. Can't I, Clarence?"

The royal retainer nodded solemnly at the wide-eyed group. " 'Course he can!"

"Why," spouted Jimmie, "you just ought to see me ride once! You just ought to see me! Why, I can go like the wind! Can't I, Clarence? And I can ride far, too—oh, awful far! Can't I, Clarence? Why, I wouldn't have that one! 'Tain't any good! You just ought to see mine once!"

The overwhelmed Horace attempted to re-construct his battered glories. "I can ride right over the kerb-stone—at some of the crossin's," he announced brightly.

Jimmie's derision was a splendid sight. " '*Right over the kerb-stone*'! Why, that wouldn't be *nothin'* for me to do! I've rode mine down Bridge Street hill. Yessir! Ain't I, Clarence? Why, it ain't nothin' to ride over a kerb-stone—not for *me*! Is it, Clarence?"

"Down Bridge Street hill? You never!" said Horace hopelessly.

"Well, didn't I, Clarence? Didn't I, now?"

The faithful retainer again nodded solemnly at the assemblage.

At last Horace, having fallen as low as was possible, began to display a spirit for climbing up again. "Oh, you can do wonders," he said laughing. "You can do wonders. I s'pose you could ride down that bank there?" he asked with art. He had indicated a grassy terrace some six feet in height which bounded one side of the walk. At the bottom was a small ravine in which the reckless had flung ashes and tins. "I s'pose you could ride down that bank?"

All eyes now turned upon Jimmie to detect a sign of his weakening but he instantly and sublimely arose to the occasion. "That bank?" he asked scornfully. "Why, I've ridden down banks like that many a time. Ain't I, Clarence?"

This was too much for the company. A sound like the wind in the leaves arose; it was the song of incredulity and ridicule.

"O—o—o—o—o!" And on the outskirts, a little girl suddenly shrieked out: "Story-teller!"

Horace had certainly won a skirmish. He was gleeful. "Oh, you can do wonders!" he gurgled. "You can do wonders!" The neighborhood's superficial hostility to foreigners arose like magic under the influence of his sudden success and Horace had the delight of seeing Jimmie persecuted in that manner known only to children and insects.

Jimmie called angrily to the boy on the velocipede: "If you'll lend me yours, I'll show you whether I can or not."

Horace turned his superior nose in the air. "Oh, no, I don't ever lend it." Then he thought of a blow which would make Jimmie's humiliation complete. "Besides," he said airily, " 'tain't really anythin' hard to do. I could do it—easy—if I wanted to."

But his supposed adherents, instead of receiving this boast with cheers, looked upon him in a sudden blank silence. Jimmie and his retainer pounced like cats upon their advantage.

"Oh," they yelled, "you *could*, eh? Well, let's see you do it, then! Let's see you do it! Let's see you do it! Now!" In a moment the crew of little spectators were jibing at Horace.

The blow that would make Jimmie's humiliation complete! Instead, it had boomeranged Horace into the mud. He kept up a sullen muttering. " 'Tain't really anythin'! I could if I wanted to."

"Dare you to!" screeched Jimmie and his partisans. "Dare you to! Dare you to! Dare you to!"

There were two things to be done—to make gallant effort or to retreat. Somewhat to their amazement, the children at last found Horace moving through their clamor to the edge of the bank. Sitting on the velocipede he looked at the ravine and then with gloomy pride at the other children. A hush came upon them for it was seen that he was intending to make some kind of an antemortem statement.

"I—" he began. Then he vanished from the edge of the walk. The start had been unintentional—an accident.

The stupefied Jimmie saw the calamity through a haze. His first clear vision was when Horace with a face as red as a red flag arose bawling from his tangled velocipede. He and his retainer exchanged a glance of horror and fled the neighborhood. They did not look back until they had reached the top of the hill near the lake. They could see Horace walking slowly under the maples toward his home, pushing his shattered velocipede before him. His chin was thrown high and the breeze bore them the sound of his howls.

Shame

D ON'T COME IN HERE botherin' me," said the cook, intolerantly. "What with your mother bein' away on a visit, an' your father comin' home soon to lunch, I have enough on my mind—and that without bein' bothered with *you*. The kitchen is no place for little boys, anyhow. Run away, and don't be interferin' with my work." She frowned and made a grand pretence of being deep in herculean labors; but Jimmie did not run away.

"Now—they're goin' to have a picnic," he said, half audibly.

"What?"

"Now—they're goin' to have a picnic."

"Who's goin' to have a picnic?" demanded the cook, loudly. Her accent could have led one to suppose that if the projectors did not turn out to be the proper parties, she immediately would forbid this picnic.

Jimmie looked at her with more hopefulness. After twenty minutes of futile skirmishing, he had at least succeeded in introducing the subject. To her question he answered, eagerly:

"Oh, everybody! Lots and lots of boys and girls. Everybody."

"Who's everybody?"

According to custom, Jimmie began to singsong through his nose in a quite indescribable fashion an enumeration of the prospective picnickers: "Willie Dalzel an' Dan Earl an' Ella Earl an' Wolcott Margate an' Reeves Margate an' Walter Phelps an' Homer Phelps an' Minnie Phelps an'—oh—lots more girls an'—everybody. An' their mothers an' big sisters too." Then he announced a new bit of information: "They're goin' to have a picnic."

"Well, let them," said the cook, blandly.

Jimmie fidgeted for a time in silence. At last he murmured, "I—now—I thought maybe you'd let me go."

The cook turned from her work with an air of irritation and amazement that Jimmie should still be in the kitchen. "Who's stoppin' you?" she asked, sharply. "I ain't stoppin' you, am I?"

"No," admitted Jimmie, in a low voice.

"Well, why don't you go, then? Nobody's stoppin' you."

"But," said Jimmie, "I—you—now—each feller has got to take somethin' to eat with 'm."

"Oh ho!" cried the cook, triumphantly. "So that's it, is it? So that's what you've been shyin' round here fer, eh? Well, you may as well take yourself off without more words. What with your mother bein' away on a visit, an' your father comin' home soon to his lunch, I have enough on my mind—an' that without bein' bothered with *you*."

Jimmie made no reply, but moved in grief toward the door. The cook continued: "Some people in this house seem to think there's 'bout a thousand cooks in this kitchen. Where I used to work b'fore, there was some reason in 'em. I ain't a horse. A picnic!"

Jimmie said nothing, but he loitered.

"Seems as if I had enough to do, without havin' *you* come round talkin' about picnics. Nobody ever seems to think of the work I have to do. Nobody ever seems to think of it. Then they come and talk to me about picnics! What do I care about picnics?"

Jimmie loitered.

"Where I used to work b'fore, there was some reason in 'em. I never heard tell of no picnics right on top of your mother bein' away on a visit an' your father comin' home soon to his lunch. It's all foolishness."

Little Jimmie leaned his head flat against the wall and began to weep. She stared at him scornfully. "Cryin', eh? Cryin'? What are you cryin' fer?"

"N-n-nothin'," sobbed Jimmie.

There was a silence, save for Jimmie's convulsive breathing. At length the cook said: "Stop that blubberin', now. Stop it! This kitchen ain't no place fer it. Stop it! . . . Very well! If you don't stop, I won't give you nothin' to go to the picnic with—there!"

For the moment he could not end his tears. "You never said," he sputtered—"you never said you'd give me anything."

"An' why would I?" she cried, angrily. "Why would I—

with you in here a-cryin' an' a-blubberin' an' a-bleatin' round?
Enough to drive a woman crazy! I don't see how you could
expect me to! The idea!"

Suddenly Jimmie announced: "I've stopped cryin'. I ain't
goin' to cry no more 't all."

"Well, then," grumbled the cook—" well, then, stop it. I've
got enough on my mind." It chanced that she was making for
luncheon some salmon croquettes. A tin still half full of pinky
prepared fish was beside her on the table. Still grumbling, she
seized a loaf of bread and, wielding a knife, she cut from this
loaf four slices, each of which was as big as a six-shilling
novel. She profligately spread them with butter, and jabbing
the point of her knife into the salmon-tin, she brought up
bits of salmon, which she flung and flattened upon the bread.
Then she crashed the pieces of bread together in pairs, much
as one would clash cymbals. There was no doubt in her own
mind but that she had created two sandwiches.

"There," she cried. "That'll do you all right. Lemme see.
What 'll I put 'em in? There—I've got it." She thrust the
sandwiches into a small pail and jammed on the lid. Jimmie
was ready for the picnic. "Oh, thank you, Mary!" he cried,
joyfully, and in a moment he was off, running swiftly.

The picnickers had started nearly half an hour earlier, ow-
ing to his inability to quickly attack and subdue the cook, but
he knew that the rendezvous was in the grove of tall, pillar-
like hemlocks and pines that grew on a rocky knoll at the lake
shore. His heart was very light as he sped, swinging his pail.
But a few minutes previously his soul had been gloomed in
despair; now he was happy. He was going to the picnic,
where privilege of participation was to be bought by the con-
tents of the little tin pail.

When he arrived in the outskirts of the grove he heard a
merry clamor, and when he reached the top of the knoll he
looked down the slope upon a scene which almost made his
little breast burst with joy. They actually had two camp fires!
Two camp fires! At one of them Mrs. Earl was making some-
thing—chocolate, no doubt—and at the other a young lady
in white duck and a sailor hat was dropping eggs into boiling
water. Other grown-up people had spread a white cloth and

were laying upon it things from baskets. In the deep cool shadow of the trees the children scurried, laughing. Jimmie hastened forward to join his friends.

Homer Phelps caught first sight of him. "Ho!" he shouted; "here comes Jimmie Trescott! Come on, Jimmie; you be on our side!" The children had divided themselves into two bands for some purpose of play. The others of Homer Phelps's party loudly endorsed his plan. "Yes, Jimmie, you be on *our* side." Then arose the usual dispute. "Well, we got the weakest side."

" 'Tain't any weaker'n ours."

Homer Phelps suddenly started, and looking hard, said, "What you got in the pail, Jim?"

Jimmie answered, somewhat uneasily, "Got m' lunch in it."

Instantly that brat of a Minnie Phelps simply tore down the sky with her shrieks of derision. "Got his *lunch* in it! In a *pail!*" She ran screaming to her mother. "Oh, mamma! Oh, mamma! Jimmie Trescott's got his picnic in a pail!"

Now there was nothing in the nature of this fact to particularly move the others—notably the boys, who were not competent to care if he had brought his luncheon in a coalbin; but such is the instinct of childish society that they all immediately moved away from him. In a moment he had been made a social leper. All old intimacies were flung into the lake, so to speak. They dared not compromise themselves. At safe distances the boys shouted, scornfully: "Huh! Got his picnic in a pail!" Never again during that picnic did the little girls speak of him as Jimmie Trescott. His name now was Him.

His mind was dark with pain as he stood, the hang-dog, kicking the gravel, and muttering as defiantly as he was able, "Well, I can have it in a pail if I want to." This statement of freedom was of no importance, and he knew it, but it was the only idea in his head.

He had been baited at school for being detected in writing a letter to little Cora, the angel-child, and he had known how to defend himself, but this situation was in no way similar. This was a social affair, with grown people on all sides. It would be sweet to catch the Margate twins, for instance, and hammer them into a state of bleating respect for his pail; but that was a matter for the jungles of childhood, where grown folk seldom penetrated. He could only glower.

The amiable voice of Mrs. Earl suddenly called: "Come, children! Everything's ready!" They scampered away, glancing back for one last gloat at Jimmie standing there with his pail.

He did not know what to do. He knew that the grown folk expected him at the spread, but if he approached he would be greeted by a shameful chorus from the children—more especially from some of those damnable little girls. Still, luxuries beyond all dreaming were heaped on that cloth. One could not forget them. Perhaps if he crept up modestly, and was very gentle and very nice to the little girls, they would allow him peace. Of course it had been dreadful to come with a pail to such a grand picnic, but they might forgive him.

Oh no, they would not! He knew them better. And then suddenly he remembered with what delightful expectations he had raced to this grove, and self-pity overwhelmed him, and he thought he wanted to die and make every one feel sorry.

The young lady in white duck and a sailor hat looked at him, and then spoke to her sister, Mrs. Earl. "Who's that hovering in the distance, Emily?"

Mrs. Earl peered. "Why, it's Jimmie Trescott! Jimmie, come to the picnic! Why don't you come to the picnic, Jimmie?" He began to sidle toward the cloth.

But at Mrs. Earl's call there was another outburst from many of the children. "He's got his picnic in a pail! In a *pail*! Got it in a pail!"

Minnie Phelps was a shrill fiend. "Oh, mamma, he's got it in that pail! See! Isn't it funny? Isn't it dreadful funny?"

"What ghastly prigs children are, Emily!" said the young lady. "They are spoiling that boy's whole day, breaking his heart, the little cats! I think I'll go over and talk to him."

"Maybe you had better not," answered Mrs. Earl, dubiously. "Somehow these things arrange themselves. If you interfere, you are likely to prolong everything."

"Well, I'll try, at least," said the young lady.

At the second outburst against him Jimmie had crouched down by a tree, half hiding behind it, half pretending that he was not hiding behind it. He turned his sad gaze toward the

lake. The bit of water seen through the shadows seemed per-
pendicular, a slate-colored wall. He heard a noise near him,
and turning, he perceived the young lady looking down at
him. In her hand she held plates. "May I sit near you?" she
asked, coolly.

Jimmie could hardly believe his ears. After disposing herself
and the plates upon the pine-needles, she made brief expla-
nation. "They're rather crowded, you see, over there. I don't
like to be crowded at a picnic, so I thought I'd come here. I
hope you don't mind."

Jimmie made haste to find his tongue. "Oh, I don't mind! I
like to have you here." The ingenuous emphasis made it appear
that the fact of his liking to have her there was in the nature
of a law-dispelling phenomenon, but she did not smile.

"How large is that lake?" she asked.

Jimmie, falling into the snare, at once began to talk in the
manner of a proprietor of the lake. "Oh, it's almost twenty
miles long, an' in one place it's almost four miles wide! an'
it's *deep*, too—awful deep—an' it's got real steamboats on
it, an'—oh—lots of other boats, an'—an'—an'—"

"Do you go out on it sometimes?"

"Oh, lots of times! My father's got a boat," he said, eying
her to note the effect of his words.

She was correctly pleased and struck with wonder. "Oh,
has he?" she cried, as if she never before had heard of a man
owning a boat.

Jimmie continued: "Yes, an' it's a grea' big boat, too, with
sails, real sails; an' sometimes he takes me out in her, too; an'
once he took me fishin', an' we had sandwiches, plenty of 'em,
an' my father he drank beer right out of the bottle— *right out
of the bottle!* "

The young lady was properly overwhelmed by this amazing
intelligence. Jimmie saw the impression he had created, and
he enthusiastically resumed his narrative: "An' after, he let me
throw the bottles in the water, and I throwed 'em 'way, 'way,
'way out. An' they sank, an'—never comed up," he con-
cluded, dramatically.

His face was glorified; he had forgotten all about the pail;
he was absorbed in this communion with a beautiful lady
who was so interested in what he had to say.

She indicated one of the plates, and said, indifferently: "Perhaps you would like some of those sandwiches. I made them. Do you like olives? And there's a deviled egg. I made that also."

"Did you really?" said Jimmie, politely. His face gloomed for a moment because the pail was recalled to his mind, but he timidly possessed himself of a sandwich.

"Hope you are not going to scorn my deviled egg," said his goddess. "I am very proud of it." He did not; he scorned little that was on the plate.

Their gentle intimacy was ineffable to the boy. He thought he had a friend, a beautiful lady, who liked him more than she did anybody at the picnic, to say the least. This was proved by the fact that she had flung aside the luxuries of the spread cloth to sit with him, the exile. Thus early did he fall a victim to woman's wiles.

"Where do you live?" he asked, suddenly.

"Oh, a long way from here! In New York."

His next question was put very bluntly. "Are you married?"

"Oh, no!" she answered, gravely.

Jimmie was silent for a time, during which he glanced shyly and furtively up at her face. It was evident that he was somewhat embarrassed. Finally he said, "When I grow up to be a man—"

"Oh, that is some time yet!" said the beautiful lady.

"But when I *do*, I—I should like to marry you."

"Well, I will remember it," she answered; "but don't talk of it now, because it's such a long time; and—I wouldn't wish you to consider yourself bound." She smiled at him.

He began to brag. "When I grow up to be a man, I'm goin' to have lots an' lots of money, an' I'm goin' to have a grea' big house, an' a horse an' a shot-gun, an' lots an' lots of books 'bout elephants an' tigers, an' lots an' lots of ice-cream an' pie an'—caramels." As before, she was impressed; he could see it. "An' I'm goin' to have lots an' lots of children—'bout three hundred, I guess—an' there won't none of 'em be girls. They'll all be boys—like me."

"Oh, my!" she said.

His garment of shame was gone from him. The pail was dead and well buried. It seemed to him that months elapsed as he dwelt in happiness near the beautiful lady and trumpeted his vanity.

At last there was a shout. "Come on! we're going home." The picnickers trooped out of the grove. The children wished to resume their jeering, for Jimmie still gripped his pail, but they were restrained by the circumstances. He was walking at the side of the beautiful lady.

During this journey he abandoned many of his habits. For instance, he never travelled without skipping gracefully from crack to crack between the stones, or without pretending that he was a train of cars, or without some mumming device of childhood. But now he behaved with dignity. He made no more noise than a little mouse. He escorted the beautiful lady to the gate of the Earl home, where he awkwardly, solemnly, and wistfully shook hands in good-by. He watched her go up the walk; the door clanged.

On his way home he dreamed. One of these dreams was fascinating. Supposing the beautiful lady was his teacher in school! Oh, my! wouldn't he be a good boy, sitting like a statuette all day long, and knowing every lesson to perfection, and—everything. And then supposing that a boy should sass her. Jimmie painted himself waylaying that boy on the homeward road, and the fate of the boy was a thing to make strong men cover their eyes with their hands. And she would like him more and more—more and more. And he—he would be a little god.

But as he was entering his father's grounds an appalling recollection came to him. He was returning with the bread-and-butter and the salmon untouched in the pail! He could imagine the cook, nine feet tall, waving her fist. "An' so that's what I took trouble for, is it? So's you could bring it back? So's you could bring it back?" He skulked toward the house like a marauding bush-ranger. When he neared the kitchen door he made a desperate rush past it, aiming to gain the stables and there secrete his guilt. He was nearing them, when a thunderous voice hailed him from the rear: "Jimmie Trescott, where you goin' with that pail?"

It was the cook. He made no reply, but plunged into the shelter of the stables. He whirled the lid from the pail and dashed its contents beneath a heap of blankets. Then he stood panting, his eyes on the door. The cook did not pursue, but she was bawling: "Jimmie Trescott, what you doin' with that pail?"

He came forth, swinging it. "Nothin'," he said, in virtuous protest.

"I know better," she said, sharply, as she relieved him of his curse.

In the morning Jimmie was playing near the stable, when he heard a shout from Peter Washington, who attended Doctor Trescott's horses: "Jim! Oh, Jim!"

"What?"

"Come yah."

Jimmie went reluctantly to the door of the stable, and Peter Washington asked: "Wut's dish yere fish an' brade doin' unner dese yer blankups?"

"I don't know. I didn't have nothin' to do with it," answered Jimmie, indignantly.

"Don' tell *me!*" cried Peter Washington, as he flung it all away—"don' tell *me!* When I fin' fish an' brade unner dese yer blankups, I don' go an' think dese yer ho'ses er yer pop's put 'em. I *know.* An' if I caitch enny more dish yer fish an' brade in dish yer stable, *I'll* tell yer pop."

.

The Carriage-Lamps

IT WAS THE FAULT of a small nickel-plated revolver, a most incompetent weapon, which, wherever one aimed, would fling the bullet as the devil willed, and no man, when about to use it, could tell exactly what was in store for the surrounding country. This treasure had been acquired by Jimmie Trescott after arduous bargaining with another small boy. Jimmie wended homeward, patting his hip pocket at every three paces.

Peter Washington, working in the carriage-house, looked out upon him with a shrewd eye. "Oh, Jim," he called, " wut you got in yer hind pocket?"

"Nothin'," said Jimmie, feeling carefully under his jacket to make sure that the revolver wouldn't fall out.

Peter chuckled. "S'more foolishness, I raikon. You gwine be hung one day, Jim, you keep up all dish yer nonsense."

Jimmie made no reply, but went into the back garden, where he hid the revolver in a box under a lilac-bush. Then he returned to the vicinity of Peter, and began to cruise to and fro in the offing, showing all the signals of one wishing to open treaty. "Pete," he said, "how much does a box of cartridges cost?"

Peter raised himself violently, holding in one hand a piece of harness, and in the other an old rag. "Ca'tridgers! *Ca'tridgers!* Lan' sake! wut the kid want with ca'tridgers? Knew it! Knew it! Come home er-holdin' on to his hind pocket like he got money in it. An' now he want ca'tridgers."

Jimmie, after viewing with dismay the excitement caused by his question, began to move warily out of the reach of a possible hostile movement.

"Ca'tridgers!" continued Peter, in scorn and horror. "Kid like you! No bigger'n er minute! Look yah, Jim, you done been swappin' round, an' you done got hol' of er pistol!" The charge was dramatic.

The wind was almost knocked out of Jimmie by this display of Peter's terrible miraculous power, and as he backed away his feeble denials were more convincing than a confession.

"I'll tell yer pop!" cried Peter, in virtuous grandeur. "I'll tell yer pop!"

1206

In the distance Jimmie stood appalled. He knew not what to do. The dread adult wisdom of Peter Washington had laid bare the sin, and disgrace stared at Jimmie.

There was a whirl of wheels, and a high lean trotting-mare spun Doctor Trescott's buggy toward Peter, who ran forward busily. As the doctor climbed out, Peter, holding the mare's head, began his denunciation:

"Docteh, I gwine tell on Jim. He come home er-holdin' on to his hind pocket, an' proud like he won a tuhkey-raffle; an' I sure know what he been up to, an' I done challenge him, an' he nev' say he didn't."

"Why, what do you mean?" said the doctor. "What's this, Jimmie?"

The boy came forward, glaring wrathfully at Peter. In fact, he suddenly was so filled with rage at Peter that he forgot all precautions. "It's about a pistol," he said, bluntly. "I've got a pistol. I swapped for it."

"I done tol' 'im his pop wouldn' stand no fiah-awms, an' him a kid like he is. I done tol' 'im. Lan' sake! he strut like he was a soldier! Come in yere proud, an' er-holdin' on to his hind pocket. He think he was Jesse James, I raikon. But I done tol' 'im his pop stan' no sech foolishness. First thing— *blam*—he shoot his haid off. No, seh, he too tinety t' come in yere er-struttin' like he jest bought Main Street. I tol' 'im. I done tol' 'im—shawp. I don' wanter be loafin' round dish yer stable if Jim he gwine go shootin' round an' shootin' round— *blim— blam— blim— blam!* No, seh. I retiahs. I re-tiahs. It's all right if er grown man got er gun, but ain't no kids come foolishin' round *me* with fiah-awms. No, seh. I retiahs."

"Oh, be quiet, Peter!" said the doctor. "Where is this thing, Jimmie?"

The boy went sulkily to the box under the lilac-bush and returned with the revolver. "Here 'tis," he said, with a glare over his shoulder at Peter. The doctor looked at the silly weapon in critical contempt.

"It's not much of a thing, Jimmie, but I don't think you are quite old enough for it yet. I'll keep it for you in one of the drawers of my desk."

Peter Washington burst out proudly: "I done tol' 'im th'

docteh wouldn' stan' no traffickin' round yere with fiah-awms. I done tol' 'im."

Jimmie and his father went together into the house, and as Peter unharnessed the mare he continued his comments on the boy and the revolver. He was not cast down by the absence of hearers. In fact, he usually talked better when there was no one to listen save the horses. But now his observations bore small resemblance to his earlier and public statements. Admiration and the keen family pride of a Southern negro who has been long in one place were now in his tone.

"That boy! He's er devil! When he get to be er man—wow! He'll jes take an' make things whirl round yere. Raikon we'll all take er back seat when he come erlong er-raisin' Cain."

He had unharnessed the mare, and with his back bent was pushing the buggy into the carriage-house.

"Er pistol! An' him no bigger than er minute!"

A small stone whizzed past Peter's head and clattered on the stable. He hastily dropped all occupation and struck a curious attitude. His right knee was almost up to his chin, and his arms were wreathed protectingly about his head. He had not looked in the direction from which the stone had come, but he had begun immediately to yell: "You Jim! Quit! Quit, I tell yer, Jim! Watch out! You gwine break somethin', Jim!"

"Yah!" taunted the boy, as with the speed and ease of a light-cavalryman he manoeuvred in the distance. "Yah! Told on me, did you! Told on me, hey! There! How do you like that?" The missiles resounded against the stable.

"Watch out, Jim! You gwine break somethin', Jim, I tell yer! Quit yer foolishness, Jim! Ow! Watch out, boy! I—"

There was a crash. With diabolic ingenuity, one of Jimmie's pebbles had entered the carriage-house and had landed among a row of carriage-lamps on a shelf, creating havoc which was apparently beyond all reason of physical law. It seemed to Jimmie that the racket of falling glass could have been heard in an adjacent county.

Peter was a prophet who after persecution was suffered to recall everything to the mind of the persecutor. "*There!* Knew it! Knew it! *Now* I raikon you'll quit. Hi! jes look ut dese yer lamps! Fer lan' sake! Oh, now yer pop jes break ev'ry bone in yer body!"

In the doorway of the kitchen the cook appeared with a startled face. Jimmie's father and mother came suddenly out on the front veranda. "What was that noise?" called the doctor.

Peter went forward to explain. "Jim he was er-heavin' rocks at me, docteh, an' erlong come one rock an' go *blam* inter all th' lamps an' jes skitter 'em t' bits. I declayah—"

Jimmie, half blinded with emotion, was nevertheless aware of a lightning glance from his father, a glance which cowed and frightened him to the ends of his toes. He heard the steady but deadly tones of his father in a fury: "Go into the house and wait until I come."

Bowed in anguish, the boy moved across the lawn and up the steps. His mother was standing on the veranda still gazing toward the stable. He loitered in the faint hope that she might take some small pity on his state. But she could have heeded him no less if he had been invisible. He entered the house.

When the doctor returned from his investigation of the harm done by Jimmie's hand, Mrs. Trescott looked at him anxiously, for she knew that he was concealing some volcanic impulses. "Well?" she asked.

"It isn't the lamps," he said at first. He seated himself on the rail. "I don't know what we are going to do with that boy. It isn't so much the lamps as it is the other thing. He was throwing stones at Peter because Peter told me about the revolver. What are we going to do with him?"

"I'm sure I don't know," replied the mother. "We've tried almost everything. Of course much of it is pure animal spirits. Jimmie is not naturally vicious—"

"Oh, I know," interrupted the doctor, impatiently. "Do you suppose, when the stones were singing about Peter's ears, he cared whether they were flung by a boy who was naturally vicious or a boy who was not? The question might interest him afterward, but at the time he was mainly occupied in dodging these effects of pure animal spirits."

"Don't be too hard on the boy, Ned. There's lots of time yet. He's so young yet, and— I believe he gets most of his

naughtiness from that wretched Dalzel boy. That Dalzel
boy—well, he's simply awful!" Then, with true motherly in-
stinct to shift blame from her own boy's shoulders, she pro-
ceeded to sketch the character of the Dalzel boy in lines that
would have made that talented young vagabond stare. It was
not admittedly her feeling that the doctor's attention should
be diverted from the main issue and his indignation divided
among the camps, but presently the doctor felt himself burn
with wrath for the Dalzel boy.

"Why don't you keep Jimmie away from him?" he de-
manded. "Jimmie has no business consorting with abandoned
little predestined jail-birds like him. If I catch him on the
place I'll box his ears."

"It is simply impossible, unless we kept Jimmie shut up all
the time," said Mrs. Trescott. "I can't watch him every minute
of the day, and the moment my back is turned, he's off."

"I should think those Dalzel people would hire somebody
to bring up their child for them," said the doctor. "They
don't seem to know how to do it themselves."

Presently you would have thought from the talk that one
Willie Dalzel had been throwing stones at Peter Washington
because Peter Washington had told Doctor Trescott that Wil-
lie Dalzel had come into possession of a revolver.

In the meantime Jimmie had gone into the house to await
the coming of his father. He was in rebellious mood. He had
not intended to destroy the carriage-lamps. He had been
merely hurling stones at a creature whose perfidy deserved
such action, and the hitting of the lamps had been merely
another move of the great conspirator Fate to force one Jim-
mie Trescott into dark and troublous ways. The boy was be-
ginning to find the world a bitter place. He couldn't win
appreciation for a single virtue; he could only achieve quick
rigorous punishment for his misdemeanors. Everything was
an enemy. Now there were those silly old lamps—what were
they doing up on that shelf, anyhow? It would have been just
as easy for them at the time to have been in some other place.
But no; there they had been, like the crowd that is passing
under the wall when the mason for the first time in twenty
years lets fall a brick. Furthermore, the flight of that stone
had been perfectly unreasonable. It had been a sort of freak

in physical law. Jimmie understood that he might have thrown stones from the same fatal spot for an hour without hurting a single lamp. He was a victim—that was it. Fate had conspired with the detail of his environment to simply hound him into a grave or into a cell.

But who would understand? Who would understand? And here the boy turned his mental glance in every direction, and found nothing but what was to him the black of cruel ignorance. Very well; some day they would—

From somewhere out in the street he heard a peculiar whistle of two notes. It was the common signal of the boys of the neighborhood, and judging from the direction of the sound, it was apparently intended to summon him. He moved immediately to one of the windows of the sitting-room. It opened upon a part of the grounds remote from the stables and cut off from the veranda by a wing. He perceived Willie Dalzel loitering in the street. Jimmie whistled the signal after having pushed up the window-sash some inches. He saw the Dalzel boy turn and regard him, and then call several other boys. They stood in a group and gestured. These gestures plainly said: "Come out. We've got something on hand." Jimmie sadly shook his head.

But they did not go away. They held a long consultation. Presently Jimmie saw the intrepid Dalzel boy climb the fence and begin to creep amongst the shrubbery, in elaborate imitation of an Indian scout. In time he arrived under Jimmie's window, and raised his face to whisper: "Come on out! We're going on a bear-hunt."

A bear-hunt! Of course Jimmie knew that it would not be a real bear-hunt, but would be a sort of carouse of pretension and big talking and preposterous lying and valor, wherein each boy would strive to have himself called Kit Carson by the others. He was profoundly affected. However, the parental word was upon him, and he could not move. "No," he answered, "I can't. I've got to stay in."

"Are you a prisoner?" demanded the Dalzel boy, eagerly.

"No-o—yes—I s'pose I am."

The other lad became much excited, but he did not lose his wariness. "Don't you want to be rescued?"

"Why—no—I dunno," replied Jimmie, dubiously.

Willie Dalzel was indignant. "Why, of course you want to be rescued! We'll rescue you. I'll go and get my men." And thinking this a good sentence, he repeated, pompously, "I'll go and get my men." He began to crawl away, but when he was distant some ten paces he turned to say: "Keep up a stout heart. Remember that you have friends who will be faithful unto death. The time is not now far off when you will again view the blessed sun-light."

The poetry of these remarks filled Jimmie with ecstasy, and he watched eagerly for the coming of the friends who would be faithful unto death. They delayed some time, for the reason that Willie Dalzel was making a speech.

"Now, men," he said, "our comrade is a prisoner in yon— in yond—in that there fortress. We must to the rescue. Who volunteers to go with me?" He fixed them with a stern eye.

There was a silence, and then one of the smaller boys remarked, "If Doc Trescott ketches us trackin' over his lawn—"

Willie Dalzel pounced upon the speaker and took him by the throat. The two presented a sort of a burlesque of the wood-cut on the cover of a dime novel which Willie had just been reading—*The Red Captain: A Tale of the Pirates of the Spanish Main.*

"You are a coward!" said Willie, through his clinched teeth.

"No, I ain't, Willie," piped the other, as best he could.

"I say you are," cried the great chieftain, indignantly. "Don't tell *me* I'm a liar." He relinquished his hold upon the coward and resumed his speech. "You know me, men. Many of you have been my followers for long years. You saw me slay Six-handed Dick with my own hand. You know I never falter. Our comrade is a prisoner in the cruel hands of our enemies. Aw, Pete Washington? He dassent. My pa says if Pete ever troubles me he'll brain 'im. Come on! To the rescue! Who will go with me to the rescue? Aw, come on! What are you afraid of?"

It was another instance of the power of eloquence upon the human mind. There was only one boy who was not thrilled by this oration, and he was a boy whose favorite reading had been of the road-agents and gun-fighters of the great West, and he thought the whole thing should be conducted in the Deadwood Dick manner. This talk of a "comrade" was silly;

"pard" was the proper word. He resolved that he would make a show of being a pirate, and keep secret the fact that he really was Hold-up Harry, the Terror of the Sierras.

But the others were knit close in piratical bonds. One by one they climbed the fence at a point hidden from the house by tall shrubs. With many a low-breathed caution they went upon their perilous adventure.

Jimmie was grown tired of waiting for his friends who would be faithful unto death. Finally he decided that he would rescue himself. It would be a gross breach of rule, but he couldn't sit there all the rest of the day waiting for his faithful-unto-death friends. The window was only five feet from the ground. He softly raised the sash and threw one leg over the sill. But at the same time he perceived his friends snaking among the bushes. He withdrew his leg and waited, seeing that he was now to be rescued in an orthodox way. The brave pirates came nearer and nearer.

Jimmie heard a noise of a closing door, and turning, he saw his father in the room looking at him and the open window in angry surprise. Boys never faint, but Jimmie probably came as near to it as may the average boy.

"What's all this?" asked the doctor, staring. Involuntarily Jimmie glanced over his shoulder through the window. His father saw the creeping figures. "What are those boys doing?" he said, sharply, and he knit his brows.

"Nothin'."

"Nothing! Don't tell me that. Are they coming here to the window?"

"Y-e-s, sir."

"What for?"

"To—to see me."

"What about?"

"About—about nothin'."

"What about?"

Jimmie knew that he could conceal nothing. He said, "They're comin' to—to—to rescue me." He began to whimper.

The doctor sat down heavily.

"What? To rescue you?" he gasped.

"Y-yes, sir."

The doctor's eyes began to twinkle. "Very well," he said presently. "I will sit here and observe this rescue. And on no account do you warn them that I am here. Understand?"

Of course Jimmie understood. He had been mad to warn his friends, but his father's mere presence had frightened him from doing it. He stood trembling at the window, while the doctor stretched in an easy-chair near at hand. They waited. The doctor could tell by his son's increasing agitation that the great moment was near. Suddenly he heard Willie Dalzel's voice hiss out a word: "S-s-silence!" Then the same voice addressed Jimmie at the window: "Good cheer, my comrade. The time is now at hand. I have come. Never did the Red Captain turn his back on a friend. One minute more and you will be free. Once aboard my gallant craft and you can bid defiance to your haughty enemies. Why don't you hurry up? What are you standin' there lookin' like a cow for?"

"I—er—now—you—" stammered Jimmie.

Here Hold-up Harry, the Terror of the Sierras, evidently concluded that Willie Dalzel had had enough of the premier part, so he said: "Brace up, pard. Don't ye turn white-livered now, fer ye know that Hold-up Harry, the Terrar of the Sarahs, ain't the man ter—"

"Oh, stop it!" said Willie Dalzel. "He won't understand that, you know. He's a pirate. Now, Jimmie, come on. Be of light heart, my comrade. Soon you—"

"I 'low arter all this here long time in jail ye thought ye had no friends mebbe, but I tell ye Hold-up Harry, the Terrar of the Sarahs—"

"A boat is waitin'—"

"I have ready a trusty horse—"

Willie Dalzel could endure his rival no longer.

"Look here, Henry, you're spoilin' the whole thing. We're all pirates, don't you see, and you're a pirate too."

"I ain't a pirate. I'm Hold-up Harry, the Terrar of the Sarahs."

"You ain't, I say," said Willie, in despair. "You're spoilin' everything, you are. All right, now. You wait. I'll fix you for this, see if I don't! Oh, come on, Jimmie. A boat awaits us at the foot of the rocks. In one short hour you'll be free forever from your ex—excwable enemies, and their vile plots. Hasten, for the dawn approaches."

The suffering Jimmie looked at his father, and was surprised at what he saw. The doctor was doubled up like a man with the colic. He was breathing heavily. The boy turned again to his friends. "I—now—look here," he began, stumbling among the words. "You—I—I don't think I'll be rescued to-day."

The pirates were scandalized. "What?" they whispered, angrily. "Ain't you goin' to be rescued? Well, all right for you, Jimmie Trescott. That's a nice way to act, that is!" Their upturned eyes glowered at Jimmie.

Suddenly Doctor Trescott appeared at the window with Jimmie. "Oh, go home, boys!" he gasped, but they did not hear him. Upon the instant they had whirled and scampered away like deer. The first lad to reach the fence was the Red Captain, but Hold-up Harry, the Terror of the Sierras, was so close that there was little to choose between them.

Doctor Trescott lowered the window, and then spoke to his son in his usual quiet way. "Jimmie, I wish you would go and tell Peter to have the buggy ready at seven o'clock."

"Yes, sir," said Jimmie, and he swaggered out to the stables. "Pete, father wants the buggy ready at seven o'clock."

Peter paid no heed to this order, but with the tender sympathy of a true friend he inquired, "Hu't?"

"Hurt? Did what hurt?"

"Yer trouncin'."

"Trouncin'!" said Jimmie, contemptuously. "I didn't get any trouncin'."

"No?" said Peter. He gave Jimmie a quick shrewd glance, and saw that he was telling the truth. He began to mutter and mumble over his work. "Ump! Ump! Dese yer white folks act like they think er boy's made er glass. No trouncin'! Ump!" He was consumed with curiosity to learn why Jimmie had not felt a heavy parental hand, but he did not care to lower his dignity by asking questions about it. At last, however, he reached the limits of his endurance, and in a voice pretentiously careless he asked, "Didn' yer pop take on like mad erbout dese yer cay'ge-lamps?"

"Carriage-lamps?" inquired Jimmie.

"Ump."

"No, he didn't say anything about carriage-lamps—not that I remember. Maybe he did, though. Lemme see. . . . No, he never mentioned 'em."

The Knife
I

S I BRYANT'S PLACE was on the shore of the lake and his garden patch, shielded from the north by a bold little promontory and a higher ridge inland, was accounted the most successful and surprising in all Whilomville town-ship. One afternoon, Si was working in the garden patch when Doctor Trescott's man, Peter Washington, came trudging slowly along the road, observing nature. He scanned the white man's fine agricultural results. "Take your eye off them there melons, you rascal," said Si placidly.

The negro's face widened in a grin of delight. "Well, Mist' Bryant, I raikon I ain't on'y make m'se'f covertous er-lookin' at dem yere mellums, sure 'nough. Dey suhtainly is grand."

"That's all right," responded Si with affected bitterness of spirit. "That's all right. Just don't you admire 'm too much— that's all."

Peter chuckled and chuckled. "Ma Lode, Mist' Bryant, y-y-you don' think I'm gwine come prowlin' in dish yer gawden?"

"No, I know you hain't," said Si with solemnity. "B'cause if you did, I'd shoot you so full of holes you couldn't tell yourself from a sponge."

"Um—no seh! No seh! I don' raikon you'll git chance at Pete, Mist' Bryant. No seh. I'll take an' run 'long an' rob er bank 'fore I'll come foolishin' 'roun' *your* gawden, Mist' Bryant."

Bryant, gnarled and strong as an old tree, leaned on his hoe and laughed a Yankee laugh. His mouth remained tightly closed but the sinister lines which ran from the sides of his nose to the meetings of his lips developed to form a comic oval and he emitted a series of grunts while his eyes gleamed merrily and his shoulders shook. Peter, on the contrary, threw back his head and guffawed thunderously. The effete joke in regard to an American negro's fondness for water-melons was still an admirable pleasantry to them and this was not the first time they had engaged in badinage over it. In fact, this venerable survival had formed between them a friendship of casual roadside quality.

Afterward, Peter went on up the road. He continued to chuckle until he was far away. He was going to pay a visit to old Alek Williams, a negro who lived with a large family in a hut clinging to the side of a mountain. The scattered colony of negroes which hovered near Whilomville was of interesting origin being the result of some contrabands who had drifted as far north as Whilomville during the great civil war. The descendants of these adventurers were mainly conspicuous for their bewildering number and the facility which they possessed for adding even to this number. Speaking for example of the Jacksons—one couldn't hurl a . stone into the hills about Whilomville without having it land on the roof of a hut full of Jacksons. The town reaped little in labor from these curious suburbs. There were a few men who came in regularly to work in gardens, to drive teams, to care for horses, and there were a few women who came in to cook or to wash. These latter had, usually, drunken husbands. In the main the colony loafed in high spirits and the industrious minority gained no direct honor from their fellows unless they spent their earnings on raiment—in which case, they were naturally treated with distinction. On the whole, the hardships of these people were the wind, the rain, the snow and any other physical difficulties which they could cultivate. About twice a year, the lady philanthropists of Whilomville went up against them, and came away poorer in goods but rich in complacence. After one of these attacks, the colony would preserve a comic air of rectitude for two days and then relapse again to the genial irresponsibility of a crew of monkeys.

Peter Washington was one of the industrious class who occupied a position of distinction for he surely spent his money on personal decoration. On occasion, he could dress better than the mayor of Whilomville himself, or at least in more colors, which was the main thing to the minds of his admirers. His ideal had been the late gallant Henry Johnson whose conquests in Watermelon Alley as well as in the hill shanties had proved him the equal if not the superior of any Pullman-car porter in the country. Perhaps Peter had too much Virginia laziness and humor in him to be a wholly adequate successor to the fastidious Henry Johnson but at any rate he admired his memory so attentively as to be openly termed a dude by envious people.

On this afternoon he was going to call on old Alek Williams because Alek's eldest girl was just turned seventeen and, to Peter's mind, was a triumph of beauty. He was not wearing his best clothes because on his last visit Alek's half-breed hound, Susie, had taken occasion to forcefully extract a quite large and valuable part of the visitor's trousers. When Peter arrived at the end of the rocky field which contained old Alek's shanty, he stooped and provided himself with several large stones, weighing them carefully in his hand and finally continuing his journey with three stones of about eight ounces each. When he was near the house, three gaunt hounds, Rover and Carlo and Susie, came sweeping down upon him. His impression was that they were going to climb him as if he were a tree but at the critical moment they swerved and went growling and snapping around him, their heads low, their eyes malignant. The afternoon caller waited until the Susie presented her side to him. Then he heaved one of his eight-ounce rocks. When it landed, her hollow ribs gave forth a drum-like sound and she was knocked sprawling, her legs in air. The other hounds at once fled in horror and she followed as soon as she was able, yelping at the top of her lungs. The afternoon caller resumed his march.

At the wild expressions of Susie's anguish, old Alek had flung open the door and come hastily into the sunshine. "Yah, you Suse, come erlong outa dat now. What fer you—oh, how'do, how'do, Mist' Wash'ton, how'do."

"How'do, Mist' Willums. I done foun' it necessa'y fer ter damnearkill dish yer dawg a' your'n, Mist' Willums."

"Come in, come in, Mist' Wash'ton. Dawg no 'count, Mist' Wash'ton." Then he turned to address the unfortunate animal. "Hu't, did it? Hu't? 'Pears like you gwine lun some saince by time somebody brek yer back. 'Pears like I gwine club yer inter er frazzle 'fore you fin' out some saince. Gw'on 'way f'm yah."

As the old man and his guest entered the shanty, a body of black children spread out in crescent-shaped formation and observed Peter with awe. Fat old Mrs. Williams greeted him turbulently while the oldest girl, Mollie, lurked in a corner

and giggled with finished imbecility; gazing at the visitor
with eyes that were shy and bold by turns. She seemed at
times absurdly over-confident; at times, foolishly afraid; but
her giggle consistently endured. It was a giggle on which an
irascible but right-minded judge would have ordered her
forthwith to be buried alive.

Amid a great deal of hospitable gabbling, Peter was con-
ducted to the best chair out of the three the house contained.
Enthroned therein, he made himself charming in talk to the
old people who beamed upon him joyously. As for Mollie, he
affected to be unaware of her existence. This may have been
a method for entrapping the sentimental interest of that
young gazelle or it may be that the giggle had worked upon
him.

He was absolutely fascinating to the old people. They could
talk like rotary snow-ploughs and he gave them every chance
while his face was illumined with appreciation. They pressed
him to stay to supper and he consented after a glance at the
pot on the stove which was too furtive to be noted.

During the meal, old Alek recounted the high state of
Judge Oglethorpe's kitchen garden which Alek said was due
to his unremitting industry and fine intelligence. Alek was a
gardener whenever impending starvation forced him to cease
temporarily from being a lily of the field.

"Mist' Bryant he suhtainly got er grand gawden," observed
Peter.

"Dat so, dat so, Mist' Wash'ton," assented Alek. "He got
fine gawden."

"Seems like I nev' *did* see sech mellums; big as er bar'l,
layin' dere. I don't raikon an'body in dish yer county kin hol'
it with Mist' Bryant when comes ter mellums."

"Dat so, Mist' Wash'ton."

They did not talk of water-melons until their heads held
nothing else, as the phrase goes. But they talked of water-
melons until when Peter started for home that night over a
lonely road, they held a certain dominant position in his
mind. Alek had come with him as far as the fence in order to
protect him from a possible attack by the mongrels. There
they had cheerfully parted, two honest men.

The night was dark and heavy with moisture. Peter found

it uncomfortable to walk rapidly. He merely loitered on the road. When opposite Si Bryant's place, he paused and looked over the fence into the garden. He imagined he could see the form of a huge melon lying in dim stateliness, not ten yards away. He looked at the Bryant house. Two windows, down stairs, were lighted. The Bryants kept no dog, old Si's favorite child having once been bitten by a dog and having since died, within that year, of pneumonia.

Peering over the fence, Peter fancied that if any low-minded night-prowler should happen to note the melon, he would not find it difficult to possess himself of it. This person would merely wait until the lights were out in the house and the people presumably asleep. Then he would climb the fence, reach the melon in a few strides, sever the stem with his ready knife, and in a trice be back in the road with his prize. There need be no noise and, after all, the house was some distance.

Selecting a smooth bit of turf, Peter took seat by the roadside. From time to time he glanced at the lighted windows.

II

When Peter and Alek had said good-bye, the old man turned back in the rocky field and shaped a slow course toward that high dim light which marked the little window of his shanty. It would be incorrect to say that Alek could think of nothing but water-melons. But it was true that Si Bryant's water-melon patch occupied a certain conspicuous position in his thoughts.

He sighed; he almost wished that he was again a conscienceless pickaninny instead of being one of the most ornate, solemn and look-at-me-sinner deacons that ever graced the handle of a collection-basket. At this time, it made him quite sad to reflect upon his granite integrity. A weaker man might perhaps bow his moral head to the temptation but for him such a fall was impossible. He was a prince of the church and if he had been nine princes of the church, he could not have been more proud. In fact, religion was to the old man a sort of a personal dignity. And he was on Sundays so obtrusively good that you could see his sanctity through a door.

He forced it on you until you would have felt its influence even in a fore-castle.

It was clear in his mind that he must put water-melon thoughts from him and, after a moment, he told himself with much ostentation that he had done so. But it was cooler under the sky than in the shanty and as he was not sleepy he decided to take a stroll down to Si Bryant's place and look at the melons from a pinnacle of spotless innocence. Reaching the road he paused to listen. It would not do to let Peter hear him because that graceless rapscallion would probably misunderstand him. But assuring himself that Peter was well on his way, he set out walking briskly until he was within four hundred yards of Bryant's place. Here he went to the side of the road and walked thereafter on the damp yielding turf. He made no sound.

He did not go on to that point in the main road which was directly opposite the water-melon patch. He did not wish to have his ascetic contemplation disturbed by some chance wayfarer. He turned off along a short lane which led to Si Bryant's barn. Here he reached a place where he could see, over the fence, the faint shapes of the melons.

Alek was affected. The house was some distance away, there was no dog and doubtless the Bryants would soon extinguish their lights and go to bed. Then some poor lost lamb of sin might come and scale the fence, reach a melon in a moment, sever the stem with his ready knife and in a trice be back in the road with his prize. And this poor lost lamb of sin might even be a bishop but no one would ever know it. Alek singled out with his eye a very large melon and thought that the lamb would prove his judgment if he took that one.

He found a soft place in the grass, and arranged himself comfortably. He watched the lights in the windows.

III

It seemed to Peter Washington that the Bryants absolutely consulted their own wishes in regard to the time for retiring; but at last he saw the lighted windows fade briskly from left to right and after a moment a window on the second floor blazed out against the darkness. Si was going to bed. In five minutes, this window abruptly vanished and all the world was night.

Peter spent the ensuing quarter-hour in no mental debate. His mind was fixed. He was here and the melon was there. He would have it. But an idea of being caught appalled him. He thought of his position. He was the beau of his community, honored right and left. He pictured the consternation of his friends and the cheers of his enemies if the hands of the redoubtable Si Bryant should grip him in his shame.

He arose and going to the fence, listened. No sound broke the stillness, save the rhythmical incessant clicking of myriad insects and the guttural chanting of the frogs in the reeds at the lakeside. Moved by sudden decision, he climbed the fence and crept silently and swiftly down upon the melon. His open knife was in his hand. There was the melon, cool, fair to see, as pompous in its fatness as the cook in a monastery.

Peter put out a hand to steady it while he cut the stem. But at the instant he was aware that a black form had dropped over the fence lining the lane in front of him and was coming stealthily toward him. In a palsy of terror he dropped flat upon the ground, not having strength enough to run away. The next moment he was looking into the amazed and agonized face of old Alek Williams.

There was a moment of loaded silence and then Peter was overcome by a mad inspiration. He suddenly dropped his knife and leaped upon Alek. "I got'che!" he hissed. "I got'che! I got'che!" The old man sank down as limp as rags.

"I got'che! I got'che! Steal Mist' Bryant's mellums, hey?"

Alek in a low voice began to beg. "Oh, Mist' Peteh Wash'ton, don' go fer ter be too ha'd on er ole man. I nev' come yere fer ter steal 'em. 'Deed, I didn't, Mist' Wash'ton. I come yere jes fer ter *feel* 'em. Oh, please, Mist' Wash'ton—"

"Come erlong outa yere, you ol' rip," said Peter. "An' don' trumple on dese yer baids. I gwine put you wah you won' ketch col'."

Without difficulty he tumbled the whining Alek over the fence to the road-way, and followed him with sheriff-like expedition. He took him by the scruff. "Come erlong, deacon. I raikon I gwine put you wah you kin pray, deacon. Come erlong, deacon."

The emphasis and reiteration of his layman's title in the church produced a deadly effect upon Alek. He felt to his marrow the heinous crime into which this treacherous night had betrayed him. As Peter marched his prisoner up the road toward the mouth of the lane, he continued his remarks. "Come erlong, deacon. Nev' see er man so anxious-like er-bout er mellum-paitch, deacon. Seem like you jes' must see 'em er-growin' an' *feel* 'em, deacon. Mist' Bryant he'll be s'prised, deacon, findin' out you come fer ter *feel* his mellums. Come erlong, deacon. Mist' Bryant he expectin' some ole rip like you come soon."

They had almost reached the lane when Alek's cur Susie who had followed her master approached in the silence which attends dangerous dogs; and seeing indications of what she took to be war she appended herself swiftly but firmly to the calf of Peter's left leg. The melee was short but spirited. Alek had no wish to have his dog complicate his already serious misfortunes and went manfully to the defense of his captor. He procured a large stone and by beating this with both hands down upon the resounding skull of the animal, he induced her to quit her grip. Breathing heavily Peter dropped into the long grass at the roadside. He said nothing.

"Mist' Wash'ton," said Alek at last in a quavering voice, "I raikon I gwine wait yere see what you gwine do ter me."

Whereupon Peter passed into a spasmodic state in which he rolled to and fro and shook.

"Mist' Wash'ton, I hope dish yer dog ain't gone an' give you fitses?"

Peter sat up suddenly. "No, she ain't," he answered, "but she gin me er big skeer an' fer yer 'sistance with er cobble-stone, Mist' Willums, I tell you waht I gwine do—I tell you what I gwine do." He waited an impressive moment. "I gwine 'lease you."

Old Alek trembled like a little bush in a wind. "Mist' Wash'ton?"

Quoth Peter deliberately: "I gwine 'lease you."

The old man was filled with a desire to negotiate this statement at once but he felt the necessity of carrying off the event without an appearance of haste. "Yes, seh; thank'e, seh; thank'e, Mist' Wash'ton. I raikon I ramble home pressenly."

He waited an interval and then dubiously said: "Good evenin', Mist' Wash'ton?"

"Good evenin', deacon. Don' come foolin' roun' *feelin'* no mellums and I say troof. Good evenin', deacon."

Alek took off his hat and made three profound bows. "Thank'e, seh. Thank'e, seh. Thank'e, seh."

Peter underwent another severe spasm but the old man walked off toward his home with a humble and a contrite heart.

IV

The next morning, Alek proceeded from his shanty under the complete but customary illusion that he was going to work. He trudged manfully along until he reached the vicinity of Si Bryant's place. Then, by stages, he relapsed into a slink. He was passing the garden patch under full steam when, at some distance ahead of him he saw Si Bryant leaning casually on the garden fence.

"Good mornin', Alek."

"Good mawnin', Mist' Bryant," answered Alek with a new deference. He was marching on when he was halted by a word—"Alek."

He stopped. "Yes, seh."

"I found a knife this mornin' in th' road," drawled Si, "an' I thought maybe it was your'n."

Improved in mind by this divergence from the direct line of attack, Alek stepped up easily to look at the knife. "No, seh," he said scanning it as it lay in Si's palm while the cold steel-blue eyes of the white man looked down into his stomach, " 'tain't no knife er mine." But he knew the knife. He knew it as if it had been his mother. And at the same moment a spark flashed through his head and made wise his understanding. He knew everything. " 'Tain't much of er knife, Mist' Bryant," he said, deprecatingly.

" 'Tain't much of a knife, I know that," cried Si in sudden heat, "but I found it this mornin' in my water-melon patch—hear?"

"Watah-mellum paitch?" yelled Alek, not astounded.

"Yes, in my water-melon patch," sneered Si, "an' I think you know something about it, too!"

"Me?" cried Alek. "Me?"

"Yes—you," said Si with icy ferocity. "Yes—you!" He had become convinced that Alek was not in any way guilty but he was certain that the old man knew the owner of the knife and so he pressed him at first on criminal lines. "Alek, you might as well own up, now. You've been meddlin' with my water-melons!"

"Me?" cried Alek again. "Yah's *ma* knife. I done cah'e it foh yeahs."

Bryant changed his ways. "Look here, Alek," he said confidentially, "I know you and you know me and there ain't no use in any more skirmishin'. *I* know that *you* know whose knife that is. Now, whose is it?"

This challenge was so formidable in character that Alek temporarily quailed and began to stammer. "Er—now—Mist' Bryant—you—you—frien' er mine—"

"I know I'm a friend of yours, but," said Bryant inexorably, " who owns this knife?"

Alek gathered unto himself some remnants of dignity and spoke with reproach. "Mist' Bryant, dish yer knife ain' mine."

"No," said Bryant, "it ain't. But you know who it belongs to an' I want you to tell me—quick."

"Well, Mist' Bryant," answered Alek scratching his wool, "I won't say's I *do* know who b'longs ter dish yer knife an' I won't say's I *don't*."

Bryant again laughed his Yankee laugh but this time there was little humor in it. It was dangerous.

Alek seeing that he had gotten himself into hot water by the fine diplomacy of his last sentence, immediately began to flounder and totally submerge himself. "No, Mist' Bryant," he repeated, "I won't say's I *do* know who b'longs ter dish yer knife an' I won't say's I *don't*." And he began to parrot this fatal sentence again and again. It seemed wound about his tongue. He could not rid himself of it. Its very power to make trouble for him seemed to originate the mysterious Afric reason for its repetition.

"Is he a very close friend of your'n?" said Bryant softly.

"F-frien'?" stuttered Alek. He appeared to weigh this question with much care. "Well, seems like he *was* er frien' an', then agin, it seems like he—"

" 'It seems like he *wasn't*'?" asked Bryant.

"Yes, seh, jest so, jest so," cried Alek. "Sometimes it seems like he *wasn't*. Then agin—" He stopped for profound meditation.

The patience of the white man seemed inexhaustible. At length his low and oily voice broke the stillness. "Oh, well, of course, if he's a friend of your'n, Alek! You know I wouldn't want to make no trouble for a friend of your'n."

"Yes, seh," cried the negro at once. "He's er frien' er mine. He is dat."

"Well, then, it seems as if about the only thing to do is for you to tell me his name so's I can send him his knife and that's all there is to it."

Alek took off his hat and in perplexity ran his hand over his wool. He studied the ground. But several times he raised his eyes to take a sly peep at the imperturbable visage of the white man. "Y-y-yes, Mist' Bryant. . . . I raikon dat's erbout all what kin be done. I gwine tell you who b'longs ter dish yer knife."

"Of course," said the smooth Bryant, "it ain't a very nice thing to have to do but—"

"No, seh," cried Alek brightly, "I'm gwine tell you, Mist' Bryant. I gwine tell you erbout dat knife. Mist' Bryant," he asked solemnly, "does you know who b'longs ter dat knife?"

"No. I—"

"Well, I gwine tell. I gwine tell who. Mist' Bryant—" The old man drew himself to a stately pose and held forth his arm. "I gwine tell who. Mist' Bryant, *dish yer knife b'longs ter Sam Jackson!*"

Bryant was startled into indignation. "Who in hell is Sam Jackson?" he growled.

"He's a nigger," said Alek impressively, "an' he wuks in er lumbeh-yawd up yere in Hoswego."

The Trial, Execution, and Burial
of Homer Phelps

FROM TIME TO TIME, an enwearied pine-bough let fall to
the earth its load of melting snow and the branch swung
back glistening in the faint wintry sun-light. Down the gulch
a brook clattered amid its ice with the sound of a perpetual
breaking of glass. All the forest looked drenched and for-
lorn.

The sky-line was a ragged enclosure of grey cliffs and hem-
locks and pines. If one had been miraculously set down in
this gulch one could have imagined easily that the nearest hu-
man habitation was hundreds of miles away if it were not for
an old half-discernible wood-road that led toward the brook.

"Halt! Who's there?"

This low and gruff cry suddenly dispelled the stillness
which lay upon the lonely gulch but the hush which followed
it seemed even more profound. The hush endured for some
seconds and then the voice of the challenger was again raised,
this time with a distinctly querulous note in it.

"Halt! Who's there? Why don't you answer when I holler?
Don't you know you're likely to get shot?"

A second voice answered: "Oh, you knew who I was, easy
enough."

"That don't make no diff'rence." One of the Margate twins
stepped from a thicket and confronted Homer Phelps on the
old wood-road. The majestic scowl of official wrath was upon
the brow of Reeves Margate; a long stick was held in the
hollow of his arm as one would hold a rifle and he strode
grimly to the other boy. "That don't make no diff'rence.
You've got to answer when I holler, anyhow. Willie says so."

At the mention of the dread chieftain's name, the Phelps
boy daunted a trifle but he still sulkily murmured: "Well, you
knew it was me."

He started on his way through the snow but the twin stur-
dily blocked the path. "You can't pass less'n you give the
counter-sign."

"Huh?" said the Phelps boy. "Counter-sign?"

"Yes—counter-sign," sneered the twin, strong in his sense of virtue.

But the Phelps boy became very angry. "Can't I, hey? Can't I, hey? I'll show you whether I can or not. I'll show you, Reeves Margate."

There was a short scuffle and then arose the anguished clamor of the sentry: "Hey, fellers! Here's a man tryin' to run a-past the guard. Hey, fellers! Hey!"

There was a great noise in the adjacent under-brush. The voice of Willie could be heard exhorting his followers to charge swiftly and bravely. Then they appeared—Willie Dalzel, Jimmie Trescott, the other Margate twin, and Dan Earl. The chieftain's face was dark with wrath. "What's the matter? Can't you play it right? Ain't you got any sense?" he asked the Phelps boy.

The sentry was yelling out his grievance. "Now—he come along an' I hollered at 'im, an' he didn't pay no 'tention an' when I ast 'im for the counter-sign, he wouldn't say nothin'. That ain't no way."

"Can't you play it right?" asked the chief again with gloomy scorn.

"He knew it was me, easy enough," said the Phelps boy.

"That ain't got nothin' to do with it," cried the chief furiously. "That ain't got nothin' to do with it. If you're goin' to play, you've got to play it right. It ain't no fun if you go spoilin' the whole thing this way. Can't you play it right?"

"I forgot the counter-sign," lied the culprit weakly.

Whereupon the remainder of the band yelled out with one triumphant voice: "War to the knife! War to the knife! I remember it, Willie. Don't I, Willie?"

The leader was puzzled. Evidently he was trying to develop in his mind a plan for dealing correctly with this unusual incident. He felt, no doubt, that he must proceed according to the books but unfortunately the books did not cover the point precisely. However he finally said to Homer Phelps: "You are under arrest." Then with a stentorian voice he shouted: "Seize him!"

His loyal followers looked startled for a brief moment but directly they began to move upon the Phelps boy. The latter clearly did not intend to be seized. He backed away, expostulating wildly. He even seemed somewhat frightened. "No; no; don't you touch me, I tell you; don't you dare touch me."

The others did not seem anxious to engage. They moved slowly watching the desperate light in his eyes. The chieftain stood with folded arms, his face growing darker and darker with impatience. At length, he burst out: "Oh, seize him, I tell you! Why don't you seize him! Grab him by the leg, Dannie! Hurry up, all of you. Seize him, I keep a-sayin'."

Thus adjured, the Margate twins and Dan Earl made another pained effort while Jimmie Trescott manoeuvred to cut off a retreat. But, to tell the truth, there was boyish law which held them back from laying hands of violence upon little Phelps under these conditions. Perhaps it was because they were only playing whereas he now was undeniably serious. At any rate they looked very sick of their occupation.

"Don't you dare," snarled the Phelps boy, facing first one and then the other; he was almost in tears—"don't you dare touch me."

The chieftain was now hopping with exasperation. "Oh, seize him, can't you! You're no good at all." Then he loosed his wrath upon the Phelps boy: "Stand still, Homer, can't you? You've got to be seized, you know. That ain't the way. It ain't any fun if you keep a-dodgin' that way. Stand still, can't you? You've got to be seized."

"I don't *want* to be seized," retorted the Phelps boy, obstinate and bitter.

"But you've *got* to be seized," yelled the maddened chief. "Don't you see? That's the way to play it."

The Phelps boy answered promptly: "But I don't want to play that way."

"But that's the *right* way to play it. Don't you see? You've got to play it the right way. You've got to be seized an' then we'll hold a trial on you an'—an' all sorts of things."

But this prospect held no illusions for the Phelps boy. He continued doggedly to repeat: "I don't want to play that way."

Of course in the end the chief stooped to beg and beseech this unreasonable lad. "Oh, come on, Homer. Don't be so mean. You're a-spoilin' everything. We won't hurt you any.

Not the tintiest bit. It's all just playin'. What's the matter with you?"

The different tone of the leader made an immediate impression upon the other. He showed some signs of the beginning of weakness. "Well," he asked, "what you goin' to do?"

"Why, first we're goin' to put you in a dungeon or tie you to a stake or something like that—just pertend, you know," added the chief hurriedly, "an' then we'll hold a trial, awful solemn, but there won't be anything what'll hurt you. Not a thing."

And so the game was re-adjusted. The Phelps boy was marched off between Dan Earl and a Margate twin. The party proceeded to their camp which was hidden some hundred of feet back in the thickets. There was a miserable little hut with a pine-bark roof which so frankly and constantly leaked that existence in the open air was always preferable. At present it was noisily dripping melted snow into the black mouldy interior. In front of this hut, a feeble fire was flickering through its unhappy career. Under-foot, the watery snow was of the color of lead.

The party having arrived at the camp, the chief leaned against a tree and, balancing on one foot, drew off a rubber boot. From this boot, he emptied about a quart of snow. He squeezed his stocking which had a hole from which protruded a lobster-red toe. He resumed his boot. "Bring up the prisoner," said he. They did it. "Guilty or not guilty?" he asked.

"Huh?" said the Phelps boy.

"Guilty or not guilty?" demanded the chief peremptorily. "Guilty or not guilty? Don't you understand?"

Homer Phelps looked profoundly puzzled. " 'Guilty or not guilty'?" he asked slowly and weakly.

The chief made a swift gesture and turned in despair to the others. "Oh, he don't do it right. He does it all wrong." He again faced the prisoner with an air of making a last attempt. "Now, lookahere, Homer, when I say, 'Guilty or not guilty,' you want to up an' say, 'Not guilty.' Don't you see?"

"Not guilty," said Homer at once.

"No—no—no. Wait 'til I ask you. Now wait." He called out, pompously: "Pards, if this prisoner before us is guilty, what shall be his fate?"

All those well-trained little infants with one voice sung out: *"Death!"*

"Prisoner," continued the chief, "are you guilty or not guilty?"

"But, lookahere," argued Homer, "you said it wouldn't be nothin' what would hurt. I—"

"Thunder an' lightnin'," roared the wretched chief. "Keep your mouth shut, can't ye? What in the mischief—"

But there was an interruption from Jimmie Trescott who shouldered a twin aside and stepped to the front. "Here," he said very contemptuously, "let *me* be the prisoner. I'll show 'im how to do it."

"All right, Jim," cried the chief delighted. "You be the prisoner then. Now all you fellers with guns stand there in a row. Get out of the way, Homer." He cleared his throat and addressed Jimmie. "Prisoner, are you guilty or not guilty?"

"Not guilty," answered Jimmie firmly. Standing there before his judge—unarmed, slim, quiet, modest—he was ideal.

The chief beamed upon him and looked aside to cast a triumphant and withering glance upon Homer Phelps. He said: "There! That's the way to do it."

The twins and Dan Earl also much admired Jimmie.

"That's all right so far, anyhow," said the satisfied chief. "An' now we'll—now we'll—we'll perceed with the execution."

"That ain't right," said the new prisoner suddenly. "That ain't the next thing. You've got to have a trial first. You've got to fetch up a lot of people first who'll say I done it."

"That's so," said the chief. "I didn't think. Here, Reeves, you be first witness. Did the prisoner do it?"

The twin gulped for a moment in his anxiety to make the proper reply. He was at the point where the roads forked. Finally he hazarded, "Yes."

"There," said the chief, "that's one of 'em. Now, Dan, you be a witness. Did he do it?"

Dan Earl having before him the twin's example did not hesitate. "Yes," he said.

"Well, then, pards, what shall be his fate?"

Again came the ringing answer, *"Death!"*

With Jimmie in the principal role, this drama hidden deep

in the hemlock thicket neared a kind of perfection. "You must blindfold me," cried the condemned lad briskly, "an' then I'll go off an' stand an' you must all get in a row an' shoot me."

The chief gave this plan his urbane countenance and the twins and Dan Earl were greatly pleased. They blindfolded Jimmie under his careful directions. He waded a few paces into snow and then turned and stood with quiet dignity, awaiting his fate. The chief marshalled the twins and Dan Earl in line with their sticks. He gave the necessary commands: "Load! Ready! Aim! Fire!" At the last command the firing party all together yelled, "Bang!"

Jimmie threw his hands high, tottered in agony for a moment and then crashed full length into the snow—into, one would think, a serious case of pneumonia. It was beautiful.

He arose almost immediately and came back to them wondrously pleased with himself. They acclaimed him joyously.

The chief was particularly grateful. He was always trying to bring off these little romantic affairs and it seemed, after all, that the only boy who could ever really help him was Jimmie Trescott. "There," he said to the others, "that's the way it ought to be done."

They were touched to the heart by the whole thing and they looked at Jimmie with big smiling eyes. Jimmie, blown out like a balloon-fish with pride of his performance, swaggered to the fire and took seat on some wet hemlock-boughs. "Fetch some more wood, one of you kids," he murmured negligently. One of the twins came fortunately upon a small cedar tree the lower branches of which were dead and dry. An armful of these branches flung upon the sick fire soon made a high, ruddy, warm blaze which was like an illumination in honor of Jimmie's success.

The boys sprawled about the fire and talked the regular language of the game. "Waal, pards," remarked the chief, "it's many a night we've had together here in the Rockies among the b'ars an' the Indy-uns, hey?"

"Yes, pard," replied Jimmie Trescott, "I reckon you're right. Our wild free life is—there ain't nothin' to compare with our wild free life."

Whereupon the two lads arose and magnificently shook hands while the others watched them in an ecstasy. "I'll allus stick by ye, pard," said Jimmie earnestly. "When yer in trouble, don't forget that Lightnin' Lou is at yer back."

"Thanky, pard," quoth Willie Dalzel deeply affected. "I'll not forget it, pard. An' don't you forget, either, that Deadshot Demon, the leader of the Red Raiders, never forgits a friend."

But Homer Phelps was having none of this great fun. Since his disgraceful refusal to be seized and executed he had been hovering unheeded on the outskirts of the band. He seemed very sorry; he cast a wistful eye at the romantic scene. He knew too well that if he went near at that particular time he would be certain to encounter a pitiless snubbing. So he vacillated modestly in the background.

At last the moment came when he dared venture near enough to the fire to gain some warmth for he was now bitterly suffering with the cold. He sidled close to Willie Dalzel. No one heeded him. Eventually, he looked at his chief and with a bright face said, "Now—if I was seized now to be executed, I could do it as well as Jimmie Trescott, I could."

The chief gave a crow of scorn in which he was followed by the other boys. "Ho!" he cried, "why didn't you do it then? Why didn't you do it?" Homer Phelps felt upon him many pairs of disdainful eyes. He wagged his shoulders in misery.

"You're dead," said the chief frankly. "That's what you are. We executed you, we did."

"When?" demanded the Phelps boy with some spirit.

"Just a little while ago. Didn't we, fellers? Hey, fellers, didn't we?"

The trained chorus cried: "Yes, of course we did. You're dead, Homer. You can't play any more. You're dead."

"That wasn't me. It was Jimmie Trescott," he said in a low and bitter voice, his eyes on the ground. He would have given the world if he could have retracted his mad refusals of the early part of the drama.

"No," said the chief, "it was you. We're playin' it was you, an' it *was* you. You're dead, you are." And seeing the cruel effect of his words he did not refrain from administering some advice: "The next time, don't be such a chuckle-head."

Presently the camp imagined that it was attacked by Indians and the boys dodged behind trees with their stick-rifles shouting out, "Bang!" and encouraging each other to resist until the last. In the meantime the dead lad hovered near the fire looking moodily at the gay and exciting scene. After the fight the gallant defenders returned one by one to the fire where they grandly clasped hands, calling each other "old pard," and boasting of their deeds.

Parenthetically, one of the twins had an unfortunate inspiration. "I killed the Indy-un chief, fellers. Did you see me kill the Indy-un chief?"

But Willie Dalzel, his own chief, turned upon him wrathfully: "*You* didn't kill no chief. *I* killed 'im with me own hand."

"Oh!" said the twin, apologetically, at once. "It must have been some other Indy-un."

"Who's wounded?" cried Willie Dalzel. "Ain't anybody wounded?" The party professed themselves well and sound. The roving and inventive eye of the chief chanced upon Homer Phelps. "Ho! Here's a dead man! Come on, fellers, here's a dead man! We've got to bury him, you know." And at his bidding they pounced upon the dead Phelps lad. The unhappy boy saw clearly his road to rehabilitation but mind and body revolted at the idea of burial even as they had revolted at the thought of execution. "No!" he said stubbornly. "No! I don't want to be buried! I don't want to be buried!"

"You've *got* to be buried!" yelled the chief passionately. " 'Tain't goin' to hurt ye, is it? Think you're made of glass? Come on, fellers, get the grave ready!"

They scattered hemlock-boughs upon the snow in the form of a rectangle and piled other boughs near at hand. The victim surveyed these preparations with a glassy eye. When all was ready, the chief turned determinedly to him: "Come on now, Homer. We've got to carry you to the grave. Get him by the legs, Jim!"

Little Phelps had now passed into that state which may be described as a curious and temporary childish fatalism. He still objected but it was only feeble muttering as if he did not know what he spoke. In some confusion they carried him to the rectangle of hemlock-boughs and dropped him. Then they piled other boughs upon him until he was not to be seen. The chief stepped forward to make a short address but before proceeding with it he thought it expedient, from certain indications, to speak to the grave itself. "Lie still, can't ye? Lie still until I get through." There was a faint movement of the boughs and then a perfect silence.

The chief took off his hat. Those who watched him could see that his face was harrowed with emotion. "Pards," he began brokenly—"pards, we've got one more debt to pay them murderin' red-skins. Bowie-knife Joe was a brave man an' a good pard but—he's gone now—gone." He paused for a moment, overcome, and the stillness was only broken by the deep manly grief of Jimmie Trescott.

The Fight

I

THE CHILD LIFE of the neighborhood was sometimes moved in its deeps at the sight of wagon-loads of furniture arriving in front of some house which with closed blinds and barred doors had been for a time a mystery or even a fear. The boys often expressed this fear by stamping bravely and noisily on the porch of the house and then suddenly darting away with screams of nervous laughter as if they expected to be pursued by something uncanny. There was a group who held that the cellar of a vacant house was certainly the abode of robbers, smugglers, assassins, mysterious masked men in council about the dim rays of a candle and possessing skulls, emblematic bloody daggers, and owls. Then, near the first of April, would come along a wagon-load of furniture and children would assemble on the walk by the gate and make serious examination of everything that passed into the house and taking no thought whatever of masked men.

One day, it was announced in the neighborhood that a family was actually moving into the Hannigan house, next door to Doctor Trescott's. Jimmie was one of the first to be informed and by the time some of his friends came dashing up, he was versed in much.

"Any boys?" they demanded eagerly.

"Yes," answered Jimmie proudly. "One's a little feller and one's 'most as big as me. I saw 'em, I did."

"Where are they?" asked Willie Dalzel as if under the circumstances he could not take Jimmie's word but must have the evidence of his senses.

"Oh, they're in there," said Jimmie carelessly. It was evident he owned these new boys.

Willie Dalzel resented Jimmie's proprietary way. "Ho," he cried scornfully. "Why don't they come out then? Why don't they come out?"

"How'd I know?" said Jimmie.

"Well," retorted Willie Dalzel, "you seemed to know so thundering much about 'em."

At the moment, a boy came strolling down the gravel walk

which led from the front door to the gate. He was about the
height and age of Jimmie Trescott but he was thick through
the chest and had fat legs. His face was round and rosy and
plump but his hair was curly black and his brows were natu-
rally darkling so that he resembled both a pudding and a
young bull.

He approached slowly the group of older inhabitants and
they had grown profoundly silent. They looked him over; he
looked them over. They might have been savages observing
the first white man or white men observing the first savage.
The silence held steady.

As he neared the gate, the strange boy wandered off to the
left in a definite way which proved his instinct to make a cir-
cular voyage when in doubt. The motionless group stared at
him. In time, this unsmiling scrutiny worked upon him some-
what and he leaned against the fence and fastidiously exam-
ined one shoe.

In the end, Willie Dalzel authoritatively broke the stillness.
"What's your name?" said he gruffly.

"Johnnie Hedge, 'tis," answered the new boy. Then came
another great silence while Whilomville pondered this intelli-
gence.

Again came the voice of authority—"Where'd you live
b'fore?"

"Jersey City."

These two sentences completed the first section of the
formal code. The second section concerned itself with the es-
tablishment of the newcomer's exact position in the
neighborhood.

"I kin lick you," announced Willie Dalzel and awaited the
answer.

The Hedge boy had stared at Willie Dalzel but he stared at
him again. After a pause he said: "I know you kin."

"Well," demanded Willie, "kin *he* lick you?" And he indi-
cated Jimmie Trescott with a sweep which announced plainly
that Jimmie was the next in prowess.

Whereupon the new boy looked at Jimmie respectfully but
carefully and at length said: "I dunno."

This was the signal for an outburst of shrill screaming and
everybody pushed Jimmie forward. He knew what he had to

say and as befitted the occasion he said it fiercely. "Kin you lick me?"

The new boy also understood what he had to say and, despite his unhappy and lonely state, he said it bravely. "Yes."

"Well," retorted Jimmie bluntly, "come out and do it then! Jest come out and do it!" And these words were greeted with cheers. These little rascals yelled that there should be a fight at once. They were in bliss over the prospect. "Go on, Jim! Make 'im come out. He said he could lick you! Aw-aw-aw! He said he could lick you!" There probably never was a fight among this class in Whilomville which was not the result of the goading and guying of two proud lads by a populace of urchins who simply wished to see a show.

Willie Dalzel was very busy. He turned first to the one and then to the other. "You said you could lick him. Well, why don't you come out and do it then? You said you could lick him, didn't you?"

"Yes," answered the new boy, dogged and dubious.

Willie tried to drag Jimmie by the arm. "Aw, go on, Jimmie. You ain't afraid, are you?"

"No," said Jimmie.

The two victims opened wide eyes at each other. The fence separated them and so it was impossible for them to immediately engage but they seemed to understand that they were ultimately to be sacrificed to the ferocious aspirations of the other boys and each scanned the other to learn something of his spirit. They were not angry at all. They were merely two little gladiators who were being clamorously told to hurt each other. Each displayed hesitation and doubt without displaying fear. They did not exactly understand what were their feelings and they moodily kicked the ground and made low and sullen answers to Willie Dalzel who worked like a circus-manager.

"Aw, go on, Jim! What's the matter with you? You ain't afraid, are you? Well, then, say something." This sentiment received more cheering from the abandoned little wretches who wished to be entertained and in this cheering there could be heard notes of derision of Jimmie Trescott. The latter had a position to sustain; he was well-known; he often bragged of his willingness and ability to thrash other boys; well, then, here was a boy of his size who said that he could not thrash him. What was he going to do about it? The crowd made these arguments very clear and repeated them again and again.

Finally Jimmie, driven to aggression, walked close to the fence and said to the new boy, "The first time I catch you out of your own yard, I'll lam the head off'n you." This was received with wild plaudits by the Whilomville urchins.

But the new boy stepped back from the fence. He was awed by Jimmie's formidable mien. But he managed to get out a semi-defiant sentence. "Maybe you will and maybe you won't," said he.

However, his short retreat was taken as a practical victory for Jimmie and the boys hooted him bitterly. He remained inside the fence, swinging one foot and scowling while Jimmie was escorted off down the street amid acclamations. The new boy turned and walked back toward the house, his face gloomy, lined deep with discouragement, as if he felt that the new environment's antagonism and palpable cruelty were sure to prove too much for him.

II

The mother of Johnnie Hedge was a widow and the chief theory of her life was that her boy should be in school on the greatest possible number of days. He himself had no sympathy with this ambition but she detected the truth of his diseases with an unerring eye and he was required to be really ill before he could win the right to disregard the first bell, morning and noon. The chicken-pox and the mumps had given him vacations—vacations of misery, wherein he nearly died between pain and nursing. But bad colds in the head did nothing for him and he was not able to invent a satisfactory hacking cough. His mother was not consistently a tartar. In most things he swayed her to his will. He was allowed to have more jam, pickles and pie than most boys; she respected his profound loathing of Sunday-School; on summer evenings he could remain out of doors until 8.30; but in this matter of school she was inexorable. This single point in her character was of steel.

The Hedges arrived in Whilomville on a Saturday and on the following Monday Johnnie wended his way to school with a note to the principal and his Jersey City school-books. He knew perfectly well that he would be told to buy new and different books but in those days mothers always had an idea that old books would "do" and they invariably sent boys off to a new school with books which would not meet the selected and unchangeable views of the new administration. The old books never would "do." Then the boys brought them home to annoyed mothers and asked for ninety cents or sixty cents or eighty-five cents or some number of cents for another out-fit. In the garret of every house holding a large family there was a collection of effete school-books with Mother rebellious because James could not inherit his books from Paul who should properly be Peter's heir while Peter should be a beneficiary under Henry's will.

But the matter of the books was not the measure of Johnnie Hedge's unhappiness. This whole business of changing schools was a complete torture. Alone, he had to go among a new people, a new tribe, and he apprehended his serious time. There were only two fates for him. One meant victory. One meant a kind of serfdom in which he would subscribe to every word of some superior boy and support his every word. It was not anything like an English system of fagging because boys invariably drifted into the figurative service of other boys whom they devotedly admired and if they were obliged to subscribe to everything, it is true that they would have done so freely in any case. One means to suggest that Johnnie Hedge had to find his place. Willie Dalzel was a type of the little chieftain and Willie was a master but he was not a bully in a special physical sense. He did not drag little boys by the ears until they cried nor make them tearfully fetch and carry for him. They fetched and carried but it was because of their worship of his prowess and genius. And so all through the strata of boy life were chieftains and sub-chieftains and assistant-sub-chieftains. There was no question of little Hedge being towed about by the nose; it was, as one has said, that he had to find his place in a new school. And this in itself was a problem which awed his boyish heart. He was a stranger cast away upon the moon. None knew him, understood him, felt for him. He would be surrounded for this initiative time by a horde of jackal-creatures who might turn out in the end to be little boys like himself but this last point his philosophy could not understand in its fullness.

He came to a white meeting-house sort of a place in the squat tower of which a great bell was clanging impressively. He passed through an iron gate into a play-ground worn bare as the bed of a mountain brook by the endless runnings and scufflings of little children. There was still a half-hour before the final clangor in the squat tower but the play-ground held a number of frolicsome imps. A loitering boy espied Johnnie Hedge, and he howled: "Oh, oh! Here's a new feller! Here's a new feller!" He advanced upon the strange arrival. "What's your name?" he demanded belligerently, like a particularly offensive custom-house officer.

"Johnnie Hedge," responded the new-comer shyly.

This name struck the other boy as being very comic. All new names strike boys as being comic. He laughed noisily. "Oh, fellers, he says his name is Johnnie Hedge! Haw-haw-haw."

The new boy felt that his name was the most disgraceful thing which had ever been attached to a human being.

"Johnnie Hedge! Haw-haw! What room you in?" said the other lad.

"I dunno," said Johnnie. In the meantime a small flock of interested vultures had gathered about him. The main thing was his absolute strangeness. He even would have welcomed the sight of his tormentors of Saturday; he had seen them before at least. These creatures were only so many incomprehensible problems. He diffidently began to make his way toward the main door of the school and the other boys followed him. They demanded information.

"Are you through subtraction yet? We study jogerfre—did you, ever? You live here now? You goin' to school here now?"

To many questions he made answer as well as the clamor would permit and at length he reached the main door and went quaking unto his new kings. As befitted them, the rabble stopped at the door. A teacher strolling along a corridor found a small boy holding in his hand a note. The boy palpably did not know what to do with the note but the teacher knew and took it. Thereafter this little boy was in harness.

A splendid lady in gorgeous robes gave him a seat at a double desk in the end of which sat a hoodlum with grimy finger-nails who eyed the inauguration with an extreme and personal curiosity. The other desks were gradually occupied by children who first were told of the new boy and then turned upon him a speculative and somewhat derisive eye. The school opened; little classes went forward to a position in front of the teacher's platform and tried to explain that they knew something. The new boy was not requisitioned a great deal; he was allowed to lie dormant until he became used to the scenes and until the teacher found, approximately, his mental position. In the meantime, he suffered a shower of stares and whispers and giggles as if he were a man-ape, whereas he was precisely like other children. From time to time, he made funny and pathetic little overtures to other boys but these overtures could not yet be received; he was not known; he was a foreigner. The village school was like a nation. It was tight. Its amiability or friendship must be won in certain ways.

At recess he hovered in the school-room around the weak lights of society and around the teacher in the hope that somebody might be good to him but none considered him save as some sort of a specimen. The teacher of course had a secondary interest in the fact that he was an additional one to a class of sixty-three.

At twelve o'clock, when the ordered files of boys and girls marched toward the door, he exhibited—to no eye—the tremblings of a coward in a charge. He exaggerated the lawlessness of the play-ground and the street.

But the reality was hard enough. A shout greeted him. "Oh, here's the new feller! Here's the new feller!" Small and utterly obscure boys teased him. He had a hard time of it to get to the gate. There never was any actual hurt but everything was competent to smite the lad with shame; it was a curious, groundless shame but nevertheless it was shame. He was a newcomer and he definitely felt the disgrace of the fact.

In the street he was seen and recognized by some lads who had formed part of the group of Saturday. They shouted: "Oh, Jimmie! Jimmie! Here he is! Here's that new feller!"

Jimmie Trescott was going virtuously toward his luncheon

when he heard these cries behind him. He pretended not to hear and in this deception he was assisted by the fact that he was engaged at the time in a furious argument with a friend over the relative merits of two Uncle Tom's Cabin companies. It appeared that one company had only two blood-hounds while the other had ten. On the other hand, the first company had two Topsys and two Uncle Toms while the second had only one Topsy and one Uncle Tom.

But the shouting little boys were hard after him. Finally they were even pulling at his arms.

"Jimmie—"

"What?" he demanded turning with a snarl. "What d'you want? Leggo my arm."

"Here he is! Here's the new feller! Here's the new feller! Now!"

"I don't care if he is," said Jimmie with grand impatience. He tilted his chin. "I don't care if he is."

Then they reviled him. "Thought you was goin' to lick him first time you caught him. Yah! You're a 'fraid-cat!" They began to sing: " 'Fraid-cat! 'Fraid-cat! 'Fraid-cat!" He expostulated hotly, turning from one to the other, but they would not listen. In the meantime the Hedge boy slunk on his way, looking with deep anxiety upon this attempt to send Jimmie against him. But Jimmie would have none of the plan.

III

When the children met again on the play-ground, Jimmie was openly challenged with cowardice. He had made a big threat in the hearing of comrades and when invited by them to take advantage of an opportunity, he had refused. They had been fairly sure of their amusement and they were indignant. Jimmie was finally driven to declare that as soon as school was out for the day, he would thrash the Hedge boy.

When finally the children came rushing out of the iron gate, filled with the delights of freedom, a hundred boys surrounded Jimmie in high spirits for he had said that he was determined. They waited for the lone lad from Jersey City. When he appeared, Jimmie wasted no time. He walked straight to him and said: "Did you say you kin lick me?"

Johnnie Hedge was cowed, shrinking, affrighted, and the roars of a hundred boys thundered in his ears but again he knew what he had to say. "Yes," he gasped in anguish.

"Then," said Jimmie resolutely, "you've got to fight." There was a joyous clamor by the mob. The beleaguered lad looked this way and that way for succor as Willie Dalzel and other officious youngsters policed an irregular circle in the crowd. He saw Jimmie facing him; there was no help for it; he dropped his books—the old books which would not "do."

Now it was the fashion among tiny Whilomville belligerents to fight much in the manner of little bear-cubs. Two boys would rush upon each other, immediately grapple and—the best boy having probably succeeded in getting the coveted "under-hold"—there would presently be a crash to the earth of the inferior boy and he would be probably mopped around in the dust or the mud or the snow or whatever the material happened to be, until the engagement was over. Whatever havoc was dealt out to him was ordinarily the result of his wild endeavors to throw off his opponent and arise. Both infants wept during the fight, as a common thing, and if they wept very hard, the fight was a harder fight. The result was never very bloody but the complete dishevelment of both victor and vanquished was extraordinary. As for the spectacle, it more resembled a collision of boys in a fog than it did the manly art of hammering another human being into speechless inability.

The fight began when Jimmie made a mad bear-cub rush at the new boy amid savage cries of encouragement. Willie Dalzel, for instance, almost howled his head off. Very timid boys on the outskirts of the throng felt their hearts leap to their throats. It was a time when certain natures were impressed that only man is vile.

But it appeared that bear-cub rushing was no part of the instruction received by boys in Jersey City. Boys in Jersey City were apparently schooled curiously. Upon the onslaught of Jimmie, the stranger had gone wild with rage—boy-like. Some spark had touched his fighting blood and in a moment he was a cornered, desperate, fire-eyed little man. He began to swing his arms, to revolve them so swiftly that one might have considered him a small working model of an extra-fine patented wind-mill which was caught in a gale. For a moment, this defense surprised Jimmie more than it damaged him but, two moments later, a small knotty fist caught him squarely in the eye and with a shriek he went down in defeat. He lay on the ground so stunned that he could not even cry; but if he had been able to cry he would have cried over his prestige—or something—not over his eye.

There was a dreadful tumult. The boys cast glances of amazement and terror upon the victor and thronged upon the beaten Jimmie Trescott. It was a moment of excitement so intense that one cannot say what happened. Never before had Whilomville seen such a thing—not the little tots. They were aghast, dumbfounded, and they glanced often over their shoulders at the new boy who stood alone, his clenched fists at his side, his face crimson, his lips still working with the fury of battle.

But there was another surprise for Whilomville. It might have been seen that the little victor was silently debating against an impulse. But the impulse won, for the lone lad from Jersey City suddenly wheeled, sprang like a demon and struck another boy.

A curtain should be drawn before this deed. A knowledge of it is really too much for the heart to bear. The other boy was Willie Dalzel. The lone lad from Jersey City had smitten him full sore.

There is little to say of it. It must have been that a feeling worked gradually to the top of the little stranger's wrath that Jimmie Trescott had been a mere tool, that the front and centre of his persecutors had been Willie Dalzel, and being rendered temporarily lawless by his fighting blood, he raised his hand and smote for revenge.

Willie Dalzel had been in the middle of a vandal's cry which screeched out over the voices of everybody. The new boy's fist cut it in half, so to say. And then arose the howl of an amazed and terrorized walrus.

One wishes to draw a second curtain. Without discussion, or enquiry or brief retort, Willie Dalzel ran away. He ran like a hare, straight for home, this redoubtable chieftain. Following him at a heavy and slow pace, ran the impassioned new boy. The scene was long remembered.

Willie Dalzel was no coward; he had been panic-stricken into running away from a new thing. He ran as a man might run from the sudden appearance of a vampire or a ghoul or a gorilla. This was no time for academics—he ran.

Jimmie slowly gathered himself and came to his feet. "Where's Willie?" said he first of all. The crowd sniggered. "Where's Willie?" said Jimmie again.

"Why he licked him, *too*," answered a boy suddenly.

"He did?" said Jimmie. He sat weakly down on the roadway. "He did?" After allowing a moment for the fact to sink into him, he looked up at the crowd with his one good eye and his one bunged eye, and smiled cheerfully.

The City Urchin and the Chaste Villagers

AFTER THE BRIEF ENCOUNTERS between the Hedge boy and Jimmie Trescott and the Hedge boy and Willie Dalzel, the neighborhood which contained the homes of the boys was, as far as child life is concerned, in a state resembling anarchy. This was owing to the signal over-throw and shameful retreat of the boy who had for several years led a certain little clan by the nose. The adherence of the little community did not go necessarily to the boy who could whip all the others but it certainly could not go to a boy who had run away in a manner that made his shame patent to the whole world. Willie Dalzel found himself in a painful position. This tiny tribe which had followed him with such unwavering faith, was now largely engaged in whistling and cat-calling and hooting. He chased a number of them into the sanctity of their own yards but from these coigns they continued to ridicule him.

But it must not be supposed that the fickle tribe went over in a body to the new light. They did nothing of the sort. They occupied themselves with avenging all which they had endured—gladly enough, too—for many months. As for the Hedge boy, he maintained a curious timid reserve, minding his own business with extreme care and going to school with that deadly punctuality of which his mother was the genius. Jimmie Trescott suffered no adverse criticism from his fellows. He was entitled to be beaten by a boy who had made Willie Dalzel bellow like a bull-calf and run away. Indeed he received some honors. He had confronted a very superior boy and received a bang in the eye which for a time was the wonder of the children and he had not bellowed like a bull-calf. As a matter of fact, he was often invited to tell how it had felt and this he did with some pride, claiming arrogantly that he had been superior to any particular pain.

Early in the episode he and the Hedge boy had patched up a treaty. Living next door to each other, they could not fail to have each other often in sight. One afternoon they wandered together in the strange indefinite diplomacy of boy-hood. As they drew close the new boy suddenly said: "Napple?"

"Yes," said Jimmie and the new boy bestowed upon him an apple. It was one of those green-coated winter apples which lie for many months in safe and dry places and can at any time be brought forth for the persecution of the unwary and inexperienced. An older age would have fled from this apple but to the unguided youth of Jimmie Trescott it was a thing to be possessed and cherished. Wherefore this apple was the emblem of something more than a truce despite the fact that it tasted like wet Indian-meal. And Jimmie looked at the Hedge boy out of one good eye and one bunged eye. The long-drawn animosities of men have no place in the life of a boy. The boy's mind is flexible; he readjusts his position with an ease which is derived from the fact—simply—that he is not yet a man.

But there were other and more important matters. Johnnie Hedge's exploits had brought him into such prominence among the school-boys that it was necessary to settle a number of points once and for all. There was the usual number of boys in the school who were popularly known to be champions in their various classes. Among these Johnnie Hedge now had to thread his way, every boy taking it upon himself to feel anxious that Johnnie's exact position should be soon established. His fame as a fighter had gone forth to the world but there were other boys who had fame as fighters and the world was extremely anxious to know where to place the newcomer. Various heroes were urged to attempt this classification. Usually it is not accounted a matter of supreme importance but in this boy life it was essential.

In all cases the heroes were backward enough. It was their followings who agitated the question. And so Johnnie Hedge was more or less beset.

He maintained his bashfulness. He backed away from altercation. It was plain that to bring matters to a point he must be forced into a quarrel. It was also plain that the proper person for the business was some boy who could whip Willie Dalzel. There were not many boys in the school who could whip Willie Dalzel and these formidable warriors were distinctly averse to undertaking the new contract. It is a kind of a law in boy life that a quiet, decent, peace-loving lad is able to thrash a wide-mouthed talker. And so it had transpired that by a peculiar system of elimination most of the real chiefs were quiet, decent, peace-loving boys and they had no desire to engage in a fight with a boy on the sole grounds that it was not known who could whip. Johnnie Hedge attended his affairs; they attended their affairs; and around them waged this discussion of relative merit. Jimmie Trescott took a prominent part in these arguments. He contended that Johnnie Hedge could thrash any boy in the world. He was certain of it and to any one who opposed him he said: "You just get one of those smashes in the eye and then you'll see." In the meantime there was a grand and impressive silence in the direction of Willie Dalzel. He had gathered remnants of his clan but the main parts of his sovereignty were scattered to the winds. He was an enemy.

Owing to the circumspect behavior of the new boy, the commotions on the school-grounds came to nothing. He was often asked: "Kin you lick him?" And he invariably replied: "I dunno." This idea of waging battle with the entire world appalled him.

A war for complete supremacy of the tribe which had been headed by Willie Dalzel was fought out in the country of the tribe. It came to pass that a certain half-dime blood-and-thunder pamphlet had a great vogue in the tribe at this particular time. This story relates the experience of a lad who began his career as cabin-boy on a pirate-ship. Throughout the first fifteen chapters, he was rope's-ended from one end of the ship to the other end and very often he was felled to the deck by a heavy fist. He lived through enough hardships to have killed a battalion of Turkish soldiers, but in the end he rose upon them. Yes, he rose upon them. Hordes of pirates fell before his intrepid arm and in the last chapters of the book he is seen jauntily careering on his own hook as one of the most gallows pirate-captains that ever sailed the seas.

Naturally when this tale was thoroughly understood by the tribe, they had to dramatize it although it was a dramatization that would gain no royalties for the author. Now it was plain that the urchin who was cast for the cabin-boy's part would lead a life throughout the first fifteen chapters which would attract few actors. Willie Dalzel developed a scheme by which some small lad would play cabin-boy during this period of misfortune and abuse and then when the cabin-boy came to the part where he slew all his enemies and reached his zenith that he, Willie Dalzel, should take the part.

This fugitive and disconnected rendering of a great play opened in Jimmie Trescott's back garden. The path between the two lines of gooseberry-bushes was elected unanimously to be the ship. Then Willie Dalzel insisted that Homer Phelps should be the cabin-boy. Homer tried the position for a time and then elected that he would resign in favor of some other victim. There was no other applicant to succeed him. Whereupon it became necessary to press some boy. Jimmie Trescott was a great actor as is well known, but he steadfastly refused to engage for the part. Ultimately they seized upon little Dan Earl whose disposition was so milky and docile that he would do whatever anybody asked of him. But Dan Earl made the one firm revolt of his life after trying existence as cabin-boy for some ten minutes. Willie Dalzel was in despair. Then he suddenly sighted the little brother of Johnnie Hedge who had come into the garden and in a poor-little-stranger sort of a fashion was looking wistfully at the play. When he was invited to become the cabin-boy he accepted joyfully thinking that it was his initiation into the tribe. Then they proceeded to give him the rope's-end and to punch him with a realism which was not altogether painless. Directly he began to cry out. They exhorted him not to cry out, not to mind it, but still they continued to hurt him.

There was a commotion among the gooseberry-bushes, two branches were swept aside and Johnnie Hedge walked down upon them. Every boy stopped in his tracks. Johnnie was boiling with rage. "Who hurt him?" he said ferociously. "Did *you*?" He had looked at Willie Dalzel.

Willie Dalzel began to mumble. "We was on'y playin'. Wasn't nothin' fer him to cry fer."

The new boy had at his command some big phrases and he used them. "I am goin' to whip you within an inch of your life. I am goin' to tan the hide off'n you." And immediately there was a mixture—an infusion of two boys which looked as if it had been done by a chemist. The other children stood

back, stricken with horror. But out of this whirl they pres-
ently perceived the figure of Willie Dalzel seated upon the
chest of the Hedge boy.

"Got enough?" asked Willie hoarsely.

"No," choked out the Hedge boy. Then there was another
flapping and floundering and finally another calm.

"Got enough?" asked Willie.

"No," said the Hedge boy. A sort of a war-cloud again
puzzled the sight of the observers. Both combatants were
breathless, bloodless in their faces, and very weak.

"Got enough?" said Willie.

"No," said the Hedge boy. The carnage was again renewed.
All the spectators were silent but Johnnie Hedge's little brother
who shrilly exhorted him to continue the struggle. But it was
not plain that the Hedge boy needed any encouragement for he
was crying bitterly and it has been explained that when a boy
cried it was a bad time to hope for peace. He had managed
to wriggle over upon his hands and knees. But Willie
Dalzel was tenaciously gripping him from the back and it seemed
that his strength would spend itself in futility. The bear-cub
seemed to have the advantage of the working model of the
wind-mill. They heaved; uttered strange words; wept; and the
sun looked down upon them with steady, unwinking eye.

Peter Washington came out of the stable and observed this
tragedy of the back garden. He stood transfixed for a moment
and then ran toward it, shouting: "Hi! What's all dish yere?
Hi! Stopper dat, stopper dat, you two! For lan' sake, what's
all dish yere?" He grabbed the struggling boys and pulled
them apart. He was stormy and fine in his indignation. "For
lan' sake! You two kids act like you gwine mad-dogs. Stopper
dat." The whitened, tearful, soiled combatants, their clothing
all awry, glared fiercely at each other as Peter stood between
them, lecturing. They made several futile attempts to circum-
vent him and again come to battle. As he fended them off
with his open hands he delivered his reproaches at Jimmie.
"I'se s'prised at *you*! I suhtainly is!"

"Why?" said Jimmie. "I ain't done nothin'. What have I
done?"

"Y-y-you done 'courage dese yere kids ter scrap," said Peter
virtuously.

"Me!" cried Jimmie. "I ain't had nothin' to do with it."

"I raikon you ain't," retorted Peter with heavy sarcasm. "I raikon you been er-prayin', ain't you?" Turning to Willie Dalzel, he said: "You jest take an' run erlong outer dish yere or I'll jest nachually take an' damnearkill you." Willie Dalzel went. To the new boy, Peter said: "You look like you had some saince but I raikon you don't know no more'n er rabbit. You jest take an' trot erlong off home an' don' lemme caitch you round yere er-fightin' or I'll break yer back." The Hedge boy moved away with dignity followed by his little brother. The latter when he had placed a sufficient distance between himself and Peter, played his fingers at his nose and called out: "Nig-ger-r-r! Nig-ger-r-r!"

Peter Washington's resentment poured out upon Jimmie. " 'Pears like you never would unnerstan' you ain't reg'lar common trash. You take an' 'sociate with an'body what done come erlong."

"Aw, go on," retorted Jimmie profanely. "Go soak your head, Pete."

The remaining boys retired to the street whereupon they perceived Willie Dalzel in the distance. He ran to them. "I licked him!" he shouted exultantly, "I licked him! Didn't I, now?"

From the Whilomville point of view, he was entitled to a favorable answer. They made it. "Yes," they said, "you did."

"I run in," cried Willie, "an' I grabbed 'im an' afore he knew what it was, I throwed 'im. An' then it was easy." He puffed out his chest and smiled like an English recruiting sergeant. "An' now," said he, suddenly facing Jimmie Trescott, " whose side were you on?"

The question was direct and startling. Jimmie gave back two paces. "He licked you once," he explained haltingly.

"He never saw the day when he could lick one side of me. I could lick him with my left hand tied behind me. Why, I could lick him when I was asleep." Willie Dalzel was magnificent.

A gate clicked and Johnnie Hedge was seen to be strolling toward them.

"You said," he remarked coldly, "you licked me, didn't you?"

Willie Dalzel stood his ground. "Yes," he said stoutly.

"Well, you're a liar," said the Hedge boy.

"You're another," retorted Willie.

"No, I ain't, either, but *you're* a liar."

"You're another," retorted Willie.

"Don't you dare tell *me* I'm a liar or I'll smack your mouth for you," said the Hedge boy.

"Well, I did, didn't I?" barked Willie. "An' whatche goin' to do about it?"

"I'm goin' to lam you," said the Hedge boy.

He approached to attack warily and the other boys held their breaths. Willie Dalzel winced back a pace. "Hol' on a minute," he cried, raising his palm. "I'm not—"

But the comic wind-mill was again in motion and between gasps from his exertions, Johnnie Hedge remarked: "I'll show—you—whether—you kin—lick me—or not."

The first blows did not reach home on Willie for he backed away with expedition keeping up his futile cry: "Hol' on a minute." Soon enough, a swinging fist landed on his cheek. It did not knock him down but it hurt him a little and frightened him a great deal. He suddenly opened his mouth to an amazing and startling extent, tilted back his head, and howled, while his eyes, glittering with tears, were fixed upon this scowling butcher of a Johnnie Hedge. The latter was making slow and vicious circles evidently intending to renew the massacre.

But the spectators really had been desolated and shocked by the terrible thing which had happened to Willie Dalzel. They now cried out: "No, no, don't hit 'im anymore! Don't hit 'im anymore!"

Jimmie Trescott, in a panic of bravery, yelled: "We'll all jump on you if you do."

The Hedge boy paused, at bay. He breathed angrily and flashed his glance from lad to lad. They still protested: "No, no, don't hit 'im anymore! Don't hit 'im no more."

"I'll hammer him until he can't stand up," said Johnnie observing that they all feared him. "I'll fix him so he won't know hisself an' if any of you kids bother with *me*—"

Suddenly he ceased, he trembled, he collapsed. The hand of one approaching from behind had laid hold upon his ear and it was the hand of one whom he knew.

The other lads heard a loud iron-filing voice say: "Caught ye at it again, ye brat, ye!" They saw a dreadful woman with grey hair, with a sharp red nose, with bare arms, with spectacles of such magnifying quality that her eyes shone through them like two fierce white moons. She was Johnnie Hedge's mother. Still holding Johnnie by the ear, she swung out swiftly and dexterously and succeeded in boxing the ears of two boys before the crowd regained its presence of mind and stampeded. Yes; the war for supremacy was over and the question was never again disputed. The supreme power was Mrs. Hedge.

ENGLAND: LAST WORKS

Contents

The Kicking Twelfth

THE SPITZBERGEN ARMY was backed by traditions of centuries of victory. In its chronicles, occasional defeats were not printed in italics but were likely to appear as glorious stands against overwhelming odds. A favorite way to dispose of them was to frankly attribute them to the blunders of the civilian heads of government. This was very good for the army and probably no army had more self-confidence. When it was announced that an expeditionary force was to be sent to Rostina to chastise an impudent people, a hundred barrack-squares filled with excited men and a hundred serjeant-majors hurried silently through the groups and succeeded in looking as if they were the repositories of the secrets of empire. Officers on leave sped joyfully back to their harness and recruits were abused with unflagging devotion by every man from colonels to privates of experience.

The Twelfth Regiment of the Line—the Kicking Twelfth—was consumed with a dread that it was not to be included in the expedition and the regiment formed itself into an informal indignation meeting. Just as they had proved that a great outrage was about to be perpetrated, warning orders arrived to hold themselves in readiness for active service abroad—in Rostina, in fact. The barrack-yard was in a flash transformed into a blue and buff pandemonium and the official bugle itself hardly had the power to quell the glad disturbance.

Thus it was that early in the spring the Kicking Twelfth—sixteen hundred men in service equipment—found itself crawling along a road in Rostina. They did not form part of the main force but belonged to a column of four regiments of foot, two batteries of field-guns, a battery of mountain howitzers, a regiment of horse and a company of engineers. Nothing had happened. The long column had crawled without amusement of any kind through a broad green valley. Big white farm-houses dotted the slopes but there was no sign of man nor beast and no smoke came from the chimneys. The column was operating from its own base and its general was expected to form a junction with the main body at a given point.

A squadron of the cavalry was fanned out ahead, scouting, and day by day the trudging infantry watched the blue uniforms of the horsemen as they came and went. Sometimes there would sound the faint thuds of a few shots but the cavalry was unable to find anything to seriously engage.

The Twelfth had no record of foreign service and it could hardly be said that it had served as a unit in the great civil war when His Majesty the King had whipped the Pretender. At that time the regiment had suffered from two opinions. So that it was impossible for either side to depend upon it. Many men had deserted to the standard of the Pretender and a number of officers had drawn their swords for him. When the King, a thorough soldier, looked at the remnant he saw that they lacked the spirit to be of great help to him in the tremendous battles which he was waging for his throne. And so this emaciated Twelfth was sent off to a corner of the kingdom to guard a dock-yard where some of the officers so plainly expressed their disapproval of this policy that the regiment received its steadfast name, the Kicking Twelfth.

At the time of which I am writing the Twelfth had a few veteran officers and well-bitten serjeants but the body of the regiment was composed of men who had never heard a shot fired excepting on the rifle-range. But it was an experience for which they longed and when it came the moment for the corps' cry—"Kim up, the Kickers"—there was not likely to be a man who would not go tumbling after his leaders.

Young Timothy Lean was a second-lieutenant in the First Company of the third battalion and just at this time he was pattering along at the flank of the men, keeping a fatherly look-out for boots that hurt and packs that sagged. He was extremely bored. The mere far-away sound of desultory shooting was not war as he had been led to believe it.

It did not appear that behind that freckled face and under that red hair there was a mind which dreamed of blood. He was not extremely anxious to kill somebody but he was very fond of soldiering—it had been the career of his father and of his grandfather—and he understood that the profession of arms lost much of its point unless a man shot at people and had people shoot at him. Strolling in the sun through a practically deserted country might be a proper occupation for a divinity student on a vacation but the soul of Timothy Lean was in revolt at it. Sometimes at night he would go morosely to the camp of the cavalry and hear the infant subalterns laughingly exaggerate the comedy side of adventures which they had had when out with small patrols far ahead. Lean would sit and listen in glum silence to these tales and dislike the young officers—many of them old military-school friends—for having had experience in modern warfare. "Anyhow," he said savagely, "presently you'll be getting in a lot of trouble and then the Foot will have to come along and pull you out. We always do. That's history."

"Oh, we can take care of ourselves," said the cavalry, with good-natured understanding of his mood.

But the next day even Lean blessed the cavalry for excited troopers came whirling back from the front, bending over their speeding horses and shouting wildly and hoarsely for the infantry to clear the way. Men yelled at them from the roadside, as courier followed courier and from the distance ahead sounded in quick succession six booms from field-guns. The information possessed by the couriers was no longer precious. Everybody knew what a battery meant when it spoke. The bugles cried out and the long column jolted into a halt. Old Colonel Sponge went bouncing in his saddle back to see the general and the regiment sat down in the grass by the roadside and waited in silence. Presently the second squadron of the cavalry trotted off along the road in a cloud of dust and in due time old Colonel Sponge came bouncing back and palavered his three majors and his adjutant. Then there was a bit more talk by the majors and gradually through the correct channels spread information which in due time reached Timothy Lean. The enemy, 5,000 strong, occupied a pass at the head of the valley some four miles beyond. They had three batteries well posted. Their infantry was intrenched. The ground in their front was crossed and lined with many ditches and hedges but the enemy's batteries were so posted that it was doubtful if a ditch would ever prove convenient as shelter for the Spitzbergen infantry. There was a fair position for the Spitzbergen artillery 2,300 yards from the enemy. The cavalry had succeeded in driving the enemy's skirmishers back upon the main body but of course had only tried to worry them a little. The position was almost inaccessible on the enemy's right owing to high, steep hills which had been crowned by small parties of infantry. The enemy's left although guarded by a much larger force was approachable and might be flanked. This was what the cavalry had to say and it added briefly a report of two troopers killed and five wounded.

Whereupon, Major-General Richie, commanding a force of 7,500 men of His Majesty of Spitzbergen, set in motion with a few simple words the machinery which would launch his army at the enemy. The Twelfth understood the orders when they saw the smart young aide approaching old Colonel Sponge and they rose as one man, apparently afraid that they would be late. There was a clank of accoutrements. Men shrugged their shoulders tighter against their packs and thrusting their thumbs between their belts and their tunics they wriggled into a closer fit with regard to the heavy ammunition equipment. It is curious to note that almost every man took off his cap and looked contemplatively into it as if to read a maker's name. Then they replaced their caps with great care. There was little talking; and it was observable that not a single soldier handed a token or left a comrade with a message to be delivered in case he should be killed. They did not seem to think of being killed; they seemed absorbed in a desire to know what would happen and what it would look like when it was happening. Men glanced continually at their officers in a plain desire to be quick to understand the very first order that would be given and officers looked gravely at their men, measuring them, feeling their temper, worrying about them.

A bugle called; there were sharp cries; and the Kicking Twelfth was off to battle.

The regiment had the right of the line in the infantry brigade and as the men tramped noisily along the white road every eye was strained ahead, but after all there was nothing to be seen but a dozen farms—in short, a country-side. It resembled the scenery in Spitzbergen; every man in the Kicking Twelfth had often confronted a dozen such farms with a composure which amounted to indifference. But still down the road there came galloping troopers who delivered informations to Colonel Sponge and then galloped on. In time the

Twelfth came to the top of a rise and below them on a plain was the heavy black streak of a Spitzbergen squadron and back of the squadron loomed the grey bare hills of the Rostina position. There was a little of skirmish firing. The Twelfth reached a knoll which the officers easily recognized as the place described by the cavalry as suitable for the Spitzbergen guns. The men swarmed up it in a peculiar formation. They resembled a crowd coming off a race-track but nevertheless there were no stray sheep. It is simply that the ground on which actual battles are fought is not like a chess-board. And after them came swinging a six-gun battery, the guns wagging from side to side as the long line turned out of the road and the drivers using their whips as the leading horses scrambled at the hill. The halted Twelfth lifted its voice and spake amiably but with point to the battery. "Go on, Guns! We'll take care of you. Don't be afraid. Give it to them." The teams—lead, swing and wheel—struggled and slipped over the steep and uneven ground and the gunners as they clung to their springless positions wore their usual and natural airs of unhappiness. They made no reply to the infantry. Once upon the top of the hill, however, these guns were unlimbered in a flash and directly the infantry could hear the loud voice of an officer drawling out the time for the fuses. A moment later the first three-point-two bellowed out and there could be heard the swish and the snarl of a fleeting shell. Colonel Sponge and a number of officers climbed to the battery's position but the men of the regiment sat in the shelter of the hill like so many blindfolded people and wondered what they would have been able to see if they had been officers. Sometimes the shells of the enemy came sweeping over the top of the hill and burst in great brown explosions in the fields to the rear. The men looked after them and laughed. To the rear could be seen also the mountain-battery coming at a comic trot with every man obviously in a deep rage with every mule. If a man can put in long service with a mule battery and come out of it with an amiable disposition, he should be presented with a medal weighing many ounces. After the mule battery came a long black winding thing which was three regiments of Spitzbergen infantry and back of them and to the right was an inky square which was the remaining

Spitzbergen guns. General Richie and his staff clattered up to the hill. The blindfolded Twelfth sat still. The inky square suddenly became a long racing line. The howitzers joined their little bark to the thunder of the guns on the hill and the three regiments of infantry came on. The Twelfth sat still.

Of a sudden a bugle rang its warning and the officers shouted. Some used the old cry, "Attention! Kim up, the Kickers!" and the Twelfth knew that it had been told to go in. The majority of the men expected to see great things as soon as they rounded the shoulder of the hill but there was nothing to be seen save a complicated plain and the grey knolls occupied by the enemy. Many company commanders in low voices worked at their men and said things which do not appear in the written reports. They talked soothingly; they talked indignantly; and they talked always like fathers. And the men heard no sentence completely. They heard no specific direction, these wide-eyed men. They understood that there was being delivered some kind of exhortation to do as they had been taught and they also understood that a superior intelligence was anxious over their behavior and welfare.

There was a great deal of floundering through hedges, a climbing of walls, a jumping of ditches. Curiously original privates tried to find new and easier ways for themselves instead of following the men in front of them. Officers had short fits of fury over these people. The more originality they possessed the more likely they were to become separated from their companies. Colonel Sponge was making an exciting progress on a big charger. When the first faint song of the bullets came from above, the men wondered why he sat so high. The charger seemed as tall as the Eiffel Tower. But if he was high in air, he had a fine view and that is supposedly why people ascend the Eiffel Tower. Very often he had been a joke to them but when they saw this fat old gentleman so coolly treating the strange new missiles which hummed in the air, it struck them suddenly that they had wronged him seriously and that a man who could attain the command of a Spitzbergen regiment was entitled to general respect. And they gave him a sudden quick affection, an affection that would make them follow him heartily, trustfully, grandly—this fat old gentleman, seated on a too-big horse. In a flash his towselled grey head, his short thick legs, even his paunch, had become specially and humorously endeared to them. And this is the way of soldiers.

But still the Twelfth had not yet come to the place where tumbling bodies begin their test of the very heart of a regiment. They backed through more hedges, jumped more ditches, slid over more walls. The Rostina artillery had seemed to have been asleep but suddenly the guns aroused like dogs from their kennels and around the Twelfth there began a wild swift screeching. There arose cries to hurry, to come on, and, as the rifle bullets began to plunge into them, the men saw the high formidable hills of the enemy's right and perfectly understood that they were doomed to storm them. The cheering thing was the sudden beginning of a tremendous uproar on the enemy's left.

Every man ran, hard, tense, breathless. When they reached the foot of the hills they thought they had won the charge already but they were electrified to see officers above them waving their swords and yelling with anger, surprise and shame. With a long murmurous out-cry the Twelfth began to climb the hill. And as they went and fell, they could hear frenzied shouts. "Kim up, the Kickers." The pace was slow. It was like the rising of a tide. It was determined, almost relentless in its appearance, but it was slow. If a man fell there was a chance that he would land twenty yards below the point where he was hit. The Kickers crawled, their rifles in their left hands as they pulled and tugged themselves up with their right hands. Ever arose the shout, "Kim up, the Kickers." Timothy Lean, his face flaming, his eyes wild, yelled it back as if he was delivering the Gospel.

The Kickers came up. The enemy—they had been in small force, thinking the hills safe enough from attack—retreated quickly from this preposterous advance and not a bayonet in the Twelfth saw blood. Bayonets very seldom do.

The homing of this successful charge wore an unromantic aspect. About twenty windless men suddenly arrived and threw themselves upon the crest of the hill and breathed. And these twenty were joined by others and still others until almost 1,100 men of the Twelfth lay upon the hill-top while the regiment's track was marked by body after body, in groups and singly. The first officer—perchance the first man—one never can be certain—the first officer to gain the top of the hill was Timothy Lean, and such was the situation that he had the honor to receive his colonel with a bashful salute.

The regiment knew exactly what it had done. It did not have to wait to be told by the Spitzbergen newspapers. It had taken a formidable position with the loss of about 500 men and it knew it. It knew too that it was great glory for the Kicking Twelfth and as the men lay rolling on their bellies they expressed their joy in a wild cry. "Kim up, the Kickers." For a moment there was nothing but joy and then suddenly company commanders were besieged by men who wished to go down the path of the charge and look for their mates. The answers were without the quality of mercy. They were short, snapped, quick words. "No; you can't."

The attack on the enemy's left was sounding in great rolling crashes. The shells in their flight through the air made a noise as of red-hot iron plunged into water and stray bullets nipped near the ears of the Kickers.

The Kickers looked and saw. The battle was below them. The enemy was indicated by a long noisy line of gossamer smoke, although there could be seen a toy battery with tiny men employed at the guns. All over the field the shrapnel was bursting, making quick bulbs of white smoke. Far away two regiments of Spitzbergen infantry were charging and at the distance this charge looked like a casual stroll. It appeared that small black groups of men were walking meditatively toward the Rostina intrenchments.

There would have been orders given sooner to the Twelfth but unfortunately Colonel Sponge arrived on top of the hill without a breath of wind in his body. He could not have given an order to save the regiment from being wiped off the earth. Finally he was able to gasp out something and point at the enemy. Timothy Lean ran along the line yelling to the men to sight at 800 yards and like a slow and ponderous machine the regiment again went to work. The fire flanked a great part of the enemy's trenches.

It could be said that there were only two prominent points of view expressed by the men after their victorious arrival on the crest. One was defined in the exulting use of the corps' cry. The other was a grief-stricken murmur which is invariably heard after a hard fight. "My God, we're all cut to pieces!"

Colonel Sponge sat on the ground and impatiently waited for his wind to return. As soon as it did, he arose and cried out: "Form up and we'll charge again! We will win this battle as soon as we can hit them!" The shouts of the officers sounded wild like men yelling on ship-board in a gale. And the obedient Kickers arose for their task. It was running down hill this time. The mob of panting men poured over the stones.

But the enemy had not been at all blind to the great advantage gained by the Twelfth and they now turned upon them a desperate fire of small arms. Men fell in every imaginable way and their accoutrements rattled on the rocky ground. Some landed with a crash, floored by some tremendous blow; others drooped gently down like sacks of meal; with others it would positively appear that some spirit had suddenly seized them by the ankles and jerked their legs from under them. Many officers were down but Colonel Sponge, stuttering and blowing, was still upright. He was almost the last man in the charge but not to his shame, rather to his stumpy legs. At one time it seemed that the assault would be lost. The effect of the fire was somewhat as if a terrible cyclone was blowing in the men's faces. They wavered, lowering their heads and shouldering weakly as if it were impossible to make headway against the wind of battle. It was the moment of despair, the moment of the heroism which comes to the chosen of the war-god. The colonel's cry broke and screeched absolute hatred. Other officers simply howled and the men silent, debased, seemed to tighten their muscles for one last effort. Again they pushed against this mysterious power of the air and once more the regiment was charging. Timothy Lean, agile and strong, was well in advance and afterward he reflected that the men who had been nearest to him were an old grizzled serjeant who would have gone to hell for the honor of the regiment and a pie-faced lad who had been obliged to lie about his age in order to get into the army.

There was no shock of meeting. The Twelfth came down on a corner of the trenches and as soon as the enemy had ascertained that the Twelfth was certain to arrive, they scuttled out, running close to the earth and spending no time in glances backward. In these days it is not discreet to wait for a charge to come home. You observe the charge, you attempt to stop it, and if you find that you can't, it is better to retire immediately to some other place. The Rostina soldiers were not heroes perhaps but they were men of sense. A maddened and badly frightened mob of Kickers came tumbling into the trench and shot at the backs of fleeing men. And at that very moment the action was won, and won by the Kickers. The enemy's flank was entirely crumpled and knowing this, he did not await further and more disastrous information. The Twelfth looked at themselves and knew that they had a record. They sat down and grinned patronizingly as they saw the batteries galloping to advanced positions to shell the retreat and they really laughed as the cavalry swept tumultuously forward. The Twelfth had no more concern with the battle. They had won it and the subsequent proceedings were only amusing.

There was a call from the flank and the men wearily adjusted themselves as General Richie and his staff came trotting up. The young general, cold-eyed, stern and grim as a Roman, looked with his straight glance at a hammered and thin and dirty line of figures which was His Majesty's Twelfth Regiment of the Line. When opposite old Colonel Sponge, a pudgy figure standing at attention, the general's face set in still more grim and stern lines. He took off his helmet. "Kim up, the Kickers," said he. He replaced his helmet and rode off. Down the cheeks of the little fat colonel rolled tears. He stood like a stone for a long moment and then wheeled in supreme wrath upon his surprised adjutant. "Delahaye, you damn fool, don't stand there staring like a monkey. Go tell young Lean I want to see him." The adjutant jumped as if he was on springs and went after Lean. That young officer presented himself directly, his face covered with disgraceful smudges, and he had also torn his breeches. He had never seen the colonel in such a rage. "Lean, you young whelp, you—you're a good boy." And even as the general had turned away from the colonel, the colonel turned away from the lieutenant.

The Shrapnel of Their Friends

F ROM FAR over the knolls came the tiny sound of a cavalry
bugle singing out the recall, and later, detached parties of
His Majesty's Second Hussars came trotting back to where
the Spitzbergen infantry sat complacently on the captured
Rostina position. The horsemen were well pleased, and they
told how they had ridden thrice through the helter-skelter of
the fleeing enemy. They had ultimately been checked by the
great truth that when a good enemy runs away in daylight he
sooner or later finds a place where he fetches up with a jolt
and turns to face the pursuit—notably if it is a cavalry pur-
suit. The Hussars had discreetly withdrawn, displaying no
foolish pride of corps at that time.

There was a general admission that the Kicking Twelfth
had taken the chief honors of the day, but the Artillery added
that if the guns had not shelled so accurately the Twelfth's
charge could not have been made so successfully, and the
three other regiments of infantry of course did not conceal
their feeling that their attack on the enemy's left had with-
drawn many rifles that otherwise would have been pelting at
the Twelfth. The Cavalry simply said that but for them the
victory would not have been complete.

Corps prides met each other face to face at every step, but
the Kickers smiled easily and indulgently. A few recruits
bragged, but they bragged because they were recruits. The
older men did not wish it to appear that they were surprised
and rejoiced at the performance of the regiment. If they were
congratulated they simply smirked, suggesting that the ability
of the Twelfth had long been known to them and that the
charge had been a little thing, you know, just turned off in
the way of an afternoon's work. Major-General Richie en-
camped his troops on the position which they had taken from
the enemy. Old Colonel Sponge of the Twelfth redistributed
his officers, and the losses had been so great that Timothy
Lean got command of a company. It was not too much of a
company. Fifty-three smudged and sweating men faced their
new commander. The company had gone into action with a
strength of eighty-six. The heart of Timothy Lean beat high

with pride. He intended to be some day a general, and if he ever became a general that moment of promotion was not equal in joy to the moment when he looked at his new possession of fifty-three vagabonds. He scanned the faces and recognized with satisfaction one old serjeant and two bright young corporals. "Now," said he to himself, "I have here a snug little body of men with which I can do something." In him burned the usual fierce fire to make them the best company in the regiment. He had adopted them; they were his men. "I will do what I can for you," he said. "Do you the same for me."

The Twelfth bivouacked on the ridge. Little fires were built and there appeared among the men innumerable blackened tin cups, which were so treasured that a faint suspicion in connection with the loss of one could bring on the grimmest of fights. Meantime certain of the privates silently re-adjusted their kits as their names were called out by the serjeants. These were the men condemned to picket duty after a hard day of marching and fighting. The dusk came slowly, and the color of the countless fires, spotting the ridge and the plain, grew in the falling darkness. Far-away pickets fired at something.

One by one the men's heads were lowered to the earth until the ridge was marked by two long shadowy rows of men. Here and there an officer sat musing in his dark cloak with a ray of a weakening fire gleaming on his sword hilt. From the plain there came at times the sound of battery horses moving restlessly at their tethers, and one could imagine he heard the throaty grumbling curse of the aroused drivers. The moon dived swiftly through flying light clouds. Far-away pickets fired at something.

In the morning the infantry and guns breakfasted to the music of a racket between the cavalry and the enemy which was taking place some miles up the valley. The ambitious Hussars had apparently stirred some kind of a hornet's nest, and they were having a good fight with no officious friends near enough to interfere. The remainder of the army looked toward the fight musingly over the tops of tin cups. In time the column crawled lazily forward to see. The Twelfth, as it crawled, saw a regiment deploy to the right, and saw a battery dash to take position. The cavalry jingled back, grinning with pride and expecting to be greatly admired. Presently the Twelfth was bidden to take seat by the roadside and await its turn. Instantly the wise men—and there were more than three—came out of the east and announced that they had divined the whole plan. The Kicking Twelfth was to be held in reserve until the critical moment of the fight, and then they were to be sent forward to win a victory. In corroboration they pointed to the fact that the general in command was sticking close to them in order, they said, to give the word quickly at the proper moment. And in truth, on a small hill to the right Major-General Richie sat his horse and used his glasses, while back of him his staff and the orderlies bestrode their champing, dancing mounts.

It is always good to look hard at a general, and the Kickers were transfixed with interest. The wise men again came out of the east and told what was inside the Richie head, but even the wise men wondered what was inside the Richie head.

Suddenly an exciting thing happened. To the left and ahead was a pounding Spitzbergen battery, and a toy suddenly appeared on the slope behind the guns. The toy was a man with a flag—the flag was white save for a square of red in the centre. And this toy began to wig-wag wag-wig, and it spoke to General Richie under the authority of the captain of the battery. It said: "The Eighty-eighth are being driven on my centre and right."

Now when the Kicking Twelfth had left Spitzbergen there was an average of six signal-men in each company. A proportion of these signalers had been destroyed in the first engagement, but enough remained so that the Kicking Twelfth read, as a unit, the news of the Eighty-eighth. The word ran quickly. "The eighty-eighth are being driven on my centre and right."

Richie rode to where Colonel Sponge sat aloft on his big horse, and a moment later a cry rang along the column. "Kim up, the Kickers." A large number of the men were already in the road, hitching and twisting at their belts and packs. The Kickers moved forward.

They deployed and passed in a straggling line through the battery and to the left and right of it. The gunners called out to them cheerfully, telling them not to be afraid.

The scene before them was startling. They were facing a country cut up by many steep-sided ravines, and over the resultant hills were retreating little squads of the Eighty-eighth. The Twelfth laughed in its exultation. The men could now tell by the volume of fire that the Eighty-eighth were retreating for reasons which were not sufficiently expressed in the noise of the Rostina shooting. Held together by the bugle, the Kickers swarmed up the first hill and laid on the crest. Parties of the Eighty-eighth went through their lines, and the Twelfth told them coarsely its several opinions. The sights were clicked up to 600 yards, and with a crashing volley the regiment entered its second battle.

A thousand yards away on the right the cavalry and a regiment of infantry were creeping onward. Sponge decided not to be backward, and the bugle told the Twelfth to go ahead once more. The Twelfth charged, followed by a rabble of rallied men of the Eighty-eighth, who were crying aloud that it had been all a mistake.

A charge in these days is not a running match. Those splendid pictures of leveled bayonets dashing at headlong pace toward the closed ranks of the enemy are absurd as soon as they are mistaken for the actuality of the present. In these days charges are likely to cover at least the half of a mile, and to go at the pace exhibited in the pictures, a man would be obliged to have a little steam engine inside of him.

The charge of the Kicking Twelfth somewhat resembled the advance of a great crowd of beaters who for some reason passionately desired to start the game. Men stumbled; men fell; men swore. There were cries: "This way! Come this way! Don't go that way! You can't get up that way." Over the rocks the Twelfth scrambled, red in the face, sweating and angry. Soldiers fell because they were struck by bullets and because they had not an ounce of strength left in them. Colonel Sponge, with a face like a red cushion, was being dragged windless up the steeps by devoted and athletic men. Three of the older captains lay afar back, and swearing with their eyes because their tongues were temporarily out of service.

And yet—and yet the speed of the charge was slow. From the position of the battery, it looked as if the Kickers were taking a walk over some extremely difficult country.

The regiment ascended a superior height and found trenches and dead men. They took seat with the dead, satisfied with this company until they could get their wind. For thirty minutes purple-faced stragglers rejoined from the rear. Colonel Sponge looked behind him and saw that Richie, with his staff, had approached by another route, and had evidently been near enough to see the full extent of the Kickers' exertions. Presently Richie began to pick a way for his horse toward the captured position. He disappeared in a gully between two hills.

Now it came to pass that a Spitzbergen battery on the far right took occasion to mistake the identity of the Kicking Twelfth and the captain of these guns, not having anything to occupy him in front, directed his six 3.2's upon the ridge where the tired Kickers lay side by side with the Rostina dead. A shrapnel shell came swinging over the Kickers, seething and fuming. It burst directly over the trenches and the shrapnel, of course, scattered forward, hurting nobody. But a man screamed out to his officer, "By God, sir. That is one of our own batteries." The whole line quivered with fright. Five more shells streaked overhead and one flung its hail into the middle of the third battalion's line and the Kicking Twelfth shuddered to the very centre of its heart—and arose like one man—and fled.

Colonel Sponge, fighting, frothing at the mouth, dealing blows with his fist right and left, found himself confronting a fury on horseback. Richie was as pale as death and his eye sent out sparks. "What does this conduct mean?" he flashed out from between his fastened teeth.

Sponge could only gurgle, "The battery—the battery—the battery——"

"The battery?" cried Richie in a voice which sounded like pistol shots. "Are you afraid of the guns you almost took yesterday? Go back there, you white-livered cowards! You swine! You dogs! Curs!—curs!—curs! Go back there!"

Most of the men halted and crouched under the lashing tongue of their maddened general. But one man found desperate speech and he yelled: "General, it is our own battery that is firing on us!"

Many say that the general's face tightened until it looked

like a mask. The Kicking Twelfth retired to a comfortable place where they were only under the fire of the Rostina artillery. The men saw a staff officer riding over the obstructions in a manner calculated to break his neck directly.

The Kickers were aggrieved but the heart of the old colonel was cut in twain. He even babbled to his majors, talking like a man who is about to die of simple rage. "Did you hear what he said to me? Did you hear what he called us? *Did you hear what he called us?*"

The majors searched their minds for words to heal a deep wound.

The Twelfth received orders to go into camp upon the hill where they had been insulted. Old Sponge looked as if he were about to knock the aide out of the saddle but he saluted and took the regiment back to the temporary companionship of the Rostina dead.

Major-General Richie never apologized to Colonel Sponge. When you are a commanding officer you do not adopt the custom of apologizing for the wrongs done to your subordinates. You ride away. And they understand and are confident of the restitution to honor. Richie never opened his stern young lips to Sponge in reference to the scene near the hill of the Rostina dead but in time there was a General Order No. 20 which spoke definitely of the gallantry of His Majesty's Twelfth Regiment of the Line and its colonel. In the end Sponge was given a high decoration because he had been badly used by Richie on that day. Richie knew that it is hard for men to withstand the shrapnel of their friends.

A few days later the Kickers, marching in column on the road, came upon their friend the battery halted in a field. And they addressed the battery. And the captain of the battery blanched to the tips of his ears. But the men of the battery told the Kickers to go to the devil—frankly, freely, placidly, told the Kickers to go to the devil.

And this story proves that it is sometimes better to be a private.

"And If He Wills, We Must Die"

A SERJEANT, a corporal and fourteen men of the Twelfth Regiment of the Line had been sent out to occupy a house on the main highway. They would be at least a half of a mile in advance of any other picket of their own people. Serjeant Morton was deeply angry at being sent on this duty. He said that he was over-worked. There were at least two serjeants, he claimed furiously, whose turn it should have been to go on this arduous mission. He was treated unfairly; he was abused by his superiors; why did any damned fool ever join the army; as for him he would get out of it as soon as possible; he was sick of it; the life of a dog. All this he said to the corporal who listened attentively, giving grunts of respectful assent. On the way to this post, two privates took occasion to drop casually to the rear and pilfer in the orchard of a deserted plantation. When the serjeant discovered this absence, he grew black with a rage which was an accumulation of all his irritations. "Run, you!" he howled. "Bring them here! I'll show them——" A private ran swiftly to the rear. The remainder of the squad began to shout nervously at the two delinquents whose figures they could see in the deep shade of the orchard hurriedly picking fruit from the ground and cramming it within their shirts, next to their skins. The beseeching cries of their comrades stirred the criminals more than did the barking of the serjeant. They ran to rejoin the squad, while holding their loaded bosoms and with their mouths open with aggrieved explanations.

Jones faced the serjeant with a horrible cancer marked in bumps on his left side. The disease of Patterson showed quite around the front of his waist in many protuberances. "A nice pair!" said the serjeant with sudden frigidity. "You're the kind of soldiers a man wants to choose for dangerous out-post duty, ain't you?"

The two privates stood at attention, still looking much aggrieved. "We only——" began Jones huskily.

"Oh, you 'only'!" cried the serjeant. "Yes, you 'only'! I know all about that. But if you think you are going to trifle with me——"

A moment later, the squad moved on toward its station. Behind the serjeant's back Jones and Patterson were slyly passing apples and pears to their friends while the serjeant expounded eloquently to the corporal. "You see what kind of men are in the army now! Why, when I joined the regiment it was a very different thing, I can tell you. *Then*, a serjeant had some authority and if a man disobeyed orders, he had a very small chance of escaping something extremely serious. But now! Good God! If I report these men, the captain will look over a lot of beastly orderly sheets and say"—here the serjeant wrathfully imitated the voice of his captain—" 'Haw, eh, well, Serjeant Morton, these men seem to have very good records; very good records indeed. I can't be too hard on them; no; not too hard.' " Continued the serjeant: "I tell you, Flagler, the army is no place for a decent man."

Flagler, the corporal, answered with a sincerity of appreciation which with him had become a science. "I think you are right, serjeant," he answered.

Behind them the privates mumbled discreetly. "Damn this serjeant of ours. He thinks we are made of wood. I don't see any reason for all this strictness when we are on active service. It isn't like being at home in barracks. This is very different. He hammers us now worse than he did in barracks. There is no great harm in a couple of men dropping out to raid an orchard of the enemy when all the world knows that we haven't had a decent meal in twenty days."

The reddened face of Serjeant Morton suddenly showed to the rear. "A little more marching and much less talking," he said.

When he came to the house he had been ordered to occupy, the serjeant sniffed with disdain. "These people must have lived like cattle," he said angrily. To be sure, the place was not alluring. The ground-floor had been used for the housing of cattle and it was dark and terrible. A flight of steps led to the lofty first floor which was denuded but respectable. The serjeant's visage lightened when he saw the strong walls of stone and cement. "Unless they turn guns on us, they will never get us out of here," he said cheerfully to the squad. The men, anxious to keep him in an amiable mood, all hurriedly grinned and seemed very appreciative and pleased. "I'll make this into a fortress," he announced. He sent Jones and Patterson, the two orchard-thieves, out on sentry-duty. He worked the others then until he could think of no more things to tell them to do. Afterward he went forth, with a major-general's serious scowl, and examined the ground in front of his position. In returning he came to a sentry, Jones, munching an apple. He sternly commanded him to throw it away.

The men spread their blankets on the floors of the bare rooms, and putting their packs under their heads and lighting their pipes, they lived in lazy peace. Bees hummed in the garden and a scent of flowers came through the open window. A great fan-shaped bit of sunshine smote the face of one man and he indolently cursed as he moved his primitive bed to a shadier place.

Another private explained to a comrade: "This is all nonsense anyhow. No sense in occupying this post. They——"

"But of course," said the corporal, " when she told me herself she cared more for me than she did for him, I wasn't going to stand any of his talk——" The corporal's listener was so sleepy that he could only grunt his sympathy.

There was a sudden little spatter of shooting. A cry from Jones rang out. With no little intermediate scrambling, the serjeant leaped straight to his feet. "Now," he cried, "let us see what you are made of! If," he added bitterly, "you are made of anything."

A man yelled: "Good God, can't you see you're all tangled up in my cartridge belt?"

Another man yelled: "Keep off my legs! Can't you walk on the floor?"

To the windows there was a blind rush of slumberous men, who brushed hair from their eyes even as they made ready their rifles. Jones and Patterson came stumbling up the steps, crying dreadful information. Already the enemy's bullets were spitting and singing over the house.

The serjeant suddenly was stiff and cold with a sense of the importance of the thing. "Wait until you see one," he drawled loudly and calmly, "then shoot."

For some moments the enemy's bullets swung swifter than lightning over the house without anybody being able to discover a target. In this interval a man was shot in the throat.

He gurgled and then lay down on the floor. The blood slowly waved down the brown skin of his neck while he looked meekly at his comrades.

There was a howl. "There they are! There they come!" The rifles crackled. A light smoke drifted idly through the rooms. There was a strong odor as from burnt paper and the powder of fire-crackers. The men were silent. Through the windows and about the house the bullets of an entirely invisible enemy moaned, hummed, spat, burst and sang.

The men began to curse. "Why can't we see them?" they muttered through their teeth. The serjeant was still frigid. He answered soothingly as if he were directly reprehensible for this behavior of the enemy. "Wait a moment. You will soon be able to see them. There! Give it to them!" A little skirt of black figures had appeared in a field. It was really like shooting at an upright needle from the full length of a ball-room. But the men's spirits improved as soon as the enemy—this mysterious enemy—became a tangible thing, and far off. They had believed the foe to be shooting at them from the adjacent garden.

"Now," said the serjeant ambitiously, "we can beat them off easily if you men are good enough."

A man called out in a tone of quick great interest. "See that fellow on horse-back, Bill? Isn't he on horse-back? I thought he was on horse-back."

There was a fusilade against another side of the house. The serjeant dashed into the room which commanded that situation. He found a dead soldier on the floor. He rushed out howling: "When was Knowles killed? When was Knowles killed? Damn it, when was Knowles killed?" It was absolutely essential to find out the exact moment this man died. A blackened private turned upon his serjeant and demanded: "How in hell do I know?" Serjeant Morton had a sense of anger so brief that in the next second he cried: "Patterson!" He had even forgotten his vital interest in the time of Knowles' death.

"Yes?" said Patterson, his face set with some deep-rooted quality of determination. Still, he was a mere farm-boy.

"Go in to Knowles' window and shoot at those people," said the serjeant hoarsely. Afterward he coughed. Some of the fumes of the fight had made way to his lungs.

Patterson looked at the door into this other room. He looked at it as if he suspected it was to be his death-chamber. Then he entered and stood across the body of Knowles and fired vigorously into a group of charming plum-trees.

"They can't take this house," declared the serjeant in a contemptuous and argumentative tone. He was apparently replying to somebody. The man who had been shot in the throat looked up at him. Eight men were firing from the windows. The serjeant detected in a corner three wounded men talking together feebly. "Don't you think there is anything to do?" he bawled. "Go and get Knowles' cartridges and give them to somebody that can use them! Take Simpson's too." The man who had been shot in the throat looked at him. Of the three wounded men who had been talking, one said: "My leg is all doubled up under me, serjeant." He spoke apologetically.

Meantime the serjeant was re-loading his rifle. His foot slipped in the blood of the man who had been shot in the throat and the military boot made a greasy red streak on the floor.

"Why, we can hold this place," shouted the serjeant jubilantly. "Who says we can't?"

Corporal Flagler suddenly spun away from his window and fell in a heap.

"Serjeant," murmured a man as he dropped to a seat on the floor out of danger, "I can't stand this. I swear I can't. I think we should run away."

Morton, with the kindly eyes of a good shepherd, looked at the man. "You are afraid Johnston, you are afraid," he said softly. The man struggled to his feet, cast upon the serjeant a gaze full of admiration, reproach and despair, and returned to his post. A moment later he pitched forward and thereafter his body hung out of the window, his arms straight and the fists clenched. Incidentally this corpse was pierced afterward by chance three times by bullets of the enemy.

The serjeant laid his rifle against the stone-work of the window-frame and shot with care until his magazine was empty. Behind him, a man simply grazed on the elbow was wildly sobbing like a girl. "Damn it, shut up," said Morton without turning his head. Before him was a vista of a garden, fields, clumps of trees, woods, populated at the time with little stealthy fleeting figures.

He grew furious. "Why didn't he send me orders?" he cried aloud. The emphasis on the word "he" was impressive. A mile back on the road, a galloper of the Hussars lay dead beside his dead horse.

The man who had been grazed on the elbow still set up his bleat. Morton's fury veered to this soldier. "Can't you shut up? Can't you shut up? Can't you shut up? Fight! That's the thing to do. Fight!"

A bullet struck Morton and he fell upon the man who had been shot in the throat. There was a sickening moment. Then the serjeant rolled off to a position upon the bloody floor. He turned himself with a last effort until he could look at the wounded who were able to look at him.

"Kim up, the Kickers," he said thickly. His arms weakened and he dropped on his face.

After an interval, a young subaltern of the enemy's infantry, followed by his eager men, burst into this reeking interior. But just over the threshold he halted before the scene of blood and death. He turned with a shrug to his serjeant. "God! I should have estimated them as at least one hundred strong."

The Upturned Face

"WHAT WILL WE DO now?" said the adjutant, troubled and excited.

"Bury him," said Timothy Lean.

The two officers looked down close to their toes where lay the body of their comrade. The face was chalk-blue; gleaming eyes stared at the sky. Over the two upright figures was a windy sound of bullets, and on the top of the hill, Lean's prostrate company of Spitzbergen infantry was firing measured volleys.

"Don't you think it would be better——" began the adjutant. "We might leave him until to-morrow."

"No," said Lean, "I can't hold that post an hour longer. I've got to fall back, and we've got to bury old Bill."

"Of course," said the adjutant at once. "Your men got intrenching tools?"

Lean shouted back to his little firing line, and two men came slowly, one with a pick, one with a shovel. They stared in the direction of the Rostina sharpshooters. Bullets cracked near their ears. "Dig here," said Lean gruffly. The men, thus caused to lower their glances to the turf, became hurried and frightened merely because they could not look to see whence the bullets came. The dull beat of the pick striking the earth sounded amid the swift snap of close bullets. Presently the other private began to shovel.

"I suppose," said the adjutant, slowly, " we'd better search his clothes for . . . things."

Lean nodded; together in curious abstraction they looked at the body. Then Lean stirred his shoulders, suddenly arousing himself. "Yes," he said, " we'd better see . . . what he's got." He dropped to his knees and approached his hands to the body of the dead officer. But his hands wavered over the buttons of the tunic. The first button was brick-red with drying blood, and he did not seem to dare to touch it.

"Go on," said the adjutant hoarsely.

Lean stretched his wooden hand, and his fingers fumbled blood-stained buttons. . . . At last he arose with a ghastly face. He had gathered a watch, a whistle, a pipe, a tobacco pouch, a handkerchief, a little case of cards and papers. He looked at the adjutant. There was a silence. The adjutant was feeling that he had been a coward to make Lean do all the grizzly business.

"Well," said Lean, "that's all, I think. You have his sword and revolver."

"Yes," said the adjutant, his face working. And then he burst out in a sudden strange fury at the two privates. "Why don't you hurry up with that grave? What are you doing, anyhow? Hurry, do you hear? I never saw such stupid——"

Even as he cried out in this passion, the two men were laboring for their lives. Ever overhead, the bullets were spitting.

The grave was finished. It was not a masterpiece—poor little shallow thing. Lean and the adjutant again looked at each other in a curious silent communication.

Suddenly the adjutant croaked out a weird laugh. It was a terrible laugh which had its origin in that part of the mind which is first moved by the singing of the nerves. "Well," he said humorously to Lean, "I suppose we had best tumble him in."

"Yes," said Lean. The two privates stood waiting bent over on their implements. "I suppose," said Lean, "it would be better if we laid him in ourselves."

"Yes," said the adjutant. Then apparently remembering that he had made Lean search the body, he stooped with great fortitude and took hold of the dead officer's clothing. Lean joined him. Both were particular that their fingers should not feel the corpse. They tugged away; the corpse lifted, heaved, toppled, flopped into the grave, and the two officers, straightening, looked again at each other—they were always looking at each other. They sighed with relief.

The adjutant said: "I suppose we should . . . we should say something. Do you know the service, Tim?"

"They don't read the service until the grave is filled in," said Lean, pressing his lips to an academic expression.

"Don't they?" said the adjutant, shocked that he had made the mistake. "Oh, well," he cried suddenly, "let us . . . let us say something while . . . while he can hear us."

"All right," said Lean. "Do you know the service?"

"I can't remember a line of it," said the adjutant.

Lean was extremely dubious. "I can repeat two lines but——"

"Well, do it," said the adjutant. "Go as far as you can. That's better than nothing. And . . . the beasts have got our range exactly."

Lean looked at his two men. "Attention!" he barked. The privates came to attention with a click, looking much aggrieved. The adjutant lowered his helmet to his knee. Lean, bare-headed, stood over the grave. The Rostina sharpshooters fired briskly.

"*O, Father, our friend has sunk in the deep waters of death, but his spirit has leaped toward Thee as the bubble arises from the lips of the drowning. Perceive, we beseech, O, Father, the little flying bubble and——*"

Lean, although husky and ashamed, had suffered no hesitation up to this point, but he stopped with a hopeless feeling and looked at the corpse.

The adjutant moved uneasily. "*And from Thy superb heights——*" he began, and then he, too, came to an end.

"*And from Thy superb heights,*" said Lean.

The adjutant suddenly remembered a phrase in the back part of the Spitzbergen burial service, and he exploited it with the triumphant manner of a man who has recalled everything and can go on.

"*O, God, have mercy——*"

"*O, God, have mercy——*" said Lean.

"*'Mercy,'*" repeated the adjutant in a quick failure.

"*'Mercy,'*" said Lean. And then he was moved by some violence of feeling, for he turned suddenly upon his two men and tigerishly said: "Throw the dirt in."

The fire of the Rostina sharpshooters was accurate and continuous.

II

One of the aggrieved privates came forward with his shovel. He lifted his first shovel load of earth and for a moment of inexplicable hesitation it was held poised above this corpse which from its chalk-blue face looked keenly out from the grave. Then the soldier emptied his shovel on—on the feet.

Timothy Lean felt as if tons had been swiftly lifted from off his forehead. He had felt that perhaps the private might empty the shovel on—on the face. It had been emptied on the feet. There was a great point gained there—ha, ha!—the first shovelful had been emptied on the feet. How satisfactory!

The adjutant began to babble. "Well, of course . . . a man we've messed with all these years . . . impossible . . . you can't, you know, leave your intimate friends rotting on the field. . . . Go on, for God's sake, and shovel, *you*."

The man with the shovel suddenly ducked, grabbed his left arm with his right hand and looked at his officer for orders. Lean picked the shovel from the ground. "Go to the rear," he said to the wounded man. He also addressed the other private. "You get under cover, too. I'll . . . I'll finish this business."

The wounded man scrambled hastily for the top of the ridge without devoting any glances to the direction from whence the bullets came and the other man followed at an equal pace but he was different in that he looked back anxiously three times. This is merely the way—often—of the hit and the unhit.

Timothy Lean filled the shovel, hesitated, and then in a movement which was like a gesture of abhorrence, he flung the dirt into the grave and as it landed it made a sound— plop. Lean suddenly paused and mopped his brow—a tired laborer.

"Perhaps we have been wrong," said the adjutant. His glance wavered stupidly. "It might have been better if we hadn't buried him just at this time. Of course, if we advance to-morrow, the body would have been——"

"Damn you," said Lean. "Shut your mouth." He was not the senior officer.

He again filled the shovel and flung in the earth. Always the earth made that sound—plop. For a space Lean worked frantically like a man digging himself out of danger.

Soon there was nothing to be seen but the chalk-blue face. Lean filled the shovel. . . . "Good God," he cried to the adjutant. "Why didn't you turn him somehow when you put him in? This——" Then Lean began to stutter.

The adjutant understood. He was pale to the lips. "Go on, man," he cried, beseechingly, almost in a shout. . . . Lean swung back the shovel; it went forward in a pendulum curve. When the earth landed it made a sound—plop.

A Poker Game

USUALLY A POKER GAME is a picture of peace. There is no drama so low-voiced and serene and monotonous. If an amateur loser does not softly curse there is no orchestral support. Here is one of the most exciting and absorbing occupations known to intelligent American manhood, here a year's reflection is compressed into a moment of thought, here the nerves may stand on end and scream to themselves, but a tranquility as from heaven is only interrupted by the click of chips. The higher the stakes, the more quiet the scene; this is a law that applies everywhere save on the stage.

And yet sometimes in a poker game things happen. Everybody remembers the celebrated corner on bay rum that was triumphantly consummated by Robert F. Cinch of Chicago assisted by the United States courts and whatever other federal power he needed. Robert F. Cinch enjoyed his victory four months. Then he died and young Bobbie Cinch came to New York in order to more clearly demonstrate that there was a good deal of fun in twenty-two million dollars.

Old Henry Spuytendyvil owns all the real estate in New York save that previously appropriated by the hospitals and Central Park. He had been a friend of Bob's father. When Bob appeared in New York, Spuytendyvil entertained him correctly. It came to pass that they just naturally played poker.

One night they were having a small game in an up-town hotel. There were five of them, including two lawyers and a politician. The stakes depended on the ability of the individual fortune.

Bobbie Cinch had won rather heavily. He was as generous as sunshine and when luck chases a generous man it chases him hard, even though he cannot bet with all the skill of his opponents.

Old Spuytendyvil had lost a considerable amount. One of the lawyers from time to time smiled quietly because he knew Spuytendyvil well and he knew that anything with the name of loss attached to it sliced the old man's heart into sections.

At midnight, Archie Bracketts, the actor, came into the room. "How you holding 'em, Bob?" said he.

"Pretty well," said Bob.

"Having any luck, Mr. Spuytendyvil?"

"Blooming bad," grunted the old man.

Bracketts laughed and put his foot on the round of Spuy-tendyvil's chair. "There," said he. "I'll queer your luck for you." Spuytendyvil sat at the end of the table. "Bobbie," said the actor presently, as young Cinch won another pot, "I guess I better knock your luck." So he took his foot from the old man's chair and placed it on Bob's chair. The lad grinned good-naturedly and said he didn't care.

Bracketts was in a position to scan both of the hands. It was Bob's ante and old Spuytendyvil threw in a red chip. Everybody passed out up to Bobbie. He filled in the pot and drew a card.

Spuytendyvil drew a card. Bracketts, looking over his shoulder, saw him holding the ten, nine, eight and seven of diamonds. Theatrically speaking, straight flushes are as frequent as berries on a juniper tree but as a matter of truth the reason that straight flushes are so admired is because they are not as common as berries on a juniper tree. Bracketts stared; drew a cigar slowly from his pocket and placing it between his teeth, forgot its existence.

Bobbie was the only other stayer. Bracketts flashed an eye for the lad's hand and saw the nine, eight, six and five of hearts. Now there are but six hundred and forty-five emotions possible to the human mind and Bracketts immediately had them all. Under the impression that he had finished his cigar, he took it from his mouth and tossed it toward the grate without turning his eyes to follow its flight.

There happened to be a complete silence around the green-clothed table. Spuytendyvil was studying his hand with a kind of contemptuous smile but in his eyes there perhaps was to be seen a cold stern light expressing something sinister and relentless.

Young Bob sat as he had sat. As the pause grew longer, he looked up once inquiringly at Spuytendyvil.

The old man reached for a white chip. "Well, mine are worth about that much," said he, tossing it into the pot. Thereupon he leaned back comfortably in his chair and renewed his stare at the five straight diamonds. Young Bob extended his hand leisurely toward his stack. It occurred to Bracketts that he was smoking but he found no cigar in his mouth.

The lad fingered his chips and looked pensively at his hand. The silence of these moments oppressed Bracketts like the smoke from a conflagration.

Bobbie Cinch continued for some moments to coolly observe his cards. At last he breathed a little sigh and said: "Well, Mr. Spuytendyvil, I can't play a sure thing against you." He threw in a white chip. "I'll just call you. I've got a straight flush." He faced down his cards.

Old Spuytendyvil's roar of horror and rage could only be equaled in volume to a small explosion of gasolene. He dashed his cards upon the table. "There!" he shouted glaring frightfully at Bobbie. "I've got a straight flush, too! And mine is Jack high!"

Bobbie was at first paralyzed with amazement but in a moment he recovered and apparently observing something amusing in the situation he grinned.

Archie Bracketts, having burst his bond of silence, yelled for joy and relief. He smote Bobbie on the shoulder. "Bob, my boy," he cried exuberantly, "you're no gambler but you're a mighty good fellow and if you hadn't been you would be losing a good many dollars this minute."

Old Spuytendyvil glowered at Bracketts. "Stop making such an infernal din, will you, Archie," he said morosely. His throat seemed filled with pounded glass. "Pass the whiskey."

Manacled

IN THE FIRST ACT there had been a farm scene, wherein real horses had drunk real water out of real buckets, afterward dragging a real wagon off stage, L. The audience was consumed with admiration of this play, and the great Theatre Nouveau rang to its roof with the crowd's plaudits.

The Second Act was now well advanced. The hero, cruelly victimized by his enemies, stood in prison garb, panting with rage while two brutal warders fastened real handcuffs on his wrists and real anklets on his ankles. And the hovering villain sneered.

" 'Tis well, Aubrey Pettingill," said the prisoner. "You have so far succeeded, but, mark you, there will come a time——"

The villain retorted with a cutting allusion to the young lady whom the hero loved.

"Curse you," cried the hero, and he made as if to spring upon this demon, but, as the pitying audience saw, he could only take steps four inches long.

Drowning the mocking laughter of the villain came cries from both the audience and the people back of the wings. "Fire! Fire! Fire!" Throughout the great house resounded the roaring crashes of a throng of human beings moving in terror, and even above this noise could be heard the screams of women more shrill than whistles. The building hummed and shook; it was like a glade which holds some bellowing cataract of the mountains. Most of the people who were killed on the stairs still clutched their play-bills in their hands as if they had resolved to save them at all costs.

The Theatre Nouveau fronted upon a street which was not of the first importance, especially at night, when it only aroused when the people came to the theatre and aroused again when they came out to go home. On the night of the fire, at the time of the scene between the enchained hero and his tormentor, the thoroughfare echoed with only the scraping shovels of some street-cleaners who were loading carts with blackened snow and mud. The gleam of lights made the shadowed pavements deeply blue, save where lay some yellow plum-like reflection.

Suddenly a policeman came running frantically along the street. He charged upon the fire-box on a corner. Its red light touched with flame each of his brass buttons and the municipal shield. He pressed a lever. He had been standing in the entrance of the theatre chatting to the lonely man in the box-office. To send an alarm was a matter of seconds.

Out of the theatre poured the first hundreds of fortunate ones, and some were not altogether fortunate. Women, their bonnets flying, cried out tender names; men, white as death, scratched and bleeding, looked wildly from face to face. There were displays of horrible blind brutality by the strong. Weaker men clutched and clawed like cats. From the theatre itself came the howl of a gale.

The policeman's fingers had flashed into instant life and action the most perfect counter-attack to the fire. He listened for some seconds and presently he heard the thunder of a charging engine. She swept around a corner, her three shining enthrilled horses leaping. Her consort, the hose-cart, roared behind her. There were the loud clicks of the steel-shod hoofs, hoarse shouts, men running, the flash of lights, while the crevice-like streets resounded with the charges of other engines.

At the first cry of fire, the two brutal warders had dropped the arms of the hero and run off the stage with the villain. The hero cried after them angrily. "Where you going? Here, Pete—Tom—you've left me chained up, damn you!"

The body of the theatre now resembled a mad surf amid rocks, but the hero did not look at it. He was filled with fury at the stupidity of the two brutal warders, in forgetting that they were leaving him manacled. Calling loudly, he hobbled off stage, L, taking steps four inches long.

Behind the scenes he heard the hum of flames. Smoke, filled with sparks sweeping on spiral courses, rolled thickly upon him. Suddenly his face turned chalk-color beneath his skin of manly bronze for the stage. His voice shrieked. "Pete—Tom—damn you—come back—you've left me chained up."

He had played in this theatre for seven years, and he could find his way without light through the intricate passages which mazed out behind the stage. He knew that it was a long way to the street door.

The heat was intense. From time to time masses of flaming wood sung down from above him. He began to jump. Each jump advanced him about three feet, but the effort soon became heart-breaking. Once he fell, and it took time to get upon his feet again.

There were stairs to descend. From the top of this flight he tried to fall feet first. He precipitated himself in a way that would have broken his hip under common conditions. But every step seemed covered with glue, and on almost every one he stuck for a moment. He could not even succeed in falling down stairs. Ultimately he reached the bottom, windless from the struggle.

There were stairs to climb. At the foot of the flight he lay for an instant with his mouth close to the floor trying to breathe. Then he tried to scale this frightful precipice up the face of which many an actress had gone at a canter.

Each succeeding step arose eight inches from its fellow. The hero dropped to a seat on the third step and pulled his feet to the second step. From this position he lifted himself to a seat on the fourth step. He had not gone far in this manner before his frenzy caused him to lose his balance, and he rolled to the foot of the flight. After all, he could fall down stairs.

He lay there whispering. "They all got out but I. All but I." Beautiful flames flashed above him, some were crimson, some were orange, and here and there were tongues of purple, blue, green.

A curiously calm thought came into his head. "What a fool I was not to foresee this! I shall have Rogers furnish manacles of papier-mâché to-morrow."

The thunder of the fire-lions made the theatre have a palsy.

Suddenly the hero beat his handcuffs against the wall, cursing them in a loud wail. Blood started from under his finger-nails. Soon he began to bite the hot steel, and blood fell from his blistered mouth. He raved like a wolf.

Peace came to him again. There were charming effects amid the flames. . . . He felt very cool, delightfully cool. . . . "They've left me chained up."

POEMS

Contents

The Black Riders and Other Lines

I

Black riders came from the sea.
There was clang and clang of spear and shield,
And clash and clash of hoof and heel,
Wild shouts and the wave of hair
In the rush upon the wind:
Thus the ride of sin.

II

Three little birds in a row
Sat musing.
A man passed near that place
Then did the little birds nudge each other.

They said: "He thinks he can sing."
They threw back their heads to laugh.
With quaint countenances
They regarded him.
They were very curious
Those three little birds in a row.

III

In the desert
I saw a creature, naked, bestial,
Who, squatting upon the ground,
Held his heart in his hands,
And ate of it.
I said, "Is it good, friend?"
"It is bitter—bitter," he answered;
"But I like it
"Because it is bitter,
"And because it is my heart."

IV

Yes, I have a thousand tongues,
And nine and ninety-nine lie.
Though I strive to use the one,
It will make no melody at my will,
But is dead in my mouth.

V

Once there came a man
Who said,
"Range me all men of the world in rows."
And instantly
There was terrific clamor among the people
Against being ranged in rows.
There was a loud quarrel, world-wide.
It endured for ages;
And blood was shed
By those who would not stand in rows,
And by those who pined to stand in rows.
Eventually, the man went to death, weeping.
And those who staid in bloody scuffle
Knew not the great simplicity.

VI

God fashioned the ship of the world carefully.
With the infinite skill of an all-master
Made He the hull and the sails,
Held He the rudder
Ready for adjustment.
Erect stood He, scanning His work proudly.
Then—at fateful time—a wrong called,
And God turned, heeding.
Lo, the ship, at this opportunity, slipped slyly,
Making cunning noiseless travel down the ways.
So that, forever rudderless, it went upon the seas
Going ridiculous voyages,
Making quaint progress,

Turning as with serious purpose
Before stupid winds.
And there were many in the sky
Who laughed at this thing.

VII

Mystic shadow, bending near me,
Who art thou?
Whence come ye?
And—tell me—is it fair
Or is the truth bitter as eaten fire?
Tell me!
Fear not that I should quaver,
For I dare—I dare.
Then, tell me!

VIII

I looked here
I looked there
No where could I see my love.
And—this time—
She was in my heart.
Truly then I have no complaint
For 'though she be fair and fairer
She is none so fair as she
In my heart.

IX

I stood upon a high place,
And saw, below, many devils
Running, leaping,
And carousing in sin.
One looked up, grinning,
And said, "Comrade! Brother!"

X

Should the wide world roll away
Leaving black terror
Limitless night,
Nor God, nor man, nor place to stand
Would be to me essential
If thou and thy white arms were there
And the fall to doom a long way.

XI

In a lonely place,
I encountered a sage
Who sat, all still,
Regarding a newspaper.
He accosted me:
"Sir, what is this?"
Then I saw that I was greater,
Aye, greater than this sage.
I answered him at once,
"Old, old man, it is the wisdom of the age."
The sage looked upon me with admiration.

XII

"And the sins of the fathers shall be visited upon the
heads of the children, even unto the third and fourth
generation of them that hate me."

Well, then, I hate Thee, unrighteous picture;
Wicked image, I hate Thee;
So, strike with Thy vengeance
The heads of those little men
Who come blindly.
It will be a brave thing.

XIII

If there is a witness to my little life,
To my tiny throes and struggles,
He sees a fool;
And it is not fine for gods to menace fools.

XIV

There was crimson clash of war.
Lands turned black and bare;
Women wept;
Babes ran, wondering.
There came one who understood not these things.
He said, "Why is this?"
Whereupon a million strove to answer him.
There was such intricate clamor of tongues,
That still the reason was not.

XV

"Tell brave deeds of war."

Then they recounted tales,—
"There were stern stands
"And bitter runs for glory."

Ah, I think there were braver deeds.

XVI

Charity, thou art a lie,
A toy of women,
A pleasure of certain men.
In the presence of justice,
Lo, the walls of the temple
Are visible
Through thy form of sudden shadows.

XVII

There were many who went in huddled procession,
They knew not whither;
But, at any rate, success or calamity
Would attend all in equality.

There was one who sought a new road.
He went into direful thickets,
And ultimately he died thus, alone;
But they said he had courage.

XVIII

In Heaven,
Some little blades of grass
Stood before God.
"What did you do?"
Then all save one of the little blades
Began eagerly to relate
The merits of their lives.
This one stayed a small way behind
Ashamed.
Presently God said:
"And what did you do?"
The little blade answered: "Oh, my lord,
"Memory is bitter to me
"For if I did good deeds
"I know not of them."
Then God in all His splendor
Arose from His throne.
"Oh, best little blade of grass," He said.

XIX

A god in wrath
Was beating a man;
He cuffed him loudly
With thunderous blows
That rang and rolled over the earth.

All people came running.
The man screamed and struggled,
And bit madly at the feet of the god.
The people cried,
"Ah, what a wicked man!"
And—
"Ah, what a redoubtable god!"

XX

A learned man came to me once.
He said, "I know the way,—come."
And I was overjoyed at this.
Together we hastened.
Soon, too soon, were we
Where my eyes were useless,
And I knew not the ways of my feet.
I clung to the hand of my friend;
But at last he cried, "I am lost."

XXI

There was, before me,
Mile upon mile
Of snow, ice, burning sand.
And yet I could look beyond all this,
To a place of infinite beauty;
And I could see the loveliness of her
Who walked in the shade of the trees.
When I gazed,
All was lost
But this place of beauty and her.
When I gazed,
And in my gazing, desired,
Then came again
Mile upon mile,
Of snow, ice, burning sand.

XXII

Once I saw mountains angry,
And ranged in battle-front.
Against them stood a little man;
Aye, he was no bigger than my finger.
I laughed, and spoke to one near me,
"Will he prevail?"
"Surely," replied this other;
"His grandfathers beat them many times."
Then did I see much virtue in grandfathers,—
At least, for the little man
Who stood against the mountains.

XXIII

Places among the stars,
Soft gardens near the sun,
Keep your distant beauty;
Shed no beams upon my weak heart.
Since she is here
In a place of blackness,
Not your golden days
Nor your silver nights
Can call me to you.
Since she is here
In a place of blackness,
Here I stay and wait.

XXIV

I saw a man pursuing the horizon;
Round and round they sped.
I was disturbed at this;
I accosted the man.
"It is futile," I said,
"You can never——"

"You lie," he cried,
And ran on.

XXV

Behold, the grave of a wicked man,
And near it, a stern spirit.

There came a drooping maid with violets,
But the spirit grasped her arm.
"No flowers for him," he said.
The maid wept:
"Ah, I loved him."
But the spirit, grim and frowning:
"No flowers for him."

Now, this is it——
If the spirit was just,
Why did the maid weep?

XXVI

There was set before me a mighty hill,
And long days I climbed
Through regions of snow.
When I had before me the summit-view,
It seemed that my labor
Had been to see gardens
Lying at impossible distances.

XXVII

A youth in apparel that glittered
Went to walk in a grim forest.
There he met an assassin
Attired all in garb of old days;
He, scowling through the thickets,
And dagger poised quivering,
Rushed upon the youth.
"Sir," said this latter,
"I am enchanted, believe me,
"To die, thus,
"In this medieval fashion,

"According to the best legends;
"Ah, what joy!"
Then took he the wound, smiling,
And died, content.

XXVIII

"Truth," said a traveller,
"Is a rock, a mighty fortress;
"Often have I been to it,
"Even to its highest tower,
"From whence the world looks black."

"Truth," said a traveller,
"Is a breath, a wind,
"A shadow, a phantom;
"Long have I pursued it,
"But never have I touched
"The hem of its garment."

And I believed the second traveller;
For truth was to me
A breath, a wind,
A shadow, a phantom,
And never had I touched
The hem of its garment.

XXIX

Behold, from the land of the farther suns
I returned.
And I was in a reptile-swarming place,
Peopled, otherwise, with grimaces,
Shrouded above in black impenetrableness.
I shrank, loathing,
Sick with it.
And I said to him,
"What is this?"

He made answer slowly,
"Spirit, this is a world;
"This was your home."

XXX

Supposing that I should have the courage
To let a red sword of virtue
Plunge into my heart,
Letting to the weeds of the ground
My sinful blood,
What can you offer me?
A gardened castle?
A flowery kingdom?

What? A hope?
Then hence with your red sword of virtue.

XXXI

Many workmen
Built a huge ball of masonry
Upon a mountain-top.
Then they went to the valley below,
And turned to behold their work.
"It is grand," they said;
They loved the thing.

Of a sudden, it moved:
It came upon them swiftly;
It crushed them all to blood.
But some had opportunity to squeal.

XXXII

Two or three angels
Came near to the earth.
They saw a fat church.
Little black streams of people

Came and went in continually.
And the angels were puzzled
To know why the people went thus,
And why they stayed so long within.

XXXIII

There was One I met upon the road
Who looked at me with kind eyes.
He said: "Show me of your wares."
And this I did
Holding forth one.
He said: "It is a sin."
Then held I forth another.
He said: "It is a sin."
Then held I forth another.
He said: "It is a sin."
And so to the end
Always He said: "It is a sin."
And, finally, I cried out:
"But I have none other."
Then did He look at me
With kinder eyes.
"Poor soul," He said.

XXXIV

I stood upon a highway,
And, behold, there came
Many strange pedlers.
To me each one made gestures,
Holding forth little images, saying,
"This is my pattern of God.
"Now this is the God I prefer."

But I said, "Hence!
"Leave me with mine own,
"And take you yours away;
"I can't buy of your patterns of God,
"The little gods you may rightly prefer."

XXXV

A man saw a ball of gold in the sky;
He climbed for it,
And eventually he achieved it——
It was clay.

Now this is the strange part:
When the man went to the earth
And looked again,
Lo, there was the ball of gold.
Now this is the strange part:
It was a ball of gold.
Aye, by the heavens, it was a ball of gold.

XXXVI

I met a seer.
He held in his hands
The book of wisdom.
"Sir," I addressed him,
"Let me read."
"Child——" he began.
"Sir," I said,
"Think not that I am a child,
"For already I know much
"Of that which you hold.
"Aye, much."

He smiled.
Then he opened the book
And held it before me.—
Strange that I should have grown so suddenly blind.

XXXVII

On the horizon the peaks assembled;
And as I looked,
The march of the mountains began.
As they marched, they sang,
"Aye! We come! We come!"

XXXVIII

The ocean said to me once,
"Look!
"Yonder on the shore
"Is a woman, weeping.
"I have watched her.
"Go you and tell her this,—
"Her lover I have laid
"In cool green hall.
"There is wealth of golden sand
"And pillars, coral-red;
"Two white fish stand guard at his bier.

"Tell her this
"And more,—
"That the king of the seas
"Weeps too, old, helpless man.
"The bustling fates
"Heap his hands with corpses
"Until he stands like a child
"With surplus of toys."

XXXIX

The livid lightnings flashed in the clouds;
The leaden thunders crashed.
A worshipper raised his arm.
"Hearken! Hearken! The voice of God!"

"Not so," said a man.
"The voice of God whispers in the heart
"So softly
"That the soul pauses,
"Making no noise,
"And strives for these melodies,
"Distant, sighing, like faintest breath,
"And all the being is still to hear."

XL

And you love me?

I love you.

You are, then, cold coward.

Aye; but, beloved,
When I strive to come to you,
Man's opinions, a thousand thickets,
My interwoven existence,
My life,
Caught in the stubble of the world
Like a tender veil,—
This stays me.
No strange move can I make
Without noise of tearing.
I dare not.

If love loves,
There is no world
Nor word.
All is lost
Save thought of love
And place to dream.
You love me?

I love you.

You are, then, cold coward.

Aye; but, beloved——

XLI

Love walked alone.
The rocks cut her tender feet,
And the brambles tore her fair limbs.
There came a companion to her,

But, alas, he was no help,
For his name was Heart's Pain.

XLII

I walked in a desert.
And I cried,
"Ah, God, take me from this place!"
A voice said, "It is no desert."
I cried, "Well, but——
"The sand, the heat, the vacant horizon."
A voice said, "It is no desert."

XLIII

There came whisperings in the winds:
"Good-bye! Good-bye!"
Little voices called in the darkness:
"Good-bye! Good-bye!"
Then I stretched forth my arms.
"No— No——"
There came whisperings in the wind:
"Good-bye! Good-bye!"
Little voices called in the darkness:
"Good-bye! Good-bye!"

XLIV

I was in the darkness;
I could not see my words
Nor the wishes of my heart.
Then suddenly there was a great light——

"Let me into the darkness again."

XLV

Tradition, thou art for suckling children,
Thou art the enlivening milk for babes;

But no meat for men is in thee.
Then——
But, alas, we all are babes.

XLVI

Many red devils ran from my heart
And out upon the page.
They were so tiny
The pen could mash them.
And many struggled in the ink.
It was strange
To write in this red muck
Of things from my heart.

XLVII

"Think as I think," said a man,
"Or you are abominably wicked;
"You are a toad."

And after I had thought of it,
I said, "I will, then, be a toad."

XLVIII

Once there was a man,—
Oh, so wise!
In all drink
He detected the bitter,
And in all touch
He found the sting.
At last he cried thus:
"There is nothing,—
"No life,
"No joy,
"No pain,—
"There is nothing save opinion,
"And opinion be damned."

XLIX

I stood musing in a black world,
Not knowing where to direct my feet.
And I saw the quick stream of men
Pouring ceaselessly,
Filled with eager faces,
A torrent of desire.
I called to them,
"Where do you go? What do you see?"
A thousand voices called to me.
A thousand fingers pointed.
"Look! Look! There!"

I know not of it.
But, lo! in the far sky shone a radiance
Ineffable, divine,—
A vision painted upon a pall;
And sometimes it was,
And sometimes it was not.
I hesitated.
Then from the stream
Came roaring voices,
Impatient:
"Look! Look! There!"

So again I saw,
And leaped, unhesitant,
And struggled and fumed
With outspread clutching fingers.
The hard hills tore my flesh;
The ways bit my feet.
At last I looked again.

No radiance in the far sky,
Ineffable, divine;
No vision painted upon a pall;
And always my eyes ached for the light.
Then I cried in despair,
"I see nothing! Oh, where do I go?"

The torrent turned again its faces:
"Look! Look! There!"

And at the blindness of my spirit
They screamed,
"Fool! Fool! Fool!"

L

You say you are holy,
And that
Because I have not seen you sin.
Aye, but there are those
Who see you sin, my friend.

LI

A man went before a strange god,—
The god of many men, sadly wise.
And the deity thundered loudly,
Fat with rage, and puffing,
"Kneel, mortal, and cringe
"And grovel and do homage
"To my particularly sublime majesty."

The man fled.

Then the man went to another god,—
The god of his inner thoughts.
And this one looked at him
With soft eyes
Lit with infinite comprehension,
And said, "My poor child!"

LII

Why do you strive for greatness, fool?
Go pluck a bough and wear it.
It is as sufficing.

My lord, there are certain barbarians
Who tilt their noses
As if the stars were flowers,
And thy servant is lost among their shoe-buckles.
Fain would I have mine eyes even with their eyes.

Fool, go pluck a bough and wear it.

LIII

I

Blustering god,
Stamping across the sky
With loud swagger,
I fear you not.
No, though from your highest heaven
You plunge your spear at my heart,
I fear you not.
No, not if the blow
Is as the lightning blasting a tree,
I fear you not, puffing braggart.

II

If thou can see into my heart
That I fear thee not,
Thou wilt see why I fear thee not,
And why it is right.
So threaten not, thou, with thy bloody spears,
Else thy sublime ears shall hear curses.

III

Withal, there is one whom I fear;
I fear to see grief upon that face.
Perchance, friend, he is not your god;
If so, spit upon him.
By it you will do no profanity.
But I——
Ah, sooner would I die
Than see tears in those eyes of my soul.

LIV

"It was wrong to do this," said the angel.
"You should live like a flower,
"Holding malice like a puppy,
"Waging war like a lambkin."

"Not so," quoth the man
Who had no fear of spirits;
"It is only wrong for angels
"Who can live like the flowers,
"Holding malice like the puppies,
"Waging war like the lambkins."

LV

A man toiled on a burning road,
Never resting.
Once he saw a fat, stupid ass
Grinning at him from a green place.
The man cried out in rage,
"Ah! do not deride me, fool!
"I know you——
"All day stuffing your belly,
"Burying your heart
"In grass and tender sprouts:
"It will not suffice you."
But the ass only grinned at him from the green place.

LVI

A man feared that he might find an assassin;
Another that he might find a victim.
One was more wise than the other.

LVII

With eye and with gesture
You say you are holy.

I say you lie;
For I did see you
Draw away your coats
From the sin upon the hands
Of a little child.
Liar!

LVIII

The sage lectured brilliantly.
Before him, two images:
"Now this one is a devil,
"And this one is me."
He turned away.
Then a cunning pupil
Changed the positions.
Turned the sage again:
"Now this one is a devil,
"And this one is me."
The pupils sat, all grinning,
And rejoiced in the game.
But the sage was a sage.

LIX

Walking in the sky,
A man in strange black garb
Encountered a radiant form.
Then his steps were eager;
Bowed he devoutly.
"My lord," said he.
But the spirit knew him not.

LX

Upon the road of my life,
Passed me many fair creatures,
Clothed all in white, and radiant.
To one, finally, I made speech:

"Who art thou?"
But she, like the others,
Kept cowled her face,
And answered in haste, anxiously,
"I am Good Deed, forsooth;
"You have often seen me."
"Not uncowled," I made reply.
And with rash and strong hand,
Though she resisted,
I drew away the veil
And gazed at the features of Vanity.
She, shamefaced, went on;
And after I had mused a time,
I said of myself,

     "Fool!"

LXI

I

There was a man and a woman
Who sinned.
Then did the man heap the punishment
All upon the head of her,
And went away gayly.

II

There was a man and a woman
Who sinned.
And the man stood with her.
As upon her head, so upon his,
Fell blow and blow,
And all people screaming, "Fool!"
He was a brave heart.

III

He was a brave heart.
Would you speak with him, friend?

Well, he is dead,
And there went your opportunity.
Let it be your grief
That he is dead
And your opportunity gone;
For, in that, you were a coward.

LXII

There was a man who lived a life of fire.
Even upon the fabric of time,
Where purple becomes orange
And orange purple,
This life glowed,
A dire red stain, indelible;
Yet when he was dead,
He saw that he had not lived.

LXIII

There was a great cathedral.
To solemn songs,
A white procession
Moved toward the altar.
The chief man there
Was erect, and bore himself proudly.
Yet some could see him cringe,
As in a place of danger,
Throwing frightened glances into the air,
A-start at threatening faces of the past.

LXIV

Friend, your white beard sweeps the ground.
Why do you stand, expectant?
Do you hope to see it
In one of your withered days?
With your old eyes
Do you hope to see

The triumphal march of justice?
Do not wait, friend.
Take your white beard
And your old eyes
To more tender lands.

LXV

Once, I knew a fine song,
—It is true, believe me,—
It was all of birds,
And I held them in a basket;
When I opened the wicket,
Heavens! They all flew away.
I cried, "Come back, little thoughts!"
But they only laughed.
They flew on
Until they were as sand
Thrown between me and the sky.

LXVI

If I should cast off this tattered coat,
And go free into the mighty sky;
If I should find nothing there
But a vast blue,
Echoless, ignorant,—
What then?

LXVII

God lay dead in Heaven;
Angels sang the hymn of the end;
Purple winds went moaning,
Their wings drip-dripping
With blood
That fell upon the earth.
It, groaning thing,
Turned black and sank.

Then from the far caverns
Of dead sins
Came monsters, livid with desire.
They fought,
Wrangled over the world,
A morsel.
But of all sadness this was sad,—
A woman's arms tried to shield
The head of a sleeping man
From the jaws of the final beast.

LXVIII

A spirit sped
Through spaces of night;
And as he sped, he called,
"God! God!"
He went through valleys
Of black death-slime,
Ever calling,
"God! God!"
Their echoes
From crevice and cavern
Mocked him:
"God! God! God!"
Fleetly into the plains of space
He went, ever calling,
"God! God!"
Eventually, then, he screamed,
Mad in denial,
"Ah, there is no God!"
A swift hand,
A sword from the sky,
Smote him,
And he was dead.

War Is Kind

Do not weep, maiden, for war is kind.
Because your lover threw wild hands toward the sky
And the affrighted steed ran on alone,
Do not weep.
War is kind.

Hoarse, booming drums of the regiment
Little souls who thirst for fight,
These men were born to drill and die
The unexplained glory flies above them
Great is the battle-god, great, and his kingdom——
A field where a thousand corpses lie.

Do not weep, babe, for war is kind.
Because your father tumbled in the yellow trenches,
Raged at his breast, gulped and died,
Do not weep.
War is kind.

Swift, blazing flag of the regiment
Eagle with crest of red and gold,
These men were born to drill and die
Point for them the virtue of slaughter
Make plain to them the excellence of killing
And a field where a thousand corpses lie.

Mother whose heart hung humble as a button
On the bright splendid shroud of your son,
Do not weep.
War is kind.

. . . .

"What says the sea, little shell?
"What says the sea?
"Long has our brother been silent to us
"Kept his message for the ships
"Awkward ships, stupid ships."

"The sea bids you mourn, oh, pines
"Sing low in the moonlight.
"He sends tale of the land of doom
"Of place where endless falls
"A rain of women's tears
"And men in grey robes
"—Men in grey robes—
"Chant the unknown pain."

"What says the sea, little shell?
"What says the sea?
"Long has our brother been silent to us
"Kept his message for the ships
"Puny ships, silly ships."

"The sea bids you teach, oh, pines
"Sing low in the moonlight.
"Teach the gold of patience
"Cry gospel of gentle hands
"Cry a brotherhood of hearts
"The sea bids you teach, oh, pines."

"And where is the reward, little shell?
"What says the sea?
"Long has our brother been silent to us
"Kept his message for the ships
"Puny ships, silly ships."
"No word says the sea, oh, pines
"No word says the sea.
"Long will your brother be silent to you
"Keep his message for the ships
"Oh, puny pines, silly pines."

     . . . .

To the maiden
The sea was blue meadow
Alive with little froth-people
Singing.

To the sailor, wrecked,
The sea was dead grey walls
Superlative in vacancy
Upon which nevertheless at fateful time,
Was written
The grim hatred of nature.

.   .   .   .

A little ink more or less!
It surely can't matter?
Even the sky and the opulent sea,
The plains and the hills, aloof,
Hear the uproar of all these books.
But it is only a little ink more or less.

What?
You define me God with these trinkets?
Can my misery meal on an ordered walking
Of surpliced numbskulls?
And a fanfare of lights?
Or even upon the measured pulpiting
Of the familiar false and true?
Is this God?
Where, then, is hell?
Show me some bastard mushroom
Sprung from a pollution of blood.
It is better.

Where is God?

.   .   .   .

"Have you ever made a just man?"
"Oh, I have made three," answered God
"But two of them are dead
"And the third——
"Listen! Listen!
"And you will hear the thud of his defeat."

. . . .

I explain the silvered passing of a ship at night
The sweep of each sad lost wave
The dwindling boom of the steel thing's striving
The little cry of a man to a man
A shadow falling across the greyer night
And the sinking of the small star.

Then the waste, the far waste of waters
And the soft lashing of black waves
For long and in loneliness.

Remember, thou, oh ship of love
Thou leavest a far waste of waters
And the soft lashing of black waves
For long and in loneliness.

. . . .

"I have heard the sunset song of the birches
"A white melody in the silence
"I have seen a quarrel of the pines.
"At nightfall
"The little grasses have rushed by me
"With the wind-men.
"These things have I lived," quoth the maniac,
"Possessing only eyes and ears.
"But, you——
"You don green spectacles before you look at roses."

. . . .

Fast rode the knight
With spurs, hot and reeking
Ever waving an eager sword.
"To save my lady!"

Fast rode the knight
And leaped from saddle to war.
Men of steel flickered and gleamed
Like riot of silver lights
And the gold of the knight's good banner
Still waved on a castle wall.

*   *   *

A horse
Blowing, staggering, bloody thing
Forgotten at foot of castle wall.
A horse
Dead at foot of castle wall.

.   .   .   .

Forth went the candid man
And spoke freely to the wind——
When he looked about him he was in a far strange
    country.

Forth went the candid man
And spoke freely to the stars——
Yellow light tore sight from his eyes.

"My good fool," said a learned bystander
"Your operations are mad."

"You are too candid," cried the candid man
And when his stick left the head of the learned bystander
It was two sticks.

.   .   .   .

You tell me this is God?
I tell you this is a printed list,
A burning candle and an ass.

. . . .

On the desert
A silence from the moon's deepest valley.
Fire-rays fall athwart the robes
Of hooded men, squat and dumb.
Before them, a woman
Moves to the blowing of shrill whistles
And distant-thunder of drums
While slow things, sinuous, dull with terrible color
Sleepily fondle her body
Or move at her will, swishing stealthily over the sand.
The snakes whisper softly;
The whispering, whispering snakes
Dreaming and swaying and staring
But always whispering, softly whispering.
The wind streams from the lone reaches
Of Arabia, solemn with night,
And the wild fire makes shimmer of blood
Over the robes of the hooded men
Squat and dumb.
Bands of moving bronze, emerald, yellow,
Circle the throat and the arms of her
And over the sands serpents move warily
Slow, menacing and submissive,
Swinging to the whistles and drums,
The whispering, whispering snakes,
Dreaming and swaying and staring
But always whispering, softly whispering.
The dignity of the accursèd;
The glory of slavery, despair, death
Is in the dance of the whispering snakes.

. . . .

A newspaper is a collection of half-injustices
Which, bawled by boys from mile to mile,
Spreads its curious opinion
To a million merciful and sneering men,

While families cuddle the joys of the fireside
When spurred by tale of dire lone agony.
A newspaper is a court
Where every one is kindly and unfairly tried
By a squalor of honest men.
A newspaper is a market
Where wisdom sells its freedom
And melons are crowned by the crowd.
A newspaper is a game
Where his error scores the player victory
While another's skill wins death.
A newspaper is a symbol;
It is fetless life's chronicle,
A collection of loud tales
Concentrating eternal stupidities,
That in remote ages lived unhaltered,
Roaming through a fenceless world.

.   .   .   .

The wayfarer
Perceiving the pathway to truth
Was struck with astonishment.
It was thickly grown with weeds.
"Ha," he said,
"I see that none has passed here
"In a long time."
Later he saw that each weed
Was a singular knife.
"Well," he mumbled at last,
"Doubtless there are other roads."

.   .   .   .

A slant of sun on dull brown walls
A forgotten sky of bashful blue.

Toward God a mighty hymn
A song of collisions and cries
Rumbling wheels, hoof-beats, bells,
Welcomes, farewells, love-calls, final moans,
Voices of joy, idiocy, warning, despair,
The unknown appeals of brutes,
The chanting of flowers
The screams of cut trees,
The senseless babble of hens and wise men——
A cluttered incoherency that says at the stars:
"O, God, save us!"

.   .   .   .

Once a man clambering to the house-tops
Appealed to the heavens.
With strong voice he called to the deaf spheres;
A warrior's shout he raised to the suns.
Lo, at last, there was a dot on the clouds,
And—at last and at last—
—God—the sky was filled with armies.

.   .   .   .

There was a man with tongue of wood
Who essayed to sing
And in truth it was lamentable
But there was one who heard
The clip-clapper of this tongue of wood
And knew what the man
Wished to sing
And with that the singer was content.

. . . .

The successful man has thrust himself
Through the water of the years,
Reeking wet with mistakes,
Bloody mistakes,
Slimed with victories over the lesser
A figure thankful on the shore of money.
Then, with the bones of fools
He buys silken banners
Limned with his triumphant face;
With the skins of wise men
He buys the trivial bows of all.
Flesh painted with marrow
Contributes a coverlet
A coverlet for his contented slumber.
In guiltless ignorance, in ignorant guilt
He delivers his secrets to the riven multitude.
     "Thus I defended: Thus I wrought."
Complacent, smiling,
He stands heavily on the dead.
Erect on a pillar of skulls
He declaims his trampling of babes;
Smirking, fat, dripping,
He makes speech in guiltless ignorance,
Innocence.

. . . .

In the night
Grey heavy clouds muffled the valleys
And the peaks looked toward God, alone.
     "Oh, Master that movest the wind with a finger
     "Humble, idle, futile peaks are we.
     "Grant that we may run swiftly across the world
     "To huddle in worship at Thy feet."

In the morning
A noise of men at work came the clear blue miles
And the little black cities were apparent.
    "Oh, Master that knowest the meaning of rain-drops
    "Humble, idle, futile peaks are we.
    "Give voice to us we pray oh, Lord
    "That we may sing Thy goodness to the sun."

In the evening
The far valleys were sprinkled with tiny lights.
    "Oh, Master
    "Thou that knowest the value of kings and birds
    "Thou hast made us humble, idle, futile peaks.
    "Thou only, needest eternal patience;
    "We bow to Thy wisdom, oh, Lord——
    "Humble, idle, futile peaks."

In the night
Grey heavy clouds muffled the valleys
And the peaks looked toward God, alone.

    . . . .

The chatter of a death-demon from a tree-top.

Blood—blood and torn grass—
Had marked the rise of his agony——
This lone hunter.
The grey-green woods impassive
Had watched the threshing of his limbs.

A canoe with flashing paddle
A girl with soft searching eyes,
A call: "John!"

Come, arise, hunter!
Can you not hear?

The chatter of a death-demon from a tree-top.

.   .   .   .

The impact of a dollar upon the heart
Smiles warm red light
Sweeping from the hearth rosily upon the white table,
With the hanging cool velvet shadows
Moving softly upon the door.

The impact of a million dollars
Is a crash of flunkeys
And yawning emblems of Persia
Cheeked against oak, France and a sabre,
The outcry of old Beauty
Whored by pimping merchants
To submission before wine and chatter.
Silly rich peasants stamp the carpets of men,
Dead men who dreamed fragrance and light
Into their woof, their lives;
The rug of an honest bear
Under the feet of a cryptic slave
Who speaks always of baubles
Forgetting place, multitude, work and state,
Champing and mouthing of hats
Making ratful squeak of hats,
Hats.

.   .   .   .

A man said to the universe:
"Sir, I exist!"
"However," replied the universe,
"The fact has not created in me
"A sense of obligation."

.   .   .   .

When the prophet, a complacent fat man,
Arrived at the mountain-top
He cried: "Woe to my knowledge!

"I intended to see good white lands
"And bad black lands——
"But the scene is grey."

.   .   .   .

There was a land where lived no violets.
A traveller at once demanded: "Why?"
The people told him:
"Once the violets of this place spoke thus:
" 'Until some woman freely gives her lover
" 'To another woman
" 'We will fight in bloody scuffle.' "
Sadly the people added:
"There are no violets here."

.   .   .   .

There was one I met upon the road
Who looked at me with kind eyes.
He said: "Show me of your wares."
And I did,
Holding forth one.
He said: "It is a sin."
Then I held forth another.
He said: "It is a sin."
Then I held forth another.
He said: "It is a sin."
And so to the end.
Always he said: "It is a sin."
At last, I cried out:
"But I have none other."
He looked at me
With kinder eyes.
"Poor soul," he said.

.   .   .   .

Aye, workman, make me a dream
A dream for my love.
Cunningly weave sunlight,
Breezes and flowers.
Let it be of the cloth of meadows.
And—good workman—
And let there be a man walking thereon.

.   .   .   .

Each small gleam was a voice
—A lantern voice—
In little songs of carmine, violet, green, gold.
A chorus of colors came over the water;
The wondrous leaf-shadow no longer wavered,
No pines crooned on the hills
The blue night was elsewhere a silence
When the chorus of colors came over the water,
Little songs of carmine, violet, green, gold.

Small glowing pebbles
Thrown on the dark plane of evening
Sing good ballads of God
And eternity, with soul's rest.
Little priests, little holy fathers
None can doubt the truth of your hymning
When the marvelous chorus comes over the water
Songs of carmine, violet, green, gold.

.   .   .   .

The trees in the garden rained flowers.
Children ran there joyously.
They gathered the flowers
Each to himself.

Now there were some
Who gathered great heaps—
—Having opportunity and skill—
Until, behold, only chance blossoms
Remained for the feeble.
Then a little spindling tutor
Ran importantly to the father, crying:
"Pray, come hither!
"See this unjust thing in your garden!"
But when the father had surveyed,
He admonished the tutor:
"Not so, small sage!
"This thing is just.
"For, look you,
"Are not they who possess the flowers
"Stronger, bolder, shrewder
"Than they who have none?
"Why should the strong—
"—The beautiful strong—
"Why should they not have the flowers?"

Upon reflection, the tutor bowed to the ground.
"My Lord," he said,
"The stars are displaced
"By this towering wisdom."

"INTRIGUE"

Thou art my love
And thou art the peace of sundown
When the blue shadows soothe
And the grasses and the leaves sleep
To the song of the little brooks
Woe is me.

Thou art my love
And thou art a storm
That breaks black in the sky
And, sweeping headlong,
Drenches and cowers each tree
And at the panting end
There is no sound
Save the melancholy cry of a single owl
Woe is me!

Thou art my love
And thou art a tinsel thing
And I in my play
Broke thee easily
And from the little fragments
Arose my long sorrow
Woe is me.

Thou art my love
And thou art a weary violet
Drooping from sun-caresses.
Answering mine carelessly
Woe is me.

Thou art my love
And thou art the ashes of other men's love
And I bury my face in these ashes
And I love them
Woe is me.

Thou art my love
And thou art the beard
On another man's face
Woe is me.

Thou art my love
And thou art a temple
And in this temple is an altar
And on this altar is my heart
Woe is me.

Thou art my love
And thou art a wretch.
Let these sacred love-lies choke thee
For I am come to where I know your lies as truth
And your truth as lies
Woe is me.

Thou art my love
And thou art a priestess
And in thy hand is a bloody dagger
And my doom comes to me surely
Woe is me.

Thou art my love
And thou art a skull with ruby eyes
And I love thee
Woe is me.

Thou art my love
And I doubt thee
And if peace came with thy murder
Then would I murder.
Woe is me.

Thou art my love
And thou art death
Aye, thou art death
Black and yet black
But I love thee
I love thee
Woe, welcome woe, to me.

    . . . .

Love forgive me if I wish you grief
For in your grief
You huddle to my breast
And for it
Would I pay the price of your grief.

You walk among men
And all men do not surrender
And thus I understand
That love reaches his hand
In mercy to me.

He had your picture in his room
A scurvy traitor picture
And he smiled
—Merely a fat complacence
Of men who know fine women—
And thus I divided with him
A part of my love.

Fool, not to know that thy little shoe
Can make men weep!
—Some men weep.
I weep and I gnash
And I love the little shoe
The little, little shoe.

God give me medals
God give me loud honors
That I may strut before you, sweetheart
And be worthy of—
—The love I bear you.

Now let me crunch you
With full weight of affrighted love
I doubted you
—I doubted you—
And in this short doubting
My love grew like a genie
For my further undoing.

Beware of my friends
Be not in speech too civil
For in all courtesy

My weak heart sees spectres,
Mists of desires
Arising from the lips of my chosen
Be not civil.

The flower I gave thee once
Was incident to a stride
A detail of a gesture
But search those pale petals
And see engraven thereon
A record of my intention.

.   .   .   .

Ah, God, the way your little finger moved
As you thrust a bare arm backward
And made play with your hair
And a comb, a silly gilt comb
Ah, God—that I should suffer
Because of the way a little finger moved.

.   .   .   .

Once I saw thee idly rocking
—Idly rocking—
And chattering girlishly to other girls,
Bell-voiced, happy.
Careless with the stout heart of unscarred womanhood
And life to thee was all light melody.
I thought of the great storms of love as I knew it
Torn, miserable and ashamed of my open sorrow,
I thought of the thunders that lived in my head
And I wish to be an ogre
And hale and haul my beloved to a castle
And there use the happy cruel one cruelly
And make her mourn with my mourning.

. . . .

Tell me why, behind thee,
I see always the shadow of another lover?
Is it real
Or is this the thrice-damned memory of a better happiness?
Plague on him if he be dead
Plague on him if he be alive
A swinish numskull
To intrude his shade
Always between me and my peace.

. . . .

And yet I have seen thee happy with me.
I am no fool
To poll stupidly into iron.
I have heard your quick breaths
And seen your arms writhe toward me;
At those times
—God help us—
I was impelled to be a grand knight,
And swagger and snap my fingers,
And explain my mind finely.
Oh, lost sweetheart,
I would that I had not been a grand knight.
I said: "Sweetheart."
Thou said'st: "Sweetheart."
And we preserved an admirable mimicry
Without heeding the drip of the blood
From my heart.

. . . .

I heard thee laugh,
And in this merriment
I defined the measure of my pain;

I knew that I was alone,
Alone with love,
Poor shivering love,
And he, little sprite,
Came to watch with me,
And at midnight
We were like two creatures by a dead camp-fire.

     ·   ·   ·   ·   ·   ·   ·   ·   ·   ·   ·

I wonder if sometimes in the dusk,
When the brave lights that gild thy evenings
Have not yet been touched with flame,
I wonder if sometimes in the dusk
Thou rememberest a time,
A time when thou loved me
And our love was to thee thy all?
Is the memory rubbish now?
An old gown
Worn in an age of other fashions?
Woe is me, oh, lost one,
For that love is now to me
A supernal dream,
White, white, white with many suns.

     ·   ·   ·   ·   ·   ·   ·   ·   ·   ·   ·

Love met me at noonday,
—Reckless imp,
To leave his shaded nights
And brave the glare,—
And I saw him then plainly
For a bungler,
A stupid, simpering, eyeless bungler,
Breaking the hearts of brave people
As the snivelling idiot-boy cracks his bowl,
And I cursed him,
Cursed him to and fro, back and forth,

Into all the silly mazes of his mind,
But in the end
He laughed and pointed to my breast,
Where a heart still beat for thee, beloved.

. . . .

I have seen thy face aflame
For love of me,
Thy fair arms go mad,
Thy lips tremble and mutter and rave.
And—surely—
This should leave a man content?
Thou lovest not me now,
But thou didst love me,
And in loving me once
Thou gavest me an eternal privilege,
For I can think of thee.

There is a grey thing that lives in the tree-tops
None know the horror of its sight
Save those who meet death in the wilderness
But one is enabled to see
To see branches move at its passing
To hear at times the wail of black laughter
And to come often upon mystic places
Places where the thing has just been.

"LEGENDS"

I

A man builded a bugle for the storms to blow.

The focussed winds hurled him afar.
He said that the instrument was a failure.

II

When the suicide arrived at the sky,
The people there asked him: "Why?"
He replied: "Because no one admired me."

III

A man said: "Thou tree!"
The tree answered with the same scorn: "Thou man!
Thou art greater than I only in thy possibilities."

IV

A warrior stood upon a peak and defied the stars.
A little magpie, happening there, desired the soldier's plume,
And so plucked it.

V

The wind that waves the blossoms
Sang, sang, sang from age to age.
The flowers were made curious by this joy.
"Oh, wind," they said, "why sing you at your labour,
While we, pink beneficiaries, sing not,
But idle, idle, idle from age to age?"

. . . .

Tell me not in joyous numbers
We can make our lives sublime
By—well, at least, not by
Dabbling much in rhyme.

. . . .

When a people reach the top of a hill
Then does God lean toward them,
Shortens tongues, lengthens arms.
A vision of their dead comes to the weak.
       The moon shall not be too old
       Before the new battalions rise
            —Blue battalions—
       The moon shall not be too old
       When the children of change shall fall
       Before the new battalions
            —The blue battalions—

Mistakes and virtues will be trampled deep
A church and a thief shall fall together
A sword will come at the bidding of the eyeless,
The God-led, turning only to beckon.
       Swinging a creed like a censer
       At the head of the new battalions
            —Blue battalions—
       March the tools of nature's impulse

Men born of wrong, men born of right
Men of the new battalions
   —The blue battalions—

The clang of swords is Thy wisdom
The wounded make gestures like Thy Son's
The feet of mad horses is one part,
—Aye, another is the hand of a mother on the brow
    of a son.
   Then swift as they charge through a shadow,
   The men of the new battalions
     —Blue battalions—
   God lead them high. God lead them far
   Lead them far, lead them high
   These new battalions
     —The blue battalions—.

    . . . .

A man adrift on a slim spar
A horizon smaller than the rim of a bottle
Tented waves rearing lashy dark points
The near whine of froth in circles.
                God is cold.

The incessant raise and swing of the sea
And growl after growl of crest
The sinkings, green, seething, endless
The upheaval half-completed.
                God is cold.

The seas are in the hollow of The Hand;
Oceans may be turned to a spray
Raining down through the stars
Because of a gesture of pity toward a babe.
Oceans may become grey ashes,
Die with a long moan and a roar
Amid the tumult of the fishes

And the cries of the ships,
Because The Hand beckons the mice.

A horizon smaller than a doomed assassin's cap,
Inky, surging tumults
A reeling, drunken sky and no sky
A pale hand sliding from a polished spar.

                              God is cold.

The puff of a coat imprisoning air.
A face kissing the water-death
A weary slow sway of a lost hand
And the sea, the moving sea, the sea.

                              God is cold.

              .   .   .   .

There exists the eternal fact of conflict
And—next—a mere sense of locality.
Afterward we derive sustenance from the winds.
Afterward we grip upon this sense of locality.
Afterward, we become patriots.
The godly vice of patriotism makes us slaves,
And—let us surrender to this falsity
Let us be patriots

Then welcome us the practical men
Thrumming on a thousand drums
The practical men, God help us.
        They cry aloud to be led to war
        Ah—
        They have been poltroons on a thousand fields
        And the sacked sad city of New York is their record
Furious to face the Spaniard, these people, and crawling
    worms before their task
They name serfs and send charity in bulk to better men
They play at being free, these people of New York
Who are too well-dressed to protest against infamy.

"THE BATTLE HYMN"

All-feeling God, hear in the war-night
The rolling voices of a nation;
Through dusky billows of darkness
See the flash, the under-light, of bared swords—
—Whirling gleams like wee shells
Deep in the streams of the universe—
Bend and see a people, O, God,
A people rebuked, accursed,
By him of the many lungs
And by him of the bruised weary war-drum
(The chanting disintegrate and the two-faced eagle)
Bend and mark our steps, O, God.
Mark well, mark well, Father of the Never-Ending Circles
And if the path, the new path, lead awry
Then in the forest of the lost standards
Suffer us to grope and bleed apace
For the wisdom is Thine.
Bend and see a people, O, God,
A people applauded, acclaimed,
By him of the raw red shoulders
The manacle-marked, the thin victim
(He lies white amid the smoking cane)
—And if the path, the new path, leads straight—
Then—O, God—then bare the great bronze arm;
Swing high the blaze of the chained stars
And let them look and heed
(The chanting disintegrate and the two-faced eagle)
For we go, we go in a lunge of a long blue corps
And—to Thee we commit our lifeless sons,
The convulsed and furious dead.
(They shall be white amid the smoking cane)
For, the seas shall not bar us;
The capped mountains shall not hold us back
We shall sweep and swarm through jungle and pool,
Then let the savage one bend his high chin
To see on his breast, the sullen glow of the death-medals

For we know and we say our gift.
His prize is death, deep doom.
(He shall be white amid the smoking cane.)

.   .   .   .

A naked woman and a dead dwarf;
Wealth and indifference.
Poor dwarf!
Reigning with foolish kings
And dying mid bells and wine
Ending with a desperate comic palaver
While before thee and after thee
Endures the eternal clown—
—The eternal clown—
A naked woman.

.   .   .   .

A grey and boiling street
Alive with rickety noise.
Suddenly, a hearse,
Trailed by black carriages
Takes a deliberate way
Through this chasm of commerce;
And children look eagerly
To find the misery behind the shades.
Hired men, impatient, drive with a longing
To reach quickly the grave-side, the end of solemnity.

Yes, let us have it over.
Drive, man, drive.
Flog your sleek-hided beasts,
Gallop—gallop—gallop.
Let us finish it quickly.

Chronology

1871   Born November 1 in Newark, New Jersey, fourteenth and last child of Reverend Jonathan Townley Crane, Methodist minister and religious publicist (*The Arts of Intoxication*, 1870), and Mary Helen Peck, daughter of George Peck, prominent Methodist minister. Eight brothers and sisters survive infancy: Mary Helen (b. 1849), George Peck (b. 1850), Jonathan Townley (b. 1852), William Howe (b. 1854), Agnes Elizabeth (b. 1856), Edmund Brian (b. 1857), Wilbur Fiske (b. 1859), and Luther Peck (b. 1863).

1874   Family moves to Bloomington, New Jersey, when father accepts pastorate there. Mother active in New Jersey temperance movement.

1875   Without parents' knowledge, joins boys at Raritan River swimming hole and almost drowns.

1876   Family moves to Paterson, New Jersey, when father is appointed pastor of Cross Street Church.

1878   Father, chosen pastor of Drew Methodist Church, moves family to Port Jervis, New York, on the Delaware River. Sullivan County north of town, and Pike County, Pennsylvania, just across the river, include large hilly tracts of forest where, over the years, Crane goes exploring, riding, fishing, hunting, camping, and listens to the yarns of outdoorsmen. Enters school in September.

1879   "Will, one of my brothers, gave me a toy gun and I tried to shoot a cow with it over at Middleton when father was preaching there and that upset him wonderfully."

1880   Father dies February 16. Mother earns extra money to support family by writing for Methodist journals, New York *Tribune*, and Philadelphia *Press* with Crane's help. (Crane later says, "After my father died, mother lived in and for religion. My brother Will used to try to argue with her on religious subjects such as hell but he always gave it up. Don't understand that mother was bitter or mean but it hurt her that any of us should be slipping from Grace and giving up eternal damnation or salvation or those things.")

1883   Mother moves to Asbury Park, New Jersey, with younger children. Brother William remains in Port Jervis, New York, where he practices law and becomes a founding member of the Hartwood Club, a Sullivan County vacation resort of 6,000 acres.

1884   Sister Agnes Elizabeth, pious schoolteacher who nurtured Crane's early literary interest, dies in May.

1885   Writes short story "Uncle Jake and the Bell-Handle." In September, enters Pennington (N.J.) Seminary, a Methodist boarding school, where his father had been principal 1849–58.

1886   Brother Luther crushed to death between two freight cars while working for the Erie Railroad.

1888   Transfers in January to Claverack (N.Y.) College–Hudson River Institute, a military boarding school. During summer writes for Asbury Park news bureau run by his brother Townley.

1890   Leaves Claverack with rank of cadet captain. Enters Lafayette College in September as an engineering student. Leaves at mid-year because of "academic delinquencies."

1891   Becomes special student in January at Syracuse University, co-founded by mother's uncle, Bishop Jesse Truesdell Peck. Writes sketches and stories, serves as stringer for the New York *Tribune*, plays shortstop and catcher on the baseball team, gets an "A" in English literature. In August, writes report of a Hamlin Garland lecture on realism that leads to acquaintance with the older writer. Falls in love with Helen Trent (who later rejects him). Decides to write instead of going back to college in September. Lives with brother Edmund in Lake View (now part of Paterson), and often stays with artist friends in New York. Studies the saloons, flophouses, and people of the Bowery ("the most interesting place in New York"). Mother dies of cancer December 7. Crane writes draft of *Maggie* ("in two days before Christmas," as he later recalls).

1892   Working as a free lance, publishes fourteen Sullivan County sketches and other pieces in the *Tribune*. Among reports submitted through Townley's bureau, "Parades and Entertainments" (August 21) offends both the Junior Order of United American Mechanics and the *Tribune* publisher, Whitelaw Reid, Republican candidate for vice-president. The *Tribune* cancels its arrangement with Townley for coverage of the New Jersey resorts. Crane lives in New York and at the homes of brothers Wilbur, Edmund, and William. Falls in love with Mrs. Lily Brandon Munroe. Rewrites *Maggie* with no hope of finding a publisher. Borrows against inheritance from mother to print novel at his own expense.

1893   Applies for copyright for "A Girl of the Streets, A Story of New York" on January 16. Publishes *Maggie: A Girl of the Streets* under the pseudonym Johnston Smith in March. Though not widely reviewed, the book is read by Hamlin Garland and recommended by him to William Dean Howells, who admires it and invites Crane to tea. Reads extensively in Civil War memoirs and begins *The Red Badge of Courage* in the spring.

1894   Writes stories (including "An Experiment in Misery") and poems. Shows some of this writing, as well as *The Red Badge of Courage*, to Garland in March or April. After further revision, gives novel in May to S. S. McClure, who holds it till October without making a decision. Despite poverty and anxiety, begins intensive work on *George's Mother* in May and reports its completion to Garland in November. Sends book of poems to the Boston publisher Copeland and Day and during summer, fall, and winter conducts protracted negotiations over contents and layout. Sends title poem, "The Black Riders," on October 30. Retrieves manuscript from McClure and sells *The Red Badge of Courage* to Irving Bacheller in November, who buys it for ninety dollars and syndicates shortened version as newspaper serial appearing December 3 through 8. The staff of the Philadelphia *Press*, one of the newspapers that runs the serial version, asks Bacheller to bring Crane to Philadelphia to receive their congratulations in person.

D. Appleton and Company accepts the novel for book publication in December.

1895   Travels to the West and Mexico in January under contract with Bacheller newspaper syndicate. Meets Willa Cather, college senior on staff of *Nebraska State Journal* in February; she notes his depressed state. From New Orleans in early March, sends final revisions of *The Red Badge of Courage* to editor at Appleton; the contract gives him ten percent royalty. Stays in Mexico City for a few weeks in March and early April, then goes south into the provinces. *The Black Riders* published May 11. Returns to Port Jervis, New York, the next week and lives during the summer (and most of the next year) at nearby Hartwood, where brother Edmund has become stationmaster, postmaster, and odd-jobs entrepreneur. Crane also has easy access to household of brother William in Port Jervis. Goes to New York City for poker, partying, and business, but writes Mexican stories and *The Third Violet* at Hartwood. *The Red Badge of Courage,* published October 5, becomes a bestseller and establishes his reputation.

1896   January, agrees to supply McClure syndicate with war stories and other short works. In June, Appleton brings out revised version of *Maggie,* and Edward Arnold (London) publishes *George's Mother.* Meets Police Commissioner Theodore Roosevelt in New York and lets him read "A Man and Some Others" in manuscript. After interviewing chorus girl Dora Clark, witnesses her arrest for soliciting September 16 and appears in court for the defense. Testifying against arresting officer makes him *persona non grata* with the police, including Roosevelt. After several out-of-town assignments, leaves November 13 for Jacksonville, Florida, on his way to cover the Cuban revolution. On November 29 writes brother William about the will he meant to have put in order and suggests as literary executors Howells, Hamlin Garland, friend Willis Hawkins, and Appleton editor Ripley Hitchcock; also writes: "I almost forgot to mention the Dora Clark case. If I should happen to be detained upon my journey, you must always remember that your brother in that case acted like a man of honor and a gentleman and you need not fear to hold your head up to anybody and defend his name." Meets Cora Howorth Steward ("Cora Taylor"), six years his senior, proprietress of the Hotel de Dream. Gives her a copy of *George's Mother* inscribed "To an unnamed sweetheart." McClure's serialization of *The Third Violet* begins October 5 (book published May 15, 1897). *The Little Regiment and Other Episodes of the American Civil War* published December 5. Departs Jacksonville December 31 on the steamship *Commodore* with cargo of arms for Cuban rebels.

1897　　The *Commodore* founders and sinks January 2; ordeal at sea becomes source of "The Open Boat." Further effort to go to Cuba frustrated by Coast Guard blockade; stays with Cora in Florida. Returns to New York in March and takes passage for England and from there to Greece to cover the Greco-Turkish war. Joined by Cora who has been hired by the New York *Journal* as their "first and only woman war correspondent"; she signs herself "Imogene Carter." After war ends in June, they return to London as man and wife and take a house in Oxted, Surrey. With new friends, writer Harold Frederic and Kate Lyon, they visit Ireland for a working vacation in September. Through his English publisher William Heinemann, Crane meets Joseph Conrad, who becomes a close friend. *The Monster*, "The Bride Comes to Yellow Sky," and "Death and the Child" date from this autumn.

1898　　Spends at least six weeks writing "The Blue Hotel"—for him an unusually long period of composition for any work—and finishes it February 7. Financial anxiety, a tangle of literary commitments beyond his ability to fulfill, and war fever aroused by the sinking of the *Maine* on February 15 impel him to return to New York. Fails physical examination for the navy in April and then signs on as a correspondent for Joseph Pulitzer's *World* to cover the Cuban campaign. Under fire at Guantánamo, Las Guásimas, San Juan Hill, he wins, according to fellow correspondent Richard Harding Davis, "the first place among correspondents." Suffers from fever (typhoid, malaria, flare-up of tuberculosis are all possible causes) and exhaustion and is sent back from the war zone to recuperate at Old Point Comfort, Virginia. Fired by Pulitzer, contracts with Hearst's *Journal* to cover the Puerto Rico campaign. Goes to Havana at war's end in August, stays first at Hotel Pasaje, then at boardinghouse of Mary Horan. Grinds out newspaper sketches and begins novel of the Greek war, *Active Service*; writes "His New Mittens" and a series of poems. Does not communicate with Cora or his brothers, who react to his virtual disappearance by initiating official inquiries. Finally, after General J. F. Wade in Havana has been involved, he decides to leave and sails November 17 for New York City. Remains in the United States visiting friends and family. Sails for England December 31.

1899   Reads David Garnett's essay ("Stephen Crane: An Appreciation," *Academy*, Dec. 17, 1898) when he returns to England. Becomes friends with Garnett, Henry James, H. G. Wells. In February the Cranes move to partially restored baronial manor, Brede Place, rented by Cora from Moreton Frewen and his American wife, Clara Jerome Frewen, sister of Lady Randolph Churchill; although rent is low, upkeep and entertainment of guests stretch tenants' means to the limit. They take in two of the children of Kate Lyon and Harold Frederic, who has recently died. Crane completes *Active Service*; writes a series of stories about children (*Whilomville Stories*, published Aug. 1900); plans historical romance of the American Revolution; starts Irish romance, *The O'Ruddy* (published 1903); begins a popular series, *Great Battles of the World* (published 1901), relying on Kate Lyon for research and eventually for much of the writing; composes his Western tales, "Twelve O'Clock" and "Moonlight on the Snow." *War Is Kind*, second book of poems, published May 20. *Active Service* published October 14. *The Monster and Other Stories* (including "The Blue Hotel" and "His New Mittens") published December 9. Final copy of *Wounds in the Rain* (Spanish-American war stories) sent to publisher. Gives three-day house party at Brede Place, concluding with a ball December 29; as festivities end, suffers first tubercular hemorrhage of the lungs.

1900   Beset by debts and deadlines, continues to work on battle articles and Irish romance and tries to conceal the seriousness of his tuberculosis. Massive hemorrhages April 1 and 2. Writes new will April 21, and arranges with Robert Barr to finish *The O'Ruddy*. In May travels as a litter patient to a sanitarium at Badenweiler, in the Black Forest, where he dies June 5. Cora Crane takes the body to the United States for burial at Hillside, New Jersey.

Note on the Texts

Stephen Crane wrote the more than one hundred works included in this volume, except for two early newspaper reports and one story that may date from 1900, in the eight years from 1892 to 1899. Because he wrote so much so quickly and published under so many different circumstances, often after disheartening delays, the pattern of development in his work has often been obscured. In the present volume his five short novels, *Maggie: A Girl of the Streets*, *The Red Badge of Courage*, *George's Mother*, *The Third Violet*, and *The Monster*, grouped together at the beginning, help define the range of his imaginative world. His two books of verse, *The Black Riders and Other Lines* (1895), and *War Is Kind* (1899), together with selections from Crane's uncollected poems, are placed at the end of this volume. The short stories, sketches, and reportage which comprise the rest of the volume are arranged in topical and chronological order and display the phases that are distinguishable even in so brief and crowded a career.

Maggie: A Girl of the Streets was privately printed in 1893. Exactly when Stephen Crane wrote it is unclear. Fraternity brothers at Syracuse University later recalled seeing a version during the spring semester of 1891. A niece was one day to confirm Crane's recollection of writing it in one intensive spurt after the death of his mother in December of that same year. A version of the story was shown to Richard Watson Gilder, editor of the *Century*, in March 1892—and immediately rejected. Crane worked on the novel in the fall of 1892, in the free-lance period after he had been fired from the New York *Tribune*. In January 1893, when he applied to the Librarian of Congress for copyright, its title was "A Girl of the Streets, A Story of New York"; the revision which gave names to the characters and to the book was yet to come. Discouraged at the prospects for commercial publication, Crane paid to have it printed by a firm that according to Crane usually specialized in religious and medical books. This firm refused to allow its name to appear on the title page, and

Crane himself used the pseudonym of Johnston Smith. The book appeared probably in March, and it had almost no sale.

Three years later, after his next novel, *The Red Badge of Courage*, had clearly become a success, Crane's editor at D. Appleton and Company gave him the chance to revise *Maggie* and publish it commercially. Unfortunately, the 1896 edition was not only revised, but was also bowdlerized, and it is not always possible to tell whether the changes reflect Crane's own literary judgment or the external pressure of censorship. When Crane reported to his editor, Ripley Hitchcock, that he had "dispensed with a goodly number of damns" (R. W. Stallman and Lillian Gilkes, editors, *Stephen Crane: Letters*, New York, 1960, p. 112), he was clearly following instructions about cutting profanity. When he reported a few days later that he had "carefully plugged at the words which hurt," he could have been referring to taboo words or to repetitious usages of *red* and *crimson* as epithets—for example, "Suddenly Pete swore redly"—that were stylistic marks of his new way of writing. In the 1893 text, on Maggie's last night she solicits "a huge fat man in torn and greasy garments" (see page 72). This passage does not appear in the 1896 text. It may be that the maturer Crane found the passage too lurid, or it may be, as the patched transition suggests, that Crane also removed this passage under pressure from others. How Crane, the more experienced novelist of 1896, might have revised *Maggie* without this pressure is now impossible to know. The 1893 text, reprinted here, represents the twenty-one-year-old writer who was just discovering his powers.

The earliest states of *The Red Badge of Courage*, those of the draft and final manuscript versions, still exist, and throw light on the evolution of the first published version (New York, D. Appleton & Co., 1895), reprinted here. At successive stages of revision, Crane deleted the proper names of his three main characters except in direct discourse and made them over into the "youth," the "tall soldier," and the "loud soldier." At the suggestion of Hamlin Garland, he changed their speech in many passages from dialect to normal usage and spelling, concentrating in particular on his protagonist, Henry Fleming. Finally, he eliminated much of Henry Fleming's rhetorical quasi-philosophical soliloquizing. There seems to be no evidence that Crane did this revising for other than his own artistic reasons. The nature of the revisions made would not imply any form of censorship. That Crane took some advice from Garland is documented, but while still working on *The Red Badge of Courage*, he refused to accept editorial advice from Copeland & Day, publishers of *The Black Riders* (*Letters*, pp. 39–40), and he dedicated that volume to Hamlin Garland (*Letters*, pp. 47, 59–60). In 1896, at the same time that he made out his will in anticipation of seeing hostilities in Cuba, he informally named Garland and Hitchcock as literary executors (*Letters*, p. 134). In 1899, he singled out Garland as having his gratitude for "sound advice about 'The Red Badge'" (*Letters*, p. 226). However, there may be two places that were inadvertently affected by outside editorial intervention. Fredson Bowers, in his manuscript studies for the Virginia edition, discovered two brief passages which Garland crossed out as suggested deletions but which Crane indicated by his later revisions that he intended to keep (Bowers, ed., Stephen Crane, *The Red Badge of Courage: A Facsimile Edition of the Manuscript*, Washington, D.C., 1973, I, 33; compare in Volume II, manuscript pages 22 and 29). These passages are provided in the *Notes* at the appropriate points of Chapters II and III of this edition.

Therefore, for these two novels that Crane revised at different stages, the texts of the first published versions are printed here instead of any of the texts prepared by later editors. For the remaining works, this volume adopts the texts of the University of Virginia Edition of the Works of Stephen Crane (University Press of Virginia, Charlottesville, 1969–76, 10 ols.), edited by Fredson Bowers, which is the most comprehensive edition of Crane that has been made and the first consistently to provide texts based on a thorough study of the textual history. Working from a massive collection of relevant documents—manuscripts, fragments of manuscripts, author's notes when they could be found, newspaper syndications, periodical publications, and books printed in both Great Britain and the United States—Bowers tried to establish precisely what Crane wrote: not only his substantive language, but also his spelling, capitalization, word-division, and punctuation. The editorial principles that have been applied are described in the prefatory "Text of the Virginia Edition" (I, xi–xxix), and the ten volumes of the edition provide textual introductions and notes to all the works included.

The following list records the volumes of the Virginia edition in which each of the pieces used in this volume appears: Volume I, *Bowery Tales* (1969), *George's Mother*; Volume III, *The Third Violet and Active Service* (1976), *The Third Violet*; Volume V, *Tales of Adventure* (1970), "The Pace of Youth," "One Dash—Horses," "The Wise Men," "The Five White Mice," "A Man and Some Others," "The Bride Comes to Yellow Sky," "The Blue Hotel," "Twelve O'Clock," "Moonlight on the Snow," "The Open Boat," "Flanagan and His Short Filibustering Adventure," "Death and the Child," "A Poker Game"; Volume VI, *Tales of War* (1970), "A Mystery of Heroism," "A Grey Sleeve," "The Little Regiment," "The Veteran," "An Episode of War," "The Price of the Harness," "The Clan of No-Name," "Marines Signaling Under Fire at Guantanamo," "'God Rest Ye, Merry Gentlemen,'" "The Revenge of the *Adolphus*," "Virtue in War," "The Second Generation," "This Majestic Lie," "The Kicking Twelfth," "The Shrapnel of Their Friends," "'And If He Wills, We Must Die,'" "The Upturned Face"; Volume VII, *Tales of Whilomville* (1969), "'The Monster,'" "'His New Mittens,'" "Lynx-Hunting," "The Angel-Child," "The Lover and the Tell-Tale," "'Showin' Off,'" "Shame," "The Carriage-Lamps," "The Knife," "The Trial, Execution, and Burial of Homer Phelps," "The Fight," "The City Urchin and the Chaste Villagers"; Volume VIII, *Tales, Sketches, and Reports* (1973), "Avon's School by the Sea," "Howells Discussed at Avon-by-the-Sea," "On the Boardwalk," "Parades and Entertainments," "The Last of the Mohicans," "Hunting Wild Hogs," "Four Men in a Cave," "The Octopush," "A Ghoul's Accountant," "The Black Dog," "Killing His Bear," "A Tent in Agony," "The Mesmeric Mountain," "The Broken-Down Van," "An Ominous Baby," "A Great Mistake," "A Dark-Brown Dog," "An Experiment in Misery," "An Experiment in Luxury," "Mr. Binks' Day Off," "The Art Students' League Building," "Stories Told by an Artist," "The Men in the Storm," "Coney Island's Failing Days," "In a Park Row Restaurant," "The Fire," "When Man Falls, a Crowd Gathers," "In the Depths of a Coal Mine," "Howells Fears the Realists Must Wait," "An Excursion Ticket," "Nebraska's Bitter Fight for Life," "Seen at Hot Springs," "Galveston, Texas, in 1895," "Stephen Crane in Texas," "Stephen Crane in Mexico (II)," "The Mexican Lower Classes," "Opium's Varied Dreams," "New York's Bicycle Speedway," "An Eloquence of Grief," "Adventures of a Novelist," "London Impressions," "Ballydehob," "The Royal Irish Constabulary," "A Fishing Village," "Harold Frederic," "Concerning the English 'Academy'," "Manacled"; Volume IX, *Reports of War* (1971), "Stephen Crane's Own Story," "Greek War Correspondents," "Crane at Velestino," "Stephen Crane Tells of War's Horrors," "Stephen Crane's Vivid Story of the Battle of San Juan," "Regulars Get No Glory"; Volume X, *Poems and Literary Remains* (1975), *The Black Riders and Other Lines*, *War Is Kind*, Uncollected Poetry.

Crane's inconsistencies of spelling, usage, and punctuation are most visible in the text of the 1893 *Maggie,* in part because he was so young as not to have fully formed literary habits, in part because the privately printed volume was least subjected to the standardization imposed by professional editing. There, as in the texts of the Virginia edition, the object has been to preserve the nineteenth-century practice whereby a word might be spelled in more than one way even in the same work. Nineteenth-century printing practice preserved other kinds of variation as well. Commas were sometimes used expressively to suggest the movements of voice, capitals were sometimes meant to give significances to a word beyond those it might have in its uncapitalized form, dialect was rendered by various spelling and punctuation devices. Since modernization would remove such effects, this volume has preserved the spelling, punctuation, capitalization, and wording of Stephen Crane in the texts reprinted here.

The present edition is concerned only with preserving the *texts* of these editions; it does not attempt to reproduce features of their typographical design—such as display capitalization of chapter openings or the itemized numbering used in the Virginia edition. Open contractions are retained when they appear in the editions used. Typographical errors have been corrected in this edition and are listed here by page and line number: 8.8, mahood; 8.33, foward; 9.26, Jimmy; 11.32, distainfully; 20.38, it; 21.7, chrisanthemums; 21.17, breath; 26.1, similiar; 26.21, See."; 27.3, sight,'; 27.36–37, of world; 32.3, it; 35.2, amirable; 35.12, oblgied; 35.27, trash; 35.30, monkeys; 36.18, ecstastic; 38.10, He gray; 39.19, missles; 39.22, tin a; 39.29, yer; 39.32, framed; 40.13, dam; 40.29, "Dere; 40.30, now, door; 41.30, riddance.; 42.20, be; 42.21–22, "Oh, . . . yes," . . . "Oh, . . . yes."; 44.14, 'im.; 44.37, use!"; 46.22, begrimmed; 48.12, Billie?; 48.29, eyes; 50.5, missles; 50.13, missles; 55.6, home; 56.17, wont; 56.25, anyway,; 58.12, a immense; 62.32, gone; 66.10, her; 67.12, fer?; 69.18, did'nt; 69.25, sterness; 70.2–3, chapter; 70.33, forgetness; 71.36, hand; 72.20, eyet; 73.35, treata; 74.9, magnificently; 74.27, me'; 75.7, quiverering; 75.24, didn't?; 75.25, me,"; 76.26, glasss; 82.31, bank; 96.24, peeked; 106.6, would; 108.1, Se; 111.20, knitting; 116.24, emblem; 118.26, gate; 122.33, aid; 125.10, guilt and; 126.1, with a; 131.27, different; 135.14, shoulders; 139.38, see 'a; 139.40, Hurt; 140.1, much?; 144.10, way; 144.31, weight like; 154.19, recognzied; 156.3, draw; 163.14, a; 167.5, continued; 168.15, somtimes; 170.7, yellings; 171.28, burlike; 175.13, bur; 176.2, 4, an'; 177.28, onto; 190.21, panicstricken; 190.32, illusions; 197.37, laughin,'; 198.30, major generals; 198.30, -generals.'; 200.26, up.; 201.20, friends; 205.8, savage religion mad.; 410.34, cortége; 420.28, er-saying'; 552.35, that; 725.20, archeologist; 750.40, kids; 868.27, prostitue; 1029.25, though; 1058.26, habor; 1150.14, dinner."; 1239.25, sacrified; 1271.2, Ffom; 1350.28, distintegrate. Errors corrected second printing: 427.29, overhead (Library of America error). Errors corrected fourth printing: 1114.21, where in; 1325.21, slaugther (*LOA*).

Notes

For more detailed notes, references to other studies, and further biographical background, see the relevant volumes of the Virginia Edition of the Works of Stephen Crane. In the notes below, the numbers refer to page and line of this volume (the line count includes chapter headings). No note is made for material included in a standard desk-reference book. Notes at the foot of the page in the text are Crane's own.

NOVELS AND NOVELLAS

7.3   Rum Alley]   Crane's equivalent of Beer Street and Gin Lane, in William Hogarth's eighteenth-century London. The model is the Bowery area, named for a principal street of New York's Lower East Side.

55.25   squdgy]   This apparently invented word has been variously interpreted; it evidently passed Crane's own ability to recall and emend, for he deleted it from the 1896 edition.

79.3   *An Episode . . . War*]   With regard to any particular terrain or action, Crane expected he would run into carping critics, but, he wrote, "I evaded them in the Red Badge because it was essential that I should make my battle a type and name no names. . . ." However, in the sequel story, "The Veteran," Henry Fleming says of this Civil War episode, "That was at Chancellorsville" (see p. 667.9). The events of the novel seem very closely to follow the battle of May 1–3, 1863.

94.15   perception.]   MS addition: "I told you so, didnt I?" (Crane's typist, misled by Hamlin Garland's tentative crossing-out, failed to transcribe this sentence. Crane showed his intention to retain by making later changes: he canceled *yeh* and wrote *you* above, and he inserted closing quotation marks, which he placed before the question mark.)

95.4   blatant]   Changed to "loud" in manuscript but overlooked by typist.

99.27   and ammunition.]   MS continues: "You can now eat, drink, sleep, and shoot," said the tall soldier to the youth. "That's all you need. What do you want to do—carry a hotel?" (Crane's typist, again misled by Hamlin Garland's tentative crossing-out, seems not to have transcribed the sentences as written, although Crane showed his intention to retain by making the later insertion of closing quotation marks, which he placed before the question mark.)

213.1   GEORGE'S MOTHER]   The novel earlier had had the title: *A Woman Without Weapons* (*Bookman* 1 [1895], 230).

279.1   THE THIRD VIOLET] Although the resort could be in the Catskills or the Poconos, not far from Port Jervis, the unpretentious family of the hero—and their big orange and white setter—are much like the household of Edmund Crane at Hartwood.

389.1   THE MONSTER] Whilomville, where *The Monster* is set, appears in a number of stories as the town of Stephen Crane's reminiscence of childhood. Despite the false clue which suggests somewhere between Syracuse and Rochester, it is modeled on Port Jervis, New York.

ASBURY PARK

449.1   ASBURY PARK] Of the contiguous seaside towns that Crane knew from childhood, Asbury Park, New Jersey, was the most developed and even had amusement rides and night life; Ocean Grove, just to the south, was a Methodist meeting area where many of the summer residences were built on old tent sites; Avon-by-the-Sea was a middle-class summer colony, quieter than Asbury Park and more secular than Ocean Grove.

457.4   Hamlin Garland] (1860–1940) Wisconsin-born, raised on the Great Plains frontier, and self-educated in the Boston Public Library; published his realistic stories of the Middle Border in *Main-Travelled Roads* (1891).

463.3   Junior . . . Mechanics] A patriotic workingmen's organization, dedicated to restricting immigration and protecting public schools from sectarian interference, had been active since the first Nativist movements of the 1850s. A convention representing its 160,000 members met at Asbury Park and held its American Day parade on August 17. New Jersey newspapers raised the initial protest against Crane's report because, said the Asbury Park *Journal*, "he thought it smart to sneer at the Juniors for their personal appearance and marching."

SULLIVAN COUNTY

484.8   William H. Crane] Stephen Crane's older brother.

NEW YORK CITY, 1892–94

538.1   *An Experiment in Misery*] As printed in the New York *Press*, April 22, 1894, this story had a framing narrative which Crane removed when revising for book publication in 1898. The original version began:

Two men stood regarding a tramp.

"I wonder how he feels," said one, reflectively. "I suppose he is homeless, friendless, and has, at the most, only a few cents in his pocket. And if this is so, I wonder how he feels."

The other being the elder, spoke with an air of authoritative wisdom. "You can tell nothing of it unless you are in that condition yourself. It is idle to speculate about it from this distance."

"I suppose so," said the younger man, and then he added as from an inspiration: "I think I'll try it. Rags and tatters, you know, a couple of dimes, and hungry, too, if possible. Perhaps I could discover his point of view or something near it."

"Well, you might," said the other, and from those words begins this veracious narrative of an experiment in misery.

The youth went to the studio of an artist friend, who, from his store, rigged him out in an aged suit and a brown derby hat that had been made long years before. And then the youth went forth to try to eat as the tramp may eat, and sleep as the wanderers sleep. It was late at night, and a fine rain was swirling softly down, covering the pavements with a bluish luster. He began a weary trudge toward the downtown places, where beds can be hired for coppers. By the time he had reached City Hall Park he was so completely plastered with yells of "bum" and "hobo," and with various unholy epithets that small boys had applied to him at intervals that he was in a state of profound dejection, and looking searchingly for an outcast of high degree that the two might share miseries. But the lights threw a quivering glare over rows and circles of deserted benches that glistened damply, showing patches of wet sod behind them. It seemed that their usual freights of sorry humanity had fled on this night to better things. There were only squads of well dressed Brooklyn people, who swarmed toward the Bridge.

The young man loitered about for a time, and then went shuffling off down Park row. In the sudden descent in style of the dress of the crowd he felt relief. He began to see others whose tatters matched his tatters. In Chatham square there were aimless men strewn in front of saloons and lodging houses. He aligned himself with these men, and turned slowly to occupy himself with the pageantry of the street.

The mists of the cold and damp night made an intensely blue haze, through which the gaslights in the windows of stores and saloons shone with a golden radiance. The street cars rumbled softly, as if going upon carpet stretched in the aisle made by the pillars of the elevated road. Two interminable processions of people went along the wet pavements, spattered with black mud that made each shoe leave a scar like impression. The high buildings lurked a-back, shrouded in shadows. Down a side street there were mystic curtains of purple and black, on which lamps dully glittered like embroidered flowers.

548.11   convictions.]   Following this word, the newspaper version concluded:

"Well," said the friend, "did you discover his point of view?"

"I don't know that I did," replied the young man; "but at any rate I think mine own has undergone a considerable alteration."

At a time about halfway between the original and the revision, Crane commented: "In a story of mine called 'An Experiment in Misery' I tried to make plain that the root of Bowery life is a sort of cowardice. Perhaps I mean a lack of ambition or to willingly be knocked flat and accept the licking."

594.1   *The Fire*]   First appeared in the New York *Press*, November 25, 1894, under the headline "When Every One Is Panic Stricken" and subtitled "A Realistic Pen Picture of a Fire in a Tenement." No evidence has been found to suggest that it is the news report of an actual fire.

605.1   *In the . . . Mine*]   This article, as well as illustrations for it by Crane's artist friend Corwin Linson, was commissioned by the famous muck-raker S. S. McClure. Crane and Linson visited Scranton, Pennsylvania, in June 1894. The newspaper syndicate version came out on July 22, and *Mc-Clure's Magazine* ran the article in its August issue.

615.1   *Howells . . . Wait*]   At the suggestion of Hamlin Garland, Crane sent a copy of *Maggie* to Howells (1837–1920), the leading novelist and critical advocate of the American realist movement. Howells' enthusiastic response led to an early meeting and eventually to this interview, reported on October 28, 1894. Earlier, Crane in a letter had referred to "my literary fathers—Howells and Garland." He told of discovering "that my creed was identical with the one of Howells and Garland and in this way I became involved in the beautiful war between those who say that art is man's substitute for nature and we are the most successful in art when we approach the nearest to nature and truth, and those who say—well, I don't know what they say. They don't, they can't say much but they fight villianously and keep Garland and I out of the big magazines. Howells, of course, is too powerful for them." Stephen Crane to Lily Brandon Munroe [March 1894?].

THE WEST AND MEXICO

681.2   *An Excursion Ticket*]   When this article appeared in the New York *Press*, May 20, 1894, it was headlined "Billy Atkins Went to Omaha."

772.1   *A Man . . . Others*]   Crane met New York City Police Commissioner Theodore Roosevelt in the summer of 1896. Roosevelt was a particular admirer of *The Red Badge of Courage*, had a professional interest in Crane's Bowery tales, and to a degree lived out the legendary popular enthusiasm for the West. Shared interest evidently led to his reading "A Man and Some Others" in manuscript some weeks before it was sent to Crane's literary agent, but he could offer only qualified response to the young writer's departures from popular convention: "Some day I want you to write another story of the frontiersman and the Mexican Greaser in which the frontiersman shall come out on top; it is more normal that way!" (August 18, 1896)

NEW YORK CITY, 1896

865.1   *Adventures of a Novelist*]   Crane's journalistic investigation of New York's Tenderloin district led to his witnessing the arrest of Dora Clark for soliciting on September 16, 1896. Since Crane had just interviewed her and had been walking with her to the cable car, he could testify to her innocence. The story was featured in all the New York papers during the week; "Adventures of a Novelist" received a full-page spread in the New York *Journal* on Sunday, September 20.

FLORIDA

875.1   *Stephen . . . Story*]   The Ten Years' War for Cuban independence (1868–78) ended in suppression by the Spanish military governor. When revolution broke out again in 1895, there was widespread sympathy in the United States despite official neutrality. The *Commodore*, with its contraband cargo and filibusters (participants in a foreign insurrection), sailed December 31, 1896, with Crane on board as a reporter for the New York *World*. The ship sank January 2, 1897.

GREECE

931.1   *Greek War Correspondents*]   Crane's sense of the tangle of journalistic coverage of the Greco-Turkish war was well-founded: although he went to Greece as correspondent for William Randolph Hearst's New York *Journal*, this piece was distributed to American newspapers by the McClure syndicate in what was apparently a separate arrangement. His contempt for grand-scale political expertise on "the Eastern question" stemmed from his having completely identified with the cause of Greek nationalism. At Soudha Bay in Crete he had seen the array of warships of the major European powers, which served to prevent Greek armed forces from landing to support irregular Greek rebels in the hills. He forgot that the same "Concert of Powers" had made possible the revision of borders whereby Thessaly had been ceded to the Greek monarchy by the Turks in 1881.

934.1   *Crane at Velestino*]   Hostilities opened April 9, 1897, when Greek irregulars crossed from Thessaly into Macedonia to the north. Regular Greek armed forces became engaged a week later. The expected uprising of Macedonian Greeks did not take place. Instead, a general Turkish advance began on April 18, and a series of Greek retreats followed. On April 17 Larissa, the capital of Thessaly, fell. The Turkish probe toward Volos, the main port of Thessaly, was stopped at the railway junction of Velestino, a few miles to the west, on April 27, and again on April 29–30. But the main Turkish advance through Pharsala and Domoko towards Lamia necessitated the abandonment of Velestino on May 5 in order to reinforce defenses on the route to Athens. (Through intercession of the czar, an armistice was arranged May 20 before Volos was taken.) With this dispatch, it is possible to see how two different rewrite men for the New York *Journal* made different texts of Crane's cabled story. For example, the first three paragraphs of the city edition, reprinted in this volume, are paralleled by the opening long paragraph of the out-of-town edition, as follows:

Stephen Crane at Velestino

By courier from volo to athens, May 10.—Velestino will surely be famous as one of the greatest battles of this war. The Greek reverse began at Larissa, and the world expected a quick conclusion, but Velestino proved that Greek soldiers could, when well led, successfully cope with the overwhelming numbers of Turks. It proved them good fighters and long fighters and stayers. It must have been generally surprising after Larissa, and it occasioned general rejoicing throughout Greece, and its effect upon the Greek soldiers was great. It made them perfectly happy. To be sure the army retreated from Velestino, but it was not the fault of this army. The commander bit his fingers and cursed when the order came to retreat. He was at that time perfectly confident of success. For three days he had been holding the Turks beautifully in check and inflicting heavy loss. Then came the orders to fall back, due to reverses or something else in other places.

938.1   Ephzones] Evzones (in modern transliteration), distinguished by their white Macedonian kilts, are the crack infantry of the Greek army.

ENGLAND AND IRELAND, 1897

984.1   *Harold Frederic*] (1856–1898) London correspondent of *The New York Times*, lived in suburban Kenley, a few miles from Crane at Oxted. Their friendship was that of journalistic cronies, and despite their having vacationed together in Ireland, where Crane was working on *The Monster*, Frederic had no taste for that novel or for Crane's literary friends Joseph Conrad and Henry James. Nevertheless, in this piece he elicited Crane's most sustained effort at literary comment.

CUBA

997.1   I. FROM . . . FIELD] The Spanish-American War began with the joint resolution of Congress approved by President McKinley on April 20, 1898, demanding Spanish withdrawal from Cuba. Although Dewey's victory at Manila Bay was the first major battle of the war, Cuba was the principal scene of action. There, after Admiral Sampson had bottled up Cervera's fleet in Santiago harbor, General Shafter began supporting operations by landings east of Santiago at Daiquiri beginning June 22 and at Siboney June 23. Most of the troops were regular army; of the newly enlisted regiments taking part, the most famous was the First Volunteer Cavalry, the "Rough Riders," under Colonel Leonard Wood and Lieutenant-Colonel Theodore Roosevelt. Behind the landing area was a ridge with Spanish blockhouses; the battle for Las Guásimas, described in the first report, secured passage of the ridge for the United States forces.

1001.2   *Battle of San Juan*] On July 1, the United States forces attacked El Caney and the hill of San Juan, the Spanish strongholds outside Santiago.

The dateline of the story indicates that Crane filed it on the day he reached Old Point Comfort (Fort Monroe), to which he was invalided from Cuba.

1001.5   like Inkerman]   The battle of Inkerman (1854) in the Crimean War was a "soldier's battle," in which general command is largely lost and units are forced to engage self-directed.

1010.29–30   Guantanamo]   Located a few miles east of the beachhead where the Marines established the supply base for the Cuban operations.

CATALOGING INFORMATION

Crane, Stephen, 1871–1900.
    Prose and poetry.

    (The Library of America; 18)
    "J. C. Levenson wrote the notes and selected the texts for this volume."—Prelim. p. v.
    Includes Bibliographical references and index.
    Contents: Maggie: a girl of the streets—The red badge of courage—Stories and sketches—Poetry.
    I. Title.   II. Maggie: a girl of the streets.   III. The red badge of courage.   IV. Series.
PS1449.C85A6   1984   813'.4   83–19908
ISBN 0–940450–17–8

Index of Prose Titles

Index of Poetry: First Lines and Titles

THE LIBRARY OF AMERICA SERIES

This book is set in 10 point Linotron Galliard,
a face designed for photocomposition by Matthew Carter
and based on the sixteenth-century face Granjon. The paper
is acid-free Ecusta Nyalite and meets the requirements for perma-
nence of the American National Standards Institute. The binding
material is Brillianta, a 100% woven rayon cloth made by
Van Heek-Scholco Textielfabrieken, Holland. The com-
position is by Haddon Craftsmen, Inc., and The
Clarinda Company. Printing and binding
by R. R. Donnelley & Sons Company.
Designed by Bruce Campbell.